PENGUIN CLASSICS

THE ARABIAN NIGHTS
TALES OF 1001 NIGHTS
VOLUME 1

MALCOLM C. LYONS, sometime Sir Thomas Adams Professor of Arabic at Cambridge University and a life Fellow of Pembroke College, Cambridge, is a specialist in the field of classical Arabic Literature. His published works include the biography *Saladin: The Politics of the Holy War*, *The Arabian Epic: Heroic and Oral Story-telling, Identification and Identity in Classical Arabic Poetry* and many articles on Arabic literature.

URSULA LYONS, formerly an Affiliated Lecturer at the Faculty of Oriental Studies at Cambridge University and, since 1976, an Emeritus Fellow of Lucy Cavendish College, Cambridge, specializes in modern Arabic literature.

ROBERT IRWIN is the author of *For Lust of Knowing: The Oriental-ists and Their Enemies*, *The Middle East in the Middle Ages*, *The Arabian Nights: A Companion* and numerous other specialized studies of Middle Eastern politics, art and mysticism. His novels include *The Limits of Vision*, *The Arabian Nightmare*, *The Mysteries of Algiers* and *Satan Wants Me*.

The Arabian Nights

Tales of 1001 Nights

Volume 1
Nights 1 to 294

Translated by MALCOLM C. LYONS,
with URSULA LYONS
Introduced and Annotated by ROBERT IRWIN

PENGUIN BOOKS

PENGUIN CLASSICS

Published by the Penguin Group
Penguin Books Ltd, 80 Strand, London WC2R ORL, England
Penguin Group (USA) Inc., 375 Hudson Street, New York, New York 10014, USA
Penguin Group (Canada), 90 Eglinton Avenue East, Suite 700, Toronto, Ontario, Canada M4P 2Y3
(a division of Pearson Penguin Canada Inc.)
Penguin Ireland, 25 St Stephen's Green, Dublin 2, Ireland (a division of Penguin Books Ltd)
Penguin Group (Australia), 250 Camberwell Road, Camberwell, Victoria 3124, Australia
(a division of Pearson Australia Group Pty Ltd)
Penguin Books India Pvt Ltd, 11 Community Centre, Panchsheel Park, New Delhi – 110 017, India
Penguin Group (NZ), 67 Apollo Drive, Rosedale, North Shore 0632, New Zealand
(a division of Pearson New Zealand Ltd)
Penguin Books (South Africa) (Pty) Ltd, 24 Sturdee Avenue, Rosebank,
Johannesburg 2196, South Africa

Penguin Books Ltd, Registered Offices: 80 Strand, London WC2R ORL, England

www.penguin.com

This translation first published in Penguin Classics hardback 2008
Published in paperback 2010

011

Translation of Nights 1 to 294, Note on the Translation and Note on the Text
copyright © Malcolm C. Lyons, 2008
Translation of 'The story of Ali Baba and the forty thieves killed by a slave girl' and 'Translating Galland'
copyright © Ursula Lyons, 2008
Introduction, Glossary, Further Reading and Chronology copyright © Robert Irwin, 2008
All rights reserved

The moral right of the translators and editor has been asserted

Text illustrations design by Coralie Bickford-Smith; images: Gianni Dagli Orti/Museo Correr,
Venice/The Art Archive

Printed in England by Clays Ltd, St Ives plc

ISBN: 978-0-140-44938-9

www.greenpenguin.co.uk

Contents

Editorial Note

This new English version of *The Arabian Nights* (also known as *The Thousand and One Nights*) is the first complete translation of the Arabic text known as the Macnaghten edition or Calcutta II since Richard Burton's famous translation of it in 1885–8. A great achievement in its time, Burton's translation nonetheless contained many errors, and even in the 1880s his English read strangely.

In this new edition, in addition to Malcolm Lyons's translation of all the stories found in the Arabic text of Calcutta II, Ursula Lyons has translated the tales of Aladdin and Ali Baba, as well as an alternative ending to 'The seventh journey of Sindbad', from Antoine Galland's eighteenth-century French. (For the Aladdin and Ali Baba stories no original Arabic text has survived and consequently these are classed as 'orphan stories'.)

The text appears in three volumes, each with an introduction, which, in Volume 1, discusses the strange nature of the *Nights*; in Volume 2, their history and provenance; and, in Volume 3, the influence the tales have exerted on writers through the centuries. Volume 1 also includes an explanatory note on the translation, a note on the text and an introduction to the 'orphan stories' ('Editing Galland'), in addition to a chronology and suggestions for further reading. Footnotes, a glossary and maps appear in all three volumes.

As often happens in popular narrative, inconsistencies and contradictions abound in the text of the *Nights*. It would be easy to emend these, and where names have been misplaced this has been done to avoid confusion. Elsewhere, however, emendations for which there is no textual authority would run counter to the fluid and uncritical spirit of the Arabic narrative. In such circumstances no changes have been made.

Introduction

The story collection of *The Arabian Nights* has drawn on many cultures and sources – Indian, Persian, Greek. One of its parallel sources, which drew on the same ancient Indian materials, is a Sanskrit text known as the *Kathasaritsagara*, or 'The Ocean of the Streams of Story', compiled by the eleventh-century author Somadeva. *The Arabian Nights* is, like the *Kathasaritsagara*, a vast storytelling ocean in which the readers can lose themselves. One story, like a wave, is absorbed into the one that follows. The drift of the narrative tides carries us, like Sindbad, to strange places, and the further from home, the stranger those places are. Within the stories themselves, the sea operates as the agent of destiny which carries ships, men and magically sealed bottles and casts them upon unexpected shores: the Island of Waq-Waq where the women grow from trees, the island of the Magnetic Mountain presided over by its talismanic statue, the Black Islands of the Ensorcelled Prince and the islands of China. The tides are unpredictable, and men's fortunes founder and are wrecked upon the sea of destiny.

The vastness and complexity of the *Nights* is mesmerizing. In her story 'The Djinn in the Nightingale's Eye' (1994), A. S. Byatt has written:

> What delights above all in the *Arabian Nights* is its form. Story is embedded in story, story sprouts out of the midst of story, like the Surinam toads out of the back of their mother toad, which Coleridge used as a metaphor for his unruly imagination. The collection resembles both a group of Russian dolls, formally similar, faces and colours different, and a maze or spider-web with threads and passages leading in all directions, both formless and orderly at once.

Plot motifs within the *Nights* combine and recombine: the ageing and childless couple who, having prayed for a son, find that their wish is granted; the merchant who sits minding his business when a veiled woman enters his shop and summons him to follow her; the man who is told that he may explore every room in the palace save only one room, which is locked; the squandering of his deceased father's fortune by a feckless youth; the fisherman who casts his net upon the waters but at first has no luck; the young man who is smuggled into the caliph's harem; the curiously assembled queue of people each of whom swears that he or she can tell a tale yet more remarkable than the one they have just heard. The stories are full of echoes and half echoes of one another, like recurrent dreams in which the landscape is thoroughly familiar, though what is to come is utterly unpredictable. The stories' devices are recombined, inverted or truncated in what comes to seem like a complete spectrum of storytelling possibilities.

Those Surinam toads . . . one story frames another, which in turn contains yet another within it, and so on and so on. The French refer to this sort of framing procedure as the *mise en abîme*, the thrust into the abyss. Shahrazad, talking in an attempt to save her life, tells the tale of the hunchback, and that includes the tale of the tailor, and the tailor tells the tale of the barber, and the barber tells his own tale, and within that are the tales of his various unlucky brothers. Such a Chinese-box structure as an organizing device in fiction has its counterpart in real life, wherein we are all of us the stories we carry within us, but that master story contains also the stories of our family and friends, and perhaps the newsagent and the postman, and perhaps what the postman told you about his brother and the story the brother was told by a tourist he met in Italy, and so on. To look at it from the opposite direction, each of us embodies a life story and our stories get inserted into the overarching master stories of other people we know – just as, without having any choice in the matter, we may appear in the dreams of people we know.

Shahrazad tells stories in order to postpone her death. But death, 'the destroyer of delights', is implicitly or explicitly the terminator of all the stories she tells and, in this sense, whether a prince marries a princess or a poor fisherman wins his just reward from the caliph, all stories will end unhappily if carried through to their inevitable conclusion. The Angel of Death, a protagonist in several stories, is unfailingly intransigent. The calender dervishes, whom Shahrazad has relating the stories of their adventures, are nothing other than the stories that they tell about themselves. The same is true of Sindbad, and of the sequence of people that manhandled the corpse of the hunchback from place to place and then, in order to save themselves from being executed for the hunchback's murder, tell the stories of their strange adventures. As in medieval fiction, so, in real life, we are the stories we tell about ourselves. And our tales are told in order to postpone the coming of 'the destroyer of all delights'.

The stories that Shahrazad relates in order to delay her execution are told at night, and they cease abruptly when dawn breaks. Stories are best told at night. Since listening to stories in Arab society was regarded as less sinful after the day's work was done, stories were known as *asmar*, 'things of the evening' or 'tales related in the night for amusement'. Stories told at night often feature adventures that take place at night: the caliph Harun al-Rashid disguises himself and wanders the streets of Baghdad at night; the singing girls entertain the caliph's courtiers at night; lovers' assignations happen at night; so does housebreaking, and the thief was known as the *Sahib al-Layl*, or 'Master of the Night'. In the darkness it is easy to get lost in the warren of streets in Baghdad or Cairo and so find oneself in an alleyway one has never set foot in before, and in that alleyway there is a house where the lights are still on and something strange is about to happen. The *jinn* are on the move when darkness falls.

The night cloaks many mysteries. The Arabic for 'mystery' or 'secret' is *sirr*, but *sirr* is one those numerous Arabic words which also comprehends its opposite meaning, so that *sirr* also means 'a thing that is revealed, appears or made manifest'. Many stories open strangely and they will only close when that strangeness is resolved and the truth 'appears or is made manifest'. One night the caliph Harun ventures out in disguise and hires a boat on the Tigris. Only a little time passes before a torch-lit barge approaches and on it Harun sees a man enthroned and robed as the caliph and waited upon by servants and courtiers in the robes of the caliph's court . . . Or consider the tale in which, once again, Harun ventures out in disguise and makes his way to the Tigris, where he encounters a fisherman who is pulling a large box out of the water. The box contains the body of a mutilated woman. Harun tells his vizier Ja'far that the crime must be solved in three days or his life will be forfeit . . . Much stranger yet is the adventure of Judar who used to fish on Lake Qarun. One day he is approached by a Maghribi – that is, a North African – who asks Judar to tie his hands behind his back and throw him into the lake. If the Maghribi drowns, Judar is to go to a certain

Jew and give him the Maghribi's mule and saddlebag, for which he will receive one hundred dinars . . . 'These are mysteries that are worthy to be graven on the corner of an eye with a needle.' For some readers the atmosphere of deep mystery in such *Nights* stories may summon memories of the similarly atmospheric and mystifying openings of stories by Arthur Conan Doyle or G. K. Chesterton.

Then consider the case of the multi-coloured fish caught in the net of a poor fisherman which he then presents to the king and for which he is well rewarded. These fish are sent down to the royal kitchens, where they are scaled and put in a frying pan with oil. They are fried on one side and then turned over. Whereupon a beautiful maiden, her eyes darkened with kohl, bursts through the wall of the kitchen and, having stuck her wand in the frying pan, addresses the fish: 'Fish, are you faithful to the covenant?' The cook faints, but the frying fish raise their heads and reply: 'Yes, yes. If you return, we return; if you keep faith, then so do we . . .' What is the meaning of this? There is no answer. Some of the mysteries of *The Arabian Nights* are destined never to be solved.

The mystery of the locked room is particularly important. Within the *Nights* there are many locked rooms that should not be entered. Just one will serve as an example here. After the third dervish has departed from the palace of the ten one-eyed men, he follows their guidance and comes to a palace inhabited by forty moon-faced, amorous young women. After a year at the palace sleeping with different girls, he is woken by the wailing of the women. They tell him they must be away on business for forty days. He has very nearly the free run of the palace and he can go into every room except the fortieth, which on no account must he enter. And then the women ride off. What now? As the reader, one does not want the dervish to enter that last room, because there is obviously something evil or dangerous in it; one wants him to carry on dallying with the moon-faced women for ever. But at the same time the reader wants the dervish to enter the forbidden chamber, because the reader is, like the dervish, curious and wishes to know what is within it. Besides, unless the dervish crosses the forbidden threshold, there will be no more story. The third dervish's dilemma is the same as that of Peter Rabbit, whose mother tells him: 'Whatever you do, do not go into Mr McGregor's garden.' The reader both wants and does not want to see the rabbit venture into the garden. A horrible tension has been set up.

In the event, on the fortieth day, the dervish, unable to contain his curiosity any longer, enters the fortieth chamber, where he finds a horse waiting, saddled and bridled. He mounts the horse and whips it into action. The magic horse flies him to the roof of another palace and, as the dervish dismounts, the horse lashes out with its tail, striking out his right eye. The dervish finds that he has been brought back to the palace of the ten one-eyed men. His story has been a warning to the curious. It is as if the storyteller is teasing the audience, saying to them: 'Beware. You should not be listening to my stories.' Also, perhaps, the interdiction 'Whatever you do, do not do this' acts as a kind of dam, slowing the narrative stream of the plot. It holds the story back for a while, but, when the narrative flow breaks through, it does so with redoubled force.

The stories of the *Nights* are suffused by sex. Their protagonists languish and faint from excess of desire. They waste away from love, and they improvise verses to celebrate their melancholy passions. All the emotions are heightened. Those who listen to poems or to music on the lute are liable to tear their robes in ecstasy; a good joke may cause the caliph to fall over with laughter. The stories are full of competing eloquences, as men and women debate before caliphs or *jinn* and engage in a rhetoric of persuasion that draws on stories, maxims and pious examples. Envy is one of the powerful passions to fuel the plotting of the stories, and the eye of envy seeks out the beautiful child or the magic key to wealth. The storytellers have a ruthlessly mocking attitude towards mutilation and misfortune. The streets of Baghdad, Cairo and Damascus teem with one-eyed, one-handed men and hunchbacks, and each mutilation or deformity has its own story. People hunger for justice, even if that justice may be summary and arbitrary. When they bring their story and complaint before the caliph, they cannot know whether the end of it will be a purse of gold or being thrust down on to the executioner's leather mat to be beheaded. Though religious belief and practice are rarely the subject of the stories, invocations to God – 'In the Name of God', 'Praise be to God', 'I take refuge in God', 'From God we come and to Him do we return' – come as easily to the Muslims in the street as breathing. However, it is fate, not God, which governs their destinies.

There are many stories about richly apparelled and libidinous princes and princesses and their hunting, feasting and music making, designed, in part, to stir up envy. But one should not ignore the fact there are other stories in the *Nights* which suggest that there is a mystical meaning to the way the world works and which call their audience to repentance. There are tales in praise of hermits and renunciation of the pleasures of the world. There are also stories of virtuous deeds done by stealth and tales of divine favour. In one lengthy story, a small encyclopedia in its own right, the slave girl Tawaddud lectures her audience on the Quran, traditions concerning the Prophet, Islamic law and other edifying matters. In the story of Buluqiya, we are introduced to the fantastic structures of Islamic cosmology: the cosmic mountain, Qaf, at the end of the world; the archangels that preside over the procession of night and day, earthquakes, famine and prosperity; the angel who carries the seven worlds and who stands on a bull who stands on a fish who swims in the sea of infinity.

Although it is missing at the beginning of the Arabic text from which this translation has been made, the manuscript from which Antoine Galland made his translation opens with an address to the reader. The first part runs:

> Praise be to God, the Beneficent King, the creator of the world and man, who raised the heavens without pillars and spread out the earth as a place of rest and erected the mountains as props and made the water flow from the hard rock and destroyed the race of Thamud, 'Ad and Pharaoh of the vast domain . . .

Thamud was the name of a pagan people who dwelt in north-western Arabia and rejected the call of Allah's prophet Salih to repent and turn to monotheism, and who were consequently destroyed in an earthquake. The 'Ad were an ancient and arrogant tribe that dwelt among the sand dunes. Their fate is recounted in the *Nights* in the tale of Iram, 'City of the Columns'. Their ruler, Shaddad ibn 'Ad, ordered the building of a city in imitation of Paradise. Its building took three hundred years, but no sooner was it completed than God destroyed it with a rushing single wind, the 'Cry of Wrath'. Centuries later, a certain 'Abd Allah ibn Abi Qilaba stumbled across its ruins. Pharaoh appears in the Bible and in the Quran as the ruler who, having rejected Moses' mission, was punished together with his people. The reader was expected to take warning from such stories: power and wealth are transitory and all things perish before the face of God.

The storytellers of the *Nights* and their audiences lived in the vicinity of ruins. Tales were told in the shadows of Tadmur, Petra, Ikhmim, Luxor and Giza. In the story of al-Ma'mun and the Pyramids of Egypt, the 'Abbasid caliph orders his workmen to break into a Pyramid, but after an awful lot of digging he discovers a cache of money that is exactly equivalent to the amount that he has expended in digging towards it. In the story of the City of Brass, the Umaiyad caliph 'Abd al-Malik commissions an expedition to North Africa to seek out one of the stoppered vases that were reputed to contain the *jinn* imprisoned by Solomon centuries earlier. The expedition led by the emir Musa sets off into the desert, but loses its way for a year before entering the ancient lands of Alexander and, after several strange encounters, they arrive at the City of Brass. After reciting verses from the Quran, Musa's party enters the city only to find that it is populated by the dead, while at the heart of the labyrinth that is the royal palace they find the mummified corpse of the queen to whom the deceptive semblance of life has been given by quicksilver in her eyeballs. This was once the city of Qush, son of Shaddad ibn 'Ad, and all its wealth could not save it when God declared its doom. So take warning from that. Inside the City of Brass the expedition finds a gold tablet with the following inscription: 'Where are the kings of China, the masters of might and power? Where is 'Ad, son of Shaddad,* and the buildings he raised up? Where is Nimrod, the mighty tyrant?' The dead and their ruined habitations are present in the world of the living to guide men to repentance.

At a more mundane level, the stories of *Nights* carry warnings against dissemblers, charlatans, tricksters and adulterers. They give lessons on how to detect cheats, deal with gate-crashers and how to avoid the wiles of women. The cunning of women is not the least of the many marvels of the *Nights*, and many of the stories that are superficially about sex are more profoundly about cunning and the celebration of cunning. As the opening address of the Galland manuscript has it: 'This book, which I have called *The Thousand and One Nights*, abounds also with splendid biographies that teach the reader to detect deception and to protect himself from it . . .' The importance of not being cheated loomed large in the minds of the shopkeepers of Cairo and Damascus and the frequenters of the coffee houses who were the primary audience of the *Nights*.

Let us return to the merchant who sits minding his business when a veiled woman enters his shop and summons him to follow her. He is a man who has been waiting for a story to happen to him. *The Arabian Nights* should be understood as the collective dreaming of commercial folk in the great cities of the medieval Arab world. It seems clear from the marginal jottings made on manuscripts of the *Nights* that have

---

* In reality, Shaddad ibn 'Ad; the inscription is wrong.

survived that most of their borrowers and readers were shopkeepers and other people engaged in trade in the big cities – Aleppo, Baghdad, Basra, Cairo and Damascus. It is not surprising that there are as many merchants and sons of merchants in these stories as there are princes and princesses. Money, debts and loans play a much larger part here than they do in European fairy stories. A number of tales celebrate the entrepreneurial and innovative qualities of the Muslims. And, despite the impression given by Hollywood films, Sindbad was not a sailor but a merchant.

At times, the stories go into some detail about commercial transactions. There is, for example, the Christian broker's tale, in which the Christian trading in Cairo is offered by a young man the brokerage on a large quantity of sesame at the rate of one *ardabb* for a hundred dirhams, but before going round to collect it from the Khan al-Jawali (a warehouse and hostel for visiting merchants), he checks the going rate for sesame with other buyers and finds it to be a hundred and twenty dirhams for a single *ardabb*. He is then offered a brokerage commission of ten dirhams on every *ardabb*, from a total of fifty *ardabbs* of sesame that he will be handling for the young man. The details of this mundane transaction serve as the frame for the young man's tale of sexual ensnarement, financial ruin and mutilation.

Some stories pander to the tradesmen's fascination with commodities. Consider the porter of Baghdad who is hired by a dark-eyed young woman to load his basket with the things that she is going to purchase: first 'an olive-coloured jar of strained wine'; then in a fruiterer's shop 'where she bought Syrian apples, Uthmani quinces, Omani peaches, jasmine and water lilies from Syria, autumn cucumbers, lemons, *sultani* oranges, scented myrtle, privet flowers, camomile blossoms, red anemones, violets, pomegranate blooms and eglantine'. The lovingly catalogued shopping spree continues at the butcher's, the grocer's, with the sweetmeat seller and the perfume seller. Or consider the shop that 'Ala' al-Din Abu'l-Shamat buys and which was 'furnished with rugs and cushions, and stored there he discovered sails, spars, ropes and chests, together with bags filled with beads, shells, stirrups, axes, maces, knives, scissors and other such things, as the previous owner had been a second-hand dealer'. Among later storytellers perhaps only H. G. Wells, himself the son of a shopkeeper, has given so much prominence to the small shopkeeper in fiction. Wells, and before him the anonymous storytellers of the *Nights*, celebrated the culture of tradesmen who wish for something better than minding the store and dream of making something of themselves in a world from which routine has been banished.

The stories of the *Nights* were composed and collected for the entertainment of city dwellers, and the city is the usual setting for those stories. The streets are narrow and the upper storeys often have corbelled and enclosed projecting balconies. High *mashrabiyya* windows allow the inhabitants to observe the street without being seen. Narrow, densely packed alleyways often end in cul-de-sacs. Parts of the city consisted of *harat*, or secure quarters, whose gates were closed at night. In the daytime, the streets are crowded. The shopkeepers usually sit on *mastabas* (stone platforms) at the front of their stores. The mosque is more than a place for prayer; it is where public business is conducted and where travellers, unable to find lodgings elsewhere, sleep (as did the man who became rich again because of a dream). The *hammam*, or public bath, is usually close to the mosque. Visiting merchants lodge in caravanserais, hotels-cum-warehouses, in which their goods are usually stored on the ground floor while they sleep in the upper galleries. Prosperous domestic houses usually present austere outer façades that belie the wealth and ornamentation to be found within. The more prosperous dwellings are often built around a central courtyard with the reception room on the first floor. The poor sleep in tenement buildings, shanties or holes in the ground.

Less frequently, the adventures of the *Nights* take place outside the city. The storytellers had only a slight interest in the lives of the *fellahin* or peasants (though there are a few stories about them). Beyond the walls of the city of the storytellers lay mostly wasteland and desert, populated by huntsmen, woodcutters, bandits and *ghuls*. The storytellers and their listeners rarely ventured beyond the city and into the desert. It was rarely that they entered a palace, and never its harem; certainly they never visited the Valley of Diamonds or the Island of Waq-Waq with its trees bearing human fruit. The wastelands, as much as the palaces and remote islands, were sites of improbable adventures – places urban shopkeepers and artisans could only dream about.

In 'The Djinn in the Nightingale's Eye', the heroine (who is a narratologist)

was accustomed to say in lectures that it was possible that the human need to tell tales about things that were unreal originated in dreams and that memory had certain things in common with dreams; it rearranged, it made clear, simple narratives, certainly it invented as well as recalling.

Ultimately it is the dream-like quality of *The Arabian Nights* which appeals. The dream, like Shahrazad, can only continue in existence as long as it tells a story. Once things stop happening in a dream, that dream, perforce, is ended.

Robert Irwin
London

A Note on the Translation

The life of the fictional Shahrazad depended on her ability to produce stories night after night, leaving them carefully unfinished at appropriate points so as to be asked to complete them later. In real terms throughout the Arab world, the reciters of such tales were concerned not with life but livelihood, for their audiences had to be encouraged to return, night after night, to attend the performances and reward the performers. As can be seen in the search for a text of the tale of Saif al-Muluk in Volume 3, the stories had manuscript backing, although sadly many of these manuscripts have been destroyed, lost or left unstudied and unedited. Edward Lane noted in his *Manners and Customs of the Modern Egyptians* (1836) how the reciters would allow themselves to take liberties with whatever texts they had to suit the taste of their audience. Successful accretions could be added to the conflated versions, so adding to the repetitions, non sequiturs and confusions that mark the present text. Except where textual justification can be found, no attempt has been made to superimpose on the translation changes that would be needed to 'rectify' these. This leaves a representation of what is primarily oral literature, appealing to the ear rather than the eye.

Success for the reciters did not depend merely on creativity, important as this is, but on the introduction of ingredients that their audiences would recognize and find attractive. Tautology, standard phrases and repetition help this process, while colours add to and at times replace imagery – 'brown' is applied to a spear, for instance, and 'white' to a sword. Such details can be multiplied at will but behind them lie universal questions of narrative technique. Specifically, in *The Arabian Nights* the structure of the language itself did much to point the way. Arabic, with its infusion of words from surrounding cultures, has a vast vocabulary, providing a range of virtual synonyms and almost unlimited access to rhyme words. Its clauses are characteristically attached rather than subordinated to one another, and sentences resemble an accumulation of wavelets rather than the sound of single breakers. Assonance and rhyme duplicate sounds, and the strength of the linguistic effect these produce derives characteristically from repetition rather than innovation.

In Arabic popular literature, this effect is designed to mesmerize the audience by the use of rhythm and sound, adapted to a pace that is deliberately slow. The hypnotized listeners are not encouraged to look forward or back, but to immerse themselves in the reciter's present. By contrast, a reader not only can assimilate more words in a given space of time, but he is in control of his own pages and can look wherever he wants. For example, more often than not, characters of the *Nights* are introduced with their full names and descriptions whenever they occur – A son of B, the king of C, and so on. For identification the reader will find this unnecessary, as, even if he has forgotten to whom a name refers, he can look back and find out. Similarly, one of the main effects of rhymed prose, as well as the introduction of poetry, is not only its direct appeal to the ear but its ability to slow down the pace of the narrative, the opposite of what is attempted here.

The translators Richard Burton and Enno Littmann have shown in their versions of the *Nights* that it is by no means impossible to reproduce the element of rhyme, but whether this helps to duplicate the mesmeric force of the original is more doubtful, and in the present translation no such attempt has been made. Here the object has been to speed up the pace of the narrative to what is hoped to be more nearly adapted to the eye rather than the ear of the modern reader. In no case has the sense been deliberately falsified, but, where possible, its presentation has been simplified and accelerated. This does not apply to the poetry, which some translators have curtailed, thinking it inessential. It does, however, form so important a part of the reciters' presentation that it has been included in full, although no attempt has been made to risk further distortion by imposing on the English version rhyme schemes omnipresent in Arabic.

What has been sacrificed is the decorative elaboration of the original, as well as the extra dimension of allusiveness that it provides. In the latter case, it is not merely that one incident will recall another, either within the *Nights* themselves or, more widely, in the huge corpus of Arabic popular literature, but a single phrase, one description or one line of poetry must have served to call other contexts to the mind of the original audience. To explore these intricacies, however, is the task of a commentary rather than of a translation.

Beneath the elaboration of the text are fundamental patterns of the genre of storytelling. Not only are these responsible for the basic structure of the *Nights*, but it is they that serve to underline the importance of the work, firstly as an immediate source of popular literature and, more generally, in the universal history of storytelling. It is these patterns that, it is hoped, this translation will help to make more accessible.

In any English version, the transliteration of Arabic names and words presents familiar problems. Here it has been decided not to enter in most cases the diacritical markings that distinguish matching consonants as well as long and short vowels. For Arabists these are unnecessary and for the general reader they may be thought to add confusion rather than clarity. Similarly, on a more restricted point, academic rectitude suggests that in many cases *y* should be used in place of *i*, as in the case of *Zayd* for *Zaid*, but here *i* has been preferred throughout as appearing simpler and less exotic.

A Note on the Text

The purely academic problems connected with the compilation of *The Arabian Nights* lie outside the scope of this work. It represents accretive literature, changing from place to place and from age to age, and so there can be no 'perfect' text. Although it would be possible to produce a conflated version, adding and subtracting from manuscripts and printed texts, here a choice has been made of the Macnaghten text (Calcutta 1839–42 or Calcutta II). This has been translated in full, and to it have been added stories from Galland's French version. For those interested in individual points, the notes of the translators Edward Lane and Richard Burton, with their wide-ranging experience in this field, are of prime importance. In this translation, notes have been reduced to a minimum and have only been added to help with the reading or, in the case of the Quran, to provide references. In most cases these cover individual points. More generally, entries in the Glossary supply information on characters and terms found throughout the text.

No translator can fail to acknowledge a debt of gratitude to his predecessors, and, in the present case, to contemporary translators of the *Nights* such as Husain Haddawy. Unfortunately, the recent Pléiade edition of *Les Mille et une nuits* by Jamel Eddine Bencheikh and André Miquel (2005) came to my attention in time to be admired but too late to be used. Particular use has been made of the excellent German version, *Erzählungen aus den Tausendundein Nächten*, by Enno Littmann (1921–8). Finally, all scholars in this field owe an especial debt to R. Dozy, who used the *Nights* as one of the sources of his magisterial *Supplément aux dictionnaires arabes* (1877–81), in which almost all its obscure words are explained. In general, the sense of the Arabic is clear, but there are occasions when even Dozy admits that he does not know what a word means, and others in which it is impossible to be certain of what was the original meaning of an idiomatic phrase or term.

*

My own most grateful thanks are owed to Robert Irwin, the protagonist of this project, who has not only helped with checking the translation, but has added introductions, a glossary and notes of his own. A similar debt of gratitude must happily be acknowledged to Hilary Laurie of Penguin Books, whose friendly skills and editorial encouragement have helped to smooth difficulties at every stage in the work's production. Unstinted gratitude is also owed to Kate Parker and Caroline Pretty, who have been confronted with the Herculean task of cleaning the Augean stable of the text. Finally, my wife Ursula is responsible not only for the translation of Galland's French but has used her Arabic expertise to add invaluable help to what would otherwise have been an infinitely slower and more tedious task. *Quae mihi praestiteris memini.*

Malcolm C. Lyons
Pembroke College
Cambridge

Translating Galland

The translation from the French of two of the best-known tales in the *Nights* ('Aladdin' and 'Ali Baba'), called 'orphan stories' because they were not included among the three manuscripts used by Antoine Galland and because they lacked a surviving text, presents problems of another kind. Both are essentially retold by Galland to suit the audience and society of his time, and consequently the contrast is stark between the Arabic of the Calcutta text and the sophisticated and elegant French of Galland. 'Aladdin' was first read by Galland in 1709/10 in an Arabic version written for him by Hanna Diab, and he himself admitted his version was '*toute différente de ce que lui avait été raconté jusqu'alors*'. Galland makes Shahrazad conclude her story by pointing out the moral it contained, and he also added an ending where the king asks Shahrazad if she has finished her story. In his version, Galland's sultan and courtiers act as though they are at the court of the Sun King, with its etiquette, language and customs. The language of deference is even used by Aladdin's mother, who, despite her description as a poor woman of humble origins, Galland makes speak in language quite out of character, giving her long monologues containing a complex sentence structure of subordinate clauses when she tries to dissuade her son from daring to seek the hand of the sultan's daughter in marriage. Moreover, she asks him, anachronistically, what he has done for his sultan (whom she describes as '*un si grand monarque*') and for his country ('*patrie*') – concepts alien to *Nights* society – to deserve this. Here the translation remains as faithful as possible to the eighteenth-century French, but it has been necessary to simplify the sentence structure and shorten the sentences. Some of the idioms have had to be altered, together with some of the modes of address (such as *mon bonhomme*, *ma bonne femme*), and such concepts as *honnêteté*, the *honnête homme* and the *beau monde*, which all need reinterpreting.

Galland's version of 'Ali Baba' was developed from a summary he entered in his journal and, again, was originally written down in French after he had heard it from Diab. Galland's treatment here is more straightforward. The story is much shorter and is told in a more direct manner. The action is faster; the dialogue is in keeping with the characters, though he cannot resist making the wily Marjana more representative of a cultivated Frenchwoman, allowing her space in which to describe her actions. Here, interestingly, we find the origin of the phrase 'Open, Sesame!' or 'Sesame, open!' (or 'close'), which Galland has translated from the Arabic in which he was told the story as *'Sésame, ouvre-toi!'* and *'Sésame, referme-toi!'*

As for the proper names in the French versions of 'Ali Baba' and 'Aladdin', these have been changed to follow the conventions for transliterating Arabic names that are used in the rest of the translation, but without any diacritical marks. (Hence 'Husain' is used instead of 'Houssain'; 'Qasim' instead of 'Cassim'; 'Badr al-Budur' instead of 'Badroulboudour'; and so on.)

To these two tales has been added an alternative ending for 'The seventh journey of Sindbad' as it is given in Galland, but which is also found in the translations by Enno Littmann and Edward Lane.

Ursula Lyons
Lucy Cavendish College
Cambridge

The Arabian Nights

Nights 1 to 294

Among the histories of past peoples a story is told that in the old days in the islands of India and China there was a Sasanian king, a master of armies, guards, servants and retainers, who had two sons, an elder and a younger. Although both of them were champion horsemen, the elder was better than his brother; he ruled over the lands, treating his subjects with justice and enjoying the affection of them all. His name was King Shahriyar, while his younger brother, who ruled Persian Samarkand, was called Shah Zaman. For ten years both of them continued to reign justly, enjoying pleasant and untroubled lives, until Shahriyar felt a longing to see Shah Zaman and sent off his vizier to fetch him. 'To hear is to obey,' said the vizier, and after he had travelled safely to Shah Zaman, he brought him greetings and told him that his brother wanted a visit from him.

Shah Zaman agreed to come and made his preparations for the journey. He had his tents put up outside his city, together with his camels, mules, servants and guards, while his own vizier was left in charge of his lands. He then came out himself, intending to leave for his brother's country, but at midnight he thought of something that he had forgotten and went back to the palace. When he entered his room, it was to discover his wife in bed with a black slave. The world turned dark for him and he said to himself: 'If this is what happens before I have even left the city, what will this damned woman do if I spend time away with my brother?' So he drew his sword and struck, killing both his wife and her lover as they lay together, before going back and ordering his escort to move off.

When he got near to Shahriyar's city, he sent off messengers to give the good news of his arrival, and Shahriyar came out to meet him and greeted him delightedly. The city was adorned with decorations and Shahriyar sat talking happily with him, but Shah Zaman remembered what his wife had done and, overcome by sorrow, he turned pale and showed signs of illness. His brother thought that this must be because he had had to leave his kingdom and so he put no questions to him until, some days later, he mentioned these symptoms to Shah Zaman, who told him: 'My feelings are wounded,' but did not explain what had happened with his wife. In order to cheer him up, Shahriyar invited him to come with him on a hunt, but he refused and Shahriyar set off by himself.

In the royal palace there were windows that overlooked Shahriyar's garden, and as Shah Zaman was looking, a door opened and out came twenty slave girls and twenty slaves, in the middle of whom was Shahriyar's very beautiful wife. They came to a fountain where they took off their clothes and the women sat with the men. 'Mas'ud,' the queen called, at which a black slave came up to her and, after they had embraced each other, he lay with her, while the other slaves lay with the slave girls and they spent their time kissing, embracing, fornicating and drinking wine until the end of the day.

When Shah Zaman saw this, he told himself that what he had suffered was less serious. His jealous distress ended and, after convincing himself that his own misfortune was not as grave as this, he went on eating and drinking, so that when Shahriyar returned and the brothers greeted one another, Shahriyar saw that Shah Zaman's colour had come back; his face was rosy and, following his earlier loss of appetite, he was eating normally. 'You were pale, brother,' Shahriyar said, 'but now you have got your colour back, so tell me about this.' 'I'll tell you why I lost colour,' his brother replied, 'but don't press me to tell you how I got it back.' 'Let me know first how you lost it and became so weak,' Shahriyar asked him, and his brother explained: 'When you sent your vizier to invite me to visit you, I got ready and had gone out of the city when I remembered a jewel that was intended as a present for you, which I had left in my palace. I went back there to find a black slave sleeping in my bed with my wife, and it was after I had killed them both that I came on to you. I was full of concern about the affair and this was why I became pale and sickly, but don't make me say how I recovered.' Shahriyar, however, pressed him to do this, and so Shah Zaman finally told him all that he had seen.

'I want to see this with my own eyes,' said Shahriyar, at which Shah Zaman suggested that he pretend to be going out hunting again and then hide with him so that he could test the truth by seeing it for himself.

Shahriyar immediately announced that he was leaving to hunt; the tents were taken outside the city and the king himself went out and took his seat in one of them, telling his servants that nobody was to be allowed in to visit him. Then secretly he made his way back to the palace where his brother was and sat down by the window overlooking the garden. After a while the slave girls and their mistress came there with the slaves and they went on acting as Shah Zaman had described until the call for the afternoon prayer.

Shahriyar was beside himself and told his brother: 'Come, let us leave at once. Until we can find someone else to whom the same kind of thing happens, we have no need of a kingdom, and otherwise we would be better dead.' They left by the postern gate and went on for some days and nights until they got to a tall tree in the middle of a meadow, where there was a spring of water by the seashore. They drank from the spring and sat down to rest, but after a time the sea became disturbed and from it emerged a black pillar, towering up into the sky and moving towards the meadow. This sight filled the brothers with alarm and they climbed up to the top of the tree to see what was going to happen. What then appeared was a tall *jinni*, with a large skull and a broad breast, carrying a chest on his head. He came ashore and went up to sit under the tree on top of which the brothers were hiding. The *jinni* then opened the chest, taking from it a box, and when he had opened this too, out came a slender girl, as radiant as the sun, who fitted the excellent description given by the poet 'Atiya:

> She shone in the darkness, and day appeared
> As the trees shed brightness over her.
> Her radiance makes suns rise and shine,
> While, as for moons, she covers them in shame.
> When veils are rent and she appears,
> All things bow down before her.
> As lightning flashes from her sanctuary,
> A rain of tears floods down.

The *jinni* looked at her and said: 'Mistress of the nobly born, whom I snatched away on your wedding night, I want to sleep for a while.' He placed his head on her knee and fell asleep, while she, for her part, looked up at the tree, on top of which were the two kings. She lifted the *jinni*'s head from her knee and put it on the ground, before gesturing to them to come down and not to fear him. 'For God's sake, don't make us do this,' they told her, but she replied: 'Unless you come, I'll rouse him against you and he will put you to the cruellest of deaths.' This so alarmed them that they did what they were told and she then said: 'Take me as hard as you can or else I'll wake him up.' Shahriyar said fearfully to his brother: 'Do as she says.' But Shah Zaman refused, saying: 'You do it first.'

They started gesturing to each other about this and the girl asked why, repeating: 'If you don't come up and do it, I'll rouse the *jinni* against you.' Because they were afraid, they took turns to lie with her, and when they had finished, she told them to get up. From her pocket she then produced a purse from which she brought out a string on which were hung five hundred and seventy signet rings. She asked them if they knew what these were and when they said no, she told them: 'All these belonged to lovers of mine who cuckolded this *jinni*, so give me your own rings.' When they had handed them over, she went on: 'This *jinni* snatched me away on my wedding night and put me inside a box, which he placed inside this chest, with its seven heavy locks, and this, in turn, he put at the bottom of the tumultuous sea with its clashing waves. What he did not know was that, when a woman wants something, nothing can get the better of her, as a poet has said:

> Do not put your trust in women
> Or believe their covenants.
> Their satisfaction and their anger
> Both depend on their private parts.
> They make a false display of love,
> But their clothes are stuffed with treachery.
> Take a lesson from the tale of Joseph,
> And you will find some of their tricks.
> Do you not see that your father, Adam,
> Was driven out from Eden thanks to them?

Another poet has said:

> Blame must be matched to what is blamed;
> I have grown big, but my offence has not.
> I am a lover, but what I have done
> Is only what men did before me in old days.
> What is a cause for wonder is a man
> Whom women have not trapped by their allure.'

When the two kings heard this, they were filled with astonishment and said to each other: '*Jinni* though he may be, what has happened to him is worse than what happened to us and it is not something that anyone else has experienced.' They left the girl straight away and went back to Shahriyar's city, where they entered the palace and cut off the heads of the queen, the slave girls and the slaves.

Every night for the next three years, Shahriyar would take a virgin, deflower her and then kill her. This led to unrest among the citizens; they fled away with their daughters until there were no nubile girls left in the city. Then, when the vizier was ordered to bring the king a girl as usual, he searched but could not find a single one, and had to go home empty-handed, dejected and afraid of what the king might do to him.

This man had two daughters, of whom the elder was called Shahrazad and the younger Dunyazad. Shahrazad had read books and histories, accounts of past kings and stories of earlier peoples, having collected, it was said, a thousand volumes of these, covering peoples, kings and poets. She asked her father what had happened to make him so careworn and sad, quoting the lines of a poet:

Say to the careworn man: 'Care does not last,
And as joy passes, so does care.'

When her father heard this, he told her all that had happened between him and the king from beginning to end, at which she said: 'Father, marry me to this man. Either I shall live or else I shall be a ransom for the children of the Muslims and save them from him.' 'By God,' he exclaimed, 'you are not to risk your life!' She insisted that it had to be done, but he objected: 'I'm afraid that you may experience what happened to the donkey and the bull with the merchant.' 'What was that,' she asked, 'and what happened to the two of them?' HER FATHER TOLD HER:

You must know, my daughter, that a certain merchant had both wealth and animals and had been given by Almighty God a knowledge of the languages of beasts and birds. He lived in the country and had at home a donkey and a bull. One day the bull went to the donkey's quarters and found them swept out and sprinkled with water; there was sieved barley and straw in his trough, while the donkey was lying there at his ease. At times his master would ride him out on some errand, but he would then be taken back.

One day the merchant heard the bull say to the donkey: 'I congratulate you. Here am I, tired out, while you are at your ease, eating sieved barley. On occasion the master puts you to use, riding on you but then bringing you back again, whereas I am always ploughing and grinding corn.' The donkey replied: 'When they put the yoke on your neck and want to take you out to the fields, don't get up, even if they beat you, or else get up and then lie down again. When they bring you back and put beans down for you, pretend to be sick and don't eat them; for one, two or three days neither eat nor drink and you will have a rest from your hard labour.'

The next day, when the herdsman brought the bull his supper, the creature only ate a little and next morning, when the man came to take the bull out to do the ploughing, he found him sick and said sadly: 'This was why he could not work properly yesterday.' He went to the merchant and told him: 'Master, the bull is unwell and didn't eat any of his food yesterday evening.' The merchant realized what had happened and said: 'Go and take the donkey to do the ploughing all day in his place.'

When the donkey came back in the evening after having been used for ploughing all day, the bull thanked him for his kindness in having given him a day's rest, to which the donkey, filled with the bitterest regret, made no reply. The next morning, the herdsman came and took him out to plough until evening, and when the donkey got back, his neck had been rubbed raw and he was half dead with tiredness. When the bull saw him, he thanked and praised him, but the donkey said: 'I was sitting at my ease, but was unable to mind my own business.' Then he went on: 'I have some advice to give you. I heard our master say that, if you don't get up, you are to be given to the butcher to be slaughtered, and your hide is to be cut into pieces. I am afraid for you and so I have given you this advice.'

When the bull heard what the donkey had to say, he thanked him and said: 'Tomorrow I'll go out with the men.' He then finished off all his food, using his tongue to lick the manger. While all this was going on, the merchant was listening to what the animals were saying. The next morning, he and his wife went out and sat by the byre as the herdsman arrived and took the bull out. When the bull saw his master, he flourished his tail, farted and galloped off, leaving the man laughing so much that he collapsed on the ground. His wife asked why, and he told her: 'I was laughing because of something secret that I saw and heard, but I can't tell you or else I shall die.' 'Even if you do die,' she insisted, 'you must tell me the reason for this.' He repeated that he could not do it for fear of death, but she said: 'You were laughing at me,' and she went on insisting obstinately until she got the better of him. In distress, he summoned his children and sent for the *qadi* and the notaries with the intention of leaving his final instructions before telling his wife the secret and then dying. He had a deep love for her, she being his cousin and the mother of his children, while he himself was a hundred and twenty years old.

When all his family and his neighbours were gathered together, he explained that he had something to say to them, but that if he told the secret to anyone, he would die. Everyone there urged his wife not to press him and so bring about the death of her husband and the father of her children, but she said: 'I am not going to stop until he tells me, and I shall let him die.' At that, the others stayed silent while the merchant got up and went to the byre to perform the ritual ablution, after which he would return to them and die.

The merchant had a cock and fifty hens, together with a dog, and he heard the dog abusing the cock and saying: 'You may be cheerful, but here is our master about to die.' When the cock asked why this was, the dog told him the whole story. 'By God,' exclaimed the cock, 'he must be weak in the head. I have fifty wives and I keep them contented and at peace while he has only one but still can't keep her in order. Why doesn't he get some mulberry twigs, take her into a room and beat her until she either dies or repents and doesn't ask him again?'

The vizier now said to his daughter Shahrazad: 'I shall treat you as that man treated his wife.' 'What did he do?' she asked, AND HE WENT ON:

When he heard what the cock had to say to the dog, he cut some mulberry twigs and hid them in a room, where he took his wife. 'Come,' he said, 'so that I can speak to you in here and then die with no one looking on.' She went in with him and he locked the door on her and started beating her until she fainted. 'I take it all back,' she then said, and she kissed his hands and feet, and after she had repented, she and her husband went out to the delight of their family and the others there. They lived in the happiest of circumstances until their deaths.

Shahrazad listened to what her father had to say, but she still insisted on her plan and so he decked her out and took her to King Shahriyar. She had given instructions to her younger sister, Dunyazad, explaining: 'When I go to the king, I shall send for you. You must come, and when you see that the king has done what he wants with me, you are to say: "Tell me a story, sister, so as to pass the waking part of the night." I shall then tell you a tale that, God willing, will save us.'

Shahrazad was now taken by her father to the king, who was pleased to see him and said: 'Have you brought what I want?' When the vizier said yes, the king was about to lie with Shahrazad but she shed tears and when he asked her what was wrong, she told him: 'I have a young sister and I want to say goodbye to her.' At that, the king sent for Dunyazad, and when she had embraced Shahrazad, she took her seat beneath the bed, while the king got up and deflowered her sister. They then sat talking and Dunyazad asked Shahrazad to tell a story to pass the waking hours of the night. 'With the greatest pleasure,' replied Shahrazad, 'if our cultured king gives me permission.' The king was restless and when he heard what the sisters had to say, he was glad at the thought of listening to a story and so he gave his permission to Shahrazad.

Night 1

SHAHRAZAD SAID:

I have heard, O fortunate king, that a wealthy merchant, who had many dealings throughout the lands, rode out one day to settle a matter of business in one of them. When it became hot, he sat down under a tree and put his hand in his saddlebag, from which he took out a piece of bread and a date. He ate and when he had finished with the date he threw away its stone, at which a huge *'ifrit* appeared, with a drawn sword in his hand. This *'ifrit* came up to the merchant and said: 'Get up so that I can kill you as you killed my son.' 'How did I kill your son?' asked the merchant, and the *'ifrit* told him: 'When you ate that date and threw away the stone, it struck my son in the chest as he was walking, and he died instantly.' 'We belong to God and to Him do we return,' recited the merchant, adding: 'There is no might and no power except with God, the Exalted, the Omnipotent. If I killed him, this was by accident, so please forgive me.' 'I must kill you,' insisted the *'ifrit*, and he dragged off the merchant, threw him down on the ground and raised his sword to strike.

With tears in his eyes, the merchant exclaimed: 'I entrust my affair to God!' and he then recited these lines:

Time is two days, one safe and one of peril,
And our lives are of two halves, one fair, one overcast.
Say to those who reproach us for what Time has done:
'Does Time oppose any but great men?'
Do you not see that when the storm winds blow,
It is the tall trees that they strike?
Corpses rise to the surface of the sea,
While it is in its depths that pearls lie hid.
It may be that Time will mishandle us,
Subjecting us to constant harm.
Though in the heavens there are countless stars,
Only the sun and moon suffer eclipse.
There are both green and dry boughs on the earth,
But we throw stones only at those with fruit.
You think well of the days when they are fine,
So do not fear the evil that fate brings.

When he had finished, the *'ifrit* said: 'Stop talking, for, by God, I am most certainly going to kill you.' '*Ifrit*,' the merchant said, 'I am a wealthy man, with a wife and children; I have debts and I hold deposits, so let me go home and give everyone their due before returning to you at the start of the new year. I shall take a solemn oath and swear by God that I shall come back to you and you can then do what you want with me. God will be the guarantor of this.' The *'ifrit* trusted him and let him go, after which he went home, settled all his affairs, and gave everyone what was owed them. He told his wife and children what had happened, gave them his injunctions and stayed with them until the end of the year, when he got up, performed the ritual ablution and, with his shroud under his arm, said goodbye to his family and all his relations as well as his neighbours, and set off reluctantly, while they all wept and wailed. He came to the orchard on what was New Year's Day, and as he sat there weeping over his fate, a very old man approached him, leading a gazelle on a chain. The newcomer greeted him and asked him why he was sitting there alone, when the place was a haunt of *jinn*. The merchant told the story of his encounter with the *'ifrit*, and the old man exclaimed: 'By God, brother, you are a very pious man and your story is so wonder-ful that were it written with needles on the corners of men's eyes, it would be a lesson for those who take heed.'

He took his seat by the merchant's side and promised not to leave until he had seen what happened to him with the *'ifrit*. As the two of them sat there talking, the merchant was overcome by an access of fear together with ever-increasing distress and apprehension. It was at this point that a second old man arrived, having with him two black Salukis. After greeting the two men, he asked them why they were sitting in this haunt of *jinn* and they told him the story from beginning to end. No sooner had he sat down with them than a third old man, with a dappled mule, came up, greeted them and asked why they were there, at which they repeated the whole story – but there is no point in going over it again.

As soon as the newcomer had sat down, a huge dust-devil appeared in the middle of the desert, clearing away to show the *'ifrit* with a drawn sword in his hand and sparks shooting from his eyes. He came up to the three, dragged the merchant from between them and said: 'Get up so that I can kill you as you killed my beloved son.' The merchant sobbed and wept, while the three old men shed tears, wailed and lamented. Then the first of them, the man with the gazelle, left the others, kissed the *'ifrit*'s hand and said: '*Jinni*, royal crown of the *jinn*, if I tell you the story of my connection with this gazelle, will you grant me a third share in this merchant's blood?' The *'ifrit* agreed to do this if he found the story marvellous, AND SO THE OLD MAN BEGAN HIS TALE:

Know, *'ifrit*, that this gazelle is my cousin, my own flesh and blood. I married her when she was still young and stayed with her for thirty years without her bearing me a child. So I took a concubine and she bore me a son, the perfection of whose eyes and eyebrows made him look like the full moon when it appears. He grew up and when he was fifteen I had occasion to travel to a certain city, taking with me a great quantity of trade goods. My wife, now this gazelle, had studied sorcery since her youth and she turned the boy into a calf and his mother into a cow, handing them over to the herdsman. When, after a long absence, I got back from my journey, I asked about the two of them and my wife told me that the woman had died and that the boy had run away, where she did not know.

For a year I remained sad at heart and tearful until 'Id al-Adha came round and I sent to tell the herdsman to bring me a fat cow. What he brought me was my slave girl whom my wife had enchanted. I tucked up my clothes, took the knife in my hand and was about to slaughter her, when she gave a cry, howled and shed tears. This astonished me and, feeling pity for her, I left her and told the herdsman to fetch me another. At that my wife called out: 'Kill this one, as I have no finer or fatter cow.' I went up again to do the killing and again the cow gave a cry, at which I told the herdsman to slaughter her and then skin her. He did this, only to discover that there was neither flesh nor fat in the carcass, but only skin and bone. I was sorry for what I had done at a time when regret was of no use, and I gave the cow to the herdsman, telling him to bring me a fat calf. He brought me my son, and when this 'calf' caught sight of me, he broke his tether and rolled in the dust in front of me, howling and shedding tears. Again I felt pity and told the herdsman to leave the calf and fetch me a cow, and again my wife, now this gazelle, called to me, insisting that I must slaughter the calf that day. 'This is a noble and a blessed day,' she pointed out. 'The sacrifice must be a good one and we have nothing fatter or finer than this calf.' 'Look at what happened with the cow that you told me to kill. This led to a disappointment and we got no good from it at all, leaving me full of regret at having slaughtered it. This time I am not going to do what you say or kill this calf.' 'By God the Omnipotent, the Compassionate, the Merciful, you must do this on this noble day, and if you don't, then you are not my husband and I am not your wife.' On hearing these harsh words, but not realizing what she intended to do, I went up to the calf with the knife in my hand.

Morning now dawned and Shahrazad broke off from what she had been allowed to say. 'What a good, pleasant, delightful and sweet story this is!' exclaimed Dunyazad, at which Shahrazad told her: 'How can this compare with what I shall tell you this coming night, if I am still alive and the king spares me?' 'By God,' the king said to himself, 'I am not going to kill her until I hear the rest of the story,' and so they spent the rest of the time embracing one another until the sun had fully risen. The king then went to his court as the vizier came with the shroud under his arm, and he gave his judgements, appointing some officials and dismissing others, until evening, but to the vizier's great surprise he gave no instructions about his daughter. The court was then dismissed and King Shahriyar returned to his palace.

Night 2

When it was the second night, Dunyazad said to Shahrazad: 'Sister, finish your story of the merchant and the *'ifrit* for us.' 'With pleasure,' replied Shahrazad, 'if the king gives me permission,' and when the king gave it, SHE WENT ON:

I have heard, O fortunate king and rightly guided ruler, that when the merchant was about to cut the throat of the calf, he was moved by pity and told the herdsman to keep the calf among the other beasts.

The *'ifrit* was listening with astonishment to what the old man with the gazelle was saying, AND THE MAN WENT ON:

Lord of the kings of the *jinn*, while all this was going on, my wife, now this gazelle, was looking on and telling me to kill the calf, because it was fat, but I could not bring myself to do this and so I told the herdsman to take it away, which he did. The next day, as I was sitting there, he came back to me and said: 'I have something to tell you that will please you, and you owe me a reward for my good news.' I agreed to this and he went on: 'Master, I have a daughter who, as a young girl, was taught magic by an old woman we had staying with us. Yesterday when you gave me the calf, I went to the girl and, when she saw it, she covered her face, shed tears but then burst into laughter. Then she said: "Father, do you hold me so cheap that you bring strange men in to me?" "Where are these strange men," I asked, "and why are you laughing and crying?" She said: "This calf you have with you is our master's son, who is under a spell laid upon him and his mother by his father's wife. This is why I was laughing, but the reason why I wept was that his father killed his mother." I was astonished by this and as soon as I found that it was morning, I came to tell you.'

When I heard what the man had to say, I went out with him, drunk, although not on wine, with the joy and delight that I was feeling. When I got to his house his daughter welcomed me, kissing my hands, while the calf came and rolled on the ground in front of me. I asked her: 'Is what you say about this calf true?' 'Yes, master,' she assured me. 'This is your darling son.' 'Girl,' I told her, 'if you free him, you can have all the beasts and everything else that your father looks after.' She smiled and said: 'Master, I only want this on two conditions, the first being that you marry me to him and the second that I be allowed to put a spell on the one who enchanted him and keep her confined, for otherwise I shall not be safe from her scheming.'

When I heard what she had to say, I promised to give her what she wanted as well as everything that was in her father's charge, adding that I would even give her permission to kill my wife. At that, she took a bowl, filled it with water and recited a spell over it, after which she sprinkled the water over the calf, saying: 'If you are a calf and this is how Almighty God created you, stay in this shape and don't change, but if you are under a spell, then return to your original shape with the permission of Almighty God.' The calf shuddered and became a man, at which I fell on him and said: 'For God's sake, tell me what my wife did to you and your mother.' He told me what had happened, and I said: 'My son, God has sent you a rescuer to restore your rights.' I then married the herdsman's daughter to him and she transformed my wife into this gazelle, saying: 'This is a beautiful shape and not a brutish one, repellent to the sight.'

The girl stayed with us for some time until God chose to take her to Himself and my son went off to India, the country of the man with whom you have had this experience. I myself took my wife, this gazelle, and have travelled from place to place looking for news of him until fate brought me here and I saw this merchant sitting weeping. This is my story.

'It is indeed a marvellous tale,' the *'ifrit* agreed, 'and I grant you a third share in his blood.'

At this point, the old man with the two Salukis came up and asked the *'ifrit*: 'If I tell you what happened to me and my brothers, these two dogs, and you find it the most amazing and astonishing of stories, will you transfer to me a third of this man's offence?' The *'ifrit* agreed AND THE MAN BEGAN:

Lord of the kings of the *jinn*, these two dogs are my brothers, I being the third. On his death my father left us three thousand dinars and each one of us opened a shop for trade. I had not been there for long before my eldest brother, now one of these dogs, sold the contents of his shop for a thousand dinars, bought trade goods and set off on his travels.

He had been away for a whole year when one day as I was in my shop a beggar came up to me and stopped. I wished him well, but he said, in tears: 'Don't you know me any more?' When I looked at him closely, I saw that this was my brother and so I got up to welcome him and brought him into the shop. I asked him how he was and he said: 'Don't ask. My wealth has gone and my circumstances have changed.' I took him to the baths, gave him some of my own clothes and then brought him back home. Then I checked my accounts and the sales figures of my shop and I found that I had made a profit of a thousand dinars on a capital of two thousand. I divided this with my brother, telling him to forget that he had ever travelled abroad. He took the money gladly and opened another shop.

Some time later, my second brother, now this other dog, sold everything he had, with the intention of travelling. We tried unsuccessfully to stop him, but he bought trade goods and set out with some others. He too spent a whole year away before coming back to me in the same state as his brother. 'Brother,' I told him, 'didn't I tell you not to go?' But he replied: 'This was something decreed by fate, and here am I, a poor man, penniless and without even a shirt.' I took him to the baths and gave him a new suit of my own clothes to put on, before bringing him to my shop, where we then ate and drank. I told him: 'Brother, I check the accounts of my shop once every new year and any surplus I find I shall share with you.' When I did my audit, I found that I had two thousand dinars, and after praising the Exalted Creator, I gave him a thousand and kept the other thousand myself.

My brother opened another shop, but after a time he and my other brother proposed that I should go off with them on a voyage. I refused, asking: 'What did you get from your travels to make me imagine that I could make a profit?' I refused to listen to them and we stayed there trading in our shops. Every year they would make the same proposal to me and I would not agree, until after six years I finally accepted and told them I would go with them. I asked them to show me what money they had, only to find that they had nothing at all, having squandered everything on food, drink and entertainment. I didn't say a word to them but checked the accounts of my shop and sold what I owned together with all my shop goods, leaving me, to my delight, with a total of six thousand dinars. I divided this in half, telling my brothers that they and I could have three thousand dinars with which to trade, while I would bury the remaining three thousand in case the same thing happened to me as had happened to them. In that case I would have money left over to allow us to reopen our shops. They agreed to this and I handed each of them a thousand dinars, keeping a thousand for myself.

We provided ourselves with what we had to have in the way of trade goods and made our preparations for travel, hiring a ship and loading our goods on board. After a whole month's journey we brought them to a city, where they fetched us a ten-fold profit. We were about to sail off again when on the shore we came across a girl dressed in rags and tatters. She kissed my hand and asked if I was a charitable man, in which case she would reward me. 'I love charity and good deeds,' I told her, 'even if you give me no reward.' 'Marry me, master,' she said, 'and take me to your country. I have given myself to you; treat me kindly, for I am someone who deserves kindness and generosity. I shall pay you back for this and don't be misled by the state I am in now.'

When I heard this, I felt a yearning for her, as God, the Great and Glorious, had decreed, and so I took her, gave her clothes and provided her with elegantly furnished accommodation on the ship. I treated her with respect and as our journey went on I fell so deeply in love with her that I could not bear to leave her by night or by day. In my concern for her I neglected my brothers, who grew jealous of me, envying my wealth and the quantity of my goods. They spent their time eyeing all this, and they discussed killing me and taking what I had, saying: 'Let us kill our brother and then all this will be ours.' Satan made this seem good to them and so, finding me alone and asleep by the side of my wife, they picked us both up and threw us overboard.

My wife woke; a shudder ran through her and she became an *'ifrita*. She then carried me to an island where she left me for a time before coming back at dawn and saying: 'I am your servant and it was I who saved your life by carrying you off, with the permission of Almighty God. You must know that I am one of the *jinn* and when I saw you I fell in love with you, as God had decreed. For I believe in Him and in His Apostle, may God bless him and give him peace. I came to you wearing rags, as you saw, but you married me and now I have saved you from drowning. I am angry with your brothers and will have to kill them.'

I was astonished to hear this and I thanked her for what she had done but forbade her to kill my brothers. I then told her the whole story of my dealings with them and this prompted her to say: 'Tonight I shall fly off to them, sink their ship and destroy them.' I implored her in God's Name not to do that, reminding her of the proverb that tells those who do good to those who wrong them – 'The evil-doer's own deeds are punishment enough for him' – and pointing out that, at all events, they were my brothers. She continued to insist, despite my pleading with her, and she then flew off with me and put me down on the roof of my own house. I opened the doors, brought out the money that I had buried and opened up my shop, after greeting the people there and buying goods for trade.

When I went home that evening, I found these two dogs tied up and when they caught sight of me they came up with tears in their eyes and attached themselves to me. Before I realized what was happening, my wife told me: 'These are your brothers.' 'Who did this to them?' I asked, and she said: 'I sent a message to my sister; it was she who transformed them, and they will not be freed from the spell for ten years.' My brothers have now been like this for ten years and I was on my way to get them released when I came across this man. He told me his story and I decided not to leave him until I saw what was going to happen between you and him. This is my tale.

'It is a marvellous one,' agreed the *'ifrit*, adding: 'I grant you a third share in the blood he owes for his crime.'

The third old man, with the mule, now said: 'If I tell you a more amazing story than these two, will you grant me the remaining share?' The *'ifrit* agreed AND THE MAN WENT ON:

Sultan and leader of the *jinn*, this mule was my wife. I had been away for a year on my travels, and when I had finished I came back to her. This was at night and I saw a black slave lying in bed with her; the two of them talked, flirted, laughed, kissed and played with each other. My wife caught sight of me and came to me with a jug of water over which she uttered a spell. She sprinkled the water over me and said: 'Leave this shape of yours and take the form of a dog.' Immediately I became a dog and she drove me out through the door of the house.

I went on until I came to a butcher's shop, where I started gnawing bones. The butcher saw me and took me into his house, where his daughter covered her face from me and said: 'Are you bringing a man in to me?' 'Where is there a man?' asked her father, and she said: 'This dog is a man over whom his wife has cast a spell, but I can free him from it.' 'Do that, for God's sake,' said her father, and she took a jug of water, spoke some words over it and sprinkled some of it on me. 'Go back to your original shape,' she said, and that is what I did.

I kissed the girl's hand and said: 'I would like you to use your magic to do to my wife what she did to me.' She gave me some water and told me: 'When you find her asleep, sprinkle this water over her and say what you like, for she will become whatever you want.' I took the water and went to my wife, whom I found sleeping. I sprinkled her with the water and said: 'Leave this shape and become a mule,' which she did there and then, and it is she whom you can see, sultan and chief of the kings of the *jinn*.

*

'Is that true?' the man asked the mule, at which it nodded its head, conveying by gesture the message: 'That is my story and that is what happened to me.' When the old man had finished his tale, the *'ifrit*, trembling with delight, granted him a third of the merchant's blood.

Morning now dawned and Shahrazad broke off from what she had been allowed to say. 'What a good, pleasant, delightful and sweet story this is!' exclaimed Dunyazad, at which Shahrazad told her: 'How can this compare with what I shall tell you this coming night, if I am still alive and the king spares me?' 'By God,' the king said to himself, 'I am not going to kill her until I hear the rest of this remarkable story,' and so they spent the rest of the time embracing one another until the sun had fully risen. The king then went to his court; the troops arrived together with the vizier, and when everyone was there, he gave his judgements, appointing some officials, dismissing others, and issuing orders and prohibitions until evening. The court was then dismissed and the king returned to his palace, where, when night came, he lay again with Shahrazad.

Night 3

When it was the third night, Dunyazad asked her sister to finish the story. 'With pleasure,' said Shahrazad and went on: 'I have heard, O fortunate king, that the third old man told the *'ifrit* a more remarkable story than the other two, and that in his astonishment and delight the *'ifrit* granted him the remaining share of the blood debt and allowed the merchant to go free. For his part, the merchant went and thanked the old men, who congratulated him on his safety, after which each of them went home. This, however, is not more surprising than the tale of the fisherman.' When the king asked what that was, SHE WENT ON:

I have heard, O fortunate king, that there once was a poor, elderly fisherman with a wife and three children, who was in the habit of casting his net exactly four times each day. He went out to the shore at noon one day, put down his basket, tucked up his shirt, waded into the sea and cast his net. He waited until it had sunk down before pulling its cords together and then, finding it heavy, he tried unsuccessfully to drag it in. He took one end of it to the shore and fixed it to a peg that he drove in there, after which he stripped and dived into the sea beside it, where he continued tugging until he managed to get it up. He climbed out delightedly, put his clothes back on and went up to the net, only to find that what was in it was a dead donkey, and that the donkey had made a hole in the net. The fisherman was saddened by this and recited the formula: 'There is no might and no power except with God, the Exalted, the Omnipotent,' before saying: 'This is a strange thing that God has given me by way of food!' and then reciting:

> You who court danger, diving in the dark of night,
> Give up; your efforts do not win your daily bread from God.
> The fisherman rises to earn his keep;
> There is the sea, with stars woven in the sky.
> He plunges in, buffeted by waves,
> His eyes fixed on his billowing net.
> Happy with his night's work, he takes back home
> A fish, its jaw caught up on his pronged hook.
> This fish is bought from him by one who spent his night
> Out of the cold, enjoying his comforts.
> Praise be to God, Who gives and Who deprives;
> For one man eats the fish; another catches it.

He encouraged himself, saying that Almighty God would show favour and reciting:

> When you are faced with hardship, clothe yourself
> In noble patience; that is more resolute.
> Do not complain, then, to God's servants; you complain
> To those who have no mercy of the Merciful.

He freed the donkey from the net, which he then wrung out before spreading it out again and going back into the sea. Invoking the Name of God, he made another cast, waited until the net had settled, and found it heavier and more difficult to move than before. Thinking that it must be full of fish, he fastened it to his peg, stripped off his clothes and dived in to free it. After tugging at it he got it up on shore, only to discover that what was in it was a large jar full of sand and mud. Saddened by this sight, he recited:

> Troubles of Time, give up!
> Stop, even if you have not had enough.
> I came out looking for my daily bread,

But I have found there is no more of this.
How many a fool reaches the Pleiades!
How many wise men lie hidden in the earth!

The fisherman threw away the jar, wrung out his net, cleaned it and went back a third time to the sea, asking God to forgive him. He made his cast and waited for the net to settle before drawing it in, and this time what he found in it were bits of pots, bottles and bones. He was furious and, shedding bitter tears, he recited:

You have no power at all over your daily bread;
Neither learning nor letters will fetch it for you.
Fortune and sustenance are divided up;
One land is fertile while another suffers drought.
Time's changes bring down cultured men,
While fortune lifts the undeserving up.
Come, death, and visit me, for life is vile;
Falcons are brought down low while ducks are raised on high.
Feel no surprise if you should see a man of excellence
In poverty, while an inferior holds sway.
One bird circles the earth from east to west;
Another gets its food but does not have to move.

He then looked up to heaven and said: 'O my God, You know that I only cast my net four times a day. I have done this thrice and got nothing, so this time grant me something on which to live.' He pronounced the Name of God and cast his net into the sea. He waited until it had settled and then he tried to pull it in, but found that it had snagged on the bottom. He recited the formula: 'There is no power and no might except with God,' and went on:

How wretched is this kind of world
That leaves us in such trouble and distress!
In the morning it may be that things go well,
But I must drink destruction's cup when evening comes.
Yet when it is asked who leads the easiest life,
Men would reply that this was I.

The fisherman stripped off his clothes and, after diving in, he worked his hardest to drag the net to shore. Then, when he opened it up, he found in it a brass bottle with a lead seal, imprinted with the inscription of our master Solomon, the son of David, on both of whom be peace. The fisherman was delighted to see this, telling himself that it would fetch ten gold dinars if he sold it in the brass market. He shook it and, discovering that it was heavy as well as sealed, he said to himself: 'I wonder what is in it? I'll open it up and have a look before selling it.' He took out a knife and worked on the lead until he had removed it from the bottle, which he then put down on the ground, shaking it in order to pour out its contents. To his astonishment, at first nothing came out, but then there emerged smoke which towered up into the sky and spread over the surface of the ground. When it had all come out, it collected and solidified; a tremor ran through it and it became an 'ifrit with his head in the clouds and his feet on the earth. His head was like a dome, his hands were like winnowing forks and his feet like ships' masts. He had a mouth like a cave with teeth like rocks, while his nostrils were like jugs and his eyes like lamps. He was dark and scowling.

When he saw this 'ifrit the fisherman shuddered; his teeth chattered; his mouth dried up and he could not see where he was going. At the sight of him the 'ifrit exclaimed: 'There is no god but the God of Solomon, His prophet. Prophet of God, do not kill me for I shall never disobey you again in word or in deed.' ''Ifrit,' the fisherman said, 'you talk of Solomon, the prophet of God, but Solomon died eighteen hundred years ago and we are living in the last age of the world. What is your story and how did you come to be in this bottle?' To which the 'ifrit replied: 'There is no god but God. I have good news for you, fisherman.' 'What is that?' the fisherman asked, and the 'ifrit said: 'I am now going to put you to the worst of deaths.' 'For this good news, leader of the 'ifrits,' exclaimed the fisherman, 'you deserve that God's protection be removed from you, you damned creature. Why should you kill me and what have I done to deserve this? It was I who saved you from the bottom of the sea and brought you ashore.'

But the 'ifrit said: 'Choose what death you want and how you want me to kill you.' 'What have I done wrong,' asked the fisherman, 'and why are you punishing me?' The 'ifrit replied: 'Listen to my story,' and the fisherman said: 'Tell it, but keep it short as I am at my last gasp.' 'Know, fisherman,' the 'ifrit told him, 'that I was one of the apostate jinn, and that together with Sakhr, the jinni, I rebelled against Solomon, the son of David, on both of whom be peace. Solomon sent his vizier, Asaf, to fetch me to him under duress, and I was forced to go with him in a state of humiliation to stand before Solomon. "I take refuge with God!" exclaimed Solomon when he saw me, and he then offered me conversion to the Faith and proposed that I enter his service. When I refused, he called for this bottle, in which he imprisoned me, sealing it with lead and imprinting on it the Greatest Name of God. Then, at his command, the *jinn* carried me off and threw me into the middle of the sea.

'For a hundred years I stayed there, promising myself that I would give whoever freed me enough wealth to last him for ever, but the years passed and no one rescued me. For the next hundred years I told myself that I would open up all the treasures of the earth for my rescuer, but still no one rescued me. Four hundred years later, I promised that I would grant three wishes, but when I still remained imprisoned, I became furiously angry and said to myself that I would kill whoever saved me, giving him a choice of how he wanted to die. It is you who are my rescuer, and so I allow you this choice.'

When the fisherman heard this, he exclaimed in wonder at his bad luck in freeing the *'ifrit* now, and he went on: 'Spare me, may God spare you, and do not kill me lest God place you in the power of one who will kill you.' 'I must kill you,' insisted the *'ifrit*, 'and so choose how you want to die.' Ignoring this, the fisherman made another appeal, calling on the *'ifrit* to show gratitude for his release. 'It is only because you freed me that I am going to kill you,' repeated the *'ifrit*, at which the fisherman said: 'Lord of the *'ifrits*, I have done you good and you are repaying me with evil. The proverbial lines are right where they say:

We did them good; they did its opposite,
And this, by God, is how the shameless act.
Whoever helps those who deserve no help,
Will be like one who rescues a hyena.'

'Don't go on so long,' said the *'ifrit* when he heard this, 'for death is coming to you.' The fisherman said to himself: 'This is a *jinni* and I am a human. God has given me sound intelligence which I can use to find a way of destroying him, whereas he can only use vicious cunning.' So he asked: 'Are you definitely going to kill me?' and when the *'ifrit* confirmed this, he said: 'I conjure you by the Greatest Name inscribed on the seal of Solomon and ask you to give me a truthful answer to a question that I have.' 'I shall,' replied the *'ifrit*, who had been shaken and disturbed by the mention of the Greatest Name, and he went on: 'Ask your question but be brief.' The fisherman went on: 'You say you were in this bottle, but there is not room in it for your hand or your foot, much less all the rest of you.' 'You don't believe that I was in it?' asked the *'ifrit*, to which the fisherman replied: 'I shall never believe it until I see it with my own eyes.'

Morning now dawned and Shahrazad broke off from what she had been allowed to say.

Night 4

When it was the fourth night, Dunyazad asked her to finish the story, if she was not sleepy, AND SO SHE WENT ON:

I have heard, O fortunate king, that when the fisherman told the *'ifrit* that he would not believe him until he saw this with his own eyes, a shudder ran through the *'ifrit* and he became a cloud of smoke hovering over the sea. Then the smoke coalesced and entered the jar bit by bit until it was all there. Quickly the fisherman picked up the brass stopper with its inscription and put it over the mouth of the bottle. He called out to the *'ifrit*: 'Ask me how you want to die. By God, I am going to throw you into the sea and then build myself a house in this place so that I can stop anyone who comes fishing by telling them that there is an *'ifrit* here who gives anyone who brings him up a choice of how he wants to be killed.'

When the *'ifrit* heard this and found himself imprisoned in the bottle, he tried to get out but could not, as he was prevented by Solomon's seal, and he realized that the fisherman had tricked him. 'I was only joking,' he told the fisherman, who replied: 'You are lying, you most despicable, foulest and most insignificant of *'ifrits*,' and he took up the bottle. 'No, no,' called the *'ifrit*, but the fisherman said: 'Yes, yes,' at which the *'ifrit* asked him mildly and humbly what he intended to do with him. 'I am going to throw you into the sea,' the fisherman told him. 'You may have been there for eighteen hundred years, but I shall see to it that you stay there until the Last Trump. Didn't I say: "Spare me, may God spare you, and do not kill me lest God place you in the power of one who will kill you"? But you refused and acted treacherously towards me. Now God has put you in my power and I shall do the same to you.' 'Open the bottle,' implored the *'ifrit*, 'so that I can do you good.' 'Damned liar,' said the fisherman. 'You and I are like the vizier of King Yunan and Duban the sage.' 'What is their story?' asked the *'ifrit*, AND THE FISHERMAN REPLIED:

You must know, *'ifrit*, that once upon a time in the old days in the land of Ruman there was a king called Yunan in the city of Fars. He was a wealthy and dignified man with troops and guards of all races, but he was also a leper, who had taken medicines of various kinds and used ointments, but whose illness doctors and men of learning had been unable to cure.

There was an elderly physician known as Duban the sage, who had studied the books of the Greeks, the Persians, the Arabs and the Syrians. He was a master of medicine and of astronomy and was conversant with the fundamental principles of his subject, with a knowledge of what was useful and what was harmful. He knew the herbs and plants that were hurtful and those that were helpful, as well as having a mastery of philosophy, together with all branches of medicine and other sciences. When this man arrived at the city, within a few days he had heard that the king was suffering from leprosy and that no doctor or man of learning had been able to cure him. He spent the night thinking over the problem, and when dawn broke he put on his most splendid clothes and went to the king, kissing the ground before him and calling eloquently for the continuance of his glory and good fortune. After introducing himself, he went on: 'I have heard, your majesty, of the disease that has afflicted you and that, although you have been treated by many doctors, they have been unable to remove it. I shall cure you without giving you any medicine to drink or applying any ointments.'

Yunan was amazed to hear what he had to say and asked how he was going to do that, promising to enrich him and his children's children. 'I shall shower favours on you,' he said, 'and grant you all your wishes, taking you as a boon companion and a dear friend.' He then presented Duban with a robe of honour and treated him with favour, before asking: 'Are you really going to cure my leprosy without medicines or ointment?' Duban repeated that he would and the astonished king asked when this would be, urging him to be quick. 'To hear is to obey,' replied Duban, promising to do this the very next day.

Duban now went to the city, where he rented a house in which he deposited his books, his medicines and his drugs. He took some of the latter and placed them in a polo stick, for which he made a handle, and he used his skill to design a ball. The next day, after he had finished, he went into the presence of the king, kissed the ground before him, and told him to ride out to the polo ground and play a game. The king was accompanied by the emirs, chamberlains, viziers and officers of state, and before he had taken his seat on the ground, Duban came up to him and handed him the stick. 'Take this,' he said. 'Hold it like this and when you ride on to the field, hit the ball with a full swing until the palm of your hand begins to sweat, together with the rest of your body. The drug will then enter through your palm and spread through the rest of you. When you have finished and the drug has penetrated, go back to your palace, wash in the baths and then go to sleep, for you will have been cured. That is all.'

At that, the king took the stick from him and mounted, holding it in his hand. He threw the ball ahead of him and rode after it, hitting it as hard as he could when he caught up with it, and then following it up and hitting it again until the palm of his hand and the rest of his body became sweaty because of his grip on the stick. When Duban saw that the drug had penetrated into the king's body, he told him to go back to his palace and bathe immediately. The king went back straight away and ordered that the baths be cleared for him. This was done, and house boys and mamluks hurried up to him and prepared clothes for him to wear. He then entered the baths, washed himself thoroughly and dressed before coming out, after which he rode back to his palace and fell asleep.

So much for him, but as for Duban the sage, he returned to spend the night in his house, and in the morning he went to ask permission to see the king. On being allowed to enter, he went in, kissed the ground before him and addressed him with these verses which he chanted:

Virtues are exalted when you are called their father,
A title that none other may accept.
The brightness shining from your face removes
The gloom that shrouds each grave affair.
This face of yours will never cease to gleam,
Although the face of Time may frown.
Your liberality has granted me the gifts
That rain clouds shower down on the hills.
Your generosity has destroyed your wealth,
Until you reached the heights at which you aimed.

When Duban had finished these lines, the king stood up and embraced him, before seating him by his side and presenting him with splendid robes of honour. This was because when he had left the baths he had looked at his body and found it, to his great delight and relief, pure and silver white, showing no trace of leprosy. In the morning, he had gone to his court and taken his seat on his royal throne, the chamberlains and officers of state all standing up for him, and it was then that Duban had come in. The king had risen quickly for him, and after the sage had been seated by his side, splendid tables of food were set out and he ate with the king and kept him company for the rest of the day. The king then made him a present of two thousand dinars, in addition to the robes of honour and other gifts, after which he mounted him on his own horse.

Duban went back to his house, leaving the king filled with admiration for what he had done and saying: 'This man treated me externally without using any ointment. By God, that is skill of a high order! He deserves gifts and favours and I shall always treat him as a friend and companion.' The king passed a happy night, gladdened by the soundness of his body and his freedom from disease. The next day, he went out and sat on his throne, while his state officials stood and the emirs and viziers took their seats on his right and his left. He asked for Duban, who entered and kissed the ground before him, at which the king got up, greeted him, seated him by his side and ate with him. He then presented him with more robes of honour as well as gifts, and talked with him until nightfall, when he gave him another five robes of honour together with a thousand dinars, after which Duban went gratefully home.

The next morning, the king came to his court, where he was surrounded by his emirs, viziers and chamberlains. Among the viziers was an ugly and ill-omened man, base, miserly and so envious that he was in love with envy. When this man saw that the king had taken Duban as an intimate and had rewarded him with favours, he was jealous and planned to do him an injury. For, as the sayings have it: 'No one is free of envy' and 'Injustice lurks in the soul; strength shows it and weakness hides it.'

This vizier came up to King Yunan, kissed the ground before him and said: 'King of the age, I have grown up surrounded by your bounty and I have some serious advice for you. Were I to conceal it from you, I would show myself to be a bastard, but if you tell me to give it to you, I shall do so.' Yunan was disturbed by this and said: 'What is this advice of yours?' The vizier replied: 'Great king, it was a saying of the ancients that Time was no friend to those who did not look at the consequences of their actions. I have observed that your majesty has wrongly shown favour to an enemy who is looking to destroy your kingdom. You have treated this man with generosity and done him the greatest honour, taking him as an intimate, something that fills me with apprehension.'

Yunan was uneasy; his colour changed and he asked the vizier who he was talking about. 'If you are asleep, wake up,' the vizier told him, and went on: 'I am talking about the sage Duban.' 'Damn you!' exclaimed Yunan. 'This is my friend and the dearest of people to me, for he cured me through something that I held in my hand from a disease that no other doctor could treat. His like is not to be found in this age or in this world, from west to east. You may accuse him, but today I am going to assign him pay and allowances, with a monthly income of a thousand dinars, while even if I divided my kingdom with him, this would be too little. I think that it is envy that has made you say this, reminding me of the story of King Sindbad.'

Morning now dawned and Shahrazad broke off from what she had been allowed to say.

Night 5

When it was the fifth night, Dunyazad asked her sister to finish the story if she was not too sleepy, AND SHAHRAZAD SAID:

I have heard, O fortunate king, that King Yunan accused his vizier of being jealous of Duban and wanting to have him killed. 'Then after that I would regret it,' Yunan added, 'as King Sindbad regretted killing his falcon.' 'Excuse me, your majesty,' said the vizier, 'but how was that?' YUNAN WENT ON:

You must know that there was a Persian king with a passion for enjoyment and amusement, who had a fondness for hunting. He had reared a falcon which was his constant companion by night and by day, and which would spend the night perched on his wrist. He would take it hunting with him and he had a golden bowl made for it which he hung round its neck and from which it could drink. One day the chief falconer came to where he was sitting and told him that it was time to go out hunting. The king gave the orders and went off with the falcon on his wrist until he and his party reached a *wadi*, where they spread out their hunting cordon. Trapped in this was a gazelle and the king threatened that anyone who allowed it to leap over his head would be put to death. When the cordon was narrowed, the gazelle came to where the king was posted, supported itself on its hindlegs and placed its forelegs on its chest as though it was kissing the ground before him. He bent his head towards it and it then jumped over him, making for the open country. He noticed that his men were looking at him and winking at each other and when he asked his vizier what this meant, the man explained: 'They are pointing out that you said that if anyone let the gazelle jump over his head, he would be killed.'

The king then swore that he would hunt it down and he rode off in pursuit, following the gazelle until he came to a mountain. There it was about to pass through a cleft when the king loosed his falcon at it and the bird clawed at its eyes, blinding and dazing it, so that the king could draw his mace and knock it over with a single blow. He then dismounted and cut its throat, after which he skinned it and tied it to his saddlebow. As this was in the noonday heat and the region was desolate and waterless, both the king and his horse were thirsty by now. The king scouted round and discovered a tree from which what looked like liquid butter was dripping. Wearing a pair of kid gloves, he took the bowl from the falcon's neck, filled it with this liquid and set it in front of the bird, but it knocked the bowl and overturned it. The king took it and filled it again, thinking that the falcon must be thirsty, but the same thing happened when he put it down a second time. This annoyed him and he went a third time to fill the bowl and take it to his horse, but this time the falcon upset it with its wing. The king cursed it, exclaiming: 'You unluckiest of birds, you have stopped me drinking, and have stopped yourself and the horse.' He then struck off its wing with a blow from his sword, but the bird raised its head as though to say by its gesture: 'Look at the top of the tree.' The king raised his eyes and what he saw there was a brood of vipers whose poison was dripping down. Immediately regretting what he had done, he mounted his horse and rode back to his pavilion, bringing with him the gazelle, which he handed to the cook, telling him to take it and roast it. As he sat on his chair with the falcon on his wrist, it drew its last breath and died, leaving its master to exclaim with sorrow for having killed it, when it had saved his life. So ends the story of King Sindbad.

'Great king,' the vizier said, 'Sindbad acted out of necessity and I can see nothing wrong in that. I myself am acting out of sympathy for you, so that you may realize that I am right, for otherwise you may meet the same fate as the vizier who schemed against the prince.' 'How was that?' the king asked, AND THE VIZIER SAID:

You must know, your majesty, that there was a vizier in the service of a certain king with a son who was passionately fond of hunting. This vizier had been ordered to accompany the prince wherever he went, and so, when he went off to hunt one day, the vizier rode with him. While they were riding they caught sight of a huge beast and the vizier encouraged the prince to pursue it. The prince rode after it until he was out of sight and the beast then vanished into the desert, leaving the prince with no idea of where to go. Just then, ahead of him he saw a weeping girl and when he asked her who she was, she told him: 'I am the daughter of one of the kings of India and while I was in this desert I became drowsy. Then, before I knew what was happening, I had fallen off my beast and was left alone, not knowing what to do.'

When the prince heard this, he felt sorry for the girl and took her up behind him on the back of his horse. On his way, he passed a ruined building and the girl said she wanted to relieve herself. He set her down, but she was taking so long that he followed her, only to discover that, although he had not realized it, she was a female *ghul* and was telling her children: 'I have brought you a fat young man today.' 'Fetch him to us, mother,' they said, 'so that we can swallow him down.' On hearing this, the prince shuddered, fearing for his life and certain that he was going to die. He went back and the *ghula* came out and, seeing him panic-stricken and shivering, she asked why he was afraid. 'I have an enemy whom I fear,' he told her. 'You call yourself a prince?' she asked, and when he said yes, she went on: 'Why don't you buy him off with money?' 'He won't accept money but wants my life,' he told her, adding: 'I am afraid of him and I have been wronged.' 'In that case, if what you say is true, then ask help from God,' she said, 'for He will protect you against your enemy's evil and the evil that you fear from him.' At that the prince lifted his head towards heaven and said: 'God Who answers the prayers of those in distress when they call on You, and Who clears away evil, may You help me against my enemy and remove him from me, for You have power to do what You wish.'

After hearing the prince's prayer, the *ghula* left him. He went back to his father and when he told him about the vizier's advice, his father summoned the man and had him killed. As for you, your majesty, if you put your trust in this sage, he will see to it that you die the worst of deaths, and it will be the man whom you have well treated and taken as a friend who will destroy you. Don't you see that he cured your disease externally through something you held in your hand, so how can you be sure that he won't kill you by something else you hold?

'What you say is right, vizier, my sound advisor,' agreed the king, 'for this man has come as a spy to destroy me and if he could cure me with something I held, it may be that he can kill me with something that I smell.'

Then he asked the vizier what was to be done about Duban. The vizier said: 'Send for him immediately, telling him to come here, and when he does, cut off his head and then you will be safe from any harm he may intend to do you. Betray him before he betrays you.' The king agreed with the vizier, and sent for Duban, who came gladly, not knowing what God the Merciful had ordained. This was as the poet said:

> You who fear your fate, be at your ease;
> Entrust your affairs to Him Who has stretched out the earth.
> What is decreed by fate will come about,
> And you are safe from what is not decreed.

Duban the wise came into the presence of the king and recited:

> If I do not show gratitude
> In accordance with part, at least, of your deserts,
> Tell me for whom I should compose my poetry and my prose.
> Before I asked, you granted me
> Favours that came with no delay and no excuse.
> Why then do I not give you your due of praise,
> Lauding your generosity in secret and in public?
> I shall record the benefits you heaped on me,
> Lightening my cares, but burdening my back.

He followed this with another poem:

> Turn aside from cares, entrusting your affairs to fate;
> Rejoice in the good that will come speedily to you,
> So that you may forget all that is past.
> There is many a troublesome affair
> Whose aftermath will leave you in content.
> God acts according to His will;
> Do not oppose your God.

He also recited:

> Leave your affairs to God, the Gentle, the Omniscient,
> And let your heart rest from all worldly care.
> Know that things do not go as you wish;
> They follow the decree of God, the King.

He then recited:

> Be of good cheer, relax; forget your cares;
> Cares eat away the resolute man's heart.
> Planning is no help to a slave who has no power.
> Abandon this and live in happiness.

The king asked him: 'Do you know why I have sent for you?' 'No one knows what is hidden except for God,' Duban replied. 'I have sent for you,' said the king, 'in order to kill you and take your life.' This astonished Duban, who said: 'Why should you kill me, your majesty, and what is my crime?' 'I have been told that you are a spy,' answered the king, 'and that you have come to murder me. I am going to kill you before you can do the same to me.' The king then called for the executioner and said: 'Cut off this traitor's head, so that we may be freed from his evil-doing.' 'Spare me,' said Duban, 'and God will spare you; do not kill me, lest He kill you.'

He then repeated what I repeated to you, *'ifrit*, but you would not give up your intention to kill me. Similarly, the king insisted: 'I shall not be safe unless I put you to death. You cured me with something that I held in my hand, and I cannot be sure that you will not kill me with something that I smell or in some other way.' Duban said: 'My reward from you, O king, is the reward of good by evil,' but the king insisted: 'You must be killed without delay.'

When Duban was certain that the king was going to have him killed, he wept in sorrow for the good that he had done to the undeserving, as the poet has said:

> You can be sure that Maimuna has no sense,
> Though this is what her father has.
> Whoever walks on dry or slippery ground,
> And takes no thought, must fall.

The executioner then came up, blindfolded him and unsheathed his sword, asking the king's permission to proceed. Duban was weeping and imploring the king: 'Spare me and God will spare you; do not slay me lest God slay you.' He recited:

I gave my good advice and yet had no success,
While they succeeded, but through treachery.
What I advised humiliated me.
If I live, never shall I give advice again;
If not, after my death let all advisors be accursed.

Then he said to the king: 'If this is how you reward me, it is the crocodile's reward.' The king asked for the story of the crocodile, but Duban replied: 'I cannot tell it to you while I am in this state. I conjure you by God to spare me so that God may spare you.' At that one of the king's courtiers got up and asked the king for Duban's life, pointing out: 'We have not seen that he has done you any wrong, but only that he cured you of a disease that no wise doctor was able to treat.' The king said: 'You do not know why I have ordered his death, but this is because, if I spare him, I shall certainly die. A man who cured me of my illness by something that I held in my hand is able to kill me by something that I smell. I am afraid that he has been bribed to murder me, as he is a spy and this is why he has come here. He must be executed, and after that I shall be safe.'

Duban repeated his plea for mercy, but on realizing that he could not escape execution, he said to the king: 'If I must be killed, allow me a delay so that I may return to my house, give instructions to my family and my neighbours about my funeral, settle my debts and give away my books of medicine. I have a very special book which I shall present to you to be kept in your treasury.' 'What is in the book?' asked the king. 'Innumerable secrets,' Duban replied, 'the least of which is that, if you cut off my head and then open three pages and read three lines from the left-hand page, my head will speak to you and answer all your questions.' The astonished king trembled with joy. 'When I cut off your head, will you really talk to me?' he asked. 'Yes,' said Duban. 'This is an amazing thing!' exclaimed the king, and he sent him off under escort.

Duban returned to his house and settled all his affairs, and then the next day he came back to the court, where all the viziers, chamberlains, deputies and officers of state assembled, until the place looked like a garden in flower. He entered and was brought before the king, carrying with him an old book together with a collyrium case containing powder. He sat down and asked for a plate, which was brought. He then poured the powder on it and spread it out, after which he said: 'King, take this book, but don't open it until you cut off my head. When you have done that, set the head on the plate and have it pressed into the powder. At that, the flow of blood will halt and you can then open the book.'

The king took the book from him and gave orders for his execution. The executioner cut off his head, which fell on the plate, where it was pressed down into the powder. The blood ceased to flow and Duban the wise opened his eyes and said: 'O king, open the book.' The king did this, but he found the pages stuck together, so he put his finger into his mouth, wet it with his spittle, and with difficulty he opened the first, the second and the third pages. He opened six pages in all, but when he looked at them, he could find nothing written there. 'Wise man,' he said, 'there is no writing here.' 'Open more pages,' said Duban. The king opened three more, but soon afterwards he felt the poison with which the book had been impregnated spreading through him. He was wracked by convulsions and cried out that he had been poisoned, while Duban recited:

> They wielded power with arrogance,
> But soon it was as though their power had never been.
> If they had acted justly, they would have met with justice,
> But they were tyrants and Time played the tyrant in return,
> Afflicting them with grievous trials.
> It was as though here fate was telling them:
> 'This is a return for that, and Time cannot be blamed.'

As soon as Duban's head had finished speaking, the king fell dead. Know then, 'ifrit, that had he spared Duban, God would have spared him, but as he refused and looked to have him killed, God destroyed him. Had you spared me, God would have spared you . . .

Night 6

Morning now dawned and Shahrazad broke off from what she had been allowed to say. Then, when it was the sixth night, her sister, Dunyazad, told her to finish the story and Shahrazad said: 'If the king permits me.' 'Go on,' he replied, AND SHE CONTINUED:

I have heard, O fortunate king, that the fisherman told the 'ifrit: 'Had you spared me, I would have spared you, but you wanted nothing but

my death and so now I am going to destroy you by throwing you into
the sea here, imprisoned in this bottle.' The *'ifrit* cried out: 'I implore
you, in God's Name, fisherman, don't do this! Spare me and don't punish
me for what I did. If I treated you badly, do you for your part treat me
well, as the proverb says: "You who do good to the evil-doer, know that
what he has done is punishment enough for him." Do not do what
'Umama did to 'Atika!' 'What was that?' asked the fisherman, but the
'ifrit said: 'I cannot talk while I am imprisoned, but if you let me out, I
shall tell you the story.' The fisherman said: 'Stop talking like this, for
I shall certainly throw you into the sea and I am never going to release
you. I pleaded with you and begged you, but all you wanted to do was
to kill me, although I had done nothing at all to deserve this and, far
from doing you any harm, I had helped you by freeing you from your
prison. When you did that to me, I realized that you were an evil-doer.
Be sure that, when I throw you into the sea, if anyone brings you out, I
will tell him what you did to me and warn him, so that he may throw
you back again and there you will stay until the end of time or until you
perish.' 'Free me,' pleaded the *'ifrit*. 'This is a time for generosity and I
promise you that I shall never act against you again but will help you by
making you rich.'

At this, the fisherman made the *'ifrit* promise that were he freed, far
from hurting his rescuer, he would help him. When the fisherman was
sure of this and had made the *'ifrit* swear by the greatest Name of God,
he opened the bottle and the smoke rose up, until it had all come out
and had formed into a hideous shape. The *'ifrit* then picked the bottle
up and hurled it into the sea, convincing the watching fisherman that he
was going to be killed. The man soiled his trousers, crying: 'This is not
a good sign!' but then his courage came back and he said: 'God Almighty
has said: "Fulfil your promise, for your promise will be questioned."*
You gave me your word, swearing that you would not act treacherously
to me, as otherwise God will do the same to you, for He is a jealous God
Who bides His time but does not forget. I say to you what Duban the
wise said to King Yunan: "Spare me and God will spare you."'

The *'ifrit* laughed and told the fisherman to follow him as he walked
ahead. This the fisherman did, scarcely believing that he was safe. The
pair of them left the city, climbed a mountain and then went down into
a wide plain. There they saw a pool, and after the *'ifrit* had waded into

* Quran 17.36.

the middle of it, he asked the fisherman to follow him, which he did. When the *'ifrit* stopped, he told the fisherman to cast his net, and the man was astonished to see that the pond contained coloured fish – white, red, blue and yellow. He took out his net, cast it and when he drew it in he found four fish, each a different colour. He was delighted by this, and the *'ifrit* said: 'Present these to the sultan and he will enrich you. Then I ask you in God's Name to excuse me, since at this time I know no other way to help you. I have been in the sea for eighteen hundred years and this is the first time that I have seen the face of the land.' After advising the fisherman not to fish the pool more than once a day, he took his leave, speaking words of farewell. Then he stamped his foot on the earth and a crack appeared into which he was swallowed.

The fisherman returned to the city, full of wonder at his encounter. He took the fish to his house, where he brought out an earthenware bowl, filled it with water and put them in it. As they wriggled about in the water, he placed the bowl on his head and went to the palace as the *'ifrit* had told him. When he came to the king and presented him with the fish, the king was astonished, for never in his life had he seen anything like them. He gave orders that they were to be handed over to a slave girl who was acting as cook but whose skill had not yet been tested, as she had been given him three days earlier by the king of Rum. The vizier told her to fry the fish, adding that the king had said that he was testing her only in the hour of need, and that he was putting his hopes in her artistry and cooking skills, for the fish had been given him as a present.

After issuing these instructions, the vizier went back to the king, who told him to hand the fisherman four hundred dinars. After he had passed over the money, the man stowed it inside his clothes and set off back home at a run, falling, getting up and then stumbling again, thinking that this was all a dream. He bought what was needed for his family and then returned to his wife in joy and delight.

So much for him, but as for the slave girl, she took the fish and cleaned them. Then, after setting the frying pan on the fire, she put the fish in it and when one side was properly cooked, she turned them on to the other. All of a sudden, the kitchen wall split open and out came a girl, with a beautiful figure and smooth cheeks, perfect in all her attributes. Her eyes were darkened with kohl and she had on a silken *kaffiyeh* with a blue fringe. She was wearing earrings; on her wrists were a pair of bracelets, while her fingers were adorned with rings set with precious gems, and in her hand she held a bamboo staff. Thrusting this into the pan, she asked: 'Fish, are you still faithful to your covenant?' at which the cook fainted. The girl repeated her question a second and a third time and the fish raised their heads from the pan and said: 'Yes, yes,' in clear voices, and then they recited:

> If you return, we return;
> If you keep faith, then so do we,
> But if you go off, we are quits.

At that, the girl turned the pan upside down with her staff and left through the hole from which she had come, after which the wall closed up behind her. The cook recovered from her faint and saw the four fish burned like black charcoal. She exclaimed: 'His spear was broken on his very first raid!' and fell unconscious again on the floor. While she was in this confused state, the vizier came and saw that something had gone badly wrong with her, so much so that she could not even tell what day of the week it was. He nudged her with his foot, and when she had recovered her senses, she explained to him, in tears, what had happened. He was astonished, and exclaimed: 'This is something wonderful!' He then sent for the fisherman and, when he was brought in, the vizier told him to fetch another four fish like the first ones.

The fisherman went to the pool, cast his net and when he drew it in, there were four fish like the first. He took them to the vizier, who brought them to the cook and said: 'Fry these in front of me so that I can see what happens.' The cook got up, prepared the fish, put the pan over the fire and threw them into it. As soon as she did, the wall split open and out came the girl, looking as she had done before, with a staff in her hand. She prodded the pan and asked: 'Fish, fish, are you true to your old covenant?' At this, all the fish raised their heads and repeated the lines:

> If you return, we return;
> If you keep faith, then so do we,
> But if you go off, we are quits.

Night 7

Morning now dawned and Shahrazad broke off from what she had been allowed to say. Then, when it was the seventh night, SHE CONTINUED:

I have heard, O auspicious king, that, when the fish spoke, the girl overturned the pan with her staff and then left by the way she had come, with the wall closing behind her. At that, the vizier got up and said: 'This is something which must not be kept from the king.' So he went to the king and told him the story, explaining what he had seen for himself. 'I must see this with my own eyes,' said the king, and at that the fisherman was sent for and told to bring another four fish like the others. He went down to the pool with three guards as an escort and brought the fish immediately. The king ordered him to be given four hundred dinars, after which he turned to the vizier and told him: 'Come and cook these fish in my presence.' The vizier did as he was told, brought the pan and, after preparing the fish, he put the pan over the fire and threw them into it. As soon as he did so, the wall split open and out came a black slave, tall as a mountain or like a survivor of the race of 'Ad. In his hand was a green bough and he asked in a hectoring voice: 'Fish, fish, are you true to your old covenant?' The fish raised their heads from the pan and replied: 'Yes, yes, we keep to our covenant.

If you return, we return;
If you keep faith, then so do we,
But if you go off, we are quits.'

The slave came up to the pan, overturned it with the branch that he was holding, and left by the way that he had come. The vizier and the king looked at the fish and saw that they were now like charcoal. The king was amazed and said: 'This is something that cannot be kept quiet and there must be some secret attached to them.' So he gave orders for the fisherman to be summoned and when the man came, the king asked him where the fish came from. 'From a pool surrounded by four mountains,' replied the fisherman, 'and it is under the mountain outside the city.' The king turned and asked: 'How many days' journey is it?' and the fisherman told him that it was half an hour away.

This astonished the king and he ordered his troops to mount and ride immediately, with the fisherman at their head, while the fisherman, in his turn, as he accompanied the king, spent his time cursing the *'ifrit*.

The riders climbed up the mountain and then went down into a broad plain that they had never seen before in their lives. Everyone, including the king, was filled with wonder when they looked at it and at the pool in its centre, set as it was between four mountains, with its fish of four colours – red, white, yellow and blue. The king halted in astonishment and asked his soldiers and the others there whether they had ever seen the pool before. 'King of the age,' they replied, 'never in all our lives have we set eyes on it.' The elderly were asked about it, but they too said that they had never before seen the pool there.

The king then swore by God: 'I shall not enter my city or sit on my throne again until I find out the secret of this pool and of these fish.' He gave orders for his men to camp around the mountains, and then summoned his vizier, a learned, wise and sensible man, with a knowledge of affairs. When he came into the king's presence, the king said to him: 'I am going to tell you what I want to do. It has struck me that I should go out alone tonight and investigate the secret of this pool and of these fish. I want you to sit at the entrance of my tent and to tell the emirs, viziers, chamberlains and deputies, as well as everyone who asks about me, that I am unwell and that you have my instructions not to allow anyone to come in to see me. Don't tell anyone what I am planning to do.'

The vizier was in no position to disobey and so the king changed his clothes and strapped on his sword. He climbed down from one of the mountains and walked on for the rest of the night until morning. He spent all the next day walking in the intense heat, and carried on for a second night until morning. At that point, he was pleased to see something black in the distance, and he said to himself: 'Perhaps I shall find someone to tell me about the pool and the fish.' When he went nearer he found a palace made of black stones plated with iron, one leaf of whose gate was open and the other shut. Joyfully he stood by the door and knocked lightly; on hearing no reply, he knocked a second and a third time, and when there was still no answer, he knocked more loudly. When no one answered, he was sure that the palace must be empty and so, plucking up his courage, he went through the gate to the passage that led from it, and called out: 'People of the palace, here is a passing stranger. Have you any food?'

He repeated this a second and a third time, and when there was still no reply, emboldened and heartened, he went through the passage to the centre of the palace. This was furnished with silks, starry tapestries and other hangings, but there was no one there. In the centre was an open space, leading to four halls. There was a stone bench, and one hall next to another, then an ornate fountain and four lions of red gold, from whose mouths water poured, glittering like pearls or gems. Round and about were birds and over the top of the palace there was a net of gold that kept them from flying away, but the king was astonished and saddened that he had not seen anyone whom he could ask about the plain, the pool, the fish, the mountains and the palace.

He was sitting between the doors, sunk in thought, when suddenly he heard a plaintive sound coming from a sorrowful heart, with a voice chanting these verses:

I try to hide what I suffer at your hands, but this is clear,
With my eyes exchanging sleep for sleeplessness.
Time, you neither spare me nor cease your work,
And it is between hardship and danger that my heart lies.
Have you no mercy on one whom love's law has abased,
Or on the wealthy who is now made poor?
I was jealous of the breeze as it blows over you,
But when fate pounces, then men's eyes are blind.
What can the archer do if, as he meets the foe,
His bow-string snaps just when he wants to shoot?
When cares mass to assault a man,
Where can he flee from destiny and fate?

When the king heard this lament, he got up and, following the sound, he found a curtain lowered over the door of a room. He lifted it and behind it he found a handsome young man, well made, eloquent, with a bright face, ruddy cheeks and a mole on his cheek like a disc of amber. He was seated on a couch raised one cubit from the ground and he fitted the poet's description:

There is many a slender one whose dark hair and bright forehead
Have made mankind to walk in dark and light.
Do not find fault with the mole upon his cheek:
I would sell my brother in exchange for such a speck.

The king was glad to see him and greeted him. He, for his part, was sitting there wearing a silk gown embroidered with Egyptian gold, and on his head was a crown studded with gems. He was showing signs of grief, but when the king greeted him, he replied with the utmost courtesy:

'Your dignity deserves that I should rise for you, but I have an excuse for not doing so.' 'I excuse you, young man,' said the king. 'I am your guest and I am also here on an important errand. I want you to tell me about the pool, the fish, this palace, the reason why you are here alone and why you are weeping.'

When the young man heard this, tears coursed down his cheeks and he wept bitterly until his breast was drenched. He then recited:

Say to the one to whom Time grants sleep,
How often misfortunes subside only to rise up!
While you may sleep, God's eye remains sleepless.
For whom is Time unclouded and for whom do worldly things
    endure?

He sighed deeply and continued to recite:

Entrust your affair to the Lord of all mankind;
Abandon care and leave aside anxious thoughts.
Do not ask how what happened has occurred,
For all things come about through the decree of fate.

The king, filled with wonder, asked the youth why he was weeping. 'How can I not shed tears,' he replied, 'when I am in this state?' and he reached down to the skirts of his robe and raised it. It could then be seen that the lower half of his body, down to his feet, was of stone, while from his navel to the hair of his head he was human. When he saw this condition of his, the king was filled with grief and regret. He exclaimed in sorrow: 'Young man, you have added another care to my cares! I was looking for information about the fish, but now I see I must ask both about them and about you.' He went on to recite the formula: 'There is no power and no strength except with God, the Exalted, the Omnipotent,' and added: 'Tell me at once what your story is.'

'Listen and look,' said the young man. 'My ears and eyes are ready,' replied the king, and the young man continued: 'There is a marvellous tale attached to the fish and to me, which, were it written with needles on the corners of the eyes, would be a lesson for all who can learn.' 'How is that?' asked the king, AND THE YOUNG MAN REPLIED:

You must know that my father was the ruler of this city. His name was Mahmud and he was the king of the Black Islands and of these four mountains. He died after a reign of seventy years and I succeeded him on the throne. I married my cousin, who loved me so deeply that, if I left her, she would neither eat nor drink until my return. She stayed with me for five years but then one day she went in the evening to the baths. I told the cook to prepare a quick supper for me and then I came to these apartments and lay down to sleep in our usual place, telling the slave girls to sit, one at my head and one at my feet. I was disturbed because of my wife's absence, and although my eyes were shut, I could not sleep and I was still alert.

It was then that I heard the slave girl who was sitting at my head saying to her companion: 'Mas'uda, how unfortunate our master is and how miserable are the days of his youth! What damage he suffers at the hands of that damned harlot, our mistress!' 'Yes,' answered the other, 'may God curse treacherous adulteresses. A man like our master is too young to satisfy this whore, who every night sleeps outside the palace.' The girl at my head said: 'Our master is dumb and deluded in that he never asks questions about her.' 'Do you think that he knows about her and that she does this with his consent?' exclaimed the other, adding: 'She prepares him a drink that he takes every night before he goes to sleep and in it she puts a sleeping drug. He knows nothing about what happens or where she goes. After she has given him the drink, she puts on her clothes, perfumes herself and goes out, leaving him till dawn. Then she comes back to him and burns something under his nose so that he wakes from his sleep.'

When I heard what the girls were saying, the light became darkness in my eyes, although I could not believe that night had come. Then my wife returned from the baths; our table was spread and we ate, after which we sat for a time talking, as usual. Then she called for my evening drink and when she had given me the cup which she had poured out, I tipped the contents into my pocket, while pretending to be drinking it as usual. I lay down immediately and, pretending to be asleep, I heard her saying: 'Sleep through the night and never get up. By God, I loathe you and I loathe your appearance. I am tired of living with you and I don't know when God is going to take your life.' She then got up, put on her most splendid clothes, perfumed herself and, taking my sword, she strapped it on and went out through the palace gates, while for my part I got up and followed her out. She made her way through the markets until she reached the city gate. She spoke some words that I could not understand, at which the bolts fell and the gate opened.

My wife went out, without realizing that I was following her, and passed between the mounds until she came to a hut with a brick dome.

As she went in through its door, I climbed on to the roof and looked down to see her enter and go up to a black slave. One of his lips looked like a pot lid and the other like the sole of a shoe – a lip that could pick up sand from the top of a pebble. The slave was lying on cane stalks; he was leprous and covered in rags and tatters. As my wife kissed the ground before him, he raised his head and said: 'Damn you, why have you been so slow? My black cousins were here drinking, and each left with a girl, but because of you I didn't want to drink.' She said: 'My master, my darling, delight of my eyes, don't you know that I am married to my cousin, whose appearance I hate and whose company I loathe? Were it not that I am afraid for you, I would not let the sun rise before the city had been left desolate, echoing to the screeches of owls and the cawing of crows, the haunt of foxes and wolves, and I would move its stones to behind Mount Qaf.' 'You are lying, damn you,' said the black man. 'I swear by the chivalry of the blacks – and don't think that our chivalry is like that of the whites – that if you are as late as this once more, I will never again keep company with you or join my body to yours. You are playing fast and loose with me. Am I here just to serve your lust, you stinking bitch, vilest of the whites?'

As I looked on and listened to what they were saying, the world turned black for me and I didn't know where I was. My wife was standing weeping, humbling herself before the slave and saying: 'My darling, fruit of my heart, if you are angry with me, who will save me, and if you throw me out, who will shelter me, my darling and light of my eyes?' She went on weeping and imploring him until, to her delight, she managed to conciliate him. She then got up and took off all her clothes. 'My master,' she said, 'is there anything for your servant to eat?' 'Lift the pan cover,' he said. 'There are some cooked rat bones beneath it that you can eat, and you can then go to this jar and drink the remains of the beer there.'

After my wife had eaten and drunk, she washed her hands and her mouth before lying down naked on the cane stalks with the slave, and getting in with him beneath the rags and tatters. When I saw what she had done, I lost control of myself and, climbing down from the top of the roof, I drew the sword that I had brought with me, intending to kill them both. First I struck the neck of the slave, and thought that he was dead . . .

Night 8

Morning now dawned on Shahrazad and she broke off from what she had been allowed to say. Then, when it was the eighth night, SHE CONTINUED:

I have heard, O auspicious king, that THE YOUNG MAN SAID:

I struck the slave with the intention of cutting off his head but I had failed to sever his jugular and only cut his gullet, skin and flesh. He let out a loud snort and as my wife stirred, I stepped back, returned the sword to its sheath and went back to the city, where I entered the palace and lay down on my bed until morning. There was my wife coming to wake me, with her hair shorn, wearing mourning. She said: 'Cousin, don't object to what I am doing, as I have had news that my mother has died and that my father has been killed fighting the infidels, while one of my brothers has died of a fatal sting and the other of a fall. It is right for me to weep and grieve.'

When I heard this, I did not tell her what I knew but said: 'Do what you think proper and I shall not oppose you.' From the beginning to the end of a whole year she remained miserable and in mourning, and then she said to me: 'I want you to build me a tomb shaped like a dome beside your palace, which I shall set aside for grief and call the House of Sorrows.' 'Do as you please,' I said, and she built her House of Sorrows, over which was a dome, covering what looked like a tomb. She brought the slave there and installed him in it, but he could no longer be of any service to her. He went on drinking wine, but since the day that I had wounded him he could no longer speak, and he was alive only because his allotted span had not yet come to an end. Every day, morning and evening, my wife would go to the tomb weeping and lamenting for him, and she would give him wine and broth.

Things went on like this until it came to the second year. I had been long-suffering and had paid no attention to her, until one day, when I came to her room unexpectedly, I found her exclaiming tearfully: 'Why are you absent from my sight, my heart's delight? Talk to me, O my soul; speak to me, my darling.' She recited:

If you have found consolation, love has left me no endurance.
My heart loves none but you.
Take my bones and my soul with you wherever you may go,

And where you halt, bury me opposite you.
Call out my name over my grave and my bones will moan in answer,
Hearing the echo of your voice.

Then she went on:

My wishes are fulfilled on the day I am near you,
While the day of my doom is when you turn from me.
I may pass the night in fear, threatened with destruction,
But union with you is sweeter to me than safety.

Next she recited:

If every blessing and all this world were mine,
Together with the empire of the Persian kings,
To me this would not be worth a gnat's wing,
If my eyes could not look on you.

When she had finished speaking and weeping, I said to her: 'Cousin,
that is enough of sorrow, and more weeping will do you no good.' 'Do
not try to stop me doing what I must do,' she said, 'for in that case, I
shall kill myself.' I said no more and left her to do what she wanted,
and she went on grieving, weeping and mourning for a second year
and then a third. One day, I went to her when something had put
me out of temper and I was tired of the violence of her distress. I found
her going towards the tomb beneath the dome, saying: 'Master, I
hear no word from you. Master, why don't you answer me?' Then she
recited:

Grave, grave, have the beloved's beauties faded?
And has the brightness and the radiance gone?
Grave, you are neither earth nor heaven for me,
So how is it you hold both sun and moon?

When I heard what she said and the lines she recited, I became even
angrier than before and I exclaimed: 'How long will this sorrow last?'
Then I recited myself:

Grave, grave, has his blackness faded?
And has the brightness and the foulness failed?
Grave, you are neither basin nor a pot,
So how is it you hold charcoal and slime?

When she heard this, she jumped up and said: 'Damn you, you dog. It was you who did this to me and wounded my heart's darling. You have caused me pain and robbed him of his youth, so that for three years he has been neither dead nor alive.' To which I replied: 'Dirty whore, filthiest of the fornicators and the prostitutes of black slaves, yes, it was I who did that.' Then I drew my sword and aimed a deadly blow at her, but when she heard what I said and saw that I was intending to kill her, she burst out laughing and said: 'Off, you dog! What is past cannot return and the dead cannot rise again, but God has given the man who did this to me into my power. Because of him there has been an unquenchable fire in my heart and a flame that cannot be hidden.'

Then, as she stood there, she spoke some unintelligible words and added: 'Through my magic become half stone and half man.' It was then that I became as you see me now, unable to stand or to sit, neither dead nor alive. After this, she cast a spell over the whole city, together with its markets and its gardens. It had contained four different groups, Muslims, Christians, Jews and Magians, and these she transformed into fish – the white fish being the Muslims, the red the Magians, the blue the Christians and the yellow the Jews – and she transformed the four islands into four mountains that surround the pool. Every day she tortures me by giving me a hundred lashes with her whip until the blood flows down over my shoulders. Then she dresses me in a hair shirt of the kind that I am wearing on my upper half, over which she places this splendid gown.

The young man then wept and recited:

O my God, I must endure Your judgement and decree,
And if that pleases You, I shall do this.
Tyrants have wronged me and oppressed me here,
But Paradise may be my recompense.
My sufferings have left me in sad straits,
But God's choice as His favoured Prophet intercedes for me.

The king then turned to the youth and said: 'Although you have freed me from one worry, you have added another to my cares. Where is the woman and where is the tomb with the wounded slave?' 'He is lying in his tomb beneath the dome,' said the young man, 'and she is in that chamber opposite the door. She comes out once each day at sunrise, and the first thing she does is to strip me and give me a hundred lashes. I weep and call out but I cannot move to defend myself, and after she has tortured me, she takes wine and broth to the slave. She will come early tomorrow.' 'By God, young man,' said the king, 'I shall do you a service for which I shall be remembered and which will be recorded until the end of time.' He then sat talking to him until nightfall, when they both slept.

Close to dawn the king rose, stripped off his clothes, drew his sword and went to where the slave lay, surrounded by candles, lamps, perfumes and unguents. He came up to the slave and killed him with one blow, before lifting him on to his back and throwing him down a well in the palace. After that, he wrapped himself in the slave's clothes and lay down in the tomb with the naked sword by his side. After an hour, the damned sorceress arrived, but before she entered the tomb, she first stripped her cousin of his clothes, took a whip and beat him. He cried out in pain: 'The state that I am in is punishment enough for me, cousin; have pity on me.' 'Did you have pity on me,' she asked, 'and did you leave me, my beloved?' She beat him until she was tired and the blood flowed down his sides; then she dressed him in a hair shirt under his robe, and went off to carry the slave a cup of wine and a bowl of broth.

At the tomb she wept and wailed, saying: 'Master, speak to me; master, talk to me.' She then recited:

How long will you turn away, treating me roughly?
Have I not shed tears enough for you?
How do you intend abandoning me?
If your object is the envious, their envy has been cured.

Shedding tears, she repeated: 'Master, talk to me.' The king lowered his voice, twisted his tongue, and speaking in the accent of the blacks, he said: 'Oh, oh, there is no might and no power except with God, the Exalted, the Omnipotent!' When she heard this, she cried out with joy and then fainted. When she had recovered, she said: 'Master, is this true?' The king, in a weak voice, said: 'You damned woman, do you deserve that anyone should talk to you or speak with you?' 'Why is that?' she asked. 'Because all day long you torture your husband, although he cries for help, and from dusk to dawn he stops me from sleeping as he calls out his entreaties, cursing both me and you. He disturbs me and harms me, and but for this I would have been cured. It is this that keeps me from answering you.' 'With your permission,' she replied, 'I shall release him.' 'Do that,' said the king, 'and allow me to rest.' 'I hear and obey,' she replied and, after going from the tomb to the palace, she took a bowl, filled it with water and spoke some words over it. As the water boiled and bubbled, like a pot boiling on the fire, she sprinkled her husband with it and said: 'I conjure you by the words that I have recited, if you are in this state because of my magic, revert from this shape to what you were before.'

A sudden shudder ran through the young man and he rose to his feet, overjoyed at his release, calling out: 'I bear witness that there is no god but God and that Muhammad is the Apostle of God – may God bless him and give him peace.' His wife shouted at him, saying: 'Go, and don't come back, or else I shall kill you!' He left her and she went back to the tomb, where she said: 'Master, come out to me, so that I may see your beautiful form.' In a weak voice the king replied: 'What have you done? You have brought me relief from the branch but not from the root.' 'My beloved, my black darling,' she said, 'what is the root?' 'Curse you, you damned woman!' he replied. 'It is the people of the city and of the four islands. Every night at midnight the fish raise their heads asking for help and cursing me and you. It is this that stops my recovery. Go and free them quickly and then come back, take my hand and help me to get up, for I am on the road to recovery.'

On hearing these words and thinking that he was the slave, the sorceress was delighted and promised in God's Name willingly to obey his command. She got up and ran joyfully to the pool, from which she took a little water . . .

Night 9

Morning now dawned and Shahrazad broke off from what she had been allowed to say. Then when it was the ninth night, SHE CONTINUED:

I have heard, O auspicious king, that after the sorceress had taken water from the pool and spoken some unintelligible words over it, the fish danced, lifted their heads and immediately rose up, as the magic spell was removed from the city. It became inhabited again, the merchants buying and selling and each man practising his craft, while the islands were restored to their former state. The sorceress went straight away to the tomb and said to the king: 'Give me your noble hand, my darling, and get up.' In a low voice, the king replied: 'Come to me.' When she did this he, with the drawn sword in his hand, struck her in the breast as she clung on to him, so that it emerged gleaming from her back. With another blow he cut her in two, and threw the two halves on the ground.

When he came out he found the young man whom she had enchanted standing waiting for him, congratulating him on his escape, kissing his hand and thanking him. The king asked him whether he would prefer to stay in his own city, or to go with him to his. 'King of the age,' said the young man, 'do you know how long a journey it is to your city?' 'Two and a half days,' replied the king. 'If you have been sleeping,' said the young man, 'wake up. Between you and your city is a full year's worth of hard travelling. You only got here in two and a half days because this place was under a spell. But I shall not part from you for the blink of an eye.' The king was glad and said: 'Praise be to God, Who has given you to me. You shall be my son, for all my life I have been granted no other.'

They embraced with great joy and then walked to the palace. Here the young man told his courtiers to make ready for a journey and to collect supplies and whatever was needed. This took ten days, after which the young man and the king set off, the latter being in a fever of anxiety to get back his own city. They travelled with fifty mamluks and magnificent gifts, and their journey continued day and night for a whole year until, as God had decreed their safety, they eventually reached their goal. Word was sent to the vizier that the king had arrived safe and sound, and he, together with his soldiers, who had despaired of him, came to greet him, kissing the ground before him and congratulating him on his safe arrival.

The king then entered the city to take his seat on his throne, and the vizier, on presenting himself and hearing of all that had happened to the young man, added his own congratulations. Then, when things were settled, the king presented gifts to many people and he told the vizier to fetch the man who had brought him the fish and who had been responsible for saving the people of the enchanted city. A messenger was sent to him and when he was brought to the palace, the king presented him with robes of honour and asked him about his circumstances, and whether he had any children. The fisherman replied that he had two daughters and one son. The king sent for them and married one of the girls himself, giving the other to the young man. The fisherman's son was made treasurer, while the vizier was invested and sent off as ruler of the capital of the Black Islands, the young man's city. With him were sent the fifty mamluks who had come with the king, and he was given robes of honour to take to the emirs of the city. He kissed the king's hands and started out immediately, while the king remained with the young man. The fisherman, meanwhile, had become the richest man of his age, while his daughters remained as wives of kings until they died.

This, however, is not more remarkable than what happened to the porter. There was an unmarried porter who lived in the city of Baghdad. One day, while he was standing in the market, leaning on his basket, a woman came up to him wrapped in a silken Mosuli shawl with a floating ribbon and wearing embroidered shoes fringed with gold thread. When she raised her veil, beneath it could be seen dark eyes which, with their eyelashes and eyelids, shot soft glances, perfect in their quality. She turned to the porter and said in a sweet, clear voice: 'Take your basket and follow me.' Almost before he was sure of what she had said, he rushed to pick up the basket. 'What a lucky day, a day of good fortune!' he exclaimed, following her until she stopped by the door of a house. She knocked at it and a Christian came down to whom she gave a dinar, taking in exchange an olive-coloured jar of strained wine. She put this in the basket and said to the porter: 'Pick this up and follow me.' 'By God,' repeated the porter, 'this is a blessed and a fortunate day!' and he did what she told him.

She then stopped at a fruiterer's shop, where she bought Syrian apples, Uthmani quinces, Omani peaches, jasmine and water lilies from Syria, autumn cucumbers, lemons, *sultani* oranges, scented myrtle, privet flowers, camomile blossoms, red anemones, violets, pomegranate blooms and eglantine. All these she put into the porter's basket, telling him to pick it up. This he did and he followed her until she stopped at the butcher's, where she got the man to cut her ten *ratls'* weight of meat. He did this, and after paying him, she wrapped the meat in banana leaves and put it in the basket, giving the porter his instructions. He picked up the basket and followed her to the grocer, from whom she bought pistachio kernels for making a dessert, Tihama raisins and shelled almonds. The porter was told to pick them up and to follow her. Next she stopped at the sweetmeat seller's shop. This time she bought a bowl and filled it with all that he had – sugar cakes, doughnuts stuffed with musk, 'soap' cakes, lemon tarts, Maimuni tarts, 'Zainab's combs', sugar fingers and '*qadis*' snacks'.

Every type of pastry was piled on to a plate and put into the basket,

at which the porter exclaimed: 'If you had told me, I'd have brought a
donkey with me to carry all this stuff.' The girl smiled and gave him a
cuff on the back of the neck. 'Hurry up,' she said. 'Don't talk so much
and you will get your reward, if God Almighty wills it.' Then she stopped
at the perfume seller's where she bought ten types of scented water –
including rosewater, orange-flower water, waters scented with water lilies
and with willow flowers – two sugar loaves, a bottle of musk-scented
rosewater, a quantity of frankincense, aloes, ambergris, musk and Alexandrian candles. All of these she put in the basket, telling the porter to
pick it up and follow her.

He carried his basket and followed her to a handsome house, overlooking a spacious courtyard. It was a tall, pillared building, whose door
had two ebony leaves, plated with red gold. The girl halted by the
door, raised the veil from her face and knocked lightly, while the porter
remained standing behind her, his thoughts occupied with her beauty. The
door opened and, as its leaves parted, the porter looked at the person
who had opened it. He saw a lady of medium height, with jutting breasts,
beautiful, comely, resplendent, with a perfect and well-proportioned
figure, a radiant brow, red cheeks and eyes rivalling those of a wild cow
or a gazelle. Her eyebrows were like the crescent moon of the month of
Sha'ban; she had cheeks like red anemones, a mouth like the seal of
Solomon, coral red lips, teeth like camomile blossoms or pearls on a
string, and a gazelle-like neck. Her bosom was like an ornate fountain,
with breasts like twin pomegranates; she had an elegant belly and a navel
that could contain an ounce of unguent. She was as the poet described:

> Look at the sun and the moon of the palaces,
> At the jewel in her nose and at her flowery splendour.
> Your eye has not seen white on black
> United in beauty as in her face and in her hair.
> She is rosy-cheeked; beauty proclaims her name,
> Even if you are not fortunate enough to know of her.
> She swayed and I laughed in wonder at her haunches,
> But her waist prompted my tears.

As the porter stared at her, he lost his wits and the basket almost fell
from his head. 'Never in my life,' he repeated, 'have I known a more
blessed day than this!' The girl who had answered the door said to the
other, who had brought the provisions: 'Come in and take the basket
from this poor porter.' So the two girls went in, followed by the porter,

and they went on until they reached a spacious, well-designed and beautiful courtyard, with additional carvings, vaulted chambers and alcoves, and furnished with sofas, wardrobes, cupboards and curtains. In the middle of it was a large pool filled with water on which floated a skiff, and at its upper end was a couch of juniper wood studded with gems over which was suspended a mosquito net of red satin, the buttons of whose fastenings were pearls as big as or bigger than hazelnuts.

From within this emerged a resplendent girl of pleasing beauty, glorious as the moon, with the character of a philosopher. Her eyes were bewitching, with eyebrows like bent bows; her figure was slender and straight as the letter *alif*; her breath had the scent of ambergris; her lips were carnelian red, sweet as sugar; and her face would shame the light of the radiant sun. She was like one of the stars of heaven, a golden dome, an unveiled bride or a noble Bedouin lady, as described by the poet:

> It is as though she smiles to show stringed pearls,
> Hailstones or flowers of camomile.
> The locks of her hair hang black as night,
> While her beauty shames the light of dawn.

This third girl rose from the couch and walked slowly to join her sisters in the centre of the hall. 'Why are you standing here?' she said. 'Take the basket from the head of this poor porter.' The provision buyer or housekeeper came first, followed by the doorkeeper, and the third girl helped them to lower the basket, after which they emptied out its contents and put everything in its place. Then they gave the porter two dinars and told him to be off. For his part, he looked at the lovely girls, the most beautiful he had ever seen, with their equally delightful natures. There were no men with them and, as he stared in astonishment at the wine, the fruits, the scented blossoms and all the rest, he was reluctant to leave. 'Why don't you go?' asked the girl. 'Do you think that we didn't pay you enough?' and with that, she turned to her sister and said: 'Give him another dinar.' 'By God, lady,' said the porter, 'it was not that I thought that the payment was too little, for my fee would not come to two dirhams, but you have taken over my heart and soul. How is it that you are alone with no men here and no pleasant companion? You know that there must be four to share a proper feast and women cannot enjoy themselves except with men. As the poet says:

Do you not see that four things join for entertainment –
Harp, lute, zither and pipe,
Matched by four scented flowers –
Rose, myrtle, gillyflower, anemone.
These only become pleasant with another four –
Wine, gardens, a beloved and some gold.

There are three of you and so you need a fourth, who must be a man of intelligence, sensible, clever and one who can keep a secret.'

The three girls were surprised by what the porter said, and they laughed at him and asked: 'Who can produce us a man like that? We are girls and are afraid of entrusting our secrets to someone who would not keep them. We have read in an account what the poet Ibn al-Thumam once said:

Guard your secret as you can, entrusting it to none,
For if you do, you will have let it go.
If your own breast cannot contain your secret,
How is it to be held by someone else?

And Abu Nuwas has said:

Whoever lets the people know his secret
Deserves a brand imprinted on his forehead.'

When the porter heard what they said, he exclaimed: 'By God, I am an intelligent and a trustworthy man; I have read books and studied histories; I make public what is good and conceal what is bad. As the poet says:

Only the trustworthy can keep a secret,
And it is with the good that secrets are concealed.
With me they are kept locked inside a room
Whose keys are lost and whose door has been sealed.'

When the girls heard this quotation, they said: 'You know that we have spent a great deal of money on this place. Do you have anything with you which you can use to pay us back? We shall not let you sit with us as our companion and to look on our comely and beautiful faces until you pay down some money. Have you not heard what the author of the proverb said: "Love without cash is worthless"?' The doorkeeper said: 'My dear, if you have something, you are someone, but if you have nothing, then go without anything.' At that point, however, the house-keeper said: 'Sisters, let him be. For, by God, he has not failed us today, whereas someone else might not have put up with us, and whatever debt he may run up, I will settle for him.' The porter was delighted and thanked her, kissing the ground, but the girl who had been on the couch said: 'By God, we shall only let you sit with us on one condition, which is that you ask no questions about what does not concern you, and if you are inquisitive you will be beaten.' 'I agree, lady,' said the porter. 'I swear by my head and my eye, and here I am, a man with no tongue.'

The housekeeper then got up, tucked up her skirts, set out the wine bottles and strained the wine. She set green herbs beside the wine-jar and brought everything that might be needed. She then brought out the wine-jar and sat down with her two sisters, while the porter, sitting between the three of them, thought he must be dreaming. From the wine-jar that she had fetched she filled a cup, drank it, and followed it with a second and a third. Then she filled the cup and passed it to her sister and finally to the porter. She recited:

Drink with pleasure and the enjoyment of good health,
For this wine is a cure for all disease.

The porter took the cup in his hand, bowed, thanked her and recited:

Wine should be drunk beside a trusted friend,
One of pure birth from the line of old heroes.
For wine is like the wind, sweet if it passes scented flowers,
But stinking if it blows over a corpse.

Then he added:

Take wine only from a fawn,
Subtle in meaning when she speaks to you,
Resembling the wine itself.

After he had recited these lines, he kissed the hand of each of the girls. Then he drank until he became tipsy, after which he swayed and recited:

The only blood we are allowed to drink
Is blood that comes from grapes.
So pour this out for me, and may my life
And all I have, both new and old,
Serve to ransom your gazelle-like eyes.

Then the housekeeper took the cup, filled it and gave it to the door-keeper, who took it from him with thanks and drank it. She then filled it for the lady of the house, before pouring another cup and passing it to the porter, who kissed the ground in front of her, thanked her and recited:

Fetch wine, by God; bring me the brimming glass.
Pour it for me; this is the water of life.

He then went up to the mistress of the house and said: 'Lady, I am your slave, your mamluk and your servant.' He recited:

By the door there stands a slave of yours,
Acknowledging your kindly charity.
May he come in, fair one, to see your loveliness?
I swear by love itself I cannot leave.

She replied: 'Enjoy yourself, drink with pleasure and the well-being that follows the path of health.' He took the cup, kissed her hand and chanted:

I gave her old wine, coloured like her cheeks,
Unmixed and gleaming like a fiery brand.
She kissed it and said, laughingly:
'How can you pour us people's cheeks?'
I said: 'Drink: this comes from my tears;
Its redness is my blood;
My breath has heated it within the glass.'

She replied with the line:

Companion, if you have wept blood for me,
Pour it obediently for me to drink.

She then took the cup, drank it and sat down with her sister. They continued to drink, with the porter seated between them, and as they drank, they danced, laughed and sang, reciting poems and lyrics. The porter began to play with them, kissing, biting, rubbing, feeling, touching and taking liberties. One of them would give him morsels to eat, another would cuff him and slap him, and the third would bring him scented flowers. With them he was enjoying the pleasantest of times, as though he was seated among the houris of Paradise.

They went on in this way until the wine had taken its effect on their heads and their brains. When it had got the upper hand of them, the doorkeeper stood up, stripped off her clothes until she was naked, and letting down her hair as a veil, she jumped into the pool. She sported in the water, ducking her head and then spitting out the water, after which she took some in her mouth and spat it over the porter. She washed her limbs and between her thighs, after which she came out from the water and threw herself down on his lap. 'My master, my darling, what is the name of this?' she said, pointing to her vagina. 'Your womb,' he replied. 'Oh!' she said. 'Have you no shame?' and she seized him by the neck and started to cuff him. 'Your vagina,' he said, and she cuffed him again on the back of his neck, saying: 'Oh! Oh! How disgusting! Aren't you ashamed?' 'Your vulva,' he replied. 'Do you feel no shame for your honour?' and she struck him a blow with her hand. 'Your hornet,' he said, at which the lady of the house pounced on him and beat him, saying: 'Don't speak like that.'

With every new name that he produced, the girls beat him more and more, until the back of his neck had almost dissolved under their slaps. They were laughing among themselves, until he asked: 'What do you call it, then?' 'The mint of the dykes,' replied the doorkeeper. 'Thank God, I am safe now,' said the porter. 'Good for you, mint of the dykes.' Then the wine was passed round again, and the housekeeper got up, took off her clothes and threw herself on to the porter's lap. 'What is this called, light of my eyes?' she asked, pointing at her private parts. 'Your vagina,' he said. 'Oh, how dirty of you!' she exclaimed, and she struck him a blow that resounded around the hall, adding: 'Oh! Oh! Have you no shame?' 'The mint of the dykes,' he said, but blows and slaps still rained on the back of his neck. He tried another four names, but the girls kept on saying: 'No, no!' 'The mint of the dykes,' he repeated, and they laughed so much that they fell over backwards. Then they fell to beating his neck, saying: 'No, that's not its name.' He said: 'O my sisters, what is it called?' 'Husked sesame,' they said. Then the housekeeper put her clothes back on and they sat, drinking together, with the porter groaning at the pain in his neck and shoulders.

After the wine had been passed round again, the lady of the house, the most beautiful of the three, stood up and stripped off her clothes. The porter grasped the back of his neck with his hand and massaged it, saying: 'My neck and my shoulders are common property.' When the girl was naked, she jumped into the pool, dived under water, played around and washed herself. To the porter in her nakedness she looked like a sliver of the moon, with a face like the full moon when it rises or the dawn when it breaks. He looked at her figure, her breasts and her heavy buttocks as they swayed, while she was naked as her Lord had created her. 'Oh! Oh!' he said, and he recited:

If I compare your figure to a sappy branch,
I load my heart with wrongs and with injustice.
Branches are most beautiful when concealed with leaves,
While you are loveliest when we meet you naked.

On hearing these lines, the girl came out of the pool and sat on the porter's lap. She pointed at her vulva and said: 'Little master, what is the name of this?' 'The mint of the dykes,' he replied, and when she exclaimed in disgust, he tried 'the husked sesame'. 'Bah!' she said. 'Your womb,' he suggested. 'Oh! Oh! Aren't you ashamed?' and she slapped the back of his neck. Whatever name he produced, she slapped him, saying: 'No, no,' until he asked: 'Sisters, what is it called?' 'The *khan* of Abu Mansur,' they replied. 'Praise God that I have reached safety at last,' he said. 'Ho for the *khan* of Abu Mansur!' The girl got up and put on her clothes and they all went back to what they had been doing.

For a time the wine circulated among them and the porter then got up, undressed and went into the pool. The girls looked at him swimming in the water and washing under his beard and beneath his armpits, as they had done. Then he came out and threw himself into the lap of the lady of the house, with his arms in the lap of the doorkeeper and his feet and legs in the lap of the girl who had bought the provisions. Then he pointed to his penis and said: 'Ladies, what is the name of this?' They all laughed at this until they fell over backwards. 'Your *zubb*,' one of them suggested. 'No,' he said, and he bit each of them. 'Your *air*,' they said, but he repeated 'No', and embraced each of them.

Night 10

Morning now dawned and Shahrazad broke off from what she had been allowed to say. Then, when it was the tenth night, her sister Dunyazad said: 'Finish your story.' 'With pleasure,' she replied, AND SHE CONTINUED:

I have heard, O fortunate king, that the girls produced three names for the porter, while he kissed, bit and embraced them until he was satisfied. They went on laughing until they said: 'What is its name, then, brother?' 'Don't you know?' 'No.' 'This is the mule that breaks barriers, browses on the mint of the dykes, eats the husked sesame and that passes the night in the *khan* of Abu Mansur.' The girls laughed until they fell over backwards and then they continued with their drinking party, carrying on until nightfall.

At this point, they told the porter that it was time for him to get up, put on his gaiters and go – 'Show us the width of your shoulders.' 'By God,' said the porter, 'if the breath of life were to leave me, it would be easier for me to bear than having to part from you. Let me link night with day, and in the morning we can all go our separate ways.' The girl who had bought the provisions pleaded with the others: 'Let him sleep here so that we can laugh at him. Who knows whether in all our lives we shall meet someone else like him, both wanton and witty.' They then said: 'You can only spend the night with us on condition that you accept our authority and that you don't ask about anything you see or the reason for it.' The porter agreed to this, and they then told him: 'Get up and read what is written over the door.' He went to the door and there he found written above it in gold leaf: 'Whoever talks about what does not concern him will hear what will not please him.' 'I call you to witness,' he said, 'that I shall not talk about what is no concern of mine.'

The housekeeper got up and prepared a meal for them, which they ate, and then they lit candles and lamps, dipping ambergris and aloes into the candles. They sat drinking and talking of past loves, after having reset the table with fresh fruits and more wine. They continued for a time, eating, drinking, carousing together over their dessert, laughing and teasing each other, when suddenly there was a knock on the door. This did not disrupt the party, however, and one of the girls went by herself to the door and returned to report: 'Our happiness is complete tonight.' 'How is that?' the others asked. She told them: 'At the door are three Persian dervishes, with shaven chins, heads and eyebrows. By a very remarkable coincidence, each of them has lost his left eye. They have only just arrived after a journey; they are showing the signs of travel and this is the first time that they have been to our city, Baghdad. They knocked on our door because they couldn't find a lodging for the night and they had said to themselves: "Perhaps the owner of this house would give us the key to a stable or to a hut in which we could pass the night." For they had been caught out by nightfall, and, being strangers, they had no acquaintance who might give them shelter – and, sisters, each of them is of a ludicrous appearance.'

She continued to persuade and cajole until the others agreed to let the

Persians come in on condition that they would not talk about what did not concern them lest they hear what would not please them. The girl went off joyfully and came back with the three one-eyed men, with shaven beards and moustaches. They spoke words of greeting, bowed and hung back. The girls got up to welcome them and, after congratulating them on their safe arrival, told them to be seated.

What the visitors saw was a pleasant and clean room, furnished with greenery, where there were lighted candles, incense rising into the air, dessert, fruits and wine, together with three virgin girls. 'This is good, by God,' they all agreed. Then they turned to the porter and found him cheerfully tired out and drunk. They thought, on seeing him, that he must be one of their own kind and said: 'This is a dervish like us, either a foreigner or an Arab.' Hearing this, the porter glowered at them and said: 'Sit down and don't be inquisitive. Didn't you read what is written over the door? It is not for poor men who arrive like you to let loose your tongues at us.' The newcomers apologized submissively, and the girls laughed and made peace between them and the porter, after which food was produced for the new arrivals, which they ate.

They then sat drinking together, with the doorkeeper pouring the wine and the wine cup circulating among them. The porter then asked the visitors whether they had some story or anecdote to tell. Heated by wine, they, in their turn, asked for musical instruments and were brought a tambourine, a lute and a Persian harp by the doorkeeper. They then got up and tuned the instruments, after which each one took one of them, struck a note and began to sing. The girls added a shrill accompaniment and the noise rose. Then, while this was going on, there was a knock at the door and the doorkeeper got up to see what was going on.

The reason for this knocking was that the caliph Harun al-Rashid was in the habit of going around disguised as a merchant and he had come down from his palace that night on an excursion to listen to the latest news, accompanied by his vizier, Ja'far, and Masrur, his executioner. On his way through the city, he and his companions had happened to pass that house, where they heard music and singing. He had said to Ja'far: 'I want to go in here so that we may listen to these voices and see their owners.' Ja'far had replied: 'Commander of the Faithful, these people are drunk and I am afraid that they may do us some harm.' The caliph had then said: 'I must enter and I want you to think of some scheme to get us in.' 'To hear is to obey,' Ja'far had replied, before going up and knocking on the door. When it was opened by the doorkeeper,

Ja'far advanced and kissed the ground. 'Lady,' he said, 'we are traders from Tiberias who have been in Baghdad for ten days. We have sold our goods and are staying at the merchants' *khan*, but this evening we were invited out by a colleague. We went to his house and, after he had given us a meal, we sat drinking with him for a time, but when he let us go night had fallen and, as we are strangers here, we could not find our way back to our hostel. Of your charity, and may God reward you, would you let us come in and spend the night with you?'

The girl looked at them and saw that they were dressed as merchants and appeared to be respectable people. So she went back to her sisters and passed on Ja'far's message. The others sympathized with the visitors' plight and told her: 'Let them in,' after which she went back and opened the door. The caliph, Ja'far and Masrur came in and when the girls saw them, they stood up, seated their visitors and ministered to their needs, saying: 'Welcome to our guests, but we lay a condition on you.' 'What is that?' they asked. 'That you do not speak of what does not concern you, lest you hear what will not please you.' 'We agree,' they replied, and they sat down to drink together.

Looking at the three dervishes, the caliph was surprised to find that each of them had lost his left eye. He was also thrown into confusion by the beauty and grace of the girls, which prompted his admiration. They began to drink together and to talk, but when the girls invited the caliph to drink, he said: 'I am proposing to go on the pilgrimage to Mecca.' The doorkeeper then got up and brought him an embroidered table cloth on which she set a china jar in which she poured willow-flower water, adding some snow and a sugar lump. The caliph thanked her and said to himself: 'By God, I shall reward her tomorrow for the good that she has done me.'

Then they all occupied themselves with drinking, and when the drink had gained the upper hand, the lady of the house got up, bowed to the company and then, taking the housekeeper by the hand, she said: 'Sisters, come, we must settle our debt.' 'Yes,' agreed the other two girls, and at that, the doorkeeper got up in front of them and first cleared the table, removed the debris, replaced the perfumes and cleared a space in the middle of the room. The dervishes were made to sit on a bench on one side of the room and the caliph, Ja'far and Masrur on a bench on the other side. Then the lady of the house called to the porter: 'Your friendship does not amount to much. You are not a stranger, but one of the household.' The porter got up, tightened his belt and asked: 'What do you want?' 'Stay where you are,' she said. Then the housekeeper stood up and set a chair in the middle of the room, opened a cupboard and said to the porter: 'Come and help me.'

In the cupboard he saw two black bitches, with chains around their necks. 'Take them,' said the girl, and he took them and brought them to the centre of the room. Then the lady of the house got up, rolled back her sleeves and took up a whip. 'Bring one of them,' she told the porter, and he did this, pulling the bitch by its chain, as it whimpered and shook its head at the girl. It howled as she struck it on the head, and she continued to beat it until her arms were tired. She then threw away the whip, pressed the bitch to her breast and wiped away its tears with her hand, kissing its head. Then she said to the porter: 'Take this one away and bring the other.' This he did and she treated the second bitch in the same way as the first.

The caliph was concerned and troubled by this. Unable to contain his curiosity about the story of the two bitches, he winked at Ja'far, but the latter turned to him and gestured to him to remain silent. Then the lady of the house turned to the doorkeeper and said: 'Get up and do your duty.' 'Yes,' she replied and, getting up, she went to the couch, which was made of juniper wood with panels of gold and silver. Then the lady of the house said to the other two girls: 'Bring out what you have.' The doorkeeper sat on a chair by her side, while the housekeeper went into a closet and came out with a satin bag with green fringes and two golden discs. She stood in front of the lady of the house, unfastened the bag and took from it a lute whose strings she tuned and whose pegs she tightened, until it was all in order. Then she recited:

You are the object of my whole desire;
Union with you, beloved, is unending bliss,
While absence from you is like fire.
You madden me, and throughout time
In you is centred the infatuation of my love.
It brings me no disgrace that I love you.
The veils that cover me are torn away by love,
And love continues shamefully to rend all veils.
I clothe myself in sickness; my excuse is clear.
For through my love, you lead my heart astray.
Flowing tears serve to bring my secret out and make it plain.
The tearful flood reveals it, and they try

To cure the violence of this sickness, but it is you
Who are for me both the disease and its cure.
For those whose cure you are, the pains last long.
I pine away through the light shed by your eyes,
And it is my own love whose sword kills me,
A sword that has destroyed many good men.
Love has no end for me nor can I turn to consolation.
Love is my medicine and my code of law;
Secretly and openly it serves to adorn me.
You bring good fortune to the eye that looks
Its fill on you, or manages a glance.
Yes, and its choice of love distracts my heart.

When the lady of the house heard these lines, she cried: 'Oh! Oh! Oh!', tore her clothes and fell to the ground in a faint. The caliph was astonished to see weals caused by the blows of a whip on her body, but then the doorkeeper got up, sprinkled water over her and clothed her in a splendid dress that she had fetched for her sister. When they saw that, all the men present were disturbed, as they had no idea what lay behind it. The caliph said to Ja'far: 'Don't you see this girl and the marks of a beating that she shows? I can't keep quiet without knowing the truth of the matter and without finding out about this girl and the two black bitches.' Ja'far replied: 'Master, they made it a condition that we should not talk about what did not concern us, lest we hear what we do not like.'

At this point, the doorkeeper said: 'Sister, keep your promise and come to me.' 'Willingly,' said the housekeeper, and she took the lute, cradled it to her breasts, touched it with her fingers and recited:

If I complain of the beloved's absence, what am I to say?
Where can I go to reach what I desire?
I might send messengers to explain my love,
But this complaint no messenger can carry.
I may endure, but after he has lost
His love, the lover's life is short.
Nothing remains but sorrow and then grief,
With tears that flood the cheeks.
You may be absent from my sight but you have still
A settled habitation in my heart.
I wonder, do you know our covenant?
Like flowing water, it does not stay long.

Have you forgotten that you loved a slave,
Who finds his cure in tears and wasted flesh?
Ah, if this love unites us once again,
I have a long complaint to make to you.

When the doorkeeper heard this second poem, she cried out and said:
'That is good, by God.' Then she put her hand to her clothes and tore
them, as the first girl had done, and fell to the ground in a faint. The
housekeeper got up and, after sprinkling her with water, clothed her in
a new dress. The doorkeeper then rose and took her seat before saying:
'Give me more and pay off the debt you owe me.' So the housekeeper
brought her lute and recited:

How long will you so roughly turn from me?
Have I not poured out tears enough?
How long do you plan to abandon me?
If this is thanks to those who envy me,
Their envy has been cured.
Were treacherous Time to treat a lover fairly,
He would not pass the night wakeful and wasted by your love.
Treat me with gentleness; your harshness injures me.
My sovereign, is it not time for mercy to be shown?
To whom shall I tell of my love, you who kill me?
How disappointed are the hopes of the one who complains,
When faithfulness is in such short supply!
My passion for you and my tears increase,
While the successive days you shun me are drawn out.
Muslims, revenge the lovesick, sleepless man,
The pasture of whose patience has scant grass.
Does love's code permit you, you who are my desire,
To keep me at a distance while another one
Is honoured by your union? What delight or ease
Can the lover find through nearness to his love,
Who tries to see that he is weighted down by care?

When the doorkeeper heard this poem, she put her hand on her dress
and ripped it down to the bottom. She then fell fainting to the ground,
showing marks of a beating. The dervishes said: 'It would have been
better to have slept on a dunghill rather than to have come into this
house, where our stay has been clouded by something that cuts at the

heart.' 'Why is that?' asked the caliph, turning to them. 'This affair has distressed us,' they replied. 'Do you not belong to this household?' he asked. 'No,' they replied. 'We have never seen the place before.' The caliph was surprised and said, gesturing at the porter: 'This man with you may know about them.' When they asked him, however, he said: 'By Almighty God, love makes us all equal. I have grown up in Baghdad but this is the only time in my life that I ever entered this house and how I came to be here with these girls is a remarkable story.'

The others said: 'By God, we thought that you were one of them, but now we see that you are like us.' The caliph then pointed out: 'We are seven men and they are three women. There is no fourth. So ask them about themselves, and if they don't reply willingly, we will force them to do so.' Everyone agreed except for Ja'far, who said: 'Let them be; we are their guests and they made a condition which we accepted, as you know. It would be best to let the matter rest, for there is only a little of the night left and we can then go on our ways.' He winked at the caliph and added: 'There is only an hour left and tomorrow we can summon them to your court and ask for their story.' The caliph raised his head and shouted angrily: 'I cannot bear to wait to hear about them; let the dervishes question them.' 'I don't agree,' said Ja'far, and the two of them discussed and argued about who should ask the questions until they both agreed that it should be the porter.

The lady of the house asked what the noise was about and the porter got up and said to her: 'My lady, these people would like you to tell them the story of the two bitches and how you come to beat them and then to weep and kiss them. They also want to know about your sister and why she has been beaten with rods like a man. These are their questions to you.' 'Is it true what he says about you?' the lady of the house asked the guests, and all of them said yes, except for Ja'far, who stayed silent. When the lady heard this, she told them: 'By God, you have done us a great wrong. We started by making it a condition that if any of you talked about what did not concern him, he would hear what would not please him. Wasn't it enough for you that we took you into our house and shared our food with you? But the fault is not so much yours as that of the one who brought you in to us.'

Then she rolled her sleeve back above the wrist and struck the floor three times, saying: 'Hurry.' At this, the door of a closet opened and out came seven black slaves, with drawn swords in their hands. 'Tie up these men who talk too much,' she said, 'and bind them one to the other.'

This the slaves did, after which they said: 'Lady, give us the order to cut off their heads.' She replied: 'Let them have some time so that I may ask them about their circumstances before their heads are cut off.' 'God save me,' said the porter. 'Don't kill me, lady, for someone else's fault. All the rest have done wrong and have committed a fault except me. By God, it would have been a pleasant night had we been saved from these dervishes who entered a prosperous city and then ruined it.' He recited:

How good it is when a powerful man forgives,
Particularly when those forgiven have no helper.
By the sanctity of the love we share,
Do not spoil what came first by what then follows it.

When the porter had finished reciting these lines, the girl laughed . . .

Night 11

Morning now dawned and Shahrazad broke off from what she had been allowed to say. Then, when it was the eleventh night, SHE CONTINUED:

I have heard, O auspicious king, that the girl laughed in spite of her anger. She then went up to the men and said: 'Tell me about yourselves, for you have no more than one hour to live, and were you not people of rank, leaders or governors among your peoples, you would not have been so daring.' 'Damn you, Ja'far,' the caliph said. 'Tell her about us or else we shall be killed by mistake, and speak softly to her before we become victims of misfortune.' 'That is part of what you deserve,' replied Ja'far, but the caliph shouted at him: 'There is a time for joking, but now is when we must be serious.' The lady then went to the dervishes and asked them whether they were brothers. 'No, by God,' they said, 'we are only *faqirs* and foreigners.' She next asked one of them whether he had been born one-eyed. 'No, by God,' he said, 'but I have a strange and wonderful story about the loss of my eye, which, were it written with needles on the inner corners of the eyeballs, would serve as a warning to those who take heed.' The second and the third dervish, when asked, made the same reply, and they then said: 'By God, lady, each of us comes from a different country and each is the son of a king and is a ruler over lands and subjects.'

She turned to them and said: 'Each of you is to tell his story and explain why he came here and he can then touch his forelock and go on his way.' The first to come forward was the porter, who said: 'Lady, I am a porter and this girl, who bought you your provisions, told me to carry them from the wine seller to the fruiterer, from the fruiterer to the butcher, from the butcher to the grocer, from the grocer to the sweetmeat seller and the perfumer, and then here. You know what happened to me with you. This is my story, and that's all there is.' The girl laughed and said: 'Touch your forelock and go.' 'By God,' he said, 'I am not going to leave until I have heard the stories of my companions.' THE FIRST DERVISH THEN CAME FORWARD AND SAID:

Lady, know that the reason why my chin is shaven and my eye has been plucked out is that my father was a king, who had a brother, also a king, who reigned in another city. His son and I were born on the same day. Years later, when we had grown up, I had got into the habit of visiting my uncle every so often, and I would stay with him for some months. My cousin treated me with the greatest generosity, and would kill sheep for me and pour out wine that he strained for me. Once, when we were sitting drinking and were both under the influence of the wine, he said to me: 'Cousin, there is something that I need from you. Please don't refuse to do what I want.' 'I shall obey you with pleasure,' I said. After binding me with the most solemn of oaths, he got up straight away and left for a short while. Back he came then with a lady, veiled, perfumed and wearing the most expensive of clothes, who stood behind him as he turned to me and said: 'Take this woman and go ahead of me to such-and-such a cemetery' – a place that I recognized from his description. 'Take her to the burial enclosure and wait for me there.'

Because of the oath that I had sworn, I could not disobey him or refuse his request and so I went off with the woman and we both went into the enclosure. While we were sitting there, my cousin arrived with a bowl of water, a bag containing plaster, and a carpenter's axe. Taking this axe, he went to a tomb in the middle of the enclosure and started to open it up, moving its stones to one side. Then he used the axe to prod about in the soil of the tomb until he uncovered an iron cover the size of a small door. He raised this, revealing beneath it a vaulted staircase. Turning to the woman, he said: 'Now you can do what you have chosen to do,' at which she went down the stairs. My cousin then looked at me and said: 'In order to complete the favour that you are doing me, when I go down there myself, I ask you to put back the cover and to replace the soil on top of it as it was before. Use the mortar that is in this bag and the water in the bowl to make a paste and coat the circle of the stones in the enclosure so that it looks as it did before, without anyone being able to say: "The inner part is old but there is a new opening here." I have been working on this for a full year and no one but God knows what I have been doing. This is what I need from you.' He then took his leave of me, wishing me well, and went down the stairs. When he was out of sight, I got up and replaced the cover and followed his instructions, so that the place looked just as it had before.

I then went back like a drunken man to the palace of my uncle, who was away hunting. In the morning, after a night's sleep, I thought of what had happened to my cousin the evening before and, when repentance was of no use, I repented of what I had done and of how I had obeyed him. Thinking that it might have been a dream, I started to ask after my cousin, but nobody could tell me where he was. I went out to the cemetery, looking for the enclosure, but I could not find it. I kept on going round enclosure after enclosure and grave after grave until nightfall, but I still failed in my search. I returned to the palace, but I could neither eat nor drink, for my thoughts were taken up with my cousin, as I did not know how he was, and I was intensely distressed. I passed a troubled night until morning came, when I went for a second time to the cemetery, thinking over what my cousin had done and regretting that I had listened to him. I went round all the enclosures but, to my regret, I still could not find the right one or recognize the grave.

For seven days I went on with my fruitless quest, and my misgivings increased until I was almost driven mad. The only relief I could find was to leave and go back to my father, but as soon as I reached the gate of his city, I was attacked by a group of men who tied me up. I was astonished, seeing that I was the son of the city's ruler and they were my father's servants, and in my alarm I said to myself: 'What can have happened to my father?' I asked my captors why they were doing this. At first they did not answer, but after a time one of them, who had been a servant of mine, said: 'Your father has fallen victim to the treachery of Time. The army conspired against him and he was killed by the vizier, who has taken his place. It was on his orders that we were watching out for you.'

I was stunned by what I heard about my father and fearful because I had a long-standing quarrel with the vizier, before whom my captors now brought me. I had been passionately fond of shooting with a pellet bow and the quarrel arose from this. One day when I was standing on the roof of my palace, a bird settled on the roof of the palace of the vizier. I intended to shoot it, but the pellet missed and, as had been decreed by fate, it struck out the eye of the vizier. This was like the proverb expressed in the old lines:

> We walked with a pace that was decreed for us,
> And this is how those under fate's control must walk.
> A man destined to die in a certain land
> Will not find death in any other.

When the vizier lost his eye, he could not say anything because my father was the king of the city, and this was why he was my enemy. When I now stood before him with my hands tied, he ordered my head to be cut off. 'For what crime do you kill me?' I asked. 'What crime is greater than this?' he replied, pointing to his missing eye. 'I did that by accident,' I protested. 'If you did it by accident,' he replied, 'I am doing this deliberately.' Then he said: 'Bring him forward.' The guards brought me up in front of him, and sticking his finger into my right eye, the vizier plucked it out, leaving me from that time on one-eyed, as you can see. Then he had me tied up and put in a box, telling the executioner: 'Take charge of him; draw your sword and when you have brought him outside the city, kill him and let the birds and beasts eat him.'

The executioner took me out of the city to the middle of the desert and then he removed me from the box, bound as I was, hand and foot. He was about to bandage my eyes before going on to kill me, but I wept so bitterly that I moved him to tears. Then, looking at him, I recited:

> I thought of you as a strong coat of mail
> To guard me from the arrows of my foes,
> But you are now the arrow head.
> I pinned my hopes on you in all calamities
> When my right hand could no longer aid my left.
> Leave aside what censurers say,
> And let my enemies shoot their darts at me.
> If you do not protect me from my foes,
> At least your silence neither hurts me nor helps them.

There are also other lines:

> I thought my brothers were a coat of mail;
> They were, but this was for the enemy.
> I thought of them as deadly shafts;
> They were, but their points pierced my heart.

The executioner had been in my father's service and I had done him favours, so when he heard these lines, he said: 'Master, what can I do? I am a slave under command.' But then he added: 'Keep your life, but don't come back to this land or else you will be killed and you will destroy me, together with yourself. As one of the poets has said:

> If you should meet injustice, save your life
> And let the house lament its builder.
> You can replace the country that you leave,
> But there is no replacement for your life.
> I wonder at those who live humiliated
> When God's earth is so wide.
> Send out no messenger on any grave affair,
> For only you yourself will give you good advice.
> The necks of lions would not be so thick
> Were others present to look after them.'

I kissed his hands, scarcely believing that I had escaped death, in comparison with which I found the loss of my eye insignificant. So I travelled to my uncle's city and, after presenting myself to him, I told him what had happened to my father, as well as how I had come to lose my eye. He burst into tears and said: 'You have added to my cares and my sorrows. For your cousin disappeared days ago and I don't know what has happened to him, nor can anyone bring me news.' He continued to weep until he fainted and I was bitterly sorry for him. He then wanted to apply some medicaments to my eye, but when he saw that it was like an empty walnut shell, he said: 'Better to lose your eye, my boy, than to lose your life.'

At that, I could no longer stay silent about the affair of my cousin, his son, and so I told him all that had happened. When he heard my news, he was delighted and told me to come and show him the enclosure. 'By God, uncle,' I said, 'I don't know where it is. I went back a number of times after that and searched, but I couldn't find the place.' Then, however, he and I went to the cemetery and, after looking right and left, to our great joy I recognized the place. The two of us went into the enclosure and, after removing the earth, we lifted the cover. We climbed down fifty steps and when we had reached the bottom, we were met by blinding smoke. 'There is no might and no power except with God, the Exalted, the Omnipotent,' exclaimed my uncle – words that can never put to shame anyone who speaks them. We walked on and found ourselves in a hall filled with flour, grain, eatables and so on, and there in the middle of it we saw a curtain hanging down over a couch. My uncle looked and found his son and the woman who had gone down with him locked in an embrace, but they had become black charcoal, as though they had been thrown into a pit of fire.

On seeing this, my uncle spat in his son's face and said: 'You deserve this, you pig. This is your punishment in this world, but there remains the punishment of the next world, which will be harsher and stronger.'

Night 12

Morning now dawned and Shahrazad broke off from what she had been allowed to say. Then, when it was the twelfth night, SHE CONTINUED:

I have heard, O auspicious king, that the dervish said to the lady of the house, to Ja'far and the caliph and the rest of the company that were listening: 'My uncle struck his son with his shoe, as he lay there, burned black as charcoal.' HE WENT ON:

This astonished me and I was filled with grief for my cousin and at the fate that had overtaken him and the girl. 'By God, uncle,' I said, 'remove rancour from your heart. My heart and mind are filled with concern; I am saddened by what has happened to my cousin, and by the fact that he and this girl have been left like charcoal. Is their fate not enough for you that you strike your son with your shoe?' He said: 'Nephew, from his earliest days this son of mine was passionately in love with his sister. I used to keep him away from her and I would tell myself: "They are only children," but when they grew up they committed a foul sin. I heard of this and, although I did not believe it, I seized him and reproached him bitterly, saying: "Beware of doing what no one has done before you or will do after you and which will remain as a source of disgrace and disparagement among the kings until the end of time, as the news is carried by the caravans. Take care not to act like this or else I shall be angry with you and kill you."

'I kept him away from her and kept her from him, but the damned girl was deeply in love with him and Satan got the upper hand and made their actions seem good to them. When my son saw that I was keeping him from his sister, he constructed this underground chamber, set it in order and provisioned it, as you see. Then, taking me unawares when I had gone out hunting, he came here, but the Righteous God was jealous

of them and consumed them both with fire, while their punishment in
the next world will be harsher and stronger.'

He then wept and I wept with him, and he looked at me and said:
'You are my son in his place.' I thought for a time about this world and
its happenings and of how my father had been killed by his vizier, who
had then taken his place and who had plucked out my eye, and I thought
of the strange fate of my cousin. I wept and my uncle wept with me.
Then we climbed back up and replaced the cover and the earth and
restored the tomb as it had been, after which we returned to the palace.
Before we had sat down, however, we heard the noise of drums, kettle-
drums and trumpets, the clatter of lances, the shouting of men, the clink
of bridles and the neighing of horses. The sky was darkened by sand and
dust kicked up by horses' hooves and we were bewildered, not knowing
what had happened. When we asked, we were told that the vizier who
had taken my father's kingdom had fitted out his troops, collected men,
hired Bedouin, and come with an army like the sands that could not be
numbered and which no one could withstand. They had made a surprise
attack on the city, which had proved unable to resist and which had
surrendered to them.

After this, my uncle was killed and I fled to the edge of the city, saying
to myself: 'If I fall into this man's hands, he will kill me.' Fresh sorrows
were piled on me; I remembered what had happened to my father and
to my uncle and I wondered what to do, for if I showed myself, the
townspeople and my father's men would recognize me and I would be
killed. The only way of escape that I could find was to shave off my beard
and my moustache, which I did, and after that I changed my clothes and
went out of the city. I then came here, hoping that someone might take me
to the Commander of the Faithful, the caliph of the Lord of creation, so
that I might talk to him and tell him the story of what had happened to me.
I got here tonight and was at a loss to know where to go when I came to
where this dervish was standing. I greeted him and told him that I was a
stranger, at which he said: 'I too am a stranger.' While we were talking,
our third companion here came up to us, greeted us, introducing himself
as a stranger, to which we made the same reply. We then walked on as
darkness fell and fate led us to you. This is the story of why my beard
and moustache have been shaved and of how I lost my eye.

The lady said: 'Touch your forelock and go.' 'Not before I hear someone
else's tale,' the man replied. The others wondered at his story and the

caliph said to Ja'far: 'By God, I have never seen or heard the like of what has happened to this dervish.' The second dervish then came forward and kissed the ground. HE SAID:

Lady, I was not born one-eyed and my story is a marvellous one which, were it written with needles on the inner corners of the eyes of men, would serve as a warning to those who take heed. I was a king, the son of a king. I studied the seven readings of the Quran; I read books and discussed them with men of learning; I studied astronomy, poetry and all other branches of knowledge until I surpassed all the people of my time, while my calligraphy was unrivalled. My fame spread through all lands and among all kings. So it was that the king of India heard of me and he sent a messenger to my father, together with gifts and presents suitable for royalty, to ask for me. My father equipped me with six ships and after a full month's voyage we came to land.

We unloaded the horses that we had taken on board with us and we loaded ten camels with presents, but we had only travelled a short way when suddenly we saw a dust cloud which rose and spread until it filled the sky. After a while, it cleared away to show beneath it fifty mail-clad horsemen like scowling lions, and on closer inspection we could see that they were Bedouin highwaymen. When they saw our small numbers, and that we had ten camels laden with gifts for the king of India, they rushed at us with levelled lances. We gestured to them with our fingers and said: 'We are envoys on our way to the great king of India, so do not harm us.' 'We don't live in his country,' they told us, 'and are no subjects of his.' Then they killed some of my servants, while the rest took flight. I was badly wounded and I too fled, but the Bedouin did not pursue me, being too busy sorting through the money and the gifts that we had brought with us.

Having been cast down from my position of power, I went off with no notion of where I was going, and I carried on until I reached the top of a mountain, where I took refuge in a cave until daybreak. I continued travelling like this until I came to a strong and secure city, from which cold winter had retreated, while spring had come with its roses. Flowers were blooming; there were gushing streams and the birds were singing. It fitted the description of the poet:

A place whose citizens are subject to no fear,
And safety is the master there.
For its people it is a decorated shield,
Its wonders being plain to see.

As I was tired out with walking and pale with care, I was glad to get there. With my changed circumstances, I had no idea where to go. Passing by a tailor in his shop, I greeted him and he returned my greeting and welcomed me with cheerful friendliness. When he asked me why I had left my own country, I told him what had happened to me from beginning to end. He was sorry for me and said: 'Young man, don't tell anyone about yourself, as I am afraid lest the king of this city might do you some harm as he is one of your father's greatest enemies and has a blood feud with him.' He then produced food and drink and he and I ate together. I chatted with him that night and he gave me a place to myself at the side of his shop and fetched me what I needed in the way of bedding and blankets.

I stayed with him for three days, and he then asked: 'Do you know any craft by which to make your living?' I told him: 'I am a lawyer, a scientist, a scribe, a mathematician and a calligrapher.' 'There is no market for that kind of thing here,' he replied. 'No one in this city has any knowledge of science or of writing and their only concern is making money.' 'By God,' I said, 'I know nothing apart from what I have told you.' He said: 'Tighten your belt, take an axe and a rope and bring in firewood from the countryside. This will give you a livelihood until God brings you relief, but don't let people know who you are or else you will be killed.' He then brought me an axe and a rope and handed me over to some woodcutters, telling them to look after me. I went out with them and collected wood for a whole day, after which I carried back a load on my head and sold it for half a dinar. With part of this I bought food and the rest I saved.

I went on like this for a year, and then when the year was up, I came out to the countryside one day, as usual, and as I was wandering there alone I found a tree-filled hollow where there was wood aplenty. Going down into the hollow, I came across a thick tree stump and dug round it, removing the soil. My axe then happened to strike against a copper ring and, on clearing away the earth, I discovered a wooden trapdoor, which I opened. Below it appeared a flight of steps, and when I reached the bottom of these, I saw a door, on entering which I saw a most beautiful palace set with pillars. In it I found a girl like a splendid pearl, one to banish from the heart all trace of care, sorrow and distress, while her words would dispel worries and would leave a man, however intelligent and sensible, robbed of his senses. She was of medium height, with rounded breasts and soft cheeks; she was radiant and beautifully formed, with a face shining in the black night of her hair, while the gleam of her mouth was reflected on her breast. She was as the poet said:

> Dark-haired and slim-waisted,
> Her buttocks were like sand dunes
> And her figure like that of a *ban* tree.

There is another verse:

> There are four things never before united
> Except to pierce my heart and shed my blood:
> A radiant forehead, hair like night,
> A rosy cheek, and a slim form.

When I looked at her, I praised the Creator for the beauty and loveliness that He had produced in her. She looked at me in turn and asked: 'What are you, a human or one of the *jinn*?' 'A human,' I told her, and she asked: 'Who brought you to this place where I have been for twenty-five years without ever seeing a fellow human?' I found her speech so sweet that it filled my heart, and I said, 'It was my lucky stars that brought me here, my lady, to drive away my cares and sorrows.' Then I told her from beginning to end what had happened to me and she found my plight hard to bear and wept. 'I, for my part,' she said, 'will now tell you my own story. You must know that I am the daughter of King Iftamus, lord of the Ebony Islands. He had given me in marriage to my cousin, but on my wedding night I was snatched away by an *'ifrit* named Jirjis, son of Rajmus, the son of the maternal aunt of Iblis. He flew off with me and brought me down into this place, where he fetched everything that was needed – clothes, ornaments, fabrics, furniture, food, drink and everything else. He comes once every ten days, sleeps here for the night and then goes on his way, as he took me without the permission of his own people. He has promised me that if I need anything night or day, and if I touch with my hand these two lines inscribed on the inside of this dome, before I take my hand away he shall appear before me. Today is the fourth day since he was here, and so there are six left until he comes again. Would you like to stay with me for five days and you can then leave one day before he returns?' 'Yes,' I replied. 'How splendid it is when dreams come true!'

This made her glad and, rising to her feet, she took me by the hand and led me through an arched door to a fine, elegant bath. When I saw this, I took off my clothes and she took off hers. After bathing, she stepped out and sat on a bench with me by her side. Then she poured me out wine flavoured with musk and brought food. We ate and talked, until she said: 'Sleep, rest, for you are tired.' Forgetting all my troubles, I thanked her and fell asleep. When I woke, I found her massaging my feet. 'God bless you,' I said and we sat there talking for a time. 'By God,' she said, 'I was unhappy, living by myself under the ground, with no one to talk to me for twenty-five years. Praise be to God, Who has sent you to me.' Then she asked me whether I would like some wine, and when I said yes, she went to a cupboard and produced old wine in a sealed flask. She then set out some green branches, took the wine and recited:

> Had I known you were coming, I would have spread
> My heart's blood or the pupils of my eyes.
> My cheeks would have been a carpet when we met
> So that you could have walked over my eyelids.

When she had finished these lines, I thanked her; love of her had taken possession of my heart and my cares and sorrows were gone. We sat drinking together until nightfall, and I then passed with her a night the like of which I had never known in my life. When morning came we were still joining delights to delights, and this went on until midday. I was so drunk that I had lost my senses and I got up, swaying right and left, and I said: 'Get up, my beauty, and I will bring you out from under the earth and free you from this *'ifrit.'* She laughed and said: 'Be content with what you have and stay silent. Out of every ten days he will have one and nine will be for you.' But drunkenness had got the better of me and I said: 'I shall now smash the dome with the inscription; let him come, so that I may kill him, for I am accustomed to killing *'ifrits.'* On hearing this, she turned pale and exclaimed: 'By God, don't do it!' Then she recited:

> If there is something that will destroy you,
> Protect yourself from it.

She added more lines:

> You look for separation, but rein in
> The horse that seeks to head the field.
> Patience, for Time's nature is treacherous,
> And at the end companions part.

She finished her poem but, paying no attention to her words of warning, I aimed a violent kick at the dome.

Night 13

Morning now dawned and Shahrazad broke off from what she had been allowed to say. Then, when it was the thirteenth night, SHE CONTINUED:

I have heard, O auspicious king, that THE SECOND DERVISH SAID TO THE LADY OF THE HOUSE:

As soon as I had delivered my violent kick, it grew dark; there was thunder and lightning; the earth shook and everything went black. My head cleared immediately and I asked the girl: 'What has happened?' 'The *'ifrit* has come,' she said. 'Didn't I warn you? By God, you have brought harm on me, but save yourself and escape by the way that you came.' I was so terrified that I forgot my shoes and my axe. Then, when I had climbed up two steps, I turned to look back and I caught sight of a cleft appearing in the earth from which emerged a hideous *'ifrit*. 'Why did you disturb me?' he asked the girl, 'and what has happened to you?' 'Nothing has happened to me,' she said, 'but I was feeling depressed and I wanted to cheer myself by having a drink. So I drank a little, and then I was about to relieve myself, but my head was heavy and I fell against the dome.' 'Whore, you are lying,' said the *'ifrit*, and he looked through the palace, right and left, and caught sight of the shoes and the axe. 'These must belong to a man!' he exclaimed. 'Who was it who came to you?' 'I have only just seen these things,' she said. 'You must have brought them with you.' 'Nonsense; that doesn't deceive me, you harlot!' he cried.

Then he stripped her naked and stretched her out, fastening her to four pegs. He started to beat her to force her to confess, and as I could not bear to listen to her weeping, I climbed up the staircase, trembling with fear, and when I got to the top I put the trapdoor back in its place and covered it with earth. I bitterly repented what I had done, and I remembered how beautiful the girl was and how this damned *'ifrit* was torturing her, how she had been there for twenty-five years and what had happened to her because of me. I also thought about my father and his kingdom, and how I had become a woodcutter, and how my cloudless days had darkened. I then recited:

If one day Time afflicts you with disaster,
Ease and hardship come each in turn.

I walked away and returned to my friend the tailor, whom I found waiting for me in a fever of anxiety. 'My heart was with you all last night,' he said, 'and I was afraid lest you had fallen victim to a wild beast or something else, but praise be to God that you are safe.' I thanked him for his concern and entered my own quarters, where I started to think over what had happened to me, blaming myself for the impulsiveness that had led me to kick the dome. While I was thinking this over, the tailor came in to tell me that outside there was a Persian *shaikh* looking for me, who had with him my axe and my shoes. He had taken them to the woodcutters and had told them that, at the call of the muezzin, he had gone out to perform the dawn prayer and had found the shoes when he had got back. As he did not know whose they were, he asked about their owner. 'The woodcutters recognized your axe,' said the tailor, 'and so told him where you were. He is sitting in my shop and you should go to thank him and take back your axe and your shoes.'

On hearing these words, I turned pale and became distraught. While I was in this state, the floor of my room split open and from it emerged the 'Persian', who turned out to be none other than the *'ifrit*. In spite of the severest of tortures that he had inflicted on the girl, she had made no confession. He had then taken the axe and the shoes and had told her: 'As certainly as I am Jirjis of the seed of Iblis, I will fetch the owner of this axe and these shoes.' He then went with his story to the woodcutters, after which he came on to me. Without pausing, he snatched me up and flew off with me into the air, and before I knew what was happening he came down and plunged under the earth. He took me to the palace where I had been before and my eyes brimmed with tears as I saw the girl, staked out naked with the blood pouring from her sides.

The *'ifrit* took hold of her and said: 'Whore, is this your lover?' She looked at me and said: 'I don't recognize him and I have never seen him before.' 'In spite of this punishment, are you not going to confess?' he asked. She insisted: 'I have never seen this man in my life and God's law does not allow me to tell lies against him.' 'If you don't know him,' said the *'ifrit*, 'then take this sword and cut off his head.' She took the sword, came to me and stood by my head. I gestured to her with my eyebrows, while tears ran down my cheeks. She understood my gesture and replied with one of her own, as if to say: 'You have done all this to us.' I made a sign to say: 'Now is the time for forgiveness,' and inwardly I was reciting:

My glance expresses the words that are on my tongue,
And my love reveals what is concealed within.
We met as the tears were falling;
Though I was silent, my eyes spoke of you.
She gestured and I understood the meaning in her eyes;
I signed to her with my fingers and she understood.
Our eyebrows settled the affair between us,
And we kept silence, but love spoke.

When I had finished the poem, the girl threw down the sword and said:
'How can I cut off the head of someone whom I do not know and who
has done me no harm? My religion does not allow this.' Then she stepped
back, and the *'ifrit* said: 'It is not easy for you to kill your lover, and
because he spent a night with you, you endure this punishment and do
not admit what he did. Like feels pity for like.' Then he turned to me
and said: 'Young man, I suppose that you too don't recognize her?' I
said: 'Who is she? I have never seen her before.' 'Then take this sword,'
he said, 'and cut off her head. By this, I shall be sure that you don't
know her at all, and I shall then allow you to go free without doing you
any harm.' 'Yes,' I said, and taking the sword, I advanced eagerly and
raised my hand, but the girl gestured to me with her eyebrows: 'I did not
fail you. Is this the way that you repay me?' I understood her meaning
and signed to her with my eyes: 'I shall ransom you with my life,' and it
was as though our inner tongues were reciting:

How many a lover has used his eyes to tell
His loved one of the secret that he kept,
With a glance that said: 'I know what happened.'
How beautiful is the glance! How elegant the expressive eye!
The one writes with his eyelids;
The other recites with the pupil of the eye.

My eyes filled with tears and I threw away the sword and said: 'O
powerful *'ifrit*, great hero, if a woman, defective as she is in understanding and in religious faith, thinks that it is not lawful to cut off my head,
how can it be lawful for me to cut off hers when I have not seen her
before? I shall never do that even if I have to drain the cup of death.'
The *'ifrit* said: 'The two of you know how to pay each other back for
favours, but I shall show you the consequence of what you have done.'
Then he took the sword and cut off one of the girl's hands, after which

he cut off the other. With four blows he cut off her hands and her feet, as I watched, convinced that I was going to die, while she took farewell of me with her eyes. 'You are whoring with your eyes,' said the *'ifrit*, and he struck off her head.

Then he turned to me and said: 'Mortal, our code allows us to kill an unfaithful wife. I snatched away this girl on her wedding night when she was twelve years old and she has known no one but me. I used to visit her for one night in every ten in the shape of a Persian. When I was sure that she had betrayed me, I killed her. As for you, I am not certain that you have played me false, but I cannot let you go unscathed, so make a wish.' Lady, I was delighted and asked: 'What wish shall I make?' 'You can tell me what shape you want me to transform you into,' he said, 'that of a dog, an ass or an ape.' I was hoping that he would forgive me and so I said: 'By God, if you forgive me, God will forgive you, because you have spared a Muslim who has done you no harm.' I went on to implore him with the greatest humility, and, standing before him, I cried: 'I am wronged.' 'Don't talk so much,' he said. 'I am not far from killing you, but I will give you one chance.' 'Forgiveness befits you better, *'ifrit*,' I said, 'so forgive me as the envied forgive the envier.' 'How was that?' he asked, AND I REPLIED:

It is said, O *'ifrit*, that in a certain city there were two men living in two houses joined by a connecting wall. One of these two envied the other and because of this he used the evil eye against him and did all he could to injure him. So far did this envy increase that the envier lost appetite and no longer enjoyed the pleasure of sleep, while the man whom he envied grew more and more prosperous, and the more the envier tried to gain the upper hand, the more the other's prosperity increased and spread. On hearing of his neighbour's envy and of his attempts to injure him, he moved away from the district, leaving the country and saying: 'By God, I shall abandon worldly things for his sake.' He settled in another city and bought a piece of land there in which was a well with an old water wheel. On this land he endowed a small mosque for which he bought everything that was needed, and there he devoted himself with all sincerity to the worship of Almighty God. *Faqirs* and the poor flocked there from every quarter, and his fame spread in that city until eventually his envious neighbour heard how he had prospered and how the leading citizens would go to visit him. So he came to the mosque where the object of his envy gave him a warm welcome and showed him the greatest honour.

The envier then said: 'I have something to tell you and this is why I have made the journey to see you. So get up and come with me.' The other did this and, taking the envier's hand, he walked to the farthest end of the mosque. 'Tell the *faqirs* to go to their rooms,' said the envier, 'for I can only speak to you in private where no one can hear us.' This the envied did, and the *faqirs* went to their rooms as they were told. The two then walked on a little until they came to the old well and there the envier pushed his victim into it without anyone knowing. He himself then left the mosque and went on his way, thinking that he had killed his former neighbour.

The well, however, was inhabited by *jinn*, who caught the falling man and lowered him gently on to the bedrock. They then asked each other whether any of them knew who he was. Most said no, but one of them said: 'This is the man who fled from his envier and who settled in this city where he founded this mosque. We have listened with delight to his invocations and to his reading of the Quran. The envier travelled to meet him and by a trick threw him down into our midst. But news of him has reached the king, who is intending to visit him tomorrow on the matter of his daughter.' 'What is wrong with his daughter?' asked one of the *jinn*. 'She is possessed by an evil spirit,' replied the other, 'for the *jinni* Marwan ibn Damdam is in love with her. If this man knew how to treat her, he could cure her, for the treatment is the easiest possible.' 'What is it?' asked the other. 'The black cat that he has with him in the mosque has a white spot as big as a dirham at the end of its tail. If he takes seven of its white hairs and uses them to fumigate the girl, the evil spirit will leave her head and never return and she will be cured there and then.'

The man was listening to all this, and so it was that the next morning, when dawn broke and the *faqirs* came, they found the *shaikh* rising out of the well, and as a result he became a figure of awe to them. Since he had no other medicines, he took seven hairs from the white spot at the end of the black cat's tail and carried them away with him. The sun had scarcely risen when the king arrived with his escort and his great officers of state. He told his men to wait and went in to visit the *shaikh*, who welcomed him warmly and said: 'Shall I tell you why you have come to me?' 'Please do,' replied the king. The man said: 'You have come to visit me in order to ask me about your daughter.' 'That is true, good *shaikh*,' the king agreed. 'Send someone to fetch her,' said the man, 'and I hope, if God Almighty wills it, that she will be cured immediately.' The king gladly sent for his daughter, who was brought tied up and manacled.

The man sat her down and spread a curtain over her, after which he produced the seven cat hairs and used them to fumigate her. The evil spirit that was in her head cried out and left. She then recovered her senses, covered her face and said: 'What is all this? Who has brought me here?'

The joy that the king felt was not to be surpassed. He kissed his daughter's eyes and then the hands of the *shaikh*, after which he turned to his state officials and said: 'What do you say? What does the man who cured my daughter deserve?' 'He should marry her,' they said. 'You are right,' said the king, and he married the man to his daughter, making him his son-in-law. Shortly afterwards, the vizier died and when the king asked who should replace him, the courtiers said: 'Your son-in-law.' So he was appointed vizier and when, soon after that, the king himself died and people asked who should be made king, the answer was: 'The vizier.' Accordingly he was enthroned and ruled as king.

One day, as he was riding out, the envier happened to be passing by and saw the man he envied in his imperial state among his emirs, viziers and officers of state. The king's eye fell on him and, turning to one of his viziers, he said: 'Bring me that man, but do not alarm him.' When his envious neighbour was brought to him, he said: 'Give this man a thousand *mithqals* of gold from my treasury; load twenty camels for him with trade goods, and send a guard with him to escort him to his land.' Then he took his leave of the man who envied him, turned away from him and did not punish him for what he had done.

'See then, *'ifrit*, how the envied forgave the envious, who had started by envying him, then injured him, followed him, and eventually threw him into the well, intending to kill him. His victim did not pay him back for these injuries but forgave and pardoned him.' At this point, lady, I wept most bitterly before him and recited:

> Forgive those who do wrong, for the wise man
> Forgives wrongdoers for their evil deeds.
> If every fault is mine,
> Every forgiveness should be yours.
> Who hopes that his superior will pardon him
> Has to forgive inferiors their faults.

The *'ifrit* said: 'I shall not kill you, but neither shall I forgive you. Instead, I shall cast a spell on you.' Then he plucked me from the ground and flew up into the air with me until I could see the earth looking like a bowl set in the middle of water. He set me down on a mountain and, taking some earth, he muttered over it, cast a spell and scattered it over me, saying: 'Leave this shape of yours and become an ape.' Instantly, I became a hundred-year-old ape, and when I saw myself in this ugly form, I wept over my plight, but I had to endure Time's tyranny, knowing that no one is Time's master. After climbing down from the mountain top, I found a wide plain across which I travelled for a month before ending at the shore of the salt sea. I stayed there for some time until suddenly I caught sight of a ship out at sea that was making for the shore with a fair breeze. I hid myself behind a rock and waited until it came by, when I jumped down into it. 'Remove this ill-omened beast,' cried one of the merchants on board. 'Let's kill it,' said the captain. 'I'll do that with this sword,' said another. I clung to the hem of the captain's clothes and wept copious tears.

The captain now felt pity for me and told the merchants: 'This ape has taken refuge with me and I have granted it to him. He is now under my protection, so let no one trouble or disturb him.' He then began to treat me with kindness, and as I could understand whatever he said, I did everything that he wanted and acted as his servant on the ship, so that he became fond of me. The ship had a fair wind for fifty days, after which we anchored by a large city, with a vast population. As soon as we had arrived and the ship had anchored, mamluks sent by the local king came on board. They congratulated the merchants on their safe voyage and passed on further congratulations from the king. Then they said: 'The king has sent you this scroll of paper, on which each one of you is to write one line. The king's vizier was a calligrapher and as he is now dead, the king has taken the most solemn of oaths that he will only appoint as his successor someone who can write as well as he did.'

The merchants were then handed a scroll which was ten cubits long and one cubit in breadth. Every last one of them who knew how to write, did so, and then I, in my ape's form, snatched the scroll from their hands. They were afraid that I was going to tear it and they tried to stop me, but I gestured to them to tell them I could write, and the captain signalled to them to leave me alone. 'If he makes a mess of it,' he said, 'we can drive him away, but if he can write well, I shall take him as a son, for I have never seen a more intelligent ape.' Then I took the pen, dipped it in the inkwell and wrote in the *ruka'i* script:

Time has recorded the excellence of the generous
But up till now your excellence has not been written down.
May God not orphan all mankind of you,
Who are the mother and father of every excellence.

Then I wrote in the *raihani* script:

He has a pen that serves every land;
Its benefits are shared by all mankind.
The Nile cannot rival the loveliness
That your five fingers extend to every part.

Then in the *thuluth* script I wrote:

The writer perishes but what he writes
Remains recorded for all time.
Write only what you will be pleased to see
When the Day of Resurrection comes.

I then wrote in *naskh*:

When we were told you were about to leave,
As Time's misfortunes had decreed,
We brought to the mouths of inkwells with the tongues of pens
What we complained of in the pain of parting.

Then I wrote in *tumar* script:

No one holds the caliphate for ever:
If you do not agree, where is the first caliph?
So plant the shoots of virtuous deeds,
And when you are deposed, no one will depose them.

Then I wrote in *muhaqqaq* script:

Open the inkwell of grandeur and of blessings;
Make generosity and liberality your ink.
When you are able, write down what is good;
This will be taken as your lineage and that of your pen.

I then handed over the scroll and, after everyone had written a line, it was taken and presented to the king. When he looked at it, mine was the only script of which he approved and he said to his courtiers: 'Go to the one who wrote this, mount him on a mule and let a band play as you

bring him here. Then dress him in splendid clothes and bring him to me.'
When they heard this, they smiled. The king was angry and exclaimed:
'Damn you, I give you an order and you laugh at me!' 'There is a reason
for our laughter,' they said. 'What is it?' he asked. 'You order us to bring
you the writer, but the fact is that this was written by an ape and not a
man, and he is with the captain of the ship,' they told him. 'Is this true?'
he asked. 'Yes, your majesty,' they said.

The king was both amazed and delighted. He said: 'I want to buy this
ape from the captain,' and he sent a messenger to the ship, with a mule,
a suit of clothes and the band. 'Dress him in these clothes,' he said,
'mount him on the mule and bring him here in a procession.' His men
came to the ship, took me from the captain, dressed me and mounted
me on the mule. The people were astonished and the city was turned
upside down because of me, as the citizens flocked to look at me. When
I was brought before the king, I thrice kissed the ground before him, and
when he told me to sit, I squatted on my haunches. Those present were
astonished at my good manners and the most astonished of all was the
king. He then told the people to disperse, which they did, leaving me
with him, his eunuch and a young mamluk.

At the king's command, a table was set for me on which was everything
that frisks or flies or mates in nests, such as sandgrouse, quails, and all
other species of birds. The king gestured to me that I should eat with
him, so I got up, kissed the ground in front of him and joined him in the
meal. Then, when the table cloth was removed, I washed my hands seven
times, took the inkwell and the pen, and wrote these lines:

> Turn aside with the chickens in the spring camp of the saucers
> And weep for the loss of fritters and the partridges.
> Mourn the daughters of the sandgrouse,
> Whom I do not cease to lament,
> Together with fried chickens and the stew.
> Alas for the two sorts of fish served on a twisted loaf.
> How splendid and how tasty was the roasted meat,
> With fat that sank into the vinegar in the pots.
> Whenever hunger shakes me, I spend the night
> Applying myself to a pie, as bracelets glint.
> I am reminded of this merry meal when I eat
> On tables strewn with various brocades.
> Endure, my soul; Time is the lord of wonders.
> One day is straitened, but the next may bring relief.

I then got up and took my seat some way off. The king looked at what I had written and read it with astonishment. 'How marvellous!' he exclaimed. 'An ape with such eloquence and a master of calligraphy! By God, this is a wonder of wonders.' Then some special wine was brought in a glass, which he drank before passing it to me. I kissed the ground, drank and then wrote:

> They burned me with fire to make me speak,
> But found I could endure misfortune.
> For this reason, hands have lifted me,
> And I kiss the mouths of lovely girls.*

I added the lines:

> Dawn has called out to the darkness, so pour me wine
> That leaves the intelligent as a fool.
> It is so delicate and pure that I cannot tell
> Whether it is in the glass or the glass is in it.

When the king read the lines, he sighed and said: 'Were a man as cultured as this, he would surpass all the people of his age.' He then brought out a chessboard and asked whether I would play with him. I nodded yes and came forward to set out the pieces. I played two games with him and beat him, to his bewilderment. Then I took the inkwell and the pen and wrote these lines on the chessboard:

> Two armies fight throughout the day,
> The battle growing fiercer every hour,
> But when night's darkness covers them,
> Both sleep together in one bed.

On reading this, the king was moved to wonder, delight and astonishment and told a servant: 'Go to your mistress, Sitt al-Husn, and tell her that I want her to come here to see this wonderful ape.' The eunuch went off and came back with the lady. When she saw me, she covered her face and said: 'Father, how can you think it proper to send for me in order to show me to men?' 'Sitt al-Husn,' he said, 'there is no one here except for this little mamluk, the eunuch who brought you up, and I, your father. So from whom are you veiling your face?' She said: 'This ape is a young man, the son of a king, who has been put under a spell by the

---

* The speaker here is the wine.

'*ifrit* Jirjis, of the stock of Iblis, who killed his own wife, the daughter of King Iftamus, the lord of the Ebony Islands. You think that he is an ape, but in fact he is a wise and intelligent man.'

The king was astonished by his daughter and he looked at me and said: 'Is what she says about you true?' I nodded yes and broke into tears. 'How did you know that he was under a spell?' the king asked his daughter. 'When I was young,' she replied, 'I had with me a cunning old woman who had a knowledge of magic, a craft she passed on to me. I remembered what she taught me and have become so skilled in magic that I know a hundred and seventy spells, the least of which could leave the stones of your city behind Mount Qaf and turn it into a deep sea, with its people swimming as fish in the middle of it.' 'By my life, daughter,' said the king, 'please free this young man so that I can make him my vizier, for he has wit and intelligence.' 'Willingly,' she replied, and taking a knife in her hand, she cut out a circle . . .

Night 14

Morning now dawned and Shahrazad broke off from what she had been allowed to say. Then, when it was the fourteenth night, SHE CONTINUED:

I have heard, O auspicious king, that THE DERVISH SAID TO THE LADY OF THE HOUSE:

The princess took in her hand a knife inscribed with Hebrew characters and with this she cut a circle in the middle of the palace. Over this she wrote names, talismans and spells, and she recited words, some intelligible and some unintelligible. After a time, everything grew dark and the '*ifrit* came down on us in his own shape. His arms were like winnowing forks, his legs like the masts of ships and his eyes like firebrands. We shrank from him in fear, and the princess said: 'There is no welcome for you,' at which he turned into a lion and said: 'Traitress, you have broken the covenant and the oath. Did we not swear that neither of us would oppose the other?' 'You accursed '*ifrit*,' she said, 'am I bound to one like you?' 'Take what comes to you,' said the '*ifrit*, and in his lion shape he opened its mouth and sprang at the girl. She quickly took one of her hairs, shook it in her hand and muttered a spell, so that the hair became a sharp sword. With this she struck a blow at the lion which cut it in two, but its head turned into a scorpion. For her part, the princess turned into a huge snake which attacked the damned '*ifrit* in his scorpion form.

There was a fierce fight, and the scorpion turned into an eagle while the snake became a vulture. For some time the vulture pursued the eagle until it turned into a black cat. The princess then became a brindled wolf and for a time the two creatures fought together in the palace. Then the cat, finding itself beaten, became a large red pomegranate in the middle of the palace fountain. When the wolf came up to it, it rose in the air and fell on the palace floor where it burst, its seeds scattered, each in a different place, until they covered the floor. A shiver ran through the wolf and it became a cock, which started to pick the seeds so as not to leave a single one, but, as was fated, one of them was hidden by the side of the fountain.

The cock then started to crow and to flap its wings, gesturing to us with its beak. We could not understand what it meant and it crowed so loudly that we thought that the palace had fallen in on us. Then it went all around the floor until it saw the grain concealed beside the fountain. It pounced on this to peck it up, but the grain slipped into the middle of the water in the fountain and became a fish which dived down to the bottom. The cock turned into a bigger fish and went down after it. This second fish vanished from sight for some time and then suddenly we heard a loud cry and a scream, which made us shudder. Then out came the *'ifrit* like a firebrand, with fire coming from his open mouth and fire and smoke from his eyes and nose. He was followed by the princess in the form of a huge burning coal and the two fought for a time until both were covered by thick flames and the palace was choked with smoke. We were terrified and were about to plunge into the water, fearing we might be burned to death. The king recited the formula: 'There is no might and no power except with God, the Exalted, the Omnipotent. We belong to God and to Him do we return.' He added: 'I wish that I had not forced her to do this in order to rescue this ape, placing so huge a burden on her to confront this damned *'ifrit*, who cannot be matched by all the *'ifrits* to be found in the world. I wish that I had never known this ape – may God give him no blessing now or ever. I had wanted to do him a favour for God's sake and to free him from his spell, but my heart has been weighed down by misfortune.'

Meanwhile, I myself, lady, was tongue-tied and could not say anything to him. Then, before we knew what was happening, there was a shout from beneath the flames and the *'ifrit* was there in the hall with us, blowing fire into our faces. The princess caught up with him and blew back fire at him, while we were struck by sparks from both of them. Her sparks did us no harm, but one of his caught me in the eye while I was still in my ape form and blinded it. Another spark struck the king's face, half of which it burned, together with his beard and lower jaw, while all his lower teeth fell out. Yet another fell on the chest of the eunuch and he was immediately burned to death.

We were sure that we were about to die, but in the midst of our despair we heard a voice extolling God and adding: 'He has given victory and aid and has confounded those who disbelieve in the religion of Muhammad, the radiant moon.' This voice belonged to none other than the princess, who had burnt the *'ifrit*, reducing him to a pile of ashes. She came up to us and said: 'Bring me a cup of water.' When this had been fetched, she spoke some incomprehensible words over it, sprinkled me with the water and said: 'I conjure you by the Truth, and by the greatest Name of God, return freely to your original shape.' A shudder ran through me and suddenly I had gone back to being a man, although I had lost one eye.

The princess then cried out: 'The fire, father, the fire! I have not much longer to live. I have not been used to fighting with a *jinni*, although, had he been human, I would have killed him long ago. I was not in difficulty until the pomegranate burst and I picked up the seeds, but I forgot the one which contained the *'ifrit*'s life. Had I picked it up in time, he would have died instantly, but I did not know what fate had ordained. Then he came back and we fought a hard battle under the earth, in the sky and in the water. Every time I tried a spell, he would reply with another, until he tried the spell of fire, and there are few who escape when this is used against them. Then destiny came to my aid and I burned him up before he could burn me, after I had summoned him to accept the religion of Islam. But now I am a dead woman – may God recompense you for my loss.' Then she cried for help against the fire and went on crying as a black spark leapt up to her breast and from there to her face. When it got there, she wept and recited: 'I bear witness that there is no god but God and that Muhammad is the Prophet of God.' We looked at her and all of a sudden she had become a pile of ashes lying beside those of the *'ifrit*. We grieved for her and I wished that I could have taken the place of my benefactress rather than see her beautiful face reduced to ashes, but God's decrees are not to be revoked.

On seeing what had happened to his daughter, the king plucked out what was left of his beard, struck his face and tore his clothes, as did I, and we both wept for her. The chamberlains and officers of state arrived to find the two piles of ashes and the king lying unconscious. For a time they stood around him in amazement and when he recovered and told what had happened to the princess in her encounter with the *'ifrit*, they were filled with distress and the women and the slave girls all screamed.

After seven days of mourning, the king gave orders for a huge dome to be built over his daughter's ashes, which was lit with candles and lamps, while the *'ifrit*'s ashes were scattered in the air, subject to God's wrath. The king then fell ill and was at the point of death, but he recovered after a month and his beard grew again. He sent for me and said: 'Young man, I passed my days living at ease, protected from the calamities of time, until you came here. How I wish that I had never set eyes on you or your ugly face, for it is you who have brought me to ruin. Firstly, I have lost my daughter, who was worth a hundred men. It was you whom my daughter rescued at the cost of her own life. Secondly, I was injured by fire; I lost my teeth, and my servant died. I recognize that none of this was your fault: all that happened to you and to me came from God – to Whom be praise. But now, my son, leave my land, for you have caused enough suffering, as was fated for me and for you. Go in peace, but if you come back and I see you again, I shall kill you.'

He shouted at me and I left his presence, scarcely believing that I had escaped and without knowing where to go. I thought over what had happened to me – how I had been abandoned on my journey, how I had escaped from my attackers, how I had walked for a month before entering the city as a stranger, how I had met the tailor and then the girl in the underground chamber, and how I had escaped from the *'ifrit* who had wanted to kill me. I relived all my emotions from the beginning to the end and I gave praise to God, saying: 'It has cost me my eye but not my life.' Before quitting the city, I went to the baths and shaved off my beard, after which I put on a black hair shirt and poured dust over my head. There is not a day on which I do not weep, thinking of the disasters that have struck me and of the loss of my eye. Every time I think of this, I shed tears and recite these lines:

By God, the Merciful, surely my affair bewilders me;
I do not know the source of sorrows that have surrounded me.
I shall endure until endurance itself cannot match mine,
Continuing until God closes my affairs.
I may be conquered, but I shall not show pain,
As a thirsty man endures in a hot valley.

I shall endure until endurance itself learns
I can endure what is more bitter than aloes,
Itself the bitterest of all,
But bitterer than all this would be for patience to betray me.
The secrets of my secret heart are its interpreter;
At the heart of the secret is my heart's secret love for you.
Were mountains to feel my sorrow, they would be crushed;
Fire would be quenched and winds would cease to blow.
Whoever claims that Time holds sweetness
Must sometime meet a day more bitter than aloes.

After that, I wandered through the world visiting cities and making for Baghdad, the House of Peace, in the hope of reaching the Commander of the Faithful and telling him what had happened to me. I arrived at the city tonight and there I found this first companion of mine standing in perplexity. I greeted him and talked to him and then our third companion arrived, greeted us and told us that he was a stranger. 'So are we,' the two of us said, 'and we have only just come on this blessed night.' The three of us then walked together without knowing each other's stories until fate brought us to this door and we came into your presence. This, then, is the reason why my beard and moustache have been shaven and my eye gouged out.

'Yours is a strange story,' said the lady of the house. 'You can touch your forelock and go on your way.' 'Not before I have heard my companions' stories,' he replied, at which THE THIRD DERVISH STEPPED FORWARD AND SAID:

Great lady, my tale is not like theirs but is more wonderful and more marvellous, and it explains the reason for the shaving of my beard and the plucking out of my eye. They both were victims of fate, but I brought this fate upon myself, burdening my own soul with sorrow. I was a king and the son of a king. After my father's death, I succeeded to the throne, ruled justly and treated my subjects well. I was fond of sailing and my city lay on the shore of a broad sea, in the middle of which many large islands were scattered, and I had fifty merchant ships, fifty smaller pleasure boats and a hundred and fifty warships. It so happened, that I decided to go on a pleasure trip to the islands and I set out with ten ships, taking provisions for a whole month. We had been sailing for twenty days when, one night, cross winds blew against us and the sea became very rough, with tumultuous waves, and we were plunged into thick darkness. Despairing of life, I said: 'A man who courts danger is not to be praised, even if he comes out safely.' We called on Almighty God and implored His help, but the wind continued to shift and the waves to clash together until daybreak. The wind then dropped; the sea became calm and the sun came out.

Looking out, we found ourselves by an island and so we landed on the shore, cooked and ate a meal and rested for two days. We then sailed on for another twenty days, when the currents turned against us and, as the captain of my ship did not recognize where we were, we told the lookout to climb to the crow's-nest to scan the sea. He went up the mast and shouted to the captain that to the right he could see fish on the surface, while at some distance away there was a dark shape, showing sometimes as black and sometimes as white. When the captain heard this, he dashed his turban on the deck, tore out hairs from his beard and said: 'Good news! We are all dead men; not one of us can escape.' He started to cry, and we all joined in, weeping for ourselves.

I then asked the captain what it was that the lookout had seen. 'Master,' he said, 'we went off course on the day of the gale when the wind did not die down until the following morning. That meant that we were off course for two days, and since that night we have been astray for eleven days, with no wind to blow us back on course. Tomorrow evening we shall come to an island of black stone that is called the Magnetic Mountain. The currents will force us under its lee and the ship will split apart, nails being drawn out to attach themselves to the rock. This is because God Almighty has set in it a secret power that attracts everything made of iron and God only knows how much of the metal is there, thanks to the many ships that have been wrecked on the rock over the course of time. By the shore there is a vaulted dome of brass set on ten columns and on top of this is a rider and his horse, both made of brass. In his hand the rider carries a brass lance and to his breast is fixed a lead tablet inscribed with names and talismans. It is this rider, O king,' he went on, 'who kills everyone who comes his way, and there is no escape unless the rider falls from his horse.'

At that, my lady, the captain wept bitterly and we were convinced that we were doomed. Each of us said farewell to his comrades and left his final instructions in case one should escape. We had no sleep that night and when morning came, we found ourselves close to the mountain. Then the force of the currents took us and when our ships were under the cliffs, they split apart, the nails and every iron object aboard being drawn towards the magnetic rock, to which they stuck. By the end of the day, we were drifting in the water around the mountain, and although some of us still lived, most were drowned, while the survivors could scarcely recognize each other, stunned as they were by the force of the waves and the gusts of wind. As for me, Almighty God preserved my life as it was His intention to distress, torture and afflict me further. I clung to a plank that was driven by the wind until it was blown ashore. There I found a beaten track, like a staircase carved in the mountain, leading to the summit. I pronounced the Name of Almighty God . . .

Night 15

Morning now dawned and Shahrazad broke off from what she had been allowed to say. Then, when it was the fifteenth night, SHE CONTINUED:

I have heard, O auspicious king, that, while the other guests waited, tied up with slaves standing by their heads with drawn swords, THE THIRD DERVISH SAID:

I pronounced the Name of God and called on Him with supplication. Then, gripping the cracks in the rock, I gradually managed to climb up. At that point, by God's permission, the wind died down and He helped me to make my way in safety until I reached the summit, where the only path that I could take led to the dome. I went in and then performed the ritual ablution as well as two *rak'as* in gratitude to God for bringing me to safety, after which I fell asleep under its shelter. In my sleep, I heard a voice saying: 'Ibn Khadib, when you wake, dig beneath your feet and you will find a bow of brass with three lead arrows, on which are inscribed talismans. Take the bow and the arrows and shoot the rider on top of the dome, for in this way you will rescue people from great distress. When you shoot him, he will fall into the sea and the bow will drop at your feet. Take it and bury it where you found it, and when you do this the sea will swell higher and higher, until it comes level with the mountain top. A little boat will then come up in which will be a man of brass – but not the one whom you shot. He will come to you with an oar in his hand and you must board his boat, but you are not to pronounce the Name of Almighty God. The man will row you for ten days and bring you to the Sea of Safety, where you will find someone to take you back to your own land, but all this will happen only if you do not mention the Name of God.'

When I awoke, I got up eagerly and did what the voice had told me. I shot the horseman and when he fell into the sea, the bow dropped at my feet and I took it and buried it. The sea then stirred and rose higher until it was level with me on the mountain, and before I had waited long, I saw a little boat making its way towards me, at which I called down praises on Almighty God. When it arrived, I found in it a man of brass with a lead tablet on his breast, inscribed with names and talismans. I boarded it silently, without speaking, and the brass sailor rowed day after day for the full ten days. Then, looking out, to my great joy, I saw the Islands of Safety. Because of the intensity of my joy, I invoked the Name of God, reciting the formula: 'There is no god but God,' and crying: '*Allahu akbar!*' As soon as I did this, the boat tipped me into the sea and then itself overturned.

I knew how to swim, however, and so I swam all that day until nightfall, by which time my arms could no longer support me and my shoulders were tired. Exhausted and in mortal danger, I recited the confession of faith, being sure that I was about to die. A violent wind stirred up the sea and I was carried on by a wave as big as a castle, which hurled me on to the land in accordance with God's will. I climbed up on the shore, where I squeezed out my wet clothes, spreading them out on the ground to dry overnight. The next morning, I put them on and went to see where I could walk. I came to a valley, only to discover, after walking round the edge of it, that I was on a small island surrounded by sea. 'Every time that I escape from one predicament,' I said to myself, 'I fall into another that is worse.'

While I was thinking over my plight and wishing that I was dead, at a distance I caught sight of a ship with people on it which was making for my island. I got up and sat in a tree, and from there I saw that the ship had come to land, and out of it emerged ten black slaves, each carrying a spade. They walked to the centre of the island where they dug until they had uncovered a trapdoor, which they raised up. They then went back to the ship and returned with bread, flour, butter, honey, sheep and utensils that someone living in the underground chamber would need. The slaves kept on going to and fro from the ship until they had moved all its cargo to the chamber. They then came back bringing the very finest of clothes and in the middle of them was a very old man, a skeletal figure, crushed by Time and worn away. He was wearing a tattered blue robe through which the winds blew west and east, as the poet has said:

> What shudders are produced by Time,
> And Time is strong and violent!
> I used to walk without weakness,
> But now I am weak and cannot walk.

The old man's hand was being held by a youth cast in the mould of splendour and perfection to the extent that his beauty deserved to be proverbial. He was like a tender branch, enchanting every heart with his grace and enslaving all minds with his coquetry. As the poet has said:

> Beauty was brought to be measured against him,
> But bowed its head in shame.
> It was asked: 'Have you seen anything like this,
> Beauty?' It answered: 'No.'

They walked on, lady, until they reached the underground chamber and went down into it. They stayed out of sight for an hour or more, and then the slaves and the old man came up, but the youth was not with them. They closed the door of the chamber as it had been before, after which they got into the boat and sailed out of sight. I climbed down from my tree and walked to the pile of earth, where I excavated the soil, removed it and worked patiently until I had cleared it all away. There was the trapdoor, made of wood and as big as a millstone. When I lifted it, I could see under it, to my astonishment, a vaulted stone staircase. Down this I went until I reached the bottom and there I found a clean chamber furnished with rugs and silks in which the youth was sitting on a raised dais, leaning back against a round cushion, holding a fan in his hand, with nosegays and scented herbs set before him. He was alone and when he saw me, he turned pale. I greeted him and said: 'Calm yourself; don't be alarmed. I mean you no harm. I am a mortal like you, and the son of a king, who has been brought to you by fate to cheer you in your loneliness. What is your story and how is it that you come to be living alone underground?'

When he was sure that I was a man like himself, his colour returned and he let me approach him. Then he said: 'My brother, my story is a strange one. My father is a merchant jeweller, who engages in trade, with slaves, black and white, acting for him, sailing to the furthest of lands with his goods, travelling with camels and carrying vast stores of wealth. He had never had a son, but then in a dream he saw that, although he would have one, this son would be short-lived. He woke in the morning after his dream, crying and weeping, and it was on the following night that my mother conceived me, a date that my father noted. When the period of her pregnancy ended, she gave birth to me, to his delight. He gave banquets and fed the mendicants and the poor because, so near the end of his life, he had been granted this gift. Then he summoned all the astrologers and astronomers, the sages and those who could cast a horoscope. They investigated my horoscope and told my father: "Your son will live for fifteen years, after which he will be faced by a danger, but if he escapes, his life will be a long one. The cause of his death will be as follows. In the Sea of Destruction is the Magnetic Mountain on top of which stands a horse of brass with a rider on whose chest is a lead tablet. Fifty days after this rider falls from his horse, your son will die, killed by the man who shoots the rider, his name being 'Ajib ibn Khadib." This caused my father great distress, but he gave me the best of upbringings until I reached the age of fifteen. Then, ten days ago, he heard that the rider had fallen into the sea and that the name of the man who had shot him was 'Ajib, son of King Khadib. In his fear lest I be killed, my father brought me here. This is my story and this is why I am here all alone.'

When I heard this, I was astonished and I said to myself: 'I was the man who shot the rider, but by God I shall never kill this youth.' Speaking aloud, I said: 'Master, may you be preserved from disease and destruction, and if God Almighty wills it, you shall not see care, sorrow or confusion. I shall sit with you and serve you and then, having kept company with you throughout this period, I shall go on my way and you can take me to some of your mamluks, with whom I can travel back to my own lands.' I sat talking to him until nightfall, when I got up, set light to a large candle and lit the lamps. After having brought out some food, we sat down to a meal, and we then ate some sweetmeats which I had produced. We sat talking until most of the night had passed, when the youth went to sleep. I put a covering over him and settled down to sleep myself.

In the morning, I got up, heated some water and gently woke my companion. When he was awake, I brought him the hot water and he washed his face and thanked me. 'By God,' he said, 'when I am free from my present danger and safe from 'Ajib ibn Khadib, I shall ask my father to reward you, but if I die, may my blessing be on you even so.' I replied:

'May there never be a day on which evil strikes you and may God will it that the day of my death comes before yours.' I produced some food and we ate and I got him to perfume himself with incense. Then I made a draughts board for him and, after eating some sweetmeats, he and I started to play, going on until nightfall, when I got up, lit the lamps and brought out some more food. I sat talking to him until only a little was left of the night, when he fell asleep, after which I covered him up and slept myself. I went on doing this for a period of days and nights, becoming fond of him and forgetting my cares. 'The astrologers lied,' I said to myself, 'for by God I shall never kill this boy.'

I continued to serve him, to act as his companion and to talk with him for thirty-nine days until the night of the fortieth day. The youth was full of gladness and said to me: 'Thanks be to God, my brother, Who has saved me from death, and this is because of your blessing and the blessing brought by your arrival. I pray that God may restore you to your own land.' He then asked me to heat him water for a bath, which I willingly agreed to do. I warmed up a great quantity of water and brought it to him. He had a good bath, using lupin flour,* and I helped by rubbing him down and bringing him a change of clothes, after which I made up a high couch for him. He came and lay down to sleep there after his bath, saying: 'Brother, cut me up a melon and dissolve some sugar in its juice.' I went to the store cupboard and found a fine melon, which I put on a plate. 'Master,' I said to him, 'do you have a knife?' 'It is on this high shelf above my head,' he replied. So I got up quickly, took the knife and drew it from its sheath, but as I went back, I tripped. With the knife in my hand, I fell on top of the youth and, in accordance with the eternal decree, it quickly penetrated his heart and he died on the spot.

When this happened and I realized that I had killed him, I uttered a loud cry, beat my face and tore my clothes, saying: 'To God we belong and to Him do we return. O Muslims, this handsome youth had only a single night left of the dangerous period of forty days that the astrologers and sages had predicted for him, and his death came at my hands. How I wish I had not tried to cut this melon. This is an agonizing disaster, but it came about in order that God's decree might be fulfilled.'

* Used for soap.

Night 16

NIGHT 16

Morning now dawned and Shahrazad broke off from what she had been allowed to say. Then, when it was the sixteenth night, SHE CONTINUED:

I have heard, O auspicious king, that THE DERVISH TOLD THE LADY OF THE HOUSE:

When I knew for certain that I had killed him, I got up, climbed the stairs and replaced the soil. Then I looked out to sea and caught sight of the ship making for the shore. I said fearfully: 'Now they will come and find the boy dead. They will know that it was I who killed him and they will be bound to kill me.' I made for a high tree, which I climbed, concealing myself among the leaves, and scarcely had I settled there than the black slaves and the youth's old father disembarked and went towards the hidden chamber. They cleared away the earth, found the trapdoor and went down. There they found the youth apparently asleep, his face glowing with the effect of his bath, dressed in clean clothes but with the knife plunged into his breast. They shrieked, wept, struck their faces, wailing and lamenting. The old man fainted for so long that the slaves thought that he would not survive his son. They wrapped the corpse of the youth in his clothes, covered him in a silken sheet and returned to the boat. Behind them came the old man, but when he saw his son laid out, he fell to the ground, poured earth on his head, struck his face and plucked out his beard, while the thought that his son had been killed caused his tears to flow faster and he fainted again. One of the slaves got up and spread a piece of silk on a couch, upon which they laid the old man and then sat by his head.

While all this was going on, I was in the tree above them, watching what was happening. Because of the cares and sorrows that I had suffered, my heart turned grey before my hair and I recited:

How many hidden acts of grace does God perform
Whose secrets are too subtle to be grasped by clever men?
How often in the morning trouble comes,
While in the evening follows joy?
How many times does hardship turn to ease,
As pleasure follows the sad heart's distress?

The old man did not recover from his swoon until it was close to evening. Then, looking at the body of his son, he saw that what he had feared had come to pass. He slapped his face and his head and recited these lines:

> The loved ones left me with a broken heart,
> And floods of tears rain from my eyes.
> My longing is for what lies distant, but, alas,
> How can I reach this? What can I say or do?
> I wish that I had not set eyes on them.
> What can I do, my masters, in these narrow paths?
> How can I find my solace in forgetfulness?
> The blazing fire of love plays with my heart.
> I wish we had been joined by death
> In an inseparable link.
> In God's Name, slanderer, go slow;
> Join me with them while this can still be done.
> How pleasantly we were sheltered by one roof,
> Living a life of constant ease, until
> Arrows of separation struck and parted us.
> And who is there with power to endure them?
> A blow struck us through the dearest of all men,
> Perfect in beauty, unique in his age.
> I called him – but the silent voice preceded me.
> My son, would that your fate had not arrived.
> How may I rush to ransom you, my son,
> With my own life, were that acceptable?
> I say: he is the sun, and the sun sets.
> I say: he is the moon, and moons decline.
> The days bring sorrow and distress for you.
> I cannot do without you. None can take your place.
> Your father longs for you, but you are dead,
> And he is helpless. The envious look at us today
> To see what they have done; how evil was their deed!

At that, with a deep sigh his soul parted from his body. 'O master,' cried the slaves, and, pouring dust on their heads, they wept more and more bitterly. Then they put his body on the ship beside that of his son and, unfurling the sail, they passed out of sight. I came down from the tree, went through the trapdoor and thought about the youth. Seeing some of his belongings, I recited:

I see their traces and so melt with longing,
Weeping in places where they used to dwell.
I ask God, Who decreed that they should leave,
That one day He may grant that they return?

I then went out and passed my time wandering around the island by
day and going into the underground chamber by night. In this way a
month went by and, as I looked out over the western tip of the island, I
could see that with every day that passed the water was drying up.
Eventually there was very little of it left to the west and there was no
longer any current. By the end of the month, to my joy, the sea had dried
up in that direction and, sure that I was now safe, I got up and waded
through what water was left until I reached the mainland. There I encountered sand dunes in which camels would sink up to their hocks, but,
steeling myself, I managed to cross them, and then far off I caught a
glimpse of a fire burning brightly. I made for it, hoping to find relief.
Meanwhile I recited:

It may perhaps be that Time will direct its reins
Towards some good – but Time is envious.
Were it to aid hopes and fulfil my needs,
It might bring pleasure after this distress.

When my course brought me nearer, I saw a palace with a door of
brass which, when the sun shone on it, gleamed from a distance like fire.
I was delighted at the sight and sat down opposite the door. Scarcely
had I taken my seat when there came towards me ten young men, wearing
splendid clothes, with a very old companion. All the young men had lost
their right eyes, and I was astonished by their appearance and at this
coincidence. When they saw me they greeted me and asked me about
myself and about my story. They were amazed when I told them what
had happened to me and of my misfortunes, and they then brought me
into the palace. Ranged around the hall were ten couches, each spread
with and covered in blue material. In the middle of these was a small
couch whose coverings, like those of the others, was also blue.

When we entered the room, each of the young men went to his own
couch and the old man went to the small one in the middle. He told me
to sit down, but warned me not to ask questions about him and his
companions or why they were one-eyed. He then brought food for each
man in one container and drink in another and he did the same for me.

After that, they sat asking me about my circumstances and my adventures, and their questions and my replies took up most of the night. Then they said: '*Shaikh*, bring us our due.' 'Willingly,' the old man replied, and after going away into a closet, he came back carrying on his head ten trays, each with a covering of blue, and gave one to each of the young men. Then he lit ten candles, fixing one to each tray, and removed the covers. There beneath the covers on the trays was nothing but ashes and grime from cooking pots. All the young men rolled up their sleeves and, with tears and sobs, they smeared and slapped their faces, tore their clothes and beat their breasts, saying: 'We were seated at our ease but our inquisitiveness did not leave us.' They went on doing this until it was nearly morning, when the old man got up and heated water for them with which they washed their faces before putting on fresh clothes.

When I saw this, I said: 'I am astonished, amazed and afire with curiosity.' I forgot what had happened to me and, unable to keep silent, I asked them: 'Why have you done this, after we had become pleasantly tired? You are men of sound minds – praise be to God – and it is only madmen who act like this. I implore you by what you hold dearest to tell me your story and why you have lost your eyes and why you smear your faces with ashes and grime.' They turned to me and said: 'Young man, do not be led astray by your youth and do not press your question.' Then they got up and so did I, after which the old man brought out food, and when we had eaten and the plates had been removed, they sat talking until nightfall. The old man then rose and lit candles and lamps, before bringing us food and drink.

We sat talking in a friendly way to one another until midnight. 'Bring us our due,' they then told the old man, 'as it is time for sleep.' He brought the trays with the black ashes and they did what they had done on the first night. The same thing went on for a whole month while I stayed with them, as every night they would smear their faces with ashes before washing them and then changing their clothes. I was astonished at this and became more and more uneasy, to the extent that I could neither eat nor drink. 'Young men,' I said, 'you must satisfy my concern and tell me why it is that you smear your faces.' They said: 'It is better to keep our secret hidden,' but as I was too perplexed to eat or drink, I insisted that they tell me. 'This will go hard with you,' they replied, 'as you will become like us.' 'There is no help for it,' I said, 'unless you allow me to leave you and go back to my family, so that I may no longer have to watch all this. As the proverb has it, it is better for me to be far away from you, for what the eye does not see the heart does not grieve over.' At this, they took a ram, slaughtered it and skinned it, then told me to take a knife, wrap the skin around me and sew it up. They went on: 'A bird called a *rukh* will swoop on you and lift you up, before setting you down on a mountain, where you should slit open the skin and come out. The bird will be scared away from you and will go off, leaving you alone. Walk on for half a day and you will find in front of you a strange-looking palace. Enter it and you will have achieved what you wanted, as it was because we went into it that we blacken our faces and each of us has lost an eye. It would take a long time to explain all this, as each of us has a tale to tell of how his right eye was plucked out.'

I was pleased when I heard this, and after I had done what they had instructed, the bird came and carried me off, leaving me on the mountain top. I got out of the skin and walked on until I reached the palace, where I found forty girls, beautiful as moons, at whom no one could tire of looking. On seeing me, they all greeted me warmly. 'We have been expecting you for a month,' they said, 'and praise be to God Who has brought us one who deserves us and whom we deserve.' They seated me on a high dais and said: 'Today you are our lord and master and we are your slave girls, under your command, so give us your orders.' I was astonished by all this, but they brought me food and we ate together, after which they fetched drink. They clustered around me and five of them spread out a mat around which they set out quantities of scented flowers, together with fruits, fresh and dried. Then they brought wine and we sat down to drink as they sang to the music of the lute.

The wine circulated and such was my delight that I forgot all worldly cares. 'This is the life,' I said, and I stayed with them until it was time to sleep. 'Take whichever of us you choose to sleep with you,' they said. So I took one of them, with a beautiful face, dark eyes, black hair, well-spaced teeth, perfect in all aspects, with joining eyebrows, like a supple bough or a sprig of sweet basil, astonishing and amazing the mind. As the poet has said:

It shows ignorance to compare her to a tender branch,
And how far is she unlike a gazelle!
How can the dear gazelle have a form like hers
Or honeyed lips like hers – how sweet a drink –
Or her wide eyes, that act as murderers,
Capturing the desperate lover, tortured and then slain?

I yearn for her; mine is a heathen love;
No wonder that the lovesick is in love.

I recited to her:

My eyes see nothing but your loveliness;
Apart from you no thought enters my heart,
For every thought of mine is fixed on you;
In your love is my death and my rebirth.

I then got up and spent a night of unsurpassed pleasure sleeping with her. In the morning, the girls took me to the baths, washed me and gave me the most splendid of clothes to wear. Then they brought out food and drink and we ate and drank, the wine circulating until nightfall. This time I chose another lovely, pliant girl. As the poet describes:

I saw upon her breast two caskets sealed with musk,
Withheld from any lover's grasp,
Guarded with arrows she shoots from her eyes –
Arrows that strike down any who attack.

I passed the most delightful of nights, sleeping with her until dawn. In short, my lady, I spent a whole year with these girls, enjoying a carefree life, but as the next year began, they said: 'Would that we had never known you, but if you listen to us you can save yourself.' They then started to weep and when I asked them what the matter was, they explained: 'We are the daughters of kings, and we have been gathered together here for a period of years. We go away for forty days and then stay here for a year, eating, drinking, enjoying ourselves and taking our pleasure, after which we go off again. This is our custom and we are afraid that when we leave you, you will not do what we tell you. Here are the keys of the palace, which we are handing over to you. In the palace are forty rooms, thirty-nine of which you may enter, but you must take care not to open the door of the fortieth, or else you will be forced to leave us.' 'If that is so,' I said, 'then I shall certainly not open it.'

One of them then came to me, embraced me, wept and recited the lines:

If after separation we come close again,
The frown upon Time's face will turn into a smile.
If a sight of you serves as kohl for my eyes,
I shall forgive Time all its evil deeds.

Then I recited:

When she came close to say farewell, she and her heart
Were allies there to longing and to love.
She wept moist pearls, while my tears, as they flowed,
Were like carnelians, forming a necklace on her breast.

On seeing the girls' tears, I swore that I would never open the forbidden room, and after I had said goodbye, they went outside and flew away. So I sat in the palace by myself and when evening approached, I opened the door to the first chamber and went in. There I found a virtual paradise, a garden with green trees, ripe fruits, tuneful birds and gushing waters. I felt at rest as I walked among the trees, smelling sweet-scented flowers and listening to the song of the birds as they glorified the One God, the Omnipotent. I looked at apples whose colour was midway between red and yellow, as the poet has said:

An apple's nature has combined two shades –
The beloved's cheek and the complexion of the timorous lover.

Then I looked at quinces that put to shame the scent of musk and ambergris, as the poet has said:

Within the quince are all mankind's delights;
Its fame surpasses every other fruit.
Its taste is wine and its scent diffused musk,
Golden in colour, shaped like the full moon.

I then looked at apricots whose beauty delighted the eye like polished rubies, and after that I left the chamber and locked the door again. Next day I opened the door to the second chamber, went in and found a large space, with date palms and a flowing stream whose banks were carpeted with rose bushes, jasmine, marjoram, eglantine, narcissus and gilly-flowers. Breezes passed over these scented flowers and the scent spread in all directions, filling me with perfect happiness. I left this chamber, locked the door behind me and opened the third. Here I found a hall, paved with coloured marble, valuable minerals and precious stones. In it were cages of sandalwood and aloes wood, with singing birds, such as the nightingale, the ringdove, blackbirds, turtledoves and the Nubian song thrush. I was delighted by this; my cares were dispelled and I slept there until morning. Then I opened the fourth door to discover a large chamber with forty closets whose doors were standing open. I went in and saw an indescribable quantity of pearls, sapphires, topazes, emeralds and other precious stones. In my astonishment I exclaimed: 'I do not think that there is a single king who has all this in his treasury.' Joy filled me, my cares leaving me, and I said: 'I am the supreme ruler of the age; my wealth is a gift granted me by God's grace; the forty girls are under my authority, and they have no other man besides me.' I went from place to place until thirty-nine days had passed, during which time I had opened all the rooms except for the one whose door I had been told not to open.

This one, which made the number up to forty, preoccupied me and, in order to bring me misery, Satan incited me to open it. I could not hold out against this, and so with only one day left before the girls were due to return, I went to the chamber, opened the door and went in. I found a fragrance the like of which I had never smelt before. It overcame my senses and I fell down in a faint, which lasted for an hour. Then I plucked up my courage and went further into the room, whose floor I found spread with saffron. Light was given by lamps of gold and candles from which was diffused the scent of musk and ambergris, and I saw two huge censers, each filled with aloes wood, ambergris and honeyed perfume whose scent filled the room. I saw a horse, black as darkest night, in front of which was a manger of clear crystal, filled with husked sesame, together with a similar manger filled with rosewater scented with musk. The horse was harnessed and bridled and its saddle was of red gold.

When I saw this, I was astonished and said to myself: 'There must be something of great importance here.' Satan led me further astray and so I took hold of the horse and mounted it. It didn't move and so I kicked it, and when it still refused to move, I took the whip and struck it. As soon as it felt the blow, it neighed with a sound like rumbling thunder and, opening up a pair of wings, it flew off with me, carrying me up into the sky way above the ground. After a time, it set me down on a flat roof and whisked its tail across my face, striking out my right eye and causing it to slide down my cheek. It then left me and I came down from the roof to find the ten one-eyed youths. 'No welcome to you,' they said. 'Here I am,' I replied. 'I have become like you, and I want you to give me a tray of grime with which to blacken my face and to let me sit with you.' 'No, by God,' they said, 'you may not do that. Get out!'

They drove me away, leaving me in dire straits, thinking over the misfortunes that had overtaken me. I was sad at heart and tearful when I parted from them, and I said to myself in a low voice: 'I was resting at my ease, but my inquisitiveness would not leave me.' So I shaved off my beard and whiskers and wandered from place to place. God decreed that I should remain safe and I reached Baghdad yesterday evening, where I found these two men standing in perplexity. I greeted them and introduced myself as a stranger. 'We too are strangers,' they said, so we agreed to go together, all of us being dervishes and all being blind in the right eye. This, lady, is why I am clean shaven and have lost my eye.

'You can touch your forelock and go,' she told him, but he replied: 'Not before I have heard what these other people have to say.'

The lady of the house then turned to the caliph, Ja'far and Masrur and said: 'Tell me your story.' Ja'far came forward and told her the story that he had told to the doorkeeper when they entered and when she heard this, she allowed them all to leave. In the lane outside, the caliph asked the dervishes where they were proposing to go as dawn had not yet broken. When they said that they did not know, he told them to come and spend the night with him. 'Take them,' he said to Ja'far, 'and bring them to me in the morning, so that we may write down what has happened.' Ja'far did as he was told and the caliph went up to his palace, but found himself unable to sleep that night.

In the morning, he took his seat on the imperial throne, and when his officials had assembled, he turned to Ja'far and told him to bring the three ladies, the two bitches and the three dervishes. Ja'far got up and brought them all, the ladies being veiled. Ja'far turned to them and said: 'You are forgiven because of your earlier kindness, although you did not know who we were. I can tell you now that you are standing before the fifth of the caliphs of the Banu 'Abbas, Harun al-Rashid, the brother of Musa al-Hadi and son of al-Mahdi Muhammad, the son of Abu Ja'far al-Mansur, the son of Muhammad, the brother of al-Saffah, son of Muhammad. You are to tell nothing but the truth.'

When the ladies heard what Ja'far had said as spokesman for the Commander of the Faithful, the eldest of them came forward and said to the caliph: 'Commander of the Faithful, mine is a story which, were it written with needles on the inner corners of the eyeballs of mankind, would serve as a warning to those who take heed and counsel to those who profit from counsel.'

Night 17

Morning now dawned and Shahrazad broke off from what she had been allowed to say. Then, when it was the seventeenth night, SHE CONTINUED:

I have heard, O auspicious king, that when the lady of the house stood before the caliph, SHE SAID:

Mine is a strange story. The two black bitches are my sisters. Three of us were full sisters and these two, the doorkeeper and the housekeeper, were born of a different mother. When our father died, each of us took her share of the inheritance. Some days later, my mother died, leaving us three thousand dinars, and so each of us, I being the youngest, inherited a thousand dinars. My sisters were thus equipped with dowries and each married. Their husbands stayed for a time, but then they collected trade goods and, each of them taking a thousand dinars from his wife, they all went off on a voyage together, leaving me behind. They were away for five years, during which time the men lost their money and were ruined, abandoning their wives in foreign parts.

After five years, my eldest sister came to me in the most squalid of states, dressed as a beggar, with tattered clothes and a dirty old shawl. When I saw her, I didn't recognize her at first and took no notice of her. Then, realizing who she was, I asked her what had happened, but she said: 'It is no use talking, sister, the pen of fate has written God's decree.' So I sent her to the baths, gave her clothes to wear and said: 'Sister, you have been given to me in exchange for my father and mother. My share of what the three of us inherited has been blest by God and it has allowed me to thrive and become prosperous. You and I are equal partners.' I treated her with all kindness and she stayed with me for a whole year.

We were concerned about our other sister, but it was not long before she too arrived in an even worse plight than the eldest. I treated her even better than I had treated her sister and both of them shared in my wealth. Some time later, they told me that they wanted to marry again as they could not bear to remain without husbands. 'My dears,' I said, 'there is no longer any benefit to be got from marriage and good men are hard to find now. I don't see any advantage in your proposal and you have already had experience of marriage.' My sisters did not accept that and married without my approval although I covered all their costs. They then left with their husbands, who very soon afterwards played them false, took all that they had and went off, abandoning them.

Once again they came back to me, covered in shame, apologized and said: 'Don't blame us. You may be younger than us but you are more intelligent; we shall never again mention marriage, so take us as your slave girls that we may have a bite to eat.' 'Welcome, sisters,' I said. 'No one is dearer to me than you.' And I kissed them and honoured them even more than before. This went on for a full year, after which I decided to fit out a ship to go to Basra. I chose a large one and loaded it with goods, merchandise and everything needed for the voyage. I asked my sisters whether they would prefer to sit at home until I returned from my voyage or whether they would like to come with me. 'We will go with you,' they said, 'as we cannot bear to be parted from you,' and so I took them along.

I had divided my wealth in two, taking half with me and leaving the other half behind, with the idea that, were the ship to be wrecked and we survived, there would be something to support us on our return. We sailed for some days and nights, but the ship then went astray as the captain had not kept to the right course, and without realizing it, we were sailing in the wrong direction. This went on for some time and over a period of ten days we had fair winds. After that, the lookout climbed up to investigate; he called out: 'Good news!' and came down full of joy and told us that he had seen what looked like a city resembling a dove. We were delighted and, within an hour, we could see the place in the distance. We asked the captain its name, but he said: 'By God, I don't know. I have never seen it before and never in my life have I sailed on this sea. But things have turned out safely and all we have to do is put in to harbour. Look out your merchandise and if you can sell, sell and then buy up whatever is there; if that does not work, we can rest here for two days, buy provisions and go on with our voyage.'

We put in and the captain went up to the city. He was away for a time and when he came back he told us: 'Come up and wonder at what God has done to those He created, and seek refuge from His anger.' We went to the city and when we came to the gate, we saw that it was guarded by men with sticks in their hands, but when we got nearer we found that they had been turned to stone, while in the city itself we found that everyone had been transformed to black stone and there was no trace of life. We were astonished, but as we threaded our way through the markets, we discovered that the traders' wares and the gold and silver had remained unchanged. This delighted us and, thinking that there must be some mystery here, we split up and walked through the city streets, each concerned to collect her own booty, money and fabrics.

I myself went to the castle, which turned out to be strongly fortified, and I then entered the royal apartments, where all the utensils were made of gold and silver. There I saw the king wearing robes of bewildering splendour, seated with his chamberlains, officers and viziers. When I approached, I found that he was sitting on a throne studded with pearls and gems, wearing cloth of gold, with every jewel gleaming like a star. Standing around him were fifty mamluks, dressed in silks of various kinds, with drawn swords in their stone hands – an astonishing sight. I then walked into the hall of the harem, whose walls were covered with hangings of silk with gold-embroidered branches. The queen was there asleep, wearing a robe ornamented with fresh pearls. On her head was a crown studded with gemstones of all kinds, while around her neck were necklaces of all sorts. Everything she was wearing, dress and ornaments, was unchanged, but she herself had been transformed to black stone.

I then found an open door and went up to it. There were seven steps and these led to a chamber whose marble floor was spread with gold-embroidered carpets. In it there was a couch made of juniper wood, inset with pearls and precious stones, together with two large emeralds, covered by a pearl-studded hanging. There was also a door from which I could see a light shining. I went to stand over it and there in the centre on a small chair I found a jewel the size of a duck's egg, burning like a candle and shedding light, while spread over the couch was an amazing array of silks. The sight filled me with astonishment. On looking further, I saw lighted candles. 'Someone must have lit these,' I said to myself, and I then went to another room and proceeded to search all through the building, forgetting myself in my astonishment at all this and plunged in thought.

I continued exploring until nightfall, but then, wishing to leave, I found I had lost my way and had no idea where the gate was. So I went back to the chamber with the lighted candles, sat down on the couch and, after reciting a portion of the Quran, wrapped myself in a coverlet, trying in vain to sleep but becoming uneasy. Then at midnight I heard a beautiful voice reciting the Quran. This filled me with joy and I followed the sound until I came to a small room whose door was shut. I opened it and looked inside, to find a chapel with a prayer niche in which hung lighted lamps together with two candles. In this chapel a prayer rug had been put down and on this sat a handsome young man with, before him, a copy of the holy Quran from which he was reading.

Wondering how he alone had been saved from out of all the inhabitants of the city, I entered and greeted him. He looked up and returned my greeting, at which I said: 'By the truth of what you have recited from the Book of God, I implore you to answer my question.' He looked at me, smiling, and replied: 'Servant of God, do you tell me why you came here and I will tell you what happened to me and the people of this city and how it was that I escaped.' So I told him my story, which filled him with wonder, and then I asked him about the townspeople. 'Wait, sister,' he said, and he then closed the Quran and put it into a bag of satin, before making me sit beside him. When I looked at him, I saw him to be the moon when it comes to the full, excellent in his attributes, supple and handsome; his appearance was like a sugar stick, with a well-proportioned frame. As the poet has said:

To the astrologer watching by night
Appeared a beautiful form dressed in twin robes.
Saturn had granted him black hair,
Colouring his temples with the shade of musk.
From Mars derived the redness of his cheek,
While Sagittarius shot arrows from his eyelids.
Mercury supplied keenness of mind
While the Bear forbade the slanderers to look at him.
The astrologer was bewildered by what he saw
And the ground before him was kissed by the full moon.

Almighty God had clothed him in the robe of perfection and embroidered it with the beauty and splendour of the down of his cheek, as the poet has said:

I swear by the intoxication of his eyelids,
By his waist and by the arrows that his magic shoots,
By the smoothness of his flanks, the sharpness of his glance,
His white complexion and the darkness of his hair,
His eyebrow that denies sleep to my eye,
Controlling me as he orders and forbids,
By his rosy cheek and the myrtle of its down,
By the carnelian of his mouth, his pearly teeth,
By his neck and by the beauty of his form,

With pomegranates showing on his chest,
By his haunches that quiver whether he moves or is still,
By his slender waist and by his silken touch,
The lightness of his spirit and all the beauty he encompasses.
I swear by his generous hand and by his truthful tongue,
His high birth and his lofty rank.
For those who know of musk, it is his scent,
And he it is who spreads the scent of ambergris.
Compared with him the radiant sun
Is nothing but the paring of a fingernail.

The glance that I gave him was followed by a thousand sighs and love for him was fixed in my heart. 'My master,' I said, 'answer my question.' 'Willingly,' he replied, and he went on: 'Know, servant of God, that this is my father's city and he is the king whom you saw sitting on the throne turned into black stone, while the queen whom you saw in the hall is my mother. All the people of the city were Magians, worshipping fire rather than Almighty God. They would swear by fire, light, shadows, the heat of the sun and the circling sphere. After my father had for long been without a son, late in his life I was born to him. He brought me up until I was a grown man, and good fortune always preceded me. With us there was an old Muslim woman who believed in God and His Apostle in secret, while in public she followed the practices of my people. My father had faith in her because he saw that she was trustworthy and chaste, and he showed her great respect, thinking that she was his co-religionary. When I grew older he entrusted me to her, saying: "Take him; give him a good upbringing; ground him in the tenets of our faith and look after him." When she had taken me, she taught me about the religion of Islam with the obligations of ritual purification and of prayer, and she made me learn the Quran by heart, telling me to worship none but Almighty God. When she had done all this, she told me to keep it hidden from my father and not to tell him lest he kill me. So I kept the secret for a few days, but then the old woman died and the people of the city sank ever further into unbelief and presumptuous error.

'While they were in this state, suddenly they heard a mighty voice like the rumbling of thunder, calling out in tones that could be heard far and near: "Citizens, turn away from the worship of fire and worship God, the Merciful King." The people were startled and they all came to my father, the king, and asked: "What is this alarming voice that we have heard, astounding and terrifying us?" "Do not be alarmed or frightened by it," he replied, "and do not let it turn you from your religion." Their hearts inclined to what he said; they persisted in their worship of fire and they acted even more wickedly until a year had passed from the first time that they had heard the voice. They then heard it for a second time and, after three years, for a third time – once each year – but they still clung to their beliefs. Then, at dawn one day, divine wrath descended and they, together with their animals and their flocks, were turned to black stone. I was the only one to escape and since that happened, I have been living like this – praying, fasting and reciting the Quran – but I can no longer endure being alone, with no one to keep me company.'

I had lost my heart to him, so I asked him whether he would go to Baghdad with me where he could meet the men of learning and the *faqihs*, and so add to his knowledge, understanding and grasp of religious law. 'Know,' I went on, 'that the slave who stands before you is the mistress of her people, with command over men, eunuchs and slaves. I have a ship laden with merchandise and it was fate that led us here in order that we should see these things, and it was ordained by destiny that you and I should meet.'

I continued to prompt him to leave with me, flattering him and using my wiles until he agreed to accept.

Night 18

Morning now dawned and Shahrazad broke off from what she had been allowed to say. Then, when it was the eighteenth night, SHE SAID:

I have heard, O auspicious king, that the lady continued to prompt him to leave with her until he said yes. THE LADY WENT ON:

I spent the night at his feet, unable to believe what had happened to me because of my joy. In the morning, we got up and, going to the treasuries, we took what was both light to carry and valuable, after which we left the castle and went down to the city. There we met the slaves and the ship's captain, who were searching for me and who were filled with joy when they saw me. I told them, to their astonishment, what I had seen and explained to them the story of the young man and the reason for the curse that had struck the city, as well as what had happened to its people. When my sisters, now these two bitches, saw me with the young man, they became jealous of me and angry, and they secretly schemed against me. We boarded the ship gaily, overjoyed at the profit we had made, although I was more pleased because of the young man. We stayed waiting for a wind, and when it blew fair, we made sail and set off. My sisters sat with me and we started to talk. 'What are you going to do with this handsome young man?' they asked. 'I intend to take him as my husband,' I replied. Then, turning, I went up to him and said: 'Sir, I want to say something to you and I would ask you not to refuse me. When we reach Baghdad, our city, I shall propose myself to you in marriage; you shall be my husband and I shall be your wife.' He agreed to this, and I turned to my sisters and said: 'This young man is enough for me, so whatever profit others have made, they can keep.' 'That is well done of you,' they said, but secretly they continued to plot against me.

On we sailed with a fair wind until we left the Sea of Fear and reached safety. After a few more days of sailing, we came in sight of the walls of Basra. Evening fell and we settled down to sleep, but then my sisters got up, carried me on my mattress and threw me into the sea. They did the same thing with the young man, and as he could not swim well, he was drowned and God entered him in the roll of the martyrs. I wish that I had drowned with him, but God decreed that I should be saved, and so while I was floating in the sea, He provided me with a plank of wood on to which I climbed. The waves then swept me along until they threw me up on the shore of an island. There I walked for the rest of the night and, when morning came, I saw a track just broad enough for a human foot that connected the island to the mainland.

The sun had now risen and I dried my clothes in the sunlight, ate some of the island fruits and drank from its water. Then I set off on the track and went on walking until I was close to the mainland and only two hours away from the city. Suddenly, I saw a snake as thick as a palm tree darting towards me, and as it came I could see it swerving to right and to left until it reached me. Its tongue was trailing along the ground for the length of a span and it was sweeping aside the dust with the whole length of its body. It was being pursued by a dragon, thin and long as a lance. In its flight the snake turned to the right and the left, but the dragon seized its tail. The snake shed tears and its tongue lolled out because of its violent efforts to escape. Feeling sorry for it, I picked up a stone and threw it at the dragon's head, killing it instantly, after which the snake unfolded a pair of wings and flew up into the sky until it passed out of my sight.

I sat there in amazement, but I was tired and sleepy and so, for a time, I fell asleep where I was. When I awoke I found at my feet a girl with two bitches who was massaging my feet. I felt embarrassed by her presence and so I sat up and said: 'Sister, who are you?' 'How quickly you have forgotten me,' she replied. 'I am the one to whom you did a service, killing my foe and sowing the seed of gratitude. I am the snake whom you saved from the dragon. I am one of the *jinn*, as was the dragon. He was my enemy and it was only because of you that I escaped from him. After that, I flew on the wind to the ship from which your sisters threw you overboard, and after taking all its cargo to your house, I sank it. As for your sisters, I turned them into two black bitches, for I know the whole story of their dealings with you, but as for the young man, he had already drowned.' She then carried me off, together with the bitches, and set me down on the roof of my house, in the middle of which I could see all the goods that had been on the ship, not one thing being missing.

Then the snake girl said: 'By the inscription on the ring of our lord Solomon, on whom be peace, if you do not give each of these bitches three hundred lashes every day, I shall come and turn you into a bitch like them.' I told her that I would obey, and so, Commander of the Faithful, I have gone on beating them, although I feel pity for them and they realize that this is not my fault and accept my excuse. This is my story.

The caliph was filled with wonder, and he then asked the doorkeeper the reason for the whip scars on her body. 'Commander of the Faithful,' she replied, 'when my father died he left a great quantity of wealth, and soon afterwards I married the wealthiest man of his time.' SHE WENT ON:

I stayed with him for a year, but he too then died and from him I inherited eighty thousand gold dinars, this being my portion in accordance with Islamic law. I was then exceedingly rich; my reputation spread, and I had ten costumes made, each worth a thousand dinars. As I was sitting one day, in came an old woman with pendulous cheeks, thinning eyebrows, popping eyes, broken teeth and a blotched face. She was bleary-eyed, with a head that looked as though it had been covered in plaster, grey hair and a bent body covered in scabs. Her skin was discoloured and she was dribbling mucus, as the poet has described:

An old woman of evil omen – may God have no mercy on her youth
Or pardon her sins the day she comes to die –
She could lead a thousand bolting mules
With a spider's web for reins, so domineering is she.

On entering, this woman greeted me and after she had kissed the
ground before me, she said: 'I have a fatherless daughter and tonight is
her wedding and the ceremony of her unveiling. We are strangers with
no acquaintances in this city and our hearts are broken. Were you to
come to the wedding, you would win reward and recompense from God,
as the ladies of the city would hear that you were going and would come
themselves. You would then mend my daughter's broken heart, for her
only helper is God.' She then wept, kissed my feet and recited the lines:

Your presence there would honour us,
And that we would acknowledge.
While if you do not come,
We have no substitute and no replacement.

Moved by pity and compassion, I agreed, saying: 'I shall do something
for her, if God wills, and she shall be married in my clothes with my
jewellery and my finery.' The old woman was delighted: she bent down
to kiss my feet and said: 'May God reward you and mend your heart as
you have mended mine. But do not trouble yourself to do this service
now. If you are ready in the evening, I will come and fetch you.' She
then kissed my hand and left. I was ready when she came back and she
said: 'My lady, the women of the town have come. I told them that you
were going to be there and they were delighted and are waiting for you
to arrive.' So I drew my veil and got up, taking my maids with me, and
I went on until we came to a lane that had been swept and sprinkled
with water, and where a cool breeze was blowing. There we arrived at
an arched gate with a strongly built marble dome, leading to the door
of a palace that soared from the ground to touch the clouds. Over the
gate these lines were inscribed:

I am a house built for pleasure
And consecrated for all time to joy and relaxation.
In my centre is a fountain with gushing waters
That clear away all sorrows.
Flowers border it – anemones and the rose,
Myrtle, narcissus blooms and camomile.

When we got to the door, the old woman knocked, and when it was opened, we went in to find a hall spread with carpets, in which lighted lamps were hanging and candles were ranged, with gems and precious stones. We walked through the hall until we came to a room of unparalleled splendour, spread with silken rugs and lit by hanging lamps and two rows of candles. In the centre of it there was a couch of juniper wood studded with pearls and gems and covered with a buttoned canopy of satin. Before we knew what was happening, out came a girl. I looked at her, Commander of the Faithful, and saw that she was more perfect than the moon at its full, with a forehead brighter than daybreak, as the poet has said:

> In the palaces of the Caesars she is a maiden
> From among the bashful ones of the Chosroes' courts.
> On her cheeks are rosy tokens;
> How beautiful are those red cheeks.
> A slender girl with a languid, sleepy glance,
> She encompasses all beauty's graces.
> The lock of hair that hangs above her forehead
> Is the night of care set over joyful dawn.

She emerged from beneath the canopy and greeted me as her dear and revered sister, giving me a thousand welcomes and reciting:

> Were the house to know who comes to visit it,
> It would kiss in joyfulness the place where you have trod.
> And call out with its silent voice:
> 'Welcome to the generous and noble one.'

She then sat down and said: 'Sister, I have a brother who has seen you at a number of weddings and festivals. He is a young man more handsome than I am, and he is deeply in love with you because of the richness of beauty and grace that you possess. He has heard that you are the mistress of your people, as he is the master of his. Because he wished to attach himself to you, he played this trick in order that I should meet you. He wants to marry you in accordance with the ordinance of God and of His Apostle, and there is no disgrace in what is lawful.' When I heard what she had to say and saw that I was now inside the house, I told her that I would agree. She was delighted and, after clapping her hands, she opened a door from which emerged a young man in the bloom of his youth, immaculately dressed, well built, handsome, graceful, splendid and perfect, with engaging manners. His eyebrows were like an archer's bow and his eyes could steal hearts with licit magic, as the poet's description has it:

> His face is like a crescent moon,
> Where marks of good fortune are like pearls.

How excellent also are the lines:

> Blessed is his beauty and blessed is our God.
> How great is He who formed and shaped this man!
> Alone he has acquired all loveliness,
> And in his beauty all mankind strays lost.
> Upon his cheek beauty has written these words:
> 'I testify there is no handsome man but he.'

When I looked at him, my heart turned to him and I fell in love. He sat beside me and I talked to him for an hour, after which the girl clapped her hands for a second time. The door of a side room opened and from it emerged a *qadi* with four witnesses, who greeted us and then sat down. The marriage contract between me and the young man was drawn up, after which the others withdrew. 'May this be a blessed night,' said my bridegroom, turning to me. 'But, my lady,' he added, 'I impose one condition on you.' 'What is that?' I asked. He got up and fetched a copy of the Quran and said: 'Swear that you will not look at any other man but me, or incline to him.' I swore to that, to his great joy. He embraced me and my whole heart was filled with love for him. Servants then set out a table and we ate and drank our fill. Night fell and he took me to bed, where we continued to kiss and embrace until morning.

We continued in this state for a month, living in happiness and joy, and at the end of that time I asked my husband's leave to go to market to buy some material. After he had given me permission, I put on an outdoor mantle, and taking with me the old woman and a servant girl, I went down to the market. There I sat in the shop of a young merchant who was known to the old woman. She told me that he was a youth whose father had died, leaving him a huge amount of money. 'He has a great stock of goods,' she added. 'You will find whatever you want, and no trader in the market has finer fabrics.' Then she told the man to produce for me the most expensive stuff that he had and he replied: 'To hear is to obey.' The old woman then began to sing his praises, but I told her: 'There is no necessity for this. All we want is to get what we need and then to go back home.'

The man brought out what we were looking for and we produced the money for him, but he refused to take anything and said: 'This is a guest gift for you today from me.' I said to the old woman: 'If he refuses to accept the money, then give him back the stuff.' 'By God,' he said, 'I shall not accept anything from you, and all this is a gift from me in exchange for a single kiss, which is of more value to me than everything that is in my shop.' 'What good will a kiss do you?' asked the old woman, but then she told me: 'You heard what he said, daughter. What harm will a kiss do you, and you can then take what you want?' 'Don't you know that I have sworn an oath?' I asked, but she went on: 'Stay silent and let him kiss you. You will have done nothing wrong and you can take back this money.' She continued to inveigle me, until I fell into the trap and agreed. I then covered my eyes and hid myself from the passers-by with the edge of my veil. He put his mouth on my cheek beneath my veil and, after kissing me, he bit me hard, piercing the skin of my cheek so that I fainted.

The old woman held me to her breast and when I recovered my senses, I found the shop closed, with her grieving over me and saying: 'God has averted what could have been worse.' Then she said to me: 'Come back to the house with me and pull yourself together, lest you be shamed. When you get home, go to bed, pretend to be sick and cover yourself up. I will fetch you something with which to treat this bite and it will soon be better.' After a while, I got up, full of care and extremely fearful, and I walked very slowly home, where I acted as though I was sick. At nightfall, in came my husband. He asked: 'My lady, what happened to you while you were out?' 'I'm not well,' I said, 'and I have a headache.' He looked at me, lit a candle and came up to me. 'What is this wound on your tender cheek?' he asked. 'After receiving your permission to go out today to buy materials, I left the house but was pushed by a camel carrying firewood; my veil was torn and, as you can see, I got this wound on my cheek, for the streets are narrow here.' 'Tomorrow I will go to the governor,' he said, 'and tell him to hang everyone who sells firewood in the city.' I implored him not to burden himself with the guilt of wronging someone, adding: 'I was riding on a donkey which threw me and I fell on the ground where I struck a piece of wood which grazed my cheek and wounded me.' He said: 'Tomorrow I shall go to Ja'far the Barmecide and tell him what happened to you, so that he may put every donkey driver in this city to death.' 'Are you going to kill everyone because of me?' I asked. 'What happened was a matter of fate and destiny.' 'It must be done,' he said, and he kept on insisting on this until, when he got up, I turned around and spoke sharply to him.

At that, Commander of the Faithful, he realized what had happened to me. 'You have been false to your oath,' he said, letting out a great cry. The door opened and seven black slaves came in. On his orders, they dragged me from my bed and threw me down in the middle of the room. He told one of them to hold my shoulders and to sit on my head, while another was to sit on my knees and hold my feet. A third came with a sword in his hand and my husband ordered him to strike me with the sword and cut me in two and then said: 'Let each of you take a piece and throw it into the Tigris as food for the fish. This is the reward of those who betray their oaths and are false to their love.' He grew even more angry and recited these verses:

If I must have a partner in my love,
Even though passion slay me, I shall drive love from my soul.
I say to my soul: 'Die nobly,
For there is no good in a love that is opposed.'

Then he told the slave: 'Strike, Sa'd.' When the slave was sure that his master meant what he said, he sat over me and said: 'Lady, recite the confession of faith, and if there is anything that you want done, tell me, for this is the end of your life.' 'Wait a little, good slave,' I said, 'so that I can give you my last instructions.' Then I raised my head and saw the state that I was in and how I had fallen from greatness to degradation. My tears flowed and I wept bitterly, but my husband recited angrily:

Say to one who has tired of union and turned from me,
Being pleased to take another partner in love:
'I had enough of you before you had enough of me,
And what has passed between us is enough for me.'

When I heard that, Commander of the Faithful, I wept and, looking at him, I recited:

You have abandoned me in my love and have sat back;
You have left my swollen eyelids sleepless and have slept.
You made a pact between my eyes and sleeplessness.
My heart does not forget you, nor are my tears concealed.
You promised to be faithful in your love,
But played the traitor when you won my heart.

I loved you as a child who did not know of love,
So do not kill me now that I am learning it.
I ask you in God's Name that, if I die,
You write upon my tomb: 'Here lies a slave of love.'
It may be that a sad one who knows love's pangs
Will pass this lover's heart of mine and feel compassion.

On finishing these lines, I shed more tears, but when my husband heard them and saw my tears, he became even angrier and recited:

I left the darling of my heart not having tired of her,
But for a sin that she was guilty of.
She wanted a partner to share in our love,
But my heart's faith rejects a plural god.

When he had finished his lines, I pleaded with him tearfully, telling myself that if I could get round him with words, he might spare my life, even if he were to take everything that I had. So I complained to him of my sufferings and recited:

Treat me with justice and do not kill me;
The sentence of separation is unjust.
You loaded me with passion's heavy weight,
Although even one shirt is too much for my strength.
I am not surprised that my life should be lost;
My wonder is how, after your loss, my body can be recognized.

I finished the lines weeping, but he looked at me and rebuffed and reviled me, reciting:

You left me for another and made clear
You were forsaking me; this is not how we were.
I shall abandon you as you abandoned me,
Enduring without you as you endure my loss.
I cease to occupy myself with you,
For you have occupied yourself with someone else.
The severance of our love is set at your door, not at mine.

On finishing these lines, he shouted at the slave: 'Cut her in half and let us be rid of her, for there is no good to be got from her.' While we were sparring with each other in this exchange of verses and I had become certain I would die, despairing of life and commending my affair to

Almighty God, suddenly in came the old woman, who threw herself at my husband's feet, kissed them and said tearfully: 'My son, I have brought you up and served you. I conjure you by this to spare this girl, for she has not committed a crime that deserves death. You are very young and I am afraid lest she involve you in sin – as the saying goes, "Every killer is killed." What is this slut? Cast her off from you, from your mind and from your heart.' Then she wept and she kept on pressing him until he agreed and said: 'I shall spare her life, but I must mark her in a way that will stay with her for the rest of her life.' On his orders, the slaves then dragged me off, stripped me of my clothes and stretched me out. They sat on me while he fetched a rod from a quince tree and set about beating me. He went on striking my back and sides so severely that I lost consciousness, giving up hope of life. He then told the slaves that when night fell they should take the old woman with them as a guide, carry me off and throw me into my old house. They did as they were told and after throwing me into the house, they went off.

It was not until daybreak that I recovered from my faint and I then tried to soothe my wounds, treating my body with salves and medicines. As you can see, my ribs continued to look as though they had been struck with clubs, and for four months I remained weak and bedridden, tending to my own wounds until I recovered and was cured. I then went to the house that had been the scene of my downfall, only to find it ruined and reduced to a pile of rubble, with the lane in which it stood totally demolished. I could find no news of what had happened and so I came to my half-sister, with whom I found these two black bitches. After greeting her, I told her everything that had happened to me. 'My sister,' she said, 'who is unscathed by the misfortunes of Time? Praise be to God who brought a safe ending to this affair,' and she started to recite:

This is how Time acts, so show endurance
Whether you be stripped of wealth or parted from your love.

She then told me her own story, of what had happened to her with her sisters and how they had ended up. I stayed there with her and the word 'marriage' never crossed our lips. We were then joined by this girl who acts as our housekeeper, going out each day to buy what we need for the next twenty-four hours. Things went on like this until last night. Our sister had gone out as usual to buy our food when she returned with the porter, and the three dervishes arrived shortly afterwards. We talked with them, brought them in and treated them well. After only a little of the night had passed, we were joined by three respectable merchants from Mosul. They told us their story and we talked with them, but we had imposed a condition on all our visitors, which they broke. We paid them back for this breach and asked them all for their stories, which they recited. We then forgave them and they left. Today, before we knew what was happening, we were brought before you. This is our story.

The caliph was filled with amazement at this and had the account written down and placed in his archives.

Night 19

Morning now dawned and Shahrazad broke off from what she had been allowed to say. Then, when it was the nineteenth night, SHE CONTINUED:

I have heard, O auspicious king, that the caliph ordered their story to be written down in the records and placed in the royal archives. He then asked the first girl: 'Have you any news of the *jinn* lady who bewitched your sisters?' 'Commander of the Faithful,' she replied, 'she gave me a lock of her hair and told me that when I wanted her I should burn a single hair and she would come quickly, even if she were on the far side of Mount Qaf.' The caliph asked her to produce the lock of hair, which she did, and he then took a single strand and burned it. When the smell of the burning spread, the palace was rocked by a tremor; there was a sound like a peal of thunder and there stood the lady. As she was a Muslim, she greeted the caliph, who replied: 'Peace be on you and the mercy and blessings of God.' 'Know,' she went on, 'that this girl sowed the seed of gratitude for a good deed that she did me, for which I could not repay her, when she saved me from death and killed my enemy. I then saw what her sisters had done to her. At first I wanted to kill them but I was afraid that this might distress her, so then I thought that I should take revenge by turning them by magic into dogs. If you now want them to be set free, Commander of the Faithful, I shall release them as a favour to you and to her, for I am a Muslim.' 'Do so,' he said, 'and after that I shall begin to investigate the affair of the girl who was beaten. If it turns out that she was telling the truth, we shall avenge her on whoever wronged her.'

'Commander of the Faithful,' said the lady, 'I shall release the two and then tell you who it was who wronged this girl and seized her wealth – someone who is your closest relation.' She then took a bowl of water, cast a spell over it and recited some unintelligible words. She sprinkled water on the faces of the two bitches and said: 'Return to your former shapes as humans,' which they did. 'Commander of the Faithful,' she then said, 'the young man who beat the girl is your own son, al-Amin, the brother of al-Ma'mun. He had heard of her great beauty and set a trap for her. But he married her legally and was within his rights to beat her, as he had imposed a condition on her and got her to swear a solemn oath that she would do nothing to break it. Break it she did, however, and he was going to kill her, but for fear of God he beat her instead and sent her back to her own house. This is the story of the second girl, but God knows better.'

When the caliph heard what she had to say and learned how the girl had come to be beaten, he was filled with astonishment and said: 'Glory be to God, the Exalted, the Omnipotent, Who has granted me the favour of learning this girl's history and rescued these two others from sorcery and torture. By God, I shall do something that will be recorded after me.' Then he had his son al-Amin brought before him and he questioned him about the second girl, questions to which al-Amin returned a truthful answer. He then brought in *qadis* and notaries, as well as the three dervishes, together with the first girl and her two sisters who had been bewitched. He married the three of them to the three dervishes, who had told him that they were kings, and whom he now appointed as chamberlains at his court, giving them all they needed and assigning them allowances, as well as lodgings in the palace of Baghdad. He returned the girl who had been beaten to his son al-Amin, renewing their marriage contract, giving her a great store of wealth and ordering that their house should be rebuilt with the greatest splendour. He himself married the housekeeper and slept with her that night and in the morning he gave her a chamber of her own among his concubines, together with slave girls to serve her and regular allowances. The people were astonished at his magnanimity, generosity and wisdom. His orders were that all these stories should be written down.

Dunyazad said to her sister: 'Shahrazad, by God, no one has heard so fine and pleasant a story, but tell me another to pass what remains of this wakeful night.' 'Willingly,' Shahrazad replied, 'if the king gives me leave.' 'Tell your story at once,' he said, AND SHE BEGAN:

It is said, king of the age and lord of our times, that one night the
caliph Harun al-Rashid summoned his vizier Ja'far and said: 'I want to
go down into the city to ask the common people about the governors
who have charge of them, so as to depose any of whom they complain
and promote those to whom they are grateful.' 'To hear is to obey,'
replied Ja'far.

So the caliph, Ja'far and Masrur left the palace and made their way
through the city, walking in the markets and streets until they passed a
lane. There they saw a very old man carrying on his head a fishing net
and a basket, and holding a stick in his hand. He was walking slowly
and reciting:

They said to me: 'Among mankind
You with your wisdom are a moonlit night.'
I said: 'Do not say this to me;
There is no wisdom without power.
Were they to try to pawn me and my wisdom,
Together with my books and my inkstand,
For one day's worth of food, it would not work
And such a bargain would be thought contemptible.
The poor, their state, their life,
How dark they are with troubles!
In summer they cannot find food, and in the cold
They have to warm themselves over a brazier.
Street dogs attack them and they are the butt
Of every despicable man.
When one of them complains about his lot,
There is none to excuse him among all mankind
Such is the life of the poor man;
It will be best for him when he is in his grave.'

When the caliph heard what the man was reciting, he said to Ja'far:
'Look at this man and note his verses, which show that he is in need.'
The caliph then went up to the man and said: 'Shaikh, what is your
craft?' 'I am a fisherman,' he replied. 'I left home at midday, but up till
now God has not provided me with anything with which I can feed my
family. I am tired of life and I wish that I were dead.' 'Would you go
back with us to the Tigris, stand on the bank and trust in my luck as
you cast your net. Whatever comes up I will buy for a hundred dinars.'
When he heard this, the old man agreed with delight. He went with the

three of them back to the river, cast his net and waited before pulling in the cord and dragging it in. Up it came with a heavy, locked chest. The caliph looked at the chest, handled it and noted its weight, after which he gave the fisherman his hundred dinars, and the man went off.

The caliph himself then left, accompanied by Masrur, who was carrying the chest, and they brought it up to the palace. Candles were lit and after the chest had been placed in front of the caliph, Ja'far and Masrur came forward and broke it open. In it they found a basket of palm leaves sewn up with threads of red wool, and after they had cut this open, they found a carpet. When they had lifted this out, they discovered a shawl and wrapped in this was a girl like a silver ingot, who had been killed and cut in pieces – a sight that so distressed the caliph that his tears flowed over his cheeks. He turned to Ja'far and said: 'Dog of a vizier, are people to be murdered and thrown into the river during my reign, so that I am to be held responsible for them on the Day of Judgement? By God, I must make the murderer pay for this girl's death and I shall put him to the most cruel of deaths.' He then told Ja'far in his furious rage: 'It is as true as is my descent from the 'Abbasid caliphs that if you do not produce the murderer for my justice, I will hang you at the palace gate together with forty of your cousins.'

Before leaving his presence, Ja'far asked for a three-day delay, which the caliph granted. He then went down sadly into the city, saying to himself: 'How can I find out who killed this girl and bring him to the caliph? If I bring the wrong person, I shall be held responsible for him. I don't know what to do.' For three days, he sat at home and on the fourth the caliph sent a chamberlain to fetch him. When he came to the caliph and was asked where the murderer was, he said: 'Commander of the Faithful, am I the monitor of murder victims that I should know who killed the girl?' The caliph was enraged and gave orders that he should be hanged below the palace. A town crier was ordered to call out in the streets of Baghdad: 'Whoever wants to see the hanging of Ja'far the Barmecide, the caliph's vizier, and the hanging of his Barmecide cousins at the palace gate, let him come to watch.' People came out from all quarters of the city to see the execution, although they did not know why the Barmecides were being hanged. The gallows were set up and the victims were made to stand beneath.

The executioners were waiting for the agreed signal from the caliph and the crowd was weeping for Ja'far and his cousins. At this point, however, out came a young man – handsome, well dressed, with a face bright as the moon, dark eyes, radiant forehead, red cheeks and a mole like a disc of ambergris. He cleared a way for himself through the people and kept on until he stood before Ja'far. 'Lord of the emirs and shelterer of the poor,' he said, 'you are saved from this plight. The killer of the murdered girl whom you found in the chest is I, so hang me in retaliation for her death and take revenge for her on me.'

When Ja'far heard this, he was glad that he himself had escaped death, but he felt sorry for the young man. While they were talking, an old man, stricken in years, made his way through the crowd until he reached the two of them. He greeted them and said: 'My lord, great vizier, don't believe what this young man says. No one but I killed the girl, so avenge her death on me; if you do not, I will demand justice from you in the presence of Almighty God.' 'Vizier,' said the youth, 'this is the maundering of an old man who doesn't know what he is saying. It was I and I alone who killed her, so make me pay for her death.' 'My son,' said the old man, 'you are young and this world is still attractive to you, while I am old and have had my fill of it. I shall give my life to ransom you and I shall ransom the vizier and his cousins, for I killed the girl and I conjure you by God to hang me quickly, as there is no life for me now that she is dead.'

The vizier was astonished to see what was happening and he took the young man and the old one to the caliph. He kissed the ground and said: 'Commander of the Faithful, I have brought you the murderer of the girl.' 'Which is he?' asked the caliph. 'This young man says that he killed her, while the old man here says that that is a lie and that he himself is the killer. Here are the two of them before you.' The caliph looked at them and asked: 'Which of you did kill her?' 'I did,' said the young man. 'I am the killer,' protested the old man. 'Take the two of them,' said the caliph to Ja'far, 'and hang them both.' 'If only one of them killed her,' said Ja'far, 'then to hang the other would be unjust.' The young man insisted: 'By the truth of the One God Who raised up the heavens and spread out the earth, it was I who killed her and this was how she was killed.' He described what the caliph had found, which made him sure that the young man was indeed the murderer.

Filled with wonder at what the two had said, the caliph asked the young man: 'Why was it that you unjustly killed this girl and what led you to confess to the murder without being beaten? Why did you come yourself just now to tell me to avenge her on you?' THE YOUNG MAN REPLIED:

You must know, Commander of the Faithful, that this girl was my cousin and my wife, while this old man is her father and my uncle. I married her when she was a virgin and God gave me three sons by her. She used to love me and wait on me and I saw no fault in her, while I for my part loved her dearly. At the beginning of this month, she fell seriously ill, but I brought her doctors and gradually she got better. I wanted to take her to the baths but she said that before going, there was something that she wanted for which she had been longing. I said that I would willingly get it and asked what it was. 'I have a longing for an apple,' she said, 'that I can smell and from which I can take a bite.' I went straight away to the city and searched for apples, but I couldn't find a single one to buy, even for a dinar. I went back home in distress and told my wife of my failure. This upset her; she had been weak before, and that night she became much weaker.

I spent the night brooding over the problem and when morning came, I left my house and did the rounds of the orchards, one after the other, without finding any apples in them. Then I met an old gardener and, when I asked him, he told me: 'There are few or no apples to be found, except in Basra, in the orchard of the Commander of the Faithful, where they are in the charge of his gardener who keeps them for his master.' I went back home and my love and affection for my wife led me to make myself ready to set out on a journey to Basra. I travelled for fifteen days and nights there and back, bringing my wife three apples which I had bought from the gardener at Basra for one dinar each. I went in and gave them to her, but they gave her no pleasure and she put them aside. Her weakness and fever had grown worse and this went on for ten days, after which she recovered.

I then left my house and went to my shop, where I sat buying and selling. At midday, while I was sitting there, a black slave passed by holding one of those three apples in his hand and playing with it. When I asked him about the apple, pretending that I wanted to get one like it, he laughed and told me that he had got it from his mistress. 'I had been away,' he explained, 'and when I got back, I found her sick. She had three apples with her and she told me that her cuckold of a husband had gone to Basra for them and had bought them for three dinars. It was one of these that I took.'

When I heard what the slave had to say, Commander of the Faithful, the world turned black for me. I got up, closed my shop and returned home, out of my mind with anger. Looking at the apples, I could see only two. 'Where is the third?' I asked my wife, and when she said: 'I don't know,' I was certain that the slave had told me the truth, so I picked up a knife, and coming from behind her, without a word I knelt on her breast and slit her throat with the knife. Then I cut off her head and quickly put her in a basket, covering her with a shawl. I wrapped her in a piece of carpet, sewed the whole thing up and put it in a chest, which I locked. I then loaded it on to my mule and threw it with my own hands into the Tigris. In God's Name, Commander of the Faithful, I implore you to hang me quickly, as I am afraid that my wife will demand restitution from me on the Day of Judgement. For when I had thrown her into the river without anyone knowing what I had done, I went back home and there I found my eldest son in tears, although he did not know what I had done to his mother. When I asked him why he was crying, he told me that he had taken one of his mother's apples and had gone into the lane to play with his brothers. He said: 'But a tall black slave snatched it from me and asked me where I had got it. I told him that my father had gone to Basra to bring it for my mother who was sick and that he had bought three apples for three dinars. The slave took the apple and paid no attention to me, even though I told him this a second and a third time, and then he hit me and went off with it. I was afraid that my mother would beat me because of it and so my brothers and I went off out of the city. Evening came and I was still afraid of what she might do to me. For God's sake, father, don't say anything to her that may make her ill again.'

When I heard what the boy had to say, I realized that this slave was the one who had made up a lying story to hurt my wife and I was certain that I had killed her unjustly. While I was weeping bitterly, this old man, her father, arrived and, when I told him what had happened, he sat down beside me and wept. We went on weeping until midnight, and for five days until now we have been mourning her and regretting her unjust death. All the blame for this rests on the slave and it is he who is responsible for her death. I implore you, by your ancestors' honour, to kill me quickly, as there is no life for me now she is dead. So avenge her death on me.

When the caliph heard the young man's story, he was filled with astonishment and said: 'By God, I shall hang no one except this damned slave and I shall do a deed which will cure the sick and please the Glorious King.'

Night 20

Morning now dawned and Shahrazad broke off from what she had been allowed to say. Then, when it was the twentieth night, SHE CONTINUED:

I have heard, O auspicious king, that the caliph swore that he would hang no one but the slave, as what the young man had done was excusable. Then he turned to Ja'far and said: 'Fetch me this damned slave who was responsible for all this, and if you fail, you will take his place.' Ja'far went away weeping and saying: 'Twice I have been threatened with death; the pitcher does not always escape unbroken. There is nothing that I can do about this but hope that He who saved me on the first occasion may save me on the second. By God, I shall not leave my house for three days, and the True God will do what He sees fit.'

Accordingly, he stayed inside for three days and on the fourth he brought in the *qadis* and the notaries and took a tearful farewell of his children. At that moment, a messenger arrived from the caliph, saying: 'The Commander of the Faithful is furiously angry and has sent for you, saying that before the day is over you will be hanged.' When Ja'far heard that, he wept, as did his children, his slaves and his whole household. When he had finished taking leave of the others, he went up to his youngest daughter, whom he loved more than all his other children, to say goodbye to her. He clasped her to his breast, kissed and wept at parting from her. In her pocket he could feel something round and he asked her what it was. 'An apple, father,' she told him, 'inscribed with the name of our lord, the caliph. Our slave Raihan brought it four days ago and would not give it to me until I paid him two dinars.'

When Ja'far heard about the slave and the apple, he was overjoyed. Putting his hand into his daughter's pocket, he brought out the apple and recognized it, exclaiming: 'O God, Whose deliverance is near at hand!' He then ordered the slave to be brought, and when he had come, Ja'far asked him where he had got the apple. 'By God, master,' he replied, 'if lies can save a man once, truth can save him twice. I didn't steal it from your palace, from the imperial palace or from the Commander of the Faithful's orchard. Five days ago, while I was out walking, I went into a lane in the city where I saw some children playing. One of them had this apple and I snatched it away from him and hit him. He cried and told me that it belonged to his sick mother. "She wanted my father to get her an apple," he told me, "and my father went to Basra and bought her three of them, for which he paid three dinars. I stole one of the three to play with." I paid no attention to the child's tears and took the apple and came here. Then my little mistress paid two gold dinars for it. That is my story.'

When Ja'far heard this, he was amazed that the mischief involving the death of the girl had been caused by his own slave. He was sorry for his connection with him but delighted at his own escape, reciting these lines:

When a slave brings disaster on you,
Use him as a ransom for your life.
You can get many other slaves,
But you will never find another life.

Grasping the slave by the hand, he brought him to the caliph and told him his story from beginning to end. The caliph was full of astonishment and laughed until he fell over. He ordered that the story should be written down and spread among the people, but Ja'far said: 'Do not wonder at this tale for it is not more astonishing than the story of the vizier Nur al-Din 'Ali, the Egyptian, and Shams al-Din Muhammad, his brother.' 'Tell it to me,' said the caliph, 'although what can be more wonderful than the story we have just heard?' 'I shall not tell it to you,' said Ja'far, 'unless you promise not to execute my slave.' 'If it is really more remarkable than what has just happened, I shall grant you his life, but if not, then I shall have him killed.' JA'FAR BEGAN:

Know then, Commander of the Faithful, that in the old days there was in Egypt a just and upright sultan who loved the poor and would sit with men of learning. He had an intelligent and experienced vizier, with a knowledge of affairs and of administration. This vizier was a very old man and he had two sons, fair as moons, unequalled in comeliness and beauty. The name of the elder was Shams al-Din Muhammad, while the younger was Nur al-Din 'Ali. Nur al-Din was more conspicuously graceful and handsome than his brother, so much so that his fame had spread in other lands, and people came to Egypt to see his beauty.

It then happened that their father died. He was mourned by the sultan, who went to the sons, brought them close to him and gave them robes of honour. 'Do not be distressed,' he said, 'for you will take your father's place.' This delighted them and they kissed the ground in front of him. After a month of mourning for their father, they entered into office as joint viziers, sharing between themselves the power that had been in their father's hands, with one of them accompanying the sultan whenever he went on his travels.

It happened that the sultan was about to leave on a journey in the morning and it was the turn of the elder brother to go with him. On the night before, the two brothers were talking together and the elder said to the younger: 'Brother, it is my intention that you and I should marry on the same night.' 'Do what you want,' said his brother, 'for I agree to your suggestion.' When they had made this agreement, the elder said: 'If God so decrees, we shall marry two girls and consummate the marriage on one and the same night. Then they will give birth on the same day and, God willing, your wife will produce a boy and mine a girl. We shall then marry them to each other and they will be husband and wife.' 'What dowry will you ask from my son for your daughter?' asked Nur al-Din. 'I shall take from your son,' replied Shams al-Din, 'three thousand dinars, three orchards and three estates. On no other terms will the marriage contract be valid.'

When he heard this, Nur al-Din said: 'What is this dowry that you want to impose as a condition on my son? Don't you know that we two are brothers and that both of us, by God's grace, are joint viziers, equal in rank? You should give your daughter to my son without asking for any dowry at all, and if there must be one, then it should be fixed at something that will merely show people that a payment has been made. You know that the male is better than the female. My son is a male and it is through him and not through your daughter that we shall be remembered.' 'What about my daughter, then?' asked Shams al-Din. 'It will not be through her that we shall be remembered among the emirs,' his brother told him, and added: 'You want to deal with me like the man in the story who approached one of his friends to ask for something. "I swear by the Name of God," said his friend, "that I shall do what you ask, but tomorrow." In reply, the other recited:

If favours are put off until next day,
For those who know, that is rejection.'

Shams al-Din said: 'I see that you are selling me short and making out that your son is better than my daughter. It is clear that you lack intelligence and have no manners. You talk about our shared vizierate, but I only let you share out of pity for you, so that you might help me as an assistant and I might not cause you disappointment. Now, by God, after what you have said, I shall not marry my daughter to your son, even if you were to pay out her weight in gold.' Nur al-Din was angry when he heard this and said: 'I'm no longer willing to marry my son to your daughter.' 'And I'm not prepared to accept him as a husband for her,' repeated Shams al-Din, adding: 'Were I not going off on a journey I would make an example of you, but when I get back, I shall let you see what my honour requires.'

On hearing what his brother had to say, Nur al-Din was beside himself with anger, but he managed to conceal this. The two of them spent the night in separate quarters and in the morning the sultan set out on his journey, going by Giza and making for the Pyramids, accompanied by the vizier Shams al-Din. As for Shams al-Din's brother, Nur al-Din, after spending the night in a furious rage, he got up and performed the morning prayer. Then he went to his strongroom and, taking out a small pair of saddlebags, he filled them with gold. Remembering his brother's contemptuous remarks, he started to recite these lines:

Go, and you will replace the one you leave behind;
Work hard, for in this lies life's pleasure.
The stay-at-home is humble, arriving at no goal
Except distress, so leave your land and go.
I see that water left to stand goes bad;
If it flows, it is sweet, but if not, it is not.
Were the full moon not to wane,
The watcher would not always follow it.
Lions that do not leave their lair will find no prey;
Arrows not shot from bows can strike no target.
Gold dust when in the mine is worth no more than earth,
And aloes wood in its own land is merely used for fires.
When taken from the mine, gold is a precious object of demand,
While elsewhere in the world it is outranked by aloes wood.

When Nur al-Din had finished these lines, he told one of his servants to prepare the official mule with its quilted saddle. This beast, coloured like a starling, had a high, dome-like back; its saddle was of gold and its stirrups of Indian steel; its trappings were like those of the Chosroes; and it looked like a bride unveiled. Nur al-Din ordered that a silk carpet and a prayer rug should be put on it, with the saddlebags being placed under the rug. He then told his servants and slaves that he was going on a pleasure trip outside the city. 'I shall go towards Qalyub,' he said, 'and spend three nights away. None of you are to follow me, for I am feeling depressed.'

He quickly mounted the mule, taking with him only a few provisions, and he then left Cairo, making for open country. By noon he had reached Bilbais, where he dismounted, rested and allowed the mule to rest too. He took and ate some of his provisions, and in Bilbais he bought more food for himself and fodder for his mule. He then set out into the country, and when night fell, he had come to a place called al-Sa'diya. Here he spent the night, getting out some food, placing the saddlebags beneath his head and spreading out the carpet. He slept there in the desert, still consumed with anger, and after his night's sleep, he rode off in the morning, urging on his mule until he came to Aleppo. There he stayed for three days in one of the *khans*, looking around the place at his leisure until both he and the mule were rested. Then he decided to move on and, mounting his mule, he rode out of the city without knowing where he was heading. His journey continued until, without knowing where he was, he reached Basra. He stopped at a *khan*, unloaded the saddlebags from the mule and spread out the prayer mat. He then handed over the mule with all its gear to the gatekeeper of the *khan*, asking him to exercise it, which he did.

It happened that the vizier of Basra was sitting at the window of his palace. He looked at the mule with its costly trappings and thought that it might be a ceremonial beast, the mount of viziers or kings. Perplexed by this, he told one of his servants to bring him the gatekeeper of the city. The servant did as he was told, and the gatekeeper came to him and kissed the ground. The vizier, who was a very old man, asked him who the mule's owner might be and what he was like. 'Master,' said the gatekeeper, 'the owner of this mule is a very young man of the merchant class, impressive and dignified, with elegant manners, the son of a merchant.' On hearing this, the vizier got up and after riding to the *khan*, he approached Nur al-Din who, seeing him coming, rose to meet him. He greeted the vizier who, in turn, welcomed him, dismounted from his horse, and embraced him, making him sit beside him. 'My son,' he said, 'where have you come from and what do you want?' 'Master,' replied Nur al-Din, 'I have come from Cairo. I was the son of a vizier there, but my father moved from this world to the mercy of Almighty God.' He then told his story from beginning to end, adding: 'I have made up my mind that I shall never return until I have passed through every city and every land.' 'My son,' said the vizier when he heard this, 'do not obey the promptings of pride or you will destroy yourself. The lands are desolate and I am afraid lest Time bring misfortunes on you.'

He then had Nur al-Din's saddlebags placed on the mule and, taking the carpet and the prayer mat, he brought him to his house where he lodged him in elegant quarters and showed him honour, kindness and much affection. 'My boy,' he said to him, 'I am an old man and I have no son, but God has provided me with a daughter who is your match in beauty and whose hand I have refused to many suitors. I have conceived love for you in my heart and so I ask whether you would be willing to take her to serve you, while you become her husband. If you accept, I shall bring you to the sultan of Basra and tell him that you are the son of my brother, and I shall get him to appoint you as his vizier in my place. I shall then stay at home, for I am an old man.'

When Nur al-Din heard what he had to say, he bowed his head and said: 'To hear is to obey.' The vizier was delighted and he told his servants to set out food and to decorate the main reception hall where the weddings of the emirs were held. He collected his friends and invited the great officials of state together with the merchants of Basra. When they came, he told them: 'I had a brother, the vizier of Egypt. God provided him with two sons, while, as you know, He gave me a daughter. My brother had enjoined me to marry her to one of his sons. I agreed to this, and when the appropriate time for marriage came, he sent me one of his sons – this young man who is here with us. Now that he has arrived, I want to draw up the marriage contract between him and my daughter that the marriage may be consummated here, for he has a greater right to her hand than a stranger. After that, if he wants he can stay here, or if he prefers to leave, I shall send him and his wife off to his father.'

Everyone there approved of the plan and, looking at Nur al-Din, they admired what they saw. The vizier then brought in the *qadis* and the notaries, who drew up the contract. Incense was scattered, sugared drinks served and rosewater sprinkled, after which the guests left. The vizier then told his servants to take Nur al-Din to the baths. He gave him a special robe of his own and sent him towels, bowls and censers, together with everything else that he might need. When he left the baths wearing the robes, he was like the moon when it is full on the fourteenth night. He mounted his mule and rode on until he reached the vizier's palace, where he dismounted. Entering the vizier's presence, he kissed his hand and was welcomed . . .

Night 21

Morning now dawned and Shahrazad broke off from what she had been allowed to say. Then, when it was the twenty-first night, SHE CONTINUED:

I have heard, O auspicious king, that the vizier got up to greet him, saying: 'Go in to your wife tonight and tomorrow I will take you to the sultan. I hope that God will grant you every blessing.' Nur al-Din then did as the vizier had said.

So much for him, but as for Shams al-Din, his brother, when he came back from his journey with the sultan of Cairo and failed to find Nur al-Din, he asked the servants about him. They replied: 'The day that you left with the sultan, he mounted his mule with its ceremonial trappings and told us that he was going in the direction of Qalyub and would be away for a day or two. No one was to follow him for he was depressed, and from that day to this we have heard no news of him.' Shams al-Din was disturbed by the departure of his brother and bitterly sorry to have lost him. 'This is because of my angry words to him that night,' he said to himself. 'He must have taken them to heart and gone off on his travels. I must send after him.' He went to the sultan and told him what had happened, and he then wrote notes and posted instructions to his agents throughout the lands. As it happened, however, in the twenty days that Shams al-Din had been away with the sultan, Nur al-Din had travelled to distant regions, and although Shams al-Din's agents searched, they had to come back with no news of him. Shams al-Din then despaired of his brother and said: 'I went too far in what I said to him about our children's marriage. I wish that I hadn't done this; it was due to my stupidity and mismanagement.'

Shortly after this, he proposed to the daughter of a Cairene merchant and after the contract had been drawn up, the marriage was consummated. As it happened, this coincided with the wedding of Nur al-Din to the daughter of the vizier of Basra, as God Almighty had willed it, in order that what He had decreed might be fulfilled among His creatures. What the brothers had said in their conversation came about, in that both their wives became pregnant. The wife of Shams al-Din, the Egyptian vizier, gave birth to the most beautiful girl who had ever been seen in Cairo, while the wife of Nur al-Din gave birth to a son as handsome as any of the people of his age. He was as the poet described:

A slender youth whose hair and whose forehead
Leave mankind to enjoy both dark and light.
Find no fault with the mole upon his cheek;
Every corn-poppy has its own black spot.

Another poet has produced these lines:

If beauty comes to be measured against him,
It must hang down its head in shame.
Asked: 'Have you ever seen a sight like this?'
It answers: 'No, I never have.'

Nur al-Din named his son Badr al-Din Hasan and his grandfather was
overjoyed at his birth and gave banquets and feasts worthy of the sons
of kings. He then took Nur al-Din and brought him to the sultan. When
he appeared before the sultan, Nur al-Din kissed the ground and, being
as eloquent as he was courageous, handsome and generous, he recited:

My lord, may your prosperity endure,
And may you live while dark and dawn remain.
When men talk of your high-mindedness,
Time itself dances as it claps its hands.

The sultan rose to greet his two visitors, thanked Nur al-Din for what
he had said and asked the vizier who he was. The vizier told him Nur
al-Din's story from beginning to end, adding that he was his own nephew.
'How can he be your brother's son,' asked the sultan, 'when we have
never heard of him?' 'My lord, the sultan,' replied the vizier, 'I had a
brother who was vizier of Egypt. On his death, he left two sons, the elder
of whom has taken his father's place as vizier, while this, the younger
son, has come to me. I swore that I would marry my daughter to no one
else, and when he arrived, this is what I did. He is young and I am very
old. I am hard of hearing and my control of affairs is weak, and so I
would ask my master to appoint him in my place. He is my nephew, the
husband of my daughter, someone well fitted to be vizier, as he is a man
of judgement and a good manager.'

The sultan found what he saw of Nur al-Din to be to his taste and so
he granted the vizier's request and promoted Nur al-Din to the vizierate.
On his orders, the new vizier was given a robe of honour and one of the
special mules, as well as pay and allowances. He kissed the sultan's hand
and he and his father-in-law went back joyfully to their house, saying:

'This is due to the good luck brought by baby Hasan.' The next day, Nur al-Din went to the sultan, kissed the ground and recited:

Happiness is renewed on every day
Together with good fortune, confounding envious schemes.
May the whiteness of your days not cease,
While the days of your enemies are black.

The sultan ordered him to take the vizier's seat, which he did, and he then took in hand the duties of his office, investigating the affairs of the people and their lawsuits, as is the habit of viziers. Watching him, the sultan was astonished at what he was doing, his intelligence and powers of administration, all of which won him the sultan's affection and his intimate regard. When the court was dismissed, Nur al-Din went home and delighted his father-in-law by telling him what had happened. The young man continued to act as vizier until, both by night and by day, he became inseparable from the sultan. His pay and allowances were increased and he became rich; he owned shops that traded on his account, slaves, mamluks, and many flourishing estates with water wheels and gardens.

When Hasan was four years old, the old vizier, Nur al-Din's father-in-law, died and Nur al-Din gave him the most lavish of funerals. He then concerned himself with the upbringing of his son, and when the boy grew strong and had reached the age of seven, his father brought in a tutor to teach him at home, telling the man to give him the best instruction. The tutor taught Hasan to read and made him commit to heart many useful branches of learning, as well as getting him to memorize the Quran, over a period of years.

Hasan became ever more beautiful and well formed, as the poet puts it:

A moon reaches its full in the heavens of his beauty,
While the sun shines from his blooming cheeks.
All beauty is his and it is as though
All that is fair in men derives from him.

He was brought up in his father's palace, which throughout his early years he never left, until one day his father took him, clothed him in one of his most splendid robes, mounted him up on one of the best of his mules and brought him to the sultan. The sultan looked at the boy with admiration and felt affection for him. As for the townspeople, when he passed for the first time on his way to the sultan with his father, they were astonished at his beauty and they sat in the street waiting for him to come back so that they could have the pleasure of looking at his comely and well-shaped form. This was as the poet puts it:

One night as the astronomer watched, he saw
The form of a graceful youth wandering in his twin robes.
He observed how Gemini had spread for him
The graceful beauty that his flanks displayed.
Saturn had granted him black hair,
Colouring his temples with the shade of musk.
From Mars derived the redness of his cheeks,
While Sagittarius shot arrows from his eyelids.
Mercury supplied keenness of mind,
And the Bear forbade slanderers to look at him.
The astronomer was bewildered at what he saw
And then ran forward to kiss the earth before him.*

When the sultan saw Hasan, he conferred his favour and affection on him and told his father that he must always, and without fail, bring the boy with him to court. 'To hear is to obey,' replied Nur al-Din, after which he took him back home. Every day from then on he went with him to the sultan until the boy reached the age of fifteen. It was then that Nur al-Din fell ill and, sending for his son, he said: 'Know, my son, that this world is transitory, while the next world is eternal. I wish to give you various injunctions, so try to understand what I have to say and take heed of it.' He then started to tell Hasan how to deal well with people and how to manage his affairs. Then he remembered his brother and his native land and he wept for the loss of loved ones. Wiping away his tears, he recited:

If I complain of distance, what am I to say,
And if I feel longing, what way of escape is there?
I might send messengers to speak for me,
But none of them can convey a lover's complaint.
I might show endurance, but after the beloved's loss
The life span of the lover is not long.
Nothing is left except yearning and grief,
Together with tears that stream down my cheeks.
Those whom I love are absent from my sight,

* cf. Night 17.

But they are found still settled in my heart.
Do you not see, though I have long been spurned,
My covenant is subject to no change?
Has her distance led you to forget your love?
Have tears and fasting given you a cure?
We are of the same clan, both you and I,
But you still try me with long-lasting censure.

When Nur al-Din, in tears, had finished reciting this, he turned to his son and said: 'Before I give you my injunctions, you must know that you have an uncle who is vizier of Egypt. I parted from him and left him without his leave. Take a scroll of paper and write down what I shall dictate.' Hasan took the paper and started to write, while his father dictated an account of what had happened to him from start to finish. He noted the date of the consummation of his marriage with the old vizier's daughter, explaining how he had arrived at Basra and met his father-in-law, adding: 'Many years have passed since the day of our quarrel. This is what I have written to him, and may God now be with him in my stead.'

He folded the letter, sealed it, and said: 'Hasan, my son, keep this testament, for in it is an account of your origin and your genealogy. If anything happens to you, go to Egypt, ask for your uncle and tell him that I have died in a foreign land, longing for him.' Hasan took the paper, folded it and sewed it up in a fold of material, before placing it in the wrapper of his turban, all the while shedding tears at the thought of being parted from his father while he himself was still young. Nur al-Din then said: 'I give you five injunctions. The first is: do not be on intimate terms with anyone, for in this way you will be safe from the evil they may do you. Safety lies in seclusion, so do not be too familiar with anyone. I have heard what the poet says:

There is no one in this age of yours for whose friendship you can
    hope;
When Time is harsh to you, no friend will stay faithful.
Live alone and choose no one in whom to trust.
This, then, is my advice; it is enough.

The second injunction, my son, is to injure no man, lest Time injure you, for one day it will favour you and the next day it will harm you, and this world is a loan to be repaid. I have heard what the poet says:

Act slowly; do not rush to what you want.
Be merciful and be known for your mercy.
No power surpasses that of God,
And every wrongdoer will be oppressed.

The third injunction is to keep silent and to concern yourself with your own faults and not with those of others. The saying goes: "Whoever stays silent, escapes," and I have heard the poet say:

Silence is an adornment which affords you safety,
But if you speak, refrain from babble.
If you regret your silence once,
You will regret having spoken many times.

The fourth injunction, my son, is this: be on your guard against drinking wine, for wine is the root of all discord and it carries away men's wits, so I repeat, guard against it. I have heard the poet say:

I gave up drinking wine and have become
A source of guidance for its censurers.
Drink makes the drunken stray from the right path,
And opens the door to evil.

The fifth injunction is this: guard your wealth and it will guard you; protect it and it will protect you. Do not overspend or you will find yourself in need of help from the most insignificant people. Look after your money, for it will be a salve for your wounds. I have heard the poet say:

If I lack money, then I have no friends,
But all men are my friends when I have wealth.
How many friends have helped me spend,
But when the money went, they all deserted me.'

Nur al-Din went on delivering his injunctions to Hasan until his soul left his body, after which Hasan stayed at home mourning for him, with the sultan and all the emirs joining in his grief. His mourning extended for two months after the funeral, during which time he did not ride out, attend court or present himself before the sultan. This earned him the sultan's anger, as a result of which one of the chamberlains was appointed vizier in his place, with orders to set his seal on Nur al-Din's properties, wealth, buildings and possessions.

The new vizier set out to do this and to arrest Hasan and take him to the sultan to deal with the young man as he saw fit. Among his soldiers was one of the dead vizier's mamluks, and when he heard what was about to happen, he quickly rode to Hasan, and found him sitting by the door of his house, broken-hearted and with his head bowed in sorrow. The mamluk dismounted, kissed his hand and said: 'My master and son of my master, quick, quick, run away before you are doomed.' 'What is the matter?' asked Hasan, trembling. 'The sultan is angry with you and has ordered your arrest,' replied the mamluk. 'Misfortune is hot on my heels, so flee for your life.' 'Is there time for me to go inside to fetch some money to help me in exile?' Hasan asked. 'Get up now, master,' urged the mamluk, 'and leave at once.'

So Hasan got up, reciting these lines:

If you meet injustice, save your life
And let the house lament its builders.
You can replace the country that you lose,
But there is no replacement for your life.
Send out no messenger on any grave affair,
For only you yourself will give you good advice.
The lion's neck is only thick
Because it looks after all its own affairs.*

Then, heeding the mamluk's warning, he covered his head with the skirt of his robe and walked off until he got outside the city. He heard the people saying that the sultan had sent the new vizier to the old vizier's house, to set his seal on his wealth and his properties and to arrest his son, Hasan, in order to bring him for execution, and they were sorry for this because of the young man's beauty.

On hearing what they were saying, Hasan left the city immediately, without knowing where he was going, until fate led him to his father's grave. He entered the cemetery and made his way among the tombs until he reached that of his father. There he sat down, unwinding the skirt of his robe from his head. On the cloth were embroidered in gold the lines:

You whose face gleams
Like stars and dew,
May your fame last for ever
And your exalted glory stay eternally.

* cf. Night 11.

As he was sitting there, a Jew, who appeared to be a money-changer, came up to him, carrying saddlebags containing a great quantity of gold. After approaching him, this Jew said: 'Master, why is it that I see that you are drained of colour?' Hasan replied: 'I was sleeping just now, when in a dream I saw my father reproaching me for not having visited him. I got up in alarm, and I was afraid that if I did not pay him a visit before the end of the day, it might go hard with me.' 'Master,' said the Jew, 'your father sent out trading ships, some of which have just arrived and I want to buy the cargo of the first of them from you for this thousand dinars of gold.' He then brought out a purse filled with gold, from which he counted out a thousand dinars and gave them to Hasan in return for which he asked for a signed bill of sale. Hasan took a piece of paper, on which he wrote: 'The writer of this note, Hasan, son of Nur al-Din, has sold to Ishaq the Jew for a thousand dinars the cargo of the first of his father's ships to come to port, the sale price having been paid in advance.'

After Ishaq had taken the note, Hasan began to weep as he remembered the glory that had been his, and he recited:

The dwelling is no dwelling since you left,
And since you left, we have no neighbours there.
My old familiar friends are now no friends,
Nor are the moons still moons.
You left and this has made the world a wilderness,
And the wide lands are now all dark.
Would that the crow that croaked of your going
Were stripped of feathers and could find no nest.
I have scant store of patience. Now that you have gone,
My body is gaunt and many a veil is torn.
Do you think that those past nights will ever come again
As we once knew them, and the same home shelter us?

He wept bitterly, and as night drew in, he rested his head on his father's tomb and fell asleep. As he slept, the moon rose: his head slipped from the tombstone and he slept on his back, with his face gleaming in the moonlight. It so happened that the cemetery was frequented by *jinn* who believed in God. A *jinniya* came and looked at the sleeping Hasan and, struck by wonder at his beauty, she exclaimed: 'Glory to God, it is as though this youth is one of the children of Paradise.' She then flew off, making her customary circuit in the air. Seeing an *'ifrit* flying by, she greeted him and asked him where he had come from. 'From Cairo,' he said, and she asked: 'Would you like to go with me to see the beauty of this youth asleep in the cemetery?' The *'ifrit* agreed and they flew down to the tomb. 'Have you ever in your life seen anything to match this?' the *jinniya* asked. 'Glory be to the Matchless God!' the *'ifrit* exclaimed. 'But sister,' he added, 'would you like me to tell you what I have seen?' 'What was that?' she asked. 'I have seen someone who is like this youth in the land of Egypt. This is the daughter of Shams al-Din, a girl about twenty years old, beautiful, graceful, splendid, perfectly formed and proportioned. When she passed this age, the sultan of Egypt learned of her, sent for Shams al-Din, her father, and said: "Vizier, I hear that you have a daughter and I would like to ask you for her hand in marriage." "My master," said Shams al-Din, "accept my excuse and have pity on the tears that I must shed. You know that my brother Nur al-Din left us and went away we don't know where. He was my partner in the vizierate and the reason that he left in anger was that we had sat talking about marriage and children and this caused the quarrel. From the day that her mother gave birth to her, some eighteen years ago, I have sworn that I shall marry my daughter to none but my brother's son. A short time ago, I heard that my brother married the daughter of the vizier of Basra, who bore him a son, and out of respect for my brother I shall marry my daughter to no other man. I have noted the date of my own marriage, my wife's pregnancy and the birth of this girl. She is the destined bride of her cousin; while for the sultan there are girls aplenty."

'When he heard this, the sultan was furiously angry and said: "When someone like me asks for a girl's hand from a man like you, do you refuse to give her to me and put forward an empty excuse? I swear that I shall marry her off to the meanest of my servants to spite you." The sultan had a hunchbacked groom, with a hump on his chest and another on his back. He ordered this man to be brought to him and he has drawn up a contract of forced marriage between him and Shams al-Din's daughter, ordering him to consummate the marriage tonight. The sultan is providing the groom with a wedding procession and when I left him he was surrounded by the sultan's mamluks, who were lighting candles around him and making fun of him at the door of the baths. Shams al-Din's daughter, who bears the greatest resemblance to this young man, is sitting weeping among her nurses and maids, for her father has been ordered not to go to her. I have never seen anything more disgusting than the hunchback, while the girl is even more lovely than this youth.'

Night 22

Morning now dawned and Shahrazad broke off from what she had been allowed to say. Then, when it was the twenty-second night, SHE CONTINUED:

I have heard, O auspicious king, that when the 'ifrit told the jinniya that the sultan, to the girl's great distress, was marrying her off to the hunchbacked groom and that, apart from Hasan, he had never seen her match for beauty, the jinniya replied: 'You are lying, for this young man is the most beautiful of all the people of his age.' The 'ifrit contradicted her, saying: 'By God, sister, the girl is more lovely than he is, but he is the only fit mate for her, for they resemble one another like siblings or cousins. How sad will be her fate with the hunchback!' 'My brother,' said the jinniya, 'let us lift him from beneath and carry him to the girl you are talking about to see which of them is the more beautiful.' 'To hear is to obey,' replied the 'ifrit. 'You are right, and there can be no better plan, so I shall carry him myself.' This he did, flying off into the air with Hasan, while the jinniya at his heels kept pace with him until he came to land in Cairo, where he set Hasan down on a bench and roused him.

When Hasan awoke and found that he was not by his father's grave in Basra, he looked right and left and discovered that he was in some other city. He was about to cry out when the 'ifrit struck him. He had brought for him a splendid robe and made him put it on. Then he lit a candle for him, saying: 'Know that I have brought you here and am going to do you a favour for God's sake. Take this candle and go to these baths, where you are to mix with the people and walk along with them until you reach the bridal hall. Then go on ahead, entering the hall without fear, and once you are inside, stand to the right of the hunch-backed bridegroom. Whenever any of the maids, singing girls and attend-ants approaches you, put your hand in your pocket, which you will find filled with gold. Take a handful of the gold and throw it to them: you needn't fear that when you do this you will ever find your pocket empty, so you can scatter coins for everyone who comes up. Put your trust in your Creator, for this does not come about through any power of yours but at God's command.'

When Hasan heard what the 'ifrit had to say, he wondered who the bride might be and why the 'ifrit was doing him such a favour, but he lit the candle, went to the baths and found the hunchbacked bridegroom mounted on a horse. He joined the crowd in all the splendour of his beauty, wearing, as has been described, a tarboosh with a white covering and a mantle woven with gold. He continued to walk in the bridal procession and every time the singing girls stopped so that people might throw them money, he would put his hand in his pocket, find it filled with gold and, to the girls' astonishment, he would throw a handful into their tambourines, filling these up with dinars. His beauty moved the crowd, and they went on like this until they reached the house of Shams al-Din. Here the chamberlains turned back the crowd and would not let them enter, but the singing girls said: 'By God, we will not go in unless this young man comes too, for he has overwhelmed us with his generosity and we will not help display the bride unless he is there.'

At that, they entered the festal hall; Hasan was seated to the right of the hunchbacked bridegroom, while the wives of the emirs, viziers and chamberlains were drawn up in two lines, each carrying a large lighted candle and wearing a mouth-veil. The lines were drawn up to the right and left beneath the bridal throne, extending to the top of the hall beside the room from which the bride was to emerge. When the ladies saw Hasan's graceful beauty, with his face gleaming like the crescent moon, they were all drawn to him. The singing girls told them that the handsome young man had given them nothing but red gold: 'So be sure to serve him as best you can and do whatever he says.' The ladies crowded around him with their torches, looking at his beauty and envying him his gracefulness. There was not one of them who did not wish that they could enjoy his embrace for an hour or a year, and so far out of their senses were they that they let down their veils, exclaiming: 'Happy is she who has this young man as husband or master.' They then cursed the hunchback and the one who was responsible for his marriage to so beautiful a girl, while every blessing that they invoked upon Hasan was matched by a curse for the hunchback.

Then the singing girls beat their tambourines; the flutes shrilled and out came the maids with Shams al-Din's daughter in the middle of them. They had covered her with perfume, dressed her hair beautifully and scented it, and robed her in clothes splendid enough for the kings of Persia. On top of these she wore a gown woven with red gold on which were embroidered pictures of beasts and birds, and round her throat was a Yemeni necklace worth thousands of dinars, comprising gemstones such as no king of Yemen or Byzantine emperor had ever possessed. She was like the moon when it is full on the fourteenth night, and when she came forward she was like a houri of Paradise – praise be to God, Who created her in beauty. The ladies surrounding her were like stars, while in their midst she was like the moon shining through clouds. Hasan was sitting there, the cynosure of all eyes, when she appeared and moved forward, swaying as she did so.

The hunchbacked bridegroom rose to greet her, but she turned from him and moved away until she stood before her cousin Hasan. The people laughed, and when they saw that she had turned towards Hasan, they shouted, while the singing girls raised a cry. Hasan put his hand in his pocket and, to their joy, he threw a handful of gold once more into their tambourines. 'Would that this was your bride,' they said. He laughed, and all those there pressed around him, while the bridegroom was left on his own, sitting hunched up like a monkey. Every time they tried to light a candle for him, he could not keep it alight, and as he could find nothing to say, he sat in the darkness looking down at the floor.

As for Hasan, he was confronted by people carrying candles, and when he looked at the bridegroom sitting alone in the shadows, he was filled with perplexity and astonishment, but this changed to joy and delight when he looked at his cousin. He saw her face shining radiantly in the candlelight, and he looked at the red satin dress that she was wearing, the first to be removed by her maids. As they unveiled her, this allowed Hasan to see her, swaying as she moved with artful coquetry, bewitching both men and women, and fitting the description of the poet:

> A sun on a branch set in a sand hill,
> Appearing in a dress of pomegranate blossom –
> She let me drink the wine of her lips and with the gift
> Of her cheeks she quenched the greatest fire.

The maids then changed her dress and clothed her in a blue gown, so that she looked like the gleaming full moon, with her black hair, smooth cheeks, smiling mouth, jutting breasts and beautiful hands and wrists. When they showed her in this second dress, she was as the sublime poets have written:

> She came forward in a gown of azure blue,
> The colour of the sky.
> I looked and saw within this gown
> A summer moon set in a winter night.

They then changed that for another dress, using some of her hair as a veil and letting the remaining long, black locks hang loose. The length and blackness of this hair resembled the darkness of night and she shot at hearts with the magic arrows of her eyes. Of the third dress in which they showed her, the poet has written:

Veiled by hair draped over cheeks,
She was a temptation strong as burning fire.
I said: 'You have used night to veil the dawn.'
'No,' she replied, 'but I have veiled the moon in darkness.'

They then showed her in a fourth dress, and she came forward like the rising sun, swaying coquettishly and looking from side to side like a gazelle, while transfixing hearts with the arrows of her eyelids, as the poet has said:

The watchers saw a sun of loveliness,
Radiant in coquetry, adorned with bashfulness.
She turned her smiling face to the sun of day,
Since when the sun has veiled itself in cloud.

In her fifth dress, the adorable girl was like the branch of a *ban* tree or a thirsty gazelle. Her curls crept like scorpions and she showed the wonders of her beauty as she shook her hips and displayed the locks of hair covering her temples, as has been described in the lines:

She appeared as the full moon on a lucky night,
With tender hands and slender figure.
Her eye enslaves men with its loveliness;
The redness of her cheeks rivals the ruby.
Her black hair falls over her hips;
Beware the snakes that form those curling locks.
Her flanks are soft, but though they may be smooth,
Her heart is harder than the solid rock.
Her eyebrows shoot the arrows of her glance.
Even from far away, they strike unerringly.
If we embrace, I press against her belt,
But her breasts keep me from holding her too close.
Oh for her beauty which surpasses every grace!
Oh for her figure which shames the tender bough!

The sixth dress in which they showed her was green. Her upright posture put to shame the brown spear and her comeliness surpassed that of the beauties of every land. Her gleaming face outshone the shining moon; beauty yielded to her every wish; she captivated the boughs with her softness and suppleness, and she shattered hearts with her qualities, as has been described in the lines:

A girl trained in shrewdness –
You see that the sun is borrowed from her cheeks.
She came in a green dress,
Like pomegranate blossom veiled by leaves.
I asked her for its name and her reply
Was phrased with elegance:
'With it I cut men's hearts and so
The name I give it is "the bitter cut".'

The seventh dress in which they displayed her was part safflower red and part saffron. As the poet has said:

She sways in a dress part safflower, part saffron,
Scented with ambergris and musk and sandalwood –
A slender girl; youth urges her to rise;
Her buttocks tell her: 'Sit or move slowly.'
If I ask her for union, her beauty says:
'Be generous,' but coquetry says: 'Refuse.'

When the bride opened her eyes, she said: 'O God, make this my husband and free me from this hunchbacked groom.' So it was that she was shown in all her seven robes to Hasan of Basra, while the hunchbacked groom was left sitting by himself. When this had been done, the guests were allowed to leave, and all the women and children who had attended the wedding went out, leaving only Hasan and the hunchback. The maids took the bride to her room to change her ornaments and her clothes and make her ready for the bridegroom. At that, the hunchback approached Hasan and said: 'Sir, you have been kind enough to favour us with your company this evening but it is time for you to get up and go.' 'In the Name of God,' said Hasan, and he got up and went out of the door. There, however, the *'ifrit* met him and told him to stop, saying: 'When the hunchback goes out to the latrine, enter at once and sit down in the alcove. When the bride comes, tell her: "I am your husband and the sultan only played this trick on you for fear that you might be hurt by the evil eye. The man whom you saw is one of our grooms.' After this, go up to her and uncover her face. As far as we are concerned, this is a matter of honour.'

While Hasan was talking with the *'ifrit*, out came the hunchback and went to the latrine. As he sat down, the *'ifrit* in the form of a mouse emerged from the water bowl and said *'ziq'*. 'What is the matter with you?' said the hunchback. Then the mouse grew bigger until it became a cat, which said *'miya, miya'*, after which it grew bigger still and turned into a dog, which said *"awh, 'awh"*. At this, the hunchback became frightened and said: 'Go away, you ill-omened beast,' but the dog grew bigger and swelled up until it became an ass, which brayed and bellowed *'haq, haq'* in his face. The hunchback was even more frightened and called for help, but the donkey grew even larger until it was the size of a buffalo. Blocking the hunchback's retreat, it called to him in a human voice: 'You stinking fellow.' The hunchback could not control his bowels and sat down on the outlet of the latrine, still wearing his clothes, and with his teeth chattering. 'Do you find the world so narrow,' asked the *'ifrit*, 'that you can find no one to marry except my beloved? Answer me,' he went on, as the hunchback stayed silent, 'or else I shall put you in your grave.' 'By God,' said the hunchback, 'none of this is my fault. They forced me to marry the girl and I didn't know that she had a buffalo for a lover. I repent of the match to God and to you.' 'I swear to you,' said the *'ifrit*, 'that if you leave this place or speak a single word before the sun rises, I shall kill you. At sunrise you can go on your way, but never come back to this house.' Then he took hold of the hunchback and put him head first into the outlet of the latrine. 'I shall leave you here,' he said, 'but I shall be watching over you until sunrise.'

This is what happened to the hunchback, but as for Hasan, leaving the hunchback and the *'ifrit* quarrelling, he went into the house and took his seat in the middle of the alcove. At that moment, the bride appeared, accompanied by an old woman, who said: 'You well-made man, rise up and take what God has entrusted to you.' Then she turned back, while the bride, whose name was Sitt al-Husn, came into the alcove. She was heartbroken, saying: 'I shall never let him have me, even if he kills me.' But when she entered and saw Hasan, she exclaimed: 'Darling, are you still sitting here? I had told myself that you could share me with the hunchback.' 'How can the hunchback approach you?' said Hasan. 'And how could he share you with me?' 'But who is my husband,' she asked, 'you or he?' 'Sitt al-Husn,' said Hasan, 'we only did this as a joke to

mock him. When the maids and the singing girls and your family saw
your beauty being unveiled for me, they were afraid of the evil eye and
your father hired this fellow for ten dinars to turn it away from us, and
now he has gone.' When Sitt al-Husn heard this from Hasan, she smiled
with joy and laughed gently. 'By God,' she said, 'you have quenched my
fire, so I ask you to take me and crush me to your breast.'

She was without any outer clothing and when she now raised her shift
up to her neck, her private parts and her buttocks were revealed. At this
sight, Hasan's passion was aroused and, getting up, he stripped off his
clothes. He took the purse of gold with the thousand dinars that he had
got from the Jew and wrapped it in his trousers, placing it under the end
of the mattress, and he took off his turban and set it on a chair, leaving
him wearing only a fine shirt embroidered with gold. At that, Sitt al-Husn
went up to him and drew him to her as he drew her to him. He embraced
her and placed her legs around his waist. He then set the charge, fired
the cannon and demolished the fortress. He found his bride an unbored
pearl and a mare that no one else had ridden, so he took her maidenhead
and enjoyed her youth. Then he withdrew from her and after a restorative
pause, he returned fifteen times, as a result of which she conceived.

When he had finished, he put his hand beneath her head and she did
the same to him, after which they embraced and fell asleep in each other's
arms. This was as the poet has described:

> Visit your love; pay no heed to the envious:
> For such are of no help in love.
> God in His mercy makes no finer sight
> Than of two lovers on a single bed,
> Embracing one another and clothed in content,
> Pillowed on one another's wrists and arms.
> When hearts are joined in love,
> The iron is cold on which all others strike.
> When your age has provided you a single friend,
> How good a friend is this! Live for this one alone.
> You who blame the lovers for their love,
> Have you the power to cure the sick at heart?

This is what took place between Hasan and his cousin, Sitt al-Husn.
As for the 'ifrit, he said to the jinniya: 'Get up and go in beneath this
young man so that we may take him back to where he came from lest
morning overtakes us. It is almost dawn.' The jinniya did this as Hasan

slept, still wearing his shirt and nothing else, and taking hold of him she flew off. She continued on her way, while the *'ifrit* kept pace with her, but midway through their journey they were overtaken by the dawn. The muezzin called to prayer and God permitted his angels to hurl a shooting star at the *'ifrit*, who was consumed by fire. The *jinniya* escaped, but she set Hasan down in the place where the *'ifrit* had been struck by the star, as she was too afraid for his safety to take him any further. As fate had decreed, they had reached Damascus and it was by one of the city gates that she left him, before flying away.

When the gates were opened in the morning, the people came out and there they found a handsome youth clothed only in a shirt and a woollen skullcap. Because of his wakeful night, he was sunk in sleep. When the people saw him, they said: 'How lucky was the one with whom this fellow spent the night, but he should have waited to put on his clothes.' Another said: 'They are poor fellows, these rich men's sons. This one must have just come out of the wine shop to relieve himself, when his drunkenness got the better of him, and as he couldn't find the place he was making for, he arrived instead at the city gate, only to find it locked. Then he must have fallen asleep here.'

As they were talking, a gust of wind blew over Hasan, lifting his shirt above his waist. Beneath it could be seen his stomach, a curved navel, and two legs and thighs like crystal. The people exclaimed in admiration and Hasan woke up to find himself by the city gate, surrounded by a crowd. 'Where am I, good people?' he said. 'Why have you gathered here and what have I to do with you?' 'When the muezzin gave the call to morning prayer,' they said, 'we saw you stretched out asleep, and that is all we know about the business. Where did you sleep last night?' 'By God,' replied Hasan, 'I slept last night in Cairo.' 'You've been eating hashish,' said one of them. 'You're clearly mad,' said another. 'You go to sleep in Cairo and in the morning here you are asleep in Damascus.' 'Good people,' he replied, 'I have not told you a lie. Last night I was in Egypt and yesterday I was in Basra.' 'Fine,' said one. 'He is mad,' said another, and they clapped their hands over him and talked among themselves, saying: 'What a shame for one so young, but he is undoubtedly mad.' Then they said to him: 'Pull yourself together and return to your senses.' 'Yesterday,' insisted Hasan, 'I was a bridegroom in Egypt.' 'Maybe you were dreaming,' they said, 'and it was in your dream that you saw this.' Hasan thought it over to himself and said: 'By God, that was no dream, nor did I see it in my sleep. I went there and they unveiled the bride before me, and there was a third person, a hunchback, sitting there. By God, brothers, this was not a dream, and had it been one, where is the purse of gold that I had with me and where is my turban and the rest of my clothes?'

He then got up and went into the city, with the people pressing around him and accompanying him as he made his way through the streets and markets. He then entered the shop of a cook, who had been an artful fellow, that is to say, a thief, but had been led to repent of his evil-doing by God, after which he had opened a cookshop. All the people of Damascus were afraid of him because of his former violence, and so when they saw that Hasan had gone into his shop, they dispersed in fear. The cook, looking at Hasan's grace and beauty, felt affection for him enter his heart. 'Where have you come from, young man?' he said. 'Tell me your story, for you have become dearer to me than my life.'

Hasan told him what had happened to him from beginning to end, and the cook exclaimed at how remarkable and strange it was. 'But, my son,' he added, 'keep this affair concealed until God relieves your distress. Stay with me here, and I shall take you as a son, for I have none of my own.' Hasan agreed to this and the cook went to the market and bought fine material for him, with which he clothed him. The two of them went off to the *qadi* and Hasan declared himself to be the cook's son. This is how he became known in Damascus, and he sat in the shop taking the customers' money, having settled down with the cook.

So much for him, but as for his cousin, Sitt al-Husn, when dawn broke and she awoke from her sleep, she did not find Hasan, and thinking that he must have gone to the latrine, she sat for a time waiting for him. Then in came Shams al-Din, her father, who was distressed at what the sultan had done to him and at how he had forced Sitt al-Husn to marry one of his servants, a mere groom and a hunchback. He said to himself that he would kill the girl if she had allowed that damned man to have her. So he walked to her room, stopped at the door and called out to her. 'Here I am, father,' she said, and she came out, swaying with joy. She kissed the ground and her face shone with ever more radiant beauty, thanks to the embrace of that gazelle-like youth.

When her father saw her in this state, he said: 'Are you so pleased with that groom, you damned girl?' When she heard this, she smiled and said: 'By God, what happened yesterday was enough, with people laughing at me and shunning me because of this groom who is not worth the paring of my husband's fingernail. I swear that never in my life have

I spent a more delightful night than last night, so don't make fun of me or remind me of that hunchback.' When her father heard this, he glared at her in anger and said: 'What are you talking about? It was the hunchback who spent the night with you.' 'For God's sake, don't mention him, may God curse his father, and don't jest. The groom was hired for ten dinars and he took his fee and left. Then I arrived and when I went into the room I found my husband sitting there. This was after the singing girls had unveiled me for him and he had scattered enough red gold to enrich all the poor who were present. I passed the night in the embrace of my charming husband, with the dark eyes and the joining eyebrows.'

When her father heard this, the light before him turned to darkness. 'You harlot,' he said, 'what are you saying? Where are your wits?' 'Father,' she replied, 'you have broken my heart – enough of this ill humour. This is my husband who took my virginity. He has gone to the latrine, and he has made me pregnant.' Her father got up in astonishment and went to the latrine, where he found the hunchback with his head stuck in the hole and his legs sticking out on top. He was amazed and said: 'Surely this is the hunchback.' He called to the man, who mumbled in reply, thinking that it was the *'ifrit* who was speaking to him. Shams al-Din then shouted to him: 'Speak or else I shall cut your head off with this sword.' 'By God, *shaikh* of the *'ifrits*,' said the hunchback, 'since you put me here I have not raised my head, and I implore you by God to be kind to me.' 'What are you talking about?' said Shams al-Din when he heard this. 'I am the father of the bride and not an *'ifrit*.' 'Enough of that,' said the hunchback, 'for you are on the way to getting me killed, so go off before the *'ifrit* who did this to me comes back. What you have done is to marry me to the mistress of buffaloes and *'ifrits*. May God curse the man who married me to her and the one who was the cause of this.'

Night 23

Morning now dawned and Shahrazad broke off from what she had been allowed to say. Then, when it was the twenty-third night, SHE CONTINUED:

I have heard, O auspicious king, that the hunchback started to talk to Shams al-Din, the father of the bride, saying: 'May God curse the man who was the cause of this.' 'Get up,' said Shams al-Din, 'and come out.' 'Do you think that I am mad,' said the hunchback, 'that I should go with you without the *'ifrit'*s permission? He told me to come out and leave at sunrise. So has the sun risen or not, for I can't come out of here until it has?' Shams al-Din then asked who had put him there. 'I came here last night to relieve myself,' the man replied, 'and suddenly a mouse came out of the water and squeaked, and then it went on growing bigger and bigger until it was as large as a buffalo. It spoke to me in tones that rang through my ears, after which it left me and went away. May God curse the bride and the man who married me to her!'

Shams al-Din went up and removed him from the latrine, after which he ran off, not believing that the sun had risen, and going to the sultan, he told him what had happened to him with the *'ifrit*. As for Shams al-Din, the bride's father, he went back in a state of perplexity, not understanding what had happened to his daughter, and he asked her to explain the matter again. She replied: 'The bridegroom, for whom I was unveiled yesterday, spent the night with me, took my virginity and has made me pregnant. If you don't believe me, here is his turban, in its folds, lying on the chair, and here are his other clothes underneath the bed, with something wrapped up in them, although I don't know what it is.' On hearing this, her father came into the alcove, where he found the turban of his nephew, Hasan. He took it in his hands, turned it over and said: 'This is a vizier's turban and it is of muslin.' He then looked and saw an amulet sewn into the tarboosh, which he took and opened, and he picked up the outer clothes, in which he found the purse containing the thousand dinars. Opening it, he found inside it a sheet of paper, which he read and which turned out to be the Jew's contract of sale, with the name of Badr al-Din Hasan, the son of Nur al-Din 'Ali, the Egyptian. He also found the thousand dinars.

On reading the paper, he uttered a loud cry and fell down in a faint. When he recovered and grasped what this all meant, he was filled with wonder and exclaimed: 'There is no god but God, Who has power over all things.' Then he said: 'Daughter, do you know who it was who deflowered you?' 'No,' she replied. 'It was my brother's son, your cousin,' he said, 'and these thousand dinars are your dowry. Glory be to God, but I wish I knew how this came about.' Then he reopened the amulet and in it he found a note in the handwriting of his brother Nur al-Din. After looking at his brother's handwriting, he recited:

I see the traces they have left and melt with longing,
And I pour down my tears over their former dwellings.
I ask the One who afflicted me with separation
That one day He might favour me with their return.

On finishing these lines, Shams al-Din read through what was in the amulet and there he found the date of Nur al-Din's marriage to the daughter of the vizier of Basra, its consummation, the date of Hasan's birth, and an account of Nur al-Din's life up until the time of his death. This astonished him; he trembled with joy and, on comparing what had happened to his brother with his own history, he found that they matched exactly, that the consummation of his marriage and that of his brother had happened on the same date, as had the birth of Hasan and that of his own daughter, Sitt al-Husn. Taking the paper, he brought it to the sultan and told him all that had happened from start to finish. The astonished sultan ordered that an account of this should be written down immediately.

Shams al-Din waited, expecting his nephew to come, but he did not come that day, or on the next, or on the third, and after seven days had passed, there was still no news of him. So Shams al-Din said: 'By God, I shall do something that no one has ever done before,' and taking an inkwell and a pen, he produced on a piece of paper a sketch plan of the whole house, with the alcove here, such-and-such a hanging there, and so on, including everything in the house. He then folded the paper and gave orders for all Hasan's things to be collected. He took the turban, the tarboosh, the mantle and the purse, which he locked up in his own room with a lock of iron, setting a seal on it to await his nephew's arrival.

As for his daughter, at the end of the months of her pregnancy, she gave birth to a boy, splendid as the moon, resembling his father in beauty, perfection, splendour and grace. The midwives cut the umbilical cord, spread kohl on his eyelids and then handed him over to the nurses, naming him 'Ajib. In one day he grew as much as other children grow in a month, and in a month as much as they do in a year. When he was seven years old, he was handed over to a teacher who was told to give him a good education and to teach him to read. He stayed at school for four years, but he began to fight with the other children and abuse them, saying: 'Which of you is my equal? I am the son of Shams al-Din of Egypt.' The other children went together to the monitor to complain of his rough behaviour. The monitor told them: 'When he arrives to-morrow, I'll teach you something to say to him that will make him give up coming to school. Tomorrow, when he arrives, sit around him in a circle and say to each other: "By God, no one may play this game with us unless he can tell us the names of his mother and father." Anyone who doesn't know these names is a bastard and won't be allowed to play.'

The next morning, they came to school and when 'Ajib arrived, they surrounded him and said: 'We are going to play a game but no one may join in with us unless he can tell us the names of his mother and father.' They all agreed to this, and one of them said: 'My name is Majid; my mother is 'Alawiya and my father is 'Izz al-Din.' A second boy did the same and so did the others until it came to 'Ajib's turn. He then said: 'My name is 'Ajib; my mother is Sitt al-Husn and my father is Shams al-Din of Egypt.' 'By God,' they said to him, 'Shams al-Din isn't your father.' 'Yes, he is,' insisted 'Ajib, and at that the boys laughed at him, clapped their hands, and said: 'He doesn't know who his father is; go away and leave us. We will only play with those who know their father's name.'

At that, the children around him went off laughing and leaving him angry and choked with tears. The monitor told him: 'We know that your grandfather, Shams al-Din, is not your father but the father of your mother, Sitt al-Husn; as for your own father, neither you nor we know who he is. The sultan married your mother to the hunchbacked groom, but a *jinni* came and slept with her and you have no father we know of. You won't be able to compare yourself with the other boys in this school unless you find out who your father is, for otherwise they will take you for a bastard. You can see that the trader's son knows his father, but although your grandfather is Shams al-Din of Egypt, as we don't know who your father is, we say that you have no father. So act sensibly.'

When 'Ajib heard what the monitor and the boys had to say and how they were insulting him, he went away immediately and came to his mother, Sitt al-Husn, to complain, but he was crying too hard to speak. When she heard his sobs, her heart burned and she said: 'What has made you cry? Tell me.' So he told her what he had heard from the children and from the monitor, and he asked her: 'Who is my father?' She said: 'Your father is Shams al-Din of Egypt.' But he said: 'Don't tell me lies. Shams al-Din is your father, not mine, so who is my father? If you don't tell me the truth, I'll kill myself with this dagger.' When his mother heard him talk of his father, she burst into tears, remembering her cousin Hasan and how she had been unveiled for him and what he had done with her. She recited these lines:

> They stirred up longing in my heart and left.
> Those whom I love have now gone far away.
> They left and with them has my patience gone.
> After this loss, patience is hard to find.
> They left, and were accompanied by my joy.
> Nothing stays fixed; there is no fixity.
> By leaving me, they brought tears to my eyes,
> And thanks to this, my tears flow down in floods.
> I yearn to see them, and for long
> I have been yearning and awaiting them.
> I call up pictures of them, and my inmost heart
> Is home to passion, longing and to care.
> Your memory has now become my cloak,
> And under it I wear my love for you.
> Beloved, for how long will this go on?
> How long will you stay distant and shun me?

She wept and wailed, as did 'Ajib, and at that point suddenly in came Shams al-Din. When he saw their tears, his heart was burned and he asked what was the reason for all this grief. Sitt al-Husn told him what had happened to 'Ajib with the boys at his school, and Shams al-Din himself wept, remembering his brother and what had happened to the two of them, as well as what had happened to his daughter, the real truth of which he did not know. He then immediately got up and went to the court, where he came into the sultan's presence and told him his story, asking leave to travel to the east in order to make enquiries about his nephew in Basra. He also asked the sultan to give him written instructions addressed to all lands, allowing him to take his nephew with him wherever he might be found. He then burst into tears before the sultan, who was moved with pity for him and wrote him the orders for which he had asked. This delighted Shams al-Din, who called down blessings on his master, and then took his leave.

He immediately went home and made his preparations for the journey, taking with him all that he, his daughter and 'Ajib might need. They travelled day after day until they arrived at Damascus, which they found full of trees and watered by streams, as the poet has described it:

I passed a day and a night in Damascus, and Time swore
That with a city like this it could make no mistake.
I spent the night while night's wing paid no heed,
And dawn was smiling with grey hair.
On the branches there dew gleamed like pearls,
Touched gently by the zephyr and then falling.
The pool was like a page read by the birds,
Written by wind, with clouds as punctuation.

Shams al-Din halted in the Maidan al-Hasa, where he pitched his tents, telling his servants that they would rest there for two days. For their part, they then went into the city to do as they pleased, one selling, one buying, one going to the baths and another to the Umaiyad Mosque, whose like is to be found nowhere in the world. 'Ajib went out accompanied by a eunuch and they entered the city to look at the sights, with the eunuch walking behind holding a cudgel so heavy that were he to use it to strike a camel, the beast would never rise again. The people of Damascus looked at 'Ajib, his well-formed figure, his splendour and his beauty, for he was a remarkably handsome boy with soft manners, more delicate than the northern breeze, sweeter than cold water to the thirsty man and more delightful than the recovery of health to the sick. As a result, he was followed by a large crowd, some running behind him and others going on ahead and sitting in the road looking at him as he passed.

This went on until, as had been decreed by fate, the eunuch stopped at the shop of his father Hasan. In the twelve years that he had spent in Damascus, Hasan's beard had grown long and he had matured in intelligence. The cook had died and he had taken over his wealth and his shop, having been acknowledged before the judges and the notaries as his son. When 'Ajib and the eunuch halted by his shop that day, Hasan looked at 'Ajib, his son, and, taking note of how extremely handsome he was, his heart beat fast, blood sensed the pull of blood, and he felt linked to the boy by affection. He happened to have cooked a dish of sugared pomegranate seeds and as God had inspired him with love for his son, he called out to him: 'My master, who has taken possession of my heart and for whom I yearn, would you enter my shop, mend my broken heart and eat of my food?' Then, spontaneously, his eyes filled with tears and he thought of what he had been and what he now was.

As for 'Ajib, when he heard what his father had said, he felt drawn to him. He told this to the eunuch, adding: 'It is as though this cook is a man who has parted from his son. Let us go into his shop, so that we may comfort him and eat what he gives us as guests. It may be that, if I do this for him, God may unite me with my father.' 'A fine thing, by God!' exclaimed the eunuch when he heard this. 'Do viziers' sons stay eating in a cookshop? I use this stick to keep people away from you lest they even look at you, and I shall never feel safe in letting you go in here.' When Hasan heard this, he was astonished and turned to the eunuch with tears running down his cheeks, while 'Ajib said: 'My heart is filled with love for this man.' 'Don't say that,' the eunuch replied, 'for you are never going in there.' Hasan himself then turned to the eunuch and said: 'Great one, why do you not mend my broken heart by entering my shop yourself, you who are like a chestnut, dark but with a white heart, you who fit the description of the poet?' 'What is this you say?' said the eunuch, laughing. 'Produce the description but keep it short.' So Hasan started to recite these lines:

Were he not educated and reliable,
He would hold no office in the royal palace
Or be given charge of the harem. Oh what a servant,
Who, for his beauty, heavenly angels serve!

The eunuch was filled with admiration when he heard this and, taking 'Ajib with him, he entered the shop. Hasan then ladled into a bowl an excellent mixture of pomegranate seeds, almonds and sugar and they both ate after Hasan had welcomed them, saying: 'You have done me a favour, so enjoy your meal.' 'Ajib then said to his father: 'Sit and eat with us, and it may be that God will bring us together with those whom we wish to meet.' 'My boy,' said Hasan, 'have you, young as you are, had to suffer the loss of dear ones?' 'Yes, uncle,' replied 'Ajib. 'This has caused me bitter distress, and the one whom I have lost is my father. My grandfather and I have come to search for him through all the lands, and I am filled with sad longing for him.' He then wept bitterly and his father wept because of his loss and because of the boy's tears, remembering the loss of his own loved ones and his separation from his father and his mother, while the eunuch shared his sorrow. They then ate their fill, after which the two got up, and when they left the shop, Hasan felt as though his soul had parted from his body and gone with them.

He could not endure to be parted from them for the blink of an eye and so he locked up his shop and followed, without realizing that 'Ajib was his son. He hurried on until he caught up with them before they had gone out of the main gate. The eunuch turned and asked what he wanted. 'When you left my shop,' replied Hasan, 'I felt that my soul had gone with you and, as I have an errand in the suburbs outside the gate, I wanted to go with you, do my errand, and then go back.' The eunuch was angry. 'This is what I was afraid of,' he told 'Ajib. 'The bite that we had to eat was unfortunate in that it has put us under an obligation, and here is that fellow following us from place to place.' 'Ajib turned, and finding Hasan walking behind him, he became angry and his face flushed red. To the eunuch he said: 'Let him walk on the public road, but if, when we come out to our tents, we find that he is still following us, then we can drive him away.'

He then lowered his head and walked on, with the eunuch behind him and Hasan trailing them, as far as the Maidan al-Hasa. When they were close to the tents, they turned and saw him still behind them. 'Ajib was afraid that the eunuch might tell his grandfather, and he became very angry for fear lest he be reported as having entered the cookshop and having been followed by the cook. So he turned and found Hasan's eyes fixed on his, while Hasan himself looked like a body without a soul. To 'Ajib it seemed as though his eyes were those of a pervert or that he was a debauchee, and so, in a fit of rage, he took a stone and hit his father with it, knocking him unconscious, with the blood running down over his face. He and the eunuch then went to the tents.

When Hasan recovered consciousness, he wiped away the blood, and after cutting off a strip of his turban, he bandaged his head. He blamed himself and said: 'I wronged the boy by shutting up my shop and following him, making him think that I was a pervert.' So he went back to the shop and went on selling his food, but he started to yearn for his mother in Basra and he recited in tears:

You wrong Time if you ask it to be fair.
Do not blame it; it was not created for fair dealing.
Take what comes easily and leave care aside.
Time must contain both trouble and happiness.

He carried on with his business, while his uncle, Shams al-Din, after spending three days in Damascus, left for Homs, which he entered, and while he was on his journey he made enquiries wherever he went. He went to Diyar Bakr, Mardin and Mosul, and he kept on travelling until he reached Basra. After entering the city and settling himself there, he went to the sultan. When they met, the sultan treated him with respect and honour and asked him the reason for his visit. Shams al-Din told him his story and that his brother was Nur al-Din 'Ali. 'May God have mercy on him,' interjected the sultan, adding: 'He was my vizier and I loved him dearly, but he died fifteen years ago. He left a son, but the son only stayed for a month after his death before going missing and we have never heard any more news of him, although his mother, the daughter of my old vizier, is still with us.'

When Shams al-Din heard that the mother of his nephew was well, he was delighted and told the sultan that he would like to meet her. Permission was immediately granted and he went to visit her in his brother's house. He let his gaze wander around it, and kissing its threshold, he thought of his brother and of how he had died in exile. So he shed tears and recited these lines:

> I pass by the dwellings, the dwellings of Laila,
> And I kiss first one wall and then another.
> It is not love for the dwellings that wounds my heart,
> But love for the one who lived in them.

He passed through the door into a large hall where there was another door, arched and vaulted with flint inset with marble of different kinds and different colours. He walked through the house, and as he looked at it and glanced around, he found the name of his brother inscribed in letters of gold. He went up to the inscription, kissed it and wept as he remembered his separation from his brother. He then recited these lines:

> Every time it rises, I ask the sun for news of you,
> And I question the lightning about you when it flashes.
> Longing folds and unfolds me in its hands
> All night, but I do not complain of pain.
> Dear ones, for long, after you went,
> Separation from you has left me cut to pieces.
> Were you to grant my eyes a sight of you –
> It would be better still if we could meet.
> Do not think I am busied with another;
> My heart has no room for another love.

He then walked on until he reached the room of his brother's widow, the mother of Hasan, who throughout her son's disappearance had been weeping and wailing constantly, night and day. When long years had passed, she had made a marble cenotaph for him in the middle of the hall, where she would shed tears, and it was only beside this that she would sleep. When Shams al-Din came to her room, he heard the sound of her voice, and standing behind the door, he listened to her reciting:

> In God's Name, grave, are his beauties now gone,
> And has that bright face changed?
> Grave, you are neither a garden nor a sky,
> So how do you contain both branch and moon?*

While she was reciting this, Shams al-Din came in. He greeted her and told her that he was her husband's brother, and he then explained what had happened, giving her the full story, that her son Hasan had spent a whole night with his daughter ten years earlier and had then disappeared at dawn. 'He left my daughter pregnant,' Shams al-Din added, 'and she gave birth to a son who is here with me, and he is your grandson, the son of your son by my daughter.'

When she looked at her brother-in-law and heard the news that her son was still alive, she got up and threw herself at his feet, kissing them and reciting:

> How excellent is the man who brings good tidings of your coming!
> He has brought with him the most delightful news.
> Were he to be contented with a rag, I would give him
> A heart that was torn in pieces when you said goodbye.

Shams al-Din then sent a message telling 'Ajib to come, and when he did, his grandmother got up, embraced him and wept. 'This is no time for tears,' Shams al-Din told her. 'This is the time for you to make your preparations to travel with us to Egypt, and perhaps God will allow us and you to join your son, my nephew.' She agreed to leave and instantly got up to collect what she needed, together with her treasures and her maids. As soon as she was ready, Shams al-Din went to the sultan of Basra and took leave of him, while the sultan, in his turn, sent gifts and presents with him to take to the sultan of Egypt.

Shams al-Din then left immediately and travelled to Damascus, where he halted and pitched camp at al-Qanun. He told his entourage that they would stay there for a week so that they could buy gifts for the sultan. 'Ajib went out, telling his servant, Layiq, that he wanted to look around the place, adding: 'Come with me and we shall go down to the market

---

* cf. Night 8.

and pass through the city to see what has happened to that cook whose
food we ate and whose head I hurt. He had been kind to me and I
harmed him.' Layiq agreed and the two of them left the camp, 'Ajib
being drawn to his father by the ties of kinship.

After entering the city, they went on until they came to the cookshop,
where they found Hasan. It was close to the time of the afternoon prayer
and, as luck would have it, he had cooked a dish of pomegranate seeds.
When they approached him, 'Ajib looked at him with a feeling of affection, while noting the scar on his forehead left by the blow from the
stone. He greeted Hasan affectionately, while, for his part, Hasan was
agitated: his heart fluttered, he hung his head towards the ground and
he tried without success to move his tongue around his mouth. Then
looking up at his son, with meekness and humility he recited these lines:

> I wished for my beloved, but when he came in sight,
> In my bewilderment I could not control tongue or eyes.
> I bowed my head in reverence and respect;
> I tried to hide my feelings, but in vain.
> I had whole reams of blame to give to him,
> But when we met I could not speak a word.

Then he said to 'Ajib: 'Mend my broken heart and eat of my food. By
God, when I look at you, my heart races and it was only because I had
lost my wits that I followed you.' 'You must indeed be fond of me. I
took a bite to eat with you, after which you followed me, wanting to
bring shame on me. I shall only eat your food on condition that you
swear not to come out after me or follow me again, for otherwise I shall
never come back here, although we are staying for a week so that my
grandfather can buy gifts for the sultan.' Hasan agreed and 'Ajib entered
with his servant. Hasan presented them with a bowl of pomegranate
seeds and 'Ajib asked him to give them the pleasure of eating with him.
He accepted gladly, but as his heart and body were concentrated on
'Ajib, he kept staring fixedly at his face. 'Ajib objected, saying: 'Didn't
I tell you that you are an unwelcome lover, so stop staring at my face.'
When Hasan heard what his son said, he recited these lines:

> You have a hidden secret in men's hearts,
> Folded away, concealed and not spread out.
> Your beauty puts to shame the gleaming moon
> While your grace is that of the breaking dawn.

The radiance of your face holds unfulfillable desires,
Whose well-known feelings grow and multiply.
Am I to melt with heat, when your face is my paradise,
And shall I die of thirst when your saliva is Kauthar?*

Hasan kept filling 'Ajib's plate and then that of the eunuch. They ate
their fill and then got up. Hasan rose himself and poured water over
their hands, after which he unfastened a silk towel from his waist on
which he dried their hands before sprinkling them with rosewater from
a flask that he had with him. Then he left his shop and came back
with a jug of sherbet mixed with musk-flavoured rosewater, which he
presented to them, saying: 'Complete your kindness.' 'Ajib took it and
drank, after which he passed it to the eunuch. They then drank from it
in turns until their stomachs were full, as they had had more than usual.

After leaving, they hurried back to their camp, where 'Ajib went to see
his grandmother. She kissed him and then, thinking of her son, she
sighed, shed tears and recited:

I hoped that we might meet, and, after losing you,
There was nothing for me to wish for in my life.
I swear that there is nothing in my heart except your love,
And God, my Lord, knows every secret thing.

She then asked 'Ajib where he had been, to which he replied that he had
gone into the city of Damascus. She got up and brought him a bowl of
pomegranate seeds that had only been sweetened a little, and she told
the eunuch to sit down with his master. 'By God,' said the eunuch to
himself, 'I have no urge to eat,' but he sat down. As for 'Ajib, when he
took his seat, his stomach was full of what he had already eaten and
drunk, but he took a morsel, dipped it among the pomegranate seeds
and ate it. Because he was full, he found it undersweetened and he
exclaimed: 'Ugh, what is this nasty food?' 'My son,' said his grandmother, 'are you blaming my cooking? I cooked this myself and no one
can cook as well as I can, except for your father Hasan.' 'By God,
grandmother,' replied 'Ajib, 'this dish of yours is disgusting. We have
just come across a cook in the city who cooked a dish of pomegranate
seeds whose smell would open up your heart. His food makes one
want to eat again, while, in comparison, yours is neither one thing nor
another.'

* Kauthar is the water of Paradise.

On hearing this, his grandmother became very angry and, looking at the eunuch . . .

Night 24

Morning now dawned and Shahrazad broke off from what she had been allowed to say. Then, when it was the twenty-fourth night, SHE CONTINUED:

I have heard, O auspicious king, that on hearing this, his grandmother became very angry and, looking at the eunuch, she reproached him, telling him that he had spoiled her son by taking him into a cookshop. The apprehensive eunuch denied this, saying: 'We didn't go into the shop but merely passed by it.' 'Ajib, however, insisted that they had gone in and had eaten, adding: 'And it was better than your food.' His grandmother got up and told her brother-in-law about this, turning him against the eunuch, who was then brought before him. 'Why did you take my grandson into the cookshop?' Shams al-Din asked. In his fear, the eunuch again denied this, but 'Ajib insisted: 'We did go in and we ate pomegranate seeds until we were full, after which the cook gave us a drink with snow and sugar.' Shams al-Din became even angrier with the eunuch and asked him again. He again denied it, at which Shams al-Din said: 'If you are telling me the truth, then sit down and eat in front of me.' The eunuch came forward and tried to do this but failed and had to throw away what he had taken. 'Master,' he explained, 'I am still full from yesterday.' Shams al-Din then realized that he had indeed eaten in the cookshop. He ordered the slaves to throw him down, which they did, and he then started to beat him painfully. The eunuch called for help. 'Don't beat me, master,' he cried, 'and I'll tell you the truth.' After this, Shams al-Din stopped beating him and demanded the truth. 'We did go into the shop,' he said, 'and the cook was preparing a dish of pomegranate seeds. He gave us some of it and, by God, never in my life have I tasted anything like it, while I have never tasted anything nastier than this stuff that is before us.'

Hasan's mother was angry and told him: 'You must go to this cook and fetch us a bowl of pomegranate seeds that he has prepared. You can then show it to your master and he can then say which is better and more tasty.' The eunuch agreed and was given a bowl and half a dinar. He went to the shop and said to Hasan: 'In my master's house we have laid a bet on your cooking. They have pomegranate seeds there, so for this half dinar give me some of yours, and take care over it, for your cooking has already cost me a painful beating.' Hasan laughed and said: 'By God, this is a dish that nobody can cook properly except for my mother and me, and she is now in a distant land.' He then ladled the food into the bowl and took it to put the finishing touches on it using musk and rosewater.

The eunuch carried it back quickly to the camp, where Hasan's mother took it and tasted it. When she noted how flavoursome it was and how well it had been cooked, she realized who must have cooked it and gave a shriek before falling in a faint, to the astonishment of Shams al-Din. He sprinkled rosewater over her and after a time she recovered. 'If my son is still in this world,' she exclaimed, 'it was he and no one else who cooked these pomegranate seeds. It has to have been my son, Hasan. No one else can cook it except him, for I taught him the recipe.' When Shams al-Din heard this, he was overjoyed and exclaimed: 'How I long to see my brother's son! Will time unite me with him? But it is only from Almighty God that I may seek a meeting with him.'

He got up immediately and went to his escort, ordering twenty men to go the cookshop, demolish it, and tie up the cook with his own turban. 'Then,' he said, 'drag him here by force, but without injuring him in any way.' The men agreed to do this, and Shams al-Din himself rode immediately to the palace of the governor of Damascus, whom he met and to whom he showed the letters that he had brought with him from the sultan. The governor kissed them and then placed them on his head, before asking: 'Where is the man you are looking for?' 'He is a cook,' replied Shams al-Din, and the governor instantly ordered his chamberlains to go to his shop. They went and found the shop demolished with all its contents smashed, for when Shams al-Din had gone to the governor's palace, his men had carried out his orders. They sat there waiting for him to return, while Hasan was asking: 'What could they have seen in the dish of pomegranate seeds that led to all this?'

Shams al-Din returned with the governor's permission to carry away Hasan. When he entered his tent, he ordered the cook to be produced and he was brought in, tied up with his own turban. Hasan wept bitterly on seeing his uncle and said: 'Master, what offence do you charge me with?' 'Was it you,' asked Shams al-Din, 'who cooked these pomegranate seeds?' 'Yes,' said Hasan, 'and did you find anything in them that entitles you to cut off my head?' 'For you this would be the best and lightest

punishment,' said Shams al-Din. 'Master,' said Hasan, 'are you not going
to tell me what I did wrong?' 'Yes, immediately,' said Shams al-Din, but
he then called to the servants to bring the camels. They took Hasan with
them, put him in a box, locked it and set off, travelling until nightfall.
Then they halted and ate some food. They took Hasan out of his box,
gave him something to eat and then put him back in it. They followed
this pattern until they reached Qamra, when Hasan was taken out of
his box and was again asked whether it was he who had cooked the
pomegranate seeds. When he still said yes, Shams al-Din ordered him to
be fettered, which was done and he was put back in the box.

The party then travelled on to Cairo, where they halted at the Raid-
aniya camping ground. Shams al-Din ordered Hasan to be taken out and
he ordered a carpenter to be fetched whom he told to make a wooden
cross. 'What are you going to do with it?' asked Hasan. 'I will garrotte
you on it and then nail you to it, before parading you around the whole
city,' Shams al-Din told him. 'Why are you doing this to me?' asked
Hasan. 'Because of your ill-omened cooking of the pomegranate seeds,
for you cooked them without enough pepper,' replied Shams al-Din.
'Are you really doing all this to me because the dish lacked pepper?' said
Hasan. 'Was it not enough for you to keep me shut up, giving me only
one meal a day?' 'There was not enough pepper,' said Shams al-Din,
'and the only punishment for you is death.' Hasan was both astonished
and sorry for himself. 'What are you thinking about?' asked Shams
al-Din. 'About superficial minds like yours,' replied Hasan, 'for if you
had any intelligence you would not treat me like this.' 'We have to punish
you,' said Shams al-Din, 'so as to see that you don't do this kind of thing
again.' 'The least part of what you have done to me is a punishment,'
said Hasan, but Shams al-Din insisted that he must be strangled.

While all this was going on, the carpenter was preparing the wood
before his eyes. This went on until nightfall when Shams al-Din took
Hasan and threw him into the box, saying: 'The execution will take
place tomorrow.' He then waited until he was sure that Hasan was
asleep, when he got up, lifted the chest and, after mounting his horse, he
placed the box in front of him. He entered the city and rode on until he
came to his house. To his daughter, Sitt al-Husn, he said: 'Praise be to
God who has reunited you with your cousin. Get up and arrange the
furnishings of the house as they were on your wedding night.' The
household was roused and the candles were lit, while Shams al-Din
produced the paper on which he had drawn a plan showing how the

furniture was to be arranged. Everything was put in its place, so that anyone looking at it would be in no doubt that this was as it had been on the actual wedding night.

Shams al-Din gave instructions that Hasan's turban should be placed where he himself had left it, as should his trousers and the purse that was beneath the mattress. He then told his daughter to wear no more than she had been wearing when left alone with her bridegroom on her wedding night. 'When your cousin comes in,' he said, 'tell him that he has been a long time in his visit to the latrine and then invite him to pass the rest of the night with you. Talk with him until daybreak, and I shall then explain the whole affair to him.' Next, he took Hasan out of the chest, having first removed the fetters from his feet. He stripped off the clothes that he was wearing, so that he was left in a thin nightshirt with no trousers.

The sleeping Hasan knew nothing about what was happening, but, as fate had decreed, he turned over and woke up to find himself in a brilliantly lit hallway. 'This is a confused dream,' he said to himself, but he then walked a short way to a second door, and, on looking, he found himself in the room in which his bride had been unveiled for him. There was the alcove and the chair and he could see his turban and his other things. He was astonished at this sight and hesitated, moving forwards and then backwards. 'Am I asleep or awake?' he asked himself, wiping his forehead and saying in amazement: 'By God, this is the room of the bride who was unveiled for me; but where am I, for I was in a box?'

While he was talking to himself, Sitt al-Husn suddenly lifted the bottom of the alcove curtain and said: 'Master, are you not going to come in? You have been a long time in the latrine.' When he heard her voice and looked at her face, he laughed and said: 'I am in a confused dream.' He went into the alcove, where he sighed, and, thinking over his experiences, he was filled with confusion, particularly at the sight of the turban, his trousers and the purse with the thousand dinars, and was at a loss to grasp what had happened. 'God knows better,' he said, 'but this is a muddled dream.' 'What are you so astonished about?' asked Sitt al-Husn. 'You weren't like that at the beginning of the night.' Hasan laughed and asked: 'How long have I been away from you?' 'Bless you,' she said, 'and may the Name of God encompass you, you left to attend to yourself and then come back. Are you out of your mind?' Hasan laughed when he heard that and said: 'You are right, but when I left you I took leave of my senses in the latrine and dreamt that I was a cook in

Damascus and had been there for ten years, when a boy, a great man's son, came in with a eunuch.'

At that, he rubbed his hand over his forehead and found the scar on it. 'By God, lady,' he said, 'that almost seems to be true, because he struck me on the forehead and broke the skin, and it seemed as though I was awake at the time.' He went on: 'It was as though we had just gone to sleep in each other's arms and then I had this dream and I appeared to have arrived in Damascus with no turban and no trousers and then worked as a cook.' After remaining perplexed for a time, he said: 'By God, I seemed to see that I had cooked a dish of pomegranate seeds and had put on too little pepper, but I suppose that I must have been asleep in the latrine and I must have seen all this in a dream.' 'What else did you see?' asked Sitt al-Husn. Hasan told her, and then he said: 'By God, if I had not woken up, they would have crucified me.' 'What for?' she asked. 'Because there was too little pepper on the pomegranate seeds,' he replied. 'It seemed as though they had wrecked my shop and broken up my utensils and put me in a box. Then they brought a carpenter to make a cross for me and they were going to garrotte me. Thank God that all this happened in a dream and not in real life.' Sitt al-Husn laughed and clasped him to her breast as he clasped her to his, but then he thought for a while and said: 'By God, it seemed as though it was real, but I don't know why that should be.' He was still perplexed when he fell asleep, muttering alternately 'I was asleep' and 'I was awake'.

That went on until morning, when his uncle Shams al-Din came in and greeted him. Hasan looked at him and said: 'By God, aren't you the man who ordered me to be tied up and crucified and ordered my shop to be wrecked because there was not enough pepper on the pomegranate seeds?' 'Know, my son,' said Shams al-Din, 'that the truth is now revealed and what was hidden has been made clear. You are the son of my brother and I only did all this to make sure that it was you who slept with my daughter that night. I could only be certain of this because you recognized the room and recognized your turban and your trousers, your gold, the note that you wrote and the one that your father, my brother, wrote. For I had never seen you before and could not identify you. I have brought your mother with me from Basra.' He then threw himself on Hasan in tears. When Hasan heard what his uncle had to say, he was lost in astonishment and, embracing his uncle, he wept from excess of joy.

'The reason for all this,' Shams al-Din told him, 'was what happened between me and your father.' He then told him the story of this and of why Hasan's father, Nur al-Din, had gone to Basra. He sent for 'Ajib, and when his father saw him, he said: 'This is the one who hit me with the stone.' 'He is your son,' Shams al-Din told him. Hasan threw himself on the boy and recited these lines:

> I have wept over our separation, and for long
> Tears have been pouring from my eyes.
> I vowed, were Time to join us once again,
> My tongue would never speak the word 'parting'.
> Delight has now launched its attack on me,
> And my great joy has made me weep.

As soon as he had finished speaking, in came his mother, who threw herself on him and recited:

> On meeting, we complained of the great suffering of which we
>   speak.
> It is not good to send complaints by messengers.

She then told him what had happened to her after he had vanished, and he told her of his own sufferings, and they then gave thanks to God for having reunited them. Two days after his arrival, Shams al-Din went to the sultan. On entering, he kissed the ground before him and greeted him with a royal salute. The sultan, who was glad to see him, smiled at him and told him to come nearer. He then asked him what he had seen in his travels and what had happened to him. Shams al-Din told him the story from beginning to end. 'Praise be to God,' said the sultan, 'for the achievement of your desire and your safe return to your family and children. I must see your nephew, Hasan of Basra, so bring him to court tomorrow.' Shams al-Din agreed to this – 'If God Almighty wills' – and then took his leave and went out. When he got home he told his nephew that the sultan wanted to see him. 'The servant obeys the order of his master,' said Hasan, and he accompanied his uncle to the sultan's court. When he was in the sultan's presence, he greeted him with the greatest respect and courtesy, and began to recite:

> The one you have ennobled now kisses the ground,
> A man whose quest has been crowned with success.
> You are the lord of glory; those who rest their hope on you
> Obtain what will exalt them in this world.

The sultan smiled, motioning him to sit, and so he took his seat near his uncle, Shams al-Din. The sultan then asked him his name, to which he replied: 'The meanest of your servants is known as Hasan of Basra, and night and day he invokes blessings on you.' The sultan was pleased with what he said and wanted to put his apparent knowledge and good breeding to the test. 'Do you remember any poetry that describes a mole?' he asked. 'Yes,' said Hasan, and he recited:

> There is a dear one at the thought of whom
> My tears fall and I wail aloud.
> He has a mole, in beauty and in colour
> Like the pupil of the eye or the heart's core.

The sultan approved of these lines and courteously asked him to produce more. So he recited:

> Many a mole has been compared to a musk grain,
> But this comparison is not to be admired.
> Rather, admire the face encompassing all its beauty,
> So that no single part is missing from the whole.

The sultan rocked with delight and said: 'Give me more, may God fill your life with blessing.' Hasan then recited:

> You, on whose cheek the mole
> Is like a grain of musk set on a ruby,
> Grant me your union, and do not be harsh,
> You who are my heart's wish and its nourishment.

'Well done, Hasan,' said the sultan. 'You have shown great proficiency. Now explain to us how many meanings does the word *khal*, or "mole", have in Arabic.' 'Fifty-eight,' was his reply, 'although some say fifty.' 'Correct,' said the sultan, who then asked him if he knew how beauty can be particularized. 'Yes,' he replied. 'It comprises brightness of face, clear skin, a well-shaped nose, sweet eyes, a lovely mouth, a witty tongue, an elegant frame and the qualities of refinement, while its perfection is found in the hair. The poet al-Shihab al-Hijazi has combined all these in a poem written in the *rajaz* metre:

> Say, brightness is in the face; the skin is clear.
> Let that be what you see.
> Beauty is rightly ascribed to the nose,

While sweetness is attributed to eyes.
Yes, and men talk of mouths as beautiful.
Learn this from me, and may you not lack rest.
The tongue has wittiness and the frame elegance,
Whereas refinement lies in the qualities,
And perfect loveliness, they say, is in the hair.
Listen to my verse, and hold me free from blame.'

The sultan was pleased with what Hasan had said and felt well disposed towards him. He then asked him to explain the meaning of the proverbial expression 'Shuraih is more cunning than the fox'. 'Know, your majesty,' replied Hasan, 'may God Almighty aid you, that in the plague days Shuraih went to Najaf. Whenever he was going to pray, a fox would come and stand opposite him, imitating what he was doing and distracting him from his prayer. When that had gone on for a long time, one day he took off his shirt and put it on a cane, with its sleeves spread out. He then put his turban on top of the cane, tied a belt around the middle and set it up in the place where he prayed. The fox came up as usual and stood in front of it, at which Shuraih came up from behind and seized the animal. This is the explanation of the saying.'

When the sultan heard his explanation, he said to Shams al-Din: 'This nephew of yours is a man of perfect breeding, and I do not believe that his match is to be found in all Egypt.' Hasan rose, kissed the ground before the sultan, and took his seat like a mamluk in front of his master, and the sultan, delighted at having discovered the extent of his knowledge of the liberal arts, gave him a splendid robe of honour and invested him with an office that would help him to live well.

Hasan rose and, after kissing the ground again, he prayed for the sultan's enduring glory, and then asked permission to leave with his uncle Shams al-Din. When this was granted, he left and he and his uncle returned home. Food was brought and after they had finished eating a pleasant meal, Hasan went to his wife's apartment and told her what had happened to him in the sultan's court. She said: 'He is bound to make you one of his intimate companions and shower gifts and presents on you. By God's grace, you are like a great light spreading the rays of your perfection, wherever you may be, on land or sea.' He said to her: 'I want to compose an ode in his honour, so as to increase the love that he feels for me in his heart.' 'A good idea,' she agreed. 'Produce good concepts and elegant expressions and I'm sure that he will find your poem acceptable.'

Hasan then went off by himself and wrote some well-formed and elegantly expressed lines. They ran as follows:

I have a heroic patron, soaring to the heights of greatness,
And treading on the path of generous and noble men.
His justice brings security to every land,
And for his enemies he has barred the path.
He is a lion, pious and astute;
If you call him king or angel, he is both.*
Those who ask him for favours are sent back rich.
There are no words to sum him up.
On the day of generosity, he is the shining dawn,
While on the day of battle, he is darkest night.
Our necks are fettered with his generosity,
And by his favours he masters the freeborn.
God grant us that he may enjoy long life,
Defending him from all that may bring harm.

When he had finished composing this piece, he sent it to the sultan with one of his uncle's slaves. The sultan studied it with delight and read it out to those who were in attendance on him. They were enthusiastic in their praise, and the sultan summoned Hasan and told him when he came: 'From this day on, you are my intimate companion, and I have decreed for you a monthly allowance of a thousand dirhams, in addition to what I have already assigned you.' Hasan rose and thrice kissed the ground before the sultan, praying for his lasting glory and long life. From then on, he enjoyed lofty status; his fame spread throughout the lands, and he lived in the greatest comfort and ease with his uncle and his family until he was overtaken by death.

When Harun al-Rashid heard this story from Ja'far, he was astonished and said: 'These accounts should be written down in letters of gold.' He then freed the slave and provided the young man with a monthly allowance to allow him to live in comfort. He also gave him one of his own concubines and enrolled him among his intimates.

'This tale, however, is not more wonderful than the story of what happened in the case of the tailor, the hunchback, the Jew, the inspector

---

* An Arabic pun on *malik* ('king') and *malak* ('angel').

and the Christian.' 'What was that?' asked the king, AND SHAHRAZAD
EXPLAINED:

I have heard, O fortunate king, that once upon a time, in the old days,
in the city of China there lived a tailor, an open-handed man with a
liking for pleasure and entertainment. He used to go out with his wife
from time to time to see the sights. One afternoon, the two of them went
early and came back home towards evening. On their way home, they
found a hunchback whose strange appearance would raise a laugh even
from a man who had been cheated in a bargain and which would dispel
the grief of the sad. The tailor and his wife went over to look at him, and
they then invited him to come home with them to keep them company
that night. He agreed and accompanied them.

Night had now fallen and the tailor went off to the market, where he
bought a fried fish, together with bread, lemons and a milky dessert. On
returning, he set the fish before the hunchback and they ate. His wife
then took a large bit of fish and crammed it into her guest's mouth,
which she covered with her hand, telling him that he had to swallow it
in one gulp. 'And I shall not allow you time to chew it.' The hunchback
did swallow it, but it contained a solid bone which stuck in his throat
and, his allotted span having come to an end, he died.

Night 25

Morning now dawned and Shahrazad broke off from what she had been
allowed to say. Then, when it was the twenty-fifth night, SHE CONTINUED:
I have heard, O auspicious king, that when the tailor's wife gave the
hunchback a mouthful of fish to eat, as his allotted span had ended, he
died instantly. 'There is no might and no power except with God,'
exclaimed the tailor. 'Poor man, that he should die like this at our hands!'
'Why are you wasting time?' said his wife. 'Haven't you heard what the
poet says:

Why do I try to console myself with the impossible,
When I have never met a friend to bear my sorrows?
How can one sit on a fire before it is put out?
To sit on fire brings harm.'

'What am I to do?' asked her husband. 'Get up,' she said. 'Carry the
man in your arms and spread a silk covering over him. We must do this

tonight, and I shall go in front, with you following behind. You are to say: "This is my son and this is his mother, and we are taking him to see the doctor."' On hearing this, the tailor got up and carried the hunchback in his arms, while his wife kept saying: 'My son, may you recover; what is paining you and where are the symptoms of smallpox showing?' Everyone who saw them said: 'These people have a child with smallpox.' They continued on their way, asking for the doctor's house, until they were directed to the house of a Jewish physician. They knocked on the door and down came a black slave girl, who opened it. When she saw a man carrying a child and accompanied by a woman, she asked: 'What's the matter?' The tailor's wife replied: 'We have a child with us and we would like the doctor to have a look at him. Take this quarter dinar, give it to your master, and let him come down to see my sick son.' The girl went up and the tailor's wife came through the door and said to her husband: 'Leave the hunchback here and then let's make our escape.' The tailor agreed, and propping the hunchback against the wall, he and his wife made off.

The slave girl went to the Jew and told him: 'There is someone at the door with a sick person. His wife is with him and he has handed me a quarter dinar for you to go down to look at him and to prescribe something suitable.' The Jew, delighted to see the money, got up quickly and went off in the dark, but as soon as he put his foot down, he stumbled over the corpse. 'O Ezra!' he cried. 'O Moses and the Ten Commandments! O Aaron and Joshua, son of Nun! I seem to have stumbled over this sick man and he has fallen down the stairs and died. How can I get the corpse out of my house?' He carried it inside and told his wife what had happened. She said: 'Why are you sitting there? If you wait until daybreak, then both you and I will lose our lives. We have to take him up to the roof and drop him into the house of our neighbour, the Muslim. As he is an inspector in charge of the king's kitchens, he often brings home fat, which the cats and the rats eat. If the corpse is left there overnight, the dogs will come down from the roofs and drag it off, for they do a great deal of damage to all the stuff that he brings home.'

So the Jew and his wife went up to their roof, carrying the hunchback, and they then lowered him to the ground by his arms and legs, leaving him by the wall, before going off. No sooner had they done this than the inspector came home, opened the door and went up, carrying a lighted candle. He noticed a man standing in the corner under the ventilation shaft. 'By God!' he exclaimed. 'This is a fine thing! It must have been a man who has been stealing my stores!' Turning to the corpse, he said: 'It was you who has been stealing the meat and the fat, when I thought it was the cats and dogs of the neighbourhood. I have put myself in the wrong by killing them, when all the time it was you, coming down from the roof.' He took up a large hammer and, brandishing it, he went up to the corpse and struck it on the breast. When he found that the man was dead, he was moved with grief, and, fearing for his own life, he exclaimed: 'There is no might and no power except with God Almighty! May God curse the fat and the sheep's tail!' He then added: 'How was it that I brought this man's life to an end with my own hand?' The inspector looked at his victim and found that he was a hunchback. 'Wasn't it enough for you to be a hunchback,' he asked, 'that you had to become a thief and steal meat and fat? O God, the Shelterer, cloak me with Your gracious covering.' He then hoisted the corpse on to his shoulders as the night was ending and took it out of his house. He continued to carry it until he reached the edge of the market, where he propped it up at the side of a shop at the head of an alley. He then left the corpse and made off.

A Christian, the king's broker, was the next to appear on the scene. He was drunk and had come out to go to the baths, realizing, in his drunkenness, that it was nearly time for matins. He went on, staggering as he walked, until, when he was near the corpse, he squatted down to urinate. Then, casting a sideways glance, he saw someone standing there. As it happened, at the beginning of that night his turban had been stolen and when he saw the hunchback leaning against the wall, he imagined the man meant to steal the one that he now had on. So he balled his fist and struck the hunchback on the neck, felling him to the ground. He called to the market watchman, and then, in the excess of his drunkenness, he set about belabouring the corpse and trying to strangle it. The watchman came up and found the Christian kneeling on the Muslim and hitting him. 'What has he done?' he asked. The Christian said: 'He wanted to steal my turban.' 'Get away from him,' ordered the watchman, and when the Christian had got up, he went to the hunchback and found him dead. 'By God,' he said, 'this is a fine thing – a Christian killing a Muslim,' and after having tied the Christian's hands, he took him to the house of the *wali*. All the while the Christian was saying to himself: 'O Messiah, O Holy Virgin, how could I have killed this man and how quickly he died from a single blow!' Drunkenness vanished, to be replaced by care, and the Christian together with the hunchback spent the rest of the night until morning in the *wali*'s house.

In the morning, the *wali* sentenced 'the killer' to be hanged. The executioner was ordered to proclaim his crime; a gallows was set up under which the Christian was made to stand, and the executioner came and put a rope around his neck. He was on the point of hanging him when the inspector made his way through the crowd. When he saw the Christian about to be hanged, he cleared a way for himself and then said: 'Don't do it; it was I who killed him.' 'Why did you do that?' asked the *wali*. 'I came home last night,' he said, 'and found that he had come down through the ventilation shaft and had stolen my goods, so I struck him on the chest with a hammer and he died. I carried him off to the market and propped him up in a lane nearby.' He added: 'Is it not enough for me to have killed a Muslim that I should kill a Christian as well? I am the one to be hanged.' On hearing this, the *wali* freed the Christian and told the executioner to hang the inspector on his own confession. The executioner took the rope from the neck of the king's broker and put it round that of the inspector, who was made to stand under the gallows.

He was about to be hanged when, all of a sudden, the Jewish doctor came through the crowd, shouting to them and to the executioner: 'Don't do it! It was I and I alone who killed him. I was at home last night when a man and a woman knocked at my door bringing with them this hunchback, who was sick. They gave my servant girl a quarter of a dinar. She told me about them and handed me the money, but it turned out that the pair had brought the hunchback into the house, left him on the stairs and gone off. I came down to look at him, but in the darkness I tripped over him and he fell down to the bottom of the stairs, killing himself on the spot. My wife and I carried him up to the roof and lowered him into the ventilation shaft of this inspector, who lives next door to us. The man was dead, but when the inspector came and found him in his house, he took him for a thief and struck him with a hammer so that he fell to the ground, leaving the inspector to think that he had killed him. Isn't it enough for me to have unknowingly killed one Muslim that I should knowingly be responsible for the death of another?'

When the *wali* heard this, he told the executioner to release the inspector and to hang the Jew. The executioner took him and put the rope round his neck, but at that the tailor came through the crowd and told him to stop: 'It was I and I alone who killed the man. Yesterday I went out to see the sights, and in the evening I met this hunchback, drunk and singing at the top of his voice to his tambourine. I invited him home and bought a fish, which we sat down to eat. My wife took a piece of it and making it into a mouthful, she crammed it into his gullet where a bit of it stuck, killing him instantly. Then my wife and I took him to the Jew's house. The servant girl came down and opened the door for us, and I told her to tell her master that a woman and a man were at the door with a sick person and to ask him to come and look at him. I gave her a quarter of a dinar and while she went up to her master, I carried the hunchback to the head of the stairs and propped him up there, after which my wife and I went away. The Jew came down and tripped over the hunchback and thought that he had killed him. Is that right?' he asked the Jew. 'Yes,' said the Jew, at which the tailor turned to the *wali* and said: 'Release the Jew and hang me.'

When the *wali* heard what he had to say, he was astonished by the whole affair, which he said should be recorded in books. Then he told the executioner to release the Jew and to hang the tailor on his own confession. 'I'm tired of this,' complained the executioner. 'I bring one man forward and put another one back and no one gets hanged.' Then he put the rope round the tailor's neck.

So much for these people, but as for the hunchback, the story goes that he was the king's fool and that the king could not bear to be parted from him. After getting drunk, he had left the king and had been away all night. As he was still not back by midday the next day, the king asked some of his courtiers about him, and they replied: 'Master, his dead body was brought to the *wali*, who ordered his killer to be hanged. Then a second and a third person arrived, each of them claiming to have killed him and each telling the *wali* the reason for it.' When the king heard this, he called to his chamberlain, telling him to go to the *wali* and to fetch him all those concerned.

When the chamberlain went there, he found the executioner about to hang the tailor. 'Don't do it!' he shouted, and he told the *wali* what the king had said. He then brought everyone, the *wali*, the tailor, the Jew, the Christian and the inspector, and had the corpse of the hunchback carried along with them. When the *wali* stood before the king, he kissed the ground and told him what had happened to each of them – but there is nothing to be gained from repetition. The king himself was filled with amazement and delight at the story, and gave orders that it should be recorded in letters of gold. He then asked those present whether they had ever heard anything more astonishing than the story of that hunchback.

At that, the Christian came forward and said: 'Your majesty, if you give me leave, I will tell you of something that happened to me which was more remarkable, stranger and more entertaining than the story of the hunchback.' When the king told him to produce his story, HE SAID:

King of the age, I came to these lands as a trader and it was fate that brought me to you. I was born in Cairo and am a Cairene Copt. I was brought up there and my father was a broker. He died when I had reached manhood and I took his place as a broker. One day when I was sitting there, up came a most handsome young man, wearing splendid clothes and riding on a donkey. When he saw me, he greeted me and I rose as a mark of respect. He then produced a kerchief in which there was a quantity of sesame. 'How much would an *ardabb* of this be worth?' he asked. 'A hundred dirhams,' I replied. 'Bring donkey men and grain measurers and go to Bab al-Nasr and then on to Khan al-Jawali, where you will find me,' he instructed.

He then went on his way, leaving me with the kerchief containing the sample. I went round the buyers and got a price of a hundred and twenty dirhams for an *ardabb*, after which I took four donkey men and went to find the young man waiting for me. When he saw me, he went to the storeroom, opened it and cleared out its contents. We measured them and they amounted to fifty *ardabbs*, totalling five thousand dirhams. The young man told me: 'You can have ten dirhams in every *ardabb* as your brokerage fee, so take the fee and keep four thousand five hundred dirhams for me. When I have finished selling my goods, I will come and collect it.' I agreed to this, kissed his hand and left him, having made a total profit of a thousand dirhams that day.

After a month's absence, the young man turned up and asked me for his money. I got up and, after greeting him, I asked if he would care to have something to eat in my house, but he refused and told me to have the money ready so that he could go off and collect it on his return. He then left and I fetched the money and sat waiting for him. He stayed away for a month and then when he came back, he asked where it was. I got up, greeted him and again invited him to eat with me, but again he refused and told me to have the money ready for him to take when he returned. When he had gone, I went and fetched it and sat waiting for him and again he stayed away for a month. 'This young man,' I said, 'is the perfection of liberality.'

A month later, he came riding on a mule, splendidly dressed and looking like the moon on the night when it comes to the full. It seemed as though he had emerged from the baths, with his face like the moon, red cheeks, radiant brow and a mole like a speck of ambergris, as the poet says:

> Sun and moon have met in the same zodiac sign,
> Rising with supreme beauty and good fortune.
> This beauty shows us why men envy them;
> How lovely they are when the call of joy rings out.
> Beauty and grace complete their charms,
> Which intelligence adorns and modesty distinguishes.
> God be praised; how wonderful is His creation!
> His wishes with regard to His creation are what He carries out.

When I saw him, I got up, kissed his hand and called down blessings on him. 'Sir,' I said, 'are you not going to take your money?' 'What's the hurry?' he asked. 'I shall finish my business and then take it from you,' after which he turned away. 'By God,' I said, 'when he comes next, I must offer him hospitality because I have made a fortune out of trading with his dirhams.'

It was at the end of the year that he came, wearing clothes even more splendid than before, and I swore to him that he had to stay with me and taste my hospitality. 'On condition that whatever you spend on me comes out of the money that you are holding for me,' he replied. I agreed to this and made him sit down, while I went and prepared the necessary food, drink, and so on, which I then presented to him, inviting him to eat in the Name of God. He went to the table and stretched out his left hand, after which he ate with me. This surprised me, and when we had finished, I washed his hand and gave him something to dry it with. We then sat down to talk, after I had offered him some sweetmeats. 'Sir,' I said to him, 'you would relieve me of a worry were you to tell me why you ate with your left hand. Is there perhaps something in your other hand that causes you pain?' When he heard this, he recited:

> Friend, do not ask what burns within my heart,
> Lest you should bring to light my sickness.
> Not of my own free will have I kept company with Salma
> In place of Laila, but necessity has its own laws.

He then took out his right arm from his sleeve and there I could see that the hand had been amputated from the arm. This astonished me, but he told me: 'Don't be astonished and don't say to yourself that it was out of pride that I used my left hand to eat with you. There is a remarkable reason for the loss of my right hand.' When I asked him what that was, he explained: 'You must know that I come from Baghdad and my father was one of the leading men of that city. When I grew up, I heard pilgrims, travellers and merchants talking about Egypt. That made a lasting impression on me, and so when my father died, I took a large quantity of money and prepared trade goods, consisting of fabrics from Baghdad and Mosul, all of which I loaded up before setting out. As God had decreed, I arrived safely in this city of yours.' Here the young man broke into tears and recited:

> The blind man may escape a pit
> In which the man of keen sight will be trapped.
> The ignorant may not be injured by a word
> That brings destruction on learned and clever men.
> A believer may find it hard to earn his daily bread,
> Unlike the unbeliever and the libertine.
> Of what use are man's actions and his schemes?
> What happens is what fate decrees for him.

When he had finished his recitation, HE WENT ON:
I entered Cairo, where I set down my goods at Khan Masrur, undoing the bales and stowing them away there. I gave my servant money to buy us something to eat, and I then had a short nap. When I got up, I walked down Bain al-Qasrain street, and then came back and passed the night in my lodgings. In the morning I opened up a bale and thought to myself that I would go through some of the markets to see what conditions were like. So I selected some fabrics, giving them to a number of my slaves to carry, and I went as far as the covered market of Jirjis, where the brokers, who had learned of my arrival, came to meet me. They took my goods and tried to auction them, but I was saddened to find that they failed to reach their capital cost. The senior auctioneer told me: 'I can give you useful advice. Do what the merchants do and sell your goods on credit for a fixed term of months, using a scribe, an inspector and a money-changer. You will get your money every Monday and Thursday; for each of your dirhams you will get back two, and what is more, you will be able to enjoy the sights of Cairo and the Nile.' 'That is a sound idea,' I said, so I took the brokers with me and went to the *khan*. They took my goods to the covered market, where I had a deed of sale

prepared, giving the price. I took the document to a money-changer from whom I got a receipt, and after that I went back to the *khan*.

There I stayed for a period of days, breakfasting every day on a glass of wine, mutton and sweetmeats. This went on until the month when the money was due, and then I would go every Monday and Thursday to the covered market and sit by the merchants' shops. The money-changer and the scribe would bring me what was due from the merchants until it was past the time for the afternoon prayer. I would then count it out, set my seal on its container and take it off with me to the *khan*. One Monday, after a visit to the baths, I went back to the *khan* and entered my room where I broke my fast with a glass of wine. Then I fell asleep and, on waking, I ate a chicken. After perfuming myself, I went to the shop of a merchant called Badr al-Din al-Bustani. When he saw me, he greeted me and chatted with me for a time until the market opened.

Just then, on to the scene came a woman with a proud carriage and a haughty gait. She wore a head-covering of extraordinary beauty, different perfumes wafting from her, and when she raised her veil, I found myself looking into her black eyes. She greeted Badr al-Din, who returned her greeting and got up to talk with her. When I heard her voice, love for her took hold of my heart. 'Have you a piece of embroidered silk decorated with hunting scenes?' she asked Badr al-Din, and he brought out for her one of the ones that he had bought from me and he sold it to her for twelve hundred dirhams. 'I'll take it now,' she said, 'and send you the money later.' 'I can't wait for it,' he said, 'for here is the owner of the material and I owe him a share in the sale.' 'Bad luck to you,' she replied. 'I am in the habit of buying quantities of material from you for high prices, giving more than you ask and sending you the money.' 'Agreed,' he said, 'but I have to have it today.' She then took the piece and threw it at him, saying: 'People like you don't know how to value anyone.'

She then rose to leave and, thinking that my soul was going with her, I got up and stopped her, saying: 'Lady, as a favour to me, be generous enough to retrace your steps.' She turned back, smiling, and said: 'It is for your sake that I have come back.' She took a seat opposite me in the shop and I asked Badr al-Din for what price the piece had been sold to him. 'Eleven hundred dirhams,' he said. 'You can have a hundred dirhams' profit,' I told him. 'Bring me a piece of paper and I shall write down its price.' I then took the material and wrote a receipt for Badr al-Din in my own hand, after which I gave the material to the lady and said: 'Take it with you, and if you like, you can pay me for it next market day, or, if you prefer, take it as a guest gift from me.' 'May God give you a good reward,' she said, 'endowing you with my wealth and making you my husband' – a prayer which was accepted by God. Then I said to her: 'Lady, accept this piece of silk and you can have another like it, but let me see your face.'

One glance at this was followed by a thousand sighs, and love for her was fixed so firmly in my heart that I took leave of my senses. She then lowered her veil, took the silk and said: 'Sir, do not leave me desolate,' after which she turned away. I sat in the covered market until after the afternoon prayer, out of my mind thanks to the domination of love. Consumed by the violence of this passion, I got up and asked Badr al-Din about the lady. He told me that she was a wealthy woman, the daughter of an emir who had died, leaving her a large amount of money. I then left him and went off back to the *khan*. When supper came, I was unable to eat anything for thinking of her; when I tried to sleep, sleep would not come, and I remained wakeful until morning. I then got up, changed into different clothes, drank a glass of wine and had a small breakfast, after which I went to Badr al-Din's shop.

I greeted him and sat with him, and then the lady came as usual, dressed more splendidly than before and accompanied by a maid. She greeted me and not Badr al-Din, and then, speaking eloquently in as sweet and delightful a voice as I had ever heard, she said: 'Send someone with me to take the twelve hundred dirhams, the price of the silk.' 'What is the hurry?' I asked. 'May we never be deprived of you,' she replied, and she then paid over the purchase price to me. I sat talking to her and my gestures led her to understand that I wanted union with her. At this, she got up hurriedly and shied away from me, leaving my heart caught in her toils. I followed her out of the market and was suddenly confronted by a servant girl, who said: 'Master, come and speak to my mistress.' Taken aback, I replied: 'There is nobody here who knows me.' She replied: 'How quickly you have forgotten her – my lady who was at the shop of Badr al-Din, the merchant, today,' and I then walked with her to the money-changer.

When the lady saw me, she brought me over to her side and said: 'My darling, you have been in my thoughts, and love for you has taken possession of my heart. Since the moment that I saw you I have not been able to enjoy sleep or food or drink.' 'I suffered twice as much,' I replied, 'and my present condition speaks for itself without needing to voice it.'

'My darling,' she asked, 'shall it be your house or mine?' 'I am a stranger,' I replied, 'and I have no place to go except the *khan*, so if you would be so good, let it be with you.' 'Yes,' she said, 'but this is Friday night and so there is nothing to be done until tomorrow after prayers. When you have prayed, get on your donkey and ask for the Habbaniya quarter. Then, when you get there, ask for the house of Barakat the *naqib*, who is known as Abu Shama, for that is where I am living. Don't be late, for I shall be expecting you.'

I was overjoyed at this; we parted and I went to my *khan*, where I spent a sleepless night. As soon as dawn had broken, I got up, changed my clothes, perfumed and scented myself and, taking with me fifty dinars wrapped up in a kerchief, I walked from Khan Masrur to Bab Zuwaila. There I got on a donkey and told its owner to take me to the Habbaniya quarter. He set off instantly and in no time he had come to a street called Darb al-Munqari. I told him to go into the street and ask for the house of the *naqib*. He was only away for a short time before coming back to tell me to dismount. I asked him to lead the way to the house, and then I said: 'Come for me here tomorrow morning and take me back.' When he had agreed to this, I gave him a quarter of a dinar and, after taking it, he went off.

I then knocked at the door and out came two young girls with swelling breasts, virgins like moons. 'Come in,' they said. 'Our mistress is expecting you, and she did not sleep last night, so pleased was she with you.' I entered a vaulted hall with seven doors, round which were windows overlooking a garden with fruits of all kinds, gushing waters and singing birds. The walls were treated with *sultani* gypsum in which a man could see his own face, while the ceiling was ornamented with gold, showing inscriptions in lapis lazuli, encompassing all the qualities of beauty and dazzling those who looked at it. The floor was laid with variegated marble and strewn with carpets, coloured silks and mattresses, while in the centre was a fountain, at whose corners were birds made of pearls and other gems. I entered and sat down . . .

Night 26

Morning now dawned and Shahrazad broke off from what she had been allowed to say. Then, when it was the twenty-sixth night, SHE CONTINUED:

I have heard, O auspicious king, that THE YOUNG MERCHANT TOLD
THE CHRISTIAN:

When I entered and sat down, before I knew it, the lady had come
forward, ornamented with henna and wearing a crown studded with
pearls and other gems. When she saw me, she smiled at me, hugged me
to her breast, and setting her mouth on mine she started to suck my
tongue as I sucked hers. 'Have you really come to me?' she said. 'I am
your slave,' I replied. She said: 'You are welcome. From the day that I
saw you, I have enjoyed neither sleep nor food.' 'It is the same with me,'
I told her, and we sat and talked, while I kept my head bent downwards
out of bashfulness. It was not long before she produced a meal with the
most splendid of foods, ragouts, and meats fried with honey, together
with stuffed chickens. We both ate until we had had enough and the
servants then brought me a bowl and a jug. I washed my hands and we
used musk-infused rosewater to perfume ourselves, after which we sat
talking. She then recited these lines:

> Had I known of your coming, I would have spread out
> My heart's blood and the pupils of my eyes.
> I would have strewn my cheeks to welcome you,
> So that you might have walked on my eyelids.*

She kept telling me of her sufferings, while I told her of mine, and her
love had so strong a grip on me that all my wealth was as nothing beside
it. We then started to play, dallying with each other and exchanging
kisses until nightfall. At this point, the maids produced us a complete
meal with food and wine, and we drank until midnight, when we went
to bed. I slept with her until morning, and never in my life have I
experienced a night like that. In the morning I got up and threw the
kerchief with the dinars under the bed for her. I then said goodbye and
went out, leaving her in tears. 'Sir,' she said, 'when shall I see this
handsome face again?' 'I shall be with you in the evening,' I replied.

When I left, I met the donkey man who had brought me there the day
before. He was standing at the door waiting for me and so I got on the
donkey and went with him to Khan Masrur, where I dismounted and
gave him half a dinar. 'Come at sunset,' I told him, and he agreed. I then
had breakfast and went out to collect the money for my goods. I prepared
a roast lamb for the lady and took some sweetmeats, after which I

* cf. Night 12.

summoned a porter, put the food in his basket and paid him his hire, before going back to my own affairs, tending to them until sunset. The donkey man turned up, and taking fifty dinars in a kerchief, I went to the lady's house, where I found that the servants had washed down the marble, polished the brass, filled the lamps and lit the candles, as well as making ready the food and straining the wine.

When the lady saw me, she threw her arms around my neck and said: 'You left me desolate.' The meal was then produced and we ate our fill, after which the maids cleared away the table and brought out the wine. We went on drinking until midnight, and then we went to the bedroom and slept until morning. Then I got up, gave her the fifty dinars as before and left. The donkey man was there and I rode to the *khan*, where I slept for an hour. After getting up, I made preparations for the evening meal, getting ready walnuts and almonds on a bed of peppered rice, together with fried colocasia roots, and I bought fruits, fresh and dried, as well as sweet-smelling flowers. When I had sent these off, I went back to the *khan*, and later I rode as usual with the donkey man to the house, taking fifty dinars wrapped in a kerchief. After I had entered, we ate, drank and then slept until morning, when I got up, gave the lady the kerchief and then rode back as usual to the *khan*.

Things went on like this for a time, until I woke up one morning and found that I had no money left at all. 'The devil has done this,' I said to myself, and I recited these lines:

When the rich man becomes poor, his splendour goes,
Just as the setting sun turns pale.
If he is absent, no one talks of him;
When present, he has no standing in his clan.
He walks through the markets covering his face,
While in the desert he sheds copious tears.
By God, he may be with his own people,
But even so, the poor man is a stranger.

I went out of the *khan* and walked up Bain al-Qasrain street, going on until I reached Bab Zuwaila. There I found a great crowd of people blocking the gate. As was fated, I saw a soldier and jostled him unintentionally. I touched his pocket with my hand, and on feeling it, I discovered that my fingers were resting on a purse there. Realizing that this was within my grasp, I removed it, but the soldier felt that his pocket had become lighter, and when he put his hand into it, he found it empty. He turned towards me, lifted his club and struck me on the head, knocking me to the ground. I was surrounded by people, who held on to the bridle of the man's horse, exclaiming: 'Do you strike this young man like that because you have been jostled?' 'He's a damned thief!' the soldier shouted at them. I then came to my senses and found people saying: 'This is a handsome young man and he has not taken anything.' Some of them believed this but others did not, and there was a great deal of argument. People were pulling me and wanting to free me from the soldier but, as fate had decreed, the *wali*, the police chief and his men came through the gate and found the people crowding around me and the soldier.

When the *wali* asked what the trouble was, the soldier said: 'Sir, this man is a thief. I had in my pocket a blue purse with twenty dinars in it and while I was stuck in the crush, he took it.' The *wali* asked whether there had been anyone with him. 'No,' he said, and the *wali* shouted to his police chief, who laid hold of me, leaving me no place to hide. 'Strip him,' ordered the *wali*, and when they did, they found the purse in my clothes. The *wali* took it, opened it and when he counted the money, he found in it twenty dinars, just as the soldier had said. He shouted angrily to the guards, who brought me before him. 'Tell the truth, young man,' he said. 'Did you steal this purse?' I hung my head and said to myself: 'I can say that I didn't steal it, but it has been found on me, and yet, if I confess that I did steal it, then I am in trouble.' So I raised my head and said: 'Yes, I took it.'

The *wali* was astonished when he heard me say this and he called for witnesses who, when they came, testified to what I had said. All this was happening by the Zuwaila gate. The *wali* then gave orders to the executioner, who cut off my right hand. Afterwards the soldier felt pity for me and, thanks to his intercession, the *wali* left me and went on his way. The people stayed around me and gave me a glass of wine, while the soldier gave me his purse, saying: 'You are a handsome young man and you should not be a thief.' I recited the lines:

> By God, I am no robber, my trusty friend,
> And neither am I a thief, O best of men.
> The misfortunes of Time cast me down suddenly,
> As my cares, temptation and poverty increased.
> It was not you but God Who shot the arrow
> That struck the royal crown from off my head.

After he had given me the purse, the soldier left me, while I went off myself, after wrapping my hand in a scrap of cloth and putting it inside the front of my clothes. I wasn't feeling well and I had turned pale as the result of my experience; I walked unsteadily to the lady's house, where I threw myself down on the bed. The lady looked at my altered colour and asked: 'What is paining you? Why do I see that your manner has changed?' 'I have a headache,' I replied, 'and I'm not well.' She was distressed and disturbed on my behalf. 'Don't distress me,' she said, 'but sit up, raise your head and tell me what has happened to you today, as it is clear from your face that you have a tale to tell.' 'Please don't talk,' I said, but she wept and said: 'I fear that you have finished with me, for I can see that you are not your usual self.' I kept silent, and although she went on talking, I made no reply. This went on until nightfall, when she brought me food, but I would not eat it lest she see me eating with my left hand. 'I don't want to eat just now,' I told her, but she persisted: 'Tell me what happened to you today, and why you are careworn and broken-hearted.' 'I shall tell you soon in my own time,' I said. Then she brought me wine and said: 'Take this, for it will remove your cares. You have to drink and then you can tell me your news.' 'Must I really tell you?' I asked. 'Yes,' she replied. 'If that is so,' I said, 'then give me to drink with your own hand.' She filled a glass and drank it and then filled it again and handed it to me. I took it from her with my left hand and, with tears pouring from my eyes, I recited:

When God wills some fate to befall a man –
A man of intelligence, having all his senses –
He deafens him and blinds his heart,
Drawing out his intelligence as one pulls a hair.
When what He has decreed then comes to pass,
He gives it back that its owner may take note.

On finishing these lines, I took the glass in my left hand and wept. She gave a loud shriek and asked: 'Why are you weeping, and so distressing me? Why did you take the glass in your left hand?' 'I have a boil on my right hand,' I said. 'Show it to me,' she said, 'and I will burst it for you.' 'It's not ready for that,' I said, adding: 'Don't pester me, for I'm not going to show it to you yet.' I then drank the glass, and she went on pouring out wine for me, until I was overcome by drunkenness and fell asleep on the spot. She then looked and saw an arm without a hand; on searching me, she found the purse with the gold. She felt more grief than anyone had ever experienced before, and the pain of this grief for me stayed with her until morning.

When I woke up, I found that she had prepared me a dish of four boiled chickens, and she gave me a glass of wine. I ate and drank and then laid down the purse and was about to go out, when she said: 'Where are you going?' 'To wherever it may be,' I replied. 'Don't go,' she said, 'but sit down.' I did as she said, and she asked: 'Have you loved me so much that you have spent all your money and lost your hand? I take you as my witness – and God is the truest witness – that I shall never leave you, and you shall see that what I say is true.' Then she sent for the notaries, and when they came she said: 'Draw up a marriage contract for me and this young man and bear witness that I have already received my dowry.' They did as they were told, and then she said: 'Bear witness that all my wealth, which is in this chest, and that all my slaves and servant girls are his property.' This they did, and I accepted the transfer of ownership, after which they took their fee and left.

She then took me by the hand and led me to a closet, where she opened a large chest, telling me to look at its contents. I looked and saw that it was full of kerchiefs. 'This is your money which I took from you, for all the kerchiefs that you gave me, each with its fifty dinars, I put together and dropped into this chest. Take your money, for it has been returned to you, and today you have become a great man. It was because of me that you became a victim of fate and lost your hand. For this I can make you no fair return, as even if I gave my life, it would not be enough by way of repayment.' Then she added: 'Take charge of your wealth,' and so I transferred what was in her chest to mine and added my money to what I had given her. I was filled with joy; my cares left me and I got up, kissed her and thanked her. 'You have given your hand out of love for me,' she said, 'so how can I repay you?' And she repeated: 'If I gave my life in love for you, it would not be enough and I would not have settled the debt that I owe you.'

Then she made over to me by formal deed all that she owned – dresses, jewellery and everything else. She spent the night with me, distressed by my own distress, until I told her all that had happened to me. After we had had less than a month together, she became very sick, and her illness intensified, until after only fifty days she was removed to the next world. I made the funeral preparations for her, buried her, arranged for the Quran to be recited over her grave, and distributed money and alms in her name, after which I went away from her tomb. I then found out that she had left a huge store of money, together with properties and estates, and among the storehouses was one filled with sesame, some of which I sold to you. I have been too busy to settle with you over this period because I have been selling off the rest of the goods, together with everything that was in the storehouses, and up till now I have not finished collecting the purchase price. As for you, you must not refuse what I propose. I have eaten your food and so I make you a present of the price of the sesame that you have with you. You now know why my right hand was cut off and why I eat with my left.

'You have done me a very great kindness,' I said. The young merchant then asked: 'Would you like to go with me to my own country? I have bought trade goods from Cairo and Alexandria, so will you come?' I agreed to this and arranged to meet him on the first day of the next month. I then sold all that I had and used the price to buy more trade goods, after which the young man and I travelled to this country of yours. The young man sold his goods, bought replacement stock and went back to Egypt, while it was my fate to be sitting here tonight when all this happened to me, a stranger. Is this not more remarkable than the story of the hunchback, O king of the age?'

The king replied: 'I must very certainly hang you all.'

Night 27

Morning now dawned and Shahrazad broke off from what she had been allowed to say. Then, when it was the twenty-seventh night, SHE CONTINUED:

I have heard, O auspicious king, that the king replied: 'I must very certainly hang you all.' At that, the king's inspector came forward and said: 'With your permission, I will tell you a story of what happened to me just before I found this hunchback. If it is more remarkable than the previous tale, will you spare all our lives?' The king agreed, AND THE INSPECTOR WENT ON:

You must know, your majesty, that last night I was with a group who had organized a recitation of the Quran, for which the *faqihs* had been brought together. When the reciters had performed their task and finished, a table was set out and among the foods that were produced was a dish made with sugar, almonds and vinegar. We came forward to eat, but one of our number held back and refused to join in. We urged him, but he swore that he would not eat any of it, and when we pressed him, he said: 'Don't force me. What happened to me the last time I ate this is enough for me,' and he recited:

Shoulder your belongings and be on your way;
If you like this kohl, anoint yourself with it.

When he had finished speaking, we urged him to tell us why he had refused the dish. 'If I have to eat it,' he said, 'I can only do that after I have washed my hands forty times with soap, forty times with potash and forty times with galingale; that is, a total of a hundred and twenty times.' At that, our host gave orders to his servants, who brought water and the other things for which he had asked, after which he washed his hands as I have described. He then came reluctantly, sat down and stretched out his hand, apparently in fear, plunged it into the dish and started to force himself to eat, filling us with surprise. His hand was shaking and when he raised it up, we could see that the thumb was missing and that he was eating with four fingers. We asked what had happened to his thumb, whether he had been born like that or whether he had suffered an accident. 'Brothers,' he replied, 'it is not only this thumb, but the other one as well, together with both my big toes. Wait till you see.' He then uncovered his left hand, and we found that it was like the right, and similarly that the big toes were missing from his feet. This sight added to our astonishment and we told him that we could not wait to hear his story, the reason for his mutilation, and why he washed his hands a hundred and twenty times. HE BEGAN:

Know that my father was one of the leading merchants of Baghdad in the days of Harun al-Rashid, and he was passionately fond of drinking wine and listening to the lute and other musical instruments. As a result, on his death he had nothing to leave. I arranged for the funeral and had the Quran recited over his grave. After a period of mourning, I opened up his shop, but I found that there was very little there and that he was in debt. I placated his creditors and persuaded them to wait, after which I started to trade, making them a weekly payment. Things went on like this for a time until I had paid off the debts and had added to my capital.

Then one day as I was sitting there, before I knew what was happening, a girl appeared, wearing jewellery and fine clothes, riding on a mule, with one slave in front of her and another behind. I had never seen

anything more lovely. She halted the mule at the entrance to the covered
market and went in, with her eunuch following and protesting: 'Come
out, my lady, and don't let anyone know, lest we find ourselves in the
fire.' He stood guarding her from sight as she looked at the merchants'
shops, of which, as she found, mine was the only one open. She walked in,
with the eunuch behind her, and sat down. The girl greeted me in the
loveliest and sweetest voice that I had ever heard, and when she uncovered
her face, I saw that she was as radiant as the moon. The glance that I threw
her was followed by a thousand sighs, and love for her became fixed in my
heart. Looking again and again at her face, I recited:

> Say to the lovely girl in the veil of the ringdove's colouring:
> 'It is certain that only death will relieve me from the torture you
>   inflict.
> Grant me union, that may perhaps give me life.
> Here is my hand stretched to you, hoping for bounty.'

On hearing this, she replied:

> I cannot bear the pangs of love, but may you find relief,
> Whereas my heart loves none but you.
> If my eyes look at any loveliness but yours,
> May this parting lead to no delight.
> I have sworn an oath never to forget your love;
> My heart is sad, though proud that we once met.
> Passion has poured a brimming glass of love.
> Would that it poured for you what it has poured for me.
> Take my corpse with you on your travels,
> And where you halt, bury me facing you.
> Call my name by my grave, and then my bones
> Will groan in answer when they hear your call.
> If I were asked what I desire from God, I would reply:
> 'His favour, Merciful is He, followed by yours.'

When she had finished these lines, she asked me whether I had attractive
materials for sale. 'My lady,' I replied, 'your servant is poor, but if you
wait until the other merchants open up their shops, I shall fetch you
what you want.' We then talked together, with me drowning in the sea
of love and lost in my passion for her, until the other merchants opened
their shops. I went to them and fetched her all that she wanted, at a price
of five thousand dirhams, after which the eunuch took the purchases

that she handed to him, and they both left the covered market. Her mule was brought up and she mounted, without having told me where she came from, something that I was too bashful to ask. The merchants made me guarantee the purchase price, and so I shouldered the debt of five thousand dirhams, and went back home, drunk with love. My servants brought me my evening meal but I only ate a mouthful, thinking of the girl's beauty and grace. I tried to sleep but no sleep would come, and I stayed in this restless state for a week.

At that point, the merchants asked me for their money, but I persuaded them to wait for another week. At the end of this, the girl appeared, riding on her mule, accompanied by a eunuch and two slaves. She greeted me and said: 'Sir, I have been slow in paying you for the materials. Bring the money-changer and take the cash.' The money-changer duly came and the eunuch produced the money, which then I took. The girl and I talked together until the market opened, when she told me to get her other materials. I fetched these for her from the merchants, and she then went off without having said anything to me about the price. This was something I regretted after she had gone, since it had cost me a thousand dinars to get what she wanted, and as soon as she was out of sight, I asked myself: 'What is this love? She gave me five thousand dirhams but I have just spent a thousand dinars.' I was sure that I would find myself reduced to poverty thanks to what I owed the merchants. 'I am the only one whom they know,' I said to myself, 'and this woman is nothing but a swindler who has used her beauty and grace to fool me. She thought of me as a little boy and laughed at me and I never even asked her where she lived.'

These misgivings stayed with me, and for more than a month she did not return. The merchants came to press me for their money and they forced me to sell my property, leaving me facing ruin. I was sitting, lost in thought, when before I knew it, there she was, dismounting at the gate of the market. She came into my shop and, when I saw her, my cares left me and I forgot my troubles. She came up and talked to me sweetly and then said: 'Fetch the money-changer and have your money weighed out,' after which she gave me the price of the goods that she had taken and added in a profit. Then she talked with me in so relaxed a way that I almost died of joy and delight. 'Have you a wife?' she asked. 'No,' I told her, 'I know no women at all,' and I burst into tears. 'Why are you crying?' she asked, and I replied: 'It's all right.'

I then took some of the dinars and gave them to the eunuch, asking him to act as my go-between in the affair, but he laughed at me and said: 'She loves you more than you love her. She didn't need the stuff that she bought from you and she bought it only because of her love for you. Ask her whatever you want; she will not say no to you.' The lady saw me giving money to him, and she came back and sat down. Then I said to her: 'Be generous to your servant and give him what he asks.' I told her what was in my heart and she agreed to my request. 'Do you bring my messages,' she told the eunuch, and to me she said: 'Do what the eunuch tells you.' She got up and left, while I went and handed over their money to the merchants, being left with a profit.

I then received no further news of her, and such was my regret I could not sleep at night, but after a few days the eunuch came back. I welcomed him with respect and asked him about his mistress. 'She is ill,' he said, and I asked him to explain her position to me. 'This girl,' he told me, 'was brought up by the Lady Zubaida, the wife of the caliph Harun al-Rashid, and she is one of her maidservants. She asked to be allowed to come and go as she pleased, and she has reached a position of authority. She talked about you to her mistress and asked whether she would marry her to you. "No, I shall not," replied Lady Zubaida, "until I see the young man, and then, if he is a suitable match for you, I shall give consent." We need to smuggle you into the palace now; if you succeed, you will be able to marry the girl, but if you are found out, your head will be cut off. What do you say?' 'I will go with you,' I said, 'and endure the fate you have described.' The eunuch said: 'Go tonight to the mosque, pray and spend the night there – that is the mosque which the Lady Zubaida built by the Tigris.'

I willingly agreed and in the evening I went to the mosque, performed my prayers and spent the night there. At daybreak, eunuchs arrived in a little boat, bringing with them several empty chests, which they brought to the mosque, before going off again. One of them stayed behind and, when I looked at him, I recognized him as my go-between. A little later, the girl arrived. When she came forward, I got up and embraced her; she kissed me and burst into tears, after which we talked for some time. Then she took me and put me in a chest, which she locked. She approached the eunuch, who had with him a large quantity of goods, and these she started to take and pack in the other chests, locking them one after the other until she had packed them all. The servants then loaded them on the boat and set off for Lady Zubaida's palace.

I became anxious, saying to myself that my lust would lead to my death, and wondering whether I would or would not succeed. I started to weep inside the chest and prayed God to deliver me from my plight. The servants continued their journey until they had brought all the chests to the gate of the caliph's palace, carrying in mine together with the others. They passed by a number of eunuchs entrusted with the protection of the harem, together with some of the harem women, until they came to a senior eunuch. Roused from his sleep, he shouted to the girl: 'What is in these chests?' 'They are full of goods for Lady Zubaida,' she said. 'Open them up one by one,' he ordered, 'so that I can look at the contents.' 'Why do you want them opened?' she objected, but he shouted at her: 'Don't waste time; these chests must be opened!'

He got to his feet and the first chest that he wanted to be opened was the one in which I was hidden. When it was brought to him, I lost my senses; I was so afraid that I was unable to control myself and my urine seeped from the chest. The girl cried to the eunuch: 'You have destroyed me and destroyed yourself, as you have spoiled something worth ten thousand dinars. In this chest are coloured dresses and four *manns*' of Zamzam water. The container has just fallen open and the water has leaked out over the clothes in the chest, ruining their colours.' 'Take your chests and go, God damn you,' said the eunuch. So the servants hurriedly carried off the chest that I was in, bringing the others with it.

While they were on their way, I heard someone saying: 'Woe, woe, the caliph, the caliph!' When I heard that, I almost died of fright, exclaiming: 'There is no might and no power except with God, the Exalted, the Omnipotent' – words which never bring shame on those who repeat them. To which I added: 'This is a disaster that I have brought on myself.' I then heard the caliph asking my mistress what was in the chests. 'Clothes belonging to the Lady Zubaida,' she said. 'Open them for me,' he ordered, and when I heard that, I felt that I had truly died, saying to myself: 'By God, this is the last day of my life in this world. If I escape, I shall marry her – no question about it – but if I am found out, then my head will be cut off.' I started to recite: 'I bear witness that there is no god but God and Muhammad is the Apostle of God.'

Night 28

Morning now dawned and Shahrazad broke off from what she had been allowed to say. Then, when it was the twenty-eighth night, SHE CONTINUED:

I have heard, O auspicious king, that the young man recited the confession of faith. HE WENT ON:

I heard the girl say: 'The contents of these chests has been left in my charge. There are some dresses for the Lady Zubaida and she wants no one to look at them.' 'The chests must be opened,' said the caliph, 'and I shall inspect what is in them.' Then he shouted to the eunuchs: 'Bring them to me,' at which I was so certain that I was going to die that I lost consciousness.

Meanwhile, the eunuchs began to bring forward the chests one by one, and the caliph looked at their contents: rare perfumes, costly materials and splendid dresses. They carried on opening the chests as the caliph inspected the dresses and whatever else was in them, until the only one left was the chest which contained me. The eunuchs had reached out to open it when the girl rushed up to the caliph and said: 'This chest in front of you is only to be opened in the presence of Lady Zubaida, for it is the one that contains her secret.' When the caliph heard this, he ordered that they should all be taken into her quarters. The eunuchs came and carried me in my chest before setting it down in the middle of the hall among the other ones. My mouth was dry, but the girl let me out and said: 'All's well; don't be afraid. You can relax happily. Sit down until the Lady Zubaida comes, and it may be your good fortune to win me.'

I sat there for a time, until suddenly ten maidens like moons came forward, and formed two lines of five, facing each other. They were followed by twenty more swelling-breasted virgins and in the middle of them was Lady Zubaida, wearing such a quantity of jewellery and such splendid robes that she could scarcely walk. When she came forward, the maids round about her dispersed and I went up and kissed the ground before her. She gestured to me to sit, and when I had taken my place in front of her, she began to question me. She asked about my family background and she was pleased at my answers to all her questions. She said to the girl: 'The way that I brought you up has not proved a failure,' and to me she said: 'Know that this girl is like a daughter to me and she is entrusted by God to your protection.'

I kissed the ground before her, happy that I was to be allowed to marry. On Lady Zubaida's orders, I stayed in the palace for ten days, during which I did not see the girl but was brought my meals morning and evening by a servant. At the end of this period, the Lady Zubaida consulted the caliph about the girl's marriage, and he gave his permission, as well as providing the girl with ten thousand dinars. Lady Zubaida sent for the notaries and the *qadi* and they drew up her marriage contract. After that the servants prepared sweetmeats and splendid dishes, which they distributed among all the rooms in the harem. Ten more days passed like this and after a total of twenty days, the girl went to the baths.

The servants then brought a small table, on which among other dishes was a plate of sugared almonds and vinegar, on top of which had been poured rosewater scented with musk. It contained roasted chicken breasts and an astonishing variety of other ingredients. I didn't wait but set upon it and ate my fill, but although I wiped my hands, I forgot to wash them. I sat there until nightfall, when the candles were lit and the singing girls came in with their tambourines. They went round the whole palace, displaying the bride and being showered with gold coins, after which they brought her forward, having taken off her outer clothes.

I found myself alone with her on the bed, and I embraced her, scarcely believing that I was going to enjoy union with her. Then, on my hand, she caught the scent of the dish I had eaten and she screamed aloud. The maids came in from all sides, while I trembled, not knowing what was happening. 'What is the matter with you, sister?' they asked. 'Remove this madman from me,' she said, 'for I had thought that he was a person of sense.' 'What symptom of madness have you seen in me?' I asked her. 'Madman,' she said, 'how is it that you ate the almond dish without washing your hands? By God, I shall repay you for what you have done. Is someone like you to sleep with someone like me?' Then from beside her she took a plaited whip and started to beat my back and then my buttocks with so many strokes that I fainted. 'Take him,' she ordered the maids, 'and bring him to the city magistrate to cut off the hand with which he ate the almond dish and which he failed to wash.'

When I heard this, I exclaimed: 'There is no might and no power except with God! Is my hand to be cut off simply because I ate that dish and didn't then wash my hands?' The maids interceded with her and said: 'Sister, don't punish him this time for this fault.' 'I must cut off some of his extremities,' she said, after which she went away. She stayed away for ten days, during which I didn't see her, but after that she came back to me and said: 'Black face, I'll teach you how to eat without washing your hands!' Then she called to the maids, who tied me up, and taking a sharp razor she cut off my thumbs and my big toes, as you all can see. I fainted, but she sprinkled powder over me, which stopped the flow of blood. I started to say that I would never again eat that dish without first washing my hands forty times with potash, forty times with galingale and forty times with soap. She made me swear to do this, as I have said, and that is why, when you produced this dish, I changed colour and said to myself that this was why I had lost my thumbs and my big toes, and when you forced it on me, I said that I must keep the oath that I had sworn.

The man was then asked what had happened after that. 'When I swore that oath for her,' he said, 'she calmed down and she and I slept together. We stayed there for a time, but after that she said that the caliph's palace was not a good place for us to be. "No man apart from you has ever entered it and you only did that because of the care taken by the Lady Zubaida. She has given me fifty thousand dinars, so take the money and go out to buy us a house." I went and bought one that was both handsome and spacious, and into this she moved all the elegant possessions she had in the palace, together with all the wealth, materials and treasures that she had stored up. This, then, is the reason why I lost my thumbs and my toes.'

We finished eating following our recitation and left, and it was after this that I had my encounter with the hunchback. This is the end of my story.

The king said: 'This was no more agreeable than the tale of the hunchback, and, in fact, his was more agreeable than yours, so I must certainly hang you all.' At that, the Jewish doctor came forward and said: 'Lord of the age, I can tell you a more remarkable story than that of the hunchback.' 'Then produce it,' said the king, AND THE JEW SAID:

The most remarkable thing that happened to me in my youth took place when I was in Damascus, where I was studying. While I was sitting in my lodgings one day, up came a mamluk from the palace of the governor of the city, who told me to come to his master. I went out with him to the palace, and when I entered I saw at the upper end of the hall a couch of juniper wood plated with gold, on which a sick person was lying. This turned out to be a young man, the most handsome to be seen.

I took my seat by his head and uttered a prayer for his recovery. He made a sign to me with his eyes and I asked him to be so good as to give me his hand. I was surprised when he produced his left hand and I said to myself: 'By God, how remarkable. Here is a handsome young man, from a great house, but he lacks manners. This is strange.' I felt his pulse and wrote him a prescription, after which I paid him regular visits for ten days until he recovered. He then went to the baths and came out after having washed himself. The governor presented me with a fine robe and appointed me as one of his superintendents in the Damascus hospital.

When I went to the baths with my patient, these had been completely cleared for him. The servants brought him in and took his clothes, and when he was stripped I saw that his right hand had recently been amputated, that being the cause of his illness. The sight filled me with surprise and I was feeling sorry for him when I looked at his body and could see from his scars that he had been beaten with whips and treated with salves. This troubled me and my concern showed on my face. Looking at me, he understood what I was feeling. 'Physician of the age,' he said to me, 'don't be surprised at my condition, and I will tell you my story when we leave the baths.' We left and went to the palace, where we ate and then rested. 'Would you like to look at the upper room?' he asked me, and when I said yes, he ordered the slaves to take the furnishings upstairs, as well as to roast a lamb and to bring us fruit. When the fruit had been fetched, we ate, the young man using his left hand. I then asked him to tell me his story. 'Physician of the age,' he said, 'listen to what happened to me.' HE WENT ON:

You must know that I was born in Mosul and when my grandfather died, he left ten sons, of whom my father was the eldest. They all grew up and married, but while my father produced me, his nine brothers had no children. I grew up among my uncles and they took the greatest pleasure in me. When I had grown to man's estate, I sat one day in the mosque of Mosul at the time of the Friday prayer. My father was there, and when we had performed the prayer, the congregation all left, while my father and my uncles sat talking about the wonders of the world and the marvels of foreign cities, until they mentioned Cairo. My uncles said: 'Travellers claim that on the face of the earth there is no city more beautiful than Cairo by the Nile.'

When I heard this, I felt a longing to see Cairo and my father said: 'Whoever has not seen Cairo has not seen the world. Its soil is gold; its river is a wonder; its women are houris; its houses are palaces; its climate is mild; and its scent surpasses that of frankincense, which it puts to shame. There is nothing surprising about this, as Cairo is the whole world. How eloquent was the poet who said:

Am I to leave Cairo, with its comforts and delights?
What other place is there to rouse my longing?
Am I to leave a land which is itself perfume,
Rather than what is found in the partings of perfumed hair?
How could I do this when this is a paradise of loveliness,
Strewn with rich carpets and cushions,
A land whose splendour fills eye and heart with longing,
Holding all that the godly and ungodly can desire?
Here are true brothers united in their merit,
Meeting within the confines of its gardens.
People of Cairo, if God decrees that I must leave,
Covenants and compacts still remain between us.
Do not mention her to the zephyr lest it may
Steal from her gardens scent to give elsewhere.'

My father went on: 'Were you to see its gardens in the evening in the slanting shadows, you would see a wonder and be filled with delight.' He and his brothers started to describe Cairo and the Nile, and when they had finished and I had listened to the description of the place, my mind remained fixed on it. At the end of this, each one got up and left for his own home, while I could not sleep that night because I had conceived a passion for Cairo, as a result of which I could enjoy neither food nor drink. A few days later, my uncles made preparations to go to Cairo and I wept bitterly until my father provided me with some trade goods and I went off with them, although his instructions were that I should not to be allowed to enter Cairo but was to be left to sell my goods in Damascus.

I took leave of my father and we set out on our journey from Mosul, carrying on until we reached Aleppo, where we stopped for a few days. Then we continued to Damascus, where we found a city of trees, streams and birds, like a paradise, with fruits of all kinds. We stopped at one of the *khans* and my uncles stayed in the city to trade. They also sold my goods and delighted me by making a profit of five hundred per cent, before going on to Egypt, while I stayed behind in a house so attractively built that it beggared description. The rent was two dinars a month and

I stayed there eating and drinking until I had spent all the money that I had with me.

One day, as I was sitting by the door of the house, a girl came up, wearing as splendid a dress as I had ever seen. I winked at her and without hesi tation she passed through the door. I followed her in and closed the door behind us. She then removed her cloak and the veil from her face, and I found that she was astonishingly beautiful. Love for her took possession of my heart and I went off and brought a tray of the tastiest foods and fruits and all that the occasion required. When I had fetched this, we ate, and then, after an interval for play, we drank until we became drunk. I then got up and slept with her, passing the most delightful of nights.

The following day, I gave her ten dinars, but she frowned, knitting her brows, and exclaiming indignantly: 'Shame on you, Mosuli! Do you think that I want your money?' Out of the pocket of her dress she produced fifteen dinars and left them in front of me, saying: 'By God, if you don't take them, I shall never come back to you.' I took the money and she said: 'Darling, expect me in three days' time and I shall come between sunset and supper. Use the money to prepare us another meal like the last.' Then she took her leave of me and went away, taking my senses with her. Three days later, she came back dressed in brocade, jewels and robes more splendid than those she had worn the first time. Before she came I had made my preparations, and we ate, drank and slept until morning, as we had done before. As before, she gave me fifteen dinars, and promised to come back after three days.

Again I made preparations for her visit, and she came dressed even more splendidly than on her first and second visit. 'Am I not beautiful?' she asked me. 'Yes, by God, you are,' I replied. 'Will you let me bring with me a girl who is more beautiful as well as younger than I am,' she asked, 'so that she can play with us, and you and she can laugh together and she can enjoy herself, as for a long time she has been sad? She has asked to come out with me and to spend the night with me.' On hearing this, I agreed willingly, and then we got drunk and slept until morning. When she produced the fifteen dinars this time, before leaving she told me to provide extra provisions for the girl who was to come with her. On the fourth day, I made my preparations as usual, and after sunset she arrived with a girl wrapped in a mantle. They came in and sat down, and at this sight, I recited:

How pleasant and delightful it is now,
When the censurer is absent and unaware.
Love of pleasure and drunkenness –
One of these is enough to steal our wits.
The full moon appears veiled;
The branch bends in a gown, and on the cheeks
The rose blooms in its freshness, while in the eyes
Languishes the narcissus.
Life, as I wish it, is without a cloud;
Because of the beloved, pleasure is complete.

Filled with delight, I lit the candles and received the girls joyfully. They took off their outer clothes and the new girl showed me a face like the moon at its full. I had never seen anyone more beautiful. I then rose and brought food and wine, after which we ate and drank our fill. I was giving mouthfuls of food to the new girl, filling up her glass and drinking with her until her companion became secretly jealous and asked me whether the girl was not prettier than she was. 'Yes, by God,' I replied. 'I would like you to sleep with her,' she told me and when I agreed she got up and spread out bedding for us. I went over to the girl and slept with her until morning.

When I stirred, I found that I was very damp and I thought that I must have been sweating. I sat up to rouse the girl and shook her by the shoulders, at which her head rolled off the pillow. Losing control of myself, I cried out: 'Kind Shelterer, shelter me!' I saw that her throat had been cut and I sprang up, finding that the world had turned black for me. I looked for my former mistress but when I could not find her, I realized that it must have been she who had murdered the other out of jealousy. 'There is no power and no might except with God, the High, the Almighty!' I exclaimed. 'What am I to do?' I thought for a time and then I got up and stripped off my clothes. In the middle of the house I dug a hole and then I took the girl, jewels and all, and put her into it, after which I covered it with earth and then with marble. Next, I washed, put on clean clothes and, taking what money I still had, I left the house, locked it up, and went to its owner. Summoning up my courage, I paid him a year's rent, telling him that I was going off to join my uncles in Cairo.

When I reached Cairo, I met my uncles who were glad to see me and they had, as I found, finished selling their goods. When they asked me why I had come, I told them that it was because I had missed them. I stayed with them for a year, seeing the sights of Cairo and the Nile, but concealing the fact that I still had some money with me. Then, taking my store of money, I started to spend it, using it on food and drink, until the time had come for my uncles to leave. At this point, I ran off and hid from them so that, although they looked, they could get no news of me. Thinking that I must have gone back to Damascus, they left.

I came out of hiding and stayed in Cairo for three years until all my money had run out. Every year I had been sending the rent to the owner of the house in Damascus, but after three years I found myself at a standstill and could not afford more than the one year's rent. So I set off for Damascus and when I got there I stopped at my old house. The owner was glad to see me and I found the storerooms sealed up as I had left them. So I opened them and removed my belongings. Then, under the bed on which I had slept that night with the murdered girl, I found a gold necklace set with jewels. I took it, and after wiping it clean of her blood, I stared at it, shedding tears for some time. For two days I waited and then on the third I went to the baths, where I changed my clothes. I had no money at all with me and, on going to the market one day, I listened to the promptings of the devil, so that what was fated came to pass.

Taking the jewelled necklace, I gave it to the market auctioneer, who got up and asked me to sit beside the owner of the house. Waiting until the market was crowded, he then secretly, and without my knowledge, called for buyers. It turned out that the necklace was valuable enough to bring in two thousand dinars, but the auctioneer came to me and said: 'It is a copper piece, of Frankish work, which will fetch a thousand dirhams.' 'Yes,' I said, 'we had it made for a woman as a joke, and now my wife has inherited it, so we want to sell it. Accept the thousand dirhams for it.'

Night 29

Morning now dawned and Shahrazad broke off from what she had been allowed to say. Then, when it was the twenty-ninth night, SHE CONTINUED:

I have heard, O auspicious king, that he told the auctioneer to accept a thousand dirhams. HE WENT ON:

When the auctioneer heard that, he realized that something was not right and he went to the market superintendent and gave him the necklace. He, in turn, went to the *wali* and said: 'This necklace was stolen from my house and we have found the thief dressed as a merchant.' Before I knew what was happening, I was surrounded by guards, who seized me and brought me to the *wali*. He asked me about the necklace, and I told him the story that I had told the auctioneer. The *wali* laughed and said: 'This is not true.' Before I knew it, I was stripped of my clothes and beaten on my sides with whips. Because of the burning pain of the beating, I said: 'I stole it,' telling myself that it was better to confess to theft than to say that the girl who owned the necklace had been killed in my house, lest I be killed in retaliation for her murder. They wrote down that I had stolen the necklace and they then cut off my hand and cauterized it with oil. I fainted, but they poured wine down my throat and I recovered. Taking my hand, I went back to the house, but the owner said: 'After what has happened, you must leave and find another place for yourself, for you have been charged with robbery.' 'Sir,' I asked him, 'let me have two or three days to look for a place.'

He agreed to this and went off, leaving me. I stayed sitting there, weeping and saying: 'How can I go back to my family now that I have lost my hand and they don't know that I am innocent? It may be that God will bring something to pass after this,' and I went on to shed bitter tears. After the owner of the house had left me, I spent two days in a state of great distress and agitation. Then, on the third day, before I knew what was happening, he came back with a number of guards as well as the market superintendent, the man who claimed that I had stolen the necklace. I went out to meet them and asked: 'What is the matter?' Giving me no time to answer, they tied my arms and threw a chain around my neck. Then they told me that the necklace that had been in my possession had been taken to the governor of Damascus, who ruled the city as its vizier, and it appeared to have vanished from his palace three years ago, together with his daughter.

When I heard this, my heart sank, and I said to myself: 'There is no doubt that I am a dead man. I must tell the governor my story, and if he wants, he can kill me, or otherwise he may pardon me.' When we came to him, I was made to stand before him. Looking at me out of the corner of his eye, he said to the people there: 'Why did you cut his hand off? This is an unfortunate man who has committed no crime and you have wronged him by doing this.' When I heard what he said, I took courage and my spirits rose. 'By God, sir,' I said, 'I am no thief. They brought this grave accusation against me and beat me with whips in the middle of the market, forcing me to confess. So I told a lie against myself and admitted the theft, although I was innocent.' 'No harm shall come to you,' he said, and then he ordered the market superintendent to pay me compensation for my hand: 'Or else I shall hang you and confiscate all your property.' He then shouted to the officers, who seized the man and dragged him off, leaving me with the governor.

With his permission, guards removed the chain from my neck and untied my bonds. The governor looked at me and said: 'My son, tell me the truth and explain to me how you got this necklace,' and he recited:

> You must speak the truth, even if this truth
> Burns you with the promised fire of hell.

Promising that I would do this, I then told him what had happened to me with the first girl and how she had brought me the second, whose throat she had then cut in a fit of jealousy. When he had listened to the whole story as I told it, he shook his head, struck his right hand against his left and covered his face with his kerchief. For a time he wept and then he recited the lines:

> I see the ills of this world crowding in on me.
> Their victim remains sick until he dies.
> Meetings of friends must end in their parting,
> And the time before parting is short indeed.

He then came up to me and said: 'My son, you must know that the elder girl was my daughter. I brought her up in strict seclusion and when she reached maturity, I sent her to Cairo, where she married her cousin. After his death she came back to me, but she had learned evil ways from the Egyptians and so it was that she went to you four times, finally bringing you her younger sister. They were full sisters and they loved each other deeply. After the elder had met you, she told her secret to her sister, who asked to go with her. When the elder came back alone, I asked her about her sister, and I found her weeping for her. Then she told her mother and myself in private how she had murdered the girl, and she kept on shedding tears and saying: 'By God, I shall go on weeping for her until I die.' That is how the matter stood, and now that you have seen what happened, I want you to agree to what I propose, which is to marry you to my youngest daughter. She is not a full sister of the other two and is a virgin. I shall not take any dowry from you; instead I shall make you an allowance and you can stay with me as my son.' I agreed to this, saying: 'How can it be that I have found such good fortune?' The governor sent at once for the *qadi* and the notaries and he drew up the marriage contract, after which I consummated the marriage. He got a large amount of money for me from the market superintendent, and I occupied an honoured place at his court. My father died this year and the governor of Mosul sent a courier to bring me the money that he had left, and so today I am living in the greatest prosperity. This, then, is how I came to lose my right hand.

I was astonished at this story and I stayed with him for three days, after which he gave me a large sum of money. When I left him, I travelled to this city of yours, where I have enjoyed a good life, until I had this adventure with the hunchback.

'This is no more wonderful than the tale of the hunchback,' said the king of China, 'and I must hang you – except that there is still the tailor who was responsible for the whole thing.' He then told the tailor that if he produced a tale more remarkable than that of the hunchback he would pardon their crimes. At that the tailor came forward, AND HE SAID:

Know, king of the age, that my most remarkable experience happened yesterday. At the beginning of the day, before I met the hunchback, I was at a banquet given by one of my friends, at which about twenty guests had been collected from among the citizens of this place – craftsmen such as tailors and carpenters, together with silk merchants and others. At sunrise, food was set out for us to eat, and in came our host with a handsome young man, a stranger from Baghdad. He was wearing the finest of clothes and was remarkably good-looking, but he was lame. We stood up for him as he came in and greeted us, and he was about to take his seat when he caught sight of a barber who was with us. On seeing the man, he refused to sit down and attempted to leave. We tried to restrain him and the host held on to him, swearing that he should not go and asking: 'Why do you come in and then go out?' 'By God, sir,' replied the young man, 'don't try to stop me. I am going because of this ill-omened barber who is sitting there.' The host was astonished to hear this and said: 'How is it that this young man comes from Baghdad and yet is so upset by this barber?' We looked at him and said: 'Tell us why it is that you are angry with him.'

The young man then addressed us and said: 'I had an encounter with this man in Baghdad, my native city, and it is he who is responsible for my lameness and for the breaking of my leg. I swore that I would never associate with him in any place or in any town in which he was living. I then left Baghdad and travelled away from it until I settled here, but this very night I shall set out again on my travels.' We pressed him to tell us his story and the barber turned pale as the young man started to speak. 'You should know,' the young man explained to us, 'that my father was one of the leading merchants of Baghdad and I was his only son.' HE WENT ON:

When I had grown up and reached man's estate, my father died, moving from this world to the mercy of Almighty God. He bequeathed me money, eunuchs and servants, and I began to dress and to eat well. God had endowed me with a hatred of women and so one day, when I was in one of the lanes of Baghdad and a group of women approached from the opposite direction, I ran off and went into a cul-de-sac, at the end of which I sat down on a stone bench.

Before I had been there for long, a window opened in the house opposite me and from it a girl like the full moon looked out, whose equal I had never seen in all my life. She was watering plants on her windowsill, and, after looking right and left, she shut the window and disappeared from view. Fire was kindled in my heart and my mind was consumed by her, my hatred for women turning to love. I went on sitting there in a trance until sunset, when the *qadi* of Baghdad rode up, with his black slaves before him and his eunuchs behind. On dismounting, he went into the house from which the girl had gazed, and I realized that this must be her father.

I went back sorrowfully to my own house and fell on my bed, full of care. My servant girls came in and sat around me, but they could not understand what was wrong with me and, as I said nothing to them, they wept over me and grieved. Then in came an old woman who, when she saw me, realized at once what the matter must be. She sat down by my head and spoke gently to me, saying: 'My son, tell me about it and I shall see to it that you are united with her.' I told her my story and she said: 'My son, this is the daughter of the *qadi* of Baghdad and she is kept in seclusion. The window where you saw her is on her floor of the building, while her father lives in a great hall beneath it. She sits by herself, but I often go to visit the house, and it is only through me that you can achieve union with her, so pluck up your courage.'

I took heart from her words – that was a day of joy for my household – and in the morning I felt better. The old woman went off, but when she came back, her colour had changed. 'My son,' she said. 'Don't ask what happened between me and the girl. When I had spoken to her about you, she said: "You ill-omened old woman. If you don't stop talking like this, I shall treat you as you deserve." But I must go back to her a second time.'

When I heard that, my sickness worsened, until after some days the old woman came back. 'My son,' she said. 'You must reward me for bringing good news.' This restored me to life and I said: 'You may have everything that is good.' At that, she went on: 'I went to visit the girl yesterday and she could see that I was sad and tearful. "Aunt," she asked, "why do you look so unhappy?" I wept and replied: "My lady, I have come to you from a young man who loves you and who is near to death because of you." Her heart softened at this and she asked: "Where does he come from, this young man whom you have mentioned?" "He is like a son to me and the fruit of my heart. Some days ago, he saw you in the window when you were watering your plants, and after looking at your face, he fell deeply in love with you. The first time that I told him what you had said to me, his love sickness grew worse; he kept to his bed, and there can be no doubt that he is going to die." She turned pale. "Is all this because of me?" she asked. "Yes, by God," I said, "so what should I do?" She said: "Go to him; greet him from me and let him know that my love is twice as great as his. Then tell him to come to the house on Friday before prayers. When he gets here, I shall go down and open the door and bring him up to my room. He and I can be together for a time and he can leave before my father gets back from prayers."'

When I heard what the old woman had to say, the pain that I was feeling left me and my spirits recovered. I gave her the clothes that I was wearing and she went off, telling me to be of good heart. 'I have no pain left at all,' I replied, and my household and my friends were delighted by my recovery. I stayed like that until Friday, when the old woman came in and asked me how I was. I told her that I was in good health, and then I put on my clothes, perfumed myself and stayed waiting for the people to go to the mosque for prayers, so that I could then visit the girl. The old woman said: 'You have plenty of time, so why not go to the baths and have your hair cut, especially after your serious illness? That would restore you.' 'A good idea,' I said, 'but I shall have my head shaved first and after that I will go to the baths.'

I then sent for a barber to shave my head, and I told my servant to fetch me an intelligent man, who would not be inquisitive and would not give me a headache with his constant chatter. My servant went off and the barber whom he fetched was this calamitous old man. He greeted me when he came in and I returned the greeting. 'I see that you are very thin,' he said. 'I have been ill,' I replied. 'May God remove all your cares, your sorrows, your distress and your griefs,' he said. 'May He accept your prayer,' I said. 'Be of good cheer,' he went on, 'for good health has come to you. Do you want your hair to be trimmed or do you want to be bled? It is reported on the authority of Ibn 'Abbas – may God be pleased with him – that the Prophet said: "Whoever has his hair cut on a Friday is kept free of seventy diseases." It is also recorded of him that he said: "Whoever is cupped on a Friday is preserved from loss of sight and from many diseases."' 'Stop talking,' I told him, 'and start shaving my head immediately, for I have been sick.'

He got up, stretched out his hand and, bringing out a kerchief, he unfolded it, revealing an astrolabe with seven plates set with silver. Taking this, he went to the middle of the house and raised his head towards the sun's rays. After a long look, he said to me: 'You must know that this day is Friday, that is the tenth of the month of Safar in the year 653 of the Prophet* – on whom be peace and the best of blessings – and the year 7320 dating from Alexander the Great, the ascendant planet, according to arithmetical calculation, being Mars. Of the day, eight degrees and six minutes have passed and, as it happens, Mars is in conjunction with Mercury. That shows that this is a good time for hair cutting and it also shows me that you are looking for union with someone and that this will be fortunate, but afterwards there will be words and something that I won't mention to you.' 'By God,' I told him, 'you have driven me to distraction, lowered my spirits and produced an omen for me that is not good. I only asked you to cut my hair, so get on and do it and stop talking so much.' 'By God,' he said, 'if you know what is coming to you, you would not do anything today, and my advice is that you should act as I tell you, on the basis of my reading of the stars.' 'You are the only astrological barber whom I have ever met,' I told him. 'I can see that you have a fund of jokes, but I only asked you here to look after my hair, and instead you have produced all this rubbish.'

* The year 653 *hijri* corresponds to AD 1255–6. (The date that follows, 7320, is imaginary.)

'Do you need any more advice?' he asked. 'God in His bounty has provided you with a barber who is also an astrologer, a chemist, an expert in natural magic, grammar, morphology, philology, rhetoric, eloquence, logic, arithmetic, astronomy, geometry, religious law, the traditions of the Prophet and the interpretation of the Quran. I have read the relevant books and studied them; I have a practical knowledge of affairs; I have committed to heart a perfect knowledge of the sciences; I am a theoretical and practical master of technical skill. There is nothing that I have not organized and undertaken. I was a favourite with your father because I am lacking in curiosity and it is because of this that I feel it an obligation to serve you. Whatever you think, I am not inquisitive and this is why I am known as "the silent and serious one". What you should do is to praise God and not to oppose me, for the advice that I have to offer is good. I feel sympathy for you and I would like to be in your service for a whole year so that you might value me as I deserve, and I would not want any wages from you for that.' When I heard that, I said: 'Without a doubt you will be the death of me today.'

Night 30

Morning now dawned and Shahrazad broke off from what she had been allowed to say. Then, when it was the thirtieth night, SHE CONTINUED:

I have heard, O auspicious king, that the young man said: 'You will be the death of me today.' HE WENT ON:

'Sir,' the barber replied, 'I am the man the people call the Silent because, unlike my six brothers, I speak so little. My eldest brother is known as the Babbler; the second is the Bellower; the third is the Jabberer; the fourth is the Aswan Jug; the fifth is the Talker; the sixth is the Prattler; while I, the seventh, am the Silent.' While he kept on talking at me, I felt as though my gall bladder had split. I told my servant to give him quarter of a dinar, adding: 'And for God's sake, see that he leaves me, as I don't need to have my head shaved after all.' 'What is this, master?' the barber said when he overheard what I had been saying. 'By God, I will take no fee from you until I have done something for you. I must do this, as it is my duty to serve you and do what you want, and I don't care whether I get anything from you at all. Even if you don't know how to value me, I know how to value you, and your father – may God Almighty have mercy on him – was generous to me, for he was a munificent man. He once sent for me on a fortunate day such as this, and when I came in, I found that he had a number of friends with him. He wanted me to bleed him, but I took my astrolabe and measured the angle of the ascendant star, which I found to be unlucky, making blood-letting under its influence to be inappropriate. I told him that, and he followed my advice and waited, and so I recited in his praise:

> I went to my master to draw his blood,
> But I found that the time did not conduce to health.
> I sat and talked to him of wonders of all kinds,
> Unfolding before him my store of knowledge.
> He admired what he heard from me and said:
> "You have passed the bounds of understanding, you mine of
>   learning."
> I said to him: "Lord of mankind, had you not poured
> Understanding over me, mine would not have increased.
> You are, it seems, a master of merit, generous and bountiful,
> A treasure house of knowledge, understanding and clemency
>   for all."

Your father was pleased and told his servant to give me a hundred and three dinars as well as a robe of honour, which was handed to me, and when a propitious time came, I bled him. He did not ignore my recommendations but thanked me, as did all the company. After I had bled him, I could not stay silent, and I asked him to tell me why he had told the servant to give me a hundred and three dinars. 'One dinar,' he explained, 'was for your astronomical observation and another for your conversation, the third was the fee for the blood-letting, and the hundred dinars and the robe of honour were the reward for your eulogy of me.'

'May God have no mercy on my father,' I exclaimed, 'for knowing a man like you!' The barber laughed and said: 'There is no god but God, and Muhammad is the Apostle of God, Who causes change but is not changed. I had thought that you were an intelligent man, but your illness has made you feeble-minded. God has referred in His Holy Book to "those who suppress their anger and those who forgive others".* At any rate, you are forgiven, but I don't know why you are in such a hurry. You know that neither your father nor your grandfather would do anything except on my advice. There is a common saying that "the

* Quran 128.1.

advisor is to be trusted" and "whoever asks for advice is not disappointed". There is also a proverb: "Whoever has no elder to help him will not himself be an elder." As the poet has said:

> When you intend some action, take advice
> From one who knows, and do not disobey.

You will not find anyone who knows more about worldly matters than I do, and I am on my feet here to serve you. I am not irritated by you, so how can you be irritated by me? I put up with you patiently because of the favours that your father did me.' 'By God, you donkey's tail,' I said, 'you go on and on speechifying and talking more and more, while all I want is for you to cut my hair and leave.' After that, he dampened my hair and said: 'I realize that you have become irritated with me, but I shall not hold it against you, because your intellect is weak and you are a young boy. It was only yesterday that I used to carry you on my shoulder and take you to school.' 'For God's sake, brother,' I said, 'let me finish my business and be on your way,' and then I tore my clothes.

When he saw me do that, he took his razor and went on and on sharpening it until I was almost out of my mind with impatience. Then he came up, but after he had shaved part of my head, he raised his hand and said: 'Master, haste comes from the devil and patience from the Merciful God.' He then recited:

> Act slowly and not with haste in what you want;
> Be merciful to men, and you shall meet the Merciful.
> God's power is greater than all other powers,
> And the unjust will suffer from injustice.

'Master,' he added, 'I don't think you are aware of my status. This hand of mine touches the heads of kings, emirs, viziers, together with men of wisdom and excellence. It could have been about me that the poet said:

> Crafts are like necklaces, and here this barber
> Is like the pearl hung on a necklace string,
> Standing above all men of wisdom,
> While under his hand are the heads of kings.'

'Stop busying yourself with what is no concern of yours,' I said, 'for you have made me angry and distracted.' 'I think you must be in a hurry,' he said. 'Yes, yes, yes,' I told him. 'Allow yourself to slow down,' he insisted, 'for haste comes from the devil and it leaves behind repentance and loss. The Prophet – upon whom be blessing and peace – said: "The best affair is the one that proceeds slowly." I am uneasy about your affairs and I wish you would tell me what you are planning to do. It may be something good, but I fear that it might turn out to be something else.'

There were still three hours to go before the time of prayer, but he said: 'I want to be in no doubt about that. Rather, I would like to know the time exactly, for guesswork leads to shame, especially in the case of a man like me, whose merits are clear and celebrated among the people. I cannot speak by conjecture as the common run of astrologers do.' So he threw down his razor, took the astrolabe and went out into the sun. He stayed there for a long time and when he came back, he said: 'There are exactly three hours to go, neither more nor less.' 'I implore you, in God's Name,' I said, 'don't speak to me. You have broken my heart.' So, as before, he took his razor, sharpened it, and shaved part of my head. Then he said: 'I am worried by your hastiness. If you told me the reason for it, it would be better for you, since you know that your father and your grandfather never did anything except on my advice.'

When I realized that I couldn't get rid of him, I told myself: 'Prayer time has come and I want to go before the people leave the mosque, as if I delay at all, I don't know how I can get in to see the girl.' So I said: 'Cut this short and stop all this chattering and inquisitiveness. I want to go to a party to which I have been invited by a friend of mine.' When the barber heard me talk of an invitation, he said: 'This is a fortunate day for me. Yesterday I invited a group of my friends, but I forgot to see to it that they had something to eat. I have only just thought of that, and how ashamed I shall be.' 'Don't worry about it,' I said. 'I have already told you that I have been invited out today, so you can have all the food and drink in my house, if only you finish the job and shave my head quickly.' 'May God reward you,' he said, but then added: 'Tell me what you have for my guests, so that I may know.' I told him: 'There are five different types of food, ten grilled chickens and a roasted lamb.' 'Bring them out, so that I may inspect them,' he said. I produced all of this, but, after looking at it, he said: 'There is still the wine.' 'I have some,' I said, and when he told me to fetch it out, I did so. He praised my generosity, but added: 'There is still the incense and the perfumes.' I fetched him a container with *nadd*, aloes, ambergris and musk worth fifty dinars.

Time was getting short, as was my temper, and so I said: 'Finish shaving my head, by the life of Muhammad – may God have mercy on him and give him peace.' 'By God,' said the barber, 'I cannot take this container until I have seen all its contents.' On my orders, my servant opened it, and putting away his astrolabe, the barber sat on the ground turning over its contents, so adding to my annoyance. He then came forward and, taking his razor, he then shaved a small bit of my head. Then he recited:

> The child grows up to resemble his father,
> And the tree grows from its roots.

'By God, my son,' he went on, 'I don't know whether to thank you or to thank your father. My party today will be all the result of your kindly generosity. None of my guests is worthy of that, but the people who are coming are respected citizens, such as Zantut the bath keeper, Sali' the grain merchant, Sulit the bean seller, 'Ikrisha the greengrocer, Humaid the street sweeper, Sa'id the camel driver, Suwaid the porter, Abu Makarish the bath man, Qasim the guard and Karim the groom. None of these are heavy-going, quarrelsome, inquisitive or otherwise troublesome men. Each one of them has a dance that he can perform and verses that he can recite, and the best thing about them is that, like your humble servant, they are ignorant of verbosity and are without curiosity. The bath keeper sings a magical song to the tambourine: "Mother I am going to fill my jar". The grain merchant, bringing to it more skill than anyone else, dances and recites "My lady, you hired mourner, you have given no short measure", stealing all hearts as people laugh at his antics. The street sweeper stops the birds in their flight by his singing, and he dances and recites "What my wife knows is shut in a box". He is an able fellow, smart and bold. In praise of his handsomeness I say:

> My life is the ransom for a street sweeper who has roused my
>   passion.
> Sweet-natured, he is like a swaying branch.
> When time granted him to me one night, my passion
> Wore me away as it increased, and I told him:
> "You have kindled your fire within my heart."
> "No wonder," he replied, "when sweeper turns stoker."

Each one of my guests has in full measure what entertains and amuses.' Then he added: 'But hearing is not the same as seeing. Were you to choose to come to our party, both you and we would prefer it. Don't go to the friends you are thinking of visiting, for you are still showing the traces of your illness and it may be that you will find yourself with chatterboxes who talk about what is no concern of theirs, and you might find some inquisitive fellow there who would give you a headache while you are still depressed as a result of your illness.' 'Another time, perhaps,' I said, with an angry laugh. Then I added: 'Finish your job and let me go under the protection of Almighty God, while you go to your friends who are expecting you.' 'Master,' he said, 'I only want to let you enjoy the company of these clever people, men of good background, none of them being long-winded or inquisitive. From my earliest days, I have never been able to associate with anyone who asks about what is no concern of his; my only associates are men of few words like me. If you came to meet them and saw them one single time, you would abandon all your own companions.' 'May God complete your happiness with them,' I said, 'and one day I must certainly come to meet them.' 'May that be today,' he replied. 'If you make up your mind to go with me to my friends, let me take your generous gifts, but if you have to go to your own friends today, I shall carry away the gifts and leave them with my companions, who can start eating and drinking without waiting for me. Then I can come back for you and go with you to your friends. I don't stand on ceremony with mine, as this might stop me leaving them and coming back to you quickly and going with you wherever you want to go.' 'There is no might and no power except with God, the Exalted, the Almighty!' I exclaimed. 'Off you go to your own friends and enjoy yourself with them and let me go to mine, who are expecting me, so that I can be with them today.' The barber said: 'I cannot let you go by yourself.' 'No one but I can enter the place where I am going,' I told him, which prompted him to say: 'I think that you have an assignation with some woman, for otherwise you would be taking me with you, and yet I am the most suitable of people to help you get what you want. I am afraid, however, that you may want to meet some foreign woman, at the cost of your life. For this is Baghdad and no one can do things like that here, especially on a day like this, and the *wali* is a very stern man.' 'You foul old fellow,' I said, 'take yourself off!' 'Why are you talking to me like this, you silly man?' he replied. 'I'm ashamed to listen to you. You're hiding something from me; I know it; I'm certain of it, and I only wanted to help you today.'

I became afraid that my family and my neighbours might hear what he was saying, and so I fell into a deep silence. We had reached the hour of the Friday prayer, and the sermon was due by the time that he had finished cutting my hair. I told him to take the food and the drink to his friends, saying that I would wait for him until he came back, when he could go with me. I went on flattering and trying to mislead the damned man, in the hope that he might leave me, but he said: 'You're trying to deceive me so that you can go alone and involve yourself in a disaster from which you won't be able to escape. For God's sake, don't leave until I get back, so that I can go with you, to see how your affair turns out.' 'Yes,' I said, 'but don't be long.'

He then took all the food, the drink and the rest of what I had given him, and left my house. But what the wretched fellow did was to give all this to a porter to take to his house, while he himself hid in a lane nearby. I got up at once, as the muezzin had already finished the service, put on my clothes and went out. I then came to the lane and stopped at the house where I had seen the girl. There I found the old woman waiting for me, and I went up with her to the floor on which the girl lived. My entry, however, coincided with the return of the master of the house from Friday prayers. He came into the hall and shut the door, and when I looked out of the window, I saw this very same barber – God damn him – sitting by the door, and I asked myself: 'How did this devil know where I was?'

It happened just then, as God intended my secret to be uncovered, that a maidservant had committed some fault. The master of the house beat her, and when she shrieked, a slave rushed to her rescue. He for his part was also beaten and he, too, cried out. The damned barber thought that it was I who was being beaten, and so he shouted, tore his clothes and poured earth on his head. He continued to yell and cry for help until he was surrounded by a crowd. He kept repeating: 'My master has been killed in the *qadi*'s house,' and then, still shouting, he went to my house, followed by the crowd. He told my family and my servants, and before I knew what was happening, there they came with their clothes torn and their hair loosed, crying: 'Woe for our master!' In the forefront was the barber, with his torn clothes and his cries, accompanied by the crowd. My family kept on shouting and so did he from among the front ranks of the crowd. Crying: 'Woe, woe, for the murdered man!' they made for the house where I was.

Hearing the disturbance and the shouting at his door, the *qadi* told one of his servants to see what the matter was. The man came out and then went back to his master and said: 'Sir, there are more than ten thousand people, men and women, at the door. They are shouting: "Woe for the murdered man!" and pointing at our house.' When the *qadi* heard this, he thought that this was a monstrous business and, getting up angrily, he went to open the door. He was astonished to see the huge crowd and asked them what the matter was. 'You damned man, you dog, you pig!' shouted my servants. 'You have killed our master.' 'What has your master done that I should kill him?' he asked . . .

Night 31

Morning now dawned and Shahrazad broke off from what she had been allowed to say. Then, when it was the thirty-first night, SHE CONTINUED:

I have heard, O auspicious king, that the *qadi* said to the servants: 'What has your master done that I should kill him?' THE YOUNG MAN WENT ON:

'Here is my house standing open before you,' added the *qadi*. 'You beat him just now with whips,' said the barber, 'and I heard him screaming.' 'What had he done that I should kill him?' repeated the *qadi*. 'Who brought him to my house? Where did he come from? Where did he go?' 'Don't play the sinister old man,' said the barber. 'I know the whole story. Your daughter loves him and he loves her. When you found out that he had come into your house, you ordered your servants to beat him. I shall get the caliph to judge which of us is right, unless you produce our master so that his family can take him off, before I go in and bring him out, putting you to shame.' The *qadi*'s tongue was bridled and, feeling himself shamed before the crowd, he said: 'If you are telling the truth, come in yourself and fetch him out.'

Encouraged by this, in came the barber, and when I saw this, I looked for a way to escape, but could not find one. Then in the part of the house where I was I saw a large chest and I got into this, closing the lid on top of me and holding my breath. The barber came into the hall, but scarcely had he entered it, when he came up to the room where I was, and after turning right and then left, he came up to my chest and carried it off on his head, driving me out of my mind. He started off in a hurry and, realizing that he would not leave me alone, I pulled myself together, opened the chest and threw myself out on to the ground, so breaking my leg. The door was open, and I saw a crowd of people there. In my sleeve,

I was carrying a quantity of gold in readiness for a day or a crisis like this. So I began to scatter it among the people to distract their attention, which it did, as they picked it up. Then I started to make my way through the lanes of Baghdad, turning right and left, but always with this damned barber on my heels. Into whatever place I went, on he came after me, repeating: 'They wanted to rob me of my master. Praise be to God who gave me the upper hand over them and freed my master from their hands!'

Then he told me: 'You continued to distress me by what you were planning and eventually you brought all this on yourself. If God in His grace had not sent me to you, you would never have escaped from the disaster into which you had fallen, but would have fallen into another, from which you would not have escaped. You wanted to go by yourself, but I don't hold your folly against you, as you are an impatient young man of limited intelligence.' I said: 'Isn't what you have done enough for you, that you run after me and talk to me like this in the market?' My soul had almost left my body, so enraged was I, and going into the shop of a weaver in the centre of the market, I asked for his help. The weaver kept the barber away from me, while I sat in the storeroom and said to myself: 'I shall never be able to get away from this damned man. He will stay with me night and day and if I have to look at him I shall have no breath of life left in me.'

So, on the spot, I sent for the notaries and drew up a legal document for my family, dividing up my wealth and appointing a trustee for them, instructing him to sell my house and my properties and to look after the members of the household, both young and old. From that day on, I have been off on my travels so as to escape from this pimp. I came and settled down in your city, where I have been for some time. Then you invited me and I came, only to see the pimp – damn him – sitting with you at the head of the table. How can I stay here cheerfully among you with a man who has done all this to me and who was the cause of my broken leg?

The young man refused to take a seat and when we had heard his story, we asked the barber: 'Is what he says about you true?' HE REPLIED:
I acted like that with him out of knowledge, intelligence and a sense of chivalry. Had it not been for me, he would be dead, and the fact that he escaped is due to me alone. It was lucky for him that it was his leg that was broken and he did not lose his life. Were I a man of many

words, I would not have done him this favour, and now I shall tell you a story of something that happened to me, so that you may know for certain that I am a man of few words without curiosity, unlike my six brothers.

I was in Baghdad in the time of al-Mustansir bi'llah, who was then caliph. He loved the poor and the unfortunate, and would sit with men of learning and virtue. It happened that one feast day he became angry with ten men and ordered the prefect of Baghdad to bring them to him, they being thieves and highwaymen. The prefect went out, arrested them, and sent them off in a boat. I saw this and said to myself: 'These people must have gathered together for a banquet. I suppose that they are going to spend the day eating and drinking on their boat, and no one but I shall be their companion.' So I got up, and thanks to my sense of chivalry and the soundness of my intellect, I boarded this boat and mixed with them. They crossed the river and disembarked on the far bank. Then the watch and the guards brought chains which they placed round their necks, and they did the same to me. All this, my friends, was caused by my sense of chivalry and the fact that, as a man of few words, I kept silence and did not allow myself to speak.

The guards then took us by our chains and brought us before al-Mustansir bi'llah, the Commander of the Faithful, who gave orders that the ten should have their heads cut off. The executioner made us sit before him on the execution mat and, having drawn his sword, he cut off the heads of the ten, one after the other, leaving me. The caliph looked and said to the executioner: 'Why have you only cut off nine heads?' 'God forbid that I should only cut off nine after you had ordered me to cut off ten,' the man replied. 'I think that you have only cut off nine,' insisted the caliph, 'and this man in front of you is the tenth.' 'By your favour,' said the executioner, 'there were ten of them.'

The caliph ordered a count to be made, and it turned out that there were ten. He then looked at me and said: 'What led you to stay silent at a time like this? How did you come to be with these criminals, and what is the reason for this, you being an old man of little brain?' When I heard what he said, I told him: 'You must know, Commander of the Faithful, that I am the silent *shaikh*. I have a large store of wisdom, and the soundness of my intelligence, the excellence of my understanding and my taciturnity are without bounds. By profession I am a barber. Early yesterday morning, I saw these ten men on their way to a boat, and I joined them, thinking that they had gathered together for a banquet.

Shortly afterwards, the guards came and put chains around their necks, and they chained me together with the others. Because of my great sense of chivalry, I stayed silent and did not say a word, this being a simple matter of honour. They then took us off and brought us before you and you ordered the execution of the ten. I stayed there in front of the executioner without telling you who I was. It was a hugely honourable act on my part to share in their execution, but all my days I have been doing favours of this kind to people, in spite of the fact that they repay me in the most brutish of ways.'

On hearing this, the caliph saw at once that I was a taciturn man with a great sense of chivalry, lacking in inquisitiveness, contrary to the claim made by this young man whom I saved from fearful danger. In fact, the caliph laughed so much that he fell over, and he asked me: 'Silent man, are your six brothers as wise, learned and taciturn as you?' 'May they not stay alive,' I said, 'if they are like me. You are denigrating me, Commander of the Faithful, and you should not compare my brothers to me, as thanks to their loquacity and lack of honour, each of them has some physical deformity. One of them has lost an eye, while another is completely blind, a third is semi-paralysed, a fourth has had his ears and a fifth his lips cut off, while the sixth is a hunchback. You should not think, Commander of the Faithful, that I am a man of many words, but I must explain to you that I have a greater sense of honour than they do, and each of them has a story, which I must tell you, explaining how he came to be disabled.' AND I WENT ON:

The first of them, the hunchback, was by trade a tailor in Baghdad. He used to do his sewing in a shop which he rented from a wealthy man who lived over the shop, while in the basement another man worked a mill. One day, when my brother the hunchback was sitting sewing in his shop, he raised his head and saw in the window of the house a woman like the full moon as it rises. She was looking out at the passers-by and when my brother saw her, love for her became fixed in his heart. He spent that day staring at her and doing no more work until evening. The next morning, he opened his shop and sat sewing, but after every stitch he would glance up at the window and see her looking out as before, so strengthening his love.

On the third day, as he sat in his place looking at her, the woman caught sight of him and realized that he had been captivated by love for her. She smiled at him and he smiled at her. She then disappeared from sight and sent her maid to him with a bundle containing a quantity of red figured silk. When the maid came, she said: 'My mistress greets you and asks you to use your skill to cut out a shift for her from this material and to sew it elegantly.' My brother agreed to this and he cut out the shift and finished sewing it on that same day. Early the next morning, the maid came to him and said: 'My mistress greets you and asks how you passed the night, as she herself was not able to sleep because she was concerned for you.' Then she produced for him some yellow satin and said: 'My mistress asks you to cut out for her from this material a pair of harem trousers and to sew them up today.' My brother agreed and said: 'Give her many greetings from me and tell her: "Your slave is obedient to your commands, so give him what orders you wish."'

Then he started to cut out the material and he worked hard sewing up the trousers. Some time later, she looked out at him from her window and gestured a greeting, at times lowering her eyes and at times smiling at him, leading him to think that he would make a conquest of her. She then disappeared from view, and the maid came and took away the trousers which he handed to her. When night came, he threw himself down on his bed and spent the hours until morning twisting and turning. When morning came, he got up and sat in his place. This time, when the maid came to him, she said: 'My master summons you.' When my brother heard that, he was extremely afraid. Noticing this, the maid reassured him: 'No harm will come to you, but only good, for my mistress has told my master about you.'

My brother was delighted and, after accompanying the maid, he came into the presence of her master, the husband of her mistress, and kissed the ground. The man returned his greeting and then gave him a quantity of material, telling him to cut out a shirt from it and to sew it up. My brother agreed and he went on working, without stopping for anything to eat, until he had cut out twenty shirts by supper time. When he was asked what his fee was for this, he said: 'Twenty dirhams,' and the husband called to the maid to fetch the money. My brother said nothing, but the lady made signs to him that he should take none of it. So he said: 'By God, I shall not ask anything from you,' after which he took his work things and went out.

In fact, he had not a penny to his name and for three days he had been working so hard at sewing those clothes that he had had little to eat and drink. The maid had then come and asked him how the work was going. 'The shirts are finished,' he had replied, and he had then taken them to the people upstairs, handing them over to the husband and leaving immediately. Although my brother hadn't known it, the lady had told her husband about the state that my brother was in, and the two of them had agreed to make him the butt of a joke by getting him to sew things for them without charge. So the next morning, when my brother went to his shop, the maid came to tell him to have another word with her master. He went with her and was asked by the man to cut out five mantles for him. He did this and then left, taking the material with him. When he had sewed the mantles, he brought them to the man, who admired his work and called for a purse. There was money in it and my brother had stretched out his hand when the lady, standing behind her husband, gestured to him not to take anything. So my brother said to the husband: 'There is no need to hurry, sir; there is ample time.'

He then went out more submissively than a donkey, urging himself on in spite of the fact that he was suffering from five things – love, bankruptcy, hunger, nakedness and drudgery. When he had finished all the work that they wanted done, they played another trick on him and married him to the maid. On the night that he was due to sleep with her, they told him: 'It will be better if you spend the night in the mill and wait for tomorrow.' My brother believed that this was sound advice and so he spent the night alone in the mill, but the lady's husband maliciously told the miller about him in order to get him to turn the millwheel. At midnight, the miller came in and started to say: 'This bull is lazy; he has stopped and isn't turning the wheel tonight, in spite of the fact that we have a great deal of corn.' He came down to the mill, filled the trough with grain, and then went up to my brother carrying a rope which he tied round his neck. 'Hup,' he cried, 'turn the millstone over the grain. All you do is eat and leave your droppings and your urine.' He then took up a whip and lashed my brother with it. My brother wept and cried out, but could find no one to help him, and the grinding continued until it was almost morning.

The owner of the house then came but went off again after seeing my brother tethered to the millwheel. Early in the day, the maid arrived and professed to be shocked by what had happened to him: 'My mistress and I were worried about you.' Because of his tiredness and the severity of his beating, my brother could give no answer in return. When he got back to his lodging, in came the official who had drawn up the marriage contract. The man greeted him and said: 'God give you long life. This is a face that tells of delights, dalliance and night-long embraces.' 'May God give no blessing to the liar, you thousand-time cuckold,' retorted my brother. 'By God, I have been doing nothing but grind corn in place of the bull until morning.' The official asked him to tell his story, which he did, and the man then said: 'Your star did not match hers, but if you like, I can alter the contract for you.' He then added: 'Watch out lest they play another trick on you.'

After that, he left my brother, who went to his shop to see if anyone would bring him work from which he could get money to buy food. Again, the maid came and asked him to go to her mistress, but this time he said: 'Go away, my good girl; I will have no further dealings with your mistress.' The girl went off and told her mistress of this, and before my brother knew what was happening, she was looking out at him from her window, weeping and saying: 'My darling, why will you have nothing more to do with me?' He made no reply, and she then swore that nothing that had happened in the mill had been of her choosing and that she hadn't had anything to do with it.

When my brother looked at her loveliness and grace and listened to her sweet words, he forgot his sufferings, accepted her excuse and took pleasure in gazing at her. He greeted her and talked with her, after which he sat for a time doing his sewing. When the maid came this time, she said: 'My mistress greets you and tells you that her husband is intending to spend the night with friends. When he goes to them, you can come to us and pass the most delicious of nights with her until morning.' In fact, her husband had asked her how they could get my brother to leave her alone, and she had said: 'Let me play another trick on him and I will see that his shame is known throughout this city.'

My brother knew nothing of women's wiles, and so when the maid came that evening, he went off with her. When the lady saw him, she said: 'I am full of passionate longing for you.' 'For God's sake,' he said, 'give me a kiss at once,' but before he had finished speaking, in came her husband from another room. 'By God,' he said to my brother, 'I'm going to take you straight to the chief of police.' Paying no attention to my brother's pleadings, he carried him off to the *wali*, who had him beaten with whips, mounted on a camel and taken round the city, with the people shouting at him: 'This is the reward of someone who violates the harems of others!' He was banished from the city and went out without knowing where to go, but, as I was afraid for him, I caught up with him and stayed with him. Then I brought him back and lodged him in my house, where he still is.

*

The caliph laughed at my story and said: 'Well done, you silent and taciturn man.' He ordered me to be rewarded and to leave, but I said that I would not accept anything from him until I had told him what happened to my other brothers, adding: 'But do not think that I am loquacious.' I CONTINUED:

You must know, Commander of the Faithful, that my second brother is called the Babbler and it is he who is semi-paralysed. One day when he was walking along on some errand of his, he met an old woman who asked him to stop for a moment so that she could propose something to him, adding: 'And if you like the sound of it, then do it for me, with God's guidance.' He stopped and she went on: 'I shall tell you of something and guide you to it, but you must not question me too much.' 'Tell me,' said my brother, and she asked: 'What do you say to a beautiful house with a pleasant garden, flowing streams, fruit, wine, a beautiful face and someone to embrace you from evening until morning? If you do what I shall suggest to you, you will find something to please you.'

When my brother heard this, he said: 'My lady, how is it that you have singled me out from everybody else in this affair, and what is it about me that has pleased you?' 'Didn't I tell you not to talk too much?' she said. 'Be quiet and come with me.' She then turned back and my brother followed her, hoping to see what she had described. They entered a spacious house with many servants, and after she had taken him from the bottom to the top of it, he saw that it was an elegant mansion. When the members of the household saw him, they asked: 'Who has brought you here?' 'Don't talk to him,' said the old woman, 'and don't worry him. He is a craftsman and we need him.'

She then took him to a beautifully decorated room, as lovely as eye had ever seen. When they entered, the women there got up, welcomed him and made him sit beside them. Immediately he heard a great commotion, and in came maids, in the middle of whom was a girl like the moon on the night it comes to the full. My brother turned to look at her and then got up and made his obeisance. She welcomed him, telling him to sit down, and after he had done this, she went up to him and said: 'May God honour you, is all well with you?' 'Very well indeed,' replied my brother. Then she ordered food to be brought, and a delicious meal was produced for him. She sat and joined him in eating it, but all the while she could not stop laughing, although whenever he looked at her, she turned away to her maids as though she was laughing at them.

She made a show of affection for him and joked with him, while he, donkey that he is, understood nothing. He was so far under the influence of desire that he thought that the girl was in love with him and that she would allow him his wish. After they had finished eating, wine was produced, and then ten maids like moons came with stringed lutes in their hands and they started to sing with great emotion. Overcome by delight, my brother took a glass from the girl's hand and drained it, before standing up. The girl then drank a glass. 'Good health,' said my brother, and he made her another obeisance. She then gave him a second glass to drink, but when he did this, she slapped him on the nape of his neck. At that my brother left the room as fast as he could, but the old woman followed him and started winking at him, as if to tell him to go back. So back he went, and when the girl told him to sit down, he sat without a word. She then slapped him again on the nape of his neck and, not content with that, she ordered all her maids to slap him. All the while he was saying to the old woman: 'I have never seen anything finer than this,' while she was exclaiming to her mistress that that was enough.

But the maids went on slapping him until he was almost unconscious. When he had to get up to answer the call of nature, the old woman caught up with him and said: 'A little endurance and you will get what you want.' 'How long do I have to endure,' he asked, 'now that I have been slapped almost unconscious?' 'When she gets drunk,' the old woman told him, 'you will get what you want.' So my brother went back and sat down in his place. All the maids stood up and their mistress told them to perfume my brother and to sprinkle rosewater over his face. When they had done this, the girl said: 'May God bring you honour. You have entered my house and endured the condition I imposed. Whoever disobeys me, I expel, but whoever endures reaches his goal.' 'I am your slave, lady,' said my brother, 'and you hold me in the palm of your hand.' 'Know,' she replied, 'that God has made me passionately fond of amusement, and those who indulge me in this get what they seek.'

On her orders, the maids sang with loud voices until all present were filled with delight. She then said to one of them: 'Take your master, do what needs to be done to him and then bring him back immediately.' The maid took my brother, little knowing what was going to be done to him. He was joined by the old woman, who said: 'Be patient; you will not have to wait long.' His face cleared and he went with the maid, heeding the words of the old woman telling him that patience would bring him his desire. He then asked: 'What is the maid going to do?' 'No harm will come to you,' said the old woman, 'may I be your ransom.

She is going to dye your eyebrows and pluck out your moustache.' 'Dye on the eyebrows can be washed away,' said my brother, 'but plucking out a moustache is a painful business.' 'Take care not to disobey her,' said the old lady, 'for her heart is fixed on you.' So my brother patiently allowed his eyebrows to be dyed and his moustache plucked. The maid went to her mistress and told her of this, but her mistress said: 'There is one thing more. You have to shave his chin so as to leave him beardless.'

The maid returned to tell my brother of her mistress's order, and he, the fool, objected: 'But won't this make me a public disgrace?' The old woman explained: 'She only wants to do that to you so that you may be smooth and beardless, with nothing on your face that might prick her, for she has fallen most deeply in love with you. So be patient, for you will get what you want.' Patiently my brother submitted to the maid and let his beard be shaved. The girl then had him brought out, with his dyed eyebrows, his shorn moustache, his shaven chin and his red face. At first, the lady recoiled from him in alarm, but then she laughed until she fell over. 'My master,' she said, 'you have won me by your good nature.' Then she urged him to get up and dance, which he did, and there was not a cushion in the room that she did not throw at him, while the maids began to pelt him with oranges, lemons and citrons, until he fell fainting from the blows, the cuffs that he had suffered on the back of his neck and the things that had been thrown at him.

'Now,' said the old woman, 'you have achieved your goal. There will be no more blows, and there is only one thing left. It is a habit of my mistress that, when she is drunk, she will not let anyone have her until she has stripped off her clothes, including her harem trousers, and is entirely naked. Then she will tell you to remove your own clothes and to start running, while she runs in front of you as though she was trying to escape from you. You must follow her from place to place until you have an erection, and she will then let you take her.'

She told him to strip, and he got up in a daze and took off all his clothes until he was naked ...

Night 32

Morning now dawned and Shahrazad broke off from what she had been allowed to say. Then, when it was the thirty-second night, SHE CONTINUED:

I have heard, O auspicious king, that the old woman told the barber's brother to strip and he got up in a daze and took off all his clothes until he was naked. THE BARBER WENT ON:

'Get up now,' the lady told my brother, 'and when you start running, I'll run, too.' She, too, stripped and said: 'If you want me, then come and get me.' Off she ran, with my brother following. She started to go into one room after another, before dashing off somewhere else, with my brother behind her, overcome by lust, his penis rampant, like a madman. In she went to a darkened room, but when my brother ran in after her, he trod on a thin board that gave way beneath him, and before he knew what was happening, he was in the middle of a lane in the market of the leather sellers, who were calling their wares and buying and selling. When they saw him in that state, naked, with an erection, a shaven chin, dyed eyebrows and reddened cheeks, they cried out against him, slapped him with their hands and started to beat him in his naked-ness with leather straps, until he fainted. Then they sat him on a donkey and took him to the *wali*. When the *wali* asked about him, they said: 'He fell down in this state from Shams al-Din's house.' The *wali* sen-tenced him to a hundred lashes and banished him from Baghdad, but I went out after him and brought him back in secret. I have given him an allowance for his food, but were it not for my sense of honour, I could not put up with a man like him.

My third brother is called the Jabberer, and he is blind. One day, fate led him to a large house, at whose door he knocked, hoping to speak to its owner and to beg some alms from him. The owner called out: 'Who is at the door?' but he made no reply. He then heard the owner calling loudly: 'Who is there?' but again he made no answer. He heard footsteps as the owner came to the door, opened it and asked him what he wanted. 'Alms for the love of God Almighty,' my brother replied. 'Are you blind?' the man asked and my brother said yes. 'Give me your hand,' the man told him, and my brother did this, thinking that he was going to give him something. Instead, holding him by the hand, the man led him into the house and, taking him up stair after stair, he brought him to the flat roof. My brother was saying to himself: 'Surely he will give me some food or some money?' But when the owner reached the top of the house, he repeated: 'What do you want, blind man?' 'Alms for the love of Almighty God,' replied my brother. 'May God open the gates of profit for you,' the man said. 'Why didn't you tell me that when I was downstairs?' said my brother. 'Scum, why didn't you speak the first time that I called?' replied the man. 'What are you going to do with me now?' asked my brother. 'I have nothing in the house to give you,' said the man. 'At least take me down the stairs,' said my brother. 'The way is in front of you,' replied the man. So my brother moved forward and went on down the stairs until there were only twenty steps left between him and the door, but then his foot slipped and he fell down as far as the door, breaking open his head.

He went out, dazed and not knowing where he was going, until he was joined by two blind companions of his. 'What did you get today?' they asked, and he told them what had happened. Then he said: 'Brothers, I want to take out some of the money that I still have and spend it on myself.' His companions agreed to do the same. The owner of the house was following them and listening to what they said, although neither my brother nor his companions realized this. My brother then came to his lodgings and as he entered, unbeknown to him, the man slipped in behind. My brother sat down, waiting for his companions, and when they came in he told them to lock the door and to search the house, in case they had been followed by some stranger. On hearing this, the man got up and clung to a rope that was dangling from the roof. As a result, although the blind men went around the whole room, they found no one. Then they went back and took their seats by my brother, after which they brought out what money that they had and this, when they counted it, turned out to be twelve thousand dirhams. They left it in a corner of the room; each man took what he needed, and what remained was buried. They then produced some food and sat eating, but my brother heard the sounds of a stranger chewing beside him. He warned his companions of this and, stretching out his hand, he caught hold of the house owner and he and the others fell to beating him.

After a time, they called out: 'Muslims, a thief has got in, wanting to steal our money.' A large crowd gathered, but, for his part, the house owner seized hold of the blind men, accusing them of what they had accused him. He closed his eyes until he looked so like one of them that no one doubted that he was blind. 'Muslims,' he cried out, 'I appeal to God and to the sultan. I appeal to God and to the *wali*. Listen to what I have to tell.' Before my brother knew what was happening, all of them had been surrounded and taken to the *wali*'s house.

When they were brought before him, the *wali* asked what the matter was. The house owner said: 'Ask as much as you like, but you will find out nothing except by torture. So start by torturing me and this fellow, who is our leader' – and he pointed at my brother. They stretched the man out and gave him four hundred painful strokes on the backside. He then opened one eye, and when they went on beating him, he opened the other. 'What's this, you damned fellow?' said the *wali*. 'Give me a guarantee of protection,' said the man, and he went on: 'We four pretend to be blind and we prey on people, entering their homes, looking at their women and corrupting them. This has proved very profitable and we have collected twelve thousand dirhams. I told my companions to give me my share, that is three thousand dirhams, but instead, they beat me and took my money. I take refuge with God and with you, but I have a greater right to my share. I want you to realize that I am telling you the truth, so beat each one of them more than you beat me and they will open their eyes.'

At that, the *wali* ordered the blind men to be beaten, starting with my brother. They tied him to a whipping frame and the *wali* said to them all: 'You evil men, do you deny the grace of God and pretend to be blind?' 'God, God, by God,' cried my brother, 'not one of us can see,' but they beat him until he fainted. 'Leave him until he recovers,' said the *wali*, 'and then beat him again.' He went on to order that each of the others be given more than three hundred lashes, while the house owner kept urging: 'Open your eyes, or else you will be beaten again.' Then he said to the *wali*: 'Send someone with me to fetch the money, for these men will not open their eyes as they are afraid of public disgrace.' The *wali* did this and, after getting the money, he gave the house owner three thousand dirhams which he had claimed as his share, keeping the rest for himself, and he then exiled the three blind men. I went out and caught up with my brother and asked him what had happened to him. When he told me the story that I have just told you, I took him back into the city secretly and, still in secret, I gave him an allowance for food and drink.

The caliph laughed at the story and ordered that I should be given a reward and allowed to leave, but I told him: 'By God, I will not take anything until I tell the Commander of the Faithful what happened to my other brothers, for I am a taciturn man.' THEN I SAID:

My fourth brother, who is now one-eyed, was a butcher in Baghdad who sold meat and raised rams. Men of importance and wealth used to seek him out and buy meat from him, as a result of which he became very wealthy and acquired both riding beasts and houses. This good fortune lasted for a long time. Then one day, when he was sitting in his shop, an old man with a long beard stopped beside him, gave him some money and asked for its value in meat. When the exchange of money and meat had been made, the old man went off.

On looking at the silver that he been given, my brother saw that the dirhams were glistening white, so he stored them by themselves. For five months, the old man kept coming back and my brother went on putting his dirhams in a box by themselves. He then wanted to take them out in order to buy some sheep, but when he opened the box, he found that all it contained was white paper cut in pieces. He struck his face and cried out, and when a crowd gathered around him he told them his story, which filled them with astonishment. Following his usual practice, my brother then got up and slaughtered a ram whose carcass he hung up in his shop, while the meat that he had sliced from it he hung up outside, saying as he did so: 'O God, let that ill-omened old man come.' In fact, some time later, the man did arrive, bringing silver with him. My brother got up and, holding on to him, shouted: 'Muslims, come here and listen to what I have to tell you about this evil-doer.' When the old man heard this, he said to my brother: 'Which would you prefer – to leave me alone or to be publicly shamed by me?' 'How can you shame me?' asked my brother. 'By showing that you are selling human flesh as mutton,' said the old man. 'You are lying, you damned fellow,' my brother replied. 'The one who is damned is the one who has a man hung up in his shop.' 'If that is so,' said my brother, 'then my money and my blood are lawfully yours.'

At that, the old man called to the bystanders: 'If you want to check what I say to find that I am telling the truth, then come into his shop.' The people surged forward and found that the ram had become a man, whose corpse was hanging there. When they saw that, they laid hold of my brother and shouted at him: 'Infidel, villain,' while his dearest friend started hitting and slapping him and saying: 'Do you give us human flesh to eat?' The old man struck him on the eye and knocked it out. Then the people took the corpse to the chief of police, to whom the old man said: 'Emir, this man slaughters people and sells their flesh as mutton. We have brought him to you, so do you punish him in accordance with the law of the Omnipotent and All-powerful God.' My brother tried to defend himself, but the police chief would not listen and ordered him to be given five hundred lashes. All his money was confiscated, and had it not been for the money, he would have been killed.

He then fled away as fast as he could and eventually he reached a large city where he thought it best to set up as a shoemaker. He opened a shop and sat working for his daily bread. One day, he went out on some errand. Hearing the sound of horses' hooves, he asked what was happening, and he was told that the king was going out hunting. My brother was gazing at his splendour when, on noticing him, the king lowered his head and said: 'God is my refuge from the evil of this day.' He turned his horse about and rode back with all his retinue. He then gave orders to his servants, who got hold of my brother and beat him so painfully that he almost died.

My brother didn't know why they had done this and returned home in a state of near collapse. Later he approached one of the king's household and told him what had happened. The man laughed until he fell over and then said: 'Brother, you must know that the king cannot bear to look at a one-eyed man, especially if it is the right eye that he has lost, in which case he doesn't let him go free, but kills him.' On hearing this, my brother made up his mind to flee from the city. He got up and left for another part where no one knew him, and there he stayed for a long time. Then, while thinking over his situation, he went out one day to see the sights, but on hearing the sound of horses behind him, he cried: 'My fate has come upon me!' He looked for a place to hide, but could find nothing until he caught sight of a door. Pushing it open, he went in. There he saw a long hallway, which he entered, but before he knew what was going on, two men had laid hold on him. 'Praise to God,' they said, 'for thanks to Him we have laid our hands on you, you enemy of God. For three nights now, thanks to you, we have had no sleep and no rest, and you have given us a taste of the pangs of death.' 'What is the matter with you people?' asked my brother. 'You have been raiding us,' they said, 'wanting to disgrace us, scheming and trying to murder the owner of the house. Isn't it enough for you that you and your friends have ruined him? Hand over the knife that you have been using to threaten us each night.' They then searched my brother and found a knife in his waistband. 'For God's sake, show mercy,' implored my brother, 'for you must know that mine is a strange story.'

They asked what his story might be, and he told them in the hope that they would free him, but when they heard what he had to say, they paid no attention but struck him and tore his clothes. When they found the scars of the beating on his sides, they said: 'You damned man. These are the marks of a beating.' They took him to the *wali* and my brother said to himself: 'My sins have caught up with me and only Almighty God can save me.' 'You villain,' said the *wali* to him, 'what led you to do this, to enter this house with intent to kill?' 'Emir,' said my brother, 'I ask you in God's Name to listen to what I have to say and not to judge me hastily.' 'Am I to listen to a thief,' asked the *wali*, 'a man who has reduced people to poverty and who still bears the scars of a beating on his back? You would not have been beaten like this except for some serious crime.' On his orders, my brother then received a hundred lashes, after which he was mounted on a camel, with guards proclaiming: 'This is the reward, and the least of the rewards, for one who attacks the houses of others.' He was then expelled from the city and he fled away. When I heard of this, I went out to him and asked him what had happened. He told me his story and I stayed with him. People kept shouting at him, but they eventually let him go and I took him off and brought him secretly to the city, where I have made him an allowance for food and drink.

As for my fifth brother, whose ears have been cut off, Commander of the Faithful, he was a poor man who used to beg from the people by night and spend what he got by day. Our father was a very old man and when he fell ill and died, he left us seven hundred dirhams, of which each of us took a hundred. When my fifth brother got his share, he was bewildered and didn't know what to do with it. Still in a state of confusion, it occurred to him to get glassware of all kinds and make a profit from it. He spent a hundred dirhams on buying this glass, which he set out on a large tray and, to sell it, he sat down beside a wall. As he sat, leaning against the wall, he thought to himself: 'This glass represents my capital of a hundred dirhams. I shall sell it for two hundred and then use the two hundred to buy more, which I shall sell for four hundred. I shall go on buying and selling until I have great wealth, and then I shall buy all kinds of goods, jewels and perfumes, and make an enormous profit. After that, I shall buy a fine house, with mamluks, horses and saddles of gold. I shall eat and drink and invite home every singer in the city, whether male or female. My capital, God willing, will come to a hundred thousand dirhams.'

All this was going through his mind while his glassware was spread out on its tray in front of him. He went on to musing to himself: 'When my capital reaches a hundred thousand dirhams, I shall send out the marriage brokers who can arrange alliances with the daughters of kings and viziers. It is the hand of Shams al-Din's daughter for which I shall ask, as I hear that her beauty is perfect and that she is marvellously graceful. I shall offer a dowry of a thousand dinars for her, and if her father accepts, well and good, but if he does not, then I shall take her by force to spite him. When I have her in my house, I shall buy ten little eunuchs for myself, together with a robe such as is worn by kings and sultans, and I shall have a golden saddle made, studded with precious gems. I shall mount, with my mamluks walking around and in front of me, and as I go about the city, people will greet me and call down blessings on me. I shall come into the presence of Shams al-Din, the girl's father, with my mamluks behind and in front of me, as well as to my right and my left. When he sees me, Shams al-Din will get up and seat me in his place, while he himself sits below me, as he is to be my relative by marriage. With me will be two eunuchs carrying two purses, each of which will contain a thousand dinars. I shall give him a thousand as his daughter's dowry and then I shall hand him another thousand so that he may learn of my chivalry, generosity and magnanimity, as well as my scorn for worldly things. If he addresses me in ten words, I shall reply in two.

'Then I shall go to my own house, and if any messenger comes to me from my bride, I shall give him money and a robe of honour, while if he brings me a gift, I shall return it to him, refusing to accept it, so that people may know that I am a proud man and only allow myself to relax when it is appropriate. My servants will then be told to dress me suitably and when they have done that, I shall order them to arrange for the wedding ceremony. My house will be splendidly decorated and when the time comes for the unveiling of the bride, I shall wear my most sumptuous clothes and recline in a robe of brocade, looking neither to right nor to left because of the greatness of my mind and the soundness of my understanding.

'My bride, with her jewellery and her robes, will be standing before me like a full moon, but in my pride and haughtiness, I shall not glance at her until all those present say: "Master, your wife, your servant, is standing before you. Spare her a glance, because this standing is tiring her." They will kiss the ground before me a number of times and at that I shall lift my head, cast a single glance at her, and then look down towards the ground. They will then take me to the bedroom, where I shall change my clothes and put on something even more splendid. When they bring the bride a second time, I shall not look at her until they beg me many times, and after looking, I shall again look down towards the ground and I shall continue in this way until her unveiling has been completed.'

Night 33

Morning now dawned and Shahrazad broke off from what she had been allowed to say. Then, when it was the thirty-third night, SHE CONTINUED:

I have heard, O auspicious king, that the barber's brother said: 'I shall again look down towards the ground and I shall continue in this way until her unveiling has been completed.' THE BARBER WENT ON:

'I shall then order one of the eunuchs to bring a purse with five hundred dinars,' my brother thought to himself, 'and when he has brought it, I shall give it to the bride's attendants and tell them to bring me into the bride. When they do this, I shall not look at her or deign to speak to her, so that people may say: "What a great-souled man this is!" Then her mother will come and kiss my head and my hand and say: "Master, look at your servant. She wants you to approach her, to mend her broken heart." When she sees that I make no reply, she will come and shower kisses on my feet before pleading: "Master, my daughter is a beautiful girl who has never seen a man. If she finds you shunning her, her heart will be broken, so please turn to her and speak to her." She will then get up and fetch a glass of wine, which her daughter will take and bring to me. I shall leave her standing in front of me as I recline on a brocaded cushion, and such will be my pride that I shall not glance at her, so that she will take me for a mighty sultan and will say: "Master, I implore you by God not to reject this glass from my hand, who am your servant." I shall still not speak to her and she will press me and say: "You must drink it," and she will put it to my mouth. I shall shake my fist in her face and kick her with my foot, like this.' My brother then kicked with his foot and the tray with the glasses fell to the ground, so that everything on it was smashed.

'All this is the result of my pride,' cried my brother. He pummelled his face, tore his clothes and started to weep as he struck himself. The passers-by on their way to the Friday prayer were staring at him. Some of them looked at him with pity, while others felt no concern for him; as for my brother himself, he was in the position of having lost both his capital and his expected profit. After he had been weeping for some time, up came a beautiful lady, accompanied by a number of eunuchs. She was riding on a mule with a saddle of gold and from her spread the scent of musk as she made her way to the Friday prayer. When she saw the broken glasses and the state that my weeping brother was in, she felt pity for him and asked about him. She was told that a tray full of glassware, which represented his livelihood, had been broken and it was this that had brought him to his present state. Summoning one of her eunuchs, she said: 'Give what money you have with you to this poor man,' at which the eunuch handed my brother a purse in which he found five hundred dinars.

When he had laid his hand on this, he almost died of the excess of joy. He called down blessings on his benefactress and went back home, a rich man. As he sat there thinking, he heard a knock on the door. He got up and opened it, to find an old woman whom he did not know. 'My son,' she said to him, 'it is almost time for the prayer, but I have not performed the ritual ablution. Would you let me in to your house so that I may do it?' My brother agreed and, going in himself, he told the old woman to follow, which she did, and he handed her a jug for her ablution. He then sat, still overjoyed because of the money, which he stowed away in his belt. When he had finished doing this and the old woman had completed her ablution, she came to where he was sitting and prayed, performing two *rak'as*, after which she called down blessings on him.

He thanked her for that and, reaching for his money, he gave her two dinars, saying to himself: 'This is a charitable gift on my part.' When she saw the money, she exclaimed: 'Why do you take those who love you for beggars? Take back your money, as I don't need it, or else give it back to the lady who gave it to you. If you want to meet her, I can arrange that for you, as she is my mistress.' 'Mother,' said my brother, 'how can I get to her?' 'My son,' she replied, 'the lady is attracted to you, but she is the wife of a wealthy man. So take all your money with you and follow me and I shall lead you to her. When you meet her, use all your charm and every fair word at your command, and in that way you will be able to enjoy all you want of her beauty and her wealth.'

My brother took all his money and got up and went with her, scarcely believing what was happening. She walked on, with my brother at her heels, until she came to an imposing door. She knocked and out came a Rumi slave girl, who opened the door for her. The old woman entered and told my brother to come in with her. He entered a spacious mansion, going into a large room whose floor was strewn with wonderful carpets and whose walls were covered in hangings. My brother sat down with his gold in front of him and his turban on his knee. Before he knew what was happening, in came a lady as beautiful as any he had ever seen, wearing a most splendid dress. My brother rose to his feet and she smiled at him and showed pleasure at their meeting. She motioned to him to sit, ordered the door to be closed and then took him by the hand. Together they went into a separate room, strewn with various types of brocade. My brother sat down with the lady beside him and she played with him for a time.

Then she got up and said: 'Don't move from here until I come back,' after which she went away. While my brother was sitting there, in came an enormous black slave holding a drawn sword. 'Miserable man,' he said, 'who brought you here and what are you doing?' At the sight of this slave, my brother's tongue was tied and he could make no reply. So the man took him, stripped him of his clothes and went on beating him with the flat of his sword until he fell on the ground, fainting because of the violence of the beating. The ill-omened slave thought that he was dead and my brother heard him say: 'Where is the girl with the salt?' A slave girl then came up to him carrying a large dish on which there was a great quantity of salt. The slave kept on pouring this on my brother's wounds as he lay motionless for fear that if the slave realized that he was still alive, he would kill him.

After the girl had gone, the slave called for the cellar keeper and this time it was the old woman who came to my brother and dragged him by his feet to a cellar into which she threw him on top of a pile of corpses. He stayed where he was for two whole days, but thanks to God's providence, the salt saved his life, as it stopped the flow of blood. When he found that he had strength enough to move, he left the cellar, opened its trapdoor in spite of his fear, and came out on the other side. God granted him shelter; it was dark as he walked and he hid himself in the entrance hall until dawn. In the morning, the damned old woman came out in search of another victim while, unknown to her, my brother followed behind. He then made for his own house, where he treated his hurts until he had recovered.

Meanwhile, he had been keeping a constant watch over the old woman as she took people, one by one, to her house. During this time he uttered no word, but when he had regained his spirits and his strength, he got hold of a strip of material and made it into a purse, which he then filled with glass, tying it around his waist. He disguised himself as a Persian so that no one could recognize him, and he hid a sword beneath his clothes. When he saw the old woman, he accosted her in a Persian accent, saying: 'Old woman, I am a stranger and have just come today to this city where I know nobody. Do you have some scales that will take nine hundred dinars? If so, I would give you some of the money.' 'I have a son,' she replied, 'who is a money-changer and who has scales of all kinds. Come with me before he leaves his place of business so that he can weigh your gold.' 'Lead the way,' said my brother, and she walked off followed by him until she came to the door. When she knocked, out came the same lady and the old woman smiled at her and said: 'I have brought you some fat meat today.' The lady took my brother by the hand and brought him into the room in which he had been before. She sat with him for a time and then left, telling him to wait until she came back. Before my brother knew it, in came the damned slave, with his drawn sword. 'Get up, damn you,' he told my brother, and when my brother had risen, the slave went on ahead with my brother behind him. My brother then reached for the sword beneath his clothes, struck at the slave and cut his head from his body, after which he dragged him by the feet to the cellar. 'Where is the girl with the salt?' he cried, and when she came with the salt dish, she saw him with the sword in his hand and turned in flight. He followed and with a blow struck off her head. Then he called out: 'Where is the old woman? Do you recognize me, you ill-omened creature?' he asked when she came. 'No, master,' she replied. 'I am the man with the dirhams,' he said. 'You came to my house, performed your ablution and prayed there, and then trapped me here.' 'Fear God,' she cried, 'and don't judge me hastily.' My brother paid no attention to this and continued to strike until he had cut her into four pieces.

He then went out to look for the lady. When she saw him, she became distraught and cried: 'Spare me!' He did, and then asked her: 'What brought you here with this black man?' She said: 'I was in the service of a merchant. This old woman often used to visit me and I became friendly with her. One day, she said to me: "We are having a wedding feast of unparalleled splendour at our house. Would you like to see it?" "Yes," I replied, and I got up, put on my best clothes and my jewellery, and taking with me a purse containing a hundred dinars, I went here with her. When I came in, before I knew what was happening, the black man had seized me, and here I have been for three years because of the wiles of this damned old woman.' 'Is there anything of his in the house?' asked my brother. 'A great deal,' she replied, adding: 'Carry it off if you can, asking God for guidance.' My brother got up and went with her as she opened chests that were full of purses. My brother was bewildered, but the lady said: 'Leave me here and go and get someone to carry away the money.' So out he went and hired ten men, but when he got back he found no trace of the lady, and there was nothing left except a few of the purses and the household goods. He realized then that he had been tricked and so he took the money that was left and he opened the storerooms, taking their contents and leaving nothing in the house.

He spent a happy night, but in the morning he found twenty soldiers at the door, who laid hands on him and said: 'You are wanted by the *wali*.' They took him off and although he pleaded with them to be permitted to pass by his house, they would not allow him the time. He promised them money, but they refused to accept and bound him tightly with ropes and carried him off. On the way he came across a friend of his, to whose robe he clung, pleading with him to stay with him and to help free him from the soldiers. The man stopped and asked the soldiers what the matter was. 'The *wali* has ordered us to bring this man before him and we are on our way with him now.' My brother's friend asked them to let him go, promising to give them five hundred dinars and suggesting that when they got back to the *wali* they could tell him that they had not found my brother. They would not listen to this, but started to drag my brother along on his face until they brought him to the *wali*.

When the *wali* saw him, he asked him where he had got the goods and the money. My brother said: 'I want a guarantee of immunity,' at which the *wali* gave him the kerchief that was a sign of this. My brother then told of his adventure with the old woman from beginning to end and of the flight of the lady. He added: 'Take what you want from what I got, but leave me enough to live on.' The *wali*, however, took all the goods and the money, and as he was afraid that this might come to the ears of the sultan, he summoned my brother and threatened to hang him if he did not leave the city. My brother agreed to go, but when he left for another town, he was set upon by thieves, who stripped him, beat him and cut off his ears. When I heard of this, I went out to take him clothes and then I brought him into the city secretly, and gave him an allowance for food and drink.

As for my sixth brother, Commander of the Faithful, the one whose lips have been cut off, he had become poor, and one day he went out in search of something with which to keep body and soul together. On his way, he caught sight of a fine house, with a wide and lofty portico and eunuchs at the door, having all the trappings of authority. In answer to his question, a bystander told him that the house belonged to one of the Barmecides. He approached the doorkeepers and asked them for alms. 'Go in through the main door,' they said, 'and you will get what you want from the owner.' So my brother entered the portico and walked through until he came to a most beautiful and elegant building, paved with marble and adorned with hangings, in the middle of which was a garden whose like he had never seen before. He looked round in bewilderment, not knowing where to go, and he then advanced to the head of the room, where he saw a man, bearded and with a handsome face, who stood up to greet him. The man asked him how he was, and my brother told him that he was in need. On hearing this, the other showed great concern, and stretching out his hand to his clothes, he tore them, saying: 'Are you to be hungry in a town in which I live? I cannot bear the thought of it.'

He promised my brother all manner of good things and said: 'You must share my salt with me.' 'Sir,' said my brother, 'I am at the end of my endurance, for I am desperately hungry.' 'Boy,' shouted the man to a servant, 'bring the basin and the jug.' Then, to my brother he said: 'Come and wash your hands.' My brother got up to do this but saw neither basin nor jug. The man went through the motions of hand washing, after which he shouted: 'Bring out the table.' Again, my brother saw nothing, although his host invited him to eat and not to be ashamed, after which he himself pretended to be eating. He kept saying to my brother: 'I am surprised at your lack of appetite. Don't eat too little, for I know how hungry you must be.' My brother started to make a pretence of eating as his host urged him on, saying: 'Eat up and try this beautiful white bread.' As my brother could see nothing, he said to himself: 'This fellow likes making a fool of people.' Out loud he said: 'Never in my life, sir, have I come across whiter or more delicious bread.' 'It was baked,' replied the host, 'by a slave girl whom I bought for five hundred dinars.'

He then called out: 'Bring the first course, the pie, and put lots of fat on it.' Turning to my brother, he asked whether he had ever seen anything more delicious, urging him again to eat up and not be ashamed. Next, he called for 'the stew with the fatted sandgrouse'. 'Guest,' he said to my brother, 'start eating, for you are hungry and you need this.' My brother started moving his jaws and munching, while the host kept calling for one type of dish after another. Nothing came, but he kept on urging my brother to eat. Eventually he told the servant to fetch the chickens stuffed with pistachio nuts. 'By your life, my guest,' he said, 'these chickens have been fattened on pistachio nuts. You will have never tasted the like before, so eat up.' 'This is excellent, sir,' agreed my brother, and the man began to move his hand towards my brother's mouth, as though he was giving him mouthfuls to eat.

He kept on enumerating particular types of food and describing them to my hungry brother, who grew even hungrier and longed for a barley loaf. 'Have you come across anything more tasty than the seasoning of these dishes?' asked his host, and when my brother said no, he urged him to eat heartily and not to be ashamed. When my brother said that he had had enough food, the servants were told to remove the dishes and bring in the desserts. 'Take some of this to eat. It is good,' said the man. 'Eat some of these doughnuts. Take this one before the syrup runs out of it.' 'Sir, may I never be deprived of you,' said my brother, and he then started to ask his host about the amount of musk in the doughnuts. 'This is my custom,' replied the other. 'My people put a *mithqal* of musk in each doughnut, together with half a *mithqal* of ambergris.' All the while my brother was moving his head and his mouth and waggling his jaws. He was then invited to help himself to almonds – 'Don't be shy' – but my brother said that he had had enough and could not eat another thing. 'If you want to eat and enjoy yourself, my guest,' said the host, 'then for God's sake don't stay hungry.' 'Sir,' said my brother, 'how can anyone who has eaten all these various dishes be hungry?'

Then he thought to himself that he would do something to make his host sorry for what he had done. 'Bring the wine,' said the man, and the servants moved their hands in the air as though they were doing this. The man then gave my brother a cup and said: 'Take this and tell me if you like it.' 'It has a fine bouquet,' said my brother, 'but I am in the habit of drinking wine that is twenty years old.' 'Then here is the stuff for you,' said the host. 'You will not find any better to drink.' My brother thanked him, and moved his hand as though he was drinking. 'Cheers and good health,' he said, and the host, too, pretended to drink. Then he gave my brother another cup to drink, and my brother, pretending to be drunk, took him unawares, and lifting his arm until his armpit was bared, he gave him a resounding slap on the nape of the neck, following this up with another one. 'What's this, you scum?' said the man. 'Sir,' replied my brother, 'you have been generous to your servant. You have taken him into your house, given him food to eat and old wine to drink, but he has become drunk and attacked you like a hooligan. As a man of nobility you will put up with such folly and pardon his fault.'

When the man heard this, he laughed loudly and said: 'For a long time now I have been making fun of people and playing jokes on my friends, but you are the only man whom I have ever met with the ability and understanding to bear his part with me in all this. Now you have my forgiveness, so join me as my real companion and never leave me.' He then ordered a number of the dishes that he had mentioned earlier to be brought out and he and my brother ate until they had had their fill. They then moved to the drinking room, where slave girls like moons sang tunes of all kinds to a variety of instruments, and they drank until drunkenness overcame them. The man became so friendly with his guest that the two of them were like brothers. Out of his deep affection for him, the host gave my brother robes of honour and in the morning they went back again to their eating and drinking.

They continued like this for twenty years, but the host then died and the sultan seized his wealth together with my brother's possessions, and as a result of this my brother was left poor and powerless. Accordingly, he fled away, but in the course of his journey he was set upon by Bedouin, who took him prisoner and brought him to their tribe. His captor started to torture him and to say: 'Buy your life from me with cash, or else I'll kill you.' My brother began to weep and say: 'By God, I have nothing at all. I am your captive so do what you want.' The Bedouin brought out a knife, cut off my brother's lips and pressed him hard again for money.

This man had a beautiful wife, and when he went out, she would flaunt herself at my brother and try to seduce him. He kept on refusing her, until one day she had her way. He started to play with her and sat her on his lap, but when they were in this position, in burst her husband. 'You miserable, damned man,' he said, 'so now you want to corrupt my wife,' and he took out a knife and cut off my brother's penis. Then he carried him off on a camel and threw him down on a mountain, where he left him. Some travellers passed by who recognized him; they gave him food and drink and then told me what had happened to him. I went to him, carried him off and brought him to the city, where I gave him an allowance sufficient for his needs. Here I have come before you,

Commander of the Faithful, fearing to leave before telling you my story, as that would be a mistake, since in my shadow stand six brothers, whom I have to support.

When the caliph heard what I had to tell him about my brothers, he laughed and said: 'You told the truth, silent man, when you said that you are a man of few words, lacking in inquisitiveness, but now leave this city and settle somewhere else.' He banished me by official decree, and as a result I went to other parts and travelled around various regions until I heard that he had died and that the caliphate had passed to someone else. So I went back to Baghdad, where I found that my brothers were dead. Then I met this young man for whom I did a very great service, and had it not been for me he would have been killed. He has accused me of something that is not in my nature and what he has said about my being inquisitive is false. It is because of him that I have wandered around many lands before arriving here, where I have found him with you. Is this not, good people, an example of my sense of honour?

'When we heard the barber's story, listened to his long-windedness and realized the injury that he had done to the young man, we laid hands on him and imprisoned him,' said the tailor to the king of China. HE WENT ON:

We then sat peacefully eating and drinking and finishing our banquet until the call for the afternoon prayer. I then left and went home, where my wife was scowling. 'You have been enjoying yourself with your friends,' she said, 'while I have been left in sadness. If you don't take me out to see the sights for the rest of the day, I shall cut my ties with you and leave you.' So I took her and went out with her and we looked at the sights until evening. On our way back we met the hunchback, who was overflowingly drunk and was reciting these lines:

The glass is clear and so is the wine;
They are like one another, and so is this affair.
It looks as though there is wine without a glass,
Or as though there is a glass with no wine.

I invited him home and went out to buy a fried fish. We sat eating and then my wife gave him a mouthful of bread and a piece of fish. She put them both into his mouth which she closed, and he then choked to death.

I carried him off and as a ruse I threw him into the house of this Jewish doctor, who, as a ruse, threw him into the inspector's house. The inspector, as a ruse, threw him into the path of the Christian broker. This is my story and this is what happened to me yesterday. Is it not more wonderful than the story of the hunchback?

When the king of China heard this tale, he shook his head in delight and showed his astonishment, saying: 'The tale of what happened between the young man and the inquisitive barber is pleasanter and better than the story of the hunchback.' He then gave orders to one of his chamberlains to go with the tailor and fetch the barber from prison. 'I want to listen to what he has to say,' he added, 'for he is the reason why I am letting you all go free. We shall then bury the hunchback . . .

Night 34

Morning now dawned and Shahrazad broke off from what she had been allowed to say. Then, when it was the thirty-fourth night, SHE CONTINUED:

I have heard, O auspicious king, that the king of China said: 'Fetch me the barber, for he is the reason why I am letting you all go free. We shall then bury the hunchback for he has been dead since yesterday, and we shall have a tomb made for him.' It did not take long for the chamberlain and the tailor to reach the prison. They brought out the barber and took him before the king, who studied him and saw an old man of ninety, with a dark face, white beard and eyebrows, small ears, a long nose and a foolish expression.

The king laughed at his appearance and said: 'O silent man, I want you to tell me something of your story.' The barber replied: 'King of the age, what is the story of this Christian, this Jew, this Muslim and this hunchback who lies dead here, and what is the reason for this gathering?' 'Why do you ask?' said the king. 'I ask,' he replied, 'so that the king may know that I am not an inquisitive man, that I am not guilty of the charge of loquacity, that I am known as the Silent and that I have my share in the quality this name indicates. As the poet says:

You seldom find a man with a soubriquet
Which, if you look, does not contain his quality.'

The king then ordered that everything should be explained to the barber – the affair of the hunchback and what happened to him at supper time, and the tales of the Christian, the Jew, the inspector and the tailor, but there is nothing to be gained in repetition. The barber shook his head and said: 'By God, this is a wonder indeed. Uncover the hunchback for me.' This was done and the barber sat by his head, which he then moved on to his lap. He looked at the hunchback's face and then laughed until he fell over backwards. 'Every death is a wonder,' he said, 'but the death of this hunchback deserves to be written in letters of gold.' Those present were bewildered by what he said and the king was astonished. 'Silent man,' he said, 'tell us about this.' 'King of the age,' he replied, 'I swear by the truth of your grace that there is still life in this lying hunchback.'

He then took a bag from his belt and brought out a bottle of ointment, with which he rubbed the neck and the neck veins of the hunchback. Next, he took a pair of iron forceps and after putting them into the hunchback's throat, he drew out the slice of fish with its bone, all covered in blood. The hunchback sneezed and then immediately leapt to his feet. He passed a hand over his face and said: 'I bear witness that there is no god but God and that Muhammad is the Apostle of God.' The king and all those present were astonished at what they saw, and laughed so much that they almost lost consciousness. 'By God,' said the king, 'this is something remarkable and I have never seen anything more strange. You Muslims, you soldiers, have you ever in your lives seen a man die and then come back to life? Had not God provided him with this barber who restored him to life, he would be dead.' 'By God,' they said, 'this is a wonder of wonders.' The king ordered the story to be written down, and when this had been done, it was stored away in the royal treasury. The king then gave the Jew, the Christian and the inspector a splendid robe of honour each, and, at his command, they then left. Another splendid robe was given to the tailor, who was appointed as the royal tailor and given official allowances. He was reconciled with the hunchback, who received a gorgeous robe as well as the grant of allowances and was taken as a companion by the king. Gifts, together with a robe of honour, were given to the barber, as well as a regular salary. He was appointed court barber and taken as a companion by the king. They all continued to lead the most pleasant and delightful of lives until they met death, the destroyer of delights and the parter of companions.

*

'This is not more remarkable,' said Shahrazad, 'than the story of the two viziers and Anis al-Jalis.' 'How was that?' asked Dunyazad. SHAHRAZAD BEGAN:

I have heard, O auspicious king, that in Basra was a certain sultan who loved the poor, the beggars and all his subjects, distributing his wealth to those who believed in Muhammad – may God bless him and give him peace. He fitted the description given of him by a poet:

A king who, when squadrons circled round,
Cut through his foes with sharp and piercing blades.
His writing could be read upon their breasts,
When he assailed the riders with his spear.

The name of the sultan was Muhammad ibn Sulaiman al-Zaini and he had two viziers, one called al-Mu'in ibn Sawa and the second al-Fadl ibn Khaqan. The latter was a man of good conduct, the most generous person of his time. All loved him; all came to him for counsel and everyone prayed that he be granted a long life, for he encouraged good and eliminated evil and wrongdoing. Al-Mu'in ibn Sawa, on the other hand, disliked the people, did not love what is good but encouraged evil. As the poet has it:

Take refuge with the noble, sons of noble men,
For these in turn will father noble sons.
Abandon the mean, descendants of the mean,
For those whom these produce are mean as well.

The love that the people felt for al-Fadl ibn Khaqan was matched by their hatred of al-Mu'in ibn Sawa. God's providence decreed that one day the sultan was seated on his royal throne, surrounded by his officers of state, when he summoned al-Fadl and said: 'I want a slave girl unsurpassed in beauty by anyone in this age, perfect in her grace, splendidly proportioned, with praiseworthy qualities.' 'A girl like that cannot be got for less than ten thousand dinars,' said his officials. At that, the sultan called for his treasurer and told him to take this sum to the house of al-Fadl, which he did, and al-Fadl had the sultan's orders to go to the market each day, passing on to the brokers the instructions that he had received. According to these orders, no slave girl priced at over a thousand dinars was to be sold without having first been shown to al-Fadl.

The brokers carried out this instruction, but none of their girls won al-Fadl's approval. Then one day a broker came to al-Fadl's house, and finding that he was about to ride off to the royal palace, he put his hand on al-Fadl's stirrup and recited:

> You who unfold royal commands,
> You who enjoy continued happiness,
> Your generosity has brought life to the dead,
> And God rewards your efforts with His favour.

Then he added: 'The one for whom the royal decree ordered us to search has been found.' 'Bring her to me,' said al-Fadl. The man went off for a time and then came back with a slender girl with jutting breasts, kohl-dark eyes, smooth cheeks, a slender waist and heavy buttocks. Her clothes were of the loveliest; her saliva was sweeter than rosewater; her figure was more perfectly proportioned than a swaying branch; and her voice was sweeter than the dawn breeze. She was as a poet has described:

> Wonderful in her beauty, with a face like the full moon;
> The people's darling, sweet as raisins and as juice.
> The Lord of Heaven has exalted her,
> With charm and understanding, and a slender form.
> The heavens of her face hold seven stars
> That guard her cheeks against all those who watch.
> If someone tries to steal a glance at her,
> The devils in her eyes burn him with meteors.

When al-Fadl saw the girl, he was filled with admiration and, turning to the broker, he asked her price. 'It has been fixed at ten thousand dinars,' said the man, 'and her owner swears that this does not cover the cost of the chickens she has eaten, what she has drunk and the robes of honour that have been given to her teachers. For she has studied calligraphy, grammar, philology, Quranic interpretation, the foundations of jurisprudence, religion, medicine, precise calculation and how to play musical instruments.' 'Bring the owner over to me,' said al-Fadl. This was immediately done, the man turning out to a Persian of whom the assault of Time had left no more than a husk, as the poet puts it:

> Time has shaken me, and what a shaking!
> For Time, the powerful, acts with violence.
> I used to walk and not be tired,
> But now I tire and cannot walk.

Al-Fadl asked him whether he was willing to accept ten thousand dinars for the girl from the sultan Muhammad ibn Sulaiman al-Zaini. 'By God,' said the Persian, 'if I gave her for nothing, this would only be my duty.' Al-Fadl then ordered the money to be brought and when this had been done, it was weighed out for the Persian. The broker then approached al-Fadl and asked permission to speak, and when this had been granted, he said: 'My advice is that you should not take this girl to the sultan today. She has just come from a journey which has tired her out, and she is suffering from the change of air. You should keep her in your house for ten days until she recovers. After that, take her to the baths, dress her in the finest of dresses and then you can bring her to the sultan. That will best for you.' Al-Fadl thought over this advice and considered it sound. So he took the girl to his house, assigned her a room and provided her every day with what she needed in the way of food, drink, and so on, and she stayed like this for a time.

Al-Fadl had a son, Nur al-Din 'Ali, like the moon at its full, with a bright face, red cheeks and a downy mole like a speck of ambergris, as the poet has fully described:

> A moon, whose glances, when he looks, are murderous,
> A branch whose figure breaks hearts when he bends.
> His locks are Negroid black and his complexion gold;
> His character is sweet; his frame is a spear shaft.
> Hard of heart and soft of waist –
> Why not move quickly from one to the other?
> Were the softness of his waist found in his heart,
> He would never injure or offend his lover.
> You who blame me for loving him, absolve me from all guilt.
> Who will help me now my body is worn away?
> The fault belongs to my heart and to my eye –
> Stop blaming me; leave me in my distress.

This young man did not know about the slave girl, but his father had warned her about him. 'Know, my daughter,' he had said, 'that I have bought you as a concubine for the sultan, Muhammad ibn Sulaiman al-Zaini, and that I have a son who takes every girl in the district. Beware of him and take care not to let him see your face or hear your voice.' 'To hear is to obey,' said the girl, after which he left her and went away. One day, as had been fated, it happened that the girl went to the house baths, where maids washed her. She put on splendid clothes, looking even more beautiful and graceful, after which she went to the lady of the house, al-Fadl's wife, and kissed her hand. 'Bless you, Anis al-Jalis,' said the lady, 'are our baths not lovely?' 'The only thing that I missed,' said the girl, 'was your presence there.'

At that, the lady told her maids to come with them to the baths and they rose obediently, with her between them. She had put two little slave girls to guard over the door to Anis al-Jalis's room, telling them not to let anyone in to see her, to which they had said: 'To hear is to obey.' While Anis al-Jalis was sitting in her room, al-Fadl's son, Nur al-Din 'Ali, came in to ask about his mother and the family. The two girls said: 'They have gone to the baths.' From inside her room, Anis al-Jalis heard the sound of Nur al-Din's voice and she said to herself: 'What do you suppose this young man is like, who, according to al-Fadl, has left no girl in the district without taking her? By God, I should like to have a look at him.' She got up, still glowing from her bath, went towards the door of her room and looked out at Nur al-Din. There he was, like a full moon, and his glance left her the legacy of a thousand sighs. Nur al-Din turned and noticed her and he, too, was left a thousand sighs when he looked at her. Each of them was ensnared by love for the other.

Nur al-Din then advanced towards the two little girls and shouted at them. They ran away, but stopped at a distance, watching him to see what he would do. He went to the room door, opened it and went in to meet Anis al-Jalis. 'Are you the girl whom my father bought for me?' he asked. When she said yes, he went up to her, and, under the influence of wine, he took hold of her legs and wound them around his waist. She twined her arms round his neck and received him with kisses, sighs and coquetry. He sucked her tongue and she sucked his, and he then took her maidenhead. When the two little girls saw their master going in to Anis al-Jalis, they shrieked and cried out, but he had already had his way with her and had fled away, fearing the consequences of what he had done.

When the lady of the house heard the girls shriek, she got up and came out of the bath with sweat dripping from her. 'What is this noise?' she asked, and coming up to the two girls whom she had stationed at Anis al-Jalis's door, she asked them what was the matter. When they saw her, they said: 'Our master, Nur al-Din, came to us and hit us so we ran away from him. Then he went into Anis al-Jalis's room and embraced her; we don't know what he did then, but when we called out to you, he ran off.' The lady then went to Anis al-Jalis and asked: 'What happened?' 'I was sitting here, my lady,' she replied, 'when a handsome young man came in and said: "Are you the girl whom my father has bought for me?" I said yes, for by God, my lady, I thought what he said was true. At that he came up to me and embraced me.' 'Did he say anything else to you?' she asked. 'Yes,' said Anis al-Jalis, 'and he took three kisses from me.' 'He certainly did not leave you without deflowering you,' said the lady, and she burst into tears and both she and the maids slapped their faces, for fear that his father kill Nur al-Din.

While they were in this state, al-Fadl came in and asked what had happened. 'Swear that you will listen to what I have to say,' she said. 'Yes,' he replied, and she then repeated to him what his son had done. He tore his clothes in grief, slapped his face and plucked out his beard. 'Don't kill yourself,' urged his wife. 'I shall give you ten thousand dinars of my own money as her price.' He raised his head and looked at her. 'I don't need her purchase price,' he said. 'My fear is that I shall lose both my life and my money.' 'How is that, master?' she asked. 'Don't you know,' he told her, 'that in the background is my enemy, al-Mu'in ibn Sawa. When he hears of this, he will go to the sultan . . .'

Night 35

Morning now dawned and Shahrazad broke off from what she had been allowed to say. Then, when it was the thirty-fifth night, SHE CONTINUED:

I have heard, O auspicious king, that al-Fadl said to his wife: 'Don't you know that in the background is my enemy, al-Mu'in ibn Sawa. When he hears of this, he will go to the sultan and say: "This vizier of yours, whom you think loves you, has taken ten thousand dinars from you and has used it to buy a slave girl of unequalled beauty. Then when she pleased him, he told his son: 'Do you take her, for you have a better right to her than the sultan.' So he took her and deflowered her and she is now in his house." When the sultan says: "This is a lie," he will ask permission to raid my house and take the girl to him. The sultan will give permission and he will make a surprise attack and carry the girl off to the royal palace. When the sultan asks her, she will not be able to deny what happened. Then al-Mu'in will say: "Master, you know that I gave you sound advice, but I find no favour with you." The sultan will make an example of me with everyone looking on, and I shall lose my life.'

'There is no need to tell anyone about this,' said his wife, 'for it happened in private, and so, as far as this is concerned, leave the affair in the hands of God.' This quieted al-Fadl's agitation, but as for Nur al-Din, he was afraid of what might happen. He stayed all day long in the orchard and at the end of the day he came to his mother and spent the night in her apartments, getting up before dawn and going back to the orchard. For a month, he carried on like this, not showing his face to his father. Then his mother said to his father: 'Master, are we going to lose our son as well as the girl? If this goes on for too long, he will run away from us.' 'What are we to do?' he asked. She said: 'Stay awake tonight and when he comes, take hold of him, reconcile yourself with him and give him the girl, for she loves him and he loves her. I will pay you her price.'

Al-Fadl waited patiently until nightfall, and when Nur al-Din arrived, he seized him and was about to cut his throat. His mother then came up and cried: 'What are you going to do to our son?' 'I shall cut his throat,' he answered. 'Am I of so little value to you?' asked Nur al-Din. Al-Fadl's eyes filled with tears and he said: 'My son, how was it that the loss of my wealth and my life was unimportant to you?' Nur al-Din said: 'Listen to the words of the poet, father:

I may have sinned but men of understanding
Continue to give a general pardon to the sinner.
What is there for your enemy to hope
When he is at the nadir and you at the zenith?'

At that, al-Fadl let go of his son and, moved by pity, told him that he was forgiven, at which Nur al-Din rose and kissed his father's hand. His father said: 'If I knew that you would treat Anis al-Jalis fairly, I would give her to you.' 'How could I not treat her fairly?' asked Nur al-Din. 'I enjoin you,' replied his father, 'not to take another wife or a concubine and not to sell her.' 'I swear to you that I will not take another wife or sell her,' said Nur al-Din, and he swore an oath on this. He then went in to join Anis al-Jalis and stayed with her for a year, while God Almighty caused the king to forget that he had wanted a slave girl.

As for al-Mu'in, the story had come to his ears, but since his fellow vizier stood so high in the sultan's favour, he did not dare to speak about it. At the end of a year, al-Fadl went to the baths, but he was still sweating when he came out and the fresh air proved harmful to him. He took to his bed and spent long sleepless hours as his illness grew worse and worse. He then summoned Nur al-Din and, when he came, he said: 'Know, my son, that what God gives us as our daily bread is apportioned to us, that our allotted time is decreed by fate and that every living soul must drink of the cup of death.' Then he recited:

I am a mortal: great is the Immortal God!
I know for sure that I shall die.
No mortal keeps his kingdom when he dies;
The kingdom belongs to Him Who does not die.

'I have no instruction to give you, my son, except to fear God, to think about the consequences of your actions, and to do what I told you about the slave girl, Anis al-Jalis.' 'Father,' said Nur al-Din, 'who is your equal? You are known for your charitable acts, and preachers bless you from their pulpits.' 'My son,' his father said, 'I hope to find acceptance with Almighty God.' Then he pronounced the two confessions of faith and was enrolled among the blessed. At that, his palace was turned upside down with cries of mourning. News reached the sultan; the people heard of al-Fadl's death and children wept for him in their schools. Nur al-Din, his son, got up and made preparations for the funeral, which was attended by the emirs, officers of state and the people of the city, while among those who came was the vizier al-Mu'in.

When the funeral cortège left the house, someone recited:

On Thursday I parted from my friends;
They washed me on a stone slab by the door.
They stripped me of the clothes that I had on,
Dressing me in what was not my own.
On the shoulders of four men they carried me
To the chapel, where people prayed for me,
Using a prayer where there is no prostration.
All my friends prayed over me, and then
They went with me into a vaulted house,
Whose door shall not be opened, though Time wears all away.

When the earth had been heaped over the corpse and his family and friends had left, Nur al-Din went back home, sobbing and tearful, and reciting in his distress:

They left on a Thursday evening;
I said goodbye to them and they to me.

When they had turned away, my soul went with them.
'Return,' I told it, but it said: 'To where should I return –
To a bloodless body with no breath of life,
That is no more than rattling bones?
My eyes are blinded by the violence of my tears;
My ears are deaf and cannot hear.'

For a long time, he remained in deep mourning for his father, until one day, when he was seated in his father's house, a knock came at the door. He rose and opened it, to find one of his father's intimate friends and companions. The man came in, kissed his hand and said: 'One who has left behind a son like you is not dead, and this is a path trodden by Muhammad, the master of all generations of mankind, earlier and later. Be of good heart, sir, and abandon your mourning.' At that, Nur al-Din got up, went to the reception room and brought there all that was needed. His companions gathered around him, including ten young merchants, and he took his slave girl and began to eat and drink and to hold one entertainment after another, making generous gifts. His agent then came to him and said: 'Sir, have you not heard it said that whoever spends without keeping a reckoning, becomes poor before he knows it? As the poet says:

I act as guardian and defend my cash,
For this, I know, serves as my sword and shield.
If I spend it on my most bitter foes,
I exchange good fortune among men for bad.
I spend on food and drink with happiness,
Giving away no single coin.
I guard my money from mean-natured folk,
Those people who are no true friends of mine.
I like this more than saying to some low man:
"Give me a dirham till tomorrow in exchange for five."
He would shun me, turning away his face,
While my soul would be like that of a dog.
Men without money are disgraced,
Even if their virtues shine out like the sun.'

The agent went on: 'Master, this enormous expenditure and these huge gifts are destroying your wealth.' When Nur al-Din heard what his agent had to say, he looked at him and said: 'I shall not pay attention to a single word of yours, for I have heard what the poet says:

If I have money which I do not give away,
May my hand wither and my foot not stir.
Find me a man whose meanness won him fame,
Or one who died of generosity.'

Then he told the man: 'If you have enough left for my morning meal,
then don't worry me about what to eat in the evening.' The agent left
him, while he himself set about enjoying the life of pleasure on which he
had embarked. Whenever one of his companions said: 'This is a beautiful
thing,' he would say: 'It is yours as a gift,' and if someone else said:
'Such-and-such a house is beautiful,' he would reply: 'I give it to you.'
Both first thing and last thing each day, he would give entertainments,
and for a whole year he continued in this way. Then, after a year was
up, Anis al-Jalis came and recited:

You thought well of Time when Time was kind,
You did not fear the evils fate might bring.
The nights kept peace with you; you were deceived.
It is when the nights are undisturbed that distress comes.

When she had finished these lines, there was a knock on the door. Nur
al-Din got up, followed, although he did not know it, by one of his
companions. When he opened the door, he found his agent, and when
he asked what news he had, the agent said: 'What I feared for you has
happened.' 'How is that?' asked Nur al-Din. 'Know,' replied the man,
'that I have nothing at my disposal worth a dirham, neither more nor
less. Here are the account books showing your expenditure, and these
are the ones that show your original capital.' On hearing this, Nur al-Din
looked down at the ground and exclaimed: 'There is no might and no
power except with God!' The man who had secretly followed him was
there to spy on him, and when he had heard what the agent had to say,
he returned to his companions and told them: 'Mind what you do, for
Nur al-Din is bankrupt.'

When Nur al-Din returned, his distress was plainly written on his face.
One of his drinking companions then got to his feet, looked at him, and
asked politely for leave to go. 'Why do you want to go?' asked Nur
al-Din. 'My wife is giving birth and I cannot be away from her. I would
like to go and see her,' replied the man. When Nur al-Din gave him
leave, another stood up and said that he wanted to go to his brother,
who was circumcising his son, and then everyone produced some excuse

to leave, until eventually they had all gone and Nur al-Din was left alone. He called for Anis al-Jalis and said: 'Do you see what has happened to me?'

He told her about the agent's news and she said: 'For some nights now I have been thinking of talking to you about this, but I heard you reciting:

> If the world is generous to you, be generous with your worldly
> goods,
> And give to everyone before good fortune goes.
> Generosity will not destroy your luck,
> Nor will meanness retain it when it turns away.

When I heard you speak these lines, I stayed silent and said nothing.'

Nur al-Din then pointed out: 'You know that it is only to my companions that I have given away my wealth. They have left me with nothing, but I don't think that they will abandon me without giving me something in return.' 'By God,' said Anis al-Jalis, 'they will be of no help at all to you.' 'I shall go to them at once,' said Nur al-Din, 'and knock on their doors. They may supply me with what I can use as trading capital, and I will then abandon pleasure and idle pastimes.'

He got up immediately and walked to the lane in which all ten of his companions lived. When he knocked on the first door, a slave girl came out and asked him who he was. He said to her: 'Tell your master that Nur al-Din 'Ali is standing at the door and that he says to you: "Your slave kisses your hand and awaits your generosity."' The girl went in and told her master, but he shouted at her and told her to go back and tell Nur al-Din that he was not there, which she did. Nur al-Din turned away, saying to himself: 'If this bastard pretends not to be there, perhaps one of the others may be more generous.' So he went to the door of the second man and repeated what he had said before, but this man, too, pretended not to be in. So Nur al-Din recited:

> They have gone, those who when you were standing at their door
> Would generously give you meats and roasts.

When he had finished these lines, he said: 'By God, I must test every one of them, for it may be that one of them may stand in place of all the rest.' So he went round all ten, but not one opened his door, showed himself or broke a loaf for him. So he recited:

> In his time of fortune man is like a tree;
> People surround it while it bears its fruit.

But when the fruit it bore has gone,
They leave it to endure the heat and dust.
May ill befall the children of this age;
Not one in ten of them has proved sincere.

He then returned with redoubled concern to Anis al-Jalis, who said:
'Didn't I tell you, master, that these people would do you no good at
all?' 'By God,' he replied, 'not one of them would show me his face and
no one would acknowledge me.' 'Master,' she then advised him, 'sell the
furniture and the household goods and wait for God's providence, but
dispose of them bit by bit.'

So Nur al-Din started to sell what he had and he went on until he had
disposed of everything in the house and had nothing left. Then he looked
at Anis al-Jalis and said: 'What shall we do now?' 'My advice, master,
is that you should get up at once, take me down to the market and sell
me. You know that your father bought me for ten thousand dinars, and
it may be that God will open the way for you to get something like that
price. Then later, if God decrees that we should meet, meet we shall.'
'By God, Anis al-Jalis,' he said to her, 'I would not find it easy to part
from you for a single hour.' 'Nor I, master,' she replied, 'but necessity
has its own laws, as the poet says:

Necessity forces men in their affairs
To follow paths that do not fit good manners.
When someone brings himself to do something,
The reason for it matches what he does.'

At that Nur al-Din got to his feet and embraced Anis al-Jalis, with
tears running down his cheeks like rain. He recited in his grief:

Stop; give me a glance before you go,
To distract a heart close to destruction as you leave.
But if you find this burdensome, then let me die
Of love; do not burden yourself.

He then went to the market and handed over Anis al-Jalis to the
auctioneer. 'Hajji Hasan,' he said, 'you know the value of what you are
offering for sale.' 'Master,' the auctioneer said, 'I know the principles of
my trade.' Then he added: 'Isn't this Anis al-Jalis, whom your father
bought from me for ten thousand dinars?' 'It is,' said Nur al-Din, and
Hasan then went to the merchants and, finding that they were not all

there, he waited until they had arrived. The market was packed with slave girls of all races – Turks, Franks, Circassians, Abyssinians, Nubians, Takruris, Rumis, Tartars, Georgians and others. When he saw this, he came forward, took up his position and cried: 'Merchants, men of wealth, not everything round is a walnut; not everything long is a banana; not everything red is meat; and not everything white is fat. But here is a unique pearl beyond all price. How much am I bid for her?' 'Four thousand five hundred dinars,' said one, and the auctioneer opened the bidding at this sum.

As he was calling it out, al-Mu'in ibn Sawa, who happened to be passing, caught sight of Nur al-Din standing at the edge of the market. 'What is Ibn Khaqan's son doing here?' he asked himself. 'Does this good-for-nothing have anything left over for buying slave girls?' He looked then heard the auctioneer in the market, surrounded by merchants, calling for bids. 'I think that Nur al-Din must be bankrupt,' he said to himself, 'and that he has brought Anis al-Jalis to sell her. How refreshing this is for me!'

He summoned the auctioneer, who came and kissed the ground before him. 'I want this girl whom you are auctioning,' al-Mu'in said. The auctioneer could not oppose him and replied: 'Sir, let it be in God's Name.' Then he brought the girl and showed her to him. The vizier approved of her and said: 'Hasan, how much have you been bid for the girl?' 'Four thousand five hundred dinars was the opening bid,' the man replied. 'My bid is four thousand five hundred,' said al-Mu'in, and when they heard that, none of the merchants was able to advance the bidding by a single dirham. They knew al-Mu'in's evil nature and so held back. Al-Mu'in then said to the auctioneer: 'What are you waiting for? Go and bid four thousand dinars for me and you can have five hundred for yourself.' The man went to Nur al-Din and said: 'Master, you have lost the girl for nothing.' 'How is that?' Nur-al-Din asked. 'We opened the auction at four thousand five hundred,' the auctioneer explained, 'and then this tyrant, al-Mu'in, came by the market and admired the girl when he saw her. He told me to get her for four thousand dinars, promising me five hundred for myself. I think that he knows that she belongs to you. Were he to hand over the cash immediately, that would be fine, but I know his evil ways. He will write you a note of hand to get the money from his agents, and then when you have gone he will send a man to tell them not to pay you anything. Every time you go to ask them for the money, they will say: "We'll give it to you soon," and they will put you off like this, day after day. You are a proud man and when they get tired of your coming to press them, they will say: "Show us the note." Then, when you hand it over, they will tear it up, and you will have lost the price of the girl.'

When Nur al-Din heard what the auctioneer had to say, he looked at him and asked what to do. The man replied: 'I can give you advice which, if you accept it, will turn out to your best advantage.' 'What is that?' Nur al-Din asked. 'I suggest,' he replied, 'that you come up to me now as I am standing in the middle of the market and that you snatch the girl from me, slap her and say: "Whore, now that I have brought you to the market, I am released from the oath that I swore to bring you here and to get the auctioneer to call for bids for you. This I have now done." It may be that this ruse will work with al-Mu'in and with the others, and they will think that you only brought her here to fulfil an oath.'

Nur al-Din approved of this strategy. The auctioneer then left him and went to the centre of the market, took the girl by the hand and gestured to al-Mu'in. 'Master,' he said, 'here is her owner just coming.' Nur al-Din then came up to him, snatched the girl from his hands, slapped her and cried: 'Evil take you, you whore! I have brought you to the market to fulfil my oath. So go back home and don't disobey me again. Am I in need of the price you would fetch that I should sell you? If I sold the house furnishings, they would fetch many times more than what I could get for you.' When al-Mu'in saw this, he said: 'Damn you, have you anything left to trade?' and he was about to attack Nur al-Din.

The merchants were all looking on, and Nur al-Din said to them: 'I am in your hands; you know al-Mu'in's tyrannical ways.' 'By God,' said al-Mu'in, 'if it were not for you people, I would kill this fellow.' The merchants were fond of Nur al-Din and they all looked meaningfully at him, as if to say: 'Get your own back on him; none of us will interfere.' At that, Nur al-Din, who was a brave man, went up to the vizier, dragged him from his saddle and threw him to the ground, where there was a kneading trough for clay and it was into the middle of this that he fell. Nur al-Din started to strike him and punch him, and when a blow landed on his teeth, his beard became stained with his blood. Al-Mu'in had with him ten mamluks, and when they saw this happening to their master, their hands went to their sword hilts and they were about to draw their weapons and attack Nur al-Din in order to cut him down when the bystanders called to them: 'One of these is a vizier and the other is the

son of a vizier. It may be that at some time in the future they may become
reconciled, in which case both of them would hate you, or a blow might
strike your master and then you would all die the worst of deaths. The
best advice is for you not to interfere.'

When Nur al-Din had finished drubbing al-Mu'in, he took Anis al-Jalis
and went back home. As for al-Mu'in, he left immediately with his
clothes stained in three colours – the black of the mud, the red of his
blood and the colour of ashes. When he saw the state he was in, he took
a piece of matting and placed it round his neck, and taking two handfuls
of esparto grass, he went to stand beneath the sultan's palace, where he
called out: 'King of the age, I have been wronged.' He was brought
before the sultan, who saw that this was his chief vizier and asked who
had done this. With tears and sobs, the vizier recited:

Can an age in which you live wrong me,
And can wolves devour me when you are a lion?
The thirsty are given water from your trough;
Am I to thirst under your protection when you are the rain?

He added: 'Master, are all those who love you and serve you to suffer
like this?' 'Be quick,' said the sultan, 'and tell me how this happened to
you and who treated you like this, when the respect owed to me covers
you as well.' Al-Mu'in replied: 'You must know, master, that I went
today to the slave girls' market to buy a cook. There I saw the most
beautiful girl that I have ever seen in my life. I wanted to buy her for you
and I asked the auctioneer about her and about her owner. He told me
that she belonged to Nur al-Din 'Ali, the son of al-Fadl ibn Khaqan. You,
master, had earlier given his father ten thousand dinars with which to
buy a pretty slave girl. This was the one whom he bought, but because
he admired her, he was reluctant to see her go to you, and so he gave
her to his son. On his father's death, Nur al-Din sold all his properties,
his orchards and his household goods until he became bankrupt. Then
he took the girl to the market to sell her. He handed her over to the
auctioneer, who put her up for sale, and the merchants bid against each
other until her price reached four thousand dinars. I said to myself: "I
will buy her for my master, the sultan, as it was he who paid the price
for her originally." So I said to Nur al-Din: "My son, take four thousand
dinars from me as her price." When he heard this, he looked at me and
said: "You ill-omened old man, I shall sell her to Jews and Christians,
but I will not sell her to you." "I am not buying her for myself," I said,

"but for our master, the sultan, who is our generous patron." When he heard me say this, he became angry and dragged me from my horse, old man that I am. He struck me and went on punching me until he left me as you see me. The only reason for this was that I had come to buy the girl for you.'

Al-Mu'in then threw himself on the ground and started to weep and to shake. When the sultan saw the state that he was in and heard what he had to say, the vein of anger stood out between his eyes. He turned to the officers of his court and ordered forty men armed with swords who were standing before him to go at once to the house of Nur al-Din, which they were to plunder and then to destroy. 'Tie him and the girl with their hands behind their backs, drag them on their faces and bring them to me.' 'To hear is to obey,' they replied, and they armed themselves and left the palace to set off for Nur al-Din's house.

The sultan had a chamberlain named 'Alam al-Din Sanjar, who had originally been one of the mamluks of al-Fadl ibn Khaqan, Nur al-Din's father. He had risen in rank until he had been employed as a chamberlain by the sultan. When he heard the sultan's orders and saw how his enemies were getting ready to kill his old master's son, he was not prepared to let this be. Leaving the sultan's presence and mounting his horse, he rode to Nur al-Din's house, where he knocked on the door. Nur al-Din came out and recognized him as soon as he saw him. 'Alam al-Din then told him: 'Master, this is not a time for greetings or for words. Listen to what the poet said:

If you meet injustice, save your life,
And let the house lament its builder.
You can replace the country you have left,
But there is no replacement for your life.'*

'What is the news?' asked Nur al-Din. 'Get up and save yourself, you and the girl,' replied 'Alam al-Din. 'Al-Mu'in has laid a trap for you both, and if you fall into his hands, he will kill you. The sultan has sent forty swordsmen to take you, and my advice is to fly before you are harmed.' He put his hand into the pocket of his sash, where he found forty dinars, and these he gave to Nur al-Din, saying: 'Take these, master, and use them for your journey. If I had more, I would give it to you, but this is no time for reproaches.'

* cf. Night 11.

At that, Nur al-Din went in and told Anis al-Jalis, who was almost paralysed with fear. The two of them left the city at once, God covering them with the cloak of His shelter, and after they had walked to the river bank, they found a ship ready to sail. The captain was standing amidships and calling out: 'If anyone needs to fetch provisions or to say goodbye to his family, or if anyone has forgotten anything, they should see to it now, for we are about to sail.' All those on board replied: 'We have nothing left to do,' and at that the captain shouted to the crew: 'Cast off the moorings and up with the poles.' 'Where are you heading for, captain?' asked Nur al-Din. 'The House of Peace, Baghdad,' came the answer.

Night 36

Morning now dawned and Shahrazad broke off from what she had been allowed to say. Then, when it was the thirty-sixth night, SHE CONTINUED:

I have heard, O auspicious king, that the captain told Nur al-Din that he was bound for Baghdad. So Nur al-Din, together with Anis al-Jalis, went aboard. The vessel cast off, and when its sails were unfurled it moved like a bird on the wing, as has been well described by a poet:

> Look at a ship, a captivating sight,
> Racing the wind as it follows on its course,
> Like a bird that has spread its wings,
> Swooping from the air to skim the water.

It carried them off on a fair wind.

So much for them, but as for the mamluks, they came to Nur al-Din's house and broke down the door, but when they entered and went through all the rooms, they could find no trace of their quarry, so they destroyed the house and went back to tell the sultan. 'Search for them wherever they may be,' he ordered, to which they replied: 'To hear is to obey.' Al-Mu'in then went home with a robe of honour which the sultan had given him. He was in a calm state of mind for the sultan had told him: 'No one will take vengeance on your behalf but me.' In return, he had prayed that the sultan would enjoy a long life.

The sultan then made a proclamation to the entire population of the city that whoever found Nur al-Din 'Ali and brought him to him would receive a robe of honour and a gift of a thousand dinars, whereas if anyone hid him or knew where he was but failed to report him, he would bring down on himself an exemplary punishment. A thorough search was then made for Nur al-Din, but no trace of him or news of his whereabouts could be found.

So much for them, but as for Nur al-Din and Anis al-Jalis, they reached Baghdad without mishap. The captain said: 'This is Baghdad, a safe city. The cold of winter has gone; spring has come with its roses; the blossom is on the trees, and the streams are flowing.' Nur al-Din disembarked with Anis al-Jalis, and after he had given the captain five dinars, they walked for a while until, as fate had decreed, they found themselves in the middle of a garden. They came to a place which they found to have been swept out and sprinkled with water. There were benches running lengthways along it and hanging pots filled with water. A reed trellis sheltered the length of the path, and at the head of it was a garden gate, but this was locked. 'This is a beautiful place,' said Nur al-Din to Anis al-Jalis, and she suggested that they sit down on one of the benches to rest. They did this, and then they washed their faces and their hands, after which, as the breeze fanned them, they fell asleep – glory be to Him who does not sleep!

This garden was called the Garden of Pleasure and in it was a palace known as the Palace of Delight and of Statues, the property of Caliph Harun al-Rashid, who would come to the garden and the palace when he was feeling depressed, and sit there. The palace had eighty windows, with eighty hanging lamps, and in the middle there was a great candelabrum made of gold. When the caliph came in, he would tell the slave girls to open the windows. Then he would order the singing girls and his boon companion, Ishaq ibn Ibrahim, to sing, until his depression was relieved and his cares dispelled.

In charge of the garden was a very old man, Shaikh Ibrahim by name. When he went out on some errand, he had very often found pleasure seekers there accompanied by prostitutes, and that made him furiously angry. He waited until one day he had found an opportunity to tell this to the caliph, who had given him permission to do whatever he wanted with anyone he found on the benches by the garden gate. On that particular day, he had gone out to do something and by the gate he found Nur al-Din and Anis al-Jalis covered by a single mantle. 'Good, by God,' he said to himself. 'These people don't know that the caliph has given me official permission to kill anyone I find here. I shall give this pair an ignominious beating, so that no one else will ever come near this gate.' So saying, he cut a green palm branch and went over to the two sleepers. He raised his arm until the white of his armpit could be seen and was on the point of striking them when he thought to himself: 'Ibrahim, how can you strike them when you know nothing about them? They may be strangers or wanderers brought here by fate. I shall uncover their faces and take a look at them.' So he lifted the mantle and then exclaimed: 'What a handsome pair! I must not beat them.' He covered up their faces again and began to massage Nur al-Din's foot.

Nur al-Din opened his eyes, to find at his feet a venerable and dignified old man. In a state of embarrassment, he tucked in his feet and, sitting up, he took Ibrahim's hand and kissed it. Ibrahim asked: 'My son, where do you come from?' Nur al-Din replied: 'Sir, we are strangers,' and his eyes brimmed with tears. Shaikh Ibrahim said: 'Know, my son, that the Prophet – may God bless him and give him peace! – enjoined us to treat strangers hospitably.' Then he added: 'Why don't you get up and go into the garden to enjoy yourselves and relax there?' 'Sir,' asked Nur al-Din, 'who owns this garden?' In reply, Ibrahim told him that he himself had inherited it from his family, his intention being to put his visitors' minds to rest and to encourage them to stroll round the garden.

When Nur al-Din heard this, he thanked him, after which he and Anis al-Jalis got up and, with Ibrahim leading the way, they went further into the garden – and what a garden it was! Its gate was arched like a vaulted hall, covered with vines, whose grapes varied in colour from ruby red to ebony black. They walked beneath a trellis where fruits hung in pairs or singly. On the branches birds sang tunefully, with the nightingale repeating her melodies and the turtledove filling the garden with song, the blackbird warbling like a human singer, and the ringdove singing like one drunk with wine. All kinds of edible fruits were there. There were camphor apricots, almond apricots and the apricots of Khurasan. There were plums coloured like beautiful girls, cherries that keep the teeth from turning yellow, and figs of two colours, red and white. There were flowers like pearls and coral. The redness of the rose put to shame the cheeks of the beautiful women; the violets were like sulphur to which fire has been put at night; and there was myrtle along with gillyflowers, lavender and red anemones. The leaves were bedewed with the tears of the clouds; the mouths of the camomiles smiled. The narcissus looked at the rose with its Negro's eyes; the citrons were like cups and the lemons like nuts of gold. The ground was strewn with flowers of all kinds. Spring had come and its splendour added radiance to the garden. The streams murmured; the notes of the birds filled the air and the wind rustled, so temperate was the season.

Shaikh Ibrahim then took Nur al-Din and Anis al-Jalis into a vaulted hall. As they gazed upon its beauty and at the candles in the windows, Nur al-Din remembered past entertainments and said: 'By God, this is a pleasant place!' He and Anis al-Jalis sat down and Ibrahim brought out food, of which they ate their fill. Nur al-Din went to a window and called to Anis al-Jalis, who joined him there and they looked out at the trees with their various fruits. He then turned to Ibrahim and asked him whether he had anything to drink: 'For people drink after they have eaten.' Ibrahim brought him water, pleasant, cool and sweet, but he said: 'This is not the type of drink that I want.' 'Perhaps you would prefer wine?' asked Ibrahim, and when Nur al-Din said yes, he added: 'I take refuge with God from wine. For thirteen years I have not drunk it, as the Prophet – may God bless him and give him peace! – cursed those who drink it as well as those who press its grapes, those who sell it and those who buy it.' 'Listen to a couple of words from me,' said Nur al-Din, and when he was urged to go on, he said: 'If this damned donkey is cursed, will the curse hurt you at all?' 'No,' replied Ibrahim. 'Then take this dinar,' Nur al-Din told him, 'and these two dirhams, get on the donkey and stop some distance away. When you come across someone making purchases, call to him and say: "Take these two dirhams and use this dinar to buy wine." Then set the wine on the donkey, and as you will not have carried it or bought it, no harm will come to you from it.'

Ibrahim laughed when he heard this and said: 'By God, my son, I have not met anyone with a more penetrating wit or more pleasant speech than you.' So he did as Nur al-Din had asked him, and Nur al-Din thanked him and said: 'We are now your responsibility and, as you must agree to what we ask, bring us what we need.' 'My son,' said Ibrahim, 'here in front of you is my pantry, a storeroom made ready for the Commander of the Faithful. Go and take what you like, for there is more there than you can need.' Nur al-Din went in and found utensils of gold, silver and crystal, studded with gems of all kinds. He took them out, set them in a row, and poured wine into jugs and bottles. He was pleased by what he saw to the point of astonishment. Shaikh Ibrahim brought fruits and scented flowers, and then went and sat at some distance from the couple. They drank with enjoyment, and, as the wine took hold of them, their cheeks grew red, they exchanged amorous glances, and their hair hung down as their colour changed.

Shaikh Ibrahim said to himself: 'Why am I sitting so far away? Why don't I sit with them, and when else am I going to find myself in the company of two shining moons like these?' He went up to sit at the edge of the dais, and when Nur al-Din urged him to come and sit with them, he came forward. The young man filled a glass and, addressing Ibrahim, said: 'Drink this, so that you can see what it tastes like.' 'I take refuge with God,' Ibrahim replied. 'For thirteen years I have not touched a drop.' Nur al-Din then drank the glass himself and threw himself on the ground, as though he was drunk. Anis al-Jalis then looked at him and said: 'See how he treats me, Shaikh Ibrahim.' 'What is wrong with him, lady?' asked Ibrahim. 'He always does this to me,' she replied. 'He drinks for a time and then falls asleep, leaving me on my own with no one to share my glass with me, and no one for whom I can sing as he drinks.'

Filled with tenderness and sympathy towards her because of what she had said, Ibrahim exclaimed: 'By God, that is not good.' She filled a glass and, looking at him, she said: 'By my life, please take this and drink it. Don't reject it, but mend my broken heart.' So Ibrahim put out his hand, took the glass and downed it. She then filled a second one, and setting it by a candle, she said: 'There is still this one here for you.' 'By God, I cannot drink it,' he replied. 'The one that I had was enough for me.' But when she insisted, he took it and drank it, after which she gave him a third, which he also took. He was about to drink when Nur al-Din stirred, sat up . . .

Night 37

Morning now dawned and Shahrazad broke off from what she had been allowed to say. Then, when it was the thirty-seventh night, SHE CONTINUED:

I have heard, O auspicious king, that Nur al-Din sat up and said: 'What is this, Shaikh Ibrahim? Didn't I press you to drink some time ago only for you to refuse, saying that you hadn't drunk for thirteen years?' Ibrahim was ashamed and said: 'By God, it wasn't my fault. It was she who told me to do it.' Nur al-Din laughed and they all sat down to drink together. Anis al-Jalis then turned and whispered privately to her master: 'Drink up but don't press the *shaikh*, and I'll show you what he does.' So she started to fill Nur al-Din's glass and gave it to him to drink, while he did the same for her. They did this time after time until Ibrahim looked at them and said: 'What kind of good fellowship is this? God curse the greedy! You don't pour me a drink, brother, when it is my turn. What is all this, bless you?' Nur al-Din and Anis al-Jalis laughed until they fell over, and they then drank up and poured wine for Ibrahim.

They went on drinking together until a third of the night had passed. Then Anis al-Jalis asked Ibrahim: 'Have I your permission to get up and light one of this row of candles?' 'Get up,' he said, 'but only light a single one of them.' She got to her feet and, beginning with the first, she lit all eighty candles in the row before sitting down again. Nur al-Din then asked the *shaikh*: 'What share are you going to allow me? Won't you let me light one of these lamps?' 'Get up and light one,' said Ibrahim, 'but don't you make trouble, too.' So Nur al-Din got up and, beginning with the first, he lit all eighty lamps, until the place danced with light. 'You two are bolder than I am,' said Ibrahim, who was under the influence of drink. He got to his feet, opened all the windows, and then took his place with his guests, after which they sat drinking together and exchanging lines of verse, while the house was filled with flickering light.

As had been decreed by God Almighty, Who assigns to everything a cause, the caliph was looking out in the moonlight towards one of the windows on the Tigris side, and he saw the lights of the lamps and the candles reflected in the river. On seeing the garden palace flickering with light, he ordered Ja'far the Barmecide to be brought to him. He came immediately, and the caliph said: 'Dog of a vizier, are you taking the city of Baghdad from me without saying?' When Ja'far asked him what he was talking about, he said: 'Unless the city had been taken from me, the Palace of Statues would not be lit by lamps and candles, with all the windows open. Who would dare to do this had I not been stripped of the caliphate?' In fear and trembling, Ja'far asked: 'Who told you that lights were lit in the Palace of Statues and that its windows were open?' 'Come over here,' said the caliph, 'and look out.'

When Ja'far looked out towards the garden, he found that lights from the garden palace were illumining the darkness. He wanted to find an excuse for the gardener, Shaikh Ibrahim, thinking that perhaps this had been done with his permission for what he had thought to be a good reason. So he said: 'Commander of the Faithful, last Friday Shaikh Ibrahim told me that he wanted to hold a party for his sons during the lifetime of the Commander of the Faithful and my own life. "What do you need?" I asked him. "I want you to get me an order from the caliph," he replied, "allowing me to circumcise my sons in the palace." "Go ahead and arrange this," I said, "and I shall approach the caliph and tell

him about it." So he left me, and I forgot to tell you.' 'You were guilty
of one offence against me, Ja'far, and then it became two. Of your two
mistakes, the first was that you failed to tell me about this, and the
second was that you did not give Shaikh Ibrahim what he wanted. He
only approached you and said what he said as a hint that he was in need
of money. You neither gave him anything nor did you tell me.' 'I forgot,
Commander of the Faithful,' said Ja'far. 'I swear by my fathers and my
forefathers,' said the caliph, 'that I shall not spend the rest of the night
anywhere else but with him. He is a good man who entertains *shaikhs*
and *faqirs*, and as they are gathered at his home, it may be that one of
them may give us a blessing that will help us, both in this world and the
next. Some good may come if I visit him and I may give him pleasure.'
'Commander of the Faithful,' said Ja'far, 'it is late and they must be
nearly finished.' The caliph, however, insisted on going, and Ja'far kept
silent, being at a loss and not knowing what to do.

So the caliph got up, and with Ja'far going on ahead and accompanied
by Masrur, the eunuch, all disguised as merchants, he walked from the
royal palace through the lanes until they came to the garden gate. When
the caliph went up to it, he was surprised to find it open. 'See how Shaikh
Ibrahim has left the gate open and at such a late hour,' he said to Ja'far,
adding: 'He is not in the habit of doing this.' They entered and, on
reaching the end of the garden, they stood beneath the palace wall. 'I
want to spy out the ground,' said the caliph, 'before I show myself to
them, so that I can see what they are doing and take a look at the *shaikhs*.
For up till now I have not heard any sound from them, or from any *faqir*
reciting the Name of God.' He then noticed a high walnut tree and said:
'Ja'far, I shall climb this tree, as its branches are near the windows and
I can look in at the company.'

Up he went, and he went on climbing from one branch to the next
until he reached one opposite a window. Looking through the window,
he saw a girl and a young man, radiant as moons – praise be to Him
Who created them and formed them! He saw Shaikh Ibrahim sitting
glass in hand and heard him saying: 'Queen of the beauties, it is no good
drinking without music. I have heard that the poet says:

Pass round the glasses, great and small;
Take them from the hand of a resplendent moon,
But do not drink without music.
A horse will only drink when whistled to.'

When the caliph saw what Shaikh Ibrahim was doing, the vein of anger rose between his eyes. He climbed down the tree and told Ja'far: 'I have never seen pious men behaving like this, so climb the tree yourself and have a look, in case you lose the benefit of the blessings of the pious.' Ja'far was taken aback by this, but he climbed to the top of the tree and, looking in, he saw Nur al-Din, Shaikh Ibrahim and the girl. The *shaikh* was holding a glass in his hand, and when Ja'far saw this, he was certain that death awaited him. He climbed down and stood before the caliph, who said to him: 'Praise be to God Who has placed us among those who follow the literal meaning of the revealed law!' As Ja'far was too abashed to speak, he went on: 'Who do you suppose brought these people here and who took them into my palace?' and he added: 'But I have never seen beauty like that of this young man and this girl.'

Ja'far, hoping to placate the caliph, agreed with him, and the caliph told him to climb up with him to the branch opposite the window to get a view of what was going on. The two climbed up the tree, and when they looked through the window, they heard Ibrahim saying: 'I have abandoned my dignity by drinking wine, but it only becomes pleasant when it is accompanied by music.' 'Shaikh Ibrahim,' said Anis al-Jalis, 'if we had with us any musical instrument, then our pleasure would indeed be complete.' Ibrahim got up when he heard this. 'What do you suppose he is going to do?' the caliph asked Ja'far. 'I don't know,' replied Ja'far, but when Ibrahim left and then came back with a lute, the caliph recognized it as belonging to his boon companion, Abu Ishaq. 'By God,' he said, 'if this girl sings badly, I will crucify you all, and if she sings well, I will only crucify you.' 'May God make her sing badly!' exclaimed Ja'far. 'Why?' asked the caliph. 'So that, if you crucify us all, we can keep each other company,' Ja'far replied, at which the caliph laughed.

Anis al-Jalis then took the lute, inspected it, tuned the strings and struck up a strain that moved hearts with longing. Then she recited the lines:

You who bring poor lovers aid,
The fires of love and longing consume me.
Whatever you may do, this I deserve.
You are my refuge; do not laugh at my misfortune.
I am abashed and wretched; do what you want with me.
It is no cause for pride to kill me in your camp;
My fear is that you sin by killing me.

'Excellent, by God, Ja'far,' said the caliph. 'Never in my life have I heard a voice as delightful as this.' Ja'far then asked whether his anger had left him. 'Yes, it has gone,' he replied, after which the two of them climbed down from the tree. The caliph then said to Ja'far: 'I want to go and sit with them and listen to the girl singing in front of me.' 'If you do,' said Ja'far, 'it may disturb them, while as for Shaikh Ibrahim, he will die of fear.' 'Then, Ja'far,' said the caliph, 'you must teach me how to trick them, so that I can meet them without their knowing who I am.'

As the two of them went towards the Tigris, thinking over the problem, they came across a fisherman, who was casting his net beneath the palace windows. Some time earlier, the caliph had called to Ibrahim to ask him what the noises were that he could hear beneath the windows of his palace. On being told that these were the voices of fishermen, he had told Ibrahim to go down and stop them fishing there, and as a result, fishermen had been ordered to keep away. That night, however, one of them, called Karim, had come and found the garden gate open. He had said to himself that somebody must have been careless and that it was time to take advantage of it. He had taken his net and cast it into the river, but then all of a sudden he saw the caliph standing beside him.

The caliph had recognized him and addressed him by name. On hearing himself being addressed as 'Karim', the fisherman had turned, and at the sight of the caliph, he began to tremble. 'Commander of the Faithful,' he said, 'I have not done this out of disrespect for your orders, but poverty and the needs of my family have led me to do what you see me doing.' 'Try a cast in my name,' said the caliph, and the fisherman came up joyfully, cast his net and waited until it had opened to its fullest extent and settled on the bottom, before drawing it in. It turned out to be filled with all kinds of fish, which pleased the caliph. He then told Karim to take off his clothes, a smock with a hundred patches of rough wool, full of long-tailed lice, and on his head a turban that he had not unwound for three years and on to which he had sewn every rag that he could find. The caliph then stripped off two robes of Alexandrian and Baalbaki silk, as well as an over-mantle and a mantle. He told Karim to take these and put them on, while he in turn put on Karim's smock and turban, veiling the lower part of his face. 'Now go about your business,' he told Karim, who kissed his foot, thanked him and started to recite:

You have granted favours, for which I proclaim my gratitude,
And you have aided me in all affairs of mine.
Throughout my life I shall give you thanks, and if I die
My bones will proclaim their gratitude from my grave.

Before the fisherman had finished his poem, the lice started crawling
over the caliph's skin and he had to use both hands to pull them off his
neck and throw them away. 'You wretched fisherman,' he exclaimed,
'there are swarms of lice in this smock!' 'They may annoy you just now,
master,' said Karim, 'but after a week you won't notice them or think
about them.' The caliph laughed and said: 'Am I to go on wearing this
smock?' 'I would like to say something,' said Karim. 'Say on,' replied
the caliph. 'It has struck me, Commander of the Faithful,' said Karim,
'that if you want to learn how to fish so as to be master of a useful trade,
this smock will suit you.' The caliph laughed at this and the fisherman
went on his way.

The caliph then picked up the basket of fish, placed a few green leaves
on top of it and approached Ja'far. When he stood before him, Ja'far
believed that he was Karim the fisherman and was afraid for the man's
safety. 'Karim,' he said, 'what has brought you here? Save yourself, for
the caliph is in the garden tonight, and if he sees you, you will lose your
life.' On hearing this, the caliph laughed, and Ja'far, recognizing him by
his laugh, said: 'Perhaps you are the caliph, our master?' 'Yes, Ja'far,' he
replied, 'and you are my vizier. You and I came here together and yet
you didn't recognize me, so how is Shaikh Ibrahim going to recognize
me when he is drunk? Stay here until I come back to you.' 'To hear is to
obey,' said Ja'far.

The caliph then went to the door of the garden palace and knocked
on it softly. 'Somebody is knocking on the door,' said Nur al-Din to
Ibrahim. 'Who is there?' asked Ibrahim. 'It is I, Shaikh Ibrahim,'
answered the caliph. 'Who are you?' repeated Ibrahim, and the caliph
told him: 'Karim, the fisherman,' adding: 'I heard that you have guests,
so I have brought you some fresh fish.' When Nur al-Din heard him say
'fish', both he and Anis al-Jalis were delighted and they asked Ibrahim
to open the door and let the man in. Ibrahim did that and the caliph, in his
disguise as a fisherman, came in and began by greeting them. 'Welcome to
the thief, the robber, the gambler,' said Ibrahim. 'Come and show us
what fish you have.' The fish the caliph showed them were still alive and
wriggling, and Anis al-Jalis said: 'Sir, these are fine fish, but I wish they

were fried.' 'You're right, lady,' said Ibrahim, and he then asked the caliph: 'Why didn't you bring these fish fried? Go off at once, fry them and then fetch them back to us.' 'At your command,' said the caliph. 'I'll fry them for you and then bring them back.' 'Get on with it,' they told him, so he ran off until he reached Ja'far.

'Ja'far,' he called. 'Yes, Commander of the Faithful,' said the vizier, 'is everything all right?' 'They have asked for the fish to be fried,' replied the caliph. 'Hand them over, Commander of the Faithful,' said Ja'far, 'and I shall do the frying for them.' 'By the graves of my fathers and my forefathers,' swore the caliph, 'no one else is going to fry these fish. I shall do it with my own hand.' He then went to the gardener's hut, and after rummaging through it, he found everything that he needed, including salt, saffron, thyme and other seasonings. He went to the brazier, set the frying pan on it and fried the fish nicely. When they were ready, he put them on a banana leaf, and after collecting some windfalls and some lemons from the garden, he took the fish and presented them to the three in the palace.

All three came forward and ate, and when they had finished and had washed their hands, Nur al-Din said: 'Fisherman, this is a very good turn you have done us tonight.' He put his hand in his pocket and brought out three of the dinars that Sanjar had given him when he left on his travels. 'Excuse me, fisherman,' he said, 'for, by God, had you known me before I fell from fortune, I would have removed the bitterness of poverty from your heart, but take what matches my present state.' He then threw the coins towards the caliph, who took them, kissed them and put them away.

What the caliph had wanted, by doing this, was to hear Anis al-Jalis sing. So he said: 'You have bestowed a generous favour on me, but what I want from your all-embracing bounty is to hear this girl sing a song for us.' 'Anis al-Jalis,' called Nur al-Din, and when she answered, he asked her: 'Sing something to please this fisherman, for he wants to listen to you.' On hearing this, Anis al-Jalis took the lute, tuned the strings, struck up a melody and sang:

There is many a girl whose fingers have held the lute,
Stealing away men's souls as she touched the strings.
As she sang, her singing cured the deaf,
While the dumb cried out: 'Well done, indeed!'

She then began a remarkable and bewitching strain, to which she sang:

> We are honoured that you have visited our land,
> And your splendour has driven away our gloomy dark.
> It is only right I should perfume my house
> With camphor, musk and rosewater.

The caliph was moved and overcome by emotion, so much so that in his delight he could not control himself. 'Good, by God! Good, by God! Good, by God!' he kept saying. 'Does the girl please you, fisherman?' asked Nur al-Din. 'Yes, by God,' replied the caliph. 'Then she is a present to you from me,' said Nur al-Din, 'the gift of a generous man who does not reclaim or take back what he gives.' He then got to his feet, took an over-mantle and threw it round the fisherman, telling him to go off with the girl. Anis al-Jalis looked at him and said: 'Master, are you going without saying goodbye? If this has to be, stay until I take my leave of you and find relief.' Then she started to recite these lines:

> I suffer longing, memories and sorrow,
> That make my wasted body like a ghost.
> Beloved, do not say I shall forget;
> Despair comes from despair and my grief will not cease.
> If anyone could swim in his own tears,
> The first to do so would be I.
> Your love holds sway within my heart
> As water and wine are mixed in the same glass.
> This is the separation which I feared,
> O you, whose love is in my inmost heart.
> O Ibn Khaqan, you are my wish and hope;
> Your love can never leave my heart.
> It was because of me that our sultan
> Became your enemy and you were driven out.
> May God not cause you to regret my loss.
> You have given me to a generous man who earns our praise.

When she had finished, Nur al-Din replied to her with the lines:

> She took her leave of me the day we parted;
> The pangs of longing made her weep and say:
> 'What will you find to do when I have gone?'
> I said: 'Say this to one who stays alive.'

When the caliph heard Anis al-Jalis say: 'You have given me to a generous man,' his desire for her increased, but he found it hard to think of parting the two. So he said to Nur al-Din: 'Sir, in her verses this girl said that you had made an enemy of her master and owner. Tell me, who is this enemy of yours and who has a claim against you?' 'By God, fisherman,' answered Nur al-Din, 'this girl and I share a strange and remarkable story which, were it written with needles on the corners of the eyes, would serve as a lesson for those who can learn.' 'Please tell me what happened to you and let me know your story,' said the caliph. 'It may be that you will find relief from your plight, as relief sent by God is close at hand.'

Nur al-Din asked him whether he wanted to hear the story in prose or verse. 'Prose,' said the caliph, 'is only speech, but poetry is strung pearls.' At that, Nur al-Din looked down at the ground and recited:

Friend, I have abandoned sleep;
Exile has made my cares increase.
My father was affectionate,
But he left me and went down to the grave.
With him my fortune perished,
And I became broken in heart.
He bought for me a girl,
Whose pliant figure put the boughs to shame.
All my inheritance I spent on her,
And I gave generously to the generous.
My cares increased; I offered her for sale,
Though pangs of parting were not what I wished.
When bids were called for by the auctioneer,
The highest came from a depraved old man.
At this, my anger blazed up and I snatched
Her hand away from that old scoundrel's grasp.
The wretch struck me in anger, and the fire
Of evil-doing kindled in his heart.
I hit him with my right hand and my left
In anger, until my distress was cured.
I was afraid and went back to my house,
Hiding away for fear of enemies.
The ruler of the land ordered me to be seized;
His chamberlain, a man of rectitude,

Warned me that I should flee out of their reach,
Thus saddening my jealous enemies.
Sheltered by darkness we then left our house,
Looking to come and stay here in Baghdad.
Fisherman, I have no treasures I can give,
Except for what I have already given.
But here you have the darling of my heart;
Be sure it is my own heart that I give.

When he had finished these lines, the caliph asked him to explain the affair, and Nur al-Din told him what had happened from beginning to end. When the caliph understood the situation, he asked: 'Where are you making for now?' and Nur al-Din replied: 'God's lands are wide.' The caliph then said: 'I shall write you a note to take to the sultan Muhammad ibn Sulaiman al-Zaini and when he reads it, he will do you no harm or injury.'

Night 38

Morning now dawned and Shahrazad broke off from what she had been allowed to say. Then, when it was the thirty-eighth night, SHE CONTINUED:

I have heard, O auspicious king, that the caliph said: 'I shall write you a note to take to the sultan Muhammad ibn Sulaiman al-Zaini and when he reads it, he will do you no harm or injury.' 'Is there in this world a fisherman who writes to kings?' asked Nur al-Din. 'This is something that can never be.' 'That is true,' replied the caliph, 'but I shall tell you the reason. Muhammad and I studied in the same school with one and the same teacher, and I was his monitor. He then enjoyed good fortune and became a sultan, while God demoted me and made me a fisherman, but every time I write to ask him for something, he does what I ask, and this would be true even if I sent him a thousand requests a day.' 'That is good,' said Nur al-Din. 'Write and let me see it.' So the caliph took an inkstand and a pen and wrote: 'In the Name of God, the Compassionate, the Merciful. To continue: this letter is sent from Harun al-Rashid ibn al-Mahdi to Muhammad ibn Sulaiman al-Zaini, who enjoys my gracious favour and whom I have appointed as my lieutenant in one part of my kingdom. This letter is brought to you by Nur al-Din 'Ali, son of the vizier Ibn Khaqan. As soon as it reaches you, depose yourself from your sultanate and invest him with it. Do not disobey my order. Peace be on you.' The caliph then gave the letter to Nur al-Din, who kissed it, placed it in his turban and set off at once on his journey.

So much for him, but as for the caliph, Shaikh Ibrahim looked at him dressed as he was as a fisherman, and said: 'You vilest of fishermen, you take three dinars for bringing us a couple of fish worth twenty *nusfs*, and then you want to take off the girl as well?' When he heard this, the caliph shouted at him and made a sign to Masrur, who came out of hiding and attacked Ibrahim. Ja'far, meanwhile, had sent one of the gardener's boys to the gatekeeper of the palace to fetch some royal robes. The boy, having carried out the errand, kissed the ground in front of the caliph, who took off what he was wearing, handed it to the boy, and then put on the clothes that had been brought for him. Ibrahim, who had been looking on, was flabbergasted at what he saw and sat biting his nails distractedly and saying: 'Am I asleep or awake?' The caliph looked at him and said: 'Shaikh Ibrahim, what is this state that you are in?' At that, Ibrahim recovered from his drunkenness, threw himself on the ground and recited:

> Forgive the crime that caused my foot to slip.
> The servant seeks generosity from his master.
> I admit that I have followed the demands of sin,
> But where are those of forgiveness and generosity?

The caliph forgave him and ordered that the girl be taken to the royal palace, where he gave her a room of her own and assigned her servants. 'Know,' he told her, 'that I have sent your master to be sultan of Basra, and, if God Almighty wills it, I shall despatch him a robe of honour, and shall send you to join him.'

So much for them, but as for Nur al-Din, he travelled on to Basra, where he went up to the sultan's palace and gave a loud shout. The sultan heard him and sent for him. On entering Nur al-Din kissed the ground, and then produced his note and handed it over. When he saw that the Commander of the Faithful had addressed it in his own hand, the sultan rose to his feet, kissed it three times, and said: 'To hear is to obey Almighty God and the Commander of the Faithful.' He then summoned the four *qadis* and the emirs, and was about to abdicate when al-Mu'in arrived. The sultan handed him the note, but when he saw it he tore it into pieces, took the pieces in his mouth, chewed them and then spat them out.

The sultan was angry and said: 'Wretch, what prompted you to do this?' 'By your life, master,' said al-Mu'in, 'this fellow has never met the caliph or his vizier; he is the spawn of a scheming devil, who has come across a blank sheet of paper signed by the caliph, and has used it for his own ends. The caliph cannot have sent him to take the sultanate from you without an official rescript or a diploma of investiture. He has never, never, never come from the caliph! Had the tale been true, the caliph would have sent a chamberlain with him, or a vizier, but he has come alone.' 'What is to be done, then?' asked the sultan. 'Send him with me,' said al-Mu'in. 'I will take him off your hands and despatch him with a chamberlain to Baghdad. If what he says is true, he can come back to us with a rescript and a diploma, and if he cannot produce these, I shall punish him as his crime deserves.'

When the sultan heard what al-Mu'in had to say, he agreed to hand over Nur al-Din to him. Al-Mu'in then took him to his house and shouted to his servants, who stretched him out and beat him until he fainted. He then had heavy fetters put on his feet and took him to the prison, where he called out for the gaoler, a man named Qutait, who came and kissed the ground before him. 'Qutait,' said al-Mu'in, 'I want you to take this man and throw him into one of your underground dungeons and torture him night and day.' 'To hear is to obey,' said the gaoler. He took Nur al-Din into the prison and shut the door on him, but then gave orders for the stone bench behind the door to be swept, and on it he laid a mattress and a leather mat. He let Nur al-Din sit on this, loosed his fetters and treated him well. Every day al-Mu'in would send word to him, telling him to beat Nur al-Din, but instead he protected him, and this went on for forty days.

On the forty-first day, a gift came from the caliph. When the sultan saw it, he admired it and consulted his viziers about it. 'It may be meant for the new sultan,' said one of them, but al-Mu'in said: 'The right thing to have done would have been to kill him as soon as he came.' 'By God,' said the sultan, 'you have reminded me of him. Go and fetch him and then cut off his head.' 'To hear is to obey,' said al-Mu'in, and he added: 'I wish to have it proclaimed in the city that whoever wants to enjoy the spectacle of the execution of Nur al-Din 'Ali should come to the palace. Everyone, high or low, will come to watch and I shall have had my revenge as well as bringing distress to those who envy me.'

The sultan gave him permission to do as he wanted, and so al-Mu'in, glad and happy, went to the *wali* and ordered him to have the proclamation made. When the people heard it, they all shed tears of grief, even the children in their schools and the common people in the shops. Some raced to get places to watch the spectacle, while others went to the prison in order to accompany Nur al-Din. Al-Mu'in, escorted by ten mamluks, went there, and he was asked by Qutait what he wanted. 'Bring me this wretch,' replied the vizier. 'He is in the worst of states because of his frequent beatings,' said Qutait, and he then went in and found Nur al-Din reciting:

> Who will help me in my affliction?
> My disease has increased and its cure is hard to find.
> Separation has affected my heart's blood and my last breath of life,
> While Time has changed my friends, making them foes.
> Are there any here with pity and compassion
> To weep for my state or answer to my cry?
> The pangs of death are easy for me to bear;
> I have abandoned all hopes of a pleasant life.
> O Lord, in the name of our guide, the chosen bringer of good news,
> Ocean of knowledge, lord of intercessors,
> I call on You to rescue me and to forgive my fault,
> Removing from me hardship and distress.

When he had finished speaking, the gaoler removed his clean clothes and, after giving him dirty ones to put on, he brought him to al-Mu'in. At the sight of his enemy who wanted to kill him, Nur al-Din wept and said: 'Do you feel secure against the blows of time? Have you not heard the words of the poet:

> Where are the mighty Persian kings? They hoarded treasures,
> But the treasures are gone, as are the kings.'

'Know, vizier,' he added, 'that it is God, Great and Glorious, who acts according to His wish.' 'Are you trying to frighten me by saying this?' asked al-Mu'in. 'Today I shall have you executed in spite of all the people of Basra, without any thought for the consequences. Let Time do what it wants, for I shall not listen to your advice but rather to the words of another poet:

> Let the days act as they will; be content with your present fate.

How well another poet has written:

> He who outlives his enemy by a day has won his heart's desire.'

Al-Mu'in then ordered his servants to place Nur al-Din on the back
of a mule. They were unhappy with this order and said to Nur al-Din:
'Let us stone this man and cut him to pieces, even if this costs us our
lives.' 'No, never,' replied Nur al-Din. 'Have you not heard what the
poet said:

Inevitably I have an allotted time to live,
And when its days are finished, I shall die.
Were lions to drag me to their lair,
They could not end my life, if time were still assigned to me.'

As Nur al-Din was being led along, it was proclaimed: 'This is the
least of requitals for those who invent lies against kings.' They continued
to lead him around Basra until they halted with him under the window
of the palace and set him on the execution mat. The executioner came
up to him and said: 'Master, I am a slave acting under orders in this
matter. If you have any needs, let me know so that I may fulfil them for
you, as your life must end when the sultan shows his face from that
window.' Nur al-Din looked right and left, before and behind, and then
recited:

I see the sword, the swordsman and the mat,
And I lament humiliation and my great misfortune.
Do I see no compassionate friend to give me help?
I have asked you; now reply to me.
The span of my life is over and my death is near.
Will none show mercy and win God's reward for this,
Looking at my plight, relieving my distress
With a drink of water, to lessen my suffering?

The people wept for him and the executioner brought a drink of water
which he was offering to him when al-Mu'in rose from his place and
dashed the jug from his hand, breaking it. He shouted to the executioner,
ordering him to strike off Nur al-Din's head. Nur al-Din was blindfolded
and the people were in uproar, shouting at al-Mu'in. Then there was a
tumultuous noise and the people all turned to each other, wondering
what to do. While they were in this state of confusion, suddenly a dust
cloud could be seen rising and filling the sky and the open country. The
sultan, sitting in his palace, noticed it and told his servants to find out
what was happening. 'First, let us execute this man,' said al-Mu'in, but
the sultan told him to wait until they had learned the news.

The dust was that of Ja'far the Barmecide, the caliph's vizier, who was riding with his retinue. The reason for his coming was that the caliph had spent thirty days without thinking of the story of Nur al-Din and without being reminded of it by anyone. Then, one night he came to Anis al-Jalis's room where he heard her sobbing and reciting in a beautiful and charming voice the lines of the poet:

Whether you are far from me or near,
Your image never leaves me, and your name
Is never absent from my tongue.

She then wept even more, and when the caliph opened the door of her room, he saw her sitting there in tears. When she caught sight of him, she threw herself on the ground, kissed his feet three times and recited:

You of pure race, well-born,
Well-planted, ripe and fruitful branch,
I remind you of the promise that you made,
In your great generosity. God forbid that you forget!

'Who are you?' asked the caliph. 'I am the gift given you by Nur al-Din 'Ali and I want you to fulfil the promise that you made me, when you said that you would send me to him with a letter of appointment. Thirty days have now passed, during which I have not tasted sleep.' At that, the caliph summoned Ja'far and said: 'For thirty days I have heard no news of Nur al-Din, and I cannot but think that the sultan may have killed him. I swear by my head and by the graves of my fathers and my forefathers, if any harm has been done to him, I shall destroy whoever caused it, even if he were my dearest friend. I want you to go at once to Basra and to find out what the sultan has done with Nur al-Din. If you spend any longer away than the length of the journey warrants, I will cut off your head. You are to tell my cousin, the sultan, the story of Nur al-Din, and that I sent him off with a letter from me. If you find that he has done anything other than what I ordered in my letter, then you are to bring him and al-Mu'in in whatever state you find them, and you are not to be away for any longer than the journey requires.' 'To hear is to obey,' replied Ja'far.

The vizier made his preparations immediately and travelled to Basra, where news of his coming preceded him to the sultan. When he arrived, he noticed the disturbance and the thronging crowds. He asked what the matter was and was told about Nur al-Din. When he heard this, he hurried to the sultan and explained his errand, adding that if Nur al-Din had come to any harm, the caliph would execute whoever was responsible. He then arrested both the sultan and al-Mu'in, keeping them confined, while he ordered the release of Nur al-Din, whom he installed as the new ruler.

Ja'far stayed in Basra for three days, this being the fixed period for hospitality, and on the morning of the fourth day, Nur al-Din turned to him and said: 'I should like to see the Commander of the Faithful.' Ja'far instructed the ex-sultan, Muhammad ibn Sulaiman al-Zaini, to make ready to leave, telling him that they would set out for Baghdad after the morning prayer, to which Muhammad replied: 'To hear is to obey.' After the prayer, they all started off, taking with them al-Mu'in, who was beginning to regret what he had done. Nur al-Din rode beside Ja'far and they went on to Baghdad, the House of Peace, where they came into the caliph's presence. When the caliph was told about Nur al-Din and how he had been found on the point of death, he went up to him and said: 'Take this sword and cut off the head of your enemy.' Nur al-Din took the sword and advanced towards al-Mu'in, who looked at him and said: 'I acted according to my nature, so do you act according to yours.' Nur al-Din then threw away the sword, looked at the caliph and said: 'He has got round me by these words.' Then he recited:

> When he came, he deceived me by a trick;
> The noble man is deceived by soft words.

'Leave him, then,' said the caliph and, turning to Masrur, he said: 'Masrur, do you cut off his head,' at which Masrur rose and beheaded al-Mu'in. The caliph then promised to grant Nur al-Din a wish. 'Master,' he replied, 'I have no need of the sultanate of Basra. My only wish is to have the honour of serving you and to see your face.' The caliph willingly granted his request and he then sent for Anis al-Jalis. When she came, he showered gifts on them both, gave them one of the palaces of Baghdad and assigned them allowances. Nur al-Din was made one of his boon companions, and he stayed with him, enjoying the most pleasurable of lives until the time of his death.

'This story,' said Shahrazad, 'is no more remarkable than that of the merchant and his sons.' 'How is that?' asked the king. 'I have heard, O auspicious king,' she replied, 'that once upon a time there was a wealthy merchant who had a son like the full moon, with an eloquent tongue, named Ghanim ibn Ayyub, known as the slave of love, whose wits had been stolen away. Ghanim had a sister named Fitna, who was unique in her beauty. Their father died, leaving them great wealth.'

Night 39

Morning now dawned and Shahrazad broke off from what she had been allowed to say. Then, when it was the thirty-ninth night, SHE CONTINUED:

I have heard, O auspicious king, that their father left great wealth to the two of them. Among this were a hundred loads of silk, brocade and containers of musk, with a note attached to them to say that they were destined for Baghdad, where Ghanim's father had been intending to go. Some time after his death, Ghanim took the goods himself and made the journey to Baghdad, this being in the time of the caliph Harun al-Rashid. Before he left, he took his leave of his mother, his relatives and the townspeople, after which he set off with a group of merchants, entrusting his affairs to Almighty God, Who granted him a safe journey to Baghdad. In Baghdad, he rented a fine house, furnishing it with carpets, cushions and hangings, and here he stored his bales and stabled his mules and his camels. He stayed there until he was rested, and the merchants and the chief men of Baghdad came to greet him. He then took a bundle containing ten different sorts of precious materials, with their prices written on them, to the traders' market. Here the traders greeted him warmly, showed him honour and brought him to the shop of their superintendent, where they seated him. He then handed over his bundle to this man, who opened it and took out the materials, which he sold for Ghanim at a profit of a hundred per cent.

Ghanim was delighted and he started to sell his materials and the individual items bit by bit, over the period of a full year. At the start of the second year, he came to the covered hall in the market, only to find its doors closed. When he asked why that was, he was told that one of the merchants had died and that all the others had gone to walk in the funeral procession. He was asked whether he would like to go with them and so acquire a heavenly reward. 'Yes,' he replied, and, in answer to his question, he was told where the funeral was being held. He then performed the ritual ablution and walked with the others until they came to the chapel, where prayers were said over the dead man. Then all the merchants walked in front of the bier to the burial ground, with Ghanim modestly following them. The bier was carried out of the city and the procession threaded its way between the tombs until it reached the grave.

They found that the dead man's family had pitched a tent over the grave and had brought candles and lamps. The corpse was buried and the Quran reciters sat to recite verses over the grave. The merchants took their seats, as did Ghanim, but he was overcome by shyness, telling himself: 'I cannot leave them, and will have to go back with them.' They sat listening to the Quran until evening, when supper and sweetmeats were produced for them. The guests ate their fill, washed their hands and then sat down again in their places. Ghanim, however, was preoccupied by thoughts of his house and his goods. He was afraid of thieves and said to himself: 'I am a stranger and suspected of being wealthy. If I spend the night away from home, thieves will steal my money and my goods.'

Such was his fear for his possessions that he finally got up and left the company, excusing himself to them on the grounds of the call of nature. He started to walk, following the waymarks until he came to the city gate, but as it was now midnight, he found the gate shut. He could see nobody coming or going and the only sounds to be heard were the barking of dogs and the howls of jackals. He turned back, exclaiming: 'There is no might and no power except with God! I was afraid for my wealth, which is why I came here, but now that I have found the gate shut, it is my life for which I fear.' He went back in search of a place in which to sleep until morning and found a burial plot, surrounded by four walls, with a palm tree in the middle of it and a stone gateway, whose door stood open.

He went in with the intention of sleeping there, but before he could fall asleep, he started to tremble, feeling the desolation of his situation among the tombs. So he got to his feet, went through the door and looked out. There in the distance, in the direction of the city gate, he could see a light. He walked a short way and then saw that the light was on the track leading to the burial plot where he was. Fearing for his life, he quickly shut the gate and climbed to the top of the palm tree, concealing himself among its branches.

Little by little the light came nearer until, when it was close by, Ghanim looked towards it and saw three black slaves, two carrying a chest and one carrying a lantern and an axe. When they got near the tomb, one of the two carrying the chest said: 'What's the matter with you, Sawab?'

while the other one said: 'What's the matter with you, Kafur?' 'Weren't we here at supper time and didn't we leave the door open?' said the first. 'Yes, that's true,' replied the second. 'Well, here it is locked and bolted,' said his companion. 'What fools you two are,' said the third man, whose name was Bukhait and who was carrying the axe and lantern. 'Don't you know that the owners of gardens are in the habit of coming out of Baghdad to look after their property here, and if they are still here in the evening, they come in and shut the door, for fear of being caught, roasted and eaten by black men like us?' 'You're right,' said the others, 'but by God, neither of us is feebler-witted than you.' 'You won't believe me,' Bukhait said, 'until we go into the tomb and find someone there. I think that when they saw the light and caught sight of us, they would have tried to escape up the palm tree for fear of us.'

When Ghanim heard this, he said to himself: 'You doubly damned black slave. May God give you no shelter, you with your cleverness and all this knowledge of yours. There is no might and no power except in the Exalted and Omnipotent God. What can I do now to save myself from these slaves?' The two who were carrying the box then said to the man with the axe: 'Bukhait, do you climb the wall and open the door, for we're tired from carrying this chest over our shoulders. When you open up for us, bring us one of the people inside and we'll roast him for you so skilfully that no drop of his fat will be wasted.' Bukhait replied: 'Because of my silliness, I'm afraid of something I've thought of, and I think the best thing to do is to throw in the chest behind the door, for it holds our treasure.' The other two said: 'It'll break if we throw it.' 'What I'm afraid of,' said Bukhait, 'is that there may be robbers in the graveyard, the kind who kill people and steal things. In the evening, they go into places like this and divide up their booty.' 'You stupid fellow,' said the two with the chest, 'how can they get in here?' They then lifted up the chest, climbed the wall and got down and opened the door. Bukhait, the third slave, was waiting for them with the lantern, the axe and a basket containing some watermelons. They then bolted the door and sat down.

'Brothers,' said one of them, 'we are tired out by walking, picking up the chest, putting it down, and then opening and shutting the door. It's now midnight and we have no energy left for opening up the tomb and burying the chest. Rather, let us rest for three hours and then get up and do our business. Meanwhile, let each of us tell the story of why he was castrated and what happened to him from beginning to end. This will help pass the night and we can relax.' The first of them, Bukhait, the man who had carried the lantern, then said: 'I'll tell you my story.' 'Go on,' they said, AND HE BEGAN:

You must know, brothers, that when I was small a slave dealer brought me from my own country – I was five years old at the time – and I was bought by a sergeant. He had a three-year-old daughter with whom I was brought up, and people would laugh at me as I played with her and danced and sang for her. This went on until I was twelve years old and she was ten, and they still did not keep me away from her.

One day, I went in to see her and found her sitting by herself, looking as though she had just come from the bath that they had in the house, for she smelt of perfume and incense and her face was like the rounded moon on the fourteenth night. She started to play with me and I with her. I had just reached puberty and my penis stood up like a large key. She pushed me on to the floor where I lay on my back as she sat on my chest, and she started to sprawl on top of me until my penis was uncovered. When she saw it, rampant as it was, she took it in her hand and started rubbing it against the lips of her vagina on the outside of her clothes. I became heated with lust and so I clasped her in my arms, while she laced her hands together behind my neck and then started squeezing me as hard as she could. Before I knew what was happening, my penis had pierced her dress, entered her vagina and deflowered her.

When I saw that, I ran off to one of my friends. The girl's mother then came into her room, and when she saw the state her daughter was in, she almost went out of her mind, but then she put things to rights and concealed the girl's condition from her father. She waited for two months, during which time the members of the household were calling to me and showing kindness to me, until they got me to come out of the place where I'd been hiding. Nobody told the girl's father anything of this because they were fond of me. Her mother then arranged to marry the girl off to a young barber who used to shave her father, providing the dowry from her own funds. She made all the bridal preparations without the father knowing of his daughter's condition, and great efforts were made to deck her out. It was then that I was taken unawares and castrated. When they brought the bride to her bridegroom, they concealed the loss of her virginity by killing a young pigeon in order to show blood on her shift. I was made her eunuch and wherever she went, I walked before her, whether this was to the baths or to her father's house. I stayed in that position for a long time – enjoying her beauty and grace, kissing, embracing and sleeping with her – until she died, together with her husband and both her parents. I was then taken as the property of the state treasury, and eventually I came here and became your companion. This, my brothers, is the reason for my castration. That is all.

The second slave, Kafur, then said: 'Know, my brothers, that at the start of my career, when I was an eight-year-old boy, I used to tell the slave dealers one lie each year, to get them to quarrel with one another.' HE WENT ON:

My owner lost patience with me and handed me over to the auctioneer, telling him to call out: 'Who will buy this slave in spite of his defect?' When he was asked: 'What is this defect?' he replied: 'Every year he tells one lie.' A merchant approached the auctioneer and asked: 'What is his price, blemish and all?' 'Six hundred dirhams,' said the auctioneer. 'I'll give you another twenty, as your profit,' the man promised. The auction-eer then brought the merchant to meet the slave dealer and got the money from him. He fetched me to the man's house, took his commission and went off. The merchant gave me suitable clothes to wear and I served him for the rest of the year.

The new year began auspiciously; it was one of blessings and fertility. Every day, the merchants held a banquet, which was provided by each of them in turn. When it came to my master's turn, the banquet was to be held in a garden outside the city. My master went there with the other merchants, and he brought them all the food and the other things that they might need. They sat eating, drinking and carousing until noon. Then my master needed something from the house, and so he told me to get on the mule, go back home and fetch it from my mistress, before hurrying back. I did as I was told and set off home, but when I was near the house, I let out a cry and started to weep. The people of the district, old and young, gathered round, and when my master's wife and her children heard my voice, they opened the door for me and asked me what had happened. I said: 'My master was sitting with his companions under an old wall and it collapsed on them. As soon as I saw what had happened to them, I got on the mule and came as fast as I could to tell you.'

When my master's daughters and his wife heard that, they shrieked, tore their clothes and struck their faces. The neighbours came, but my mistress turned the furniture of the house upside down, smashed the shelves, broke the windows and the lattices, and smeared the walls with mud and indigo. 'Come and help me, Kafur, damn you,' she cried.

'Smash the cupboards and break these vases and the china and everything else.' So I went to her and with her I smashed the shelves in the house with everything that stood on them. Then I went round the roof terraces and everywhere else, destroying things. All the china and anything else in the house I smashed, calling out: 'Alas for my master!'

Then my mistress went out with her face uncovered, wearing only a shawl around her head, and with her went the children, girls and boys. 'Go ahead of us, Kafur,' they said, 'and show us where your master lies dead under the wall, so that we can bring him out from the rubble and carry him on a bier. Then we shall take him back to the house and give him a fine funeral.' I walked in front of them, crying out: 'Alas for my master!' while the rest of them followed behind, with their faces and heads uncovered, shouting: 'Alas, alas for the poor man!' There was no one in the quarter, man, woman, young or old, who did not come with us, all of them joining us and striking themselves in a frenzy of weeping. As I took them through the city, people asked what had happened, and the others told them what they had heard from me. Some people said: 'There is no might and no power except with God,' while others said: 'He was a man of importance. We must go to the *wali* and tell him.'

Night 40

Morning now dawned and Shahrazad broke off from what she had been allowed to say. Then, when it was the fortieth night, SHE CONTINUED:

I have heard, O auspicious king, that when they went and told the *wali*, he rose, mounted and took with him workmen with shovels and baskets. KAFUR WENT ON:

They went off after me, accompanied by a large crowd. I was walking in front, slapping my face and crying out, while behind me walked my mistress and her children screaming. I then ran on ahead of them, crying out, pouring dust on my head and striking my face. When I went into the garden, my master saw me striking myself, while I now cried out: 'Alas for my mistress, woe, woe, woe! Who will now pity me, now that my mistress is gone? Would that I could have been her ransom!' On seeing me, my master was startled and turned pale. 'What's wrong with you, Kafur?' he said. 'What's the news?' 'When you sent me to the house,' I told him, 'I went in and saw that the wall of the hall had fallen on my mistress and her children.' 'Didn't your mistress escape?' he asked me. 'No, by God, master,' I told him. 'Not one of them escaped and the first to die was my lady, your eldest daughter.' 'Did my youngest daughter escape?' 'No,' I said. 'And what about my riding mule? Was it saved?' 'No, by God, master,' I said, 'for the house walls and the stable walls collapsed, burying everything there, even the sheep, the ducks and the hens. They have all become one pile of flesh. The dogs ate them and not one of them is left.' 'Is my eldest son, your master, safe?' he asked. 'No, by God,' I said, 'no one survived, and now there is no house, no inhabitants and no trace of them, while the sheep, the geese and the hens have been eaten by cats and dogs.'

When my master heard what I said, the light turned to darkness for him. He was unable to control himself and was out of his mind, unable to stand. His legs seemed crippled and his back broken. He tore his clothes, plucked his beard and threw off his turban from his head, while he went on beating his face until the blood flowed. 'Alas for my children!' he cried out. 'Alas for my wife! Alas for my misfortune! Who has ever suffered a disaster like this?' His cries were echoed by his companions, the merchants, who wept with him, lamented his fate and tore their clothes. My master then left the garden, still striking himself because of the violence of his grief, and so hard were the blows on his face that he was like a drunken man.

While he and the other merchants were going out of the garden gate, they saw a great cloud of dust and heard cries and wailing. They looked at the people coming towards them, and saw the *wali* with his officers, the townspeople and a crowd of spectators. Behind them came the merchant's family, calling out and shrieking amidst storms of tears. The first to meet my master was his wife, together with his children. When he saw them he was astonished; he laughed hysterically and stood stock still. Then he said: 'How are you? What happened to the house? And what happened to you?' When they saw him, they said: 'Praise be to God that you are safe!' They threw themselves on him; the children clung to him, crying out: 'Daddy, praise to God that you are safe.' His wife said: 'Are you all right? Praise be to God, Who has preserved you and shown me your face!'

She was astonished and almost out of her mind at seeing him, and she asked him: 'How did you come to survive, you and your companions, the merchants?' 'But what happened to you in the house?' he asked. 'We were fine and well,' she said, 'and there was nothing wrong with the house. Your slave, Kafur, came to us, bare-headed and with torn clothes, crying out: "Alas for the master, alas for the master!" When we asked him what was wrong, he told us that you and your companions had all been killed when a wall fell on you in the garden.' 'By God,' said my master, 'Kafur has just come to me calling out: "Alas for my mistress, alas for the children!" and telling me that you and the children were all dead!'

Then he looked towards me and saw me with a torn turban on my head, crying out, weeping violently and pouring dust on my head. He shouted at me, and when I went up to him, he said: 'Damn you, you ill-omened slave, you son of a whore coming from an accursed race, what is all this you have done? By God, I will flay the skin from your flesh and cut the flesh from your bones.' 'By God,' I told him, 'you can't do anything to me because you bought me, fault and all. This was the condition and there are witnesses to testify that you bought me in spite of my fault. You know about it – the fact that I tell one lie each year. This is half a lie, and when the year is up, I shall tell the other half and it will be one full lie.' 'Dog, son of a dog,' he shouted, 'you damnedest of slaves, is all this just half a lie? Rather, it is an enormous calamity. Leave me at once. I free you in the Name of God.' 'By God,' I said, 'even if you free me, I can't free you until the year is up and I have told my other half lie. When I have completed it, you can take me to the market and sell me for what you bought me, defect and all. You are not to free me, as I have no craft by which I could earn my living. This point is found in *shari'a* law and is mentioned by lawyers in their discussion of the emancipation of slaves.'

While we were talking, up came the whole crowd, together with the people of the quarter, men and women alike, who had come to mourn, accompanied by the *wali* and his escort. My master and the merchants went to the *wali* and told him about the affair and that this constituted half a lie. When he and the others heard that, they were struck by the enormity of the lie and were filled with astonishment, cursing and abusing me. I stood there laughing and saying: 'How can my master kill me when he bought me knowing I had this defect?'

When he got home, he found his house a wreck; it was I who had done most of the damage, and what I had broken was worth a large sum of money. His wife had broken things as well, but she told him that it was I who had smashed the vases and the china. My master grew even angrier, striking one hand against the other and saying: 'By my life, I have never seen a bastard to match this black slave. He says that this is half a lie. If it were a full one, he would have destroyed a whole city or even two.' In the heat of his anger he took me to the *wali*, who gave me a fine beating until I lost consciousness and fainted. My master left me unconscious, and brought a barber to me, who castrated me and cauterized the wound. When I came to my senses, it was to find myself a eunuch. My master said: 'As you burned my heart with regret for the things I held dearest, so I have made your heart burn for the loss of the dearest part of your body.' Then he took me and sold me for an exorbitant price as a eunuch, and I have gone on stirring up trouble in the households to which I have been sold, moving from emir to emir and great man to great man, being bought and sold until I came to the palace of the Commander of the Faithful, with a broken spirit, having lost my strength as well as my testicles.

When the other two heard his story, they laughed and said: 'You are dung, the son of dung, and you tell abominable lies.' Then the remaining slave, Sawab, was told to tell them his story. 'Cousins,' he said, 'what you have said is worthless stuff. I'll tell you how I came to lose my testicles, and I deserved an even worse punishment, for I lay with my mistress as well as with my master's son. But it is a long story and this is not the time to tell it, for it is getting close to dawn and if day breaks while we still have this chest with us, we'll be exposed and lose our lives. So go and open the door and once we've done this and got back to the palace, I'll tell you the story of my castration.'

He then climbed the wall, dropped down and opened the door. The others came in, set down the lantern and dug a hole between four graves to match the length and breadth of the box. Kafur did the digging and Sawab carried away the earth in the basket, until they had dug down three feet. Then they lowered the chest into the hole, put the earth back on top of it and left the graveyard.

When they were out of Ghanim's sight and he was sure that the place was deserted and that he was alone again, he turned his attention to the contents of the chest, saying to himself: 'What do you suppose is in it?' He waited until dawn had broken and the light had spread. He then climbed down from his palm tree and removed the soil with his hands until he had uncovered the chest and freed it from the hole. With a big stone he struck and broke its lock and, after lifting the lid, he looked inside. There he saw a girl in a drugged sleep, with her breast rising and falling as she breathed. She was very beautiful, and was wearing ornaments, gold jewellery and jewelled necklaces, priceless stuff worth a sultan's kingdom.

When Ghanim saw her, realizing that someone must have entrapped her and drugged her, he set about removing her from the chest, laying her down on her back. When she sniffed the breeze, the air entered her nostrils and lungs, and she sneezed, then choked and coughed. A pill of Cretan *banj* fell out of her throat, a drug so strong that one sniff could put an elephant to sleep for twenty-four hours. She opened her eyes and looked around, before saying in a sweet, clear voice: 'Ill wind, you cannot give drink to the thirsty nor do you show friendship to those who have drunk their fill. Where is Zahr al-Bustan?' When no one answered her, she turned and cried: 'Subiha, Shajarat al-Durr, Nur al-Huda, Najmat al-Subh, are you awake? Nuzha, Hulwa, Zarifa, speak.' Again, no one answered, and she looked round and said sorrowfully: 'Am I buried among the tombs? You, Who know the secrets of the hearts, and rewards and punishes all on the Day of Resurrection, who was it who brought me from the harem and placed me between four graves?'

While she was speaking, Ghanim was standing by her. 'Lady,' he said, 'there are no boudoirs here, and no palaces or graves, but only your slave whose wits you have stolen, Ghanim ibn Ayyub, brought here by Him Who knows the unseen, to rescue you from this distress and to bring you to your heart's desire.' He then stayed silent, and when she had checked how things stood with her, she repeated the confession of faith: 'I bear witness that there is no god but God and I bear witness that Muhammad is the Apostle of God.' Then she turned to Ghanim and, putting her hands over her face, she asked him in a sweet voice: 'Blessed young man, who brought me here? Please tell me for I have now recovered my senses.' 'My lady,' he replied, 'three black eunuchs came carrying this chest,' and he went on to tell her everything that happened to him and how he had found himself there the previous evening, this being what had led to her rescue, for otherwise she would have been smothered to death. He then asked her for her own story, but she said: 'Praise be to God Who brought me into the hands of a man like you! Get up now, put me back in the chest and go out on to the road. When you find a donkey man or a muleteer, hire him to carry the chest and then bring me to your house. When I am there, all will be well and I shall tell you the whole of my story and good will come to you through me.'

Ghanim gladly went out from the graveyard as the rays of dawn were spreading and light was filling the sky. People were on the move, and on the road he hired a muleteer, brought him to the graveyard and then lifted up the chest, into which he had already put the girl. Love for her had entered his heart and he went off with her happily. As a slave girl she was worth ten thousand dinars, while her ornaments and robes were enormously valuable. No sooner had he got to his house than he set the chest down, opened it . . .

Night 41

Morning now dawned and Shahrazad broke off from what she had been allowed to say. Then, when it was the forty-first night, SHE CONTINUED:

I have heard, O auspicious king, that when Ghanim brought the chest to his house, he opened it and brought the girl out. On looking around, she saw that she was in a handsome house, spread with carpets and adorned in attractive hangings and so forth. On seeing bundles and bales of materials and other such things, she realized that here was a merchant of substance, a man of great wealth. She uncovered her face, looked at him and, discovering him to be a handsome young man, she fell in love with him at first sight. 'Sir,' she said, 'bring us something to eat.' 'Willingly,' he replied, and he then went down to the market, where he bought a roast lamb and a dish of sweetmeats. He also brought with him dried fruits, candles, wine and glasses, together with other such things needed for drinking, as well as perfumes. When he brought all this back home, the girl was glad to see him and laughed. She kissed him and embraced him and started to caress him. His love for her increased and took possession of his heart. The two of them then ate and drank until nightfall. Each of them had fallen in love with the other, as they were not only of the same age, but were matched in beauty.

When night fell, Ghanim got up and lit the candles and the lamps, filling the room with light. He brought out the drinking glasses and set out a dinner table. The two of them then sat, and as he filled her glass and gave her wine to drink, she did the same for him. They were playing, laughing and reciting poetry as their gaiety increased, and each became more deeply in love with the other – glory be to God Who unites hearts! They kept on in this way until it was nearly dawn, when they were overcome by sleep and they slept where they were until morning came. Then Ghanim got up and went to the market, where he bought the food and drink that they needed – vegetables, meat, wine, and so on. He took these to the house, and the two of them sat down to eat until they had had enough. Then he produced the wine and they drank and played with each other until their cheeks grew red and their eyes darkened.

Ghanim longed to kiss the girl and to sleep with her. 'Lady,' he said, 'allow me once to kiss your mouth, so that this may cool the fire of my heart.' 'Ghanim,' she replied, 'wait until I am drunk and unconscious, and then steal a kiss from me secretly, so that I don't know that you have kissed me.' She then stood up and took off some of her clothes, so that she was left sitting in a delicate shift, with a silken head covering. At that, Ghanim felt the stirrings of lust, and he said: 'Lady, won't you let me do what I asked you?' 'By God,' she said, 'that cannot be, as there is a hard word written on the waistband of my drawers.' Ghanim was downcast, but as his goal became more distant, so the ardour of his love increased, and he recited:

I asked the one who caused my sickness
For a kiss to cure the pain.
'No, no, never!' the beloved said.
But 'Yes, yes!' I replied.
She smiled and said:
'Take it with my goodwill by lawful means.'
'By force?' I asked, and she said, 'No,
But with my generous consent.'
Do not enquire what happened then.
Ask pardon from the Lord, for it is done.
Think what you like of us;
Suspicion makes love sweet,
And after this, I do not care
Whether a foe gives it away or keeps it hidden.

His love now increased and the fires of passion spread through his heart's blood. She kept on repulsing him and saying: 'You cannot have me,' but they continued to drink together as lovers. Ghanim was drowning in a sea of passion, while the girl became ever stricter in her modesty, until night brought its darkness and lowered the skirts of sleep on them. Ghanim got up to light the lamps and the candles, and he set the room and the table to rights. He then took her feet and kissed them, and, finding them like fresh butter, he rubbed his face on them. 'Have pity, lady,' he said, 'on one enslaved by your love and slain by your eyes. But for you, my heart would have stayed whole.' He then wept a little, and she said: 'My master and light of my eyes, by God I love you and trust you, but I know that you cannot have me.' 'What is the hindrance?' he asked. 'Tonight,' she said, 'I shall tell you my story so that you may accept my excuse.' Then she threw herself on him and kissed him, winding her arms around his neck as she comforted him and gave him promises of union. They continued to play and laugh until love for the other was firmly entrenched in each of their hearts.

Things went on like this for a whole month. Every night they slept on the same bed, but every time that he asked her for union she rejected him, in spite of the fact that they loved each other and could scarcely endure to be kept apart. It happened then one night that, when the two of them were drunk and were lying there, Ghanim reached out and caressed her body. His hand went to her belly and down to her navel. This roused her and she sat up, inspected her drawers, but when she found that they were still fastened, she went to sleep again. He stroked her with his hand which slipped down to the waistband of her drawers. When he pulled at it, she woke up again and sat up, with Ghanim sitting by her side. 'What do you want?' she asked. 'To sleep with you,' he replied, 'and that we should be frank with one another.' 'The time has now come,' she said, 'for me to tell you about myself so that you may know my standing, discover my secret and see plainly my excuse.' 'Yes,' he said, and at that she tore open the bottom of her shift and put her hand on the waistband of her drawers. 'Master,' she said, 'read what is written on the border of this waistband.' Ghanim took it in his hand and when he looked at it he found written on it in letters of gold: 'I am yours and you are mine, cousin of the Prophet.'

When he read this, he removed his hand and said: 'Tell me your story.' 'I will,' she replied, and went on: 'You must know that I am the concubine of the Commander of the Faithful. My name is Qut al-Qulub and I was brought up in the caliph's palace. When I grew up and the caliph saw my qualities and the beauty and grace with which God had endowed me, he fell deeply in love with me. He took me and installed me in an apartment of my own, giving me ten slave girls to serve me, and he then presented me with the jewellery which you see that I have with me. One day when he had left on a journey to some part of his lands, the Lady Zubaida approached one of my slave girls, telling her that she wanted her to do something. 'What is that, my lady?' asked the girl. 'When your mistress Qut al-Qulub is asleep, put this piece of *banj* in her nostrils or her drink and I will give you all the money that you want.'

The girl willingly agreed and took the *banj* from her, delighted by the thought of the money, and also because originally she had been one of Zubaida's maids. She came to me and put the drug in the drink which

I took that night. When it had lodged within me, I fell head over heels, conscious only of being in some other world. When her ruse had succeeded, Zubaida had me placed in a chest and summoned the black slaves in secret, bribing them, together with the gatekeepers. Then she sent me off with them on the night that you were hiding on top of the palm tree. You saw what they did to me; it is you who saved me and you who brought me here and treated me with the utmost kindness. This is my story and I don't know what has happened to the caliph in my absence. So you have to acknowledge my high standing, and you must not let anyone know what has happened to me.'

When Ghanim heard what Qut al-Qulub had to say and realized that she was the caliph's concubine, fear of the caliph made him draw back and he sat by himself in a corner of the room, blaming himself, thinking over his position and telling himself to be patient. He remained bewildered because of his love for an unattainable beloved, and the violence of his passion caused him to weep as he complained of the hostile assaults of Time – Glory be to the One Who kindles hearts with love for the beloved! He recited:

The heart of the lover wearies for his beloved;
Unique in beauty, the loved one steals his wits.
Men ask me: 'What is the taste of love?'
'Sweet,' I reply, 'but it contains torture.'

At that, Qut al-Qulub got up, embraced Ghanim and kissed him. Love for him was firmly rooted in her heart; she had told him her secret and shown how deeply she felt for him. Winding her arms around his neck she kissed him again, while he tried to keep away from her, for fear of the caliph. They talked for a while, drowning as they were in the ocean of their love. When day broke, Ghanim got up, dressed and went out as usual to the market. He bought all that was needed and then came back to the house, where he found Qut al-Qulub in tears. When she saw him, she stopped crying and smiled. 'I was lonely because of you, heart's darling,' she said. 'The hour that you have been away from me has been like a year because of our parting. Thanks to my deep love for you, I told you how things are with me, so come now, forget the past, and take me as you want.' 'God forbid,' he said. 'This can never be. How can the dog sit in the lion's place? What belongs to the master is forbidden to the slave.'

Dragging himself away from her, he sat down in the corner on a mat.

His abstinence increased her love for him, and she sat beside him, drinking with him and playing with him. They became drunk and she longed to be possessed by him. So she sang these lines:

> The infatuated lover's heart is almost shattered;
> How long, how long, will you turn away from me?
> You shun me though I am guilty of no fault;
> It is the habit of gazelles to play.
> Shunning, remoteness, constant separation –
> All this is more than a young man can bear.

Ghanim wept, and she shared his tears and they continued to drink until night, when Ghanim got up and spread two beds, each in a place by itself. 'For whom is the second bed?' asked Qut al-Qulub. 'For me,' he replied, 'and the other is for you, as from this night on, this is the way in which we shall sleep; for everything that belongs to the master is forbidden to the slave.' 'No more of this,' she said. 'Everything happens by the decree of fate.' He refused to yield and her heart burned with love. As her passion increased, she clung to him and said: 'By God, we are going to sleep together.' 'God forbid,' he exclaimed, and getting the better of her persistence, he slept alone until morning, with her love and passion increasing and her longing becoming still more violent.

For three long months they went on like this; every time she approached him, he would draw away from her, repeating that what belonged to the master was unlawful for the slave. Because of this prolonged delay in her union with him, Qut al-Qulub's sorrow and distress increased, and she recited these lines with a sad heart:

> Peerless in your beauty, what false charges do you bring,
> And who incited you to turn away from me?
> Yours is the ideal grace and every elegance.
> You move each heart to passion and empower
> Sleeplessness over all eyelids.
> Fruit has been plucked from branches before you;
> Branch of the thorn bush, how do you wrong me?
> I used to hunt gazelles, so how is it
> I see them hunting hunters, armed with shields?
> The strangest thing I have to tell of you is that
> I am infatuated, but you know nothing of my moans.
> Never allow me union; if I am

Jealous for you of yourself, how much more, then, of me?
While life remains, I shall not say again:
'Peerless in your beauty, what false charges do you bring?'

They stayed like this for a time, with Ghanim being kept from Qut al-Qulub out of fear. So much for him, the slave of love, the man robbed of his wits. As for Lady Zubaida, after she had done what she did to Qut al-Qulub in the caliph's absence, she remained perplexed, wondering to herself what she could say when he came back and asked about the girl. So she called an old woman who was in her service, told her the secret and asked her what she should do, now that Qut al-Qulub had died an untimely death. The old woman grasped the position and said: 'Know, mistress, that the caliph will soon be here. Send for a carpenter and tell him to make what looks like a corpse out of wood. Then we can dig a grave for it in the middle of the palace, bury it, and make a shrine, where we can burn candles and lamps. Everyone in the palace should wear black, and the slave girls and the eunuchs must be told that, when they hear that the caliph has returned from his journey, they are to spread straw in the halls. When the caliph comes in and asks about this, they are to say: "Qut al-Qulub is dead, may God compensate you amply for her. So highly did our mistress regard her that she had her buried in her own palace."

'When the caliph hears this, he will weep, finding the loss hard to bear, and he will have the Quran recited for her and keep vigil by her grave. If he says to himself: "My cousin Zubaida must have contrived to kill Qut al-Qulub out of jealousy," or if he is overcome by passionate love and orders her to be exhumed, you need have no fears. When the workmen dig up the grave and come upon what looks like a human form, the caliph will see that it is wrapped in splendid grave clothes. If he wants to remove these in order to look at her, you must stop him or let some other woman do that, saying: "It is forbidden to look at her nakedness." He will then believe that she really is dead and will put her back in the grave, thanking you for what you have done. In this way, if God Almighty wills it, you will escape from your predicament.'

When Lady Zubaida heard what the old woman had to say, she thought that the advice was good. She gave her a robe of honour, together with a large sum of money, and told her to see that this was done. The old woman set to work at once. She asked the carpenter to make a figure, as described, and when this was done, she brought it to Lady Zubaida, who provided it with grave clothes and buried it. She then had candles and lamps lit and spread out carpets around the grave. She herself wore black and she ordered the slave girls to do the same, as word spread in the palace that Qut al-Qulub was dead.

After a while, the caliph returned from his journey and went to the palace, his only concern being for Qut al-Qulub; there he saw the servants, eunuchs and slave girls wearing black. With a quaking heart he went to Lady Zubaida and found that she too was in black. When he asked about this, he was told that Qut al-Qulub had died. He fell down in a faint and when he recovered, he asked where she was buried. 'Know, Commander of the Faithful,' said Lady Zubaida, 'that, because of my high regard for her, I had her buried in the palace.' The caliph, still wearing his travelling clothes, went in to visit the grave, and he found the carpets laid down and the candles and lamps lit. When he saw this, he thanked Zubaida for what she had done, but he remained perplexed, neither believing nor refusing to believe. Eventually, overcome by suspicion, he ordered the grave to be opened and the corpse to be exhumed. When he saw the shroud, he wanted it to be removed so that he might look at Qut al-Qulub, but he was afraid of the anger of Almighty God, and the old woman said: 'Put her back in her grave.' He then immediately ordered the *faqihs* and Quran reciters to be brought, and he had the Quran recited over her grave, while he sat beside it weeping until he fainted. He continued to sit there for a whole month.

Night 42

Morning now dawned and Shahrazad broke off from what she had been allowed to say. Then, when it was the forty-second night, SHE CONTINUED:

I have heard, O auspicious king, that the caliph kept visiting the grave for a month. It then happened one day, after the emirs and viziers had gone home, that he visited the harem, where he fell asleep for a time. At his head a slave girl sat fanning him, while another sat massaging his feet. After his sleep, he woke up and opened his eyes, but closed them again as he heard the girl at his head say to the other at his feet: 'Khaizaran.' 'Yes, Qudib al-Ban,' replied the other. 'Our master doesn't know what happened,' said Qudib al-Ban. 'He keeps vigil over a grave that contains nothing but a piece of wood carved by a carpenter.' 'What happened to Qut al-Qulub?' asked the other. Her companion told her: 'Lady Zubaida sent a slave girl to drug her with a *banj* pill, and after that, Lady Zubaida had her put in a chest and sent her off with Sawab and Kafur, telling them to throw her out in a graveyard.' Khaizaran said: 'Isn't Qut al-Qulub dead then?' 'No, by God,' replied the other, 'and may a young girl like her be preserved from death! I have heard Lady Zubaida saying that she is with a young merchant, Ghanim ibn Ayyub of Damascus. She has now been there with him for four months, and here is our master weeping and keeping vigil at night by a tomb in which there is no corpse.'

The two girls went on talking like this while the caliph listened. By the time that they had finished, he knew all about the affair – that the tomb was a fake and that Qut al-Qulub had been with Ghanim for four months. In a violent rage he got up and went to see his officers of state. Ja'far the Barmecide came forward and kissed the ground before him. 'Go down with a group of men,' the caliph told him angrily, 'find out where the house of Ghanim ibn Ayyub may be, break in and bring me my slave girl, Qut al-Qulub. As for Ghanim, I must punish him.' 'To hear is to obey,' replied Ja'far, and he set off, accompanied by a large crowd, including the *wali*.

When they got to Ghanim's house, he had come back with some meat and he and Qut al-Qulub were just about to eat it, when she happened to look round and saw that disaster had overtaken them and that the house was surrounded on all sides. There was Ja'far, the *wali*, the guards and the mamluks with drawn swords encircling the place as the white of the eye surrounds its pupil. She knew at once that word of her presence must have reached her master, the caliph. Certain that this meant death, she turned pale and her beauty faded. She looked at Ghanim and said: 'My darling, save yourself.' 'What am I to do,' he said, 'and where can I go? All my means of livelihood are here in this house.' She insisted: 'Don't waste time or you will die, and all your wealth will be lost.' 'Darling and light of my eyes,' he asked, 'how can I manage to get out of the house, now that it is surrounded?' 'Have no fear,' she replied, at which she stripped him of his clothes and dressed him in old rags. Then she fetched the pot that contained the meat, added some broken pieces of bread round it, together with a bowl of food, and putting this all in a basket she set it on his head. 'Trick your way out with this,' she said, 'and don't worry about me, for I know how to deal with the caliph.'

Following her advice, Ghanim went out through the middle of Ja'far's men, carrying his basket with its contents, and, as God the Shelterer sheltered him, he escaped from the evils that were plotted against him by virtue of his innocence. When Ja'far got near the house, he dismounted from his horse and, on entering, he found Qut al-Qulub dressed in all her finery. She had filled a chest with gold, jewellery, gems and such treasures as were light to carry but of great value. She rose to her feet when Ja'far came and kissed the ground before him. 'Master,' she said, 'God's decrees have been written down since past eternity.' When Ja'far saw all this, he said: 'By God, lady, my orders are only to arrest Ghanim ibn Ayyub.' 'He picked up some merchandise,' she said, 'and left with it for Damascus. That is all that I know about him, but I would like you to look after this chest for me and bring it up to the palace of the Commander of the Faithful.' 'To hear is to obey,' he replied, after which he took the chest and gave orders that it should be carried up, while Qut al-Qulub herself went with the escort to the caliph's palace, being treated with honour and respect. This was after Ja'far's men had plundered Ghanim's house, before setting off to the caliph.

Ja'far told the caliph all that had happened, and on his orders Qut al-Qulub was given a dark room in which to live, with an old woman to see to her needs, because he believed that Ghanim must have seduced her and slept with her. He wrote instructions to Muhammad ibn Sulaiman al-Zaini, his deputy in Damascus, instructing him that, as soon as the order came, he was to arrest Ghanim ibn Ayyub and send him to Baghdad. When this order did arrive, Muhammad kissed it and placed it on his head. He then had a proclamation made in the markets that whoever wanted plunder should go to the house of Ghanim ibn Ayyub. When the crowd got there, they found Ghanim's mother and his sister sitting weeping by a tomb that they had had made for him in the middle of the house. The two of them were arrested and the house was plundered, without their knowing what the matter was. They were brought before the sultan, who asked them about Ghanim, but they said that for a year or more they had heard no word of him. They were then sent back home.

So much for them, but as for Ghanim, when he had lost all his riches and saw the state that he was in, he wept for himself until his heart almost broke. He went on his way, wandering until the end of the day with ever-increasing hunger, tired out with walking. On coming to a town, he entered it and went to a mosque, where he sat on a mat, leaning his back on the mosque wall until he collapsed on the ground through hunger and fatigue. He stayed there until morning, his heart palpitating with hunger, while lice, attracted by the sweat, crawled over his body. His breath stank and his appearance was quite changed. When the townsfolk came for the morning prayer, they found him stretched out there, weak and emaciated by hunger, but with signs of his previous prosperity still visible. After they had finished the prayer, they went up to him and, finding him cold and hungry, they gave him an old coat with ragged sleeves and asked: 'Where are you from, stranger, and what is the reason for your weakness?' He opened his eyes to look at them, and wept but made no reply. One of them, seeing that he was starving, went off and brought him a bowl of honey and two loaves of bread. He ate a little and the people stayed with him until the sun was up, when they left to go about their own business.

Things went on like this for a month, during which he grew weaker and more ill. The townsfolk wept out of sympathy for him and consulted one another about his affair, agreeing at last to take him to the hospital of Baghdad. While he was in this state, two beggar women arrived, and these turned out to be his mother and his sister. When he saw them, he gave them the bread that was placed by his head, and they slept there with him that night, although he did not recognize them. The next day, the people came with a camel and they told the camel driver to take the sick man on its back, bring him to Baghdad and leave him at the door of the hospital, in the hope that he might be cured. The camel man would then be rewarded. 'To hear is to obey,' the man said, so they then brought Ghanim out of the mosque and placed him on the camel, together with the mat on which he was sleeping.

Among those who were looking on were his mother and his sister, who had not recognized him. They now looked more closely and said: 'This looks like our Ghanim. Do you suppose that he is this sick man or not?' Ghanim himself did not wake up until he found himself tied on by a rope to the back of the camel. He wept and complained and the townspeople saw the two women, his mother and sister, weeping for him, although they had not recognized him. The two of them set off and made the journey to Baghdad, while the camel driver set Ghanim down at the hospital door, before taking his camel and leaving.

Ghanim slept until morning and when people started to move to and fro along the road, they looked at him. There he lay, thin as a tooth-pick, with a crowd staring at him, when the superintendent of the market came up and sent them on their way. He then said to himself: 'This poor fellow will get me entrance to Paradise, for if they take him into the

hospital, they will kill him off in a single day.' He ordered his servants
to carry Ghanim to his house, where he spread out fresh bedding and
gave him a new pillow, telling his wife to look after him well. She
willingly agreed and, rolling up her sleeves, she heated water and washed
his hands, feet and body. She then dressed him in a gown belonging to
one of her slave girls and gave him a glass of wine to drink, in which
rosewater had been sprinkled. He recovered his senses but then began to
utter mournful complaints, and as he thought of his beloved Qut al-
Qulub, his sorrows increased.

So much for him, but as for Qut al-Qulub, the caliph was angry with
her . . .

Night 43

Morning now dawned and Shahrazad broke off from what she had been
allowed to say. Then, when it was the forty-third night, SHE CONTINUED:

I have heard, O auspicious king, that the caliph was angry with Qut
al-Qulub and had placed her in a dark room. Things stayed like this for
eighty days, but then one day, as he happened to be passing by, he heard
Qut al-Qulub reciting poetry. When she had finished, she said: 'Ghanim,
my darling, how good you are and how chaste! You did good to one
who wronged you; you preserved the honour of one who dishonoured
you; you guarded his womenfolk, while he took you and your family as
prisoners. There must come a time when you and the Commander of the
Faithful will stand before a Righteous Ruler. You will demand justice
against him on a day when the judge will be the Lord God, Great and
Glorious, and the witnesses will be the angels.' When the caliph heard
this and understood the nature of her complaint, he realized that she
had been wronged.

He went back to his quarters and sent Masrur, the eunuch, to fetch
her. When she came before him, she lowered her head, tearful and sad
at heart. 'Qut al-Qulub,' he said, 'I find that you claim to have been
wronged by me and you accuse me of injustice. You claim that I have
harmed one who has done good to me. Who is this who has preserved
my honour, while I have dishonoured him, and has guarded my womenfolk, while I have imprisoned his?' 'He is Ghanim ibn Ayyub,' she replied.
'He never led me to commit any shameful or foul act. I swear this by
your grace, Commander of the Faithful.' 'There is no might and no

power except with God,' exclaimed the caliph, and he promised to grant
Qut al-Qulub whatever she wished. 'I wish you to grant me my beloved,
Ghanim ibn Ayyub,' she replied, and the caliph agreed. 'Commander of
the Faithful,' she said, 'bring him here and give him to me.' 'If he comes,'
he replied, 'I will present you to him as a gift from one who does not
take back what he has given.' 'Give me permission, Commander of the
Faithful,' she said, 'to go round looking for him, for it may be that God
will unite me with him.' He allowed her to do this, and she left joyfully,
taking with her a thousand gold dinars.

She visited the *shaikhs*, giving alms in Ghanim's name, and on the
next day she went to the traders' market. Here she gave the superintendent money which she told him to distribute as alms to any strangers.
On the following Friday, she went back, bringing with her the thousand
dinars. She came to the market of the goldsmiths and jewellers and called
for the superintendent, to whom she gave the money, telling him to give
it as alms to strangers. The superintendent, who was the senior merchant
of the market, looked at her and said: 'Lady, would you care to come to
my house to see a young stranger, one of the most graceful and perfectly
formed of men?' This stranger was none other than Ghanim ibn Ayyub,
the slave of love, the man bereft of his wits, but the superintendent did
not know this and took him for a poor debtor who had been stripped of
his goods, or a lover parted from his beloved. When Qut al-Qulub heard
what he said, her heart beat faster and she suffered inner disquiet. She
asked the superintendent to send someone with her to take her to his
house. He provided a young boy, who brought her to where the superintendent's 'stranger' was. She thanked him, went in and greeted the
superintendent's wife. She, in her turn, got up and, recognizing Qut
al-Qulub, she kissed the ground before her. 'Where is the sick man you
have with you?' asked Qut al-Qulub. The woman wept and said: 'Here
he is, lady. By God, he must come from a good family, and he shows
signs of earlier prosperity. There he is on the bed.'

Qut al-Qulub turned and looked at him. She saw that he was like
Ghanim, but he was so wasted and emaciated that he was like a tooth-
pick and therefore unrecognizable. She could not be sure that he was, in
fact, Ghanim, but she pitied him nonetheless and shed tears, exclaiming:
'Strangers are wretched, even if in their own country they are emirs!'
Even though she did not recognize him, she felt concern for him and in
her sadness of heart she arranged for him to be provided with wine and
with medicines. She then sat for a time by his head, after which she rode

back to the palace and set about visiting every market in search of Ghanim.

Later, the superintendent brought her Ghanim's mother and his sister, and said to her: 'Mistress of the benefactors, today this woman and her daughter have come to our city. They have beautiful faces and they show signs of having previously been prosperous and fortunate, but each of them is wearing a hair shirt, with a food bag around her neck. Their eyes are tearful and their hearts are sad, so I have brought them to you for shelter so that you may save them from beggary, as they are unsuited to a beggar's life. If God wills it, they may be our passport to Paradise.' 'By God, sir,' she said, 'you have made me want to help them. Where are they? Bring them to me.'

The superintendent told his eunuch to bring the two women to Qut al-Qulub. So Ghanim's sister Fitna entered with her mother, and when Qut al-Qulub saw how beautiful they were, she wept for them and said: 'By God, these have come from a prosperous family and they show signs of having been wealthy.' 'Lady,' said the superintendent's wife, 'we love the poor and needy because of the heavenly reward promised us. It may be that these were attacked by evil-doers who robbed them of their wealth and destroyed their house.' Meanwhile, mother and daughter shed bitter tears, thinking of the prosperity that they had enjoyed and the sorrowful poverty to which they had been reduced, and then their thoughts turned to Ghanim. Qut al-Qulub shed tears to match theirs, and heard them pray God to unite them with the one whom they were seeking: 'our Ghanim'.

Hearing this, Qut al-Qulub realized that one of these women must be the mother of her beloved and the other his sister. She wept until she fainted and, when she had recovered, she approached them and said: 'No harm shall come to you. This is the first day of your good fortune and the last of your misery. So do not grieve.'

Night 44

Morning now dawned and Shahrazad broke off from what she had been allowed to say. Then, when it was the forty-fourth night, SHE CONTINUED:

I have heard, O auspicious king, that Qut al-Qulub told them not to grieve. She then told the superintendent to take them home and get his wife to bring the two of them to the baths, to give them fine clothes to wear, to look after them and to treat them with the greatest respect. She gave him money and on the following day she rode to his house and went in to see his wife, who rose to greet her, kissed her hand and thanked her for her generosity. She looked at Ghanim's mother and sister, who had been taken to the baths and given a change of clothes. The signs of their prosperity were clear and Qut al-Qulub sat talking to them for a time. Then she asked the superintendent's wife about her sick patient. 'He is still in the same state,' she said. 'Come with us and let us visit him,' said Qut al-Qulub, and so she, the superintendent's wife, together with Ghanim's mother and his sister, went into his room and sat with him. Ghanim heard them mention the name Qut al-Qulub, and although his body was emaciated and his bones wasted, at this his spirit returned, and raising his head from his pillow, he called: 'Qut al-Qulub!' She looked at him and now realized for certain that this was Ghanim. 'Yes, my darling,' she called out. 'Come near me,' he said. 'Are you perhaps Ghanim ibn Ayyub, the slave of love, the man robbed of his wits?' she asked, and when he answered: 'Yes, I am,' she fell down in a faint.

On hearing this, Ghanim's sister Fitna and his mother cried out in joy and fell fainting. When they had recovered, Qut al-Qulub said to Ghanim: 'Praise be to God who has united me with you and with your mother and sister.' Then she went up to him to tell him all that had happened to her regarding the caliph. 'I told him the truth,' she said, 'and he believed me and approved of your conduct. He now wants to see you,' and she added: 'He has given me to you.' Ghanim was filled with delight and Qut al-Qulub said to them all: 'Don't leave until I come back.' She got up immediately and went to her apartments. She took the chest that she had brought from Ghanim's house, and taking out some dinars, she gave them to the superintendent. 'Take these,' she said, 'and bring each of these people four complete sets of clothes of the finest materials, as well as twenty kerchiefs and whatever else they need.'

She then took the two ladies to the baths, together with Ghanim, where she ordered them to be bathed, and when they came out and had put on their clothes, she prepared soup for them, together with galingale water and apple juice. She stayed with them for three days, feeding them on chicken and soup and giving them drinks made from refined sugar. After three days, their spirits were restored and she took them to the baths again, giving them fresh clothes when they came out. She then left them in the house of the superintendent and went to the palace, where she asked for an audience with the caliph.

When she was given leave to enter his presence, she kissed the ground before him and told him the story, explaining that her master Ghanim had arrived, as had his mother and his sister. When the caliph heard what she had to say, he told the eunuchs to bring him Ghanim. In fact, it was Ja'far who went, but Qut al-Qulub forestalled him. She came to Ghanim and told him that the caliph had sent for him, and she advised him to speak eloquently and sweetly and to be of good courage. She dressed him in a splendid robe and gave him a large quantity of money, telling him to give it away liberally to the caliph's attendants as he entered his presence. At this point, Ja'far arrived, mounted on his mule of state. Ghanim got up to greet him, saluted him and kissed the ground before him. He shone brightly like a star of good omen and Ja'far went off with him until they came into the presence of the Commander of the Faithful.

When he arrived there, he looked at Ja'far, the emirs, the chamberlains, the deputies, the officers of state and the military commanders. He turned to the caliph, lowered his head to the ground and recited with agreeable eloquence:

> Greetings to you, king of great majesty,
> Whose generous deeds follow on one another.
> None else can be extolled as holding such a rank,
> Whether he be a Caesar or a Persian Lord of the Hall.
> At your threshold kings on greeting you
> Set on the ground the jewels of their crowns.
> When you appear before their eyes,
> In awe of you they fall prostrate on their beards.
> Should they win your favour as they stand there,
> They gain high rank and splendid sultanates.
> The deserts and all the world cannot contain your army,
> So pitch your camp on Saturn's heights.
> May the King of kings preserve you with His might;
> You are the excellent director, the man of steadfast mind.
> Your justice spreads through all the world,
> And in it the farthest parts are equal to the nearest.

When he finished his poem, the caliph was delighted and admired his eloquence and the sweetness of his speech.

Night 45

Morning now dawned and Shahrazad broke off from what she had been allowed to say. Then, when it was the forty-fifth night, SHE CONTINUED:

I have heard, O auspicious king, that the caliph was delighted and admired his eloquence and the sweetness of his speech. 'Approach,' he said, and when Ghanim drew near, he asked him for his story and an account of what had happened to him. Ghanim sat and told him of his experiences in Baghdad, how he had gone to sleep in the graveyard and how he had taken the chest left by the slaves after they had gone. He went through the whole tale from beginning to end, but there is no advantage to be got from repetition. When the caliph saw that he was telling the truth, he presented him with a robe of honour, brought him up to him and said: 'Forgive me my debt.' 'I forgive it, master,' said Ghanim, 'for the slave with all that he owns is still the property of the master.'

This pleased the caliph and he ordered that Ghanim should be given a palace of his own, with pay, allowances and gifts assigned to him in generous quantities. He moved there with his sister and his mother, and when the caliph heard that his sister Fitna lived up to the meaning of her name as a girl of enticing beauty, he asked Ghanim for her hand in marriage. 'She is your maidservant,' said Ghanim, 'and I am your mamluk.' The caliph thanked him and gave him a hundred thousand dinars. The notaries and the *qadi* were then fetched and marriage contracts were drawn up on the same day, one for the caliph and Fitna and one for Ghanim ibn Ayyub and Qut al-Qulub. Both marriages were consummated on the same night, and in the morning the caliph gave orders that the history of Ghanim from beginning to end should be written down and given a permanent place in his treasury, so that future generations might read it, wonder at the turns of fortune and entrust their affairs to God, the Creator of night and day.

'This, however, is not more wonderful than the story of King 'Umar ibn al-Nu'man and his sons Sharkan and Dau' al-Makan, and the strange and remarkable things that happened to them.' 'What is this story?' asked the king, AND SHAHRAZAD SAID:

I have heard, O fortunate king, that in Baghdad, the City of Peace, before the caliphate of 'Abd al-Malik ibn Marwan, there was a king called 'Umar ibn al-Nu'man. He was a ruler of great power, who had conquered the kings of Persia and of Byzantium. No one could endure his battle fire or rival him in the field, while in his anger sparks would fly from his nostrils. His conquests had spread to all parts; God had caused all His servants to obey him; his rule had spread to all cities; his armies had reached the farthest parts; and east and west were under his command, together with what lay between – India with its islands, Sind, China and its islands, the Hijaz, Yemen, the northern territories, Diyar Bakr, the lands of the blacks, the islands of the oceans, and the famous rivers, such as the Saihun, the Jaihun, the Nile and the Euphrates. He sent his messengers to the farthest cities to bring him news, and they came back to tell him that there throughout the lands there was justice, obedience and security, and that his people were praying for him. He was of high lineage, and gifts, presents and tribute came to him from all parts.

He had a son named Sharkan, who most closely resembled him. He was one of the scourges of the age, a man who overcame the brave and destroyed his enemies. His father loved him very dearly and named him as his successor. When Sharkan reached man's estate at twenty years of age, God caused all His servants to obey him because of his force and hardiness. His father 'Umar had four legal wives, but only one of them had given him a son, Sharkan, while the rest were barren and had produced no child. He also had three hundred and sixty concubines, equalling the number of the days of the Coptic year. They were of all nationalities, and each of them had an apartment made for her within a palace, twelve of which the king had built, one for every month of the year, each containing thirty apartments to make the number up to three hundred and sixty. The concubines who lived in them were each assigned one night which the king would spend with her, and it would be a full year before he came back to her.

Things continued like this for a period of time, during which the fame of Sharkan spread throughout the lands, to the delight of his father. His strength increased and he acted tyrannically and violently, capturing castles and cities. Then, in accordance with the decree of fate, one of 'Umar's concubines became pregnant. When this became known and the king learned of it, he was delighted and said: 'I trust that all my descendants will be males.' He took note of the day on which the girl conceived and began to treat her with favour. When Sharkan heard of her pregnancy, he was distressed, thinking that this was a blow for him, and that he might have a rival for the throne. 'If this girl gives birth to a boy,' he said to himself, 'I shall kill her,' but he kept this to himself.

So much for Sharkan, but as for the girl, she was a Byzantine who had been sent to 'Umar as a gift from the emperor of Byzantium, overlord of Caesarea, together with many gifts. Her name was Sophia and she was the most beautiful and most chaste of women, with the loveliest face, while in addition to her dazzling beauty she had great intelligence. During her attendance on the king on the night that he spent with her, she said: 'O king, I wish that the God of heaven would provide you with a son by me so that I may bring him up well and that through my training he may become a highly cultivated and modest young man.' This pleased and gladdened the king.

Things went on like this until Sophia reached the term of her pregnancy and sat on the birthing chair. During this period she had been assiduous in performing good deeds and in serving God to the best of her power, while calling on Him to give her a virtuous son and allow her an easy labour, a prayer which God accepted. The king had entrusted a eunuch with the duty of telling him whether she had given birth to a boy or a girl, and Sharkan, too, had sent someone to bring him news. When Sophia did give birth, the midwives inspected the child and they found that it was a girl with a face more splendid than the moon. They told this to all who were present, and the messengers both of the king and of Sharkan went back to let their masters know. Sharkan was delighted when he heard, but after the eunuch had left, Sophia told the midwives to wait for a while, as she felt that there was still something in her womb. With another cry she went into labour again. God made this easy for her and she produced a second child, which, when the midwives looked at it, turned out to be a boy like the full moon, with a gleaming forehead and rosy cheeks. Sophia was filled with joy, as were the eunuchs, the attendants and everyone else who was there. When she was freed of the placenta, trills of joy resounded in the palace, and at the sound of them, all the other concubines were filled with jealousy.

When the news reached 'Umar, he was pleased and happy. He got up and came to see Sophia. He kissed her on the head and then, looking at the newborn boy, he bent down and kissed him, as the slave girls beat their tambourines and played musical instruments. On his instructions the boy was named Dau' al-Makan and his sister Nuzhat al-Zaman. He arranged for the children to have assigned their own wet nurses, attendants and children's nurses to look after them, and he provided them with quantities of sugar, drinks, ointments, and so on, such as would tire the tongue to describe. When the people of Baghdad heard of what God had granted him, the city was adorned and drums were beaten to spread the good news. The emirs, viziers and officers of state came to congratulate him on the birth of his son and daughter, for which he thanked them, giving them robes of honour, together with additional favours, and he gave generous gifts to everyone present, both high and low.

Things went on like this for four years, with the king every few days asking about Sophia and her children. After four years, he ordered that a great quantity of jewellery, ornaments, robes and money should be given to her, with instructions that she was to bring the children up with a good education. While all this was happening, Prince Sharkan never knew that his father had had another son, as he had only been told of the birth of Nuzhat al-Zaman, while news of Dau' al-Makan had been kept from him.

Days and years passed as he busied himself battling against the brave and riding out to challenge horsemen. Then, one day when the king was seated on his throne, his chamberlains entered, kissed the ground before him and told him of the arrival of envoys from the emperor of Byzantium, the lord of the great city of Constantinople, who were requesting an audience with him. 'If the king admits them to his presence, we shall bring them in, but if not, his orders cannot be countermanded.' The king gave his permission for the envoys to enter, and when they did, he received them courteously, asking them how they were and why they had come. They kissed the ground before him, saying: 'Great and mighty king, know that we have been sent by Emperor Afridun, lord of the lands of Greece and of the armies of Christendom, whose royal seat is at Constantinople. He informs you that he is now waging a bitter war with an obdurate tyrant, the lord of Caesarea. The reason for this war is this. In former times, a king of the Arabs found on one of his conquests a treasure dating to the age of Alexander. From this he removed un-countable wealth, among which were three rounded gems, as big as ostrich eggs, from a mine of pure white jewels whose like is nowhere to be found. Each of these is inscribed with secret formulae in Greek characters. They have many powers of their own; indeed, if one of them is hung around the neck of a newborn child, as long as it stays in place, that child will never suffer pain, be stricken by fever or have cause to groan. When they fell into the hands of the Arab king and he discovered their secret powers, he sent the three of them to Emperor Afridun, together with other gifts and treasures. He fitted out two ships, one containing the treasure and the other crewed with men who were to guard it from attack while they were at sea. He himself had been certain that no one would be able to interfere with the ships as he was the king of the Arabs, while the course that they would follow to their destination led them across a sea controlled by Afridun, emperor of Constantinople, whose shores were peopled only by his subjects. When they had been fitted out, the ships sailed off, but as they came near our shores, they were attacked by pirates, including soldiers in the pay of the lord of Caesarea. These men seized everything that was in them – the gifts, the money and the treasures, including the three gems – and they killed the king's men. When our emperor heard of this, he sent an army against them, which they defeated, and when he sent a second force, stronger than the first, they routed that too.

'At this, Afridun in his anger swore that he himself would go out against them with all his men and that he would not return until he had left Armenian Caesarea as a ruin and had ravaged its lands, together with all the towns that were under the control of its king. The emperor's request to the lord of the age, King 'Umar ibn al-Nu'man, the ruler of Baghdad and of Khurasan, is that he should aid him by sending an army, so as to add to his own glory.' The envoys added: 'We have brought you from our emperor gifts of various kinds; he asks you to be graciously pleased to accept them, and to grant him aid.' They then kissed the ground before him.

Night 46

Morning now dawned and Shahrazad broke off from what she had been allowed to say. Then, when it was the forty-sixth night, SHE CONTINUED:

I have heard, O auspicious king, that the escort and the envoys from the emperor of Constantinople kissed the ground before 'Umar, after having told him their story, and then produced the gifts, which comprised fifty slave girls – the most select to be found in the lands of Byzantium – together with fifty mamluks dressed in gowns of brocade with girdles of gold and silver. Each of them was wearing a golden earring in which was set a pearl equal in value to a thousand *mithqals* of gold. The same was true of the slave girls, whose dresses were made of the costliest materials.

When he saw them, King 'Umar accepted them gladly and gave orders that the envoys were to be treated with honour. He then went to ask the advice of his viziers as to what he should do. From among them one very old man, named Dandan, got up and, after kissing the ground before him, spoke as follows: 'Your majesty, the best thing to do here is for you to fit out a large army under the command of your son Sharkan, which we would accompany as his servants. This counsel is to be preferred for two reasons, the first being that the emperor of Byzantium has asked you for protection and has sent you a present, which you have accepted; the second reason is that no enemy dares attack our lands and if your army protects the emperor of Byzantium so that his foes are defeated, the victory will be attributed to you and word of this will spread throughout the regions. In particular, when the news reaches the islands of the ocean and the people of the west hear of it, they will send you offerings of gifts and money.'

When 'Umar heard what his vizier had to say, it pleased him and he decided that this was the right course to follow. He gave Dandan a robe of honour and said: 'You are the kind of man whose advice should be sought by kings. You must go with the advance guard, while my son Sharkan follows with the rear guard.' He then ordered Sharkan to be brought to him and he, on his arrival, kissed the ground in front of his father and took his seat. 'Umar then told him what had happened, what the envoys had said and what the vizier Dandan had recommended. He ordered him to collect his equipment and to prepare for a campaign, adding that whatever he did, he was not to act against Dandan's advice. He was told to pick from his army ten thousand riders, fully armed and capable of enduring the hardships of war.

Sharkan obeyed his father's instructions and, rising immediately, he selected his ten thousand. He then returned to his palace, reviewed his troops, provided them with money and ordered them to be ready in three days. Obediently, they kissed the ground in front of him, before leaving to collect their battle gear and put their affairs in order. Sharkan then went to the armoury, from which he took all the equipment and weapons that he needed, before visiting the stable to make his choice from among the best horses.

After three days, the army moved out of Baghdad and King 'Umar came to say goodbye to his son, who kissed the ground before him and was given seven chests of money. Next, Dandan was visited by 'Umar and instructed to take care of Sharkan's army, and he too kissed the ground and replied: 'To hear is to obey.' 'Umar then returned to Sharkan and told him to consult Dandan on everything, to which he agreed. After this, 'Umar re-entered the city and Sharkan ordered the officers to parade the troops for inspection, which they did, the total coming to ten thousand, not counting the camp followers. The baggage was loaded, drums were beaten, trumpets blared, banners and flags were unfurled, and Prince Sharkan rode out, with Dandan at his side, banners fluttering over their heads.

They continued on their way, preceded by the Byzantine envoys, until the day drew to a close and night fell. They then dismounted to rest for the night, remounting and moving out the following morning. They continued to press on with their march, guided by the envoys, for twenty days. On the twenty-first, they looked down into a wide valley, well wooded, fertile and extensive. As it was night when they arrived, Sharkan ordered them to dismount and to stay there for three days, and after dismounting, the soldiers pitched camp before dispersing right and left. Dandan and the Byzantine envoys stayed in the middle of the valley, while Sharkan waited behind for a time until they had all dismounted and were scattered throughout the valley. He then rode off with a loose rein to reconnoitre, taking the guard duties on himself, because of the instructions given him by his father, for the army was now on the edge of Byzantine territory and this was hostile land.

He set off alone, after ordering his mamluks and his personal guard to pitch camp with Dandan. His path took him along the side of the valley until a quarter of the night had passed, by which time he was tired and so overcome by sleep that he was unable to control his horse. He was in the habit of sleeping while on horseback, and so when he felt sleepy and then dozed off, the horse continued on its way until midnight, when it entered a thicket of trees. Sharkan only woke as it stamped its hoof on the ground, and on being roused he found himself among trees, with the whole sky illumined by moonlight. He was taken aback and exclaimed: 'There is no might and no power except with God, the Exalted, the Omnipotent!' – words which never bring shame on those who use them. While he was in this state, fearful of wild beasts, he saw in the moonlight, spread out before him, a meadow like one of the fields of Paradise, from which there came the sound of pleasant speech, loud voices and laughter of the sort that would captivate a man's mind. He dismounted and, after tying his horse to a tree, he walked on until he came upon a stream. He heard a woman speaking in Arabic and saying:

'By the truth of the Messiah, this is not good on your part. If anyone says anything at all, I shall throw her down and tie her up with her own girdle.'

While this was happening, Sharkan was walking in the direction of the voices, until he reached the edge of the meadow. He could see the stream, with birds singing gaily, gazelles roaming freely and wild beasts pasturing. Pleasure was expressed in the varied songs of the birds and the place was abloom with plants of all kinds, as a poet has described in these lines:

> The beauty of the land lies in its flowers,
> And the water that flows freely over it,
> Created by the power of the Almighty God,
> The Giver of gifts, Generous to the generous.

When Sharkan looked at the place, he saw a convent within whose bounds was a castle that towered in the moonlight. Through the grounds a stream flowed into the meadow, and there, by the stream, was a lady in front of whom stood ten girls like moons, wearing ornaments and robes of all kinds such as dazzled the eyes. All of them were virgins, as the poet describes:

> The meadow gleams with beautiful white girls.
> Beauty and grace are added by their unique attributes –
> All fascinating virgins, flirtatious coquettes,
> Their hair loose flowing like grapes on a trellis.
> Their eyes enchant; their glances dart as arrows.
> Swaying as they walk, they slaughter valiant heroes.

When he looked, Sharkan saw among them a girl like the full moon, with curling hair, a clear forehead, large black eyes and a curving forelock. She was perfect in all her delightful qualities, fitting the description of the poet:

> She is lovely to me with her wonderful gaze;
> Her figure puts to shame Samhari spears.
> Her cheeks, as I look at them, are rosy red,
> And she is mistress of all the charms of grace.
> It is as though the hair above her face
> Is night surmounting the dawn of delights.

Sharkan heard her say to the girls: 'Come here so that I can wrestle with you before the moon goes down and the day breaks.' Each of them went to challenge her, but she immediately forced each girl to the ground and tied her up with her girdle, before turning to the old woman who was there with her. This woman asked her angrily: 'Harlot, are you pleased to have got the better of these girls? Here am I, an old woman, but I have wrestled them down forty times, so how is it that you are so pleased with yourself? If you have strength enough to wrestle with me, then come here so that I may set about you and put your head between your legs.' The girl made a show of smiling, but inwardly she was furious. She went to the old woman and said: 'By the truth of the Messiah, do you really mean to wrestle with me, Dhat al-Dawahi, or are you joking?' 'Yes, I am serious,' replied the other.

Night 47

Morning now dawned and Shahrazad broke off from what she had been allowed to say. Then, when it was the forty-seventh night, SHE CONTINUED:

I have heard, O auspicious king, that the girl said to the old woman: 'By the truth of the Messiah, do you really mean to wrestle with me, Dhat al-Dawahi, or are you joking?' 'I will certainly wrestle with you,' came the reply. As Sharkan was watching, the girl said to the old woman: 'Then come and do it, if you have the strength.' At this, the old woman became furiously angry and all the hairs on her body stood out like the prickles of a hedgehog. She jumped forward and, as the girl rose to meet her, the old woman said: 'By the truth of the Messiah, harlot, I shall only wrestle against you naked.' She took a silk kerchief, unloosed her drawers and then, grasping her clothes with both hands, she stripped them from her body. She then picked up the kerchief and tied it round her waist until she looked like a hairless 'ifrit or a spotted snake. Turning to the girl, she told her to do the same.

Sharkan was watching all this and laughing as he looked at the misshapen form of the old woman. When her opponent had stripped, the girl in a leisurely way took a Yemeni towel and twisted it twice round herself. She tucked up her harem trousers, revealing two thighs of marble, surmounted by a crystal sand hill, soft and plump, a belly from whose folds wafted the scent of musk, looking as though it was covered with anemones, and a chest with two breasts like a pair of luxuriant pomegranates. The old woman leaned towards her and the two of them grappled, while Sharkan gazed up to heaven and prayed to God that the girl would get the better of the old woman. The girl, meanwhile, got under her, put her left hand on her girdle, with her right around the old woman's windpipe, and then lifted her up with both hands. The old woman slipped out of her grip, but in trying to get free, she fell over with her legs in the air, showing her pubic hair in the moonlight. She farted twice, the first fart scattering the dust on the ground and the second raising a stench to heaven.

Sharkan laughed so much that he fell over, but then he got up and drew his sword, looking to right and left. He saw nobody except the old woman lying on her back and he said to himself: 'Whoever called you Dhat al-Dawahi* did not lie; you should have known the girl's strength by what she did to the others.' He then went nearer to the two opponents to listen to what they were saying. The girl came up and threw an elegant silk wrap over the old woman, clothed her, and excused herself for what she had done, saying: 'I only meant to throw you, lady; nothing that happened to you was intended, but you slipped out of my hands. God be thanked that you are unhurt.' The old woman made no reply, but got up and walked off shamefacedly until she was out of sight. The others were still tied up on the ground and the girl was left standing alone.

'Every piece of good fortune has its cause,' said Sharkan to himself. 'It was thanks to my good luck that I fell asleep and that my horse brought me here, and it may be that this girl and her companions will be my booty.' He went to his horse, mounted it and touched its sides with his spurs. It shot off with him like an arrow from a bow and, after unsheathing his sword, he shouted: '*Allahu akbar!*' When the girl saw him, she got up to stand on the bank of the stream, which was six cubits wide, and she then jumped across and took up her stance on the other side. She called in a loud voice: 'Who are you, fellow? You have interrupted our pleasures and have brandished your sword as though you were charging against an army. Where do you come from and where are you going? Don't try to lie, for lying is one of the qualities of base men, but tell the truth, for this will do you more good. No doubt you have lost your way in the night and that is why you have come to a place where the most you can hope for is to escape unscathed. You are now in a meadow where, were I to give a single cry, four thousand

* 'Mistress of Disasters'.

knights would come to my aid. Tell me what you want. If you need to be directed to your road, I shall guide you and if you want help, I shall help you.'

When Sharkan heard what she said, he replied: 'I am a Muslim stranger and I came here alone tonight looking for plunder. I have found no better booty in this moonlight than these ten girls and I shall take them and bring them to my companions.' 'You have found no booty at all,' the other replied, 'for, by God, these girls are no prey of yours. Didn't I tell you that it is a disgrace to lie?' 'The wise man,' Sharkan told her, 'is one who learns his lesson from others.' 'By the truth of the Messiah,' she said, 'were I not afraid that your blood would be on my hands, you would find to your cost that my shout would fill this meadow with horse and foot. But I have pity on strangers, and if it is booty you want, then dismount and swear to me by your religion that you will use no weapon against me. Then you and I can wrestle together, and if you throw me, then put me on your horse and take us all, but if I throw you, you will be at my command. Swear to that, as I am afraid of treachery on your part, for, as it is noted, treachery comes naturally, and to trust everyone is a sign of weakness. If you do swear, then I shall cross over the stream and come to meet you.'

Sharkan was eager to capture her, and said to himself: 'She doesn't know that I am a champion.' Out loud he called to her: 'I shall take whatever oath you want and are prepared to trust, swearing that I will not move against you in any way until you are ready and tell me to come and wrestle. Then I shall come and if you throw me, I have enough money to ransom myself, while if I throw you, then I shall take great booty.' 'I am happy with that,' replied the girl. Sharkan was taken aback, but said: 'By the truth of the Prophet – may God bless him and give him peace! – so am I.' She then said: 'Swear by the One Who has set the breath of life in bodies and has given laws to mankind that, if you harm me in any way except by wrestling, you will die as one who has been excommunicated from Islam.' 'By God,' said Sharkan, 'were a *qadi*, or even the supreme *qadi*, to get me to swear, he would not try to make me take an oath like this,' but he then did as she had said, after which he tied his horse to a tree.

Drowning in an ocean of thought, he said to himself: 'Praise be to God who has formed her from vile sperm.'* He then summoned up his

* Quran 22.5.

strength and prepared himself for wrestling, before telling the girl to cross the stream. 'I am not going to cross over to you,' she said. 'You must cross over to me.' 'I can't do that,' he replied, at which she tucked up her skirts and jumped over to him on the far bank. He then approached her, bent forward and clapped his hands. Dazzled by her beauty and grace, he saw a form tanned by the hand of divine power with leaves used for tanning by the *jinn*, and nurtured by the hand of providence, over which the breezes of happiness had breathed, and for whom a star of good fortune had acted as midwife.

The girl came up to him and called: 'Muslim, come on and wrestle before dawn breaks.' With her sleeves tucked up, she showed a forearm glowing like fresh curds, casting radiance over the place. Sharkan, in a state of confusion, bent forward and clapped his hands, and she did the same. They gripped each other and grappled, holding and struggling. As Sharkan put his hand on her slender waist, his fingers sunk into the folds of her belly. His limbs relaxed and he discovered himself weakening, as he had found a place that induced languor. He started to shake like a Persian reed in a storm wind, at which the girl lifted him up, threw him to the ground and then sat on his chest, with buttocks like sand dunes, driving him out of his wits. 'Muslim,' she said, 'you think that you are permitted to kill Christians, so what do you say about my killing you?' 'Mistress,' he said, 'when you talk about killing me, this is forbidden, for our Prophet Muhammad – may God bless him and give him peace! – forbade the killing of women, children, old men and monks.' 'If this is part of your Prophet's revelation,' she said, 'we should return the favour. So get up, I grant you your life. No one loses by acting generously.'

She got off his chest and he stood up, shaking the dust from his head, ashamed at having been beaten by a crooked-ribbed woman.* 'Don't be ashamed,' she said, 'but when a man enters the lands of Byzantium in search of booty and to help kings against kings, how is it that he cannot defend himself against a crooked-ribbed one?' 'This was not through lack of power on my part,' he said, 'nor did you throw me because of your own strength. Rather, it was your beauty that overcame me. Perhaps in your generosity you would favour me with another bout.' She agreed, laughing, but said: 'The girls have been tied up for a long while and their hands and arms will be getting tired. I must untie them, as it may be that

---

* A reference to Eve being created from Adam's rib.

the next bout with you will be a long one.' She then went up to the girls and as she released them, she said to them in Greek: 'Go off to a safe place, so that this Muslim may stop coveting you.'

They went away, Sharkan staring after them, while they in turn were looking back at the wrestlers. The two approached each other and Sharkan set his belly against that of the girl. When she felt this, she lifted him up with her hands faster than a lightning flash and threw him to the ground. He fell on his back and she told him: 'Get up, for I give you your life a second time. The first time I was generous to you because of your Prophet, as he did not allow the killing of women, and this second time is because of your own weakness, your youth and the fact that you are a stranger. If the Muslim army that 'Umar ibn al-Nu'man has sent to help the emperor of Constantinople has in it anyone stronger than you, I would advise you to send him to me and to tell him about me. There are as many positions and holds in wrestling as can be imagined, such as the first grip, the grapple, the seizing of the legs, biting the thighs, cross-buttock throws and the leg lock.'

Sharkan was even angrier with her and swore: 'Even if the champions al-Safadi or Muhammad Qaimal or Ibn al-Saddi in his prime were here, I would pay no heed to the refinements you mentioned. By God, it was not by your strength that you threw me, but by the seduction of your buttocks. We Iraqis are fond of large thighs, and this robbed me of my wits and of my sight. But if you wish, you can wrestle with me again when I have my wits about me, and this will be the last bout for me, according to the rules of wrestling. My vigour has now returned to me.' 'Why do you want to try again, loser?' she taunted. 'But come on if you must, although I'm sure that this bout will be enough.' So saying, she leaned forward, challenging him to wrestle, and he did the same, beginning to exert himself and taking care not to weaken. They grappled for a time and the girl found in him a strength that she had not met before. 'You are taking care, Muslim,' she said. 'Yes,' he agreed, 'for you know that this is our last bout and afterwards we shall go our own ways.' She laughed, and he laughed back, but at that she forestalled him, taking him unawares and gripping him by the thigh. She then threw him to the ground so that he fell on his back. Laughing at him, she said: 'Do you eat nothing but bran? You're like a Bedouin's cap that falls off at a single blow or a child's toy blown away by the wind. What an unfortunate man you are! Go back to your Muslim army, and send someone else, for you are not capable of exertion. Proclaim among the Arabs, the

Persians, the Turks and the Dailamis that if there is any strong man, he should come to me.'

With this, she jumped over to the other side of the stream and said laughingly to Sharkan: 'It is hard for me to part from you, master, but you should go back to your companions before dawn, lest the knights come and take you at lance point. As you don't have the strength to defend yourself against women, how could you cope with them?' Sharkan was at a loss, but after she had turned away from him on her way back to the convent, he exclaimed: 'My lady, are you going to abandon me, the slave of love, the stranger, the wretched, the broken-hearted?' She turned to him with a laugh and asked him what he wanted, adding: 'For I shall grant your request.' He replied: 'How can I tread on your land and taste the sweets of your kindness and then go back without eating your food – and I have become one of your servants?' 'Only the mean refuse to act with generosity,' she replied. 'In the Name of God, please come and you will be very welcome. Mount your horse and ride along the bank opposite me, for you are my guest.'

Sharkan was delighted: hurrying to his horse, he mounted and, moving at a walk, he kept pace opposite her as she led the way to a drawbridge of poplar beams, where pulleys with iron chains were fastened with locks to hooks. Sharkan looked at the drawbridge and saw the girls who had been wrestling with his opponent standing there watching him. She went up to them and said to one of them in Greek: 'Go to him, take the reins of his horse and bring him across to the convent.' She herself went ahead as Sharkan followed over the drawbridge in a state of bewilderment at what he saw. 'I wish that Dandan were with me here,' he said to himself, 'and that he could see these lovely faces with his own eyes.' He then turned to his opponent and said: 'Most beautiful lady, I have now two inviolable claims on you – one is that of companionship, and the second is that I have come to your home and accepted your hospitality, as a result of which I am now under your authority and direction. Would you perhaps do me the favour of coming with me to the lands of Islam so that you can look at all our gallant heroes and learn who I am?'

When she heard this, she grew angry and said: 'By the truth of the Messiah, I had thought that you were a man of sound intelligence, but I now see the wickedness in your heart. How can you say something that shows you to be so deceitful, and how could I do what you suggest? I know that if I fell into the hands of your king, 'Umar ibn al-Nu'man, I

would never be freed since there is no one to match me within his walls
or his palaces, even though he is lord of Baghdad and Khurasan, with
twelve palaces for the number of the months of the year and in each of
them a concubine for every day of the year. Were I in his power, he
would not be held back by any fear of me since, according to your creed,
I would be lawfully yours, as is shown in your books by the words "or
what your right hands have possessed".* How is it, then, that you can
talk to me like this? As for what you say about looking at the Muslim
heroes, by the truth of the Messiah, that is a silly point. I watched your
army when you came to our lands two days ago, and when they
advanced, I saw no signs that they had been trained by kings. Rather,
they looked like a collection of scattered groups. When you say "You
will learn who I am", I am not doing you a favour in order to get to
know you, but to add to my own glory. Someone like you cannot speak
like this to one like me, not even if you were Sharkan, the son of King
'Umar ibn al-Nu'man, the illustrious hero of the age.' 'Do you know
Sharkan?' he asked. 'Yes,' she said, 'and I knew that he was coming here
with an army of ten thousand men. His father, 'Umar ibn al-Nu'man,
sent his army with him to help the emperor of Constantinople.'

'Lady,' said Sharkan, 'I ask you to swear by your religious faith that
you will tell me what is behind all this, so that I may be able to distinguish
truth from falsehood and learn who is responsible for the evil.' 'By the
truth of the Messiah,' she said, 'were I not afraid lest word would spread
that I was a Byzantine girl, I would risk my life by riding out against
the ten thousand Muslims, killing their leader, the vizier Dandan, and
overcoming the champion, Sharkan. I would bring no shame on myself
by this, as I have read Arabic books and studied what they have to say
about good manners. I am not going to describe myself to you as brave,
as you have already seen my trained skill and strength when I showed
you my proficiency at wrestling. Had Sharkan been in your place tonight
and had he been told to jump this stream, he could not have done it and
I would like the Messiah to bring him before me in this convent so that I
could come out against him, dressed as a man, capture him and put him
in chains.'

* Quran 4.3, 28, 29.

Night 48

Morning now dawned and Shahrazad broke off from what she had been allowed to say. Then, when it was the forty-eighth night, SHE CONTINUED:

I have heard, O auspicious king, that Sharkan listened to the Christian girl saying: 'If I had Sharkan here, I would come out against him dressed as a man, capture him as he sat in his saddle and put him in chains.' Sharkan was filled with a burning sense of pride and the self-respect felt by champions. He wanted to reveal himself to her and to strike out at her, but he was kept back from this by her beauty, and he recited:

When the lovely girl commits a single fault,
Her beauty supplies a thousand intercessions.

She then climbed up the path and, as he followed her, looking at her from behind, he saw her buttocks moving against each other like waves in a tumultuous sea, and he recited these lines:

In her face is worthy intercession,
Erasing her wrongdoing from the hearts to which it pleads.
At the sight of her I exclaim in wonder:
'A full moon has risen on a perfect night.
Were the Queen of Sheba's *'ifrit* to wrestle with her,
For all his reported strength, he would promptly be thrown down.'

The two of them went on walking until they came to a doorway arched with marble. The lady opened the door and she and Sharkan entered a long hallway vaulted with ten connected arches, each with a crystal lamp gleaming in it. At the end of the hallway they were met by girls carrying perfumed candles and wearing headbands embellished with gems of all kinds. The lady went ahead, followed by Sharkan, and when they reached the convent hall, Sharkan found it ringed with couches facing one another, covered with hangings adorned with gold. The floor was covered with tesselated marble of all kinds; in the middle was a pool with twenty-four golden fountains from which gushed water shining like silver. At the head of the hall was a throne spread with silks fit for a king. 'Mount to this throne, master,' said the lady.

When Sharkan had done this, she went off and was absent for some time. He asked some of the servants about her and they told him: 'She

has gone to her bedroom, and we are at your service, as she has ordered.'
They then produced various types of exotic foods and Sharkan ate until
he had had enough, after which they brought him a golden bowl and a
silver ewer. He washed his hands, but his thoughts were with his army,
as he did not know what had happened to them in his absence. He also
thought of how he had forgotten his father's instructions and he
remained in a state of perplexity, regretting what he had done, until
dawn broke and day appeared. Sighing in distress over his actions and
drowning in a sea of care, he recited these lines:

> I do not lack resolve, but now misfortune
> Has overtaken me in my affair; what can I do?
> Could someone clear away this love from me,
> I would use my own might and power to cure myself,
> But as my heart has gone astray in love,
> God is my only hope in my distress.

When he had finished these lines, a sight of great magnificence suddenly
presented itself, and he saw more than twenty maids like moons grouped
around the lady, who shone among them like the moon amidst stars as
they screened her. She was wearing a regal brocade and around her waist
was a woven girdle studded with every type of gem. This confined her
waist but made her buttocks stand out until it looked as if here was a
crystal sand hill beneath a silver branch, while her breasts were like two
luxuriant pomegranates. When Sharkan saw that, such was his joy that
his wits almost flew from him and he forgot his army and the vizier. He
looked at her head and saw that she was wearing a chaplet of pearls
interspersed with gems of all kinds. The maids to her right and left were
holding up her train and she was swaying entrancingly.

At the sight of her beauty and grace, Sharkan sprang to his feet and
cried out: 'Beware, beware of this girdle!' Then he recited:

> She sways with heavy buttocks,
> And is soft, with tender breasts;
> While she hides the passion that she feels,
> My own passion cannot be hidden.
> With her maids following behind,
> She is like a king with powers to loose and bind.

The lady gave him a long look and then did this again until she was
certain that she had recognized him. Then she advanced towards him

and said: 'You have brought honour and light to the place, Sharkan. How did you pass the night, hero, after we went away and left you?' Then she added: 'Lying is a shameful defect among rulers, and especially among great kings. You are Sharkan, son of King 'Umar ibn al-Nu'man. Do not hide the secret of your rank, and after this let me hear nothing from you but the truth, as lying leaves a legacy of hatred and enmity. The arrow of fate has pierced you and it is for you to give in and accept.' He could not deny what she said and had to admit that she was right. 'I am Sharkan, son of 'Umar ibn al-Nu'man,' he agreed, 'a man tortured by fate and cast up here, so do what you want with me now.'

She stood for a long time with her head bent, before turning to him and saying: 'Take heart and console yourself. You are my guest and we are linked by the ties of bread and salt. You are covered by my protection, and so you can set your mind at rest. By the truth of the Messiah, were all the people of the land to wish to injure you, they could only reach you after I had lost my life in your defence. You are here under the protection of the Messiah and of me.' Then she sat beside him and joked with him until his fear left him and he realized that, had she wanted to kill him, she would have done so the previous night.

She spoke in Greek to a girl, who went off for a time and came back with a glass and a table laden with food. Sharkan held back from eating, saying to himself that there might be something in the food, but the lady, realizing what he was thinking, said: 'It is not like that; there is nothing in this food to suspect. Had I wanted to kill you, I would have done it by now.' She went to the table and ate one mouthful of every dish. To her delight, Sharkan then ate and she ate with him until they both had had enough. They washed their hands, and she told the maid to bring scented herbs, as well as drinking cups of gold, silver and crystal, together with every kind of wine. When these had been fetched, the lady filled the first cup and drank the wine before him, as she had done with the food. She then filled a second and gave it to him and he drank. 'See, Muslim,' she said, 'how you are enjoying the sweetest of pleasures.' She went on drinking with him and pouring him drink until he lost control of his senses . . .

Night 49

Morning now dawned and Shahrazad broke off from what she had been allowed to say. Then, when it was the forty-ninth night, SHE CONTINUED:

I have heard, O auspicious king, that she went on drinking with him and pouring him drink until he lost control of his senses, both because of the wine and out of the drunkenness of love. 'Marjana,' she then said, addressing the maid, 'fetch us some musical instruments.' 'To hear is to obey,' replied the girl, who left for a moment and came back with a Damascene lute, a Persian harp, a Tartar flute and an Egyptian zither. She took the lute, tuned it, tightening its strings, and then sang to it in a melodious voice – softer than the zephyr and sweeter than the water of Paradise – from a wounded heart:

God forgive your eyes; how much blood have they shed!
How many arrows have your glances shot!
I honour a beloved who mistreats the lover;
Pity and mercy are not for the lover to receive.
Fortunate is the eye sleepless because of you,
And blessed is the heart your love enslaves.
You are my owner and decree my death;
I ransom with my life the judge who passes this decree.

After this, every one of the maids got up, each with her own instrument, and recited for the lady verses in Greek, filling Sharkan with pleasure. Then it was the turn of their mistress to sing herself. 'Muslim,' she asked, 'can you understand what I am saying?' 'No,' he answered, 'but I take pleasure in the beauty of your fingers.' She laughed and said: 'If I sing to you in Arabic, what will you do?' 'I would go out of my mind,' he replied. So she took an instrument and sang in a different tempo:

How bitter is the taste of parting; can it be endured?
I faced three things: aversion, distance and abandonment.
I love a graceful one whose beauty captured me,
And so abandonment is bitter.

When she had finished these lines, she looked at Sharkan and found that he had indeed lost his senses and was lying at full length among the maids. After a time, he recovered and, remembering the song, he swayed with pleasure. The two of them then started to drink and they continued jesting and amusing themselves until the day had flown and night had lowered its wing. The lady then got up and when Sharkan asked about her, her maids told him that she had gone to her bedroom. 'May God guard and protect her,' he said. In the morning, a maid came to him and said: 'My mistress invites you to go to her.' He got up and followed her, and when he came near the place, the other maids accompanied him in a procession with tambourines and flutes until they came to a large door of ivory, studded with pearls and other gems.

When they entered, Sharkan found a large apartment, at the top end of which was a great hall, adorned with silks of all kinds. Within it were open windows looking out over trees and streams, together with lifelike images into which the wind could enter, setting in motion machinery inside them which gave the impression that they were speaking. The lady was seated watching them, and when she saw Sharkan, she got to her feet, took his hand and seated him beside her. She asked what kind of a night he had passed, and after he had invoked blessings on her, they sat talking. 'Do you know anything relating to lovers and the slaves of love?' she asked. 'Yes, I know some poetry,' he replied. 'Let me hear it,' she told him, and he recited:

> Health and delight, untainted by disease,
> To 'Azza – how much of my honour is in her hands!
> By God, whenever I came near, she sternly kept away,
> And when I gave her much, she gave me little.
> What was between us is now at an end,
> And in my love for 'Azza I am like a man
> Who hopes a dwindling cloud will shade his midday sleep.

When she heard this, the lady said: 'Kuthaiyir was a chaste man of clear eloquence, and how well he described 'Azza in the lines:

> Were 'Azza to dispute on the point of beauty with the morning sun
> Before a judge, he would rule in her favour.
> Women have slandered her to men,
> But may God set their cheeks beneath her feet.

'Azza is said to have been extremely beautiful,' the lady added, and she went on to ask Sharkan to recite some lines by Jamil Buthaina, if he knew any. 'Yes,' he said, 'I know his poetry better than anyone.' Then he recited Jamil's lines:

They say: 'Fight in the Holy War, Jamil; go on a raid.'
But what war do I want to wage except the war of women?
In every talk of theirs is joy,
And all their victims die a martyr's death.
When I tell her my love is killing me,
She answers: 'Stand firm and it will increase.'
'Return some of my wits,' I tell her, 'so I may
Live amongst people.' She says: 'Far be it from you!'
You want to kill me and none other, while I see
No other goal to aim at except you.

'Well done, prince,' said the lady, 'and this was well spoken by Jamil.
But what did Buthaina want with Jamil to make him produce the half
line "You want to kill me and none other"?' 'Lady,' said Sharkan, 'she
wanted what you want with me, and even that will not content you.' She
laughed at his words and they went on drinking until the day ended with
the coming of the darkness of night. She then got up and went to her
bedroom, where she slept, while Sharkan slept in his own place. When
he awoke, the maids came to him as usual, with their tambourines and
musical instruments. They kissed the ground before him and said: 'In
the Name of God, please answer our lady's summons to come to her.'
He got up and walked between them as they beat their tambourines and
played their instruments until, on leaving the first apartment, he entered
another, larger one, filled with statues and pictures of birds and beasts,
that surpassed all description. Struck with wonder at the works of art
that he saw there, he recited:

Has the watcher plucked fruits of necklaces –
Pearls set in gold from around throats,
Gleaming eyes made from ingots of silver,
And rosy cheeks in faces of topaz?
It is as though the colour of the violet
Matches the blue of eyes, daubed with antimony.

At the sight of Sharkan, the lady got up, took him by the hand and
sat him beside her. 'Prince,' she asked, 'are you any good at chess?' 'Yes,
I am,' he replied, 'but don't be as the poet said:

Passion folds and unfolds me as I speak;
A draught of love's saliva slakes my thirst.
I came to play chess with her, and she played

With both the white and black, not pleasing me.
It was as though the king was next to the rook,
While looking for a game with the two queens.
If I try to establish what her glances mean,
Their coquetry, I tell you, destroys me.'

She then brought out a chess set for him and played with him, but every time that he was about to study her moves, he was distracted by her face, and put his knight where the bishop should have gone, and vice versa. She laughed and said: 'If this is how you play, you know nothing.' 'This is the first game,' he replied, 'so don't count it.' When she had beaten him, he set out the pieces and played again, but she beat him a second time and then a third, a fourth and a fifth. Turning to him, she said: 'You are beaten at every turn.' 'My lady,' he replied, 'how can anyone who plays with someone like you fail to be beaten?' She then ordered food to be brought, and after they had both eaten and washed their hands, wine was produced and they drank. Taking a zither, she touched it skilfully and recited:

Time is both wrapped away and then spread out,
Now an extended line and now a cone.
Drink to its beauty if you can be sure
That you will not leave or abandon me.

They went on like this until night fell, and this second day was better than the first. When night came, the lady went to her bedroom, leaving only the maids with Sharkan, who threw himself on the ground and slept until morning. The maids then came to him as usual, with their tambourines and musical instruments. When he saw them, he got up and they walked with him to meet the lady. She got up when she saw him, took him by the hand and set him down by her side. She asked him what kind of night he had spent, and in return he wished her long life. She then took the lute and recited the lines:

Do not leave or part from me,
For parting's taste is bitter.
When the sun sets, it is the pain
Of parting that has made it pale.

While they were occupied like this, there was a sudden commotion, with men crowding in and knights with drawn swords flashing in their hands, shouting in Greek: 'You have fallen into our hands, Sharkan; be sure that we shall kill you.' When Sharkan heard this, he said to himself: 'This girl has played a trick on me and has kept me here until her men could come. These are the riders with whom she threatened me, but it was I who brought the danger on myself.' He turned to reproach her but found that she had turned pale, and she then leapt to her feet, saying: 'Who are you?' The leader of the knights replied: 'Noble princess, pearl without equal, do you know who this man is who is with you?' 'No,' she replied, 'who is he?' 'He is the ravager of lands, the master of riders, Sharkan, son of King 'Umar ibn al-Nu'man, the conqueror of castles, who has taken every strong fortress. News of him was brought to your father, King Hardub, by the old woman Dhat al-Dawahi and the king checked that what she had reported was true. You have brought help to the army of Byzantium by capturing this ill-omened lion.'

When the lady heard this, she looked at the leader and asked him for his name. 'I am Masura, the son of your slave Mawsura, son of Kashardah, the champion of the knights.' 'How is it that you have entered without my leave?' she asked. 'My lady,' he replied, 'when I came to the door, no chamberlain or gatekeeper stopped me. Rather, they all got up and walked ahead of us, as is the custom, whereas when anyone else comes they leave him standing by the gate until they get leave for him to enter. But this is no time for talking. The king is waiting for us to return with this prince, who is the thorn of the army of Islam, so that he may kill him and send his army back to where they came from without putting us to the trouble of having to fight them.'

When the lady heard this, she said: 'What you say is not good. Dhat al-Dawahi lied and what she said was untrue, as she did not know the truth of the matter. I swear by the Messiah that this man who is with me is not Sharkan, nor is he a prisoner. He is someone who came here, approached us and asked for hospitality, which we granted him. Even if I was sure that he was Sharkan himself and this was established beyond doubt, it would not accord with my honour to allow you to take someone who is under my protection. Do not force me to betray my guest or put me to open shame, but go back to the king, my father, kiss the ground before him and tell him that the matter is not as Dhat al-Dawahi said.' 'Princess Abriza,' said Masura the knight, 'I cannot go back to the king without taking his enemy with me.' 'Damn you,' said the lady in a rage, 'go back to him with my answer and you will not be blamed.' 'I will not go off without him,' replied Masura.

The lady's colour changed. 'Don't be ridiculous,' she said. 'This man only came in here because he was sure that he, by himself, could attack a hundred riders. Were I to say to him: "You are Sharkan, son of King 'Umar ibn al-Nu'man," he would say yes, but I shall not allow you to interfere with him. If you do, he will not leave you until he has killed everyone here. He is here with me and I shall bring him out before you with his sword and his shield.' Masura replied: 'Your anger will not hurt me but your father's anger will. When I see Sharkan, I shall give the sign to my men, and when they have captured him, we shall take him as a humiliated prisoner to the king.' 'This shall not be,' she said. 'It is pure folly. Here is a single man and there are a hundred of you. If you want to fight him, go out to meet him one by one, so that the king may see which of you is the champion.'

Night 50

Morning now dawned and Shahrazad broke off from what she had been allowed to say. Then, when it was the fiftieth night, SHE CONTINUED:

I have heard, O auspicious king, that Princess Abriza told Masura: 'He is one single man and you are a hundred knights. If you want to fight him, go out to meet him one by one, so that the king may see who is the champion among you.' Masura replied: 'By the truth of the Messiah, what you say is right, but the first to go out against him will be no one except me.' 'Wait, then,' she said, 'until I go and tell him about this to see what his reply will be. If he agrees, well and good, but if he refuses, you cannot touch him for I and everyone in this convent, including my maids, will be his ransom.' She then went and explained to Sharkan what had happened. He smiled when he learned that she had not told anyone about him and that it was not due to her that word of his being there had reached the king, but he went back to blaming himself, wondering how he came to have risked his life in Byzantine territory.

After listening to what the princess had to say, he told her: 'To make them come out against me one at a time would be to wrong them. Why not let them come out in groups of ten?' 'It's a mistake to be too clever,' she said. 'It must be one to one.' At that, Sharkan leapt to his feet and went to confront them with his sword and the rest of his battle gear. Masura rushed in to attack him, but Sharkan met him like a lion and struck him on the shoulder with his sword, which came out gleaming from his back and his innards. When the lady saw this, her opinion of Sharkan rose and she realized that it had been her beauty and not her strength that had allowed her to throw him. She went up to the knights and told them to avenge their comrade, at which the dead man's brother, a huge and stubborn fighter, came out against Sharkan, who with no delay struck him on the shoulder, the sword coming out gleaming from his innards. She called to the others to avenge him and they came one after the other, but Sharkan's sword play left fifty of them dead, as she looked on. God then struck fear into the hearts of the survivors, who hung back and did not dare challenge him singly, but all attacked together. For his part, Sharkan charged against them with a heart harder than stone and crushed them as though on a threshing floor, robbing them of their wits and their lives.

The princess called to her maids: 'Who is left in the convent?' 'No one,' they answered, 'except for the gatekeepers.' She then went to meet Sharkan and embraced him, and as he had finished fighting, he went with her back to her apartments. There were still a few knights left, hiding in corners, and when she saw them she left Sharkan and came back, wearing a closely knit coat of mail, with an Indian sword in her hand. 'By the truth of the Messiah,' she said, 'I shall not grudge to give my life for my guest, and I shall not desert him, even if that brings me disgrace throughout the lands of Byzantium.' When she looked at the knights, she found that he had killed eighty of them, while twenty had taken to their heels. When she saw what he had done to them, she said to him: 'Men like you are the boast of the riders. How excellent you are, Sharkan!' Wiping his sword clean of the blood, he recited:

How many a host have I scattered in battle,
Leaving their armoured men as food for the wild beasts.
Ask all mankind about both me and them,
When I attack on the day of battle.
I have left their lions overthrown in war,
Among those plains upon the burning ground.

When he had finished these lines, the princess came up to him smiling, kissed his hand and took off the mail coat that she was wearing. He asked her: 'Why did you put this on and draw your sword?' 'Because I wanted to help you against those wretches,' she said. Then she summoned the gatekeepers and said: 'How did you come to let the king's companions enter my house without my leave?' 'Princess,' they answered, 'it is not usual for us to need your permission for royal messengers and, in particular, the leader of the knights.' 'I think that what you wanted,' she said, 'was to dishonour me and to kill my guest,' and she then ordered Sharkan to cut off their heads, and when he had done that, she told her other servants that these had deserved an even worse fate.

She then turned to Sharkan and said: 'What was hidden has now become clear to you and so I shall tell you my story. You must know that I am the daughter of Hardub, king of Rum; my name is Abriza and the old woman known as Dhat al-Dawahi is my grandmother on my father's side. It was she who told my father about you and she will certainly try to have me killed, particularly now that you have killed my father's men and word has spread that I have left and gone to the bad among the Muslims. The sensible thing for me to do is to leave here while Dhat al-Dawahi is on my heels. I would like you to repay me the kindness that I did you, as it is thanks to you that I am on hostile terms with my father. So do everything that I say, for you are the cause of all this.'

When Sharkan heard this, he was out of his mind with joy and filled with happiness. 'By God,' he said, 'no enemy is going to touch you as long as I have breath in my body, but can you bear to part from your father and your people?' 'Yes,' she said, and Sharkan swore an oath for her, after which they made a pact. 'Now I am at ease,' she said, 'but I have one more condition for you.' 'What is that?' he asked. 'That you lead your army back to your own country,' she told him. 'My lady,' he said, 'my father, 'Umar ibn al-Nu'man, has sent me to fight against your father because of the treasure that he took, including three large jewels, which can bring great good fortune.' 'You can set your heart at rest,' she said, 'and console yourself, for I'll tell you about them and explain the reason for the feud with the emperor of Constantinople. We have an annual festival, called the Feast of the Convent, to which kings come from all parts, together with the daughters of the great, as well as merchants and their wives, and they stay for seven days.

'I used to be one of those who went there, but after we had become enemies, my father stopped me from going to the festival for seven years. It happened one year that the daughters of the great came there as usual from all parts. One of them was the daughter of the emperor of Constantinople, a beautiful girl named Sophia. They stayed in the convent for six days and on the seventh, when everyone left, Sophia insisted on going back to Constantinople by sea, and so a ship was made ready for her, which she boarded with her own attendants. They set sail and put out to sea, but while they were on their way, a wind got up and blew the ship off course. As fate would have it, a Christian ship from the Island of Camphor was there with five hundred armed Franks on board. They had been at sea for a long time and when they saw the sails of the ship carrying Sophia and her maids, they quickly gave chase. In less than an hour, they had caught up with it and had thrown grappling irons on board. After lowering its sails, they towed it towards their island, but soon they met a contrary wind which dragged them on to a reef and tore their sails. Their ship was then driven on to our shore, and as we saw that this was booty that had been brought to us, we seized the men and killed them, and then we found the wealth, the gifts and the forty girls, among whom was the emperor's daughter, Sophia.

'The girls were taken and brought to my father, but we didn't know that one of them was Afridun's daughter. My father chose ten of them, among them being Sophia, and the rest he distributed among his retainers. Out of the ten, my father picked five, including Sophia, whom he sent to your father, 'Umar ibn al-Nu'man, together with broadcloth, woollen clothing and Byzantine silks. Your father accepted the gift and chose Sophia from out of the five. At the beginning of the year, her father wrote a letter to mine in terms that cannot be repeated, with threats and abuse, saying: "Two years ago, you plundered a ship of ours which had been taken by Frankish pirates. On board was my daughter Sophia, together with about sixty maids. You did not tell me or send any messenger to bring me the news. I did not make this public, for fear that, had my daughter had been dishonoured, this would be a source of shame for me among my peers. I kept the affair hidden until this year when I wrote a message to a number of Frankish pirates to ask whether there was any word of my daughter among the kings of the islands." They replied: "By God, we did not take her from your lands, but we have heard that she was captured from some pirates by King Hardub," and they told him the story. The emperor added in his letter: "Unless you want to be on hostile terms with me, and unless your intention is to disgrace me and dishonour my daughter, as soon as you receive my letter you are to return her to me. If you ignore this message and disobey my command, then I shall have to pay you back for your foul and evil actions."

'When the letter reached my father and he had read it and grasped its contents, he was distressed, regretting that he had not known that the emperor's daughter had been among the girls, so that he could have sent her back to her father. He was at a loss to know what to do, as after all this time it was no longer possible for him to write to King 'Umar ibn al-Nu'man and ask for her return, more especially since we had recently heard that a concubine of his, called Sophia, had given birth to children. When we had confirmed this, we realized that this letter spelt disaster and my father had no recourse except to send a reply to the emperor, excusing himself and swearing on oath that he had not known that his daughter had been among the girls on that ship, and he told him that she had been sent to King 'Umar ibn al-Nu'man, by whom she had borne children.

'When my father's letter reached the emperor, he flew into a rage, frothing and foaming. "How dared he make a captive of my daughter," he cried, "so that she became like a slave girl, passed from hand to hand, and given to kings who sleep with her without any marriage contract? By the truth of the Messiah and the true religion, I shall not take this insult sitting down, but I shall seek revenge and clear away this shame, doing a deed that people will talk about after I am dead." He waited until he had concocted a clever plan, sending an embassy to your father, 'Umar ibn al-Nu'man, with the message that you heard, which led your father to send you out with your army. As for the three gems that he told your father about when he asked for help, there is no truth in his story. They were with Sophia, his daughter, and my father took them from her when she and her companions fell into his hands. He gave them to me and I have them now. So go to your men and lead them back before they advance too far into the lands of the Franks and the Byzantines. For if you go on, they will close in on you and you won't be able to escape from them until the Day of Judgement. I know that your men are still where you left them because you told them to stay for three days, and also, as they have not been able to find you during this time, they have not known what to do.'

When Sharkan heard this, he went off for a time, deep in thought. Then he kissed the hand of Princess Abriza and said: 'Praise be to God Who has favoured me with you and has sent you to save me and my companions. I find it difficult to part from you and I don't know what will happen to you after I leave.' 'Go to your army now,' she said, 'and withdraw them. If the envoys are with them, arrest them so as to learn the facts of the matter while you are still near your own country. After three days, I shall join you and we shall enter Baghdad together.' Then, when Sharkan was about to leave, she added: 'Don't forget the pact between us.'

She got up to stand with him, embrace him, say goodbye and quench the fire of her longing. After her farewell embrace, she wept bitterly and recited:

I said farewell, as my right hand wiped away my tears,
While my left hand folded her in my embrace.
'Do you not fear disgrace?' she said, and I said no.
The day of parting is the lovers' disgrace.

Sharkan then left her and went down from the convent. They brought him his horse and he rode out on his way to the drawbridge, which he crossed before entering the trees. Having passed through them, he rode across the meadow, to be confronted by three riders. He was wary of them and, drawing his sword, he rode towards them, but when they came nearer, they recognized him, while, for his part, he saw that one of them was the vizier Dandan, accompanied by two emirs. When they saw and recognized him, they dismounted and greeted him. In answer to Dandan's question why he had been away, he told them everything that had happened to him with Princess Abriza from beginning to end. Dandan gave praise to God and then said to Sharkan: 'Lead us out of these lands, for the envoys who were with us have gone to tell their king that we have arrived and it may be that they will come in a hurry to seize us.' They all moved as fast as they could until they reached the floor of the valley. Meanwhile, the envoys had brought their king news of Sharkan's arrival, and he had prepared a force to seize him and his companions.

So much for them, but as for Sharkan, Dandan and the two emirs, they had already given urgent orders to the army to march. The Muslims left at once and travelled for five days before halting to rest for a while in a wooded valley and then pressing on. After twenty-five days, they were on the edge of the borders of their own land, and there, thinking themselves safe, they dismounted to rest again. The locals brought out guest provisions for them, fodder for their beasts and food for the men. After a two-day halt, they set off for home, Sharkan staying in the rear with a hundred riders, while Dandan led off the rest of the army.

When Dandan's men were a day's march ahead, Sharkan decided to move and he and his hundred riders mounted and rode for two *parasangs* until they came to a narrow mountain pass. There in front of them they suddenly caught sight of a dust cloud. They reined in their horses and paused until the dust cleared and there beneath it they saw a hundred iron-clad horsemen, like grim lions. Approaching Sharkan and his men, they shouted: 'By the truth of John and Mary, we have got what we hoped for. We have been pressing on in pursuit of you, night and day, until we got here before you. Dismount, hand over your weapons and surrender yourselves to us, so that we may spare your lives.'

When Sharkan heard that, his eyes started from his head, his cheeks flushed and he exclaimed: 'Christian dogs, how have you dared come to our lands and to tread on our soil, let alone speak to us with such effrontery! Do you think that you will escape us and return to your own country?' He then shouted to his riders: 'Attack these dogs; the numbers are equal.' Drawing his sword, he charged them and his hundred men joined in the attack. The Franks met them with hearts harder than stone; men clashed with men and champion with champion. There was ferocious fighting in the mêlée; among the dire terrors of battle there was no time for speech. They continued to fight, struggle and exchange sword blows, until the day ended and they were parted by the darkness of night.

Sharkan collected his force and found that the only casualties were four men, whose wounds he could see were not fatal. 'By God,' he said, 'all my life I have been plunging into the boisterous seas of battle and fighting against men, but I have never met any with greater endurance of war and combat than these champions.' 'Know, prince,' his men told him, 'that there is a Frank with them, their leader, a brave man, who deals slashing blows, but, by God, he has spared us, both great and small. He ignores all those who fall before him and does not fight them, whereas, by God, if he wanted to kill us, he would slaughter us all.'

Sharkan was taken aback by what he had seen of this man's feats and what he heard of him. 'Tomorrow morning,' he said, 'we shall draw up in formation and go out to meet them, a hundred against a hundred, and we shall pray to the Lord of heaven for victory over them.' Having agreed on this, they spent the night there, while the Franks gathered round their leader and said: 'We did not get what we wanted from those men today.' He told them: 'Tomorrow morning, we shall form up and challenge them one by one.' They agreed and during the night both sides kept watch until morning came at the command of Almighty God.

Sharkan mounted, together with his hundred riders, and when the whole force had come to the battlefield, they found the Franks drawn up and ready. Sharkan said to his men: 'Our foes intend to fight as they did yesterday, so prepare to charge them.' Then a Frankish herald called out: 'Today let us fight in turn, with one champion of yours challenging one of ours.' On hearing this, one of Sharkan's companions came out to fight, shouting: 'Will anyone dare to challenge me? Let no sluggish or weak man come forward.' Before he had finished speaking, out rode a Frankish rider, armed from head to foot, wearing a golden surcoat and mounted on a grey horse, and with no hair on his face. He rode out and halted in the middle of the battlefield, after which the two began to exchange cuts and thrusts, but it was not long before the Frank unhorsed the Muslim with a thrust with his spear and took him prisoner, leading him off in humiliation.

The Franks were delighted by his feat, but they stopped him from going out again and sent out another rider. Out came a second Muslim, the brother of the captive; the two halted on the battlefield and then charged each other and fought for a short time. Then the Frank bore down on his opponent and tricked him by striking him with the butt of his spear, so unhorsing him and capturing him. The Muslims continued to come out one by one and the Franks went on capturing them, until the day waned and night darkened, by which time twenty Muslims had been taken.

When Sharkan saw this, he found it hard to bear, and collecting his companions, he said to them: 'What has happened to us? Tomorrow morning I shall go out to the battlefield, challenge their leader and find out what it was that brought him to our lands. I shall warn him against fighting us; if he refuses to listen, we shall fight, and if he offers peace, we shall make peace with him.' They spent the night like this until Almighty God caused dawn to break. Both sides then mounted and formed up their ranks. Sharkan was about to go out to the battlefield when more than half the Franks dismounted before one of their riders and walked in front of him until they came to the middle of the ground. Sharkan looked at this man and saw that he was the Frankish commander. He wore a robe of blue satin, over which was a close-meshed mail coat. His face was like the full moon when it rises; in his hand was an Indian sword and he was mounted on a black horse with a blaze the size of a dirham on its face. His own face was hairless.

This rider spurred his horse until he reached the centre of the field and then, pointing at the Muslims, he said in fluent Arabic: 'Sharkan, son of 'Umar ibn al-Nu'man, you who have taken fortresses and laid waste lands, I challenge you to fight one who shares the field with you. You are the leader of your people and I am the leader of mine. Let whichever one of us overcomes the other command the obedience of the other's men.' Before he had finished speaking, Sharkan came out, his heart filled with rage. He spurred on his horse until he was close to the Frank and he then closed with him like an angry lion. The Frank met him with skill and power and struck him with a true horseman's blow. The two of them then started to cut and thrust, and kept on charging and retreating, receiving and returning blows, like two mountains clashing or the collision of two oceans. They continued to fight until day was done and night fell. They then withdrew from each other, each returning to his own people.

When Sharkan had rejoined his companions, he said to them: 'I have never before seen a rider like this. He has one particular trick which I have never seen anyone else use. When his opponent leaves himself open, rather than deal a fatal blow, he reverses his spear and strikes with the butt. I don't know what the outcome of our duel will be, but I wish that we had people like him and his men in our own army.' Sharkan then spent the night there, and in the morning the Frank came out again to meet him, stopping in the middle of the field. Sharkan advanced against him and they started to fight. The duel was prolonged and the necks of the spectators craned towards the fighters, who continued to fight, struggle and thrust with their spears until the day was over and it had grown dark. They then parted and each returned to his own side, to whom they started to tell of their experiences in the duel.

The Frank told his companions that the result would be decided next day. After a night's rest, in the morning the two rode out and charged against one another. They continued to fight until midday, but then the Frank played a trick. He spurred on his horse, but then pulled it up with the reins so that it stumbled, throwing off its rider. Sharkan pounced on him and was about to strike him with his sword, fearing to prolong the affair, but the Frank shouted at him: 'Sharkan, this is not knightly behaviour, but the deed of a man who has been overcome by women.' When Sharkan heard that, he looked up, stared at his opponent, and found that this was none other than Princess Abriza, whom he had earlier met in the convent. When he recognized her, he threw away his sword, kissed the ground before her and said: 'What led you to do this?' 'I wanted to test you on the field,' she answered, 'and to see how you could stand up to blows given in battle. All my companions are virgin girls. They have overcome your riders on the battlefield and had my horse not stumbled and brought me down, you would have seen how strongly I can fight.' Sharkan smiled at this and said: 'Praise be to God for our safety and for my meeting with you, queen of the age!'

Abriza then called to her girls and told them to dismount, after releasing the twenty Muslims whom they had captured from Sharkan's band. The girls obeyed her orders and then kissed the ground before Sharkan and Abriza, as Sharkan told them: 'People like you should be treasured by kings to help in times of peril.' He then gestured to his men, telling them to greet the princess. They all dismounted and kissed the ground before her, for they had realized what the position was. Then all two hundred of them mounted and rode day and night for six days, by which time they were near Muslim territory. Sharkan told Abriza and her girls to remove their Frankish clothes . . .

Night 51

Morning now dawned and Shahrazad broke off from what she had been allowed to say. Then, when it was the fifty-first night, SHE CONTINUED:

I have heard, O auspicious king, that Sharkan told Abriza and her girls to remove their Frankish clothes and to dress as Rumi girls, which they did. He then sent a number of his companions to Baghdad to tell his father of his arrival and that with him was Princess Abriza, daughter of Hardub, king of Rum, so that 'Umar might send someone to meet her. The rest immediately dismounted where they were, as did Sharkan, and there they passed the night. When Almighty God sent morning, Sharkan and his companions, together with Abriza and hers, rode out and were approaching the city when they were met by Dandan who had come out with a thousand riders to meet the two of them on the instructions of King 'Umar.

When the vizier and his men had come close, they went up to Sharkan and Abriza, kissed the ground before them, and acted as an escort for them as they rode into the city and up to the palace. Sharkan then went into his father's presence, and his father rose to embrace him, asking him what news he had brought. Sharkan told him what Princess Abriza had said, as well as of his encounter with her and of how she had come to leave her kingdom and part from her father. He explained: 'She chose to leave with us in order to stay here. The emperor of Constantinople wanted to trick us out of revenge for his daughter Sophia, as the king of Rum told him what had happened to her, explaining why she had been given to you, and assuring him that he had not known that she was his daughter, while, had he known that, he would not have passed her to you but would have returned Sophia to him.' Sharkan then added: 'We only escaped from this adventure because of this girl Abriza, and I have never seen anyone braver than her.'

He then began to tell his father what she had done with him, from beginning to end, including their wrestling match and their duel. When his father heard all this, Abriza rose in his estimation and he began to wish to see her. He asked that she come to be questioned, and at that, Sharkan went to her to tell her of the summons. 'To hear is to obey,' she said, and Sharkan brought her before the king. 'Umar, for his part, was seated on his throne and he sent away his courtiers, so that only the eunuchs were present. Abriza entered, kissed the ground before him and addressed him in fair words. He was astonished at her eloquence and, after thanking her for what she had done for his son Sharkan, he told her to sit.

She sat down and uncovered her face, at the sight of which the king's wits flew from him. He made her come nearer and promised her a palace of her own for herself and her girls, assigning allowances to each of them. He then began to ask her about the three gems that were mentioned earlier. 'I have them with me, king of the age,' she said, and she then went to her quarters, opened her baggage and brought out a case from which she took a golden box. She opened this and took from it the three gems which she kissed before giving them to the king. She then left, taking his heart with her.

After she had gone, the king sent for Sharkan, and when he had come, the king gave him one of the three gems. Sharkan asked about the other two and the king said: 'I will give one to your brother, Dau' al-Makan, and the other to Nuzhat al-Zaman, your sister.' Sharkan knew about his sister Nuzhat al-Zaman, but when he heard that he had a brother called Dau' al-Makan, he turned to his father and asked: 'Your majesty, do you have another son apart from me?' 'Yes,' replied the king, 'and he is now six years old.' He then told Sharkan that the child's name was Dau' al-Makan, his sister being Nuzhat al-Zaman, and that they were twins. Sharkan found this hard to bear, but he concealed his secret feelings and said to his father: 'God bless you.' Then he threw away the gem he was holding and shook the dust from his clothes. 'Why do I see this change in you,' asked his father, 'now that you have heard this news? You are still the heir to my throne: I have made the army take an oath of loyalty to you and the emirs of the state are pledged to support you. Of the three gems, this one is for you.' Sharkan bowed his head towards the ground and, being ashamed to dispute with his father, he accepted the gem and got up.

He was so angry, however, that he did not know what to do and he walked on until he entered Abriza's palace. When he came to her, she rose to greet him and thanked him for what he had done, calling down blessings on him and on his father. She then sat down and made him sit beside her, but when he was seated, she saw the anger in his face and asked him about it. He told her that Sophia had given birth to two children by his father, a boy called Dau' al-Makan and a girl, Nuzhat al-Zaman. He went on: 'He gave them two of the gems and handed me one, which I left behind. It is only now that I have heard about this, although the children are six years old, and when my father told me, I was furious. Now I have explained the reason for my anger; I have kept nothing hidden from you and I am afraid for you lest my father marry you, for he loves you and I saw that he was showing his desire for you. What would you say if he wants this?' 'You must know, Sharkan,' she said, 'that your father has no authority over me and cannot take me against my will, while if he were to take me by force, I would kill myself. As for the three gems, it had not occurred to me that he would give any of them to any one of his children, for I thought that he would store them among his treasures. Now, of your kindness, I would like you to make me a present of the gem that your father gave you, if you accepted it from him.' 'To hear is to obey,' he said, after which he handed it over to her. She told him to have no fear, and after talking to him for a time, she said: 'I am afraid that if my father hears that I am with you, he will not let me be, but will make efforts to recover me. He and the emperor will come to terms, because of the emperor's daughter Sophia, and the two of them will lead their armies against you and there will be a huge outcry.' 'My lady,' said Sharkan, 'if you are content to stay with us, there is no need to think about them, even if all the peoples of land and sea unite against us.' 'Nothing but good will result,' she said, adding: 'If you treat me well, I shall stay with you, while if you treat me badly, I shall leave.' She then ordered the girls to bring food. This came on a table, but after eating a little, Sharkan went to his own apartments, full of worries and cares.

So much for him, but as for his father, 'Umar ibn al-Nu'man, after Sharkan had left, he got up and went to his concubine Sophia, taking with him the two gems. When she saw him, she rose and remained standing until he sat down. Then his children, Dau' al-Makan and Nuzhat al-Zaman, came to him and when he saw them, he kissed them and fastened one of the gems round each of their necks. They were delighted with the gift, kissed his hands and went to their mother, who was glad and prayed that the king might enjoy a long life. He, in his turn, asked: 'Why, in all this time, did you not tell me that you were the daughter of Afridun, emperor of Constantinople, so that I might have honoured you more, as well as being more liberal to you and giving you higher rank?'

When Sophia heard that, she said: 'O king, what would I want with anything more or with a higher rank than what I already have, when I am submerged by your favours and your goodness, and when God has given me two children by you, a boy and a girl?' The king was pleased with her answer, and after he had left her, he set aside a splendid palace for her and her children, assigning them eunuchs, attendants, *faqihs*, philosophers, astronomers, doctors and surgeons, with instructions to look after them. He showed them increased favour and treated them with the greatest generosity. He then returned to the royal palace, the seat of his administration.

So much for Sophia and her children, but as for Princess Abriza, the king was on fire with love for her and he spent his nights and days in a state of infatuation. Every night he would go to visit her and talk with her, using words that hinted at his feelings. She made no reply to this, but would only say: 'King of the age, at this time there is nothing that I want from men.' When he saw that she was keeping herself from him, his infatuation and his burning passion increased until he became unable to cope with it. He then summoned Dandan his vizier and told him of his love for Abriza, adding that she would not submit to his wishes and that, although his love for her was killing him, he had got nothing in return from her. When Dandan heard that, he said: 'When it grows dark at night, take a *mithqal* of *banj* and go to visit her. Drink some wine with her, and when the two of you have almost finished drinking together, put the *banj* in the last glass and let her drink it. Before she retires to bed, it will have overpowered her and you can then come in and have your way with her. This is the advice that I have to give.'

The king approved of this and from his cabinet he took some refined *banj*, whose scent would put an elephant to sleep for a whole year. He put it in his pocket and waited until a brief part of the night had passed.

He then visited Princess Abriza in her palace and when she saw him, she rose to her feet and told him to be seated. She then sat down and he sat with her, proposing, as they talked, that they should drink. She brought out a table with drinks, set out the drinking glasses, lit the candles, and ordered fruits, dried and fresh, sweetmeats and whatever else that might be needed. The two of them drank, with the king keeping her company, until the wine went to her head. When he saw this, he took the drug out of his pocket and put it between his fingers. He then filled a glass with his own hand, which he drank, and after that he filled it again, pledging her with it, and into it, without her knowledge, he dropped the *banj*. Abriza took it and drank, and when in less than an hour he saw that it had overcome her and robbed her of her senses, he got up and went to her, finding her stretched out on her bed. She had taken off her harem trousers and the breeze had lifted the hem of her shift.

When the king saw her like that with a candle at her head and another at her feet, casting light on what was between her thighs, he lost his wits. The devil tempted him and as he was unable to control himself, he stripped off his trousers, fell on her and deflowered her. He then got up from on top of her and went to one of her maids, named Marjana, whom he told to answer a summons from her mistress. The maid went in and found Abriza lying on her back with blood flowing over her thighs. She fetched a kerchief and used it to set things to rights, wiping away the blood. She then spent the night with her, and when Almighty God brought morning, she washed her mistress's face, hands and feet; after which she brought rosewater, which she used on her face and mouth.

The princess sneezed and yawned before vomiting out the *banj* from her stomach in the form of a pill. After washing her mouth and her hands, she asked her maid what had happened to her and when Marjana told her the story, she realized that the king must have slept with her and that his ruse had been successful. In her great sorrow she went into seclusion and told her maids not to allow anyone to visit her – 'Tell them that I am ill' – until she saw what God would do with her. Word reached the king that she was sick, and he sent her drinks, sugar and electuaries. She stayed like this for some months, during which the king's passion cooled. His desire for her had been satisfied, and he kept away.

Abriza had become pregnant by him and with the passage of the months her pregnancy was shown by her swollen belly. In her distress she said to Marjana: 'You must know that it is not these people who have harmed me, but I have wronged myself by leaving my father, my mother and my kingdom. I am tired of life and my spirit is broken; I have no resolution or strength. I used to be able to control my horse, but now I cannot ride. When I give birth here, I will be an object of shame among my maids and everyone in the palace will know that I lost my virginity to fornication. Were I to go home, how could I face my father and how could I go back to him? How excellent is the line of the poet:

> What relief is there for one without family or homeland,
> Who has no boon companion, no wine glass and no dwelling?'

Marjana said: 'It is for you to command and I shall obey.' The princess said: 'I want to leave at once in secret. No one is to know of this except you. I shall go to my father and mother, for when flesh is putrid, no one but the family can help and God will do what He wills with me.' 'What you are doing is good, princess,' said Marjana. Abriza then made her preparations in secret and she waited for some days until the king had gone out to hunt and Sharkan had left to spend some time in the castles. She then went to Marjana and told her: 'I want to set off tonight, but what can I do against fate? I already feel my labour pains, and if I wait for four or five days, I shall give birth here and will not be able to go home. This is my destined fate.'

She thought for a time and then said to Marjana: 'Look for a man to travel with me and to act as my servant on the journey, for I don't have the strength to carry arms.' 'By God, my lady,' said Marjana, 'I know of no one apart from a black slave called Ghadban, one of the slaves of King 'Umar. He is a brave man – he told me earlier that he used to be a highwayman – and has been assigned to guard the door of our palace with orders from the king to serve us. We have overwhelmed him with generosity, and I shall go out and speak to him about this. I shall promise him money and tell him that, if he wants to stay with us, I shall marry him off to whoever he wants. If he agrees to this, we shall get what we want and reach our own lands.' 'Tell him to come to me,' said the princess, 'so that I can talk to him.' Marjana went out and called: 'Ghadban, God will bring you prosperity if you accept what my mistress is going to propose to you.' Taking him by the hand, she led him to the princess. When he saw her he kissed her hands, whereas she disliked him on sight, but said to herself: 'Necessity has its own laws.' So, in spite of her feelings, she went up to him and talked to him, asking: 'Ghadban, will you help us against Time's treachery, and if I tell you my secret, will you keep it hidden?' When he looked at her, she took possession of his heart and he fell in love with her on the spot. All he could say was: 'My lady, I shall obey any command that you give me.' She told him: 'I want you immediately to take me and this maid of mine and to saddle two camels, as well as two of the king's horses. Each horse is to have a saddlebag with some money and some provisions, and then I want you to come with us to our own country. If you want to stay there, I shall marry you to whichever of my maids you choose, but if you prefer to go back home, we shall give you a wife and whatever else you want to take back with you, in addition to enough money to satisfy your needs.'

When Ghadban heard this, he was delighted, and he said: 'My lady, I would give my eyes to serve the two of you. I shall go with you, and I shall saddle the horses for you both.' He went off joyfully, saying to himself: 'I have got what I want from them and if they don't do what I say, I shall kill them and take the money that they are bringing with them.' Keeping this to himself, he went off and returned with two camels and three horses, on one of which he rode himself. He brought up one of the others to the princess, and after mounting this, she got Marjana to mount the other. She herself was suffering from birth pangs and was unable to control herself because of the violence of the pain. Ghadban led them on through the mountain passes, travelling by day and night until they were within a day's journey of their own lands. The princess then went into labour, and being unable to hold back, she told Ghadban to help her from her horse as she was about to give birth. She then called to Marjana, telling her to dismount, sit at her feet and act as her midwife. Both Marjana and Ghadban dismounted while Ghadban secured the reins of his horse and that of the princess, who, by the time that she dismounted, had almost lost consciousness because of the pain.

When Ghadban saw her get down, at the prompting of the devil he brandished his sword in her face and said: 'Lady, have pity on me and allow me to enjoy you.' When she heard this, she said: 'All that is left for me is to give myself to black slaves, I who have refused valiant kings!'

Night 52

Morning now dawned and Shahrazad broke off from what she had been allowed to say. Then, when it was the fifty-second night, SHE CONTINUED:

I have heard, O auspicious king, that the princess said to Ghadban: 'All that is left for me is to give myself to black slaves, I who have refused valiant kings!' She then added in anger: 'Damn you, what are you saying to me? Do not speak of this in my presence, you wretch. I shall not agree to what you say, even if I die for it. But once I have given birth and tended to the child and to myself, and have rid myself of the afterbirth, then, if you can overcome me, do what you want with me. But if you don't stop talking in this obscene way now, I shall take my own life, leave this world and find rest from all this.' Then she recited:

> Leave me alone, Ghadban. I have had enough
> In my struggles against the miseries of Time.
> God has forbidden me fornication and has said:
> 'Hellfire is the abode of those who disobey My words.'
> I have no inclination to do wrong,
> As this is impious; leave and do not look at me.
> Give up your foul approach and join with those
> Who show respect towards my chastity,
> Or I shall shriek out to my own clansmen,
> Summoning them from far and near.
> Though I were cut in pieces with a Yemeni sword,
> I would allow no fornicator to gaze at me,
> From all the ranks of freemen and the great,
> So how much less a whoreson slave?

When Ghadban heard that, he became furiously angry. His eyes reddened, his colour paled, his nostrils flared, his lips drooped and he became even more repulsive. He then recited to Abriza:

> Do not leave me as one slain by your love,
> With a glance like a Yemeni sword.
> My heart is cut in pieces by your harshness;
> My body wastes away and my endurance vanishes.
> The magic of your eyes has captured hearts;

My wits are absent but my desire is close at hand.
Bring all the inhabitants of earth to fight for you,
But I shall take what I want now.

When Abriza heard this, she wept bitterly and said: 'Damn you,
Ghadban, are you in a position to speak to me like this, whoreson, child
of filth? Do you think that all men are equal?' When the ill-omened slave
heard that, his eyes reddened with rage; he approached her and struck
her on the neck with his sword, killing her. He then took the money and
rode off for safety among the hills.

So much for him, but as for Princess Abriza, she gave birth to a boy
as beautiful as the moon. Marjana took him, attended to him and placed
him beside his dead mother, whose teat he sucked. Meanwhile, Marjana
herself screamed loudly, tore her clothes, poured dust on her head and
slapped her cheeks until her face was bloodied. 'Oh my mistress!' she
cried. 'Oh disaster! You, for all your valour, have fallen at the hand of
a worthless black slave.' She was still weeping, when suddenly a dust
cloud appeared, covering the land, and when it cleared away, beneath it
could be seen a huge army.

This was the army of Abriza's father, King Hardub, and the reason
for its arrival was that Hardub had heard that his daughter and her
maids had fled to Baghdad and were with King 'Umar ibn al-Nu'man.
He had ridden out with his men to sniff out news from travellers, to find
if they had seen her with the king. When he was a day's journey from
his capital, he had seen in the distance three riders, whom he wanted to
approach in order to ask where they had come from, and to try to get
news of his daughter. In fact, the three whom he had seen were none
other than his daughter, her maid and the slave Ghadban. When he
approached them, Ghadban made his escape, fearing for his life because
he had killed Abriza,* and as the army came up Hardub saw his daughter
lying dead, with her maid weeping over her. He threw himself from his
saddle and fell fainting on the ground. All the knights, emirs and viziers
who were with him dismounted. They immediately pitched camp there
among the mountains, setting up a circular pavilion for the king, outside
which the officers of state took their post.

When Marjana saw her master, she recognized him and wept even
more bitterly. The king recovered consciousness and asked her what had
happened, at which she told him the story. 'Your daughter's murderer,'

* The text gives: 'fearing for his life, he killed her'.

she said, 'is a black slave belonging to King 'Umar ibn al-Nu'man,' and she went on to tell him how King 'Umar had treated the princess. The world grew dark in Hardub's eyes when he heard this and he wept bitterly. On his orders a litter was then fetched, on which the body of the princess was placed and taken to his palace in Caesarea.

The king himself went to visit his mother, Dhat al-Dawahi, and said: 'Is this how the Muslims treat my daughter? King 'Umar deflowers her by force and then one of his black slaves kills her. I swear by the Messiah, I shall have vengeance for her on him and clear my honour of this disgrace. If I fail, I shall kill myself by my own hand.' He then burst into tears. His mother said: 'It was Marjana who killed your daughter, as she nursed a secret dislike for her.' Then she added: 'Don't distress yourself about avenging her. By the truth of the Messiah, I shall not come back from King 'Umar before I have killed him and killed his sons. I shall do something that will be beyond the powers of the heroes and the men of wiles, something that people will talk of in every region and place, but you will have to obey me in everything I say. The man who makes up his mind to do what he wants achieves what he wants.'

When the king had sworn that he would never disobey her orders, she said: 'Fetch me virgins with swelling breasts and then bring the wisest men of the age to teach them philosophy, courtly behaviour and poetry, and how to consort with kings. The teachers are to talk with them on philosophical and religious subjects and these teachers must be Muslims so that they can teach the girls the histories of the Arabs, of the caliphs and of the old kings of Islam. If this is done over a period of four years, then we shall have reached our goal. You must show patience and endurance, for it is an Arab saying that to wait forty years for revenge is a small matter, and by teaching those girls we shall get what we want from our enemy. 'Umar is naturally disposed towards loving girls. He has three hundred and sixty-six of them, to which were added a hundred whom you picked to accompany your late daughter. When the ones I want have been trained as I told you, I shall take them and go off with them myself.'

The king was glad when he heard this and, getting up, he kissed his mother's head before immediately sending out agents to travel to the farthest lands in order to bring him Muslim sages. In accordance with his orders, the agents went to distant parts and brought him the wise men for whom he was looking. When these appeared before him, he showed them the greatest respect, gave them robes of honour, assigned

them salaries and allowances and promised them huge sums of money
in return for teaching the girls, whom he then fetched for them.

Night 53

Morning now dawned and Shahrazad broke off from what she had been
allowed to say. Then, when it was the fifty-third night, SHE CONTINUED:
I have heard, O auspicious king, that when the sages and wise men
had come to the king, he showed them the greatest honour and brought
them the girls. When the girls had been produced, he ordered the sages
to teach them philosophy and general culture, which they did.

So much for King Hardub, but as for King 'Umar, when he got back
from hunting he went to his palace and looked for Princess Abriza, but
failed to find her. No one could tell him anything about her or give him
any news of her, something that he found hard to bear. 'How can a girl
leave the palace without anyone knowing anything about her? If this is
the state of my kingdom, then it is badly run with no one to control it. I
shall not go out hunting again until I have sent officers to take charge of
the gates.' The loss of the princess was a great sadness and grief to him
and, while he was in this state, his son, Sharkan, returned from his
journey. His father gave him to news, telling him, to his deep distress,
that the princess had run away while he was hunting.

The king then took to paying daily visits to his children and showing
them his favour. He had brought wise and learned teachers for them,
whom he provided with salaries. On seeing this, Sharkan became very
angry, and he was so envious of the children's treatment that the marks
of his anger were visible on his face and he became chronically ill. One
day his father said to him: 'Why is it that I see you getting weaker and
weaker and why is your complexion so pale?' 'Father,' replied Sharkan,
'every time I see you showing close affection for my brother and sister
and favouring them, I am filled with jealousy. I'm afraid that this may
grow worse until it leads me to kill them, in return for which you will
kill me. This is why I am sick and my colour has changed. So, of your
kindness, I would like you to give me one of your more distant castles,
where I can stay for the rest of my life. As the proverb says: "It is better
for me to be far from my beloved. What the eye does not see, the heart
does not grieve over."' He then bent his head towards the ground.

When the king heard what Sharkan had to say, he realized what it was that had caused his decline and said reassuringly: 'My son, I shall grant your request. There is no greater citadel in my kingdom than that of Damascus, and from this day on it is yours.' He immediately summoned the registrars and ordered them to draw up a document investing his son Sharkan with authority over the city. This was done; preparations were made and Sharkan took Dandan with him, after his father had given Dandan instructions about the administration of the province, giving him control of affairs of state and instructing him to stay with Sharkan. He then said goodbye to his son, as did the emirs and the chief officers of state. Sharkan set off for Damascus with his troops, and on his arrival the inhabitants beat drums, blew their trumpets and adorned the city. They met him in a great procession and those officials whose place was on the right of the throne rode on his right, while those whose place was on the other side rode on his left.

So much for Sharkan, but as for his father, after Sharkan had left, the wise teachers came to tell him that his children were now masters of learning, with a full grasp of philosophy, together with a knowledge of general culture and decorum. The king was delighted and rewarded them generously. Dau' al-Makan was now well grown and developed. At the age of fourteen, he had mastered the art of horsemanship; he concerned himself with matters of religion and worship; he loved the poor as well as men of learning and Quranic scholars; and he was beloved by the people of Baghdad, both men and women.

The *mahmal* of Iraq now made a circuit in Baghdad on its way to the pilgrimage and the grave of the Prophet – may God bless him and give him peace. When Dau' al-Makan saw the procession, he felt a longing to go on the pilgrimage, and he went to ask his father's permission. His father refused and said: 'Wait till next year and then you and I can go together.' Dau' al-Makan thought that this was too long a delay and he went to see his sister, Nuzhat al-Zaman, whom he found standing in prayer. When she had finished, he explained: 'I long to go on pilgrimage to the sacred House of God and to visit the Prophet's grave – may God bless him and give him peace. This longing is killing me, but when I asked leave from my father, he refused to let me go and so I propose to take some money and to leave secretly without telling him.' 'I ask you in God's Name,' she replied, 'to take me with you and not to deprive me of the chance of visiting the Prophet's grave,' and so he told her: 'When it gets dark, come from here without telling anyone.'

At midnight Nuzhat al-Zaman got up, and dressed as a man, being of the same age as Dau' al-Makan. She took some money with her and walked as far as the palace gate, where she found that her brother had provided camels. He mounted his and helped her to mount, after which they set off in the night and mixed with the pilgrims, going on until they were in the middle of the Iraqi contingent. They continued on the journey until by God's decree they reached the noble city of Mecca in safety. They stood at 'Arafat and performed the ceremonies of the pilgrimage, after which they went on to pay their visit to the grave of the Prophet. They had intended after that to go back with the pilgrims to their own country, but Dau' al-Makan told his sister that he had a mind to visit Jerusalem as well as the city of Abraham, the Friend of God. 'So do I,' she said, and this is what they agreed to do, after which Dau' al-Makan went out and bought a passage for the two of them with the Jerusalem pilgrims. They set off with their caravan, and that night Nuzhat al-Zaman succumbed to a fever, but after a period of illness she recovered. Next it was her brother who fell ill and she nursed him tenderly. The two of them went on until they got to Jerusalem, but Dau' al-Makan's illness became worse and he became weaker and weaker. They stopped at a *khan* there and hired a room for themselves in which they stayed as Dau' al-Makan became more and more seriously ill until he was emaciated and unconscious. This distressed his sister and she exclaimed: 'There is no might and no power except with God, the Exalted, the Omnipotent! This is God's decree.'

She stayed there with her brother, nursing him as he grew weaker and spending her money on him and on herself. Eventually, all she had was used up and she was reduced to absolute penury, having not a single dirham left. She sent the servant boy of the *khan* to the market with some of her clothes, which he sold, and she spent the money on her brother. Then she sold another item, and she went on selling what she had, bit by bit, until the only thing left was a tattered mat. She wept and said: 'God ordains the past and the future.' Her brother said to her: 'Sister, I feel that I am getting better and I think that I would like some roast meat.' 'By God, brother,' she replied, 'I am ashamed to beg, but tomorrow I will enter some great man's house, act as a servant and work to get something to feed us both.'

She thought for a while and then said: 'It is not easy for me to leave you while you are in this state, but I shall go even so.' 'Are you to fall from grandeur to humiliation?' he asked, adding: 'There is no might and power except with God.' He then burst into tears and so did she, and

she said to him: 'We are strangers here, brother, and we have stayed for
a whole year without anyone knocking on our door. Are we to die of
hunger? I cannot think of anything else to do except to go out and get a
job as a servant so that I can fetch food to support us until you get better,
after which we can go back to our own country.'

For a time she stayed there in tears and he lay back and wept, but
then she got up and covered her head with a piece from a cloak that had
belonged to one of the camel drivers, who had left it with them and
forgotten about it. She kissed her brother's head, embraced him and then
went out. She was in tears and did not know where to go, but she
continued on her way. Her brother waited expectantly for her until
evening, but she did not come back, and although he went on waiting
until daybreak, she still had not returned. Things went like this for two
days and he was greatly distressed, shuddering with fear for his sister,
while the pangs of hunger grew worse and worse. Finally he left his
room and called to the servant boy, asking to be carried to the market.
The boy carried him and put him down there.

The people of Jerusalem gathered around him and shed tears when
they saw the state he was in. He made signs to show that he wanted
something to eat and one of the merchants from the market provided
some money with which food was bought and given to him. Then they
carried him off and set him down in a booth where they had spread a
piece of matting. By his head they placed a water jar, but when night
fell, they all left, although they were still concerned about him.

Halfway through the night, he remembered his sister. His illness
worsened; he neither ate nor drank but lost consciousness. The market
folk collected thirty silver dirhams for him from the merchants and they
hired a camel for him, telling the camel driver to take him to Damascus
and deliver him to the hospital, in the hope that he might recover his
health. The camel driver agreed, while to himself he said: 'Am I to go
off with this sick man, who is on the point of death?' So he took him to
a hiding place where he kept him until nightfall, after which he threw
him on a rubbish heap attached to the furnace of a bath house, and went
on his way.

In the morning, when the furnace man of the bath house came to
work, he found Dau' al-Makan lying on his back. 'Why do they have to
throw this corpse here?' he said to himself and he kicked the body with
his feet. It moved and he said to himself: 'Someone has been chewing
hashish and has thrown himself down in the first place he came to.' Then

he looked at Dau' al-Makan's face and found that he had no hair on his cheeks and was marked by splendour and beauty. He was moved to pity and realized that this was a sick man and a stranger. 'There is no might and no power except with God!' he exclaimed. 'I was wrong about this boy. The Prophet told us to honour strangers, especially if they are ill.' So he picked up Dau' al-Makan and brought him to his house, where he took him to his wife, telling her to look after him and to spread out a rug for him. This she did, and she placed a pillow under his head, heated water for him and used it to wash his hands, feet and face. The furnace man then went off to the market where he bought some rosewater and some sugar. He sprinkled the rosewater over Dau' al-Makan's face, gave him a sugar drink and brought out a clean shirt, which he put on him.

Dau' al-Makan sniffed the scent of good health and, beginning to recover, he propped himself up on the pillow. This delighted the furnace man, who praised God for the boy's recovery and said: 'God, I implore You by Your hidden secret, that You allow me to save this youth.'

Night 54

Morning now dawned and Shahrazad broke off from what she had been allowed to say. Then, when it was the fifty-fourth night, SHE CONTINUED:

I have heard, O fortunate king, that the furnace man said: 'God, I implore You by Your hidden secret, that you allow me to save this youth.' For three days he continued to look after Dau' al-Makan, giving him drinks made with sugar, willow-flower and rosewater, and nursing him with tender care until his body was suffused with good health. He opened his eyes, and when the furnace man came in to visit him, he saw him sitting up and looking animated. 'How are you now, my boy?' he asked. 'Praise be to God,' Dau' al-Makan replied. 'I am now well and in good health, if God Almighty wishes it.' The furnace man praised God for this and went off to the market where he bought ten chickens for the boy. He brought these to his wife, telling her to kill two of them each day, one early in the morning and one in the evening. She got up and killed one, which she boiled and brought to her patient to eat, making him drink the chicken broth. When he had finished his meal, she fetched him hot water. He washed his hands and propped himself up on his pillow, after which she covered him with a sheet. He slept until afternoon when she boiled him another chicken, brought it and cut it up for him, saying: 'Eat, my son.'

While he was eating, the furnace man came in and found her feeding him. He sat down by his head and asked him how he was now. 'Praise be to God, I am well,' Dau' al-Makan replied, 'and may God reward you well on my behalf.' The furnace man was glad to hear that and he went out and brought a drink flavoured with violets and rosewater, which he gave him. This man used to work in the baths for a daily wage of five dirhams. For Dau' al-Makan he would spend every day one dirham on sugar, rosewater, violet sherbet and willow-flower water, while for another dirham he would buy chickens.

He went on ministering to Dau' al-Makan for a month, until the signs of illness had vanished and he was restored to health. This delighted both the furnace man and his wife, and he then asked whether Dau' al-Makan would like to go with him to the baths. When he said that he would, the furnace man went to the market and fetched a donkey man. He mounted the convalescent on the donkey and supported him on the saddle until he had taken him to the baths, where he made him sit down while he took the donkey man into the furnace room. He himself went off to the market where he bought lotus leaves and lupin flour for him. 'Master,' he then said, 'in God's Name, go in and I shall wash your body.' So the two of them went into the baths and the furnace man began to rub Dau' al-Makan's legs, after which he started to bathe his body with the lotus leaves and the lupin flour.

An attendant, sent by the supervisor of the baths for Dau' al-Makan, then arrived and found the furnace man washing him and rubbing his legs. The newcomer went up and told him that he was infringing the supervisor's rights, to which the furnace man replied: 'The supervisor has overwhelmed us with his generosity.' The attendant then started to shave Dau' al-Makan's head, after which he and the furnace man bathed.

The furnace man took Dau' al-Makan back to his house and clothed him in a fine shirt, with some of his own clothes, an excellent turban and fine belt, winding a scarf around his neck. His wife had killed and cooked two chickens for him, and when he came in and sat on the bed, the furnace man melted some sugar in willow-flower water and gave it him to drink. He then brought up a table and started to carve the chickens for him to eat, giving him the broth to drink, until he had had enough. Dau' al-Makan then washed his hands and gave thanks to Almighty God for having restored his health.

To the furnace man he said: 'It is you who have been given to me as a favour by Almighty God, Who made you the instrument of my survival.' 'Don't talk like that,' said the furnace man, 'but tell me what brought you to this city and where you came from, for I see in your face signs of prosperity.' 'Tell me how you came across me,' said Dau' al-Makan, 'and then I shall tell you my story.' 'As far as that goes,' the furnace man exclaimed, 'I was on my way to work and I found you when it was almost dawn, lying on a rubbish heap by the door of the furnace room. I didn't know who had thrown you down there and so I took you to my house. That is my story.'

'Glory to God, Who gives life to dry bones!' exclaimed Dau' al-Makan. 'You have befriended one who is worthy of your kindness, and you will reap the fruits of that.' He went on to ask the man where he was. 'You are in the city of Jerusalem,' was the reply. At that, Dau' al-Makan remembered how he had left home and, thinking about his parting from his sister, he wept. He then revealed his secret to the furnace man, told him his story and recited the lines:

> They burdened me with a love I cannot bear;
> Because of them I cannot control myself.
> You who are leaving, be gentle with my heart's blood:
> When you have gone, malicious enemies will pity me.
> Do not grudge me one single glance
> To lighten my lot and the excess of my love.
> I asked endurance from my heart, but it replied:
> 'It is not my habit to endure.'

He then shed more tears and the furnace man told him: 'Don't weep, but praise Almighty God for your preservation and the recovery of your health.' 'How far is it from here to Damascus?' Dau' al-Makan asked. 'Six days,' he replied. 'Can you send me there?' Dau' al-Makan asked, but the furnace man said: 'Master, how could I let you go by yourself, when you are a young boy and a stranger? If you want to go there, I am the one who will go with you and, if my wife is willing to listen obediently and to go with me, I shall stay there, for I would not find it easy to part from you.' He then asked his wife whether she would go with him to Damascus, or would prefer to stay in Jerusalem until he had brought Dau' al-Makan to Damascus and then come back to her. 'He wants to go to Damascus,' he added, 'and it would be difficult for me to part from him, as I'm afraid that he might meet with highwaymen.' His wife agreed to come with them. 'Praise be to God that we are agreed,' he said. 'The matter is settled.' He then went and sold his possessions and those of his wife.

Night 55

Morning now dawned and Shahrazad broke off from what she had been allowed to say. Then, when it was the fifty-fifth night, SHE CONTINUED:

I have heard, O fortunate king, that the furnace man and his wife agreed with Dau' al-Makan to go with him to Damascus. The man then went and sold his possessions and those of his wife. He bought a camel and hired a donkey, on which he mounted Dau' al-Makan. They then set off and after a journey of six days they came to Damascus towards evening, after which the furnace man went and bought food and drink for them as usual. They stayed like that for five days, but then, after a few days' illness, the furnace man's wife passed on, to the mercy of Almighty God. This was a blow to Dau' al-Makan because he had become used to her and she had attended to his needs, while her death caused her husband bitter grief. Dau' al-Makan turned to him and, finding him sad, he said to him: 'Do not grieve; this is a door through which all shall enter.' 'May God reward you,' the man replied, 'and may He compensate us in His grace and remove sorrow from us. Would you like to cheer yourself by going out with me and looking around Damascus?' 'As you wish,' said Dau' al-Makan, and the furnace man got up and took Dau' al-Makan's hand in his, after which they went off until eventually they came to the stable of the governor of Damascus.

Here they found milling crowds, camels laden with chests, carpets and brocades, as well as saddled-up horses, Bactrian camels, black slaves and mamluks. 'Who do you suppose owns these mamluks, as well as the camels and all the goods?' wondered Dau' al-Makan. He asked one of the eunuchs where the presents were being sent, and the man replied that this was a gift from the governor of Damascus which was being forwarded, together with the Syrian tribute, to King 'Umar ibn al-Nu'man. When he heard this, Dau al-Makan's eyes filled with tears and he recited the lines:

You who are beyond the range of sight,
But are still lodged within my heart,

I can no longer see your loveliness; my life holds
No sweetness, but my longing does not change.
If God decrees that I meet you again,
I have a long story of my passion to tell you.

On finishing these lines, he burst into tears. His companion said: 'My son, we could scarcely believe that you had recovered, so be cheerful and do not weep, or else I'm afraid you might have a relapse.' He went on speaking gently and joking with him, while Dau' al-Makan kept sighing in regret for his exile and the parting from his sister and his kingdom. He then recited the following lines in tears:

Acquire provisions of piety in this world, for you will leave,
And know there is no doubt that death is on its way.
The comfort you have here is all deceit and grief;
Your worldly life is absurd vanity.
This world is like a traveller's camping ground;
He halts there in the evening and in the morning he is gone.

Dau' al-Makan continued to weep, lamenting his exile, while his companion wept for the loss of his wife, but still kept comforting Dau' al-Makan until morning. When the sun rose, he said: 'You seem to have remembered your own land.' 'Yes,' replied Dau' al-Makan, 'I cannot stay here. I must say goodbye to you, for I am going to set out with these people and accompany them by short stages until I reach my own country.' 'I will go with you,' said the other, 'for I cannot bear to part from you. I have done you a favour and I want to complete it by serving you.' 'May God reward you well on my behalf,' said Dau' al-Makan, who was delighted that he was coming with him. The man went off immediately and bought another donkey, selling the camel and buying provisions for the journey. Then he told Dau' al-Makan: 'Ride on this donkey, and when you are tired of riding, you can dismount and walk.' 'God bless you,' said Dau' al-Makan, 'and may He help me to repay you, for you have treated me better than a man treats his own brother.' They waited for the darkness of night, when they loaded their provisions on to the donkey and then set off.

So much for Dau' al-Makan and the furnace man. As for his sister, Nuzhat al-Zaman, she had left their *khan* in Jerusalem, wrapped in a cloak and hoping to find someone who would take her as a servant, so that she could buy the roast meat that her brother wanted. She was in tears; she had no idea where she was going and her mind was preoccupied with thoughts of her brother. Thinking of her family and her homeland, she started to implore Almighty God to ward off her misfortunes, and she recited these lines:

The night is dark; passion has stirred up sickness,
While longing has aroused the pains I feel.
The pangs of parting settled in my heart –
And thanks to passion nothing of me is left –
Disturbing me, while longing burns my heart,
As tears reveal the secret that was hidden.
I know no way by which I can reach union,
So as to banish the weakness disease has brought.
The fire of my heart is kindled by this longing
While its blaze leaves the lover in distress.
You blame me for my suffering; it is enough.
I endure what the pen of destiny has decreed.
I swear by love that I shall never be consoled,
And oaths that lovers take remain inviolate.
Night, carry news of me to those who tell of love;
Bear witness that you know I have not slept.

Then, shedding more tears, she started to walk, turning from one side to the other, until suddenly she came across an old man on his way from the desert with five Bedouin. He turned towards her and saw that although she was beautiful, her head was covered with a torn cloak. He was amazed at her beauty and said to himself: 'This is an astonishingly lovely girl, but she is in a squalid state. Whether she comes from this city or is a stranger, I must have her.' He began to follow her slowly, until in a narrow place he crossed her path. He then called out, asking her about herself, and saying: 'Little daughter, are you freeborn or are you a slave?' When she heard this, she looked at him and said: 'By your life, I implore you not to load me with any new sorrows.' He said: 'I had six daughters, but five of them are dead and only one, the youngest, is left. The reason that I came up was to ask you whether you belong to this city or are a stranger, so that I might take you off and make you my daughter's companion, in the hope that you could distract her from her grief for her sisters. If you have nobody else, I will make you like one of them and you will be a child of mine.'

When Nuzhat al-Zaman heard this, she said to herself: 'It may be that

I can trust myself to this old man.' Then, hanging her head in shame, she said: 'Uncle, I am a Bedouin girl, a stranger, and I have a sick brother. I will go to your daughter with you on condition that I stay with her by day and go back to my brother by night. If you agree to this, I shall come with you. I am a stranger here, but I was of high rank among my own people, although I am now lowly and wretched. My brother and I are from the Hijaz, and I'm afraid that he doesn't know where I am.' When the Bedouin heard this, he said to himself: 'By God, I've got what I was looking for.' He turned to her and said: 'There is no one dearer to me than you. I only want you to keep my daughter company by day, and at nightfall you can go back to your brother or, if you prefer, you can move him to my camp.' He went on speaking encouragingly and gently to her until she yielded and agreed to serve him. He walked in front of her and she followed, and he then winked at his companions, who went on ahead. They made ready the camels, loaded them, setting water and provisions on their backs, in readiness to leave as soon as the old man arrived.

Now this Bedouin was a bastard, a highway robber, a betrayer of companions, a thief and a wily schemer. He had no daughter and no son, and had merely happened to be passing when he fell in with this unfortunate girl, in accordance with God's decree. On the way, he kept on talking to her until he was outside Jerusalem and had rejoined his companions. Seeing that the camels were ready, he mounted one and took Nuzhat al-Zaman up behind him. They travelled the whole night and she soon realized that what he had said was a trick and that he had deceived her. She started to weep and shriek the whole night long, but the Bedouin rode on, making for the mountains, for fear that they be seen. When it was nearly dawn, they dismounted and the old man went up to Nuzhat al-Zaman and said: 'City girl, what's all this weeping? By God, if you don't stop, I'll beat you to death, you town whore.' When she heard what he said, life seemed unbearable and she wanted to die. She turned to him and said: 'You ill-omened old man, you greybeard from hell, how could I have looked for protection from you when you were betraying me and wanting to torture me?' On hearing this, the Bedouin replied: 'Whore, do you have a tongue to answer me back?' He went up to her with a whip and struck her, threatening to kill her if she didn't stay silent. For a time she did keep quiet, but thinking of her brother and the luxury which she had enjoyed, she wept secretly.

The following day, she turned to the Bedouin and asked: 'What is this trick that you are playing on me by bringing me to these barren mountains, and what are you going to do with me?' The man's heart was hardened when he heard this and he said: 'Ill-omened whore, do you have a tongue to answer me back?' and he struck her on the back with his whip until she fainted. Then she fell at his feet and kissed them, at which he stopped beating her and started to abuse her, saying: 'I swear by my cap that if I see or hear you crying, I'll cut out your tongue and stuff it up between your thighs, you town whore.' At that she kept quiet and did not answer him.

She was in pain because of her beating and she squatted down with her arms around her knees and her head sunk in her collar. She thought of the wretched plight that had succeeded the honour that she had enjoyed, as well as of her beating, and she thought of her brother, ill and alone, and of how they were both in a strange land. Tears ran down her cheeks and she wept in secret, reciting the lines:

It is Time's custom to go back and forth;
No single state stays fixed for mortal men.
There is a term for every worldly thing,
And each man's term must arrive at an end.
How many injuries and fears must I endure?
How sad that this is all my life contains!
May God not bless the days when I was honoured,
As folded in that honour was disgrace.
My quest has failed; my hopes are at an end;
Union is severed now by banishment.
You who pass by my dwelling, take the news
To my beloved that my tears flow down.

When she had finished her poem, the Bedouin felt sympathy and pitied her. He wiped away her tears and gave her a barley scone. 'I don't like people who answer me back when I am angry,' he told her, 'so don't use any of these ugly words in reply to me, and I'll sell you to a good man like myself who will treat you well, as I myself have done.' 'What kindness!' she exclaimed, and then, finding the night passed slowly and suffering from the pangs of hunger, she ate a small piece of her scone.

At midnight, the Bedouin ordered his party to move off . . .

Night 56

Morning now dawned and Shahrazad broke off from what she had been allowed to say. Then, when it was the fifty-sixth night, SHE CONTINUED:

I have heard, O fortunate king, that the Bedouin gave Nuzhat al-Zaman a barley scone and promised to sell her to a good man like himself. 'What kindness!' she exclaimed, and then, finding the night passed slowly and suffering from the pangs of hunger, she ate a small piece of her scone.

At midnight the Bedouin ordered his party to move off. They loaded up the camels, and the Bedouin mounted one, taking Nuzhat al-Zaman up behind him. They travelled continuously for three days, after which they halted at Damascus and lodged at Khan al-Sultan beside Bab al-Na'ib. Nuzhat al-Zaman's colour had changed because of her grief and the weariness brought on by the journey. She started to weep and the Bedouin came up to her and snarled: 'City girl, I swear by my cap that if you don't stop crying, I'll sell you to no one but a Jew!' He then took her by the hand and brought her to a room at the *khan* before going off to the market. He passed by merchants who dealt in slave girls and started talking to them and telling them: 'I have a girl whom I have brought with me. She has a sick brother whom I sent to my family in the lands of Jerusalem so that they might tend to him until he gets better. I want to sell her, but since her brother fell ill she has been weeping and finding it hard to bear being parted from him. So I'd like whoever wants to buy her from me to speak gently to her and to tell her: "Your brother is in my house in Jerusalem, sick." I'll then cut her price.'

One of the merchants asked him her age. 'She is a virgin and nubile,' he replied, 'and she is intelligent, cultured, clever and beautiful, but since I sent her brother to Jerusalem, she has been full of concern for him and has lost some of her beauty as her good looks have altered.' When the merchant heard that, he walked with the Bedouin and said: '*Shaikh* of the Arabs, I shall go with you to buy this girl whom you praise for her intelligence, culture and beauty. I shall pay you her price, but I shall lay down some conditions. If you accept them, then you can have the purchase price in ready cash, but otherwise I'll return her to you.' 'If you wanted,' said the Bedouin, 'you could take her to the sultan and lay down what conditions you liked for me. If you bring her to Sultan Sharkan, she may be to his taste and he may pay you her price and give you a good profit.' 'I have something that I want from him,' the merchant told him, 'which is that he should give me an official document freeing me from customs tolls and that he should write me a recommendation to his father King 'Umar ibn al-Nu'man. If he accepts the girl from me, I shall pay you her price on the spot.'

The Bedouin accepted the condition and the two of them went to Nuzhat al-Zaman's room. The Bedouin stood at the door and called: 'Najiya,' this being the name that he had given her. When she heard him, she burst into tears and made no answer. The Bedouin turned to the merchant and said: 'She is sitting here, so do you deal with her. Go to her, look at her and speak gently to her, as I told you.' The merchant went in and stood there politely. He found that the girl was wonderfully beautiful, and, in particular, that she knew Arabic. 'If she has the qualities you described,' he told the Bedouin, 'thanks to her I shall get what I want from the sultan.' He then greeted the girl and asked: 'Little daughter, how are you?' She turned to him and said: 'That is written in the book of fate.'

She saw that the newcomer was a respectable man with a handsome face and she said to herself: 'I think that this man has come to buy me,' adding: 'If I refuse to have anything to do with him, I shall have to stay with this evil Bedouin and he will beat me to death. At all events, this one has a handsome face, and I can hope for better treatment from him than from this boor of a Bedouin. It may be that he has only come to listen to how I speak and so I will answer him politely.' All the while her eyes had been fixed on the ground, but now she looked up at him and said sweetly: 'Peace be on you, sir, together with God's mercy and his blessings, as this is a greeting enjoined by the Prophet. As for your question about how I am, if you want to know, mine is a state which you would not wish any but your enemies to experience.'

She fell silent, leaving the merchant, who had been listening to her, beside himself with joy. He turned to the Bedouin and asked her price, saying that she was of noble blood. The man was angry and said: 'You have spoiled the girl for me by saying this. Why do you say that she is of noble blood? She is only a miserable slave girl from the dregs of the people and I won't sell her to you.' When he heard this, the merchant realized that the man was a fool. 'Don't upset yourself,' he said. 'I shall buy her from you in spite of the defects that you have mentioned.' 'How much will you pay me for her?' asked the Bedouin. 'It is only the father who names the child,' replied the merchant. 'Ask what you want.' 'It's up to you to speak,' said the Bedouin. 'This man is a hot-headed boor,' the merchant told himself. 'By God, I don't know how to set a price on her, but she has won my heart with her eloquence and her beauty. If she can read and write, this would complete the good fortune that she would bring both to herself and to whoever buys her, but this Bedouin has no notion of her value.'

So he turned to the man and said: '*Shaikh* of the Arabs, I'll give you two hundred dinars clear profit over and above the tax and the sultan's dues.' When he heard this, the Bedouin shouted furiously at him: 'Be off with you. By God, if you were to give me two hundred dinars for this bit of cloak that she is wearing, I wouldn't sell it to you. I shan't put her up for sale again, but I'll keep her with me to pasture the camels and grind the flour.' Then he shouted to her: 'Come here, you stinking girl. I'm not going to sell you.' Turning to the merchant, he said: 'I thought you were a knowledgeable man, but I swear by my cap, that if you don't leave at once, I'll say things you won't want to hear.' 'This fellow is mad,' said the merchant to himself. 'He doesn't know the girl's value, but I won't say anything about her price to him now. If he were a sensible man, he wouldn't swear by his cap. By God, the girl is worth Chosroe's kingdom. I haven't got the money with me to pay for her, but if he asks me for more, I'll give him whatever he wants, even if he takes all that I have.'

So he turned to the Bedouin and said: '*Shaikh* of the Arabs, be patient and don't upset yourself, but tell me what you have for her in the way of clothes.' 'What kind of clothes suit a whore like this? By God, this cloak in which she is wrapped is more than enough for her.' 'By your leave,' said the merchant, 'I shall unveil her and examine her, front and back, as one examines a slave girl for sale.' 'Do what you want, may God preserve your youth,' said the Bedouin. 'Examine her outside and inside, and if you want, strip off her clothes and look at her naked.' 'God forbid,' said the merchant, 'I shall only look at her face.' He then went up to her, abashed by her beauty.

Night 57

Morning now dawned and Shahrazad broke off from what she had been allowed to say. Then, when it was the fifty-seventh night, SHE CONTINUED:

I have heard, O fortunate king, that the merchant went up to her, abashed by her beauty. He sat down beside her and said: 'Lady, what is your name?' 'Do you mean my present name,' she said, 'or my earlier one?' 'Do you have one name today and another yesterday?' he asked. 'Yes,' she said. 'I used to be called Nuzhat al-Zaman, but now my name is Ghussat al-Zaman.'* When he heard this, the merchant's eyes filled with tears and he said: 'Have you a sick brother?' 'Yes, by God, sir, but time has parted us and he is in Jerusalem on his sickbed.' The merchant was astonished by the sweetness of her words and realized that the Bedouin had told the truth. Nuzhat al-Zaman then recalled her brother, his illness, his exile from home, how she had parted from him when he was sick, and how she did not know what had happened to him. She thought of her own experience with the Bedouin and of how far she was from her mother and father and her own land. The tears flowed down her cheeks, and weeping, she recited these lines:

God keep you safe wherever you may be;
You have travelled away but stay fixed in my heart.
Wherever you may be, may God protect you,
Guarding you through the changing course of Time.
You have left, and my eyes have missed your presence,
While my tears pour down in floods.
I wish I knew your spring camp or your land,
Whether you are settled in a house or with a tribe.
It may be that you drink the water of life
Within green pastures, but my drink is tears.
Though you may sleep, the coals of sleeplessness
Are here between my body and my bed.
My heart finds all else easy but to part from you,
And nothing else, except for that, is hard.

When he heard these lines of hers, the merchant wept and put up his hand to wipe the tears from her cheeks. 'God forbid!' she exclaimed, covering her face. The Bedouin sat watching her as she did this and, thinking that she was trying to stop the merchant kissing her, he ran up to her, lifting up a camel halter in his hand, with which he struck her a violent blow on the shoulders. She fell face downwards on the ground and a pebble cut open her eyebrow, so that blood poured down over her

---

* Nuzhat al-Zaman means 'Time's Delight' and Ghussat al-Zaman 'Time's Torment'.

face. She uttered a loud cry and was overcome by faintness. As she wept, the merchant wept with her. 'I must buy this girl,' he told himself, 'even if I have to pay her weight in gold, so as to rescue her from this tyrant.' He started to abuse the Bedouin as Nuzhat al-Zaman lay fainting, and when she recovered, she wiped the tears and the blood from her face and tied a cloth around her head. She then raised her eyes to the heavens and prayed to her Lord with a sorrowful heart, reciting the lines:

> Have mercy on one who was honoured, then unjustly shamed.
> With flowing tears she says: 'I can do nothing against fate.'

On finishing these lines, she turned to the merchant and said in a low voice: 'I implore you in God's Name, don't leave me with this tyrant, who knows nothing of Almighty God. If I have to spend the night with him, I shall kill myself with my own hand. Save me from him, and God will save you from hellfire.' So the merchant went to the Bedouin and said: '*Shaikh* of the Arabs, this girl will be of no use to you, so sell her to me at whatever price you want.' 'Take her,' said the Bedouin, 'and pay her price, or I'll move her to camp and leave her there to collect camel dung and herd the camels.' 'I'll give you fifty thousand dinars for her,' said the merchant. 'Not enough,' replied the Bedouin. 'Seventy thousand,' said the merchant. 'Not enough – this doesn't cover my capital costs. She has eaten barley scones with me worth ninety thousand dinars.' The merchant replied: 'You, your family and your clan have never eaten a thousand dinars' worth of barley in all your lives! I'll make you one offer and if you don't accept it, I'll lay information against you with the governor of Damascus and he will take her from you by force.' 'Say on,' said the Bedouin. 'One hundred thousand dinars,' said the merchant. 'I have sold her to you at that price,' said the Bedouin, 'and I'll be able to buy salt with what I have made from her.' On hearing this, the merchant laughed and, after fetching the money from his house, he handed it to the Bedouin. 'I shall have to go to Jerusalem,' said the old man to himself. 'I may be able to find her brother and bring him here and sell him.' So he mounted his camel and travelled on until he got to Jerusalem where he went to the *khan* and asked after Nuzhat al-Zaman's brother, but could not find him.

So much for him, but as for the merchant and Nuzhat al-Zaman, when he took her with him, he put something over her and brought her to his house.

Night 58

Morning now dawned and Shahrazad broke off from what she had been allowed to say. Then, when it was the fifty-eighth night, SHE CONTINUED:

I have heard, O fortunate king, that when the merchant bought Nuzhat al-Zaman from the Bedouin, he took her home. Here he dressed her in the most splendid of clothes and took her to the market, where he bought for her whatever jewels she wanted, wrapping them in a piece of satin and handing them over to her. 'This is all for you,' he said, 'and the only thing that I want in return is that, when I take you to the sultan, the governor of Damascus, you let him know the price for which I bought you, tiny as this was in relation to your worth. When you come to him and he buys you from me, tell him how I have treated you and ask him to give me an official letter of recommendation which I can take to his father, 'Umar ibn al-Nu'man, the ruler of Baghdad, in order to stop him levying duty on the materials and everything else in which I trade.'

When she heard what he said, she burst into tears. 'My lady,' said the merchant, 'every time that I mention Baghdad, I see that you weep. Is there someone there whom you love? If he is a merchant or someone else, tell me about him, because I know all the merchants and other such people, and if you want to send a letter, I will bring it to him.' 'By God,' she replied, 'I don't know any merchant or the like. The only person whom I do know is King 'Umar ibn al-Nu'man, the ruler of Baghdad.' When the merchant heard this, he was so pleased that he laughed aloud, saying to himself: 'By God, I have got what I wanted.' He asked: 'Have you been shown to him before?' 'No,' she replied, 'but I was brought up with his daughter; I was a favourite of his and he had great respect for me. If you want him to give you the authorization you need, bring me an inkwell and paper, and I shall write a letter for you. When you get to Baghdad, hand it to the king himself and tell him: "The changing fortunes of the nights and days have attacked your servant, Nuzhat al-Zaman, who has been sold from one place to another, and who sends you her greetings." If he asks you about me, tell him that I am with the governor of Damascus.'

The merchant admired her eloquence and his affection for her grew. He said: 'I think that you must have been tricked by men, who sold you for money. Do you know the Quran by heart?' 'Yes,' she said, 'and I have a knowledge of philosophy, medicine, the *Preface to Science* and

Galen's commentary on the *Aphorisms* of Hippocrates, on which I have commented myself. I have read the *Tadhkira*, commented on the *Burhan*, studied the *Mufradat* of Ibn al-Baitar, and can discuss the Meccan *Canon* of Avicenna.* I can solve riddles and set problems; I can talk about geometry and am proficient in anatomy. I have studied the books of the Shafi'ites, as well as the traditions of the Prophet, together with grammar. I have held debates with men of learning and have discussed all branches of knowledge. I am familiar with logic, rhetoric, arithmetic and astronomy. I know occult lore and how to establish the times of prayer. All these sciences I have mastered.'

Then she said again to the merchant: 'If you bring me an inkstand and paper, I will write you a letter which will help you in your travels and serve you in place of a passport.' 'Bravo, bravo!' exclaimed the merchant on hearing this. 'How lucky is the man in whose palace she will be!' He fetched her an inkwell, paper and a brass pen, and when he brought these to her, he kissed the ground as a mark of respect. Nuzhat al-Zaman took the scroll of paper, picked up the pen and wrote these lines:

> I see that sleep has shunned my eyes.
> Has your departure taught them wakefulness?
> Why does your memory kindle fire in me?
> Is this the way lovers remember love?
> A blessing on the days we shared; how sweet they were!
> They passed before I took full measure of delight.
> I ask a favour from the wind, which carries news
> From where you are to me, the slave of love.
> A lover with few helpers here complains
> To you; the pains of separation split the rocks.

When she had finished writing down this poem, she added: 'These are the words of one who is weakened by care and emaciated by sleeplessness. There is no light to be found in her darkness; she cannot distinguish night from day; she tosses to and fro on the bed of separation; she uses the pencil† of wakefulness to anoint her eyes; she is a guardian of the

---

* The *Tadhkira* is the *Tadhkirat al-Kahallin* ('Treatise on Ophthalmologists') by the eleventh-century Christian Arab 'Ali ibn 'Isa; Ibn al-Baitar was a botanist and pharmacologist (d. AD 1248); the *Mufradat* is al-Jami' li-mufradat al-adwiyah wa-'l-aghdiya ('The Comprehensive Book on Simple Drugs and Foods'); the Meccan *Canon* is Avicenna's al-Qanun fi'l-tibb or *The Canon of Medicine*.
† A stick used for applying kohl.

stars and marshals the dark; cares and emaciation have caused her to melt away, and it would take too long to describe her plight. Tears are her only helpers, and she has recited these lines:

> Doves calling from their branches as day breaks
> Arouse in me a sorrow that can kill.
> My grief increases every time
> A yearning lover sighs for his beloved.
> I complain of my passion to the pitiless.'

Then, with her eyes brimming over with tears, she added these lines:

> How often does love part body from soul!
> On the day of parting, love distressed my heart
> And separation robbed my eyes of sleep.
> My body is so wasted that, unless I spoke,
> I would remain invisible.

Shedding more tears, she added at the bottom of the page: 'From the one who is far from her family and her homeland, sad in heart and soul, Nuzhat al-Zaman.' Then she folded the paper and gave it to the merchant, who kissed it and noted its contents with delight. 'Glory be to the One Who fashioned you!' he exclaimed.

Night 59

Morning now dawned and Shahrazad broke off from what she had been allowed to say. Then, when it was the fifty-ninth night, SHE CONTINUED:

I have heard, O fortunate king, that Nuzhat al-Zaman wrote the letter and handed it to the merchant, who took it, read it and noted its contents. 'Glory be to the One Who fashioned you!' he exclaimed.

He treated her with even greater respect and spent the whole day indulging her. At nightfall, he went to the market and brought food for her, after which he took her to the baths and told the bath attendant, whom he fetched for her, that when she had finished washing Nuzhat al-Zaman's head and dressing her, she should send word to let him know. The attendant agreed and the merchant brought food, fruit and candles for her, setting them on the bench of the bath house. When the attendant had finished cleaning and dressing her, Nuzhat al-Zaman came out and took her seat on the bench, and the attendant sent word to the merchant. Nuzhat al-Zaman, for her part, finding the table set, joined the attendant in eating the food and the fruit, with the leftovers being given to the servants and the guard of the baths. She then slept until morning, with the merchant spending the night away from her in another room.

When he awoke, he wakened the girl and produced for her a delicate shift, a head scarf worth a thousand dinars, an embroidered Turkish dress, and shoes ornamented with red gold and studded with pearls and gems. In her ears he placed gold rings set with pearls worth a thousand dinars, while round her neck was a golden necklace that hung down between her breasts, together with an amber chain that fell below them to above her navel. On this chain were ten balls and nine crescents, with a ruby set as a ring stone in the centre of each crescent and a hyacinth gem in the centre of each ball. The value of that chain was three thousand dinars; each ball was worth twenty thousand dirhams, while the robe in which she was dressed was also hugely valuable.

When she had been dressed, the merchant told her to put on her ornaments and, decked in all her finery, she let a veil fall over her eyes, and set off with the merchant walking in front of her. At the sight of her, the people were amazed by her loveliness and exclaimed: 'Blessed is God, the finest of creators! How fortunate is whoever has this girl in his house!' The two of them walked on like this, until the merchant came into the presence of Sultan Sharkan. On entering, he kissed the ground before Sharkan and said: 'O fortunate king, I have brought you a gift of marvellous quality unique in this age, combining beauty and goodness.' 'Show it to me,' said Sharkan. The merchant then went out and brought in Nuzhat al-Zaman, who followed him until he made her stand before Sharkan. When Sharkan saw her, he felt the attraction of blood to blood, although she had been separated from him when she was little, since when he had never seen her. This was because when he had heard that he had a brother, Dau' al-Makan, as well as a sister, Nuzhat al-Zaman, he had hated them both as rivals for the kingdom and, because of this, he knew very little about them.

On presenting Nuzhat al-Zaman to him, the merchant said: 'King of the age, this girl is unique in her beauty and loveliness, with no match in her time, while, in addition, she is acquainted with all branches of knowledge – religious, secular, political and mathematical.' 'Take a price for her based on what you paid and then leave her and go on your way,' said Sharkan. 'To hear is to obey,' said the merchant, 'but write an order for me freeing me for ever from the payment of tithes on my goods.' 'I shall do that at once,' said Sharkan, 'but tell me how much you paid for her.' 'I paid out a hundred thousand dinars as her price and I then spent another hundred thousand on her clothes.' When he heard that, Sharkan said: 'I shall give you more than that for her,' and summoning his treasurer, he told him to give the merchant three hundred and twenty thousand dinars, leaving him with a profit of one hundred and twenty thousand. The four *qadis* were summoned and the money was paid over in their presence.

Sharkan then said to them: 'I call you to witness that I have freed this slave girl of mine and I want to marry her.' They drew up a document of manumission for Nuzhat al-Zaman and then a marriage contract. Sharkan scattered a great quantity of gold over the heads of all who were present, and the slaves and the eunuchs set about picking it up. After having paid the merchant his money, Sharkan then had an order written freeing him in perpetuity from having to pay tithes or taxes on his goods and ordering that no injury should be done him in any of his dominions, after which he ordered that he should be given a splendid robe of honour.

Night 60

Morning now dawned and Shahrazad broke off from what she had been allowed to say. Then, when it was the sixtieth night, SHE CONTINUED:

I have heard, O fortunate king, that after having paid the merchant his money, Sharkan then had an order written freeing him in perpetuity from having to pay tithes or taxes on his goods and ordering that no injury should be done him in any of his dominions, after which he ordered that he should be given a splendid robe of honour.

All the others then left and no one remained with Sharkan except the *qadis* and the merchant. Sharkan then said to the *qadis*: 'I want you to listen to what this girl can say to show her learning and culture in all the fields that the merchant has claimed that she can cover, so that we may check that he has spoken the truth.' They agreed to this and Sharkan ordered a curtain to be let down between him and his companions and the girl and those who were with her. All the ladies who had gathered behind the curtain with her were congratulating her and kissing her hands and feet, now that they knew that she had become the sultan's wife. They formed a circle around her and removed her robes, so as to free her from their weight, and they started to inspect her beauty and loveliness.

The wives of the emirs and the viziers had heard that the sultan had bought a slave girl who had no equal in beauty and learning, with a grasp of philosophy and mathematics, and all-embracing mastery of the sciences. He had paid out three hundred and twenty thousand dinars for her and had then freed her and drawn up a marriage contract for her, after which he had brought in the four *qadis* to test her by getting her to answer their questions and to debate with them. Having asked permission from their husbands, these ladies went to the palace where Nuzhat al-Zaman was, and on entering, they found the eunuchs standing before her.

When she saw the court ladies coming in, she stood up to greet them and her maids stood up behind her. She welcomed her visitors and smiled at them, capturing their hearts. After promising them favours of all kinds, she sat them down in order of precedence, as though she had been brought up among them, and they were astonished at her combination of intelligence and culture, as well as her beauty and loveliness. 'This is no slave girl,' they said to one another, 'but a queen and the daughter of a king.' They were deeply impressed by her as they took their seats and they said: 'Lady, you have illumined our city and added lustre to our country, our homes, our lands and our kingdom. The kingdom is your kingdom; the palace is your palace, and we are all your servants. By God, do not deprive us of your goodness and of the sight of your beauty.' She then thanked them.

This all took place with the curtain lowered between her and the other ladies on the one side and, on the other, Sharkan, beside whom were seated the four *qadis* and the merchant. Sharkan then called to her: 'Noble queen of the age, this merchant has described you as learned and cultured and has claimed that you have a grasp of all branches of knowledge, including astronomy. Let us hear something of what you told him and give us a brief account of this.' 'To hear is to obey,' she said, AND SHE WENT ON:

O king, my first topic deals with administration and the conduct of kings, of how those charged with the supervision of religious law should act, and with what is acceptable in the way of qualities that they should possess.

Know, your majesty, that beauties of character are to be found com-

bined in both religion and the secular world. This world provides the
only way to religion, and what a good path it is to the next world! The
affairs of this world are only brought into order by the acts of its people
and these can be split into four divisions – government, trade, agriculture
and manufacture. Government requires sound administration and accu-
racy of discrimination, for government is the pivotal point in the structure of this world, which, in turn, is the path to the afterlife. For Almighty
God has given His servants this world as provision for a voyage that will
allow them to reach their goal. Each man must take from it what will
enable him to come to God. In this he must not follow his own wishes,
and if mankind were only to take their just share from the world, there
would be no more enmity. Instead, however, they take unequal shares,
following their own desires, and the fact that they devote themselves to
this leads to quarrels, and so they need a ruler to settle their disputes
justly and to exercise control over their affairs. If the king did not protect
the people from one another, the strong would overcome the weak.

According to Ardashir, religion and kingship are twins; religion is a
hidden treasure and kingship is its keeper. The laws of religion and men's
intelligence show that people must appoint a ruler to ward off injustice
from those who are wronged and to bring justice to the weak in their
dealings with the strong, while checking the power of the insolent tyrant.
Know, your majesty, that the prosperity of the age depends on the good
qualities of the ruler. The Prophet of God said that if two things are
sound, all is well with the people, and if they are corrupt, the people are
corrupted. These two things are the men of learning and the rulers. A
philosopher has said: there are three types of king – a religious king, a
king who protects what is sacred, and a king who follows his own
desires.

The religious king is the one who makes his subjects follow their
religion. He must be the most pious of them all, for it is he whom they
will imitate in all religious matters. The people will be led to obey his
orders in accordance with the decrees of religious law. He will treat the
discontented in the same way as the contented, as it is necessary to
surrender to fate.

As for the king who protects what is sacred, he looks after both
religious and secular affairs; he makes his people follow religious law
and uphold manliness. He combines the pen and the sword. Whenever
anyone slips by straying from what has been written by the pen, the king
corrects his deviancy by the edge of the sword, spreading justice among

all. In the case of the king who follows his desires, his only religion is the pursuit of his lusts and he has no fear of his Lord, Who set him in authority. His kingdom is doomed to ruin and his arrogance will end in perdition.

The philosophers have said that the king stands in need of many people, but the people themselves need only one man. Because of this, the king must have a knowledge of their natures so as to be able to reconcile their differences, to treat them all with justice and to overwhelm them with his favours. You must know, your majesty, that Ardashir was known as 'Burning Coal'. He was the third king of Persia and his rule extended over all the lands, while he divided the government into four parts, with one seal ring for each of the four. Of these, one was for the sea, the police and defence, and on it was inscribed 'Officialdom'. The second was for the raising of taxes and the collection of money, and on this was inscribed 'Building'. The third was for the supply of food, which was inscribed with the word 'Abundance'. The fourth was for misdeeds, inscribed with the word 'Justice'. These regulations remained in force in Persia until the advent of Islam.

Chosroe wrote to his son, who was with the army, telling him not to be over-generous with his men, lest they should be able to do without him . . .

Night 61

Morning now dawned and Shahrazad broke off from what she had been allowed to say. Then, when it was the sixty-first night, SHE CONTINUED:

I have heard, O fortunate king, that Chosroe wrote to his son telling him not to be over-generous with his men, lest they should be able to do without him, adding: 'But do not treat them harshly lest they become discontented with you. Give them gifts in moderation; bestow favours on them. Indulge them in times of plenty, but do not stint them when times are hard.' NUZHAT AL-ZAMAN WENT-ON:

There is a story that a Bedouin came to al-Mansur and said to him: 'Starve your dog and he will follow you.' When he heard this, al-Mansur was angry, but Abu'l-'Abbas al-Tusi said: 'I'm afraid that if somebody else dangles a loaf before him, your dog will leave you and follow him.' This calmed al-Mansur's anger and, realizing that there was nothing wrong with what the Bedouin had said, he ordered him to be presented with a gift. You should also know that 'Abd al-Malik ibn Marwan wrote to his brother 'Abd al-'Aziz when he sent him to Egypt: 'Check your scribes and your chamberlains. The scribes will tell you about the inventories and the chamberlains will tell you about protocol, while the money that you spend will make you known to the army.' When 'Umar ibn al-Khattab – may God be pleased with him – engaged a servant, he made four conditions: the man was not to ride on the baggage animals, to wear fine clothes, to take a share of the plunder, or to postpone his prayers until after their proper time.

There is a saying that no possession is better than intelligence and that intelligence is best found in resolute administration. There is no resolution to match piety: the best way to approach God is through a good character; culture provides the best balancing scales; there is no profit to match success granted by God; good deeds are the best merchandise; there is no profit like God's reward; to stay within the confines of the *sunna* is the best form of piety; there is no knowledge that can rival contemplation; there is no art of worship better than the fulfilment of religious duties; there is no faith to match modesty; humility is the best type of reputation; and there is no nobility as fine as the possession of knowledge. Guard the head and what it holds and the belly and what it contains, while remembering death and tribulation. 'Ali – may God ennoble his face – said: 'Beware the evils done by women and be on your guard against them; do not consult them on any matter, but do not be stinting of your favours to them lest they be tempted to plot against you. Whoever abandons moderation finds his intellect going astray.'

There are conventions here which we shall mention later, God willing. 'Umar – may God be pleased with him – said that there are three types of women. First comes the true Muslim – pious, loving and prolific, who helps her husband against fate rather than helping fate against her husband. The second looks after her children and does no more, while the third is a fetter placed by God on the neck of whomever He wills. Similarly, there are three types of men. One is wise, acting on his own judgement. Another is wiser; he is the man who, when he does not know the probable outcome of a situation with which he is faced, approaches men of sound judgement and acts on their advice. The third is confused; he neither knows the right direction nor will he obey someone who might guide him to it.

In everything there must be justice; even slave girls need it. By way of example, one can point to highwaymen. Their lives are spent in injuring other people, but if they did not act fairly with one another and divide their booty properly, their organization would fall apart. In short, the most princely of noble qualities is generosity allied with good character. How well the poet has expressed it:

> Generosity and clemency give a man leadership,
> And so to become a leader is easy for you.

Another poet has said:

> In clemency is perfection and in forgiveness esteem,
> While truth is a safe haven for the truthful.
> Whoever uses wealth to search for praise,
> Will through his bounty win the race for glory.

After Nuzhat al-Zaman had talked of how kings should exercise power, her audience agreed that they had never heard the topic being discussed so well by anyone else, and they added: 'Perhaps she will talk to us about something else.' When she heard what they said and understood what they wanted, SHE SAID:

The topic of good manners is a broad one, as this is the compendium of perfection. One of Mu'awiya's companions happened to come into his presence and mentioned the good judgement of the people of Iraq. Mu'awiya's wife, Maisun, the mother of Yazid, was listening to their conversation, and when the man had gone, she said: 'Commander of the Faithful, I would like you to let some Iraqis come in to talk with you, so that I may listen to what they have to say.' So Mu'awiya said: 'Who is at the door?' and he was told: 'One of the Banu Tamim.' He ordered them to be brought in, and they came in, accompanied by al-Ahnaf Abu Bakr ibn Qais. Mu'awiya told him to approach and had a curtain lowered so that Maisun might hear what they said.

He then said: 'Abu Bakr, what advice have you for me?' 'Part your hair,' replied Abu Bakr, 'trim your moustache, cut your nails, pluck the hair from your armpits, shave your groin and use your tooth-pick constantly, as in this there are seventy-two merits. To make the Friday ablution expiates sins committed between one Friday and the next.'

Night 62

Morning now dawned and Shahrazad broke off from what she had been allowed to say. Then, when it was the sixty-second night, SHE CONTINUED:

I have heard, O fortunate king, that al-Ahnaf told Mu'awiya: 'Use your tooth-pick constantly, as in this there are seventy-two merits. To make the Friday ablution expiates sins committed between one Friday and the next.' NUZHAT AL-ZAMAN WENT ON:

'What advice do you give yourself?' asked Mu'awiya. 'I plant my feet on the ground, move them slowly and keep my eyes fixed on them.' 'What about when you go to visit clansmen of yours who are lower in rank than the emirs?' 'I look down modestly and am the first to say: "Peace be on you." I don't talk about what is no business of mine and I say little.' 'And when you visit your peers?' 'I listen to what they have to say, and if they want to skirmish with me, I don't reply in kind.' 'And when you visit your emirs?' 'I greet them without any gesticulation and I then wait for them to reply. If they ask me to approach, I do, but if not, I keep my distance.' 'And how about your wife?' 'Permit me not to answer this, Commander of the Faithful.' 'I insist that you tell me.' Al-Ahnaf said: 'I treat her good-naturedly and with obvious intimacy. I spend money liberally on her, for woman was created from the crooked rib.' 'And if you want to lie with her?' 'I talk her into a good mood and then I kiss her until she experiences pleasure. Then if what you know happens, I throw her on her back. If the seed settles in her womb, I say: "O God, make this blessed and not wretched, and fashion it in the best of forms." Then I leave her in order to perform the ablution. I pour water over my hands and over my body and I praise God for the favours that he has shown me.' 'These are excellent replies,' said Mu'awiya, 'so tell me what you need.' 'What I need,' said al-Ahnaf, 'is that you should fear God in your treatment of your subjects and deal justly with them all alike.' He then got up and left Mu'awiya's audience chamber. After he had gone, Maisun said: 'If he were the only man in Iraq, this would be enough for the country.'

'This,' added Nuzhat al-Zaman, 'is a small segment of the topic of good manners. Know, your majesty, that in the caliphate of 'Umar ibn al-Khattab, Mu'aiqib was in charge of the treasury.

Night 63

Morning now dawned and Shahrazad broke off from what she had been allowed to say. Then, when it was the sixty-third night, SHE CONTINUED:

I have heard, O fortunate king, that NUZHAT AL-ZAMAN SAID:

Know, your majesty, that in the caliphate of 'Umar ibn al-Khattab, Mu'aiqib was in charge of the treasury. He happened to see 'Umar's son, to whom he gave a dirham from the treasury. 'After I had done this,' he said, 'I went home and while I was sitting there, a messenger came to me from 'Umar. I went to see him fearfully and found him holding the dirham. "Damn you, Mu'aiqib," he said to me. "I have found out something about your soul." "And what is that?" I asked. "On the Day of Resurrection," he replied, "this dirham will involve you in a dispute with the people of Muhammad – may God bless him and give him peace."'

'Umar sent a letter to Abu Musa al-Ash'ari, telling him that when he received it he was to give the people what was due to them and to bring what was left over to him. He did this, and when 'Uthman became caliph, he sent Abu Musa the same message and he acted on it. This time, Ziyad came with him. When the tax money was placed before 'Uthman, his son came and took a dirham from it. Ziyad burst into tears and 'Uthman asked him why. 'I brought the tax money to 'Umar ibn al-Khattab,' he said, 'and his son took a dirham. His father ordered that it be snatched from his hand, but when your son does the same, I don't see anyone saying anything or taking it away from him.' 'And where can you find another 'Umar?' asked 'Uthman.

Zaid ibn Aslam has reported of his father that he said: 'I went out with 'Umar one night and we saw before us a fire burning. "Aslam," said 'Umar, "I think that these people must be travellers suffering from the cold, so come with me to visit them." Off we went and when we got there we found a woman who was lighting a fire under a pot and being pestered by two children. "Peace be on you, people of the light," said 'Umar, as he did not like to say "people of the fire". "What is the matter with you?" "We are suffering from the cold and it is dark," said the woman. "And why are these children crying?" "From hunger," she replied. "And what about this pot?" "It is what I use to keep them quiet, and on the Day of Resurrection God will surely ask 'Umar ibn al-Khattab about them." "What does 'Umar know about the state that they are in?"

asked 'Umar. "How can he be in charge of the affairs of the Muslims and ignore them?" replied the woman. 'Umar came up to me and told me to go off with him. We hurried off until we reached the treasury building, from which he took out a bag containing flour and a container filled with fat. "Load these on to me," he told me. "I will carry them for you, Commander of the Faithful," I said, to which he replied: "Will you carry my burden for me on the Day of Resurrection?" So I loaded the containers on to him and we rushed back and placed the bag down beside the woman, then brought out some of the flour from it. "Leave it to me," he told her, and he began to blow underneath the pot until I could see smoke coming out through his long beard. When the flour was cooked, he took some of the fat and threw it in. "Feed the children," he told the woman, "and I shall cook for them." They ate until they were full and he left the rest with the woman. Then he turned to me and said: "Aslam, I see that it was hunger that made them cry. I had not wanted to leave until I found out the reason for the light which I saw."'

Night 64

Morning now dawned and Shahrazad broke off from what she had been allowed to say. Then, when it was the sixty-fourth night, SHE CONTINUED:

I have heard, O fortunate king, that NUZHAT AL-ZAMAN SAID:

'Umar passed by a mamluk who was acting as a shepherd and asked him to sell him a sheep. 'They're not mine,' replied the mamluk. 'You are the man I want,' said 'Umar, and he bought the mamluk and then freed him. The man said: 'My God, as You have given me the lesser manumission, grant me the greater.' It is said that 'Umar used to give his servants milk, while he himself ate the curds. He would dress the servants in soft clothes, while his own were rough. He would give the people their dues and add more. He gave one man four thousand dirhams and then added another thousand. When he was asked why he had not given the same extra money to his own son, he said: 'This man's father stood fast at the Battle of Ohod.'*

According to al-Hasan, once when 'Umar came with valuable booty,

---

* The Battle of Ohod, fought outside Medina in the year 3 *hijri* (AD 625), represented a reverse for the Prophet Muhammad.

he was approached by Hafsa, who said: 'Commander of the Faithful, I ask for the due of kinship.' 'Hafsa,' he replied, 'we are told by God to pay the dues of kinship, but not from the money of the Muslims. You have pleased your family but angered your father.' Off she went, trailing her skirts. 'Umar's son said: 'One year I prayed God to let me see my dead father and I saw him, wiping sweat from his forehead. "How is it with you, father?" I asked. "Had it not been for the mercy of God, your father would certainly have perished," he replied.'

Listen, O fortunate king, to the second section of the first topic, covering accounts of the second category of the followers of the Prophet and other pious men. According to Hasan of Basra, no man's soul leaves this world without regretting three things. The first is that he did not enjoy what he had collected; the second is that he did not achieve what he had hoped for; and the third is that he had not provided himself with sufficient provisions for the journey on which he was embarked. Sufyan was asked: 'Can a man be ascetic who owns wealth?' 'Yes,' he replied, 'if he shows endurance when he is put to the test and if he is grateful when gifts are given him.' It is said that when 'Abd Allah ibn Shaddad was on the point of death, he sent for his son Muhammad and gave him his last instructions. 'My son,' he said, 'I see that I have been summoned by death. You must fear God both in private and in public. Be grateful for His mercies and tell the truth. Gratitude brings an increase in favours, and piety is the best provision for your journey. This is as a poet has said:

> I see no happiness in gathering wealth;
> The happy man is he who fears his God,
> A fear which truly is the best of all provisions,
> And it is to the pious man that God will grant increase.'

Nuzhat al-Zaman went on: 'Now listen, O king, to the anecdotes from the second section of the first topic.' 'What are they?' she was asked.
SHE SAID:

When 'Umar ibn 'Abd al-'Aziz became caliph, he went to his household and took everything that they owned, placing it in the public treasury. In alarm, the Umaiyads approached his aunt, Fatima, the daughter of Marwan, who sent a message to say that she had to see the caliph. She then came to him at night and he helped her to dismount. When she had taken a seat, he told her to speak first, as it was she who wanted something. 'Tell me what you wish,' he said. 'Commander of the Faithful,' she replied, 'it is you who must speak first, for by your judgement you see through what is hidden from the understanding of others.' The caliph then said: 'Almighty God sent Muhammad as a blessing to some and a punishment to others. He made His choice for him and then took him to Himself . . .'

Night 65

Morning now dawned and Shahrazad broke off from what she had been allowed to say. Then, when it was the sixty-fifth night, SHE CONTINUED:

I have heard, O fortunate king, that 'Umar said: 'Almighty God sent Muhammad as a blessing to some and a punishment to others. He made His choice for him and then took him to Himself, leaving the Muslims a river from which to drink. Abu Bakr al-Siddiq became caliph after Muhammad's death. He left the river as he found it and his actions were pleasing to God. He was succeeded by 'Umar, whose actions and exertions were not matched by anyone else. 'Uthman followed and caused a stream to branch off from the river. Mu'awiya as caliph diverted more streams from it, and the same process was followed by Yazid and the Banu Marwan, such as 'Abd al-Malik, al-Walid and Sulaiman, until the main stream dried up. Now that authority has passed to me, I want to restore the river to its former state.' Fatima replied: 'I only wanted to talk to you and discuss things with you, but if this is what you have to say, I have nothing to add.' She went back to the Umaiyads and said: 'Now you can taste the fruits of what you did by allying yourselves through marriage to 'Umar.' NUZHAT AL-ZAMAN WENT ON:

It is said that when 'Umar ibn 'Abd al-'Aziz was on his deathbed, he gathered his children round him. Maslama ibn 'Abd al-Malik said to him: 'Commander of the Faithful, how can you leave your children poor when you have been their guardian and in your lifetime there was nobody to stop you enriching them from the treasury? This would have been better than leaving things to your successor.' 'Umar looked at Maslama with anger and surprise and then said: 'Maslama, I have protected them throughout my life, so how can I lead them to misery after my death? My children belong to one of two types: either they are obedient to Almighty God, in which case He will see that they prosper, or else they are disobedient, and far be it from me to help them to disobedience. I was present, as were you, Maslama, at the burial of one of the Marwanids. I fell asleep there and saw him in a dream subjected to one of the punishments of God, the Great and Glorious. This filled me with terror and dread and I made a pledge to God that, if I became caliph, I would never act as he had done. All my life I have tried hard to keep to this and I hope that I may find God's forgiveness.' Maslama said: 'I attended the funeral of a man who had just died. After it was over I fell asleep and I saw him as in a dream. He was in a garden of flowing streams, wearing white clothes. He came up to me and said: "Maslama, it is for this that rulers should strive."'

There are many similar tales. A reliable man said: 'During the caliphate of 'Umar ibn 'Abd al-'Aziz I used to milk ewes and once I passed by a shepherd among whose sheep I saw a wolf or possibly more than one. I had never seen wolves before that and I thought that they were sheep-dogs. "What are you doing with these dogs?" I asked, and he told me that they were not dogs but wolves. "Doesn't having wolves in your flocks harm them?" I asked. "If the head is sound," he replied, "the body is sound."'

'Umar ibn 'Abd al-'Aziz once preached a sermon from a pulpit of clay. He praised Almighty God and glorified Him, and then he made three points. 'O people,' he said, 'set your private lives in order that this may be how you treat your brothers in public. Abstain from worldly affairs and know that between those who are alive now and Adam there is no living man, for all are dead. 'Abd al-Malik died, as did those who lived before him, and 'Umar will die as will those who live after him.'

Maslama then said to his father: 'Commander of the Faithful, if we get a cushion for you, you could prop yourself up on it a little.' 'I fear that this would be placed around my neck as a sin on the Day of Resurrection.' Then he groaned and fell down in a faint. Fatima called to various servants to attend to him and she poured water over him and wept until he recovered consciousness. He saw her weeping and asked her why. 'Commander of the Faithful,' she said, 'I saw you fall down before us and I thought of how death will cause you to fall before Almighty God, and of how you will leave this world and abandon us. It was this that made me weep.' 'Enough, Fatima,' said 'Umar. 'You have gone far enough.' He got up but fell again, and Fatima held him close and said: 'You are as dear to me as my father and mother, Commander of the Faithful, but we cannot all speak to you.'

At this point, Nuzhat al-Zaman said to Sharkan, her brother, and to the four *qadis*: 'This is the completion of the second section of the first topic.'

Night 66

Morning now dawned and Shahrazad broke off from what she had been allowed to say. Then, when it was the sixty-sixth night, SHE CONTINUED:

I have heard, O fortunate king, that Nuzhat al-Zaman said to her brother, Sharkan – whom she had not recognized – in the presence of the four *qadis*, as well as of the merchant: 'This is the completion of the second section of the first topic.' NUZHAT AL-ZAMAN WENT ON:

It happened that 'Umar ibn 'Abd al-'Aziz wrote to the Meccan pilgrims: 'In the sacred month and in the sacred city, on the day of the major pilgrimage, I call God to witness that I have played no part in wronging you or in the injuries inflicted by those who may have injured you, and that I never ordered this or intended it, nor has any news of this reached me or come within my knowledge. I hope that it may serve to win pardon for me that I have never given permission for anyone to be wronged, for if any have, I shall be questioned about them. If there is any governor of mine who has strayed from the truth and acted without the sanction of the Quran and the *sunna* of the Prophet, you should not obey him so that he may return to the way of truth.' He also said (may God be pleased with him): 'I do not want to be spared a painful death, as this is the last thing for which the believer is rewarded.'

A reliable informant has said: 'I came to 'Umar ibn al-Khattab, the Commander of the Faithful, when he was caliph, and I saw that in front of him were twelve dirhams. He ordered that these should be put in the treasury and I said: "Commander of the Faithful, you have impoverished your children and reduced them to penury and destitution. How would it be were you to make a will, leaving something to them and to the other members of your household who are poor?" He told me to come close to him, which I did, and he then said: "You have told me that I have impoverished my children and asked me to make a will in their favour and the favour of the other poor members of my household, but this is not right. God is my deputy with regard to both of these groups and He is a trustee for them. They fall into two classes – the God-fearing, who will receive their portion from God, and the inveterate sinners, whom I am not going to support in their disobedience to God." He then sent for his family and had them brought before him – twelve sons in all. When he saw them, tears started from his eyes and he said: "Your father has two choices – either that you should be rich and he should enter hellfire, or that you should be poor and he should enter Paradise. He would prefer this latter than that you should be rich. Rise, then; may God protect you, for it is to Him that I have entrusted the matter.""'

Khalid ibn Safwan once said: 'I went with 'Umar's son Yusuf to 'Abd al-Malik's son, Hisham, and when I reached him, he came out with his kinsmen and his servants and halted at a place where a tent had been pitched for him. When the people had taken their seats, I came out from where the carpet was spread and looked at him. When my eye caught his, I said: "May God complete his favour to you, Commander of the Faithful, and guide aright the affairs that He has entrusted to you, allowing no trouble to mix with your joy. I can find no more profound advice than the accounts of the kings who preceded you." The caliph, who had been leaning back, sat up and told me to tell him what I had to say. I said: "Commander of the Faithful, an earlier king in an earlier age came here and asked his companions whether they had ever seen anyone to rival his splendour and whether anyone had ever made as generous gifts as he had done. With him was one of the bearers of proof, the supporters of truth, who walk in its path. 'O king,' this man said, 'you have asked a question on an important matter. Will you allow me to reply to it?' 'Yes,' said the king. 'Do you think that the state in which you are is eternal or transient?' the man asked. 'It is transient,' replied the king. 'Why is it then that I see you taking pride in a state which you will enjoy briefly and be asked about for long, and for which you will be held to account?' 'How can I escape,' asked the king, 'and where can I find what I must look for?' 'If you remain king,' replied the man, 'then you must act in obedience to God. Otherwise, you should dress in rags and spend the rest of your life in His worship. At dawn I shall come to you.' The man knocked on the king's door at dawn and found that he had laid aside his crown and was prepared to live as a wandering ascetic because of the strength of the admonition." At that, Hisham ibn 'Abd al-Malik wept so much that his beard was soaked. He ordered that his robes should be removed and he stayed within his palace, while his freedmen and servants came to Khalid, complaining about what he had done to the Commander of the Faithful, ruining his pleasure and spoiling his life.'

'How many good counsels are there in this topic,' said Nuzhat al-Zaman to Sharkan. 'I cannot produce all that is to be found here in one session . . .'

Night 67

I have heard, O fortunate king, that Nuzhat al-Zaman said to Sharkan: 'How many good counsels are there in this topic. I cannot produce all that is to be found here in one session, but good will come of it if it is spread over a period of days.' 'O king,' said the *qadis*, 'this girl is the wonder of the age, unique in her time. Never at any time throughout our lives have we heard the like of this.' They then called down blessings on the king and left.

Sharkan turned to his servants and told them to start getting ready for the wedding and to prepare a banquet with foods of all kinds, which they did in obedience to his orders. He told the wives of the emirs, the viziers and government officials not to leave until they had seen the unveiling of the bride and shared in the wedding feast. It was hardly time for the noon prayer before the tables were laid with delicious, eye-tempting food, roast meats, geese and chickens, of which the guests ate their fill. All the singing girls of Damascus had been ordered to attend, together with all the adult slave girls of the sultan who could sing. They all came to the palace and in the evening, when it grew dark, candles were lit on both sides of the road from the gate of the citadel to that of the palace.

Then the emirs, viziers and grandees processed before Sultan Sharkan, while the singing girls and the tire-women took Nuzhat al-Zaman in order to dress and adorn her, although they saw that she needed no embellishment. Sharkan had gone to the baths, after which he took his seat on the dais. The bride was displayed to him in seven different dresses, after which the attendants relieved her of the weight of her clothes and gave her the advice that is given to girls on their wedding night. Sharkan then went in to her and deflowered her, at which she immediately conceived. He was delighted when she told him and he ordered the wise men to note down the date of conception. In the morning, when he took his seat on the throne, his officials came to congratulate him. He ordered his private secretary to write to his father 'Umar ibn al-Nu'man to tell him that he had bought a learned and cultured slave girl, a mistress of all branches of wisdom, whom he would have to send to Baghdad so that she could visit his brother Dau' al-Makan and his sister Nuzhat al-Zaman. He had freed her, married her, lain with her, and she had conceived his child. He eulogized her intelligence and sent his greetings to his brother and sister and to the vizier Dandan, as well as to all the other emirs. He then sealed the letter and sent it off by courier to Baghdad.

The courier was away for a whole month, after which he returned with an answer, which he handed to Sharkan. Sharkan took it and read it. After the invocation of God's Name, the letter went on: 'From King 'Umar ibn al-Nu'man, the bewildered and distracted man who has lost his children and parted from his country, to his son, Sharkan: know that since you left me, I have found this place oppressive and have not been able to show endurance. I cannot keep my secret. Dau' al-Makan asked me to allow him to go to the Hijaz, but I was afraid lest he might meet with some disaster and so I stopped him from going until the next year or the year after that. Then I went off hunting, and I was absent for a whole month . . .'

Night 68

Morning now dawned and Shahrazad broke off from what she had been allowed to say. Then, when it was the sixty-eighth night, SHE CONTINUED:

I have heard, O fortunate king, that King 'Umar said in his letter that he had been away hunting for a full month. He went on: 'When I got back, I found that your brother and sister had taken some money and gone off secretly with the pilgrims on the pilgrimage. When I learned that, I was distressed, but I waited for the pilgrims' return in the hope that the two would come back with them. Then when the pilgrims arrived, I asked about my children, but no one could give me any news of them. So, grieved at heart, I put on mourning for them, unable to sleep and drowned in tears.' He quoted the lines:

Their image never leaves me for an instant;
It holds the place of honour in my heart.
Did I not hope for their return, I would not stay alive;
Were it not for visions of them in my dreams, I would not sleep.

He then added in his letter: 'After sending you and your companions my greetings, I instruct you to spare no efforts in finding news of your brother and sister, for this brings shame on us.'

When Sharkan read the letter, he was sorry for his father but pleased to hear that his siblings were missing, and he took the letter to his wife, Nuzhat al-Zaman, whom he did not know to be his sister, while she in turn did not know that he was her brother. He kept coming back to her night and day, until the months of her pregnancy were ended and she sat on the birthing stool. God allowed her an easy labour and she gave birth to a girl. She then sent for Sharkan and when she saw him, she said: 'This is your daughter, so give her whatever name you choose.' 'It is the general custom,' he replied, 'to name children seven days after their birth.' Then, as he bent over the baby and kissed her, he saw hung round her neck one of the three jewels that Princess Abriza had brought from Byzantium. When he saw this hanging on his daughter's neck, his wits left him. He became angry, with staring eyes, and, recognizing the jewel, he looked at Nuzhat al-Zaman and demanded: 'Slave girl, where did you get this jewel?' To which she replied: 'I am your lady and the mistress of all who are in your palace. Aren't you ashamed to address me as "slave girl" when I am a queen and the daughter of a king? Concealment is now at an end and it can be revealed that I am Nuzhat al-Zaman, the daughter of King 'Umar ibn al-Nu'man.'

On hearing this, Sharkan trembled and bent his head towards the ground . . .

Night 69

Morning now dawned and Shahrazad broke off from what she had been allowed to say. Then, when it was the sixty-ninth night, SHE CONTINUED:

I have heard, O fortunate king, that on hearing this, Sharkan's heart quaked; he turned pale, trembled and bent his head towards the ground, realizing that this was his half-sister. He fainted, and when he recovered, he remained in astonishment, but did not tell Nuzhat al-Zaman who he was. 'Lady,' he said, 'are you really the daughter of King 'Umar ibn al-Nu'man?' 'Yes,' she replied. 'Tell me how and why you left your father and came to be sold,' he said, and she told him all that happened to her from beginning to end, including how she had left her sick brother in Jerusalem, and how she had been kidnapped by the Bedouin and sold by him to the merchant. When Sharkan heard that, he realized that she was indeed his half-sister. 'How could I have married my sister?' he said to himself. 'By God, I shall have to marry her off to one of my chamberlains, and if word of the affair gets out, I shall claim that I divorced her before consummating the marriage and married her to my principal chamberlain.'

He then raised his head and confessed sorrowfully: 'Nuzhat al-Zaman, you are, in fact, my sister, and I ask God's forgiveness for the sin into which we have fallen. I am Sharkan, son of King 'Umar ibn al-Nu'man.' She looked at him and realized that this was true. Then she lost her senses, wept and struck her face, exclaiming: 'There is no might and no power except with God! We have fallen into a grave sin. What are we to do and what can I say to my father and my mother when they ask who was the father of this child?' 'What I think,' said Sharkan, 'is that I should marry you to my chief chamberlain and let you raise my daughter with him in his household, so that no one will know that you are my sister. This is something that has been decreed by Almighty God for some purpose of His own, and the only way we can conceal the matter is for you to be married to the man before anyone knows.' He then began to comfort her and to kiss her head, and when she asked what name he would give the baby, he said 'Qudiya-fa-Kana'.* He then married her to the chief chamberlain and transferred her to his house, together with her baby, who was brought up in the care of slave girls and dosed with potions and powders.

While all this was happening, Dau' al-Makan was in Damascus with the furnace man. One day a courier arrived from King 'Umar ibn al-Nu'man with a letter for Sharkan, which he took and read. After the invocation of God's Name, it ran: 'Know, glorious king, that separation from my children has left me in the depth of distress. I cannot sleep and am forced to remain wakeful. As soon as you receive this letter which I am sending to you, make your preparations to forward the tax revenues and send with them the slave girl whom you have bought and married, as I want to see her and to listen to what she has to say. That is because a pious old woman has come to us from the lands of Byzantium with five swelling-breasted virgins, who have a compendious knowledge of science, culture and all the forms of wisdom that should be studied. No tongue can describe this old woman and her companions, such is their knowledge of all branches of learning, virtue and wisdom. I loved them as soon as I saw them and I wanted to have them in my palace and under my control, since no other king has anyone to match them. When I asked

---

* 'It was decreed and it happened'.

the old woman for their price, she said that she would only sell them for the tribute of Damascus, and, by God, I do not think that this is too much, for any one of them is worth it all. I agreed to the sale and have taken them to my palace, where they remain in my possession. So send the tribute quickly, so that the old woman may return to her own country, and send me the slave girl so that she may debate with these five in the presence of the learned doctors, and if she gets the better of them, I shall send her back to you, together with the tribute of Baghdad.'

Night 70

Morning now dawned and Shahrazad broke off from what she had been allowed to say. Then, when it was the seventieth night, SHE CONTINUED:

I have heard, O fortunate king, that in his letter the king had told Sharkan to send the girl to debate with the five in the presence of the learned doctors, saying: 'If she gets the better of them, I shall send her back to you, together with the tribute of Baghdad.'

When Sharkan read this, he went to his brother-in-law and said: 'Bring me the girl whom I married to you.' When she came, he showed her the letter and asked her how he should reply to it. 'Do as you think fit,' she said, but, feeling a longing for her family and her homeland, she added: 'Send me off with my husband, the chamberlain, so that I may tell my father my story and let him know what happened to me with the Bedouin who sold me to the merchant and how the merchant sold me to you, and how you freed me and married me to the chamberlain.' Sharkan agreed to this, and taking his daughter, Qudiya-fa-Kana, he gave her into the charge of wet nurses and eunuchs. He then started to prepare the tribute, which he gave to the chamberlain, telling him to take it to Baghdad, together with Nuzhat al-Zaman, providing a palanquin for him to sit in and another for Nuzhat al-Zaman. The chamberlain accepted his mission, and Sharkan fitted out camels and mules. He wrote a letter which he entrusted to the chamberlain, and he said goodbye to Nuzhat al-Zaman, his sister. He had taken the jewel from her and put it once again round the neck of his daughter, set on a chain of pure gold. The chamberlain set out that same night.

As it happened, Dau' al-Makan had come out with the furnace man and the two were watching from below the outer buildings. They saw camels, including ones from Bactria, as well as laden mules, torches and

lighted lanterns, and when Dau' al-Makan asked what was being transported and to whom it belonged, he was told that this was the tribute of
Damascus on its way to King 'Umar ibn al-Nu'man, the ruler of Baghdad,
in the charge of the head chamberlain, the man who had married the slave
girl who had studied science and philosophy. At that, Dau' al-Makan
burst into tears, remembering his mother and father, his sister and his
homeland. He told the furnace man that he could stay in Damascus no
longer, but would go with the caravan, travelling by short stages until he
reached his own land. 'I didn't trust you to go by yourself from Jerusalem
to Damascus,' said his companion, 'so how can I let you go to Baghdad?
I shall come with you and accompany you until you reach your goal.'

Dau' al-Makan welcomed his offer and the man began to get ready,
preparing a donkey and loading it with saddlebags containing provisions.
He then tightened his belt and waited until the baggage train passed by,
with the chamberlain riding on a dromedary, surrounded by footmen.
Dau' al-Makan mounted and told his companion: 'Get up with me.' 'I
am not going to ride,' the man said, 'for I am acting as your servant.'
'You must ride for a while,' said Dau' al-Makan. 'I shall if I'm tired,'
was the reply. 'When I come to my own people,' said Dau' al-Makan,
'you will see how I shall reward you.'

The caravan continued on its way until sunrise, and at siesta time the
chamberlain ordered a halt. The travellers stopped, rested and watered
their camels, after which the order was given to move out. Five days
later, they reached the city of Hama, where they halted for three days.

Night 71

Morning now dawned and Shahrazad broke off from what she had
been allowed to say. Then, when it was the seventy-first night, SHE
CONTINUED:

I have heard, O fortunate king, that they halted in Hama for three
days. They then travelled on to another city, where they halted again for
three days, and from there they moved to Diyar Bakr, where the breezes
of Baghdad blew over them and Dau' al-Makan remembered Nuzhat
al-Zaman, his sister, as well as his mother and father and his native land.
He wondered how he could go back to his father without his sister and
he wept, groaned and lamented, suffering from the pangs of regret. Then
he recited these lines:

Dear one, how long must I endure delay?
No messenger comes from you to bring me news.
The days of union were not long;
Would that the days of parting were as short.
Take my hand, open my cloak and you will see
How wasted is the form which I conceal.
'Forget your love,' they tell me. I reply:
'By God, not until Resurrection Day.'

'Stop this weeping,' said the furnace man, 'as we are close to the tent of the chamberlain.' 'I must recite some poetry,' replied Dau' al-Makan, 'in the hope that the fire in my heart may be quenched.' 'For God's sake,' said the other, 'leave aside this grief until you reach your own country and then you can do what you like. I shall stay with you wherever you go.' 'By God,' said Dau' al-Makan, 'I cannot stop,' and he turned his face towards Baghdad in the rays of the moon. Nuzhat al-Zaman was restless and had not been able to sleep that night, remembering her brother. She wept and, as she did so, she heard Dau' al-Makan reciting through his tears:

Lightning gleams in the south, stirring my sorrows,
For a loved one who used to pour me the cup of pleasure,
Reminding me of one who left me, forbidding my approach.
Lightning flash, will the days return when we were close?
Censurers, do not blame me; it is God Who has afflicted me
With a time of misery and a beloved who has left.
Delight has left my heart and Time has turned its back on me,
Pouring for me a cup of unmixed care.
Before we can meet again, Time shows that I shall die.
Time, I implore you by my love, quickly bring happiness again,
With joy and safety from care's arrows that have struck.
Who will help a wretched stranger, passing the night afraid at heart,
Spending his days alone in sorrow for the loss of Time's Delight?*
I have now fallen into the hands of miserable scum.

When he had finished his recitation, he gave a cry and fell fainting.

So much for him, but as for the wakeful Nuzhat al-Zaman, full of memories of her brother, when she heard the sound, her heart was eased and in her joy she called the chief eunuch. He asked what she wanted,

---

* 'Time's Delight' is what Nuzhat al-Zaman means in Arabic.

and she told him to fetch whoever was reciting this poem. He said: 'I did not hear him . . .'

Night 72

Morning now dawned and Shahrazad broke off from what she had been allowed to say. Then, when it was the seventy-second night, SHE CONTINUED:

I have heard, O fortunate king, that when Nuzhat al-Zaman heard her brother's poem, she summoned the chief eunuch and told him to fetch her the man who had recited it. He said: 'I did not hear him, and I don't know who he was. The people are all asleep.' 'If you find someone awake,' said Nuzhat al-Zaman, 'it must be the man who recited the poem.' So the eunuch went to investigate, and the only person whom he found awake was the furnace man, as Dau' al-Makan was still unconscious. The furnace man was alarmed to see the eunuch standing beside him, and when he was asked whether it was he who had been reciting the lines that his mistress had heard, he was sure that she had been angered by the recitation. 'By God,' he said fearfully, 'it wasn't me.' 'Well, who was it then?' said the eunuch. 'Show him to me. You must know him, as you are awake.' The furnace man was afraid for Dau' al-Makan, saying to himself that the eunuch might do him some injury, so he swore again that he did not know. 'You're lying,' said the eunuch. 'There is no one else here sitting awake, so you must know.' 'By God,' said the furnace man, 'I'm telling you the truth. The reciter was a passing wanderer, who roused me and disturbed me – may God repay him.' 'If you can recognize him, show him to me,' said the eunuch, 'so that I can take him and bring him to the entrance of my lady's palanquin, or else you can take him yourself.' 'Do you go off,' said the furnace man, 'and I'll bring him to you.'

The eunuch left him and went away. He then entered the presence of his mistress and told her what he had learned. 'No one knows him,' he explained, 'for he was only a passing wanderer.' Nuzhat al-Zaman remained silent, but as for Dau' al-Makan, when he recovered consciousness, he saw that the moon had reached the mid-point of the sky and the dawn breeze was blowing over him. His heart was troubled and sorrowful, so he cleared his throat and was about to recite, when his companion asked him what he was going to do. 'To recite some poetry,' he replied, 'so as to quench the fire in my heart.' 'You don't know what happened to me. I only escaped death by managing to calm the eunuch.' Dau' al-Makan asked what had happened and he said: 'Master, while you were unconscious, a eunuch came to me with a long stick of almond-tree wood. He started looking at the faces of the sleepers and he was asking who it was who had been reciting poetry. I was the only one whom he found awake and so he asked me and I told him that it had been a passing wanderer. He went off, and had God not saved me from him, he would have killed me. He told me that if I heard the man again, I was to produce him.'

When Dau' al-Makan heard this, he wept and said: 'Who can stop me reciting poetry? I shall do it whatever happens to me, for I am near my own land and I don't care about anyone.' 'You want to get yourself killed,' said his companion. 'I must recite,' Dau' al-Makan insisted. 'Then we shall part now,' said the other, 'in spite of the fact that I had not meant to leave you until you had reached your own city and had been reunited with your father and mother. You have been with me for a year and a half, and I have done nothing to injure you. What is making you recite poetry when we are worn out with walking and sleeplessness, and people are sleeping because they are tired and need their rest?' 'I shall not change my mind,' said Dau' al-Makan, and then, moved by grief, he revealed his secret sorrow once again and started to recite these lines:

Halt by the dwellings; greet the abandoned camp.
Call to it and maybe, maybe, it will reply.
If desolate night has covered you,
Kindle a brand of longing in its darkness.
If the snake hisses on the beloved's cheeks,*
No wonder that it bites me, should I kiss red lips.
O paradise that the soul has left unwillingly,
If not consoled by immortality, I shall die of grief!

He also added these lines:

There was a time when the days were in our service,
While we were with each other in the happiest of lands.
Who will now bring me to the house of the dear ones,
Where the place is illumined† and there is Time's Delight?

---

* A lock of hair is often compared to a snake.
† A play on the name Dau' al-Makan, literally 'light of the place'.

When he had finished his poem, he cried thrice and fell on the ground in a faint, after which the furnace man got up and covered him. When Nuzhat al-Zaman heard the first poem, she remembered her father, her mother and her brother. Then, on hearing the second, containing as it did a mention of her name and that of her brother, together with their familial home, she burst into tears and called to the eunuch, reproaching him and saying: 'The man who recited earlier has done it again. I heard him close by and if you don't bring him to me, I shall report you to the chamberlain and he will have you beaten and driven away. Take this hundred dinars and give it to him, and then bring him to me gently, doing him no harm. If he refuses to come, then give him this purse which contains a thousand dinars, and if he still refuses, leave him, but find out where he is staying, what is his profession and where he comes from. Then come back to me quickly and don't be away long.'

Night 73

Morning now dawned and Shahrazad broke off from what she had been allowed to say. Then, when it was the seventy-third night, SHE CONTINUED:

I have heard, O fortunate king, that Nuzhat al-Zaman sent the eunuch to look for the reciter and said: 'Don't come back to me and say that you haven't found him.'

The eunuch went off, peering at the people there and stamping through their tents, but failing to find anyone awake, as they were all sleeping soundly. He then came upon the furnace man, whom he found sitting with his head uncovered, and approaching him, he seized his hand. 'You are the man who was reciting poetry,' he exclaimed. 'No, by God, leader of the people,' said the frightened furnace man, 'it wasn't me.' 'I'm not going to let you go until you show me who it was,' said the eunuch, 'as I'm afraid of what my mistress will do if I go back to her without him.' When he heard this, the man was afraid for Dau' al-Makan and repeated, weeping bitterly: 'By God, it wasn't me and I don't know the man. I only heard some passer-by reciting. Don't do me wrong, for I am a stranger from Jerusalem. May Abraham, the Friend of God, be with you.' 'Do you come with me,' said the eunuch, 'and tell this to my mistress yourself, for I have found no one else awake except you.' The furnace man said: 'You have come and seen where I am sitting and you know where it is.

No one can move from his place without being arrested by the guards, and if after this you hear anyone reciting poetry, near at hand or far away, it will be me or someone that I know and you will only find out who he is through me.' He then kissed the eunuch's head and calmed him.

The eunuch then left him, but circled round and concealed himself behind the furnace man, as he was afraid to return to his mistress with nothing to show for his search. The furnace man got up and roused Dau' al-Makan. 'Sit up,' he told him, 'so that I can tell you what has just happened.' He did this, but Dau' al-Makan insisted: 'I'm not going to worry about this; I don't care about anyone, for my own country is near at hand.' 'Why do you follow your own wishes and obey the devil?' asked his friend. 'You may not fear anyone, but I fear for you and for myself, and I ask you, for God's sake, don't recite any more poetry until you are home. I didn't think that you were like this. Don't you realize that this lady, the chamberlain's wife, wants to reprimand you for disturbing her, as she may be sick or wakeful because of the fatigue of the journey and the distance that she has travelled? This is the second time that she has sent the eunuch to look for you.'

Paying no attention to him, Dau' al-Makan cried out for a third time and recited:

I have abandoned every censurer whose blame disturbed me;
He blames me but he does not know he has incited me.
'He has found consolation,' slanderers say,
And I reply: 'This is because of love for my own land.'
'What makes it beautiful?' they ask.
I tell them: 'That which has evoked my love.'
'And what is it that makes it great?' they say.
The answer is: 'That which has humbled me.'
Far be it from me ever to leave it,
Even if I must drink the cup of grief,
And I shall not obey a censurer
Who condemns me for loving it.

The eunuch, who was listening as Dau' al-Makan finished his poem, came out of hiding and stood beside him. On seeing this, the furnace man ran off and stopped at a distance to watch what was happening between them. 'Peace be on you, master,' said the eunuch. 'And on you be peace and the mercy and blessing of God,' replied Dau' al-Makan.

Night 74

Morning now dawned and Shahrazad broke off from what she had
been allowed to say. Then, when it was the seventy-fourth night, SHE
CONTINUED:

I have heard, O fortunate king, that the eunuch said to Dau' al-Makan:
'Master, I have come to you three times tonight, because my mistress
summons you to come to her.' 'Where does this bitch come from who
wants me? God damn her and her husband as well!' exclaimed Dau'
al-Makan. He then started to abuse the eunuch, who was not able to
reply as his mistress had told him to do the man no injury and only to
fetch him if he was willing to come. Otherwise, he was to give him a
hundred dinars. So the eunuch started talking gently to him and saying:
'Master, take this money and come with me. My son, we have done you
no mischief or harm. I would like you to be good enough to accompany
me to my mistress. She will answer your queries; you will return in all
safety and you will find that we have great news for you.' On hearing this,
Dau' al-Makan got up and walked through the people, stepping over their
sleeping bodies, with the furnace man following behind, watching him
and saying to himself: 'Alas for this youth: they will hang him tomorrow.'
He walked on until he came close to them, without their seeing him, and
when he stopped, he said to himself: 'How mean it would be of him
were he to accuse me of having told him to recite the verses.'

So much for him, but as for Dau' al-Makan, he walked on with the
eunuch who then entered into the presence of Nuzhat al-Zaman and
said: 'My lady, I have brought you the man you were looking for. He is
a handsome young fellow, who looks as though he comes from a wealthy
background.' When she heard that, her heart beat fast and she said: 'Let
him recite some poetry so that I may listen to it from close at hand. Then
ask him his name and where he comes from.' The eunuch went out to
Dau' al-Makan and said: 'Recite your poetry, for the lady is here nearby
to listen to you, and after that I am to ask you your name, country and
condition.' 'Willingly,' answered Dau' al-Makan, 'but if you ask me my
name, it has been blotted out; my traces are effaced and my body is worn
away. The beginning of my story cannot be known, nor can its end be
described. I am here like a drunkard who has drunk too much and has
not spared himself. He has been afflicted by hardships; his wits have left
him and he is bewildered, drowning in a sea of cares.'

When Nuzhat al-Zaman was told this, she burst into tears and then wept and moaned even more bitterly. 'Ask him,' she told the eunuch, 'whether he has been parted from someone he loves, such as his mother or his father.' The eunuch followed her orders and put the question to Dau' al-Makan. 'Yes,' he said, 'I have been parted from everyone, but the dearest of them to me was my sister, who was separated from me by fate.' When Nuzhat al-Zaman heard this, she said: 'May Almighty God reunite him with those he loves.'

Night 75

Morning now dawned and Shahrazad broke off from what she had been allowed to say. Then, when it was the seventy-fifth night, SHE CONTINUED:

I have heard, O fortunate king, that when Nuzhat al-Zaman heard this, she said: 'May Almighty God reunite him with those he loves.' Then she told the eunuch: 'Let him recite me some lines about his parting from his family and his native land.' The eunuch did as he was told, and Dau' al-Makan, sighing deeply, recited:

The lover is bound by the compact of this love;
I honour a dwelling in which Hind once lived.
Love for her is the only love known to man;
There is no past or future to be found in it.
The valley smells of musk and ambergris,
If one day it is visited by Hind.
Greetings to a beloved in the guarded heights,
The mistress of the tribe for whom all those surrounding her are
    slaves.
My two companions, after this evening there is no halting place;
Rest; here is the *ban* tree and the lone waymark.
Question none other than my heart;
It is love's ally, not to be turned back.
May God cause clouds to rain on Time's Delight,
As thunder rolls with no break from their depths.

When Nuzhat al-Zaman had listened to the end of his poem, she drew back the skirt of the curtain from her palanquin and looked at him. As soon as her eyes fell on his face, she recognized him and was certain that it was he. 'Brother!' she cried out. 'Dau' al-Makan!' He in his turn looked at her, recognized her and said: 'My sister, Nuzhat al-Zaman!' She threw herself into his arms and he clasped her to him, after which they both fell down in a faint. The astonished eunuch threw a covering over them and waited until they had recovered consciousness. When they had, Nuzhat al-Zaman was full of joy; care and sadness left her and their place was taken by delight. She recited these lines:

Time swore it would not cease to sadden me;
Time, you are forsworn, so expiate your sin.
Happiness has come; the beloved has helped me.
So rise, tuck up your robe and meet the summoner of happiness.
I did not trust old tales of Paradise
Until I came to taste the nectar of red lips.

On hearing this, Dau' al-Makan clasped his sister to his breast, while tears of joy poured from his eyes and he recited:

We two are equal in our love, but she
Shows hardiness at times, while I have none.
She fears malicious threats, but when I am held back
And threatened, then my love for her becomes madness.

They sat for a time at the entrance to the palanquin, after which Nuzhat al-Zaman invited her brother to come in with her so that he could tell her his story and she could tell him hers. They entered and he said: 'Do you tell me yours first.' She told him all that had happened to her since she left him in the *khan*: her encounter with the Bedouin and with the merchant who had bought her from him; how the merchant had taken her to her brother, Sharkan; how Sharkan had set her free after buying her, drawn up a marriage contract and consummated the marriage, after which her father had heard about her and sent word to Sharkan to ask for her. Then she said: 'Praise be to God, Who has given me to you. As we were together when we left our father, so we shall go back to him together.' She added that Sharkan had married her to the chamberlain in order that he might take her to her father. 'This is everything that happened to me from beginning to end, so do you tell me what happened to you after I left you.'

Dau' al-Makan told her the whole tale from start to finish – how God had granted him the help of the furnace man, who had travelled with him, spent his money on him and looked after him, night and day. When

Nuzhat al-Zaman expressed her gratitude for this, Dau' al-Makan added: 'Sister, this man has done me such services as no one would do for one of his loved ones, and no father for his son. He went hungry to feed me and walked while making me ride. I owe him my life.' 'If God Almighty wills,' said Nuzhat al-Zaman, 'we shall repay him as far as is in our power.' She then called for the eunuch, who kissed the hand of Dau' al-Makan when he came in. 'Take the reward for good news, you bringer of luck,' Nuzhat al-Zaman said to him. 'It is through you that I have been reunited with my brother. The purse that you have with you and its contents are yours. So now go and bring me your master quickly.'

The delighted eunuch made his way to the chamberlain's presence and asked him to come to his mistress. When he arrived with the eunuch, he found Dau' al-Makan with Nuzhat al-Zaman, and in reply to his question, she told him everything that had happened to the two of them from beginning to end. 'You must know, chamberlain,' she said, 'that it was no slave girl whom you took, but the daughter of King 'Umar ibn al-Nu'man. For I am Nuzhat al-Zaman and this is my brother, Dau' al-Makan.' When the chamberlain heard the story, he recognized the truth of what she had said; the whole affair was clear to him and he realized that he had indeed become the son-in-law of the king. 'I shall be made the governor of a province,' he said to himself, after which he went up to Dau' al-Makan, congratulating him on his safe return and his reunion with his sister. He immediately told his servants to prepare a tent for him and to bring one of his best horses.

Nuzhat al-Zaman then said to him: 'We are close to our own country. I want to be alone with my brother so that we may relax in each other's company and take our fill of it before we reach home, since we have been parted for so long.' 'As you wish,' said the chamberlain. He then sent them candles, together with sweetmeats of various sorts and left them. He sent Dau' al-Makan three splendid suits of clothes and walked back to his own palanquin, savouring his good fortune. 'Send for the eunuch,' Nuzhat al-Zaman told him, 'and tell him to fetch the furnace man. He is to be given a horse to ride; meals are to be provided for him morning and evening, and he is to be told not to leave us.' At that, the chamberlain sent for the eunuch and passed on these instructions. 'To hear is to obey,' replied the eunuch, and he then took his own servants and went off in search of the furnace man. He found him at the far end of the caravan, saddling his donkey and preparing for flight, with tears running down his cheeks out of fear for his own life and sorrow at being parted from Dau' al-Makan. 'I warned him in God's Name,' he was saying to himself, 'but he wouldn't listen to me. I wonder what state he is in.' Before he had finished speaking, the eunuch was standing beside him, with his servants all around him. When the furnace man turned and saw this, he grew pale with fear.

Night 76

Morning now dawned and Shahrazad broke off from what she had been allowed to say. Then, when it was the seventy-sixth night, SHE CONTINUED:

I have heard, O fortunate king, that the furnace man was saddling his donkey and preparing for flight, wondering what was happening to Dau' al-Makan, when before he had finished speaking, the eunuch was standing beside him, with his servants all around him. When the furnace man turned and saw this, he shivered with fear. Then he said aloud: 'He didn't acknowledge the good that I did him and I think he must have accused me falsely to the eunuch and these servants, saying that I was his partner in this crime.' The eunuch shouted at him and asked: 'Who was it who recited the verses? You liar, how can you say: "I didn't do it and I don't know who did" when he was your companion? I am going to stay with you from here to Baghdad, so that everything that happens to your companion will happen to you.'

When the man heard that, he said to himself: 'What I was afraid of has happened.' Then he recited the line:

What I feared has come about; to God do we return.

At the eunuch's shouted order, the servants made the man get down from his donkey and they then brought him a horse, which he mounted, and he moved off with the caravan, surrounded by servants. 'If he loses a single hair,' the eunuch told them, 'one of you will pay for it,' for he had secretly instructed them to treat him with respect and not to humiliate him. Seeing the servants all around him, the furnace man despaired of life. He turned to the eunuch and said: 'Sir, I am not his brother or any relation of his. He has no connection with me or I with him; I am a furnace man in a bath house and I found him when he was ill and had been thrown on to a dung heap.'

The caravan set off on its way, with the furnace man weeping, prey to a thousand regrets, and the eunuch walking by his side. The eunuch had told him nothing of what had happened, but kept saying: 'You disturbed my mistress with your reciting, you and the young man, but don't fear for yourself,' while all the while he was secretly laughing at him. When they halted, food would be produced and he and the furnace man ate from the same dish. He would then tell the servants to bring a jug of sherbet, from which he would drink and which he would offer to the furnace man, who never stopped weeping out of fear for himself and sorrow at being parted from Dau' al-Makan and for what had happened to them on their journey from home. At times the eunuch waited on Dau' al-Makan and Nuzhat al-Zaman at the entrance of the palanquin, while at other times he kept his eye on the furnace man.

As for Nuzhat al-Zaman and her brother, they continued to pass the time talking and going over their sufferings until they were within three days of Baghdad. The caravan camped in the evening and rested there until dawn. The people had woken and were about to load up, when suddenly a great cloud of dust appeared. The sky darkened and it became black as night. 'Wait,' shouted the chamberlain, 'don't load the baggage!' And he and his mamluks mounted and rode out towards the dust cloud. When they got near it they could see beneath it a huge army like a swelling sea, with banners, standards, drums, horsemen and champions. The chamberlain was astonished, but when the army saw them, a detachment of some five hundred horse split away from it and approached him and his men, surrounding them and outnumbering them five to one. 'What is going on?' the chamberlain asked them. 'Where have the troops come from and why are they treating us like this?' 'Who are you?' they asked in reply. 'Where are you from and where are you going?' 'I am the chamberlain of the governor of Damascus, Sultan Sharkan, son of King 'Umar ibn al-Nu'man, the lord of Baghdad and ruler of Khurasan,' the chamberlain answered. 'I have come from him bringing tribute and gifts and am on my way to his father in Baghdad.' When they heard this, they covered their faces with their kerchiefs and wept. ''Umar ibn al-Nu'man is dead,' they said. 'He has died of poison, but you may go on in safety to meet the grand vizier, Dandan.'

At this news the chamberlain wept bitterly, exclaiming: 'How our hopes have been dashed on this journey!' He and his companions went on shedding tears until they joined the main body of the troops. Permission was asked for them to approach the vizier Dandan and this was granted. Dandan ordered a tent to be pitched and, having taken his seat on a couch in the middle of it, he told the chamberlain to be seated. When he had done so, Dandan asked him for his news, and on hearing that this was the chamberlain of the sultan of Damascus and that he had come with gifts and with the Damascene tribute, he broke into tears at a reference to 'Umar ibn al-Nu'man. 'The king has died of poison,' he said, 'and because of his death, there is a dispute about who should succeed him. There has been some killing, but the factions have been kept apart by men of standing and distinction, helped by the four *qadis*. Everyone agreed that no one was to oppose the *qadis'* recommendation, and that I should go to Damascus, seek out the king's son, Sharkan, and then bring him back and set him on his father's throne. There are some who want the king's second son, Dau' al-Makan, the brother of Nuzhat al-Zaman, but the two of them went to the Hijaz and it is five years since anyone heard of them.'

When the chamberlain heard that, he realized that the story of his wife's adventures was true. He was greatly saddened by the death of 'Umar, but his sadness was mixed with joy, particularly because of the arrival of Dau' al-Makan, who would become ruler of Baghdad in his father's place.

Night 77

Morning now dawned and Shahrazad broke off from what she had been allowed to say. Then, when it was the seventy-seventh night, SHE CONTINUED:

I have heard, O fortunate king, that when Sharkan's chamberlain heard about King 'Umar ibn al-Nu'man from the vizier Dandan, he was saddened, but his sadness was mixed with joy for his wife and her brother, Dau' al-Makan, who was to succeed his father as king of Baghdad. He turned to Dandan and said: 'Your tale is a wonder of wonders. You must know, great vizier, that because you happened to meet me now, God has given you rest from labour, and things have turned out as you would wish in the simplest of ways. For God has restored to you Dau' al-Makan, together with his sister, Nuzhat al-Zaman, and the affair can be settled easily.'

The vizier was delighted when he heard this and he asked the chamberlain to tell him what had happened to the pair and why they had been absent. The chamberlain told him about Nuzhat al-Zaman, and that she had become his wife, and he also repeated the story of Dau' al-Makan from beginning to end. When he had finished, Dandan sent to the emirs, viziers and great officers of state to tell them about this. Both delighted and amazed by the coincidence, they all came to the chamberlain, made their obeisance and kissed the ground in front of him, while Dandan went up and stood in front of him. On that day, the chamberlain held a grand council meeting, at which he and the vizier Dandan sat on a dais with all the emirs, grandees and officers of state ranged before them, according to their ranks. Sugar was dissolved in rosewater and they drank this, after which the emirs sat down to take counsel, while the rest of the army was allowed to ride off, moving on slowly until the council was finished, so that the others could catch them up.

Accordingly, the troops kissed the ground before the chamberlain and rode off, preceded by their battle flags. When the great officers had finished their deliberations, they mounted and rejoined the others, and it was then that the chamberlain came up to the vizier Dandan and said: 'I think that I should go on ahead to prepare a suitable place for the king, letting him know of your arrival and telling him that you have chosen him as your ruler over the head of his brother Sharkan.' The vizier approved of this, after which the chamberlain got up, as did the vizier to show respect for him. The vizier gave him gifts, begging him to accept them, as did the great emirs and the officers of state, who called down blessings on him and asked him to talk on their behalf to the king, Dau' al-Makan, with a request that they may continue in their offices. The chamberlain agreed to this. He then ordered the servants to set off, and Dandan sent tents with him, ordering that they be pitched at a distance of a day's journey from Baghdad.

They obeyed his command and the chamberlain rode off in a state of delight, saying to himself: 'What a lucky journey this has been!' His wife gained in importance in his eyes, as did Dau' al-Makan. He pressed on with his journey until he came within a day's distance of Baghdad, where he ordered his men to halt for a rest and to prepare a place for King Dau' al-Makan, son of King 'Umar, to sit. He and his mamluks dismounted at a distance, and he ordered the eunuchs to ask Lady Nuzhat al-Zaman's permission for him to enter her presence. When this had been given, he went in and joined her and her brother. He told them of their father's death and that the leaders had chosen Dau' al-Makan as their ruler in his father's place, congratulating them both on their kingdom. They wept at the loss of their father and asked how he had been killed. 'It is the vizier Dandan who knows about this,' said the chamberlain, 'and he and the whole army will be here tomorrow. Nothing remains, your majesty, except for you to follow their advice. They have unanimously chosen you as king. If you do not accept, they will appoint someone else and your life will not be safe from him. Either he will kill you, or things will go wrong between you, and the kingdom will slip from the hands of you both.'

Dau' al-Makan bent his head down for a time, before saying: 'I accept, as I cannot free myself of this office.' Convinced that the chamberlain had given him sound advice, he then said: 'Uncle, what am I to do with my brother Sharkan?' 'My son,' said the chamberlain, 'your brother will be sultan of Damascus and you are to be king of Baghdad, so be resolute and make your preparations.' Dau' al-Makan accepted this advice and the chamberlain fetched him a royal robe that Dandan had brought, as well as the ceremonial dagger. He then left Dau' al-Makan and told the servants to pick a high place for the erection of an enormous pavilion in which the king could sit when the emirs came to meet him. The cooks were ordered to prepare and present a splendid meal, while the water carriers were to provide water troughs.

Some time passed and then a dust cloud could be seen filling all parts, and when it cleared away, beneath it could be seen a huge army like a swelling sea.

Night 78

Morning now dawned and Shahrazad broke off from what she had been allowed to say. Then, when it was the seventy-eighth night, SHE CONTINUED:

I have heard, O fortunate king, that orders were given for the erection of an enormous pavilion such as was customary for kings and where the people could gather in the king's presence. When this had been done, a dust cloud appeared, blotting out the sky, and beneath it could be seen a huge army. This was the army of Baghdad and Khurasan, led by Dandan, and all were full of joy that the kingdom had passed to Dau' al-Makan. He himself was wearing royal robes and was girt with the processional sword. The chamberlain brought up his horse and, after mounting, he moved off with his mamluks, while all those who were in the tents walked in attendance on him until he entered the great pavilion.

There he took his seat, with his dagger on his thigh, and the chamberlain in attendance before him. The mamluks, with drawn swords in their hands, were in the outer section of the pavilion, and it was now that the regular troops and levies arrived and asked permission to enter. The chamberlain went in to pass their request to Dau' al-Makan, who ordered that they should come in groups of ten. When the chamberlain told them that, they agreed and they all stood at the outer entrance. Ten of them then entered and the chamberlain took them through and brought them into the sultan's presence.

When they saw Dau' al-Makan they were filled with awe; he greeted them with the greatest courtesy and promised them all manner of favours. They congratulated him on his safe return, invoked blessings on him and swore a faithful oath that they would do nothing against his will, after which they kissed the ground before him and left. They were followed by another ten, whom he treated in the same way, and the rest kept on coming in, ten at a time, until no one was left except the vizier Dandan. He entered and kissed the ground in front of Dau' al-Makan, who rose for him, came up to him and said: 'Welcome to the vizier, the venerable father. Your acts are those of a noble counsellor and the administration is in the hands of a man of subtlety and experience.'

He then told the chamberlain to go out immediately to order tables to be laid, to which all the soldiers were to be summoned. They came up, ate and drank, and Dau' al-Makan told Dandan to order them to stay there for ten days so that the two of them might have a private meeting in which he could find out the cause of his father's death. Dandan obeyed his instructions, saying: 'I shall certainly do that,' and after going to the middle of the camp, he gave orders that his men were to rest there for ten days. They were given leave to amuse themselves, and for three days none of the orderly officers were to enter to present their services to the king. They all expressed their humble duty and prayed for Dau' al-Makan's continued glory, after which Dandan went to him and told him of this.

Dau' al-Makan himself waited until nightfall and he then visited Nuzhat al-Zaman and asked her whether or not she knew how it was that their father had met his death. When she had said that she did not, she let down a silken curtain and Dau' al-Makan, seated on the far side of it, ordered the vizier Dandan to be brought to him. When he came, Dau' al-Makan told him that he wanted to know the details of his father's death. 'You must know, your majesty,' said Dandan, 'that when

King 'Umar ibn al-Nu'man returned from his hunting trip and came to the city, he asked about you and your sister, but could not find you. He realized that you must have gone on the pilgrimage and was distressed and exceedingly angry. For six months he asked for news from all stray comers, but no one could tell him anything. Then one day, a full year after the loss of you both, while I was with him an old woman came to us, showing the marks of asceticism. With her were five slave girls, swelling-breasted virgins like moons, whose beauty and loveliness no tongue could describe. Not only were they beautiful, but they could recite the Quran and had a knowledge of philosophy and the histories of past generations.' HE WENT ON:

The old woman asked for and received permission to have an audience with the king. I was sitting there by his side as she came in and kissed the ground before him. He allowed her to approach because of the signs of pious asceticism that she displayed, and when she had settled, she turned to him and said: 'Your majesty, with me are five slave girls, the like of whom no king possesses. They are intelligent, beautiful and perfect; they can recite the Quran with its variant readings; they are acquainted with the sciences and the histories of past peoples. They are here before you, standing in attendance on you, king of the age. It is by examination that a man is honoured or scorned.' Your late father looked at the girls and was pleased by what he saw, so he told each of them to produce for him something that she knew of the histories of the past.

Night 79

Morning now dawned and Shahrazad broke off from what she had been allowed to say. Then, when it was the seventy-ninth night, SHE CONTINUED:

I have heard, O fortunate king, that the vizier Dandan told King Dau' al-Makan: 'Your lamented father looked at the girls and was pleased by what he saw, so he told each of them to produce for him something that she knew of the histories of the past.' HE WENT ON:

One of them came forward, kissed the ground before him and said: 'You have to know, O king, that every man of culture must avoid officiousness, adorn himself with virtues, perform his religious duties and avoid mortal sin. He must keep to this pattern of behaviour, believing that to abandon it would destroy him. The foundation of culture is nobility of character. You must also know that what we seek through most of the ways in which we make our living is life, and the purpose of life is to worship God. You must behave well towards men and never abandon this practice. Those who occupy the highest rank are most in need of sound planning, and so kings require this more than common people, who may plunge without restraint into affairs, with no thought for the consequences. You must freely offer your life and your wealth in God's cause. Know that your enemy is an opponent with whom you can argue, whom you can convince with proofs and against whom you can guard yourself, while between you and your friend the only judge who can adjudicate is good character. Test your friend before choosing him. If he is one of those who lives for the next world, let him follow faithfully the externals of the law, while knowing its secret meaning, as far as this is possible. If he is an adherent of this world, he should be liberal and truthful, and neither ignorant nor wicked. His own parents should flee from the ignorant man, while the liar cannot be a friend, as the word "friend" derives from "truth".* This comes from the depth of the heart, so how can it apply to one whose tongue speaks falsehood?

'Know that to follow God's law is of advantage to those who do it. Love your brother if this is what he is like, and do not break with him. If you see in him something you dislike, he is not like a wife to whom you can return after divorcing her. Rather, his heart is like glass which, when broken, cannot be mended. How eloquent was the poet who said:

> Take care not to wrong hearts;
> When they have shied off, they will not return,
> For then they are like shattered glass
> Which cannot be repaired.'

Before ending her speech, the girl gestured to us and said: 'Wise men have said that the best of brothers are the most severe in their advice; the best actions are those that lead to the fairest results and the best of praise is what is on the mouths of men. It has been said that the worshipper should not neglect to thank God for two favours in particular – health and intelligence. It has also been said that whoever has a sense of his own honour despises his lusts; whoever magnifies small misfortunes will be afflicted by God with great ones; whoever obeys his own desires fails to perform his duties; and whoever follows the slanderer loses his

---

* In Arabic the word for 'friend' is *sadiq* and the word for 'truth' is *sidq*.

friend. If a man thinks well of you, see to it that his opinion is justified; whoever takes enmity too far, commits a sin; and whoever does not guard against injustice is not safe from the sword.

'I shall now tell you something of the good qualities of judges. A sound judgement is of no use until the case has been proved. A judge must treat all people alike, so that the upper classes may not be tempted to do wrong and the weak may not despair of justice. The burden of proof should be on the claimant and the defendant should be made to swear an oath. Compromise is possible between Muslims except where it leads to the permitting of a forbidden act or the banning of what is allowed. If you have a problem today, turn your mind to it again and you will find the right way to lead you back to truth. Truth is an obligation and to return to it is better than to persist in error. You should take note of precedents, understand what has been said, and treat both sides equally, fixing your eyes on the truth and entrusting your affair to the Great and Glorious God. The burden of proof is on the claimant and if he produces this, the case should be settled in his favour, while, if not, the defendant should be made to swear an oath. This is the decree of God. Accept the evidence of upright Muslims, one against the other, for Almighty God has ordered judges to judge by externals, while He Himself is responsible for what is secret. No judge should make decisions while suffering from extreme pain or hunger. In the decisions that he gives his object must be to serve Almighty God. If his intentions are pure and he is honest with himself, God will protect him in his dealings with the people.

'According to al-Zuhri, there are three faults for which a judge should be dismissed: if he shows honour to the ignoble, if he is fond of praise, and if he dislikes the thought of being dismissed. 'Umar ibn 'Abd al-'Aziz once dismissed a judge, who then asked him why. "I have heard," replied 'Umar, "that you talk more loftily than your position warrants." It is said that Alexander the Great said to his judge: "I have given you a position in which I have entrusted you with my soul, my honour and my manhood. Guard it with your life and your intelligence." To his cook he said: "You are in charge of my body; treat it as well as you would treat yourself." He told his secretary: "You are in charge of my intelligence. Protect me in whatever you write on my behalf."'

The first girl then withdrew and the second came forward.

Night 80

Morning now dawned and Shahrazad broke off from what she had been allowed to say. Then, when it was the eightieth night, SHE CONTINUED:

I have heard, O fortunate king, that the vizier Dandan told Dau' al-Makan that the first girl then withdrew and the second came forward. HE WENT ON:

She kissed the ground seven times in front of the king, your father, and said: 'Luqman told his son: "There are three types of man that can only be recognized in three contexts – the clement man in the context of anger, the brave man in war, and your brother when you need him. The wrongdoer, it is said, will be filled with regret, even if people praise him, while whoever is wronged will be unhurt even if people blame him." God Almighty has said: "Do not consider that those who rejoice in their deeds and like to be praised for what they have not done are secure from punishment. Theirs is a painful punishment."* The Prophet – on whom be blessing and peace – has said: "Actions are judged by intentions and to each man is attributed what he intended." He also said: "In the body there is one part whose soundness means that the whole body is sound, but if it is corrupt, the whole body is subject to corruption. This is the heart, the most marvellous organ of man, as it is by means of it that he controls his affairs. If he is moved by covetousness, he will be destroyed by greed; if he is under the sway of grief, sorrow will kill him; if his anger rages, he will fall prey to violent destruction; and if he is fortunate enough to win approval, he is secure against anger. If he is afraid, he will be preoccupied by sorrow; if he is overtaken by some misfortune, he will be in the grip of anxiety; should he gain wealth, he may be distracted from the recollection of his Lord; if poverty chokes him, care will distract him; and if anxiety wears him out, weakness will hold him back. In all circumstances, he can only thrive through the remembrance of God, busying himself with earning his living and striving for salvation." A learned man was asked: "Who is the happiest of men?" He answered: "He whose manliness overcomes his lust, whose ambition reaches far into the heights, whose knowledge is extensive, and who makes few excuses." How excellent are the lines of Qais:

* Quran 3.285.

I am far removed from being a busybody
Who thinks others wrong while he himself is not right.
Wealth and natural qualities are loans;
Each man is clothed by what he conceals within his heart.
When you approach an affair through what is not its proper gate,
You go astray, while, entering by the gate, you will be rightly
    guided.'

The girl continued: 'As for accounts of the ascetics, Hisham ibn Bishr
has said: "I asked 'Umar ibn 'Ubaid what was true asceticism. He replied:
'This was shown clearly by the Apostle of God – may God bless him and
give him peace – where he said: "The ascetic is one who has not forgotten
the corruption of the grave and who chooses what remains in preference
to what passes away; who does not consider tomorrow to be one of the
days of his life and who numbers himself among the dead."'" Abu
Dhurr is quoted as saying: "Poverty is dearer to me than riches and
sickness than health."

'To which one of his audience replied: "May God have mercy on Abu
Dhurr! My own view is that whoever relies on the excellence of the choice
made by Almighty God should be content with whatever condition God
has chosen for him." A reliable authority has said: "Ibn Abi Aufa led us
in the morning prayer and recited: 'You who are enwrapped'* until,
when he reached God's words 'when the trumpet sounds', he fell down
dead." Thabit ibn Bunani is said to have wept until he almost lost his
eyesight. A man brought in to treat him said that he would do this only
on condition that Thabit would obey him. "In what?" asked Thabit. "In
agreeing to stop weeping," said the doctor. "What virtue is there in
my eyes," asked Thabit, "if they cannot weep?" A man once asked
Muhammad ibn 'Abd Allah for counsel . . .'

Night 81

Morning now dawned and Shahrazad broke off from what she had
been allowed to say. Then, when it was the eighty-first night, SHE
CONTINUED:

I have heard, O fortunate king, that THE VIZIER DANDAN SAID TO
DAU' AL-MAKAN:

* Quran 74.

The second girl told your late father: 'A man once asked Muhammad ibn 'Abd Allah for counsel. To which he replied: "I counsel you to be an ascetic king in this world and a greedy slave with regard to the next." "How is that?" the man asked. "Whoever is an ascetic in this world," replied Muhammad, "possesses both this world and the next." Ghauth ibn 'Abd Allah has said: "There were two brothers among the Israelites, one of whom asked the other: 'What is the most perilous thing that you have ever done?' His brother replied: 'I once passed by a chicken coop from which I took a chicken. I put it back, but not among the ones from whom I had taken it. This is what has caused me most fear.' He then asked his brother what he had done and his brother said: 'When I rise to pray, I am afraid lest I only do that for the reward.' Their father, who had been listening to what they were saying, then said: 'Oh my God, if they are telling the truth, take them to Yourself.' These two, according to one of the wise men, were among the most virtuous of children."

'Sa'id ibn Jubair has said: "I was in the company of Fudala ibn 'Ubaid and I asked him for counsel. 'Remember these two points that I tell you,' he said: 'Do not associate anything with God and do not injure any of God's creatures.' He then recited these lines:

Be as you wish, for God is generous;
Banish care, for here there is no harm
Except in two crimes which you must not commit:
To associate anything with God and to do people harm."

'How excellent are the words of the poet:

If you have not provision of piety,
And when you die you meet with one who has,
You will regret that you were not like him,
And did not watch the future as he did.'

The second girl now withdrew and the third girl came forward and said: 'The field of asceticism is vast, but I shall mention some of what I know about the pious men of old. A master of religious lore once said: "I look forward to death, although I am not certain that it will give me rest. But I know that death is interposed between a man and his works, and I hope that my good deeds may be doubled and my evil deeds cut away." When 'Ata al-Sulami ended an exhortation, he would shiver, tremble and weep bitterly. When he was asked why, he said: "This is a grave action on which I am embarking, for I shall have to stand before

Almighty God to be judged as to whether I acted in accordance with the counsel that I gave." This was why 'Ali Zain al-'Abidin used to tremble when he stood up to perform the prayer. He said, on being asked about this: "Do you know for Whom I am standing and Whom I am addressing?"

'It is said that a blind man lived near Sufyan al-Thauri. In the month of Ramadan, he would go out to join with those who were praying, but he would stay silent and hang behind. Sufyan said: "On the Day of Resurrection this man will come with the people of the Quran and they will be distinguished by marks of special honour from all others." Sufyan also said: "Were the soul properly lodged in the heart, the heart would flutter for joy and longing for Paradise and for grief and fear of hellfire." It is reported of Sufyan that he also said: "It is a sin to look on the face of an evil-doer."'

The third girl then retired and the fourth came forward and announced that she was going to tell some stories that she knew of the pious. She went on: 'It is reported of Bishr al-Hafi that he said: "I heard Khalid saying: 'Beware secret polytheism.' 'What is that?' I asked him. He replied: 'It is when one man goes on bowing and prostrating himself for so long that he becomes ritually impure.'" A master of religious lore has said: "The doing of good deeds expiates evil ones." Ibrahim ibn Adham once said: "I asked Bishr al-Hafi to teach me some of the hidden truths. 'My son,' he said, 'this knowledge is not to be taught to everyone but only to five in every hundred, like the alms tax on cash.'" Ibrahim went on: "I thought that this was a good and excellent reply. Then, while I was praying, I suddenly saw Bishr, who was also praying, and so I stood behind him, bowing until the call of the muezzin. Then a shabby-looking man stood up and said: 'O people, beware of truth that brings harm, while there is no harm in a lie that brings some benefit; necessity allows no choice; speech is of no help when coupled with privation; and silence does no harm in the presence of generosity.'" Ibrahim continued: "I saw Bishr drop a *daniq*, so I came to him and handed him a dirham in its place. He refused to accept it, although I told him that I had come by it perfectly legally. He said: 'I am not going to exchange the goods of this world for those of the next.'" There is a story that Bishr's sister went to Ahmad ibn Hanbal . . .'

Night 82

Morning now dawned and Shahrazad broke off from what she had been allowed to say. Then, when it was the eighty-second night, SHE CONTINUED:

I have heard, O fortunate king, that THE VIZIER DANDAN TOLD DAU' AL-MAKAN:

The fourth girl told your father: 'Bishr's sister once went to Ahmad ibn Hanbal and said to him: "Imam of the Faith, we are people who spin at night and work for our living by day. Sometimes the torches of the officers of the city guards pass by while we are on the house roof and we spin by their light. Is this something that is forbidden us?" "Who are you?" he asked. "I am the sister of Bishr al-Hafi," she answered. "I can always see the light of piety in the hearts of your family," he said. A master of religious lore has said: "When God wishes to confer good on one of His servants, He provides an opportunity for him to act." When Malik ibn Dinar went through the market and saw something he wanted, he used to say: "Patience, my soul. I shall not agree to what you want." He also said (may God be pleased with him): "Your soul's salvation lies in your refusing its wishes, and its misfortune lies in your following them."

'Mansur ibn 'Ammar has said: "I went on pilgrimage one year, approaching Mecca by the road from Kufa. It was a dark night and suddenly I heard a voice crying out in the darkness: 'My God, I swear by Your glory and grandeur that I never intended to disobey You by my recalcitrance, nor am I ignorant of You. From past eternity You decreed that I should commit this fault, so forgive me for what has happened, as it was through my ignorance that I transgressed.' On finishing his prayer, he recited the Quranic verse: 'You who believe, protect yourselves and your families from a fire that burns both men and rocks.'* I then heard the sound of a fall, but I did not know what it was and so I walked on. The next day, as we were going on our way, out came a funeral procession behind which walked a feeble old woman. I asked her about the dead man and she replied: 'On this bier is a man who passed us yesterday when my son was standing praying. My son recited a verse of the holy Quran, and then this man's gall bladder burst and he fell down dead.'"'

* Quran 66.6.

The fourth girl then withdrew and the fifth came forward and said: 'I shall tell you some stories that I have heard of virtuous men of past ages. Maslama ibn Dinar used to say: "If men's secret hearts are set right, then sins, small and great, will be forgiven, and when one of God's servants makes up his mind to abandon sin, he will be granted victory." He also said: "Every benefit that does not bring you closer to God is a misfortune; a small quantity of worldly goods distracts you from the great rewards of the next world, while a great quantity of them makes you forget even the small rewards to come."

'When Abu Hazim was asked: "Who is the most prosperous of men?" he replied: "The man who has passed his life in obedience to God." Then, when he was asked who was the stupidest, he said: "The man who has sold his own afterlife for the worldly goods of someone else." It is told of Moses – upon whom be peace – that when he came to the water of Midian, he said: "My Lord, I am in need of the good things that You send down on me," addressing his petition to God and not to men. Two girls then came and he drew water for them, although the shepherds had not yet finished with it. When they got home, they told this to their father, Shu'aib – upon whom be peace. "The man may be hungry," said Shu'aib, and he told one of them to go back and invite him home. When she came to him, she covered her face and said: "My father invites you home to reward you for having drawn water for us." Moses was reluctant and did not want to follow her. She was a woman with large buttocks, and as the wind was blowing her dress, Moses could see them. He lowered his eyes and said: "Follow behind me and I shall go in front." She then walked behind him until he came to Shu'aib – upon whom be peace – when supper was ready.'

Night 83

Morning now dawned and Shahrazad broke off from what she had been allowed to say. Then, when it was the eighty-third night, SHE CONTINUED:

I have heard, O fortunate king, that THE VIZIER TOLD DAU' AL-MAKAN:

The fifth girl told your father: 'Moses came to Shu'aib when supper was ready. Shu'aib told Moses that he wanted to reward him for having drawn water for the girls. "I am of a family that sells nothing that has been done to win the next world for this world's gold and silver," said Moses. "Young man," replied Shu'aib, "you are my guest, and my custom and that of my fathers is to entertain guests with food." So Moses sat down and ate. Shu'aib then hired his services for eight pilgrimage seasons – that is, eight years – promising him in return marriage to one of his daughters, with the work done by him serving as her dowry. He said, as God Almighty told of him: "I wish to marry you to one of these two daughters of mine, on condition that you serve me for eight pilgrimage seasons. If you complete ten seasons, that is your choice, as I do not wish to be hard on you."*

'A man said to one of his companions whom he had not seen for some time: "You have made me lonely, as it is long since I last saw you." "I have not been able to meet you," replied the man, "because I have been busy with Ibn Shihab. Do you know him?" "Yes," was the reply. "He has been my neighbour for thirty years, but I have never spoken to him." "You have forgotten God," said his companion, "for you have forgotten your neighbour, and if you loved God you would love your neighbour. Do you not know that the right of neighbours is like the right of kinship?" Hudhaifa has said: "I went to Mecca with Ibrahim ibn Adham in a year when Shaqiq al-Balkhi was making the pilgrimage. We met during the circumambulation and Ibrahim asked how things were with him in his country. 'When we are given food, we eat, and when we are hungry, we endure,' was the reply. 'That is what the dogs of Balkh do,' said Ibrahim. 'As for us, when food is given us, we distribute it, and when we are hungry, we thank God.' Shaqiq sat down in front of him and said: 'You are my master.'" Muhammad ibn 'Imran said: "A man once asked Hatim al-Asamm: 'What is your position with regard to reliance on God?' 'I rely on two things,' Hatim replied. 'That no one else will eat what is allotted to me, which gives me peace of mind, and the understanding that I have not been created without God's knowledge, and so I feel ashamed in front of Him.'"'

The fifth girl then withdrew and the old woman came forward and kissed the ground nine times before your father. 'O king,' she said, 'you have heard what all these girls have said about asceticism and, following on from them, I shall tell you some of the things that I have heard of the great men of old. It is said that the imam al-Shafi'i used to divide the night into three parts – one for study, one for sleep and one for religious

* Quran 28.27.

exercises. The imam Abu Hanifa used to spend half the night in worship. Once, as he was walking, a man pointed to him and said to someone else: "This man spends the whole night in worship." When Abu Hanifa heard this, he said: "I am ashamed before God that I should be described as doing something that I don't do," and after that he began to worship throughout the night.

'According to al-Rabi'a, al-Shafi'i used to recite in his prayers the whole Quran seventy times during the month of Ramadan. Al-Shafi'i – may God be pleased with him – once said: "For ten years I did not eat my fill of barley bread, for repletion hardens the heart, destroys intelligence, induces sleep and makes the eater too weak to stand up to pray." It is reported of 'Abd Allah ibn Muhammad al-Sukkari that he said: "I was talking with 'Umar, who told me that he had never seen a more pious or more eloquent man than Muhammad ibn Idris al-Shafi'i. I happened to go out with al-Harith ibn Labib al-Saffar, a pupil of al-Marzani, who had a beautiful voice. He recited the words of Almighty God: 'This is a day on which they shall not speak and shall not be permitted to excuse themselves.'* I saw al-Shafi'i change colour. He shuddered and was so violently agitated that he fell down in a faint. When he had recovered, he said: 'I take refuge with God from the station of the liars and the assemblies of the negligent. Oh my God, before You are humbled the hearts of those who know. Oh my God, of Your bounty grant me forgiveness for my sins; favour me with Your protection and forgive my shortcomings by Your magnanimity.' Then he got up and went away."

'A reliable man once said: "I came to Baghdad when al-Shafi'i was there. I sat on the river bank to perform the ritual ablution before praying. A man passed me and said: 'Young man, perform your ablution well and God will be good to you in this world and the next.' I turned and saw someone being followed by a crowd of people. I hurried through my ablution and started to follow him. He turned to me and asked me if there was anything that I needed. 'Yes,' I replied. 'I want you to teach me some of what Almighty God has taught you.' He said: 'Know that whoever believes in God will be saved and whoever preserves his religion will escape destruction. Whoever practises abstinence in this world will find happiness in the next. Shall I tell you more?' 'Yes,' I replied. He went on: 'Be abstinent in worldly things and set your desire on the world

* Quran 77.35.

to come. Be truthful in all your affairs and you will join the ranks of the saved.' He then went away, and when I asked about him I was told that he was the imam al-Shafi'i." Al-Shafi'i used to say: "I like to see people profiting from what I know, provided that none of it is attributed to me."'

Night 84

Morning now dawned and Shahrazad broke off from what she had been allowed to say. Then, when it was the eighty-fourth night, SHE CONTINUED:

I have heard, O fortunate king, that THE VIZIER DANDAN TOLD DAU' AL-MAKAN:

The old woman said to your father: 'Al-Shafi'i used to say: "I like to see people profiting from what I know, provided that none of it is attributed to me." He went on: "I have never disputed with anyone without wishing that Almighty God might aid him to find the truth and help him to reveal it. I have never held a dispute with anyone except for the purpose of revealing the truth and I don't care whether God reveals it by my tongue or by that of my opponent." He also said (may God be pleased with him): "If you fear that your knowledge may make you conceited, remember Whose approval you seek, what happiness you covet and what punishment you dread."

'Abu Hanifa was told that he had been appointed as a *qadi* by Abu Ja'far al-Mansur, with an allowance of ten thousand dirhams. He did not approve of this and on the day when the money was supposed to come to him, he performed the morning prayer and then wrapped himself in his robe and said nothing. The caliph's messenger arrived with the money, but when he came in and spoke to Abu Hanifa, Abu Hanifa made no reply. "This money is legally yours," said the messenger. "I know that," replied Abu Hanifa, "but I do not want love of tyrants to enter my heart." "Can you not associate with them," asked the man, "and yet keep yourself from loving them?" "Can I be sure that if I go into the sea my clothes will not get wet?" Abu Hanifa replied.

'Al-Shafi'i, may God be pleased with him, wrote these lines:

Soul, will you accept my words,
And prosper in eternal glory?

Abandon what you wish for and desire,
For many a wish has brought death in its wake.

'When Sufyan al-Thauri was giving counsel to 'Ali ibn al-Hasan al-Suhami, he said: "Keep to the truth and avoid lies, treachery, hypocrisy and conceit. The presence of any one of these will cause God to frustrate a good action. Do not be indebted to any except the One who is merciful towards His debtors. Take as your companion someone who will help you to abstain from the world. Remember death frequently, and frequently ask for pardon. Pray to God for safety in what remains of your life. Give advice to every believer when he asks you about his religion. Beware of betraying a believer, for whoever does this betrays God and His Apostle. Take care not to indulge in disputes and quarrels. If you abandon what causes you to doubt for what does not, you will be safe. Command what is good and forbid what is evil and you will be dear to God. If you adorn your secret heart, God will do the same to you in your outward show. Accept the excuses of those who excuse themselves to you. Do not hate any Muslim. Attach yourself to those who would break with you. If you forgive those who wrong you, you will be a companion of the prophets. Entrust your affairs to God, both in secret and openly. Fear God with the fear of one who knows that he faces death and resurrection, and that at the Last Judgement he will stand before the mighty God. Remember that you will go either to Paradise on high or to burning fire."'

After this, the old woman took her seat beside the girls. When your late father had heard what they had said, he recognized them as being the nonpareils of the age; he saw their beauty and loveliness, and the extent of their learning, and so he was prepared to shelter them. He went up to the old woman and treated her with honour, after which he assigned to her and her girls the palace where Princess Abriza, the daughter of the Byzantine emperor, had lived. All the goods that they needed were brought to them and the girls stayed there for ten days, together with the old woman. Whenever the king went to visit her, he found her occupied with her prayers, standing to pray by night and fasting by day. Affection for her filled his heart and he said to me: 'Vizier, this is a virtuous old woman, and in my heart I have a great respect for her.'

On the eleventh day, he met her in order to pay over to her the price of the slave girls. She told him: 'Your majesty, the price of these girls is too high to be covered by the common currency of mankind. It is not gold, silver or jewels that I want for them, be that little or much.' The king was astonished to hear this and asked her what then was the price. She said: 'I shall only sell them to you in return for a whole month of fasting, during which you are to fast by day and stand by night to pray to God. If you do this, then they will become yours, in your palace, to do with as you want.' The king was amazed at the extent of her virtue, asceticism and piety. He thought so highly of her that he believed that it was God who had sent him this virtuous woman to help him. He then made an agreement with her to fast for a month as she had stipulated. 'I will help you by praying for you,' she said, and she then asked for a jug of water to be brought her. When this was fetched, she took it, recited over it and muttered some words. She sat for a time, speaking in an incomprehensible tongue so that we could understand nothing. Then she covered the jug with a piece of cloth, added a seal and gave it to your father, telling him: 'When you have fasted for the first ten days, on the eleventh night break your fast with what is in this jug. It will remove from your heart love for this world and will fill you with light and faith. Tomorrow, I shall go to my brothers, the invisible men, for whom I have been longing, and then after the ten days have passed, I shall come back to you.'

Your father then took the jug and set it in a place by itself in the palace, putting the key of the room in his pocket. The next day, he fasted and the old woman went on her way.

Night 85

Morning now dawned and Shahrazad broke off from what she had been allowed to say. Then, when it was the eighty-fifth night, SHE CONTINUED:

I have heard, O fortunate king, that THE VIZIER DANDAN TOLD DAU' AL-MAKAN:

Your father fasted next day and the old woman went off on her way. The king fasted for ten days and on the eleventh he removed the covering from the jug and drank its contents, which he found had a pleasant effect on his heart. During the second period of ten days the old woman returned, bringing sweetmeats wrapped in a green leaf which did not look like the leaf of any known tree. She came to your father and greeted him. When he saw her, he rose to greet and welcome her. She said: 'O king, the unseen men give you greetings. They are pleased at what they have heard from me about you and they have sent me to bring you these sweetmeats, which are of the next world. Break your fast with them at the end of the day.' Your father was delighted and praised God for having given him friends from among the invisible men. He thanked the old woman, kissed her hands and showed her the greatest honour, as he also did to the slave girls.

Twenty days passed, during which your father fasted. At the end of the period, the old woman came to him and said: 'O king, I have told the invisible men of the affection that there is between you and me. I told them that I had left the slave girls with you and they were pleased to hear that they were with a king like you, as whenever they had seen these girls they had been in the habit of offering up fervent prayers for them, prayers which God answers. I want to take them to the invisible men, whose fragrance may spread over them. Perhaps when they return to you they will bring you one of the treasures of the earth, so that when you have completed your fast you can busy yourself with providing robes for them, using the money which they bring you to help you to your end.' When he heard this, your father thanked her and said: 'If I did not fear to disobey you, I would not consent to take the treasure or anything else.' He then asked when she was going to remove the girls, and she told him that she would take them on the twenty-seventh night and bring them back at the end of the month, 'when you have completed your fast and they are free from menstruation. They will then be yours and under your command, and I swear by God that the value of each of them is many times greater than that of your kingdom.' 'I know that, virtuous lady,' said the king, and the old woman went on: 'You must send with them from the palace someone dear to you who may enjoy the friendship of the invisible men and seek their blessing.' 'I have a Byzantine slave girl, called Sophia,' the king told her. 'She bore me two children, a girl and a boy, but they were lost some years ago. Take her with the slave girls so that she can acquire blessing.'

Night 86

Morning now dawned and Shahrazad broke off from what she had been allowed to say. Then, when it was the eighty-sixth night, SHE CONTINUED:

I have heard, O fortunate king, that THE VIZIER DANDAN TOLD DAU' AL-MAKAN:

The king told her: 'I have a Byzantine slave girl, called Sophia. She bore me two children, a girl and a boy, but they were lost some years ago. Take her with the slave girls so that she can acquire blessing. It may be that the invisible men will pray God to restore her children to her so that they can all be reunited.'

The old woman approved of this – and it was, in fact, the main purpose of her mission. Your father then started on the last part of his fast. The old woman told him that she was leaving to meet the unseen men and asked him to produce Sophia, who came as soon as she was summoned. The king handed her over to the old woman, who placed her with the five slave girls. She then entered her room and brought out a glass to which a seal had been added. She gave this to the king and told him: 'On the thirtieth day of your fast, go to the baths and when you come out, enter a private room in your palace, drink this glass and fall asleep, for you will have obtained what you seek. I now take my leave of you.' At that, the king was filled with joy and he thanked her and kissed her hands. 'I commend you to God's protection,' she said. He asked when he would see her again, adding that he did not want to be parted from her. She blessed him and set off, taking with her the slave girls and Princess Sophia.

The king waited for three days and then at the start of the new month he got up and went to the baths. When he left them, he entered a private room in the palace and closed the door, giving orders that he was not to be disturbed. Next, he drank the glass and fell asleep. We sat waiting for him till the end of the day, but he did not come out. We thought that he might be tired after bathing and after his sleepless nights and his days of fasting, and so we supposed that he might be asleep. We waited for a second day, but when he had still not come out, we stood at the door of the room and raised our voices to attract his attention and make him ask what was happening. When this failed, we took the door off its hinges and went in. There we were appalled to find him with his flesh torn and shredded and his bones crushed. We took the glass and found in what had covered it a piece of paper on which was written: 'Evil-doers are not missed when they die. This is the reward of those who scheme against the daughters of kings and rob them of their virtue. Whoever reads this should know that when Sharkan came to our country, he seduced our princess, Abriza. Not content with that, he took her from us and brought her to you and then sent her off with a black slave who killed her. We found her murdered body in the desert, thrown on to the ground. Such is not the action of a king and this is the reward of one who acts like this. Accuse no one else of the king's death, for no one else killed him but the cunning mistress of mischief, whose name is Dhat al-Dawahi. I have taken the king's wife, Sophia, and brought her to her father, Afridun, emperor of Constantinople. We shall now attack you, kill you and take your lands. Every last one of you will perish; you will have no lands left and the only inhabitants that remain will be worshippers of the Cross.'

On reading this, we realized that the old woman had deceived us and succeeded in tricking us. We cried out, slapped our faces and wept, but our tears did us no good. The army was divided as to whom they should choose as their new ruler. Some wanted you, and others your brother Sharkan. The dispute went on for a month, after which a number of us joined together with the intention of going to your brother, and we continued on our way until we found you. This, then, is how King 'Umar ibn al-Nu'man met his death.

When the vizier Dandan had finished, Dau' al-Makan, together with his sister, Nuzhat al-Zaman, burst into tears, as did the chamberlain. The chamberlain then said to Dau' al-Makan: 'Tears will do you no good. The only useful thing is for you to harden your heart, strengthen your resolve and take firm control of your kingdom. For whoever leaves behind a son like you has not died.' At this, Dau' al-Makan stopped weeping and gave orders for the throne to be placed outside the pavilion and he ordered the troops to parade before him. The chamberlain stood at his side; behind him were his personal guard; in front of him was the vizier Dandan; and all the emirs and officers of state were in their own places. Dau' al-Makan then asked Dandan to tell him about the contents of his father's treasuries. 'To hear is to obey,' replied Dandan, and he told him of the stores and jewels in the treasuries, as well as showing him the money in the pay chest. Dau' al-Makan distributed largesse to the troops, and after giving Dandan a splendid robe of honour, he told him to continue in his post. Dandan kissed the ground before him and prayed for his long life. Dau' al-Makan then distributed robes of honour to the emirs and he told the chamberlain to show him the Damascus tribute that he had with him. The chamberlain showed him the chests of money, valuables and jewels, which he then took and distributed among the troops . . .

Night 87

Morning now dawned and Shahrazad broke off from what she had been allowed to say. Then, when it was the eighty-seventh night, SHE CONTINUED:

I have heard, O fortunate king, that Dau' al-Makan told the chamberlain to show him the Damascus tribute that he had with him. The chamberlain showed him the chests of money, valuables and jewels, which he then took and distributed among the troops until nothing remained. The emirs then kissed the ground in front of him and prayed for his long life. 'We have never seen a king who gave gifts like these,' they said, before going off to their tents.

The next morning, he gave the order to march, and on the fourth day they came within sight of Baghdad. They entered the city, which they found to have been adorned with decorations for the occasion, and Dau' al-Makan went as king to the palace of his father and took his seat on the throne, while the emirs of the army, the vizier Dandan and the chamberlain of Damascus stood before him. He then gave orders to his private secretary to write a letter to his brother, Sharkan, giving an account of all that had happened from start to finish, and adding, at the end of it: 'As soon as you have read this letter, make your preparations and come with your army so that we may set out to attack the infidels, take revenge on them for our father and clear ourselves of disgrace.' He folded up the letter, sealed it and said to the vizier Dandan: 'No one else can carry this letter but you. You must be courteous in what you say to him; tell him that if he wants his father's kingdom, he can have it, and add: "And your brother, as he has told me, will be your deputy in Damascus."'

The vizier left his presence and made his preparations for the journey. Next, Dau' al-Makan ordered that the furnace man be given a magnificent residence, furnished with all splendour. There is a long story attached to this man. Dau' al-Makan himself went off hunting and, on his return to Baghdad, one of the emirs presented him with what baffles description, a present of noble horses and slave girls of indescribable beauty. One of these girls caught his fancy and so he retired with her and lay with her that same night, at which she immediately conceived. Some time later, the vizier Dandan came back from his journey with news that Sharkan was on his way. He advised Dau' al-Makan that he should go out to meet him, to which Dau' al-Makan agreed. Accompanied by his great officers of state, he moved out for the distance of a day's journey from Baghdad and pitched his tents to wait for his brother.

In the morning, Sharkan arrived, accompanied by the troops of Syria – bold riders, fierce lions and heroes of the mêlée. The squadrons approached, with the dust clouds rising; on came the troops, with the banners of the columns fluttering. Sharkan and his companions came out to meet the Baghdadis. When Dau' al-Makan caught sight of his brother, he was about to dismount to greet him, but Sharkan called out to stop him. Rather, he dismounted himself and walked for a few paces. When he was in front of Dau' al-Makan, the latter threw himself on him. Sharkan clasped him to his breast and the two wept bitterly and consoled each other for their loss. Then they both mounted and rode off, accompanied by their troops, until they came in sight of Baghdad where they dismounted, and the two of them went up to the royal palace where they spent the night.

The next morning, Dau' al-Makan came out and gave orders for troops to be collected from all quarters, and a Holy War to be proclaimed. There was then a pause for the armies to arrive from the various regions, during which everyone who came received honourable treatment and promises of future advantages. In this way a whole month passed, with men arriving in successive waves. It was at this point that Sharkan asked his brother to tell him his story and Dau' al-Makan explained everything that had happened to him from beginning to end, including the services rendered him by the furnace man. When Sharkan asked him whether he had repaid the man for these, he said: 'Brother, I have not yet done that, but, I shall, God willing, reward him when I come back from this expedition . . .'

Night 88

Morning now dawned and Shahrazad broke off from what she had been allowed to say. Then, when it was the eighty-eighth night, SHE CONTINUED:

I have heard, O fortunate king, that Sharkan asked Dau' al-Makan whether he had repaid the furnace man for his services. He replied: 'Brother, I have not yet done that, but, I shall, God willing, reward him when I return from this expedition, and have time for him.'

Sharkan now realized that all that his sister, Nuzhat al-Zaman, had told him was true. He kept secret what had happened between the two of them and sent greetings to her and her husband the chamberlain, greetings which she returned. She invoked blessings on him and asked about her daughter, Qudiya-fa-Kana. On being told that the girl was well and enjoying the best of health and well-being, she praised Almighty God and thanked Sharkan. Sharkan himself then went back to his brother to consult him about the army's march. They would move, said Dau' al-Makan, when the full tally of troops had been reached and the Bedouin had come in from all quarters. He ordered provisions to be got ready and stores to be collected.

After this, he visited his wife, who was now five months pregnant. He assigned learned men and arithmeticians to her service, providing them with salaries and allowances. Then, in the third month after the arrival of the Syrian troops, when the Bedouin and the other contingents had arrived from all parts, he set off, accompanied by the levies and the regular troops, with the columns following one after the other. The commander of the Dailami troops was Rustam, while the Turkish commander was Bahram. Dau' al-Makan rode in the centre of the army with his brother Sharkan on his right and his brother-in-law, the chamberlain, on his left. The march continued for a month, with a three-day halt every week because of the size of the army. They continued in this way until they reached Byzantine territory, where the townsfolk, together with the villagers and the poor, all fled to Constantinople.

When Emperor Afridun heard of the invasion, he went to Dhat al-Dawahi, for she had been the author of the scheme and had gone to Baghdad, killed 'Umar ibn al-Nu'man and brought back the slave girls, together with Princess Sophia, to their own land. On her return to her son, the king of Rum, and believing herself to be secure, she had said to him: 'You can be consoled, as I have avenged the death of your daughter Abriza for you; I have killed King 'Umar ibn al-Nu'man and brought back Sophia. Now get up and leave for Constantinople to return the emperor his daughter and to tell him what has happened, so that we may all be on our guard and make our preparations. I will go with you to the emperor, for I think that the Muslims will not wait for us to attack.' 'Stay until they are close to our lands,' the king replied, 'so that we have time to get ready.'

They then started to collect their men and to prepare. By the time they heard that the Muslims were on the march, they were ready, and Dhat al-Dawahi left with the advance guard. When they got to Constantinople, the emperor heard that Hardub, king of Rum, had arrived, and went out to meet him. When they met, Afridun asked Hardub how he was and why he had come. In reply, Hardub told him about the trick played by Dhat al-Dawahi and how she had killed the Muslim king and recovered Princess Sophia from him. 'The Muslims have marched with all their men,' Dhat al-Dawahi said, 'and we must all unite to face them.'

Afridun was delighted by the arrival of his daughter and the death of 'Umar, and he sent for reinforcements from all his lands, telling them why 'Umar had been killed. Christian troops hurried to join him, and within three months the muster of his armies was complete. The Franks came from their various regions, such as France, Austria, Dubrovnik, Jawarna, Venice and Genoa, together with other troops of the Banu'l-Asfar. When they had all gathered, the country was too small to hold them and so Afridun ordered them away from Constantinople. They left and the troops followed each other in succession on a column that extended for the distance of a ten-day journey. This route took them to the wide Wadi'l-Nu'man, which is close to the salt sea. Here they halted for three days, and on the fourth, when they were intending to move off, they heard news of the arrival of the armies of Islam, the defenders of the religion of the best of mankind. Accordingly, they waited for another three days and on the fourth they saw a dust cloud that rose until it had filled all quarters of the sky. Before an hour had passed it cleared away, its fragments rising into the air, and its darkness was extinguished by the stars of spearheads and lances and the gleam of white sword blades. There beneath it were the banners of Islam and the standards of Muhammadanism.

The horsemen advanced like breaking waves, wearing hauberks that looked like clouds set as chain mail over moons. The two armies moved forward against each other and met face to face. The first challenger was the vizier Dandan with the Syrians, thirty thousand riders in all, and he was accompanied by the leaders of the Turks and the Dailamis, Bahram and Rustam, with twenty thousand men. Behind them were men from the region of the salt sea, wearing armour which made them look like moons travelling through the darkness of night. The Christians started to call on Jesus, Mary and the blackened Cross, and they closed in around Dandan and his Syrians.

The plan for all this had been drawn up by the old woman, Dhat al-Dawahi. She had been approached by the emperor before he had moved out, and asked what tactics to use, for she, as he pointed out, was responsible for the crisis. 'Know, O great king and mighty priest,' she had said, 'that I shall show you a scheme that would baffle Iblis himself, even if he had all his ill-starred hosts to help him.'

Night 89

Morning now dawned and Shahrazad broke off from what she had been allowed to say. Then, when it was the eighty-ninth night, SHE CONTINUED:

I have heard, O fortunate king, that the plan for this had been drawn up by the old woman, Dhat al-Dawahi. She had been approached by the emperor before he had moved out, and asked what tactics to use, for she, as he pointed out, was responsible for the crisis. 'Know, O great king and mighty priest,' she had said, 'that I shall show you a scheme that would baffle Iblis himself, even if he had all his ill-starred hosts to help him. You should send out fifty thousand men to embark on ships and sail to the Smoke Mountain. They should stay there without moving from their position until you are confronted by the banners of Islam. You must then attack the Muslim army. The troops that have come by sea will advance and take them from the rear, while we face them on the landward side and no single one of them will escape. We shall then be free from trouble and able to enjoy lives of continuous happiness.' Afridun approved of what she said: 'What an excellent plan this is of yours, mistress of the cunning old women and refuge of the priests in time of discord!'

When the Muslims attacked the Christians in the valley, before they knew what was happening, fires were blazing among their tents, while swords were at work among the men. At that point the troops of Baghdad and Khurasan came up, a hundred and twenty thousand riders in all, with Dau' al-Makan at their head. When the sea-borne infidels saw them, they moved in from the shore and followed in their tracks. Seeing them, Dau' al-Makan shouted to his men: 'Turn back against the infidels, you followers of the chosen Prophet; fight against the impious foe in obedience to the Merciful and Compassionate God.' Sharkan advanced with another corps of the Muslim army numbering about a hundred and twenty thousand, while the infidel armies totalled some one million six hundred thousand men.

When the Muslims joined forces they became confident and called out: 'God has promised us the victory and has threatened the unbelievers with failure.' The ranks clashed together with swords and spears. Sharkan cut his way through, raging among the masses of the foe and fighting with such ferocity as to turn white the hair of children. He continued to wheel round among the infidels, striking at them with his keen sword and shouting '*Allahu akbar!*' until they were driven back to the seashore in a state of exhaustion. God granted victory to Islam and the soldiers were fighting as though drunk, but not on wine. In this battle the infidels lost forty-five thousand men, while three thousand five hundred Muslims were killed. Neither Sharkan nor his brother Dau' al-Makan slept that night, as they were busy encouraging their men, visiting the wounded and congratulating them on their victory, their survival and the reward that would be theirs on the Day of Resurrection.

So much for the Muslims. As for Afridun, the emperor of Constantinople, along with the king of Rum and his mother, Dhat al-Dawahi, they collected the army commanders and said: 'We would have achieved our goal and satisfied our desires, but we failed because we were relying on our greater numbers.' Dhat al-Dawahi said: 'The only thing that will be of use to you is to seek favour from the Messiah and to hold fast to the true faith. By the truth of the Messiah, the one thing that strengthened the Muslim army today was that devil, Sultan Sharkan.' The emperor then said: 'Tomorrow, I intend to draw up the army and then send out against the Muslims the famous knight Luqa ibn Shamlut. If he meets Sharkan in single combat, he will kill him and he will then kill the other Muslim champions until not one of them is left. I intend tonight to consecrate you with the finest incense of all.'

When his men heard this, they kissed the ground, for by the incense he meant the excrement of the Patriarch, the denier and the rejecter of the truth. The Christians used to compete with one another for this because of the value that they placed on its foulness, and the great Rumi priests would send it throughout their empire wrapped in pieces of silk and mixed with musk and ambergris. When kings heard of it, they would buy a dirham's weight of it for a thousand dinars and they would send to ask for it to use as incense at weddings, while the other priests would mix it with their own excrement, as that of the Patriarch was not enough for ten provinces. The principal kings would mix a little of it with the kohl they used as eye ointment, and they employed this in their treatment of the sick and those suffering from stomach pains.

When morning broke and light spread, the riders came out with their lances.

Night 90

Morning now dawned and Shahrazad broke off from what she had been allowed to say. Then, when it was the ninetieth night, SHE CONTINUED:

I have heard, O fortunate king, that when morning broke and light spread, the riders came out with their lances. Afridun summoned his principal officers and his ministers of state. He distributed robes of state among them, traced the sign of the Cross on their faces and perfumed them with the incense that has just been described. Having done this, he summoned Luqa ibn Shamlut, known as the Sword of the Messiah, perfumed him and then smeared him with the excrement, which he sniffed and then spread on his cheeks and moustache. Nowhere in the lands of Rum was there a greater champion than this damned Luqa, or any better archer, swordsman or spearsman on the day of battle. He was an ugly man with the face of a donkey, the shape of an ape and the appearance of a snake. To be near him was harder to bear than to part from a beloved. His was the blackness of night, the foul breath of the lion and the daring of the leopard, and he was marked with the sign of the infidels.

He now came forward to Afridun, kissed his feet and took his stand before him. The emperor told him: 'I want you to go out to challenge Sharkan, sultan of Damascus, the son of 'Umar ibn al-Nu'man, for in this way the evil will be cleared away from us and our task will become easy.' 'To hear is to obey,' replied Luqa, and the emperor made the sign of the Cross on his face, believing that victory would soon be theirs.

Luqa then left the emperor's presence and mounted a roan horse. He wore a red robe, with golden mail studded with gems, and he carried a lance with a trident head as though he was Iblis the damned at the Battle of the League.* He and his infidel followers set out, riding as though to hellfire. Among them was a herald who called out in Arabic: 'People of Muhammad, let no one come out except your champion, the Sword of Islam, Sharkan, the sultan of Damascus.'

Before he had finished speaking, there was a sound on the plain that all could hear. Galloping horses parted the ranks, calling to mind the day of wailing at the Last Judgement. Base men shrank in fear; heads turned and there was Sharkan. When Dau' al-Makan had seen Luqa the damned coming on to the battlefield and had heard the herald, he turned to his brother and said: 'They want you.' 'If that is so,' replied Sharkan, 'that is what I would most like.' When they were sure of this and heard that the herald's challenge was to Sharkan alone, they realized that the damned Luqa was the champion of the lands of Rum. He had sworn to cleanse the earth of Muslims, or else be counted as one of the greatest losers. It was he who had caused bitter grief, causing Turks, Kurds and Dailamis to take fright at the harm that he did.

So it was that Sharkan now rode out against him like an angry lion, mounted on a horse like a fleeing gazelle. He rode up to Luqa and brandished his lance as though it was a viper, reciting the lines:

I have a roan horse, obedient to the rein, a raider,
Who contents his rider with his exertions;
I have a straight lance with a smooth head:
Death itself is set within its wood.
Mine is a sharp Indian sword; when unsheathed,
You would think that lightning ripples on its blade.

Luqa understood neither the meaning of this poem nor the passion contained in it. Instead, he struck his face with his hand, to show reverence to the Cross marked on it, after which he kissed his hand, laid his lance in rest against Sharkan and charged. He tossed a javelin with one hand until it was lost to sight and then caught it again with the other hand like a juggler. He then hurled it at Sharkan like a piercing meteor, to the consternation and alarm of the Muslims, but when it was near him, Sharkan astonished everyone by plucking it out of the air. He shook

* Quran 33.

it in the hand in which he had caught it until it almost shattered, after which he threw it up into the air until it was out of sight and then caught it with his other hand faster than the blink of an eye. He cried out from the bottom of his heart: 'By the truth of God the Creator of the seven heavens, I shall expose this damned man to disgrace throughout the world.' He then threw the javelin at Luqa who, wanting to do what he had done, put out his hand to catch it in mid-air, but Sharkan forestalled him by hurling a second javelin which struck him in the middle of the Cross drawn on his face, and God hastened his soul to the Fire, an evil resting place. When the infidels saw him fall, they slapped their faces and burst into loud lamentation, imploring the help of the patriarchs of the monasteries . . .

Night 91

Morning now dawned and Shahrazad broke off from what she had been allowed to say. Then, when it was the ninety-first night, SHE CONTINUED:

I have heard, O fortunate king, that when the infidels saw him fall, they slapped their faces and burst into loud lamentation, imploring the help of the patriarchs of the monasteries and saying: 'Where are the crosses and the ascetic monks?' Then they closed formation and attacked with swords and lances. The armies met: men's chests were crushed beneath horses' hooves; lances and swords held sway; arms and wrists grew weak; and the horses looked as though they had been born without legs. The herald of war kept calling until, when men's hands were wearied, the day ended and with the fall of darkness the armies parted. Every brave man was as though drunk because of the violence of the blows and thrusts; the ground was covered with corpses; there were gaping wounds, and the wounded could not be distinguished from the dead.

Sharkan now joined his brother Dau' al-Makan, the chamberlain and the vizier Dandan, and said to them: 'God has opened a door for us to allow us to destroy the infidels – praise be to Him, the Lord of the worlds.' Dau' al-Makan replied: 'We have not ceased to praise Him for freeing Arabs and Persians from distress. Generation after generation will talk of what you did to the damned Luqa, the perverter of the Evangel, how you caught the javelin in mid-air and how you struck down the enemy of God among the armies. The story of your prowess will remain until the end of time.'

Sharkan then addressed the chamberlain, who answered that he was ready to obey. 'Take the vizier Dandan with you,' said Sharkan, 'together with twenty thousand riders, and march them for seven *parasangs* in the direction of the sea. Hurry on until you are close to the shore and two *parasangs* away from the enemy. Hide yourselves in the low ground there, and when you hear the noise of the infidel army disembarking from their ships and battle cries being raised on all sides as the swords go about their work among us, you will see our men retreating as though they were routed. The infidels will follow them from all sides, as well as from their camp by the shore. Keep watching them and when you see a banner with the words "There is no god but God and Muhammad is the Apostle of God – may God bless him and give him peace", do you raise the green banner, shout "*Allahu akbar!*" and charge them from the rear. Do your best to see that the infidels cannot get between the retreating Muslims and the sea.'

'To hear is to obey,' said the chamberlain, and after immediately agreeing to the plan, the Muslims made their preparations and set off, with the chamberlain taking with him the vizier Dandan and twenty thousand men, as Sharkan had ordered. The next morning, the soldiers mounted, drawing their swords and steadying their lances with their thighs and bearing other weapons. Troops spread over the hills and the valleys; the priests raised their voices; heads were bared; crosses were hoisted over the sails of the infidel ships and the crews made for the shore from every side. Horses were landed, with their riders determined to skirmish. Swords flashed as the armies moved; bright lances darted lightning against coats of mail; the mills of fate revolved over the heads of horse and foot; heads flew from bodies; tongues were dumb and eyes blinded; gall bladders burst as the swords went about their business; heads flew off; wrists were cut through; horses waded in blood and fighters grasped each other by the beard. The armies of Islam called out, invoking blessings and peace on the Lord of mankind and praising Merciful God for His favours. The Christians praised the Cross, the girdle, the wine, he who crushes the grapes, the priests, the monks, the palm branches and the bishop.

Dau' al-Makan drew back, together with Sharkan, and the Muslims retreated to make the enemy think that they were being routed. The Christians, believing them beaten, pressed after them, prepared for hand-to-hand fighting. The Muslims began to recite the beginning of the *sura* of the Cow, while corpses were trampled beneath the horses' hooves. The Rumi herald began to call out: 'Worshippers of the Messiah, you who follow the true religion, servants of the Primate, success has come; the armies of Islam are about to flee; don't turn back from them but pursue them with the sword. If you retire, you will be rejected by the Messiah, the son of Mary, who spoke while still in the cradle.'

Emperor Afridun, believing that his men were victorious and not realizing that this was a ruse, cleverly planned by the Muslims, sent news of this 'victory' to the king of Rum. 'It was the excrement of the Patriarch that helped us, and nothing but this, as its smell spread through the beards and moustaches of the servants of the Cross, wherever they may be. I swear by the miracles, by your daughter Abriza, the Christian, the follower of Mary, and by the waters of baptism, that I shall not leave on the face of the earth a single defender of Islam and I am determined to carry out this intention to its evil end.' His messenger set off with this message, and the infidels called to each other: 'Avenge Luqa!'

Night 92

Morning now dawned and Shahrazad broke off from what she had been allowed to say. Then, when it was the ninety-second night, SHE CONTINUED:

I have heard, O fortunate king, that the infidels called to each other: 'Avenge Luqa!' while the king of Rum shouted: 'Avenge Abriza!'

At that moment, King Dau' al-Makan cried: 'Servants of God the Judge, strike the infidels who rebel against God, with your white swords and brown spears.' The Muslims turned back against the infidels, using their sharp swords, and the Muslim herald began to call out: 'Turn on the enemies of faith, you who love the chosen Prophet. This is the time to win the favour of God, the Generous, the Merciful. You who hope for salvation on the dreadful Day of Judgement, Paradise lies under the shadow of the swords.' It was then that Sharkan charged with his men, cutting off the enemy's escape route, wheeling and circling between the ranks.

Suddenly, a fine rider cut a path through the infidels and circled round, cutting and thrusting. He filled the ground with heads and bodies; the infidels shrank from encountering him and their necks reeled from under his thrusts and blows. He had two swords, his sabre and his glances, and carried two lances, his spear and his erect frame, while his long hair served him in place of numbers of men; as the poet has said:

> Long hair is of no use except when it streams out
> On both sides of the head on the day of battle,
> Belonging to a young hero with a straight lance,
> That drinks the blood of the moustachioed enemy.

Another poet says:

> When he girds on his sword, I say:
> 'The swords of your eyes serve you in place of steel.'
> He answered: 'The sword of my eyes is for those I love;
> My steel is for those who do not know love's sweetness.'

When Sharkan saw him, he said: 'Champion, who are you? May God preserve you through the Quran and God's verses. Your actions have pleased the Judge, Who is not distracted from one affair by another, because you have routed the impious infidels.' The rider called back to him: 'You are the man who made a compact with me yesterday; how quickly you have forgotten me.' He then removed his mouth-veil, showing the beauty that lay hidden, and it turned out that here was Dau' al-Makan. Sharkan's pleasure at the sight was mixed with fear for his brother because of the thick press of heroes around him.

There were two reasons for this, the first being that Dau' al-Makan was still young and needed to be protected from the evil eye, and the second that his life was of prime importance to the kingdom. So he said: 'King, you are risking your life. Keep your horse close to mine, for I don't think that you are safe from the enemy. It would be better if you did not ride out from our lines, so that we may shoot at the enemies with our arrows that fly true.' 'I want to match you in battle,' replied his brother, 'and I don't grudge risking my life by fighting before you.'

The armies of Islam then closed in on the infidels from all sides, fighting hard and overcoming their might and their stubbornness in evil-doing. Afridun was filled with sorrow when he saw the disaster that had overtaken his men, who had turned their backs and taken flight, making for their ships, at which point a Muslim force had come out from the shore, led by the vizier Dandan, the overthrower of champions. He fought with sword and spear, as did the emir Bahram, lord of the Syrian provinces, with twenty thousand heroes like lions. The Christians were surrounded, front and rear, and a body of Muslims attacked those who were in the ships, spreading destruction among them so that they threw themselves into the sea. A huge number of them, more than a hundred thousand, were killed, and none of their champions, small or great, escaped, while all but twenty of their ships, with the wealth, stores and baggage they contained, were captured. The Muslims won more booty that day than anyone had ever taken in earlier times, nor had anyone ever heard of a battle like this. Among their prizes were fifty thousand horses, and that was to say nothing of the stores and spoils, which passed all counting. The delight of the Muslims at the victory and the help given them by God could not have been surpassed.

So much for them, but as for the routed Christians, they came to Constantinople, where the people had earlier been told that it was Emperor Afridun who had been victorious over the Muslims. The old woman Dhat al-Dawahi said: 'I know my son, the king of Rum, is not a man to be beaten. He has no fear of the armies of Islam and he will restore the people of the world to the religion of Christ.' She had told the emperor to have the city adorned with decorations. The inhabitants showed their joy and drank wine, not knowing what fate had brought them. Then, in the middle of their celebration, the crow of sorrow and distress began to croak. The twenty ships that had escaped arrived with the king of Rum. The emperor met them on the shore and they told him what had happened to them when they met the Muslims, weeping bitterly and sobbing aloud. News of success was replaced by sorrow for the harm they had suffered. The emperor was told that Luqa ibn Shamlut had met with misfortune and had been struck down by the unerring arrow of fate.

Afridun was horrified, realizing that the disaster could not be undone. People came together to mourn their dead; resolve was weakened; the mourning women lamented; and from every quarter rose loud sounds of sobbing and weeping. The king of Rum, having met Afridun, gave him a report of the battle, explaining that the supposed rout of the Muslims was only a cunning trick, and adding: 'Do not look for any more of the army to return, apart from those who have already come.' When Afridun heard that, he fell down in a faint, with his nose under his feet. When he had recovered, he said: 'It may be that the Messiah was angry with them and so brought the Muslims down on them.' The Patriarch approached the emperor sorrowfully, and Afridun said to him: 'Father, our army has been destroyed as a punishment from the Messiah.' 'Do not grieve or mourn,' said the Patriarch. 'One of you must have sinned against the Messiah and it was for his sin that everyone was punished. Now, however, we will recite prayers for you in the churches so that these Muhammadan armies may be driven back.'

The old woman Dhat al-Dawahi then came and said: 'O king, the Muslim armies are large and it is only by a ruse that we can deal with them. I intend to play a cunning trick and I shall go to them in the hope that I can succeed in what I plan to do to their leader and kill him, their champion, as I killed his father. If my plan succeeds, not one man from among his armies will get back to his own country, as they all derive their strength from him. I need help from the Christians living in Syria who go out every month and every year to sell their goods, for it is through them that I shall achieve my goal.' 'That will be done whenever you want,' said the emperor, and so she gave orders for a hundred men to be fetched from Syrian Najran. They were brought to Afridun, who asked them if they knew of the disaster suffered by the Christians at the hands of the Muslims. When they said yes, he told them: 'This woman has dedicated herself to the Messiah and now she intends to go with you, all disguised as Muslims, to carry out a stratagem that will help us and stop the Muslim army from reaching us. Will you dedicate yourselves to the Messiah? If so, I shall give you a *qintar* of gold. Whoever survives will get the gold and whoever dies will be rewarded by the Messiah.' 'We all give ourselves to the Messiah,' they told him, 'and we will be your ransom.'

The old woman then took all the drugs she needed, put them in water and boiled them up over a fire, dissolving their black core. She waited until the mixture had cooled and then lowered the end of a long kerchief over it. Over her clothes she put on an embroidered mantle, while in her hand she held a rosary. When this was done and she came out into the emperor's presence, neither he nor any of those sitting with him recognized her. She then uncovered her face and all who were present praised her cunning. Her son was delighted and prayed that the Messiah might never deprive them of her. She then left with the Najrani Christians, making for the army of Baghdad.

Night 93

Morning now dawned and Shahrazad broke off from what she had been allowed to say. Then, when it was the ninety-third night, SHE CONTINUED:

I have heard, O fortunate king, that when Afridun heard of the disaster, he fell down in a faint with his nose under his feet; and when he had recovered, trembling with fear, he complained to the old woman Dhat al-Dawahi.

This damned woman was a sorceress, skilled in magic and in lies, unchaste, wily, debauched and treacherous, with foul breath, red eyelids, sallow cheeks in a dark face, bleary eyes, and a body covered with scabs. Her hair was grey; she was hunchbacked; her complexion was pallid and her nose streamed with mucus. She had, however, read Islamic texts and had travelled to the Haram of Mecca – all this in order to study religions and to become acquainted with the verses of the Quran. For two years she had claimed to follow Judaism in Jerusalem in order to possess herself of all the wiles of men and *jinn*. She was a disaster and an affliction, with no sound faith and no adherence to any religion. It was because of his virgin slave girls that she spent most of the time with her son Hardub, king of Rum, for she was a passionate lesbian, and if deprived of her pleasure for long, she would wilt away. If any slave girl pleased her, she would teach her this art, crush saffron over her, and fall into a lengthy faint on top of her as a result of the pleasure she received. Those who obeyed her she treated well and commended to her son, but she schemed to destroy any who did not.

Abriza's maids, Marjana, Raihana and Utrujja, knew about this, while Abriza herself had disliked Dhat al-Dawahi and found it unpleasant to sleep in the same bed as her because of the fetid smell of her armpits and her flatulence, which was worse than a corpse, while her body was rougher than palm fibres. She would try to seduce lovers by offering jewels and instruction, but Abriza used to shun her, taking refuge with God, the All-wise, the Omniscient. How well the poet puts it:

> You who grovel in abasement to the rich
> And lord it proudly over the poor,
> Adorning your repulsiveness by money-grubbing,
> Perfume does not make up for an ugly woman's stench.

Let us return to the tale of the trickery and the calamities she planned. She left, accompanied by the Christian leaders and their forces, making for the Muslim army. After she had gone, King Hardub visited Emperor Afridun and said: 'O king, we have no need for the Patriarch or his prayers. We should act on the advice of my mother, Dhat al-Dawahi, and see what she can do to the Muslim army with her boundless powers of deception. They are advancing on us with their force and will soon be here, surrounding us.' When Afridun heard that, he was so frightened that he wrote immediately to all Christian lands, telling them that no Christian follower of the Cross was to hold back, in particular the garrisons of forts and castles, and that all of them, horse and foot, women and children, were to come to Constantinople. He added: 'The Muslim army is already trampling over our land, so hurry, hurry, before what we dread takes place.'

So much for them, but as for Dhat al-Dawahi, she left the city with her companions, whom she had dressed as Muslim merchants. She had taken with her a hundred mules, laden with materials from Antioch, such as Ma'dani satin, regal brocades and so forth. She had been given by the emperor a letter to say the merchants were Syrians who had been in Byzantine territory, and that no one was to harm them or to demand a tithe from them until they had safely returned to their own land. 'Trade brings prosperity,' the letter added, 'and these are neither men of war nor evil-doers.' The damned woman then told her companions that she wanted to destroy the Muslims by a trick. 'Give us what orders you want, O queen,' they said, 'for we are at your command, and may the Messiah not frustrate what you plan to do.'

She then put on robes of soft white wool and rubbed her forehead until it acquired a large mark which she smeared with an unguent that she had prepared which gleamed brightly. She was a thin woman, with sunken eyes, and she now tied her legs, above the feet, and only untied the bonds when she had reached the Muslim army, by which time they had left weals, which she smeared with red juice. Then she told her companions to give her a severe beating and put her in a chest. They were to cry aloud: 'There is no god but God,' and this, she assured them, would bring no great harm on them. 'How can we beat you,' they exclaimed, 'when you are our mistress and the mother of our splendid king?' 'A man who goes off to relieve himself is not blamed or treated harshly,' she said, 'as necessity knows no laws. When you have placed me in the chest, put it with the rest of your goods, load it on the mules and take it through the Muslim army. You need fear no blame, and if you are confronted by any of the Muslims, you are to hand over to them the mules, together with the goods they are carrying, and then go to their king, Dau' al-Makan, asking him to help you. Say: "We have come from the land of the infidels where, far from anyone taking anything from us, they wrote an order for us saying that no one was to molest us. How is it, then, that you take our goods when here is a letter from the king of Rum saying that we are not to be harmed?" If Dau' al-Makan asks you what profit you made from trading in the lands of Rum, tell him: "Our profit was the release of an ascetic who had been held in a subterranean chamber for fifteen years, tortured by the infidels night and day and crying for help but not being answered. We had known nothing of this, but we stayed in Constantinople for a time, where we sold our goods, bought replacements and then made our preparations for the return journey to our own land. We spent the last night talking about our journey, and in the morning, drawn on the wall, we saw a picture, which moved when we came up to look at it more closely. Then a voice from the picture said: 'Muslims, is there anyone among you who will serve the Lord of the worlds?' 'How is that?' we asked. The voice replied: 'God has let me speak to you so that your faith may be strengthened and you may be inspired to aid your religion. Leave the lands of the infidels and make for the Muslim army. In that army is the Sword of the Merciful, the champion of the age, Sultan Sharkan. It is through him that Constantinople will be captured and the Christians destroyed. After you have travelled for three days, you will find a monastery known as the monastery of Matruhina. In it there is a cell which you must seek out with pure hearts, using the strength of your resolution to help you get to it. It contains an anchorite from Jerusalem, named 'Abd Allah, one of the most godly of men, who has performed miracles that remove all doubts and confusion. One of the monks tricked him and imprisoned him in an underground chamber, where he has been for a very long time. To rescue him would be to please God, the Lord of His servants, as this would be the best contribution to the Holy War.'"'

After having agreed with them on what they were to say so far, the old woman went on: 'When you have caught the attention of Sultan Sharkan, say to him: "When we heard what the picture said, we realized that the anchorite . . ."'

Night 94

Morning now dawned and Shahrazad broke off from what she had been allowed to say. Then, when it was the ninety-fourth night, SHE CONTINUED:

I have heard, O fortunate king, that when Dhat al-Dawahi had told this to her companions, she went on: 'When you have caught the attention of Sultan Sharkan, say to him: "When we heard what the picture said, we realized that the anchorite must be one of the great saints from among God's pure servants. So we travelled for three days, after which we came in sight of the monastery and turned aside to go to it. We stayed there for a day, buying and selling in the way that merchants do. That evening, when the shades of night had fallen, we went to the cell with the underground chamber and there we heard the anchorite reciting verses from the Quran, followed by these lines:

I wrestle with my heart and am downcast;
A sea of sorrows sweeps away my heart and then drowns it.
If there is no relief, then I wish for sudden death:
Death would be kinder to me than my misfortunes.
Lightning flash, if you come to my lands and to their folk,
And if you see rising above you the brightness of good news,
Tell me how I may meet them, while wars part us,
And while the door of ransom has stayed closed.
Take greetings to my loved ones and tell them
I am a distant captive, in a Rumi cell."'

The old woman went on: 'When you bring me to the Muslim army and I am within their ranks, you will see how I shall produce a trick to deceive them and destroy every last one of them.' On hearing this, the Christians kissed her hands and put her in a chest, after having given her a violent and painful beating by way of showing respect for her, as they thought they must obey her commands. They then set off with her to the Muslim army, as we have said.

So much for Dhat al-Dawahi, the damned, and her companions. As for the Muslim army, after God had granted them victory over their enemies and they had taken the money and the stores that had been on the ships, they sat talking together. 'It was because of our just dealings and the fact that we were prepared to follow each other's lead that God helped us,' said Dau' al-Makan to his brother, adding: 'So obey my commands in obedience to God, the Great and Glorious. For what I intend to do is to kill ten kings in revenge for my father, to slaughter fifty thousand Rumis and to enter Constantinople.' 'May my own life ransom you from death,' Sharkan replied. 'I must myself fight in the Holy War, even if I have to stay in their country for years, but in Damascus I have a daughter, whose name is Qudiya-fa-Kana and to whom I am deeply attached. She is one of the wonders of the age and is destined for fame.' 'I, too,' said Dau' al-Makan, 'have left a slave girl on the point of giving birth and I don't know what sex of child God will provide for me. So make a pact with me that if it turns out to be a boy, you will allow me the hand of your daughter in marriage to my son, binding yourself to this with an oath.' Sharkan willingly agreed and shook his brother's hand, saying: 'If you have a son, I will give you my daughter, Qudiya-fa-Kana.'

This pleased Dau' al-Makan and they started to congratulate each other on their victory over the enemy. The vizier Dandan congratulated both of them and said: 'Know, your majesties, that God gave us victory because we devoted ourselves to Him, the Lord of majesty and glory, leaving our families and our homeland. My advice is that we should follow the retreating enemy, besiege them and fight in the hope that God may allow us to achieve our goal and exterminate them. If you are willing, take the ships and set out by sea, while we march by land and endure the heat of combat in battle.' He kept on urging them to fight, reciting the lines of the poet:

'My greatest pleasure is to kill my foe,
When I am mounted on a noble horse,
Or when a promise comes from a beloved,
Or when a beloved comes without a tryst.

Another poet has said:

If I am given life, I take war as a mother,
The spears as brothers and the sword as a father,
With all dishevelled heroes smiling in the face of death,
As though by being killed they win their heart's desire.'

Having finished this poem, Dandan added: 'Glory be to Him who gave us His mighty aid and allowed us to take spoils of silver and gold!'

Dau' al-Makan then ordered the army to move out and they set off for Constantinople, pressing on with their march until they reached a broad stretch of pasture full of good things, with wild beasts disporting themselves and passing herds of gazelles. They had crossed many deserts and had not found water for six days, so when they came to the pasture land and looked at the springs that gushed up there and the ripe fruits, the land, so decorated and adorned, looked to them like a paradise. It seemed as though the tree branches were drunken and reeling with the wine of the dew, combining the sweetness of the fountain of Paradise with the languor of the zephyr. Both mind and sight were astonished; it was as the poet has said:

> Look at the verdant garden and it is as though
> It has been covered with a robe of green.
> If you allow your eye to roam, all you will see
> Will be a pool in which the water swirls.
> You will see yourself as glorious among the trees,
> Since everywhere you go a banner floats above your head.

Another poet has said:

> The river is a cheek reddened by the sun's rays,
> Over which creeps the down of the *ban* tree's shade.
> Water is like silver anklets around the trunks of trees,
> While the flowers there resemble crowns.

When Dau' al-Makan saw this meadow with its closely packed trees, its flowers in bloom and singing birds, he called to Sharkan and said: 'Brother, there is no place like this in Damascus. We shall wait for three days to rest before leaving it so that the soldiers of Islam may be refreshed and heartened before meeting the vile infidels.'

They halted and, while they were there, they heard the sound of far-off voices. On asking about this, Dau' al-Makan was told that a caravan of Syrian merchants had stopped there for a rest and that perhaps the soldiers had come across them and taken some of their goods, as they had been in infidel territory. Some time later, the merchants came up, crying out and calling for help from the king. Dau' al-Makan ordered them to be brought to him, and when they came, they said: 'O king, when we were in the lands of the infidels, no one plundered any of our goods, so how is it that our Muslim brothers rob us while we are in their own lands? When we saw your men, we went up to them and they seized all we had. Now we have told you what has happened to us.'

They then produced for him the letter from the emperor of Constantinople. Sharkan took this and read it, after which he told them that their goods would be handed back to them, but that they should not trade in the lands of the infidel. 'Master,' they said, 'it was God who sent us to their lands to win a prize such as no *ghazi* has ever won, not even in one of your raids.' When Sharkan asked what this prize might be, they said: 'We can only tell you in private, because if word of it spread and someone found out, it could lead to our destruction and the destruction of every Muslim who goes to the land of Rum.'

The merchants had hidden away the chest in which the damned Dhat al-Dawahi had been placed, and when Dau' al-Makan and his brother took them off by themselves, they explained the story of the anchorite and started to shed tears, causing the two brothers to weep with them.

Night 95

Morning now dawned and Shahrazad broke off from what she had been allowed to say. Then, when it was the ninety-fifth night, SHE CONTINUED:

I have heard, O fortunate king, that when Dau' al-Makan and his brother took the merchants off by themselves, they explained the story of the anchorite and started to shed tears, causing the two brothers to weep with them. When they repeated the story that the sorceress had taught them, Sharkan felt compassion for the 'anchorite', being moved not only by pity but by zeal for the cause of Almighty God. 'Did you free this ascetic,' he asked, 'or is he still in the monastery?' 'No,' they said, 'we freed him and we killed the abbot, fearing for our lives, after which we fled in a hurry, being afraid lest we perish. We were told by a trustworthy man that in the monastery there are great stores of gold, silver and jewels.' After saying this, they produced the chest and brought out the damned old woman, black and thin as a cassia pod and laden with fetters and chains. When Dau' al-Makan and the others there saw her, they thought that she was a man, one of the best of God's servants, and a most excellent ascetic, particularly as her forehead was gleaming with the unguent that she had smeared on her face.

Dau' al-Makan and his brother both wept bitterly and, going up to her, they kissed her hands and feet, sobbing the while. She gestured to them, telling them to stop weeping and to listen to what she had to say.

They did this obediently and she said: 'Know that I am content with what my Master has done with me, for I realize that the misfortune which He brought upon me was a test on His part, Great and Glorious as He is. Whoever has not endured misfortune and trials cannot enter the garden of Paradise. I used to wish that I might return to my own land, not because I could not bear the affliction that had befallen me, but so that I might die beneath the hooves of the horses of the fighters in the Holy War who after their death are alive and not dead.' She then recited:

> The fortress is Mount Sinai; the fire of war is lit;
> You are Moses and this is the appointed time.
> Throw down your staff to take up all they made;
> Have no fear, though their ropes have become snakes.
> Read the lines of the enemy as *suras* on the day of battle,
> For your sword in their necks will serve as verses.

When she had finished reciting these lines, her eyes filled with tears, and because of the unguent, her forehead was like a gleaming light. Sharkan went up to her, kissed her hand and had food brought for her, but she refused to take it and said: 'I have not broken my fast for fifteen years, so how should I do it now when, through my Master's bounty, I have been rescued from captivity among the infidels and saved from what was worse than the torture of fire? I shall wait until sunset.' When the time came for the evening meal, Sharkan came up with Dau' al-Makan, bringing food and telling her to eat. 'This is no time for eating,' she replied. 'Rather, this is the time to worship God, the King and Judge.' She stood praying at a shrine until the night had passed. She went on like this day for three days and nights, only sitting for the formulae of greeting at the end of the prayer.

Seeing all this, Dau' al-Makan was completely convinced of her sincerity, and he told Sharkan to have a leather tent pitched for the 'ascetic' and to assign a servant to wait on her. On the fourth day she called for food and they produced for her food of all kinds, both delicious and attractive to the eye, but of all this she would eat only a single loaf with salt, before determining to renew her fast, and standing up to pray as soon as night fell. Sharkan said to Dau' al-Makan: 'This man has taken asceticism in this world to its furthest point and, were it not for the Holy War, I would stay with him and worship God in his service until I meet Him. I want to go into his tent with him and to talk to him for some time.' 'I would like that, too,' said Dau' al-Makan. 'Tomorrow we are setting out to attack Constantinople and so we shall find no time like the present. I, too, want to visit this man, so that he may pray for me to die in the Holy War and meet my Lord, as I have no desires left in this world.'

When it was dark, they went to visit the sorceress in her tent and found her standing praying. They came close to her and started to weep out of pity for her, but she paid no attention to them until it was midnight and she had finished her prayers. Then she went up to them, greeted them and asked why they had come. They said: 'Worshipper of God, did you not hear us weeping close to you?' 'Whoever stands in the presence of God,' she answered, 'has no existence in the created world which could allow him to hear or to see anyone.' They went on: 'We want you to tell us how you came to be captured and we want you to pray for us tonight, as that would be better for us than to take Constantinople.'

'By God,' she said, 'if you were not Muslim emirs, I would never say anything about that, for it is only to God that I raise my complaint, but as it is, I shall now explain how I was captured. You must know that I was in Jerusalem with a number of the mystical saints. I did not pride myself on being superior to them, as God, the Glorious, the Exalted had granted me the grace of humility and asceticism, but it then happened one night that I went to the sea and walked on the water. I was filled with pride that came from I don't know where, and I said to myself: "Who is like me and can walk on water?"

'From that moment on, my heart became hard and God afflicted me with a love of travel. I went to the lands of Rum and travelled around its regions for a full year, worshipping God wherever I went. I reached a place where I climbed a mountain on which was the monastery of a monk called Matruhina. When this man saw me, he came out to meet me and kissed my hands and feet, saying: "You have been in my sight ever since you came to the lands of Rum and you have filled me with a longing for the lands of Islam." Taking me by the hand, he brought me into the monastery where he led me to a dark room. When I went in, before I knew what he was doing, he had shut the door on me, and he then left me there for forty days without food or drink, intending to keep me there until I died.

'One day, it happened that a patrician named Decianus came to the monastery, bringing with him ten servants together with his daughter,

Tamathil, a girl of unparalleled beauty. On their arrival, the monk Matruhina told them about me. "Bring him out," said Decianus, "for there won't be enough flesh left on him for the birds to eat." They opened the door of the dark room and found me standing in the corner, praying, reciting from the Quran, glorifying Almighty God and abasing myself before Him. When they saw me in this state, Matruhina said: "This man is a sorcerer." On hearing this, they all came in to look at me. Decianus went up to me and he and his servants gave me a violent beating, making me wish that I was dead. Then I blamed myself and said: "This is the reward of one who is proud and conceited because his Lord has granted him something which he could not achieve by himself. It was this pride and conceit that entered you, my soul. Didn't you know that pride angers the Lord, hardens the heart and leads a man to hellfire?"

'After they had beaten me, they put me back where I had been, in an underground chamber beneath that room. Every three days they would throw me a loaf of barley bread and give me some water, and every one or two months Decianus would come to the monastery. His daughter had now grown up. She was nine years old when I first saw her, and after the fifteen years I spent as a prisoner, she was twenty-four. Neither in our lands nor in those of Rum was there a more beautiful girl, but her father was afraid lest the king take her from him, as she had dedicated herself to the Messiah. Unequalled as she was in beauty, she would ride with her father dressed as a man, and no one who saw her would know that she was a girl. Her father had stored his wealth in the monastery, as this was used as a repository by all those who owned treasures. I saw in it more gold, silver and gems, as well as vessels and rarities, than any but Almighty God could count. You have more right to all this than these unbelievers, so take what is in the monastery and spend it on the Muslims, in particular those who fight in the Holy War. When these traders came to Constantinople and sold their goods, the picture on the wall spoke to them, this being a miracle with which God had honoured me. They then came to the monastery and killed the monk Matruhina, after having inflicted painful torture on him, pulling him by his beard until he showed them where I was. They took me and after that there was nothing that they could do except to flee for their lives.

'Tomorrow night, following her usual custom, Tamathil will go to the monastery and will be joined by her father and his servants, for he is afraid for her safety. If you want to see this for yourselves, take me with you and I shall hand over to you that wealth, together with the treasures of Decianus which are on that mountain. I saw them bringing out vessels of gold and silver from which to drink and I saw with them a girl who sang in Arabic – would that with her sweet voice she were to recite the Quran! If you would like to go and hide in the monastery until Decianus arrives with his daughter, you can take her, for she is fit for none but the sultan of the age, Sharkan, or King Dau' al-Makan.'

When the kings heard what Dhat al-Dawahi had to say, they were delighted, but not so the vizier Dandan, who did not believe her and was not taken in by her words. Because of the king, however, he was afraid to speak to her. He was taken aback by what she said and disbelief was clear to read on his face. Dhat al-Dawahi then added: 'If Decianus comes and sees all these troops here, I'm afraid that he will not dare to enter the monastery.' At that, Dau' al-Makan ordered his men to move off towards Constantinople. 'My plan,' he said, 'is that we should go to that mountain taking with us a hundred riders and many mules, so that we can load them with the wealth of the monastery.'

He sent at once for the grand chamberlain, who came to him, and for the leaders of the Turks and the Dailamis. 'When morning comes,' he told them, 'you are to leave for Constantinople; you, chamberlain, are to take my place as an advisor and planner, and you, Rustam, are to take my brother's place in battle. You must not tell anyone that we are not with you and we shall rejoin you after three days.' He then picked a hundred of his best men and went off with them, accompanied by his brother Sharkan and the vizier Dandan, taking along the mules and chests in which to load the treasure.

Night 96

Morning now dawned and Shahrazad broke off from what she had been allowed to say. Then, when it was the ninety-sixth night, SHE CONTINUED:

I have heard, O fortunate king, that Sharkan, his brother Dau' al-Makan and the vizier Dandan set off with the hundred riders to the monastery described to them by the damned Dhat al-Dawahi, taking with them the mules and the chests in which to load the treasure. In the morning, the chamberlain gave the army the order to march, and they set off, thinking that Sharkan, Dau' al-Makan and Dandan were with them and not knowing that they had gone to the monastery. So much for them, but as for the three leaders, they waited until the end of the day. Having asked to be allowed to go, Dhat al-Dawahi's infidel companions had left secretly, after visiting her and kissing her hands and feet. She had given them permission and told them what she wanted in order to carry out her scheme. When it grew dark, she got up and told Dau' al-Makan and the others: 'Come with me to the mountain, but take only a few soldiers with you.' They did what she told them, leaving five riders at the foot of the mountain, while the others went on with her. Delight had given her such strength that Dau' al-Makan exclaimed: 'Glory be to God who has strengthened this ascetic, the like of whom we have never seen.'

She had sent a message by pigeon to the emperor of Constantinople, telling him what had happened. At the end of this, she had added: 'I want you to send me ten thousand brave Rumi horsemen. They should move under cover by the foot of the mountain so as not to be seen by the Muslim troops, and then make their way up to the monastery, concealing themselves there until I come to them with the king of the Muslims and his brother. For I have tricked them and brought them together with the vizier Dandan and no more than a hundred riders. I shall hand over to them the crosses that are in the monastery, and I have made up my mind to kill the monk Matruhina, because otherwise my trick will not work, whereas if it does, not a single one of the Muslims will get back home. Matruhina will be a ransom for Christendom and the followers of the Cross; thanks be to the Messiah, first and last.'

When the message reached Constantinople, the keeper of the pigeon loft brought it to Emperor Afridun. When he read it, he immediately sent out a force, providing each man with a horse, a camel and a mule, as well as provisions for the journey, and ordering them to go to the monastery. On reaching its conspicuous tower, they concealed themselves in it. So much for them, but as for King Dau' al-Makan, Sharkan, his brother, the vizier Dandan and their men, when they got to the monastery they went in and there they caught sight of the monk Matruhina, who had come to see what was happening. 'Kill this damned man,' said the 'ascetic', and they struck him with their swords, giving him the cup of death to drink.

The damned Dhat al-Dawahi then led them to where the votive offerings were stored, and from there they removed even more in the way of rarities and treasures than she had described to them, putting what they had collected in chests and loading them on their mules. Neither Tama-

thil nor her father had come because of fear of the Muslims, and so Dau'
al-Makan waited for her that day, the next and then a third. 'By God,'
said Sharkan, 'I am concerned about the Muslim army and I don't know
in what state they are.' His brother said: 'We have taken this vast treasure
and I don't believe that either Tamathil or any other woman will come
to this monastery after the defeat that the Rumi army has suffered. So
we must be content with the easy spoils that God has given us and set
off in the hopes that He may allow us to take Constantinople.'

They went down from the mountain and Dhat al-Dawahi could not
oppose them for fear of giving away her deception, but when they had
reached the entrance of a ravine they found there the ten thousand
horsemen whom she had posted in ambush. When these saw the
Muslims, they surrounded them on all sides, levelled their lances,
unsheathed their white swords, shouted out the words of their unbelief
and took aim with their evil arrows. Dau' al-Makan, Sharkan and the
vizier Dandan looked, and seeing a huge army, they wondered who had
told them about their presence. 'Brother,' said Sharkan, 'this is no time
for talking but for fighting with the sword and shooting arrows, so
strengthen your resolve and take heart. This gorge is like a lane with
two gates. I swear by the Lord of the Arabs and the non-Arabs that if it
were not so narrow I would destroy them, even if there were a hundred
thousand of them.' 'Had we known about this,' said Dau' al-Makan,
'we would have taken five thousand riders with us.' But Dandan told
him: 'Even if we had ten thousand with us in this narrow place, it would
do us no good, yet God will help us against them. I know this ravine
and how narrow it is, but I also know that there are many places where
we can take refuge, as I campaigned here with King 'Umar when we laid
siege to Constantinople. We camped here and it has water colder than
snow. Lead us on, so that we may get out of this defile before the infidels
mass more troops against us and reach the mountain crest before us.
From there they could throw rocks down on us and in that case we
wouldn't be able to make head against them.'

They began to hurry out of the ravine, but on seeing this, the 'ascetic'
said: 'Why are you afraid? You have sold your lives for the sake of God
Almighty on His path. By God, I stayed as a prisoner underground for
fifteen years and never protested to God about what He had done to me.
Do you, then, fight in His path and Paradise will be the resting place of
those who fall, while whoever kills will win glory by his efforts.' When
the others heard this, their cares and distress vanished and they stood

their ground until the infidels attacked them on all sides. The swords played with men's necks and the cups of death circulated among them. The Muslims exerted themselves to the utmost, fighting in God's service and using their spears and swords against the enemy. Dau' al-Makan cut at men, overthrew champions, striking off their heads, five or ten at a time, until he had destroyed more than could be numbered or counted. While he was fighting, he caught sight of the damned Dhat al-Dawahi, who was pointing with a sword to the infidels and encouraging them. All those who had been stricken with fear fled to her, and she signalled to them to kill Sharkan. Squadron after squadron attacked him, and as each one came on, he would charge it and rout it, after which another would charge and be driven back by his sword. Thinking that his victory was due to the blessing of the 'ascetic', he said to himself: 'God has looked at this pious man with the eye of His concern, and has strengthened my resolve against the infidels because of the purity of his intent. I see that they are afraid of me and cannot advance against me; every time they start to charge, they turn back and take refuge in flight.'

The Muslims continued to fight for the rest of the day, and when night fell, they halted at a cave in the ravine because of the hail of arrows and stones aimed at them. During the day, they had lost forty-five men. When the remainder assembled, they looked for the 'ascetic' but could find no trace of her. They took this as a serious misfortune and wondered whether she had died a martyr. 'I saw him encouraging the riders with gestures inspired by God,' said Sharkan, 'and protecting them with verses from the Quran.' Then, while they were talking, they suddenly saw the damned Dhat al-Dawahi coming forward, holding in her hand the head of the chief patrician, the commander of twenty thousand men. He had been a huge and a stubborn man, a rebellious devil: a Turk had killed him with an arrow and God had promptly despatched his soul to hell. When the infidels saw what the Muslims had done to their leader, they all rushed at him, wounding him and then cutting him to bits with their swords, with God giving him a swift passage to Paradise.

It was after that that the damned woman had cut off the infidel's head, which she brought and threw down in front of Sharkan, King Dau' al-Makan and the vizier Dandan. When Sharkan saw her, he jumped to his feet and said: 'Praise be to God that we see you safe, O worshipper of God, ascetic and fighter in the Holy War.' 'My son,' 'she said, 'I looked for martyrdom today, throwing myself between the ranks of the infidels, but they shrank from me in fear. Then, when you broke off the fight, zeal overcame me and I attacked the great patrician, their leader, who was reckoned as a match for a thousand riders. With a blow I severed his head from his body; none of the infidels was able to come near me and so I have brought the head to you . . .'

Night 97

Morning now dawned and Shahrazad broke off from what she had been allowed to say. Then, when it was the ninety-seventh night, SHE CONTINUED:

I have heard, O fortunate king, that the damned Dhat al-Dawahi took the head of the chief patrician, the commander of twenty thousand men, and threw it down before Dau' al-Makan and Sharkan. She said: 'When I saw the state that you were in, I was moved by zeal and I attacked the great patrician. With a blow I severed his head from his body; none of the infidels was able to come near me and so I have brought the head to you to encourage you to fight in the Holy War and to please the Lord of mankind with your swords. I now want to leave you busied with the holy war and go myself to your army, even if they are at the gates of Constantinople, in order to fetch you twenty thousand of their riders to destroy these infidels.' 'How can you get to them,' asked Sharkan, 'now that the valley is blocked on all sides by the infidels?' 'God will shelter me from their eyes,' said the damned woman, 'and they will not see me, or if anyone does see me, he will not dare to approach, for at that moment I shall have passed into the presence of God and He will protect me from His foes.' 'You have spoken the truth, ascetic,' said Sharkan, 'for I have seen that with my own eyes. If you can go in the first part of the night, it will be better for us.' 'I shall go now,' she said, 'and if you want to come with me without anyone seeing you, come. If your brother wants to join us, we can take him but no one else, for the shadow of a saint can cover no more than two.'

'As for me,' said Sharkan, 'I cannot leave my companions, but if my brother is willing, there would be no harm in his going with you and escaping from this dangerous position, for he is the fortress of the Muslims and the sword of the Lord of the worlds. If he wants, he could take the vizier Dandan with him, or anyone else he chooses, and he could send us ten thousand riders to help us against these vile men.' They agreed on this plan and then the old woman said: 'Wait and let me go first to reconnoitre among the unbelievers, to see whether they are asleep or awake.' 'We shall go out with you,' they said, 'entrusting our affairs to God.' She said: 'If I agree to this, then don't blame me but blame yourselves, for my advice is that you should give me time to investigate first.' 'Go to them quickly,' said Sharkan, 'and we shall wait for you.'

At that, she left and when she had gone, Sharkan said to his brother: 'This ascetic is a miracle worker, for otherwise he could not have killed that giant. This is enough to show his miraculous power, and the death of that man has broken the power of the infidels, for he was a huge and stubborn man and a rebellious devil.' While they were discussing the miracles of the 'ascetic', the damned Dhat al-Dawahi came to them, promising them victory over the infidels, and they thanked her, without realizing that this was trickery and deceit. The damned woman then said: 'Where is Dau' al-Makan, the king of the age?' He came at her call and she said: 'Take your vizier with you and walk behind me so that we can set out for Constantinople.'

In fact, she had told the infidels of the trick that she had played. They were overjoyed and said: 'We shall not be consoled until we have killed this king in exchange for the death of our leader, as we had no better rider.' When she told them that she would bring them the king, they replied to her, ill-omened old woman that she was: 'When you fetch him, we will take him to the emperor.' She now set off, together with Dau' al-Makan and the vizier Dandan. She went ahead of them, saying: 'Walk on with the blessing of Almighty God.' They obeyed and were pierced by the arrow of fate. She led them on until they were in the middle of the Rumi army and had reached the narrow defile that has already been mentioned. The Rumis were watching them, but, in accordance with the damned woman's instructions, they were making no move to harm them.

Dau' al-Makan and Dandan looked at the infidels and saw that they were watching but not trying to interfere with them. 'By God,' said Dandan, 'this is a miracle performed by the ascetic and there is no doubt that he is one of the great saints.' 'By God,' replied Dau' al-Makan, 'I think that the infidels are blind, as we see them and they don't see us.' Then, while they were praising the 'ascetic' and listing her miracles, together with her abstinence and acts of worship, the infidels suddenly attacked and surrounded them. When they had seized them, they asked: 'Is there anyone else, apart from the two of you, for us to take?' 'Don't you see this other man in front of you?' said Dandan. 'By the truth of the Messiah, the monks, the Primate and the Metropolitan,' they replied, 'we have not seen anyone but you.' 'By God,' said Dau' al-Makan, 'what has happened to us is a punishment from Almighty God.'

Night 98

Morning now dawned and Shahrazad broke off from what she had been allowed to say. Then, when it was the ninety-eighth night, SHE CONTINUED:

I have heard, O fortunate king, that when the infidels seized King Dau' al-Makan and the vizier Dandan, they asked: 'Is there anyone else, apart from the two of you, for us to take?' 'Don't you see this other man in front of you?' said Dandan. 'By the truth of the Messiah, the monks, the Primate and the Metropolitan,' they replied, 'we have not seen anyone but you.' The infidels then fettered their feet and set guards over them in their bivouac.

Dhat al-Dawahi had vanished from the sight of the two Muslims, who were saying sadly to one another: 'To oppose the pious leads to worse fates than this, and the straits in which we now find ourselves are our reward.' So much for Dau' al-Makan, but as for Sharkan, when morning came, he got up and performed the morning prayer, after which he and the rest of his men began to prepare for battle with the infidels. He encouraged them and made them fair promises and they moved off to meet the enemy. But when the infidels saw them in the distance, they called out: 'Muslims, we have captured your sultan, as well as the vizier who organized your affairs. Either stop fighting us, or we will kill every last one of you. Surrender to us and we will take you to our king, who will make peace with you on condition that you leave our lands and return to your own, and if you do us no harm, we shall do none to you. If you agree, it will be lucky for you, and if you refuse, we shall have no choice but to kill you. We have told you our terms and this is our last word.'

When Sharkan heard what they had to say and realized that his brother and the vizier had been captured, he found it hard to bear. He shed tears, lost heart and felt certain that he faced destruction. He wondered what had led to their capture and whether they had been guilty of some rudeness towards the 'ascetic' and had opposed her wishes, or whether something else had happened. He and his men, however, advanced against the infidels and killed large numbers of them. That was a day on which the brave were distinguished from the cowards. Swords and spears were stained with blood and the infidels swarmed around the Muslims from every side like flies around juice. Sharkan and his companions fought like men who have no fear of death and who let pass no opportunity, until the valley ran with streams of blood and the earth was piled with corpses.

At nightfall, both sides parted and each returned to their own camp. The Muslims went back to their cave, looking like men who were on the point of total defeat. Just a few of them were left and their only reliance was on God and on their swords. Thirty-five of the leading emirs had been killed that day, although they themselves had killed thousands of the infidels, both horse and foot. When Sharkan saw this, he was distressed and he asked his companions what was to be done. 'Only what Almighty God wills,' was their reply.

The next day, Sharkan said to them: 'If you go out to fight, none of you will survive, as we have only a little water and food. The right thing to do, in my opinion, is to draw your swords and to go and stand at the entrance to the cave in order to stop the enemy from breaking in. It may be that the ascetic will get to the Muslim army and bring us ten thousand reinforcements to help fight the infidels, for perhaps they did not see him and his companions.'

The Muslims agreed that without any doubt this was the right plan, and so they went out and occupied the cave entrance, standing on either side of it and killing any of the enemy who tried to enter. They defended the entrance and resisted the infidels until the day ended and night darkened.

Night 99

Morning now dawned and Shahrazad broke off from what she had been allowed to say. Then, when it was the ninety-ninth night, SHE CONTINUED:

I have heard, O fortunate king, that the Muslims held the entrance to the cave, standing on both sides of it and resisting the infidels, killing all who attacked and continuing to resist until the day ended and night darkened. By that time, Sharkan had no more than twenty-five men left, while the infidels were wondering when this was going to end as they were tired of battling against the Muslims. 'Come on,' said one of them, 'let us attack them, for there are only twenty-five of them left and if we can't defeat them we can prepare to burn them out. If they agree to surrender, we can take them prisoner, but if they refuse, we shall leave them as fuel for the fire, and they will be a warning for those who have eyes to see – may the Messiah have no mercy on them or lead them to the Paradise of the Christians!' They then carried firewood to the cave's entrance and set it alight, after which Sharkan and his men, seeing that they were certain to be destroyed, surrendered.

When they had done this, one of the infidels advised that they be put to death, but their leader turned to him and said: 'They can only be killed in the presence of the emperor Afridun to satisfy his thirst for revenge. We must keep them with us as prisoners and tomorrow we can take them to Constantinople and hand them over to the emperor, who can do what he wants with them.' His men agreed that this was the right thing to do. Orders were given for the prisoners to be fettered and a guard was mounted over them. When it grew dark, the infidels occupied themselves with pleasure. They ate and called for wine, which they drank until every one of them had fallen over. Sharkan and Dau' al-Makan, his brother, were tied up, as were the valiant Muslims who were with them, and Sharkan looked at Dau' al-Makan and said: 'Brother, how are we going to escape?' 'By God,' replied Dau' al-Makan, 'I don't know. We are like birds in a cage.'

Sharkan's breast swelled in anger, and as he stretched, his bonds broke. When he was free, he went to the guard commander and took the keys of the fetters from his pocket, after which he released Dau' al-Makan and Dandan and then the other Muslims. Having done this, he turned to Dau' al-Makan and Dandan and said: 'I want to kill three of these guards so that we can take their clothes, which the three of us can put on and then we can walk through them disguised as Rumis, without anyone knowing who we are, and we can then set off for own army.' 'That is not a good idea,' said Dau' al-Makan. 'If we kill them, I'm afraid that someone might hear their death groans, which would draw the attention of the unbelievers to us and they would kill us. The best plan is for us to leave this ravine.' The others agreed and when they had gone a little way outside it, they saw horses tethered and their owners asleep. 'Each of us,' said Sharkan to his brother, 'must take one of these horses.' There were twenty-five of the Muslims and so they took twenty-five horses, God having caused the infidels to sleep, through His wise foreknowledge. Sharkan then set about stealing weapons from the infidels, both swords and lances, until he had found enough, and they then mounted the horses that they had taken and set off.

The infidels had thought that no one could free Dau' al-Makan, his brother and their companions, and that it was impossible for them to escape. When they all had managed to do this and were at a safe distance from the enemy, Sharkan rejoined his men and found them waiting for him in a fever of anxiety and full of concern. He turned to them and said: 'Have no fear, for God has sheltered us. I have a plan which may work.' When they asked what it was, he said: 'I want you to climb to the mountain top and then every one of you is to shout out all together: "*Allahu akbar!*" Then call out: "The armies of Islam have come" and follow it with another combined shout of "*Allahu akbar!*" This will make the infidels disperse; they will not be able to think of what to do on the spur of the moment, as they are drunk and will imagine that the Muslim army have surrounded them on all sides and have got in among them. As a result, they will start fighting one another, bemused by drink and sleep, and we can then cut them down and put them to the sword until morning.' 'That is not a good plan,' said Dau' al-Makan. 'What we should do is to go off to our own army without saying a word, for if we cry "*Allahu akbar!*", this will alert the infidels. They will catch up with us and none of us will escape.' 'By God,' said Sharkan, 'even if they were alerted, that would do us no harm. I want you to agree to my plan, as nothing but good will come of it.'

They then agreed and climbed to the mountain top, where they cried '*Allahu akbar!*' and the fear of God caused the mountains, trees and rocks to re-echo the shout. The infidels heard it and cried out . . .

Night 100

Morning now dawned and Shahrazad broke off from what she had been allowed to say. Then, when it was the one hundredth night, SHE CONTINUED:

I have heard, O fortunate king, that Sharkan said: 'I want you to agree to my plan, as nothing but good will come of it.' They then agreed and climbed to the mountain top, where they cried '*Allahu akbar!*' and the fear of God caused the mountains, trees and rocks to re-echo the shout. The infidels heard it and cried out to one another, arming themselves and saying: 'By the truth of the Messiah, the enemy has attacked us.' Of their own men they killed a number known only to God Almighty and when morning came they looked for the prisoners but found no trace of them. Their leaders then said: 'It was the prisoners whom we captured who did this to you, so pursue them until you catch up with them and then exterminate them, and don't be afraid or startled.' So they mounted and rode after the Muslims, losing no time in catching up with them and surrounding them. When Dau' al-Makan saw this, he became very frightened and he told his brother: 'This is what I feared would happen, and we have no option but to fight.' Sharkan said nothing and Dau' al-Makan came down from the mountain top and shouted '*Allahu akbar!*' as did his men, and they all made up their minds to fight, selling their lives in the service of the Lord of mankind.

While this was happening, suddenly they heard voices reciting the formulae of unity and glorification and calling down blessings and peace on Muhammad, the evangelist, the warner. Turning towards the direction of the sound, they saw advancing the armies of Islam, the mono-theists. This strengthened their hearts, and Sharkan charged the infidels with his men, all proclaiming the unity and greatness of God. The ground trembled as with an earthquake shock; the infidels scattered across the mountainsides and the Muslims followed them, cutting and thrusting, striking their heads from their bodies. Dau' al-Makan and the Muslims with him kept cutting at the necks of the infidels until the day waned and it grew dark. Then they drew off and regrouped, passing the whole night in great joy.

When the light of morning dawned, they saw Rustam, the leader of the Dailamis, and Bahram, the leader of the Turks, advancing towards them with twenty thousand riders like frowning lions. On seeing Dau' al-Makan, the riders dismounted to greet him and to kiss the ground in front of him. 'There is good news for you,' he said. 'The Muslims are victorious and the infidels have been destroyed.' They congratulated each other on coming safely through and on the great reward that would be theirs on the Day of Resurrection.

The reason why these reinforcements had arrived was that when Bahram, Rustam and the chamberlain had marched with the Muslim armies to Constantinople, with their banners fluttering overhead, they saw that the infidels were on the walls, manning the towers and the citadels. On learning of the advance of the armies of Islam under the banners of Muhammad, the infidels had made their preparations in every strong fortress. Then they had heard the clashing of arms and the noise of shouting and, looking out, they had seen the Muslims and heard the noise of their horses' hooves beneath the dust. The Muslims were like a swarm of locusts or flooding rain clouds, and the infidels could hear their voices as they recited the Quran and glorified the Compassionate God.

They had known that the Muslims were on their way, thanks to a scheme laid by Dhat al-Dawahi, untruthful, depraved, false and wily as she was, and so Christian armies had risen like a swelling sea, with hordes of foot and horse, together with women and children. The emir of the Dailamis then said to the Turkish leader: 'We are in danger from these men on the walls. Look at those towers and this horde of defenders, like a boisterous sea with clashing waves. They outnumber us by a hundred to one and we cannot be sure that some spy may not tell them that we are without a king. As a result, we are in danger from an enemy whose numbers cannot be counted and whose reinforcements we cannot cut off, more especially in the absence of King Dau' al-Makan, his brother and the grand vizier Dandan. Their absence will encourage the Rumis to attack us and to put us all to the sword, with none of us escaping. The best plan would be for you to take ten thousand Mosulis and Turks and to lead them to the monastery and the plain of Malukhina in search of our brothers and their companions. If you obey me, it will be thanks to us that they will be rescued if the infidels are pressing them, and if you don't, then I am not to be blamed. If you do set off, you must come back quickly, for it is prudent to expect the worst.' The Turkish emir agreed with his proposal, and after the two of them had chosen twenty thousand riders, they set off along the roads, making for the plain and the monastery. This was the reason for their timely arrival.

As for the old woman, Dhat al-Dawahi, when she had succeeded in getting Dau' al-Makan, his brother Sharkan and the vizier Dandan to fall into the hands of the infidels, she took a horse and mounted it, harlot that she was, telling the infidels that she wanted to go to the Muslim army and plot their destruction. 'They are at Constantinople,' she said, 'and when they hear from me that their companions are dead, their combined force will split up; they will disintegrate and their army will disperse. I shall then go to see Emperor Afridun, the lord of Constantinople, and my son, Hardub, king of Rum, and tell them what has happened, so that they will lead their men out against the Muslims and destroy every last one of them.'

She then rode across country all night long, and when dawn broke, she caught sight of the force led by Bahram and Rustam. She went into a wood, where she hid her horse, and then she walked for a short way, saying to herself that the Muslims might be coming back after having been defeated at Constantinople. When she got a closer look at them and could make out their banners, she could see that they had not been lowered, and she realized that this was no defeated force nor one that was afraid for its king and his companions. On seeing this, she ran swiftly towards them, like a rebellious devil, and when she got to them she called out: 'Quickly, quickly, followers of the Merciful God; come and fight the adherents of the devil.'

When Bahram saw her, he went up to her, dismounted and kissed the ground in front of her, saying: 'Saint of God, what is behind you?' 'Don't ask about what was a terrible misfortune,' she replied. 'When our companions took the treasure from the monastery of Matruhina, they intended to set out for Constantinople, but at that point a huge and powerful infidel force came out against them.' The damned woman then told them what had happened in order to spread alarm and fear. 'Most of them are dead,' she said, 'and only twenty-five survive.' 'O ascetic,' asked Bahram, 'when did you leave them?' 'Last night,' she answered. 'Glory be to God,' said Bahram, 'who folded up the distant land for you as you walked leaning on a palm branch. But you are one of the saints who can fly when they are under the inspiration of a sign from God.'

He then mounted his horse, perplexed and at a loss because of what he had heard from the mistress of lies and falsehood. 'There is no might and no power except with God!' he exclaimed, adding: 'Our trouble has been in vain; sorrow has overtaken us and our king and his men have been captured.' The Muslims then covered the length and breadth of the country, riding night and day. It was early dawn when they came to the head of the defile where they found Dau' al-Makan and his brother Sharkan, who were reciting the formulae of God's unity and grandeur, as well as calling down blessings and peace on Muhammad, the evangelist, the warner. Bahram and his companions charged and surrounded the infidels as a rain torrent spreads over the desert, raising a shout which terrified brave champions and split the mountains. When morning came and the dawn light spread, the sweet scent of Dau' al-Makan and his brother Sharkan spread over them and both groups recognized each other, as has already been told.

The newcomers kissed the earth before Dau' al-Makan and his brother, and Sharkan astonished them by telling them what had happened in the cave. Then they said to one another: 'We must hurry to Constantinople because we have left our companions there and our hearts are with them.' They pressed on with their journey, entrusting themselves to God, the Gracious, the Omniscient. Dau' al-Makan, encouraging the Muslims to steadfastness, recited the lines:

To You be praise, Who deserve both praise and thanks;
My Lord, may You not cease to aid me in my affairs.
You nurtured me as a stranger in the land,
Protecting me and helping me by Your decree.
You gave me wealth, kingdom and favour,
Girding me with the sword of courage and of aid.
You have shaded me with kingship and prolonged my days,
And overwhelmed me with Your flooding bounty.
You saved me from every danger that I feared
By the counsel of the grand vizier, the hero of the age.
It was with Your favour we assailed the Rumis,
And our blows sent them back in robes of red.
I made it seem that I had been defeated,
Before returning like a raging lion.
I left them cast down like drunkards on the plain,
But drunk with the cup of death, not that of wine.
Their ships are now all ours and we possess
The double sovereignty of land and sea.
There came to us the pious ascetic, whose miracles
Are known to all, nomads and settled folk alike.
Now we have come for vengeance on the infidel,
And my affair is known to every man.
They killed men of ours who now enjoy
Chambers in Paradise, above a flowing stream.

When Dau' al-Makan had finished reciting his poem, his brother Sharkan congratulated him on his safety and thanked him for what he had done, after which they pressed on with their journey . . .

Night 101

Morning now dawned and Shahrazad broke off from what she had been allowed to say. Then, when it was the one hundred and first night, SHE CONTINUED:

I have heard, O fortunate king, that Sharkan congratulated his brother on his safety and thanked him for what he had done, after which they pressed on with their journey back to their armies.

So much for them, but as for the old woman, Dhat al-Dawahi, after meeting the troops of Bahram and Rustam, she went back to the wood, where she took her horse, mounted it and rode at speed until she reached a point overlooking the Muslim armies that were besieging Constantinople. There she dismounted and led her horse to the pavilion of the chamberlain. When he saw her, he rose to greet her and, gesturing towards her, he said: 'Welcome to the pious ascetic.' He then asked her what had happened, and she told him her alarming tale with its destructive lies. She went on: 'I fear for the emir Rustam and the emir Bahram. I met them on the way with their force and I sent them on to the king and his companions. They had twenty thousand riders, but the infidels outnumbered them. I want you to send some of your troops at once to catch up with them as soon as possible, lest they all be lost. Hurry, hurry,' she added.

When the chamberlain and the other Muslims heard this, their resolution weakened and they shed tears. 'Take refuge in God,' she told them, 'and endure this misfortune. You have an example in earlier generations of Muslims, and God has prepared Paradise with its palaces for those who die as martyrs. Everyone must die, but death in the Holy War is more laudable.' When the chamberlain heard what the damned woman had to say, he summoned the brother of the emir Bahram, a skilled horseman named Tarkash. He picked out for him ten thousand riders, grim champions, and ordered him to set off. After riding for the whole of that day and through the night, Tarkash came near the Muslims.

In the morning, Sharkan saw the dust and feared for his own men, saying: 'There are troops approaching us. If they are Muslims, we shall clearly be victorious, while if they are infidels, there is nothing that we can do to oppose fate.' He went to his brother Dau' al-Makan and said: 'There is nothing at all for you to fear, for I will ransom you from death with my own life. If these men are from our army, this would be the greatest of God's favours, while if they are enemies, we shall have to fight them. I would like to meet the ascetic to ask him to pray for me that I be granted a martyr's death.'

While the two of them were talking, the banners of the newcomers appeared, inscribed with the words: 'There is no god but God and Muhammad is the Apostle of God.' 'How are you, Muslims?' shouted Sharkan. 'We are safe and well,' was the reply, 'and we have only come because we were fearful for you.' Their commander dismounted and kissed the ground in front of Sharkan. He asked whether the king, the vizier Dandan, Rustam and his own brother, Bahram, were all safe. Sharkan assured him that they were and then asked: 'Who told you about us?' 'The ascetic,' he replied. 'He said that he had met Rustam and my brother Bahram and had sent them on to you, saying that you were surrounded by large numbers of infidels, but the opposite is true from what I can see, and you are victorious.' On being asked how the 'ascetic' had come to him, he replied: 'On his own two feet and in a day and a night he covered what for a man riding at speed would have been a ten-day journey.' 'There is no doubt that he is one of God's saints,' said Sharkan, and he then asked where the 'ascetic' was now. 'We left him with our army, the soldiers of the true faith,' was the reply, 'urging them on to fight the tyrannical infidels.'

This news delighted Sharkan, and they all praised God that both they and the 'ascetic' were safe, and invoking God's mercy on their dead, they exclaimed: 'This was written in the book of fate!' Then they pressed on with their journey. While they were on the march, they saw a rising dust cloud that blocked the regions of the sky, blotting out the day. Looking at it, Sharkan said: 'I am afraid that the infidels have broken the Muslim army, for this cloud has blocked the east and the west, filling both horizons.' At that point, beneath the dust appeared a pillar of darkness, blacker than the gloom of dark days, coming nearer and nearer, more awesome than the terrors of the Day of Resurrection. Horse and foot hurried towards it to find what had caused this evil, and there they saw the 'ascetic'. They crowded round to kiss her hands, and she called out: 'Followers of the best of men, the light in darkness; the infidels have taken the Muslims unawares. Go and save them from the vile unbelievers, who attacked them in their tents, inflicting shameful punishment on them while they thought themselves secure in their camp.'

When Sharkan heard that, his heart almost flew out of his chest, so violently did it beat. He dismounted in a state of bewilderment and then kissed the hands and feet of the 'ascetic'. His brother Dau' al-Makan followed his example, as did the rest of the army, both horse and foot, with the exception of the vizier Dandan. Dandan did not dismount but said: 'By God, my heart recoils from this ascetic for I have never known anything but evil to come from an excess of religious zealotry. Let him be, and go to join your Muslim comrades. This man is an outcast from the door of mercy of the Lord of the worlds. How many raids have I made in these parts with King 'Umar!' 'This is a false judgement; abandon it,' said Sharkan. 'Haven't you seen this ascetic urging on the Muslims to fight, taking no notice of swords or arrows? Don't slander him, for slander is blameworthy, and the flesh of the pious is poisoned. Look at the way that he encourages us to fight our enemies. If Almighty God did not love him, he would not have been able to cover these distances, after having been harshly tortured earlier.'

He then ordered that a duty mule be provided for the 'ascetic' to ride. 'Mount this, you pious, devout and God-fearing ascetic,' he said, but Dhat al-Dawahi would not accept and made a pretence of asceticism in refusing to ride, in order to achieve her goal. The Muslims did not know that this wanton was like the person described by the poet, who

> Prayed and fasted for a purpose, and then,
> Purpose achieved, he did not fast or pray.

She continued to walk between the horsemen and the infantry, like a fox planning mischief, raising her voice to recite the Quran and to glorify God, the Merciful. The Muslims continued on their way until they came within sight of the army of Islam. This army, Sharkan discovered, was being broken, with the chamberlain on the point of flight and the swords of the Rumis at work among the just and the unjust.

Night 102

Morning now dawned and Shahrazad broke off from what she had been allowed to say. Then, when it was the one hundred and second night, SHE CONTINUED:

I have heard, O fortunate king, that Sharkan discovered that the army was being broken, with the chamberlain on the point of flight and the swords of the Rumis at work among the just and the unjust. The reason for this setback was that when that enemy of religion, the damned Dhat al-Dawahi, had noted that Bahram and Rustam had gone with their men to find Sharkan and his brother Dau' al-Makan, she had gone to the Muslim army and sent off the emir Tarkash, as has already been told, intending to weaken the Muslims by dispersing them. She then left and made for Constantinople, where she called at the top of her voice to the Rumis, telling them to lower a rope on to which she could tie a letter. They were to take this to Emperor Afridun, to be read by him and by her son, the king of Rum, who were to act on the orders and prohibitions that it contained. The rope was lowered and to it she tied her letter, which read: 'From the major disaster and the greatest calamity, Dhat al-Dawahi, to Emperor Afridun. To continue: I have prepared a stratagem to enable you to destroy the Muslims. You can rest at ease. I have seen to their capture, taking their king and their vizier, and I then went to their army and gave them the news, which broke their spirit and weakened them. I tricked the besiegers of Constantinople into sending off twelve thousand riders with the emir Tarkash, to help those who had already been captured. Only a few of them are left, and I want you to lead out your whole army against them in what is left of this day, in order to attack them in their tents. You must make a simultaneous sally and kill every last man of them. You are under the eye of the Messiah; the Virgin has compassion on you, and I hope that the Messiah will not forget what I have done.'

When this message reached Afridun, he was delighted and immediately sent to fetch Dhat al-Dawahi's son, the king of Rum. When the letter was read to him, he was filled with joy and exclaimed: 'Look at the cunning of my mother, which serves in the place of swords, while her appearance is a substitute for the terrors of the dreadful Day of Judgement.' 'May the Messiah never be deprived of her,' said the emperor, and he then ordered his officers to give the word for a sally from the city. The news was passed through Constantinople; out came the Christian armies, the people of the Cross, unsheathing their sharp swords and proclaiming the formulae of their impiety and unbelief, while blaspheming God, the Lord of mankind.

On seeing this, the chamberlain said: 'The Rumis are here. They must know that our king is absent, and it may be that they have attacked us because most of our troops have set off to find Dau' al-Makan.' He then called out angrily: 'Army of Islam, defenders of the established faith, if you turn to flee, you die, and if you show endurance, you will be victorious. Know that courage means an hour's worth of endurance.

There is no difficulty that God does not resolve; may God bless you and look upon you with the eye of mercy.' At that, the Muslim monotheists raised the cry 'Allahu akbar!'; the mills of war revolved with thrusts and cuts, while swords and spears went about their work as blood filled the valleys and the plains. Priests and monks played their parts, tightening their belts and raising up their crosses, while the Muslims proclaimed the greatness of the King and Judge, calling out verses from the Quran. The armies of the Merciful God clashed with those of the devil; heads flew from bodies, while the good angels went round among the followers of the chosen Prophet. Swords did not rest until the day had ended and the darkness of night had arrived.

The infidels had surrounded the Muslims, thinking that they would escape humiliating punishment, and they remained hopeful of success against the followers of the true faith. At daybreak, the chamberlain and his men mounted, hoping for God's aid. The two sides intermingled; fighting became fierce; heads flew off; the brave stood firm and advanced, while the cowards turned back and fled. Judgements were delivered by the Judge of death; champions were thrown from their saddles and the fields were filled with the dead. The Muslims fell back from their positions and the Rumis seized some of their tents and their bivouacs. The Muslims were on the point of being broken and of taking flight in their defeat, but while they were in that state, suddenly Sharkan appeared with the armies and banners of the followers of the One Lord.

On his arrival, he charged the infidels, followed by Dau' al-Makan and after that by the emir Dandan, as well as by Bahram, the emir of the Turks, and by Rustam, together with Tarkash. When the Rumis saw that, their wits and their judgement deserted them. Dust rose until it filled all corners of the sky; the pious Muslims joined forces with their virtuous comrades, and Sharkan met the chamberlain, thanked him for having held out and congratulated him on the aid and assistance he had received. The Muslims were joyful and charged the enemy with strong hearts, dedicating themselves faithfully to God's cause in the Holy War.

When the infidels saw the banners of Islam, bearing their message of sincere devotion to God, they uttered cries of distress, invoking the help of the patriarchs of the monasteries, and calling out to John, Mary and to the Cross that they defiled, while stopping fighting. The emperor came up to the king of Rum, one of them having been on the right wing and the other on the left, while with them was a famous rider named Lawiya, whose post was in the centre of the troops. They drew up their ranks in

battle order, despite being in a state of fear and disturbance, while the
Muslims also arranged their ranks. Sharkan went up to his brother Dau'
al-Makan and said: 'King of the age, there can be no doubt that they are
going to offer a challenge to single combat and this is what we want
most. I would like to post men of firm resolution in front of our army,
for planning is half the battle in life.' 'Whatever you want, O wise
advisor,' said the king. 'I want to be opposite the enemy centre,' said
Sharkan, 'with Dandan to the left and you to the right, the emir Bahram
on the right flank and Rustam on the left. You, mighty king, must take
your post beneath the standards and the banners, for you are our buttress
and after God it is on you that we rely. All of us will give our lives to
protect you from any hurt.' Dau' al-Makan thanked him for that and a
shout was then raised and swords drawn.

At this point, a rider suddenly appeared from among the Rumi ranks.
When he came near, the Muslims saw that he was mounted on a slow-
paced mule that shied away with its rider from the clash of swords. Its
saddle cloth was of white silk, over which was a rug of Kashmiri work.
Its rider was a handsome grey-haired old man of obvious dignity, wearing
a tunic of white wool. He came on fast, until, when he was near the
Muslims, he said: 'I am a messenger sent to you all. A messenger's only
duty is to deliver his message. Give me safe conduct and permission to
speak so that I may deliver you mine.' 'You have safe conduct,' said
Sharkan, 'so fear neither sword cut nor spear thrust.'

At that the old man dismounted, and taking the cross from his neck
before the sultan, he performed the obeisance of one who was hoping
for favour. 'What news do you bring?' the Muslims asked him. 'I am a
messenger from Emperor Afridun,' he replied. 'I advised him to abstain
from the destruction of these human forms, which are the temples of
God's mercy. I showed him that the right course was to prevent blood-
shed and to confine the battle to two riders. He agreed to that, saying:
"I shall ransom my army with my own life, and let the king of the
Muslims follow my example and do the same for his men. If he kills me,
my army will not be able to stand, nor will the Muslims if I kill him."'

When Sharkan had heard this, he said: 'Monk, I agree to his proposal;
this is a fair solution, about which there can be no disagreement. It is I
who will come out to meet him and ride against him, for I am the Muslim
champion, just as he is the champion of the infidels. If he kills me, victory
will be his and flight will be the only recourse of the Muslims. So do you
go back to him, monk, and tell him that the meeting will take place

tomorrow. We are tired today, as we have just arrived after our journey, but when we have rested there will be no grounds for reproach or blame.' The monk went back joyfully, and when he reached the emperor and the king of Rum, he told them what had happened.

Afridun was delighted and his care and sorrow left him. He told himself: 'There is no doubt that Sharkan is the best of the Muslims when it comes to sword blows and spear thrusts, and if I kill him they will lose heart and be weakened.' Dhat al-Dawahi had earlier written to him about this, warning him that Sharkan was the champion of the brave and the bravest of the champions. Afridun, however, was himself a great fighter, a master of the various arts of combat, who could hurl rocks, shoot arrows and strike blows with an iron mace, and who had no fear of even the strongest opponent. So when he heard the monk saying that Sharkan had agreed to meet him in single combat, he was almost beside himself with joy, as he was confident of his prowess, knowing that no one could overcome him.

The infidels passed a happy and joyful night drinking wine, and when morning came, the riders rode forward with their brown spears and white swords. They saw a rider who rode out on to the field, mounted on an excellent horse with strong legs, in full battle gear. Its rider wore a coat of mail made to withstand violent blows; on his chest was a jewelled mirror, while he held a sharp sword together with a lance of *khalanj* wood of wonderful Frankish workmanship. Uncovering his face, he said: 'Whoever recognizes me knows enough of me and whoever has not recognized me will soon see who I am. I am Afridun, a man encompassed by the blessing of the keen eyes of Dhat al-Dawahi.'

Before he had finished speaking, Sharkan, the champion of the Muslims, rode out to face him, mounted on a roan horse worth a thousand dinars of red gold, whose harness was studded with pearls and gems. He himself was equipped with a jewelled Indian sword that could sever necks and for which hard tasks were easy. He rode out between the ranks, with the riders watching him, and he called to Afridun: 'Woe to you, you damned man, do you think that I am like those riders whom you have met, who cannot stand against you in the field of battle?' Each of them then charged the other and they were like two mountains colliding or two seas clashing. They closed with each other and then parted, fighting at close quarters and then separating, charging and retreating, toying with each other and then fighting in earnest, striking and thrusting, under the eyes of both armies. 'Sharkan is winning,' said some, while others said: 'It is Afridun.' They continued to fight, until there was no more talking; the dust rose high, and as the day waned, the sun paled.

Then the emperor called out to Sharkan: 'By the truth of the religion of the Messiah and the true faith, you are an attacking rider and a bold champion, but you are treacherous and yours is not a noble nature. I see that you act ignobly and don't fight like a courageous chief. Your people rank you as a slave, for they are bringing out another horse for you so that you can resume the fight. By the truth of my religion, fighting against you has tired me and your blows and thrusts have wearied me. If you want to fight tonight, don't change any of your harness or your horse, so as to show the riders your noble nature and how you can fight.'

When Sharkan heard this, he was angry that his companions were doing anything that might class him as a slave. He turned towards them, meaning to signal to them that they should not bring him another horse or harness, but Afridun suddenly shook a javelin and hurled it at him. When Sharkan looked behind him, he saw no one there and realizing that his damned enemy had tricked him, he turned his head in a hurry, to find that the javelin was almost on him. He swerved away from it, bending his head down to his saddlebow, but, passing by his chest, which was protuberant, the javelin pierced the skin. Sharkan gave a cry and fainted, to the delight of the damned Afridun, who was sure that his opponent had been killed. He called out to the infidels, telling them to rejoice; the tyrannical Rumis were elated, while the people of the true faith wept. When Dau' al-Makan saw his brother swaying on his horse and almost falling, he sent out his riders. The champions raced each other to reach him, and they brought him to Dau' al-Makan. The unbelievers then charged the Muslims: the two armies met, the ranks were intermixed as the sharp Yemeni swords went about their work. The first man to reach Sharkan was the vizier Dandan . . .

Night 103

Morning now dawned and Shahrazad broke off from what she had been allowed to say. Then, when it was the one hundred and third night, SHE CONTINUED:

I have heard, O fortunate king, that when Dau' al-Makan saw the damned Afridun strike his brother with a javelin, he thought that he was dead and sent out his riders. The first to reach him was the vizier Dandan, together with Bahram, the emir of the Turks, and the emir of the Dailamis. When they got to him he had fallen from his saddle, and so they propped him up and brought him back to his brother Dau' al-Makan. They then left him in the charge of the servants and returned to the battle.

The fight grew furious; blades were shattered; there was no time for talk and all that could be seen were flowing blood and lolling heads. Swords hacked at necks and the battle was fiercely contested until the greater part of the night had passed. Both sides were then too tired to fight and the order was given to break off, after which each side retired to its tents. The unbelievers went to their emperor and kissed the ground before him, while the priests and the monks congratulated him on his victory over Sharkan. He entered Constantinople and took his seat on his royal throne. King Hardub came up to him and said: 'May the Messiah strengthen your arm and never cease to help you, answering the prayers made on your behalf by my virtuous mother, Dhat al-Dawahi. Know that after the loss of Sharkan the Muslims will not be able to stand.' 'The matter will be settled tomorrow,' said Afridun, 'when I go out to challenge Dau' al-Makan to single combat and then kill him. For the Muslim army will then turn tail and take refuge in flight.'

So much for the unbelievers. As for the Muslims, when Dau' al-Makan got back to the tents, his only concern was for his brother. When he went in to see him, he found him in the worst and most perilous of states. He summoned the vizier Dandan for a consultation, together with Rustan and Bahram, and when they had come, it was decided to fetch doctors to treat him. They wept and said: 'The generosity of Time has never produced another man like him.' After they had passed a sleepless night sitting with him, the 'ascetic' came up in tears. When Dau' al-Makan saw her, he got up to greet her. The 'ascetic' brushed her hand over Sharkan's wound, reciting over him a passage from the Quran, using the lines of the Merciful God as an incantation. She then stayed with Sharkan, remaining wakeful until morning, when Sharkan recovered consciousness, opened his eyes, moved his tongue round his mouth and spoke.

Seeing this, Dau' al-Makan was delighted and said: 'The blessing of the ascetic has rested on him.' 'Praise be to God for having given me health, for I am now well,' said Sharkan, before adding: 'That damned man tricked me, and if I had not swerved faster than lightning, the javelin would have gone straight through my chest. Praise be to God who saved me!' He then asked about the Muslims, and when he was told that they were weeping for him, he said: 'I am well and healthy.' Then he asked: 'Where is the ascetic?' and Dau' al-Makan told him that the 'ascetic' was sitting by his head. He turned towards her and kissed her hands. 'My son,' said the 'ascetic', 'you must show the virtue of patience and God will reward you well, for the reward will be in proportion to the hardship.' 'Pray for me,' said Sharkan, and the 'ascetic' prayed.

When morning broke, the Muslims came to the battlefield in the light of dawn, while the infidels prepared for the fight. The Muslims advanced, drawing their swords and ready to join battle, while Dau' al-Makan and Afridun prepared to charge each other. Dau' al-Makan rode out on to the field, and with him were the vizier Dandan, the chamberlain and the emir Bahram, who told him: 'We are your ransom.' 'I swear by the Holy House, Zamzam and the Maqam of Abraham that I shall not hold back from sallying out against the unbelievers,' said Dau' al-Makan. When he reached the battlefield, he juggled with his sword and spear, astonishing the riders and amazing both sides. Then he charged the right wing and killed two officers, after which he killed another two on the left. Next, he halted in the centre of the field and called: 'Where is Afridun, that I may make him taste the torment of disgrace?'

In his folly the damned man was about to attack, but when King Hardub saw that, he urged him not to go out against Dau' al-Makan, saying: 'King, you fought yesterday, but today it is my turn and his bravery does not worry me.' He rode out, sword in hand, mounted on a roan horse like 'Antar's Abjar, matching the poet's description:

He outstripped sight on a fine race horse,
As though he wished to overtake fate.
Its colour is darkest black,
Like night when night is murky.
Its whinny delights those who hear it,
With a sound like rumbling thunder.
Were it to race the wind, the wind would be outstripped,
Nor could a lightning flash forestall it.

Each rider now charged the other, warding off blows and displaying the amazing powers that they possessed, advancing and retreating until the uneasy spectators could scarcely bear to wait for the destined end. Then Dau' al-Makan gave a shout and attacked the Armenian king, launching a blow which struck off his head and killed him. When the infidels saw that, they launched a concerted attack. Dau' al-Makan met them on the field of battle, and the cutting and thrusting went on until blood poured down in floods. The Muslims shouted the formulae of the glorification and unity of God, invoking blessing on the evangelist, the warner. The fighting was furious and God assigned victory to the Muslims and disgrace to the unbelievers. 'Take revenge for King 'Umar and for his son, Sharkan,' shouted the vizier Dandan, and baring his head he called to the Turks, more than twenty thousand of whom were at his side. They charged with him in a single body and all that the infidels could do was to turn their backs in flight. The sharp swords did their work among them; some fifty thousand riders were killed and more than that number were captured, with many being killed in the press at the entrance to the city gate.

The gate was then shut and the Rumis mounted the walls, fearing that they would be made to suffer further. The Muslims, having been granted aid and victory by God, returned to their tents. Dau' al-Makan went in to see his brother and found him full of joy. He prostrated himself in gratitude to the Generous and Exalted God and then, going up to Sharkan, he congratulated him on being restored to health. Sharkan told him: 'All of us enjoy the blessing of this devout ascetic, and you owe your victory to his prayers, which God has answered. For he has spent the whole day praying for a Muslim victory.'

Night 104

Morning now dawned and Shahrazad broke off from what she had been allowed to say. Then, when it was the one hundred and fourth night, SHE CONTINUED:

I have heard, O fortunate king, that when Dau' al-Makan came to his brother, he found him sitting with the 'ascetic'. He went up to him to congratulate him on being restored to health and Sharkan told him: 'All of us enjoy the blessing of this devout ascetic, and you owe your victory to his prayers, which God has answered. For he has spent the whole day praying for a Muslim victory. I felt myself strengthened when I heard your cry of "*Allahu akbar!*" for I realized that you had defeated the enemy. So tell me what happened to you, brother.'

Dau' al-Makan then told him the whole story of his encounter with

Hardub the damned, how he had killed him and how God's curse had taken him. Sharkan praised him and thanked him for his efforts, but when Dhat al-Dawahi, disguised as the 'ascetic', heard of the death of her son, she turned pale and her eyes brimmed with tears. Concealing this, however, she pretended to the Muslims that she was weeping from an excess of joy, but to herself she said: 'I swear by the Messiah that there will be no profit in my life if I do not cause his heart to burn with grief for his brother Sharkan, as he has burned mine in sorrow for the pillar of Christianity and the people of the Cross, King Hardub.'

She concealed her feelings, while the vizier Dandan, King Dau' al-Makan and the chamberlain stayed sitting with Sharkan, until they had produced poultices and unguents and given him medicine. To their great joy he was restored to full health, and the Muslims, delighted to be told the news, said: 'Tomorrow he will ride out with us and set about the siege.' Sharkan said to his visitors: 'You are tired after having fought today. You should go back to your own quarters and sleep, rather than staying awake.' They agreed to this and each went to his own pavilion, leaving only a few servants with Sharkan, together with Dhat al-Dawahi. He talked with her for a time during the night and then lay down to sleep, as did the servants, until, overwhelmed by drowsiness, they lay like the dead.

So much for Sharkan and his servants, but as for Dhat al-Dawahi, when they had fallen asleep, she alone was awake in the tent. Looking at Sharkan, and finding him sunk in sleep, she jumped to her feet like a hairless bear or a spotted snake. From her waistband she took a poisoned dagger which, had it been placed on a rock, would have caused it to melt away. Unsheathing this, she came to Sharkan's head and, drawing it across his throat, she slaughtered him and proceeded to cut his head from his body. She then got up and went to the sleeping servants whose heads she also cut off lest they wake. After leaving the tent, she went to that of the sultan, but here the guards were not sleeping and so she went on to the tent of the vizier Dandan, whom she found reciting the Quran. Catching sight of her, he said: 'Welcome to the pious ascetic.' Her heart fluttered when she heard this and she told him: 'I came here because I heard the voice of one of God's saints and I am on my way to him.'

She then turned away and Dandan said to himself: 'By God, I shall follow the ascetic tonight.' He got up and walked behind her, but she became conscious of his footsteps and realized that he was following her. Afraid of being exposed, she said to herself: 'If I don't manage to trick him, he will find me out.' So she turned to him from a distance and said: 'Vizier, I am following this saint to find out who he is. After that, I shall ask him to allow you to come, and then I shall return and tell you, but I'm afraid that if you come with me without his leave, he may shy away on seeing you in my company.'

When the vizier heard that, he was too ashamed to make any reply, and going back to his tent, he tried to sleep, but the pleasure of sleep eluded him and the world seemed to be closing in on him. He got up and left his tent, telling himself that he would go to Sharkan and talk with him until morning. So he went off, but when he entered Sharkan's tent, he found blood flowing in a stream, and he saw the servants lying with their necks severed. The cry that he uttered aroused the sleepers and people came hurrying up, bursting into noisy tears and sobs when they saw the streams of blood. This woke Dau' al-Makan, and when he asked what the matter was, he was told that Sharkan, his brother, and his servants had been killed. He got up quickly, went to the tent, where the vizier Dandan was screaming, and there he found the headless body of his brother. He lost consciousness, while all the troops cried out, wept and crowded around him until he came to his senses.

He then wept bitterly, looking at Sharkan, as did the vizier, Rustam and Bahram, while the chamberlain not only cried out and lamented profusely but, such was his fear, that he asked leave to go. 'Don't you know who did this to my brother?' asked Dau' al-Makan, 'and why don't I see the ascetic who has abandoned the delights of this world?' 'Who was it,' said the vizier, 'who brought these sorrows on us except this devil, the ascetic? From the beginning my heart recoiled from him as I know that all religious fanatics are evil, scheming men.' He repeated to the king the story of how he had tried to follow the 'man', and had failed. The people wept and wailed aloud, calling on God, Who is near at hand and Who answers prayer, that the 'ascetic', the denier of God's signs, might fall into their hands. They then prepared Sharkan's corpse for burial and buried it on the mountain mentioned earlier, grieving for his widely famed merit.

Night 105

Morning now dawned and Shahrazad broke off from what she had been allowed to say. Then, when it was the one hundred and fifth night, SHE CONTINUED:

I have heard, O fortunate king, that they then prepared Sharkan's corpse for burial and buried it on the mountain mentioned earlier, grieving for his widely famed merit. The Muslims then waited for the gate of Constantinople to be opened, but this did not happen and no signs could be seen of the garrison on the walls. This took them by surprise, and Dau' al-Makan said: 'By God, I shall not turn away from them even if I have to wait for years before taking revenge for my brother. I shall lay the city in ruins and kill the kings of Christendom, even if I have to die in the process and find rest from this evil world.' On his orders, the wealth taken from the monastery of Matruhina was produced and distributed to the army which had been mustered, with each man receiving a gift sufficient for his needs. He then collected three hundred riders from each division and told them to send home enough to cover their families' living expenses, repeating that it was his intention to stay where he was for years to avenge Sharkan, his brother, even if it cost him his life.

When his men heard this, they took the money that they had been given and obeyed his orders. He then summoned his couriers and gave them letters and money to be delivered to the soldiers' homes. Their families were to be told that their men were safe and at ease, and that the army was besieging Constantinople and would sack it or perish, whether this took months or years, and that it would only leave when the city had fallen. Dau' al-Makan told the vizier Dandan to write to his sister, Nuzhat al-Zaman, telling her what had happened to them and what their current situation was. She was to be asked to look after Dau' al-Makan's child, as his wife had been on the point of giving birth when he had left and the child must now have been born. He added to the courier: 'If it is a boy, as I have heard, hurry back and give me the news.' The couriers were provided with money and they set out with it immediately after the soldiers had come out to see them off and to tell them what to do with what they themselves had been given. The king then went to the vizier Dandan and told him to order the army to advance close to the city wall. They did so, but were surprised to find that no one appeared on the wall. This worried the king; he was saddened by the loss of his brother and perplexed about the treacherous 'ascetic', and the army stayed there for three days, without seeing a soul.

So much for the Muslims, but as for the Rumis, the reason that they did not fight for these three days was that when Dhat al-Dawahi had killed Sharkan, she hurried to the wall and shouted to the guards in the Rumi tongue, telling them to lower her a rope. 'Who are you?' they asked, but when she told them that she was Dhat al-Dawahi, they recognized her and let down a rope to which she tied herself. They pulled her up, and when she reached the top, she went to the emperor and said: 'What is this that I hear from the Muslims? They said that my son, Hardub, has been killed.' 'He has indeed,' said Afridun, at which she cried out and wept and went on weeping until she drew tears from Afridun himself and all who were present with him. Then she told him how she had severed the necks of Sharkan and thirty of his servants. He was pleased at this and thanked her, kissing her hands and praying that she might find patience to endure the loss of her son. 'By the Messiah,' she replied, 'I won't be content with killing one Muslim dog in revenge for one of the kings of the age. I must work a trick and think up a ruse to kill King Dau' al-Makan, together with the vizier Dandan, the chamberlain, Rustam, Bahram and ten thousand riders from the Muslim army. Sharkan's head is not and never will be a sufficient price for the head of my son.' Then she said to Afridun: 'Know, king of the age, that I wish to arrange to mourn my son, cutting my girdle and breaking the crosses.' 'Do as you wish,' said Afridun, 'for I shall not disobey you in anything. However long your mourning lasts, this will be a small matter, for even if the Muslims were to besiege us for years, they will not achieve what they want from us and they will get nothing but toil and weariness.'

When the damned woman had finished with the calamity that she had brought about and the shameful acts for which she was responsible, she took an inkstand together with paper and wrote: 'From Dhat al-Dawahi of the evil eye to the Muslims: know that I entered your lands, using my dishonour to deceive your honour. First I killed your king, 'Umar ibn al-Nu'man, in his own palace. Then, in the battle of the ravine and the cave, I killed many men, while the last of my victims was Sharkan, together with his servants. If Time aids me and the devil obeys me, I shall certainly kill your king together with the vizier Dandan. It was I who came to you disguised as an ascetic, when I worked my tricks and my wiles on you. If you want to be safe now, leave at once, but if you want to bring destruction on yourselves, stay here, and even if you stay for years, you will get nothing from us that you want. Farewell.' After having written this letter, she remained in mourning for King Hardub for three days. On the fourth, she summoned an officer and told him to take the paper, fix it to an arrow and shoot it towards the Muslims. After that, she went to the church, where she began to lament and weep for the loss of her son, telling his successor on the throne that she meant to kill Dau' al-Makan and all the Muslim emirs.

So much for her, but as for the Muslims, they spent three days filled with care and sorrow and on the fourth, when they looked towards the city wall, they saw an officer carrying an arrow to whose head was fixed a letter. They waited until he shot it towards them, and the sultan then told the vizier to read it out. When he did this and Dau' al-Makan heard what was in it, his eyes filled with tears and he cried out in anger at her trickery. 'My heart always recoiled from her,' said Dandan, while the king exclaimed: 'How did this harlot come to trick us twice? By God, I shall not turn away from here until I have filled her vagina with molten lead, caged her like a bird, tied her up by her hair and crucified her over the gate of Constantinople.' He then wept bitterly, remembering his brother, while the infidels, when Dhat al-Dawahi had told them what had happened, were glad to hear of Sharkan's death and that she herself was safe.

The Muslims went back to the gate of Constantinople and the king promised them that if he took the city, he would divide its spoils equally between them. His tears continued to flow in grief for his brother and his body became so emaciated that it was like a tooth-pick. The vizier Dandan came to visit him and said: 'Take heart and console yourself. Your brother died at his appointed time and there is no profit in this grief. The poet has put it well:

What is not to happen will never happen by a trick,
While that which is to happen will take place,
And what is fated comes at its own time,
Although the fool will always be deceived.

So give up your tears and lamentation and nerve yourself to take up arms.'

'Vizier,' replied Dau' al-Makan, 'my heart is filled with care because of my brother's death and because we are absent from our own lands, and I am concerned for my subjects.' The vizier shed tears, as did all those who were present, but they stayed for a time laying siege to

Constantinople. When they were there, news was brought from Baghdad by an emir that the wife of King Dau' al-Makan had given birth to a boy whom his sister, Nuzhat al-Zaman, had named Kana-ma-Kana.* The remarkable and marvellous qualities that he possessed showed that the child was destined for greatness. The emir continued: 'Your sister has ordered the religious scholars and the preachers to pray for you from the pulpits and at the conclusion of every prayer. We are flourishing; the rains have been plentiful; your friend the furnace man is enjoying great prosperity and has many eunuchs and servants, but he still doesn't know what has happened to you. Goodbye.' 'It has given me strength,' said Dau' al-Makan, 'to hear that I now have a son, Kana-ma-Kana.'

Night 106

Morning now dawned and Shahrazad broke off from what she had been allowed to say. Then, when it was the one hundred and sixth night, SHE CONTINUED:

I have heard, O fortunate king, that King Dau' al-Makan was delighted to hear that his wife had given birth to a son. 'It has given me strength,' he said, 'to hear that I now have a son, Kana-ma-Kana.' He then said to Dandan: 'I propose to leave aside my mourning and to arrange for recitations of the whole Quran in memory of my brother, as well as for acts of charity.' Dandan approved of this and Dau' al-Makan gave orders for tents to be pitched over Sharkan's grave. He collected from among the troops those who could recite the Quran, and while some of them did this, others glorified God until morning. Then the king came to his brother's grave, shed tears and recited these lines:

They brought him out, and every mourner following him
Swooned, as did Moses when Mount Sinai was brought low.
They brought him to a tomb, and it was as though a grave
Was dug in the heart of every follower of the One God.
Before I saw your bier, I never thought to see
Mount Radwa carried on the hands of men,
And not before your burial in the earth
Did I see stars setting within the ground.
I call to one resting in an underground cell

* 'What was, was'.

Illumined by the radiance of his face.
Praise will undertake to restore his life to him,
For it is unfolded when he is hidden away.

On finishing his poem, Dau' al-Makan wept, as did all those with him.
He then approached the grave and threw himself on it in despair, while
the vizier recited the lines of the poet:

You have left transience and won immortality,
As others did who lived before your time.
You parted from this world without misgiving,
And in its place you will be pleased with what you find.
You were a barrier against the foe
When the slender war arrows sought their marks.
I see this world as deception and as vanity;
Man's greatest goal must be the search for truth.
May the Lord of the throne grant you the gift of Paradise,
And may the Guide give you a good seat there.
Because of you I find myself in sorrow;
Both west and east are saddened by your loss.

When the vizier had finished his poem, he wept bitterly and his eyes
shed tears like rows of pearls. Then one of Sharkan's boon companions
came forward, shedding tears like rivers. He recalled Sharkan's generous
deeds and recited:

Where now is bounty, when your generous hand lies in the earth?
After your loss illness has worn away my body.
Leader of the camel litters, may you enjoy what you can see!
My tears have written lines upon my cheeks
For you to note with pleasure.
By God, I never told my inner heart of you,
Nor did your grandeur ever cross my mind
Without tears wounding the sockets of my eyes.
If I should look at anyone but you,
May passion tug at their reins as I try to sleep.

When the man had finished his poem, Dau' al-Makan shed tears, as
did the vizier Dandan, while the whole army wept noisily. They then
dispersed to their tents, while Dau' al-Makan went to Dandan and the
two of them held a war council, which continued for a period of days

and nights. Dau' al-Makan, tormented by cares and sorrows, then said: 'I would like to hear stories of people, accounts of kings and tales of infatuated lovers, in the hope that God might relieve the burden of care that has oppressed my heart, and put an end to my tears of mourning.'

The vizier said: 'If it will cure your sorrow to listen to remarkable stories and tales of lovers in days gone by, together with others, this will be an easy matter as in the lifetime of your late father my only task was to tell tales and recite poetry. Tonight I shall cheer you by telling you the story of the lover and his beloved.' When Dau' al-Makan heard this, he fixed his heart on the vizier's promise and thought of nothing but waiting for the night in order to hear what the vizier had to tell him about past kings and infatuated lovers. As soon as it was dark, he ordered the candles and lamps to be lit, and the necessary food and drink, as well as censers, to be brought. When this had been done, he sent for Dandan, who came, as well as for Bahram, Rustam, Tarkash and the grand chamberlain. When they were all there, he turned to Dandan and said: 'Know, vizier, that now night has come and lowered its robes over us, we want you to tell us the stories that you promised.' 'Willingly,' replied the vizier.

Night 107

Morning now dawned and Shahrazad broke off from what she had been allowed to say. Then, when it was the one hundred and seventh night, SHE CONTINUED:

I have heard, O fortunate king, that when King Dau' al-Makan had summoned the vizier, the chamberlain, Rustam, Bahram and Tarkash, he turned to Dandan and said: 'Know, vizier, that now night has come and lowered its robes over us, we want you to tell us the stories that you promised.' 'Willingly,' replied the vizier, AND HE WENT ON:

You must know, O fortunate king, that what I have heard of the story of the lover and his beloved, the exchanges between them and the remarkable and wonderful things that happened to them, is capable of removing care from the heart and bringing consolation even in sorrows like those of Jacob. According to the tale, in the old days, behind the mountains of Isfahan, there was what was known as the Green City. Its king, Sulaiman Shah, was generous, beneficent, just, trustworthy, virtuous and kindly. Riders came to him from all quarters and his fame spread throughout the regions. For many years he lived in his kingdom, glorious and secure, but he had neither wife nor child. He had a vizier who shared with him the same generous attributes and one day he happened to send for this man. When he came, the king told him: 'I am despondent; my patience is at an end and I am growing weak because I have no wife and no child. This is not a path to be followed by kings who rule over everyone, both high and low. These men take pleasure in leaving behind them children, adding both to their numbers and their preparedness, as the Prophet – may God bless him and give him peace – has said: "Marry, beget children and multiply, so that you may give me cause to boast over the nations on the Day of Judgement." What is your advice, vizier? Give me good counsel as to what I should do.'

When he heard this, tears streamed down from the vizier's eyes, and he replied: 'King of the age, far be it from me to speak of what is a prerogative of the Merciful God. Do you want me to anger the Omnipotent Lord and so enter hellfire? Buy a slave girl.' 'You must know,' replied Sulaiman, 'that when a king buys a slave girl, he knows nothing of her rank or her birth. He does not know whether she is to be avoided as coming from humble stock, or whether she is nobly born and so can be taken as a concubine. If he lies with her, she may conceive and the child may turn out to be a tyrannical hypocrite and a shedder of blood. She is like a salt marsh, where the seeds that are sown produce bad and weak plants. Her child may expose himself to the anger of his Lord, neither carrying out His commandments nor turning from what He has forbidden. I am not going to be responsible for this by buying a slave girl. Rather, I want you to ask the hand of a royal princess for me, whose lineage can be traced and who is characterized by beauty. If you show me a Muslim princess of high birth and sound religion, I shall ask for her hand and marry her in front of witnesses, so as to win through that the approval of the Lord of mankind.'

'Know, your majesty,' said the vizier, 'that, according to what I have heard, God has fulfilled your need and given you your desire.' He went on to explain that King Zahr Shah, lord of the White Land, had a daughter of surpassing and indescribable beauty, unrivalled in her age. 'She is perfectly made,' he added, 'symmetrically formed, with kohl-dark eyes, long hair, a slender waist and heavy buttocks. Seen from in front she fascinates, and seen from behind she kills. She ravishes both the heart and the eye, as the poet says:

She is slender, with a figure like the branch of a *ban* tree;
Neither sun nor moon can rival her in their rising.
Her saliva is like honey mixed with wine,
While in her mouth are pearls.
A houri of Paradise, built with slenderness,
Her face is lovely, with destruction in her glance.
How many of her victims died of grief,
While on the path of her love both fear and danger lie.
For my life she is death; I do not wish to mention her,
But if I die without her, my life has been of no avail.'

When he had finished describing the girl, the vizier said to King Sulaiman Shah: 'My advice, your majesty, is that you should send to her father an intelligent envoy, experienced in affairs and tested by time's vicissitudes, to present him on your behalf with a courteous request for her hand. For she has no equal in the world, far or near. If you win her, you will win a lovely face as well as the approval of the Glorious Lord, for it is told of the Prophet – may God bless him and give him peace – that he said: "There is no monkery in Islam."'

The king was overjoyed by this. He relaxed with gladness, while his cares and sorrows left him. Going up to the vizier, he said: 'Know, vizier, that no one shall undertake this mission but you, because of your consummate intelligence and your culture. Go to your house; put your affairs in order and be ready to start out tomorrow. Then ask for the hand of this girl on my behalf, for what you have said about her has preoccupied me – and do not come back to me without her.' 'To hear is to obey,' replied the vizier. He then went home and called for gifts of jewels and precious things fit for a king, together with whatever else was light to carry, but valuable. He collected Arab horses, mail coats made by Da'ud, and chests of treasure that defied description.

These were loaded on mules and camels, and the vizier set off, accompanied by a hundred mamluks, a hundred black slaves and a hundred slave girls, with flags and banners unfurled overhead. He had been ordered to return within a few days, and after he had gone, Sulaiman Shah was consumed by fire, his thoughts being centred night and day on his love for the princess. The vizier, meanwhile, travelled without a break, crossing deserts and wastes until he was within a day's march of his goal. He halted by a river bank and, summoning one of his principal officers, told him to go quickly to King Zahr Shah with news of his arrival. 'To hear is to obey,' replied the man, before hurrying off to the city.

When he got there, it happened that the king was sitting in a pleasure garden by the city gate. Seeing the messenger enter and realizing he was a stranger, he ordered him to be brought before him. When he came, the messenger told him of the arrival of the vizier of the great king, Sulaiman Shah, lord of the Green Land and the mountains of Isfahan. This pleased Zahr Shah, who welcomed the man and took him with him to his palace. 'Where did you leave the vizier?' he asked. 'I left him at dawn by the river bank,' the messenger replied, 'and he will reach you tomorrow – may God perpetuate His favours to you and receive your parents into His mercy.' Zahr Shah then ordered one of his viziers to take most of his principal officers, his chamberlains, deputies and officers of state and go to meet his visitor as a show of respect for King Sulaiman Shah, whose authority extended throughout the land.

So much for Zahr Shah, but as for the vizier, he stayed where he was until midnight and then he set off for the city. When dawn broke and sunlight spread over the hills and valleys, before he knew it, there was the vizier of King Zahr Shah, together with the chamberlains, officers of state and the leading men of the kingdom, coming towards him. They met him some *parasangs* from the city, giving him good reason to believe his mission would succeed. He greeted those who had come to welcome him and they went on ahead of him until they reached the royal palace. They preceded him through the palace gate and led him on to the seventh hall, a place that was not to be entered by anyone on horseback, as it was close to the king.

The vizier dismounted and went on foot until he arrived in a lofty room, at whose upper end was a throne of marble studded with pearls and jewels. It had four elephant tusks as legs, and it was draped with green satin embellished with red gold, while over it was a canopy, set with pearls and gems. King Zahr Shah was seated on the throne with his officers of state standing in attendance on him. The vizier, when he came in and stood before him, plucked up his courage and spoke fluently and eloquently, with practised rhetoric.

Night 108

Morning now dawned and Shahrazad broke off from what she had been allowed to say. Then, when it was the one hundred and eighth night, SHE CONTINUED:

I have heard, O fortunate king, that when the vizier of King Sulaiman Shah came to King Zahr Shah, he plucked up his courage and spoke fluently and eloquently, with practised rhetoric. Gesturing politely to the king, he recited these lines:

> He comes forward in his tunic, bending down,
> Spreading the dew of bounty over harvest and the harvesters.
> He casts a charm, and neither amulets nor spells
> Nor magic can prevail against the glances of those eyes.
> Say to the censurers: 'Do not blame me
> For staying so long without turning from his love.'
> My heart betrays me and keeps faith with him,
> While sleep loves him and has grown tired of me.
> Heart, you are not the only one with tenderness;
> Stay with him, leaving me in loneliness.
> The one sound that delights my ears
> Is praise I gather for King Zahr Shah.
> Were you to spend the whole term of your life
> In looking at his face, this would be wealth indeed.
> When you select a pious prayer for him,
> All those you meet will join in the 'amen'.
> If any hope to leave his kingdom for another,
> I do not think such men to be Muslims.

When the vizier had finished his poem, King Zahr Shah called him up and showed him the greatest honour. He seated him beside him, smiled at him and favoured him with courteous words. The audience continued until morning, when a table was set in the audience chamber. Everyone ate their fill, after which the table was removed and they all left except for the officers of state. On seeing that the chamber had been emptied, the vizier rose to his feet, bowed to the king and kissed the ground before him. He then said: 'Great king and noble lord, the mission on which I have come is one from which you should derive benefit and success. I am here as a messenger from King Sulaiman Shah, the just, the trustworthy, the virtuous and kindly, the lord of the Green Land and the mountains of Isfahan, to ask for the hand of your respected and high-born daughter. He has sent you an abundance of gifts and presents, and he wishes to become related to you through marriage. Do you want this, too?'

He then fell silent, waiting for the king's reply. For his part, on hearing this, the king rose to his feet and then kissed the ground as a sign of respect, while those present were astonished and filled with amazement that he should abase himself before the vizier. He then called down praises upon God, the Glorious, the Generous, and said, while he was still standing: 'Great and honoured vizier, listen to what I have to say. I am numbered among the subjects of King Sulaiman Shah and it will be an honour for me and the fulfilment of an aspiration to be related to him. My daughter is one of his slave girls, and this is my greatest wish, that he may be my treasure and support.'

He had the *qadis* and the notaries fetched to him, and they bore witness to the fact that King Sulaiman Shah had appointed his vizier to act as his deputy in the matter of his marriage, and that King Zahr Shah had gladly contracted his daughter to him. The *qadis* confirmed the marriage contract and prayed for the good fortune and success of both parties. The vizier then rose and produced the gifts and precious treasures, all of which he presented to the king, who, for his part, set about making preparations to send off his daughter. He treated the vizier with honour and entertained both high and low to banquets. The celebrations lasted for two months and nothing was omitted that might please the heart or delight the eye.

When everything that the bride might need had been prepared, the king ordered tents to be brought out and pitched outside the city. Fabrics were packed in chests; Rumi slave girls and Turkish maids were made ready; and the bride was given precious treasures and costly jewels to take with her. A palanquin of red gold, studded with pearls and gems, had been made for her, and twenty mules were assigned to her for the journey. The palanquin was like a chamber, the princess like a beautiful houri and her boudoir like one of the pavilions of Paradise. The treasures and money were packed up and loaded on to the mules and the camels. King Zahr Shah accompanied the party for three *parasangs* and then, after taking leave of the vizier and his companions, he went back home, feeling joyful and secure.

The vizier, together with the princess, travelled on, retracing the stages of his previous journey, crossing deserts . . .'

Night 109

I have heard, O fortunate king, that the vizier, together with the princess, travelled on, retracing the stages of his previous journey, crossing deserts and pressing on, night and day, until he was within a three-day march of his own country. He then sent word to Sulaiman Shah of the arrival of his bride, news which was quickly brought by his messenger. Sulaiman Shah was delighted; he rewarded the messenger with a robe of honour and ordered his troops to honour the bride and her entourage by filing in a grand procession, magnificently turned out with banners unfurled above their heads. The order was obeyed and a proclamation was made in the city that no girl kept in seclusion, respectable free woman or old woman broken by age should stay behind but that they were all to come out to meet the bride.

This they did and the great ladies among them exerted themselves to serve her. It was decided that she should be escorted to the royal palace by night and the officers of state agreed to adorn the road with decorations and to stand there until the bride had passed, preceded by her eunuchs, with the slave girls in front of her, wearing the robe that her father had given her. When she came, the troops flanked her on the right and the left. The litter continued on its way until it came near the palace and there was no one left who had not come to look at her. Drums were beating; lances were tossed in the air; trumpets sounded; perfume filled the air; banners fluttered; and horses raced one another until the procession reached the palace gate.

The servants then brought the palanquin to the door of the harem and the place was illumined by its splendour as every part gleamed with the ornaments that decorated it. At nightfall, the eunuchs opened the doors of the pavilion and took up their positions grouped around them. The bride then came surrounded by her slave girls like the moon among stars or a matchless pearl set among others on a string. She entered the bridal chamber, where a couch had been placed for her, made of marble studded with pearls and gems. She sat on it, and when the king came in, God caused love for her to enter his heart. He took her maidenhead, curing his own trouble and constraint, and he stayed with her for about a month, while she had conceived his child on the first night.

When the month was over, he left the harem and took his seat on his royal throne, dispensing justice among his subjects. The time of the queen's pregnancy passed and towards dawn on the last night of the ninth month she went into labour. She sat on the birthing stool; God granted her an easy delivery and she gave birth to a boy, who could be seen as marked out for good fortune. The king was overjoyed to hear of his son: he gave a huge sum of money to the bringer of the good news and, in his delight, he went to the child, kissed him between the eyes, and admired his radiant beauty, in which could be seen the truth of the poet's lines:

In him God has provided the coverts of noble deeds
With a lion, and the horizons of kingship with a star.
At his rising, the spears smile, as do the thrones,
Assemblies, armies and the edges of the sword.
Do not mount him on a woman's breasts;
To him a horse's back will seem the most comfortable of carriages.
Wean him from milk, for he will come to think
The blood of his enemies to be the sweetest of all drinks.

The midwives then took the child, cut the umbilical cord and put kohl round his eyes, after which he was named Taj al-Muluk Kharan. He was suckled by the teats of indulgence and was nurtured in the lap of favour. Days passed and years went by until he was seven years old. Then Sulaiman Shah summoned the learned doctors and philosophers and told them to teach his son calligraphy, philosophy and literary culture. They stayed for a number of years doing that until the boy had learned all that was needed. When he had mastered what the king required him to know, he was removed from the care of the *faqihs* and teachers and given an instructor to teach him horsemanship. This instruction continued until he was fourteen.

Whenever he went out on any business, all who saw him were captivated by him.

Night 110

Morning now dawned and Shahrazad broke off from what she had been allowed to say. Then, when it was the one hundred and tenth night, SHE CONTINUED:

I have heard, O fortunate king, that Prince Taj al-Muluk became a skilled horseman, surpassing all living at that time. Because of his beauty, whenever he went out on any business, all who saw him were captivated by him, poems were composed about him and freeborn women were shamefully seduced by his love. He was as described by the poet:

I became drunk on the fragrance of scent,
Embracing a moist branch the zephyr nurtured.
The lover was drunk, but not on wine.
Rather it was the beloved's saliva that intoxicated him.
All beauty is held captive by the beloved,
And because of that he holds sway over men's hearts.
By God, I will never think of consolation for his loss
As long as I am held in the bonds of life or afterwards.
If I live, I live loving him, and if I die
Because of the passion of my love, death will be welcome.

When he reached the age of eighteen, greenish down spread over a mole on his red cheek, while a beauty spot like a speck of amber was set there as an adornment. He began to captivate minds and eyes, as the poet says:

He is a successor to Joseph in his beauty;
When he appears, lovers are filled with fear.
Turn aside with me and look at him
To see on his cheeks the black banner of the caliphate.

Another poet has said:

Your eyes have never seen a finer sight
In anything that can be seen,
Than the green mole upon the cheek,
Red as it is, beneath the dark eye.

A third has said:

> I wonder at a mole that always worships your cheek's fire,
> But is not burned by it, infidel though it is.
> More wonderful is that a message from his glance
> Should confirm God's signs, although he is a sorcerer.
> How green is the crop that his cheek has produced,
> Because of the many hearts it breaks.

Yet another poet has said:

> I wonder at those who question where
> The water of life is found to flow.
> I see it on a slender gazelle's mouth
> With sweet red lips, covered by a dark moustache.
> How strange, when Moses found this water
> Flowing there, he was not content to wait.

When Prince Taj al-Muluk, enjoying such advantages, reached manhood, he became ever more handsome. He had a number of companions and favourites, and all his close associates were hoping that he would become king after his father's death and that they would be his emirs. He became attached to hunting and the chase, spending every hour that he had in its pursuit. His father, Sulaiman Shah, tried to keep him away from it, since he was afraid of his son's exposure to the dangers of the waste lands and wild beasts, but the prince would not accept any restraint.

It happened, then, that he told his servants to take with them provisions for ten days, which they did, and he left with them on a hunting trip. For four days they travelled through the wilds until they reached a spot overlooking a green land, where they saw wild beasts grazing, trees laden with ripe fruits and gushing springs. He told them to spread out their trapping ropes in a wide ring, while they themselves were to assemble at a particular spot at the head of the ring. They followed his orders, setting up the ropes in a wide circle, within which they enclosed wild beasts of many kinds, including gazelles. This caused a disturbance among the beasts, who stampeded in the face of the horses, and the prince then released the dogs, the lynxes and the falcons at them, followed by flights of arrows which inflicted mortal wounds. Before they could reach the head of the ring, many of the beasts were taken, while the rest fled.

Taj al-Muluk then dismounted by a stream, where he collected and distributed the game, setting aside the best portion for his father, Sulai-man Shah. He sent this off to him, while he assigned other portions to his principal officers, before spending the night there. In the morning a large merchant caravan arrived, with black slaves and servants. They halted in the green meadow by the water, and when he saw them, Taj al-Muluk told one of his companions to find out about them and to ask them why they were halting there. The man went to them and said: 'Tell me who you are and answer quickly.' They told him: 'We are merchants and we have stopped here to rest, as we have a long way to go before we reach the next stage on our route. We have halted here because we have confidence in Sulaiman Shah and his son; we know that all who stay in his lands can expect safe conduct, and we have expensive materials with us which we have brought for Prince Taj al-Muluk.'

The messenger went back to the prince and told him about this, relaying what he had heard from the merchants. 'If they have something that they have brought for me,' said the prince, 'I shall not leave this spot and enter the city until I have inspected it.' He mounted his horse and rode off, with his mamluks behind him, until he reached the caravan. The merchants rose to greet him, offering prayers for victory and good fortune, as well as continued glory and honour. A tent had been pitched for him of red satin embellished with pearls and gems, in which a royal couch had been placed on a silk carpet, its front studded with emeralds.

Taj al-Muluk took his seat, with his mamluks standing in attendance on him, and he then sent word to the merchants, telling them to produce everything that they had with them. They came with their goods, all of which he inspected, choosing what pleased him and paying its full price. He then mounted, intending to set off, but on happening to glance towards the caravan, he saw a handsome young man, neatly dressed and elegant, with a radiant forehead and a face like a moon, although his beauty had altered and he showed the pallor of one who has been parted from his beloved.

Night 111

Morning now dawned and Shahrazad broke off from what she had been allowed to say. Then, when it was the one hundred and eleventh night, SHE CONTINUED:

I have heard, O fortunate king, that Taj al-Muluk happened to glance towards the caravan. He saw a handsome young man, neatly dressed and elegant, with a radiant forehead and a face like a moon, although his beauty had altered and he showed the pallor of one who has been parted from his beloved. Moaning and sobbing, with tears pouring down from his eyes, he recited:

> We have long been parted; cares and passion never cease;
> Friend, the tears flow from my eyes.
> I took leave of my heart on the day of parting,
> And I have remained alone with no heart and no hope.
> Friend, stay with me as I take leave of one
> Whose words can cure all sickness and all ills.

When he had finished speaking, the young man wept for a time and then fainted, with Taj al-Muluk looking on in amazement. When he had recovered, with a wounding glance he recited:

> Beware of her glance, for it works sorcery,
> And no one can escape who is shot by her eyes.
> For all their languor, those dark eyes
> Are sharp enough to split white swords.
> Do not be deceived by her soft words,
> For love's fire can bemuse the mind.
> She is softly formed; were silk to touch her body,
> Blood would be drawn from it, as you can see.
> How far it is between her anklets and her neck!
> What fragrance rivals her sweet-smelling scent?

The young man then gave a groan and fainted. When Taj al-Muluk looked at him, he was baffled by his condition. He walked up to him, and when the young man had recovered consciousness, he saw Taj al-Muluk standing by his head. He rose to his feet and kissed the ground before him, after which the prince asked him why he had not shown him his merchandise. 'There is nothing among my goods that is suitable for your excellency,' the young man replied, but Taj al-Muluk insisted on being shown what he had, as well as on being told what was the matter with him, adding: 'I see that you are tearful and sad. If you have been wronged, I shall right the wrong, and if you are in debt, I shall pay it, for it has pained me to see you like this.'

He then ordered chairs to be set out, and they fetched him one made of ivory and ebony, draped with gold-embroidered silk, and they spread

out a silken carpet. Taj al-Muluk sat on the chair and told the young
man to be seated on the carpet, after which he said: 'Show me your
goods.' 'Please don't tell me to do that, master,' said the young man.
'My goods are not fit for you.' Taj al-Muluk insisted, however, and told
one of his servants to fetch them, whether or not he agreed. On seeing
this, tears started from the young man's eyes. He wept, groaned, complained and sighed deeply. Then he recited:

> I swear by the coquetry and the kohl of your eyes,
> By the soft lissomness of your form,
> By the wine and honey of your mouth,
> And by the gentleness and vexation of your nature:
> There came an apparition sent by you, who are my hope,
> Sweeter than safety for the craven coward.

He then opened up his goods and displayed them to Taj al-Muluk,
one after the other, piece by piece. Among the things that he brought
out was a satin robe with gold brocade worth two thousand dinars.
When he unfolded this, a piece of material fell from the middle of it,
which he quickly picked up and tucked beneath his hip. Then, in a daze,
he recited:

> When will the tortured heart find a cure for your love?
> Union with you is farther than the Pleiades.
> Distance, abandonment, longing and lovesickness,
> Delay, postponement – this is how life passes.
> Union does not bring life nor does abandonment kill me.
> Distance does not bring me near, nor are you at hand.
> It is neither fairness nor mercy that you show.
> You do not help me, but I cannot flee from you.
> All of my roads are blocked by love for you;
> I cannot make out where I am to go.

Taj al-Muluk was astonished at this recitation and wondered at the
reason for it, not knowing why the young man had picked up the scrap
of material and put it under his hip. So he asked what this was. 'You
don't need to see it, master,' replied the young man, and when the prince
insisted, he said: 'This was the reason why I refused to show you my
goods, and I cannot let you see it.'

Night 112

Morning now dawned and Shahrazad broke off from what she had been allowed to say. Then, when it was the one hundred and twelfth night, SHE CONTINUED:

I have heard, O fortunate king, that the young man said to Taj al-Muluk: 'This was the reason why I refused to show you my goods, and I cannot let you see it.' 'I must see it,' insisted Taj al-Muluk, and as he was growing angry, the young man drew it out from under his hip, weeping, moaning, complaining and uttering many groans. He then recited these lines:

> Do not blame him, for blame is hurtful.
> I spoke the truth, but he does not listen.
> I ask God to keep safe for me in the valley camping ground
> A moon that rises from the sphere of buttons.
> I said goodbye to him, but I would have preferred it
> Had pleasant life taken its leave of me before I did.
> How often did he plead with me on the morning of departure,
> As both my tears and his poured down.
> May God not give me the lie; parting from him
> Has torn my garment of excuse, but I shall patch it.
> I have no bed on which to lie, nor, since I left,
> Does any place of rest remain for him.
> Time did its best with its rough hand
> To ban me from good fortune and to ban him too.
> This was the hand that poured out unmixed grief,
> Filling the cup from which he drank what I gave him.

When he had finished, Taj al-Muluk said to him: 'I see that you are in a wretched state, so tell me why it is that you weep when you look at this piece of material.' When he heard the prince mention the material, the young man sighed and said: 'Master, my story is a remarkable one and the affair that connects me with this material, its owner and the one who embroidered it with these shapes and images, is strange.' At this, he unfolded the material and there on it was the picture of a gazelle embroidered in silk picked out with red gold, while opposite it was the picture of another gazelle, picked out in silver with a collar of red gold and three pendants of chrysolite. When Taj al-Muluk looked at this and saw its fine workmanship, he exclaimed: 'Glory be to God for teaching man what he did not know.' He then became passionately interested in the young man's story and asked him to tell him how he was connected with the lady who had embroidered the gazelles.

'Know, master,' replied the young man, 'that my father was one of the great merchants and I was his only son. I had a female cousin who was brought up with me in my father's house, as her own father had died. Before his death, he had come to an agreement with my father that they should marry me to her. When we both reached puberty, she was not kept away from me and I was not kept away from her. My father then talked with my mother and said: "This year we shall draw up the marriage contract between 'Aziz and 'Aziza." My mother agreed to this and my father started to lay in provisions for a banquet. While all this was going on, my cousin and I were sleeping in the same bed, in ignorance of all this, except that she knew more than I did, being better informed and more knowledgeable.' HE WENT ON:

My father then completed the wedding preparations and nothing remained except for the contract to be drawn up and the marriage consummated. My father wanted the contract to be signed after the Friday prayer, and he went to his friends among the merchants and others and told them about this, while my mother went and invited her women friends and her relatives. When Friday came, they washed out the hall that was prepared for the reception, cleaning the marble and spreading carpets in the house. Everything needed was set out there; the walls were adorned with brocaded hangings, and it was agreed that the guests should come to our house after the prayer. My father went off to supervise the making of the sweetmeats and the sugared dishes, and as the only thing left was the drawing up of the marriage contract, my mother made me go off to the baths, sending after me a splendid new suit of clothes. I put these on when I came out of the baths and, as they were perfumed, a pleasant odour spread from them, scenting the air.

I had meant to go to the Friday mosque, but then I remembered a friend of mine and went back to look for him in order to invite him to the signing of the marriage contract, telling myself that this would keep me busy until close to the time of prayer. I went into a lane where I had never been before, and I was sweating because of my bath and also because of the new clothes that I had on. As the sweat ran down, the scent grew stronger and I rested on a bench at the head of the lane, spreading out an embroidered kerchief that I had with me to sit on.

It grew hotter and although sweat covered my forehead and poured down my face, I could not wipe it away with the kerchief because I was sitting on it. I was about to use my gown when suddenly from above me a white kerchief fell, more delicate than the zephyr and more delightful to the eye than a sick man's cure. I caught it in my hand and looked up to see where it had come from. My gaze then fell on that of the gazelle lady . . .

Night 113

Morning now dawned and Shahrazad broke off from what she had been allowed to say. Then, when it was the one hundred and thirteenth night, SHE CONTINUED:

I have heard, O fortunate king, that THE YOUNG MAN TOLD TAJ AL-MULUK:

I looked up to see where it had come from. My gaze then fell on that of the gazelle lady, who was looking out of a window with a lattice of brass. I had never seen anyone more beautiful; indeed, my tongue cannot describe her. When she saw me looking at her, she put one finger in her mouth, and then, joining her middle finger to her index finger, she placed them on her bosom between her breasts. She then withdrew her head from the window, closing it and disappearing from sight. Fire broke out in my heart; the flames spread; my one glance was followed by a thousand regrets, and I was bewildered. I had not been able to hear anything she said, nor had I understood her gestures. I looked at the window again, but found it closed, and although I waited until sunset, I heard no sound and saw no one. Despairing of catching sight of her again, I got up from my place, taking the kerchief with me and unfolding it. The scent of musk spread from it, so delighting me that I imagined myself to be in Paradise.

As I spread it out between my fingers, a small piece of paper fell from it. I opened this up and found that it was impregnated with the purest of scents, while on it were written these lines:

I sent him a note complaining of my love,
Written in a delicate hand – and scripts are of all kinds.
My friend said: 'Why do you write like this,
So delicately and finely that it is hardly to be seen?'

I said: 'That is because I am worn away and thin;
   This is what happens to the script of lovers.'

After reading these lines, I studied the beautiful kerchief and saw the
following lines on one of its borders:

Down, that excellent calligrapher,
Wrote two lines on his cheek in ornamental script.
When he appears, the sun and moon become confused,
And when he bends, branches are put to shame.

On the opposite border were these lines:

Down wrote with ambergris upon a pearl
Two lines of jet inscribed upon an apple.
There is death in the glance of languorous eyes
And drunkenness in cheeks, not in the wine.

When I saw the verses that were embroidered on the kerchief, fire
spread through my heart and my longings and cares increased. I took
the kerchief and the note and brought them back home, not knowing
how to reach my beloved or how to particularize the generalities of love.
Some of the night had already passed before I reached the house, and
there I saw my cousin 'Aziza sitting weeping. When she saw me, she
wiped away her tears; coming up to me, she took off my robe and asked
me why I had been absent. All the emirs, she told me, together with the
great men, the merchants and others, had assembled in the house. The
qadis and the notaries had been there; they had eaten all the food and
stayed sitting for a time, waiting for me to come for the signing of the
contract. 'When finally they gave up hope of you,' she went on, 'they
dispersed and each went his way. Your father was furious at that and
swore that he would not draw up the marriage contract until next year,
because of all the money that he had spent on the wedding feast.'

   She then asked again what had happened to make me so late and to
cause all this trouble by my absence. 'Cousin,' I said to her, 'don't ask
what happened to me,' but then I told her about the kerchief and
explained things from start to finish. She took the paper and the kerchief
and read what was written on them, with tears running down her cheeks.
She then recited these lines:

If someone says: 'Love starts with choice,' tell them:
   'That is a lie; it all comes from necessity.'

Necessity is not followed by shame,
A point whose truth is shown by histories.
Sound currency cannot be falsified.
Call love sweet torture if you wish,
A throbbing in the entrails, or a blow,
A blessing, a misfortune or a goal
In which the soul finds pleasure or is lost.
Backwards or forwards – I do not know how love is to be read.
In spite of that, the days of love are feasts,
And the beloved's mouth smiles all the while.
Her spreading fragrance is a festival,
And her love cuts off all that brings disgrace,
Never alighting in the heart of a base man.

She then asked me: 'What did she say to you and what gestures did she
make at you?' 'She didn't speak at all,' I replied, 'but she put her finger
in her mouth, and she then put it together with her middle finger and
laid both of them on her breast, pointing downwards. Then she withdrew
her head and shut the window, after which I didn't see her again. She
took my heart away with her and I sat until sunset, waiting for her to
look out of the window a second time, but she didn't, and when I had
despaired of seeing her, I got up from where I was sitting and came
home. This is my story, and I wish that you would help me in my
misfortune.'

My cousin lifted her head towards me and said: 'If you asked for my
eye, cousin, I would pull it out from my eyelids for you, and I shall have
to help you get what you want, as well as helping her, for she is as deeply
in love with you as you are with her.' I asked what her gestures had
meant, and my cousin told me: 'When she put her finger in her mouth,
this was to show that you are like the soul in her body and that she
would hold on to your union with her teeth. The kerchief is the sign of
the lover's greeting to the beloved; the note signifies that her soul is
attached to you; and when she put two fingers on her bosom between
her breasts, she meant to tell you to come back after two days so as to
relieve her distress. You must know, cousin, that she is in love with you
and that she trusts you. This is the interpretation that I put on these
signs, and were I able to come and go, it would not take me long to
bring you together and shelter the two of you under my wing.'

When I heard what she said, I thanked her and I said to myself that

I would wait for two days. So I spent the days sitting at home, neither going out nor coming in and neither eating nor drinking. I put my head in my cousin's lap and she kept consoling me and telling me to be determined, resolute and of good heart.

Night 114

Morning now dawned and Shahrazad broke off from what she had been allowed to say. Then, when it was the one hundred and fourteenth night, SHE CONTINUED:

I have heard, O fortunate king, that THE YOUNG MAN TOLD TAJ AL-MULUK:

At the end of the two days, my cousin said to me: 'Be cheerful and joyful; strengthen your resolution; put on your clothes and set off for your rendezvous with her.' She then got up, brought me a change of clothing and perfumed me. I summoned up my strength, took heart and went out. I then walked on until I entered the lane, where I sat down on the bench for a time. Suddenly the window opened and I looked at the lady, but when I saw her I fell down in a faint. Then I recovered, summoned my resolve and took heart once more, but when I looked at her a second time, I lost consciousness again. When I came to myself, I saw that she had with her a mirror and a red kerchief. When she saw me, she uncovered her forearms, spread open her five fingers and struck her breast with the palm of her hand and her five fingers. Next, she raised her hands and put the mirror outside the window. She took the kerchief, went inside with it, and then, coming back again, she lowered it from the window in the direction of the lane. She did this three times, letting it down and raising it, after which she squeezed it and then folded it in her hand. She bowed her head and then drew it back from the window, which she shut. She went away without having said a single word to me, leaving me bemused, as I had no idea what her gestures meant.

I stayed sitting there until evening and it was almost midnight by the time I got home. There I found my cousin with her hand on her cheek and tears pouring from her eyes. She was reciting these lines:

Why should I harshly be abused for loving you?
How can I forget you, you the slender branch?

A beautiful face has ravished my heart and turned away –
I cannot escape my hopeless love for her.
With her Turkish glances she wounds my inner heart
More deeply than any polished and sharpened sword.
You have burdened me with a weight of passion,
While I am too weak to bear that of my shirt.
I shed tears of blood when those who blame me say:
'A sharp sword from your beloved's eyelids brings you fear.'
I wish my heart might be as hard as yours;
My withered body is as slender as your waist.
You lord it over me; your beauty is a steward
Treating me harshly, an unjust chamberlain.
To say all beauty was in Joseph is a lie.
How many Josephs are there in your loveliness!
I try to turn away from you, in fear
Of watching eyes. How difficult this is!

When I heard these lines, my cares and sorrows increased and multiplied, and I collapsed in a corner of the room. My cousin got up to come
to me. She lifted me up, took off my robe and wiped my face with her
sleeve. She then asked me what had happened and I told her everything
that the lady had done. 'Cousin,' she said, 'the gesture that she made
with the palm of her hand and her five fingers means: "Come again after
five days." As for the mirror, the lowering and raising of the red kerchief
and the fact that she put her head out of the window, this means: "Sit
in the dyer's shop until my messenger comes to you."' When I heard
what she said, fire blazed in my heart and I said: 'By God, cousin, your
interpretation of this is right, as I saw a Jewish dyer in the lane.' Then I
wept and my cousin said: 'Be resolute and firm. Others are obsessed with
love for years and endure the heat of its passion with constancy, while
you have only a week to wait, so why are you so impatient?'

She set about consoling me and she brought me food, but although I
took a morsel and tried to eat it, I failed, and I then neither ate nor drank
nor enjoyed the pleasures of sleep. My complexion turned pale and I lost
my good looks, as I had never been in love before or experienced love's
heat. I became weak and so did my cousin because of me. Every night
until I went to sleep she would try to console me by telling me stories of
lovers, and whenever I woke up, I would find her still awake thanks to
me, with tears running down her cheeks. Things went on like that for

me until the five days had passed. Then my cousin got up, heated water
for me and bathed me, after which she dressed me in my clothes. 'Go to
her,' she said, 'and may God fulfil your need and allow you to get what
you want from your beloved.'

I left and walked on until I got to the head of the lane. It was a
Saturday and I saw that the dyer's shop was shut. I sat by it until the call
for the afternoon prayer; then the sun grew pale and the muezzins called
for the evening prayer. Night fell, but I could learn nothing of my lady
and I heard nothing from her or of her. I became afraid for myself as
I sat there alone, and so I got up, staggering like a drunken man until I
got home. When I went in, I saw my cousin 'Aziza, standing alone with
one hand on a peg that had been driven into the wall and another on
her breast. She was reciting, with deep sighs, the lines:

The passion of the Arab girl, whose clan have gone,
Who longs for the *ban* tree and the sweet bay of Hijaz –
When she entertains the riders, her yearning serves
For their guest fire and her tears for their water –
This passion is no more than what I feel
For my beloved, who thinks my love a fault.

When she had finished her poem, she turned and caught sight of me.
She then wiped away her tears and mine with her sleeves and said,
smiling at me: 'May God grant you enjoyment of His gifts, cousin. Why
did you not spend the night with your beloved and get what you wanted
from her?' On hearing this, I kicked her in the chest and she fell, striking
her forehead on the edge of the raised floor of the room. There was a
peg there and it was this that struck her forehead, and when I looked at
it, I saw that the skin had been cut open and the blood was flowing.

Night 115

Morning now dawned and Shahrazad broke off from what she had been
allowed to say. Then, when it was the one hundred and fifteenth night,
SHE CONTINUED:

I have heard, O fortunate king, that THE YOUNG MAN TOLD TAJ
AL-MULUK:

I kicked my cousin in the chest and she fell, striking her forehead on
a peg at the edge of the raised floor of the room. The skin was cut open

and the blood flowed. She remained silent, not saying a single word, then, getting up immediately, she burned some rags, applying the ash to the wound, which she bandaged. She wiped away the blood that had fallen on to the carpet, and it was as though all this had never happened. Then she came up to me, smiled at me and said softly: 'By God, cousin, I didn't say this to mock you or her, but I was distracted by a headache and I was thinking of having some blood let. Now my head and my forehead feel better and so tell me what happened to you today.' I told her the whole story and then burst into tears. 'There is good news for you, cousin,' she said, 'that you will succeed in your quest and achieve what you hope for, as this is a sign of acceptance. She stayed away from you because she wants to test you and to find out whether you can show patience or not, and whether you are really in love with her or not. Go to her tomorrow, to the place where you were to start with, and see what signs she makes to you, for joy is close at hand and your sorrows are nearly over.'

She started to console me for my disappointment, but my cares and sorrows increased. Then she brought me food, but I kicked out, knocking over all the bowls, and I said: 'Every lover is mad. He has no taste for food and no enjoyment of sleep.' 'Aziza said: 'By God, cousin, these are the signs of love.' She was weeping as she picked up the broken bits of the bowls and cleaned away the food. Then she sat talking to me throughout the night, while I was praying for dawn.

When morning came and the light spread, I set off to go to the lady and quickly got to the lane, where I sat down on the bench. Suddenly the window opened and she put her head out, laughing. She then disappeared but later came back with a mirror, a bag and a pot filled with green shoots. In her hand she was carrying a lamp, and the first thing she did was to take the mirror in her hand and put it in the bag, which she then tied shut and threw into the house. She let down her hair over her face and placed the lamp for a moment on top of the plants. Then, gathering up everything, she took it away and closed the window. My heart was broken by this, by the secret gestures and cryptic signs and by the fact that she had not spoken a single word to me, but as a result, the ardour of my passionate love intensified and grew stronger.

I retraced my steps, weeping and sorrowful at heart, until I got back home, where I saw my cousin seated with her face turned to the wall. Her heart was consumed by care, sorrow and jealousy, but her love kept her from telling me anything about the passion that she felt because she could see the extent of my own infatuation. When I looked at her, I saw that she was wearing two bandages, one because of the blow to her forehead and the other over her eyes because of the pain caused by the violence of her weeping. She was in the worst of states, shedding tears and reciting:

> I count the nights, one night after another,
> But for long I lived without counting them.
> I tell you, my companions, that I do not have
> What God decreed for Laila and for me.
> Destiny gave her to another, afflicting me with her love.
> Why did it not send me some other grief?

When she had finished these lines, she looked up and saw me through her tears. Wiping them away, she came up to me, but the extent of her emotion was such that she could not speak. After staying silent for some time, she asked me to tell her what had happened to me this time with the lady. I gave her a full account and she said: 'Show patience, for the time of your union is at hand and you will get what you are hoping for. When she gestured to you with the mirror and put it in the bag, she was telling you to wait till sunset. When she loosed her hair over her face, she was saying: "When night arrives and the fall of darkness overcomes the daylight, come." The plant pot was meant to tell you that when you do, you are to enter the garden behind the lane, and by using the lamp she was telling you that when you walk into the garden, make for the place where you see a lighted lamp, sit beneath it and wait for her, for your love is killing her.'

On hearing what my cousin had to say, I shouted out because of the vehemence of my passion and said: 'How many promises do you make me, yet when I go to her, I never get what I was hoping for? I don't think that your interpretations are right.' My cousin laughed and said: 'You only have to show patience for the rest of this day until it ends and night falls. Then you will obtain union and reach the goal of your hopes. This is true and not a lie.' Then she recited:

> Allow the days to pass away;
> Do not enter the house of care.
> The goal of many a difficult quest
> Is brought near by the hour of joy.

She then came up to me and started to console me with soft words, although she did not dare to bring me any food, for fear I might be angry with her. Hoping for my affection, all she did was to come to me and take off my robe, after which she said: 'Sit down, cousin, so that I can tell you stories to distract you until the day's end, for, if God Almighty wills it, when night falls you will be with your beloved.' I paid no attention to her but set about waiting for the coming of night, exclaiming: 'Oh my Lord, make night come soon!'

When it did come, my cousin wept bitterly. She gave me a globule of pure musk, saying 'Cousin, put this in your mouth, and when you have met your beloved and have had your way with her, after she has granted you what you wanted, recite these lines to her:

Lovers, by God, tell me:
What is the desperate one of you to do?'

She then kissed me and made me swear that I would not recite these lines until I was on the point of leaving the lady. I agreed to this and went out in the evening, walking on and on until I came to the garden. I found the gate open, and when I went in I could see a light in the distance. When I got there I found a large garden room vaulted over with a dome of ivory and ebony, in the middle of which hung a lamp. The room was furnished with silk carpets, embroidered with gold and silver, while in a golden candelabrum hanging beneath the lamp was a huge lighted candle. In the middle of the room was a fountain adorned with various carved figures and beside it was a table with a silken covering, flanked by a large china jug filled with wine, together with a crystal goblet ornamented with gold. Beside all this was a large silver bowl and when I removed its cover, I found that it contained fruits of all kinds – figs, pomegranates, grapes, oranges and various sorts of citrus fruit. Among these were sweet-smelling flowers, including roses, jasmine, myrtle, eglantine, narcissus and various scented herbs.

I was enchanted and overjoyed by the place, which served to dispel my cares and sorrows, except for the fact that not one of Almighty God's creatures was there.

Night 116

Morning now dawned and Shahrazad broke off from what she had been allowed to say. Then, when it was the one hundred and sixteenth night, SHE CONTINUED:

I have heard, O fortunate king, that THE YOUNG MAN TOLD TAJ
AL-MULUK:

I was enchanted and overjoyed by the place, except for the fact that
not one of Almighty God's creatures was there. There were no slaves,
male or female, to be seen, and there was no one in charge of the
arrangements or guarding the contents of the room. I sat waiting for the
arrival of my heart's darling until the first hour of the night had passed,
and then the second and the third, but she still did not come.

I was feeling very hungry as it was a long time since I had eaten, thanks
to the violence of my passion, but when I saw that place and realized
that my cousin had interpreted the gestures of my beloved correctly,
I relaxed and then experienced hunger pangs. My appetite had been
stimulated by the aroma of the food on the table when I got there, and
certain that I was going to achieve union, I felt a longing for something
to eat. So I went to the table, removed the covering and found in the
middle of it a china dish containing four chickens, roasted and seasoned
with spices. Set around the dish were four bowls containing a mixture
of sweet and sour, one with sweetmeats, another with pomegranate
seeds, a third with baqlava and a fourth with honey doughnuts. I ate
some of the doughnuts and a piece of the meat, and I then turned to the
baqlava and ate what I could. I went on to the sweetmeats and took a
spoonful, then two and three and four, which I followed with a mouthful
of chicken. My stomach was full and my joints relaxed. Sleeplessness
had made me sluggish and so, after washing my hands, I rested my head
on a cushion and was overcome by sleep.

I don't know what happened to me after that, and I only woke up
when the heat of the sun was scorching me, as it had been days since I
had slept. When I did wake it was to find salt and charcoal scattered
over my stomach. I stood up and shook out my clothes, looking to the
right and left but seeing no one, and I found that I had been sleeping on
the bare marble. Bewilderment filled me, together with great distress.
Tears ran down my cheeks and I got up, feeling sorry for myself, and
made for home. When I got there, I found my cousin striking her breast
with her hand and shedding enough tears to rival a rain cloud. She was
reciting:

The zephyr's breath flows from the guarded land,
And as it blows, it rouses love.
Come to us, breath of the east wind,

For every lover has his own allotted fate.
Could we control passion, we would embrace,
As the lover clasps the breast of his true love.
After my cousin's face, God has outlawed for me
All pleasures in this life that time can show.
I wish I knew whether his heart, like mine,
Is melting in the burning heat of love.

When she saw me, she got up quickly, wiping away her tears and approaching me with soft words. 'Cousin,' she said, 'God has shown you kindness in your love in that He has caused your beloved to love you, while I weep in sorrow for parting from you, who both blame me and excuse me, but may God not blame you for my sake.' She smiled at me, although with exasperation, spoke gently to me and removed my robe, which she spread out. 'By God,' she said, 'this is not the scent of one who has enjoyed his beloved, so tell me all that happened to you, cousin.' I told her the whole story, and again she smiled angrily, and said: 'My heart is full of pain, but may no one live who can distress you. This woman treats you with great haughtiness and, by God, cousin, she makes me afraid for you. The salt, you should know, means that you were sunk in sleep, like unpleasant food which causes disgust, and you have to be salted lest you be spat out. You claim to be a noble lover, but lovers are forbidden to sleep and so your claim is false. In the same way, her love for you is false, as she saw you sleeping and did not wake you, which she would have done had she really loved you. By the charcoal she means to say: "May God blacken your face, in that you have falsely claimed to be in love, while in fact you are a child who thinks only of eating, drinking and sleeping." This is what she meant – may God Almighty free you from her.'

When I heard what she had to say, I struck my breast with my hand and said: 'By God, it is true; I slept, although lovers do not sleep. I wronged myself and how could I have done myself more harm than by eating and falling asleep? What am I to do?' Weeping bitterly, I asked my cousin: 'Tell me what to do. Have pity on me that God may pity you, for otherwise I shall die.' My cousin, being deeply in love with me . . .

Night 117

Morning now dawned and Shahrazad broke off from what she had been allowed to say. Then, when it was the one hundred and seventeenth night, SHE CONTINUED:

I have heard, O fortunate king, that THE YOUNG MAN TOLD TAJ AL-MULUK:

I asked my cousin: 'Tell me what to do. Have pity on me that God may pity you.' My cousin, being deeply in love with me, agreed to do this, but she added: 'I have told you many times that if I could go in and out as I pleased I would quickly bring the two of you together and take you under my protection, simply in order to please you. If God Almighty wills it, I shall do my best to unite you, but listen to what I say and obey me. Go back to the same place in the evening and sit where you were before. Take care not to eat anything, for eating induces sleep and you must not sleep. She will not come until the first quarter of the night has passed – may God protect you from her evil.'

Gladdened by hearing what she had to say, I started to pray God to bring on night. When it came, I was about to go out when my cousin reminded me that after my meeting with the lady, when I was about to leave, I was to quote the lines that she had recited earlier. I agreed to this and when I went to the garden, I found the place prepared in the same way that it had been on the first occasion, with all the necessary food and drink, dried fruits, sweet-smelling flowers, and so on. I went to the room and was attracted by what I could smell of the aroma of food. I restrained myself several times, but at last I could not resist and so I got up and went to the table. I lifted the cover and found a plate of chicken, surrounded by four bowls containing four different types of food. I took a mouthful of each and then I ate what I wanted of the sweetmeats, followed by a piece of meat. I tasted a saffron sorbet which I liked, and I drank a quantity of it with a spoon until I had had enough and my stomach was full. My eyelids closed and, taking a cushion, I placed it under my head, saying: 'I will rest on it but I shall not sleep.' Then I closed my eyes and fell asleep, not waking until the sun had risen.

On my stomach I found a large dice cube, a *tab* stick,* a date stone and a carob seed. There were no furnishings in the place or indeed

---

* A stick used in a children's game.

anything else, and it looked as though there had never been anything there the night before. I got up, brushed off what was on me and left in anger, and when I got back home, I found my cousin once again sighing deeply, and reciting these lines:

An emaciated body and a wounded heart,
With tears that flood down over cheeks,
A lover whose love is hard to harvest,
But all that beauties do is beautiful.
Cousin, you have filled my heart with passion
And my eyes' wounds are caused by tears.

I reproached her and scolded her, and she wept. Then, wiping away her tears, she came to me, kissed me and clasped me to her breast. I kept my distance from her, however, reproaching myself, and she said: 'It seems as though you went to sleep again, cousin.' 'Yes,' I replied, 'but when I woke up, I found a large dice cube, a *tab* stick, a date stone and a carob seed, and I don't know why she did this.' I then burst into tears and, going up to her, I asked her to interpret the signs for me, to tell me what I should do and to help me in my predicament. 'Willingly,' she replied. 'By the *tab* stick which she placed on your stomach she means to say that although you were present your heart was absent, and she is telling you that love is not like that and you are not to count yourself among the lovers. With the date stone she is telling you that, were you a lover, your heart would be consumed by passion and you would not enjoy the pleasure of sleep, for the pleasure of love is like a date which sets light to a coal in the heart. As for the carob seed, she is telling you that the lover's heart endures weariness, and she is saying: "Face separation from me with the patience of Job."'

When I heard this interpretation, fire spread through my heart and I became more and more sorrowful. I cried out, saying: 'God decreed that I should sleep because of my ill fortune,' and then I said: 'Cousin, by my life, I implore you to think of some scheme that will allow me to get to her.' Weeping, she said: ''Aziz, my cousin, my heart is so full of thoughts that I cannot speak, but if you go there tonight and take care not to sleep, you will get what you want. This is all the advice that I can give.' 'God willing, I shall not sleep,' I replied, 'and I shall do as you tell me.' So 'Aziza got up and fetched food, saying: 'Eat as much as you want now, so you won't have to think of it later.' I ate my fill and when night came, 'Aziza got up and brought me a splendid robe which she made me wear, and she got me to swear that I would quote to the lady the lines that she mentioned earlier. She also cautioned me again against sleeping, and I then left her and set off for the garden.

When I got to the room, I looked out at the garden and started to prop open my eyes with my fingers, shaking my head as it grew dark.

Night 118

Morning now dawned and Shahrazad broke off from what she had been allowed to say. Then, when it was the one hundred and eighteenth night, SHE CONTINUED:

I have heard, O fortunate king, that THE YOUNG MAN TOLD TAJ AL-MULUK:

I came to the garden and reached the room. Then I looked out at the garden and started to prop open my eyes with my fingers, shaking my head as it grew dark. Sleeplessness, however, had made me hungry and this hunger grew worse as the aroma of food wafted over me. So I went to the table, removed the covering and ate a mouthful of every sort of food that there was, together with a piece of meat. Then I went to the wine jug, telling myself that I would drink one glass, which I did, but I followed this with a second and a third, up to a total of ten, and when a breath of wind blew over me, I collapsed on the ground like a dead man. I stayed like that until daybreak, and when I came to my senses, I found myself outside the garden with a sharp knife and an iron dirham lying on my stomach. I shuddered and, taking the things with me, I went back home.

There I found my cousin weeping and saying: 'I am wretched and unhappy in this house and my only help is in tears.' As soon as I entered, I fell down at full length in a faint, with the knife and the dirham falling from my hand. When I had recovered, I told her what had happened to me and that I had not achieved my goal. Her sorrow increased when she saw my passionate tears, and she said: 'There is nothing that I can do. I advised you not to sleep, but you didn't listen, so what I say is of no use to you at all.' 'By God,' I said to her, 'explain to me the meaning of the knife and the iron dirham.' She replied: 'By the iron dirham, she means her right eye, and she is taking an oath by it, saying: "By the Lord of creation, and by my right eye, if you come back again and fall asleep, I shall use this knife to cut your throat." Her cunning makes me afraid for you, cousin, and my heart is so full of sorrow for you that I cannot speak. If you are sure that you will not fall asleep if you go back, then go, and if you guard against sleep, you will get what you want, but if after going back you fall asleep as usual, be sure that she will cut your throat.'

'What am I to do, then, cousin?' I asked. 'For God's sake, help me in this misfortune.' 'Willingly,' she replied, 'but I will only see your affair through if you listen to what I have to say and obey me.' When I agreed that I would do this, she said: 'I shall tell you when it is time to go,' and, taking me in her arms, she placed me on the bed and continued to massage me until I was overcome by drowsiness and fell fast asleep. She took a fan and sat by my head, fanning my face until the end of the day. She then woke me up, and when I was roused, I found her sitting by my head, fan in hand, weeping. The tears had dampened her dress. When she saw that I was awake, she wiped them away and brought me some food. When I refused this, she said: 'Didn't I tell you to listen to me? Eat,' and so I ate obediently. She started to put the food in my mouth and I chewed it until I was full. Then she gave me sugared jujube juice to drink; she washed my hands and dried them with a kerchief, after which she sprinkled me with rosewater and I sat with her, feeling in perfect health. When night fell, she gave me my robe to put on and said: 'Cousin, stay awake for the whole night and don't go to sleep. She will not come until the last part of the night, and if it is God's will, you will be united with her, but don't forget my instructions.' Then she wept, and I was pained at heart by all those tears of hers and I asked what instructions they were that she meant. 'When you leave her,' she said, 'recite the lines that I quoted to you earlier.'

I then left cheerfully and went to the garden, where I went up to the room and sat down, feeling sated and staying wakeful for the first quarter of the night. I sat there for what seemed like a year, but I still stayed awake until three quarters of it had gone and the cocks had crowed. This prolonged wakefulness made me very hungry, so I got up and went to the table, where I ate my fill. My head felt heavy and I was about to fall asleep when I saw a light approaching from a distance. I got up, washed my hands and my mouth and roused myself. It was not long before the lady came, surrounded by ten slave girls, like a moon among stars. She was wearing a dress of green satin, embroidered with red gold. She was as the poet has described:

She comes walking proudly to her lovers dressed in green,
With buttons undone and her hair unloosed.
'What is your name?' I asked her and she said:
'I am she who has burned lovers' hearts on coals of fire.'
I complained to her of love's hardships I endured;
She said: 'In your ignorance you complain to rock.'
'Although your heart be rock,' I said,
'Yet God has brought pure water out of rock.'

When she saw me, she laughed and said: 'How is it that you are awake and have not been overcome by sleep? Since you have been wakeful all night, I realize that you are a lover, for it is a characteristic of lovers that they pass sleepless nights, enduring the pains of longing.' She then went up to her slave girls and gestured to them, after which they left her. She came to me, clasped me to her breast and kissed me. I kissed her and, when she sucked my upper lip, I kissed her lower lip. I stretched out my hand to her waist and squeezed it and we both came to the ground at the same time. She undid her drawers, which slipped down to her anklets. We started our love play, with embraces, coquetry, soft words, bites, twining of legs, and a circumambulation of the House and its corners. This went on until her joints relaxed and she fainted away, losing consciousness. That night was a delight to the heart and joy to the eye, as the poet has said:

For me the pleasantest of all nights was the one
In which I did not let the wine cup slacken in its work.
I kept my eyelids from their sleep
And joined the girl's earring to her anklet.

We slept together until morning. I then wanted to leave, but she held me back and said: 'Stay, so that I can tell you something . . .'

Night 119

Morning now dawned and Shahrazad broke off from what she had been allowed to say. Then, when it was the one hundred and nineteenth night, SHE CONTINUED:

I have heard, O fortunate king, that THE YOUNG MAN TOLD TAJ AL-MULUK:

I was about to leave, but she held me back and said: 'Stay, so that I can tell you something and give you instructions.' So I stopped and she undid a knotted kerchief and took out this piece of material, which she unfolded in front of me and on which I found a gazelle pictured like this. I was filled with admiration for it and I took it, arranging with her that I should come to her every night in that garden. Then I left her, being full of joy, and in my joy I forgot the lines of poetry which my cousin had told me to recite. When the lady gave me the material with the picture of the gazelle, she had told me that this was her sister's work, and when I asked her sister's name, she said 'Nur al-Huda'. She told me to keep the piece of material, after which I said goodbye to her and left joyfully.

I walked back and went in to find my cousin lying down, but when she saw me she got up, shedding tears, and coming up to me she kissed my chest. Then she asked whether I had recited the lines as she had told me, but I said: 'I forgot it, but what distracted my attention was this gazelle,' and I threw down the piece of material in front of her. She became very agitated and, being unable to control herself, she shed tears and recited these lines:

> You, who seek for separation, go slowly,
> And do not be deceived by an embrace.
> Go slowly; Time's nature is treacherous;
> The end of companionship lies in parting.

When she had finished these lines, she asked me to give her the material, which I did, and she spread it out and read what was written on it. When the time came for me to go, she said: 'Go in safety, cousin, and when you leave her, recite the lines that I told you earlier and which you forgot.' 'Repeat them,' I asked her, and so she did, after which I went to the garden, entered the room and found the girl waiting for me. When she saw me, she got up, kissed me and made me sit on her lap. We then ate, drank and satisfied our desires as before. When morning came, I recited to her the lines:

> Lovers, by God, tell me:
> What is the desperate one of you to do?

On hearing this, her eyes brimmed over with tears and she recited:

> He must conceal his love and hide his secret,
> Showing patience and humility in all he does.

I memorized this, pleased to think that I had performed the task set by my cousin. So I left and went back to her, but I found her lying down with my mother by her head, weeping over the state that she was in. When I entered, my mother reproached me for having left my cousin in poor health without asking what was wrong with her. When she saw me, my cousin raised her head, sat up and said: ''Aziz, did you recite to her the lines that I told you?' 'Yes,' I replied, 'and when she heard them, she wept and recited other lines for me, which I memorized.' My cousin asked me to tell them to her and, when I did, she wept bitterly and produced these lines:

How can the young man hide it, when love kills him,
And every day his heart is breaking?
He tried to show fair patience but could only find
A heart that love had filled up with unease.

Then my cousin said: 'When you go to her as usual, recite these lines that you have heard.' 'To hear is to obey,' I said, and, as usual, I went to the girl in the garden and no tongue could describe the pleasure that we had. When I was on the point of leaving, I recited the lines to her, and, on hearing them, her eyes brimmed over with tears and she recited:

If he finds no patience to conceal his secret,
Nothing will serve him better than to die.

I memorized the lines and set off home, but when I went in to see my cousin, I found her lying unconscious, with my mother sitting by her head. On hearing my voice, she opened her eyes and said: ''Aziz, did you recite the lines to her?' 'Yes,' I said, 'and when she heard them, she wept and recited a couplet, beginning: "If he finds no patience."' On hearing this, my cousin fainted again, and when she had recovered, she recited these lines:

I have heard, obeyed and now I die;
So greet the one who stopped this union.
May the fortunate enjoy their happiness,
While the sad lover has to drain the glass.

When night came, I went as usual to the garden, where I found the girl waiting for me. We sat down and ate and drank, made love and then slept until morning. Before leaving, I recited my cousin's lines, and when she heard them, the girl gave a loud cry of sorrow and said: 'Oh, oh, by

God, the one who spoke these lines is dead!' Then, in tears, she asked me whether that person was related to me, to which I replied that she was my cousin. 'That is a lie, by God,' said the girl. 'If she had been your cousin, you would have loved her as much as she loved you. It is you who have killed her – may God kill you in the same way! By God, had you told me that you had a cousin, I would never have allowed you near me.' I said: 'She used to interpret for me the signs that you made to me; it was she who taught me how to reach you and to deal with you, and but for her I would never have got to you.' 'Did she know about us?' she asked, and when I said yes, she said: 'May God cause you to regret your youth as you have caused her to regret hers!' Then she added: 'Go and see her.'

So I left in a disturbed state and walked on until, reaching our lane, I heard cries of grief. When I asked about this, I was told: 'We found 'Aziza lying dead behind the door.' I went into the house and when my mother saw me, she said: 'It is you who are responsible for her loss and the guilt is all yours – may God not forgive you for her blood!'

Night 120

Morning now dawned and Shahrazad broke off from what she had been allowed to say. Then, when it was the one hundred and twentieth night, SHE CONTINUED:

I have heard, O fortunate king, that THE YOUNG MAN TOLD TAJ AL-MULUK:

I went into the house and when my mother saw me, she said: 'It is you who are responsible for her loss and the guilt is all yours – may God not forgive you for her blood! What a bad cousin you are!' My father then came and we prepared 'Aziza for her funeral and then brought her out, accompanying her bier and burying her. We arranged for recitations of the whole Quran to be given over her grave, and we stayed there for three days before returning and going home.

I was grieving for her when my mother came to me and said: 'I want to know what you were doing to 'Aziza to break her heart. I kept on asking her about the cause of her illness but she wouldn't tell me anything. I conjure you in God's Name to let me know how it was that you led her to her death.' 'I didn't do anything,' I replied.

'May God avenge her on you,' she said, 'for she told me nothing and

concealed the matter from me until the time of her death. She approved
of you; I was with her when she died and she opened her eyes and said:
"Aunt, may God not hold your son responsible for my death and may
He not punish him for what he has done to me. God has moved me from
the lower world of transience to the eternal world." "Daughter," I said,
"may you enjoy your youth in well-being," and I started to ask what
had caused her illness. At first she said nothing, but then she smiled and
said: "Aunt, tell your son that if he wants to go to the place where he
goes every day, when he leaves he is to say: 'Loyalty is good; treachery
is bad.' In this I am showing pity for him, so that I may be seen to have
been sympathetic to him both in my life and after my death." Then she
gave me something for you and made me swear that I would not hand
it over to you until I had seen you weeping for her and mourning her. I
have the thing with me and when I see you doing what she said, I shall
give it to you.'

I told her to show it to me, but she refused, and I then occupied myself
with my own pleasures, with no thought of my cousin's death, because
I was light-headed with love and wanted to spend every night and day
with my beloved. As soon as I was certain that night had come, I went
to the garden and found the girl sitting waiting for me, on fire with
anxiety. As soon as she saw me, she embraced me, hugging me round
the neck and asking me about my cousin. 'She is dead,' I replied, 'and
we held a *dhikr* ceremony for her, as well as recitations of the Quran.
She died four nights ago and this is the fifth.' When the girl heard this,
she cried out and wept. Then she said: 'It was you who killed her and
had you told me about her before her death, I would have repaid her for
the good that she did me. For she did me a service by bringing you to
me. Had it not been for her, the two of us would never have met and I
am afraid that some disaster may strike you because of her wrongful
death.' I told her: 'Before her death she absolved me from blame,' and
then I repeated for her what my mother had told me. She then conjured
me in God's Name to go to my mother and find out what 'the thing' was
that she was holding. I said: 'My mother told me that before she died
my cousin had given her instructions, saying: "When your son is about
to go to the place that he is in the habit of visiting, quote these two
sayings to him: 'Loyalty is good; treachery is bad.' " ' When the girl heard
this, she said: 'May God Almighty have mercy on her. She has saved you
from me, for I had intended to harm you and now I shall not, nor shall
I stir up trouble for you.'

I was surprised by this and asked what she had been intending to do to me before hearing these words, in view of the love that we had shared. She said: 'You are in love with me, but you are young and simple, and there is no deceit in your heart, so you don't know our wiles and our deceitfulness. Had your cousin lived, she would have helped you, for it is she who has saved you and preserved you from destruction. I advise you now not to speak to any woman and not to talk with any of us, young or old. Beware, beware, for in your inexperience you know nothing of the deceit of women and their wiles. The one who used to interpret signs for you is dead and I am afraid that you may meet with a disaster from which you will find no one to save you, now that your cousin is dead.'

Night 121

Morning now dawned and Shahrazad broke off from what she had been allowed to say. Then, when it was the one hundred and twenty-first night, SHE CONTINUED:

I have heard, O fortunate king, that THE YOUNG MAN TOLD TAJ AL-MULUK:

The girl told me that she was afraid that I would meet with a disaster from which no one would save me. 'Alas for her! I wish that I had known her before her death, so that I might have repaid her for the good that she did me, and visited her – may Almighty God have mercy on her. She kept her secret hidden and did not reveal her feelings. Had it not been for her, you would never have got to me.' She then said that she wanted me to do something, and when I asked what it was, she said: 'I want you to take me to her tomb, so that I may visit her in her grave and write some verses on it.' 'Tomorrow, God willing,' I replied. Then I slept with her that night, and after every hour she would say: 'I wish you had told me about your cousin before her death.' I asked her about the meaning of the two sayings: 'Loyalty is good; treachery is bad,' but she did not reply.

In the morning, she got up and, taking a purse with some dinars in it, she said: 'Get up and show me her grave so that I may visit it and inscribe these verses. I shall have a dome made over it, pray God have mercy on her, and I shall spend this money on alms for her soul.' 'To hear is to obey,' I said, and we walked off, I in front and she behind me, and as she walked she kept distributing alms, saying every time she did so:

'These are alms for the soul of 'Aziza, who kept her secret hidden, without revealing her love, until she drank the cup of death.' She kept on giving away money from her purse and saying: 'This is for the soul of 'Aziza,' until the purse was empty.

We came to the grave and when she saw it, she burst into tears and threw herself down on it. Then she produced a steel chisel and a light hammer, and with the chisel she carved on the headstone of the grave in small letters the following lines:

> In a garden I passed a dilapidated grave,
> On which grew seven red anemones.
> 'Whose is this grave?' I asked. The earth replied:
> 'Show respect; this is a lover's resting place.'
> I said: 'God guard you, you who died of love,
> And may He house you in the topmost heights of Paradise.
> How sad it is for lovers, that among mankind
> Their graves are covered by the soil of lowliness.
> If I could, I would plant a garden around you
> And water it with my flowing tears.'

She then left in tears and I went with her to the garden. 'Never leave me,' she said, 'I conjure by God.' 'To hear is to obey,' I replied, and I devoted myself to her, visiting her again and again. Whenever I spent the night with her, she would be kind to me and treat me well. She would ask me about the two sayings which my cousin 'Aziza had quoted to my mother and I would repeat them to her. Things went on like this with food and drink, embraces and hugs and changes of fine clothes, until I grew stout and fat. I had no cares or sorrows and I had forgotten my cousin.

This went on for a whole year. At the start of the new year, I went to the baths, groomed myself and put on a splendid suit of clothes. On coming out, I drank a cup of wine and sniffed at the scents coming from my clothes, impregnated as they were with various types of perfume. I was relaxed, not knowing the treachery of Time and the disasters that it brings. In the evening, I felt the urge to visit the girl, but I was drunk and didn't know where I was heading. I set off on my way to her but in my drunkenness I strayed into what was called the Naqib's Lane. While I was walking there, I suddenly saw an old woman walking with a lighted candle in one hand and, in the other, a folded letter.

Night 122

Morning now dawned and Shahrazad broke off from what she had been allowed to say. Then, when it was the one hundred and twenty-second night, SHE CONTINUED:

I have heard, O fortunate king, that THE YOUNG MAN TOLD TAJ AL-MULUK:

When I entered the Naqib's Lane, I caught sight of an old woman walking with a lighted candle in one hand and, in the other, a folded letter. I went up to her and found that she was weeping and reciting these lines:

Greetings and welcome to the messenger who brings news of
      consent;
How sweet and pleasant are the words you bear,
Sent as you are by one whose greeting is dear to me;
May God's peace rest on you as long as east winds blow!

When she saw me, she said: 'My son, can you read?' Inquisitiveness prompted me to reply: 'Yes, old aunt.' 'Take this letter, then,' she said, 'and read it for me.' She handed it to me and I took it from her, opened it up and read it to her. It contained greetings sent by the writer from a distant land to his loved ones. When the old woman heard this, she was happy and delighted; she blessed me and said: 'May God banish your cares as you have banished mine.' She took back the letter and walked on for a little. My bladder was overfull and I squatted down to relieve myself, after which I got up again, wiped myself, and after arranging my clothes, I was about to walk on when the old woman suddenly came back, bowed her head over my hand and kissed it. 'Master,' she said, 'may God allow you to enjoy your youth. I hope that you will walk a few steps with me to that door there. I told them what you said to me when you read the letter, but they didn't believe me. So walk a little way with me and read out the letter for them from behind the door, and accept my devout prayers.'

'What is the story behind this letter?' I asked. 'Master,' she replied, 'it comes from my son, who has been away for ten years. He went off to trade and stayed so long in foreign parts that we had abandoned hope of him and thought that he must be dead, until, some time ago, this letter came from him. He has a sister who has been weeping for him night and day. I told her that all was well with him but she didn't believe me and told me: "You must fetch someone to read the letter in my presence, so that I may be reassured and happy." You know, my son, that lovers are prone to suspicion, so do me the favour of going with me and reading her the letter. You can stand behind the curtain and I will call his sister to listen from inside the door. In this way you will free us from anxiety and fulfil our need. The Apostle of God – may God bless him and give him peace – said: "If anyone relieves an anxious man of one anxiety in this world, God will relieve him of a hundred," while another *hadith* says: "Whoever relieves his brother of one anxiety in this world, God will relieve him of seventy-two on the Day of Judgement." I have sought you out, so please don't disappoint me.'

I agreed and told her to lead the way, which she did, with me following behind. We went a little way before arriving at the door of a fine, large house, the door itself being plated with copper. I stood behind it, while the old woman called out in Persian and before I knew what was happening, a girl came out lightly and briskly, with her dress tucked up to her knees. I saw a pair of legs that bewildered thought and sight. She was as the poet described:

> You gird up your dress to show lovers your legs,
> So they may understand what the rest of you is like.
> You hurry to fetch a glass for the lover;
> It is the glass and the legs that capture them.

These legs, like twin pillars of marble, were adorned with golden anklets set with gems. Her outer robe was bunched up beneath her armpits, and her sleeves were drawn back from her forearms so that I could see her white wrists. On her arms were two bracelets, fastened with large pearls; round her neck she wore a necklace of precious gems; she had pearl earrings and on her head was a brocaded kerchief studded with precious stones. She had tucked the ends of her skirt into her waistband as though she had been busy with some task, and when I saw her, I stared in astonishment at what looked like the bright sun. In a clear, pleasant voice – I had never heard a sweeter – she asked: 'Mother, is this the man who has come to read the letter?' 'Yes,' said her mother, and so the girl stretched out her hand to me with the letter in it. She was standing some six feet or so from the door, and when I put out my hand to take the letter from her, I put my head and shoulders inside the door to get nearer her in order to read it.

As I took the letter in my hand, all of a sudden the old woman butted me in the back with her head, and before I knew what was happening, I found myself inside the hallway. Quicker than a flash of lightning, the old woman came in and the first thing she did was to lock the door.

Night 123

Morning now dawned and Shahrazad broke off from what she had been allowed to say. Then, when it was the one hundred and twenty-third night, SHE CONTINUED:

I have heard, O fortunate king, that THE YOUNG MAN TOLD TAJ AL-MULUK:

The old woman butted me and before I knew it I was inside the hall. Quicker than lightning, the old woman came in and the first thing she did was to lock the door. The girl, seeing me in the hallway, came up to me and clasped me to her breast. She then threw me down on the ground and straddled my chest, pressing my stomach with her hands until I almost lost my senses. She took my hand and the violence of her embrace was such that I couldn't free myself. The old woman then went ahead of us, carrying a lighted candle, as the girl took me through seven halls, bringing me at last to a large chamber with four galleries, big enough to serve as a polo ground.

She let me go and told me to open my eyes. I was still dizzy from the strength of her embraces, but I opened my eyes and I saw that the whole chamber had been built of the finest marble, and all its furnishings were of silk or brocade, as were the cushions and the coverings. There were two brass benches and a couch of red gold set with pearls and gems, together with other parlours and a princely chamber fit only for a king such as you.

The girl then said to me: ' 'Aziz, which do you prefer – death or life?' 'Life,' I said. 'In that case,' she replied, 'marry me.' 'I don't want to marry someone like you,' I objected, but she went on: 'If you marry me, you will be safe from the daughter of Delilah the wily.' When I asked who this might be, she laughed and said: 'The girl with whom you have now been keeping company for a year and four months – may God Almighty destroy her and afflict her with someone worse than herself! By God, there is no one more cunning than she. How many people has she killed already and what deeds she has done! How is it that you have escaped after such a long time in her company without her killing you or plunging you into confusion?'

Astonished by this, I asked her how she knew the girl. 'I know her as Time knows its calamities,' she replied, and she went on to ask me to tell her everything that had happened between us so that she could find out how I had managed to escape unharmed. I told her the full story of my dealings with the girl and with my cousin 'Aziza. She invoked God's pity on 'Aziza, shedding tears and striking her hands together at the news of her death and exclaiming: 'She sacrificed her youth in the path of God, and may He compensate you well for her loss! By God, 'Aziz, she died and it was because of her that you were saved from the daughter of Delilah the wily, for had it not been for her you would have perished. I am afraid that you may still fall victim to her evil wiles, but my mouth is blocked and I am silenced.' 'Yes, by God,' I told her, 'all this happened.' She shook her head, saying: 'There is no one now to match 'Aziza.' I replied: 'On her deathbed she told me to quote these two sayings, and nothing else, to the girl: "Loyalty is good; treachery is bad."' On hearing this, the girl said: ''Aziz, these are the two sayings that saved you from being killed by her, and now I am reassured about you, for she is not going to kill you, as your cousin has saved you both in life and in death. By God, day after day I have been wanting you, but it is only now, when I played a successful trick on you, that I have been able to get you. For you are still inexperienced, and you don't know the wiles of young women and the disasters brought about by old ones.'

I agreed with this and she told me that I could be cheerful and happy, 'For the dead have found God's mercy and the living will meet with kindness. You are a handsome young man and I only want you in accordance with the law of God and His Apostle – may God bless him and give him peace. Whatever money or materials you may want will be quickly brought to you; I shall not impose any tasks on you; in my house there is always bread baking and water in the jug. All I want you to do with me is what the cock does.' 'What is it that the cock does?' I asked. She clapped her hands and laughed so much that she fell over backwards. Then she sat up, smiled and said: 'Light of my eyes, do you really not know what the cock does?' 'No, by God, I don't,' I replied. 'His business is eating, drinking and copulating,' she said. I was embarrassed by this and said: 'Is that really so?' 'Yes,' she replied, 'and I want you to gird yourself, strengthen your resolve and copulate as hard as you can.'

She then clapped her hands and said: 'Mother, bring out the people who are with you.' The old woman then came forward with four notaries, bringing with her a piece of silk. She lit four candles and the notaries greeted me and took their seats. The girl got up and veiled herself, after which she empowered one of the notaries to act for her in drawing up the marriage contract. This was written down and she testified on her own behalf that she had received her whole dowry, both the first and the second payment, and that she was holding for me the sum of ten thousand dirhams.

Night 124

Morning now dawned and Shahrazad broke off from what she had been allowed to say. Then, when it was the one hundred and twenty-fourth night, SHE CONTINUED:

I have heard, O fortunate king, that THE YOUNG MAN TOLD TAJ AL-MULUK:

When the marriage contract was drawn up, she testified on her own behalf that she had received her whole dowry, both the first and the second payment, and that she was holding for me the sum of ten thousand dirhams. She then paid the notaries their fees and they went back to where they had come from. After that she got up, and after taking off her outer clothes, she came forward in a delicate chemise, embroidered with gold. She then pulled off her drawers and, taking me by the hand, she got up on top of the couch with me. 'There is no shame in what is legal,' she said, as she lay there, spreading herself out on her back. Dragging me down on to her breast, she moaned and followed the moan with a coquettish wriggle. She then pulled up her chemise above her breasts and when I saw her like that I could not restrain myself. I thrust into her, after sucking her lip. She cried 'Oh!' and pretended tearful submissiveness, but without shedding tears. 'Do it, my darling,' she said, reminding me as she did so of the poet's lines:

When she lifted her dress to show her private parts,
I found what was as narrow as my patience and my livelihood.
I put it half in and she sighed.
'Why this sigh?' I asked, and she said: 'For the rest.'

'Finish off, darling,' she said. 'I am your slave. Please, give me all of it; give it to me so that I can take it in my hand and put it right into me.'

She kept on uttering love cries, with tears and moans, while kissing and embracing me, until, as the noise we were making approached its climax, we achieved our happiness and fulfilment. We slept until morning, when I wanted to go out, but she came up to me laughing and said: 'Oh, oh, do you think that to enter the baths is the same as to leave them? You seem to think that I am like the daughter of Delilah the wily. Beware of any such thought. You are my lawfully wedded husband, and if you are drunk you had better sober up, for the house where you are is only open on one day in the year. Go and look at the great door.'

I went to it and found that it had been nailed shut, and when I returned and told her that, she said: ' 'Aziz, we have enough flour, grain, fruit, pomegranates, sugar, meat, sheep, poultry and so on to last for many years. The door will not be opened until a year from now, and up till then you will not find yourself outside this house.' I recited the formula: 'There is no might and no power except with God,' and she replied: 'What harm will this do you when you remember what I told you about of the work of the cock?' She laughed and I joined in her laughter. In obedience to her instructions, I stayed with her, acting the part of the cock – eating, drinking and copulating – until twelve months had passed. By the end of the year, she had conceived and given birth to my son.

At the start of the new year, I heard the sound of the door being opened and found men bringing in sweet cakes, flour and sugar. I was on the point of going out when my wife said to me: 'Wait until evening and go out in the same way that you came in.' So I waited and was again about to go out, despite being nervous and frightened, when she said to me: 'By God, I am not going to let you out until I have made you swear that you will come back tonight before the door is closed.' I agreed to this and swore a solemn oath by the sword, the Quran and the promise of divorce that I would come back to her. I then left her and went to the garden, which I found open as usual. I was angry and said to myself: 'I have been absent from here for a whole year and yet when I come unexpectedly I find it open as usual. I wonder if the girl is still as she was before or not. It is now evening and I must go in to see before I go to my mother.' So I entered the garden . . .

Night 125

Morning now dawned and Shahrazad broke off from what she had been allowed to say. Then, when it was the one hundred and twenty-fifth night, SHE CONTINUED:

I have heard, O fortunate king, that THE YOUNG MAN TOLD TAJ AL-MULUK:

I entered the garden and went to the garden room, where I found the daughter of Delilah the wily seated with her head on her knees and her hand on her cheek. Her colour had changed and her eyes were sunken, but when she saw me she exclaimed: 'Praise be to God that you are safe!' She wanted to get up but in her joy she collapsed. I was ashamed and hung my head, but then I went up to her, kissed her and asked: 'How did you know that I was going to come to you tonight?' 'I didn't know,' she replied, adding: 'By God, it is a year since I enjoyed the taste of sleep, for every night I have stayed awake waiting for you. I have been like this since the day you left me. I had given you new clothes and you had promised me that you would go to the baths and then come back. I sat waiting for you on the first night, and then the second and then the third, but it is only after this time that you have come, although I have always been expecting you, in the way that lovers do. I want you to tell me why you left me all this year.'

I told her the story and when she heard that I was married, she turned pale. Then I said to her: 'I have come to you tonight but I have to go before daybreak.' 'Wasn't it enough for her,' she said, 'to have tricked you and married you, and imprisoned you with her for a year, that she made you swear by the promise of divorce to go back to her this same night before daybreak and she could not find the generosity to allow you to spend time with your mother or with me? She couldn't bear the thought of your passing the night with either of us, away from her. How about the one whom you abandoned for a whole year, although I knew you before her? May God have mercy on your cousin 'Aziza. No one else experienced what she did and she suffered what no one else could endure. She died because of the treatment to which you subjected her, and it is she who protected you from me. I thought you loved me and I let you go on your way, although I could have seen to it that you didn't leave unscathed, or I could have kept you as a prisoner or killed you.'

Then she wept bitterly, shuddering with rage, looking at me with angry eyes. When I saw the state she was in, I trembled in fear; she was like a terrifying *ghul* and I was like a bean placed on a fire. 'You are no use any more,' she told me, 'now that you are married and have a child. You are no longer suitable company for me; only bachelors are of use, while married men serve no purpose for me at all. You sold me for a bundle of filth and I am going to make that whore sorry, as you won't be here, either for me or for her.'

She gave a loud cry, and before I knew what was happening, ten slave girls had come and thrown me on the ground. While they held me down, she got up, took a knife and said: 'I am going to cut your throat as one would kill a goat, and this is the least repayment you can expect for what you did to me and to your cousin before me.' When I saw the position I was in, held down by the slave girls, with my cheeks rubbed in the dust, and the knife being sharpened, I was sure that I was going to die.

Night 126

Morning now dawned and Shahrazad broke off from what she had been allowed to say. Then, when it was the one hundred and twenty-sixth night, SHE CONTINUED:

I have heard, O fortunate king, that the vizier Dandan told Dau' al-Makan that THE YOUNG MAN SAID TO TAJ AL-MULUK:

I found myself held down by the slave girls, with my cheeks rubbed in the dust and the knife being sharpened. Certain that I was going to die, I implored her to help me, but this only added to her mercilessness. She told the slave girls to pinion me, which they did, and they threw me on my back, sitting on my stomach and holding my head. Two of them sat on my shins while another two held my hands, and their mistress then came up with two more, whom she ordered to beat me. They did this until I lost consciousness and could not speak, and when I recovered I said to myself: 'It would be better for me to have my throat cut as this would be easier to bear than this beating.' I remembered that my cousin had been in the habit of saying: 'May God protect you from her evil,' and I shrieked and wept until my voice failed me and I was left without feeling or breath.

She sharpened the knife and told her girls to bare my throat. Then God inspired me to quote the two sayings that my cousin had told me and recommended to me, and so I said: 'My lady, don't you know that loyalty is good and treachery is evil?' On hearing this, she cried out and said: 'May God have mercy on you, 'Aziza, and reward you with Paradise in exchange for your youth.' Then she said to me: ''Aziza helped you both in her lifetime and after her death, and by these two sayings she has saved you from me. But I cannot let you go like this; I must leave a mark on you in order to hurt that shameless whore who has kept you away from me.'

She called out to her girls, telling them to tie my legs with rope and after that to sit on top of me, which they did. She left me and fetched a copper pan, which she put on top of a brazier. She poured in sesame oil and fried some cheese in it. I knew nothing of what was happening until she came up to me, undid my trousers and tied a rope round my testicles. She held the rope, but then gave it to two of her slave girls, telling them to pull. They both pulled and I fainted with the pain, losing all touch with this world. She then came with a steel razor and cut off my penis, so that I was left like a woman, and, while I was still unconscious, she cauterized the wound and rubbed it with powder.

When I came to my senses, the flow of blood had stopped and she told the slave girls to untie me. Then, after giving me a cup of wine to drink, she said: 'You can go now to the one whom you married and who grudged me one single night. May God have mercy on your cousin, who is the reason why you have escaped with your life. She never revealed her secret, and if you had not quoted her two sayings, I would have cut your throat. Go off now to anyone you want. There is nothing that I needed from you except what I have cut off. You have nothing more for me, and I neither want you or need you. Get up, touch your head and invoke God's mercy on your cousin.' She then kicked me and I got up, but I could not walk properly and so I moved very slowly to the door of my house, which I found open. I threw myself down there in a faint and my wife came out and carried me into the hall, where she found that I had been emasculated. I fell into a deep sleep and when had I recovered my senses, I found that I had been thrown down by the garden gate.

Night 127

Morning now dawned and Shahrazad broke off from what she had been allowed to say. Then, when it was the one hundred and twenty-seventh night, SHE CONTINUED:

I have heard, O fortunate king, that the vizier Dandan told Dau' al-Makan that THE YOUNG MAN SAID TO TAJ AL-MULUK:

When I had recovered my senses, I found that I had been thrown down by the garden gate. I got up and walked home, moaning with grief, and when I went in I found my mother weeping for me and saying: 'My son, I wonder in what land you are.' I threw myself on her and when she looked at me and felt me, she discovered that I was unwell, with a mixture of pallor and blackness on my face. I thought of my cousin and the good that she had done me and I was certain that she had loved me. So I wept for her, as did my mother. My mother then told me that my father had died, and as my grief and anger increased, I wept until I fainted. When I had recovered, I looked at where my cousin had used to sit, and I wept again, again almost fainting because of the violence of my grief, and I continued to weep and sob until half the night had passed.

My mother told me that it was ten days since my father had died, but I said to her: 'I cannot think of anyone except my cousin. I deserve everything that has happened to me for having neglected her in spite of the fact that she loved me.' My mother then asked: 'And what did happen to you?' so I told her the story. She wept for a time and then got up and fetched me some food. I ate a little and drank and then repeated my story, telling her everything that had happened to me. 'Praise be to God,' she said, 'that it was this rather than a cut throat that you suffered.' She then tended me and treated me until I was cured and restored to full health.

'My son,' she then said, 'I shall now fetch out what your cousin left with me as a deposit, for it is yours, and she made me swear that I would not produce it for you until I saw that you remembered her, mourned her and had cut your ties with other women. Now I know that you have fulfilled the condition.' She got up, opened a chest and produced this piece of material that has on it the picture of this gazelle, and it was the daughter of Delilah who had given it to me in the first place. When I took it, I found embroidered on it the following verses:

Mistress of beauty, who prompted you to turn away,
So that you killed a pining lover through excessive love?
If after parting you have not remembered me,
God knows that I have not forgotten you.
You torture me, falsely accusing me, but your torture is sweet.
Will you be generous to me one day and allow me to see you?
Before I fell in love with you, I did not think
That love held sickliness and torment for the soul.
This was before my heart was stirred by passion
And I became a prisoner of love, ensnared by your glance.
The censurer pitied me, lamenting the state love brought me to,
But you, Hind, never have lamented one who pined for you.
By God, were I to die, I would not be consoled for you, who are
    my hope;
Were passion to destroy me, I would not forget.

On reading these lines, I wept bitterly, slapping my face. As I opened
up the cloth, a piece of paper fell out of it, and when I opened it, I found
written on it: 'Cousin, know that I do not hold you to blame for my
death, and I hope that God will grant you good fortune in your dealings
with your beloved. But if something happens to you at the hands of the
daughter of Delilah the wily, do not go back to her or to any other
woman, but endure your misfortune. Had it not been that your allotted
span is an extended one, you would have died long ago. Praise be to
God who has allowed me to die before you. I give you my greetings.
Keep this piece of material with the picture of the gazelle and never part
from it, for the picture used to console me when you were absent . . .'

Night 128

Morning now dawned and Shahrazad broke off from what she had been
allowed to say. Then, when it was the one hundred and twenty-eighth
night, SHE CONTINUED:

I have heard, O fortunate king, that the vizier Dandan told Dau'
al-Makan that THE YOUNG MAN SAID TO TAJ AL-MULUK:

I read what my cousin had written and the instructions she had given.
She had told me to keep the picture of the gazelle and not to part with
it, as it had consoled her when I was absent. The note went on: 'I implore

you in God's Name that, if fate brings you together with the one who embroidered this gazelle, keep away from her. Don't let her make an approach to you and don't marry her. Even if you do not fall in with her and are not fated to meet her, and even if you can find no way of reaching her, do not make advances to any other woman. You must know that the embroiderer of the gazelle makes one every year and sends it off to the furthest lands to spread the fame of her beautiful workmanship, which no one else in the world can match. This one fell into the hands of your inamorata, the daughter of Delilah the wily, who used it to bemuse people, showing it to them and saying: "I have a sister who makes this." That was a lie – may God put her to shame! This is my advice, which I only give you because I know that, when I am dead, the world will be a difficult place for you and because of that you may go abroad and travel in foreign lands. It may be that you will hear of the lady who made this and want to make her acquaintance. You will remember me when it will do you no good and you will not recognize my value until after my death. Know that the girl who embroidered the gazelle is a noble princess, the daughter of the king of the Islands of Camphor.'

When I had read this note and grasped its meaning, I wept and my mother wept because of my tears. I went on looking at it and weeping until night came. I stayed in this state for a year. It was after this that these merchants, my companions in this caravan, made their preparations to leave my city on a journey. My mother advised me to get ready to travel with them, saying that I might find consolation and a cure for my sorrow. 'Relax,' she said, 'and abandon your grief. You may be away for one year or two or three before the caravan gets back, and it may be that you will find happiness and clear your mind of sorrow.' She kept on coaxing me until I prepared my trade goods and left with them. Throughout the length of the journey my tears have never dried and at every halting place I unfold this piece of material and look at its gazelle, weeping over the memory of my cousin, as you can see. For she loved me with an excessive love and she died of the sorrow that I inflicted on her. I did her nothing but harm and she did me nothing but good.

When the merchants return from their expedition, I shall go back with them. I shall have been away for a whole year, but my sorrow has increased, and what renewed it was the fact that I passed by the Islands of Camphor and the Crystal Castle. There are seven of these islands and their ruler is a king named Shahriman, who has a daughter called Dunya.

I was told that it is she who embroiders the gazelles and that the gazelle I had with me was one of hers. On hearing this, I felt a surge of longing and sank into a sea of hurtful thoughts. I wept for myself, as I was now like a woman; there was nothing I could do and I no longer had a male organ. From the day that I left the Camphor Islands I have been tearful and sorrowful at heart. I have continued in this state for a long time, wondering whether I shall be able to go back to my own land and die in my mother's house, for I have had enough of this world.

The young man then wept, groaned and complained. Looking at the image of the gazelle, with the tears running down his cheeks, he recited these lines:

> Many a man has said to me: 'Relief must come,'
> And I have answered angrily: 'How many times?'
> 'After some time,' he said, and I replied: 'How strange!
> Who guarantees me life, O faulty arguer?'

He also recited:

> God knows that, after leaving you, I wept
> Until I had to borrow tears on credit.
> A censurer once told me: 'Patience – you will reach your goal.'
> 'Censurer,' I said, 'from where will patience come?'

'This is my story, O king,' he went on. 'Have you ever heard one that is more remarkable?'

Taj al-Muluk was full of wonder, and when he heard the young man's story, fires were kindled in his heart at the mention of Princess Dunya and her beauty.

Night 129

Morning now dawned and Shahrazad broke off from what she had been allowed to say. Then, when it was the one hundred and twenty-ninth night, SHE CONTINUED:

I have heard, O fortunate king, that the vizier Dandan told Dau' al-Makan that Taj al-Muluk was full of wonder, and when he heard the young man's story, fires were kindled in his heart at the mention of Princess Dunya and her beauty. THE VIZIER WENT ON:

Realizing that it was she who had embroidered the gazelles, the passion of his love increased. The prince said to the young man: 'By God, nothing like this adventure of yours has happened to anyone before, but you have to live out your own fate. There is something that I want to ask you.' 'Aziz asked what this was and Taj al-Muluk said: 'Tell me how you came to see the girl who embroidered this gazelle.' 'Master,' replied 'Aziz, 'I approached her by a trick. When I had entered her city with the caravan, I used to go out and wander round the orchards, which were full of trees. The orchard guard was a very elderly man and when I asked him who owned the place, he told me that it belonged to the king's daughter, Princess Dunya. "We are underneath her palace here," he said, "and when she wants to take the air, she opens the postern door and walks in the orchard, enjoying the scent of the flowers." I said: "As a favour, let me sit here until she comes past, so that perhaps I may catch a glimpse of her." "There is no harm in that," agreed the old man, at which I gave him some money, saying: "Buy some food for us." He took the money gladly, opened the gate and went in, taking me with him. We kept on walking until we came to a pleasant spot where he told me to sit, saying that he would go off and come back with some fruit. He left me and went away, coming back some time later with a roasted lamb, whose meat we ate until we had had enough. I felt a longing in my heart to see the girl, and while we were sitting there, the gate suddenly opened. "Get up and hide," the old man told me, and so I did. A black eunuch then put his head out of the wicket and asked the old man whether there was anyone with him. When he said no, the eunuch told him to lock the orchard gate, which he did. Then, through the postern appeared Princess Dunya, and when I caught sight of her I thought that the moon had risen, spreading its light from the horizon. I gazed at her for a time and was filled with longing, like a man thirsting for water.

'After a while, she shut the postern and went off, at which I left the garden and went to my lodgings. I realized that I could not get to her, nor was I man enough for her, as I had become like a woman and had no male tool. She was a king's daughter and I was a merchant, and how then could I get to one like her, or indeed to any other woman? When my companions got ready to leave, I collected my things and went with them. This was where they were making for, and when we got here, I met you. You asked me questions and I replied to you. This is the story of what happened to me and that is all.'

When Taj al-Muluk heard this, his whole mind and all his thoughts were taken up with love for Princess Dunya, and he was at a loss to know what to do. He got to his feet, mounted his horse and, taking 'Aziz with him, he went back to his father's city. Here he gave 'Aziz a house of his own and supplied him with whatever he needed in the way of food, drink and clothing. He then left him and went to his palace, with tears running down his cheeks, as instead of his seeing and meeting the princess, he had to make do with what he had heard about her. He was in this state when his father came in to see him and found that his colour had changed and that he had become thin and tearful. Realizing that something had happened to preoccupy him, he said: 'My son, tell me how you are and what has happened to make you change colour and become emaciated.'

At that, Taj al-Muluk told him all that had happened, together with what he had heard from 'Aziz, and the story of Princess Dunya, adding that he had fallen in love with her by hearsay without having seen her. 'My son,' said his father, 'she is a king's daughter; his country is far distant from us, so let this matter rest and go to your mother's palace . . .'

Night 130

Morning now dawned and Shahrazad broke off from what she had been allowed to say. Then, when it was the one hundred and thirtieth night, SHE CONTINUED:

I have heard, O fortunate king, that THE VIZIER DANDAN TOLD DAU' AL-MAKAN:

Taj al-Muluk's father said: 'My son, she is a king's daughter; his country is far distant from us, so let this matter rest and go to your mother's palace where there are five hundred slave girls like moons. Take whichever of them you like, or otherwise we can set about trying to get for you the hand of a princess more beautiful than Dunya.' 'I shall never want anyone else, father,' Taj al-Muluk replied. 'She is the lady of the gazelle which I saw. I must have her, or else I shall wander off in the wastes and wildernesses and kill myself because of her.' 'Wait,' said his father, 'until I send word to her father, ask for her hand and get you what you want, as I did for myself in the case of your mother. It may be that God will bring you to your goal, but if her father refuses, I shall overturn his kingdom with an army whose rearguard will still be with me when the vanguard has reached him.'

He then summoned the young 'Aziz and said: 'My son, do you know the way?' When 'Aziz said that he did, the king said: 'I want you to go with my vizier.' 'To hear is to obey, king of the age,' replied 'Aziz. The king then summoned his vizier and said: 'Arrange things for me to help my son; go to the Camphor Islands and ask that he be given the hand of the princess.' When the vizier had agreed, Taj al-Muluk went back to his quarters. His lovelorn state had grown worse and he found the delay too long. In the darkness of night, he wept, moaned and complained, reciting these lines:

The night is dark; my tears flow more and more;
Passion springs out of my heart's raging fire.
Question the nights about me. They will tell
Whether I think of anything but care.
Thanks to my love, I shepherd the night stars,
While tears drop on my cheeks like hail.
I am alone; I have no one,
Like a lover without kin and with no child.

On finishing his poem, he fainted for a time and only recovered consciousness in the morning. One of his father's servants entered and stood by his head, telling him to come to his father. He went with the man and when his father saw him, he found that his son's colour had changed. Urging him to have patience, he promised that he would bring him together with his princess, and he then made preparations to send off 'Aziz and the vizier, supplying them with gifts.

These two travelled day and night until, when they were close to the Camphor Islands, they halted by a river bank, from where the vizier sent a messenger to the king to tell him of their arrival. The messenger had hardly been gone an hour when the king's chamberlains and his emirs came out to greet the visitors, and after meeting them at a *parasang*'s distance from the city, they escorted them into the king's presence. They presented their gifts to the king and were entertained by him for three days. On the fourth day, the vizier entered the king's presence, stood before him and told him of the errand on which he had come. The king was at a loss to know how to reply, as his daughter had no love for men and did not want to marry. For a time he bowed his head towards the ground and then, raising it again, he summoned one of the eunuchs and said: 'Go to your mistress, Dunya; repeat to her what you have heard and tell her of the errand on which this vizier has come.' The eunuch went off and was away for an hour, after which he came back to the king and said: 'King of the age, when I went in and told Princess Dunya what I had heard, she fell into a violent rage and attacked me with a stick, wanting to break my head. I ran away from her, but she said: "If my father forces me to marry, then I shall kill my husband."' Her father said to the vizier and 'Aziz: 'You have heard and understood. Tell this to your king. Give him my greetings but say that my daughter has no love for men and no desire for marriage.'

Night 131

Morning now dawned and Shahrazad broke off from what she had been allowed to say. Then, when it was the one hundred and thirty-first night, SHE CONTINUED:

I have heard, O fortunate king, that King Shahriman told 'Aziz and the vizier to give his greetings to the king and to tell him what they had heard, and that his daughter had no desire for marriage. The unsuccessful envoys then returned and, having completed their journey, they came to the king and told him what had happened. The king ordered his commanders to proclaim to the troops that they were to march out to war, but the vizier said: 'Your majesty, don't do this. It is not the fault of King Shahriman. When she learned of the proposal, his daughter sent him a message to say that if he forced her to marry, she would first kill her husband and then herself. The refusal came from her.' When the king heard what the vizier had to say, he was afraid for Taj al-Muluk and said: 'If I go to war against the father and capture the daughter, she will kill herself and it will do me no good at all.'

He told Taj al-Muluk about this, and when he learned what had happened, Taj al-Muluk said: 'Father, I cannot bear to do without her. I shall go to her and try to reach her by some ruse, even if I die. There is no other course for me to follow.' 'How will you go to her?' asked his father, and when Taj al-Muluk said that he would disguise himself as a merchant, the king said: 'If you must do this, take the vizier and 'Aziz with you.' He then took out some money for him from his treasury and prepared trade goods to the value of a hundred thousand dinars.

Both the vizier and 'Aziz agreed to go with Taj al-Muluk, and they went to 'Aziz's house and spent the night there. Taj al-Muluk, having lost his heart, could enjoy neither food nor sleep, assaulted, as he was,

by cares and shaken by longing for his beloved. He implored the Creator
to grant him a meeting with her, and with tears, moans and complaints,
he recited these lines:

Do you think that after parting we shall meet again?
I complain to you of my love and say:
'I remembered you, while night forgot;
You denied me sleep, while others were heedless.'

When he had finished his poem, he wept bitterly, while 'Aziz, remembering his cousin, wept too. They continued to shed tears until morning
came. Taj al-Muluk then got up and went to see his mother, wearing his
travelling dress. She asked him how he was, and after he had repeated
his story to her, she gave him fifty thousand dinars and said goodbye to
him. As he left, she wished him a safe journey and a meeting with his
beloved. He then went to see his father and asked leave to go. His father
granted him this and gave him another fifty thousand dinars, ordering a
tent to be pitched for him outside the city. This was done and he stayed
there for two days before setting off.

He had become friendly with 'Aziz and said to him: 'Brother, I cannot
bear to be parted from you.' 'I feel the same,' said 'Aziz, 'and I would
like to die at your feet, but, brother of my heart, I am concerned about
my mother.' Taj al-Muluk reassured him: 'When we reach our goal, all
will be well.' They then set off. The vizier had told Taj al-Muluk to be
patient and 'Aziz would talk with him at night, reciting poetry for him
and telling him histories and tales. They pressed on with their journey,
travelling night and day for two full months. Taj al-Muluk found the
journey long, and as the fires of his passion increased, he recited:

The way is long; cares and disquiet have increased;
The heart holds love, whose tortures worsen.
You who are my desire and the goal of my hopes, I have sworn an
    oath
By Him who created man from a clot of blood,
The sleepless passion I have borne, you who are my wish,
Is more than lofty mountains have to bear.
My lady Dunya, love has destroyed me,
Leaving me as a corpse deprived of life.
Did I not hope to gain union with you,
I would not leave on such a journey now.

When he had finished his recitation, he wept, as did 'Aziz, whose heart
was wounded. The vizier felt pity for their tears, saying: 'Master, set
your heart at rest and take comfort, for nothing but good will come of
this.' 'This has been a long journey, vizier,' said Taj al-Muluk, 'so tell
me how far we are from the city.' 'There is only a little way to go,' the
vizier replied, and they went on, crossing valleys, rugged ridges and
desert wastes.

One night, when Taj al-Muluk was sleeping, he dreamt that his beloved
was with him and that he was embracing her and clasping her to his
breast. Waking in alarm with his wits astray, he recited:

My two companions, my heart is astray and my tears fall;
I am filled with passion; infatuation clings to me.
My tearful lament is that of a woman who has lost her child;
In the darkness of night I moan as moans the dove.
If the wind blows from your land,
I find a coolness spreading over the earth.
I send you my greetings when the east wind blows,
As long as ringdoves fly and pigeons moan.

When he had finished reciting these lines, the vizier came up to him
and said: 'Be glad; this is a good sign, so set your heart at rest and take
comfort, for you are certain to reach your goal.' 'Aziz went up to him to
urge him to have patience, entertaining him, talking to him and telling
him stories. They continued to press on with their journey, travelling
day and night for another two months. Then one day when the sun rose
they saw in the distance something white. Taj al-Muluk asked 'Aziz what
it was and he replied: 'Master, that is the White Castle and this is the
city that you have been making for.' Taj al-Muluk was glad, and he and
the others went on until they came close to it.

At that point the prince was transported by joy, and care and sorrow
fell away from him. He and his companions entered the city disguised as
traders, with Taj al-Muluk dressed as a merchant prince. They went to
a large hostel known as the merchants' *khan* and Taj al-Muluk asked
'Aziz if it was where merchants stayed. 'Yes,' replied 'Aziz, 'and it is
where I lodged myself.' So they halted there, making their camels kneel
and unsaddling them, after which they put their goods in the storehouses
and rested for four days. The vizier then advised them to rent a larger
house. They agreed and hired a spacious property, well adapted for
feasts, and there they took up their quarters.

The vizier and 'Aziz spent their time trying to come up with a plan for Taj al-Muluk, while he himself was at a loss, with no idea what to do except to take his wares to the silk bazaar. The vizier approached him and 'Aziz, saying: 'If we stay here like this, then you can be sure that we shall not get what we want or carry out our mission. I have thought of something which, God willing, may produce a good result.' 'Do whatever occurs to you,' said the others, 'for old men are fortunate and this is especially true of you, thanks to your experience of affairs. So tell us what you have thought of.' 'My advice,' the vizier said to Taj al-Muluk, 'is that we should take a booth for you in the silk market where you should sit, buying and selling. Everyone of whatever class, upper or lower, needs pieces of silk, and if you sit there quietly, God willing, you will succeed in your affair, especially because of your good looks. Make 'Aziz your agent, so that he can sit inside the booth to hand you the various items and materials.'

When he heard this, Taj al-Muluk agreed that it was a good and sound idea. He took out a splendid set of merchant's clothes, put them on and walked off, followed by his servants, to whom he had given a thousand dinars in order to set the new place to rights. They went on until they reached the silk market, and when the merchants saw Taj al-Muluk and noted how handsome he was, they were taken aback. 'Ridwan has opened the gates of Paradise and forgotten to close them again, and so this wonderfully handsome young man has come out,' said one. 'Perhaps he is an angel!' exclaimed another. When his party came to the merchants, they asked where the market superintendent had his booth. They were given directions and walked on until they found it. They greeted him and he and the merchants who were with him rose to meet them, invited them to sit and treated them with honour. This was because of the vizier, whom they saw to be a dignified old man. On noting that he was accompanied by the young Taj al-Muluk and by 'Aziz, they said to themselves: 'There is no doubt that this old man is the father of the two young ones.'

The vizier asked which of them was the superintendent of the market. 'This is he,' they said, and the man came forward. The vizier looked at him, studied him and found him to be a venerable and dignified old man, with eunuchs, servants and black slaves. The old man gave the visitors a friendly greeting, treating them with the greatest honour, and after making them sit beside him, he asked whether they had any need that he might be able to fulfil. 'Yes,' said the vizier. 'I am an old man, stricken in years, and I have with me these two young men with whom I have travelled to many regions and countries. I have never entered a town without staying there for a whole year so that they could see its sights and get to know its people. I have now arrived at this town of yours, and as I have chosen to stay here, I want you to provide me with a fine booth in a good situation where I can set them down to trade and to inspect the city, while adapting themselves to the manners of its people, and learning how to buy and sell, give and take.' 'There is no problem with that,' said the superintendent, as he had been glad to see the two young men, for whom he felt a surge of love, he being someone who was passionately fond of murderous glances and who preferred the love of boys to that of girls, inclining to the sour rather than the sweet. To himself he said: 'This is a fine catch – praise be to Him who created and fashioned them from vile sperm!'

He got up and stood before them as a gesture of respect like a servant, after which he made ready for them a booth in the covered market. In size and splendour it was unsurpassed, being roomy and well decorated, with shelves of ivory and ebony. The keys were handed to the vizier, dressed as he was as an elderly merchant, and the superintendent said to him: 'Take these, master, and may God bless this place for your sons.' The vizier took the keys and the three of them went to the *khan* where they had left their things and told the servants to move all their goods and materials to the booth.

Night 132

Morning now dawned and Shahrazad broke off from what she had been allowed to say. Then, when it was the one hundred and thirty-second night, SHE CONTINUED:

I have heard, O fortunate king, that the vizier took the keys and the three of them went to the *khan* where they had left their things and told the servants to move all their goods, materials and treasures. There was a great deal of stuff, worth huge amounts of money; all of it was shifted and they themselves went to the booth where it was stored. They spent the night there and in the morning the vizier took the two young men to the baths. They made full use of these, washing and cleaning themselves, putting on splendid clothes and applying perfume. Each of them was dazzlingly handsome and their appearance in the baths fitted the poet's lines:

Good news it was for the bath man when his hand met
A body created from a mix of water and of light.
He continued with his delicate artistry,
Plucking musk from an image made of camphor.

When they came out, the market superintendent, who had heard where
they had gone, was sitting waiting for them. They moved forward like
gazelles, with red cheeks, dark eyes and shining faces, like two brilliant
moons or two branches laden with fruit. When the superintendent saw
them, he rose to his feet and said: 'My sons, may the baths always bring
you comfort.' In return, Taj al-Muluk said pleasantly: 'May God grant
you grace, father. Why did you not come and bathe with us?' He and
'Aziz then bent over the man's hand and kissed it, after which they
walked in front of him to the booth as a token of respect and reverence,
since he was the leader of the merchants and the superintendent of the
market, and he had already done them a favour by giving them the
booth. When he saw their buttocks swaying, his passion increased; he
snorted in his excitement and was unable to restrain himself, but staring
fixedly at them, he recited these lines:

The heart studies the chapter devoted to him,
Reading nothing that covers partnership with others.
It is not surprising that weight causes him to sway;
How many movements are there in the revolving sphere?

He also recited:

My eye saw the two of them walking on the earth,
And I wished they had been walking on my eye.

When they heard what he said, they insisted that he go a second time
with them to the baths. Scarcely able to believe this, he hurried back and
they went in with him. The vizier had not yet left and when he heard
that the superintendent was there, he came out and met him in the middle
of the bath house and invited him to enter. He refused, but Taj al-Muluk
took one of his hands and 'Aziz the other and they brought him to a
private room. The evil old man allowed himself to be led by them and
his passion increased. Taj al-Muluk swore that he and he alone should
wash him, while 'Aziz swore that none but he should pour the water over
him. Although this was what he wanted, he refused, but the vizier said:
'They are your sons; let them wash you and clean you.' May God preserve

them for you,' said the superintendent. 'By God, your arrival and that
of your companions has brought blessing and fortune to our city.' He
then recited the lines:

> You have come and our hills are clothed in green;
> Whoever looks can see they bloom with flowers.
> The earth and those who walk on it cry out:
> 'Welcome and greeting to the one who comes!'

They thanked him for that, and Taj al-Muluk continued to wash him
as 'Aziz poured water over him, leading him to think that his soul was
in Paradise. When they had finished attending to him, he blessed them
and sat down beside the vizier to talk to him, although his eyes were
fixed on the two young men. Then the servants brought towels and they
all dried themselves, put on their things and left the baths. 'Sir,' said the
vizier to the superintendent, 'baths are the delight of this world.' 'May
God grant you and your sons health,' he replied, 'and guard you from
the evil eye. Can you quote anything that eloquent men have said about
baths?' 'I can quote you some lines,' said Taj al-Muluk, and he recited:

> Life is at its pleasantest in the baths,
> But our stay there cannot be long.
> This is a paradise where we dislike to stay,
> And a hell where it is pleasant to go in.

After Taj al-Muluk had finished, 'Aziz said: 'I, too, remember some
lines about baths.' The superintendent asked him to recite them and he
quoted:

> There is many a chamber whose flowers are solid stone,
> Elegant when fires are kindled round about.
> To you it looks like a hell, but it is Paradise,
> Most of whose contents look like suns and moons.

When he had finished, the superintendent was full of admiration for
his quotation, and seeing the combination of beauty and eloquence that
the two possessed, he said: 'By God, you are both eloquent and graceful,
so now listen to me.' He then chanted tunefully the following lines:

> Beauty of hellfire, torment of Paradise,
> That gives both souls and bodies life,
> A marvellous chamber filled with fresh delight,

Although beneath it there are kindled flames.
Here pleasure lives for all those who approach,
And over it the streams have poured their tears.

Then, letting his gaze roam over the gardens of their beauty, he recited:

I went into that house and saw no chamberlain
Who did not greet me with a smiling face.
I entered Paradise and visited its hell,
Thanking Ridwan and Malik the kindly.

They were filled with admiration when they heard these lines, but
when the superintendent invited them home, they refused and went back
to their own lodgings to rest after the intense heat of the baths. Having
done this, and after eating and drinking, they spent the night there,
enjoying the fortune of perfect happiness. In the morning they woke up,
performed their ablutions and prayers and took their morning drink.
When the sun had risen and the shops and markets were open, they
walked off from the house to the market, where they opened their booth.
The servants had put this in excellent order, laying down rugs and silk
carpets, and in it they had placed two couches, each worth a hundred
dinars and each covered with a cloth fit for a king, fringed with a border
of gold, while in the middle were splendid furnishings that harmonized
with the place.

Taj al-Muluk sat on one sofa and 'Aziz on the other, while the vizier
took his place in the middle of the shop, with the servants standing
before him. Hearing about them, the townspeople crowded around, so
enabling them to sell some of their goods and their materials. The fame
of Taj al-Muluk's beauty spread through the city, and after several days,
on each of which more and more people had come hurrying up to them,
the vizier reminded Taj al-Muluk to keep his secret hidden and, after
advising him to take care of 'Aziz, he went home to concoct on his own
some plan that might turn out to their advantage.

Taj al-Muluk and 'Aziz started to talk to each other, with Taj al-Muluk
saying that perhaps someone might come from Princess Dunya. He kept
repeating this for some days and nights, and being disturbed at heart, he
was unable to sleep or rest. Love had him in its grip, and his passion and
lovesickness grew worse, while the pleasure of sleep was denied him and
he abstained from drinking and eating.

However, his beauty was like that of the moon on the night that it becomes full, and while he was sitting there, he was suddenly approached by an old woman . . .

Night 133

Morning now dawned and Shahrazad broke off from what she had been allowed to say. Then, when it was the one hundred and thirty-third night, SHE CONTINUED:

I have heard, O fortunate king, that while Taj al-Muluk was sitting there, he was suddenly approached by an old woman, followed by two slave girls. She walked up and stood by the shop and when she saw his symmetrical physique, his beauty and elegance, she admired his gracefulness and her harem trousers became damp. 'Glory to the One who created you from vile sperm and made you a temptation for those who look at you!' she exclaimed. Then, after studying him, she added: 'This is not a mortal man but a noble angel.' She approached and greeted him; he returned the greeting and rose to his feet with a smile, being prompted in all this by gestures from 'Aziz. Asking her to sit beside him, he began to fan her until she was refreshed and rested. She then turned to him and said: 'My son, you are a pattern of all perfection: do you come from these parts?' Taj al-Muluk replied eloquently, in pleasant and agreeable tones: 'My lady, this is the first time that I have ever been here in my life and I have only stopped here in order to look at the sights.' She spoke words of welcome and then asked: 'What materials have you brought with you? Show me something beautiful, for that is the only thing that can be worn by the beautiful.'

When Taj al-Muluk heard this, his heart fluttered and he could not grasp what she meant, but 'Aziz made a sign to him and he said: 'I have here everything that you could want. I have what will suit only kings or the daughters of kings, so tell me for whom it is that you need this, in order that I can put out for you everything that might be appropriate.' By saying this he hoped to find out what she really meant. In reply she said: 'I want something suitable for Princess Dunya, the daughter of King Shahriman.'

Overjoyed to hear this reference to his beloved, Taj al-Muluk told 'Aziz to fetch him a particular package. 'Aziz brought it and opened it in front of him, after which Taj al-Muluk told the old woman: 'Choose what will suit her, for this is something that you will find nowhere else.'

The old woman picked on something that was worth a thousand dinars, and asked its price, while, as she talked to him, she was rubbing the palm of her hand between her thighs. 'Am I to haggle with someone like you about this paltry price? Praise be to God who has let me come to know you,' said Taj al-Muluk. 'May God's Name guard you,' she replied. 'I ask the protection of the Lord of the dawn for your beautiful face. A beautiful face and an eloquent tongue – happy is she who sleeps in your embrace, clasps your body and enjoys your youth, especially if she is as beautiful as you!' Taj al-Muluk laughed until he fell over, exclaiming: 'You Who fulfil desires at the hands of profligate old women, it is they who satisfy needs!'

The woman asked his name and on being told that it was Taj al-Muluk, she said: 'This is a name for kings and princes, but you are dressed as a merchant.' 'Aziz said: 'It was because of the love and affection that his parents and his family had for him that they called him this.' 'That must be true,' said the old woman. 'May God protect you from the evil eye and from the evil of your enemies and the envious, even though your beauty causes hearts to break.' She then took the material and went on her way, still dazed by his beauty and symmetrical physique. She walked on until she came into the presence of Princess Dunya. 'I have brought you some fine material, lady,' she said. When the princess told her to show it to her, she said: 'Here it is, lady; turn it over and look at it.' Dunya was astonished at what she saw, saying: 'This is beautiful stuff, nurse. I have never seen its like in our city.' 'The man who sold it is more beautiful still,' said the old woman. 'It is as though Ridwan opened the gates of Paradise, and then when he forgot to close them, out came the young man who sold me this material. I wish that he could sleep with you tonight and lie between your breasts. He has brought precious stuffs to your city in order to look around it, and he is a temptation to the eyes of those who see him.'

Princess Dunya laughed at what she had to say, exclaiming: 'May God shame you, you unlucky old woman; you are talking nonsense and you have lost your wits!' Then she added: 'Bring me the material so that I can have a good look at it.' When it was given to her, she looked at it for a second time and saw that, albeit small, it was precious. She admired it, as never in her life had she seen its match, saying: 'By God, this is good material.' 'By God, lady,' said the old woman, 'if you saw its owner, you would realize that he is the most beautiful thing on the face of the earth.' The princess enquired: 'Did you ask him to tell us whether

there is any need he has that we can fulfil for him?' The old woman
shook her head and said: 'May God preserve your perspicacity. By God,
he does have a need, may your skill not desert you. Can anyone escape
from needs and be free of them?' 'Go to him,' said the princess, 'greet
him and say: "You have honoured our land and our city by coming here.
Whatever needs you have we shall willingly fulfil."'

Back went the old woman immediately to Taj al-Muluk, and when he
saw her, his heart leapt with happiness and joy. He got up, took her by
the hand and made her sit beside him. When she had rested she told him
what the princess had said to her. He was overjoyed, cheerful and relaxed;
happiness entered into his heart and he said to himself: 'I have got what
I wanted.' He asked the old woman: 'Would you carry a message from
me and bring me the reply?' 'Willingly,' she said, and he then told 'Aziz
to bring him an inkstand, paper and a brass pen. When these had been
fetched, he took the pen in his hand and wrote these lines:

> I have written you a letter, you who are my wish,
> Telling of how I suffer from the pain of separation.
> Its first line tells of the fire within my heart,
> Its second of my passion and my longing.
> The third tells how my life and patience waste away;
> The fourth says: 'All the passion still remains.'
> The fifth asks: 'When shall my eyes rest on you?'
> And the sixth: 'On what day shall we meet?'

At the end of the letter he wrote: 'This letter comes from the captive of
desire, held in the prison of longing, whose only chance of freedom lies
in union and a meeting that follows after remoteness and separation.
Parting from loved ones has left him to endure the pain and torture of
passion.' With tears pouring from his eyes, he then wrote these lines:

> I have written to you as my tears flood down,
> Falling from my eyes in ceaseless streams.
> But I am not one to despair of the grace of God;
> A day may come on which we two shall meet.

He folded the letter, sealed it and gave it to the old woman, saying:
'Take this to Princess Dunya.' 'To hear is to obey,' she said, and he then
handed her a thousand dinars, saying: 'Accept this as a friendly gift from
me, mother.' She took the money, blessed him and left, walking back to
Princess Dunya, who, when she saw her, said: 'Nurse, what did he ask

for, so that we can fulfil his request?' 'Lady,' the old woman replied, 'he sent me with this letter, but I don't know what is in it.' She handed the letter to Dunya, who took it, read it and, after having understood its meaning, exclaimed: 'What are things coming to when this trader sends me messages and writes to me?' She slapped her own face and said: 'With my position, am I to have connections with the rabble? Oh, Oh!' and she added: 'Were it not for my fear of God, I would have him killed and crucified over his shop.'

'What is in the letter that has upset and disturbed you?' asked the old woman. 'I wonder whether it is some complaint about injustice and whether he is asking payment for the material.' 'Damn you,' said Dunya, 'it is not about that. There is nothing in it but words of love. This is all thanks to you, for otherwise how could this devil have known about me?' 'Lady,' answered the old woman, 'you sit in your high palace and no one, not even the birds of the air, can reach you. May you and your youthfulness be free from blame and reproach. The dogs may bark, but this means nothing to you, who are a princess and the daughter of a king. Don't blame me for bringing you the letter, for I had no idea what was in it. My advice is that you should send him a reply, threaten him with death and tell him to give up this wild talk. That will finish the matter for him and he will not do the same thing again.' Princess Dunya said: 'I'm afraid that if I write to him, this may stir his desire for me.' 'When he hears the threats and warnings, he will draw back,' said the old woman.

The princess told her to fetch an inkstand, paper and a brass pen. When these had been brought, she wrote the following lines:

You make a pretence of love and claim sad sleeplessness,
Talking of passion and your cares;
Deluded man, do you seek union with the moon?
Has anyone got what he wanted from the moon?
I advise you to give up your quest;
Abandon it, for in it there is danger.
If you use words like these again,
You will be punished harshly at my hands.
I swear by Him Who created man from sperm
And caused the sun and the moon to spread their light,
If you should dare to talk of this again,
I shall have you crucified upon a tree.

She folded the letter, gave it to the old woman and said: 'Hand this to him and tell him to stop talking in this way.' 'To hear is to obey,' replied the old woman, who took the letter joyfully and went to her house, where she spent the night. In the morning she set off for Taj al-Muluk's shop and found him waiting for her. When he saw her, he almost flew up into the air for joy, and when she approached, he rose to meet her. He made her sit beside him, and she produced the note, handed it to him and told him to read it. 'Princess Dunya was angry when she read your letter,' she said, 'but I humoured her and joked with her until I made her laugh. Her feelings towards you softened and she wrote you a reply.' Taj al-Muluk thanked her for that and told 'Aziz to give her a thousand dinars, but when he read the note and understood what it meant, he wept bitterly. The old woman felt sympathy for him and was grieved by his tears and complaints. 'My son,' she said, 'what is in this paper that has made you weep?' 'She threatens to kill me and to crucify me,' he answered, 'and she forbids me to write to her, but if I do not, then it would be better for me to die than to live. So take the answer to her letter and let her do what she wants.' 'By your youthful life,' said the old woman, 'I must join you in risking my own life in order to get you to your goal and to help you reach what you have in mind.' 'I shall reward you for everything you do,' said Taj al-Muluk, 'and you will find it weighed out in your favour on the Day of Judgement. You are experienced in the running of affairs and you know the various types of intrigue. All difficulties are easy for you to overcome, and God has power over all things.'

He then took a piece of paper and wrote these lines on it:

She threatened me with death, alas for me,
But this would bring me rest; death is decreed for all,
And it is easier for a lover than long life
When he is kept from his beloved and oppressed.
Visit a lover who has few to help him, for God's sake;
I am your slave, and slaves are held captive.
My lady, pity me in my love for you.
All those who love the nobly born must be excused.

After writing the lines, he sighed deeply and wept until the old woman wept too. She then took the paper from him and told him to be of good cheer and to console himself, for she would bring him to his goal.

Night 134

Morning now dawned and Shahrazad broke off from what she had been allowed to say. Then, when it was the one hundred and thirty-fourth night, SHE CONTINUED:

I have heard, O fortunate king, that Taj al-Muluk wept, but the old woman told him to be of good cheer and to console himself, for she would bring him to his goal. She left him on fire with anxiety and set off for the princess. Dunya had been so enraged by Taj al-Muluk's letter that the old woman found that her colour had changed, and when she was given the second note, she grew even angrier. 'Didn't I tell you that he would desire me?' she said to the old woman. 'What is this dog that he should do such a thing?' the woman replied. 'Go to him,' ordered Dunya, 'and tell him that if he sends me another letter, I shall have his head cut off.' The old woman said: 'Write this down for him in a letter and I shall take it with me, to make him even more frightened.' Dunya then took a piece of paper on which she wrote these lines:

> You who are heedless of the blows of fate,
> You race for union, but are bound to fail.
> Do you suppose, deluded man, that you can reach a star?
> The shining moon remains outside your grasp.
> How is it that you set your hopes on me
> Hoping for union, to embrace my slender form?
> Give up this quest of yours for fear I force on you
> A day of gloom to whiten the parting of the hair.

She folded the letter and handed it to the old woman, who took it off to Taj al-Muluk. When he saw her, he got to his feet and said: 'May God never deprive me of the blessing of your coming.' The old woman told him to take the reply to his letter and when he had taken it and read it, he burst into tears. 'I would like someone to kill me now so that I might find rest, for to be slain would be easier for me to bear than my present position.' He then took the inkstand, pen and paper and wrote a note with these lines:

> You who are my wish, seek no harsh parting;
> Visit a lover drowning in his love.
> Do not think this harshness will allow me life;
> The breath of life will leave with the beloved.

He folded the letter and gave it to the old woman, saying: 'Don't reproach me for putting you to trouble without reward.' Telling 'Aziz to pay her a thousand dinars, he then said to her: 'Mother, this note will lead either to complete union or to a final break.' 'My son,' she replied, 'by God, all I want is your good and I would like you to have her, for you are the radiant moon and she is the rising sun. If I fail to bring you together, then my life is of no use. I have reached the age of ninety, having spent my days in wiles and trickery, so how can I fail to unite a pair in illicit love?' She then took her leave of him and went off, having encouraged him.

When she came into the presence of Princess Dunya, she had hidden the paper in her hair. When she sat down there, she scratched her head and asked the princess to examine her head for lice, saying that it was a long time since she had been to the baths. The princess rolled back her sleeves to the elbow, let down the old woman's hair and started to search. The note fell out and when the princess saw it, she asked what it was. 'It must have stuck to me while I was sitting in the trader's shop,' the old woman said. 'Give it to me so that I can take it back to him, as there may be a bill there which he will need.' The princess opened it up and read it, and when she had seen what was in it, she said to the old woman: 'This is one of your tricks and but for the fact that you brought me up, I would strike out at you here and now. God has plagued me with this merchant, and everything that he has done to me has been thanks to you. I don't know from what land he has come; no one else has been able to take such liberties with me, and I am afraid lest this become public, especially since it concerns a man who is not of my race and is not one of my equals.' The old woman turned to her and said: 'No one will dare talk about it for fear of your power and the awe in which your father is held. There can be no harm in sending him back an answer.' 'Nurse,' the princess said, 'this man is a devil. How has he dared to talk like this? He doesn't fear the king's power, and I don't know what to do about him. If I order him to be killed, that would not be right, but if I let him be, he will grow even more daring.' 'Write him a note,' said the old woman, 'so that he may be warned off.'

The princess asked for paper, an inkstand and a pen, after which she wrote these lines:

You have long been censured, but too much folly leads you astray;
How many verses must I write to hold you back?

The more you are forbidden, the more you covet;
If you keep this secret, that is the only thing I shall approve.
Conceal your love; never let it be known;
For if you speak, I shall not listen to you,
And if you talk of this again,
The raven of parting will croak your death-knell.
Death will soon swoop down on you,
And you will rest buried beneath the earth.
Deluded man, you will leave your family to regret your loss,
Mourning that you have gone from them for ever.

She then folded the paper and gave it to the old woman, who took it and set off to Taj al-Muluk. She gave it to him and, having read it, he realized that princess was hard-hearted and that he would not be able to reach her. He took his complaint to the vizier, asking him to devise a good plan. The vizier told him that the only thing that might be of use would be for him to write her a letter calling down a curse on her. Taj al-Muluk said: ''Aziz, my brother, write for me, as you know what to say.' So 'Aziz took a piece of paper and wrote:

Lord, by the five planets I ask You, rescue me
And lead the one who torments me to taste my grief.
You know I suffer from a burning passion;
She treats me harshly and is pitiless.
How long must I be tender in my sufferings?
How long will she oppress me in my feebleness?
I stray through endless floods of misery
And find no one to help me, oh my Lord.
How often do I try to forget her love!
It has destroyed my patience; how can I forget?
You keep me from the sweet union of love;
Are you yourself safe from the miseries of Time?
Are you not happy in your life, while, thanks to you,
I am an exile from my country and my kin?

'Aziz then folded the letter and handed it to Taj al-Muluk, who read it with admiration and handed it to the old woman. She took it and went to Princess Dunya, to whom she gave the letter. When Dunya had read it and digested its contents, she was furiously angry and said: 'This ill-omened old woman is responsible for all that has happened to me.'

She called to her slave girls and eunuchs and said: 'Seize this damned scheming old creature and beat her with your slippers.' They fell upon her and beat her until she fainted. When she had recovered consciousness, the princess said to her: 'By God, you wicked old woman, were it not for my fear of Almighty God I would kill you.' She then told the servants to beat her again, which they did until she fainted, after which on her orders they dragged her off face downwards and threw her outside in front of the door of the palace.

When she had recovered, she got up and moved off, walking and sitting down at intervals, until she reached her house. She waited until morning and then got up and went to Taj al-Muluk, to whom she told everything that had happened to her. Finding this hard to bear, he said: 'I am distressed by this, mother, but all things are controlled by fate and destiny.' She told him to be of good heart and to take comfort, adding: 'I shall not stop trying until I have brought the two of you together and fetched you to this harlot who has me beaten so painfully.' Taj al-Muluk then asked her what had caused the princess to hate men, and when he was told that this was because of a dream that she had had, he asked what the dream had been.

The old woman replied: 'One night when the princess was asleep she saw in a dream a hunter spreading out a net on the ground and scattering wheat around it. He sat down close by and all the birds there came to the net, among them being a pair of pigeons, male and female. While she was watching the net, the male pigeon got caught in it. It started to struggle and all the other birds took fright and flew off, but the female pigeon came back. She circled over him and then came down to the part of the net where her mate's foot was trapped, pulling at it with her beak until the foot was freed, after which the two of them flew off. The hunter, who had not noticed what was happening, came up and readjusted the net before sitting down at a distance from it. Within an hour, the birds had come down again, and this time it was the female pigeon that was trapped. All the birds took fright, including the male, who did not return for his mate, and so, when the hunter arrived, he took her and cut her throat. The princess woke from her dream in alarm and said: "All males are like this; there is no good in them, and no men are of any good to women."'

When she had finished her tale, Taj al-Muluk said: 'Mother, I want to look at her once, even if this means my death, so think of some way for me to do this.' The old woman said: 'Know that beneath her palace she has a pleasure garden to which she goes once a month from her postern door. In ten days, it will be time for her next visit, and when she is on the point of going out, I shall come and tell you so that you can go and meet her. Take care not to leave the garden, for it may be that if she sees how handsome you are, she may fall in love with you, and love is the most potent motive for union.' 'To hear is to obey,' said Taj al-Muluk, and he and 'Aziz then left the shop and, taking the old woman with them, they went back to their house, which they showed to her. Taj al-Muluk said to 'Aziz: 'Brother, I don't need the shop any more. I have got what I wanted from it and so I give it to you, with all its contents, as you have come with me to a foreign country, leaving your own land.'

'Aziz accepted the gift and the two sat talking, with Taj al-Muluk asking 'Aziz about the strange circumstances in which he had found himself and about his adventures, while 'Aziz gave him an account of everything that had happened to him. After that they went to the vizier and told him what Taj al-Muluk had determined to do, and asked him how they should set about it. 'Come with me to the garden,' said the vizier, and they each put on their most splendid clothes and went out, followed by three mamluks. They made their way to the garden, where they saw quantities of trees and many streams, with the gardener sitting by the gate. After they had exchanged greetings, the vizier handed the man a hundred dinars and said: 'Please take this money and buy us something to eat, as we are strangers here. I have with me these sons of mine and I want to show them the sights.' The gardener took the dinars and told them: 'Go in and look around, for it is all yours. Then you can sit down and wait for me to bring you food.'

He then went off to the market, and the vizier, Taj al-Muluk and 'Aziz entered the garden. After a while he brought back a roast lamb and bread as white as cotton, which he placed in front of them. They ate and drank, and he then produced sweetmeats, which they ate, and after this they washed their hands and sat talking. 'Tell me about this place,' the vizier then said to the gardener. 'Do you own or rent it?' 'It's not mine,' replied the gardener. 'It belongs to the king's daughter, Princess Dunya.' 'What is your monthly pay?' asked the vizier. 'One dinar, and no more,' replied the man. The vizier looked at the garden and saw that it contained a high pavilion, but that this was old. He then said to the gardener: '*Shaikh*, I would like to do a good deed by which you may remember me.' When the man asked him what he was thinking of, by way of reply he said: 'Accept these three hundred dinars.' When the gardener heard him talk of gold, he said: 'Master, do whatever you want.' The vizier gave him the money and said: 'If it is the will of Almighty God, we shall achieve something good here.'

The three then left the gardener and went back to their house, where they passed the night. The next day, the vizier summoned a house painter, an artist and a skilled goldsmith, and he produced for them all the tools they would need. He took them into the garden and told them to whitewash the pavilion and to decorate it with various kinds of pictures. He had gold and lapis lazuli fetched and he told the artist to produce on one side of the hall a picture of a hunter who had spread a net into which birds had fallen, with a female pigeon entangled by its beak. When the artist had painted this, the vizier told him to repeat the motif on the other side of the hall, with the pigeon alone captured by the hunter, who had put a knife to its throat. Opposite this there was to be the picture of a great hawk which had seized the male pigeon and sunk its claws into it. The artist completed the painting and when all three had finished the tasks set them by the vizier, he paid them their wages and they went off, as did the vizier and his companions. After taking leave of the gardener, they went home and sat talking.

Taj al-Muluk said to 'Aziz: 'Recite me some poetry, brother, so as to cheer me and to remove these cares of mine, cooling the raging fire in my heart.' At that, 'Aziz chanted the following lines:

> All the grief of which lovers talk
> Is mine alone, exhausting endurance.
> If you wish to be watered by my tears,
> Their seas will serve all those who come for water,
> And if you wish to see what lovers suffer,
> From the power of passion, then look at my body.

Shedding tears, he went on to recite:

> Whoever does not love graceful necks and eyes,
> But still lays claim to worldly pleasure, does not tell the truth.
> Love holds a concept that cannot be grasped
> By any man except for those who love.
> May God not move love's burden from my heart,
> Nor take away the sleeplessness from my eyes.

He next chanted the following lines:

In his *Canon*, Avicenna claims
That music is the lover's cure,
Together with union with one like his love,
As well as wine, a garden and dried fruits.
To find a cure, I chose a different girl,
Aided by fate and opportunity,
Only to find that lovesickness is fatal,
While Avicenna's 'cure' is senseless talk.

When 'Aziz had finished his poem, Taj al-Muluk was astonished at his eloquence and the excellence of his recitation and told him that he had removed some of his cares. The vizier then said: 'Among the experiences of the ancients are some that leave the hearer lost in wonder.' 'If you remember anything of this kind,' Taj al-Muluk said, 'let me hear what you can produce in the way of delicate poetry and long stories.' The vizier then chanted these lines:

I used to think that union could be bought
By prized possessions and payment of cattle.
In ignorance I thought your love too inconsiderable
A thing on which to waste a precious life.
That was before I saw you make your choice
And single out your beloved with choice gifts.
I realized there was no stratagem for me
To reach you, and I tucked my head beneath my wing,
Making my home within the nest of love,
Where endlessly I must pass all my days.

So much, then, for them, but as for the old woman, she remained isolated in her house. It happened that the princess felt a longing to take a walk in the garden. As she would not go out without the old woman, she sent a message and made her peace with her, reconciling her and telling her that she wanted to go out into the garden to look at the trees and their fruits and to enjoy herself among the flowers. The old woman agreed to go with her but said that she first wanted to return home to change her clothes before coming back. 'Go home, then,' the princess said, 'but don't be long.' The old woman left her and went to Taj al-Muluk. 'Get ready,' she said. 'Put on your most splendid clothes, go to the garden and, after you have greeted the gardener, hide yourself there.' 'To hear is to obey,' he replied, and they agreed between themselves on a signal, after which the old woman returned to Princess Dunya.

When she had left, the vizier and 'Aziz dressed Taj al-Muluk in the most splendid of royal robes, worth five thousand dinars, and around his waist they fastened a girdle of gold set with gems and precious stones. They then set off for the garden, and when they reached its gate, they found the gardener sitting there. When he saw Taj al-Muluk, he got to his feet and greeted him with reverence and honour, opening the gate for him and saying: 'Come in and look around the garden.' He did not know that the princess was going to visit it that day.

Taj al-Muluk went in, but he had been there for only an hour when he heard a noise, and before he knew what was happening, the eunuchs and the slave girls had come out of the postern gate. When the gardener saw them, he went to tell Taj al-Muluk, saying: 'Master, what are we going to do, for my lady, Princess Dunya, is here?' 'No harm will come to you,' said Taj al-Muluk, 'for I shall hide myself somewhere in the garden.' The man told him to be very careful, and then left him and went off.

The princess entered the garden with her maids and the old woman, who told herself: 'If the eunuchs come with us, we shall not get what we want.' She then said to the princess: 'Lady, I can tell you how best to relax,' and after the princess had told her to speak, she went on: 'We don't need these eunuchs now; you can't relax as long as they are with us, so send them off.' The princess agreed and sent the eunuchs away.

Soon after that, she began to walk, while, unbeknown to her, Taj al-Muluk was watching her in all her beauty. Every time he looked, he would lose his senses because of her surpassing loveliness. The old woman kept talking to her mistress in order to inveigle her into approaching the pavilion, which had been painted as the vizier had instructed. The princess entered it and looked at the paintings, where she saw the birds, the hunter and the pigeons. 'Glory be to God!' she exclaimed. 'This is exactly what I saw in my dream.' Looking with amazement at the pictures of the birds, the hunter and the net, she said: 'Nurse, I used to blame men and hate them, but look at how the hunter has cut the throat of the female pigeon. The male escaped, but he was going to come and rescue his mate when he was met by the hawk, which seized him.' The old woman, pretending to know nothing about this, kept her occupied with conversation until the two of them came close to Taj al-Muluk's hiding place.

She then gestured to get Taj al-Muluk to walk beneath the windows of the pavilion, and the princess, who was standing there, happened to turn. She caught sight of Taj al-Muluk and had the chance to study his beauty and his symmetrical form. 'Where has this handsome young man come from, nurse?' she asked. 'I know nothing about him,' the old woman told her, 'but I think that he must be the son of a great king, for he is handsome and beautiful to the furthest degree.' Princess Dunya fell in love; the ties of the spells that had bound her were undone, and she was dazzled by Taj al-Muluk's beauty and the symmetry of his form. Passion stirred in her and she said to the old woman: 'Nurse, this young man is handsome.' 'True,' replied the nurse, and she gestured to Taj al-Muluk to indicate that he should go home. He was on fire with love and his passion and ardour had increased, but he went off without stopping and, after saying goodbye to the gardener, he returned home. His longing had been aroused, but he did not disobey the old woman and he told the vizier and 'Aziz that she had signalled to him to go. They advised him to be patient, telling him that she would not have done that had she not thought that it would be useful.

So much for Taj al-Muluk, the vizier and 'Aziz, but as for the princess, she was overwhelmed by love, and her passion and ardour increased. She told the old woman: 'I don't know how I can meet this young man except with your help.' 'I take refuge in God from Satan the accursed,' said the old woman. 'You don't want men, so how have you come to be so disturbed by love for this one, although, by God, he is the only fit mate for your youth?' 'Help me, nurse,' said the princess, 'and if you can arrange for me to meet him, I shall give you a thousand dinars, while if you don't, I am sure to die.' 'Do you go back to your palace,' said the old woman, 'and I shall arrange your meeting and give my life to satisfy the two of you.'

Princess Dunya then returned to her palace, while the old woman went to Taj al-Muluk. When he saw her, he jumped to his feet and greeted her with respect and honour and sat her down beside him. 'The scheme has worked,' she said, and she told him what had happened with the princess. 'When can we meet?' he asked her, and when she said tomorrow, he gave her a thousand dinars and a robe worth another thousand. She took these and then left, going straight on until she reached the princess. 'Nurse,' the princess asked, 'what news do you have of my beloved?' 'I have found where he is,' she replied, 'and tomorrow I shall bring him to you.' In her delight at this, the princess gave her a thousand dinars and a robe worth another thousand. The old woman took these and went off to her house, where she spent the night.

In the morning, she went out and set off to meet Taj al-Muluk. She dressed him in women's clothes and told him: 'Follow behind me; sway as you walk; don't hurry and pay no attention to anyone who talks to you.' After giving him these instructions, she went out and he followed behind her in his women's clothes. All the way along she was telling him what to do and encouraging him to stop him taking fright. She continued to walk on ahead, with him at her heels, until they reached the palace door. She led him in and started to pass through doorways and halls, until she had taken him through seven doors. At the seventh, she said to him: 'Take heart, and when I shout to you: "Come in, girl," don't hang back but hurry. When you get into the hall, look left and you will see a room with several doors in it. Count five of them and go in through the sixth door, where you will find what you seek.' 'And where will you go yourself?' asked Taj al-Muluk. 'Nowhere,' she replied, 'but I may fall behind you, and if the chief eunuch detains me, I'll chat with him.'

She walked on, followed by Taj al-Muluk, until she came to the door where the chief eunuch was. He saw that she had a companion, this being Taj al-Muluk disguised as a slave girl, and he asked about 'her'. 'She is a slave girl. Princess Dunya has heard that she knows how to do various types of work and wants to buy her.' 'I know nothing about a slave girl or anyone else,' said the eunuch, 'but no one is going in until I search them, as the king has ordered.'

Night 135

Morning now dawned and Shahrazad broke off from what she had been allowed to say. Then, when it was the one hundred and thirty-fifth night, SHE CONTINUED:

I have heard, O fortunate king, that the eunuch said: 'I know nothing about a slave girl or anyone else, but no one is going in until I search them, as the king has ordered.' The old woman made a show of anger and said: 'I know you as a sensible, well-mannered man, but if you have changed, I shall tell the princess and let her know that you have obstructed the arrival of her slave girl.' She then shouted to Taj al-Muluk and said: 'Come on, girl,' at which he came into the hall as she had told him, while the eunuch kept silent and said nothing.

Taj al-Muluk counted five doors and went in through the sixth, where he found Princess Dunya standing waiting for him. When she saw him, she recognized him and clasped him to her breast, as he clasped her to his. The old woman then came in, having contrived to get rid of the slave girls for fear of exposure. 'You can act as doorkeeper,' the princess told her, and she then remained alone with Taj al-Muluk. The two of them continued hugging, embracing and intertwining legs until early dawn. Then, when it was nearly morning, she left him, closing the door on him and going into another room, where she sat down in her usual place. Her slave girls came to her, and after dealing with their affairs and talking to them, she told them to leave her, saying that she wanted to relax alone. When they had gone, she went to Taj al-Muluk, and the old woman brought them some food, which they ate. She then shut the door on them, as before, and they engaged in love-play until daybreak, and things went on like this for a whole month.

So much, then, for Taj al-Muluk and Dunya, but as for the vizier and 'Aziz, after Taj al-Muluk had gone to the princess's palace and stayed there for so long, they believed that he would never come out and would undoubtedly perish. 'Aziz asked the vizier what they should do. 'My son,' said the vizier, 'this is a difficult business. If we don't go back and tell his father, he will blame us for it.' They made their preparations immediately and set off for the Green Land and the Twin Pillars, the royal seat of King Sulaiman Shah. They crossed the valleys by night and by day until they reached the king, and they told him what had happened to his son, adding that since he had entered the palace of the princess they had heard no news of him.

The king was violently agitated and bitterly regretted what had happened. He gave orders that war should be proclaimed, with the troops moving out of the city, where tents were pitched for them. The king himself sat in his pavilion until his forces had gathered from all parts of his kingdom. He was popular with his subjects because of his justice and beneficence, and so when he moved out in search of his son, Taj al-Muluk, it was with an army which spread over the horizon.

So much for them, but as for Taj al-Muluk and Princess Dunya, they continued as they had been for six months, with their love for each other growing every day. The strength of Taj al-Muluk's love and his passion and ardour increased until he told the princess what was in his heart and said: 'Know, my heart's darling, that the longer I stay with you, the more my passionate love increases, for I have not fully reached my goal.' 'And what do you want, light of my eyes and fruit of my heart?' she asked. 'For if you want more than hugs and embraces and the intertwinings of legs, then do what you want, for only God is a partner in our love.' 'That is not the kind of thing that I mean,' he said, 'but rather I would like to tell you the truth about myself. You have to know that I am not a merchant but a king and the son of a king. My father's name is Sulaiman Shah, the great king, who sent his vizier to your father to ask for your hand for me, but when you heard of this, you would not agree.' Then he told her his story from beginning to end, and there is nothing to be gained from repeating it. Taj al-Muluk went on: 'I want now to go to my father to get him to send another envoy to your father to ask him again for your hand, so that we may relax.' When she heard this, the princess was overjoyed, because it coincided with what she herself wanted, and the two of them spent the night in agreement on this.

As fate had decreed, on that particular night they were overcome by sleep and they did not wake until the sun had risen. By then, King Shahriman was seated on his royal throne with the emirs of his kingdom before him. The master of the goldsmiths came into his presence carrying a large box, and, on approaching, he opened this before the king. From it he took a finely worked case which was worth a hundred thousand dinars because of what it contained in the way of gems, rubies and emeralds, such that no king of the lands could amass. When the king saw the case, he admired its beauty and he turned to the chief eunuch, Kafur, whose meeting with the old woman has already been described, and he told him to take the case and bring it to Princess Dunya.

The eunuch took the case and went to Dunya's room, where he found the door shut and the old woman sleeping on the threshold. 'Are you still asleep as late as this?' he exclaimed. When she heard his voice, the old woman woke in alarm. 'Wait until I fetch you the key,' she said, and then she left as fast as she could and fled away. So much for her, but as for the eunuch, he realized that there was something suspicious about her and, lifting the door from its hinges, he entered the room where he found Dunya asleep in the arms of Taj al-Muluk. When he saw this, he was at a loss to know what to do and he thought of going back to the king. The princess woke up and on finding him there she changed colour, turned pale and said: 'Kafur, conceal what God has concealed.' 'I cannot hide anything from the king,' he answered, and locking the door on them, he returned to the king. 'Have you given your mistress the case?' he asked. 'Take the box,' said Kafur. 'There it is; I cannot hide anything from you, and so you have to know that I saw a handsome young man sleeping with the Lady Dunya on the same bed, and they were embracing.'

The king ordered that both of them be brought before him. 'What have you done?' he said to them, and in his rage he seized a whip and was about to strike Taj al-Muluk when the princess threw herself on him and said to her father: 'Kill me before you kill him.' The king spoke angrily to her and ordered the servants to take her to her room. He then turned to Taj al-Muluk and said: 'Where have you come from, damn you? Who is your father and how did you dare to approach my daughter?' Taj al-Muluk said: 'King, know that if you kill me, you will be destroyed and you and all the inhabitants of your kingdom will have cause for regret.' When the king asked him why this was, he went on: 'Know that I am the son of King Sulaiman Shah, and before you know it, he will bring his horse and foot against you.'

When King Shahriman heard that, he wanted to postpone the execution and to keep Taj al-Muluk in prison until he could see whether what he said was true, but the vizier said: 'My advice is that you should kill this scoundrel quickly, for he has the insolence to take liberties with the daughters of kings.' So the king told the executioner: 'Cut off his head, for he is a traitor.' The executioner seized Taj al-Muluk and bound him. He then raised his hand, by way of consulting the emirs, first once and then again. In doing so, he wanted to delay things, but the king shouted at him: 'How long are you going to consult? If you do this once more, I shall cut off your head.' So the executioner raised his arm until the hair in his armpit could be seen, and he was about to strike . . .

Night 136

Morning now dawned and Shahrazad broke off from what she had been allowed to say. Then, when it was the one hundred and thirty-sixth night, SHE CONTINUED:

I have heard, O fortunate king, that the executioner raised his arm until the hair in his armpit could be seen, and he was about to strike when suddenly there were loud screams and people shut up their shops. 'Don't be too fast,' the king said to the executioner, and he sent someone to find out what was happening. When the man came back, he reported: 'I have seen an army like a thunderous sea with tumultuous waves. The earth is trembling beneath the hooves of their galloping horses, but I don't know who they are.'

The king was dismayed, fearing that he was going to lose his kingdom.

Turning to his vizier, he asked: 'Have none of our troops gone out to meet this army?' But before he had finished speaking, his chamberlains entered, escorting messengers from the newly arrived king, among them being Sulaiman Shah's vizier. The vizier was the first to greet the king, who rose to meet the envoys, told them to approach and asked them why they had come. The vizier came forward from among them and said: 'Know that a king has come to your land who is not like former kings or the sultans of earlier days.' 'Who is he?' the king asked. 'The just and faithful ruler, the fame of whose magnanimity has been spread abroad,' replied the vizier. 'He is King Sulaiman Shah, ruler of the Green Land, the Twin Pillars and the mountains of Isfahan. He loves justice and equity, hating injustice and tyranny. His message to you is that his son, who is his darling and the fruit of his heart, is with you and in your city. If the prince is safe, that is what he hopes to find, and you will be thanked and praised, but if he has disappeared from your land or if some misfortune has overtaken him, then be assured of ruin and the devastation of your country, for he will make it a wilderness in which the ravens croak. I have given you the message and so, farewell.'

When King Shahriman heard the vizier's message, he was alarmed and feared for his kingdom. He shouted a summons to his state officials, his viziers, chamberlains and deputies, and when they came, he told them to go and look for the young man. Taj al-Muluk was still in the hands of the executioner and so afraid had he been that his appearance had changed. His father's vizier happened to look around and found him lying on the execution mat. On recognizing him, he got up and threw himself on him, as did his fellow envoys. They then unloosed his bonds, kissing his hands and his feet. When Taj al-Muluk opened his eyes, he recognized the vizier and his companion 'Aziz and fainted from excess of joy.

King Shahriman was at a loss to know what to do and he was very afraid when it became clear to him that it was because of the young man that this army had come. He got up and went to Taj al-Muluk. With tears starting from his eyes, he kissed his head and said: 'My son, do not blame me; do not blame the evil-doer for what he did. Have pity on my white hairs and do not bring destruction on my kingdom.' Taj al-Muluk went up to him, kissing his hand and saying: 'No harm will come to you. You are like a father to me, but take care that nothing happens to my beloved, Princess Dunya.' 'Have no fear, sir,' said the king. 'Nothing but happiness will come to her.' He continued to excuse himself and to appease Sulaiman Shah's vizier, promising him a huge reward if he would conceal from his master what he had seen. He then ordered his principal officers to take Taj al-Muluk to the baths, give him the finest of clothes and return with him quickly. This they did, escorting him to the baths and making him put on a suit of clothes that King Shahriman had sent specially for him, before bringing him back to the audience chamber.

When he entered, the king got up for him and made all his principal officers rise to attend on the prince. Taj al-Muluk then sat down to talk to his father's vizier and to 'Aziz, telling them what had happened to him. They, in their turn, told him that during his absence they had returned to his father with the news that he had gone into the princess's apartments and not come out, leaving them unsure as to what had happened. They added: 'When he heard that, he mustered his armies and we came here, bringing great relief to you and joy to us.' 'From first to last, good continues to flow from your hands,' exclaimed Taj al-Muluk.

King Shahriman went to his daughter and found her wailing and weeping for Taj al-Muluk. She had taken a sword, fixed the hilt in the ground and placed the point between her breasts directly opposite her heart. She bent over it, saying: 'I must kill myself, for I cannot live after my beloved.' When her father came in and saw her like this, he shouted to her: 'Mistress of princesses, don't do it! Have pity on your father and your countrymen!' He then went up to her and said: 'You are not to bring down evil upon your father.' He told her that her beloved, the son of King Sulaiman Shah, wanted to marry her, adding that the betrothal and the marriage were dependent on her. She smiled and said: 'Didn't I tell you that he was a king's son? By God, I shall have to let him crucify you on a piece of timber worth two dirhams.' 'Daughter,' he said, 'have mercy on me that God may have mercy on you.' To which she replied: 'Hurry off and bring him to me quickly and without delay.'

The king then hurried away to Taj al-Muluk, to whom he whispered the news, and then the two of them went to the princess. On seeing her lover, she threw her arms around his neck in the presence of her father, embraced him and kissed him, saying: 'You left me lonely.' Then she turned to her father and said: 'Do you think that anyone could exaggerate the merits of so handsome a being? In addition, he is a king and the son of a king, one of those of noble stock who are prevented from indulging in depravity.' At that, the king went out and shut the door on them with his own hand. He then went to the vizier of Sulaiman Shah and his fellow envoys, and he told them to inform their master that his son was well and happy, living a life of the greatest pleasure with his beloved.

When they had set off to take this message to Sulaiman Shah, King Shahriman ordered that presents, forage and guest provisions should be sent out to his troops. When all this had been done, he sent out a hundred fine horses, a hundred dromedaries, a hundred mamluks, a hundred concubines, a hundred black slaves and a hundred slave girls, all of whom were led out before him as a gift, while he himself mounted and rode from the city with his chief officials and principal officers. When Sulaiman Shah learned of this, he got up and walked a few paces to meet the king. He had been delighted to hear the news brought by the vizier and 'Aziz, and he exclaimed: 'Praise be to God who has allowed my son to achieve his wish.' He then embraced King Shahriman and made him sit beside him on his couch, where they talked together happily. Food was produced and they ate their fill, after which they moved on to sweetmeats and fruit, both fresh and dried, all of which they sampled. Shortly afterwards, Taj al-Muluk arrived, dressed in his finery. His father, on seeing him, got up to embrace him and kissed him, while all those who were seated rose to their feet. The two kings made him sit between them and they sat talking for a time until Sulaiman Shah said to King Shahriman: 'I want to draw up a contract of marriage between my son and your daughter before witnesses, so that the news may spread abroad, as is the custom.' 'To hear is to obey,' said King Shahriman, and at that, he sent for the *qadi* and the notaries. When they came they drew up the contract between Taj al-Muluk and Princess Dunya, after which money and sweetmeats were distributed, incense was burned and perfume released. That was a day of happiness and delight, and all the leaders and the soldiers shared in the joy.

While King Shahriman began to prepare for his daughter's wedding, Taj al-Muluk said to his father: 'This young 'Aziz is a noble fellow who has done me a great service. He has shared my hardships, travelled with me, brought me to my goal, endured with me and encouraged me to endure until the affair was settled. For two years now he has been with me, far from his own land. I want us to equip him with merchandise from here so that he can go off joyfully, as his country is not far from here.' The king agreed that this was an excellent idea and they prepared for 'Aziz a hundred loads of the finest and most expensive materials. Taj al-Muluk then came, presented him with a huge sum of money, and said, on taking his leave of him: 'Brother and friend, take this money as a gift of friendship, and may safety attend you as you return to your own country.' 'Aziz accepted the gift and kissed the ground before him and before the king. He took his leave and Taj al-Muluk rode with him for three miles, after which 'Aziz entreated him persuasively to turn back, adding: 'Were it not for my mother, master, I would not leave you, but don't deprive me of news of you.'

Taj al-Muluk agreed to this and went back, while 'Aziz travelled on until he reached his own country. He did not stop until he had come to his mother, who, as he found, had built a tomb for him in the middle of the house, which she continually visited. When he went in, he found that she had undone her hair, which was spread over the tomb. She was weeping and reciting the lines:

> I show patience in the face of each disaster,
> But separation leaves me prey to care.
> Who can bear to lose his friend,
> And who is not brought low by the imminence of parting?

She then sighed deeply and recited:

> Why is it when I pass the tombs
> And greet my beloved's grave, he makes no answer?
> He says: 'How can I answer you,
> When I am held down here by stones and earth?
> The earth has eaten my beauties; I have forgotten you,
> Secluded as I am from my kin and my dear ones.'

While she was in this state, 'Aziz came in and, on seeing him, she fell fainting with joy. He sprinkled water on her face, and when she had recovered, she got up and took him in her arms, hugging him as he hugged her. They then exchanged greetings, and when she asked the reason for his absence, he told her the whole story of what had happened to him from beginning to end, including how Taj al-Muluk had given him money as well as a hundred loads of materials. His mother was delighted, and he stayed with her in his city, lamenting what had happened to him at the hands of the daughter of Delilah the wily, who had castrated him.

So much for 'Aziz, but as for Taj al-Muluk, he went in to his beloved, Princess Dunya, and deflowered her. King Shahriman then began to equip her for her journey with her husband and her father-in-law. He brought for them provisions, gifts and rarities, which were loaded on their beasts, and when they set off, he went with them for three days to say goodbye. On the prompting of King Sulaiman Shah, he then turned back, while Sulaiman Shah himself, Taj al-Muluk, his wife and their troops travelled on, night and day, until they were close to their city. News had kept coming in of their approach and the city was adorned with decorations for them.

Night 137

Morning now dawned and Shahrazad broke off from what she had been allowed to say. Then, when it was the one hundred and thirty-seventh night, SHE CONTINUED:

I have heard, O fortunate king, that when Sulaiman Shah arrived at his city it was adorned with decorations for him and his son. When they entered, the king took his seat on his royal throne, with Taj al-Muluk at his side. He distributed gifts and largesse, and freed all those held in his prisons. He then organized a second wedding for his son, with songs and music continuing to sound for a whole month. The dressers presented Princess Dunya in her bridal robes, and she never tired of the process and neither did the ladies tire of looking at her. Taj al-Muluk, after a meeting with his father and mother, went in to his bride and they continued to lead the most delightful and pleasant of lives until they were visited by the destroyer of delights.

At this point, Dau' al-Makan said to the vizier Dandan: 'It is men like you who bring joy to sad hearts and are the boon companions of kings, following the best of paths in what they organize.' All this took place as the Muslims were besieging Constantinople. When the siege had lasted for four years, they felt a longing for their own lands; the soldiers were restless; they were tired of sleepless nights, the siege and the fighting that went on by night and by day. So it was that Dau' al-Makan summoned Bahram, Rustam and Tarkash, and when they had come, he said: 'You know that we have been here for all these years without achieving our goal but, rather, adding to our own cares and distress. We came to free ourselves of the blood debt owed because of the death of King 'Umar ibn al-Nu'man, but we have lost my brother, Sharkan, and one sorrow and one disaster have become two. The cause of all this was the old woman, Dhat al-Dawahi, and it was she who killed the sultan in his own kingdom and took his wife, Sophia. Not content with that, she tricked us and severed the neck of my brother. I have bound myself by the solemnest of oaths to take vengeance. What have you to say? Take note of what I have told you and give me an answer.' The others bowed their heads, saying: 'It is for the vizier Dandan to give advice.' At that Dandan came forward to King Dau' al-Makan and said: 'Know, your majesty, that there is no longer anything to be got from staying here. My advice is that we should leave for home, stay there for a time and then come back and launch a raid against the idolaters.' 'This is excellent advice,' replied the king, 'as the men are longing to see their families, and I myself long to see my son, Kana-ma-Kana, and my niece, Qudiya-fa-Kana. She is in Damascus and I don't know what has happened to her.'

When the soldiers heard this, they called down blessings on the vizier Dandan in their joy and Dau' al-Makan had a proclamation made that they were to move off in three days' time. They started to make their preparations, and on the fourth day, to the sound of drums, the banners were unfurled and the vizier Dandan advanced at the head of the army, while the king was in the centre with the grand chamberlain at his side. The army continued its march, night and day, until it reached Baghdad. Its arrival delighted the inhabitants, relieving them of cares and distress; those who had stayed behind were reunited with those who had gone, and each emir went to his own house.

The king went up to his palace, where he went in to see his son, Kana-ma-Kana, who was now seven years old and had begun to go riding. When he had rested from his journey, he went to the baths with his son and then, going back, he took his seat on the royal throne. The vizier Dandan stood before him and the emirs and officers of state came and stood in attendance on him. He then sent for his companion, the furnace man, who had befriended him in foreign parts. When the man had been fetched and stood before him, the king rose to show him the respect that was his due, and then made him sit by his side. He had told the vizier of the services that the man had done him, and the emirs, together with the vizier, treated him with honour. Because of the amount that he had eaten and because of his restful life, he had become stout and fat, so much so that his neck was like that of an elephant and his face looked like a dolphin's belly. Because he never went out, his mind had become confused and he did not recognize the king. The latter came up to him, smiling and greeting him with the greatest warmth, and said: 'How fast you have forgotten me.'

At that, the furnace man came to his senses and, after taking a long look at the king, he recognized who he was and jumped to his feet, saying: 'My dear fellow, who has made you a sultan?' Dau' al-Makan laughed at this and the vizier Dandan went up to him and explained the story. 'He was your brother and your companion, and now he has become the ruler of this land. He will certainly be very good to you and my advice is that when he asks you what you want, wish for something big, for you are dear to him.' The furnace man said: 'I'm afraid that if I ask for something, he may not be willing or able to grant it me.' 'He will give you whatever you ask for,' said the vizier. 'You have no need to worry.' 'By God,' said the furnace man, 'I shall have to ask him for something that I have in mind. I dream of it every night and I hope that Almighty God may give it me.' 'Be of good heart,' said the vizier, 'for, by God, if you asked to be made sultan of Damascus in place of his brother, he would grant you this and put you in charge.' At that, the furnace man rose to his feet and, although Dau' al-Makan gestured to him to sit down, he refused, saying: 'God forbid: the days when I sat in your presence are over.' 'No,' said Dau' al-Makan, 'they are still here now. You saved my life and whatever you want to ask for, I shall give you. Make your wish first to God and then to me.' 'I'm afraid, sir,' said the man. 'Don't be,' Dau' al-Makan assured him, but he repeated: 'I'm afraid lest I ask for something and you don't give it to me.' The king laughed and said: 'If you asked for half my kingdom I would share it with you. So say what you want, with no more prevarication.' Again the man repeated: 'I'm afraid,' and when the king told him not to be, he said: 'I'm afraid that you may not be able to give me what I ask for.' At that, the king grew angry and insisted that he should say what he wanted. 'I make my wish to God and then to you, that you write a decree for me putting me in charge of all the furnace men in Jerusalem.' The king burst out laughing, as did all those who were there. 'Make another wish,' he said. 'Didn't I tell you, sir,' said the man, 'that I was afraid I might ask for something that you wouldn't or couldn't give me?' The vizier prodded him again and then again, and on each occasion he said: 'I have a wish to make.' 'Say what you want and be quick about it,' said the king. 'I want you to put me in charge of the refuse men in Jerusalem or in Damascus,' was the reply. Those present fell over laughing and the vizier struck the furnace man. 'Why are you hitting me?' the man asked. 'I have done nothing wrong. It was you who told me to ask for something big.' Then he added: 'Let me go back home.'

Dau' al-Makan then realized that he was joking and, after a short pause, he went up to him and said: 'Brother, ask me for something great that befits my status to offer you.' 'King of the age,' the man replied, 'I present my wish to God and then to you as king, that you make me sultan of Damascus in place of your brother.' 'God has granted your request,' said the king, at which the man kissed the ground in front of him. The king then ordered that a chair should be set for him in the position to which his new rank entitled him; he gave him a robe of office and wrote and signed a decree of appointment for him. He instructed Dandan to go with him to Damascus, adding that on his return journey he was to bring Sharkan's daughter, Qudiya-fa-Kana. 'To hear is to obey,' replied the vizier, and he then went off with the furnace man and made preparations for the journey. On the king's orders, the furnace man was provided with servants and retainers, together with a new palanquin, regally furnished. The king said to the emirs: 'Let whoever loves me show honour to this man and give him a great gift.' This the emirs did, each in proportion to his means, and the king named him al-Ziblkan, with the honorific title of al-Mujahid.*

When all the preparations had been made, the furnace man went with the vizier to visit the king in order to say goodbye and to ask leave to set off on his journey. The king rose for him and embraced him, charging him to act justly towards his subjects and ordering him to prepare for a war against the infidels in two years' time. They then said goodbye to each other, and al-Ziblkan al-Malik al-Mujahid left on his journey, having been instructed by Dau' al-Makan to treat his people well. The emirs provided him with five thousand mamluks and servants who rode behind him, while in front was the grand chamberlain, together with Bahram, the leader of the Dailamis, Rustam, the leader of the Persians, and the Arab leader, Tarkash. They were there in attendance on him as a parting gesture, and after accompanying him for three days, they went back to Baghdad, while the sultan al-Ziblkan, the vizier Dandan and the troops that were with them carried on until they reached Damascus.

News had come by pigeon post to the Damascenes that King Dau' al-Makan had appointed as ruler of Damascus a sultan named al-Ziblkan, to whom he had given the honorific title of al-Mujahid. When he arrived, the city was adorned with decorations and all the citizens came out to see the spectacle. The sultan entered in great procession, and after going up to the citadel, he took his seat on his royal throne,

---

* Meaning 'fighter', especially in the *jihad* or 'Holy War'.

with the vizier Dandan standing in attendance on him and informing him of the appropriate stations and ranks of the emirs as they came in to kiss his hands and to invoke blessings on him. Al-Ziblkan welcomed them, giving them robes of honour and presenting them with gifts. He then opened the treasuries and distributed their contents to all the soldiers, whatever their rank, while ruling with justice. After this he began to make preparations for the journey of Princess Qudiya-fa-Kana, the daughter of Sultan Sharkan, providing her with a silken litter. He also made preparations for the vizier and produced money for him, but Dandan refused to take it, explaining: 'You are new to the position and you may find yourself in need of money. At a later stage we shall accept it and we shall write to ask you for a subsidy for the holy war, or some other purpose.' When Dandan was ready to set off, al-Ziblkan rode out to take leave of him. He had Qudiya-fa-Kana brought and placed in her litter, sending with her ten slave girls to attend on her. When Dandan had left, he returned to administer his kingdom, concerning himself with the provision of weapons and waiting for a summons to come from King Dau' al-Makan.

So much, then, for him, but as for the vizier Dandan, he continued to traverse the various stages of his journey with Qudiya-fa-Kana until, after a month, he arrived at al-Ruhba. He then moved on to the outskirts of Baghdad, from where he sent a message to Dau' al-Makan, announcing his arrival. The king rode out to meet him, but when Dandan was about to dismount, he told him not to do so and rode up beside him instead. To his question about al-Ziblkan, Dandan replied that all was well with him, and he gave news of the arrival of Qudiya-fa-Kana, the daughter of the king's brother, Sharkan. Dau' al-Makan was delighted and said: 'Rest for three days from the hardships of your journey and then come to me.' Dandan agreed and went off to his house, while the king returned to his palace. There he went in to visit his niece, Qudiya-fa-Kana, who was now eight years old. He was filled with joy when he saw her, although this was mixed with sorrow for her father. He had clothes made for her and presented her with jewellery and great quantities of ornaments. On his instructions, she was lodged with his son, Kana-ma-Kana, and the two of them grew up to be the most intelligent of the people of their age as well as the bravest.

While Qudiya-fa-Kana was prudent and intelligent, taking note of the consequences of her actions, Kana-ma-Kana turned out to be generous and noble, but unconcerned about the future. By the time that they had

reached the age of ten, Qudiya-fa-Kana was in the habit of riding out
with him on long trips to the country, where they would practise cutting
and thrusting with sword and lance, and this went on until they were
both twelve. At that time, the king had completed his plans for the Holy
War and made all his preparations. He summoned Dandan and said:
'You must know that I have determined on a plan, which I shall set out
for you to study, and after that I want you to give me a quick answer.'
'What are you thinking of, king of the age?' asked Dandan. Dau' al-
Makan replied: 'I propose to appoint my son, Kana-ma-Kana, as king,
so that I can take pleasure in him during my life and fight in his defence
until death overtakes me. What do you think?' Dandan kissed the earth
in front of the king and said: 'Know, king of the age, that this is an
attractive idea, but this is not the right time for it, for two reasons. The
first is that your son Kana-ma-Kana is young, while the second is that
custom shows that whoever gives power to his son in his own lifetime
does not live for long afterwards. This is my answer.' 'Know, vizier,'
said the king, 'that I shall entrust my son to the care of the grand
chamberlain who, as my sister's husband, has become one of us and is
answerable to me, having taken the place of my brother.' 'Do whatever
you think right,' replied the vizier, 'for we shall obey your orders.'

The king then sent for the grand chamberlain, together with the officers
of state, and said to them: 'You know that my son, Kana-ma-Kana, is
the champion of the age, unequalled in battle and war. I have made him
your king, appointing the grand chamberlain, his uncle, as his guardian.'
The chamberlain said: 'King of the age, it is your favour that has nurtured
me.' 'Chamberlain,' replied the king, 'my son, Kana-ma-Kana, and my
brother's daughter, Qudiya-fa-Kana, are cousins, and I call all present to
witness that I intend to give her to him as a wife.' He then transferred
to his son wealth that would baffle all description, after which he went
to his sister, Nuzhat al-Zaman, and told her of this. She was delighted,
saying: 'These two are my children; may God preserve you and may you
live a long life for their sakes.' 'Sister,' he replied, 'I have achieved what
I wanted in this world and I can rely on my son, but you must keep an
eye on him and on his mother.'

He passed several nights and days in giving instructions to the chamberlain and to Nuzhat al-Zaman with regard to his son, his niece and
his wife. He then took to his bed, being certain that he was about to
drink the cup of death, while it was the chamberlain who administered
the affairs of the peoples and the lands. After a year, he summoned his

son, Kana-ma-Kana, and the vizier Dandan. 'My son,' he said, 'after my death this vizier will be your father. Know that I am leaving the transitory world for the world of eternity. I have achieved what I wanted here, but I have one heartfelt regret, which I hope that God will remove at your hands.' Kana-ma-Kana asked his father what this was, and he replied: 'It is that I should die without having taken vengeance for your grandfather, 'Umar ibn al-Nu'man, and your uncle, Sharkan, from an old woman called Dhat al-Dawahi. If God grants you victory, do not neglect to avenge this and to clear away the shame that the infidels have inflicted on us, but beware of the old woman's wiles and listen to the advice of the vizier Dandan, who for years has been the pillar of our kingdom.' Kana-ma-Kana accepted his counsel, and after this the king's eyes filled with tears as his illness grew worse. His brother-in-law, the chamberlain, an experienced man, took charge of the affairs of state, with absolute authority, and this continued for a whole year, while Dau' al-Makan was preoccupied with his disease, which continued to debilitate him for four years. The grand chamberlain's administration won the approval of the citizens of the kingdom and the officers of state, while all the lands called down blessings on him.

So much for Dau' al-Makan and the chamberlain, but as for the king's son, Kana-ma-Kana, his only concern was to ride horses, practise with lances and shoot arrows. The same was true of his cousin, Qudiya-fa-Kana, and the two of them used to be out from first light until nightfall, when they would each go back to their mothers. Kana-ma-Kana would find his mother sitting by his father's head, weeping and ministering to him all night long until morning, when he himself and his cousin would then go out again as usual. Dau' al-Makan suffered prolonged pains, and in tears he recited the following lines:

My strength has gone; my time is past;
Here I remain as you see me.
On the day of glory I outshone my people;
I was the first of them to fulfil what was wished for.
I wonder if I shall see before my death
My son as ruler of the people in my place,
Charging the enemy to take vengeance,
Cutting with the sword and thrusting with the spear.
I shall be the loser in all things, light or serious,
If God, my Master, does not mend my heart.

When he had finished his recitation, he leaned his head on his pillow, his eyes closed and he fell asleep. In a dream, he heard a voice saying: 'Good news. Your son will fill the lands with justice; he will rule over them and the people will obey him.' He woke from this dream happy at what had been revealed to him, and a few days later death struck him.

This was a source of great grief to the people of Baghdad, and high and low alike wept for him, but with the passing of time it was as though he had never been. The situation of Kana-ma-Kana changed and the Baghdadis deposed him, isolating him and his family. When his mother saw that, in her humiliation she said: 'I must go to the grand chamberlain, hoping for mercy from the Kind and All-knowing God.' She left her house and went to that of the chamberlain, who had become king and whom she found sitting on his carpet. She went to his wife, Nuzhat al-Zaman, and said, weeping bitterly: 'The dead have no friends. May God never reduce you to need with the passage of years and may you continue to rule with justice the high and the low. You heard and saw the regal dignity and rank that we enjoyed, together with the wealth and the luxurious circumstances of our life. Now time has turned against us; the passing years have betrayed us and attacked us. I have come to you to ask for your favour, after having myself conferred favours, since when a man dies, his wives and daughters are humiliated.' She then recited:

It is enough for you that death's wonders become plain,
And what is hidden in life will not be hidden from us then.
These days are only stages on a journey,
Where disasters mingle with the waters that we reach.
Nothing so saddens me as the loss of noble men,
Who have been victims of great miseries.

When Nuzhat al-Zaman heard this, she remembered her brother Dau' al-Makan and his son, Kana-ma-Kana. Inviting her visitor to approach, she went forward to meet her, saying: 'By God, I am now rich while you are poor. The only reason that we did not go to look for you was that I was afraid that you might be broken-hearted were you to think that whatever we gave you was charity, while all the good things we enjoy come from you and your husband. Our house is yours; our place is yours; our wealth is yours, together with all that we have.' She then gave the widow splendid clothes and set aside for her an apartment in the palace next to her own. The widow stayed there with her son, Kana-ma-Kana, enjoying an agreeable life. Kana-ma-Kana was dressed in kingly robes and he and his mother were assigned slave girls to serve them. Soon afterwards, Nuzhat al-Zaman told her husband about Dau' al-Makan's widow. His eyes filled with tears and he said: 'If you want to see what the world will be like after you have left it, look at it when someone else has gone. Make sure that she is given an honourable lodging here . . .'

Night 138

Morning now dawned and Shahrazad broke off from what she had been allowed to say. Then, when it was the hundred and thirty-eighth night, SHE CONTINUED:

I have heard, O fortunate king, that when Nuzhat al-Zaman told her husband about Dau' al-Makan's widow, he told her to be sure that she was given an honourable lodging and her poverty relieved.

So much for Nuzhat al-Zaman, her husband and the widow of Dau' al-Makan. As for Kana-ma-Kana and his cousin, Qudiya-fa-Kana, they grew up and flourished until, at the age of fifteen, they were like two fruit-laden branches or two shining moons. Qudiya-fa-Kana was one of the most beautiful of secluded girls, with a lovely face, smooth cheeks, a slender waist, heavy buttocks, a graceful figure, a mouth sweeter than wine, and saliva like the fountain of Paradise. A poet has described her in these lines:

> It was as though her saliva was choice wine
> And grapes were plucked from her sweet mouth.
> Were she to bend, it is grape clusters that sway –
> Glory to her Creator; none can describe her.

In her, Almighty God had united every beauty. Her figure put branches to shame; roses asked for mercy from her cheeks; while her saliva laughed the finest wine to scorn. She was a delight to both heart and eye, as the poet has said:

> A beautiful girl, perfect in loveliness,
> Whose eyebrows put to shame the use of kohl.
> To the heart of her lover her glances are like a sword
> Wielded by 'Ali, Commander of the Faithful.

As for Kana-ma-Kana, he was remarkably handsome, perfect in form, unmatched in beauty, with courage showing between his eyes and testifying for him rather than against him. Hard hearts inclined to him; his eyes were dark; and when hair started to grow around his lips and down spread on his cheeks, many lines were written about it:

> My excuse appeared only when his cheek sprouted down
> And bewildering darkness moved over it.
> He is a fawn; when others saw his beauty,
> His eyes unsheathed a dagger against them.

Another poet has said:

> The souls of lovers drew upon his cheek
> The image of an ant, perfected in red blood.
> How strange to see martyrs living in hellfire,
> Clothed in green silk of Paradise.

It so happened that, on one feast day, Qudiya-fa-Kana went out to celebrate the feast with some of her relatives at the court. She was surrounded in all her beauty by her slave girls; the roses of her cheek envied her beauty spot and camomile blossoms smiled from the lightning flashes of her mouth. Kana-ma-Kana started to walk around her, looking at her as she appeared like the shining moon. Plucking up his courage, he recited the following lines:

> When will the heart, saddened by parting, find a cure?
> When will rejection cease and the mouth of union laugh?
> I wish that I knew whether I shall spend a night
> With a beloved who feels something of my love.

When Qudiya-fa-Kana heard these lines, she made her disapproval plain to see. With a disdainful look she expressed her anger with Kana-ma-Kana and said to him: 'Is it to put me to shame among your family that you mention me in your verses? By God, if you don't stop talking like this, I shall complain of you to the grand chamberlain, the king of Khurasan and Baghdad, the just ruler, and he will bring disgrace and ignominy down on you.' Kana-ma-Kana was indignant but made no reply and went back to Baghdad in a state of anger. Qudiya-fa-Kana went to her palace and complained to her mother of her cousin's behaviour. 'Daughter,' replied her mother, 'it may be that he did not intend to do you any harm. He is, after all, fatherless, and, in addition, he did not say anything that would disgrace you. Take care not to tell anyone about it for the news might get to the king and lead him to cut short the boy's life, blotting out all memory of him and consigning him to the past.'

In spite of that, Kana-ma-Kana's love for Qudiya-fa-Kana became well known in Baghdad and was the subject of gossip among women. He himself became depressed; he lost his powers of endurance and became helpless and unable to conceal his state from those around him. He wanted to disclose the grief of separation that was in his heart, but was afraid lest Qudiya-fa-Kana reproach him and be angry with him. So he recited:

When a day comes on which I fear reproach
From one whose serene nature has been clouded over,
I bear her harshness as a man endures
Cauterization while searching for a cure.

Night 139

Morning now dawned and Shahrazad broke off from what she had been allowed to say. Then, when it was the hundred and thirty-ninth night, SHE CONTINUED:

I have heard, O fortunate king, that when the grand chamberlain became king, he was called al-Malik Sasan. He took his place on the royal throne and treated his subjects well. One day while he was seated there, he was told of the poetry recited by Kana-ma-Kana. He was filled with regret for what had passed and, going to his wife Nuzhat al-Zaman, he said: 'It is very dangerous to combine esparto grass with fire. Men are not to be trusted with women as long as eyes glance and eyelids flutter. Your nephew Kana-ma-Kana has now reached man's estate and he must be kept from visiting the ladies of the harem. It is even more necessary that your daughter be kept away from men, as girls like her should be kept in seclusion.' 'That is true, wise king,' replied his wife, and next day, when Kana-ma-Kana paid his usual visit to his aunt and they had exchanged greetings, she said to him: 'My son, there is something that I don't want to say but which I have to tell you in spite of myself.' When he told her to say it, she went on: 'Your uncle, the chamberlain, the father of Qudiya-fa-Kana, has heard of the poetry that you recited about her and he has given orders that she is to be kept away from you. If there is anything that you need, I shall send it to you from behind the door, but you are not to see Qudiya-fa-Kana or to come back here from now on.'

On hearing this, Kana-ma-Kana got up and went out without speaking a single word. He came to his mother and told her what his aunt had said. 'This is because you talked too much,' she said. 'The story of your love for Qudiya-fa-Kana has spread and is spoken of everywhere. How can you eat their food and then fall in love with their daughter?' 'Who should have her except for me?' he asked. 'She is my cousin and I have a greater right to her than any.' 'Don't talk like that,' said his mother. 'Keep quiet, lest word of this reach King Sasan and lead to your losing her. It might multiply your sorrows or even lead to your destruction. They have not sent us an evening meal tonight and we may perish of hunger. Were we in any other city we should die of starvation or from the shame of having to beg.'

When Kana-ma-Kana heard what his mother had to say, he became more distressed; his eyes filled with tears; he groaned and complained, reciting the following:

Less of this blame, which never quits me!
My heart loves one who has enslaved it;
Look for no grain of patience in me.
I swear by the Holy House, my patience is divorced.
When censurers forbid me, I disobey them,
And I am truthful in laying claim to love.
They keep me by force from visiting her,
But, by the Merciful God, I am not dissolute.
When my bones hear her mentioned,
They are like little birds pursued by hawks.
Say to all those who blame me for my love:
'I swear to you I truly love my cousin.'

When he had finished these lines, he said to his mother: 'I can no longer stay with my aunt or with these people. I shall leave the palace and find a place to live on the outskirts of the city.' His mother went out of the palace with him and they lodged near some beggars. His mother used to go to and fro to King Sasan's palace and fetch food for the two of them. Some time later, Qudiya-fa-Kana, finding herself alone with her, asked how Kana-ma-Kana was. She replied: 'My daughter, he is tearful and sad at heart, having been entrapped by love for you,' and she recited the lines that he had composed. Qudiya-fa-Kana wept and said:

'By God, I did not leave him because of what he said or because I disliked him. Rather, I did this because I was afraid that his enemies might harm him, and my longing for him is far greater than his for me. My tongue cannot describe it and had it not been for the slip of his tongue and the fluttering of his heart, my father would not have cut off his favour from him and caused him to be banished and deprived. But men's fortunes change and in all affairs endurance is best. It may be that He Who has decreed that we be parted will grant that we may meet again.' She then recited these lines:

> Cousin, my passion is like yours, but multiplied,
> Yet I hid it; why did you not hide yours?

When Kana-ma-Kana's mother heard this, she thanked Qudiya-fa-Kana and invoked a blessing on her before leaving. She then told this to her son. His desire for the princess increased and he recovered his spirits, after his strength had almost left him and he was close to breathing his last. 'By God,' he said, 'I want none but her,' and he then recited:

> Stop blaming me; I shall not listen to a word of blame.
> I have revealed the secret that I kept concealed.
> The one whose union I hope for has gone.
> My eye is wakeful and my beloved sleeps.

Days and nights passed, with the prince tossing on hot coals until he was seventeen years old – a perfect model of beauty and grace. One night, as he lay awake, he said to himself: 'Why should I stay silent until I waste away with no sight of my beloved? Poverty is my only reproach. By God, I want to leave these parts and wander in the wastes and wildernesses, for to stay here is torture. I have no friend and no beloved to console me, and so I intend to find my own consolation by staying away from home until I die and find relief from these trials and this degradation.' He then recited these lines:

> Let the throbbing of my blood increase;
> It is not for me to suffer humiliation before the foe.
> Forgive me; in my inmost heart there is a page
> For which most clearly tears provide a heading.
> My cousin seems a houri of Paradise,
> Come down to us through the favour of Ridwan.
> Whoever stands against the sword thrusts of her glance

Will find no refuge from their enmity,
So I shall travel widely through God's lands,
To win a livelihood in place of poverty.
By such a journey I shall save myself,
Exchanging my privations there for wealth,
Before returning happy and fortunate,
Having fought with heroes on the battlefield.
When I come back, it will be with booty,
And I shall conquer those who match themselves with me.

Kana-ma-Kana left, walking barefoot in a shirt with short sleeves, wearing on his head a seven-year-old felt cap, and carrying with him a three-day-old dry loaf of bread. It was pitch dark when he started out; he came to the Arij gate of the city, where he waited, and when it was opened, he was the first to go out through it. He then travelled as fast as he could by night and by day through the deserts. On the first night of his absence, his mother looked for him and when she could not find him, the wide world contracted for her and she took no pleasure in any of its delights. She waited expectantly for him first for one day, then for a second and then for a third, until ten days had passed without any news of him. In her distress she cried out and screamed, saying: 'My darling son, you have brought down sorrows on me, although I had enough of these before you left home. Now that you have gone, I have no desire for food nor can I take pleasure in sleep. All that is left for me are tears and sorrow. Oh my son, from what land shall I summon you and where have you found refuge?' Then, sighing deeply, she recited these lines:

I know that suffering awaits me now that you have gone,
And the bows of parting have shot shafts at me.
They loaded their baggage and then went,
Leaving me to the pains of death, as they crossed the sands.
In the dark of night a ringdove cooed;
'Gently,' I said to it. 'By my life, had you my grief,
You would not wear a collar nor would your foot be dyed.
My lover has left me; what meets me now
Are summoners of care that never leave.'

She neither ate nor drank but wept and sobbed more and more. Her tears became a matter of public knowledge and she caused weeping among other people and through the lands. People started to say: 'Dau' al-Makan, where are you looking?' They complained of the injustices of Time and said to each other: 'What do you suppose has happened to Kana-ma-Kana, that he has been driven away from his homeland? His father used to feed the hungry and his rule brought us justice and security.' His mother wept and wailed more and more until news of this reached King Sasan.

Night 140

Morning now dawned and Shahrazad broke off from what she had been allowed to say. Then, when it was the hundred and fortieth night, SHE CONTINUED:

I have heard, O fortunate king, that news of this reached King Sasan. It was brought to him by the leading emirs, who told him: 'He is the son of our king, of the stock of King 'Umar ibn al-Nu'man, and we have heard that he has left the country.'

When King Sasan heard this, he was angry with them and ordered one of them to be hanged, as a result of which the rest of his courtiers were filled with dread and none of them could speak. Sasan then remembered the good treatment that he had received from Dau' al-Makan and the fact that Kana-ma-Kana had been entrusted to his care. He began to feel sorry for the prince and said that a search would have to be made throughout the lands. Summoning Tarkash, he told him to pick a hundred riders and take them off to search for him, but after an absence of ten days Tarkash came back to report that he had no news of the prince nor found any trace of him nor met anyone who could tell him anything. King Sasan was sorry for how he had treated Kana-ma-Kana, while his mother could find no rest and no patience for twenty long days.

So much for them, but as for Kana-ma-Kana, when he left Baghdad he was in a state of confusion and did not know where to go. For three days he wandered alone in the desert without seeing a single soul, unable to rest and remaining constantly wakeful, thinking of his family and his own country. He fed himself on plants and drank from streams, resting in the midday heat under trees. He then left the track that he was on for another one, which he followed for three days, and after this, on the fourth day, he found himself on the edge of a grassy and fertile plain covered with beautiful plants and trees. This land had drunk from the cups of the clouds to the sound of thunder and the cooing of doves. Its borders were green and its open spaces delightful.

Kana-ma-Kana remembered Baghdad, his father's city, and expressed the excess of his emotion in these lines:

I left, hoping to return;
When this will be, I do not know.
I have become a wanderer for love,
And find no way to cure my passion.

On finishing his poem, he shed tears, but then, having wiped them away, he sustained himself by eating some of the plants there, after which he performed the ritual ablution and prayed, making up the tally of prayers that he had missed during his wanderings. He sat there to rest all through the day, and at nightfall he fell asleep. He remained asleep until midnight, and when he awoke, he heard a man's voice reciting these lines:

What is life without a lightning flash
From the beloved's mouth, and her pure face?
Let bishops in monasteries pray for her,
And vie in their prostrations before her.
For death is easier than aversion on her part,
From whom no phantom visits me at night.
How joyful is the meeting between friends,
When both the lover and his love are there,
Especially in the season of the flowery spring,
When Time speeds on with fragrant gifts.
You who drink wine, here before you
There is a happy land of gushing streams.

When Kana-ma-Kana heard this, it moved him to grief; tears streamed down his cheeks and his heart was filled with burning fire. He got up to see who was reciting the lines, but in the darkness he could not make out anyone. His passion increased but, in his alarm and distress, he went down to the bottom of the valley and walked by the bank of the stream. Then he heard the reciter of the lines sigh deeply and produce these lines:

You may conceal your love from fear,
But on the day of parting let your tears flow down.
As lovers, we are joined by covenants of love,

So for all time my longing must remain.
My heart finds rest with the beloved, and the cooling breeze
Delights me as its breath stirs up my longing.
Sa'd, will the lady of the anklets think of me
After our parting, and of our bond and covenant?
Will nights of union join us once again,
So that we may explain part of our sufferings?
She said: 'You are beguiled by love for me.' I said to her:
'God guard you; how many lovers have you beguiled?'
May God not let my eyes enjoy her loveliness,
If after she has gone they ever taste sweet sleep.
My heart is stung and I can find no cure
Except for union and to sip her lips.

When Kana-ma-Kana heard the same voice reciting poetry once again but still could not see who it was, he realized that this must be a lover like himself who had been kept from union with his beloved. He said to himself: 'It is right that we should put our heads together and that I should take him as a friend in my exile.' Clearing his throat, he called out: 'You who travel in the dark of the night, come up and tell me your story, for you may find that I can help you in your distress.' When the reciter heard this, he replied: 'Whoever you are who has answered my call and heard my tale, who are you among the riders? Are you human or *jinn*? Answer me quickly before death comes to you. I have been travelling in the desert for some twenty days without seeing anyone and yours is the only voice that I have heard.'

When Kana-ma-Kana heard this, he said to himself: 'This is a man whose story is like mine, for I, too, have been travelling for twenty days without seeing or hearing anyone.' He decided not to reply until day had broken, and so he stayed silent. The reciter shouted to him: 'You who called, if you are a *jinni*, go off in peace, but if you are human, stay awhile until dawn comes and the darkness of night clears away.' He then stayed where he was, as did Kana-ma-Kana, and the two of them went on reciting poetry to each other and shedding copious tears until night ended and the light of dawn appeared.

Kana-ma-Kana then looked at the reciter and found that he was a young Bedouin wearing tattered clothes, girt with a sword that had rusted in its scabbard, and marked out as a lover. He went up and greeted him, and the Bedouin returned his greeting, saluting him courteously, although, in fact, he despised him, seeing him to be both young and impoverished. 'Young man,' he said, 'to what people do you belong; what is your clan and what is your story? You travel by night, the action of a hero, and what you said to me at night were the words of a valiant champion. Your life is now in my hands, but I shall have mercy on you because of your tender years and I shall take you as a companion so that you can come with me as my servant.'

When Kana-ma-Kana heard these ugly words, which contrasted with the beauty of the man's poetry, he realized that the Bedouin despised him and wanted to take advantage of him. He replied with gentle eloquence: 'Chief of the Arabs, don't talk of my youth, but tell me how you come to be travelling by night through the desert, reciting poetry. I see that you say that I should act as your servant, but who are you and what prompts you to talk like this?' 'Listen, young man,' replied the Bedouin. 'I am Sabbah ibn Rammah ibn Hammam, and my clan belong to the Bedouin of Syria. I have a cousin called Najma, who brings blessings to all who see her. My father died and I was brought up with my uncle, Najma's father. When we both grew up we were kept away from each other, as my uncle saw that I was poor and penniless. The Arab chiefs and the leaders of the tribes went to see him and criticized him for this. He felt ashamed and he agreed to marry my cousin to me, but only on condition that I give him by way of dowry fifty horses, fifty camels, ten months pregnant, fifty more laden with wheat and another fifty laden with barley, ten black slaves and ten slave girls. He has asked too much, imposing a burden on me that I cannot bear, and so here am I on my way from Syria to Iraq. In twenty days, I have seen no one except you, but I intend to go into Baghdad and look to see which of the great merchants, the men of wealth, come out so that I can then follow their tracks, seize their goods, kill their men and drive off their camels with their loads. Now tell me who you are.'

'Your story is like mine,' said Kana-ma-Kana, 'except that the disease from which I suffer is more dangerous than yours, as my cousin is a king's daughter and the dowry that you mentioned, or anything like it, would not be enough to satisfy her family.' Sabbah replied: 'It may be that you are feeble-witted or the extent of your passion may have driven you out of your mind. How can your cousin be a king's daughter when, far from showing any signs of royal blood, you are nothing but a wandering beggar?' 'Chief of the Arabs,' answered Kana-ma-Kana, 'there is nothing for you to find strange about this. What has passed has passed, but if you want to know more, I am Kana-ma-Kana, son of King Dau' al-Makan, who was the son of King 'Umar ibn al-Nu'man, the ruler of Baghdad and of the land of Khurasan. Time has wronged me. My father died and King Sasan took power. I left Baghdad barefooted lest anyone see me. I have now explained how things are. In twenty days, you are the only person I have seen. Your story is like mine and so is your need.'

When he heard this, Sabbah cried out: 'O joy! I have got my wish and I have no need now of any other booty but you. You are of kingly stock, but you have come out dressed like a beggar. Your family must be looking for you and when they find you with someone, they will pay that person a huge sum to ransom you. So come on, boy, turn your back to me and walk ahead of me.' 'Don't do this, my Arab brother,' said Kana-ma-Kana. 'My family won't buy me for silver or gold or even one copper dirham. I am a poor man and I am carrying nothing with me. So give up this greed; take me as a companion and leave Iraq with me so that we can travel throughout distant lands in the hope of finding a dowry, to enable us to enjoy the kisses and embraces of our cousins.'

On hearing this, Sabbah became angry and his arrogance and irritation increased. 'Damn you,' he said. 'Are you bandying words with me, you vilest of dogs? Turn around, or else I'll punish you.' Kana-ma-Kana smiled and said: 'How should I turn my back on you? Can you not act fairly and are you not afraid of being disgraced among the Bedouin for leading a man like me as a prisoner in humiliation and disgrace without having tried me out on the field to discover whether I am a champion or a coward?' Sabbah laughed and said: 'How wonderful! In years you are a boy, but you talk big, and words like these come only from a battle-hardened champion. What "fairness" do you want?' Kana-ma-Kana replied: 'If you want me as a captive and a servant, then throw aside your weapons, strip and come to wrestle with me. Whichever of us throws the other can do what he wants with him and take him as a servant.' Sabbah laughed and said: 'All these bold words of yours show that your end is near.'

He then got up, threw down his weapons, tucked up his clothes and advanced on Kana-ma-Kana, who came up to him. They struggled with each other and the Bedouin found Kana-ma-Kana getting the better of him, as a *qintar* outweighs a dinar. He saw how firmly fixed his legs were on the ground and found that they were like two well-based minarets, two tent pegs driven into the ground or two deep-rooted mountains. Realizing that he was outmatched and regretting that he had closed with Kana-ma-Kana, he said to himself: 'I wish I'd fought him with my weapons.' Then Kana-ma-Kana grasped him, took a firm hold and shook him until the Bedouin felt as though his guts had split in his belly. 'Remove your hand, boy!' he cried, but Kana-ma-Kana paid no attention and shook him again before lifting him up and carrying him to the stream in order to throw him in. 'Hero,' shouted the Bedouin, 'what do you mean to do?' 'I'm going to throw you into this stream,' replied Kana-ma-Kana. 'It will carry you into the Tigris; the Tigris will take you to the Nahr 'Isa; the Nahr 'Isa will take you to the Euphrates; and the Euphrates will bring you to your own lands, where your people will recognize you and acknowledge your manliness and the sincerity of your love.' Sabbah cried out: 'Hero of the valleys, don't act shamefully. Let me go; I call on you by the life of your cousin, the flower of loveliness.'

At that, Kana-ma-Kana put him down on the ground, but when the Bedouin found himself free, he went to his sword and shield, picked them up and sat wondering whether to make a treacherous attack. Kana-ma-Kana saw from his eyes what he was thinking and said to him: 'I know what is in your heart now that you have got your sword and your shield. You are not a strong wrestler and you know none of the tricks, but you think that if you could have circled round on your horse and attacked me with your sword, I would long since have been a dead man. I shall allow you your choice, so that there may be no doubt left in your heart. Give me the shield and attack me with the sword, and either you will kill me or I will kill you.' 'Look out, here it is,' said Sabbah, throwing him the shield. He then drew his sword and attacked Kana-ma-Kana, who took the shield in his right hand and started warding off the blows with it. With each blow, Sabbah would say: 'This will settle it,' but the blow was never deadly, Kana-ma-Kana catching it on the shield each time, so it would be wasted.

For his part, Kana-ma-Kana did not strike Sabbah, as he had nothing with which to deliver a blow. Sabbah continued to strike with his sword until his arms grew tired, and when Kana-ma-Kana saw this, he dashed at him, seized the Bedouin in his arms, shook him and threw him to the ground. He then turned him over and tied his hands with his sword belt, after which he dragged him off by his feet towards the river. Sabbah called to him: 'What are you going to do with me, young champion of the age, hero of the battlefield?' Kana-ma-Kana replied: 'Didn't I tell you that I am going to send you to your family and your clan by the river so that you need no longer be concerned? They won't have to worry about

you and you won't have to be kept from marrying your cousin.' Sabbah
wept and cried out in distress: 'Don't do this, champion of the age. Let me
go and make me one of your servants.' In tears, he then recited these lines:

> I have left my family; how long have I been away!
> Would that I knew whether I shall die in exile.
> If I die, my family will not know that I am dead.
> I shall perish as a stranger without visiting my beloved.

At this, Kana-ma-Kana was moved to pity, saying to him: 'Promise
me, with compacts and covenants, that you will be a good companion
to me and accompany me wherever I go.' Sabbah agreed to this, and
after he had given his word, Kana-ma-Kana let him go. Sabbah got up
and wanted to kiss his hand but Kana-ma-Kana stopped him, so he then
opened his bag and took out three barley loaves and set them before
him. The two of them sat by the river bank and ate with one another.
After they had finished, they performed the ritual ablution, prayed and
sat talking to one another about their experiences with their families
and with the misfortunes of Time. 'Where do you intend to go?' asked
Kana-ma-Kana. 'To Baghdad, your city,' said Sabbah, 'and I shall stay
there until God provides me with a dowry.' 'Off you go, then,' said
Kana-ma-Kana, 'for I mean to stay here.'

Sabbah then took leave of him and set off on the way to Baghdad, while
Kana-ma-Kana stayed, wondering to himself how he could possibly go
back if he was still poor. 'By God,' he said to himself, 'I am not going to
return disappointed, and if God Almighty wills it, I shall find relief.' He
went to the river, performed the ablution and prayed. After prostrating
himself and putting his forehead on the ground, he called to his Lord,
saying: 'My God, Who sends down the rain and feeds the worms among
the rocks, I ask You through Your power and gentle mercy to provide
me with a livelihood.' He then finished the prayer, but could think of
nowhere to go.

As he was sitting there, looking to the right and the left, a horseman
came up, riding with a slack rein. Kana-ma-Kana sat up as the man
reached him, but he was at his last gasp, on the point of death thanks to
a gaping wound. When he got to Kana-ma-Kana, tears were pouring
down his cheeks as though from the mouth of a water skin, and he said:
'Chief of the Arabs, take me as a friend as long as I live, for you will not
find another like me. Give me a little water, even though it is not good
for a wounded man to drink, especially while blood is flowing and life

is ebbing. If I live I shall find something to cure your hurtful poverty, while if I die, your good intentions will bring you good fortune.'

The rider was mounted on a horse so splendid that it beggared description, with legs like marble columns. When Kana-ma-Kana looked at him and at the horse, he was smitten by love for it and said to himself: 'There is no horse to match this one in this age.' He gently helped the rider to dismount and gave him a little water to drink. Waiting until the man had rested, he went up to him and asked: 'Who has done this to you?' 'I must tell you the truth of the matter,' said the wounded man. 'I am a horse thief, jealous of my reputation, and I have spent my whole life stealthily removing horses by night and by day. My name is Ghassan, a disaster for every mare and stallion. I heard that this stallion was in the lands of Rum, with Emperor Afridun, who had named it Qatul, the Killer, with the nickname of Majnun, the Mad. Because of it I went to Constantinople and began to keep it under surveillance.

'While I was doing this, out came an old woman who is held in honour and obeyed by the Rumis. She is called Dhat al-Dawahi and is a mistress of trickery. She had with her this stallion and no more than ten slaves looking after her and it. She was on her way to Baghdad and Khurasan, hoping for an audience with King Sasan to sue for peace. I followed their tracks, in order to steal the horse, but although I went on following them, I couldn't get to it because the slaves kept so close a watch over it. They reached Iraq and I was afraid they were going to enter Baghdad, but while I was wondering how to steal the horse, a dust cloud rose up and blocked the horizon, clearing away to show a party of fifty robbers intent on intercepting merchants, led by a warrior called Kahardash – an angry lion in battle and an overthrower of champions.'

Night 141

Morning now dawned and Shahrazad broke off from what she had been allowed to say. Then, when it was the hundred and forty-first night, SHE CONTINUED:

I have heard, O fortunate king, that the wounded rider told Kana-ma-Kana: 'This man came out against the old woman and her servants, closed in on them and shouted at the top of his voice. Soon he had tied up the ten slaves, as well as the old woman, and had taken the horse from them. He took them off joyfully, while I was telling myself that

I had wasted my efforts and not got what I wanted, but I waited to see how the affair would turn out. When the old woman saw that she had been captured, she wept and said to Kahardash the chief: "Great champion and lion-like hero, what are you going to do with an old woman and her slaves, now that you have got the horse as you wanted?" She deceived him with soft words and swore that she would bring him horses and livestock, after which he freed both her and the slaves. He and his men then went off and I followed them here, watching the horse and tracking it. When I found an opportunity, I stole it; I mounted and, taking a whip from my bag, I struck it. When the robbers noticed, they caught up with me and surrounded me on all sides, shooting with arrows and throwing spears. I kept my seat as the horse defended me with its forelegs and hindlegs, until I had managed to get clear of them like a swift arrow or a shooting star. In the heat of the fight, however, I had been wounded and I have spent three nights without sleeping or enjoying food. My strength has now gone and I am no longer concerned with worldly things. You have been good to me and taken pity on me. I see that you are naked and in obvious distress, but you show signs of having been prosperous. Who are you? Where have you come from and where are you going?'

The prince answered: 'My name is Kana-ma-Kana and I am the son of King Dau' al-Makan, the son of King 'Umar ibn al-Nu'man. My father died and I was brought up as an orphan. He was succeeded by an ignoble man, who became king over both high and low.' He then told his story from the beginning to the end. The thief felt sympathy for him and said: 'You are of noble lineage and high rank. You will become a great man, the champion of the people of this age. If you can hold me up, riding behind me, so as to bring me to my own land, you will have fame in this world and the next on the Day of Judgement. I have no strength to support myself, and if this is my end, then you have a better right to the horse than anyone else.' 'By God,' said Kana-ma-Kana, 'if I could carry you on my shoulders or share my life span with you, I would do it without a thought for the horse, as I am a kindly man who helps those who are in trouble. One good deed done for the sake of Almighty God wards off seventy misfortunes from the doer. So get ready to start and put your trust in God, the Kind, the Omniscient.' He was about to mount the thief on the horse and to set off, relying on God, the source of help, but the man told him to wait a little. He then closed his eyes, spread open his hands and said: 'I testify that there is no god but God and Muhammad is the Apostle of God.' He went on: 'Great God, forgive me my great sin, for only the great can forgive great sin.' He then prepared for death, reciting these lines:

> I have wronged God's servants and travelled through the lands,
> Spending my life in drinking wine,
> Plunging in streams in order to steal horses
> And ruining houses thanks to my misdeeds.
> My affair is grave; my sin is great;
> This horse, Qatul, is the climax of my career.
> With it I hoped to get what I desired,
> But I could not bring my journey to its end.
> All my life I have been stealing horses,
> But death was decreed by God, the Omnipotent,
> And in the end the trouble that I took
> Has been to win wealth for a poor orphaned stranger.

When he had finished the poem, he shut his eyes, opened his mouth, gave a groan and left this world. Kana-ma-Kana got up, dug a grave for him and buried him in the earth. He then went up to the horse, kissed it and stroked its face with the greatest of joy. 'No one is lucky enough to have a stallion like this,' he said, 'not even King Sasan.'

So much for him, but as for King Sasan, news came to him that the vizier Dandan and half his army had cast off their allegiance, swearing that they would have only Kana-ma-Kana as king. Dandan had secured oaths of loyalty from the soldiers and had led them to the islands of India, to the Berbers and the lands of the blacks. A swelling sea of reinforcements had joined them, past all counting, and with them Dandan prepared to march on Baghdad, conquer its lands and kill anyone who opposed him. He swore that he would not sheathe his sword until Kana-ma-Kana had been made king.

When Sasan heard this, he was plunged into a sea of cares, realizing that his subjects, both great and small, had turned against him. His sorrow increased, his worries multiplied and he opened his treasuries, distributing money to the officers of state. He wished that Kana-ma-Kana would come so that he might win him over by benevolence and kindness and appoint him as commander of the troops that were still loyal to him, to quench the spark of sedition.

When Kana-ma-Kana heard the news from merchants, he hurried back to Baghdad, riding on his stallion. Sasan was sitting on his throne in a state of perplexity when he heard of his arrival. He ordered out all his troops and the leading men of Baghdad to meet him. The whole population went out and walked before him to the palace, kissing its threshold. The slave girls and eunuchs entered to give the good news of his arrival to his mother, who came to him and kissed him between the eyes. 'Mother,' he said, 'let me go to my uncle, King Sasan, who has overwhelmed me with boons and favours.' The people of the palace and the state officials were amazed at the beauty of the stallion Qatul, exclaiming that no one else owned a horse like this. Kana-ma-Kana then came out into the presence of King Sasan and greeted him. Sasan rose for him and Kana-ma-Kana kissed his hands and feet and offered him the stallion as a gift.

The king greeted him, saying: 'Welcome to my son, Kana-ma-Kana. The world has been a sad place in your absence, but praise be to God that you are safe.' Kana-ma-Kana invoked blessings on him and after this Sasan looked at Qatul and recognized that this was the stallion that he had seen many years before when he was with Kana-ma-Kana's father, Dau' al-Makan, laying siege to the Christians, on the expedition in which his uncle, Sharkan, had been killed. 'Had your father been able to get hold of it,' he said, 'he would have bought it at a cost of a thousand fine horses, but now glory has returned to the glorious. I accept the stallion, but give it to you as a gift from me. You have a better right to it than anyone else, as you are the champion of the horsemen.' He then ordered robes of honour to be brought for Kana-ma-Kana; he presented him with horses and set aside the largest apartments in the palace for his private use. He honoured him and made him glad, giving him large sums of money and treating him with the greatest respect, as he was afraid of what might come of the vizier Dandan's defection.

Kana-ma-Kana was delighted, being freed from ignominy and degradation. When he got to his room, he went to his mother and asked her how his cousin was. 'By God,' she said, 'my son, your absence distracted me from everything else, including all thought of your beloved, especially as it was she who was the cause of your exile.' Kana-ma-Kana then complained to her of his lovesickness, saying: 'Go to her, mother; approach her to see whether she will spare me a glance and cure me of this distress.' His mother replied: 'Men are humiliated by their desires. Give up this love that will only lead to disaster. I shall not go to her or give her your message.'

When he heard what his mother had to say, he told her what he had heard from the horse thief that the old woman, Dhat al-Dawahi, was on her way to their country with the intention of entering Baghdad, adding that it was she who had killed his uncle and his grandfather, and that he would have to take vengeance for this and clear away their disgrace. He then left his mother and approached an ill-omened old woman called Sa'dana, debauched, wily and guileful, to whom he complained of the state he was in and of his love for his cousin Qudiya-fa-Kana. He asked her to approach his cousin and to persuade her to look on him with favour. 'To hear is to obey,' she replied, and then she left him and went to Qudiya-fa-Kana. After succeeding in her mission, she came back and told the prince: 'Qudiya-fa-Kana sends her greetings and promises that she will come to you at midnight.'

Night 142

Morning now dawned and Shahrazad broke off from what she had been allowed to say. Then, when it was the hundred and forty-second night, SHE CONTINUED:

I have heard, O fortunate king, that the old woman came to Kana-ma-Kana and told him: 'Qudiya-fa-Kana sends her greetings and promises that she will come to you at midnight.' Kana-ma-Kana was delighted, and he sat waiting for his cousin to keep her promise. Promptly at midnight she arrived, wearing a black silk mantle, but, coming in, she had to rouse him from sleep. 'How can you claim to be in love with me,' she said, 'when you are comfortably asleep without a care?' At this, Kana-ma-Kana woke up and said: 'By God, desire of my heart, I only slept in the hope that you would appear to me in a dream.' Reproaching him gently, she recited:

If you were a true lover you would not have recourse to sleep;
You claim to follow the path of love in tender passion –
By God, cousin, the eyes of the passionate lover do not close.

When Kana-ma-Kana heard what his cousin had to say, he was filled with shame and, getting up, he apologized to her, after which they embraced and complained to each other of the pain of separation. They remained like that until the light of dawn spread over the horizon. Qudiya-fa-Kana then decided to go, at which Kana-ma-Kana wept and sighed deeply, saying:

My beloved visited me, having shunned me for too long,
And in her mouth are found pearls strung in order.
I kissed her a thousand times, embracing her,
Passing the night with my cheek under hers,
Until dawn came and parted us,
Like a sword with a gleaming edge, drawn from its sheath.

When he had finished reciting these lines, Qudiya-fa-Kana took her
leave and went back to her own chamber. However, some of her slave
girls had found out her secret and one of them went and told King Sasan.
He went to his daughter, drew his sword and was about to kill her when
her mother, Nuzhat al-Zaman, came in. 'By God,' she said, 'don't harm
her, for if you do, the news will get out and you will be disgraced among
the kings of the age. Kana-ma-Kana, as you know, is no child of adultery.
Your daughter was brought up with him and he is a man of honour and
chivalry who will do nothing disgraceful. Be patient and don't act hastily.
Everyone in the palace and all the people of Baghdad have heard the
news of the vizier Dandan, that he is leading armies from all the lands
and bringing them to install Kana-ma-Kana as king.' 'By God,' said
Sasan, 'I must bring such a disaster on Kana-ma-Kana that no land will
be able to support him and no sky will shade him. I have only shown
him favour and ingratiated myself with him because of my subjects, lest
they turn to him, but you shall see what will happen.' He then left her
and went off to deal with the affairs of his kingdom.

So much for him, but as for Kana-ma-Kana, he went to his mother
the next day and said: 'Mother, I intend to go out raiding as a highwayman, driving off horses and cattle and capturing slaves and mamluks.
When I have become wealthy and my situation improves, I shall ask
King Sasan for my cousin's hand.' 'My son,' replied his mother, 'people's
goods are not like camels left to roam freely. They are guarded by sword
blows and lance thrusts and by men who eat wild beasts, ravage lands,
hunt lions and track down lynxes.' 'I am determined,' said Kana-ma-
Kana, 'never to turn back from my resolve until I have reached my goal.'
He then sent the old woman to Qudiya-fa-Kana to say that he was going
off to win her a suitable dowry, and he told the old woman to ask her
to send him a reply. 'To hear is to obey,' she said, and, after going on
her errand, she came back to say that the princess had promised to come
to him at midnight. He stayed awake until then in a state of agitation,
and before he knew it, she had entered his room, saying: 'I shall ransom

you from sleeplessness with my life.' He got to his feet and said: 'Heart's desire, my life is your ransom from all evils.' He then told her of his resolution, and when she wept, he said: 'Don't cry, cousin, for I shall ask God, Who has decreed that we should part, to bring us together again in harmony.'

Having decided to go on this journey, he went to take leave of his mother and then, going out of the palace, he buckled on his sword and, putting on his turban and his mouth-veil, he mounted his horse, Qatul. He was like a full moon as he rode through the city. Then, coming to the city gate, he saw his companion, Sabbah ibn Rammah, going out. When Sabbah saw him, he ran up to his stirrup and greeted him. After he had returned the greeting, Sabbah asked: 'Brother, how did you get this horse and this sword, together with these clothes, while up till now I have nothing but my sword and my shield?' 'It is the hunter's purpose that determines what quarry he gets,' replied Kana-ma-Kana, 'and it was just after you left that good fortune came to me. Now, will you come with me, act as a true companion and travel with me in this desert?' 'By the Lord of the Ka'ba,' said Sabbah, 'from now on I shall call you "my master".' He then ran in front of the horse, with his sword hanging from his shoulder and his bag between his shoulder blades, followed by Kana-ma-Kana.

For four days they went further and further into the desert, living off the gazelles that they hunted and drinking from springs. On the fifth day, they came to a high hill beneath which there were meadows and a running stream, where there were camels, cows, sheep and horses, filling the hills and valleys, with little children playing in the pastures. When Kana-ma-Kana saw this, he was delighted and his heart was filled with joy. Making up his mind to fight in order to take the camels – male and female – he said to Sabbah: 'Come down with me to these flocks that are pastured away from their owners and join me in fighting all comers, from near and far, so that we may have our share of booty.' 'Master,' said Sabbah, 'the clan that owns these is numerous, and among them are skilled fighters both on horse and on foot. If we risk our lives on a matter as serious as this, we will be in grave danger. Neither of us will escape safely and each of us will lose his cousin.' Kana-ma-Kana laughed, realizing that Sabbah was a coward. He then rode down the hill to launch his attack, reciting the following lines at the top of his voice:

Clan of Nu'man, we are the ambitious heroes, the skull-strikers,
Who, when battle rages, stand on foot in the mêlée.
The poor sleep safely among us with no sight of ugly poverty.
I hope for help from the Lord of power, Creator of mankind.

He then rode against the female camels like a stallion camel in rut, driving them all off in front of him, together with the cows, the sheep and the horses. The slaves rushed out against him with sharp swords and long lances, led by a Turkish rider, a strong fighter who knew how to use both the brown spear and the white sword. He rode against Kana-ma-Kana, crying: 'Damn you, if you knew to whom these flocks belonged, you would not have done this. Their owners are the Rumi tribe, the heroes of the sea, the Circassian clan, all grim heroes, a hundred riders, who have cast off allegiance to any king. A stallion of theirs has been stolen and they have sworn that they will not leave here without it.' When Kana-ma-Kana heard this, he shouted: 'This is the stallion that you mean, you wretches, the one that you are looking for. You want to fight me for it, so come on, all of you together, and do your worst.'

He shouted from between the ears of Qatul, who charged against them like a *ghul*. Kana-ma-Kana turned in against the rider, unhorsing him with a thrust and ripping out his kidneys. He then attacked a second, a third and a fourth, killing them all. At that, the other slaves shrank from him in fear and he shouted to them: 'Drive out the cattle and the horses, you bastards, or else I shall dye my spear point in your blood.' They obeyed his order and then started to decamp, at which point Sabbah came down, shouting to Kana-ma-Kana in high glee.

Suddenly, however, a dust cloud rose, blocking out the horizon, and under it were to be seen a hundred riders like grim lions. Sabbah fled away and climbed from the valley to the top of the hill, from which he could look at the fight as a spectator, saying to himself: 'I am only a rider in play and in jest.' The hundred riders surrounded Kana-ma-Kana and circled round him. One of them came up to him and asked him where he was going with the flocks. 'I am going to take them off and rob you of them,' replied Kana-ma-Kana, adding: 'Get ready to fight, but know that between you and what you are facing is a terrible lion, a brave champion and a sword that cuts wherever it strikes.' When the rider heard what he said, he looked at him and saw that he was a horseman like a lion, but with a face like the moon on the fourteenth day of the month, with courage showing from between his eyes.

The rider, whose name was Kahardash, was the leader of the hundred, and, looking at Kana-ma-Kana, he saw that, in addition to his consummate horsemanship, he had remarkable beauty, which was like that of Fatin, his own beloved, a girl with the loveliest of faces, who had been endowed by God not only with beauty but with every noble quality and indescribable grace, so as to distract all men's hearts. The riders of her clan and the champions of that region went in fear and awe of her strength and she had sworn not to marry or to give herself to any man who could not defeat her. Kahardash was one of her suitors, but she had told her father that she would not allow anyone to approach her who had not got the better of her in a duel.

When Kahardash heard this, he had been ashamed to fight against a girl and afraid of being disgraced. One of his friends had told him: 'You have all the qualities of beauty and were she to prove stronger than you in a fight, you would still get the better of her, as she would see how handsome you are and let herself be defeated by you so that you could take her. Women have something that they want from men, as you well know.' Kahardash, however, had still refused and would not fight, and he had continued in his refusal until his encounter with Kana-ma-Kana. He was taken aback, thinking that his opponent was Fatin herself, who was, in fact, in love with him because of what she had heard of his beauty and courage. Advancing towards Kana-ma-Kana, he said: 'Damn you, Fatin, have you come to show me how brave you are? Dismount so that I can talk with you. I have driven off all these flocks, betrayed companions and intercepted warriors and champions all because of your peerless beauty. Marry me, so that the daughters of kings may serve you and you may become queen of these lands.'

When Kana-ma-Kana heard this, he became furiously angry and shouted out: 'Damn you, you Persian dog! Forget about Fatin and what you suspect her to be, and come out to fight. You will soon be on the ground.' He then began to wheel and attack, varying his tactics so that when Kahardash saw this, he realized that here was a gallant rider and a lion-like champion. His mistake was made clear to him when he saw the dark down on Kana-ma-Kana's cheek, like myrtle growing among red roses. He shrank from his attack and said to his companions: 'Damn you, charge him, one of you, and show him the sharp sword and the quivering lance. You should know that it is shameful for a group to attack a single man, even if he is a brave and powerful champion.'

At that, a strong rider charged Kana-ma-Kana, mounted on a black

horse with white fetlocks and a blaze the size of a dirham on its forehead, bewildering both mind and eye, like 'Antar's Abjar, of whom the
poet says:

> The horse has come to you, entering the battle
> Joyfully, mixing earth and sky.
> It is as though dawn has struck its forehead,
> Punishing it by plunging into its inmost parts.

He quickly charged Kana-ma-Kana and for a time they circled round
each other, striking blows that bewildered the mind and blinded the eye.
Kana-ma-Kana then forestalled him with the blow of a champion that
cut through his turban and his head-piece until it reached the head itself,
at which he toppled to the ground like a falling camel. A second rider
charged, then a third, a fourth and a fifth, only to fall as the first had
done. All the rest then attacked, upset and burning with anger, but his
spear soon picked them off like ripe fruit. When Kahardash saw this,
he was afraid to enter the fight, realizing that Kana-ma-Kana was a
stout-hearted warrior, fit to be considered unique among champions. So
he said to him: 'I grant you your own life and shall not take blood
revenge for my companions. Take what flocks you like and go on your
way. I feel pity for you because of your steadfastness and you have a
right to live.' 'May you never find yourself without the chivalry of the
noble,' said Kana-ma-Kana, 'but leave aside this kind of talk. Take your
life and fear no blame. Don't hope to recover the spoil but go straight
off to save yourself.'

At that, Kahardash became furiously and destructively angry. 'Damn
you,' he said to Kana-ma-Kana. 'If you knew who I was you would not
speak like this on the field of battle. Ask about me, for I am the strong
lion, Kahardash by name, who has plundered great kings, plagued the
roads for every traveller and seized the goods of merchants. I have been
looking for this horse that you are riding. Tell me how you got it.'
Kana-ma-Kana told him: 'This horse was on its way to my uncle, King
Sasan, led by an old woman who was attended by ten slaves. You
attacked her and took it from her. She owes me a blood debt for my
grandfather, King 'Umar ibn al-Nu'man, and my uncle, Sultan Sharkan.'
'Damn you,' said Kahardash, 'who is your father, you child without a
mother?' The prince replied: 'I am Kana-ma-Kana, the son of Dau'
al-Makan, the son of 'Umar ibn al-Nu'man.'

When Kahardash heard this, he said: 'You are undeniably a perfect blend of chivalry and beauty,' adding: 'Leave in safety, as your father was good and generous to us.' 'By God,' replied Kana-ma-Kana, 'I shall show you no respect, you contemptible fellow, until I defeat you on the battlefield.' This enraged the Bedouin and each charged the other with loud cries, while their horses pricked up their ears and raised their tails. They continued to clash until each thought that the sky had been split open. They fought like butting rams, exchanging thrusts with their spears. Kahardash tried to strike home with one such thrust, but Kana-ma-Kana avoided it and then attacked in his turn, dealing Kahardash such a blow in his chest that the spear point emerged from his back. He then collected the horses and the other spoils and ordered the servants to drive them with all speed.

It was now that Sabbah came down from the hill. He went up to Kana-ma-Kana and said: 'Well done, champion of the age. I prayed for you and the Lord answered my prayer.' He then cut off the head of Kahardash, at which Kana-ma-Kana laughed and said: 'Damn you, Sabbah. I had thought that you were a man of war.' 'Don't forget your servant when it comes to distributing these spoils,' said Sabbah, 'for with their help I may be able to marry my cousin, Najma.' 'You may certainly have a share of them, but in the meantime you must guard both the spoils and the slaves.' He then set off for his own lands and travelled night and day until he came near Baghdad. All the troops learned of his coming and they could see the spoils and the flocks that he was bringing with him, together with the head of Kahardash, mounted on Sabbah's spear. The merchants recognized it with delight, exclaiming: 'God has delivered the people from this highwayman.' They were astonished that he had been killed and they invoked blessings on his slayer.

The Baghdadis went up to Kana-ma-Kana to ask him what had happened, and when he told them, they were all struck with awe, and the riders and champions were filled with fear. He then drove his booty to the palace and planted the spear on which Kahardash's head was mounted at the palace gate. He distributed gifts to the people, giving away the horses and camels, as a result of which the Baghdadis loved and favoured him all the more. He then turned to Sabbah, assigned spacious quarters to him and gave him some of the spoils, after which he went to his mother and told her what had happened on his journey.

The news had reached King Sasan, who left his audience chamber and went off to consult his principal officers in private. 'Know,' he said to them, 'that I wish to reveal to you what I have kept hidden. It is

Kana-ma-Kana who will cause us to be dismissed from these lands. He has killed Kahardash, although Kahardash was supported by Kurdish and Turkish tribes, and thanks to this our position is doomed. Most of our troops are closely allied to him and you know what the vizier Dandan has done. Although I was good to Dandan and treated him well, he was ungrateful and broke his word to me. I am told that he has gathered the armies of the lands with the intention of making Kana-ma-Kana king, as the kingdom had belonged to his father and his grandfather, and without a doubt he is bound to kill me.' When his officers heard this, they said: 'Your majesty, Kana-ma-Kana has not the strength for this. Had we not known that he had been brought up by you, not one of us would have received him. Know that we are at your service and if you want him killed, we shall kill him, while if you want him exiled, we shall see to it that he leaves.'

When Sasan heard this, he said: 'The right thing to do is to kill him, but we must first bind ourselves by a covenant,' and so they took an oath that they would kill Kana-ma-Kana, and when the vizier Dandan came, he would hear of his death and would no longer be able to carry out what he intended. After they had made their compact and sworn to this, Sasan treated them with the greatest honour before going to his own apartments. The leaders had left him and the troops refused to obey orders until they could find out what was going to happen, as they saw that the bulk of the army had joined the vizier Dandan.

When Qudiya-fa-Kana heard what was going on, she was overcome by grief and she sent a message to the old woman who had been in the habit of bringing her news from her cousin. When the woman arrived, the princess told her to go and tell him what had happened. She went off and greeted him, and, after he had welcomed her with pleasure, she gave him the news. 'Give my greetings to my cousin,' he said when he heard this, 'and tell her that that God, the Great and Glorious, allows whom He wishes from among His servants to inherit the earth. How well has the poet put it:

Kingship belongs to God; a man may obtain his desires,
But God sends him back defeated, condemning his soul to hell.
If I, or another man, owned a finger's breadth
Of the earth, then God would not rule alone.'

The old woman went back to his cousin and told her what he had said and that he was staying in the city. King Sasan was waiting for him to leave in order to send the killers after him, and as it happened he went out on a hunting trip, accompanied by Sabbah, who never left him by night or by day. He caught ten gazelles, including one with dark eyes, which turned right and left and which he allowed to go free. When Sabbah asked him why he had done that, he laughed and let the others go as well. 'Chivalry dictates that gazelles with young should be released. The reason that one turned to one side and the other was that it had fawns, and so I let it go and I let the others go for its sake.' 'Let me go too,' said Sabbah, 'so that I can return to my family.' Kana-ma-Kana laughed and struck him over the heart with the butt of his spear, so that he fell to earth, twisting like a snake.

While the two of them were there, suddenly they caught sight of a dust cloud stirred up by galloping horses, and beneath it could be seen brave riders. The reason for this was that a number of people had told King Sasan that Kana-ma-Kana had gone out hunting, and he had sent out a Dailami emir named Jami' with orders to kill him. Jami' had with him twenty riders, to whom Sasan had given money. When they came near they attacked Kana-ma-Kana, but he for his part charged against them and killed every last man of them. King Sasan had mounted and ridden out after his men, but when he found them all dead he went back in astonishment, and the Baghdadis laid hands on him and tied him up.

Kana-ma-Kana set off from where he was, together with Sabbah, and on his way he saw a young man sitting at the door of a house. Kana-ma-Kana greeted him and after the young man had returned his greeting, he went into the house and came out again with two bowls, one filled with curds and the other with broth surrounded by melted butter. He placed them before Kana-ma-Kana, saying: 'Do us the favour of eating our food.' Kana-ma-Kana refused, and when the young man asked him why, he said: 'I have made a vow.' The young man asked him the reason for this and he said: 'Know that King Sasan has robbed me of the kingdom unjustly, although this had belonged to my father and my grandfather before me. After my father's death, he took it by force, paying no attention to me because of my youth. I then swore that I would eat no man's food until I had got satisfaction from the one who had wronged me.' 'I have good news for you,' said the young man, 'for God has honoured your vow. Sasan is being held prisoner, and I think that he will soon be dead.' 'Where is he being held?' asked Kana-ma-Kana. 'In that tall dome,' said the young man. Kana-ma-Kana looked towards the dome and saw people going in and striking Sasan, who was

enduring the pains of death. He got up and went to the dome and, after
seeing Sasan's predicament, he came back to the house and sat down to
eat. When he had had enough, he put the rest of the food in his provision
bag, and remained seated until it had grown dark.

His host, the young man, fell asleep and Kana-ma-Kana then went to
the dome. It was surrounded by guard dogs, one of whom leapt at him,
but he threw it a piece of meat from his bag. He went on throwing meat
to the other dogs until he reached King Sasan. He came up to the king
and put a hand on his head. 'Who are you?' asked Sasan in a loud voice.
'I am Kana-ma-Kana, whom you tried to kill,' he replied, 'and God has
caused you to fall victim to your own evil plot. Wasn't it enough for you
to take my kingdom and the kingdom of my father and my grandfather,
that you should try to kill me as well?' Sasan swore falsely that he had
never done this and that the charge was untrue. Kana-ma-Kana then
forgave him and said: 'Follow me.' 'I am too weak to take a single step,'
Sasan told him. 'In that case,' said Kana-ma-Kana, 'I shall fetch two
horses for us and we can both ride off into the desert.' He got the horses
and he and Sasan mounted and rode until morning. They performed the
dawn prayer and then rode on until they reached an orchard where they
sat talking. Kana-ma-Kana got up and approached Sasan. 'Is there still
anything about me that you dislike?' he asked. 'No, by God,' answered
Sasan, and they then agreed to go back to Baghdad. 'I shall go on ahead
of you,' said Sabbah the Bedouin, 'to give the good news.'

He did this, telling both women and men, and the people came out
with drums and pipes. Among them was Qudiya-fa-Kana, like the full
moon spreading its radiant light in the thick darkness. Kana-ma-Kana
went to meet her; their souls yearned for each other and one body
longed for the other. No one at that time could talk of anything but
Kana-ma-Kana, and the riders bore witness that he was the bravest
champion of the age. 'No one else should be our ruler,' they said, 'and
the kingdom of his grandfather should be restored to him.' As for Sasan,
he went in to see Nuzhat al-Zaman, who told him: 'I find that the people
are talking about nothing except Kana-ma-Kana, referring to him in a
way that beggars description.' 'To hear is not the same as to see,' her
husband replied. 'I have seen him, but I have not noticed any quality of
perfection in him. Not everything that is heard has been said, for people
follow each other's lead in eulogizing him and proclaiming their love for
him. God has caused his praise to flow over men's tongues, to win him
the hearts of the Baghdadis, together with the false and treacherous

vizier, Dandan, who has collected armies from all the lands. What ruler can be content to be under the authority of an insignificant orphan?'

'What is it that you propose to do?' asked Nuzhat al-Zaman. 'I propose to kill him,' said Sasan, 'so that the vizier Dandan's attempt may be frustrated, and he may resume his allegiance, as he will have no choice but to serve me.' 'Treachery to strangers is foul,' said Nuzhat al-Zaman, 'so how much worse it is when it comes to relatives. The right thing would be for you to marry your daughter, Qudiya-fa-Kana, to Kana-ma-Kana, and you should listen to what was said in an earlier age:

> If Time raises a man up over you,
> Although you are the more deserving,
> Give him his due, hard though this may be;
> He will reward you, whether you are near or far away.
> Do not tell what you know of him,
> Or else no benefits will come your way.
> In the women's quarters many are lovelier than the bride,
> But it is the bride whom fortune aids.'

When Sasan heard what she had to say and grasped the point of the poem, he left her in anger, saying: 'Were it not a matter of disgrace to kill you, I would cut off your head with my sword and end your life.' 'You are angry with me,' she said, 'but I am only joking with you,' and, jumping up, she kissed his head and his hands. 'You are right,' she added, 'and you and I will think of some scheme for killing him.' Sasan was glad when he heard this and said: 'Do it quickly and relieve my worry, as, for my part, I cannot think of a plan.' 'I shall work out a way,' she assured him, and when he asked how, she said: 'By means of my servant, Bakun, who is a prolific schemer.'

Bakun was one of the most ill-omened of old women, who held that it was not permissible to abandon wickedness. She had brought up Kana-ma-Kana and Qudiya-fa-Kana, Kana-ma-Kana being particularly fond of her, as a result of which he used to sleep at her feet. When Sasan heard what his wife had to say, he approved of her proposal and, having summoned Bakun, he told her what had happened and ordered her to try to kill Kana-ma-Kana, promising her favours of all kinds. 'Your orders are to be obeyed,' she replied. 'Master, I want you to give me a lethal dagger so that I may kill him quickly for you.' Sasan welcomed her agreement and produced for her a dagger that could almost forestall fate.

Bakun had heard stories and poems and had a repertoire of anecdotes and tales. After taking the dagger, she left the apartment, thinking about how to destroy Kana-ma-Kana. She went to him as he sat waiting for a rendezvous with Qudiya-fa-Kana, for, thinking of her that night, his heart was on fire with love. While he was in this state, Bakun came in to visit him, saying: 'The time of union is at hand and the days of separation are over.' When he heard this, he asked her how Qudiya-fa-Kana was and Bakun replied: 'She is preoccupied by love for you.' Kana-ma-Kana rose and put his own robes on her, promising her favours of all kinds. She said: 'Know that I shall sleep in your room tonight and tell you things that I have heard, diverting you with tales of infatuated lovers, sick with love.' Kana-ma-Kana said: 'Tell me something that will cheer me and remove my distress.' 'Willingly,' said Bakun and, sitting down beside him with the dagger hidden in her clothes, SHE CONTINUED:

Know, O prince, that the pleasantest tale that I ever heard goes as follows. A certain man used to love pretty women, on whom he spent his money, until he had lost everything and was reduced to poverty. In his destitution he started to wander through the markets, looking for something on which to feed himself. While he was walking, a nail pierced his toe, drawing blood. He sat down, wiped off the blood and bandaged his toe, after which he got up, crying out in pain. Passing by a bath house, he went in and took off his clothes. On entering he found the place clean and so he sat by the fountain and kept on pouring water over his head until he grew tired.

Night 143

Morning now dawned and Shahrazad broke off from what she had been allowed to say. Then, when it was the hundred and forty-third night, SHE CONTINUED:

I have heard, O fortunate king, that the man sat by the fountain and kept on pouring water over his head until he grew tired. He then went to the cold-water room, where he found himself alone with no companions. Taking out a piece of hashish, he swallowed it, and as the drug went to his head he toppled over on to the marble floor. The hashish led him to imagine that a high functionary was massaging him, while two slaves stood at his head, one with a bowl and the other with the utensils needed for washing in the baths. When he saw that, he said to himself: 'Either these people have mistaken who I am or else they are hashish eaters like me.' He stretched out his legs and in his delusion he thought that the bath man said to him: 'It's time for you to go up, for you are on duty today.' 'Well done, hashish,' he said to himself, laughing, and he sat there in silence. The bath man got up, took him by the hand and wrapped a band of black silk around his waist. The two slaves walked behind him with the bowl and utensils until they brought him to a private room, where they released perfumes into the air. He found the room full of fruits and scented flowers. The servants sliced a melon for him and sat him on an ebony chair, while the bath man stood washing him as the servants poured out the water. They rubbed him down expertly, saying: 'Our lord and master, may you enjoy constant happiness.' They then went out, closing the door on him, and when he imagined that, he got up, removed the band from his waist and started to laugh until he almost lost consciousness. He went on laughing for a while and then said to himself: 'I wonder why they were addressing me as though I were a vizier, calling me "lord and master". It may be that they have got things wrong for the moment but afterwards they will recognize who I am and say: "This is a good-for-nothing" and beat me on the neck to their hearts' content.'

Finding the room too hot, he opened the door and, in his dream, he saw a small mamluk and a eunuch coming in. The mamluk had with him a package which he opened and out of which he took three silk towels, placing one on the man's head, the second over his shoulders and the third round his waist. The eunuch gave him clogs, which he put on, and then other mamluks and eunuchs came up to him and supported him as he left the room, laughing, and went to the hall, which was sumptuously furnished in a way suitable only for kings. Servants hurried up to him and sat him on a dais, where they started to massage him until he fell asleep. In his sleep, he dreamt that there was a girl on his lap. He kissed her and placed her between his thighs, sitting with her as a man does with a woman. Taking his penis in his hand and drawing the girl to him, he pressed her beneath him.

At that point, someone called out: 'Wake up, you good-for-nothing! It's noon and you're still asleep.' He opened his eyes and found himself in the cold-water room surrounded by a crowd of people who were laughing at him. He had an erection and the towel had slipped from his waist. He realized, to his sorrow, that all this had been a drug-induced fantasy, and turning to the man who had woken him, he said: 'You could have waited until I put it in.' 'Aren't you ashamed, hashish eater,' the people said, 'to sleep with your penis erect?' Then they slapped him until the back of his neck was red. He was hungry but in his dream he had tasted happiness.

When Kana-ma-Kana heard this story from Bakun, he laughed until he fell over. 'Nurse,' he said, 'this is a remarkable story. I have never heard one like it. Do you have any more?' 'Yes,' she said, and she continued to tell him witty tales and amusing anecdotes until he was overcome by sleep. Bakun stayed sitting by his head until most of the night had gone. 'This is the time to seize the opportunity,' she said to herself. Standing up, she drew the dagger, leapt at Kana-ma-Kana and was about to cut his throat when in came his mother. When Bakun saw her, she went up to greet her, but in her fear she started to tremble as though she was in the grip of a fever. This surprised Kana-ma-Kana's mother, who roused her son, and when he woke up he found her sitting by his head.

It was her arrival that had saved his life, and the reason she had come was that Qudiya-fa-Kana had gone to her after overhearing her parents agreeing to have Kana-ma-Kana killed. 'Aunt,' she had said to his mother, 'go to your son before this whore Bakun kills him,' and she had told her the story from beginning to end. Kana-ma-Kana's mother had gone without further ado. She came in while her son was asleep and Bakun was on the point of cutting his throat. When he woke up, he said: 'You have come at a good time, mother. My nurse, Bakun, has been with me tonight.' He then turned to Bakun, saying: 'By my life, do you know any better story than the ones you have told me?' 'How can the ones that I have already told you compare with the even more pleasant one that I was going to tell you next? But I shall tell it to you another time.'

She got up, hardly believing that she had escaped. Kana-ma-Kana said goodbye to her, but in her cunning she could see that his mother knew what had happened. When she had gone off, Kana-ma-Kana's mother said to him: 'My son, this was a fortunate night, as Almighty God has saved you from this damned woman.' When he asked her about that, she told him the story from start to finish. 'Mother,' he said, 'a man destined to live has no killer, nor does he die if someone tries to take his life, but it would be prudent for us to leave these enemies. God acts according to His will.' The next morning, he left the city and joined the vizier Dandan, and after he had gone, an interchange took place between

King Sasan and Nuzhat al-Zaman which prompted her, too, to leave. She went to Dandan, and all Sasan's officers of state who supported their cause joined them. They sat discussing tactics and agreed to make a revenge attack on the king of Rum. They set off on their expedition, but fell into the hands of Rumzan, king of Rum, after what would take too long to describe, as will be seen in due course.

The morning after they had been captured, Rumzan ordered Kana-ma-Kana, the vizier Dandan and their companions to be brought before him. When they came, he sat them by his side and ordered tables of food to be fetched. When this had been done, they ate, drank and relaxed, although they had believed they were going to die, for when the king had ordered them to be brought, they told each other that he had only done this because he intended to have them killed. Having reassured them the king said: 'I have had a dream and when I told it to the monks, they said that the only man who could interpret it for me would be the vizier Dandan.' 'May it be something good that you saw, king of the age!' replied Dandan.

'Vizier,' said the king, 'I found myself in a pit like a black well and people were tormenting me. I wanted to get out of it, but when I tried to climb up, I fell back down and could not get free of the pit. I turned and saw on the ground beside me a girdle of gold. I put out my hand to take it, but when I picked it up, I saw that there were, in fact, two girdles. I tied them both around my waist and then found that they had become a single one. This was the dream that I had, vizier, while I was sound asleep.' 'My lord,' said Dandan, 'the meaning of your dream is that you have a brother or a nephew or a cousin, or some relation of your own flesh and blood, and he is among the best of your family.'

When the king heard this, he looked at Kana-ma-Kana, Nuzhat al-Zaman, Qudiya-fa-Kana, the vizier Dandan and their fellow captives, and he said to himself: 'If I cut off the heads of these people, their troops will be disheartened by their loss, and I shall be able to return soon to my own country, lest I lose my kingdom.' Having made up his mind to do this, he called for his executioner and told him to cut off Kana-ma-Kana's head immediately. At that moment, his nurse came forward and asked him what he was proposing to do. 'I have decided to kill these prisoners whom I am holding,' he said, 'after which I shall throw their heads to their companions. I and my men will then launch a concerted charge against them, killing some and routing the rest. This will be the decisive battle, and soon afterwards I shall go back to my own lands

before anything happens there.' When she heard this, the nurse came up
to him and said, speaking in Frankish: 'How can you think it good to
kill your nephew, your sister and your sister's daughter?'

The king was furiously angry when he heard this. 'You damned
woman,' he exclaimed, 'didn't you tell me that my mother was killed
and my father poisoned? You gave me a jewel which you said had
belonged to my father. Why didn't you tell me the truth?' 'Everything
that I said was true,' she replied, 'but my affair and yours is both strange
and wonderful. My name is Marjana. Your mother, Abriza, was beautiful
as well as famous among champions for her courage, which was proverbial. Your father was King 'Umar ibn al-Nu'man, the ruler of Baghdad
and of Khurasan. There is no shadow of doubt about this, nor is it
guesswork. King 'Umar had sent out his son, Sharkan, on a raiding
expedition in company with this vizier, Dandan. They had a number of
adventures and your brother, Sultan Sharkan, who was in command,
became separated from his men. He was entertained by your mother,
Princess Abriza, in her palace. She had gone off alone to wrestle with us,
her maids, and it was while we were doing this that Sharkan came across
us. He wrestled with your mother, who got the better of him, thanks to
her radiant beauty and her courage, after which she entertained him for
five days in her palace. Her father heard of that from his old mother,
Shawahi, whose nickname is Dhat al-Dawahi. Your mother had been
converted to Islam by Sharkan, your brother, and he took her off secretly
to Baghdad. Raihana and I, with twenty slave girls, went with her, having
ourselves been converted by Sharkan.

'When we came into the presence of your father, King 'Umar, and he
saw your mother, Princess Abriza, he fell in love with her. He went to
visit her at night and lay with her, after which she conceived you. She
had with her three jewels which she gave to your father, and he in his
turn gave one to his daughter, Nuzhat al-Zaman, the second to your
brother Dau' al-Makan and the third to your brother Sharkan. Princess
Abriza took this last one from him and kept it for you. When it was
nearly time for her to give birth, she felt a longing for her own family
and confided her secret to me. I met a black slave, named Ghadban,
whom I told about this in private, and I induced him to travel with us.
He took us out of the city and fled away with us. Your mother was close
to her time and when we had crossed the boundaries of our own lands
and were in an isolated spot, she fell into labour. It was then that the
slave thought of playing us false. He approached your mother and tried

to seduce her. She gave a great cry and recoiled from him, and so violently did she do this that she gave birth to you on the spot.

'Just then, from the direction of our own lands a dust cloud rose and spread up in the air until it blocked the horizon. The slave feared for his life and in an excess of rage he struck Princess Abriza with his sword and killed her, after which he mounted his horse and made off. When he had gone, the dust cleared away to show your grandfather, Hardub, king of Rum. The king saw your mother, his daughter, stretched out dead on the ground. He found this hard to bear and he asked me how she had come to be killed and why she had secretly left his lands. I told him the whole story from beginning to end, and this is the reason for the hostility between the people of Rum and those of the lands of Baghdad.

'We carried off the body of your dead mother and buried her, while I took you away and brought you up. I fastened Princess Abriza's jewel on you and when you grew up and reached man's estate, I could not tell you the truth of the matter, as if I had, war would have broken out between your peoples. Your grandfather, Hardub, king of Rum, told me to keep the secret and I was in no position to disobey his orders. This was why I kept the matter from you and never told you that your father was King 'Umar. When you came to the throne, I told you a little of this, but it was only now that I could give you the full story, king of the age. This is all that I know, but you know better what opinion you hold.'

When they heard all this from Marjana, the king's nurse, Nuzhat al-Zaman immediately gave a cry and said: 'This king, Rumzan, is my brother, the son of my father 'Umar. His mother was Princess Abriza, the daughter of Hardub, king of Rum, and I know this slave girl Marjana very well.' When King Rumzan heard this, he was both angry and perplexed, and he immediately had Nuzhat al-Zaman brought before him. When he saw her he felt the tie of blood and he questioned her. She repeated the same story to him and what she said agreed with Marjana's tale. He was then convinced, without a shadow of doubt, that he was an Iraqi and that his father had been King 'Umar, as a result of which he got up straight away and released his sister, Nuzhat al-Zaman, from her fetters. She went up to him and kissed his hands, with her eyes full of tears. The king wept too and he felt fraternal tenderness and sympathy for his nephew, Prince Kana-ma-Kana.

He stood up and took the sword from the hand of the executioner. When they saw this, the prisoners were sure that they were about to be killed, but when he had them brought before him, he released them from their bonds. He told Marjana: 'Explain to all of them the tale that you told me.' She replied: 'Know, your majesty, that this *shaikh* is the vizier Dandan, my principal witness, for he knows the truth of the matter.' She immediately went up to them and to the leaders of Rum and of the Franks who were there. She told them her story and Queen Nuzhat al-Zaman, the vizier Dandan and their fellow captives confirmed what she said. When she came to the end, happening to turn, she caught sight of the third jewel, the match of the other two that Princess Abriza had owned, on the neck of Prince Kana-ma-Kana. Recognizing it, she gave a great, resounding cry and said to the king: 'My son, know that now there is extra proof that I have been telling the truth. The jewel that is on the neck of this captive is the exact match of the one that I placed on your neck, and he is your brother's son, Kana-ma-Kana.' Turning to Kana-ma-Kana, she said: 'Let me see this jewel, prince of the age.' He took it from his neck and gave it to her. After she had taken it, she asked Nuzhat al-Zaman for the third one, and when this had been given her, she took them both and passed them to King Rumzan. The proof of the truth of her story was clear to him and he knew for a fact that he was the uncle of Prince Kana-ma-Kana and that his father had been 'Umar ibn al-Nu'man.

At this, he rose immediately and embraced the vizier Dandan and then Prince Kana-ma-Kana. A joyful shout arose; the good news then spread; drums of all sorts were beaten and pipes sounded, as the general gladness increased. Hearing the noise of the Rumis' celebrations, the troops of Iraq and Syria all mounted, including Sultan al-Ziblkan, who wondered to himself what could be the cause of the shouting and the joy in the army of the Rumis and the Franks. The Iraqi troops advanced to the battlefield, ready to fight, and King Rumzan turned and saw the Muslims coming out in battle order. When, in answer to his question, he was told the reason for this, he instructed Princess Qudiya-fa-Kana, the daughter of his brother Sharkan, to go at once to the Syrians and the Iraqis to tell them that King Rumzan had turned out to be the uncle of Prince Kana-ma-Kana.

She went off, released from hurtful sorrow, and came to Sultan al-Ziblkan. She greeted him and told him of the coincidence which had led to King Rumzan's being shown to be her uncle and the uncle of Kana-ma-Kana. On her arrival, she had found him weeping in fear for the emirs and the leaders, but when she had explained the affair from start to finish, the Muslims were delighted and their sadness vanished. Al-Ziblkan himself rode out with all the principal officers, led by Princess Qudiya-fa-Kana, who brought them to the pavilion of King Rumzan. When they went in they found him sitting with his nephew, Kana-ma-Kana. Rumzan had consulted him as well as the vizier Dandan about al-Ziblkan, and they had agreed to hand over Damascus to him and to leave him in charge of it, as he had been before, while they themselves went to Iraq.

As a result, al-Ziblkan was appointed sultan of Damascus and instructed to go back there, which he did, accompanied by his troops. The others went with him for a while to say goodbye, after which they returned to their quarters and a proclamation was made to the troops to set out for Iraq, at which the two armies intermingled. The kings said to one another: 'Our hearts will find no rest and our anger no cure unless we take vengeance and clear away our shame by avenging ourselves on Shawahi, the old woman known as Dhat al-Dawahi.'

Rumzan started on the journey with his principal officers and his state officials. Kana-ma-Kana was delighted with his uncle and called down blessings on Marjana for having made them known to one another. He and his men then moved off and they continued on their journey until they reached their own lands. The grand chamberlain, Sasan, having heard of their arrival came out to kiss the hand of King Rumzan, who gave him a robe of honour. Rumzan then took his seat and made his nephew Kana-ma-Kana sit beside him. 'Uncle,' said Kana-ma-Kana, 'you are the only fitting ruler for this kingdom.' 'God forbid that I should act against you in your own kingdom,' said Rumzan. The vizier Dandan then advised them to share the rule as equals, with each being in charge for one day at a time; to which they agreed.

Night 144

Morning now dawned and Shahrazad broke off from what she had been allowed to say. Then, when it was the hundred and forty-fourth night, SHE CONTINUED:

I have heard, O fortunate king, that the two kings agreed that each of them should rule for a day at a time. There was feasting, with slaughtered animals and great celebrations which continued for a long time, during which King Kana-ma-Kana was spending his nights with his cousin,

Qudiya-fa-Kana. After that, while the two kings were sitting enjoying the fact that their affairs had been set to rights, they suddenly saw a dust cloud rising – so high that it blocked the horizon. They were approached by a merchant who came to them crying out for help and saying: 'Kings of the age, how is it that in the lands of the unbelievers I am safe, but I am then robbed in your country, known for its justice and security?' King Rumzan turned to him and asked him what had happened. The man replied: 'I am a merchant and for a long time I have been in foreign parts, spending almost twenty years abroad. I have a document from Damascus, written for me by the late Sultan Sharkan, because I presented him with a slave girl. I approached your lands, bringing with me a hundred loads of Indian rarities which I was taking to Baghdad, your inviolable city, where you ensure safety and justice. My caravan was then attacked by Bedouin and Kurds gathered together from all parts. They killed my men and made off with my goods. This is why I am in such a state.' He then burst into tears in front of King Rumzan and complained brokenly.

The king was moved with pity and sympathy for him, as was his nephew Kana-ma-Kana. Swearing they would go after the raiders, they rode off with a hundred riders, each the equal of a thousand men, with the merchant going in front to show them the way. They travelled throughout the day and all the following night until dawn. The next day, they found themselves looking down on a thickly wooded valley full of streams and discovered that the raiders had come here before dispersing, having divided up the merchant's goods among themselves. Those of them who were still there were surrounded by the hundred riders; King Rumzan and his nephew Kana-ma-Kana shouted at them and it was not long before they had all been captured, three hundred of them in all, collected from the scum of the Bedouin. The goods the merchant had had with him were recovered and the men were tied up and taken to Baghdad.

King Rumzan and his nephew Kana-ma-Kana sat on one and the same throne and all the robbers were brought before them. When they were asked about their circumstances and about their leaders, they said: 'We have only three leaders, and it is they who collected us from all over the lands.' They were told to identify these men, which they did. The kings ordered that the three should be held and the others allowed to go free, after all the goods that they had with them had been seized and handed over to the merchant. After inspecting his property, the merchant found that a quarter of it was missing and the kings promised him that they would replace everything he had lost. He then produced two letters, one in the handwriting of Sharkan and the other written by Nuzhat al-Zaman. It was this merchant who had bought Nuzhat al-Zaman from the Bedouin when she was still a virgin and had presented her to her brother Sharkan, which was followed by the episode already mentioned.

King Kana-ma-Kana studied the two letters. He recognized the handwriting of his uncle, Sharkan, and he had heard the story of his aunt, Nuzhat al-Zaman. He took her the second letter which she had written for the merchant who had been robbed, telling his aunt the man's story from beginning to end. She recognized who he was and identified her own handwriting, and so she sent him guest provisions and recommended him to the care of her brother, King Rumzan, and her nephew, King Kana-ma-Kana, who ordered him to be given money, black slaves and servants to attend on him. Nuzhat al-Zaman herself sent him a hundred thousand dirhams and fifty loads of merchandise, together with other presents. She then summoned him and when he arrived, she came out, greeted him and told him that she was the daughter of King 'Umar ibn al-Nu'man, that her brother was King Rumzan and that King Kana-ma-Kana was her nephew. The merchant was overjoyed and congratulated her on her safety and on the fact that she had met her brother. He kissed her hands and thanked her for what she had done, adding: 'By God, you do not allow good deeds to be wasted.' She then retired into her private apartments.

The merchant stayed with the kings for three days, after which he took his leave of them and set off for Syria. The kings then sent for the three robbers who had led the gang of highwaymen and asked them about themselves. One of them came forward and said: 'Know that I am a Bedouin, who used to stay on the road waiting for small boys and virgin girls whom I would kidnap and sell to merchants. I did this for a long time until recently, on the prompting of the devil, I made an agreement with these two wretches to collect the scum of the Bedouin and the dregs of the lands in order to plunder goods and intercept merchants.'

The kings said to him: 'Tell us what was your most remarkable experience when you were acting as a kidnapper.' 'Kings of the age,' the man replied, 'the most remarkable thing that happened to me took place twenty-two years ago, when one day I kidnapped a Jerusalem girl. She was a beautiful creature, but she was a servant, wearing tattered clothes, with a piece of wrapping on her head. I saw her coming out of a *khan* and I immediately took her by means of a trick. I mounted her on a camel and hurried off with her, hoping to take her to my family in the desert and to keep her with me to herd the camels and to gather dung from the valley floor. She wept bitterly and I went up to her and gave her a painful beating. I then took her off to Damascus, where a merchant saw her with me and then lost his wits and wanted to buy her from me because he was so struck by her powers of expression. He went on offering me more and more for her until I sold her to him for a hundred thousand dirhams. When I handed her over, she made a great display of eloquence and I heard that he dressed her in fine clothes and presented her to the ruler of Damascus who, in turn, gave him twice as much as he paid me. This, kings of the age, is the most remarkable thing that has happened to me, and, by my life, the price paid was a small one for that girl.'

The kings were astonished when they heard this story, but when it came to the ears of Nuzhat al-Zaman, the light became darkness in her face and she cried out to her brother Rumzan: 'There is no doubt at all that this is the very same Bedouin who kidnapped me from Jerusalem.' She then told them the whole story of what had happened to her in foreign parts – the hardships, blows, hunger, humiliation and degradation – after which she said: 'I can now lawfully kill him.' She drew a sword and went to kill him, but he shouted out: 'Kings of the age, don't let her kill me until I tell you of the wonderful things that have happened to me.' 'Aunt,' said Kana-ma-Kana, her nephew, 'let him tell us a story and after that do what you want.'

She drew back and the kings said: 'Now tell us a story.' 'Kings of the age,' he asked, 'if I tell you a wonderful tale, will you pardon me?' When they had agreed to this, he began to tell them of his most remarkable experience. 'Know,' he said, 'that a short time ago I was very sleepless one night and I thought that morning was never going to come. As soon as it did, I got up, belted on my sword, mounted my horse and, with my spear resting beneath my thigh, I went out to hunt. On the way, I met a party of men who asked me what I was doing. When I told them, they said that they would come with me and so we joined forces. Then, as we were riding along, an ostrich suddenly appeared and, when we made for it, it bounded away, opening its wings. We went on after it until noon and it led us into a desert where there were no plants and no water, and where the only sounds to be heard were the hissing of snakes, the cries of the *jinn* and the screaming of *ghuls*. Here we lost sight of the ostrich and didn't know whether it had flown up into the sky or vanished into the ground. We turned our horses' heads and thought of going back, but then we saw that it was far too hot for us to start, as not only was the heat oppressive but we were parched with thirst. Our horses came to a halt and we had no doubt that we were on the point of death.' HE WENT ON:

While we were in this state, in the distance we caught sight of a wide stretch of grassland where gazelles were frolicking. A tent had been pitched there, beside which a horse was tethered and a spear with a gleaming point fixed into the ground. We had been in despair, but our spirits now revived and we turned our horses' heads towards the tent, making for the meadow and the water. As we all rode off, I was among the first and we carried on until we got to the meadow, where we halted by a spring from which we drank and watered our horses. I was then seized by the haughty spirit of the Age of Ignorance and I made for the entrance to the tent. There I saw a young man with no down on his cheeks, looking like a crescent moon, while to his right was a slender girl like the branch of a *ban* tree. When I looked at her, I fell in love with her. Exchanging greetings with the young man, I said: 'My Bedouin brother, tell me who you are and what relation to you is this girl who is with you.' The youth looked down at the ground for a time, before raising his head and saying: 'Tell me who you are and who are these riders with you.' I told him: 'I am Hammad ibn al-Fazari, the renowned rider, who is counted among the Bedouin as the equal of five hundred. We left our camp to hunt and were overtaken by thirst, as a result of which I have come to the entrance of your tent, hoping for a drink of water.' At this, he turned to the pretty girl and told her to bring me water and what food there was. She got up, trailing her skirts, with her golden anklets on her legs, tripping over her own hair. Then, soon afterwards, she came to me with a silver jug full of cold water in her right hand and in her left a bowl filled with dates, curds, as well as the meat of wild beasts.

Such was the love that I felt for her that I could take neither food nor drink, but quoted these lines:

The dye on her hand was like a crow perched on snow.
Sun and moon are joined together in her face,
The one hiding itself, the other being afraid.

After I had eaten and drunk, I said to the young man: 'Know that I have told you the truth about myself, and I now want you to tell me truthfully about your own situation.' The young man replied: 'This girl is my sister.' At which I said: 'I want you to marry her to me of your own free will, for otherwise I will kill you and take her by force.' At that, he looked down at the ground for a time, before raising his eyes to me and saying: 'You are right in claiming to be a well-known rider and a renowned champion, the lion of the desert, but if you attack me treacherously and take my sister after killing me, this will bring shame on you. If, as you say, you are riders to be counted among the champions, who face war and combat unconcernedly, then give me a little time to equip myself, buckle on my sword, take up my spear and mount my horse. Then all of you can meet me on the battlefield. If I get the better of you, I shall kill every last one of you, while if you overcome me and kill me, then this sister of mine will be yours.'

When I heard what he had to say, I told him: 'That is fair and there can be no dispute about it.' I turned back my horse's head; the mad passion of my love for the girl had increased and when I got back to my companions, I told them about her beauty and that of the young man who was with her, noting his courage and fortitude, as well as his claim to be able to face a thousand riders in battle. Then I told them of all the wealth and the treasures that were in the tent, saying: 'This youth, you must know, would not live here in isolation unless he were a man of great courage. My recommendation is that whoever kills him should take his sister.' My companions agreed to this, put on their battle gear, mounted their horses and rode out against the young man, whom they found equipped and mounted. His sister then sprang out and clung on to his stirrup, drenching her veil with tears, wailing and lamenting out of fear for him. She recited these lines:

> I complain to God of suffering and sorrow
> That the Lord of the Heavenly Throne may burden them with fear.
> Little brother, they intend to kill you,
> Although there is no reason for the fight, which is no fault of yours.
> The riders know you as a champion,
> The bravest hero in both east and west.
> You defend your sister, whose resolve is weak.
> You are her brother and for you she prays to God.
> Do not allow them to have my heart's blood,

Letting them seize and capture me by force.
By God's truth, I shall never live in any land,
Fertile though it may be, if you are not there too.
I shall then kill myself for love of you,
And go to my grave, lying on a bed of earth.

When her brother heard these lines, he wept bitterly, and, turning his
horse's head towards his sister, he recited these lines in answer to hers:

Stay here and watch the marvels I shall do
When battle is joined and I rain blows on them.
If their lion leader should come out,
The bravest and the most steadfast of them all,
I'll strike him with a blow worthy of my clan,
Leaving my spear sunk in him to its heel.
If I do not fight for you, sister, I would wish
To be struck down and left as a prey for birds.
While I can, I shall fight to do you honour,
And afterwards this story will fill books.

When he had finished his poem, he said: 'Sister, listen to what I have to
say to you and the advice I am going to give you.' 'Willingly,' she replied.
'If I die,' he went on, 'do not allow anyone to possess you.' At that, she
struck herself on the face, saying: 'God forbid, brother, that I should see
you dead and then allow myself to be taken by our enemies.' The youth
then put out his hand to her and removed the veil from her face, so that she
appeared to us like the sun coming out from below a cloud. He kissed her
between her eyes and said goodbye, after which he turned to us and said:
'Riders, are you here as guests or do you want to fight? If you are guests,
I can give you good news of guest provisions, but if it is the shining
moon that you want, come out one by one on to this battlefield.'

A brave rider then rode out and the youth said: 'What is your name
and the name of your father, for I have sworn not to kill anyone whose
name is the same as mine and whose father's name is the same as that
of my father; if this is the case with you, I will hand the girl over to you.'
'My name is Bilal,' the man said, and the youth replied with these lines:

What you say is a lie* and you have come
Acting with falsehood and with trickery.

* A pun on *bilal* in its meaning of 'doing good'.

If you are hardy, listen to my words,
For I am one who throws down heroes on the battlefield,
And my sharp sword is like a crescent moon.
Be ready for a thrust that makes the mountains shake.

The two riders charged each other and the youth struck Bilal on the
breast, with the spear point coming out from behind his back. When the
next man rode out, the youth recited:

You filthy dog, can the highly priced be equal to the low?
The noble lion pays no heed to his own life in battle.

With no delay, the youth left his opponent drowning in his own blood,
and he then called for another challenger. One of us rode out against
him, reciting:

There is fire in my heart as I come out to you,
Calling to my companions in the fight.
You have killed Arab chiefs, but not today
Will you escape from those who seek revenge.

When he heard this, the young man replied with these lines:

You evil devil, you have lied,
Coming with falsehood and untruth.
Today upon the battlefield
The deadly spear point is what you must face.

He then struck his opponent on the breast so that the spearhead came
out from his back. At his challenge, a fourth rider came out, and when
asked for his name, he replied: 'Hilal.' The youth recited:

You plunged mistakenly into my sea,
Carrying with you falsehood and all ills.
I am the one whose verses you can hear;
But before you know it, I shall snatch away your life.

The two then charged each other and exchanged blows, but the youth
struck first and killed his opponent. He continued to kill all who came
against him, and when I saw that my companions were dead, I said to
myself: 'If I fight, I shall be no match for him, but if I run away I shall
be disgraced among the Bedouin.' The youth allowed me no time to
think. He pounced on me, seized me and dragged me from my saddle.

I fell fainting, but when he raised his sword and was about to cut off my head, I clung to the skirt of his robe and he carried me off in his hand as though I were a sparrow.

When the girl saw that, she was delighted by what her brother had done and, coming up to him, she kissed him between the eyes. He handed me over to her, saying: 'Look after this man and treat him well, for he is now under our control.' She took me by the collar of my mail coat and started to lead me as one leads a dog. She then unfastened her brother's breastplate, clothed him in a robe and set out an ivory chair for him. After he had taken his seat, she said: 'May God whiten your honour and use you as a defence against misfortune.' He replied to her with these lines:

My sister says on seeing me in battle,
With my horse's blaze gleaming like the sun's rays:
'How splendid as a champion you are,
Whose prowess humbles lions in their coverts!'
I say: 'Ask heroes about me,
When warriors take to flight.
I am known for good fortune and my resolution soars aloft.
Hammad, you have come out against a lion,
Who shows you death, that strikes you as a snake.'

On hearing these lines, I was confused and, looking at my situation and the captivity into which I had fallen, I cringed, but when I saw the beauty of the young man's sister, I said to myself: 'She is the cause of the trouble.' I shed tears as I wondered at her loveliness and I recited these lines:

Friend, give up scolding and rebuking me,
For I shall pay no heed to any blame.
I am the captive of a young girl, to whose love
I was called when I first set eyes on her.
While I love her, her brother watches me,
A man of high ambition and of power.

The girl produced food for her brother and I was glad when he invited me to eat with him, feeling sure that I would not be killed. When he had finished, she brought him a jug of wine and, applying himself to this, he drank until the wine went to his head and his face grew red. He turned to me and said: 'Damn you, Hammad, do you know me or not?' 'By your life,' I replied, 'the only thing that I have in quantity is ignorance.' He said: 'I am Hammad, son of 'Abbad, son of Tamim, son of Tha'laba. God has granted you your life and spared you so that you can marry.' He then drank a toast to me, followed by a second, a third and a fourth. I drank all these down, and he drank with me and made me swear that I would never betray him. I swore by fifteen hundred oaths that I would never do this and that I would act as his helper, at which he told his sister to bring me ten robes of silk. She did this and spread them over me, among them being the one that I am wearing now. He then told her to bring me one of the best she-camels, and she brought one that was laden with treasures and provisions. The sorrel stallion was the next thing that he told her to fetch for me, and after that he presented all these things to me as a gift.

I stayed with them for three days, eating and drinking, and I still have the presents that I was given. After the three days, my host said to me: 'Hammad, my brother, I need a little sleep to rest myself. I can trust you with my life, and if you see galloping riders, don't be afraid of them, for you must know that they will be from the Banu Tha'laba, coming to fight me.' So saying, he put his sword beneath his head and dozed off. When he was sound asleep, the devil prompted me to kill him and so I got up quickly, drew out his sword from beneath his head and struck him with a blow that severed the head from his body. When his sister realized what I had done, she sprang out from the tent, threw herself on her brother, tore her clothes and recited these lines:

> Bring to my family this unhappiest of news:
> No man escapes the decrees of God, the Judge.
> My brother, you are thrown down on the ground;
> Your face in beauty matched the circle of the moon.
> You met them on a day of evil omen
> And your straight spear was broken.
> Now you are dead, no one will ride with pleasure,
> Nor shall a mother bear a son like you.
> Hammad killed you today, breaking his oaths.
> He has betrayed his covenant to reach his goal,
> But Satan is false in all that he commands.

When she had finished her poem, she said: 'You child of accursed stock, why did you betray and kill my brother? He was going to send you back to your own lands with provisions and gifts and he had also intended to marry me to you at the beginning of the month.' She then drew a sword that she had with her and, setting its hilt in the ground and its point on her breast, she fell on it until it emerged from her back and she collapsed, dead. I grieved for her and repented tearfully, when repentance was of no use. Then I went quickly to the tent and took whatever valuables could easily be carried, after which I went on my way. Because I was afraid and in a hurry, I paid no attention to any of my companions and I didn't bury the girl or the young man. This story of mine is more remarkable than my first tale of the servant girl whom I kidnapped from Jerusalem.

When Nuzhat al-Zaman heard what the Bedouin had to say, the light became dark in her eyes.

Night 145

Morning now dawned and Shahrazad broke off from what she had been allowed to say. Then, when it was the hundred and forty-fifth night, SHE CONTINUED:

I have heard, O fortunate king, that when Nuzhat al-Zaman heard what the Bedouin had to say, the light became dark in her eyes. She got up, drew a sword and struck Hammad the Bedouin on the shoulder, so that the blade came out through the tendons of his neck. When the people there asked why she had been in such a hurry to kill him, she exclaimed: 'Praise be to God, Who has permitted me to live until I could avenge myself with my own hand.' She then told the slaves to drag away the corpse by the legs and throw it to the dogs.

The kings then turned to the remaining two robbers, one of whom was a black slave. 'What is your name?' they asked him, adding, 'and tell us the truth.' 'My name is Ghadban,' he said, and he told them of his encounter with Princess Abriza, the daughter of Hardub, king of Rum, and how he had fled after killing her. Before he had finished speaking, King Rumzan had cut off his head with his sword, calling down praises on God Who had allowed him to avenge his mother with his own hand, and telling the others what he had learned about the slave from his nurse, Marjana. They then turned to the third man, who turned out to be the camel driver who had been hired by the people of Jerusalem to carry Dau' al-Makan to the hospital at Damascus, but who, instead, had taken him and thrown him down by the bath-house furnace, before going off on his way. 'Tell us your story truthfully,' they instructed him, and so he told them of his encounter with the sick Dau' al-Makan and how he had been hired by the people of Jerusalem to take him to the hospital at Damascus. He went on to explain how he had taken the money and fled, after having thrown his patient on the dunghill next to the furnace of the bath house. When he had finished his account, King Kana-ma-Kana took a sword and struck off his head, saying: 'Praise be to God, Who allowed me to live until I could repay this treacherous man for what he did to my father, for this is the very same account that I heard from my father, King Dau' al-Makan.'

The kings now said to one another: 'There only remains now Shawahi, the old woman known as Dhat al-Dawahi. She is the cause of all these troubles, for it was she who plunged us into disaster. Who will fetch her for us so that we can take vengeance on her and clear away this disgrace?' King Rumzan, Kana-ma-Kana's uncle, said: 'She must be brought here,' and immediately he wrote a letter which he sent to her, she being his great-grandmother. In this letter he told her that he had conquered the lands of Damascus, Mosul and Iraq, destroying the army of the Muslims and capturing their leaders. He added: 'I would like you to join me, bringing with you Queen Sophia, the daughter of Afridun, the emperor of Constantinople, and any of the Christian leaders you want. Do not bring any troops, for the lands are secure and under our control.'

When the letter reached Shawahi, she read it and recognized the handwriting of King Rumzan. In her delight she made immediate preparations for the journey, taking with her Queen Sophia, Nuzhat al-Zaman's mother, together with an escort. When her party reached Baghdad, a messenger went forward to tell the kings of her arrival. 'What we should do,' said Rumzan, 'is to go to meet her dressed as Franks so that we may be secure from her trickery and wiles.' The others agreed to this and put on Frankish dress. 'By the truth of the Lord we worship,' exclaimed Qudiya-fa-Kana, 'if I did not know you, I would say that you were Franks.' Rumzan went ahead of them as they started out to meet the old woman with an escort of a thousand riders. When they saw each other, Rumzan dismounted and hurried towards Shawahi. On seeing him and recognizing him, she dismounted and embraced him, but he squeezed her ribs so hard that he almost cracked them. 'What is this, my son?' she said, but before she had finished speaking, Kana-ma-Kana and the vizier Dandan came up to them, and with a shout the riders rode at her escort of slaves of both sexes, captured them all and then returned to Baghdad. On Rumzan's orders, the city was adorned with decorations for three days and then Shawahi was brought out wearing a red conical cap of palm leaves, covered with donkey's dung, preceded by a herald who called out: 'This is the reward of those who dare to attack kings and the children of kings.' She was crucified on the gate of Baghdad, and when her companions saw what had happened to her, they all embraced Islam.

Kana-ma-Kana, Rumzan his uncle, Nuzhat al-Zaman and the vizier Dandan all expressed their wonder at this remarkable sequence of events and they gave orders for the scribes to write it down in books so that it could be read in later times. They passed the rest of their lives in great pleasure and happiness until they were visited by the destroyer of delights and the parter of companions. So ends the story of the vicissitudes of Time experienced by King 'Umar ibn al-Nu'man, his sons Sharkan and Dau' al-Makan, Kana-ma-Kana his grandson, Nuzhat al-Zaman his daughter and her daughter Qudiya-fa-Kana.

King Shahriyar now told Shahrazad: 'I want you to tell me a story about birds.' Her sister said to her: 'In all this time, it is only tonight that I have seen the king looking happy, and I hope that your affair with him will turn out well.' The king then fell asleep.

Night 146

Morning now dawned and Shahrazad broke off from what she had been allowed to say. Then, when it was the hundred and forty-sixth night, SHE SAID:

I have heard, O fortunate king, that once upon a time, in an earlier age, a peacock and his mate sheltered by the seashore in a place that was full of lions and other wild beasts, but which had many trees and streams. At night, for fear of these beasts, the peacock and the peahen would take refuge in one of the trees, coming out in the morning to look for food. They carried on like this until they became so afraid that they started to look for some other place of shelter. In the course of their search, they caught sight of an island full of trees and streams. They flew down there and ate from its fruit and drank from its streams, but while they were doing this, a duck came up in a state of great alarm, rushing on until it came to the tree on which the two of them were perched, after which it became calm. The peacock was sure that there must be a strange story attached to this duck and so he asked her about herself and the reason for her fright. She told him: 'I am sick with worry and it is the son of Adam whom I fear. Beware, beware of the sons of Adam!' 'Now that you have come to us, there is no need to be afraid,' said the peacock. 'Praise be to God,' said the duck, 'Who has dispelled my cares and worries! I have come to you hoping for your friendship.'

When she had finished speaking, the peahen came down, welcomed her warmly and said: 'Don't be afraid. How can the son of Adam reach us when we are on this island in the middle of the sea? He cannot get to us by land and he cannot reach us by sea. So cheer up and tell us what has happened to you and what you have experienced at his hands.' TO WHICH THE DUCK SAID:

Know, peahen, that I have lived all my life in safety on this island without seeing anything unpleasant. Then, one night as I slept, a son of Adam appeared to me in a dream and spoke to me and I spoke to him. I heard a voice saying: 'Duck, beware of the son of Adam! Don't be deceived by what he says or by what he suggests to you, for he is full of wiles and trickery. Beware, beware of his guile, for he is a deceiver and a trickster, as the poet says:

He will offer you sweetness on the tip of his tongue,
But then he will trick you like a fox.

Know that the son of Adam works his wiles against the fish, taking them out of the sea; he shoots birds with clay pellets and brings down elephants with his cunning. Nothing is safe from the evil that he does and neither bird nor beast can escape from him. I have now told you what I have heard about the son of Adam.

I woke up from my dream in terror and up till now I have not been able to relax for fear of the son of Adam, lest he surprise me by means of some trick and catch me in his nets. By the end of the day, my strength had weakened and my spirits had failed. I wanted to eat and drink and so I went away, troubled and gloomy, and reached a mountain, where at the entrance of a cave I found a tawny lion cub who was delighted to see me, admiring my colour and my delicate shape. He called out to me and told me to come up to him. When I did, he asked me my name and what kind of creature I was. 'My name is Duck,' I replied, 'and I am a bird.' Then I asked why he kept on sitting there, and he said: 'The reason is that my father, the lion, has been warning me for days about the son of Adam, and last night in a dream this son of Adam appeared to me.'

The lion cub then told me the same story that I have told you, and having heard it, I said: 'Lion, I come to you for refuge and I implore you to make up your mind to kill the son of Adam. He has filled me with great fear for my life, and I am even more afraid because you are afraid of him, although you are the king of the beasts.' So it was, sister, that I continued to warn the lion cub about the son of Adam, advising him to kill him, until he suddenly got up and walked off with me following behind him, as he lashed his back with his tail. We went on until we came to a fork in the road and we saw rising dust which cleared away to show beneath it a stray donkey, with no trappings, galloping and running at times and at times rolling in the dust. When the lion cub saw him, he roared at him and the donkey came up submissively. 'You feeble-witted animal,' said the lion cub, 'what kind of creature are you and why have you come here?' 'Son of the sultan,' replied the donkey, 'I am a donkey and I have come here in flight from the son of Adam.' 'Are you afraid that he may kill you?' asked the lion cub. 'No, prince,' said the donkey, 'but I'm afraid that he may trick me and mount me. He has a thing called a pack saddle, which he puts on my back; things called girths, which he ties around my belly; a so-called crupper, which he sticks beneath my tail; and what he calls a bridle, which he puts in my mouth. He makes a goad for me with which he pricks me; he forces me to run more than I can; when I stumble he curses me; and if I bray he heaps abuse on me. When I grow old and cannot run, he will make a wooden pack saddle for me and hand me over to the water carriers. They will load water from the river on to my back in water skins or other containers such as jars, and I'll be degraded, humiliated and weary until I die, when they'll throw me on a rubbish dump for the dogs. What greater distress can there be than this and what greater misfortune?'

Peahen, when I heard what the donkey had to say, I shuddered in fear of the son of Adam and I said to the lion cub: 'Master, the donkey is to be excused, and what he said has made me even more afraid.' The lion cub then asked the donkey where he was going, and the donkey said: 'Before sunrise I saw the son of Adam in the distance. I took flight and I need to be off, for I have not stopped running, so great is my fear of him. I am hoping to find some place of refuge from his treachery.'

While the donkey was talking to the lion cub and wanting to take his leave of us and go, into sight came a dust cloud. The donkey brayed noisily and, looking towards the cloud, he passed wind loudly. Soon afterwards, the dust cleared away to show a black horse with a fine blaze the size of a dirham and handsome white fetlocks, good legs and a strong whinny. It went on running until it stopped in front of the lion cub, who admired it and asked: 'What kind of a creature are you, you splendid animal, and why are you straying through these broad lands?' 'Lord of the beasts,' answered the horse, 'I am one of the race of horses, and the reason that I am straying here is that I am escaping from the son of Adam.' The lion cub was astonished to hear this and exclaimed: 'Don't say that, for it brings disgrace on you – a tall, burly creature like you. How can you be afraid of the son of Adam? You are both large and swift, while in spite of my own small size, I had intended to meet the son of Adam, attack him and eat his flesh, so calming the fears of this poor duck so that she can settle back in her own land. But here you are, coming at this moment, breaking my resolution by your words, and turning me back from my purpose. For, big as you are, the son of Adam must have got the better of you, and he cannot have been afraid of your size, in spite of the fact that you could kill him with a kick. He could have had no power over you and you could pour him out his death draught.'

The horse laughed when he heard what the lion cub had to say. 'I am very, very far from being able to overcome him, prince,' he said. 'Don't be deceived by my size or my bulk in comparison with his. Through his great cunning and guile, he makes something called shackles for me from fibres twisted with felt, with which he secures my legs, and he fastens my head to a high peg, so that I have to stay standing as though crucified, unable to sit or sleep. When he wants to ride me, he makes for me iron things called stirrups that he puts on his feet. He puts something called a saddle on my back and fastens it with girths under my belly. In my mouth he puts an iron contraption called a bridle to which he fixes leather things called reins. When he rides me sitting on the saddle, he holds the reins in his hand and uses them to direct me, while he pricks my flanks with his stirrups until he makes them bleed. Don't ask me about what I suffer at his hands, prince. When I grow old and my back becomes scrawny and I can no longer run fast, he will sell me to the miller, who will use me in the mill and I will go round and round, night and day, until I become decrepit, when he will sell me to the butcher, who will kill and skin me. He will pluck my tail and sell it to the sieve maker, and he'll melt down my fat.'

When the lion cub heard what the horse had to say, he grew more and more angry and distressed. 'When did you leave the son of Adam?' he asked. 'At midday,' the horse replied, 'and he is following in my tracks.' While the two were talking, a sudden dust cloud rose up and when it cleared away, underneath it appeared an angry camel, gurgling, and trampling the ground with its legs. It went on like this until it came up to us. When the lion cub saw its size and its bulk, he thought that it must be the son of Adam and was about to spring at it, when I said to him: 'Prince, this is not the son of Adam; it is a camel and it looks as though it is fleeing from him.'

While I was talking to the lion cub, sister, the camel came up to it and they exchanged greetings. The lion cub then asked the camel why he had come, to which he replied that he was in flight from the son of Adam. 'How can a large creature like you, with your great size, be afraid of the son of Adam, whom you could kill with a single kick?' asked the lion cub. 'Prince,' answered the camel, 'know that the son of Adam is invincibly cunning and it is only death that can get the better of him. He puts a thread in my nostrils which he calls a nose ring and on my head he puts a halter. Then he hands me over to the youngest of his children, and for all my huge size this little child pulls me along by my nose ring. They make me carry the heaviest of loads and take me on long journeys, working me hard both night and day. Then when I am old and broken, the son of Adam will not keep me with him but will sell me to the butcher, who will slaughter me and then sell my hide to the tanners and my flesh to the cooks. Don't ask about the miseries that I suffer at the hands of the son of Adam.' 'When did you leave him?' asked the lion cub. 'At sunset,' replied the camel. 'I think that after I left he will be coming, and when he doesn't find me, he will pursue me. So let me go off into the trackless wilds.'

'Wait awhile, camel,' said the lion cub, 'so that you can see how I shall hunt him down, and then I shall give you his flesh to eat, while I myself shall crush his bones and drink his blood.' 'Prince,' said the camel, 'I'm afraid for you if you meet the son of Adam, for he is a master of deception and tricks.' Then he recited these lines:

When an oppressor settles in a land,
All that its people can do is to leave.

While the camel and the lion cub were talking, another dust cloud rose, clearing away after a while to show a small, thin-skinned old man, with a basket on his shoulder containing carpenter's tools. On his head he was carrying the branch of a tree, together with eight planks, and he was walking at a fast pace, leading some small children by the hand. He did not stop until he was close to the lion cub, and when I saw him, sister, I was so afraid that I fell down. As for the lion cub, he got up and walked off to meet the man. When he came up to him, the carpenter smiled at him and spoke to him eloquently: 'Great and powerful king, may God give you happiness and success and add to your courage and your power. Protect me from the misfortune that has befallen me and the evil that has overtaken me, as I can find no helper except you.' He stood before the lion cub, weeping, groaning and complaining. When the lion cub heard his laments and complaints, he said to him: 'I shall give you protection from whatever you fear. Who is it who has wronged you and who are you? Never in my life have I seen an animal like you, nor one better formed nor more eloquent. What is your business?' The man replied: 'Lord of the beasts, I am a carpenter and the one who has wronged me is the son of Adam. When morning comes at the end of this night, he will be here with you.'

When the lion cub heard what the carpenter had to say, the light turned to darkness in his eyes. He snorted and grunted; sparks flashed from his eyes and he roared out: 'By God, I shall stay awake through the night until dawn and I shall not go back to my father until I have reached my goal.' He turned to the carpenter and said: 'I see that you can only take short steps. As I am a chivalrous creature, I don't want to discourage you, but I think that you cannot keep pace with wild beasts. So tell me where you are going.' The carpenter said: 'Know that I am on my way to your father's vizier, the lynx. When the lynx heard that the son of Adam had set foot in this land, he became very afraid for himself and sent one of the wild beasts as a messenger to me, asking me to make him a house in which he could live in safety, protected from his enemies, where none of the sons of Adam could reach him. When the messenger arrived, I took these planks and set out to find his master.'

When the lion cub heard what the carpenter had to say, he became envious of the lynx and said: 'By my life, you must use these planks to make me a house before you make one for the lynx, and when you have finished the job for me, you can go on to him and make what you want for him.' After hearing this, the carpenter said: 'Lord of the beasts, I cannot make you anything until I have made what the lynx wants, and after that I shall come to serve you and make you a house to protect you from your enemies.' 'By God,' said the lion cub, 'I shall not let you leave this place until you make the planks into a house for me.' He then leapt playfully at the carpenter, struck him with his paw and knocked the basket from his shoulder, laughing as the carpenter fell down in a faint. 'You are a weak creature, carpenter,' he said. 'You have no strength and you can be excused for being afraid of the son of Adam.'

When the carpenter fell over, he became very angry, but he concealed his anger because of his fear of the lion cub. He sat up, smiled at the lion cub and agreed to make him a house. He took the planks that he had with him and nailed them as a box made to the measure of the lion cub, with its door left open like a chest. He gave it a large opening on top with a large cover, in which he bored a number of holes, with sharp-pointed nails protruding from them. He then told the lion cub to go in through the opening so that he could check the measurements. The lion cub was pleased at this, but when he came to the opening, he found it narrow. 'Go in and crouch down on all four paws,' said the carpenter. The lion cub did this but found that when he was inside, his tail was still sticking out. He wanted to back out, but the carpenter said: 'Wait; be patient and I'll see whether there is room for your tail to go in with you.' The lion cub did as he was told and the carpenter twisted his tail, stuffed it in the box and then quickly put the plank back over the opening, nailing it down. The lion cub cried out: 'Carpenter, let me out of this narrow house that you have made for me.' 'Certainly not,' replied the carpenter. 'It does no good to regret what has happened, and you are never going to get out of this.' He then laughed and added: 'You have fallen into a trap and you will never escape from its confinement, you foulest of beasts.' 'Brother,' said the lion cub, 'how do you come to address me like this?' 'Know, dog of the desert,' said the carpenter, 'that you have fallen into the very danger you feared. Fate has overthrown you, and caution can do you no good now.' When the lion cub heard that, sister, he realized that this must be the son of Adam against whom he had been warned by his father when he was awake and by the voice in his dream. I too was sure of this beyond any shadow of doubt, and being in great fear for my life, I went a little way off and stayed watching what he was going to do to the lion cub. Sister, I saw him dig a hole there near the lion cub's box, which he then threw into the hole and, piling firewood on top of it, he burned it. I was terrified and for two days now I have been fleeing from the son of Adam.

When the peahen heard what the duck had to say . . .

Night 147

Morning now dawned and Shahrazad broke off from what she had been
allowed to say. Then, when it was the hundred and forty-seventh night,
SHE CONTINUED:

I have heard, O fortunate king, that when the peahen heard what the
duck had to say she was filled with astonishment and said: 'Sister, you
are safe from the son of Adam, for you are on an island in the sea and
there is no way for him to get to it. You had better stay with us until
God smooths the way for you and for us.' 'I am afraid that some disaster
will overtake me,' said the duck, 'and no one can escape fate by fleeing.'
'Sit with us,' repeated the peahen, 'and you will be like one of us.' She
continued to insist until the duck sat down and said: 'Sister, you know
how small are my powers of endurance, and had I not seen you here, I
would not have done this.' The peahen said: 'We have to fulfil whatever
destiny is written on our foreheads. If our doom is near at hand, who
can save us? No one dies until he has had the full measure of what has
been allotted to him of both sustenance and length of life.'

While the two of them were talking to each other, they suddenly
caught sight of a cloud of dust. With a cry, the duck went down to the
sea, calling out: 'Take care, take care – even though there is no way of
escaping fate.' Then, after a time, the dust cleared away and beneath it
could be seen a gazelle. This calmed the duck as well as the peahen, who
told the duck: 'Sister, the thing that you saw and against which you were
on your guard is a gazelle, and here it is, coming towards us. It will do
us no harm; it eats the grasses that grow on the earth, and, just as you
are of the race of birds, so, for its part, it is of the race of beasts. Be calm
and don't worry, for worry makes the body thin.'

Before the peahen had finished speaking, the gazelle had come up to
them and was sheltering in the shade of a tree. When it saw the peahen
and the duck, it greeted them and told them: 'I only came to this island
today and I have never seen a more fertile spot, or a better place in which
to live.' It then asked them to take it as a true friend, and when the two
companions saw how well disposed it was to them, they approached it,
being eager for its companionship, and all three took vows of friendship.
They started to pass the night in the same spot and ate and drank
together, and they continued undisturbed in this way until a ship passed
by that had strayed from its course at sea.

It anchored close by and those on board landed, dispersing throughout the island. When they saw the gazelle, the peahen and the duck together, they made for them, but on seeing them, the peahen went up into its tree and then flew off into the air, while the gazelle made for the open country. The duck, however, was too confused to move and was caught. She cried out: 'Caution has not helped me against my destined fate,' and the sailors took her off to their ship. When the peahen saw what had happened to the duck, she left the island. 'I see that disasters are on the lookout for every one of us,' she said, adding: 'Had it not been for this ship, I would not have been parted from this duck, one of the best of my friends.' She flew off and joined the gazelle who, having greeted her and congratulated her on her escape, asked her about the duck. 'The enemy took her,' said the peahen, 'and now that she is gone, I don't want to stay on the island.' Weeping for the duck's loss, she recited:

The day of separation cut my heart in pieces;
May God cut in pieces the heart of that same day.

She then added:

I wish that union might return one day,
So I could tell the beloved what separation did.

The gazelle was exceedingly distressed, but it persuaded the peahen to change her mind about leaving. She stayed with the gazelle, eating and drinking in safety, although both were still grieved by the loss of the duck. The gazelle then said to the peahen: 'You know, sister, that the sailors who came to us from the ship were the cause of our separation and of the death of the duck, so beware of this and guard against them and against the treacherous wiles of the sons of Adam.' 'I know for a fact,' replied the peahen, 'that what killed the duck was that she gave up saying: "Glory be to God." I had told her that I was afraid for her because of this, as all God's creation must glorify Him and whoever neglects this is punished by destruction.' When the gazelle heard this, it said to the peahen: 'May God beautify you,' and it set about praising God continuously. The formula of praise used by the gazelle was said to be: 'Glory be to the Judge, the Omnipotent, the Ruler.'

It is recorded that there was a hermit who worshipped God on a mountain which was the resort of a pair of pigeons. He used to divide his food in half . . .

Night 148

Morning now dawned and Shahrazad broke off from what she had been
allowed to say. Then, when it was the hundred and forty-eighth night,
SHE CONTINUED:

I have heard, O fortunate king, that the hermit used to divide his food
in half, with half for himself and half for the pigeons. He prayed that
the pair might have many young and the prayer was answered. The
hermit's mountain was the only place to which the pigeons went, and
the reason that they associated with him was the frequency with which
they glorified God. It is said that the formula of praise used by pigeons
was: 'Glory be to the Author of all creation, the Distributor of sustenance,
the Builder of the heavens and the Unfolder of the lands.' The pigeons
lived a life of plenty with their young until the hermit died and they were
dispersed and scattered among towns, villages and mountains.

It is told that on a certain mountain there was a shepherd – a pious,
intelligent and chaste man. He owned flocks that he herded, benefiting
from their milk and their wool. His mountain was covered in trees and
pastures and there were many beasts of prey, but no wild beast had any
power over him or over his flocks. He lived a peaceful life there, un-
affected by worldly matters because of his good fortune and his concern
with prayer and worship. Then, as God had decreed, he became very ill
and went into a mountain cave from which his flock used to go out by
day to their pasture, returning to it for shelter at night. Almighty God,
wishing to test him and to try out his obedience and his powers of
endurance, sent down an angel, who sat down in front of him in the
form of a beautiful woman.

When the shepherd saw a woman sitting with him, in his revulsion
goose flesh spread all over his body. 'Woman,' he said, 'what has called
you here? I have no need of you and there is nothing between us that
should prompt you to come to me.' 'Man,' she replied, 'don't you see
my beauty and loveliness and smell the sweetness of my scent? Don't
you know what women need from men and men from women? What is
there to keep you from me? I have chosen to be near you; I want union
with you; I have come to you willingly and will not refuse myself to you.
There is no one with us whom we need fear and I want to stay with you
as long as you remain on this mountain. I will be your friend and I offer
myself to you, as you need the services of a woman. If you sleep with

me, your illness will leave you; your health will be restored and you will regret what you missed in your past life by way of intimacy with women. Accept the advice that I give you and come close to me.'

The shepherd replied: 'Leave me, you false and treacherous woman. I shall not come to you or approach you and I have no need of intimacy or union with you. Whoever desires you is without desire for the next world, and whoever desires the next world has no desire for you. You have seduced men throughout the ages. Almighty God watches over His servants and woe betide anyone who is afflicted by your company.' 'You stray from what is right,' she said, 'and you have missed the path of true guidance. Turn your face to me; look at my loveliness and take advantage of my nearness, as wise men have done before you. They had more experience than you and sounder judgement, but in spite of that they did not do what you have done in rejecting the enjoyment of women. They were eager for what you have abstained from, to be with women and to be intimate with them. That did them no harm either as regards their religion or in their worldly affairs. So change your mind and you will have cause to praise the outcome of this affair.' The shepherd replied: 'I reject with loathing all that you say and I will have nothing to do with what you are showing me. You are deceitful and treacherous, faithful to no covenant. How much ugliness lies concealed beneath your beauty! How many pious men have you seduced, leaving them with regret and loss! Get back from me, you who have prepared yourself so well to corrupt others.' He then threw his cloak over his face so as not to look at hers and he occupied himself in calling on the name of the Lord. When the angel saw how obedient he was to God, he left him and went back to heaven.

Near to the shepherd was a village in which lived a pious man who did not know where the shepherd was. In a dream, this man heard a voice saying: 'Near you, in a cave on the mountain, is a good man. Go to him and put yourself at his command.' In the morning, the man set off as he had been directed. When the heat strengthened, he came to a tree beside which was a spring of flowing water. As he rested there, sitting under the shade of the tree, he saw beasts and birds coming to drink from the stream, but when they caught sight of him, they shied away and took off. 'There is no might and no power except with God!' exclaimed the ascetic. 'All my resting here has done has been to harm the beasts and the birds.' He got up and said in self-reproach: 'Because I harmed these creatures by sitting here today, what will my excuse be to my Creator and theirs? It was I who frightened them away from their drink, their food and their pasture. How great will be my shame before my Lord on the day when He takes vengeance for the hornless sheep or the sheep with horns!' Then he wept and recited these lines:

> By God, did man but know for what was he created,
> He would not sleep the sleep of heedlessness.
> First comes death, then resurrection and then Judgement Day,
> Bringing with it rebuke and dreadful fears.
> Whether we give prohibitions or commands,
> We are like the Seven Sleepers, awake but yet asleep.

He wept in sorrow for having sat under the tree by the spring and for having kept the birds and beasts from drinking. Then he turned round and went on his way until he reached the shepherd and went in to see him. They exchanged greetings and the ascetic embraced the shepherd tearfully. The shepherd asked him: 'What has brought you to this place, where no man has ever visited me?' The ascetic replied: 'I saw in a dream one who described to me where you were and who ordered me to go to you and greet you, and it is in obedience to his orders that I am here.' The shepherd kissed him and took pleasure in his company, sitting with him on the mountain. They both worshipped God in the cave with sincere devotion and they continued to serve their Lord, eating the flesh of the sheep and drinking their milk, with no concern for wealth or children, until death, the certain, came to them. This is the end of their story.

The king said: 'Shahrazad, you have made me renounce my preoccupation with my kingdom and you have made me regret the excesses to which I went in killing women and girls. Do you have any more stories about birds?' 'Yes,' she replied, AND SHE WENT ON:

It is said, O king, that a certain bird flew high up into the sky and then swooped down to settle on a stone in the middle of a running stream. While it was perched there, a bloated human corpse, floating on the surface, was washed against the rock by the current. The bird, a water fowl, went up and, on inspecting it, found that it was the corpse of a man showing wounds made by sword blows and spear thrusts. The bird said to itself: 'I imagine that this dead man was a malefactor slain by a group of people who combined against him to rid themselves of his evil-doing.'

While it looked on, perplexed and astonished, down came vultures and kites, surrounding the body on all sides. The water fowl was very disturbed and said: 'I cannot bear to stay here.' It flew off, looking for somewhere to serve as a refuge until the corpse had time to decay and the carrion eaters had left. It went on flying until it discovered a river in the middle of which was a tree. The bird's mood had changed to sorrow and grief for its lost home, and it said to itself: 'Sorrows continue to plague me. I was pleased when I saw that corpse, and I said to myself in my joy: "This is nourishment that God has sent me." Then my joy turned to grief and my delight to sorrow and distress, for the corpse was taken and snatched away from me by predatory birds who kept me from it. How can I hope to be free from trouble in this world and how am I to rely on it with confidence? As the proverb puts it, this world is the home of those who have no home. It deceives the fool who entrusts it with his wealth, his children, his family and his clan. He continues to put his trust in it, treading proudly on the earth until he rests beneath it, with his nearest and dearest heaping soil over him. Nothing is better for a young man than patient endurance of his cares and troubles. I left my own place and my own land, and I was sad to be parted from my brothers, my friends and my companions.'

While it was plunged in thought, a male tortoise came down the stream, approached the water fowl and, after greeting it, asked: 'What has made you abandon your friends and leave your home?' The water fowl replied: 'This was because it was occupied by enemies and no intelligent man can bear to live next to his enemy. How well has the poet put it:

When an oppressor settles in a land,
All that the people there can do is leave.'

The tortoise replied: 'If that is the case and things are as you have said, then I shall stay with you and not leave you, seeing to your needs and attending on you. For, as it has been said, there is no loneliness worse than that of the stranger who has been cut off from his family and his native land. It has also been said that there is no misfortune to equal that of parting from good men, and the best consolation for people of intelligence is for them to make friends in their exile and to show patience in the face of misfortune and distress. I hope that you will approve of me as a companion, for I will be your servant and your helper.'

When the water fowl heard what the tortoise had to say, it answered: 'What you say is true and, by my life, I have experienced the pain and

sorrow of separation ever since I left home and parted from my friends
and companions. In separation there is a warning for those who take
heed and grounds for thought for those who can think. If a man fails to
find a companion to console him, what is good is cut off from him for
ever and what is bad remains in perpetuity. In all his affairs, the intelligent
man must find relief from care in his friends, and he must maintain
patience and endurance, as those are two praiseworthy qualities that
help him against misfortune and the disasters of Time, warding off fear
and anxiety in every affair.' 'Beware of anxiety,' said the tortoise, 'for it
will spoil your life and destroy your manliness.'

They went on talking to each other until the water fowl said to the
tortoise: 'I am still afraid of the misfortunes of Time and of calamitous
happenings.' On hearing this, the tortoise approached the water fowl
and, kissing it between the eyes, he said: 'The company of birds has
always derived blessings from you, and your counsel has taught them to
recognize what is good. How can they then be left with a burden of cares
and damage?'

The tortoise continued to soothe the water fowl until it was calmed.
It then flew off to where the corpse had been. There were no predatory
birds to be seen and all that was left of the corpse were the bones. The
water fowl went back and told the tortoise that his enemies had left the
place, saying: 'Know that I want to go home to enjoy the company of
my friends, for no man of intelligence can bear to be parted from his
homeland.' The two of them went there together and found nothing to
alarm them. At this, the water fowl recited:

There is many a mishap that leaves man powerless,
But God supplies him an escape from it.
It closes in, but when it has encircled him,
To my surprise, it opens up again.

The two companions settled on the island, but while the water fowl
was enjoying a happy and peaceful life, fate sent against it a ravenous
hawk which struck it in the stomach with its talons and killed it. When
its allotted span was ended, caution was no longer of use, and the reason
that it had been killed was that it had neglected to glorify God. It is said
that its formula of glorification was: 'Glory be to our Lord in what
He decrees and contrives. Glory be to our Lord, Who enriches and
impoverishes.' This is the story of the water fowl and the tortoise.

*

The king said: 'Shahrazad, through your stories you have provided me with yet more exhortations and warnings. Do you have any stories of wild beasts?' 'Yes,' she said, AND SHE WENT ON:

Know, O king, that a fox and a wolf shared the same den, to which they would go with one another for shelter, and here they would pass the night, although the wolf mistreated the fox. Things went on like this for some time, until it happened that the fox advised the wolf to behave more gently and to abandon his evil ways, adding: 'Know that if you continue to act arrogantly, God may give the son of Adam power over you, for he is wily, cunning and deceptive; he hunts down birds from the sky and takes fish from the sea; he cuts into mountains and moves them from one place to another; and all this is because of his cunning and his guile. You should act gently and fairly, abandoning evil and coercion, for this will give you a pleasanter life.' The wolf was not prepared to accept the fox's advice and said harshly: 'It is not for you to be talking about important and weighty matters.' He then felled the fox with a blow which knocked him unconscious. When the fox had recovered his wits, he laughed at the wolf and excused himself for having spoken out of turn. He then recited these lines:

If earlier in my love for you I was at fault
And did something to which you could object,
I now repent my fault, while your forgiveness
Covers the wrongdoer who asks for pardon.

The wolf accepted his apology and stopped mistreating him, while cautioning him: 'Don't talk about what does not concern you, or else you will hear what you do not like.'

Night 149

Morning now dawned and Shahrazad broke off from what she had been allowed to say. Then, when it was the hundred and forty-ninth night, SHE CONTINUED:

I have heard, O fortunate king, that the wolf said to the fox: 'Don't talk about what does not concern you, or else you will hear what you do not like.' 'To hear is to obey,' replied the fox. 'Far be it from me to do anything that displeases you. The wise man has said: "Do not talk about what you have not been asked, and if you have not been addressed, do not reply; leave what doesn't concern you for what does, and do not offer advice to evil men, for they will repay you with evil."'

Although the fox had smiled at the wolf while listening to what he had to say, he was concealing a resolve to deceive the wolf, telling himself that he must do his best to destroy him. So he put up with the wolf's maltreatment, saying to himself: 'Arrogance and falsity cause confusion and lead to destruction. It is said: arrogance is loss; the ignorant have cause to repent; he who fears is safe; justice is one of the characteristics of noble men; and the best thing that can be acquired is culture. My best course is to flatter this tyrant, for there is no doubt he will be overthrown.'

The fox then said to the wolf: 'The master pardons the servant who has done wrong and forgives him if he confesses his faults. I am a weak servant and I have gone astray in offering you advice. If you knew what pain your blow caused me, you would realize that an elephant would not have been able to withstand it, but I don't complain of that, thanks to the happiness that it brought me, for, painful as it was, it was followed by joy. The wise man has said: "The blow struck by the teacher is, to start with, very hard, but what follows is sweeter than purified honey."' The wolf said in reply: 'I have pardoned your fault and forgiven your error, but beware of my strength and acknowledge yourself to be my slave, for you know how I subdue those who oppose me.' The fox prostrated himself before him, saying: 'May God prolong your life and may you never cease to overcome your enemies.'

Because of his fear of the wolf, the fox continued to approach him with flattery and blandishment. Then one day he went to the vineyard, where he saw a gap in the wall. He was suspicious, saying to himself: 'There must be some reason for this gap. The proverb says that whoever sees a hole in the ground and does not avoid it or take care not to walk up to it, deceives and endangers himself. It is well known that some people make a figure of a fox among the vines, setting grapes on plates in front of it, so that a real fox may see that and come towards it only to fall into destruction. I think that this gap is a trick, and as the proverb has it, "Half of cleverness is caution." Caution suggests that I should take a look at it to see whether it conceals a trap, rather than that I should be led by greed to destroy myself.' So he went up to the gap in the wall and walked round carefully, studying it. What he found was a huge hole that the owner of the vineyard had dug to trap the beasts that were destroying his vines. 'You have got what you hoped for,' he said to himself.

Over the hole was a thin cover, and he drew back from this, saying:
'Praise be to God that I was wary of this, but I hope that my enemy, the
wolf, who has spoiled my life, may fall into it, leaving the vineyard free
for my sole possession so that I can live here in security.' He shook his
head, laughing aloud and reciting:

I wish that I could now see in this pit the wolf
Who has distressed me over a long time,
Forcing on me waters of bitterness.
I wish that after this I may be left
Surviving, while the wolf has met his death.
The vineyard would be free of him,
And in it I see booty for myself.

After finishing these lines, the fox went back quickly to the wolf and
said: 'God has made it easy for you to approach the vineyard without
trouble, and this is thanks to your good fortune. Congratulations on
what God has opened up for you, making it simple for you to win
easy booty and find abundant livelihood, which you can enjoy without
trouble.' 'What leads you to say this?' asked the wolf. 'I went to the
vineyard,' the fox told him, 'and found that its owner was dead, having
been killed by a wolf. I then got into the place and found the trees laden
with splendid fruit.' The wolf did not doubt that the fox was telling him
the truth and, moved by greed, he got up and went to the gap in the
wall. Greed led him on and the fox, who had thrown himself down on
the ground as though he were dead, quoted the following lines:

Do you desire union with Laila?
Desire is a harmful burden on man's neck.

When the wolf was near the gap, the fox said: 'Go into the vineyard
– this will save you the trouble of climbing the wall or knocking it down,
and it is for God to complete His favour.' So the wolf walked on in order
to enter the vineyard, but when he got to the middle of the covering of
the pit, he fell into it. The fox could not contain himself for joy; his cares
and sorrows left him and, in his delight, he chanted:

Time has had pity on my state,
Lamenting my lengthy suffering.
It has brought me what I most desired
And has removed all that I feared.

I shall forgive all its past wrongs.
The wolf has no escape from death;
The vineyard will be mine alone
With no fool to associate with me.

Looking down into the pit, he saw the wolf shedding tears of regret and sorrow for himself. The fox wept with him, and the wolf, raising his head, asked: 'Is it out of pity for me that you are shedding tears, Abu'l-Husain?' To which the fox replied: 'No, by Him Who cast you into this pit, I am weeping because of the length of your past life, regretting the fact that this did not happen earlier. Had you fallen before I met you, I would have enjoyed peace and quiet, but you have been allowed to live for the fixed time of your allotted term.'

The wolf said, as if in jest: 'Go to my mother, you evil-doer, and tell her what has happened to me. She may be able to think of a way to rescue me.' But the fox replied: 'It was the extent of your greed and covetousness that has destroyed you by causing you to fall into a pit from which you cannot escape. Don't you know, you foolish wolf, that, as the well-known proverb has it, "If a man takes no thought for the consequences of his actions, Time will not be his friend and he will not be safe from destruction"?' 'Abu'l-Husain,' said the wolf, 'you used to pretend to be my friend, to want my favour and to fear my great strength. Don't show resentment to me for what I did to you. Those who show forgiveness from a position of strength are rewarded by God. As the poet has said:

Sow the seed of good deeds even in a barren place;
Wherever this seed is sown, it will not bring disappointment.
It may take time, but none will reap the harvest of this good
Except the one who sowed it.'

'You stupidest and most foolish of the beasts of the field, have you forgotten your tyranny, your arrogance and your pride? You did not respect the dues of companionship and did not take the advice of the poet:

Do not act unjustly when you have the power;
Wrongdoers live on the edge of punishment.
You may sleep, but the one you wronged
Is still awake and cursing you, while God's eye never sleeps.'

The wolf said: 'Abu'l-Husain, don't hold my past faults against me; forgiveness is something that is sought from the noble and to do good is the best of treasures. How excellent are the poet's lines:

Be quick to do good when you can;
You may not always have the power.'

The wolf continued to humble himself before the fox, saying: 'Perhaps you can do something to free me from destruction?' 'You ignorant and deluded wolf,' said the fox, 'wily and treacherous as you are, don't hope to escape, for this is the reward and requital for your evil deeds.' He then smiled broadly, reciting these lines:

Don't try so hard to deceive me,
For you will not achieve your goal.
What you want from me is impossible;
As you have sown, so reap an evil harvest.

'Most gentle of beasts,' said the wolf, 'I think that you are too trust-worthy a friend to leave me in this pit.' Then he wept and complained, with tears streaming from his eyes, and he recited these lines:

You whose favours to me are many
And whose gifts cannot be counted,
No disaster of Time has ever struck me
Without my finding you there to hold my hand.

The fox replied: 'My foolish enemy, how is it that you now implore me meekly, abasing and humbling yourself after having shown scornful pride and haughty oppression? I associated with you in fear of your enmity and I flattered you in the hope of your favour. Now you tremble for misfortune has overtaken you.' He then recited these lines:

You who are trying to deceive me,
Your evil intentions brought you down.
Taste the evil of direst distress,
And be cut off from other wolves.

'Gentle beast,' cajoled the wolf, 'do not use the language of enmity or cast hostile glances. Be true to the covenant of friendship before the time to put things right has gone. Come and find a way of getting me a rope, so that you can tie one end of it to a tree and lower the other down for me to hold on to, so that I may escape from my present plight, after which I shall give you all the treasures that I possess.' 'You are going on about what will not save you,' said the fox. 'Have no hopes of that, for you will get nothing from me that will save your life. Think over your past misdeeds, the treachery and guile that you had in your heart towards me and how near you are to death by stoning. Know that you are about to leave this world. You are on your way from it, going to destruction and an evil resting place.' 'Abu'l-Husain,' said the wolf, 'return quickly to your former friendship and don't harbour malice. Know that whoever saves a soul from destruction has brought it to life, and if he brings it to life, it is as though he has given life to all mankind. Don't follow the path of evil-doing, for this is forbidden by the wise, and there is no clearer example of evil than my being in this pit, suffering the pains of death and looking at destruction, when you are able to free me from this trap. Grant me the gift of freedom and do me a good deed.' 'You coarse boor,' said the fox, 'with the smoothness of your outward show and your words, together with evil-ness of your intention and your deeds, I find you like the hawk with the partridge.' 'How is that?' asked the wolf. THE FOX REPLIED:

One day when I went into the vineyard to eat some grapes, I saw a hawk that had swooped down on a partridge. Although the hawk had seized it in its talons, the partridge slipped away and hid inside its nest. The hawk followed and called to it: 'You fool, I saw that you were hungry out there in the open country. I was sorry for you and picked up grain for you, taking hold of you so that you could eat it. Then you fled away from me and I don't know why, unless it was by mistake. So come out; take the grain that I brought you and eat it with pleasure and enjoyment.' When the partridge heard what the hawk said, he believed it and came out. The hawk then sank his talons into it and held it fast. 'Is this what you told me that you had brought from the field, telling me to eat it with pleasure and enjoyment?' cried the partridge. 'You lied to me and may God make my flesh, when you eat it, turn to deadly poison in your stomach.' The hawk ate the partridge, after which its feathers fell out, it lost its strength and died on the spot.

'Know, wolf, that whoever digs a pit for his brother will soon fall into it. It was you who started by acting treacherously towards me,' added the fox. 'Stop talking like this and quoting proverbs,' said the wolf, 'and don't talk to me of my past misdeeds. The evil straits that I am in at the moment are enough for me. An enemy would be sorry for me in my present plight, let alone a friend. Do something to rescue me; help me.

Even if you find that hard, a friend will put up with the severest of hardships for his friend, and risk his life to save him from destruction. It is said a sympathetic friend is better than a full brother. If I escape thanks to your help, I will gather together things that will serve you as equipment and I will teach you remarkable tricks that will allow you to open up fertile vineyards and pick what you want from fruit trees. So be happy and content.'

The fox laughed and said to him: 'How well have wise men spoken of those who, like you, are full of ignorance.' When the wolf asked what it was that they had said, the fox told him: 'They have pointed out that those with thick bodies and coarse natures are far removed from intelligence and close to stupidity. As for what you said, you deluded creature, with your foolish scheming, it is true, as you say, that a friend may endure hardship to rescue his friend, but tell me, in your ignorance and folly, how am I to treat you as a friend when you have betrayed me? Do you think of me as a friend of yours, when I am an enemy who gloats at your misfortune? Had you any sense, you would see that these words are harder to bear than death or a flight of arrows. You say that you will equip me and teach me tricks to get me into fertile vineyards and allow me to take what I want from the fruit trees. Why is it then, you treacherous deceiver, that you don't know of a trick to save yourself from destruction? How far removed are you from being able to help yourself and how far removed am I from accepting your advice! If you know any trick, then use it to rescue yourself from this situation, but I pray God to foil any chance of escape. Look at it then, fool; if you know any trick, save yourself from death, before you offer to teach others. You are like a man who fell ill and was approached by another man, suffering from the same disease, who wanted to treat him and said: "Shall I cure you?" The first man said: "Why not start with yourself?" at which the other left him and went away. It is the same with you, you ignorant wolf, so stay where you are and endure your misfortune.'

On hearing the fox's words, the wolf realized that there was no good to be got from him. Shedding tears for himself, he said: 'I have been heedless, but if God frees me from my distress, I shall repent of my haughty behaviour towards those who are weaker than me. I shall wear wool and go up to a mountain, reciting the Name of Almighty God in fear of His punishment. I shall keep away from all other beasts and bring food for the poor and for fighters in the Holy War.' He wept and sobbed until the heart of the fox softened towards him, for, on hearing his entreaties and the way in which he repented of his haughty arrogance, he felt pity for him. Jumping up in joy, the fox went to the edge of the pit and sat down on his hind paws, letting his tail dangle down into the pit. The wolf got up and, stretching out his own paw to the fox's tail, he pulled it towards him. The fox ended up in the pit with him, and the wolf said: 'Fox of little mercy, how was it that you jeered at my misfortune when you had been my companion and in my power? Now you have fallen into the pit with me and punishment will be quick to catch up with you. The wise men have said: "If one of you reproaches his brother for being suckled by a bitch, the same thing will happen to him." How well expressed are the lines of the poet:

> If Time deals harshly with some men,
> It brings distress to other men as well.
> Say to those who take pleasure in our sufferings:
> "Wake up; scoffers will taste what we have suffered."

To die in company is the best of things, and I shall certainly hurry to kill you before you see my own death.'

'Woe, woe!' said the fox to himself. 'I have fallen down here with this tyrant and must now turn to guile and deception. It is said that a woman fashions her finery for the day when it can be displayed and the proverb says: "Tears, I have stored you up to use in time of misfortune." If I don't think of some trick to use against this evil beast, I'm bound to perish. How well expressed are the lines of the poet:

> Live by deceit, for you are in an age
> Whose children are like lions of Bisha.
> Let water flow in the channels of guile
> To turn the mills of livelihood.
> Pluck fruits, but if you find these out of reach,
> Content yourself with grass.'

The fox then said to the wolf: 'Don't be in such a hurry to kill me. That is not the proper way to repay me, and you would regret it, lord of the beasts, O powerful and mighty one. If you wait for a while and consider carefully what I am going to tell you, you will see what I had intended to do, whereas if you kill me in a hurry, you will get nothing from it and both of us will die here.' 'You wily deceiver,' said the wolf. 'Is it because you hope that you and I can be saved that you ask me to delay killing you? Tell me, then, what it was that you meant to do.' 'This was something for which you should reward me generously,' replied the fox. 'When I heard the promise that you made, your acknowledgement of your past misdeeds and your sorrow for having lost the opportunity to repent and do good, and when I heard you vow that if you escaped from your present plight, you would stop harming your companions or anyone else, you would give up eating grapes and all other fruits, you would act humbly, cut your claws, break your teeth, wear wool and offer sacrifices to Almighty God, I was moved by pity for you, for the best speech is the truest. Although I was eager for you to be killed, when I heard you talk of repentance and what you vowed to do if God delivered you, I thought that I had to save you and I hung down my tail so that you could hold on to it and so escape. But you would not give up your usual roughness and violence and you made no attempt to save yourself by gentleness. Rather, you tugged me so hard that I thought my last breath had gone, and as a result both you and I are now going to die. The only way in which we can escape is through something which, if you accept it, will save us both, but after that you must keep your vow and I shall be your companion.' 'What is it that I have to accept?' asked the wolf. 'Stand upright,' said the fox, 'and I shall then get on your head, which will bring me close to the surface. I can then jump up and so get out of the pit, after which I shall fetch you something to hold on to and you in your turn will then be free.' 'I don't trust what you say,' the wolf replied, and he went on: 'The wise have told us: "Where there is hatred, it is a mistake to trust, and whoever trusts the untrustworthy is deluded; he who tries again what he has already tried will regret it and his days will be wasted; whoever cannot distinguish between cases, giving each its due, but treats them all the same, will have little fortune and many disasters." How well has the poet expressed it:

> Always think that the worst
> Suspicion is the best intelligence.
> The deadliest danger into which man can fall
> Is to do good and to expect the best.

Another poet has said:

> Be sure to be suspicious and you will be safe.
> Whoever stays alert suffers few misfortunes.
> Meet your enemy with an open, smiling face,
> But raise an army in your heart to fight him.

Yet another has said:

> Your fiercest foe is he in whom you place most trust:
> Beware of people; use deceit with them.
> It is weakness to put your hope in Time;
> Think the worst of it and remain on your guard.'

'It is not in every circumstance that suspicion is praiseworthy,' said the fox, 'while to think the best is part of a perfect character, which allows its possessor to escape from what is to be feared. You, wolf, have to think of some scheme to save you from your plight and it is better that we both escape than that we die. So abandon your suspicions and your hatred. If you take an optimistic view, one of two things can happen: either I shall bring you something to hold on to and you will make your escape; or I shall betray you, escape myself and abandon you. That, however, would be impossible, for I could not be sure that I would not fall into the same kind of misfortune that has overtaken you, as a punishment for treachery. As the proverb puts it, "Faithfulness is good and treachery is bad." You should trust me, as I am not without knowledge of the disasters that Time brings, but do not delay in thinking of some device to free us, for things are too pressing to allow us to go on talking about this for long.'

The wolf replied: 'I have no great faith in your loyalty, but I recognize what was in your mind that made you want to rescue me when you heard me talk of repentance. I said to myself: "If what he claims is true, then he will have put right what he did wrong; but if he is lying, then it is the Lord Who will repay him." So I am going to accept your advice, knowing that if you betray me, your treachery will lead to your destruction.' He then stood upright in the pit and lifted the fox on to his shoulders until he was level with the surface of the ground. The fox then jumped from his shoulders on to the ground and when he was out of the pit he fell down in a faint. 'Don't forget me, my friend,' said the wolf, 'and don't delay in rescuing me.' The fox burst into roars of laughter, saying: 'You dupe, I only fell into your hands as a result of making fun of you and laughing at you. For when I heard you talk of repentance, I was so pleased and delighted that I jumped and danced for joy, with my tail hanging down into the pit. You then pulled me in, but Almighty God rescued me from you. Why, then, should I not help in your destruction, for you are one of the devil's supporters. Yesterday I dreamt that I was dancing at your wedding and when I told this to an interpreter of dreams, he said that I was going to fall into great danger and then escape from it. I realize that my falling into your hands and then escaping is what the dream meant. You know, you foolish and deluded beast, that I am your enemy, so how can you hope in your stupidity and folly, having heard my harsh words, that I would rescue you and exert myself to save you? Wise men have said: "The death of the evil-doer brings relief to the people and purifies the land." Were it not for my fear that, if I kept faith with you, I would have to endure what is worse than the painful punishment of treachery, I would contrive your escape.'

When the wolf heard what the fox had to say, he gnawed at his paw in regret.

Night 150

Morning now dawned and Shahrazad broke off from what she had been allowed to say. Then, when it was the hundred and fiftieth night, SHE CONTINUED:

I have heard, O fortunate king, that when the wolf heard what the fox had to say, he gnawed at his paw in regret. Then he spoke softly, finding that there was nothing else to do, although it did him no good. 'You foxes,' he said in a low voice, 'are the most pleasant-spoken and the wittiest jesters among the beasts. This is a joke of yours, but not every occasion is suitable for playful jests.' 'Fool,' replied the fox, 'jokes have a limit which the joker must not pass. You need not think that God will put me in your power again after having saved me from your hands.' The wolf went on: 'You should be eager to save me because we used to live together as brothers and companions. If you free me, I shall certainly do my best to repay you.' To this the fox replied: 'Wise men have said: "Do not take a foolish and shameless man as a brother, since he will be a disgrace rather than an ornament to you, and do not take a liar as a brother, for if you do good, he will conceal it, and if you do wrong, he will spread it abroad." The wise have said: "Everything can be circumvented except for death; anything can be put right except when its essence is rotten; it is only fate that cannot be warded off." As for the repayment that you say I shall deserve at your hands, in this I think that you are like the snake that fled in alarm from the snake charmer. HE WENT ON:

*

A man saw it while it was in this state and asked what was wrong. 'I am escaping from the charmer,' said the snake. 'He is pursuing me, and if you save me from him and hide me with you, I will reward you lavishly and do you every possible favour.' The man, eager to seize the opportunity of winning a reward, took the snake and put it into his pocket. When the snake charmer had passed and had gone on his way, the snake's fear left it. The man said to it: 'I have saved you from what you feared, so where is the reward?'

To which the snake replied: 'Tell me in what limb or part of the body to bite you, for you know that this is the only reward that we snakes give.' It then bit the man, who died.

'I think that you, you fool, are like that snake with that man. Haven't you heard the words of the poet:

> Do not feel safe with one whose heart you have filled with anger
> And do not think to yourself this anger may have gone.
> Snakes are smooth to touch, but what they show is a cloak,
> While what they hide away is deadly poison.'

The wolf said: 'You eloquent beast with your handsome face, don't ignore what I am like or forget how men fear me. You know that I attack strongholds and uproot vines. Do what I tell you and attend on me as a slave attends his master.' 'You ignorant fool,' said the fox, 'your attempt is futile and I wonder at your stupidity and the brass-faced effrontery with which you tell me to serve you and to stand before you as though I were a slave you had bought with your wealth. You will see what will happen to you; your head will be smashed with stones and your treacherous teeth broken.' The fox then stood on top of a hill overlooking the vineyard and shouted to its owners, going on until he had awoken them. Seeing him, they ran towards him; he waited until they were close by and, leading them to the pit with the wolf in it, he then ran off. The people looked at the pit, saw the wolf in it and started pelting him with heavy stones. They continued to strike him with stones and bits of wood, as well as thrusting at him with spearheads, until they had killed him.

They then went off and the fox came back. Standing over the place where the wolf had been killed and seeing his corpse, he shook his head in delight, reciting these lines:

Time has destroyed the wolf, whose soul has been carried off,
Far, far away from where his heart's blood was spilled.
How often, wolf, did you try to destroy me?
But now disasters have overtaken you, bringing destruction.
You fell into a pit where all who fall
Are carried off by the storm winds of death.

He then stayed in the vineyard alone and at his ease, fearing no harm, until he died. So ends the story of the fox and the wolf.

A story is told of a mouse and a weasel that once lived in the house of a poor farmer. One of the farmer's friends fell ill and the doctor prescribed for him husked sesame seeds. He asked a companion of his for sesame as a cure for his sickness and he then gave a quantity of it to the poor farmer so that he might husk this for him. The farmer brought the sesame to his wife to prepare and she, for her part, soaked it, spread it out, husked it and prepared it. When the weasel saw the sesame, she went up to it and spent the whole day carrying off seeds to her hole, until she had removed most of what was there. The farmer's wife came back and saw, to her astonishment, that there was clearly less sesame than there had been. To find out why, she sat watching to see who would come there, and the weasel, on her way back to remove more seeds, as she had been doing, saw the farmer's wife sitting there and realized that she was on the lookout. She said to herself: 'What I have done may lead to evil consequences, for I'm afraid that this woman is lying in wait for me. Whoever does not think of the consequences of what he does will find out that Time is no friend to him. I must do something good to show my innocence and wipe away all the evil that I have done.' So she started moving the sesame that was in her hole, bringing it out and taking it to put with the rest. When the woman found her doing this, she said to herself: 'It could not have been the weasel that was responsible for this. She is taking the seeds from the hole of whoever stole them and putting them back with the rest. She has done us a favour here and the reward of one who does a favour is to have a favour done to him. As it is not the weasel who has stolen the sesame, I shall go on watching until the thief falls into the trap and I find out who he is.'

The weasel, realizing what the woman was thinking, went off to the mouse. 'Sister,' she said, 'there is no good in anyone who does not respect his duty to his neighbour, maintaining friendship.' 'Yes, my friend,' said the mouse, 'and I am glad to have you as a neighbour, but why do you say this?' The weasel went on: 'The master of the house has brought sesame; he and his family have had their fill, and having no more need of it, they have left much of it uneaten. Every living creature has taken a share of it and were you to take yours, you would have a better right to it than the others.' The mouse was pleased with this; she squeaked, danced, waggled her ears and her tail and, beguiled by her greed for the sesame, she got up straight away and left her hole. She saw the sesame dried, husked and gleaming white, with the farmer's wife sitting and watching over it. The woman had armed herself with a cudgel and the mouse, taking no thought for the consequences, fell on it unrestrainedly, scattering it to and fro and starting to eat it. The woman hit her with the cudgel, splitting her skull. Greed was the cause of her death, and the fact that she ignored the consequences of what she had done.

'This is a pleasant story, Shahrazad,' said the king. 'Have you any tales about the beauty of friendship and how its preservation in difficult circumstances has led to a rescue from death?' 'Yes,' she replied, AND SHE WENT ON:

I have heard that once a crow and a cat lived together as brothers. While they were together under a tree, suddenly they saw a panther coming towards them, and before they knew it, it was close at hand. The crow flew up to the top of the tree, but the cat stayed where it was, not knowing what to do. He called to the crow: 'My friend, is there anything you can do to save me? I hope you can.' The crow replied: 'In cases of need, when disaster strikes, it is one's brother who must be asked to find a way out. How well has the poet expressed it:

The true friend is one who goes with you,
And who hurts himself in order to help you.
When you are shattered by the blows of fate,
It is your friend who breaks himself in order to restore you.'

Near the tree were some herdsmen with dogs. The crow went and struck at the surface of the earth with his wing, cawing and screeching. He then went up to the men and struck one of the dogs in the face with his wing. Then he rose a little into the air and the dogs followed after him. Looking up, a herdsman saw a bird flying close to the ground and then falling to earth. He followed the crow, who only flew far enough ahead to avoid the dogs while still encouraging them to give chase. He then rose slightly higher, still pursued by the dogs, until he came to the tree beneath which was the panther. When the dogs saw it, they leapt at it and it turned in flight, giving up all thoughts of eating the cat. So the cat escaped because of the stratagem of its friend, the crow. This story, O king, shows that pure brotherly love can provide safety and deliverance from deadly peril.

A story is told about a fox that once lived in a den on a mountain. Every time a cub of his began to gain strength, he was driven by hunger to eat it. If he had not done this and had allowed the cub to live, staying with it and guarding it, he himself would have starved to death, but it hurt him to do what he did. A crow used to come to the peak of the mountain and the fox said to himself: 'I would like to make friends with this crow and take him as a companion in my loneliness and as a helper in my search for food, since he can do things that I cannot.' So he approached the crow, going near enough for him to hear what he said. He then greeted him, saying: 'My friend, Muslim neighbours share two rights – the right of neighbourhood and the right of Islam. Know that you are my neighbour and you have a claim on me which I must satisfy, especially since this relationship of ours has gone on for so long. The affection for you that is lodged in my heart prompts me to treat you with kindness and leads me to seek to have you as a brother. What do you have to say?' The crow told the fox: 'The best things said are the most truthful. It may be that what you say with your tongue is not in your heart. I am afraid lest your talk of brotherhood may be on the surface, while concealed in your heart is enmity. You eat and I am eaten and so we cannot join together in the union of affection. What has led you to look for something that you cannot get and to want what can never be? You are a wild beast and I am a bird, and there can be no true brotherhood between us.'

The fox said: 'He who knows where great things are to be found can make a proper choice from among them, and so he may be able to find what will help his brothers. I want to be near you and choose friendship with you so that we can help each other, and our affection may lead to success. I know a number of stories about the beauty of friendship, and if you like, I shall tell them to you.' 'You have my permission to produce them,' said the crow. 'Tell me them, so that I can listen, take heed and discover their meaning.' 'Listen then, my companion,' said the fox, 'to a story told of a flea and a mouse which illustrates the point I made to you.' 'What was that?' asked the crow, AND THE FOX REPLIED:

It is said that a mouse once lived in the house of a rich and important merchant. One night a flea went for shelter to that merchant's bed, where he found a soft body. As he was thirsty, he drank from the man's blood. The merchant, in pain, woke from his sleep, sat up and called to his maids and a number of his servants. They hurried up to him and set to work looking for the flea who, in turn, realizing what was happening, fled away. He came across the mouse's hole and went in, but when the mouse saw him, she asked: 'What has made you come to me, when you are not of the same nature or the same species as I, and you cannot be sure that I will not treat you roughly, attack you or harm you?' The flea said to her: 'I have fled into your house, escaping certain death, in order to seek refuge with you. There is nothing that I covet here; you will not have to leave because of any harm that I might do you and I hope to be able to reward you with all kinds of benefits for the service that you are doing me. You will be thankful when you discover what these words of mine will bring about.' When the mouse heard what the flea had to say . . .

Night 151

Morning now dawned and Shahrazad broke off from what she had been allowed to say. Then, when it was the hundred and fifty-first night, SHE CONTINUED:

I have heard, O fortunate king, that when the mouse heard what the flea had to say she said: 'If things are as you say, then you can rest here in peace. The rain of security will fall on you; you will only experience what will bring you joy and nothing will happen to you that will not also happen to me. I offer you my friendship. Feel no regret for the opportunity you have lost to suck the merchant's blood and don't be sorry for the nourishment that you used to get from him. Content yourself with what you can find to live on, as that will be safer for you. The following lines of poetry that I once heard were written by a preacher, who said:

> I have followed the path of contentment and solitude,
> And passed my time according to circumstance,
> With a crust of bread and water to drink,

Coarse salt and shabby clothes.
If God grants me prosperity, well and good;
If not, I am content with what He gives.'

When the flea heard what the mouse had to say, he said: 'Sister, I have listened to your advice; I shall do what you tell me, as I cannot disobey you, and I shall follow this virtuous course until the end of my days.' 'Good intentions are enough for true friendship,' replied the mouse. The two became firm friends and after that the flea would go to the merchant's bed at night but would only take enough blood for his needs, while by day he would shelter in the mouse's hole.

It happened that one night the merchant brought home a large number of dinars. He began to turn them over and over and, hearing the sound, the mouse put her head out of her hole and started to gaze at the dinars, until the merchant put them under a pillow and fell asleep. The mouse then said to the flea: 'Don't you see the chance that we have been given and what an enormous bit of luck this is? Can you think of a plan to allow us to get as many of these as we want?' 'It's no use trying to get hold of something unless you can do it,' said the flea. 'If you're not strong enough, then weakness will lead you into danger and, even if you use all your cunning, you will not get what you want, like the sparrow that picks up the grain but falls into the trapper's net and is caught. You don't have the strength to take the dinars and carry them out of the house, and neither have I. I couldn't even lift a single one of them. So do what you want about them yourself.'

The mouse said: 'I have made seventy ways out of this hole of mine from which I can leave if I want and I have prepared a safe place for treasures. If you can get the merchant out of the room by some means, then I'm sure that I can succeed if fate helps me.' 'I'll undertake to get him out,' said the flea, and he then went to the merchant's bed and gave him a fearful bite, such as he had never experienced before. The flea then took refuge in a place of safety and, although the merchant woke up and looked for him, he didn't find the flea and so went back to sleep on his other side. The flea then bit him even more savagely, and in his agitation the merchant left his bedroom and went out to a bench by the house door, where he slept without waking until morning. The mouse then set about moving the dinars until there were none left, and in the morning the merchant was left to suspect everyone around him.

*

The fox then said to the crow: 'You must know, O far-sighted, intelligent and experienced crow, that I have only told you this story so that you may get the reward for your kindness to me just as the mouse was rewarded for her kindness to the flea. You can see how he repaid her and gave her the most excellent of rewards.' The crow replied: 'The doer of good has the choice of doing good or not, as he wants, but it is not obligatory to do good to someone who tries to attach himself to you by cutting you off from others. This is what will happen to me if I befriend you, who are my enemy. You are a wily schemer, fox; creatures of your kind cannot be counted on to keep their word and no one can rely on those who are not to be trusted to do that. I heard recently that you betrayed a companion of yours, the wolf, and that you schemed against him until, thanks to your treacherous wiles, you brought about his death. You did this in spite of the fact that he was of the same species as you and you had been his companion for a long time. You did not spare him, so how can I trust in your sincerity? If this is how you act with a friend of your own race, what will you do with an enemy of a different species? Your position in regard to me is like that of the falcon with the birds of prey.' 'How was that?' asked the fox. THE CROW REPLIED:

The falcon was a headstrong tyrant . . .

Night 152

Morning now dawned and Shahrazad broke off from what she had been allowed to say. Then, when it was the hundred and fifty-second night, SHE CONTINUED:

I have heard, O fortunate king, that THE CROW REPLIED:

The falcon was a headstrong tyrant in the days of his youth, spreading fear among the birds and beasts of prey. None were safe from his evil-doing and there were many instances of his injustice and tyranny, it being his habit to harm all other birds. With the passing of the years, his powers weakened and his strength diminished. He grew hungry and the loss of his strength meant that he had to exert himself more. He decided to go to where the birds met, in order to eat what they left over. After having relied on strength and power, he now got his food by trickery.

'This is like you, fox: you may not have strength, but you have not lost your powers of deceit. I have no doubt that when you ask to become my companion, this is a trick on your part to get food. I am not one to put out my hand to clasp yours. God has given me strength in my wings, caution in my soul and clear sight. I know that whoever tries to be like someone stronger than himself finds himself in difficulties and may be destroyed. I am afraid that if you try to resemble someone stronger than yourself, what happened to the sparrow may happen to you.' 'What did happen to the sparrow?' asked the fox. 'By God, tell me the story.' THE CROW SAID:

I have heard that a sparrow was flying over a field of sheep. He looked down and as he was there watching, a great eagle swooped down on one of the young lambs and, seizing it in his talons, flew off with it. When the sparrow saw this, he fluttered his wings and said proudly: 'I can do the same kind of thing,' trying to be like something greater than him. He flew off immediately and came down on a fat, woolly ram, whose coat was matted because he had been sleeping on urine and dung, as a result of which it had become sticky. When the sparrow settled on the ram's back, he clapped his wings, but his feet stuck in the wool, and although he tried to fly off, he could not get free. While all this was going on, the shepherd had been watching, seeing first what had happened with the eagle and then what had happened to the sparrow. He came up angrily to the sparrow, seized him and pulled out his wing feathers. He then tied a string round his legs and took him off and threw him to his children. 'What is this?' one of them asked. The shepherd replied: 'This is one who tried to imitate a superior and so was destroyed.'

'This is what you are like, fox, and I warn you against trying to be like one who is stronger than you, lest you perish. This is what I have to say to you, so go off in peace.' Despairing of winning the friendship of the crow, the fox went back, groaning in sorrow and gnashing his teeth in regret. When the crow heard the sound of his weeping and groaning and saw his distress and sorrow, he asked what had come over him to make him gnash his teeth. 'It is because I see that you are a greater cheat than I am,' said the fox, and he then ran off, going back to his earth. This, O king, is the story of these two.

'How excellent and pleasant are these stories, Shahrazad,' said the king. 'Have you any other edifying tales like them?' SHE SAID:

It is told that a hedgehog made his home by the side of a palm tree which was the haunt of a ringdove and his mate who nested there and enjoyed an easy life. The hedgehog said to himself: 'The ringdove and his mate eat the fruits of this palm tree, but I can find no way to do that and so I shall have to trick them.' He then dug out a hole for himself at the foot of the tree where he and his mate went to live. Beside it he made a chapel for prayer, where he went by himself, pretending to be a devout ascetic, who had abandoned earthly things. When the ringdove saw him at his devotions, he felt pity for him because of his extreme asceticism and he asked how many years he had spent like this. 'Thirty years,' replied the hedgehog. 'What do you eat?' asked the dove. 'Whatever falls from the tree.' 'What do you wear?' 'Spikes, whose roughness is of use to me.' 'And how did you choose this place of yours rather than some-where else?' 'I chose it at random,' said the hedgehog, 'in order to guide those who are astray and to teach the ignorant.' 'I didn't think that you were like this,' said the dove, 'but I now feel a longing for your kind of life.' The hedgehog replied: 'I'm afraid that what you say is the opposite of what you do. You are like the farmer who at harvest time neglects to sow again, saying: "I am afraid that the days may not bring me what I want, and I shall have begun by wasting my money thanks to sowing too soon." Then, when harvest time comes round again and he sees people at work reaping, he regrets the opportunity that he lost by holding back and he dies of grief and sorrow.'

The dove asked him: 'What should I do to free myself of worldly attachments and devote myself solely to the worship of my Lord?' 'Begin to prepare yourself for the life to come,' said the hedgehog, 'and content yourself with eating only enough for your needs.' 'How am I to do that?' asked the dove. 'I am a bird and I cannot leave this tree which provides me with my food, and even if I could, I don't know where else to settle.' The hedgehog said: 'You can knock down enough fruit from the tree to last you and your mate for a year. Then you can settle in a nest under-neath the tree, seeking right guidance. Afterwards, go to the fruit that you have knocked down, take it all away and store it up to eat in times of want. When you have finished the fruits and you find the waiting long, make do with bare sufficiency.' 'May God give you a good reward for the purity of your intentions,' said the dove, 'in that you have reminded me of the afterlife and given me right guidance.'

The dove and his mate then worked hard, knocking down dates until there were none left on the tree. The hedgehog was delighted to find this food; he filled his lair with the fruit and stored it up to serve as his provisions, saying to himself that if the dove and his mate needed food, they would ask him for it. 'They will covet what I have,' he said, 'relying on my godly asceticism. Then, when they hear my advice and my admonitions, they will come up close to me and I can catch them and eat them. I shall then have this place to myself and I shall get enough to eat from the fruit that falls.' After the dove and his mate had knocked down all the dates, they flew down from the tree and found that the hedgehog had removed them all to his lair. 'Virtuous hedgehog,' said the dove, 'you sincere admonisher, we have not found any trace of the dates and we don't know of any other fruit on which we can live.' 'It may be that the wind blew them away,' said the hedgehog, 'but to turn away from sustenance to the Provider of sustenance is the essence of salvation. He Who created the opening in the mouth will not leave it without food.'

On he went, giving these admonitions and making a show of piety dressed in elaborate speech, until the doves approached trustingly and tried to go in through the entrance of his lair. They were sure that he would not deceive them, but he jumped up to guard the entrance, gnashing his teeth. When the dove saw his deception unveiled, he exclaimed: 'What a difference there is between tonight and yesterday! Don't you know that the victims of injustice have a Helper? Take care not to practise trickery and deceit lest you suffer the same fate as the two tricksters who schemed against the merchant.' 'How was that?' the hedgehog asked. THE DOVE SAID:

I heard that there was a wealthy merchant from a city called Sindah. He got together goods which he packed into bales and he left on a trading trip to visit a number of cities. He was followed by two swindlers who loaded up what wealth and goods they had and then accompanied him, pretending to be merchants. When they halted at the first stage, they agreed with each other to use cunning in order to take his goods, but each man planned to deceive and betray the other, saying to himself: 'Were I to betray my companion, all would be well with me and I could take all this wealth.' With these evil intentions towards one another, each of them produced food which had been poisoned before offering it to his companion. They both ate the food and both died. They had been sitting talking with the merchant, but after they had left him and been away for some time, he went in search of them to see what had happened, only to find them dead. He then realized that they were scoundrels who had been trying to double-cross him. Their cunning recoiled on their own heads, while the merchant not only escaped but took all that they had with them.

The king said: 'Shahrazad, you have drawn my attention to everything that I have been neglecting, so give me more of these examples.' SHE SAID:

O king, I have heard that there was a man who had a monkey. This man was a thief who would never pass through the markets of his city without coming away with a great profit. One day he happened to see someone carrying used clothes for sale. He was calling 'Clothes for sale!' in the market, but no one would offer him a price, and everyone to whom he showed his wares refused to buy them. When the thief with the monkey saw this man, he had bundled up the clothes and was sitting down to rest. The monkey played around in front of him and, while his attention was distracted as he looked at it, the thief stole his pack. He went off, taking the monkey, and when he got to an isolated spot, he opened up the bundle and took out the used clothes. He then put them in an expensive pack and took them to another market, where he offered the pack and its contents for sale on condition that it was not to be opened, tempting buyers by the lowness of the price he was asking. A man who saw the pack was struck by how expensive it looked and bought it on the thief's terms. He took it off home, thinking that he had got a bargain. 'What is this?' his wife asked when she saw it. 'It is something valuable that I have bought for less than its proper price in order to sell it again and make a profit.' 'You've been cheated,' she said. 'Is this stuff being sold cheaply for any reason except that it has been stolen? Don't you know that whoever buys something without examining it puts himself in the wrong, and he is like the weaver?' 'What is the story of the weaver?' her husband asked, AND HIS WIFE REPLIED:

I have heard that in a certain village there was a weaver who could only make a livelihood by working very hard indeed. It happened that a rich man in the neighbourhood gave a feast to which he invited everybody. The weaver went along and saw magnificently dressed people receiving fine foods and being treated with respect by the host because of their splendid clothes. He said to himself: 'Were I to change my trade for one that would be of less trouble, more prestigious and more rewarding, I could collect a lot of money and buy clothes like these. I would then become important; people would respect me and I would be like these others.' He looked at one of the tumblers who was at the banquet. This man got up and climbed on to a very high wall from which he threw himself down to the ground, after which he got up on his feet again. The weaver said to himself: 'I must do the same thing; it is not beyond my powers.' So he got up on the wall and threw himself down, but when he reached the ground, he broke his neck and died on the spot.

'I tell you this,' the woman went on, 'so that you may make your living from what you are familiar with and know, lest you become greedy and become attracted to what is no business of yours.' Her husband replied: 'Not every learned man is saved by his learning, nor is every fool destroyed by his folly. I have seen that snake charmers who are experienced and knowledgeable about snakes may be bitten by one and die, whereas someone who knows nothing about them and has no knowledge of how they behave may get the better of them.' He refused to listen to his wife, bought the goods and fell into the habit of buying cheaply from thieves until he fell under suspicion and perished.

In those days, there was a sparrow who used to go every day to one of the kings of the birds. He stayed with him morning and evening, as the first to visit and the last to leave. As it happened, a group of birds gathered on a high mountain. They said to one another: 'There are a lot of us and there are many disagreements between us. We must have a king who can look after our affairs, so that we can all be united and our differences may be removed.' The sparrow, who happened to pass by, advised them to choose the peacock as their king, this being the sovereign whom he was in the habit of visiting. The birds did this and made the peacock their ruler. He treated them well and made the sparrow his secretary and vizier. At times, the sparrow would interrupt his attendance on the peacock to oversee affairs, and one day, when he was absent, the peacock became very concerned. While he was in this state, the sparrow came in and the peacock asked him: 'What delayed you, who are the closest of my followers to me and the dearest of them?' 'I saw something suspicious which frightened me,' answered the sparrow. When the peacock asked him what this was, the sparrow explained: 'I saw a man with a net who spread it out by my nest, fastening it with pegs and scattering grain in the middle of it. I sat to watch what he was going to do and while I was there, fate brought a crane and his mate who fell into the middle of the net. They began to cry out and the hunter got up and caught them. This disturbed me; it is why I did not come to you, king of the age, and I shall not go on living in this nest for fear of the net.' 'Don't leave this place,' said the peacock, 'for caution will not help you against fate.'

The sparrow did what he was told, saying: 'I shall be patient and not leave, out of obedience to the king.' He went on acting cautiously, and he brought food to the peacock, who would eat his fill and wash down the food with a drink of water, after which the sparrow would fly off. One day, while he was watching, he saw two other sparrows fighting on the ground. 'How is it,' he said to himself, 'that I am the king's vizier and here are two sparrows fighting in my presence before my eyes? By God, I shall act as a peacemaker between them.' He went to them in order to do that, but the hunter tossed up the net over the three of them and the sparrow fell into the middle of it. The hunter came up, took him and handed him to his companion, saying: 'Keep a good hold of this one, for it is plump and I have never seen a finer sparrow.' The sparrow said to himself: 'I have fallen into the trap that I feared. It was the peacock who reassured me, but caution does not help against the blows of fate. The prudent man cannot escape his destiny. How well has the poet put it:

What is not to be cannot be brought about by any plan,
While that which is to be will be.
What is to happen happens at its destined time,
But foolish men delude themselves.'

The king said: 'Shahrazad, tell me more of these stories.' 'Tomorrow night,' she replied, 'if the king – may God ennoble him – spares me.'

Night 153

Morning now dawned and Shahrazad broke off from what she had been allowed to say. Then, when it was the hundred and fifty-third night, SHE SAID:

I have heard, O fortunate king, that in the old days, in the caliphate of Harun al-Rashid, there was a merchant who had a son named Abu'l-Hasan 'Ali ibn Tahir. The father was extremely rich and prosperous, while the conduct of his handsome son won universal approval. He was allowed to enter the caliph's palace without asking permission and he was a favourite with all the caliph's concubines and slave girls. He used to drink with the caliph, recite poetry to him and tell him amusing stories. For all that, he continued to buy and sell in the traders' market.

In his shop there used to sit a Persian princeling whose name was 'Ali ibn Bakkar. This young man had a fine figure and a graceful appearance; he was perfectly formed, with rosy cheeks and joining eyebrows, and he was an agreeable talker, a smiling man with a fondness for cheerful relaxation. It happened that Abu'l-Hasan and 'Ali were sitting talking and laughing together when up came ten slave girls like moons, each beautiful and symmetrically formed. In between them was a girl riding on a mule with a brocaded saddle and stirrups of gold. She was wearing a delicate veil and round her waist was a girdle of silk embellished with gold. She was as the poet has described:

> Her skin was like silk and her voice gentle;
> She spoke neither too little nor too much.
> To her eyes God said: 'Be,' and they were,
> And on men's intellects they acted as wine.
> O love for her, increase my passion every night!
> Lovers' consolation, it is the Day of Resurrection before you come.

When this group reached Abu'l-Hasan's shop, the girl dismounted from her mule and, after taking her seat in the shop, she greeted Abu'l-Hasan and he greeted her. When 'Ali ibn Bakkar saw her, she stole away his senses. He wanted to get up but she said: 'Sit where you are. We have come to you and it is not right for you to have to go.' 'By God, my lady,' he said, 'I am fleeing from what I see. The tongue of rapture says:

> She is the sun; her place is in the sky,
> So supply fair consolation to your heart.
> You can never climb to her and, as for her,
> She cannot sink to you.'

When the girl heard this, she smiled and asked Abu'l-Hasan: 'What is this young man's name and where does he come from?' 'He is a stranger,' said Abu'l-Hasan, and when she asked from what land he came, he said: 'He is a Persian prince and his name is 'Ali ibn Bakkar. It is a duty to honour strangers.' 'When my maid comes to you,' said the girl, 'she is to bring him to me.' Abu'l-Hasan agreed to this and the girl then got up and went away.

So much for her, but as for 'Ali ibn Bakkar, he did not know what to say. Then, some time later, the maid came to Abu'l-Hasan and said: 'My mistress is asking for you and your companion,' at which Abu'l-Hasan got up and took 'Ali ibn Bakkar with him. The two of them went to Harun al-Rashid's palace and the maid took them to a room where she invited them to sit down. They talked together for a time and then tables of food were set out before them. They ate and washed their hands and when wine was brought they drank deeply. The maid then told them to get up, and when they had done this, she took them to another room, set with four pillars, strewn with all kinds of furnishings and embellished with every sort of ornament, like one of the chambers of Paradise, where they were astonished by the rare treasures that they saw. While they were admiring these wonders, in came ten slave girls like moons, swaying proudly, dazzling the eyes and bewildering thought. They lined up like houris of Paradise and, after a pause, another ten came forward and greeted the two men. In their hands they were carrying lutes and other musical instruments and, after sitting down and tuning their strings, they stood in front of the visitors, playing on their lutes, singing and reciting poetry, each one of them embodying a temptation for God's servants. While this was happening, another ten of the same kind arrived, swelling-breasted, all of an age, with black eyes, rosy cheeks, joining eyebrows and languid glances – a temptation for God's servants and a delight for the onlookers. The coloured silks and ornaments that they wore were enough to bewilder the mind. When they had taken their places by the door, another ten even lovelier girls, wearing clothes too splendid to be described, entered and they too stood by the door, through which came twenty more with, in the middle of them, the girl herself, Shams al-Nahar, shining like the moon among the stars. She was swaying with haughty coquetry, with her long hair worn like a sash, dressed in a blue robe, with a veil of silk embroidered with gold and jewels, while round her waist was a girdle set with precious stones of all kinds. She advanced, swaying proudly, before taking her seat on a couch.

When 'Ali ibn Bakkar saw her, he recited these lines:

It is she who was the first cause of my illness,
Of my protracted passion and the length of my infatuation.
In her presence I see my soul melt with desire,
While all my bones are worn away.

When he had finished, he said to Abu'l-Hasan: 'It would have been kind had you told me about this before we came in here, so that I might have prepared myself and summoned up endurance to face it.' He then wept, moaned and complained, and Abu'l-Hasan said to him: 'Brother, I only meant to do you good but I was afraid that if I told you the truth, your passion would be such as to keep you away and prevent you from meeting the girl. Be happy and of good heart, for she looks on you with favour and wants to meet you.' 'What is her name?' asked 'Ali. 'Shams al-Nahar,' answered Abu'l-Hasan. 'She is one of the concubines of Harun al-Rashid, and this is the caliph's palace.'

Shams al-Nahar sat looking at the handsome 'Ali, while he too sat gazing at her beauty, and each was filled with love for the other. On her instructions, each of the slave girls sat in her place on a couch opposite a window. She told them to sing, at which one of them took a lute and recited:

Take back the message again and bring a clear reply:
I stand here, handsome prince, complaining of my lot.
Master, dear heart, my precious life,
Give me a kiss or at least lend it to me.
May you not perish; I shall give it back
Exactly in the form in which it was.
If you want more, be pleased to take it now,
And you who clothe me in emaciation,
May you enjoy the robe of health.

'Ali was delighted and said to the girl: 'Sing me more lines like these.' So she plucked the strings and recited:

My love, because you are so often absent,
You teach my eyes how long they can shed tears.
You are their pleasure and their wish,
My final goal, the object of my worship;
Mourn, then, for one whose eyes drown in the tears
Of a distracted lover in his grief.

When the girl had finished, Shams al-Nahar told another one to sing something, and so, striking up a tune, she began:

The glance of the beloved and not wine has made me drunk;
She sways and drives sleep from my eyes.
It is her locks of hair, not wine, that steal away my wits;
It is her qualities, not wine, that have uplifted me.
My resolution has been twisted by her curls;
While what is hidden by her gown destroys my mind.

When Shams al-Nahar heard the recitation, she sighed deeply in her admiration for the lines and then told another girl to sing. The girl took up her lute and recited:

A face that rivals heaven's lamp,
On which youth is distilled as water –
Down marked his cheeks with lettering,
In which love's final meaning can be found.
Beauty called out: 'When I met him,
I knew that God's embroidery had embellished him.'

When she had finished, 'Ali asked a girl sitting near him to let him hear something and, taking her lute, she recited:

The time of union is too short
For this protracted coquetry.
How many fatal rebuffs have there been,
But this is not how courteous folk behave.
When times are fortunate, make use of them
For the sweet hours of union.

The end of her recitation was followed by a flood of tears from 'Ali, and when Shams al-Nahar saw him weeping, moaning and complaining, she was burned by the fires of passion and consumed by the violence of love and desire. She got up from her couch and went to the door of the room, and when 'Ali rose to meet her, they embraced and fell down fainting. The slave girls went to them, carried them in through the door and sprinkled them with rosewater. When they had regained their senses, they could not see Abu'l-Hasan, who had concealed himself beside the couch, but when Shams al-Nahar asked where he was, he came out. Shams al-Nahar greeted him and said: 'I pray that God may enable me to reward you for the good deed that you have done.' Then, turning to 'Ali, she said: 'Master, however great your love may be, mine is twice as great, but the only thing that we can do is to endure what has overtaken us.' 'My lady,' said 'Ali, 'I cannot enjoy being with you; looking at you does not quench the fire of my passion, nor will the love for you that has taken hold of my heart leave until my soul departs from my body.' He then wept, with the tears falling over his cheeks like scattered pearls. When Shams al-Nahar saw this, she joined in his tears. 'By God,' exclaimed Abu'l-Hasan, 'I wonder at the two of you. I don't know what to make of this, as your behaviour is strange and all this is remarkable. If you weep now when you are together, how will it be when you are parted? This is not a time for sorrow and tears, but a time to rejoice that you are with one another. Relax; be happy and don't weep.'

At that, Shams al-Nahar gestured to a slave girl, who went off and then returned with maids carrying a table set with silver dishes on which were splendid foods of all kinds. They placed the table before the two lovers, at which Shams al-Nahar began to eat and to feed 'Ali. When they had had enough, the table was removed and they washed their hands. Censers were brought with incense of various types – aloes wood, ambergris and *nadd* – together with flasks of rosewater. They perfumed themselves and inhaled the incense, after which they were presented with engraved bowls of gold, filled with drinks of various sorts, and fruits, both fresh and dried, to tempt the appetite and please the eye. Next came a carnelian bowl, filled with wine.

Shams al-Nahar then chose ten maids to stay in the room together with ten singing girls, while the rest were sent back to their own quarters. Some of those who remained were told to play on their lutes, which they did, and one of them recited these lines:

> My life is ransom for the one who returns my greeting laughingly,
> And, after I had despaired of union, renews my hope.
> The force of passion brought my secrets out,
> Uncovering to the censurers what lies within my breast.
> Tears come between me and my love;
> It is as though they share in what I feel.

When the poem was finished, Shams al-Nahar got up, filled a cup and drank it, after which she filled it again and gave it to 'Ali.

Night 154

Morning now dawned and Shahrazad broke off from what she had been allowed to say. Then, when it was the hundred and fifty-fourth night, SHE CONTINUED:

I have heard, O fortunate king, that Shams al-Nahar filled a cup and gave it to 'Ali ibn Bakkar. She then called for another song and a girl chanted these lines:

My flowing tears are like my wine;
What my eyes shed is like the contents of the cup.
By God, I do not know whether my eyelids have dropped wine,
Or whether it was from my tears I drank.

When she had finished singing, 'Ali drank his cup and gave it back to Shams al-Nahar, who filled it and passed it to Abu'l-Hasan, who drank it in his turn. She then took a lute and said: 'When this cup of mine is being drunk, no one shall sing but me.' Tightening the strings, she recited these lines:

Uncommon tears clash on his cheeks,
And fires of love are kindled in his breast.
He weeps when they are near at hand, fearing departure;
But whether they are near or far away, the tears still fall.

She then quoted another poet:

Cupbearer, we are your ransom, who are clothed in beauty
From the bright parting of your hair down to your feet.
The sun shines from your hands, the Pleiades from your mouth,
And rising from your collar is the moon.
It is your glances that pass round the cup
With wine that leaves me drunk.
Is it not strange that you are a full moon,
While those who love you wane?
Are you a god, bringing both death and life,
By meeting those you choose and leaving others?
From your nature God made all loveliness,
While from your character comes the sweet zephyr.
You are no mortal creature, but you are,
Rather, an angel sent by God.

When 'Ali and Abu'l-Hasan, together with the others who were present, heard this recitation, they were beside themselves with joy, laughing gaily, but while they were in this state, in came a slave girl, trembling with fear. 'My lady,' she said, 'the eunuchs of the Commander of the Faithful are at the door – 'Afif, Masrur and Marjan, as well as others whom I don't know.' When the company heard this, they almost died of fear, but Shams al-Nahar laughed and said: 'Don't be afraid.' Then she told the girl: 'Take back an answer to them to allow us time to move from here.' She ordered the door of the room to be shut and coverings to be let down over the other entrances. The men were to stay where there were while the hall door was shut and she herself went out by her private door to the garden, where she sat on a couch that she had there. One girl was to massage her feet while the others were to return to their quarters. She then told the first slave girl to invite those who were at the door to enter. Masrur came in, together with twenty others carrying swords. They greeted Shams al-Nahar, and when she asked them why they had come, they said: 'The Commander of the Faithful greets you and is longing to see you. He sends you word that, as this is a day of great happiness and pleasure for him, he wishes to crown his pleasure by having you with him now. Will you go to him or should he come to you?' Shams al-Nahar got up, kissed the ground and said: 'To hear is to obey the orders of the Commander of the Faithful.'

On her instructions, the housekeepers and the slave girls were fetched and, when they came, she told them that she was about to follow the orders of the Commander of the Faithful. Although the place was fully prepared in all respects, she told the eunuchs: 'Go to the Commander of the Faithful and tell him that I shall expect him in a little while, after I have had time to prepare the place with furnishings and so forth.' When the eunuchs had hurried back to the Commander of the Faithful, Shams al-Nahar stripped off her outer dress, and after going to her beloved 'Ali, she clasped him to her breast and said goodbye to him. Shedding bitter tears, he said: 'My lady, this farewell will bring about my death and destruction, but I pray that God may grant me patience to endure the sufferings that my love inflicts on me.' 'By God,' replied Shams al-Nahar, 'it is I who will be destroyed. You will go out into the market and find consoling company. You will be safe and your love will be hidden, whereas I shall fall into trouble and distress without anyone to console me, especially as I have promised to receive the Commander of the Faithful. This may lead me into great danger because of my longing for you, my passionate love and the sorrow of my parting from you. How am I going to be able to sing? How can I face meeting the caliph and how am I going to talk with him? How can I look at any place if you are not there. How can I be in any company that does not include you, and how can I taste wine if you are not present?' 'Don't be dismayed,' said Abu'l-Hasan. 'Be patient; don't neglect your duty to entertain the Commander of the Faithful tonight. Don't appear to slight him, but show strength of mind.'

While they were talking, a slave girl arrived to inform her mistress that the caliph's pages had arrived. She got up, telling the girl to take Abu'l-Hasan and 'Ali to the balcony overlooking the garden and to leave them there until it was dark, after which she was to contrive to get them out. The girl took them up to the balcony, closed the door on them and went on her way. The two men were sitting there, looking at the garden, when they saw the caliph coming, escorted by a hundred eunuchs with swords in their hands, surrounded by twenty slave girls like moons, wearing the most splendid of dresses. Each of them had on her head a coronet set with gems and sapphires and each carried a lighted candle in her hand. They surrounded the caliph on all sides as he walked between them, swaying as he went, preceded by Masrur, 'Afif and Wasif.

Shams al-Nahar and all her girls got up and met him at the garden gate. They kissed the ground in front of him and walked on before him until he had taken his seat on the couch. The slave girls and eunuchs in the garden all stood before him, while other beautiful slaves and maidservants came with lighted candles, perfume and musical instruments. The caliph ordered the singers to sit down, and when they had all taken their places, Shams al-Nahar came and, having sat on a chair beside the caliph's couch, she started to talk to him.

While all this was going on, Abu'l-Hasan and 'Ali, unseen by the caliph, were watching and listening. He started to joke and play with Shams al-Nahar and, as they were happily enjoying themselves, he gave orders for the garden pavilion to be opened up. This was done; the windows were thrown open, candles were lit and, although it was night-time, the place became as bright as day. The eunuchs began to carry in what was needed to serve the drinks, at which Abu'l-Hasan said: 'I have never seen the like of these wine vessels or these treasures, beakers of gold and silver, together with other metals, as well as gems such as baffle description. So astonished am I at what I have seen that I seem to be dreaming.' As for 'Ali, since Shams al-Nahar left him, such was the force of his passionate love that he had been stretched out on the ground. When he came to himself, he started to watch this unparalleled scene. He then said to Abu'l-Hasan: 'Brother, I am afraid lest the caliph catch sight of us or find out about us. Most of my fear is for you, as I know that I myself am very certainly doomed, and what will cause my death is love, the excess of passion, and having to part from my beloved after having been close to her. I hope, however, that God may free us from this peril.'

The two of them went on watching the caliph's enjoyment from the balcony, and when the entire feast had been set before him, he turned to one of the slave girls and said: 'Gharam, produce what you have in the way of delightful song.' The girl took her lute and, having tuned it, she recited:

There is a Bedouin girl whose clan have gone;
She yearns for the *ban* tree and the sweet bay of the Hijaz.
She entertains travellers and her longing serves
For their guest fire and her tears for drinking water.
But her passion is no greater than my love,
Though my beloved thinks that this love is a fault.

When Shams al-Nahar heard this, she toppled from the chair in which she was sitting and fell fainting and unconscious to the ground. The slave girls rose and lifted her up, but when 'Ali saw her from the balcony, he, too, fainted, prompting Abu'l-Hasan to say: 'Fate has divided love equally between you.' While this was going on, the girl who had brought them to the balcony came back and said: 'Get up, Abu'l-Hasan, you and your friend, and go down. We are in a dangerous place and I'm afraid that we may be found out or that the caliph come to know about you. If you don't go down straight away, we are dead.' 'How can this young man get up and go with me?' asked Abu'l-Hasan, 'when he has not even got the strength to rise?' The girl started to sprinkle him with rosewater until he had recovered his senses, at which Abu'l-Hasan lifted him and the girl supported him as together they brought him down from the balcony and walked on a little.

The girl opened a small iron door and let them both out, after which they sat down on a stone bench that they saw by the bank of the Tigris. She then clapped her hands, and when a man came up in a small boat, she told him to take the two young men to the other bank. They got into the boat and, as the boatman rowed away from the garden with them, 'Ali looked back at the caliph's palace, the pavilion and the garden and recited these lines of farewell:

I stretched out one weak hand to say goodbye,
With the other placed above my burning heart.
May this not be the last time that we meet,
And may this not be the last of my journey food.

'Hurry them away!' said the girl to the boatman, and he rowed faster.

Night 155

Morning now dawned and Shahrazad broke off from what she had been
allowed to say. Then, when it was the hundred and fifty-fifth night, SHE
CONTINUED:

I have heard, O fortunate king, that after crossing the river, the boatman brought the two men, accompanied by the girl, to the far bank,
where they landed. The girl then took her leave of them and went back,
saying that, although she did not want to abandon them, that was as far
as she could go. As for 'Ali, he collapsed in front of Abu'l-Hasan and
was unable to rise. 'This place is not safe,' Abu'l-Hasan pointed out,
'and we are in danger of our lives here from thieves, scoundrels and
bandits.' 'Ali got up and walked a short way, but he could not go on.
Some friends of Abu'l-Hasan's lived in that district and so he went and
knocked on the door of a trustworthy man with whom he was on familiar
terms. The man came out quickly and when he saw Abu'l-Hasan and
'Ali, he greeted them, brought them inside and made them sit down.

He talked with them, asking where they had come from. Abu'l-Hasan
explained: 'We had to come here because of a man with whom I have
business dealings and who is holding some cash of mine. I had heard
that he was about to go off on a journey, taking my money with him.
So I came tonight to look for him, taking with me this friend of mine,
'Ali ibn Bakkar, for company. By the time we had arrived to see the man,
he had hidden away from us, and after failing to find him, we came away
empty-handed. We did not want to go back at this time of night and, as
we had no idea where to turn, we came to you because of what we know
of your friendliness and your kindness.' 'You are very welcome,' said
the man, and he treated them with the greatest hospitality. They stayed
with him for the rest of the night and in the morning they left and went
back to the city.

When they got there and reached Abu'l-Hasan's house, he insisted on
bringing in his friend 'Ali. They lay down for a while to sleep, and
when they woke, Abu'l-Hasan told his servants to strew the house with
splendid carpets, which they did. 'I must console this young man,' said
Abu'l-Hasan to himself, 'and take his mind off his troubles, for I know
better than anyone else what he must be feeling.' He ordered water to
be fetched for 'Ali and when this had been done, 'Ali got up, performed
the ritual ablution, together with the obligatory prayers that he had

omitted during the previous day and night, and diverted himself by talking with Abu'l-Hasan.

Abu'l-Hasan then came up to him and said: 'The best thing for you in your condition would be to stay with me tonight so that you may relax, rid yourself of the longing that is troubling you and enjoy yourself. In this way it may be that the passion that is consuming your heart may clear away.' 'Do what you want, brother,' said 'Ali. 'I cannot escape from what afflicts me, but do as you please.' Abu'l-Hasan got up, summoned his servants, collected a number of his particular friends and sent for singers and musicians. When the company was assembled, he produced food and drink for them and they sat eating, drinking and enjoying themselves for the rest of the day until evening. Then candles were lit, convivial cups circulated and pleasure reigned. A singing girl picked up her lute and chanted:

> Time has struck me with the arrow of a glance,
> Killing me on the spot as I left my beloved.
> Time has opposed me; my patience has run short,
> And this is what I thought would come to me.

When 'Ali heard this, he fell down in a faint and remained unconscious until first light. Abu'l-Hasan was in despair, but when the day dawned, 'Ali recovered. He wanted to go back home and Abu'l-Hasan did not stop him for fear of what might happen. His servants brought a mule, on which they mounted him, and he rode off accompanied by Abu'l-Hasan and a number of servants. Abu'l-Hasan took him to his house, and when he was settled there, Abu'l-Hasan gave thanks to God that he had escaped from peril. He sat with him, trying to console him, but 'Ali could not control the violence of his passionate longing. Abu'l-Hasan then got up, took his leave and went on his way.

Night 156

Morning now dawned and Shahrazad broke off from what she had been allowed to say. Then, when it was the hundred and fifty-sixth night, SHE CONTINUED:

I have heard, O fortunate king, that Abu'l-Hasan then got up, took his leave and went on his way. As he did so, 'Ali asked him to let him know if any news came, which he agreed to do. After they had parted,

Abu'l-Hasan went to his shop and opened it. He waited to hear from Shams al-Nahar, but no one brought him any news. After having spent the night in his house, the next morning he went to see 'Ali and, on going in, he found him stretched out on his bed, surrounded by his friends, with doctors in attendance. Each of these was prescribing something different and feeling his pulse. When he saw Abu'l-Hasan coming, he smiled and Abu'l-Hasan greeted him, asked him how he was and sat with him until the others had left. 'What is all this?' he asked, and 'Ali replied: 'Word spread that I was ill and my friends heard of it. I didn't have the strength to get up and walk in order to give the lie to the report, so I stayed where I was, and as you can see, my friends came to visit me. Now tell me, brother, have you seen the slave girl who accompanied us or heard any news from her?' 'I haven't set eyes on her,' said Abu'l-Hasan, 'since the time that I left her on the bank of the Tigris.' Then he added: 'Friend, beware of disgrace and stop this weeping.' 'My brother,' replied 'Ali, 'I cannot control myself,' and then he recited the following lines:

On her hand there was what my hand cannot reach –
A pattern painted on a wrist that weakened me.
Fearing lest the arrows of her eyes might harm this hand,
She clothed it with a covering of chain mail.
An ignorant doctor felt my pulse. I said:
'The pain is in my heart, so leave my hand alone.'
She asked a phantom that had visited me and left:
'By God, describe him; do not fall short or exaggerate.'
The phantom said: 'I told him as I left, though you may die of thirst,
"Don't try to come to water. It is not for you."'
She rained narcissus pearls, watering the rose,
And using hailstones to bite the jujubes.

After finishing this poem, he said: 'Abu'l-Hasan, I have been struck by a misfortune from which I thought that I was secure, and nothing can give me more relief than death.' 'Be patient,' replied Abu'l-Hasan, 'for God may bring you a cure.' He then left 'Ali and went back to open up his shop.

He had not been sitting there long when the slave girl arrived. They exchanged greetings, and when he looked at her he could see that her heart was fluttering; she was distressed and showing obvious traces of sorrow. After welcoming her, he asked after Shams al-Nahar. 'I shall tell

you about her,' said the girl, 'but first, how is 'Ali?' Abu'l-Hasan told
her the whole story of what had happened to 'Ali and she expressed her
sorrow and grief, sighing and exclaiming in wonder at his plight, before
saying: 'The case of my mistress is even more remarkable. When you
went off, I returned with my heart palpitating in fear for you both, as I
could hardly believe that you had escaped. When I got back, I found my
mistress stretched out in the pavilion, neither speaking nor replying to
anyone. The Commander of the Faithful was sitting by her head, but he
could find no one to tell him about her and he did not know what
was wrong. She remained unconscious until midnight and when she
recovered, the Commander of the Faithful asked her what the matter
was and what had come over her. When she heard his question, she
kissed his feet and said: "Commander of the Faithful, may I be your
ransom, I was attacked by a disorder which produced a burning sensation
in my body and the pain caused me to faint, after which I don't know
what happened." The caliph asked what food she had eaten that day
and she told him that she had breakfasted on something that she had
never eaten before. She then gave the impression of having recovered her
strength and called for something to drink. After having taken it, she
told the caliph to relax again. He sat down on his couch in the pavilion
and everything there returned to order.

'I went up to Shams al-Nahar, and when she asked me about the two
of you, I told her what I had done with you and I recited to her the
verses that 'Ali had spoken when we were saying goodbye. This led her
to weep secretly but she stayed silent. After the Commander of the
Faithful had taken his seat, he ordered a slave girl to sing, and she
chanted these lines:

> I swear life has no sweetness now that you have gone.
> Would that I knew how you are after leaving me.
> If it is my absence that has made you weep,
> It is right that my tears should now be of my blood.

'When my mistress heard these lines, she fell on to the sofa in a
swoon . . .'

Night 157

Morning now dawned and Shahrazad broke off from what she had been
allowed to say. Then, when it was the hundred and fifty-seventh night,
SHE CONTINUED:

I have heard, O fortunate king, that the slave girl told Abu'l-Hasan:
'When my mistress heard these lines, she fell on to the sofa in a swoon.
I took her hand and sprinkled rosewater on her face. Then, when she
had recovered, I said: "My lady, don't expose yourself and everyone else
in the palace to shame. I implore you by the life of your beloved, show
patience." "Is there anything here worse than death?" she replied. "But
it is death that I seek, as this will bring me rest." While we were talking,
a girl sang the following lines:

> They say: "Patience may lead to rest."
> I say: "But where is patience, now my love has gone?"
> When I embraced him, he confirmed our bond
> By cutting patience's ties.

'At the end of the song, Shams al-Nahar fainted again, and, on seeing
this, the caliph hurried up to her. He gave orders that the drinks were to
be removed and that the slave girls should return to their own apartments. He himself stayed with her until morning, when he summoned
doctors and physicians and instructed them to treat her, without
having any idea that what she was suffering from was love. I stayed
with her until I thought that she was better, and it was this that kept me
from coming to you. I have left her with a number of her confidantes
who are concerned about her, as she told me to come to you to get news
of 'Ali.'

Abu'l-Hasan was astonished when he heard this account and he said:
'By God, I have told you all that there is to say about 'Ali, so go back,
greet your mistress and do what you can to urge her to be patient. Tell
her to keep her secret and say that I know her affair is a difficult one
which needs careful planning.' The girl thanked him, took her leave and
went back to Shams al-Nahar.

So much for her, but as for Abu'l-Hasan, he stayed in his shop until
evening and then, when the day was over, he got up, locked up and left.
He went to 'Ali's house, where he knocked on the door and was admitted
by a servant who came out to meet him. When he entered, 'Ali smiled at

him in delight. 'Abu'l-Hasan,' he said, 'your absence today has distressed me, since for the rest of my life I shall be dependent on you.' 'Don't talk like that,' replied Abu'l-Hasan. 'Were I able to cure you, I would do it for you before you asked, and if I could, I would ransom you with my life. Shams al-Nahar's slave girl arrived today and told me that what had stopped her from coming was the fact that the caliph had been sitting with her mistress. She told me all about her mistress,' and he then passed on to 'Ali everything that the girl had told him. 'Ali himself was grief-stricken and, bursting into tears, he turned to Abu'l-Hasan and said: 'Brother, I implore you in God's Name to help me in my trouble and to tell me what to do. Do please stay the night with me so that I may enjoy your company.' Abu'l-Hasan agreed to this, and the two of them spent the time talking to one another.

When it was dark, 'Ali sighed, wept and complained and through his tears he recited these lines:

> Your image is in my eye; your name is on my lips;
> You dwell in my heart, so how can you be gone?
> My only grief is for a life that ends
> Before we have enjoyed our share of union.

From another poet he quoted:

> The sword of her glance broke through my covering;
> The lance of her figure pierced the armour of my self-control.
> Beneath the musk of her beauty spot she showed
> The camphor of dawn breaking through the night of ambergris.
> She was alarmed, biting the carnelian with pearls,
> Each of which rests within a pool of sugar.
> She sighed in her emotion, hand on breast,
> And I saw what I had never seen before –
> Pens of coral writing with ambergris
> Five lines upon a crystal page.
> You who carry a real sword, beware
> The shattering blow of her eyelids when she looks,
> And, spearsmen, guard against her thrust
> If she attacks you with her figure's lance.

When he had finished these lines, 'Ali gave a great cry and fell down fainting, leading Abu'l-Hasan to think that he was dead. He remained unconscious until daybreak, when he recovered. He then talked with

Abu'l-Hasan, who stayed sitting with him until morning was advanced, when he left to open his shop. After that, the slave girl came and stood there, and when he saw her, they exchanged greetings and she brought him greetings from her mistress. She then asked about 'Ali. 'My good girl,' Abu'l-Hasan replied, 'don't ask me how he is or about the violence of his passion. He cannot sleep at night or rest by day. Sleeplessness has emaciated him; he is overwhelmed by sorrow and his condition is not one that would give pleasure to a friend.' 'My mistress sends her greetings to you and to him,' the girl said, 'and she has written him a note. Her own plight is worse than his, and when she handed the note over to me, she told me to be sure to obey her instructions and to bring back an answer. I have the note with me and I wonder if you would go with me to him so that we can get a reply.' 'Willingly,' Abu'l-Hasan replied and, after locking up the shop, he went off with the girl by a different way.

The two of them walked on until they reached 'Ali's house, where he left her standing by the door while he went in.

Night 158

Morning now dawned and Shahrazad broke off from what she had been allowed to say. Then, when it was the hundred and fifty-eighth night, SHE CONTINUED:

I have heard, O fortunate king, that the two of them walked on until they reached 'Ali's house, where Abu'l-Hasan left her standing by the door while he went in. 'Ali was delighted to see him and Abu'l-Hasan told him: 'The reason that I am here is that a friend has sent his slave girl to you with a note in which he greets you and says that the reason he has kept away from you is that something has happened to him that serves to excuse him. The girl is standing at the door, so will you allow her to come in?' 'Bring her in,' said 'Ali, and Abu'l-Hasan winked at him to let him know that this was Shams al-Nahar's slave girl. 'Ali understood what he meant and when he saw the girl he became joyfully excited and he gestured to her, as if to say: 'How is your master – may God grant him health?' 'He is well,' she replied, and then she took out the note and passed it to him. He took it and kissed it and, after he had opened it and read it, he passed it to Abu'l-Hasan, who found the following lines written in it:

'The messenger will bring you news;
You cannot see me, so content yourself with this.
You have left behind one passionately in love,
Whose eyes cannot be closed in sleep.
I struggle with patience in my suffering,
But no created being can ward off blows of fate.
Take comfort, for my heart will not forget,
Nor will your image ever be absent from my sight.
See what has happened to your wasted form
And use this to deduce my fate.

I have written you a letter without my fingers and spoken to you without my tongue. To explain my condition – sleep has deserted my eyes and care does not leave my heart. It is as though I have never known health, never abandoned distress, never seen a beautiful sight or passed a pleasant life. It is as though I have been created out of longing and out of the pain and distress of passion. For me, one sickness follows another. My passion is doubled and my longing multiplied. The ardour of love is stirred up in my heart and I am as the poet has described:

The heart is constricted and cares spread abroad;
The eye is sleepless and the body worn away.
Patience has left; I am for ever forsaken;
With deranged wits, I am robbed of my heart.

Know that complaints cannot extinguish the fire of distress but they serve to distract those who are made sick by longing and destroyed by separation. I console myself by speaking the word "union", and how excellent are the lines of the poet:

Were there no anger nor approval in love,
Where would be the sweetness of messages and letters?'

When Abu'l-Hasan had read this, the words stirred up a turmoil of emotions and their meaning struck home to his vitals. He passed the note back to the girl, and when she had taken it, 'Ali said to her: 'Take my greetings to your mistress. Tell her of the strength of my passion and say that love for her is mixed with my flesh and my bones. Say to her that I need someone to save me from the sea of destruction and to rescue me from this confusion. Time has afflicted me with its calamities. Is there anyone to save me from the ill fortune that it brings?' He then burst into

tears and the girl wept with him. She then took her leave and went out
with Abu'l-Hasan, to whom she said goodbye before going on her way.

As for Abu'l-Hasan, he went off, opened up his shop and took his
usual place there.

Night 159

Morning now dawned and Shahrazad broke off from what she had been
allowed to say. Then, when it was the hundred and fifty-ninth night,
SHE CONTINUED:

I have heard, O fortunate king, that Abu'l-Hasan said goodbye to the
girl and went to open his shop, where he sat as usual. But when he had
settled down, he found himself depressed and gloomy. He was at a loss
to know what to do and he remained wracked by care for the rest of the
day and the following night. The next day, he went to 'Ali and sat with
him until everyone else had left. He then asked him how he was, to
which 'Ali replied by complaining of his passionate love and reciting
these lines:

> Others before me have complained of love.
> The remoteness of the beloved has prompted fears
> That terrify the living and the dead,
> But I have never seen or heard
> Of a love such as lies buried in my heart.

From another poet he quoted:

> My love for you has caused more suffering
> Than mad Qais felt for Lubna, but I have not gone
> Hunting the wild beasts as he did,
> For madness here has many forms.

Abu'l-Hasan said: 'I have never seen or heard of a lover like you. What
is all this passion and bodily weakness, when you love one who returns
your love? How would it be if your beloved was a contrary girl who
tricked you and if your affair was exposed?' According to Abu'l-Hasan's
account, 'Ali was struck by what he had said and took it seriously,
thanking him for saying it. Abu'l-Hasan went on to say that he had a
friend who was the only one to know about him and 'Ali and about their
close association. He used to come and ask Abu'l-Hasan about him, and

soon after this he asked him about the slave girl. Abu'l-Hasan told him deceptively: 'She invited 'Ali to visit her and their affair reached its climax. This is as far as it has got, but I have thought of a plan for myself which I want to submit to you.' 'What is it?' asked the friend. 'You must know, brother,' said Abu'l-Hasan, 'that I am a man well known for his many dealings in relationships between men and women. I'm afraid that if the affair between these two is discovered, it may lead to my ruin, the confiscation of my wealth and loss of my honour together with that of my family. What I propose to do is to collect all my money, make my preparations and then set out for Basra, where I shall stay without anyone's knowledge until I see what happens to 'Ali and the girl. They are deeply in love and are exchanging notes using a slave girl as a go-between. She is keeping their secret for the moment, but I'm afraid that she may become discontented and give it away to someone. Were word to spread, it might lead to my ruin and destruction, for in men's eyes I would have no excuse.'

'This is a serious matter you have told me about,' said his friend, 'enough to cause fear to a wise and experienced man. May God protect you from the evil that you fear and save you from the result you dread. Your plan, however, is a good one.' So Abu'l-Hasan went off to his house and started to put his affairs in order and make preparations for his journey to Basra. After three days, he had done all this and he then set out. Three days later, his friend came to visit him and, not finding him there, he asked one of his neighbours where he was. 'He left for Basra three days ago,' the man said. 'He had had some dealings with the Basran merchants and he went there to look for those who owe him money, but he'll be back soon.' His friend was taken aback, not knowing where to go, and he said to himself: 'I wish I had not left him.'

He then thought of a way to approach 'Ali and, after going to the latter's house, he told one of his servants to ask his master's permission for him to come in to greet him. The servant did this and returned to say permission had been granted. The man entered and finding 'Ali lying back on a pillow, he greeted him. 'Ali returned the greeting and welcomed him, after which the man apologized for not having been to see him before, adding: 'I am on friendly terms with Abu'l-Hasan. I was in the habit of entrusting him with my secrets and I used to spend all my time with him. For three days, however, I was away on business with a group of friends, and when I went to see him, I found his shop locked up. When I asked about him, his neighbours told me that he had gone to

Basra. I don't know any truer friend of his than you, so, for God's sake, tell me about him.'

When 'Ali heard this, he changed colour and became agitated. 'This is the first that I have heard of his journey,' he said, 'and if what you say is true, things will be difficult for me.' He then recited:

I used to weep for my lost joy,
While all my friends were still with me.
Now that Time parted us today,
It is for those friends that I weep.

He bent his head down towards the ground in thought. Then, after a time he looked up at one of his servants and told him to go to Abu'l-Hasan's house and to ask whether he was there or on a journey. 'If you are told that he is on a journey,' he added, 'ask where he has gone.' The servant left and came back an hour later, going to his master and saying: 'When I asked about Abu'l-Hasan, his household told me that he had started out for Basra. I found a slave girl standing by the door and, although I didn't recognize her, she knew me and asked if I was the servant of 'Ali ibn Bakkar. When I said that I was, she said: "I have a letter for him from his dearest love." She came back with me and is now at the door.' 'Ali told him to bring her in, which he did, and Abu'l-Hasan's friend looked at her and saw that she was a graceful girl.

She went up and greeted 'Ali . . .

Night 160

Morning now dawned and Shahrazad broke off from what she had been allowed to say. Then, when it was the hundred and sixtieth night, SHE CONTINUED:

I have heard, O fortunate king, that the slave girl went up and greeted 'Ali and spoke to him privately, and during the course of their conversation he kept swearing that he had not spoken a word about the matter. She then took her leave and went off.

Abu'l-Hasan's friend was a jeweller and when the girl had gone, he took the opportunity to speak. 'There is no doubt,' he said to 'Ali, 'that the caliph's palace has some call on you or that you have some dealings with it.' 'Who told you that?' said 'Ali. 'I know this girl,' the man replied. 'She belongs to Shams al-Nahar. Some time ago she brought me a note saying that she wanted a jewelled necklace and I sent her one of great value.' When 'Ali heard this, he was disturbed that his life was in danger, but, recovering his composure, he said: 'Brother, in God's Name, tell me how you came to know of her.' 'Don't press me with questions,' said the jeweller. 'I shall not let you alone,' said 'Ali, 'until you tell me the truth.'

The jeweller said: 'I'll tell you so that you need have no suspicions of me. You should not be depressed by what I have to say, and, far from hiding my secret from you, I'll tell you the truth of the whole affair on condition that you tell me what is really wrong with you and what is the cause of your illness.' So 'Ali told him his story, adding: 'I was only led to conceal my affair from everyone except you, my brother, for fear lest people uncover the secret of a certain lady.' 'The only reason that I wanted to come to you,' said the jeweller, 'was because of my affection for you and my solicitude for you in all circumstances, together with the pity that I feel for the pain that separation has inflicted on you. It may be that I can act as a comforter for you in place of my friend Abu'l-Hasan while he is away. So take heart and console yourself.' 'Ali thanked him for that, reciting:

> Were I to say I could endure her loss,
> My tears and my deep sighs would prove me false.
> How am I to hide the tears that flow
> Over my cheeks because she parted from me?

He was then silent for a time, after which he said to the jeweller: 'Do you know what the slave girl said to me in private?' When the jeweller said no, he went on: 'She thought that I had advised Abu'l-Hasan to go to Basra as a trick in order to make sure that there would be no more correspondence or contact between us. I swore to her that that was not true, but she didn't believe me. She was still suspicious as she went off to her mistress, since she had a fondness for Abu'l-Hasan and would listen to him.' The jeweller replied: 'I understand the girl's position, but if God Almighty wills, I can help you to get what you want.' 'Who is able to do that,' asked 'Ali, 'and how can you deal with her when she shies away like a wild beast of the desert?' 'By God,' said the jeweller, 'I shall have to do my best to help you and to concoct a scheme to allow you to meet her without your secret being revealed or harm being done.' He then asked 'Ali's permission to leave, and 'Ali implored him to keep his secret safe, bursting into tears while he said goodbye. The jeweller left . . .

Night 161

Morning now dawned and Shahrazad broke off from what she had been allowed to say. Then, when it was the hundred and sixty-first night, SHE CONTINUED:

I have heard, O fortunate king, that the jeweller said goodbye to him and left, although he had no idea of what he could do to help 'Ali. As he walked on, thinking the matter over, he saw a piece of paper lying in the street. He picked it up, looking to see to whom it was addressed and finding it was from 'the junior lover to the senior beloved'. After opening it up, he discovered these lines:

> The messenger came, bringing hope of union,
> But this I thought was mere illusion.
> Far from rejoicing, I became more sad,
> Knowing that he was not a man of sense.

The note went on: 'Know, my master, that I cannot understand why our correspondence has been broken off. If you are acting harshly, I meet this harshness with fidelity, and if you have ceased to love me, I still love you, distant as you are. My relationship to you is as the poet describes it:

> If you are haughty, I endure;
> If you are overbearing, I show patience;
> Be proud; I shall be humble;
> Turn back and I shall come;
> Speak and I listen; order and I shall obey.'

When the jeweller had read this, he saw the slave girl coming, turning right and left. On seeing that he had the note in his hand, she told him that it was she who had dropped it, but he made no reply and walked on. The girl followed and when he came to his house and went in, she was still behind him. 'Sir,' she said, 'give me back the note which I dropped.' He turned to her, saying: 'My good girl, don't be afraid or sad. God is the Coverer, Who loves to cover. You can tell me the true story as I am a man who keeps secrets, but swear to me that you will not hide anything from me of your mistress's affair. It may be that God will help me to get what she wants and through me will make easy what is now difficult.'

When the girl heard this, she said: 'Master, may no secret that you keep ever be revealed, and may you fail in nothing that you hope to achieve. Know that I feel drawn towards you and I will tell you about the affair, but give me back the note.' She then told him the whole story, calling God to witness that she was speaking the truth. 'I believe you,' said the jeweller, 'because I know the basic facts.' He then told her about 'Ali and how he had come to know his real feelings, telling her the whole story from beginning to end. The girl was pleased by what she heard and they agreed that she should take the note and give it to 'Ali, after which she was to come back and tell him everything that had happened. He handed over the note, which she took and sealed up as it had been sealed before, saying: 'It was sealed when my mistress Shams al-Nahar gave it to me, and when 'Ali has read it and given me a reply, I shall bring it to you.'

She then took her leave of him and went to 'Ali, whom she found waiting for her. After she had given him the note and he had read it, he wrote a reply which he gave to her. She took it and brought it to the jeweller, and when she had handed it to him, he broke the seal and read it. In it he found these lines:

'The messenger, who used to hide away
Our letters, left in anger.
Choose from your folk another trusty one,
Who prefers truth to lies.

I am not guilty of any treachery nor have I betrayed my trust. I have not acted with cruelty nor have I abandoned loyalty. I have broken no convenant; I have not severed the bonds of love. Sorrow has been my constant companion, and after we parted, I have met nothing but ruin. I know nothing at all about your accusations. I only love what you love and, by Him Who knows what is hidden in secret, my only goal is to meet the one I love. I do my best to conceal my love, even though I pine with sickness. This is the explanation of my state, and so, farewell.'

When the jeweller had read this note and found out what it contained, he wept bitterly. The girl said to him: 'Don't leave this place until I come back to you. 'Ali has excusably accused me of faithlessness, and I want by any possible means to arrange for a meeting between you and my mistress Shams al-Nahar. I left her in a state of collapse and she is expecting me to bring back an answer.' The girl went off to her mistress and the jeweller spent the night in a state of agitation. In the morning, he sat waiting for the girl and she arrived cheerfully. When she came in, he asked for her news and she told him: 'I went from you to my mistress and I passed her the note that 'Ali had written. When she had read it and grasped its meaning, she was in a state of confusion. "My lady," I said, "don't fear that your relations with 'Ali will be spoilt because of the absence of Abu'l-Hasan, as I have found a substitute for him, a better man of higher standing and someone well suited to keeping secrets." I told her about your dealings with Abu'l-Hasan; of how I had gone to him and of how I had dropped the note which you had then found. I then told her of the arrangement which you and I had made.'

The jeweller was astonished at this, but the girl went on: 'My mistress wants to hear what you have to say yourself so that you may confirm the compact that you have with 'Ali. You must make up your mind to come with me to see her at once.' When the jeweller heard this, he realized that this was a serious matter involving great danger into which he could not rush blindly. So he said to her: 'Sister, I am a common man, unlike Abu'l-Hasan, who was well known as a person of high standing, and who frequently went to the caliph's palace because of the demand for his goods there. He used to talk to me and I would shudder with fear at what he told me. If your mistress wants me to talk with her, this must be in some place other than the palace and far removed from the Commander of the Faithful, as I cannot bring myself to do what you say.'

When he refused to go with her, the girl began to say that she could guarantee his safety and that he had no need to fear any harm. She repeated this until he was on the point of getting up to accompany her, but then his legs buckled under him and his hands trembled. 'God forbid that I should go with you,' he said. 'I cannot do this.' 'Calm yourself,' she told him. 'If it is too difficult for you to go to the palace and if you can't come with me, I shall get my mistress to come to you, so don't go away until I bring her back.' She then left and, after a short absence, she returned to him and said: 'See that there is nobody here with you, either servant or slave girl.' 'There is only an old black slave woman who looks after me,' he replied. The girl got up and locked the connecting door between the jeweller and this woman, sending his servants out of the house. She then went out and came back followed by a girl whom she brought in. The house was filled with the scent of perfume and the jeweller got to his feet on seeing his visitor, for whom he set out a seat with a cushion. She sat down, and he took a seat in front of her. For some time she stayed there without speaking until she was rested. Then she unveiled her face and to the jeweller it seemed that the sun had risen in his house. 'Is this the man you told me about?' Shams al-Nahar asked the slave girl. 'Yes,' said the girl, at which the other turned to the jeweller and asked him how he was. 'I am well,' he replied, 'and I pray for your life and for that of the Commander of the Faithful.' 'You have made me come to you,' said Shams al-Nahar, 'and to tell you my secret.'

She then asked him about his family and his dependants, and he gave her a full account of all his circumstances. He told her that he had another house which he used for meetings with his friends and in which there was nobody but the slave woman about whom he had told the girl. She then asked him how he had come to know the beginning of the story, how Abu'l-Hasan was involved with this and how he had left. He told her what had passed through Abu'l-Hasan's mind, prompting him to go. She sighed at being parted from him, saying: 'My friend, men's souls are matched in their desires and people depend on each other. Nothing can be done without words; no goal can be achieved without effort; rest comes only after toil . . .'

Night 162

Morning now dawned and Shahrazad broke off from what she had been allowed to say. Then, when it was the hundred and sixty-second night, SHE CONTINUED:

I have heard, O fortunate king, that Shams al-Nahar told the jeweller: 'Rest comes only after toil and it is only manliness that brings success. I have told you of our affair and it lies with you whether you expose us or protect us. No more need be said, as you are a man of honour. You know that this slave girl of mine has kept my secret and because of this I value her highly and have picked her out to deal with my most important affairs. Respect no one more than her; tell her about your affairs and take heart, for you are secure from the dangers that you are afraid we may bring on you. If you find any approach blocked, she will open it up for you; she will bring you messages to pass to 'Ali, and you will be our intermediary.'

Shams al-Nahar then rose with difficulty and walked off, with the jeweller walking before her until she reached the house door, after which he went back and sat down on his seat. The sight of her beauty had

dazzled him and he had been bewildered by what she had said, as her
refined elegance had astonished him. He continued to think about her
until he calmed down, after which he asked for food and ate just enough
for sustenance. He then changed his clothes and left his house in order
to visit 'Ali.

Knocking on 'Ali's door, he was quickly met by his servants, who
walked ahead of him until they brought him to their master, whom he
found stretched out on his bed. On seeing him, 'Ali said: 'You have been
slow in coming, adding to my worries.' He then dismissed the servants
and ordered the doors to be shut, before saying: 'By God, brother, I have
not closed an eye from the time that you left me. The slave girl came to
me yesterday with a sealed letter from her mistress.'

After telling the jeweller all that had passed between them, he went
on: 'By God, I don't know what to do and my powers of endurance are
running out. Abu'l-Hasan was a friend and he was acquainted with the
girl.' The jeweller laughed on hearing this, at which 'Ali asked him: 'Why
do you laugh at what I said? I was pleased to see you, thinking that you
would help me in my misfortunes.' He then sighed, wept and recited
these lines:

Many a man saw me and then laughed at my tears,
But had he shared my sufferings, he would have wept.
The only one to pity what the afflicted feel
Is he who grieves like them in long distress.
My passion, longing, moaning, cares and hopeless love
Are for a beloved lodged within my heart.
Although she never leaves at any time,
Yet she is rarely to be met.
I'd take no other friend as substitute
Nor would I choose another as my love.

When the jeweller heard what he had to say and understood the point
of the poem, he burst into tears. He then told 'Ali what had happened
to him with the slave girl and her mistress after he had left him. 'Ali
listened to what he had to say and with every word his colour changed
from white to red. One moment his body would be stronger and the
next weaker. When the jeweller ended his account, 'Ali wept and said:
'Brother, I am bound to perish and I wish that my death would come
soon so that I might find rest from this pain. Of your goodness I ask you
to help me and befriend me in all my affairs until what God wills comes

about. I shall do anything you say.' 'The only thing to quench this fire of yours,' said the jeweller, 'is for you to meet the girl you love, but this cannot be done in a dangerous place like this. The rendezvous must be in my house, where the slave girl and her mistress came, this being the place that she chose for herself. What I hope to achieve is for the two of you to meet so that you can both speak of the love pains that you have suffered.' 'Do as you please,' said 'Ali, 'and may God reward you. Act as you think right, but don't delay, lest I die of this distress.'

The jeweller remained with 'Ali that night, talking to him until morning came . . .

Night 163

Morning now dawned and Shahrazad broke off from what she had been allowed to say. Then, when it was the hundred and sixty-third night, SHE CONTINUED:

I have heard, O fortunate king, that the jeweller remained with 'Ali that night, talking to him until morning came, and then, having performed the morning prayer, he left and returned to his house. Shortly after he had settled down, the slave girl arrived and when they had exchanged greetings, he told her what had happened between him and 'Ali. She said: 'Know that the caliph has gone away. There is no one in our quarters and this is a better and a safer place of concealment for us.' 'True,' replied the jeweller, 'but it is not like this house of mine, which will suit us better and provide better cover.' 'As you wish,' said the slave girl. 'I shall go to my mistress to tell her what you have said and what you propose.' She got up and went back to Shams al-Nahar, whom she told what the jeweller had said. Later, she came back to the jeweller's house and reported: 'My mistress will do what you say, so get the place ready and wait for us.'

From her pocket she took a purse full of dinars and said: 'My mistress greets you and asks you to take this purse and to make the necessary arrangements.' The jeweller swore that he would not take any of the money, and so the girl brought the purse back to Shams al-Nahar and told her that the man had refused to accept the cash and had handed it back to her, and Shams al-Nahar accepted this. Describing what then happened, THE JEWELLER SAID:

After the girl had gone, I got up and went to my second house and

moved to it all the paraphernalia and splendid furnishings that were
needed, including china dishes, glass, silver and gold, and I prepared the
food and drink that would be needed. When the slave girl came and saw
what I had done, she was pleased with it and she told me to fetch 'Ali.
'You should fetch him,' I said, and so she went and brought him back,
perfectly turned out and looking his best.

I met him, welcomed him and placed him on a suitable seat, setting
in front of him pleasant, sweet-scented flowers in vases of china and
coloured crystal, as well as a tray containing all kinds of delicacies to
delight the eye. I sat talking to him and entertaining him, while the girl
left and stayed away until evening. After sunset she came back with
Shams al-Nahar, who was accompanied by only two maids. When she
and 'Ali saw each other, he rose to his feet and the two of them embraced,
before falling to the ground in a faint which lasted for an hour. When
they had recovered, they began to exchange complaints about the pains
of separation, and they sat talking eloquently, sweetly and tenderly,
while perfuming themselves. They thanked me for my kindness to them
and I asked them whether they would like something to eat. When they
said yes, I produced food for them and, after having eaten their fill, they
washed their hands. I then led them to another room, where I brought
them wine. They drank deeply and leaned towards one another, after
which Shams al-Nahar said: 'Sir, to complete your kindness, fetch us a
lute or some other musical instrument, so as to bring our present happiness to the pitch of perfection.' 'Willingly,' I replied, and I fetched a lute
which Shams al-Nahar took and tuned. Then, placing it in her lap, she
played on it with such expertise as both to arouse sorrow and to delight
the sad, reciting these lines:

> I stayed awake as though in love with wakefulness,
> Wasting away until it was as though it was for me
> That sickness was created.
> Tears soaked my cheeks and scalded them.
> Would that I knew whether, after our parting, we shall meet again.

She began to sing in various tones songs containing delightful poetry
and which bewildered our thoughts, so that the room itself almost danced
with joy in appreciation of her singing, and our minds and thoughts
were stolen away. Then, when we were all seated and the wine cups had
passed around, the slave girl recited tunefully:

The beloved kept his promise of union on a night
Which I shall count as being worth many nights.
What a night it was that Time then granted us,
Unnoticed by those who denounce and censure us.
To my delight, he spent the night
Clasping me with his right hand while I clasped him with my left.
I embraced him and sucked his saliva's wine,
Enjoying both the honeyed drink and the honey seller.

While we were drowning in an ocean of pleasure, a small servant girl
came in, trembling with fear. 'My lady,' she said, 'look for a way to get
out. The house is surrounded; they have found you although we don't
know how this has happened.' On hearing this, I stood up in a panic,
just as the slave girl was saying: 'Disaster has overtaken you.' The wide
world seemed too narrow for me. I looked at the door and could find
no way of escape at first, but then I managed to get to the house of one
of my neighbours, where I hid myself. I found that people had gone into
my own house and were making a great disturbance, and this convinced
me that the caliph had heard about us and had ordered the police chief
to take us by surprise and to bring us to him. I had no idea what to do,
and so I stayed where I was until midnight, unable to leave my hiding
place.

The owner of the house then came, and to his great alarm he sensed
that someone was there. So he came towards me out of his room with a
drawn sword in his hand, saying: 'Who's there?' 'I'm your neighbour,
the jeweller,' I replied. On recognizing me, he went off and came back
with a light. He then approached me and said: 'Brother, I am distressed
by what has happened to you tonight.' 'Tell me who it was in my house?'
I asked him. 'Who broke down the door and went in? For I ran off
here and don't know what happened.' He said: 'Thieves visited our
neighbours yesterday and killed one of them, plundering his goods. They
saw you yesterday moving stuff here, and so they came and took what
you had, killing your guests.'

My neighbour and I went to my house and found it empty and stripped
bare. Taken aback, I said to myself: 'I don't care about the loss of the
furnishings. Some of what has gone I had borrowed from my friends,
but it doesn't matter, as they will recognize that I have the excuse that
my house was plundered and my goods taken. I'm afraid, however, that
the affair of 'Ali ibn Bakkar and the caliph's concubine may come out

and that will lead to my death.' Turning to my neighbour, I said: 'You are my brother, my neighbour and my shield against exposure, so what do you advise me to do?' 'Lie low,' he told me. 'The men who entered your house and took your goods also killed a distinguished group of palace officials, as well some of the police chief's men. State guards are on all the roads looking for them and should they happen to find them, you will get what you want without any effort on your own part.'

On hearing this, the jeweller went back to the other house where he lived.

Night 164

Morning now dawned and Shahrazad broke off from what she had been allowed to say. Then, when it was the hundred and sixty-fourth night, SHE CONTINUED:

I have heard, O fortunate king, that on hearing this, the jeweller went back to the other house where he lived. He said to himself: 'What has happened is what Abu'l-Hasan feared. He went off to Basra and it is I who have fallen into the trap.' Word of the plundering of his house now began to spread and people came up to him from all sides, some taking malicious pleasure in his misfortune, while others were helpful and sympathetic. He poured out his complaints to them and would neither eat nor drink because of his distress. Then, while he was sitting sorrowfully, one of his servants came in and told him that there was a man at the door asking for him. The jeweller went out to greet him and found someone unknown to him, who told him that he had something to say to him in private. The jeweller took him into his house, where he asked what he had to say. 'Go with me to your second house,' said the man. 'Do you know my second house?' asked the jeweller. The man replied: 'I know all about you and I have news by which God will dispel your cares.' THE JEWELLER WENT ON:

I told myself that I had better do what he wanted, and so I accompanied him to the house. When he saw it, he said: 'There is neither door nor doorman here. We can't sit in this place, so take me somewhere else.' I stayed with him as he went round from one place to another, until night fell and I had still not asked him any questions. He kept on walking with me until we came out into open country. 'Follow me,' he said, and he started to walk faster, with me hurrying behind him, encouraging myself to carry on. We then got to the river, where we were met by a small boat, and the boatman rowed us across to the far bank. The man got out and when I followed, he took my hand and led me into a street that I had never been to in my life – I didn't even know what district it was in. He stopped at the door of a house, opened it and entered, taking me in with him, after which he fastened the door with an iron lock. He then brought me into a hall and I was confronted by ten men who looked so similar that they seemed to be one and the same person. They were, in fact, brothers.

We exchanged greetings and they told us to sit down, which we did. I was almost dead with tiredness and so they brought me rosewater which they sprinkled on my face. They then poured me wine and fetched food, which some of them ate with me. 'If there were anything harmful in this food,' I said to myself, 'they would not share it with me.' When we had washed our hands, they each went back to their places, after which they asked whether I recognized them. 'No,' I said, 'I have never seen you in my life; I have never seen the man who brought me to you, and I have never seen this place.' 'Tell us about yourself and without lying,' they said. 'You must know,' I replied, 'that my case is strange and remarkable. Do you know anything about me?' 'Yes,' they said. 'It was we who took your goods last night, and we also took your friend and the girl who was singing with him.' 'May God protect you,' I said. 'Where is my friend and where is the singer?' 'Here,' they said, pointing in a certain direction and adding: 'But, by God, brother, you are the only one who knows their secret. Since we brought them here, none of us have been to see them and we have not asked them about themselves, because we saw that they had an aura of dignity about them, which is what stopped us from killing them. Tell us the truth about them and we shall spare your life and theirs.'

When I heard this, I almost died of fear and I said to them: 'Brothers, if chivalry were lost, you can be sure that it is only with you that it would be found. If I had a secret which I was afraid to make known, it is in your hearts that it would be hidden.' I went on in this exaggerated way, and then I thought that it would be better and more useful to come out with the story rather than to conceal it. So I told them everything that had happened to me, from start to finish. They listened to my tale and then asked: 'Is this young man 'Ali ibn Bakkar and is the girl Shams al-Nahar?' When I said yes, they were taken aback and went and apologized to the pair. 'Some of what we took from your house has gone, but here is the rest of it,' they said, and they returned most of my belongings, guaranteeing to bring them back to their place in my house and to restore all the rest. My fears were laid to rest, but the ten then split into two groups, one on my side and the other against me. It was then that we left the house.

So much for me, but as for 'Ali and Shams al-Nahar, they had almost died of fear before I approached them and greeted them. I asked them: 'What do you suppose has happened to the slave girl and the two maids? Where did they go?' But they said that they knew nothing about them. We then went to where a boat was anchored, and when our escort put us on board, this turned out to be the same one on which I had crossed earlier. The boatman rowed us across to the other side, where we were made to disembark, but before we had time to sit down and rest on the bank, we found ourselves encircled by horsemen who swooped down on all sides like eagles. The men who had brought us hurried to their feet; the boat came back for them and they jumped in and were ferried off by the boatman, disappearing from sight after they had reached mid-stream, while we stayed on the bank unable either to move or to sit still.

The riders asked us where we had come from and we were at a loss to know what to say. I told them: 'Those people whom you saw with us were a bunch of scoundrels whom we don't know. We ourselves are singers. They wanted to take us to sing to them, and it was only by politeness and soft words that we escaped from them. They had just let us go before going off, as you saw.' The riders looked at Shams al-Nahar and 'Ali and said to me: 'You are not telling the truth. Tell us who you are, where you have come from, where are you based and in what quarter you live.'

I had no idea what to say, but Shams al-Nahar jumped up and, after approaching their captain, she had a private word with him. He then dismounted and set her on his horse, which he started to lead by its reins. One trooper did the same for 'Ali and another for me. The captain walked on with us to a spot on the river bank where he called out in a foreign language, and a number of people came up from the land side, bringing two boats. We were then rowed up to the caliph's palace, being almost dead with fear, but we went on until we reached a place from which we could get home. There we disembarked and we walked with an escort of riders, who made friendly conversation with us until we got to 'Ali's house. Before going in, we said goodbye to them and they went off on their way. We ourselves could hardly move and could not tell morning from evening, staying like that until dawn.

At the end of the day, 'Ali collapsed in a faint, and as he lay stretched out and motionless, women and men wept over him. Some of his family came and woke me up. 'Tell us what has happened to him,' they said, 'and what is this state he is in.' 'Listen to me,' I said . . .

Night 165

Morning now dawned and Shahrazad broke off from what she had been allowed to say. Then, when it was the hundred and sixty-fifth night, SHE CONTINUED:

I have heard, O fortunate king, that the jeweller said: 'Listen to me; don't harm me, but wait patiently, for he will recover and tell you his story himself.' HE WENT ON:

I then spoke forcefully to them, threatening them with an open scandal. Then, while we were talking, to the delight of his family 'Ali suddenly stirred on his bed. The others left, but his family would not let me go. They sprinkled rosewater on his face, and when he had recovered consciousness and sniffed the air, they started to ask him questions. He tried to tell them, but his tongue was not quick enough to produce the answers and so he gestured to them to let me go home. This they did and I left, scarcely believing that I had escaped. I was accompanied by two men until I reached my own house, and when my family saw me in this state, they cried out and struck their faces, until I gestured to them to keep quiet, which they did. My escort went off, after which I lay down on my bed for the rest of the night and did not wake until morning.

When I woke, I found my family clustered around me. They asked me what misfortune had overtaken me, but I just told them to bring me something to drink. When I had drunk enough from what they brought, I said: 'What has happened has happened,' and they then left. Afterwards I made my excuses to my friends and asked them whether any of my missing goods had been returned. They said: 'Some of them have, for a man came and threw them into the doorway of the house, but we didn't catch sight of him.' I comforted myself and stayed at home for two days, unable to get up, but then I took heart and walked to the baths.

I was very tired and full of concern for 'Ali and Shams al-Nahar, since during this period I had heard no news of them. I could not go to 'Ali's house, but neither could I rest quietly at home as I was afraid for my own safety, repenting to Almighty God for what I had done and praising Him for having preserved me. After a time, I thought of making my way to a certain quarter and then coming straight back. As I was about to set off, I looked at a woman whom I saw standing nearby, and discovered that she was the slave girl of Shams al-Nahar. As soon as I recognized her, I hurried away, but she followed me. I was afraid of her, and every time I looked at her the more alarmed I became. She kept saying: 'Stop, I want to talk to you,' but, rather than turning back, I walked on until I reached a mosque in a place where there was nobody to be seen. 'Go in here,' the girl said, 'so that I can say something to you. There is nothing to be afraid of.' As she pressed me so earnestly, I went into the mosque and she followed me. I prayed, performing two *rak'as* and then I went up to her, sighing, and asked her what she wanted. She asked me how I was, and I told her what had happened to myself and to 'Ali.

I asked her about herself, and she said: 'When I saw the men breaking down the door of your house and bursting in, I was afraid, thinking that if they had been sent by the caliph to seize me and my mistress, we would face immediate death. So the two maids and I made our escape by way of the roof. We jumped down from a height and in our flight we took shelter among some people who then took us to the caliph's palace. We were in the worst of states, but we managed to conceal what had happened, although we remained tossing on coals of anxiety until it grew dark. Then I opened the river door and called to the boatman who had taken us out the night before. I told him that we had had no news of my mistress and I asked him to take me in his boat so that I could go and search for her along the river and perhaps hear some word of her. He did this and I stayed on the river until midnight, when I saw another boat approaching the door, with one man rowing, another standing and a woman lying between the two of them. The boatman rowed up to the bank; the woman got out, and when I looked at her, I saw that this was Shams al-Nahar. I disembarked to meet her, being overjoyed to see her after I had lost hope.'

Night 166

Morning now dawned and Shahrazad broke off from what she had been allowed to say. Then, when it was the hundred and sixty-sixth night, SHE CONTINUED:

I have heard, O fortunate king, that the girl told the jeweller: 'I was overjoyed to see her, after I had lost hope. When I came to her, she told me to pay a thousand dinars to the man who had brought her, and then the two maids and I carried her in and put her on her bed. She spent the night in a distressed state, and in the morning I kept the slave girls and the eunuchs from coming in to see her that day. On the following day, she had recovered although to me it seemed as though she had just emerged from a tomb. I sprinkled her face with rosewater, changed her clothes and washed her hands and feet, continuing this gentle treatment until I had given her some food to eat and something to drink. She showed no inclination for any of this, but after she had sniffed the air, she regained her health.

'I then began to reproach her, saying: "My lady, you must watch out and take care of yourself. You have seen what happened to us and you have brought down enough trouble on yourself, almost getting yourself killed." "My good girl," she said to me, "death would have been easier to bear than what happened to me. I thought that I was certain to be killed. When the thieves took me from the jeweller's house, they asked me who I was and when I told them that I was a singing girl, they believed me. They then asked 'Ali about himself, who he was and what was his position, and he told them that he was one of the common people. They took us with them to their base and such was our fear that we hurried on with them. When they got us there, they looked closely at me and noted the clothes that I was wearing, as well as my necklaces and jewels. They became suspicious and said: 'These necklaces never belonged to a singing girl, so speak the truth and tell us what your real position is.' I gave them no reply, saying to myself that they would now kill me because of my ornaments and clothing. When I stayed silent, they turned to 'Ali and said: 'You don't look like a common man – who are you and where do you come from?' But he said nothing and, still concealing our secret, we burst into tears.

'"God then softened the hearts of the robbers and they asked us who was the owner of the house in which we had been. We told them the name of the jeweller, at which one of them said: 'I know him well and I know where he is. He will be in his second house and I undertake to fetch him straight away.' They then agreed to keep me and 'Ali separate, telling us to relax and not to fear that our secret would be revealed, promising we would be safe. Their companion went and fetched the jeweller and he told them about us. We joined him and one of the robbers fetched a boat. They put us on board, took us across to the other shore, set us on the bank and then went off. Riders of the night watch came up and asked who we were. I spoke with their captain and told him that I was Shams al-Nahar, the caliph's favourite. I said that, after drinking deeply, I had gone out to visit one of my acquaintances among the vizier's wives, and had fallen into the hands of robbers who had taken me to that spot, and who had then run away when they saw the captain's men. I added that I was well able to reward him. Having heard what I had to say, he recognized me and, after dismounting, he set me on his horse and had the same thing done for 'Ali and the jeweller. I am still on fire with anxiety about them, especially 'Ali's friend, the jeweller. So go to him, greet him and ask him for news of 'Ali."

'I blamed her for what had happened and warned her, saying: "My lady, fear for your life." This annoyed her and she shouted at me, so I left her and came to you. When I couldn't find you, I was afraid to go to 'Ali and so I stood waiting for a chance to ask you about him in order to find out how he is. Please now be good enough to accept some money from me. You must have borrowed some things from your friends which have now been lost, and you will need to replace them.' THE JEWELLER WENT ON:

I told her that I would do this willingly and I asked her to come with me. We walked together until we were near my house. She then told me to wait until she came back.

Night 167

Morning now dawned and Shahrazad broke off from what she had been allowed to say. Then, when it was the hundred and sixty-seventh night, SHE CONTINUED:

I have heard, O fortunate king, that the girl told the jeweller to wait until she came back. HE WENT ON:

When she did, she was carrying the money, which she handed over to me, asking me where we could meet. 'I shall go back home immediately,' I said, 'and for your sake I shall take in hand the difficult task of planning how to get you to 'Ali, for just at the moment this is not easy.' 'Tell me where I can come to you,' she said. 'In my house,' I told her, and she then said goodbye and went off.

I carried the money back home and, when I counted it, I found that it came to five thousand dinars. I gave some of this to my household and I compensated everyone who had lent me things. Then, taking my servants with me, I went off to my other house that had been plundered. I brought in masons, carpenters and builders, who restored it to its previous state, and I installed my old slave woman in it, forgetting what I had experienced. After that, I walked to 'Ali's house. When I got there, his servants came to me and said that their master had been looking for me day and night and that he had promised to free any slave who brought me to him. They had been going around searching for me, but they did not know where I lived. They added: 'Although our master has regained some strength, he alternates between consciousness and unconsciousness. When he is conscious, he talks of you and tells us that we must bring you to him, if only for a moment, and then he relapses into his coma.'

I went with a servant to 'Ali and found him unable to speak. I sat by his head and when he finally opened his eyes and saw me, he shed tears, welcoming me. I propped him up in a sitting position and then clasped him to my breast. 'Brother,' he said, 'you should know that since I took to my bed, this is the first time that I have sat up. I praise God for allowing me to see you.' I continued to support him until I had got him on to his feet and had made him walk a few steps, after which I changed his clothes and he took something to drink. All this was done in order to cheer him up, and when I saw signs of recovery, I told him of my encounter with the slave girl in such a way that no one else could hear me. 'Be of good heart,' I said, 'for I know what is wrong with you.' He smiled and I added: 'You will find nothing but the kind of happiness that will cure your sickness.'

He then ordered food to be brought, and when this had been done, he gestured to the servants and they left. 'Brother,' he said to me, 'have you seen my misfortune?' He then apologized, asking how I had been since last we met. I told him everything that had happened to me from beginning to end. This astonished him and he told his servants to fetch a number of things that he described. They brought in costly furnishings,

rugs and articles of gold and silver that totalled more than I had lost, all
of which he gave me and which I sent to my house. I spent the night
with him and when dawn broke, he said to me: 'Everything has an end
and love must end in death or union. I am nearer to death and I wish
that I had died before what has happened. Had it not been for God's
grace, we would have been dishonoured. I don't know what can rescue
me from my present plight and, if I did not fear God, I would hasten my
own death, for I know that I am like a bird in a cage, and that distress
is bound to kill me. But there is a fixed and appointed time for this.' He
then shed tears, complaining and reciting these verses:

> Enough for the lover are his flowing tears,
> And grief removes all his endurance.
> He used to hide the secrets he collected,
> But these have now been scattered by his eyes.

When he had finished, I told him that I proposed to go home, as the
slave girl might bring me news. 'Ali agreed to this, but told me to hurry
back and pass on to him anything I heard, adding: 'You can see the state
that I am in.' I then said goodbye to him and went off to my house.

Before I had properly sat down, the girl arrived, choking with tears.
When I asked her the reason for this, she said: 'Master, the thing that
we feared has happened to us. When I left you yesterday, I met my
mistress, who was in a rage with one of the two maids who were with
us that night. She ordered her to be beaten, and in her fear the girl ran
out, but was met and seized by one of the doorkeepers. He was going to
hand her back to her mistress, but she dropped some hints and, by
treating her gently, he got her to speak and she told him about our
adventure. Word reached the caliph and he gave orders that my mistress
and all her property were to be moved to his quarters. He has put her in
the charge of twenty eunuchs, and up till now he has not been to see her
and he has not told her the reason for this. I suspect, however, that it is
because of what he has heard. I fear for my own life, and in my confusion
I don't know what to do or what to contrive for myself or for her. She
has no one better or closer at keeping secrets than me.'

Night 168

Morning now dawned and Shahrazad broke off from what she had been allowed to say. Then, when it was the hundred and sixty-eighth night, SHE CONTINUED:

I have heard, O fortunate king, that the girl told the jeweller that Shams al-Nahar had no one closer or better at keeping secrets than her. She then said: 'Go quickly to tell 'Ali of this so that he can get ready and be on his guard, and then, if the matter comes out, we can make some plan to save ourselves.' THE JEWELLER WENT ON:

I was desperately worried, for, as far as I was concerned, the girl's news had turned the world black. She was on the point of leaving when I said to her: 'What do you advise? We have no time left.' 'My advice,' she replied, 'is for you to hurry over to 'Ali, if he is your friend and you want him to escape. It is up to you to bring him the news quickly without wasting time or worrying about the distance, while I restrict myself to sniffing out news.' She said goodbye to me and left, after which I got up and followed her out. I went to 'Ali and found him occupying himself with impossible hopes of union. When he saw how quickly I had come back, he commented on this, but I said: 'Patience; don't waste time with comments, and leave aside all other concerns, for something has happened that may cost you your wealth and your life.' When he heard this, he became a changed man in his alarm, saying: 'Brother, tell me what has happened.' I repeated the story to him, adding: 'If you stay here in your house until evening, you are a dead man.' He turned pale and his soul almost left his body, but then, pulling himself together again, he asked me to advise him what he should do. 'My advice is for you to take what money you can and those servants whom you can trust,' I said, 'and then to set off with me to some other land before the end of the day.' 'To hear is to obey,' he replied.

He then jumped up, but he was in a state of confusion and bewilderment, walking on at times and then falling down. He took with him what he could, made his excuses to his household and gave instructions to his servants. Then, taking with him three laden camels, he mounted his own beast. I did the same and we left secretly and in disguise. We continued on our way for the rest of that day and throughout the night, at the end of which we unloaded the camels and hobbled them. We were so tired that we were careless of our safety and fell asleep. Before we knew it, we were surrounded by robbers who took all we had with us and killed our servants when they tried to defend us. They then left us where we were, in the worst of states, with our goods plundered and all our beasts driven off.

After we got up, we walked until morning and arrived at a town, which we entered. We made for the mosque and went in, naked as we were, and sat there in a corner for the rest of the day. Night fell and we stayed there without food or drink, and the next day we performed the morning prayer and sat down again. A man then came in who greeted us and, having performed two *rak'as*, he turned to us and asked us if we were strangers. 'Yes,' we replied, 'and we were intercepted by robbers who took our clothes. We then came to this town, but we know nobody here with whom we could shelter.' 'Would you like to come home with me?' the man asked.

I said to 'Ali: 'Come on, let's go with him. This will save us from two dangers, the first being the fear that someone might come into this mosque and recognize us, leading to our disgrace. The second is that, being strangers here, we have no place of shelter.' 'Do as you please,' said 'Ali. The man then spoke to us again, saying: 'Do what I say, you poor men, and come with me to my house.' 'To hear is to obey,' I replied, at which he took off some of his clothes and gave them to us to wear, apologizing to us and treating us with kindness. We went with him to his house and, after he had knocked on the door, a little servant came and opened it. We followed the man as he went in and, on his instructions, a package was brought to us containing clothes, which we put on, and strips of muslin which we used as turbans. When we had sat down, a slave girl brought in a table of food which she put in front of us, telling us to eat. We ate a little, after which the table was removed.

We stayed there until nightfall, but then 'Ali sighed and said: 'Brother, I know for certain that I am going to die and I want to give you my last instructions. When you see that I am dead, take the news to my mother and tell her to come here to arrange for my mourning and to be present when my body is washed. Tell her to bear my loss with patience.' He then fell down in a faint, and when he had recovered, he heard a girl singing in the distance, chanting lines of poetry. He began to listen to her voice, sinking at times into unconsciousness and then recovering and weeping sorrowfully in his affliction. The girl was chanting these lines:

Separation hastened to make us part
After we had lived as neighbours in love and harmony.
Time's misfortunes have separated us;
Would that I knew when we shall meet again.
How bitter is separation after union;
Would that it did not inflict its harm on lovers.
The pangs of death last for a moment and then end,
But separation from the beloved stays in the heart.
If I could find a way to it,
I would give separation a taste of itself.

When 'Ali heard these lines, he gave a groan and his soul parted from
his body. Seeing that he was dead, I left his body in charge of the owner
of the house, telling him that I was going to Baghdad to bring the news
to the dead man's mother and his other relatives, so that they could
come to make preparations for the funeral. When I got to Baghdad, I
changed my clothes and then went to 'Ali's house. When his servants
saw me, they came up to me, questioning me about him, but I asked
them to get permission for me to go in to see his mother. After I had
been allowed in, I entered, greeted her and then said: 'It is God Who
controls the lives of mortals by His decree. There can be no escape from
His orders, and no one can die except through the permission of God in
accordance with his appointed fate.'

These words of mine led her to suspect that her son was dead. She
wept bitterly, saying: 'For God's sake, tell me – has my son died?' My
tears and the depth of my grief kept me from replying, and when she
saw the state I was in, she herself became choked with tears and fell
fainting to the ground. When she had recovered consciousness, she asked
what had happened to her son. 'May God magnify your reward for his
loss,' I said, and then I told her the whole story from beginning to end.
She asked whether he had left any instructions. 'Yes,' I said, and after
repeating what 'Ali had said, I told her to go quickly to make the funeral
arrangements. On hearing this, she again fainted, but when she had
recovered, she made up her mind to follow my recommendations. I
myself went off to my house, and while I was on my way there, thinking
about how handsome the young 'Ali had been, a woman came up to me
and took me by the hand.

Night 169

Morning now dawned and Shahrazad broke off from what she had been allowed to say. Then, when it was the hundred and sixty-ninth night, SHE CONTINUED:

I have heard, O fortunate king, that a woman came up to the jeweller and took him by the hand. When he looked at her, he saw that she was the slave girl who had been used as a messenger by Shams al-Nahar. THE JEWELLER WENT ON:

She was obviously broken-hearted and, on recognizing each other, we both wept. When we had come to my house, I asked her whether she knew what had happened to 'Ali. 'No, by God,' she answered, and so I told her about him. We were both in tears, but I then asked her about her mistress. She said: 'The Commander of the Faithful was so deeply in love with her that he would not listen to a word said against her and everything she had done he saw in a favourable light. "Shams al-Nahar, you are dear to me," he said to her, "and I shall stand by you in spite of your enemies." He then ordered gilded apartments with a pleasant room to be furnished for her, where she lived in luxury, enjoying great favour. It happened that one day, following his usual custom, he sat drinking in the presence of his concubines, who were seated according to their status. Shams al-Nahar was placed beside him, but her powers of endurance had gone and her state had grown worse. The caliph then told one of the girls to sing and, taking her lute, she tuned it, touched the strings and struck up a melody, chanting these lines:

> A caller summoned me to love, a call I answered,
> As tears wrote lines of passion on my cheek.
> It is as though these tears tell of our state,
> Revealing the hidden and hiding what is clear.
> Can I hope to keep a secret or conceal my love,
> When an excess of passion displays what I feel?
> My death is sweet when I lose those I love;
> Would that I knew what will be sweet for them when I am gone.

When Shams al-Nahar heard what the girl was singing, she could no longer sit up but collapsed in a faint. The caliph threw aside his wine cup and drew her to him. He called out and the slave girls raised a cry, but when he turned her over and tried to move her, he found that she was dead.

So bitter was his grief that on his orders all the utensils, the lutes and the other musical instruments in the room were broken. He carried the dead Shams al-Nahar into his own room and stayed with her for the rest of the night. When morning came, he made preparations for the funeral; the corpse was washed, shrouded and then buried, while the grief-stricken caliph asked no questions about what had been the matter with her.'

The girl then asked me to tell her when 'Ali's funeral was to take place so that she could be there when he was buried. I told her that I would be wherever she wanted to reach me, and then asked where I could find her and who would be able to get to her. She replied: 'On the day Shams al-Nahar died, the Commander of the Faithful freed her slave girls, including me, and we are staying by her tomb in such-and-such a place.' I accompanied her to the grave and, having visited it, I went on my way. I then waited for 'Ali's funeral procession and, when it came, I went out to join it together with the people of Baghdad. Among the women there I found the slave girl, who was displaying the most extreme symptoms of grief. There had been no longer funeral procession in Baghdad and the huge crowd kept following until we reached the cemetery, where we buried 'Ali, entrusting him to the mercy of Almighty God. I myself have not ceased to visit his grave and that of Shams al-Nahar.

'This is their story – may Almighty God have mercy on them both,' said Shahrazad. 'The tale, however, is not more remarkable than that of King Shahriman.' The king asked her about this.

Night 170

Morning now dawned and Shahrazad broke off from what she had been allowed to say. Then, when it was the hundred and seventieth night, SHE SAID:

I have heard, O fortunate king, that in the old days there was a king called Shahriman. He had a large army, together with servants and guards, but he was an old man whose strength was fading and he had no son. This caused him concern and, in his sorrow and anxiety, he complained to one of his viziers, to whom he said: 'I fear that on my death the kingdom will be ruined as I have no son to succeed me on the throne.' The vizier replied: 'It may be that God will yet bring something about, so entrust your affair to Him, O king, and address your prayers to Him.' The king got up, performed the ritual ablution and two *rak'as*, and invoked God in all sincerity. He then called his wife to bed and lay with her immediately. Through the power of Almighty God she conceived, and at the end of her months of pregnancy she gave birth to a boy, like the moon on the night it reaches the full. The delighted king named his son Qamar al-Zaman. On his orders, the city was adorned with decorations for seven days, drums were beaten and the good news was spread.

The child was provided with nurses, wet and dry, and brought up cosseted in luxury until he was fifteen years old. He was outstandingly handsome, well formed and shapely, and such was his father's love for him that he could not bear to be parted from him, by night or by day. His father complained to one of his viziers about this excessive love, saying: 'Vizier, I am afraid for my son, Qamar al-Zaman, lest Time bring misfortunes upon him, and I want to see him married during my lifetime.' 'Marriage is an honourable state,' replied the vizier, 'and it is right that while you live you should arrange for him to wed before you entrust him with authority.' On the king's orders, Qamar al-Zaman was brought in, bowing his head towards the ground out of respect for his father. 'Qamar al-Zaman,' said the king, 'I want to see you married, so that I can arrange your wedding celebrations while I am still alive.' 'Father,' replied the prince, 'I have no wish to marry and no inclination towards women. I have found much that has been written and said about their guile and treachery. One poet has written:

Ask me about women, for here I am
A doctor who knows their circumstances.
A man with white hair or one short of cash
Has no share left in their affection.

Another poet has said:

Disobey women, for that is true obedience to God;
The young man led by women will not prosper.
They will stop him from perfecting his virtues,
Even were he to spend a thousand years in study.'

When he had finished, he went on: 'Father, to marry is something that I shall never do, even if this costs me my life.' When the king heard what his son had to say, the light turned to darkness in his eyes and he was greatly distressed . . .

Night 171

Morning now dawned and Shahrazad broke off from what she had been allowed to say. Then, when it was the hundred and seventy-first night,
SHE CONTINUED:

I have heard, O fortunate king, that when the king heard what his son had to say, the light turned to darkness in his eyes and he was greatly distressed by his son's lack of obedience to him over the matter of his marriage. Because he loved him so dearly, however, he was unwilling to repeat his demand. Rather than angering him, he went up to him, showed him honour and treated him gently in such a way as to inspire affection.

While this was going on, Qamar al-Zaman was every day becoming more handsome, more graceful and more charming. King Shahriman waited patiently for his son to finish another full year, at the end of which he found that his eloquence and elegance had reached completion: his handsome form ravished the senses of all mankind; every breeze carried news of his grace; while his beauty was a seduction for lovers and a garden of perfection for the desirous. His speech was sweet; his face put the full moon to shame; the symmetry of his form, his elegance and charm made him resemble the branch of a *ban* tree or a bamboo shoot; his cheek might serve in place of a rose or a red anemone; and with his graceful qualities he was as the poet has described:

> When he appeared, people said: 'Blessed be God;
> Great is the Lord Who fashioned and formed him.
> He is the king of all the lovely ones,
> And they are all his subjects now.
> His saliva holds melted honey and his teeth form pearls.
> He is perfect and unique in loveliness,
> In which he leads all of mankind astray.
> Beauty has written on his cheek:
> "No one is beautiful but he."'

After another full year, his father summoned him and asked if he was prepared to listen to him. Out of awe and respect for his father he fell on the ground before him, saying: 'Father, how can I not listen to you when God has commanded me to be obedient and not disobey you?'
'My son,' said the king, 'know that I want to see you married so that I can arrange for your wedding during my lifetime, after which, before

my death, I shall make you ruler over my kingdom.' When Qamar
al-Zaman heard that, he bowed his head for a time and then said: 'Father,
this is something that I shall never do, even if it costs me my life. I know
that it is true that Almighty God has placed upon me an obligation to
obey you. In God's Name, then, I ask you not to impose the duty of
marriage on me, and do not think that I shall ever get married as long
as I live. I have read books written both by old writers and their suc-
cessors and studied the seductions, disasters and endless wiles to which
they were subjected by women, as well as the calamities with which they
were afflicted. How excellent are the poet's lines:

> Whoever is tricked by harlots can find no escape.
> He may construct a thousand forts of lead,
> But this will do no good, nor will his castles help.
> Women show treachery to all, both near or far,
> With their dyed fingers and their plaited hair.
> Their eyelids may be dark with kohl,
> But men choke on the draughts they pour.

Another poet has expressed it well in the lines:

> Even if women are called on to be chaste,
> They are carrion picked over by hovering vultures.
> One night they may tell you their secrets;
> Next day another owns their legs and wrists.
> They are an inn where you spend the night and go,
> Your place then taken by one you do not know.'

When the king heard what his son had to say and understood the
point of the lines, he returned no answer because of the strength of his
affection. Rather he showed him increased favours and the assembly was
immediately dismissed. When this had been done, the king summoned
his vizier for a private meeting. 'Vizier,' he said, 'tell me what I should
do about the matter of my son's marriage.'

Night 172

Morning now dawned and Shahrazad broke off from what she had been
allowed to say. Then, when it was the hundred and seventy-second night,
SHE CONTINUED:

I have heard, O fortunate king, that the king summoned his vizier for a private meeting. 'Vizier,' he said, 'tell me what I should do about the matter of my son's marriage. I asked for your advice about arranging for him to marry, and it was you who suggested that this should be done before I put him in charge of the kingdom. I have talked to him about marriage several times, but he has disobeyed me. So tell me what to do.' 'King,' said the vizier, 'wait for another year and when you next want to talk to him about this, don't do it in private but in a court session when all the emirs and viziers are present with your soldiers standing by. When they are all there, then send for your son, and when he comes, tell him in the presence of the viziers, state officials and commanders that you want him to marry. He is bound to feel abashed in those circumstances and will not be able to disobey you while they are there.'

The king was delighted by what the vizier had said, thinking that the advice was good and rewarding him with a splendid robe of honour. He gave Qamar al-Zaman a year's grace, during every day of which he grew more handsome, splendid and perfect. When he was almost twenty years old, God had clothed him in the robe of beauty and crowned him with perfection. His eyes were more bewitching than Harut's and the coquetry of his glance more seductive than Taghut's. His cheeks gleamed red; his eyelids put sharp swords to shame; the whiteness of his forehead resembled the gleaming moon; while his black hair was like the dark of night. His waist was more slender than the thread of a girdle; his buttocks were heavier than sand dunes, causing his sides to quiver and his waist to complain. His beauties bewildered mankind, and he was as one of the poets has described:

I would swear by his cheek and by his laughing mouth,
By the arrows that he scatters through his magic,
The softness of his sides and his sharp glance,
The whiteness of his forehead and the blackness of his hair.
I swear by his eyebrow which drives sleep from my eyes,
And overwhelms me when he forbids or commands,
By the scorpion locks that curl above his temples,
Seeking to murder lovers when he deserts them,
By the roses of his cheeks, the myrtle of his down,
The carnelian of his smiling mouth and by his pearly teeth.
I swear by the sweetness of his scent and the liquid of his mouth,
That puts to shame the grapes that are pressed for wine,

By buttocks that quiver whether he moves or stays still,
By his slender waist and by his generous hand,
His truthful tongue, his noble lineage and his exalted rank.
Musk is the residue of his cheek's mole,
And from him is the scent of perfume spread.
The shining sun is his inferior,
And the crescent moon a clipping of his fingernail.

King Shahriman followed the vizier's advice for another year, until
the arrival of a festival.

Night 173

Morning now dawned and Shahrazad broke off from what she had been
allowed to say. Then, when it was the hundred and seventy-third night,
SHE CONTINUED:

I have heard, O fortunate king, that Shahriman followed the vizier's
advice for another year, until the arrival of a festival. This was a court
occasion, when the emirs, viziers, court officials, soldiers and commanders filled the king's audience chamber. Qamar al-Zaman was summoned and when he came he kissed the ground thrice in front of his
father and then stood before him with his hands folded behind his back.
'Know, my son,' said the king, 'that I have summoned you here on this
occasion before this assembly, attended, as it is, by all the state officials,
for the purpose of giving you an order, which you must not disobey. My
order is that you marry. I want to marry you to a royal princess and to
arrange for your wedding celebrations before I die.'

When Qamar al-Zaman heard what the king said, he bent his head
towards the ground for a while and then, raising it again, he looked at
his father. Juvenile folly and youthful ignorance led him to say: 'I shall
never marry, even if I die for it. You are an old man and feeble-witted.
Did you not ask me twice before to marry and I refused?' He then spread
out his hands, tucked up his sleeves as he stood before his father, and in
his angry and agitated state, he poured out a flood of words. His father
was ashamed and embarrassed that this had happened in the presence
of the state officials and the soldiers who were there for the festival. In
an outburst of regal energy, he shouted at his son, terrifying him, and he
then called to the mamluks who were standing before him. 'Seize him,'

he cried, and they rushed up to take hold of the prince, whom they then brought to his father. He ordered them to pinion him, which they did, and he was brought, hanging his head in fear, with his forehead and face beaded with sweat. He was deeply ashamed. His father poured abuse on him and said: 'Damn you, you bastard, you child of fornication, how dare you answer me like this in the presence of my men? Until now, no one has taught you manners . . .'

Night 174

Morning now dawned and Shahrazad broke off from what she had been allowed to say. Then, when it was the hundred and seventy-fourth night, SHE CONTINUED:

I have heard, O fortunate king, that Shahriman said to his son: 'How dare you answer me like this in the presence of my men? Until now, no one has taught you manners. Do you not realize that even if a common man had done this, it would have been disgraceful?'

He ordered the mamluks to unfetter the prince but to confine him in one of the towers of the palace. They took him to an ancient tower with a ruined hall in which there was an old and dilapidated well. They cleaned out the hall, sweeping the flagstones, and they set a couch for the prince on which they spread a mattress and a rug. They gave him a pillow and brought a large lantern, as well as a candle, since even in daylight the place was dark. Then they brought him in and posted a eunuch at the door. Qamar al-Zaman threw himself on the couch, broken-spirited and sad. He was full of self-reproach and he repented of how he had treated his father at a time when repentance was of no use. 'May God curse marriage,' he said, 'and curse girls and treacherous women. I wish that I had listened to my father and married, as that would have been better for me than this prison.'

So much for Qamar al-Zaman, but as for his father, he remained seated on his royal throne until evening. Then he had a private meeting with the vizier to whom he said: 'Vizier, it is you who, through your advice, caused this whole quarrel between me and my son, so what do you advise me to do now?' 'O king,' replied the vizier, 'leave your son in prison for fifteen days before having him brought to you. If you then order him to marry, he will not disobey you.'

Night 175

Morning now dawned and Shahrazad broke off from what she had been allowed to say. Then, when it was the hundred and seventy-fifth night, SHE CONTINUED:

I have heard, O fortunate king, that the vizier told the king: 'Leave your son in prison for fifteen days, and then have him brought to you. If you then order him to marry, he will not disobey you.' The king accepted this advice, but spent the night in a state of concern for his only son, whom he loved dearly. He had been in the habit of never falling asleep without putting his arm under his son's neck, and so that night, in his disturbed state, he started to twist from side to side as though he were lying on burning branches. Such was his anxiety that all night long he could not sleep. His eyes filled with tears as he recited the lines:

My night was long as the slanderers slept.
It is enough for you to have a heart terrified by parting.
After a long night of care, I say:
'Light of dawn, are you never to return?'

From another poet, he quoted:

When I saw that his eyes could not detect the Pleiades,
That the Pole Star had poured sleep over him
And that the stars of the Bear were dressed in mourning,
I knew that day would never dawn for him again.

So much for King Shahriman, but as for Qamar al-Zaman, when night fell, the eunuch brought him the lamp and lit a candle which he put in a candlestick. He also produced some food. Qamar al-Zaman ate a little, but started to reproach himself for the unmannerly way in which he had treated his father. 'Don't you know,' he said to himself, 'that a man is dependent on his tongue and that it is his tongue which plunges him into danger?' His eyes filled with tears and he wept broken-heartedly for what he had done, repenting to the full of how he had treated his father and reciting:

A man dies through a slip of his tongue,
And not through a slip of the foot.

A slip of the tongue costs him his head,
While the other can be cured at leisure.

After he had finished eating, he wanted to wash his hands, and this
the mamluk did for him. He then got up, performed the ritual ablution
and, after having completed the sunset and the evening prayers, he sat
down . . .

Night 176

Morning now dawned and Shahrazad broke off from what she had been
allowed to say. Then, when it was the hundred and seventy-sixth night,
SHE CONTINUED:

I have heard, O fortunate king, that when the prince had performed
the sunset and the evening prayers, he sat down on the couch and recited
from the Quran the *suras* of 'The Cow', 'The Family of 'Imran', 'Ya Sin',
'The Merciful', 'Blessed is the King', 'Al-Ikhlas'* and the two Talismans.
He ended with an invocation of blessing, seeking God's protection and
taking refuge with Him. He then lay down to sleep on a mattress covered
on both sides with Ma'dani satin and filled with Iraqi silk, while under
his head was a pillow stuffed with ostrich feathers. Before doing this, he
undressed, taking off his outer clothes and his drawers, leaving himself
in a fine waxed shirt, while on his head there was a blue covering from
Marv. He looked that night like a fourteen-day moon and, covered with
a silk sheet, he slept with a lighted lantern at his feet and a lighted candle
at his head.

He remained asleep for the first third of the night, not knowing what
lay hidden for him in the future and what God, the Knower of the
unseen, had decreed for him. As fate and destiny had ordained, that
ancient tower and the hall had long been left deserted. In the hall was a
well of Roman workmanship, in which lived a *jinniya*, of the stock of
Iblis the damned, whose name was Maimuna and who was the daughter
of al-Dimriyat, one of the famous kings of the *jinn*.

* 'Sincerity', cf. p. 772.

Night 177

Morning now dawned and Shahrazad broke off from what she had been allowed to say. Then, when it was the hundred and seventy-seventh night, SHE CONTINUED:

I have heard, O fortunate king, that the *jinniya*'s name was Maimuna and that she was the daughter of al-Dimriyat, one of the famous kings of the *jinn*. When Qamar al-Zaman had been asleep for the first part of the night, this Maimuna came out of her well on her way to overhear what the angels were saying in heaven. When she reached the top of the well, she noticed that, unusually, there was a light in the tower. She had been there for very many years and she told herself that this was not something that she had ever seen before. Filled with astonishment and realizing that there must be a reason for it, she went towards the light. On finding that it was coming from the hall, she entered and found the eunuch asleep by the door. Then, in the hall, she discovered that a couch had been placed on which lay a sleeping man with a lighted candle at his head and a lighted lamp at his feet. She was surprised to see the light and little by little she moved forwards towards it. Then, folding her wings, she stood beside the couch and removed the sheet from Qamar al-Zaman's face.

When she looked at him, she stayed for a time, amazed by his beauty and grace, finding the candlelight dimmed by the radiance of his face. Sleep flirted amorously with his eyes and their black pupils; his cheeks were red, his eyelids languorous and his eyebrows curved, while from him spread a sweet scent of musk. He was as the poet described:

I kissed him, and those twin seductions,
The pupils of his eyes, darkened while his cheeks grew red.
If censurers claim he has a match in loveliness,
Do you, my heart, tell them to produce him.

At the sight of him, Maimuna glorified God, saying: 'Blessed is God, the best of creators,' for she was one of the believing *jinn*. She stayed for a while looking at his face and reciting the formula: 'There is no god but God,' lost in appreciation of his beauty. 'I shall not injure him,' she said to herself, 'nor shall I allow any harm to come to him. This beautiful face deserves to be stared at so that those who look may glorify God. But how could his family have brought themselves to put him in so desolate a place? If a *marid* came now, he would kill him.' She bent over Qamar al-Zaman, kissed him between the eyes and, pulling the sheet back over his face, she covered him with it. Then, unfolding her wings, she soared up above the hall and continued to fly on upwards through the air until she had nearly reached the lowest heaven.

At that point, she heard the noise of wings beating in the air. She flew towards the source of the sound and when she got near she found that this was an *'ifrit* named Dahnash. She swooped down on him like a hawk and when he felt her grasp and recognized that she was Maimuna, daughter of the king of the *jinn*, he trembled with fear and appealed to her for protection, saying: 'By the greatest Name of God, to which honour is due, and by the noblest talisman engraved on the ring of Solomon, I call on you to treat me gently and to do me no harm.' When she heard this, she felt sympathy for him and said: 'This is a great oath with which you have conjured me, you accursed creature, but I shall not let you go until you tell me where you have come from just now.' 'Lady,' Dahnash replied, 'I have come from the farthest region of China, from within the islands. I shall tell you of a wonder that I have seen tonight, and if you find that I am telling the truth, then let me go on my way and write me a note in your own hand saying that I am your freed slave. That would mean that no one from among the races of the *jinn* could obstruct me, whether they fly, live on land or dive under the sea.' 'What was it you saw tonight, you damned liar?' asked Maimuna. 'Tell me the truth, for you are trying to escape from me by lying. I swear by what is engraved on the stone of the seal of Solomon, son of David, on both of whom be peace, that if you don't speak the truth, I shall tear out your feathers with my own hands, rip your skin to shreds and break your bones.'

The *'ifrit* agreed to this condition . . .

Night 178

Morning now dawned and Shahrazad broke off from what she had been allowed to say. Then, when it was the hundred and seventy-eighth night, SHE CONTINUED:

I have heard, O fortunate king, that the *'ifrit* accepted the condition and said: 'Know, lady, that I went out tonight from the Chinese islands, the lands of King al-Ghayur, the ruler of the islands, the seas and the seven castles. I caught sight of a daughter of his, who is more beautiful than any other creature created by God in this age. I cannot describe her for you, as my tongue is incapable of finding the right words, but I can just about tell you of some of her qualities. Her hair is black like the days of parting and separation, and her face is radiant as the days of union. She is as the poet has well described:

> One night she spread three tresses of her hair,
> And there were then four nights that could be seen.
> She turned to look up at the heavenly moon,
> Letting me see two moons at the same time.

She has a nose like a polished sword blade, cheekbones like purple wine over cheeks like red anemones and lips like coral and carnelian. Her saliva is sweeter than wine and its taste would quench the torture of hellfire. Her tongue is controlled by ample intelligence and is prompt to answer. Her bosom is a seduction for those who see it – glory be to the One Who created and formed it! Attached to it are two smoothly rounded arms, as the lovesick poet has described:

> Were these arms not held in place by bracelets,
> They would flow from her sleeves like streams.

She has two breasts like caskets of ivory, from which the sun and the moon draw light. Her stomach with its folded wrinkles is like a roll of embroidered Egyptian linen, with folds like a rolled-up scroll, ending in a waist that is more slender than imagination can dream of. This is set on buttocks like sand dunes that hinder her when she wants to get up and keep her awake when she wants to sleep. As the poet has said:

> Her buttocks are joined to a delicate waist;
> They play the tyrant over me and over her.
> The thought of them can bring me to a halt;
> They force her to sit back when she wants to get up.

They are supported by two smooth thighs and two legs like columns of pearl, all carried on two dainty feet, pointed like spearheads, the work of the Watcher, the Judge. I wondered how, being so small, they could carry what was above them. I will cut short my description of her for fear of going on too long.'

Night 179

Morning now dawned and Shahrazad broke off from what she had been allowed to say. Then, when it was the hundred and seventy-ninth night, SHE CONTINUED:

I have heard, O fortunate king, that the *'ifrit* told Maimuna: 'I will cut short my description of her for fear of going on too long.' Maimuna was astonished to hear what he had to say about the girl's beauty and grace. The *'ifrit* went on: 'The girl's father is a powerful king, a daring rider who is ready to plunge into battle by night or by day, fearless of death. He is an oppressive tyrant with irresistible force, the master of armies, provinces, islands, cities and lands. His name is King al-Ghayur, the lord of the islands, the seas and the seven castles. He is exceedingly fond of his daughter, the girl whom I have described to you, and because of his love for her he collected money from the other kings and used it to build her seven castles, each of a different kind. The first is of crystal, the second of marble, the third of Chinese iron, the fourth of precious stones and jewels, the fifth of bricks, coloured stones and gems, the sixth of silver and the seventh of gold. All seven are filled with splendid furnishings of silk, vessels of gold and silver and every kind of utensil that kings might need. Al-Ghayur told his daughter to live in each one of these castles for a certain period each year, before moving to another. Her name is Princess Budur, and when news of her beauty spread among the lands, all the kings sent to her father to ask for her hand. He consulted her and tried to tempt her to marry, but she disliked the idea and told him: "I have no intention of marrying. As a princess, I am a mistress of power and authority, ruling over the people, and I have no wish for a man to rule over me."

'The more she rejected marriage, the more eager her suitors became. So it was that all the kings of the inner islands of China sent her father gifts and presents, together with letters asking for her hand. He consulted her again and again about this, but she would not listen to him and, losing her temper, she said angrily: "Father, if you mention marriage to me once more, I shall go to my room, take a sword and fix its hilt in the ground. Then I shall put its point into my stomach and lean against it until it comes out from my back, so killing me."

'When her father heard this, the light became darkness in his eyes and he was consumed with anxiety for her as he was afraid lest she kill herself. He could not think what to do about her or about the kings who were her suitors and so he told her: "If you insist on refusing to marry, you must stop going to and fro." The princess was brought to a room and kept in seclusion there in the charge of ten elderly duennas. She was not allowed to go to her seven castles, as her father had made it plain that he was angry with her. He sent letters to all the kings telling them that she had been struck by madness and had been kept in seclusion for a year.'

Dahnash went on to add: 'I go to look at her every night, lady, so as to enjoy the sight of her face, and while she is asleep, I kiss her between the eyes, but such is my love for her that I do her no harm or injury, nor do I mount her. She has the charm of youth as well as radiant beauty, so that everyone who sees her is prepared to guard her jealously. I entreat you, lady, to come back with me and to look at her beauty and grace and the symmetry of her figure. Then, if you want, you can punish me or keep me captive, for you have authority over me.' He then lowered his head towards the ground and folded his wings.

Maimuna laughed at his words and spat in his face. 'What is this girl you talk about? She's nothing but a urine scraper. Bah! I thought that you had something wonderful or remarkable to tell, you damned *'ifrit*. What would you say if you saw my own darling? If, even in a dream, you saw the man I saw tonight, you would become paralysed and start to drool.' 'What is the story of this young man?' asked Dahnash. 'The same thing happened to him as happened to the girl you've been talking about,' Maimuna answered. 'His father told him many times to marry but he refused. His father then became angry at his disobedience and imprisoned him in the tower in which I live, and when I came out tonight I saw him.' 'Show him to me, lady,' said Dahnash, 'so that I can see whether his beauty is greater than that of my darling, Princess Budur, or not, as I don't believe that there is anyone to match her in this age.' 'You are lying, you damned creature, you foulest of *marids* and most despicable of devils!' exclaimed Maimuna. 'I am sure that my own darling has no equal in these lands . . .'

Night 180

Morning now dawned and Shahrazad broke off from what she had been allowed to say. Then, when it was the hundred and eightieth night, SHE CONTINUED:

I have heard, O fortunate king, that Maimuna said to the *'ifrit*: 'I am sure that my darling has no equal in these lands. Are you mad that you try to compare yours to mine?' 'For God's sake, lady,' said Dahnash, 'come with me and look at mine and then I shall go back with you and look at yours.' 'That is what we must do, you accursed creature,' said Maimuna, 'as you are a deceitful devil, but we shall only go with each other for a bet or on a condition. If it turns out that this girl whom you love and eulogize is lovelier than the youth I mentioned, whom I for my part love and praise, then you will have won, but if my darling is lovelier, then you will have lost the bet to me.'

Dahnash accepted the proposal and asked Maimuna to go with him to the islands. 'No,' she said. 'The place where my darling is is nearer. It is here beneath us, so come down with me to look at him and we can then go to see your princess.' 'To hear is to obey,' said Dahnash. They both then flew down and went into the hall in the tower. Maimuna made Dahnash stand beside the couch and then, stretching out her hand, she lifted the silk sheet from the face of Prince Qamar al-Zaman. The radiance of his face shone and gleamed brightly, and after looking at him, Maimuna immediately turned to Dahnash and said: 'Look, you damned creature, and don't be the foulest of madmen. This youth holds a fascination for women.' Dahnash looked and kept staring for some time, but then he shook his head and said: 'Lady, you are to be excused, but there is one point to be made against you and that is that the female is not like the male. By God's truth, however, this darling of yours most closely resembles mine in beauty and grace, splendour and perfection, so much so that it is as though they have both been cast in the same mould of loveliness.'

When Maimuna heard what he said, the light in her eyes became dark and she struck him on the head with her wing, giving him a blow so violent that it almost killed him. 'Damned creature,' she said, 'I swear by the radiance of his glorious face that you are to go at once and lift up the girl whom you love and bring her here quickly so that we can put the two together and look at them as they sleep next to each other. We can then see which is the more beautiful. If you don't do what I tell you this instant, I'll burn you with my fire, shoot you with my sparks, tear you to pieces and throw you into the desert as a lesson for all mankind.' 'I shall do that for you, lady,' said Dahnash, 'as I know that my beloved is sweeter and more beautiful.'

He flew off immediately and Maimuna went with him to watch over him. They were away for some time and when they came back they were carrying the girl. She was wearing an exquisite Venetian chemise with a double border of gold wonderfully embroidered. At the ends of the sleeves, these lines could be read:

> Three things have kept her from visiting us,
> Fearing, as she does, the watcher and those choked with envy:
> The radiance of her forehead, her clinking ornaments,
> And the scent of ambergris left clinging to her cloak.
> She could hide her forehead with the end of her sleeve,
> And take off ornaments, but what about the scent?

The two carried her in and put her down, stretching her out beside Qamar al-Zaman . . .

Night 181

Morning now dawned and Shahrazad broke off from what she had been allowed to say. Then, when it was the hundred and eighty-first night, SHE CONTINUED:

I have heard, O fortunate king, that the two carried her in and put her down, stretching her out beside Qamar al-Zaman on the couch. They uncovered both their faces and found that there was so great a resemblance between them that it looked as though they were twins or full brother and sister. They were a seduction even for the pious, as the poet has clearly expressed:

> Heart, do not fall in love with a single lovely one;
> Coquetry will bewilder you, and forced humility.
> Rather, love them all, and you will find,
> If one turns back, another will come on.

Another poet has written:

I saw two sleeping on the ground:
I would have loved them even if it were on my eyelids that they lay.

Dahnash and Maimuna looked at the pair. 'Good!' exclaimed
Dahnash. 'By God, lady, my beloved is the fairer.' 'No, mine is,' said
Maimuna. 'Damn you, Dahnash, are you blind in both eye and heart
that you can't distinguish between lean and fat? Are you trying to hide
the truth? Don't you see his beauty and the symmetry of his form? Listen
to what I have to say about my beloved and if you truly love yours, then
produce its match.' She then planted a number of kisses between Qamar
al-Zaman's eyes, reciting this poem:

Why am I so harshly abused because of you?
How can I forget you, who are a slender branch?
Your kohl-dark eye spreads magic;
There is no way of escape from 'Udhri love.
Your Turkish glances wound my inner parts
As no sharp polished sword could do.
A load of passion for you weighs me down,
While in my weakness even my shirt is now too heavy.
You know my passion for you and my lovesickness
Is natural; to love another would be by constraint.
If my heart were like yours, I would not find myself
With a body that is now thin as your waist.
Alas for a moon among mankind,
With all the attributes of grace and loveliness!
Those who find fault with love may ask:
'Who is it who has caused you your distress?'
'Find a description,' is what I reply.
Harsh heart, learn from this figure how to bend;
You may then turn to pity and compassion.
My prince, you may be grateful but your eye
Assaults me and your eyebrow knows no justice.
They lie who say all loveliness was found
In Joseph; how many Josephs does your beauty hold?
The *jinn* fear to confront me, but when I
Meet you, it is my heart that trembles.
In fear, I try to turn away from you;
The more I try, the greater grows my love.

Your hair is black, your forehead radiant;
Your eyes are dark; you have a slender form.

When Dahnash heard Maimuna's poem about her beloved, he was
delighted and filled with admiration.

Night 182

Morning now dawned and Shahrazad broke off from what she had been
allowed to say. Then, when it was the hundred and eighty-second night,
SHE CONTINUED:

I have heard, O fortunate king, that when Dahnash heard Maimuna's
poem about her beloved, he was moved to delight and said: 'How
excellently you have described your beloved in these lines. I myself must
do my very best to say something about mine.' He went up to Princess
Budur and kissed her between the eyes and then, looking at both her
and at Maimuna, although he lacked poetic sensitivity, he recited the
following poem:

They harshly blame my love for the lovely one,
But in their ignorance they are unjust.
Be generous; grant union to the slave of love,
Who perishes if you hold back from him.
I am afflicted by a tearful love,
And blood-red tears flow from my eyes.
It is no wonder I am moved by love;
The wonder is that, after you have gone,
My body then can still be recognized.
May I be kept from union if I have suspected you,
Or if my heart has tired of love, acting reluctantly.

He added other lines:

My food is the sight of their camping grounds at the waste's edge;
I lie here slain; the wadi is far away.
The wine of passion has made me drunk;
My tears dance to the camel driver's song.
I seek the happiness of union and for me
Happiness must be found in the full moons of Su'ad.
I do not know of which of these three to complain –

I have counted them up, so listen to my counting –
Her glance that is like a sword, her figure like a lance,
Or the locks covering her temples that are chain mail.
I asked townsfolk and nomads where she was. She said:
'I am here in your heart; look there and you will see.'
But I replied: 'Where is my heart?'

'Well done, Dahnash,' said Maimuna when she had heard this, 'but which is the lovelier of the two?' 'My beloved Budur is more beautiful than yours,' said Dahnash. 'That is a lie, damn you,' said Maimuna. 'Mine is lovelier than yours.' 'No, mine is lovelier,' retorted Dahnash, and they did not stop quarrelling with one another, until Maimuna shouted at Dahnash and was about to attack him. At that, he humbled himself before her, softened his language and said: 'You must not find the truth hard to bear. Put aside both our claims, for each of us bears witness that our own beloved is lovelier. Let us turn from this and look for someone who can settle the point between us and on whose word we can rely.'

Maimuna agreed to this. She struck the ground with the palm of her hand and out came an 'ifrit – one-eyed, hunchbacked, scabby, with eyes set lengthways in his face. There were seven horns on his head; he had four locks of hair that dangled down to his ankles; his hands were like winnowing forks and his legs like ships' masts. He had nails like lions' claws and hooves like those of a wild ass. When he emerged and caught sight of Maimuna, he kissed the ground before her and stood with his hands folded behind his back. 'What do you want, my lady, daughter of the king?' he asked. 'Qashqash,' she said, 'I want you to rule on a dispute between me and this damned Dahnash,' and she then told him the whole story from beginning to end. Qashqash stared at the faces of the young man and the girl and saw that they were embracing one another in their sleep, each with a wrist under the other's neck. They were equally matched in beauty and grace, and looking at them, Qashqash was filled with wonder at their loveliness. Having gazed for a long while at the two of them, he turned to Maimuna and Dahnash and recited these lines:

Visit your love; take no heed of the envious,
Who will not help you in affairs of love.
God in His mercy creates no finer sight
Than of two lovers lying on one bed

In one another's arms, clothed in contentment,
Pillowed on one another's wrists and arms.
If in your lifetime you find one true friend,
How good a friend is this; live for that one alone.
When hearts are joined in love,
The envious are striking on cold iron.
You who blame lovers for their love,
Have you the power to cure the sick at heart?
God in Your mercy, let us meet
Before death comes, if only by one day.

Qashqash then turned to Maimuna and Dahnash and said: 'If you want
the truth, I have to say that these two are an exact match in the splendour
of their beauty, grace and perfection, and they cannot be separated on
the grounds that one is male and the other female. I have another idea,
which is to wake each of them in turn without the other knowing.
Whichever then burns with love for the other must be the less beautiful.'
'That is a good plan,' said Maimuna. 'I agree,' said Dahnash, and at that
he took the shape of a flea and bit Qamar al-Zaman, who was startled
out of his sleep.

Night 183

Morning now dawned and Shahrazad broke off from what she had been
allowed to say. Then, when it was the hundred and eighty-third night,
SHE CONTINUED:

I have heard, O fortunate king, that Dahnash took the shape of a flea
and bit Qamar al-Zaman, who was startled out of his sleep. As he
scratched the painful bite on his neck, he turned on his side and there he
found a sleeper whose breath was purer than pungent musk, with a body
softer than butter. In his astonishment, he sat up and when he looked at
who it was who was sleeping beside him, he found a girl like a splendid
pearl or a well-built dome. She was slim and straight, like the letter *alif*,
not yet of full height, but with swelling breasts and rosy cheeks, as the
poet has described:

Four things have never been combined
Without shedding my blood and harming me –

A radiant forehead, hair as dark as night,
And rosy cheeks together with a gleaming smile.

Another poet has written:

She was like a moon when she appeared;
She bent as a branch of the *ban* tree,
Scented with ambergris, with eyes of a gazelle.
It seems that sorrow is enamoured of my heart;
When the beloved goes, it finds its time of union.

When Qamar al-Zaman saw the beauty and grace of Princess Budur as she lay asleep by his side, he noticed that she was wearing a Venetian chemise but no drawers, while her head was covered by a kerchief embroidered with gold and studded with gems, while in her ears were earrings that gleamed like stars, and around her neck a necklace of incomparable pearls such as no king could afford. He gazed at her in bewilderment, until his natural heat was kindled and God filled him with a desire to lie with her. 'What God wills comes about,' he said to himself, 'while what He does not, does not.' He stretched out his hand to her, turned her over and opened the collar of her chemise, so that he could see her bosom with her breasts like two caskets of ivory. His love for her deepened and, such was the strength of his desire, that he tried unsuccessfully to wake her up, as Dahnash had put her into a deep sleep. He began to shake her, saying: 'Wake up, my darling, and see who I am, for I am Qamar al-Zaman,' but she neither woke nor moved her head. He thought over the matter for a time and said to himself: 'If my guess is right, this must be the girl whom my father wants me to marry and for the past three years I have kept refusing. God willing, when morning comes I shall tell him to marry me to her so that I may possess her . . .'

Night 184

Morning now dawned and Shahrazad broke off from what she had been allowed to say. Then, when it was the hundred and eighty-fourth night,
SHE CONTINUED:

I have heard, O fortunate king, that the prince said to himself: 'When morning comes I shall tell my father to marry me to her so that I may possess her, and I shall let no more than half a day go by before I am united with her and enjoy her beauty.' He then bent over to kiss her, and while Maimuna shuddered in embarrassment, Dahnash was jubilant.

Then, just as Qamar al-Zaman was about to kiss the princess on the lips, he felt shame before Almighty God. He averted his head and turned away his face, saying to himself: 'Patience.' Thinking the matter over, he said: 'I must wait, as it may be that when my father became angry with me and imprisoned me here, he brought this girl for me and told her to sleep beside me in order to test me, and he may have told her that when I tried to rouse her she should not wake up too quickly. He would then ask her what I did with her, or it may be that he is hidden somewhere where he can see me without being seen, watching everything that I do with her. Then in the morning he will reproach me and say: "How can you say that you don't want to marry when you have been kissing and embracing that girl?" I shall hold myself back from her lest my father find out. The right thing is for me not to touch her or look at her. But I shall take something from her as a keepsake to remember her by, so that we may have something that will stay as a token between us.' He then lifted her hand and took from her little finger a seal ring of great value, as its stone was a precious jewel, inscribed with these lines:

Do not think I have forgotten your compact,
However long you may have turned from me.
Master, turn generously to me,
So I may kiss your mouth and both your cheeks.
By God, I shall never part from you,
Even if you stray across love's boundaries.

After he had taken the ring from the princess's finger, Qamar al-Zaman put it on his own, after which he turned his back on her and went to sleep. Maimuna was pleased when she saw that, saying to Dahnash and Qashqash: 'Did you see how chastely my dear Qamar al-Zaman treated this girl? This is part of his perfection, for in spite of her loveliness he neither embraced nor kissed her, and far from stretching out his hand towards her, he turned his back on her and fell asleep.' 'Yes,' said the other two, 'we saw how admirably he acted.'

At that point, Maimuna turned herself into a flea. She went into the clothes of Dahnash's beloved, Budur, and walked from her leg up to her thigh and then, going on, she bit her on a spot four inches below her navel. Budur opened her eyes and sat up. Beside her she saw a young man, breathing deeply in his sleep, one of the most beautiful of God's creatures, with eyes that would put to shame the lovely houris. His sweet-tasting saliva was a better cure than any theriac; his mouth was like the ring of Solomon; his lips were coloured like coral; and his cheeks were like red anemones. He fitted the description of the poet:

He consoled me for the loss of Zainab and Nawar,
With rosy cheeks growing the myrtle of down.
I love a tunic-wearing fawn,
And have no thoughts to love a girl with bracelets.
He is my public and my private friend;
She is my friend only within my house.
You blame me for deserting Zainab and Hind;
My excuse is clear as dawn to the night traveller.
Do you want me to be the prisoner of a girl,
Herself a captive behind walls and out of reach?

At the sight of Qamar al-Zaman, the princess fell passionately in love . . .

Night 185

Morning now dawned and Shahrazad broke off from what she had been allowed to say. Then, when it was the hundred and eighty-fifth night, SHE CONTINUED:

I have heard, O fortunate king, that at the sight of Qamar al-Zaman, the princess fell passionately in love and said to herself: 'Oh the disgrace! This young man is an unknown stranger; what is he doing sleeping next to me in the same bed?' She looked at him again and saw how handsome he was. 'By God,' she said, 'this is a beautiful young man. To my shame, my heart is almost torn in pieces through love for him. Had I known that it was he who had asked my father for my hand, rather than rejecting him I would have married him and enjoyed his beauty.' Then, looking at his face, she said: 'Master, light of my eyes, wake up and savour my loveliness.' She shook him with her hand, but Maimuna had sent sleep down on him, pressing upon his head with her wings, so that he did not wake. The princess went on shaking him and urging him to obey her: 'Wake from your sleep. Look at the narcissus and the verdure. Enjoy my belly and my navel; throw yourself on me and play with me from now until morning. By God, my master, rouse up; prop yourself on the pillow and stop sleeping.' Qamar al-Zaman made no reply but remained sunk in sleep.

'Ah, ah!' exclaimed the princess. 'Your beauty and grace, together with your powers of coquetry, have made you conceited, but, handsome as you are, I too am beautiful. What are you doing? Did they tell you to turn away from me or was it my father, that ill-omened old man, who told you, and stopped you, making you swear that you would say nothing to me tonight?'

Qamar al-Zaman neither opened his mouth nor stirred. The love that God had put into the princess's heart increased, and the glance that she cast on him was followed by a thousand sighs. Her heart fluttered, her stomach churned and her limbs trembled. 'My master,' she said to him, 'speak to me, my darling. Say something to me, my love. Answer me; tell me your name, for you have stolen away my wits.' All the time, however, Qamar al-Zaman was sunk in sleep, making no reply. The princess sighed and said: 'Ah, ah, why are you so proud?' She shook him and kissed his hand, and then, seeing her ring on his little finger, she moaned and said, with a gesture of passion: 'Oh, oh! By God, you are my darling! You love me but you seem to be turning away from me in coquetry, although you came to me while I was asleep, my darling. I don't know what you did to me, but you took my ring and I shall not take it back from your finger.' She opened the collar of his shirt, and leaning over him, she kissed him and then stretched out an exploring hand to see whether he had anything with him that she could take. When she found nothing, her hand went down to his chest and then, thanks to the smoothness of his skin, it slipped to his belly. From his navel it passed to his penis, at which her heart shook with palpitations and her lust was stirred, as lust is stronger in women than in men. This was followed by a feeling of shame and, removing the seal ring from his finger, she put it on her own as a replacement for hers. She kissed his mouth and his hands and then every part of his body, after which she took him in her arms and hugged him. With one of her arms beneath his neck and the other beneath his armpit, she embraced him and then fell asleep by his side.

Night 186

Morning now dawned and Shahrazad broke off from what she had been allowed to say. Then, when it was the hundred and eighty-sixth night,
SHE CONTINUED:

I have heard, O fortunate king, that Budur slept beside Qamar al-

Zaman. Looking on, Maimuna said to Dahnash: 'You damned creature, did you see my darling's pride and coquetry, and the passion that yours showed for him? There is no doubt that mine is more beautiful than yours, but nevertheless I forgive you.' She then wrote him a certificate setting him free, after which she turned to Qashqash and told him to help Dahnash carry the princess back home, as the night was almost gone. 'To hear is to obey,' said Qashqash, and he and Dahnash then lifted up the princess from beneath and flew home with her, setting her down on her own bed. Maimuna was left alone, gazing at the sleeping Qamar al-Zaman until only a little of the night was left, after which she went on her way.

When dawn broke, Qamar al-Zaman woke from his sleep and turned to the right and to the left, but could not find the girl. 'What is this?' he said to himself. 'It seemed as though my father was encouraging me to marry the girl who was with me but he has then removed her secretly in order to make me more eager to marry.' He then swore at the eunuch who was sleeping at the door, ordering him to get up. The eunuch did so, bemused by sleep, and brought in a ewer and a basin. Qamar al-Zaman got up, relieved himself in the privy, and then, after coming out, he performed the ritual ablution and the morning prayer, after which he sat praising Almighty God.

When he looked up, he found the eunuch standing in attendance on him. 'Sawab,' he said, 'who was it who came while I was asleep and took the girl from my side?' 'What girl, master?' asked the eunuch. 'The girl who was sleeping with me last night,' replied the prince. The eunuch was uneasy, saying: 'By God, there was no girl with you, or anyone else. How could a girl have got in when I was sleeping by the door and the door was locked? I swear to God, master, that no one, male or female, came in to you.' 'You are lying, you ill-omened slave!' cried the prince. 'Is it for you to deceive me and to hide from me where the girl who slept with me last night has gone when it was you who took her from me?' The eunuch repeated in his agitation that he had seen neither girl nor boy, at which Qamar al-Zaman exclaimed angrily: 'You damned fellow, my father has taught you trickery! Come here!' The eunuch went up to him and Qamar al-Zaman seized him by the collar and threw him to the ground. He farted and Qamar al-Zaman kneeled on him before taking him and throttling him until he lost consciousness. He then picked him up and, after tying him to the well rope, he let him down as far as the water, this being in the bitter cold of winter. After he had been dipped in the water, Qamar al-Zaman hoisted him up, before letting him down again. He went on doing this, to the accompaniment of calls for help, shrieks and cries, saying as he did so: 'You damned creature, I shall only take you out of this well when you tell me the whole story of the girl and let me know who took her while I slept.'

Night 187

Morning now dawned and Shahrazad broke off from what she had been allowed to say. Then, when it was the hundred and eighty-seventh night, SHE CONTINUED:

I have heard, O fortunate king, that Qamar al-Zaman told the eunuch: 'I shall only take you out of this well when you tell me the whole story of the girl and let me know who took her while I slept.' The eunuch, staring death in the face, replied: 'Master, let me go. I shall speak the truth and tell you the whole story.' At that, Qamar al-Zaman pulled him out of the well and released him. He was almost lost to the world because of the harshness of his sufferings, having been tortured by cold, immersion, fear of drowning, and beating. He was trembling like a storm-tossed reed; his teeth were clenched together; his clothes were soaked; and his body was filthy and scarred by the sides of the well. So revolting was his condition that Qamar al-Zaman, seeing him, found it hard to bear. Now lying on the ground, the eunuch said: 'Master, let me go and take off my clothes, wring them out and spread them out in the sun. I can then put on fresh clothes and come back to you quickly to tell you what really happened.' 'You evil slave,' said Qamar al-Zaman, 'had you not been confronted by death, you would never have acknowledged the truth or said what you did. Go off and do what you have to, but come back to me quickly and tell me what really happened.'

The eunuch left, scarcely believing that he had managed to escape. He kept running and then falling and then getting up again until he came into the presence of King Shahriman. He found the king seated with the vizier at his side and they were talking about the prince. The king was telling the vizier that, because of his concern for his son, he had not been able to sleep on the preceding night, adding: 'I'm afraid that he may come to harm in this old tower, and what useful purpose will it serve to keep him imprisoned?' 'There is no need for you to fear for him,' replied the vizier. 'Nothing will happen to him, so leave him there for a month until he is in a more malleable frame of mind, his spirit is broken and he comes to his senses.'

While they were talking, in came the eunuch in the state that has been described, which alarmed the king. The eunuch said: 'My lord the king, your son has lost his wits and gone mad. He tortured me, leaving me in the state that you can see. He kept on saying that a girl had spent the night with him before leaving secretly; he demanded to know where she was, insisting that I tell him about her and let him know who took her off. I saw neither girl nor boy; the door was locked all night long and I was sleeping beside it with the key beneath my head. I opened it for him this morning with my own hand.'

When the king heard this, he cried out in grief for his son and became furiously angry with the vizier, holding him responsible for what had happened. 'Get up,' he said, 'and find out what has happened to my son and what has affected his mind.' The vizier got up and went out, stumbling over his robes in his fear lest the king do him an injury. He went with the eunuch to the tower, the sun having now risen, and when he entered, he found Qamar al-Zaman seated on the couch, reciting the Quran. The vizier greeted him, sat down beside him and said: 'My master, this evil eunuch has told us something that has disturbed and disquieted us, making the king angry.' 'What did he tell you about me that disturbed my father, while, in fact, it was I whom he disturbed?' asked Qamar al-Zaman. 'He came to us in a sorry state,' explained the vizier, 'and he told your father something about you that you could never have done, inventing for us a cock and bull story that should never have been told about you. May God preserve your youth, your sound mind and your eloquent tongue, and far be it from you that you should commit any foul act.' 'What did this ill-omened slave say about me?' asked the prince. The vizier replied: 'He told us that your mind had gone and that you had claimed to him that you had had a girl with you last night. You had then demanded that he tell you where she had gone and you had tortured him.'

When Qamar al-Zaman heard this, he became furiously angry. 'It is clear to me,' he told the vizier, 'that it was you who instructed the eunuch to act as he did . . .'

Night 188

Morning now dawned and Shahrazad broke off from what she had been allowed to say. Then, when it was the hundred and eighty-eighth night, SHE CONTINUED:

I have heard, O fortunate king, that when Qamar al-Zaman heard this, he became furiously angry. 'It is clear to me,' he told the vizier, 'that it was you who instructed the eunuch to act as he did and you stopped him from telling me about the girl who slept with me last night. You are more intelligent than the eunuch, vizier, so tell me at once where the girl who slept in my arms last night has gone. It was you who sent her to me and told her to do this. She and I slept until morning and when I woke up, she was nowhere to be found. So where is she now?' 'My lord Qamar al-Zaman, may the Name of God encompass you. I swear by God that we sent no one to you last night. You slept alone, with the door locked on the other side and the eunuch sleeping behind it. No one came in, neither a girl nor anyone else. Take a firm grasp of your reason; return to your senses, master, and don't disturb yourself.'

This infuriated Qamar al-Zaman, who said: 'Vizier, I love that beautiful girl with the dark eyes and the rosy cheeks, whom I embraced all last night.' The vizier was astonished at his words and asked whether he had seen her with his own eyes when he was awake or in a dream. 'You ill-omened old man,' replied the prince, 'do you suppose that I saw her with my ears? Of course I saw her with my eyes while I was awake! I turned her over with my hand and stayed awake with her for half the night, looking with delight at her beauty and her grace, together with her enticing charms. But you had taught her and instructed her not to speak to me, so she pretended to be asleep and I slept by her side until morning. Then, when I woke up, I couldn't find her.' 'Master,' said the vizier, 'it may be that you saw this in a confused dream or fantasy while you slept, either as a result of eating a certain mixture of foods or as a temptation brought by evil spirits.' 'Ill-omened old man,' replied Qamar al-Zaman, 'how dare you make fun of me and tell me that this might have been a confused dream, when this eunuch confirmed to me that the girl was here and said that he would come back to me immediately and tell me her story?'

He got up straight away and, advancing on the vizier, he seized his beard in his hand. The beard was a long one and Qamar al-Zaman twisted it round his hand and used it to drag the vizier down from the couch, after which he threw him to the ground. So violently did he tear out hairs from the old man's beard that the vizier felt that his last moment had come. The prince kept on kicking him, punching him in the chest and ribs and striking the back of his neck with his hands until the vizier was close to death. He then said to himself: 'If the eunuch saved himself from this mad boy by telling a lie, I have a better right than he to do that and to tell a lie of my own, for otherwise he will kill me. I'll lie to him and save myself, for he is mad; there is no doubt about it.'

Turning to the prince, he said: 'Don't blame me, master, for it was your father who instructed me to tell you about this girl, but you have left me weak and exhausted and in pain from this beating. I am an old man with no strength left to endure blows. Give me a little respite so that I can tell you about the girl.' When the prince heard this, he stopped striking the vizier. 'Why didn't you tell me this before you were ignominiously beaten?' he said. 'Get up, then, you ill-omened old man and tell me about her.' 'Are you asking about the girl with the lovely face and fine figure?' said the vizier. 'Yes,' said the prince. 'Tell me who brought her to me, made her sleep by my side and who then removed her from me at night. Where has she gone now, so that I may go to her myself? If it was my father, the king, who did this, using this lovely girl to tempt me into marriage, I am willing to marry her so as to free myself from this distress. He can only have done all this because of my refusal to marry, and this I am now willing, and more than willing, to do. So tell that to my father and advise him to marry me to that girl. I want no one else; she is the only love of my heart. Get up and hurry to my father; advise him to speed on the marriage and then bring me back a reply immediately.' 'I will,' said the vizier, scarcely believing that he had escaped from the prince's hands. He then left him and went out of the tower, stumbling as he walked because of the violence of his fear and not stopping until he had come into the king's presence.

Night 189

Morning now dawned and Shahrazad broke off from what she had been allowed to say. Then, when it was the hundred and eighty-ninth night, SHE CONTINUED:

I have heard, O fortunate king, that the vizier left the tower and hurried on until he came into the presence of King Shahriman. 'What has happened to you, vizier?' asked the king when he arrived. 'Who has injured you? Why is it that I see you in a state of confusion, coming to me in fear?' 'I bring you good news, your majesty,' said the vizier, and when the king asked him what this was, he answered: 'Your son, Qamar al-Zaman, has lost his wits and has gone mad.' On hearing this, the light in the king's eyes became darkness and he told the vizier to explain what kind of madness this was. 'To hear is to obey,' replied the vizier and he explained what had happened, telling the king of his encounter with Qamar al-Zaman. 'In return for your good news of my son's madness,' said the king, 'I bring you good news that your happiness will come to an end and your head will be cut off, you most disastrous of viziers and vilest of emirs. It is you, I know, who are the cause of my son's condition, thanks to your counsel and the wretchedly faulty advice that you have given me from start to finish. By God, if any harm or madness affects my son, I shall bring catastrophe down on you by having you nailed to the dome of the palace.'

The king then got to his feet and took the vizier to the tower, where he went in to visit his son. When his father entered, Qamar al-Zaman jumped to his feet, quickly getting up from the couch on which he had been sitting. He kissed his father's hands and then, standing back, he bowed his head towards the ground, standing before his father with his arms folded behind his back. He stood like that for a time, and then lifted his head to look at his father, with tears falling from his eyes and running down his cheeks. He then recited these lines:

If in the past I sinned against you,
And if I have done some wrong,
I repent of my fault, and your forgiveness
Encompasses the wrongdoer when he asks for pardon.

At this, the king embraced his son and kissed him between the eyes, making him sit beside him on the couch. He then turned to the vizier and, looking at him angrily, he said: 'Dog of a vizier, how can you tell such tales of my son and frighten me about him?' He turned to Qamar al-Zaman and asked: 'My son, what day is this?' 'Today is Saturday,' answered the prince. 'Tomorrow is Sunday, followed by Monday, Tuesday, Wednesday, Thursday and Friday.' 'My son,' said the king, 'praise be to God that your mind is sound. What, then, is the Arabic name for this present month?' 'Dhu'l-Qa'da,' replied Qamar al-Zaman, 'which is followed by Dhu'l-Hijja, and then by al-Muharram, followed by Safar,

Rabi' al-awwal, Rabi' al-akhir, Jumada al-ula, Jumada al-akhira, Rajab, then Sha'ban, Ramadan, and then Shawwal.'

When the king heard this, he was delighted. He spat in the vizier's face, saying: 'You evil old man, how can you claim that my son has gone mad? If anyone is mad it is you.' The vizier shook his head and was about to speak, but then it struck him that it might be better to see what would happen. The king then asked his son: 'What is this that you told the eunuch and the vizier about sleeping with a pretty girl last night? What is this girl you mentioned?' Qamar al-Zaman laughed at this. 'Father,' he replied, 'I don't have the strength to put up with any more mockery. Don't say another word, as I am tired of what you are doing to me. You can be sure that I am willing to marry, but on condition that you marry me to the girl who slept with me last night. I know for certain that it was you who sent her to me and you who made me desire her. You then sent for her before dawn and took her away from me.'

'May God's Name encompass you, my son, and may your mind be saved from madness . . .'

Night 190

Morning now dawned and Shahrazad broke off from what she had been allowed to say. Then, when it was the hundred and ninetieth night, SHE CONTINUED:

I have heard, O fortunate king, that King Shahriman said: 'May God's Name encompass you, my son, and may your mind be saved from madness. What is this about a girl whom you say I sent to you last night and then had removed before dawn? I swear by God, my son, that I know nothing about this and I ask you in His name to tell me whether that was a confused dream or a fantasy prompted by something you ate. You spent the night obsessed with the thought of marriage, which put delusions into your head. May God damn marriage and the time of marriage, and damn the man who gave this advice! There is no doubt at all that it was this that upset your constitution and so you dreamt that a pretty girl was embracing you, and thought that you actually did see her. All this was a confused dream.' 'Stop this talk,' said Qamar al-Zaman, 'and swear to me by God, the Creator, the Omniscient, Who crushes tyrants and destroys emperors, that you know nothing about this girl or where she is.' 'By the truth of the Omnipotent God, the God of Moses and Abraham,' replied the king, 'I have neither knowledge nor information about this. It was only a muddled dream that you saw in your sleep.'

'I shall show you by analogy that this happened when I was awake,' said Qamar al-Zaman.

Night 191

Morning now dawned and Shahrazad broke off from what she had been allowed to say. Then, when it was the hundred and ninety-first night, SHE CONTINUED:

I have heard, O fortunate king, that the prince told his father: 'I shall show you by analogy that this happened when I was awake. Let me ask you whether anyone has dreamt that he was fighting in a furious battle and, on waking, found a bloody sword in his hand?' 'No, by God, my son,' replied the king. 'This has never happened.' 'Then I shall tell you what happened to me,' said Qamar al-Zaman. 'Last night I seemed to wake at midnight and found a girl sleeping beside me, whose shape and form were like mine. I hugged her and turned her over with my hands. I took her ring and put it on my finger, after which I took off my own ring and put it on hers, and then I went to sleep beside her. It was shame that I felt with regard to you that kept me from her and I was afraid that you might have sent her to test me and be hiding somewhere to see what I would do to her. Because of this feeling of shame, I was too embarrassed to kiss her on the mouth, and I thought that you were trying to fill me with a desire to marry. When I woke in the morning, I could see no trace of her nor find out anything about her. It was after that that I had my encounters with the eunuch and the vizier. How can this have been a false dream, when the affair of the ring is true? Had it not been for the ring, I would have thought it a dream, but here is her ring on my little finger. Look at it, father, and see how much it is worth.'

He handed the ring to his father, who took it, examined it and turned it over. 'There is something of great significance and importance about this,' he said, returning it to his son. 'And there is something strange about your experience last night with that girl, although I don't know where she came from. But the cause of all this trouble is the vizier. For God's sake, then, my son, show patience until He frees you from this and brings you the happiest of relief. As one of the poets has said:

Perhaps Time may pull on its reins
And bring good luck, for Time is changeable.
My hopes will happily be fulfilled, my needs accomplished,
And after hardships will come ease.

I am now certain, my son, that you are not mad, but yours is a strange tale and none but God Almighty will be able to shed light on it.' 'As a favour to me, father,' said Qamar al-Zaman, 'search for this girl on my behalf and bring her to me quickly, or else I shall die of grief and no one will know of my death.' Then, in a show of emotion, he turned to his father and recited these lines:

If your promised union was a lie,
At least join with the longing lover in his sleep or visit him.
She said: 'How can my phantom visit the eyelids
Of a young man from whom sleep is banned and kept away?'

When he had finished his poem, Qamar al-Zaman turned to his father humbly and dejectedly, and with tears in his eyes, he went on . . .

Night 192

Morning now dawned and Shahrazad broke off from what she had been allowed to say. Then, when it was the hundred and ninety-second night, SHE CONTINUED:

I have heard, O fortunate king, that when Qamar al-Zaman had recited these lines to his father, he wept, complained, moaned and, from a wounded heart, he went on:

Beware of her eyes; she is a sorceress –
None can escape whom she targets with her glance.
Do not be deceived by her soft words;
Wine overcomes the wits.
So tender is her skin that were a rose to touch her cheek,
She would weep and rain tear drops from her eyes.
Were a zephyr to pass by the country where she slept,
It would be scented that night as it left.
Her necklaces complain of the jangling of her belt,
But on her wrists the bracelets make no sound.
Her anklets long to kiss her earrings,

And to the eyes of union her secrets are made clear.
A censurer finds no excuse for my love,
But of what use are eyes that cannot see?
Censurer, God shame you, for you are unfair;
The beauty of this gazelle can deflect sight.

When he had finished his poem, the vizier said to the king: 'King of the age, how long are you going to sit with your son, inaccessible to your troops? It may be that if you stay away from your officers of state, things will go wrong with the administration of your kingdom. If there are a number of different wounds on the body, it is the most dangerous of them that the sensible man first treats. My advice is that you should move your son from here to the palace pavilion overlooking the sea. You can shut yourself away there with him, provided that you set aside two days each week, Mondays and Thursdays, for court ceremonial, when you can be approached by the emirs, viziers, chamberlains, deputies and state officials, together with the leading men of the kingdom and the rest of your troops and your subjects. They will be able to make their presentations to you and you can settle their affairs, judging between them, taking, giving, ordering and forbidding. For the rest of the week, you can stay with your son, and this can go on until God sends the two of you relief. Don't think yourself safe from the disasters of Time and the blows of fate. The wise man is always on his guard; how well has the poet expressed it:

When Time was good to you, you thought well of it,
With no fear of the evil fate might bring.
The nights kept peace with you; you were deceived,
For trouble comes when they are undisturbed.
O people, if you were helped once by Time,
It still is prudent to take care.'

When the king heard what the vizier had to say, he considered this to be good and useful advice and it had the effect of making him fear that things might go wrong with the administration of his kingdom. He got up immediately and gave orders that his son was to be moved from the tower to the pavilion in the palace overlooking the sea. The palace itself was surrounded by water and could only be approached along a causeway twenty cubits wide. All around it were windows that looked out on to the sea; its floor was surfaced with coloured marble; its roof was painted with a variety of the most gorgeous paints and embellished with gold and lapis lazuli. Splendid silk furnishings and embroidered rugs were spread out for the prince. The walls were covered with the best of embroideries and there were hangings studded with gems. In this pavilion a couch of juniper wood was placed for him, set with pearls and jewels.

The prince took his seat on this, but because of the extent of his concern and love for the girl, his colour changed, his body grew thinner, he neither ate, drank nor slept, and he looked like a man who had been ill for twenty years. His father sat by his head, plunged into the deepest sorrow, while on Mondays and Thursdays he would permit the emirs, chamberlains, deputies, state officials, soldiers and citizens to come into his presence. On entering, they would present their services and stay with him until the end of the day, when they would go on their way. Afterwards, the king would return to his son in the pavilion, not leaving him by night or by day, and this is how things continued for some time.

So much for Qamar al-Zaman, son of King Shahriman, but as for Princess Budur, daughter of King al-Ghayur, lord of the islands and of the seven castles, after the *jinn* had carried her and put her back in her bed, she went on sleeping until dawn. When she woke, she sat up and turned to the right and to the left, but could not see the young man who had lain in her arms. Her heart fluttered, her wits deserted her, and the loud cry she uttered woke all her slave girls, nurses and duennas. When they came in, the senior among them went up to her and asked: 'What has happened to you, lady?' 'You ill-omened old woman,' she replied, 'where is my darling, the handsome young man who slept in my arms last night? Tell me, where has he gone?' When her duenna heard this, the light turned to darkness in her eyes and she was terrified lest her mistress do her an injury. 'My Lady Budur,' she said, 'what is this filthy talk?' 'Damn you, you ill-omened old woman!' said Budur. 'Where is my love, the young man with the radiant face, the fine physique, the black eyes and the joining eyebrows, who slept with me last night from evening until nearly dawn?' 'By God,' answered the old woman, 'I have not seen any young man or anyone else. Don't joke with me like this; it goes beyond all bounds and might cost us our lives, for if it came to your father's ears, who could save us from him?'

Night 193

Morning now dawned and Shahrazad broke off from what she had been allowed to say. Then, when it was the hundred and ninety-third night, SHE CONTINUED:

I have heard, O fortunate king, that the duenna said: 'My lady, don't joke with me like this; it goes beyond all bounds and might cost us our lives, for if it came to your father's ears, who could save us from him?' 'There was a young man sleeping with me last night,' insisted the princess, 'and he was one of the most handsome of men.' 'May you keep your wits,' said the old woman. 'There was nobody with you here last night.'

At that point, the princess looked at her hand and found on her finger Qamar al-Zaman's ring, while she could not find her own. She said to her duenna: 'Damn you, you miserable traitress! Do you lie to me and tell me that there was nobody here with me last night, perjuring yourself before God?' 'By God,' replied the duenna, 'I have not lied to you or perjured myself.' Budur in a fury then drew a sword that she had by her and with this she struck the woman and killed her. At that, the eunuch, the slave girls and the king's concubines cried out against her and, going to her father, they told him of the state that she was in. He went immediately to see his daughter and asked her what the matter was. 'Father,' she asked, 'where is the young man who slept beside me last night?' Then she went out of her mind and started to roll her eyes right and left, after which she tore her robe from top to bottom. When her father saw this, he told the slave girls to restrain her, which they did, fettering her and placing an iron chain round her neck which was fastened to the palace window. They then left her.

So much for her, but as for her father, King al-Ghayur, when he saw what had happened to his daughter, his heart was constricted by sorrow, as his love for her meant that he could not easily deal with the situation. He had the doctors, astrologers and devisers of talismans brought to him, and he then promised his daughter's hand in marriage together with half of his kingdom to whoever could cure her, although he added: 'If anyone approaches her but fails in this, I will cut off his head and fix it to the palace gate.' Those who did fail were executed and their heads fixed to the gate until the princess had cost forty doctors their heads and forty astrologers had been crucified. No one would approach her any longer, no doctor was capable of curing her, and the problem baffled the wise men and the masters of talismans.

As for the princess, she was suffering from an excess of passion and was ravaged by the pangs of love, as a result of which she shed tears and recited:

> You who are my moon, my love for you is my antagonist;
> Your memory keeps me company in the dark of night.
> I pass the night with fire burning within my ribs,
> Its heat rivalling the fire of hell.
> I am afflicted by an excess of burning passion
> Whose torture has become excruciating for me.

She then sighed and went on:

> I send greetings to lovers, wherever they may be,
> And my wishes are directed towards my love.
> My greetings to them are not those of one who says farewell;
> They are frequent and their numbers still increase.
> I love you and I love your lands,
> But I am far from that which I desire.

When the princess had finished her recitation, she wept until her eyes became inflamed and her cheeks changed colour, and she stayed like that for three years.

Princess Budur had a foster brother named Marzuwan who had been absent all this time on a journey to the farthest parts of the lands. His affection for the princess was greater than the love of brothers and when he came back, he went to his mother and asked her about his sister. 'My son,' replied his mother, 'your sister has gone mad and for three years she has had an iron chain around her neck, as none of the doctors or the wise men have been able to cure her.' When Marzuwan heard this, he said: 'I must go to see her in the hope of finding out what is wrong with her, so that I may be able to cure her.' His mother agreed to this, but told him to wait until next day to give her time to think of a way to help him.

She then walked to Budur's palace and met the eunuch who was acting as doorkeeper, to whom she gave a present. She told him: 'I have a married daughter who was brought up with Princess Budur. When Budur suffered this misfortune, my daughter felt for her, and I want you, of your kindness, to let her come to visit her for an hour and then to go back home without anyone knowing about it.' 'That could only be done at night,' said the eunuch, 'but when the king leaves after his visit to his daughter, you may take her in.'

The old woman kissed the eunuch's hand and went home. She waited until the following evening, and then, when the time had come, she got up immediately and took her son Marzuwan, whom she had dressed in women's clothes. Holding his hand in hers, she brought him to the palace, going on until she had taken him to the eunuch after the king had left Budur's room. When the eunuch saw her, he stood up and told her to go in, but not to sit there too long. The old woman took her son in, and when he saw the state in which Budur was, he greeted her after his mother had removed his woman's dress. He then brought out some books that he had with him and, after lighting a candle, he recited some formulae of exorcism. Budur looked at him and, recognizing him, she said: 'We have heard no news of you, brother, since you went on your travels.' 'That is true,' he replied, 'but God has brought me back safely. I was going to make a second trip but I was stopped by what I heard about you. I was so distressed that I have come to see whether I can rescue you from this condition.' 'Brother,' she said, 'do you suppose that what has come over me is madness?' 'Yes,' he said, to which she replied: 'By God, it is not that but, rather, it is as the poet put it:

> They said: "Your beloved has driven you mad."
> I told them: "Only the mad can savour life's delight.
> The lover will never recover while he lives,
> And love will instantly overthrow the maddened lover.
> Yes, I am mad, so bring me the one who caused my madness,
> And if he cures it, then do not blame me."'

Realizing that she was in love, Marzuwan said: 'Tell me the story of what has happened to you, as I may be able to do something to help you.'

Night 194

Morning now dawned and Shahrazad broke off from what she had been allowed to say. Then, when it was the hundred and ninety-fourth night, SHE CONTINUED:

I have heard, O fortunate king, that Marzuwan told Budur: 'Tell me the story of what has happened to you, as it may be that God will enable me to to rescue you.'

'Listen to my tale, then, brother,' said Budur. 'I woke from my sleep in the last third of the night and when I sat up, I saw beside me a young man of indescribable beauty, like a branch of the *ban* tree or a shoot of bamboo. I thought that it must have been my father who had told him to come in order to tempt me, for he had tried to induce me to marry when the kings had asked him for my hand and I had refused. It was this suspicion that kept me from waking the young man up, for I was afraid that if I did anything or embraced him, he might tell my father. Then, in the morning, I found his ring on my finger in place of my own, which he must have taken from me. This is my story and the reason for my madness. From the moment that I saw him, my heart has been his and because of the depth of my love and my passion, I have not tasted sleep or concerned myself with anything apart from tears, weeping and the reciting of poetry by night and by day.' Then, through her tears, she recited these lines:

> Since I fell in love, are there pleasures to be enjoyed,
> While that gazelle is pasturing on lovers' hearts?
> He sets no store by lovers' blood;
> In him the heart of the emaciated lover melts away.
> Because of him, I am jealous of my eyes and thoughts,
> And one part of me keeps watch over another.
> The arrows of his eyelids strike and pierce the heart.
> Shall I see my beloved before my death,
> While in this world I still have some life left?
> I hide away his secret but my tears
> Betray my love, of which the watcher learns.
> The nearness of his union is far from me;
> While he is distant, memories are close.

The princess then said to Marzuwan: 'Brother, see what you can do to help me in my misfortune.' For a time, he kept his head bent towards the ground, not knowing, in his astonishment, what to do. He then looked up and said: 'I am sure that all this really happened to you, but the affair of the young man baffles me. So I shall explore all the lands to seek a cure for you. It may be that God will allow me to succeed, but you will have to be patient and not become anxious.' He then took his leave of her, urging her to remain steadfast, and as he left, she recited these lines:

Distant you may be, but your phantom comes
As a familiar visitor to my heart,
And wishes bring you close; the lightning flash
Is slow when set against perceptive thought.
Do not stay far from me, light of my eyes,
For if you do, no light can then anoint them.

Marzuwan walked to his mother's house, where he slept that night. In the morning, he made his preparations for travel, moving from city to city and from island to island for a whole month, before reaching a city called al-Tayrab. He walked around it, sniffing out news, in the hope of finding a cure for the princess. Up till then, whenever he entered a city or passed by one, the reports he heard were that she had gone mad. In al-Tayrab, he was told that Qamar al-Zaman, King Shahriman's son, was ill and was affected by a melancholy madness. Marzuwan asked the name of his city and was told that he lived in the Khalidan Islands, a full month's journey by sea from al-Tayrab, while by land the journey would take six months. Accordingly, he embarked on a ship that was sailing there, and after a month's voyage with a favourable wind the ship was close to its destination. Just then, however, when all that it had to do was to put to shore, a storm wind blew up, which dismasted it and tore the sails which collapsed into the sea, so that the ship with all its contents was overturned.

Night 195

Morning now dawned and Shahrazad broke off from what she had been allowed to say. Then, when it was the hundred and ninety-fifth night, SHE CONTINUED:

I have heard, O fortunate king, that when this happened, every man tried to save himself, while as for Marzuwan, he was swept on by the waves until he came beneath Qamar al-Zaman's royal palace. As had been fated, this was the day on which Shahriman's courtiers and state officials were in the habit of meeting to present their services. The king himself was seated with his son's head in his lap, while a eunuch was driving away the flies. For two days past, Qamar al-Zaman had not spoken or eaten, nor had he drunk anything, and he was now thinner than a spindle. The vizier was standing at his feet near the window that

overlooked the sea. He looked out and saw Marzuwan struggling on the
point of death with the current. Feeling pity for him, the vizier went up
to the king and said: 'Your majesty, I ask your permission to go down
to the palace courtyard and open the gate in order to rescue a drowning
man and save him from his difficulties. If I do this, it may be that God
will save your son from his own predicament.' 'Vizier,' replied the king,
'my son has suffered enough for you and because of you. If you bring in
this drowning man, he will discover what is going on here and, on seeing
the state my son is in, he will gloat over my misfortune. I swear by God
that if he comes and sees my son and then goes away and tells our secrets
to anyone at all, I shall cut off your head before I cut off his, for it is you
who are responsible for what has happened to us from beginning to end.
But do what you want.'

The vizier went and opened the postern gate of the palace leading to
the sea, and after taking twenty paces down the causeway, he went out
into the sea. Seeing Marzuwan on the point of death, he reached out his
hand towards him, grasped him by the hair and pulled him out of the
water. Marzuwan was half dead, his belly full of water and his eyes
protruding, but the vizier waited until he had recovered consciousness and then took off his clothes, giving him others to wear and providing him with one of his servant's turbans. He then said: 'Know that I
have saved you from drowning, so take care not to cause my death and
your own.'

Night 196

Morning now dawned and Shahrazad broke off from what she had been
allowed to say. Then, when it was the hundred and ninety-sixth night,
SHE CONTINUED:

I have heard, O fortunate king, that when the vizier saved Marzuwan,
he said: 'Know that I have saved you from drowning, so take care not
to cause my death and your own.' 'How is that?' asked Marzuwan. 'You
are now about to go up and move among emirs and viziers, all of whom
are keeping silent and saying nothing for the sake of the king's son,
Qamar al-Zaman.' When Marzuwan heard him mention Qamar al-
Zaman, he realized that this was the man about whom he had been
hearing throughout the lands and for whom he had come in search. He
pretended ignorance, however, asking the vizier who Qamar al-Zaman

might be. The vizier replied: 'He is the son of King Shahriman; he is ill and bedridden, but restless, and he neither eats, drinks or sleeps by night or by day. He is close to his end; we have despaired of his life and are certain that he is about to die. Take care not to look at him for any length of time or to look anywhere except at your feet, for otherwise your life and mine will be forfeited.' 'By God, vizier,' said Marzuwan, 'I hope that, of your kindness, you will tell me why it is that this young man whom you have described for me has fallen into such a state.' 'I don't know the reason,' said the vizier, 'but three years ago his father asked him to marry and he refused. His father became angry and shut him up and then next morning he claimed that, while lying in bed, he had seen by his side a lovely girl of indescribable beauty. He told us that he had exchanged the ring on her finger for his own. We don't know the real meaning of this tale, but for God's sake, my son, when you come up to the palace with me, don't look at the prince but go on your way, for the king is very angry with me.'

'By God,' said Marzuwan to himself, 'this is the one I have been looking for.' He then followed the vizier up to the palace, where the vizier took his seat at Qamar al-Zaman's feet. Marzuwan walked straight up to stand in front of him, gazing at him. The vizier almost died of fear and started to look at Marzuwan and to wink at him, trying to get him to go. Marzuwan, for his part, ignored him and kept on looking until he was certain that here was the object of his search.

Night 197

Morning now dawned and Shahrazad broke off from what she had been allowed to say. Then, when it was the hundred and ninety-seventh night, SHE CONTINUED:

I have heard, O fortunate king, that Marzuwan looked at Qamar al-Zaman and realized that here was the object of his search. 'Glory be to God,' he exclaimed, 'who has given him a figure like hers, cheeks like her cheeks and the same complexion.' Qamar al-Zaman opened his eyes and listened to what Marzuwan was saying, and when Marzuwan saw this, he recited the following verses:

You are emotional, I see, a prey to melodious sorrow,
    Swayed by accounts of beauties.

Is it love or arrows that have wounded you?
For you are like a wounded man.
Come, then, pour wine and sing for me
Of Sulaima, Rabab, Tan'um.
There is many a sun produced by grapes
Whose zodiacal sign is in the depth of the wine jug,
Rising with the cupbearer and setting in my mouth.
I am jealous of the clothes she wears,
Which she puts on over her tender skin.
I envy cups that kiss her mouth,
Set to her lips, where kisses should be placed.
You should not think a sword thrust has killed me;
I have been shot by arrows from her eyes.
We met and I found that the fingers she had dyed
Were like the juice pressed from the 'andam tree.
I asked: 'Did you dye your hands after I left?
Is this how to reward the passionate slave of love?'
She spoke, and kindled in my inmost parts the fire of love,
With the words of one who does not hide her love:
'By your life, this is not dye that I have used;
Do not suspect me falsely, without cause.
When I saw you set off, you who had been
My arm, my hand, my wrist, I wept
With tears of blood at parting, wiping them with my hand,
And so my fingers became red with blood.'
Had I forestalled her tears with my own tears of love,
I would have cured myself before feeling remorse,
But she wept first. Her weeping prompted mine;
I said: 'Merit is his who is the first to act.
Do not blame me for loving her since, by love's truth,
It is for her I endure suffering.
I have wept for one whose face beauty adorns,
Who has no match among all of mankind.
Hers is the wisdom of Luqman, the beauty of Joseph,
David's melodious voice, the chastity of Mary;
Mine are the sorrows of Jacob and Jonah's distress,
Job's tribulations as well as Adam's fate.
Do not kill her if I am killed by love for her,
But ask her, was it lawful what she did?

When Marzuwan had recited this ode, Qamar al-Zaman's feverish heart felt the coolness of recovery. He sighed and, turning his tongue round in his mouth, he asked his father to let the young man come to sit by his side.

Night 198

Morning now dawned and Shahrazad broke off from what she had been allowed to say. Then, when it was the hundred and ninety-eighth night, SHE CONTINUED:

I have heard, O fortunate king, that Qamar al-Zaman asked his father to let the young man come and sit beside him. When Shahriman heard this, he was delighted, although before that he had been ill disposed towards Marzuwan and had secretly decided to cut off his head. His mind was changed by what he heard his son say and, rising to his feet, he pulled the young man forward and made him sit next to his son. 'Praise be to God for your safe delivery,' he said, to which Marzuwan replied: 'May God preserve your son for you.' He invoked blessings on the king, who then asked him from what land he came. 'From the inner islands,' Marzuwan replied, 'in the kingdom of Ghayur, lord of the islands, the seas and the seven castles.' 'Your arrival may be a blessing for my son,' said King Shahriman, 'and serve to rescue him from his present state.' 'God willing,' said Marzuwan, 'good will come of it.'

He then approached Qamar al-Zaman and whispered in his ear so as not to attract the notice of the king and his courtiers: 'Courage, master, take heart and be comforted. As for the lady, the cause of your present condition, don't ask in what state she is because of you. You kept your affair hidden and so have fallen sick, while she let hers be known and so they said that she was mad. She is kept confined with an iron chain around her neck and is in the worst of states, but if Almighty God wills it, you will both be cured by me.' On hearing this, Qamar al-Zaman regained his spirits; he was heartened and recovered his energy. He gestured to his father to help him to sit upright and the king, almost beside himself with joy, got up and did this.

When Qamar al-Zaman sat up, the king, out of concern for him, shook his handkerchief, at which signal all the emirs and viziers dispersed. Two cushions were placed to support the prince as he sat and the king gave orders for the palace to be perfumed with saffron and then for the

city to be adorned with decorations. 'By God, my son,' he said to
Marzuwan, 'your arrival has proved a fortunate and blessed omen.'
He showed him the greatest honour and had food brought for him.
Marzuwan went up to Qamar al-Zaman and asked him to come and eat
with him, which he did. All the while, the king was calling down blessings
on Marzuwan and exclaiming: 'How good it is that you have come, my
son!' When he saw that Qamar al-Zaman was eating, his joy and delight
increased and he went out immediately and told Qamar al-Zaman's
mother and the people of the palace. Drums were beaten in the palace
to give the good news of the prince's recovery; the city was adorned with
decorations, on the king's orders; the people rejoiced and this was a
great day.

Marzuwan spent the night with Qamar al-Zaman and the king
remained with them, overjoyed . . .

Night 199

Morning now dawned and Shahrazad broke off from what she had been
allowed to say. Then, when it was the hundred and ninety-ninth night,
SHE CONTINUED:

I have heard, O fortunate king, that Shahriman spent the night with
the two young men, overjoyed that his son had been cured. When
morning came he left, and Marzuwan remained alone with Qamar al-
Zaman, to whom he told his story from beginning to end. 'I must tell
you,' he said, 'that I know the girl whom you met and she is the princess
Budur, daughter of King al-Ghayur.' He then let the prince know everything that had happened to the princess, as well as explaining how deeply
she loved him. 'Everything that happened between you and your father,'
he added, 'happened to her with hers. There is no doubt that you are
her love and she is yours. So strengthen your resolve and take heart. I
shall bring you to her and arrange for the two of you to meet soon.
I shall do as the poet has described:

> When a friend turns from his beloved and insists on shunning her,
> I reunite them, like the pin that holds scissors together.'

He continued to strengthen, encourage and console Qamar al-Zaman,
inciting him to eat and drink until he had recovered his spirits, regained
his strength and escaped from his depression. Marzuwan went on cheering

him with poems and stories until he stood up, wanting to go to the baths. Marzuwan took his hand and, after going there together, they washed themselves clean.

Night 200

Morning now dawned and Shahrazad broke off from what she had been allowed to say. Then, when it was the two hundreth night, SHE CONTINUED:

I have heard, O fortunate king, that Qamar al-Zaman went to the baths. When this happened, King Shahriman expressed his joy by ordering the release of all prisoners; he gave splendid robes of honour to his officials as well as alms to the poor and, on his instructions, the city was adorned with decorations for seven days.

Marzuwan then said to Qamar al-Zaman: 'Know, master, that this is why I have come from Princess Budur and the reason for my journey was to rescue her from her misfortune. All that remains for us is to plan how to go to her, as your father will not be able to part from you. My advice is that tomorrow you should ask his permission to go out into the country to hunt. Take a pair of saddlebags with you filled with money; mount a good horse and lead another one and I shall do the same and ride with you. Tell your father that you want to enjoy the open country and hunt there, spending a night outdoors. When we leave here, we can go off on our way, with none of the servants accompanying us.'

Qamar al-Zaman approved of this advice; he was delighted and his backbone was stiffened. He went to his father and told him about this proposal. His father gave him permission to go hunting, adding: 'May he be blest for a thousand days who gave you back your strength. I have no objection to what you ask, but don't stay away for more than one night and come back to me next day, for, as you know, it is only through you that I find pleasure in life and I can scarcely believe that you are cured. You are to me as the poet has described:

If every day and every night I had
Solomon's carpet and the empire of the Chosroes,
To me this would not be worth a gnat's wing
If I had not the power to look at you.'

He then set about equipping Qamar al-Zaman, together with Marzuwan, providing them with four horses, a dromedary to carry money for them and a camel to transport water and food. Qamar al-Zaman would not allow any servant to go with them. His father said goodbye to his son, clasping him to his breast, kissing him and calling on him in God's Name not to stay away for more than one night. 'I shall not be able to sleep tonight,' he said, 'for my position is as the poet has described:

> Your union is my height of pleasure;
> To suffer parting is the worst of pains.
> I am your ransom; if my love is sin,
> Then certainly my sin is very great.
> Do you, like me, suffer the fire of love?
> This burns me with the tortures of the damned.'

'God willing, father,' replied Qamar al-Zaman, 'I shall not be away for more than a night.' He then took his leave and went out, after which he and Marzuwan mounted their horses, taking with them the dromedary with the money and the camel with the water and food. They made for the open country . . .

Night 201

Morning now dawned and Shahrazad broke off from what she had been allowed to say. Then, when it was the two hundred and first night, SHE CONTINUED:

I have heard, O fortunate king, that the two of them made for the open country and rode from early morning until evening, when they dismounted, ate, drank, fed their beasts and rested for a time, after which they remounted and rode on. They travelled continuously for three days and on the fourth day they saw a wide stretch of country in which there was a wood, where they halted. Here Marzuwan slaughtered a camel and a horse, cutting up their flesh and stripping it from their bones. He then took Qamar al-Zaman's shirt and trousers, which he cut up and smeared with the horse's blood, after which he did the same with his mantle. He threw these down at a junction on the track, after which the two ate, drank, remounted and rode on.

Qamar al-Zaman asked Marzuwan why he had done this and Marzuwan told him: 'You must know that by staying away for one night

longer than your father, the king, has allowed us, he will ride after us
when we don't come back. When he discovers the blood that I have left
and finds your shirt and your trousers bloodied and torn, he will think
to himself that something must have happened to you, either at the hands
of highwaymen or through wild beasts. He will give up hope of finding
you unharmed and go back to his city. By this trick we shall get what
we want.' 'By God,' said Qamar al-Zaman, 'that is an excellent scheme
and you have done well.'

The two then travelled on for a period of days and nights. Whenever
he was by himself, Qamar al-Zaman would complain and weep, until
the knowledge that they were coming near the princess's country caused
him to cheer up. He recited these lines:

Will you be harsh to a lover who never has forgotten you?
Will you renounce him, eager though you once were?
May I be stripped of your approval if I betrayed your love,
And may you punish me by desertion if I lie.
I am guilty of no sin deserving harshness,
And even if I sinned, I come in penitence.
It is one of Time's wonders that you abandon me,
But wonders are produced day after day.

When Qamar al-Zaman had finished, Marzuwan said: 'Look, the
islands of King al-Ghayur are now in sight.' This delighted Qamar
al-Zaman, who thanked him for what he had done, kissed him between
the eyes and clasped him to his breast.

Night 202

Morning now dawned and Shahrazad broke off from what she had been
allowed to say. Then, when it was the two hundred and second night,
SHE CONTINUED:

I have heard, O fortunate king, that when Marzuwan said: 'Look,
these are the islands of King al-Ghayur,' Qamar al-Zaman was delighted,
thanking him for what he had done, kissing him between the eyes and
clasping him to his breast. When they reached the islands, they entered
the city and Marzuwan installed Qamar al-Zaman in a *khan* where they
rested for three days in order to recover from their journey. Marzuwan
then took him to the baths, where he dressed him as a merchant and

provided him with a geomantic table made of gold, as well as instruments and a silver astrolabe overlaid with gold. He instructed him to stand beneath the royal palace and to cry out: 'I am an arithmetician; I am a scribe; I know the seeker and what is sought; I am a skilled doctor, I am a dazzling astrologer. Who wants my services?' 'On hearing this, the king will send for you and bring you in to see his daughter, Princess Budur, your beloved,' Murzuwan went on. 'When you enter, say: "Give me three days' grace and if she recovers, marry me to her, and if not, then treat me as you treated the others who tried before me." The king will agree to that. When you get to the princess, tell her who you are, and when she sees you, she will regain her strength and her madness will leave her. One night will be enough to restore her to good health, and you must then give her food and drink. Her father will be delighted by her recovery and will marry her to you, as well as sharing his kingdom with you, as this is a condition that he laid down for himself. That is all.'

When Qamar al-Zaman heard this, he said: 'May I never be deprived of your favour,' and after taking the equipment that Marzuwan had provided, he left the *khan*, wearing his merchant's clothes. He walked on, carrying the tools of his trade, until he came to a halt beneath King al-Ghayur's palace where he cried out: 'I am an arithmetician; I am a scribe; I know the seeker and what is sought; I am an opener of books; I count up the reckoning; I am an interpreter of dreams; I trace talismans for treasure seekers. Who wants my services?' When the townspeople heard this, they flocked to him as it had been a long time since they had seen a scribe or an astrologer. When they looked at him, they saw that he was the most handsome, graceful, elegant and perfect of men. As they stood admiring his beauty and his symmetrical form, one of them went up to him and said: 'For God's sake, you handsome and eloquent young man, don't run into danger and risk your life in the hope of marrying Princess Budur, the daughter of King al-Ghayur. You can see for yourself those heads fastened there. This was why all their owners were killed.'

Qamar al-Zaman, however, paid no attention to this warning and called out at the top of his voice: 'I am a doctor and a scribe; I am an astrologer and an arithmetician.' Although all the townspeople tried to stop him, he took no notice of them at all, saying to himself: 'Only those who have to endure it know what longing is.' He went on calling out: 'I am a doctor; I am an astrologer.'

Night 203

Morning now dawned and Shahrazad broke off from what she had been
allowed to say. Then, when it was the two hundred and third night, SHE
CONTINUED:

I have heard, O fortunate king, that Qamar al-Zaman paid no attention to what the townspeople said and cried out: 'I am a scribe; I am an
arithmetician; I am an astrologer.' At this, all the townspeople grew
angry with him, saying: 'You are nothing but a stupid, conceited and
foolish young man – have some pity on your own youth and beauty.'
Qamar al-Zaman, however, continued to call: 'I am an astrologer; I am
an arithmetician. Who wants my services?' While he kept doing this in
spite of the protests of the crowd, the king heard his voice and the noise
that the crowd was making. He told the vizier to go down and fetch 'this
astrologer'. The vizier went quickly and took Qamar al-Zaman from the
crowd, bringing him to the king.

When Qamar al-Zaman stood before the king, he kissed the ground
and recited:

There are eight qualities of glory; you possess them all,
And it is thanks to these Time is your servant –
Sure knowledge, piety, nobility, generosity,
A mastery of word and meaning, grandeur, victory.

The king looked at him and, after seating him by his side, he turned to
him and said: 'For God's sake, my son, if you are not an astrologer, do not
risk your life by accepting my condition. For I have bound myself to
execute anyone who visits my daughter and fails to cure her madness,
whereas I will marry her to whoever cures her. Do not let your own good
looks lead you astray, for I swear by God that if you fail to cure her, I shall
have your head cut off.' 'You may do that with my own consent,' said
Qamar al-Zaman, 'for I knew about this before I came to you.' The king
called the *qadis* to bear witness to this, after which he handed Qamar
al-Zaman over to a eunuch with instructions to take him to Princess Budur.

The eunuch took him by the hand and led him into the hall. Qamar
al-Zaman hurried on ahead, and the eunuch ran after him, saying: 'Damn
you, don't hurry to your own death. You are the only astrologer whom
I have ever seen doing this, but you don't know what disasters lie ahead
of you.' But Qamar al-Zaman turned away from him . . .

Night 204

Morning now dawned and Shahrazad broke off from what she had been allowed to say. Then, when it was the two hundred and fourth night, SHE CONTINUED:

I have heard, O fortunate king, that the eunuch told Qamar al-Zaman not to be in such a hurry, but he turned away from him and recited these lines:

> Other things I know, but not your beauty;
> In my perplexity, I don't know what to say.
> If I call you a sun, your beauty does not sink
> Out of my sight, whereas suns set.
> Your loveliness is perfect; the eloquent
> Cannot describe it and the speaker is at a loss.

The eunuch made him stand behind the curtain covering the door. Qamar al-Zaman asked him: 'Which do you prefer? Shall I treat your mistress and cure her from here or go in and cure her from the other side of the curtain?' The eunuch was astonished by this, but replied: 'If you cure her from here, this will bring you extra credit.' At that, Qamar al-Zaman sat down behind the curtain, brought out an inkwell and a pen, took a piece of paper and wrote on it as follows: 'This letter comes from a man carried away by passion, destroyed by love and killed by grief. Misfortune has afflicted one who has despaired of life and who is sure of the approach of death. There is no helper to aid his sorrowful heart, nor can anyone visit his sleepless eyes to fight against care. His days are spent in burning passion and his nights in torture. Emaciation has scraped away his body and no messenger has come from his beloved.' He then wrote these lines:

> As I write, my heart is enamoured of your memory,
> And tears of blood drop from my wounded lids.
> My clothes are burning longing and distress,
> With the shirt of emaciation covering my broken form.
> I complain to you of love, as love has injured me,
> Leaving no place for patience.
> Be generous and merciful with sympathy,
> As my heart is torn in pieces by its love.

Under these lines he wrote in metrical prose: 'The heart's cure is the meeting with the beloved. He who is treated harshly by his beloved finds a doctor in God. Whoever acts treacherously, be it you or I, will not obtain what he wants. There is nothing finer than a lover who keeps faith with a beloved who treats him harshly.' Then by way of a signature, he wrote: 'From the distracted and confused lover, disquieted by amorous passion, the prisoner of infatuation, Qamar al-Zaman, son of King Shahriman, to the unique pearl of the age, the choice flower of the houris of loveliness, Princess Budur, daughter of King al-Ghayur. Know that I pass my nights in sleeplessness and my days in perplexity. My emaciation and sickness increase, as do my love and passion. I sigh frequently and shed copious tears, for I am held prisoner by love and slain by passion. I am a man whose heart has been seared by abandonment, passion's debtor, the boon companion of sickness. I am the sleepless one whose eyes never close, the slave of love whose tears never dry up, the fire in whose heart is never quenched, and the flames of whose longing cannot be hidden.' In the margin he wrote these fine words:

> I invoke greetings from the stores of God's grace
> On her who holds my soul and has my heart.

He also wrote:

> Give me some word from you, for it may be
> That you will pity me or bring me rest.
> The violence of my love for you makes me despise
> What I experience, which is that I am despised.
> God guard a people who are far from me,
> But whose love I conceal in my most precious part.
> Time has been gracious to me now,
> Throwing me in the dust at my beloved's door.
> I saw Budur in the bed at my side
> With the moon of my age illumined by her sun.

When he had sealed the letter, he wrote in place of an address:

> Ask my letter about what I have written;
> Its lines will tell you of my passion and my pain.
> My hand writes as my tears flow down,
> And longing complains to the paper through my pen.

My tears continue to pour out;
If they come to an end, my blood will follow them.

At the end of the letter he wrote:

I have sent your ring,
Which I exchanged on the day of union,
So send me back my own.

Qamar al-Zaman then put Budur's ring in the folded paper and handed
it to the eunuch, who took it from him and brought it in to his mistress . . .

Night 205

Morning now dawned and Shahrazad broke off from what she had been
allowed to say. Then, when it was the two hundred and fifth night, SHE
CONTINUED:

I have heard, O fortunate king, that Qamar al-Zaman then put Budur's
ring in the folded paper and handed it to the eunuch, who took it from
him and brought it in to his mistress, the princess. When she had taken
it from him and opened it, she found that it contained her own ring.
After reading the message and grasping its meaning, she realized that
here was her beloved and that he was standing behind the curtain. Her
heart bounded with joy, swelling with relief and delight, and she recited:

I regretted that we had been parted,
With tears that flooded from my eyelids;
I vowed, if Time would join us once again,
The word 'parting' would never cross my lips.
Now joy has launched itself on me,
And is so great that it has made me cry.
Tears have become so natural to my eyes
That both sorrow and joy can make them flow.

When she had finished, she got up immediately and, after planting her
feet against the wall, she strained with all her strength against the iron
ring, snapping it from her neck and breaking the chain. She then came
out from behind the curtain and threw herself on Qamar al-Zaman,
kissing him on the mouth like a dove feeding its young, and embracing
him in an ecstasy of passion. 'Master,' she said, 'am I awake or dreaming?

After our separation has God allowed us to be near each other? Praise be to Him that we are united after our despair.'

When the eunuch saw what was happening, he ran to the king and, having kissed the ground before him, he said: 'Master, know that this astrologer is the chief and the most learned of all his fellows. He managed to cure your daughter while standing behind the curtain, without going into her room.' 'Take care,' said the king. 'Is this true?' And the eunuch replied: 'Come and see for yourself how she found the strength to break the iron chain and go out to the astrologer, kissing and embracing him.' The king rose and went to his daughter who, when she saw him, got up, covered her head and recited:

> I do not love the word 'tooth-pick';
> When I pronounce it, it seems 'other than you'.*
> The *'arak* tree, however, I do love
> Since, when I say the word, it is: 'I can see you.'†

The king was almost beside himself with joy at her recovery. He kissed her between the eyes, so great was his love for her, and then, turning to Qamar al-Zaman, he asked him about himself and from what land he came. Qamar al-Zaman told him of his birth and status, saying that his father was King Shahriman. He then went through the story from beginning to end, telling the king of all that had happened to him with the princess and of how he had taken the ring from her finger, exchanging it for his own. The king was astonished by this and said: 'The story of the two of you ought to be recorded in books and recited from generation to generation after you have gone.'

He then immediately summoned the *qadis* and the witnesses and drew up the marriage contract between Princess Budur and Qamar al-Zaman. On his orders, the city was adorned with decorations for seven days; food was set out on tables; wedding celebrations were held; and, as the city was adorned, so all the troops wore their most splendid clothes. Drums were beaten to spread the good news. When Qamar al-Zaman came to Budur, her father was delighted both by her recovery and by her marriage, praising God that she had fallen in love with a handsome young prince. She was then unveiled for her bridegroom and they were seen to be alike in loveliness, grace and elegance. Qamar al-Zaman slept

---

* A pun on *al-siwaka* ('tooth-pick') and *siwaka* ('other than you').
† A pun on *al-araka* (' *'arak* tree') and *araka* ('I see you').

with her that night, having his way with her, while she satisfied her longing in the enjoyment of his beauty. They continued to embrace one another until morning, and on the next day the king gave a banquet for the whole population of the inner and outer islands. Tables were laden with splendid foods and the feasting went on for a whole month.

Then, after Qamar al-Zaman had successfully achieved his heart's desire and had spent some time with the princess, he remembered his father, King Shahriman. He saw the king in a dream, saying: 'My son, is this how you treat me?' and reciting these lines:

The full moon of night alarms me and turns away,
Leaving my eyes to herd the stars.
Go slowly, heart; he may come back to me;
Endure, my soul, the burning pain he leaves.

The morning after Qamar al-Zaman had seen his father reproaching him in a dream, he was distressed and sorrowful, and when Budur asked him, he told her what he had seen . . .

Night 206

Morning now dawned and Shahrazad broke off from what she had been allowed to say. Then, when it was the two hundred and sixth night, SHE CONTINUED:

I have heard, O fortunate king, that Qamar al-Zaman told Budur what he had seen in his dream. The two of them then went to her father and told him of this, asking his permission to leave. He gave this to Qamar al-Zaman and when Budur told him that she could not be separated from her husband, he told her that she could go with him, giving her permission to stay away for a whole year, after which she was to visit her father once each year. She kissed his hand, as did Qamar al-Zaman, and he then began to equip them for their journey. He provided them with supplies, together with the necessary paraphernalia for travelling, and gave them excellent horses and dromedaries. He supplied his daughter with a litter and had mules and camels loaded for them, as well as providing slaves and escorts for them, together with everything else that they might need on the journey.

On the day of their departure, the king said goodbye to Qamar al-Zaman and gave him ten splendid robes of honour, embroidered with gold and studded with gems, as well as ten horses, ten camels and a large sum of money. After telling him to look after his daughter, he went with them to the farthest point of the islands, where he again said goodbye to Qamar al-Zaman, and then, going into Budur's litter, he hugged her, kissed her and, starting to weep, he recited these lines:

Go slowly, you who wish to leave:
Lovers find pleasure in an embrace.
Go slowly; Time's nature is treacherous,
And companionship must end in parting.

On leaving his daughter, he went to Qamar al-Zaman, repeating his farewells and kissing him, after which he left the two of them with instructions to set off, returning himself to his kingdom with his troops. Qamar al-Zaman and his wife travelled day after day for a whole month, after which they halted in a wide meadow full of herbage. Here they camped, ate, drank and rested. The princess went to sleep and Qamar al-Zaman, coming in to see her, found her sleeping in a transparent chemise of apricot-coloured silk, with on her head a gold-embroidered kerchief set with pearls and other gems. A breeze had lifted her chemise up above her navel; her breasts were revealed as well as a belly whiter than snow, each fold of whose wrinkles could accommodate an ounce of frankincense. In an excess of passionate love, he recited:

Were I asked, as the hot flame burns
With fire inside my heart and inner parts,
'Would you prefer to see them or a cooling drink?'
I would reply: 'It is they I would prefer.'

Qamar al-Zaman put his hand on the waistband of her drawers and, in his desire for her, was tugging at it to undo it, when he caught sight of a ring with a stone as red as the dragon's blood gum that was fastened to it. On unfastening it and looking at it, he saw two lines engraved in a script that he could not read. He wondered at this, saying to himself: 'If this ring were not something of importance to her, she would not have fastened it where she did, hiding it in her most precious place so that she would never be separated from it. What do you suppose she does with it and what is its secret?' He took it outside the tent to look at it in the light.

Night 207

I have heard, O fortunate king, that Qamar al-Zaman took the ring to look at it in the light. He was holding it in his hand and starting to examine it, when suddenly a bird swooped down, seized it from him and flew off. It then put the ring back down on the ground and Qamar al-Zaman, afraid for its safety, ran after the bird, but as he ran, it took flight, and he kept on following it from place to place and from hill to hill, until the coming of night brought darkness. The bird then went to roost in a high tree and Qamar al-Zaman stood beneath it in a state of perplexity. He was sinking with hunger and weariness and felt as though he was on the point of death. He wanted to go back, but he had no idea where he had come from and the darkness had taken him by surprise. So he recited the formula: 'There is no might and no power except with God, the Exalted, the Omnipotent,' and he then slept until morning under the tree in which the bird had perched. When he woke, he discovered that the bird too had woken and had flown from its tree. He walked after it, noticing that it would make short flights, matching the distance that he walked. 'By God,' he said, smiling, 'it is wonderful that yesterday this bird flew as fast as I could run, but now it knows that I am too tired to run and so it keeps pace with me as I walk. This is marvellous indeed, but I have to go after it. Whether it leads me to life or death, I must follow it wherever it goes, and, at all events, it is bound to stop in cultivated land.'

He then started to walk underneath the flying bird, which would spend every night in a tree. This went on for ten days, during which Qamar al-Zaman would feed on plants and drink from streams, and at the end of this period he came in sight of an inhabited city. In the blink of an eye, the bird had darted off into it. Qamar al-Zaman lost sight of it, unable to see where it had gone. In his astonishment, he gave praise to God for having brought him safely to the city and he then sat down by a stream, where he washed his hands, feet and face and rested for a time. He remembered the ease and comfort he had enjoyed, together with company of his beloved, and, thinking about his present state of hunger, weariness, care, exile and separation, he shed tears and recited:

I could not hide the love you stirred in me;
My eyes have exchanged sleep for sleeplessness.
When cares weakened my heart, I called:
'Time, if you wound me, wound me mortally.'
My life lies here among distress and danger.
Were love's power fair and just,
Sleep would not be banished from my eyes.
Be gentle, masters, with a wasted lover;
Show pity to the lord whom love's law has abased
Among his people, and the rich man who is poor.
I have not followed those who censure you;
Rather, I block my ears and make them deaf.
They say: 'You love a thin girl'; I reply:
'I made this choice, abandoning all the rest.'
Stop; in fate's presence, sight is blind.

When he had finished his poem and had rested, Qamar al-Zaman got
up and walked slowly into the city . . .

Night 208

Morning now dawned and Shahrazad broke off from what she had been
allowed to say. Then, when it was the two hundred and eighth night,
SHE CONTINUED:

I have heard, O fortunate king, that when he had finished his poem
and had rested, Qamar al-Zaman got up and walked into the city with
no idea where he was going. He crossed from one end of it to the other,
having entered by the land gate and going on until he came out by the
sea gate, and during all this time he had met not a single inhabitant. The
city was on the seashore and when he had left by the sea gate, he
continued to walk on until he came to orchards and trees. He went in
among the trees and stopped at the gates of an orchard. The gardener
came out and, after they had exchanged greetings, he welcomed the
newcomer, saying: 'Praise be to God that you have got safely through
the city, but come into the orchard quickly before any of the inhabitants
catch sight of you.' Qamar al-Zaman was startled and went in to ask
the gardener to tell him about the people. 'You must know,' the man
replied, 'that they are all Magians,' and he then asked Qamar al-Zaman

to tell him how and why he had come there. Qamar al-Zaman told him everything that had happened to him, from start to finish.

The gardener was astonished and said: 'My son, the lands of Islam are a long way from here – a four-month journey by sea and a full year by land. We have a ship which carries merchandise there each year, going from here to the sea of the Ebony Islands and then to the Khalidan Islands of King Shahriman.' Qamar al-Zaman thought to himself for a while and realized that the best thing for him to do would be to stay in the orchard with the gardener, working for a quarter share of the profits. He asked the gardener whether he would agree to this and the latter accepted willingly, showing him how to divert the water to the plots where the trees were planted. Qamar al-Zaman started to do this and to hoe up the weeds, wearing a short blue smock hanging down to his knees that the gardener had given him. He stayed there, watering the trees and shedding floods of tears, finding no rest by day or by night because of his exile, and reciting poetry about his beloved. Among these poems are the lines:

> You made me a promise; why did you not keep it?
> You gave me words, but why not deeds?
> Passion decreed my wakefulness, while you have slept;
> The wakeful are not like the ones who sleep.
> We had a compact to conceal our love;
> The slanderer tempted you; he spoke and you replied.
> Beloved, whether you are angry or approve,
> However things may be, you are my only goal.
> There is one here who holds my tortured heart;
> Would that she might take pity on my state.
> Not every eye is wounded as mine is,
> Nor are all hearts enslaved like mine by love.
> You acted unjustly and said: 'Love is unjust.'
> You speak the truth, for this is what is said.
> Forget a lover, one whose promise Time
> Can never break, although fire burns in his heart.
> If my opponent is my judge in love,
> To whom can I complain of being wronged?
> Were it not for my need of love,
> I would not have a heart that love enslaves.

So much for Qamar al-Zaman, but as for his wife, the princess Budur, when she woke up she looked for her husband but failed to find him.

She discovered that her drawers had been undone and, on inspecting the fastening to which the ring had been attached, she found that the ring had gone. She said to herself in wonder: 'Where is my husband? It looks as though he took the ring stone and went off, but he doesn't know its secret. Where can he have gone? Something remarkable must have happened to make him leave, for otherwise he would not have been able to bear parting from me for a single hour. God damn the stone and the hour when it disappeared!'

She then thought the matter over and said to herself: 'If I go out and tell the servants that my husband is lost, they will lust after me and so I must think of some scheme.' She got up and dressed herself in some of Qamar al-Zaman's clothes, putting on a turban like his, wearing boots and covering her mouth with a veil. She left a slave girl in the litter and went out of the tent. She called to the servants, who brought a horse which she mounted, and after the baggage had been loaded on her orders, they all moved off after she had given the word to leave. She concealed what she had done and no one doubted that she was Qamar al-Zaman as the two of them were of the same height and similar appearance. She and her followers then travelled on for a number of days and nights, until she came within sight of a city overlooking the salt sea. She halted outside it, and had the tents pitched so that her party could rest, and when she asked about the city, she was told that it was the Ebony City, ruled by King Armanus, who had a daughter called Hayat al-Nufus.

Night 209

Morning now dawned and Shahrazad broke off from what she had been allowed to say. Then, when it was the two hundred and ninth night, SHE CONTINUED:

I have heard, O fortunate king, that when Budur halted outside the Ebony City to rest, Armanus sent a messenger to find out about the 'king' who had camped outside his city. On his arrival, the messenger asked Budur's servants, who told him that here was a prince who was making for the Khalidan Islands of King Shahriman but had lost his way. The messenger went back to King Armanus with this news, and when he heard it, he and his state officials came out to meet their visitor. When he arrived at the tents, Princess Budur came out on foot and the king met her, also on foot. After they had exchanged greetings, the king took her into his city and brought her to his palace, where on his orders food of all kinds was laid out on tables, while Budur's men were taken to his guest house. They stayed there for three days, after which the king came to visit her. She had been to the baths that day and her unveiled face shone like a full moon, so that all who saw her were reduced to a state of shameless infatuation. When the king met her, she was wearing a silk robe, embroidered with gold and studded with jewels. 'My son,' he told her, 'I am old and infirm. My only child is a daughter who resembles you in beauty and loveliness. As I can no longer govern my kingdom, I offer her to you, and if you like this land of mine and are prepared to stay and settle here, I will marry you to her and give you my kingdom so that I may rest.'

The princess bent her head with her forehead covered in the sweat of shame. She said to herself: 'How can this be done, as I am a woman? But if I don't agree and leave him, I shall not be safe, as he may send a force after me to kill me, while if I obey him, I may be disgraced. I have lost my darling Qamar al-Zaman; there is no news of him, and I have no way of escape apart from keeping silence, agreeing to the king's proposal and staying here until God brings about what has been fated.' So, raising her head, she told the king that she was willing to obey him.

In his delight, he ordered a herald to proclaim throughout the Ebony Islands that wedding celebrations were to be held and decorations brought out. He then gathered together the chamberlains, deputies, emirs, viziers and state officials, together with the *qadis* of his city, after which he abdicated, appointing Princess Budur in his place and clothing her in royal robes. All the emirs came to pay their respects and none of them had any doubt that she was a young man, while her beauty caused all those who looked at her to soil their trousers.

When she had assumed power and taken her seat on the throne, with the drums being beaten to spread the good news, King Armanus made the preparations for the wedding of his daughter, Hayat al-Nufus. A few days later, Princess Budur was brought in to her, and they looked like two moons that had risen at the same time or two suns that had met. The doors were closed on them and the curtains drawn, after candles had been lit and the marriage bed prepared. Budur sat with Hayat al-Nufus but, remembering her beloved Qamar al-Zaman, she was over-whelmed by grief and, shedding tears for his loss, she recited these lines:

Absent ones, the agitation of my heart grows worse;
Your parting leaves no breath of life within my body.
My eyes used to complain of sleeplessness,
But tears have melted them; I wish that sleeplessness had stayed.
When you left, it was love that stayed behind.
Ask it what it experienced when you went.
Were it not for tears that flood down from my eyes,
My fiery pain would burn the empty lands.
I complain to God of dear ones I have lost,
Who had no pity on my love or my distress.
I wronged them only through my love for them;
Some may be fortunate in love and others not.

When she had finished these lines, Budur sat down beside Hayat al-Nufus and kissed her on the mouth, but she then got up, performed the ritual ablution and continued to pray until Hayat al-Nufus had fallen asleep. She then got into bed with her, but kept her back turned towards her until it was morning. When the sun had risen, the king and his wife came to their daughter to ask how she was, and she told them what she had seen and the poetry that she had heard.

So much for Hayat al-Nufus and her parents, but as for Princess Budur, she went out and took her seat on the royal throne. The emirs together with all the leaders and state officials came and congratulated her on having taken power, kissing the ground before her and calling down blessings on her. She advanced towards them smilingly and distributed robes of honour among them, bestowing additional honours and lands on the emirs, officials and soldiers. They loved her and everyone prayed that her reign might continue, believing that she was a man. She issued commands and prohibitions, gave judgements, released prisoners and cancelled market dues. She continued to sit in the hall of judgement until nightfall, after which she entered the apartments that had been prepared for her. Here she found Hayat al-Nufus seated, and sitting down beside her she patted her on the back, petted her and kissed her between the eyes. She then recited the following lines:

Tears have revealed my secret;
My wasted body is an open sign of love.
I hide it, but the day of parting shows my love,
Nor is my state concealed from slanderers.
You travel from the camping ground, but leave behind

My wasted body and my anguished soul.
You dwell within my inmost parts;
My tears flow and my eyes drip blood.
My heart's blood is a ransom for the absent ones,
And that I long for them is clear to see.
The pupil of my eye rejects sleep for its love,
And its tears follow one another as they fall.
My foes may think that I endure his loss;
Far from it, and my ears are blocked to them.
Their hopes in me are not to be fulfilled;
Only Qamar al-Zaman can bring me what I wish.
In him are virtues such as no king had before.
His bounty and his kindness cause men to forget
The clemency of Mu'awiya and Ibn Za'ida the generous.
Poetry cannot describe his loveliness;
Would this not take too long, I'd leave no rhyme unused.

Budur then got to her feet, wiped away her tears, performed the ritual ablution and began to pray. Her prayers continued until Hayat al-Nufus had fallen asleep, at which point she came and slept beside her until morning. She then got up, performed the morning prayer and took her seat on the royal throne, issuing orders and prohibitions and giving equitable judgements. So much for her, but as for King Armanus, he came to his daughter to ask how she was and she told him everything that happened and recited Budur's poem for him. 'Father,' she said, 'I have never seen a more intelligent or a more modest man than my husband, but he keeps on sighing and weeping.' 'Be patient, daughter,' replied the king. 'This is the third night and if he does not go in to you and take your maidenhead, I shall have to think again and take steps, deposing him as king and banishing him from my lands.' He and his daughter agreed on what he had determined to do.

Night 210

Morning now dawned and Shahrazad broke off from what she had been allowed to say. Then, when it was the two hundred and tenth night, SHE CONTINUED:

I have heard, O fortunate king, that Armanus and his daughter agreed

on what he had determined to do. When night fell, Budur rose from the
council room and, on entering the palace, she went to the apartments
that had been prepared for her. Here she found Hayat al-Nufus sitting
with the candles lit. Thinking of her husband and how recently she had
been parted from him, with tears and deep sighs Budur recited these
lines:

I swear that the world is full of tales of me,
Like the sun rising over tamarisks.
His gestures were eloquent but hard to understand,
And so my longing grows and does not end.
Since I began to love you I have hated patience.
But have you ever seen a lover who hates love?
The beloved attacks with deadly, languorous glance.
The deadliest of glances are the languorous.
He let his hair down and unveiled his mouth;
On him I saw beauty both black and white.
For me his hands held both disease and cure;
The disease of love is cured by one who was its cause.
His belt is in love with the softness of his waist;
From jealousy his buttocks will not let him rise.
It is as though his forelock and the radiance of his brow
Were dark night held back by the light of dawn.

On finishing her poem, she was intending to get up to pray when
Hayat al-Nufus grasped the bottom of her robe, and held on to it, saying:
'Master, do you feel no shame before my father? He has treated you well
and yet you have left me alone until now.' When Budur heard this, she
sat up where she was and said: 'My darling, what are you saying?' Hayat
al-Nufus replied: 'I am saying that I have never seen anyone as pleased
with himself as you. Are all handsome people like this? It is not to make
you want me that I have said this, but because I am afraid for you
because of my father. Unless you lie with me tonight and take my
virginity, in the morning he intends to remove you from the throne and
drive you from the country. It may even be that in an excess of anger he
will kill you. It is out of pity for you that I have given you advice, but
do whatever you think fit.' On hearing this, Budur bent her head down
towards the ground in a state of perplexity. 'If I go against the king's
wishes, I am lost,' she said to herself, 'but if I obey him, I shall be
disgraced. At the moment, I am the ruler of all the Ebony Islands and

they are under my control. It is only here that I shall be able to meet Qamar al-Zaman, as he cannot reach his own country except from these islands. I don't know what to do, and so I must entrust my affairs to God, for He is the most excellent of rulers. At any rate, I am no male so as to be able to deflower this virgin.'

She then said: 'My darling, it is not because I wanted to that I have kept away from you,' and she went on to explain what had happened to her from beginning to end and showed herself to Hayat al-Nufus. 'I ask you in God's Name,' she said, 'to keep my secret concealed and hidden until God reunites me with my beloved Qamar al-Zaman, and after that what will be will be.'

Night 211

Morning now dawned and Shahrazad broke off from what she had been allowed to say. Then, when it was the two hundred and eleventh night, SHE CONTINUED:

I have heard, O fortunate king, that Budur told her story to Hayat al-Nufus and asked her to keep her secret. Hayat al-Nufus was full of astonishment when she heard this story. She felt sympathy for Budur and prayed that she would meet her beloved, adding: 'Don't fear or be alarmed, sister, but wait patiently for God to bring about what has been fated.' She then recited:

> I keep your secret inside a locked room;
> The key is lost and the room sealed.
> It is only the trustworthy who keep secrets,
> And no good man will betray them.

After finishing these lines, she went on: 'The breasts of the noble are the graves of secrets, and I shall never reveal yours.' Then the two played with each other, exchanging embraces and kisses, after which they slept until it was nearly time for the call to morning prayer. Hayat al-Nufus got up and took a young pigeon whose throat she cut over her chemise, smearing herself with its blood. She removed her drawers and gave a shriek, at which the members of her household came in, with the slave girls uttering shrill cries of joy. Her mother asked her how she was and stayed with her, looking after her until evening. As for Budur, she got up in the morning, went to the baths and washed, after which she performed the morning prayer, before going to the audience hall, where she sat on the royal throne, delivering judgements to the people. When Armanus heard the cries, he asked what they meant and was pleased and relieved to hear that his daughter had lost her virginity. He gave a great banquet and things stayed like this for some time.

So much for Budur and Hayat al-Nufus, but as for King Shahriman, when his son went out to hunt, accompanied by Marzuwan as has been described, he waited until nightfall on the day after they had left and when his son did not return he passed a long and sleepless night in a state of great agitation. His longing for his son increased and he could not believe that dawn would ever come. When it was morning, he waited expectantly for his son until midday, but when he was still absent, his father felt the pangs of separation and burned with anxiety. 'Alas for my boy,' he said, and he wept until his clothes were sodden with tears. He then recited broken-heartedly:

> I used to object to lovers
> Until I was afflicted by the sweet bitterness of love.
> I gulped down the cup of love's rejection,
> Humbling myself before its slaves and its freemen.
> Time vowed that it would make the lovers part,
> And now it has fulfilled its vow.

When he had finished his poem, he wiped away his tears and called to his men to be ready to move out on a long journey. They all mounted and he himself rode off on fire with anxiety for his son and with his heart filled with sorrow. They pressed on with their journey and the king split his force into six divisions, including a right and a left wing, a vanguard and a rearguard, telling them to rendezvous on the following day at the crossroads. The troops then split up and continued on their way for the rest of the day until it grew dark. They went on all through the night until, at midday on the following day, they reached the crossroads. They did not know which road Qamar al-Zaman would have taken, but then they saw on one of the tracks the remains of torn clothes and flesh as well as traces of blood.

When the king saw this, he gave a great cry that came from the bottom of his heart. 'O my son,' he said, striking his face, tugging hairs from his beard and tearing his clothes. Convinced that his son was dead, he wept bitterly and sobbed, and his men joined in his tears, all of them being sure that Qamar al-Zaman must be dead. They poured dust on their heads and when night fell they were still weeping, so much so that they were almost on the point of death. With his heart burning with fiery sighs, the king recited these lines:

Do not blame the sorrowful for his sorrow;
The passion of his distress is enough for him.
He weeps for his great grief and for his pain;
His suffering tells you of the fires that burn in him.
Sa'd, who helps a prisoner of love for whom grief swears
It will not halt the flow of tears from his eyelids?
He shows distress at the loss of a shining moon,
Whose radiance has outshone all other moons.
Death offered him a brimming cup
On the day he left his own country.
He left his lands and us to meet disaster,
With no friend to take leave of him.
He abandoned me by going far away,
With harsh rejection and the agony of parting.
He has left us and has gone, taking his leave,
When God welcomed him to Paradise.

When he had finished his recitation, the king returned with his men to the city . . .

Night 212

Morning now dawned and Shahrazad broke off from what she had been allowed to say. Then, when it was the two hundred and twelfth night, SHE CONTINUED:

I have heard, O fortunate king, that when King Shahriman had finished his recitation, he returned with his men to the city, convinced that his son was dead and believing that he had been attacked and carried off, either by wild beasts or by highwaymen. He had it proclaimed in the Khalidan Islands that people were to wear black as a token of mourning for Qamar al-Zaman, and he built for himself what he called the House of Sorrow. Every Monday and Thursday, he would conduct state business with his troops and his subjects, while for the rest of the week he would enter the House of Sorrow to mourn for his son and recite elegies, among them being the lines:

The day my wishes were fulfilled was when you were near me,
While the day of death was when you turned away.
Although I pass the night in fear, threatened with destruction,
Union with you is sweeter than being safe.

Other lines of his are:

May my life be the ransom for travellers, although their parting
Brought damage, ruin and disaster to my heart.
Let joy restrain itself and wait, for when they left
I divorced happiness three times.

So much for King Shahriman, but as for Princess Budur, after she had become ruler of the Ebony Islands, people started to point at her and say: 'That is King Armanus's son-in-law.' Every night she would sleep with Hayat al-Nufus, to whom she would complain of the loneliness she felt in being separated from her husband, Qamar al-Zaman, whose beauty she would describe, in tears, expressing her wish to be united with him, if only in a dream. She would recite:

God knows that when you left I wept
Until I had to borrow tears on credit.
A censurer said: 'Patience, for you will find your love again.'
'Censurer,' I asked, 'where can I find patience?'

So much for Princess Budur, while as for Qamar al-Zaman, he stayed for a time with the gardener in the orchard. He used to shed tears night and day and recite poetry, sighing with regret for happier times and for nights when his wishes were fulfilled, while the gardener kept telling him that at the end of the year a ship would sail for the lands of the Muslims. Things went on like this until one day he saw people gathering together. He was surprised, but the gardener came and told him: 'My son, there is no need to work today, so don't bother to water the trees. This is a feast day when people go to visit each other. Take a rest, but keep an eye on the garden as I want to go to look for a ship for you. Soon I shall send you off to Muslim territory.'

He then left the orchard and Qamar al-Zaman stayed there alone, thinking over his situation broken-heartedly. So bitterly did he weep that he fainted, and when he had recovered, he got up and walked in the orchard, brooding on what Time had done to him and on his long separation. While he was distracted and not paying attention, he tripped and fell on his face. His forehead struck a tree root and, as a result of the blow, blood flowed down, mingling with his tears. He wiped the blood away, dried his tears and, after bandaging his forehead with a rag, he got up and walked around the orchard, absent-mindedly, plunged in thought. He then happened to see two birds quarrelling on top of a tree. One of them attacked the other, pecking it on the throat which it cut through, and then flying off with its head. The corpse fell to the ground in front of Qamar al-Zaman, and while he was standing there, another two large birds swooped down on it. One of them stood at the top of the bird's corpse and the other at its tail, and they spread their wings and their beaks over it, stretching out their necks towards it and shedding tears. When Qamar al-Zaman saw them weeping over their companion, he too shed tears because of his separation from his wife and because of the memory of his father.

Night 213

Morning now dawned and Shahrazad broke off from what she had been allowed to say. Then, when it was the two hundred and thirteenth night, SHE CONTINUED:

I have heard, O fortunate king, that Qamar al-Zaman wept because of his separation from his wife and father. As he watched, he saw that the birds had dug a hole in which they proceeded to bury the corpse. They then flew away, but after some time they came back, bringing with them the killer, which they brought down to the grave. They settled down on top of it until they had killed it, after which they split open its stomach and pulled out its guts, with its blood pouring out over the dead bird's grave. They scattered its flesh, tore its skin and strewed the contents of its stomach here and there in different places. Qamar al-Zaman was watching in astonishment as all this was going on. He happened to turn towards the place where the bird had been killed, where he noticed something glistening, and going up to it, he discovered the bird's crop, which he took and opened. There, inside, he found the ring which had been the cause of his separation from his wife, and on seeing it and recognizing it, he fell to the ground, fainting with joy. On recovering, he exclaimed: 'Praise be to God! This is a good sign, bringing joyful news that I shall be reunited with my beloved.'

He studied the ring closely, moving it to and fro in front of him, before fastening it to his forearm, thinking that it would bring him luck. He then walked on to wait for the gardener, but when night had fallen he had still not returned, and so Qamar al-Zaman spent the night in his own quarters. In the morning, he got up to go to work, tying a fibre rope around his waist and taking with him his axe and his basket. He made his way through the orchard until he came to a carob tree at whose root he struck with the axe. The blow made a ringing sound and, on clearing away the soil, he discovered a trapdoor, which he opened.

Night 214

Morning now dawned and Shahrazad broke off from what she had been allowed to say. Then, when it was the two hundred and fourteenth night, SHE CONTINUED:

I have heard, O fortunate king, that Qamar al-Zaman opened the trapdoor. Inside he found another door and a flight of steps, and after going down these, he discovered an old chamber, dating from the time of 'Ad and Thamud, carved out of the rock, with sky-blue mouldings. Finding that it was full of glittering red gold, he said to himself: 'This marks the end of toil and the start of joy and pleasure.' After he had gone back up to the orchard, he replaced the trapdoor and then went on watering the trees until evening. At that point the gardener arrived, saying: 'Good news, my son! You can go back to your own land. The merchants are ready to go and the ship will sail in three days' time for the City of Ebony, which is the nearest of the Muslim cities, and when you get there, it is a six months' journey by land to the Khalidan Islands where you will find King Shahriman.'

In his delight, Qamar al-Zaman recited:

Do not desert one who is not accustomed to desert you,
And do not torture the innocent by turning from him.
After so long a parting, another would forget you,
And his feelings would change, but mine do not.

Qamar al-Zaman then kissed the gardener's hand, saying: 'Father, as you have given me good news, so I too have great news for you.' He then told him of the chamber that he had found and the delighted gardener said: 'My son, I have been in this orchard for eighty years without finding anything, while you have been here with me for less than a year and have come across this. It is a blessing sent by God to end your misfortunes and to help you to get back to your people and to reunite you with those whom you love.' Qamar al-Zaman insisted that the treasure must be shared and he took the gardener and brought him into the chamber, where he showed him the gold, which was stored in twenty jars. Of these he took ten and the gardener took ten. 'My son,' the gardener said, 'fill some containers with the sparrow olives that are in this orchard, for they are not to be found in any other country and merchants export them everywhere. You can use them as a covering to mix with the gold, putting the gold in the containers with the olives on top of it. Then close them up and take them on board with you.'

Qamar al-Zaman went immediately and filled fifty containers, closing them up after he had put the gold in them underneath the olives. In one of them he put the ring, after which he and the gardener then sat talking. He was sure that he was going to be reunited with his family and he told himself that after he had reached the Ebony Islands he would go on to his father's lands and ask about his beloved Budur. 'It may be,' he thought, 'that she went back to her own country or travelled on to my father's lands, unless some accident happened to her on the way.' He then recited:

> They left love in my heart and travelled off;
> Those whom I love are now far distant from me.
> The spring camps and their people are remote;
> They live too far off to be visited.
> They took my endurance with them as they went;
> Both sleep and patience have deserted me.
> My joy left me with their departure;
> There is no rest at all for me to find.
> By going, they drew tears down from my eyes,
> And these flowed freely as they went away.
> When I am filled with longing to see them,
> While yearning and expectation both increase,
> I conjure up their images, as in my heart
> Passion is joined with longing and remembrance.

As Qamar al-Zaman sat waiting for the ship to sail, he told the gardener the story of what had happened to the birds. They slept that night, but next morning the gardener woke up sick. His illness continued for two days and on the third day it was so severe that his life was despaired of. Qamar al-Zaman was deeply saddened and it was while he

was in this state that the captain came up with his sailors and asked for
the gardener. When they were told that he was sick, they said: 'Where is
the young man who wants to go with us to the Ebony Islands?' Qamar
al-Zaman replied: 'He is your servant who is standing before you.' On
his instructions, the containers were taken down to the ship and he was
told to hurry as the wind was favourable. He agreed to this, then, after
taking his provisions on board, he went back to say goodbye to the
gardener. Finding him in his death throes, he sat by his head, closing his
eyes when his soul left his body. After laying out his corpse, he buried
him, entrusting him to the mercy of Almighty God, but then, when he
went down to the ship, he found that it had set sail and put out to sea.

It sailed on until it was out of sight and Qamar al-Zaman remained
in a state of perplexity and bewilderment, neither answering any questions put to him nor volunteering any remarks. He then went back to
the orchard, care-ridden and gloomy, pouring dust on his head and
slapping his face.

Night 215

Morning now dawned and Shahrazad broke off from what she had been
allowed to say. Then, when it was the two hundred and fifteenth night,
SHE CONTINUED:

I have heard, O fortunate king, that after the ship had sailed, Qamar
al-Zaman went back to the orchard, care-ridden and gloomy. He rented
the orchard from its owner and employed a man to help him water the
trees, after which he went to the trapdoor and down into the chamber,
where he packed the remainder of the gold into fifty containers, piling
up olives on top of it. When he then asked about the ship, he was told
that it sailed only once a year, which added to his anxiety. He was
distressed by what had happened, and in particular by the loss of Princess
Budur's ring, as result of which he spent his nights and days in tears,
reciting poetry.

So much for him, but as for the ship, a fair wind took it to the Ebony
Islands, where, as fate had decreed, Princess Budur was seated at a
window overlooking the sea. She saw the ship, which had anchored off
the coast, and, with a palpitating heart, accompanied by her emirs,
chamberlains and deputies, she rode down to the shore and halted beside
the ship, whose cargo was being lifted out and shifted to the warehouses.

The captain was brought to her, and when she asked what he had brought with him, he told her: 'Your majesty, I have aromatics, cosmetics, medicinal powders, oils and ointments, together with goods, costly wares, splendid fabrics and more Yemeni mats than camels or mules could carry. There are also perfumes, spices, aloes wood, tamarinds and sparrow olives such as are rarely to be found in these lands.' When Budur heard him mention the olives, she felt a craving for them and she asked the captain what quantity he had with him. 'Fifty containers full,' the captain replied, 'and as their owner is not here with us, the king can take as many as he wants of them.' 'Bring them ashore for me to look at them,' Budur told him. The captain then shouted to his men, who brought up the fifty containers. Budur opened one, saw the olives and said: 'I'll take all fifty and pay you whatever their price may be.' 'In our country, they are valueless,' the captain said. 'The poor man who had them loaded on board was too late to sail with us.' 'How much are they worth here?' asked Budur, and when the captain quoted a thousand dirhams, she agreed to pay the price and had them carried to the palace.

That evening, she had one of the containers brought to her when she was alone in her room with Hayat al-Nufus. She put a dish down in front of her and emptied out the container on to it. When a pile of red gold fell into the plate, she exclaimed to Hayat al-Nufus: 'This is gold!' She then had the other containers fetched and, on investigating them, she found that they were all full of gold, with not as many olives as would fill a single one of them. Then, rummaging through the gold, she discovered a ring in among it and, on taking this and looking at it, she found it to be the very one that had been fastened to the waistband of her drawers and which Qamar al-Zaman had taken. When she had made sure of this, she gave a cry of joy and then fell down in a faint.

Night 216

Morning now dawned and Shahrazad broke off from what she had been allowed to say. Then, when it was the two hundred and sixteenth night, SHE CONTINUED:

I have heard, O fortunate king, that when Budur saw the ring, she gave a cry of joy and fell down in a faint. On recovering, she said to herself: 'This ring was the cause of my parting from my beloved Qamar

al-Zaman, but now it brings good news,' and she told Hayat al-Nufus
that its presence was a sign of a joyful reunion.

The next morning, she took her seat on the royal throne and had the
ship's captain brought to her. When he arrived, he kissed the ground in
front of her and she then asked him where he had left the owner of the
olives. 'King of the age,' he replied, 'we left him in the land of the
Magians, where he looks after an orchard.' 'Bring him to me,' she said,
'or else you and your ship will suffer incalculable harm.' She had the
merchants' warehouses sealed up and she told them: 'The owner of these
olives owes me a debt and if you don't bring him to me, I shall kill you
all and seize your goods as plunder.' The merchants approached the
captain, promising to pay for the hire of his ship if he made a second
voyage and imploring him to save them from such an unjust tyrant.

The captain re-embarked and set sail; God granted him a safe passage
to the island, which he reached at night, and he then went up to the
orchard. Here Qamar al-Zaman was finding that the night passed slowly;
thinking of his beloved, he sat weeping over what had happened to him
and, recalling Budur, he recited these lines:

There is many a night whose stars refuse to move
And which has not the power to go.
For one who watches in it for the dawn,
It seems as long as Judgement Day.

The captain knocked on Qamar al-Zaman's door, and when he opened
it and came out, the sailors carried him off to the ship. They then cast
off and sailed on, day and night. When Qamar al-Zaman, not knowing
the reason for this, asked them about it, they replied: 'You are wanted
by the lord of the Ebony Islands, the son-in-law of King Armanus, whose
money you stole, you ill-fated fellow.' 'By God,' he said, 'I have never in
my life been in that country and I know nothing about it.'

They sailed on to the islands and brought him to Princess Budur, who
recognized him as soon as she saw him. She ordered him to be left with
the eunuchs, who were to take him to the baths, and she then released
the merchants and gave the captain a robe of honour worth ten thousand
dinars. When she went to the palace that night, she told Hayat al-Nufus
what had happened and said: 'Keep this a secret until I get what I want
and do something that will be written down and recited after we are
dead, to kings and their subjects alike.'

Meanwhile, on her orders, Qamar al-Zaman had been taken to the baths and then clothed in royal robes. When he came out, he was like a branch of the *ban* tree or a star whose rising put the sun and moon to shame. He had recovered his spirits and, on entering the palace, he went to Budur. When she saw him, she forced herself to wait in patience until she had done what she wanted. She treated him with favour, giving him mamluks and eunuchs, camels and mules, together with a large sum of money. She continued to promote him from one grade to the next until she made him treasurer, giving him control of the revenues. She treated him as a close associate, and all the emirs, having been told of his status, were well disposed towards him. Every day, Princess Budur would increase his emoluments, while he himself could not understand why it was that she showed him such honour. The extent of his wealth allowed him to make generous gifts, and because of his services, King Armanus grew fond of him, as did the emirs and the people, both high and low, who fell into the habit of swearing by his life.

All the while, he himself was astonished at the honours Budur was showering on him, saying to himself: 'There must be some reason for this affection and it may be that the king is showing me such excessive favour for some evil purpose. I shall have to ask his permission to leave his lands.' So he went to Budur and said: 'Your majesty, you have treated me with very great favour, but the crowning favour would be permission from you for me to leave, and for you to take back everything that you have generously given me.' Budur smiled and said: 'What has led you to want to run the risk of a voyage when you are being treated with the greatest honour and ever-increasing favour?' Qamar al-Zaman replied: 'Your majesty, if this honour comes unprompted, then it is a most remarkable thing, especially as you have promoted me to ranks that are the proper preserve of the old, while I am only a juvenile.' 'The reason for this,' said Budur, 'is that I love you because of your surpassing beauty and your unique loveliness. If you let me have what I want from you, I shall honour you even further with gifts and favours, and young as you are I shall appoint you vizier, just as the people made me their ruler, although I too am young. These days, there is nothing remarkable in the young becoming leaders. How well the poet has expressed it:

It is as though our age belongs to the tribe of Lot,
Who have a passion for advancing the young.'

When Qamar al-Zaman heard this, his cheeks blushed fiery red for shame and he said: 'I have no need of this honour, which would lead me to commit a sin. Rather, I shall live poor as far as money goes but rich in perfect manliness.' Budur replied: 'I am not to be taken in by this piety of yours, which comes from pride and coquetry. How well the poet has said:

I spoke of a pledge of union and he said to me:
"How much longer will you talk in this hurtful way?"
But when I showed him a dinar, he changed his tune,
And said: "How can one escape what fate decreed?"'

When Qamar al-Zaman heard this and had understood the point of the lines, he said: 'O king, I am not accustomed to this and I have not the strength to endure such a burden. If those who are older than me cannot bear it, how can I, being only a youth?' Budur smiled on hearing this and said: 'It is remarkable how error shows itself through what is right. If you are a child, how can you be afraid of sinning by committing an unlawful act, when you have not reached the age of responsibility? A minor cannot be blamed or punished for a fault. You have proved the point against yourself by your own argument. You have to accept what is implied by the word "union", so let there be no more refusals or shying away. What God decrees is destined to come about and I have more cause than you to fear falling into error. How well the poet has expressed it:

My tool is large, but the young boy says:
"Strike like a hero to the inmost parts."
I told him: "That is not permissible," but he said:
"It is to me," and so, uncritically, I slept with him.'

When Qamar al-Zaman heard this, the light in his eyes turned to darkness. 'O king,' he said, 'you have beautiful women and slave girls whose like is to be found nowhere else in this age. Why not content yourself with them and leave me alone? Do what you want with them and let me be.' 'What you say is true,' replied Budur, 'but they cannot cure the painful agony of my love for you. When natural instincts are corrupted, they will heed no advice. Stop arguing and listen to what one poet has said:

When market fruits are set out, as you see,
Some may choose figs and others sycamores.

Another has said:

> There is many a woman whose anklets may be dumb,
> But on her girdle ornaments are tinkling.
> One man is rich; another complains of poverty.
> In her ignorance she wants me to forget you through her beauty,
> But, after true belief, I will not accept impiety.
> I swear by the down on your cheek that shames her locks of hair,
> No lovely virgin can turn me from you.

Another has said:

> You are unique in beauty; your love is my religion
> Which I prefer above all other creeds.
> Because of you I have abandoned women,
> So that people think today I am a monk.

Another has said:

> Do not compare a woman to a beardless boy,
> And do not listen to a censurer who says this is a sin.
> There is a difference between a woman whose foot the face kisses,
> And a gazelle who turns to kiss the earth.

Another has said:

> May I be your ransom; I have picked you out
> Because you neither menstruate nor ovulate.
> Were I inclined to lie with pretty girls,
> The wide land would be too narrow for my children.

Another has said:

> Coquetry left her angry and she said,
> Having invited me and been refused,
> "If you don't lie with me as man with wife,
> Do not blame me when you are cuckolded.
> Your tool is soft as wax,
> And every time I rub it, it gets flabbier."

Another has said:

> When I refused to lie with her, she said:
> "Fool, yours is the height of folly.

If you won't take my vulva as a place of prayer,
Here is another that you may prefer."

Another has said:

She offered a smooth vulva, but I said: "I don't do that."
She gave up, saying, "Whoever is turned away from it
Is turned away:* no one these days uses the front."
She then turned round for me
A backside like molten silver.
Well done, well done, my mistress!
May I never be distressed by your loss.
Well done, you who are wider spread
Than are the victories of our lord, the king.

Yet another has said:

Men ask for pardon with their hands and women with their legs.
What a good work it is God raises to the bottom.'

When Qamar al-Zaman heard all these lines and realized that he could
not avoid what Budur wanted, he said: 'King of the age, if this must be,
promise me that you will only do it with me once, even if that does not
serve to correct your perverted nature, and that you will never ask me
again. Then perhaps God may allow what I have done wrong to be put
right.' She replied: 'I promise you that, in the hope that God may forgive
us and, in His grace, wipe away our great sins. The celestial sphere that
covers us is not too narrow to contain us, and to bring forgiveness after the
heinous evils that we have done, leading us from the darkness of error to
the light of truth. The lines of the poet have been approved which run:

People have suspected us; their hearts and minds
Are set to prove it true. Come let us show them right,
So that we may save them this one time
From wronging us and then we can repent.'

She gave him guarantees and promises, swearing by God, the neces-
sarily Existent, that they would do this only one single time, adding
that passion for him was leading her to death and destruction. On this
condition, he got up and went with her to her private room in order to
quench the fires of her love, repeating the formula: 'There is no might

* Quran 51.9.

and no power except with God, the All-High, the Omnipotent, and this is the decree of the Great and Omniscient God.' Then, full of shame and shedding tears of apprehension, he undid his trousers. Budur smiled as she led him to the bed. 'After tonight you will see nothing to distress you,' she said, and she leaned towards him, kissing and embracing him and twining her legs with his. Then she said: 'Stretch out your hand between my thighs to the usual place, and maybe it will stand up.' He wept, saying: 'I am not good at any of this.' 'By my life,' she said, 'if you do what I tell you, you will find it pleasant.' So he put out his hand, with a deep sigh, and he found that her thighs were softer than butter and smoother than silk. It gave him pleasure to touch them and he moved his hand round and about to explore, until he came to a dome full of blessings and of movement. 'Perhaps this king is a hermaphrodite, neither male nor female,' he said to himself. 'O king,' he said to Budur, 'I cannot find that you have an instrument like those of men, so why do you do this?' Budur laughed out loud. 'My darling,' she said, 'how quickly you have forgotten the nights that we spent together.'

Then she revealed herself and Qamar al-Zaman recognized that this was indeed his wife, Princess Budur, daughter of King al-Ghayur, lord of the islands and the seas. He embraced her and she embraced him; they exchanged kisses and then lay with one another on the bed, reciting these lines:

When with bent elbow he came to my embrace, moving beside me,
The hardness of his heart was softened
And, after refusal and rebellion, he agreed.
He feared the censurers might see when he appeared;
He came prepared to avoid the charge of premeditated fault.
His waist complained of buttocks which, when he walked,
Burdened his feet with a full camel's load.
His glances served him as a girded sword;
The dark locks of his smooth hair were as mail.
His fragrance brought news of his happy coming,
And I ran out as a bird flies from a cage.
I laid my cheek on the ground before his shoe;
The dust he trod served as antimony for my eye.
I raised the banners of union with an embrace,
And I undid the knot of malign fortune.
I held a feast of joy and to its summons came

Delight, now purified of turbid cares.
The full moon sprinkled stars over the mouth,
These being bubbles dancing on the face of wine.
I busied myself in the prayer niche of pleasure
With that sin which never brings a sinner to repent.
I swear by the Verses of Light in his face that here
For me the *sura* of Sincerity is not forgot.

Princess Budur then told Qamar al-Zaman everything that had happened to her from beginning to end, after which, in his turn, he told her his story. He then began to reproach her, asking her what had induced her to do what she did to him that night. 'Don't blame me,' she said, 'I only did it as a joke, for amusement and pleasure.' When daylight returned, Budur sent word to King Armanus, Hayat al-Nufus's father, telling him who she really was and that she was the wife of Qamar al-Zaman. She told him their story, explaining why they had parted and adding that his daughter was still a virgin. When King Armanus heard all this, he was astonished and ordered that it should be recorded in letters of gold. Then, turning to Qamar al-Zaman, he asked whether he would be willing to become his son-in-law and to marry Hayat al-Nufus, his daughter. 'Let me first consult Princess Budur,' he replied, 'to whom my debt is greater than I can count.' He did this and she replied: 'This is a good idea. Marry her and I will be her servant, for she conferred many benefits, favours and boons on me and, in particular, we are in her country and her father has overwhelmed me with his kindliness.' Seeing that Budur was favourably inclined and was not jealous of Hayat al-Nufus, he agreed with her on the proposal.

Night 217

Morning now dawned and Shahrazad broke off from what she had been allowed to say. Then, when it was the two hundred and seventeenth night, SHE CONTINUED:

I have heard, O fortunate king, that Qamar al-Zaman agreed on the proposal with his wife, Budur. He then told King Armanus that she was in favour of the marriage and would act as a servant for Hayat al-Nufus. The king was delighted to hear this. He went out, took his seat on the royal throne and assembled all his viziers, emirs, chamberlains and officers of state, to whom he told the story of Qamar al-Zaman and his wife, Princess Budur, from start to finish. He added that he proposed to marry his daughter, Hayat al-Nufus, to Qamar al-Zaman, and to set him in the place of his wife, Budur, as ruler over them. They all said: 'As he is the husband of Princess Budur, who was our ruler before him and whom we took to be the king's son-in-law, we are all content that he should rule us. We shall be his servants and we shall not abandon our allegiance to him.' This greatly pleased King Armanus, and after assembling the *qadis*, the witnesses and the leaders of his state, he had a marriage contract drawn up between Qamar al-Zaman and his daughter, Princess Hayat al-Nufus. He organized wedding celebrations, gave magnificent banquets, distributed splendid robes of honour to all the emirs and army commanders, and gave alms to the poor and needy. Everyone rejoiced in the rule of Qamar al-Zaman and they prayed that he would enjoy continuing glory, good fortune, happiness and honour.

On coming to power, Qamar al-Zaman cancelled the market taxes and freed any who were still in prison. He conducted himself laudably and his married life was one of happiness, pleasure, faithfulness and joy. He spent alternate nights with each of his wives, and the longer this continued, his cares and sorrows cleared away, and he forgot his father, King Shahriman, and the royal dignity that he had enjoyed. Almighty God then provided him with two sons like radiant moons, one by each of his wives. Of these, the elder, Budur's son, was called al-Malik al-Amjad, while the younger, al-Malik al-As'ad, was the son of Hayat al-Nufus and he was more handsome than al-Amjad, his brother.

The two were brought up in the midst of luxury and elegance, in an atmosphere of the finest good breeding. They studied calligraphy, science, administration and horsemanship until they reached the peak of perfection and they were so handsome that men and women alike were captivated by them. By the time that they were almost seventeen, they were inseparable, eating and drinking together and not parting from each other for however short a time, to the envy of all the people. When they reached man's estate, their qualities were perfect, and when their father left on a journey, he would seat them alternately in his judgement hall, where each of them would deliver judgements to the people for one day at a time.

As fate had decreed, love for al-As'ad, Hayat al-Nufus's son, entered the heart of his father's wife Budur, while the same thing happened to Hayat al-Nufus with regard to Budur's son, al-Amjad. Each lady used to fondle the other's son, kissing him and pressing him to her heart, while, on seeing this, the mother would think that it was merely the result of affection and maternal feeling. Such was their infatuation for the two boys that both ladies fell deeply in love and each, when the other's son came in, would clasp him to her breast, wishing that he might never leave her.

When they found that things were going too slowly and they had discovered no way to achieve union, they abstained from food and drink and abandoned the pleasure of sleep. It then happened that the king went off on a hunting trip, leaving his sons to take his place as ruler, each for a day at a time, as had been the custom.

Night 218

Morning now dawned and Shahrazad broke off from what she had been allowed to say. Then, when it was the two hundred and eighteenth night, SHE CONTINUED:

I have heard, O fortunate king, that when the king went off hunting, he told his sons to take his place as ruler, each for a day at a time, as had been the custom. On the first day, it was Budur's son, al-Amjad, who sat giving judgements, issuing orders and prohibitions, appointing and dismissing officials, granting and refusing requests. Hayat al-Nufus, al-As'ad's mother, wrote him a letter of supplication in which she made it clear that she was attached to him by ties of love, disclosing her feelings and telling him that she wanted union with him. On the paper she had written in rhymed prose: 'From the unfortunate lover, the sad one parted from her beloved, whose youth has been squandered on your love and who, because of you, has suffered prolonged torment. It would take too long to describe in a letter the length of my grief, the sorrow that I endure, the passionate love that is in my heart, my tears and moans, the wounds in my sad heart, the sequence of my sorrows, the cares that follow on each other's heels, how separation pains me, my melancholy and my burning passion. These things pass all reckoning. Earth and sky are too narrow for me and I have nothing to look for or any hope except in you. I am near my end, enduring the terrors of death. My burning passion and the pains of abandonment and separation grow worse. Were I to describe my longing, there would not be enough paper to suffice. In my affliction and my emaciation, I recite these lines:

Were I to set out my burning agony,
My illness, passion and distress,
There would be no scrolls left in all the world,
No pens, no ink, no paper.'

She then folded the paper and placed it in a piece of precious silk scented
with musk and ambergris, including with it some of her hair bands whose
cost would swallow up fortunes. Wrapping everything in a kerchief, she
gave it to a eunuch with orders to take it to al-Malik al-Amjad.

Night 219

Morning now dawned and Shahrazad broke off from what she had been
allowed to say. Then, when it was the two hundred and nineteenth night,
SHE CONTINUED:

I have heard, O fortunate king, that she gave the note to a eunuch
with orders to take it to al-Malik al-Amjad. The eunuch went off, not
knowing the fate that awaited him, for He Who knows the unseen directs
affairs as He wills. When the eunuch came into al-Amjad's presence, he
kissed the ground in front of him and handed him the kerchief with the
letter. Al-Amjad took the kerchief from him and, undoing it, he saw the
letter, which he proceeded to open. When he had read it and grasped its
meaning, he realized that his father's wife was contemplating treachery
and had played his father false in her heart. In a fury, he blamed all
women for their actions, exclaiming: 'God damn women, traitresses
as they are, lacking in both intelligence and religious scruples.' Then,
unsheathing his sword, he said to the eunuch: 'Damn you, you evil slave,
do you dare to carry a message of treachery from the wife of your
master? By God, there is no good in you. Your colour is black and so is
the record of your deeds. You are ugly to look at and your nature is
despicable.' He then struck him on the neck with his sword, severing his
head from his body, after which he folded the kerchief together with its
contents and put it in his pocket. Next, he went to his mother, and after
telling her what had happened, he abused and reviled her, saying: 'Each
of you women is worse than the rest. I swear by Almighty God that were
I not afraid of acting indecorously with regard to my father and my
brother, I would go to Hayat al-Nufus and cut off her head as I did to
her eunuch.'

After this, still in a furious rage, he left his mother, Budur. Meanwhile, when Hayat al-Nufus heard what he had done to her eunuch, she reviled him and cursed him, plotting to use trickery against him. He himself spent the night sick with anger, disgust and anxiety, finding no pleasure in food, drink or sleep. The next morning, his brother, al-Malik al-Asʿad, went out and took his father's place to deliver judgements among the people. Meanwhile, his mother, Hayat al-Nufus, had fallen ill after hearing that al-Amjad had killed her eunuch. After al-Asʿad had taken his seat that day, he made just decisions, appointing and dismissing officials, giving out commands and prohibitions, and making generous gifts.

He stayed sitting there until it was nearly time for the afternoon prayer. It was then that Queen Budur, al-Amjad's mother, sent for a wily old woman and told her what was in her heart. She then took a sheet of paper on which to write to al-Asʿad, her husband's son. Complaining of the extent of love and passion that she felt for him, she wrote in rhymed prose: 'From one who is dying of passionate longing to the handsomest and best of mankind, who is proud of his beauty and boasts of his elegance, shunning those who seek union with him and abstaining from any relationship with the humble and submissive. This is sent from the distressed lover to the harsh and impatient al-Malik al-Asʿad, with his surpassing beauty and excelling loveliness, whose face is a bright moon, with a gleaming forehead and glistening radiance. The letter is addressed to one whose love has wasted away my body and split my flesh from my bones. Know that my patience is at an end; I do not know what to do. Longing and sleeplessness have made me restive; neither endurance nor sleep are kind to me, and my constant companions are sorrow and wakefulness. I am troubled by the passion of love, together with the emaciation and illness that beset me because of this. May my life be your ransom, even if you are content to kill your lover. May God preserve you and protect you from all evil.' After this, she wrote the following lines:

Time has decreed that I should love you,
Whose beauty is that of a shining moon.
Yours is all loveliness and radiance;
Your splendour is unique among mankind.
I am content that you should be my torturer,
For it may be you will spare me a glance.

How happy is the one who dies of love for you.
In those who do not love no good is to be found.

She then wrote these other lines:

To you, As'ad, I complain of the fire of passion;
Pity the slave of love who burns with longing.
How long am I to be tossed to and fro
By passion, love, care, sleeplessness and suffering?
I complain of a sea and then of fire within my heart.
This is a wonder, you who are my desire.
Blamer, abandon blame and seek to flee from love.
Tears flood down from my eyes.
How often did I cry out in distress when you abandoned me,
But my laments and cries did me no good?
You made me ill, shunning me in a way I cannot bear.
You are the doctor; help me with what I have to have as cure.
Censurer, stop; be on your guard,
Lest you yourself perish from the disease of love.

Budur then perfumed the paper of the letter with pungent musk and wrapped it in her hair bands of Iraqi silk, whose tassels were of emeralds, set with pearls and other gems. This she handed to the old woman, telling her to give it to al-As'ad. The old woman went off obligingly, and promptly came to al-As'ad, who was alone when she entered. She gave him the paper and stood for a time waiting for a reply. Al-As'ad read the letter and understood its meaning. Folding it up among the hair bands, he put it in his pocket in a state of furious anger, cursing the treachery of women. Then, getting up and unsheathing his sword, he struck the old woman on the neck, cutting off her head. After that, he walked away to his mother, Hayat al-Nufus, whom he found lying on her bed, sick because of what had happened to her with al-Amjad. Al-As'ad reviled and cursed her and then he left. Meeting his brother, al-Amjad, he told him everything that had happened to him with Budur, his mother, telling him that he had killed the old woman who had brought him the letter. 'By God, brother,' he added, 'were it not for my respect for you, I would go to Budur straight away and cut off her head.' Al-Amjad told him that, the day before, when he had been sitting on the royal throne, the same thing had happened to him and that Hayat al-Nufus had sent him the same kind of letter. After telling al-As'ad the whole story, he too added that had it not been for his respect for his brother, he would have gone to Hayat al-Nufus and treated her as he had treated the eunuch. The two of them spent the rest of the night talking and cursing the treachery of women. They advised one another that the affair should be kept secret lest their father, Qamar al-Zaman, come to hear of it and kill the two women.

After they had passed a sorrowful night, in the morning Qamar al-Zaman came back from the hunt with his men. He sat for some time on the royal throne and then, after dismissing his emirs, he got up and went to the palace. Here he found both his wives lying in bed in an enfeebled state. They had plotted against their sons and had agreed to have them killed, for they had disgraced themselves with the two young men and were afraid of being humiliated by them. When Qamar al-Zaman saw the state that they were in, he asked them what was wrong and they rose to greet him and kissed his hands. Then, reversing what had really happened, they said: 'Know, your majesty, that your two sons, whom you have reared in luxury, have betrayed you with regard to your wives and have committed a shameful act.'

When Qamar al-Zaman heard this, the light turned to darkness in his eyes and he became madly angry. He told them to explain what had happened, and Queen Budur said: 'You must know, king of the age, that for a number of days your son al-As'ad has been sending me messages and letters, attempting to seduce me. Although I tried to stop him, he would not give up. When you went away, he attacked me while he was drunk. He had a drawn sword in his hand with which he struck and killed my eunuch. He then got on top of me, still holding the sword, and I was afraid that if I tried to resist him, he would kill me as he had killed my eunuch. So he raped me and if you don't avenge me on him, as is my due, I shall kill myself with my own hand, as after this foul act there is nothing left for me to live for in this world.'

Night 220

Morning now dawned and Shahrazad broke off from what she had been allowed to say. Then, when it was the two hundred and twentieth night, SHE CONTINUED:

I have heard, O auspicious king, that Queen Hayat al-Nufus told her husband: 'The same thing happened to me with your son al-Amjad.' She then burst out weeping and wailing and told Qamar al-Zaman that if he did not take vengeance for her on al-Amjad, she would tell her father, King Armanus.

Both ladies wept bitterly in front of Qamar al-Zaman, and when he saw this and heard what they had to say, he believed that it must be true. He got up in a furious rage, intending to attack and kill his two sons, but he was met by his father-in-law, who was just coming in at that moment to greet him on his return from his hunting trip. Armanus saw him with a drawn sword in his hand and blood dripping from his nostrils because of the violence of his anger. He asked him what was wrong and Qamar al-Zaman told him what al-Amjad and al-As'ad had done, adding: 'I'm going to kill them in the vilest of ways and to make the most shameful example of them.' 'That is good, my son,' said Armanus, who was also angry with the princes. 'May God give no blessing to them or to any other sons who act like this towards their fathers. But, my son, the proverb says that whoever does not look towards the consequences will not find Time his friend. They are, after all, your sons and you shouldn't kill them with your own hand lest you yourself experience death pains and find yourself repenting of what you did when repentance is too late to be of use after you have killed them. Instead of this, send out one of your mamluks to execute them in the desert out of your sight. As the proverb has it, it is better to be far from the beloved, as what the eye does not see the heart does not grieve over.'

When Qamar al-Zaman heard what his father-in-law had to say, he thought it good advice. He sheathed his sword and returned to sit on the royal throne before sending for his treasurer, a very old man experienced in affairs and accustomed to the vicissitudes of Time. 'Go to my sons, al-Amjad and al-As'ad,' he said. 'Pinion them securely, put them in two chests and load these on a mule. Then mount and take them into the middle of the desert, where you are to cut their throats and fill two flasks with their blood. Then hurry back to me with the flasks.' 'To hear is to obey,' replied the treasurer.

He had set off at once to look for the princes, when he found them on their way out of the hall, wearing their finest clothes. They were coming to greet their father and congratulate him on his safe return from his hunting trip. When the treasurer saw them, he laid hands on them and said: 'My sons, know that I am a slave and under orders. Your father has given me a command. Are you prepared to obey it?' 'Yes,' they replied, at which he went up to them, pinioned them and put them in two chests which he loaded on the back of a mule. He then took them out of the city and rode with them into the desert until it was nearly noon. After halting in a desolate and lonely spot, he dismounted, unloaded the chests from the back of the mule and opened them, bringing out the two princes. When he looked at them, their beauty and grace caused him to weep bitterly, but he unsheathed his sword and said: 'By God, my masters, it is hard for me to treat you so badly, but I must be excused in this because I am a slave under orders. Your father, King Qamar al-Zaman, has commanded me to cut off your heads.' They said to him, 'Carry out the king's orders, emir, for we shall endure what God, the Great and Glorious, has decreed for us, and you are free of any blood guilt for us.'

They embraced one another and took their leave, after which al-As'ad said to the treasurer: 'For God's sake, uncle, I implore you not to inflict on me the death pangs of my brother, filling me with distress for him, but kill me before him so that this may be easier for me to bear.' Al-Amjad said the same thing, hoping to persuade the treasurer to kill him first. 'My brother is younger than I am,' he said, 'so don't make me suffer his pain.' Each of them then wept bitterly, prompting the treasurer to join in their tears.

Night 221

Morning now dawned and Shahrazad broke off from what she had been allowed to say. Then, when it was the two hundred and twenty-first night, SHE CONTINUED:

I have heard, O fortunate king, that the treasurer joined in their tears. The brothers then embraced and said goodbye to each other, after which one said to the other: 'This is all due to the trickery of those two treacherous women, my mother and yours, and it is a repayment for what happened to me with your mother and what happened to you with mine. There is no might and no power except with God, the Exalted, the Omnipotent. We belong to God and to him do we return.' Al-As'ad hugged his brother, sighing deeply and reciting these lines:

God of refuge, to Whom complaints are made,
You Who are ready for all we can expect,
My one resource is to knock on Your door;
If I am turned away, on whose door shall I knock?

The treasuries of Your grace are found in the word 'be'.
Show favour to me, for with You exists all good.

Al-Amjad, sharing in his brother's tears, clasped him to his breast and recited these lines:

You Who grant me favour after favour,
Whose gifts cannot be counted,
When one of Time's misfortunes comes on me,
I find You there to take me by the hand.

Al-Amjad then said to the treasurer: 'I implore you by the One God, the Almighty, the King, the Concealer, kill me before my brother al-As'ad, so that the fire in my heart may be quenched and not allowed to burn.' Al-As'ad shed tears himself and insisted that he should be the first to die, and al-Amjad then suggested that they should both embrace each other so that the sword blow could kill them both simultaneously. The two of them then held each other in a close embrace, face to face, and the treasurer tied them tightly with ropes, shedding tears as he did so. He then drew his sword and said: 'By God, masters, it is hard for me to kill you. Is there anything that you want me to do for you, any instruction that you would like me to carry out or any message that you want delivered?' 'There is nothing we need,' said al-Amjad, 'but I instruct you to put my brother al-As'ad underneath and me on top, so that the blow may fall on me first. When you have gone back to the king after having killed us and he asks you whether we said anything before we died, tell him: "Your sons sent you their greetings and said that you did not know whether they were innocent or guilty, but killed them without making sure of their guilt or looking into their case." Then recite these lines for him:

Women have been created for us as devils;
I take refuge in God from devilish wiles.
From them spring the misfortunes of mankind,
In matters of the world and in religion.'

Al-Amjad then added: 'This is all that we want you to do, to repeat to the king these lines that you have heard . . .'

Night 222

Morning now dawned and Shahrazad broke off from what she had been allowed to say. Then, when it was the two hundred and twenty-second night, SHE CONTINUED:

I have heard, O fortunate king, that Al-Amjad said: 'This is all that we want you to do, to repeat to the king these lines that you have heard. I also ask you in God's Name, to be patient until I recite these other lines to my brother.' Shedding tears, he then recited:

> There is clear proof for us among the former kings;
> How many, great and small, have passed along this road!

When the treasurer heard what al-Amjad said, he wept so bitterly that tears soaked his beard, while as for al-As'ad, tears filled his eyes and he recited:

> We saw, and Time afflicts us by what is left behind,
> But why is it we weep for shapes and images?
> What do nights suffer? God forgive whatever we have done to them;
> It is the hand of change that has betrayed them.
> They kindled a fire of cunning against Ibn Zubair,
> Without respect for his refuge at the Ka'ba and the Black Stone.
> They ransomed 'Amr with Kharija;
> Would that they had ransomed 'Ali with any man they chose.

With a flood of tears running down his cheeks, he recited:

> By nature nights and days are treacherous,
> Full of deception and of wiles.
> Desert mirages serve them as gleaming teeth,
> And the dread in every darkness serves as kohl.
> My sin against this evil-natured Time
> Is the sword's sin when the swordsman holds it back.

Sighing deeply, he recited more lines:

> You who are seeking this vile world,
> It is destruction's net, a pit of sorrows.
> It is a dwelling which may bring
> Laughter one day, but will fetch tears the next.

Evil befall it! Its attacks never cease;
No price, however great, ransoms its prisoners.
How many boasted of its vanities,
Until they passed the bounds and disobeyed their God.
It then reversed its shield and plunged its dagger home,
So it might take revenge.
Know that misfortunes take you by surprise,
Even if delays are long and fate is slow.
See that you do not waste your life in vain,
And have no victories to show.
So cut your links of love for it and end your quest,
To find right guidance and peace in your heart.

When al-As'ad had finished these lines, he and his brother embraced until they seemed to be one single person. The treasurer drew his sword and was about to strike when suddenly his horse took fright and bolted into the desert. As the horse itself was worth a thousand dinars and was carrying a magnificent and costly saddle, the treasurer threw away the sword and went after it . . .

Night 223

Morning now dawned and Shahrazad broke off from what she had been allowed to say. Then, when it was the two hundred and twenty-third night, SHE CONTINUED:

I have heard, O fortunate king, that the treasurer pursued the horse, on fire with anxiety. He kept on pursuing it, and he was still trying to catch it when it entered a wood. It made its way through the middle of the trees, drumming on the ground with its hooves, raising a high, spreading column of dust, snorting and whinnying with blood-shot eyes. In that wood was a dangerous and hideous lion, with eyes that shot out sparks, a grim face and a terrifying shape. The treasurer turned to see the lion making for him. Unable to see any way of escape and without his sword, he said to himself: 'There is no might and no power except with God, the Exalted, the Omnipotent! I have fallen into this dilemma because of the sin of al-Amjad and al-As'ad, and a journey that was ill-omened from the start.'

The princes themselves, left in the burning heat, became violently thirsty. Their tongues hung out and although they cried out for help from their thirst, there was no one to aid them. 'Would that we had been killed and so had been saved from this!' exclaimed al-Amjad. 'There is no knowing where the horse may have gone in its fright, with the treasurer following it, leaving us tied up. If he were to come back and kill us, it would be easier for us than having to endure this torture.' 'Be patient, brother,' said al-As'ad, 'and it may be that Almighty God, praise be to Him, will send us relief. It was only because of His favour to us that the horse bolted, and it is only this thirst that harms us.' He then shook himself, twisting right and left until his bonds were loosened. Getting up, he freed his brother and then, taking the treasurer's sword, he said: 'By God, we cannot leave this place until we find out about him and discover what has happened to him.'

They started to follow the trail which led them to the wood and they told each other that the horse and its master could have gone no further than that. 'Stay here,' said al-As'ad to his brother, 'while I go in and look around.' 'I am not going to let you go by yourself,' al-Amjad replied. 'We shall both go, so that whether we live or die, we shall share the same fate.' They entered together and found that the lion had attacked the treasurer, and was holding him beneath it like a little bird, while, for his part, he was pointing to the sky and imploring God for help. On seeing this, al-Amjad took the sword and attacked the lion, striking it between the eyes and killing it. As it fell on the ground, the treasurer got up, full of astonishment, and when he saw al-Amjad and al-As'ad standing there, he threw himself down at their feet. 'By God, sirs,' he said, 'it would not be right for me to commit an outrage by killing you. May no one ever kill you! I would ransom you with my life.'

Night 224

Morning now dawned and Shahrazad broke off from what she had been allowed to say. Then, when it was the two hundred and twenty-fourth night, SHE CONTINUED:

I have heard, O fortunate king, that the treasurer told the princes that he would ransom them with his life. He got to his feet immediately and embraced the princes, asking them how they had freed themselves from their bonds and had come to him. They told him that they had become thirsty and that, after one of them had managed to free himself, he had been able to release the other, thanks to their innocence. Afterwards, they had followed his trail until they had discovered him. On hearing this, the treasurer thanked them for what they had done and went with them out of the wood. There they told him to carry out their father's commands, but he said: 'God forbid that I should do you any harm. What I intend to do is to take off your clothes, dress you in mine and then fill two flasks with the lion's blood, after which I'll go to the king and tell him that I killed you. As for you, you can go off, for God's earth is wide, but know that I shall find it hard to part from you both.'

He and the princes shed tears. They then exchanged clothes and the treasurer bundled theirs up, putting them in front of him on the back of the horse together with the two flasks which he had filled with the lion's blood. Saying goodbye to the princes, he set off for the city, going on until he had come into the presence of the king. He kissed the ground in front of the king, who noticed that his colour had changed. That was because of his experience with the lion, but the king supposed it was because he had killed his sons. He was pleased, saying: 'Have you done the job?' 'Yes, master,' replied the treasurer, who then handed the king the two bundles and the flasks filled with blood. 'How did they behave,' he asked, 'and did they charge you with any commission?' 'I found them patiently resigned to their fate,' replied the treasurer. 'They told me: "Our father is to be excused. Give him our greetings and tell him that we absolve him from responsibility for our deaths. We charge you to recite these lines to him:

Women have been created for us as devils;
I take refuge in the Lord from devilish wiles.
From them spring the misfortunes of mankind,
In matters of the world and in religion."'

On hearing what the treasurer had to say, the king looked down at the ground for a time, realizing that what his sons had said showed that they had been killed unjustly. He thought of the wiles of women and the calamities that they caused, after which he took the two bundles, unfastened them and started to turn over his sons' clothes, weeping as he did so.

Night 225

Morning now dawned and Shahrazad broke off from what she had been allowed to say. Then, when it was the two hundred and twenty-fifth night, SHE CONTINUED:

I have heard, O fortunate king, that the king took the two bundles, opened them and started to turn over his sons' clothes, weeping as he did so. When he opened up al-As'ad's clothes, he found in the pocket a letter in the handwriting of his wife Budur, in which were hair bands of hers. He unfolded and read the piece of paper, and when he had understood its contents, he realized that al-As'ad had been the victim of an injustice. He then searched through al-Amjad's bundle and found in his pocket the letter written by Hayat al-Nufus, together with her hair bands. When he opened this and read it he realized that al-Amjad too had been wronged. Striking his hands together, he exclaimed: 'There is no might and no power except with God, the Exalted, the Omnipotent! I have killed my sons unjustly.' He began to strike his face, exclaiming: 'Alas for my sons. How long will be my sorrow!'

On his orders, two tombs were built in one chamber, which he named the House of Sorrows, and on these tombs were engraved the names of his sons. He then threw himself down on the tomb of al-Amjad, weeping, moaning, complaining, and reciting these lines:

A moon that has set beneath the earth;
The gleaming stars have wept for it.
O branch, after your loss, the watching eyes
Could find nothing else that bent.
My jealousy has kept you from my sight
Until I reach the world to come.
I have drowned my sleepless eyes in tears;
It is for this I find myself in hell.

Then, throwing himself on al-As'ad's tomb, he wept, moaned and complained, reciting, in a flood of tears, the lines:

I used to wish that I might share your fate,
But what God willed was not what I had wished.
Between my eyes and the heavens all is black,
While the blackness in my pupils is rubbed away.

The tears I shed are inexhaustible,
As fresh supplies are sent on by my heart.
It saddens me to see you in a place
Where worthless men and glorious are both equal.

His laments increased, but when he had finished weeping and reciting poetry, he abandoned his friends and companions and cut himself off in his so-called House of Sorrows to mourn for his sons, having parted company from his wives and his familiars.

So much for him, but as for al-Amjad and al-As'ad, they travelled on in the desert for a whole month, eating herbs and drinking from rain puddles. At the end of this time they came to a mountain range of black rock that spread out further than the eye could see. Here the track divided, with one path cutting through the middle and another climbing to the summit. This latter was the way that they took, but after having followed it for five days, they could still not see its end. They were exhausted with fatigue, not being used to walking on mountains or anywhere else, and so, despairing of reaching the end, they went back and started on the track that led through the middle of the range.

Night 226

Morning now dawned and Shahrazad broke off from what she had been allowed to say. Then, when it was the two hundred and twenty-sixth night, SHE CONTINUED:

I have heard, O fortunate king, that the princes came back from the track that led up the mountains and started on the one that led through the middle of the range. They walked all that day until nightfall. Al-As'ad, who had been tired out by the long journey, told his brother that he was too weak to walk any further. 'Take heart, brother,' said al-Amjad. 'It may be that God will bring us relief.' They walked on for some time in the night through the darkness until al-As'ad became utterly exhausted. Telling his brother that he was too tired to go any further, he threw himself down on the ground in tears. Al-Amjad picked him up and started carrying him on for a while and then sitting down for a rest. This continued until dawn, by which time they had reached the crest. Here they found a spring of water with a pomegranate tree and prayer niche. At first they could not believe their eyes, but then they sat down by the spring, drank from its water and ate pomegranates from the tree. They slept there until the sun had risen, when they sat up, washed themselves in the spring and ate more pomegranates, after which they slept until afternoon.

They now wanted to go on, but al-As'ad's feet were too swollen to allow him to move and so they stayed there for three days until they were rested. After that, for some days and nights they travelled on the mountain, walking along the summit ridge. When they were almost dead of tiredness and thirst, they caught sight of a city in the distance. They went on cheerfully and, when they got near, they gave thanks to Almighty God. 'Sit here, brother,' said al-Amjad to al-As'ad, 'and I'll go on to this city and find out what it is, to whom it belongs and where we are in God's wide world. We shall then discover how many lands we have crossed in traversing the range. Had we walked along its foot, we wouldn't have got here in a whole year, so praise be to God that we're safe.' 'By God, brother,' said al-As'ad, 'no one except me is going down there. I am your ransom and if you leave me now and go away for an hour, I shall have a thousand cares and be drowned in worries about you. I could not bear it if you left me.' 'Go down, then,' said al-Amjad, 'but don't be long.'

So al-As'ad went down from the mountain, taking with him some money and leaving his brother to wait for him. After he had reached the foot of the mountain, he went into the city and made his way through its lanes. On his way he was met by a very old man, whose forked beard hung down over his chest. He carried a staff in his hand and was wearing splendid robes, while on his head was a large red turban. Al-As'ad was astonished at seeing how he was dressed, and, going up and greeting him, he asked the way to the market. When the old man heard what he said, he smiled at him and said: 'It seems, my son, that you must be a stranger.' 'Yes, I am,' replied al-As'ad.

Night 227

Morning now dawned and Shahrazad broke off from what she had been allowed to say. Then, when it was the two hundred and twenty-seventh night, SHE CONTINUED:

I have heard, O fortunate king, that when the old man met al-As'ad, he smiled at him and said: 'It seems, my son, that you must be a stranger.'

'Yes, I am,' replied al-As'ad. 'You have brought delight to our country, my son, while leaving the lands of your family desolate. What is it that you want from the market?' 'Uncle,' answered al-As'ad, 'I have a brother whom I have left on the mountain. We have come from a distant land and have been travelling for three months. We caught sight of your city and I left my elder brother on the mountain and have come here to buy food and some provisions that I can take back to my brother.' 'I have good news for you, my son,' said the old man. 'I am giving a banquet with many guests, and have prepared the most delicious, excellent and appetizing foods. If you would like to come with me to my house, I shall give you whatever you want without taking anything at all in return, and I shall tell you all about the city. I give praise to God, my son, that it was I and no one else who fell in with you.' 'As you please,' said al-As'ad, 'but be quick; my brother is expecting me and all his thoughts are with me.'

Taking al-As'ad by the hand, the old man led him back to a narrow lane, smiling at him and saying: 'Glory to God, Who preserved you from the people of the city.' He walked on with al-As'ad, until he entered a spacious house, where there was a room, in the centre of which sat forty old men, grouped in a circle, with a fire burning in the middle of it. They were seated around the fire and were worshipping it and prostrating themselves to it. When al-As'ad saw that, he was stupefied and the hairs on his body bristled, as he did not know what they were doing. The old man cried out to the assembled company: 'Shaikhs of the Fire, what a blessed day this is!' Then he called: 'Ghadban,' and out came a tall black slave, with a fearsome form, a grim face and a flat nose. The old man gestured to him and he bound al-As'ad tightly. 'Take him to the underground chamber,' ordered the old man, 'and when you have left him there, tell the slave girl to see to it that he is tortured night and day.'

The slave took al-As'ad down to the chamber and handed him over to the slave girl, who started to torture him. She would give him a single loaf to eat early in the morning and another in the evening, with two jugs of salty water, one in the morning and the other in the evening. The *shaikhs* said to each other: 'When the time of the Fire Festival comes, we shall cut his throat on the mountain and sacrifice him to the Fire.' The slave girl set about beating him so painfully that blood flowed from his sides and he fainted. She then put down a loaf and a jug of salty water by his head, before going away and leaving him alone. When he recovered consciousness in the middle of the night, he found himself in chains and suffering from the pain of his beating. He wept bitterly, recalling his past glory and good fortune, the royal power that he had held, and how he had been parted from his father and his kingdom.

Night 228

Morning now dawned and Shahrazad broke off from what she had been allowed to say. Then, when it was the two hundred and twenty-eighth night, SHE CONTINUED:

I have heard, O fortunate king, that al-As'ad found himself in chains, suffering from the pain of his beating. He recalled his past glory and good fortune and the royal power that he had held. Weeping and sighing deeply, he recited these lines:

> Halt by the ruins of the dwelling and ask for news of us,
> But do not think that we are still where we used to be.
> Time, which disperses friends, has parted us,
> But the hearts of those who envy us are not yet cured.
> A vile slave girl has beaten me with a whip;
> Her heart was filled with hatred towards me.
> It may perhaps be that God will reunite us,
> Drive off our enemies and punish them.

When he had finished his poem, he stretched his hand up to his head, where he found the loaf and the jug of salty water. He ate a little, just enough to keep him alive, and drank some water, but swarms of bed bugs and lice kept him awake till morning. The slave girl then came down to him. She changed his clothes, which were drenched in blood and sticking to his skin. He cried out as some of his skin came off with his shirt, but then he said: 'Lord, if this is Your will, increase my torture; God, You are not unmindful of the one who wrongs me, so avenge me on him.' Then he sighed deeply and recited these lines:

> My God, may I be patient in what You decree.
> Should this please You, I shall endure my fate.
> My Lord, may I bear patiently what You decree,
> Even if I am thrown into a fire of twigs.
> With their injustice my foes have wronged me;

To compensate, perhaps You may show favour.
Far be it from You, Lord, to overlook wrongdoers.
And my help comes from You, the Lord of destiny.

From another poet he quoted:

Turn aside from your affairs;
All these depend on fate.
There is many an affair that angers you,
But whose result is satisfaction.
The narrows may be broadened,
And the empty space narrowed.
God acts according to His wish;
Do not resist.
Rejoice that good will quickly come,
Removing from your mind all that has passed.

When he had finished, the slave girl beat him until he fainted and then put down a loaf of bread and a jug of salty water for him, after which she went off, leaving him alone and miserable, with blood streaming from his sides. His fetters were of iron, he was far from his loved ones, and so he wept, remembering his brother and his former glory.

Night 229

Morning now dawned and Shahrazad broke off from what she had been allowed to say. Then, when it was the two hundred and twenty-ninth night, SHE CONTINUED:

I have heard, O fortunate king, that al-As'ad wept, remembering his brother and his former glory. Through his tears, moans and complaints, he recited these lines:

Go slowly, Time! How many injuries will you inflict on me,
And for how many days will you part me from my brothers?
Is it not now that you should pity
The length of this parting, you whose heart is hard as stone,
Who injures friends and causes enemies
To gloat because of the ruin you have brought?
The hearts of foes are comforted by what they see –
My exile, love and loneliness.

My grief, the parting from my friends, my inflamed eyes
Were not enough for them, until I was confined
In a narrow prison, on my own, biting my hand in my regret.
My tears flood down like rain pouring from clouds,
But still the fire of passion is not quenched.
Distress, love, memories – how much is there,
Allied with grief and panting sighs!
Longing and deadly sorrow must be faced,
In the abiding love that cripples me.
I meet no sympathetic friend
To pity me and come to visit me.
Does any truly love me and lament
My sickness and my lengthy sleeplessness,
To whom I might complain of my distress?
My eyes are wakeful and can find no sleep.
I pass long nights of torture and endure
The burning fire of care. Bed bugs and fleas
Have drunk my blood as one drinks wine
Passed by a red-lipped, tender girl.
Among the lice my body is an orphan's hoard,
Entrusted to an atheist *qadi*.
I live in a three-cubit grave,
Fettered and drained of blood.
Tears are my wine; my music comes from chains;
Cares serve as my dessert; sorrows spread out my bed.

When he had finished these lines, he groaned and complained, thinking over his present position and how he had been parted from his
brother.

So much for him, but as for al-Amjad, he stayed, waiting for his
brother until midday. When he had still not come back, his heart fluttered
and because of the violence of the pain of separation, he shed a flood of
tears . . .

Night 230

Morning now dawned and Shahrazad broke off from what she had been allowed to say. Then, when it was the two hundred and thirtieth night, SHE CONTINUED:

I have heard, O fortunate king, that al-Amjad stayed, waiting for his brother until midday. When he had still not come back, his heart fluttered and because of the violence of the pain of separation, he shed a flood of tears, crying out, as he wept: 'Alas for my brother, alas for my companion! How afraid I was that we would be parted!' He then came down from the mountain, with tears running down his cheeks, and entered the city. He walked through it until he reached the market, where he asked about the city's name and its inhabitants. The people told him that its name was the Magian City and that its inhabitants worshipped fire rather than the Omnipotent God. When he asked about the Ebony City they told him that it was a year's journey away by land and six months by sea. They added: 'Its king is called Armanus, but, after taking a prince as a son-in-law, he installed him in his place. The name of this ruler is Qamar al-Zaman, a just, beneficent, generous and trustworthy man.'

Al-Amjad burst into tears and lamentations on hearing his father's name. He didn't know where to go, but he had bought something to eat and, after going off into a place of concealment, he sat down. He was about to start eating when, remembering his brother, he burst into tears and could only force himself to eat enough to keep himself alive. After that, he got up and walked back to the city to look for news of his brother and, finding a Muslim tailor in a shop, he sat down with him and told him his story. 'If he has fallen into the hands of one of the Magians,' said the tailor, 'you stand little chance of seeing him again, but perhaps God may reunite you.' Then he added: 'Would you like to stay with me, brother?' To the tailor's delight, al-Amjad accepted and stayed with him for some days, during which the tailor tried to console him, urging him to be patient and teaching him tailoring until he became skilled.

One day, he went out to the seashore and washed his clothes, after which he entered the baths and put on clean clothes. On leaving the baths, he went sight-seeing in the city and on his way he came across a beautiful woman, with a symmetrical figure and outstanding loveliness, who had no equal in point of beauty. When she saw him, she lifted her veil and signalled to him with her eyes and eyebrows, giving him a flirtatious glance and reciting these lines:

> When I saw you coming, I lowered my eyes,
> As though, slender one, you were the sun's own eye.
> You are the loveliest of all who have appeared,
> More beautiful today than you were yesterday.
> Were beauty split up into lots,
> Joseph would only have one-fifth or less than that.
> The rest would all belong to you,
> With every living soul serving as your ransom.*

When al-Amjad heard what she said, he was pleased and felt affection for her, finding himself a plaything in the hands of love. He gestured towards her and recited these lines:

> The thorny lances of eyelashes guard the roses of the cheeks –
> Who will be brave enough to try to pluck them out?
> Do not reach out your hands to this beloved;
> How many times the lances thrust merely because we looked!
> In her injustice she is a seduction,
> But were she just, this quality would increase.
> Tell her: 'Your veiled face leads me further astray;
> To be unveiled, I see, better protects your beauty,
> Like the sun at which, when it shines clearly, none can look,
> But can be viewed wearing thin cloaks of cloud.'
> Young bees are guarded by the elders of the hive:
> Ask the tribe's guards what is it that I seek.
> They may want my death, but they should now forget
> Their malice and allow us free passage.
> If they come out to fight, they cannot be
> More fatal than the glances of the lady with the mole,
> If she should show herself to me.

When she had heard al-Amjad's lines, she sighed deeply and, gesturing towards him, recited:

> It was you who turned away, not I.
> Grant union; the time for redeeming promises has come.

---

* The lines 'The rest would all belong to you, / With every living soul serving as your ransom' are not in the Calcutta II text.

The light of your gleaming face is like the break of dawn,
While the locks of your hair provide night with a home.
Your form, lovely as an idol, makes me a worshipper.
You are temptation and for long have tempted me.
No wonder that the fire of love consumes my heart;
Fire is the rightful punishment of idol worshippers.
You give away lovers like me for free,
But if you must sell me, at least demand a price.

When al-Amjad heard what she said, he asked her: 'Will you come to me or shall I come to you?' She looked down at the ground modestly and recited the words of Almighty God: 'Men are the guardians of women, because of the superiority that God has granted to the one sex over the other.'* Al-Amjad grasped the point of her allusion . . .

Night 231

Morning now dawned and Shahrazad broke off from what she had been allowed to say. Then, when it was the two hundred and thirty-first night, SHE CONTINUED:

I have heard, O fortunate king, that al-Amjad grasped the point of her allusion, and realized that she wanted to accompany him wherever he was going. He felt obliged to find a place for her, but he was ashamed to take her to his master, the tailor. He walked on ahead and she followed him, and he kept on going from lane to lane and from place to place until she got tired. 'Master,' she said, 'where is your house?' 'In front of us,' he replied, adding: 'And it is not far now.' Then he turned off into a pleasant lane and walked on, still followed by her, until he reached the end of the lane, which he discovered had no exit. 'There is no might and no power except with God, the Exalted, the Omnipotent!' he exclaimed. He looked around and saw at the end of the lane a large door, flanked by two benches, but it was locked. So he took his seat on one of the benches while the girl sat down on the other. 'What are you waiting for, master?' she asked. For a time he looked down at the ground, and then, raising his head, he said: 'I am waiting for my mamluk, who has the key. I told him to get me food and drink, as well as something to go with the wine, and to be ready for me when I came from the baths.' To himself

* Quran 4.38.

he said: 'She may find it too long to wait and go off on her way, leaving me here, and then I can go on by myself.'

When she grew tired of waiting, she said: 'Master, your mamluk is slow in coming and we are left sitting in this lane.' She went up to the bolt of the door, carrying a stone. 'Don't be hasty,' said al-Amjad. 'Wait until he comes.' Paying no attention, she struck the bolt with the stone, splitting it in half and forcing the door open. 'Why have you done this?' asked al-Amjad. 'Pooh,' she said. 'What of it? It's your house.' 'Yes,' replied al-Amjad, 'but there was no need to break the bolt.' The girl then went into the house, but al-Amjad stayed where he was, in a state of perplexity, fearful of the owners of the house and not knowing what to do. 'Why don't you come in, light of my eyes and darling of my heart?' asked the girl. 'To hear is to obey,' he answered, 'but the mamluk has been slow and I don't know whether he has carried out any of the orders that I gave him or not.'

He then went in with her, although he was still very fearful at the thought of the owners. On entering he found a fine hall with four facing alcoves containing small chambers and raised seats spread with silks and brocades. In the centre was a costly fountain, by which were set plates studded with gems and filled with fruits and scented flowers, while at the side were drinking glasses. There was also a candlestick with a candle, and the place was full of precious materials, with chests and chairs set out, and a package laid on each chair, on top of which was a purse filled with gold and coins. Judging by the house, its owner was a wealthy man, as its floor was paved with marble.

Al-Amjad was taken aback when he saw this, saying to himself: 'I am a dead man. We belong to God and to Him do we return.' As for the girl, when she saw the place she was delighted and said: 'By God, master, your mamluk didn't fail. He has swept out the place, cooked the food and prepared the fruit. I have come at the best of times.' Al-Amjad, who was preoccupied by his fear of the owners, paid no attention to her. 'Pooh!' she exclaimed. 'My master and my heart, why are you standing like this?' Then, with a deep sigh, she gave al-Amjad a kiss that sounded like a walnut being cracked, and said: 'If you are expecting someone else, I'll do my best to serve her.' Al-Amjad laughed, with a heart full of anger, and he came and sat down, breathing heavily and saying to himself: 'What a miserable death I shall die when the owner comes!'

The girl sat beside him, laughing playfully, while he was frowning and full of care, turning things over and over in his mind and saying: 'The owner of this place is bound to come and what am I going to say to him? He will certainly kill me and my life will be gone.' The girl then got up, tucked up her sleeves, picked up a table, put a cloth on it and started to eat, telling al-Amjad to do the same. He came to the table to eat, but he couldn't enjoy the food and kept looking towards the door. When the girl had had enough, she removed the table and, after bringing forward the fruit, she started on the dessert. Next, she brought out the drink, opened the wine-jar and filled a drinking cup, which she handed to al-Amjad. He took it from her, saying to himself: 'Oh, oh, what will happen when the owner of the house comes and sees me?'

As he held the cup in his hand, his eyes were fixed on the hallway, and it was just then that the owner arrived. He was a mamluk and, as the king's equerry, he was one of the leading men of the city. He had got the room ready for his own pleasure as a place where he could relax in private with his chosen companions. That day, he had invited a youth whom he loved to visit him and it was for him that he had made these preparations. The mamluk's name was Bahadur and he was open-handed, generous and liberal in conferring gifts and favours.

Night 232

Morning now dawned and Shahrazad broke off from what she had been allowed to say. Then, when it was the two hundred and thirty-second night, SHE CONTINUED:

I have heard, O fortunate king, that Bahadur, the owner of the house, was the king's equerry. When he approached the door and found it open, he entered slowly and, peering in, he saw al-Amjad and the girl with a dish of fruit and a wine-jar in front of them. At that moment al-Amjad was holding the drinking cup, with his eyes fixed on the door. When his eyes caught those of Bahadur, he turned pale and began to tremble. Bahadur saw this change and put his finger to his mouth to show that he should say nothing but come over to him. Al-Amjad set down his cup and got up to go, and when the girl asked where he was going, he shook his head indicating that he wanted to relieve himself. He went out to the hallway barefooted and when he saw Bahadur he realized that this must be the owner of the house and hurried up to him. After having kissed his hands, he said: 'In God's Name, master, I implore you to do me no harm before you hear what I have to say.' He then told him his story from beginning to end, including why he had left his own kingdom and the fact that he had not come into the hall of his own free will, adding that it was the girl who had broken the lock, opened the door and done it all.

Bahadur listened to the tale of his adventures and, realizing that he was a prince, felt sympathy for him and pitied him. 'Listen to what I have to say, al-Amjad,' he said. 'Obey me and I shall guarantee not to punish you as you fear, while if you disobey me, I shall kill you.' 'Tell me to do whatever you want,' replied al-Amjad. 'I shall never disobey you, for it is your sense of chivalry that has set me free.' 'Go back to the room at once,' said Bahadur. 'Sit down quietly where you were before and I shall come in. My name is Bahadur and when I come to you, abuse me angrily and say: "Why are you so late?" Don't accept any excuse from me, but get up and beat me. If you show pity for me, I shall kill you, so go and enjoy yourself. Whatever you now ask from me, I shall produce for you instantly; you may pass this night doing what you want and tomorrow you can go off on your way, this being the courtesy that is owed to you as a stranger. I love strangers and take it as my duty to honour them.'

Al-Amjad kissed his hand and went back to the room, his face having recovered its pink and white colours. As soon as he came in, he said to the girl: 'My lady, you have brought delight to this place by your presence here and this is a blessed night.' 'It's a surprise that you're being so friendly to me now,' said the girl. 'By God, my lady,' he replied, 'I thought that Bahadur, my mamluk, had taken some jewelled necklaces of mine, each worth ten thousand dinars. I was worrying about that when I went out just now, but when I looked for them I found them in their proper place; but I don't know why he is so late and I shall have to punish him.'

The girl relaxed when she heard what he had to say and the two of them toyed with each other and drank happily, continuing to enjoy themselves until the sun had almost set. It was then that Bahadur made his entrance, having changed his clothes, wearing a belt around his waist and, on his feet, coloured shoes such as mamluks wear. He greeted the two, kissing the ground and putting his hands behind his back while bending his head towards the ground in the attitude of someone who is acknowledging a fault. Al-Amjad looked at him angrily. 'Vilest of mamluks,' he said, 'why are you so late?' 'Master,' Bahadur replied, 'I was busy washing my clothes and I didn't know that you were here. We were supposed to meet in the evening, not in the day.' 'You are lying, you vile fellow,' shouted al-Amjad, 'and I shall have to beat you.' He rose, threw Bahadur down on the ground, took a stick and began to beat him, but not hard.

Then the girl got up and, taking the stick from him, she gave Bahadur an agonizingly painful beating that reduced him to tears. He cried for help and clenched his teeth as al-Amjad called to the girl to stop. She kept saying: 'Let me work my anger off on him,' until he snatched the stick from her hand and pushed her away. Bahadur got up, wiped his tears away and stayed for a time waiting on them, after which he tidied up the room and lit the candles. Every time he went out and in, the girl would abuse and curse him. Al-Amjad was getting angry with her and implored her in the Name of Almighty God to let him be, explaining: 'He's not used to this.' The two of them continued to eat and drink, and were waited on by Bahadur, until midnight.

Bahadur, tired out by serving them and by his beating, then fell asleep in the middle of the room, breathing heavily and snoring. The girl, who was now drunk, said to al-Amjad: 'Get up. Take the sword that's hanging there and cut off this fellow's head, or else I'll see that you die.' 'What has made you think of killing my mamluk?' he asked. 'It is only with his death that our pleasure will be complete,' she answered, adding: 'And if you don't get up, I'll get up myself and kill him.' 'For God's sake, don't do it,' said al-Amjad. But she insisted: 'It has to be done.'

She took the sword, unsheathed it and was about to kill Bahadur when al-Amjad said to himself: 'This man has done us a favour, given us shelter and treated us well, pretending to be my mamluk. How can we repay him by killing him? That can never be.' So he said to the girl: 'If my mamluk has to be killed, I have a better right to do it than you.' He took the sword from her, raised his arm and struck her on the neck, severing her head from her body. The head fell on Bahadur, who woke and sat up, opening his eyes. He found al-Amjad standing sword in his hand, covered in blood, and then he looked and saw that the girl was dead. He asked al-Amjad what had happened to her and al-Amjad told him the story, saying: 'She insisted on killing you, and this is her reward.'

Bahadur got up, kissed al-Amjad's head and said: 'I wish you had spared her, but the only thing to do now is to get her out of here before morning.' He tightened his belt, took the girl and wrapped her in a cloak, after which he put her in a pannier and lifted it up. 'You're a stranger here,' he said to al-Amjad, 'and you know no one. So sit where you are and wait for me until dawn. If I come back, I shall do you much good, and try my best to get news of your brother, but if I don't, then you can be sure it is all up with me and so goodbye. The house and all the wealth and materials that it contains will be yours.'

He picked up the pannier and left the room. Threading his way through the markets, he made for the road to the sea, in order to throw the dead girl into it, but when he got near, he turned to find himself surrounded by the *wali* and his officers. They were surprised to recognize him, but when they opened up the pannier they found the dead girl and so they seized him. They kept him in chains until morning, when they took him and the pannier, just as it was, to the king, whom they told what had happened. When the king saw the pannier, he was very angry and said: 'Damn you, you are always doing this, killing people, throwing them into the sea and seizing all this wealth. How many have you managed to kill before this?' Bahadur hung his head ...

Night 233

Morning now dawned and Shahrazad broke off from what she had been allowed to say. Then, when it was the two hundred and thirty-third night, SHE CONTINUED:

I have heard, O fortunate king, that Bahadur hung his head towards the ground before the king, who cried out to him: 'Damn you, who killed this girl?' 'My lord,' Bahadur answered, 'I killed her. There is no might and no power except with God, the Exalted, the Omnipotent.' In his anger, the king ordered him to be hanged.

At the king's command, the executioner took Bahadur off, accompanied by the *wali*, with his herald, who summoned the people throughout the city streets to come and watch the execution of the king's equerry, and they paraded him around the streets and markets.

So much for him, but as for al-Amjad, when dawn had broken and the sun had risen without Bahadur having returned, he said to himself: 'There is no might and no power except with God, the Exalted, the Omnipotent. What do you think has happened to him?' While he was brooding about this, he heard the herald summoning the people to come and watch the execution of Bahadur, who was going to be hanged at midday. On hearing that, al-Amjad burst into tears and exclaimed: 'We belong to God and to Him do we return! This man is going to lose his life unjustly for my sake. It was I who killed her. By God, this shall never happen.'

He left the house, shutting it up behind him, and made his way through the middle of the city until he reached Bahadur. Standing in front of the *wali*, he said: 'Sir, don't execute Bahadur, who is innocent. By God, I was the one who killed her.' When the *wali* heard this, he took both al-Amjad and Bahadur and brought them to the king, to whom he told what he had heard al-Amjad say. The king looked at al-Amjad and asked him if he had, in fact, killed the girl. When al-Amjad admitted this, the king said: 'Tell me why you did this, and speak the truth.' 'Your majesty,' replied al-Amjad, 'mine is a strange and remarkable story, which, were it written with needles on the inner corners of the eye, would serve as a warning to those who take heed.'

He then told the king his story, explaining what had happened to him and to his brother from start to finish. This filled the king with astonishment and he said: 'I realize that you are to be excused.' He then asked al-Amjad whether he would act as his vizier, to which al-Amjad replied: 'To hear is to obey.' The king presented both him and Bahadur with splendid robes of honour and to al-Amjad he gave a fine house, together with eunuchs and servants, providing him with everything he needed, as well as assigning him pay and allowances, and telling him to search for his brother, al-As'ad. Al-Amjad sat in the place of the vizier, gave his judgements with righteousness, appointed and dismissed officers, took in money and gave it away. He sent a crier throughout the lanes of the city, calling for information about his brother, al-As'ad. For a period of days the crier went through the streets and markets, but without hearing any news or finding any trace of al-As'ad.

So much for al-Amjad, but as for al-As'ad, the Magians kept on torturing him, night and day, morning and evening, for a full year, until the time of their feast drew near. The Magian Bahram then made preparations for a journey and got ready a ship.

Night 234

Morning now dawned and Shahrazad broke off from what she had been allowed to say. Then, when it was the two hundred and thirty-fourth night, SHE CONTINUED:

I have heard, O fortunate king, that the Magian Bahram made

preparations for a journey and got ready a ship. He took al-As'ad and
put him in a chest, which he locked and had carried on board. At the
time when this was being done, fate had decreed that al-Amjad should
be standing, looking at the sea. He saw the cargo being loaded on to the
ship; his heart fluttered and he told his servants to bring him his horse,
after which he rode off with a number of his retainers, making for the
sea. Standing by the Magian ship, he ordered his men to board and
search it. This they did, going through the whole of it, but after finding
nothing they went back and said so to al-Amjad. He remounted and
rode off, heading for home. When he got there, he went into the palace
in a state of dejection and, looking around, he saw lines of poetry written
on a wall. They ran:

> My dear ones may be absent from my sight,
> But from my heart and mind they have not gone.
> You left me sick with love, and drove off sleep
> From my eyelids, while you yourselves have slept.

When al-Amjad read these lines, he wept, remembering his brother.

So much for him, but as for Bahram the Magian, he boarded the ship
and shouted to the crew to be quick to set sail. They did this and put
out to sea, sailing on, night and day, and every two days they would
take out al-As'ad and give him a little food and water. They were nearing
the Fire Mountain when they were met by a contrary wind and a rising
sea, which caused them to stray from their course, bringing them to
unknown waters. Here they arrived at a coastal city, with a castle whose
windows overlooked the sea, and which was ruled by a queen named
Marjana. The captain told Bahram: 'Master, we have gone astray and
we shall have to go into this city in order to rest, after which God will
do what He wants.' 'You have done well,' said Bahram. 'This is good
advice, so act on it.' The captain then asked: 'When the queen sends to
question us, what shall we tell her?' 'We have this Muslim here,' said
Bahram, 'but we can dress him up as a mamluk and take him out with
us. When the queen sees him she will think that that is what he is, and
I'll tell her that I'm a slave dealer who buys and sells them, adding that
of the many I had, this was the only one whom I didn't sell.'

The captain approved of this, and when they reached the city they
lowered their sails and let go the anchors, bringing the ship to a halt.
Queen Marjana came down with her men to meet them, and, halting by
the ship, she called for the captain. When he had come to her and kissed

the ground in front of her, she asked: 'What cargo is in this ship of yours and who is with you?' 'Queen of the age,' he answered, 'I have with me a merchant who sells mamluks.' 'Bring him to me,' she said, and at this Bahram came forward, with al-As'ad walking behind him dressed as a mamluk. When Bahram reached the queen, he kissed the ground and stood before her. She asked what his business was and he told her that he was a slave dealer. Then, looking at al-As'ad and thinking that he was a mamluk, she asked him his name. Choking with tears, he told her that it was al-As'ad. She felt pity for him and asked: 'Do you know how to write?' 'Yes,' he said, and so she gave him an inkstand, pen and paper, and told him to write something for her to see. He wrote these lines:

> Watcher, what is a man to do when fate
> Turns always against him?
> It throws him, with his hands tied, in the sea,
> Saying: 'Take care, take care not to get wet.'

When the queen read this, she pitied al-As'ad and told Bahram to sell him to her. 'My lady,' he replied, 'I cannot do that as I have sold all my other mamluks and this is the only one I have left.' 'I must get him from you either by sale or as a gift,' insisted the queen. 'I shall neither sell him nor give him,' Bahram told her, but she caught hold of al-As'ad's hand and took him up to the castle, after which she sent a message to the captain, telling him that if he did not set sail that night and leave her country, she would seize all his goods and break up his ship. When he heard this, he was very distressed and complained that it had not been a good voyage for him. He made his preparations, collecting all that he wanted, after which he waited for the coming of night before sailing. He told his crew to get ready, to fill their water skins, and to be prepared to put to sea at the end of the night. The men started to carry out their tasks, waiting for night to fall.

So much for them, but as for Queen Marjana, she brought al-As'ad into the castle, where she opened the windows overlooking the sea. On her orders, her slave girls brought food for the two of them, which they ate, after which she told them to fetch wine.

Night 235

Morning now dawned and Shahrazad broke off from what she had been allowed to say. Then, when it was the two hundred and thirty-fifth night, SHE CONTINUED:

I have heard, O fortunate king, that the queen ordered her slave girls to fetch wine. When this was brought, she drank with al-As'ad, and God, the Glorious, the Exalted, implanted love for him in her heart. She began filling his wine cup and giving it to him to drink, until he became fuddled and got up to relieve himself. On coming down from the castle, he went through an open door that he saw and walked on until he came to a large garden, where there were all kinds of fruits and flowers. He squatted down beneath a tree, relieved himself, and then got up and went to the garden's fountain. He lay on his back, with his clothes undone, and then went to sleep, fanned by the breeze as night fell.

So much for him, but as for Bahram, at nightfall he called to his crew, ordering them to set sail and put to sea. 'To hear is to obey,' they said, 'but wait for us to fill our water skins before we sail.' To do this, they took their water skins with them and circled around the castle, where all that they found was the garden wall. They climbed over this, and after going down into the garden they followed footprints that led to the fountain. Here they found al-As'ad lying on his back and, recognizing who he was, they carried him off joyfully, after having filled their water skins. They jumped down from the wall with him and hurried him off to Bahram. 'Good news!' they shouted. 'You have what you wanted; your heart's sorrow is cured; the pipes and drums of joy have sounded for you. We have found your prisoner, whom the queen took from you by force, and we have brought him with us.' They threw al-As'ad down before Bahram, who was overjoyed to see him, and filled with happiness and delight. He gave the men robes of honour and told them to set sail quickly. They did this and, setting a course for the Fire Mountain, they sailed on until morning.

So much for them, but as for Queen Marjana, after al-As'ad left her, she waited for some time, expecting him to come back. When he did not, she got up and looked, but could find no trace of him. So she had the candles lit and told her slave girls to search. Next, she went down herself and found the garden gate open, which made her realize that he had entered it, and when she went in herself she found his sandals beside the fountain. She searched the whole garden for him, but with no success, and after she had spent the rest of the night doing this, she asked about the ship. When she was told it had sailed in the first night watch, she realized angrily that al-As'ad must have been taken on board.

Finding this hard to bear, she ordered ten large ships to be made ready instantly, and, taking her own arms and armour, she boarded one of them, accompanied by her mamluks, slave girls and soldiers, splendidly equipped and prepared for war. The fleet set sail and she promised the captain that if they overhauled the Magian ship, she would give them robes of honour and wealth, whereas if they failed, she would kill every last one of them, so filling the sailors with a mixture of fear and great hope.

They sailed throughout that day and night and then for a second and a third day. On the fourth, Bahram's ship came into sight, and before the day had ended they had surrounded it. Just then, Bahram had brought out al-As'ad, beaten him and started to torture him. He had been crying for help and protection, but had found no one to answer his pleas, and was suffering from the violence of his beating. During the course of this, Bahram looked around to find that his ship was surrounded by others as the white of the eye surrounds the black. He was certain that he was bound to be killed, and in his distress, he said: 'Damn you, al-As'ad, you're responsible for all this.' He took him by the arm and ordered his men to throw him into the sea, saying: 'By God, I shall kill you before I die.'

They lifted him by the arms and legs and threw him in, but God, the Glorious, the Exalted, was willing that he should be saved and that his life should be preserved. Through His permission, after sinking, al-As'ad rose to the surface and struck out with his arms and legs until God facilitated his escape from danger. He was buffeted by waves which swept him far away from the Magian ship and brought him to land. He went ashore, scarcely believing that he had escaped, and when he was on dry land he took off his clothes, squeezed out the water and then spread them out. He sat there naked, weeping over his state and the misfortunes that he had suffered, the threats of death, his captivity and his exile. He then recited these verses:

My Lord, I have scant endurance or resource;
I can no longer show patience and my ropes are cut.

To whom is the poor man to complain
Except to his Lord, O Lord of lords?

When he had finished, he got up and put on his clothes, but he had no idea where to go and so he started to eat plants and fruits and to drink from streams. After travelling night and day, he came in sight of a city. He now pressed on gladly and arrived there as evening was falling . . .

Night 236

Morning now dawned and Shahrazad broke off from what she had been allowed to say. Then, when it was the two hundred and thirty-sixth night, SHE CONTINUED:

I have heard, O fortunate king, that al-As'ad arrived at the city as evening was falling and the city gate had been shut. As fate had decreed, the city turned out to be the one in which he had been held prisoner and where al-Amjad, his brother, was the king's vizier. When he saw that the gate was locked, he went back towards the tombs in the cemetery and, finding one that had no door, he went in and fell asleep, with his sleeve over his face.

As for Bahram the Magian, when Queen Marjana's ships caught up with him, he got the better of her by his magic wiles and returned safely to his city. He immediately disembarked, set off happily and, as fate would have it, while walking among the graves he saw the tomb where al-As'ad was sleeping. He was surprised to see it open and he told himself that he must look inside. When he did, he saw al-As'ad sleeping at the side of it, with his face covered by his sleeve and, looking at his face, he recognized him and exclaimed: 'Are you still alive?' He then took him off to his house, where he had an underground torture chamber for Muslims, and in this he put al-As'ad, with heavy fetters on his legs.

Bahram had a daughter, named Bustan, whom he entrusted with the task of torturing al-As'ad night and day until he died. He himself first beat him painfully and then locked the room, handing the keys to Bustan. When she opened it and went down to beat him, she discovered that here was a graceful young man, with a pleasant face, arching eyebrows and dark eyes. Love for him entered her heart and she asked him his name. 'Al-As'ad,' he replied, and she said: 'May you be happy and may your days be fortunate. You don't deserve to be tortured and beaten and I know that you have been treated unjustly.'

She started to talk to him in a friendly manner, releasing him from his fetters and asking him about the religion of Islam. 'Islam,' he told her, 'is the right and true religion; our lord Muhammad produced wonderful miracles and clear signs, whereas fire does harm and not good.' He started to tell her about the principles of Islam, and as she listened submissively to him, love for the true faith entered her heart, in which Almighty God had also instilled love for al-As'ad. She then recited the twin confessions of faith and became one of those destined for eternal happiness. After this, she started to give him food and drink; she talked with him and the two then prayed together. The chicken broth that she gave him strengthened him and, when the sickness from which he was suffering had left him, he regained his former health.

So much for his treatment at the hands of Bahram's daughter, but as for the girl herself, one day when she had left him, she was standing by her door when she heard a crier announcing: 'If anyone has with him a handsome young man of such-and-such a description and produces him, he can have all the money for which he asks. Anyone who has the man but refuses to acknowledge it will be hanged over his house door; his property will be pillaged and his blood will go unavenged.' Al-As'ad had told Bustan everything that had happened to him and when she heard this, she realized that he was the man being sought. She went to him and when she had told him her news, he came out and set off for the house of the vizier, at the sight of whom he exclaimed: 'This vizier is my brother, al-Amjad!'

Followed by the girl, he went to the palace, where, on seeing al-Amjad, he threw himself on him. Al-Amjad, recognizing him, did the same and the two brothers embraced. As the mamluks surrounding them dismounted, the brothers fainted for a time, but when they had recovered, al-Amjad took al-As'ad and brought him to the king. Having heard his story, the king gave orders that Bahram's house should be plundered . . .

Night 237

Morning now dawned and Shahrazad broke off from what she had been allowed to say. Then, when it was the two hundred and thirty-seventh night, SHE CONTINUED:

I have heard, O fortunate king, that the king gave orders that Bahram's house should be plundered, and that he himself should be hanged. Al-Amjad sent out a body of men to do that and they went to the house and looted it. They brought Bahram's daughter to al-Amjad, who received her with honour. Al-As'ad told him of how he had been tortured and of the kindness with which Bustan had treated him, leading al-Amjad to show her even greater honour. Al-Amjad then told al-As'ad of his own experiences with the other girl, how he had escaped from being hanged and how he had become vizier. Each complained to the other of the grief they had felt at being separated from the other.

The king then had Bahram the Magian brought to him and ordered him to be beheaded. 'O great king,' said Bahram, 'are you determined to kill me?' When the king said yes, Bahram asked for a brief delay and after first looking down at the ground and then raising his head, he recited the Confession of Faith and was converted to Islam at the hands of the king, to the joy of the court. The brothers then told Bahram all that had happened to them. He was astonished and said: 'My masters, prepare for a journey, for I will set off with you.' This delighted them, as did his conversion, but they burst into tears.

'Don't weep, my masters,' said Bahram, 'for you will be united with your loved ones as Ni'ma and Nu'm were united.' They asked about these two, and BAHRAM ANSWERED:

It is said – but God knows better – that one of the leading men in the city of Kufa was a certain Rabi' ibn Hatim, a wealthy man, living in comfort, who had a son, whom he named Ni'ma Allah. One day, when he was standing by the slave trader's booth, he saw a slave girl exposed for sale who was holding a little girl of remarkable beauty. He gestured to the trader and asked: 'How much for the woman and her daughter?' 'Fifty dinars,' replied the man. 'Write out the contract and then take the money and give it to her owner,' said Rabi'. He paid the purchase price together with the broker's commission and, taking charge of the slave girl and her daughter, he brought them to his house.

When his wife saw the slave, she asked him about her and he said:

'I bought her for the sake of this little girl in her arms. You can be sure that when she grows up there will be no one to match her in the lands of the Arabs and non-Arabs and no one more beautiful.' His wife agreed that he was right. She then asked the slave girl: 'What is your name?' 'Tawfiq, lady,' she replied, and when she asked her for her daughter's name, she said: 'Sa'd.'* 'There is truth in this,' said Rabi''s wife. 'You are fortunate and so is the man who bought you.' She asked her husband what he was going to call the child. 'You choose,' he replied, and she said: 'We shall call her Nu'm.' 'What a good idea,' he told her.

The baby Nu'm was then brought up with al-Rabi''s son, Ni'ma, in the same cradle; and they stayed together until they were both ten years old, and each of them seemed lovelier than the other. Ni'ma would address the girl as 'my sister', and she would call him 'brother'. Then, when Ni'ma was ten, his father came to him and said: 'My son, Nu'm is not your sister but your slave girl. I bought her on your behalf when you were still in the cradle, so from now on, don't call her "sister".' 'If that is so,' replied Ni'ma, 'I shall marry her.' He went to his mother and told her about that and she confirmed that the girl was his slave. So he lay with her and loved her and in this state they passed some years.

In all Kufa, there was no lovelier, sweeter or more graceful girl than Nu'm. When she grew up, she could recite the Quran; she had a knowledge of the sciences; she could play on a number of musical instruments, and in her brilliance as a singer and a musician she surpassed all her contemporaries. One day, as she was sitting drinking with her husband Ni'ma, she took her lute, tightened its strings and then in a mood of pleasant relaxation she recited these lines:

If you are my master, through whose grace I live,
My sword with which I can destroy misfortune,
I have no need to intercede with Zaid or 'Amr
Or anyone but you, when hardships come on me.

Ni'ma was filled with delight and said: 'By my life, sing to me using your tambourine and other instruments.' So she struck up an air and sang these lines:

By the life of him who is my guide,
In love for him I disobey the envious.
I anger censurers in my obedience to you,

* Sa'd is Arabic for 'good fortune'.

Parting from pleasure and from sleep.
I shall dig a grave for love within my inmost parts,
And my heart will not feel it.

'How eloquent you are, Nu'm!' exclaimed the young man, but while
they were enjoying the most delightful of lives, in the governor's palace
al-Hajjaj was saying: 'I must get hold of this girl, Nu'm, by some trick
or other, and send her to 'Abd al-Malik ibn Marwan, the Commander
of the Faithful, as there is no one like her in his palace or anyone who
can sing more sweetly.' He summoned an elderly duenna and told her:
'Go to the house of al-Rabi', meet the girl Nu'm and find some way for
me to take her away, for there is no one like her on the face of the earth.'
The old woman agreed to this, and in the morning she put on woollen
robes and placed around her neck a rosary with thousands of beads.
Then, taking a staff in her hand and a water bottle of Yemeni leather . . .

Night 238

Morning now dawned and Shahrazad broke off from what she had been
allowed to say. Then, when it was the two hundred and thirty-eighth
night, SHE CONTINUED:

I have heard, O fortunate king, that the old woman agreed to what
al-Hajjaj proposed; she put on woollen robes and placed around her
neck a rosary with thousands of beads. Then, taking a staff in her hand
and a water bottle of Yemeni leather, she set off, calling out: 'Glory be
to God; there is no god but God; God is greater; there is no might and
no power except with God, the Exalted, the Omnipotent!' She continued
exalting God and addressing her supplications to Him, while her heart
was filled with guile and cunning. She reached Ni'ma's house at the time
of the noon prayer and knocked on the door. This was opened by the
doorkeeper, who asked her what she wanted. 'I am a poor ascetic,' she
answered. 'The time of the noon prayer has caught me out and I should
like to perform it in this blessed place.' 'Old woman,' said the doorkeeper, 'this is the house of Ni'ma ibn al-Rabi' and not a mosque or a
chapel.' 'I know that there is no mosque or chapel to match the house
of Ni'ma ibn al-Rabi',' the old woman replied. 'I am an attendant from
the palace of the Commander of the Faithful, and I have come out on a
pious pilgrimage.' 'I shan't let you enter,' the doorkeeper insisted and

there was a long argument between them. Then the old woman took hold of the man, saying: 'Is someone like me to be stopped from entering the house of Ni'ma ibn al-Rabi', I who go into the houses of emirs and great men?'

Ni'ma came out and heard what they were saying. He laughed and told the old woman to follow him into the house. She did this and came into the presence of Nu'm, whom she greeted with the greatest courtesy. Looking at her, she was amazed and astonished by her great beauty and she said: 'My lady, God has matched you in beauty with your master and I ask Him to protect you.' She then took up her stance in the prayer niche and began to perform *rak'as* and prostrations, reciting her prayers, until the day had ended and the darkness of night had arrived. 'Mother,' said Nu'm, 'rest your feet for a little.' 'Lady,' she replied, 'those who seek the world to come must put up with weariness in this one. Those who do not do this fail to reach the dwellings of the righteous in the next world.' Nu'm brought her food and said: 'Eat of my food and pray God to grant me forgiveness and mercy.' 'I am fasting, lady,' said the woman, 'but you are a young girl and it is right for you to eat, drink and enjoy yourself. God will pardon you, for He said, Almighty is He: "All will be punished except for those who repent, believe and do good deeds."'*

Nu'm sat talking with the old woman for some time and she then told Ni'ma: 'Do your best to get this old woman to stay with us for a while, as the marks of asceticism are on her face.' He replied: 'I shall let her have a room where she can go to worship, and I shan't let anyone else go in to interrupt her. It may be that God, the Glorious, the Exalted, will favour us because of the blessing that she brings and grant that we may never be separated.' The old woman spent the night in prayer and Quranic recitation until the morning. Then she went to Ni'ma and Nu'm, wished them good morning and said: 'I leave you to the care of God.' 'Where are you going, mother?' asked Nu'm. 'My master has told me to give you a room to yourself where you can devote yourself to worship and prayer.' 'May God preserve him,' said the old woman, 'and continue to grant His favours to you both. I should like you to tell the doorkeeper not to stop me coming in to see you both. If God Almighty wills it, I shall visit the holy shrines, and after my prayers and devotions I shall call down blessings on you every day and night.'

She then went off, leaving Nu'm to weep at her departure, as she did

* Quran 25.70.

not know why she had come. As for the old woman, she went to al-Hajjaj, and when she got to him he asked for her news. 'I've seen the girl,' she said, 'and I know from looking at her that no woman in this age of ours has given birth to a more beautiful daughter.' 'If you do what I have told you to,' said al-Hajjaj, 'I shall give you a huge reward.' 'I want you to allow me a full month's delay,' she told him, and he granted her request. She then went back again and again to the house of Ni'ma and Nu'm . . .

Night 239

Morning now dawned and Shahrazad broke off from what she had been allowed to say. Then, when it was the two hundred and thirty-ninth night, SHE CONTINUED:

I have heard, O fortunate king, that she then went back again and again to the house of Ni'ma and Nu'm, and they continued to show her more and more honour, as she would come to them both in the evening and the morning, and everyone in the house used to welcome her. Then one day, when she was alone with Nu'm, she said: 'By God, lady, I pray for you when I go to the holy shrines and I wish that you were with me, so that you could see the *shaikhs* who come there and they would call down on you whatever blessings you choose.' 'For the sake of God, mother,' said Nu'm, 'take me with you.' 'I shall, if you get permission from your mother-in-law,' replied the old woman. So Nu'm said to her mother-in-law: 'Lady, please ask my master to let me go out one day with this old woman in order to pray with the *faqirs* in the holy shrines.' When Ni'ma arrived and sat down, the old woman came up to him and kissed his hands. He told her to stop, and after blessing him she left the house.

The next day she came when he was not in the house, and going up to Nu'm, she said: 'We prayed for you yesterday. If you get up immediately, you can come and look around before your husband returns.' Nu'm said to her mother-in-law: 'Please, for the sake of God, allow me to go out with this good woman so that I can enjoy the sight of God's saints in the holy places and get back quickly before my husband comes.' Her mother-in-law said: 'I am afraid he may find out about it.' 'By God,' said the old woman, 'I shall not let her sit down on the ground. She can look as she stands, and she will not be long.'

Having tricked Nu'm, she took her off to al-Hajjaj's palace, where she put her in a room and told al-Hajjaj of her arrival. He came to look at her and saw that she was the loveliest of all the people of her age and never before had he seen her like. When Nu'm saw him, she veiled her face from him, but he did not leave until he had summoned his chamberlain and ordered him to take her on a fast camel with an escort of fifty riders to Damascus, where he was to hand her over to the Commander of the Faithful, 'Abd al-Malik ibn Marwan. He wrote a letter for the chamberlain, telling him to give it to 'Abd al-Malik and to return quickly with his reply. The chamberlain hurried to mount Nu'm on a camel and to leave with her on his journey, while, for her part, she shed tears at being parted from her husband.

When they reached Damascus, the chamberlain asked leave to enter the presence of the Commander of the Faithful. This was granted and the chamberlain went in and told 'Abd al-Malik about Nu'm, who was put in a room of her own. The caliph then went to his harem and told his wife: 'Al-Hajjaj has bought a slave girl for me from one of the princesses of Kufa for ten thousand dinars. He has sent me a letter and the girl has come with it.' His wife said . . .

Night 240

Morning now dawned and Shahrazad broke off from what she had been allowed to say. Then, when it was the two hundred and fortieth night, SHE CONTINUED:

I have heard, O fortunate king, that when the caliph told his wife about the girl, she said: 'May God increase His favour to you.' His sister then went to visit Nu'm and when she saw her, she said: 'Whoever has you in his house is not going to be disappointed, even if you cost a hundred thousand dinars.' 'Lady of the beautiful face,' said Nu'm, 'which king owns this palace and what city is this?' 'This is Damascus,' replied the other, 'and the palace belongs to my brother, the Commander of the Faithful, 'Abd al-Malik ibn Marwan.' Then she added: 'It seems that you didn't know this.' 'By God, lady,' said Nu'm, 'I know nothing about it.' 'But didn't the man who sold you and took the price for you not tell you that it was the caliph who had bought you?' asked her visitor. When she heard this, Nu'm shed tears and said to herself that she had been tricked, but she added: 'If I speak out, no one will believe me. It is better to stay silent and endure patiently in the hopes that God may send me quick relief.' She bent her head in shame and her cheeks were already red from the effects of the journey and the sun.

The caliph's sister left her that day but came back on the next, with clothes and jewelled necklaces. After she had dressed Nu'm, the caliph came in and sat by her side. 'Look at this girl,' said his sister, 'in whom God has shown the perfection of beauty and loveliness.' The caliph then told her to unveil, but she refused. Although he was unable to see her face, the sight of her wrists caused love of her to enter his heart. He told his sister that he would not sleep with her for two days so that the two of them might become friends first. He then got up and left. Nu'm thought over her situation and was overcome by sorrow at having parted from her husband. When night came, she fell sick of a fever, neither eating nor drinking, until her face altered and her beauty faded. The caliph was distressed to hear about this, but although he fetched in clever doctors, no one could find a cure for her.

So much for her, but as for Ni'ma, her husband, when he came home, he sat on the bed and called 'Nu'm', but there was no reply. He got up quickly and called out, but nobody came to him and all the slave girls in the house had hidden away for fear of him. He went to his mother and found her sitting with her hand to her cheek. When he asked where Nu'm was, she told him: 'With someone who has a better right than I have to be entrusted with her, and that is the pious old woman. Nu'm went out with her to meet the *faqirs* and then come back.' 'How long has she been in the habit of doing that and when did she go out?' he asked. 'Early in the morning,' his mother replied. 'How could you have allowed her to do that?' he asked, and she said: 'It was she who suggested it to me.' 'There is no might and no power except with God, the Exalted, the Omnipotent,' he quoted, and after leaving the house in a daze, he approached the chief of police. 'Did you take my slave girl from my house by a trick?' he asked, adding: 'I shall most certainly complain of you to the Commander of the Faithful.'

The police chief asked who had taken her, to which he replied that it was an old woman of such-and-such a description, wearing wool and carrying in her hand a rosary on which were thousands of beads. 'Lead me to her,' replied the police chief, 'and I'll rescue your slave girl for you.' 'Who knows the old woman?' asked Ni'ma. 'No one knows the unseen except God, the Glorious, the Exalted,' said the police chief, although he knew that the woman was al-Hajjaj's procuress. 'It is up to

you to find my slave girl, and al-Hajjaj will judge between you and me.'
'Go to anyone you want,' said the police chief, and so Ni'ma went to
al-Hajjaj's palace, his own father being one of the leading citizens of
Kufa.

When he had arrived there, al-Hajjaj's chamberlain approached his
master and told him of the affair. 'Bring him to me,' said al-Hajjaj, and
when Ni'ma stood before him he asked him what the matter was. When
Ni'ma had told his story, al-Hajjaj said: 'Bring the police chief here and
I shall order him to look for the old woman.' In fact, he knew that the
police chief knew the woman, but when this man came before him, he
said: 'I want you to search for the slave girl of Ni'ma ibn al-Rabi'.' 'No
one knows the unseen except Almighty God,' the man said, but al-Hajjaj
told him that he must send out riders to search for the girl on the roads
and in the towns.

Night 241

Morning now dawned and Shahrazad broke off from what she had been
allowed to say. Then, when it was the two hundred and forty-first night,
SHE CONTINUED:

I have heard, O fortunate king, that al-Hajjaj told the police chief to
send out riders to search for the girl in the towns and on the roads. Then
he turned to Ni'ma and said: 'If your slave girl does not come back, I
shall give you ten from my own house and ten from that of the chief of
police.' He ordered the man to go off to start the search, which he did,
leaving Ni'ma overcome by grief and despairing of his life. He was then
fourteen years old and had no down on his cheeks. He started to weep
and moan, shutting himself away from his household, and he and his
mother kept on weeping until it was morning. Then his father came and
said: 'My son, al-Hajjaj has taken the girl by trickery, but God can bring
relief at any time.'

Ni'ma's sorrows increased; he did not know what he was saying and
he couldn't recognize those who came to see him. He remained ill for
three months and, as his condition worsened, his father despaired of
him, while the doctors who visited him said that the only thing to cure
him would be the return of Nu'm. One day, as his father was sitting
there, he heard of a clever Persian doctor, who was described as an
expert in medicine, astrology and divination. This man was summoned

by al-Rabi‘, who, when he came, sat him by his side, showed him favour and asked him to look at the condition of his son. 'Give me your hand,' he said to Ni‘ma, and when he did, the Persian felt his pulse and looked at his face. Then he laughed and, turning to his father, he said: 'The only thing wrong with your son is a disease of the heart.' 'You are right, doctor,' said al-Rabi‘, 'so use your knowledge to look at his case; tell me all about it and hide nothing from me.' 'He is attached to a slave girl,' the Persian said, 'who is either in Basra or in Damascus, and he won't be cured until he is reunited with her.' 'If you can bring this about,' said al-Rabi‘, 'I shall give you a reward that will delight you, and you will pass all your life in wealth and luxury.' 'This is an easy matter which won't take long,' claimed the Persian, and, turning to Ni‘ma, he said: 'It is all right; take heart, be cheerful and console yourself.'

He then asked al-Rabi‘ for four thousand dinars, which al-Rabi‘ produced and handed over to him. After that the Persian said: 'I want your son to come with me to Damascus and, if God Almighty wills it, I shall not come back without the girl.' Next he turned to the young man and asked him his name. When he was told that it was Ni‘ma, he said: 'Sit up, Ni‘ma; you are under the protection of Almighty God, and God will reunite you with your slave girl.' Ni‘ma sat up and the Persian repeated: 'Be of good heart. We are leaving today, so you have to eat, drink and be cheerful in order to fortify yourself for the journey.' He then started to get ready everything that he might need in the way of treasures, taking from al-Rabi‘ a total of ten thousand dinars, as well as horses, camels and whatever else he needed in order to transport the baggage. Ni‘ma then said goodbye to his father and mother and left for Aleppo with the doctor. He found no news of Nu‘m and so the two of them went on to Damascus, where they stayed for three days.

The Persian then took over a shop, filling its shelves with delicate porcelain and drapery, and embellishing them with gold and valuable pieces. In front of him he placed bottles containing ointments and potions of all kinds, surrounded by crystal goblets, and also in front of him was a divination table and an astrolabe. He put on the robes of a doctor and made Ni‘ma stand in front of him, wearing a shirt and mantle of silk with, around his waist, a silken wrapper embroidered with gold. The Persian told him: 'Ni‘ma, from today you are my son, so only address me as "father", and I shall call you "son".' 'To hear is to obey,' replied Ni‘ma.

The people of Damascus came to the Persian's shop, to look at the handsome Ni'ma, the beauty of the shop itself and the goods that it contained. The Persian spoke to Ni'ma in Persian and Ni'ma would reply in the same language, with which he was familiar, as was the custom among the sons of dignitaries. The fame of the Persian spread among the townspeople. They started to describe their ailments to him and he would give them medicines. They would also bring him flasks containing the urine of the sick and, after looking at them, he would identify the illness of the owner of each, and the patient would confirm that what the doctor said was true. As he attended to the people's needs, they flocked to him and his reputation spread throughout the city and in the houses of the great.

One day, while he was sitting in his shop, an old woman arrived, riding on a donkey whose saddle cloth was made of brocade studded with gems. She stopped at the shop, reining in the donkey, and, gesturing to the Persian, she told him: 'Take my hand.' When he did, she dismounted and asked him: 'Are you the Persian doctor from Iraq?' He told her that he was and she produced a flask, saying that she had a sick daughter. The Persian looked at its contents and then said: 'What is the girl's name, lady, so that I may work out her horoscope and find out what time will be propitious for her to take the medicine.' The old woman answered that the girl's name was Nu'm.

Night 242

Morning now dawned and Shahrazad broke off from what she had been allowed to say. Then, when it was the two hundred and forty-second night, SHE CONTINUED:

I have heard, O fortunate king, that when the Persian heard the name Nu'm he started to make his calculations, jotting notes on his hands, but he then said: 'Lady, I cannot prescribe medicine for her until I know what land she comes from, because of the change of climate. You have to tell me where she was brought up and how old she is.' 'She is fourteen,' said the old woman, 'and she was brought up in Kufa in Iraq.' 'For how many months has she been here?' he asked. 'Only a few,' was the reply. On hearing this and recognizing the girl's name, Ni'ma fainted, while the Persian told the woman that such-and-such a medicine would suit her daughter. 'Pack up what you want and give me what you have prescribed with the blessing of Almighty God,' she said, putting down ten dinars on the counter. The Persian turned to Ni'ma and told him to prepare the ingredients for the medicine. The old woman, looking at him, exclaimed: 'God be my refuge! You look just like her.' She then asked the Persian whether this was his mamluk or his son, to which he replied that he was his son. Ni'ma picked up the drugs, which he put in a box, and, taking a piece of paper, he wrote the lines:

If Nu'm grants me the favour of a glance,
Then Su'da brings no happiness
Or Juml any favour to match their names.
They said: 'Forget her and you will be given
Twenty like her,' but there is none like her,
And I shall not forget.

He slipped the paper into the box, which he sealed up, writing on its cover in Kufic script: 'I am Ni'ma ibn al-Rabi', the Kufan.' The old woman took the box, which he had put down in front of her, and after having taken leave of the two men, she set off back to the caliph's palace. She brought her purchase to Nu'm and placed the box in front of her. 'You must know, lady,' she said, 'that a Persian doctor has come to our city and I have never seen anyone with a greater or more penetrating knowledge of diseases than him. After he had looked at the flask I brought him, I told him your name. He recognized your disease and prescribed medicine for you, and, on his instructions, his son made it up for you. Nowhere in Damascus is there a more handsome and graceful young man than this son of his, nor does anyone have a shop like his.'

When Nu'm took the box, she saw written on its cover the names of her master and his father. At that her colour changed and she said to herself: 'There is no doubt that the owner of this shop has come to look for news of me.' She asked the old woman to describe the young man for her. 'His name is Ni'ma,' the woman said. 'He has a scar on his right eyebrow; he was wearing splendid clothes and is a youth of the most perfect beauty.' 'Give me the medicine,' said Nu'm, 'with the blessing of Almighty God and His aid,' and, after taking and drinking it, she laughed and told the old woman: 'This is a blessed medicine.' She then searched in the box and saw the paper, which she opened and read. When she had understood its meaning, she was certain that here was her master, and this filled her with joy and delight.

When the old woman saw her laughing, she said: 'This is a blessed day.' Nu'm told her that she wanted something to eat and drink, at which she ordered the slave girls to bring out the tables and to produce splendid foods for their mistress. They did this, and while Nu'm was sitting down to eat, in came 'Abd al-Malik. He was delighted to see her sitting and eating, and the old woman said: 'Commander of the Faithful, congratulations on the recovery of your slave girl, Nu'm. This was because a doctor came to the city whose superior in the knowledge of diseases and medicines I have never seen. I brought her medicine from him, and she recovered after a single dose.' 'Take a thousand dinars,' said the caliph, 'and see that she gets medicines to cure her.'

He then left, full of delight at Nu'm's recovery. The old woman went to the Persian's shop, where she gave him the money and told him that the patient was the caliph's slave girl. She handed him a note which Nu'm had written, and this he passed on to Ni'ma, who fell down in a faint when he recognized her handwriting. On recovering, he opened the note and found written in it: 'From the slave girl who has been deprived of her delight, cheated, and parted from her heart's darling. The arrival of your letter cheered and delighted me. It was as the poet said:

> The letter came; may the fingers that wrote it
> Be preserved for you, anointed with perfume.
> It was as though Moses had been returned
> To his mother, and Joseph's robe taken to Jacob.'

When Ni'ma read this, tears flooded his eyes. The Persian said: 'How can my son keep back his tears, when this is his slave girl and he is her master, Ni'ma ibn al-Rabi' of Kufa? The girl's health is dependent on her seeing him, as the only illness from which she suffers is love for him.'

Night 243

Morning now dawned and Shahrazad broke off from what she had been allowed to say. Then, when it was the two hundred and forty-third night, SHE CONTINUED:

I have heard, O fortunate king, that the Persian said to the old woman: 'How can my son keep back his tears, when this is his slave girl and he is her master, Ni'ma ibn al-Rabi' of Kufa? The girl's health is dependent on her seeing him, as the only illness from which she suffers is love for him. Take these thousand dinars for yourself and I'll give you more than that myself, but look on us with pity, as it is only you who can show us how to put this matter right.' 'Are you her master?' the old woman asked Ni'ma, and when he said that he was, she said: 'You must be telling the truth, for she never stops talking about you.' Ni'ma then told her what had happened to him from beginning to end. 'Young man,' she said, 'it is only through me that you will be able to meet her.'

She then rode back immediately, and after going in to see Nu'm, she looked at her face and laughed and said: 'You have good reason to weep, my daughter, and to fall ill at being parted from your master, Ni'ma.' 'The matter has been uncovered and you know the truth,' said Nu'm. 'Be happy and cheerful,' the old woman told her, 'for, by God, I'll bring the two of you together, even if it costs me my life.' She then returned to Ni'ma and told him: 'I went back and met your girl and I found that her longing for you is greater than yours for her. The Commander of the Faithful wants to sleep with her, but she does not let him. If you are steadfast and stout-hearted, I'll bring you together at the risk of my own life, and by means of a trick or a ruse I'll get you into the caliph's palace so that you can meet the girl, for she won't be able to come out.' 'May God reward you well,' said Ni'ma.

After saying goodbye to him, she went to Nu'm and told her: 'Your master is dying of love for you and he wants to come and meet you. What do you have to say about that?' 'I, too, am dying,' replied Nu'm, 'and I want to meet him.' At that, the old woman took Ni'ma a bundle containing ornaments, jewellery and a woman's dress. 'Come with me somewhere we can be alone,' she said, and he took her to a back room. When she had tattooed him, decorated his wrists and ornamented his hair, she dressed him as a slave girl with the most beautiful of slave girl's finery, until he was like one of the houris of Paradise. When the old woman saw what he looked like, she called down blessings on God, the best of creators, adding: 'By God, you are more beautiful than the girl.' Then she told him to walk with his left shoulder forward and his right back, swaying his buttocks. He walked in front of her, following her instructions, and when she saw that he had learned how to walk like a woman, she told him: 'Wait until I come for you tomorrow night, if God Almighty wills it, and I shall then take you and bring you to the palace. When you see the chamberlains and the eunuchs, be resolute. Bow your head and don't say anything to anyone, for I shall do the talking for you, and success comes from God.'

Next morning, she came and took him up to the palace, going in front, with Ni'ma following after her. The chamberlain wanted to stop him entering, but the old woman said: 'You most ill-omened of slaves, this is the slave girl of Nu'm, the caliph's favourite. How dare you stop her? Go on in, girl.' Ni'ma entered with her, and they went on until they got to the door leading to the palace courtyard. Then the old woman told Ni'ma: 'Go in with courage and steadfastness. Turn to your left, count five doors and enter the sixth, for that is the door of the place that has been prepared for you. Don't be afraid, and if anyone speaks to you, don't answer and don't stop.'

She accompanied him to the doors, but there she was confronted by the chamberlain whose duty it was to guard them. 'What is this girl?' he asked.

Night 244

Morning now dawned and Shahrazad broke off from what she had been allowed to say. Then, when it was the two hundred and forty-fourth night, SHE CONTINUED:

I have heard, O fortunate king, that the old woman was confronted by the chamberlain, who asked: 'What is this girl?' 'Our mistress wants to buy her,' replied the old woman. 'No one can go in without permission from the caliph,' said the chamberlain. 'Take her back; I shall not let her enter, for those are my orders.' 'Great chamberlain,' answered the old woman, 'see that you keep your wits about you. Nu'm is the caliph's slave girl to whom he is deeply attached. She has been restored to health, but he can scarcely believe it. She wants to buy this girl, so don't stop her from going in lest Nu'm hear that it was you who did this, in which case she may be angry with you and suffer a relapse. Her anger may then cost you your head.' She told Ni'ma: 'Go in, girl; don't listen to this man, but don't tell the queen that the chamberlain tried to stop you entering.'

Ni'ma, with his head bent downwards, entered the palace, but instead of turning left, as he had meant to do, by mistake he turned right. He had also meant to count five doors and enter the sixth, but, in fact, he counted six and went in the seventh. When he did this, he found a room spread with brocades, its walls covered with silken hangings patterned with gold. In it were censers of aloes wood, with ambergris and pungent musk, and at the end of the room he saw a couch covered with brocade. He sat down, looking at the extent of these riches, but he did not know what the future was destined to hold for him.

While he was sitting there, thinking over his position, in came the caliph's sister, together with her maid. When she saw him, she took him for a slave girl, and, going up to him, she asked who he was, what his business was and who had brought him in. Ni'ma did not speak or give any answer and the lady said: 'If you are one of my brother's concubines and he is angry with you, I shall petition him and try to win his favour for you.' Ni'ma still made no reply, and so the lady told her maid to stand at the door of the room, letting no one enter. She herself went nearer and looked at Ni'ma. His beauty astonished her and she said: 'Tell me who you are, girl. What is your name and why did you come in here, for I have never seen you before in the palace?'

When Ni'ma still did not answer, she grew angry and put her hand on his chest. Finding no breasts, she was about to remove his clothes in order to find out what he was, when he said: 'Lady, I am your mamluk; buy me; I ask for your protection, so protect me.' 'No harm shall come to you,' she replied, 'but tell me who you are and who brought you to my room.' 'O queen,' he replied, 'my name is Ni'ma ibn al-Rabi' of Kufa and I have risked my life for the sake of my slave girl, Nu'm, whom al-Hajjaj took by a trick and sent here.' 'You won't be harmed,' the lady repeated, and she then called to her maid, telling her to go to Nu'm's room. The old woman had already gone there and had asked Nu'm whether her master had come to her. 'No, by God,' said Nu'm. 'It may be that he made a mistake and went into the wrong room after losing his way,' said the old woman. 'There is no might and no power except with God, the Exalted, the Omnipotent!' exclaimed Nu'm. 'This is the end for us; we are lost.'

They both sat plunged in thought, and while they were in that state the maid of the caliph's sister came in. After greeting Nu'm, she said: 'My mistress invites you to visit her as her guest.' 'To hear is to obey,' said Nu'm. 'It may be that your master is with the caliph's sister,' the old woman said, 'and that the affair has been uncovered.' Nu'm got up straight away and went to the caliph's sister, who said to her: 'This is your master sitting here with me. It appears that he mistook the room, but, if God Almighty wills it, there is no need for either of you to be afraid.' When Nu'm heard this, her fears were calmed and she approached her master, Ni'ma. When he saw her . . .

Night 245

Morning now dawned and Shahrazad broke off from what she had been allowed to say. Then, when it was the two hundred and forty-fifth night, SHE CONTINUED:

I have heard, O fortunate king, that when he saw her, he rose to meet her and each embraced the other, before falling down in a faint. When they had recovered, the caliph's sister told them: 'Sit down, so that we may work out how to escape from the difficulty into which we have fallen.' 'To hear is to obey, mistress,' they said, 'and it is for you to command.' 'By God,' she said, 'no harm shall ever come to you from me.' She then told the servant to fetch food and drink, and when this had been done, they sat and ate their fill before starting to drink. As the wine cups passed around, so their sorrows left them. 'I wish I knew what is going to happen,' said Ni'ma. The caliph's sister then asked him: 'Do you love your slave girl, Nu'm?' 'My lady,' he replied, 'it is love for her that has brought me into my present mortal danger.' She then asked Nu'm whether she, for her part, loved her master, Ni'ma. 'It is love for him, my lady, that has wasted away my body and brought me from health to sickness,' she replied. 'Since you love each other,' said the lady, 'may no one part you. Take comfort and be at ease.'

This gladdened the two lovers and Nu'm called for a lute. When it was brought, she took it and tuned it, after which she struck up a melody to which she sang these lines:

> The slanderers insisted on parting us,
> Although they had no revenge to take from you or me.
> They launched their hostile words against our ears,
> And few there were to stand in my defence.
> I fought them with your eyes and through my tears
> And sighs, with sword and flood and fire.

Nu'm then passed the lute to Ni'ma and asked him to sing them something. He took it, tuned it and struck up a melody to which he sang:

> The full moon would resemble you, had it no spots;
> The sun would be like you, could it not be eclipsed.
> Wonder strikes me, but how many wonders does love hold,
> With its cares, passion and distress?

The way to my beloved I find short;
How long it is when I must take my leave!

When he had finished, Nu'm filled a cup and handed it to him. When he had taken it and drunk it, she filled another, which she gave to the caliph's sister. After she had drunk, she too took the lute and tuned it, tightening its strings, before reciting:

Sorrow and grief are found within my heart,
While violent love frequents my inmost parts.
My wasted form is clear to see,
For love has made my body sick.

Filling the wine cup, she passed it to Ni'ma, who drank, took and tuned the lute, and then recited:

I gave my soul to him; he tortured it,
And when I tried to free it from him, I could not.
Grant to the lover what may rescue him
Before he dies, as this is his last breath.

The three kept on reciting poetry and drinking, to the accompaniment of the notes of the lute, but while they were enjoying themselves in pleasure and delight, suddenly in came the Commander of the Faithful. When they saw him, they got up and kissed the ground before him. He looked at Nu'm, who was holding the lute, and said: 'Praise be to God, Nu'm, Who has cured you of your painful illness.' Then he turned to Ni'ma, who was still wearing his disguise, and he asked his sister who this slave girl was who was standing beside Nu'm. His sister told him: 'Commander of the Faithful, you have here a concubine slave girl, a friendly person, without whom Nu'm will neither eat nor drink.' She then recited:

They are two opposites which, when they meet,
Show separate beauties, for the loveliness of one
Is set off by the beauty of its opposite.

'By the Omnipotent God,' said the caliph, 'she is as lovely as Nu'm. Tomorrow I shall give her a room of her own next to Nu'm's. I shall have carpets and furnishings brought out, and everything that is suitable for her will be taken to her for the sake of Nu'm.' His sister then called for food to be brought, which she presented to him. He ate it, sitting there in their company, and then, after filling a wine cup, he gestured to Nu'm, inviting her to recite some poetry. She drank two glasses of wine, and then she took the lute and recited:

> When my companion pours me out again and then again
> Three cups in which the wine is heard to froth,
> I trail my skirts with pride, as though I were
> Your ruler, O Commander of the Faithful.

The caliph was delighted and filled another wine cup, which he gave to Nu'm, telling her to sing again. After drinking the cup, she touched the strings and recited:

> Noblest of all the people of this age,
> No one can claim equality with you.
> In grandeur and generosity you are unique,
> A lord and king of universal fame.
> You are king of the kings of all the earth;
> You give great gifts with no angry reproach.
> May God preserve you in spite of your foes,
> With your star adorned by fortune and by victory.

When the caliph heard these lines, he exclaimed: 'Good, by God! By God, that is fine! Well done, Nu'm; how eloquent you are and how clear is your exposition!' The four of them continued to enjoy themselves cheerfully until midnight, and at that point the caliph's sister said: 'Listen, Commander of the Faithful. I have come across a story about a certain high official.' 'What is it?' said the caliph, and his sister went on: 'In the city of Kufa there was a young man named Ni'ma ibn al-Rabi'. He had a slave girl whom he loved and who loved him. They had been reared as children together, but when they grew up and their love for each other had strengthened, Time afflicted them with misfortunes and decreed they should be parted. Traitors plotted against the girl, bringing her out of Ni'ma's house, where she was stolen. The thief sold her to a certain king for ten thousand dinars. Her love for her master was matched by his love for her, and so he left his family, his comforts and his house and set out to look for her. He found a way to meet her . . .'

Night 246

Morning now dawned and Shahrazad broke off from what she had been allowed to say. Then, when it was the two hundred and forty-sixth night, SHE CONTINUED:

I have heard, O fortunate king, that Ni'ma left his family and his country and found a way to meet her. 'But,' the caliph's sister said, 'although he succeeded in doing this at the risk of his own life, he and Nu'm – for this was her name – had scarcely settled down to sit together when the king who had bought her from the thief surprised them and immediately ordered their execution. He had not acted justly by his own lights and had not waited before giving his judgement. What is your opinion, Commander of the Faithful, about the unjust behaviour of this king?'

'This is a remarkable affair,' said the caliph, 'and the king who had the power should have pardoned them. He should have borne in mind three things: the first, that they were lovers; the second, that they were in his palace and in his power; and the third, that kings should act slowly in judging their subjects and all the more should they do this in their personal affairs. The king did not act in a manner befitting his rank.' 'Brother,' said his sister, 'by the King of heaven and earth, I ask you to tell Nu'm to sing and to listen to her song.' 'Sing, Nu'm,' said the caliph, and so she struck up a tune and recited these lines:

> Time, the ever-faithless, has been false to me.
> It wounds hearts fatally and leaves a legacy of care.
> It parts lovers, after they have been joined,
> And then you see that tears pour down their cheeks.
> There was the one I loved and there was I;
> My life was pleasant, with Time uniting us.
> Let me now pour out blood and tears in floods,
> As I must grieve for you by night and day.

These lines filled the caliph with delight. His sister told him: 'Whoever passes any judgement must abide by it himself and act in accordance with his word. You have given this judgement against yourself.' She then told both Ni'ma and Nu'm to stand up and went on: 'The girl standing here, Commander of the Faithful, is the kidnapped Nu'm, who was stolen by al-Hajjaj ibn Yusuf al-Thaqafi. He sent her to you and lied in the claim that he made in his letter that he had bought her for ten thousand dinars. Standing beside her is her master, Ni'ma ibn al-Rabi'. I beg you, by the sanctity of your pure ancestors, Hamza, al-'Aqil and al-'Abbas, to pardon them, to forgive their fault and to give them to one another so that you may win a heavenly reward for them. They are in your power and they have eaten your food and drunk your wine. I intercede for them and ask for the boon of their lives.' 'You are right,' said the caliph, 'I did give that judgement and I shall not make a decision and then go back on it.'

Then he said: 'Nu'm, is this your master?' 'Yes, Commander of the Faithful,' she replied. 'No harm shall come to the two of you, for I have given you to one another,' he told her. Then he asked Ni'ma: 'How did you find out where she was and who described this place for you?' 'Listen to the story of what happened to me, Commander of the Faithful,' said Ni'ma, 'for I swear by the line of your pure ancestors that I shall conceal nothing from you.' He then told the caliph what had happened to him, and what both the Persian doctor and the old woman had done for him, including how she had brought him into the palace and how he had then mistaken the doors. The caliph, filled with astonishment, ordered the Persian to be fetched. When this was done, he made him one of his personal attendants, giving him robes of honour, together with a handsome present, saying: 'It is right that the man who made this plan should be enrolled among our intimates.' He showed favour to Ni'ma and Nu'm, showering them with benefits and treating the old woman in the same way.

They stayed with him for seven days in the fortunate enjoyment of a life of ease, and then Ni'ma asked for permission to leave with Nu'm. When permission had been granted them to travel to Kufa, they set off, and there they rejoined Ni'ma's father and mother. They remained there, enjoying the most pleasant and easiest of lives, until they were visited by the destroyer of delights and the parter of companions.

When al-Amjad and al-As'ad heard Bahram's story, they were filled with astonishment and said: 'This is a remarkable tale.'

Night 247

Morning now dawned and Shahrazad broke off from what she had been allowed to say. Then, when it was the two hundred and forty-seventh night, SHE CONTINUED:

I have heard, O fortunate king, that when al-Amjad and al-As'ad heard this story from Bahram, the converted Magian, they spent the night filled with astonishment. The next morning, they rode out with the intention of going to see the king. They asked permission to enter his presence and, when this had been granted and they had gone in, he treated them courteously and they sat talking. While they were doing this, suddenly the townsfolk could be heard shouting, screaming and calling for help. The chamberlain came with news that another king had brought down his army against the city. They were brandishing their weapons, but no one knew what they wanted. The king passed on the chamberlain's news to al-Amjad, his vizier, and to al-As'ad, his brother. Al-Amjad said: 'I shall go out to this king and find out what is happening.' He went out of the city and found the 'king' with many men and mounted mamluks. When they saw him, they realized that he must be an envoy from the ruler of the city and so they brought him before their commander.

When he came in, he kissed the ground before 'him', only to discover that the 'king' was a queen, wearing a mouth-veil. She told him: 'Know that I have no intention of taking your city, and the only reason that I am here is to look for a beardless slave. If I find him with you, I shall do you no harm, but if I don't, there will be bloody war between us.' 'What is this mamluk like, your majesty?' asked al-Amjad. 'What is his history and what is his name?' 'His name is al-As'ad and mine is Marjana,' replied the queen. 'He came to me with Bahram, the Magian, and as Bahram refused to sell him to me, I removed him by force, but Bahram stole him away from me in a night raid.'

She proceeded to describe al-As'ad, and when he heard all the details, al-Amjad realized that this must be his brother. 'Queen of the age,' he said, 'praise be to God, Who has brought us relief! This mamluk is my own brother.' He then told her his own story, covering what had happened to him and his brother after they had left home, and why they had left the Ebony Islands. Marjana was astonished at that but was delighted to have found al-As'ad. She gave a robe of honour to al-Amjad, who returned and told the king what had happened. The news was received joyfully, and the king, together with al-Amjad and al-As'ad, came down to meet the queen. When they entered her presence they sat talking, but while they were doing this a dust cloud spread suddenly until it had covered the horizons. When it had cleared away, an army could be seen, huge as a swelling sea, clad in mail and carrying weapons. They advanced on the city until they had surrounded it as a ring surrounds the finger, with drawn swords. Al-Amjad and al-As'ad said: 'We belong to God and to Him do we return. What is this enormous army? They have to be enemies, and unless we can get this queen, Marjana, to agree to fight against them, they will take our city and kill us. The only thing that we can do is to go and find out about them.'

Al-Amjad then got up, went through the city gates, and after passing beyond Marjana's men and reaching the strange army, he found that it belonged to his grandfather, King al-Ghayur, the father of Queen Budur . . .

Night 248

Morning now dawned and Shahrazad broke off from what she had been allowed to say. Then, when it was the two hundred and forty-eighth night, SHE CONTINUED:

I have heard, O fortunate king, that when al-Amjad reached the army, he found that it belonged to his grandfather, King al-Ghayur, the lord of the islands and the seas and the seven castles. When al-Amjad came before the king, he kissed the ground in front of him and gave him the message that he was carrying. The king told him: 'My name is al-Malik al-Ghayur, and I am passing by, as fate has robbed me of my daughter Budur, who left me and never came back. I have heard no word of her or of her husband, Qamar al-Zaman. Do you have any information about them?'

On hearing this, al-Amjad looked down at the ground for a time, thinking the matter over. Then, when he was convinced that this was his maternal grandfather, he raised his head, and after kissing the ground before him, he told him that he was Budur's son. When the king heard that this was his grandson, he threw himself on him and both of them burst into tears. 'Praise be to God that you are safe, my son,' said the king, 'and that I have met you.' Al-Amjad then told him that Budur, his daughter, was well, as was his own father, Qamar al-Zaman, and that

they were living in the city of the Ebony Island. He also told him how
his father, in a rage, had ordered both him and his brother to be put to
death, and how the treasurer had pitied them and left them alive. 'I shall
go back with you and your brother to your father and make your peace
with him,' said al-Ghayur, 'and then I shall stay with you.'

Al-Amjad kissed the ground before him in his delight, and after the
king had given him a robe of honour, he returned smiling to his master
and told him about al-Malik al-Ghayur. This astonished the Magian
king, who sent out guest provisions in the form of sheep, horses, camels,
fodder and so on. He made a similar gift to Queen Marjana, who, on
being told what had happened, said that she would go with them, taking
her troops, and would help to produce a reconciliation. While they were
occupied like this, suddenly a cloud of dust rose up, filling the horizons
and darkening the daylight. From beneath it they could hear cries, shouts
and the whinnying of horses, and they saw flashing swords and levelled
spears. When the newcomers neared the city and saw the two armies
there, they beat their drums. On seeing that, the king of the city
exclaimed: 'This is a blessed day. Praise be to God, Who reconciled us
with these two armies, and if it is His will, He will reconcile us with this
one as well.'

He then spoke to al-Amjad and al-As'ad and said: 'Go and find out
about these troops, for I have never seen a larger army.' The two set off,
and as the city gates had been shut on the king's orders, for fear of the
encircling force, they had to be opened to let them go on their way. They
discovered, on reaching it, that the army which had arrived was huge,
and when they entered it they found that it belonged to the king of the
Ebony Islands and that in it was their father, Qamar al-Zaman. When
he saw them, he threw himself on them, weeping bitterly. He excused
himself and clasped them to his breast in a long embrace, after which he
told them of the extent of the loneliness which he had had to endure
after he had parted from them. The two brothers told him of the arrival
of al-Ghayur, and he mounted with his personal retinue and, taking
al-Amjad and al-As'ad with him, rode off to al-Ghayur's army. One of
his men rode ahead to the king to tell him that Qamar al-Zaman had
come, at which he came out to meet him, and when they had met,
they told of their surprise at how they had come together there. The
townspeople provided a feast for them, producing foods and sweetmeats
of all kinds, and then gave them horses, camels, guest provisions and
fodder, together with everything that armies need.

While this was going on, yet another dust cloud arose, blocking the horizons, and the earth trembled under the hooves of horses, while drums sounded like the blasts of storm winds. There was an army, fully equipped with coats of mail, all dressed in black, and in the middle of them a very old man with a beard that reached down to his chest, also dressed in black. When the townspeople saw these vast forces, the king said to the other rulers: 'Praise be to Almighty God by Whose permission you have met together on the same day and have turned out all to know each other. But what is this huge army that stretches across the land?' The others said: 'There is no need to fear it. We are three rulers, each with a large force, and if these are enemies, we would join you in fighting them, even if they were three times as many.'

While they were talking, an envoy from the newcomers came up, making for the city. He was taken before Qamar al-Zaman, al-Ghayur, Queen Marjana and the king of the city. After having kissed the ground, he said: 'My king has come from the lands of the Persians. Years ago he lost his son and he is travelling through the lands in search of him. If he finds him with you, he will do you no harm, but if he does not, then there will be war between him and you, and he will destroy your city.' 'It will not come to that,' said Qamar al-Zaman, 'but what is your king's title in the land of the Persians?' The envoy replied: 'He is called King Shahriman, lord of the Khalidan Islands. He has collected these troops from the regions through which he has passed in his search for his son.'

When Qamar al-Zaman heard what the messenger said, he gave a loud cry and fell down in a faint. He remained unconscious for some time, and when he recovered, he wept bitterly, before telling al-Amjad and al-As'ad, with their personal guards: 'Go with the envoy, my children, and greet your grandfather, my father, King Shahriman. Give him the good news that I am here, for he has been grieved by my loss and is still wearing black for my sake.' He then told the assembled kings everything that had happened to him in the days of his youth, to their great astonishment. They then accompanied Qamar al-Zaman to his father. Qamar al-Zaman greeted him and they embraced each other, before falling down in a faint from excessive joy. When they had recovered, Qamar al-Zaman told his father all that had happened to him, and the other kings gave him their greetings. They then sent Marjana home, after having married her to al-As'ad, telling her to keep in touch with them by means of letters. When she left, they married al-Amjad to Bustan, the daughter of Bahram. They all then set out for the Ebony

City, where Qamar al-Zaman went to his father-in-law, Armanus, and told him everything that had happened to him, including how he had been reunited with his sons. This delighted Armanus, who congratulated him on his safe return. Queen Budur's father, al-Ghayur, went to his daughter, greeted her and satisfied the longing that he felt for her.

They remained for a full month in the Ebony City, after which al-Ghayur set off for his own land, taking his daughter with him.

Night 249

Morning now dawned and Shahrazad broke off from what she had been allowed to say. Then, when it was the two hundred and forty-ninth night, SHE CONTINUED:

I have heard, O fortunate king, that al-Malik al-Ghayur set off for his own land with his men, taking his daughter with him. Al-Amjad accompanied them on this journey, and when al-Ghayur was again settled in his kingdom, it was al-Amjad, his grandson, whom he appointed ruler in his place. Similarly, Qamar al-Zaman set his son al-As'ad in his own place as ruler in the city of his grandfather, Armanus, with Armanus's approval. He himself then made his preparations and left with his father, King Shahriman. When they got to the Khalidan Islands, the city was adorned with decorations in their honour and drums were beaten for a whole month to give the good news. Qamar al-Zaman then ruled in his father's place until they were visited by the destroyer of delights and the parter of companies. God knows better.

'Shahrazad,' said the king, 'this is a wonderful story.' 'O king,' she replied, 'it is no more wonderful than the tale of 'Ala' al-Din Abu'l-Shamat.' 'And what was that tale?' asked the king. SHAHRAZAD WENT ON:

I have heard, O fortunate king, that in the old days there was once a Cairene merchant named Shams al-Din, one of the best and most truthful of men, who owned eunuchs, servants, slaves, slave girls and mamluks, and was possessed of vast wealth. He was the syndic of the merchants in Cairo. He had a wife whom he loved and who loved him, but he had lived with her for forty years without her having provided him with either a daughter or a son. One day, as he sat in his shop, he looked around at the other merchants, every one of whom had one, two or more sons, and these sons were seated in their shops like their fathers. As the

day was a Friday, he went to the baths and performed the Friday ablution. When he came out, he took a barber's mirror and stared at himself
in it, exclaiming: 'I bear witness that there is no god but God and
Muhammad is the Apostle of God.' Then, looking at his beard, he
saw that its white hairs had obscured the black, and white hairs, he
remembered, are a herald of death.

His wife knew the time that he would get back and so she washed and
prepared herself for him. When he came in, she said: 'Good evening,'
but he replied: 'I see nothing good.' She then told the slave girl to bring
in the evening meal and when the food was brought, she told her husband
to eat. 'I shall not eat anything,' he replied, kicking away the table
and turning his face away from her. 'What's the reason for this?' she
asked. 'And what has saddened you?' 'It is you who are the cause of my
sorrow,' he replied.

Night 250

Morning now dawned and Shahrazad broke off from what she had been
allowed to say. Then, when it was the two hundred and fiftieth night,
SHE CONTINUED:

I have heard, O fortunate king, that Shams al-Din told his wife: 'It is
you who are the cause of my sorrow.' 'Why is that?' she asked. 'When I
opened my shop today,' he answered, 'I saw that every single merchant
had one, two or more sons sitting like their fathers in their shops and I
said to myself: "Death, which took your father, will not fail to visit
you." The night on which I first lay with you I swore that I would not
marry another wife, that I would not take a concubine, be she Abyssinian,
Rumi or a slave girl of some other race; and that I would not spend a
single night away from you. The fact is, however, that you are barren,
and marriage to you is like chiselling rock.' 'As God is my witness,' his
wife replied, 'it is you who are the cause of the difficulty and not I, as
your sperm is watery.' 'What is the matter with men like that?' he asked.
'They cannot impregnate women and produce children,' she told him.
'Where is there something to thicken sperm?' he asked. 'I shall buy it to
thicken mine.' She told him to search among the apothecaries.

Next morning they were both sorry for having reproached each other,
and Shams al-Din set out for the market, where he found an apothecary.
They exchanged greetings and Shams al-Din then asked the man whether

he had anything that would thicken sperm. 'I did have,' said the man, 'but no longer. Try my neighbour.' So Shams al-Din went around asking everyone and being laughed at, after which he went back to his own shop and sat there sadly. In the market there was a poor hashish addict, the syndic of the auctioneers, Muhammad Simsim by name, who used to take opium, opium paste and green hashish. This man was in the habit of saying good morning to Shams al-Din every day, and he now came up as usual. They exchanged greetings, but Shams al-Din was irritated and Shaikh Muhammad asked him why. Shams al-Din then told him what had happened between him and his wife. 'I've been married to her for forty years,' he explained, 'but she has given me neither a son nor a daughter. I have been told that the reason she has never become pregnant is that my sperm is watery and that I should look for something to thicken it, but I haven't been able to find anything.' Shaikh Muhammad said: 'I have got something that will do that. What would you say about someone who could see to it that, after forty years, you managed to impregnate your wife?' 'If you do that,' said Shams al-Din, 'I shall shower you with favours and benefits.' 'Give me a dinar,' said the other, and when Shams al-Din produced two, he took them and said: 'Give me this china bowl.'

When Shams al-Din had done that, Muhammad took the bowl off to the hashish seller, from whom he got two ounces of Rumi opium, together with a portion of Chinese cubebs, cinnamon, cloves, cardamom, ginger, white pepper and mountain lizard. He pounded all these ingredients and boiled them up in good quality oil, after which he took three ounces of male frankincense in chunks and a cupful of cumin seeds. After having infused these, he made all this into a paste, using Rumi honey. He then put the paste in the bowl and went back and gave it to Shams al-Din. 'This,' he said, 'will thicken sperm. You must take it on a spatula after a meal of mutton and domestic pigeon seasoned with hot spices. Take the mixture on the spatula, eat your evening meal and then take a drink made with refined sugar.'

Shams al-Din took the mixture and passed it to his wife, together with the meat and the pigeons. He told her to cook them well and to take the sperm thickener and to keep it with her until he needed it and asked for it. She did as she was told and then placed the food in front of him. After his meal he asked for the bowl and ate from it. He liked it so much that he ate all the rest of it, after which he lay with his wife and she conceived that night. When her periods had ceased for three months she knew that she was pregnant. As her pregnancy came to its end and the labour pains began, the women raised cries of joy. It was a difficult delivery and by way of a charm the midwife pronounced the names of Muhammad and 'Ali over the baby, reciting the formula *Allahu akbar!* and the call to prayer in his ear. Then she wrapped him up and handed him to his mother, who gave him her breast and suckled him. He drank until he had had enough and then fell asleep. The midwife stayed there for three days and then, on the seventh day, they distributed marzipan cakes that they had made, together with sweetmeats, after which they sprinkled salt.

Shams al-Din came in and, after having congratulated his wife on her safe delivery, he asked: 'Where is the child God has entrusted to us?' She brought him a baby of surpassing beauty, the handiwork of God, the ever-present Ruler. Although he was only seven days old, anyone who saw him would have taken him for a year-old child. When his father looked at his face, he saw that it was like a radiant full moon and that he had moles on each cheek. 'What have you called him?' he asked his wife. 'Were this a girl I would have named her,' she replied, 'but as he is a boy, no one should name him but you.' At that time, people used to rely on omens in choosing their children's names. While Shams al-Din and his family were consulting about the name, someone there suddenly said to his friend: 'O my master 'Ala' al-Din.' Shams al-Din promptly said: 'We shall name the child 'Ala' al-Din Abu'-Shamat.'

'Ala' al-Din was left in the charge of nurses, both wet and dry, and after drinking milk for two years he was weaned. He grew big and began to walk, and when he was seven he was put in a room beneath a trapdoor for fear of the evil eye. He was not to leave, his father said, until his beard grew, and he was put in the charge of a slave girl and a black slave. The girl would prepare his food and the slave would carry it to him. He was circumcised and his father produced a great feast for him, after which a *faqih* was brought to teach him. This man taught him how to read and to recite the Quran, as well as instructing him in the other sciences, until he became proficient and learned.

One day it happened that the slave who brought him his food forget-fully left the trapdoor open. 'Ala' al-Din climbed through it and went to his mother. A group of the leading ladies of the city were talking with her, and when the boy came in, looking like a mamluk intoxicated by his own beauty, they veiled their faces at the sight of him and said to his mother: 'May God punish you! How can you let this mamluk, a stranger,

come in to us? Don't you know that modesty is a part of the true faith?'
'Call on the Name of God,' she replied. 'This is my son, the fruit of my
heart, fathered by Shams al-Din, the syndic of the traders, and reared in
all comfort and luxury.' 'Never in our lives did we think that you had a
son,' they exclaimed, and she explained: 'His father was afraid lest he
be hurt by the evil eye and so had him brought up in an underground
chamber.'

Night 251

Morning now dawned and Shahrazad broke off from what she had been
allowed to say. Then, when it was the two hundred and fifty-first night,
SHE CONTINUED:

I have heard, O fortunate king, that 'Ala' al-Din's mother told the
ladies: 'His father was afraid lest he be hurt by the evil eye and so
had him brought up in an underground chamber. The slave must have
forgotten and left the trapdoor open and he came out through it,
although we had not wanted him to leave his room until his beard had
sprouted.'

While the women congratulated her, 'Ala' al-Din left them and went
through the courtyard to the gate room, where he sat down. While he
was there, the slaves came in with his father's mule. He asked them
where it had come from and they told him that they had escorted his
father as he rode it to his shop and had then brought it back. 'What's
my father's profession?' he asked, and they told him that he was the
syndic of the Egyptian merchants and master of the Bedouin. He then
went to his mother and put the same question to her. She gave him the
same answer, adding: 'When it comes to selling, his slaves only consult
him on sales whose minimum value is a thousand dinars. When it is only
a matter of nine hundred dinars or less, they sell at their own discretion
without asking his advice. He has authority over all merchandise, great
or small, that arrives here, wherever it may come from, and he disposes
of it as he wants, and this authority of his also covers merchandise that
is packed up for export. Almighty God has given your father uncountable
wealth, my son.'

'Praise be to God, mother,' said 'Ala' al-Din, 'that I am the son of the
master of the Bedouin and that my father is syndic of the merchants. But
why did you put me in the underground room and leave me shut up

there?' 'We did this for fear of people's eyes,' she told him. 'The evil eye is a fact and most of those who are dead and buried have fallen victim to it.' 'But, mother,' he said, 'how can anyone escape fate? Caution is no guard against destiny and what is written in the book of fate is not to be avoided. Death, which carried off my grandfather, will not leave me, and if my father is alive today he may not be alive tomorrow. If he dies and I come out and say that I am 'Ala' al-Din, his son, no one will believe me and the old men will say: "Never in our lives did we see any son or daughter belonging to Shams al-Din." Then the public treasury will come and take my father's wealth. May God have mercy on the man who said: "When a noble man dies, his money vanishes and the vilest of people take his women." Talk to my father to make him take me with him to the market and get him to open a shop for me, where I can sit with merchandise and he can teach me the give and take of trading.'

His mother promised to do that when his father came back and, when he did, he found 'Ala' al-Din sitting with his mother. 'Why did you take him out of the underground room?' he asked her. 'I didn't do that,' she answered. 'The servants forgot to shut the trapdoor and left it open. While I was sitting with a number of important ladies, he suddenly came in.' Then she told him what 'Ala' al-Din had said, and he promised: 'Tomorrow, my son, if Almighty God wills it, I shall take you to the market with me.' But he added: 'If you want to sit in a shop in the market, you need to show perfect good manners in all circumstances.'

As a result of what his father had said, 'Ala' al-Din passed a happy night and in the morning his father took him to the baths and gave him an expensive suit of clothes to wear. Then, when they had eaten and drunk, Shams al-Din mounted his mule and placed 'Ala' al-Din on another one, leading the way as he set off to the market. The market folk saw the syndic arrive, followed by a youth who looked like a segment of a fourteen-day moon. They said to one another: 'Look at that boy behind the syndic. We used to have a good opinion of him, but he is like a leek, with white hair and a green heart.' Shaikh Muhammad Simsim, the official who was mentioned earlier, told the merchants: 'We shall no longer be prepared to accept this man as our leader.'

It had been customary, when the syndic came from his house in the morning and took his seat in his shop, for his deputy to recite the Fatiha to the merchants, who would then go with him to the syndic, where they would all recite the Fatiha, greet him and then disperse, each to his own shop. When Shams al-Din took his seat in his shop that day, as usual,

the merchants did not come to him in their normal way. He called for
Simsim and asked why this was. 'I'm not good at spreading trouble,'
Simsim said, 'but the merchants have agreed to depose you from your
office and they are not going to recite the Fatiha for you.' When Shams
al-Din asked him why this was, he explained: 'It is because of this boy
who is sitting beside you. You are an old man and the chief of the
merchants. Is he your mamluk or one of your wife's relatives? I think
myself that you are turning to him out of love.' 'Silence!' shouted Shams
al-Din. 'May God defile you and everything connected with you. This is
my son.' 'Never in all our lives,' said Simsim, 'have we seen any son of
yours.' Shams al-Din replied: 'When you brought me that sperm
thickener, my wife conceived and gave birth to him, but as I was afraid
of the evil eye, I had him brought up in an underground room. I hadn't
meant him to come out until he could hold his beard in his hand, but his
mother didn't agree. She asked me to open a shop for him, give him
some merchandise and teach him how to trade.'

Simsim then went to tell the merchants the truth of the matter. They
all came back with him to Shams al-Din and, standing in front of him,
they recited the Fatiha. They congratulated him on his son and said:
'May our Lord preserve both the root and the branch,' adding: 'But
whenever one of us, however poor, has a son or a daughter, he has to
make a dish of butter and honey gruel for his companions and invite his
acquaintances and his relatives. This is something that you have not
done.' 'I promise this to do for you,' said Shams al-Din, 'and we shall
meet in the orchard.'

Night 252

Morning now dawned and Shahrazad broke off from what she had been
allowed to say. Then, when it was the two hundred and fifty-second
night, Shahrazad's sister, Dunyazad, said: 'Sister if you are awake and
not asleep, finish off the story for us.' 'Willingly,' replied Shahrazad,
AND SHE WENT ON:

I have heard, O fortunate king, that the syndic promised to entertain
the merchants with a meal in the orchard. The next morning, he sent his
servant to the hall and the garden pavilion, telling him to spread out the
carpets, and he sent what was needed for cooking, such as sheep, butter
and so forth, as was required. He prepared two tables, one in the pavilion

and one in the hall, and then both he and 'Ala' al-Din girt up their clothes. 'My son,' Shams al-Din said, 'when any grey-haired man enters, I will receive him and seat him at the table in the pavilion, whereas, if you see a beardless boy coming in, take him into the hall and seat him at the table there.' 'Why?' asked 'Ala' al-Din. 'What is the reason for having two tables, one for men and the other for boys?' 'A beardless boy, my son,' said his father, 'is ashamed to eat with men,' an answer of which 'Ala' al-Din approved. So, when the merchants came, it was Shams al-Din who greeted the men and seated them in the pavilion, while 'Ala' al-Din met the boys and placed them in the hall.

Food was then produced and the guests ate, drank and enjoyed themselves, while perfumes were released. The elders sat discussing science and the traditions of the Prophet, but among them was a merchant named Mahmud al-Balkhi. This man was outwardly a Muslim but secretly a Magian, with a fondness for depravity, who loved boys. He looked at the face of 'Ala' al-Din with a glance that was followed by a thousand sighs. Satan had dangled a jewel before him in 'Ala' al-Din's face, and he was seized by passionate desire, as love for the boy became fixed in his heart.

He was in the habit of taking materials and other items of merchandise from 'Ala' al-Din's father. Now he got up to stroll and turned aside to the boys who rose to greet him. 'Ala' al-Din had had to relieve his bladder and so Mahmud turned to the other boys and promised that, if they managed to persuade 'Ala' al-Din to go on a journey with him, he would give each of them a robe worth a large sum of money. He then left them and returned to the men's table. 'Ala' al-Din came back to the boys who were still sitting there, and they got up and sat him at the head of their table. One of them asked a friend: 'Tell me, Hasan, that capital which you use for trading, where did you get it?' His friend said: 'When I grew up and reached manhood, I asked my father for some merchandise. He said that he had none and told me to go and borrow money from a merchant and to use this to learn the give and take of trading. So I approached a man who lent me a thousand dinars. I used this to buy material, which I took to Damascus, where I made a profit of a hundred per cent. I then took merchandise from Damascus to Aleppo, where again I doubled my profit. I did the same thing once more by taking goods from Aleppo to Baghdad and I kept on trading until my capital reached ten thousand dinars.'

Each one of the boys started to tell similar stories to their friends until it was 'Ala' al-Din's turn to speak. When they asked him, he said: 'I was brought up in an underground chamber. I only got out this week and I go to the shop and then come back home.' 'You're used to sitting at home, then,' they said, 'and you don't know the pleasures of travel – but travel is only for men.' 'I have no need to travel,' 'Ala' al-Din replied, 'and I set no value on journeys.' 'This fellow is like a fish that dies when it leaves the water,' said one of the guests to his companion. They then told him: 'The only source of pride for merchants' sons is to travel for the sake of profit.' That annoyed him and he left them, with tears in his eyes and sorrow in his heart, mounted his mule and set off back home. He was even more angry and still tearful when his mother saw him, and when she asked him what had made him cry, he said: 'All the merchants' sons have criticized me and told me that the only source of pride for them is to travel in order to make money.'

Night 253

Morning now dawned and Shahrazad broke off from what she had been allowed to say. Then, when it was the two hundred and fifty-third night, SHE CONTINUED:

I have heard, O fortunate king, that 'Ala' al-Din told his mother: 'All the merchants' sons have criticized me and told me that the only source of pride for them is to travel in order to make money.'

'Do you want to travel, my son?' asked his mother, and when he said yes, she asked him where he wanted to go. 'To Baghdad,' he told her, 'for there a man can make a hundred per cent profit.' 'My son,' his mother said, 'your father is a very wealthy man, but if he doesn't supply you with merchandise using his own money, I'll do it for you myself.' 'Ala' al-Din said: 'The best gift is the one that comes quickly. If you are going to do me a favour, now is the time for it.' So she fetched slaves and sent them to fetch packers, after which she opened up a warehouse and removed material from it, which she had packed into ten loads.

So much for his mother, but as for his father, when he looked around the orchard and failed to find 'Ala' al-Din there, he asked about him and was told that he had mounted his mule and gone back home. He rode after him and when he got to his house, he saw packed bundles. He asked about them and was told by his wife what had happened to 'Ala' al-Din with the merchants' sons. 'My boy, may God disappoint those who travel abroad!' he exclaimed. 'The Apostle of God, may God bless him and give him peace, said that he is fortunate who gets a living in his own land, while the ancients said: "Do not travel, even for a mile."'

Then he asked 'Ala' al-Din whether he was determined to go and would not change his mind. 'Ala' al-Din said: 'I must take my goods to Baghdad, otherwise I shall strip off my clothes, dress as a dervish and go wandering through the lands.' 'I am not a poor man or penniless,' said his father and, after showing 'Ala' al-Din all the wealth, trade goods and materials that he owned, he said: 'I have materials and goods suitable for every land.' Among what he showed his son were forty packed bales, each of which had its price – a thousand dinars – written on it. 'Take these forty,' he said to 'Ala' al-Din, 'together with the ten that your mother gave you, and set out under the protection of Almighty God. On your way you will come to a wood known as the Lion's Wood and a wadi known as the Wadi of the Dogs. These places make me fearful for you, as lives are lost there mercilessly.' 'Ala' al-Din asked him why that was and he said: 'Because of a Bedouin highwayman called 'Ajlan.' 'Man's sustenance comes from God,' said 'Ala' al-Din, 'and if I have a share in this, no harm will come to me.'

He and his father rode off to the beast market, where they were met by a baggage man who dismounted from his mule and kissed the syndic's hand. 'By God, master,' he said, 'it is a long time since we did any trading.' 'Each age has its own turn of fortune and its own men,' said Shams al-Din. 'May Almighty God have mercy on the poet who said:

I asked an old man walking with his beard down to his knees:
"Why are you so bent?" He waved his hands at me.
"My youth was lost on the ground," he said,
"And I am bending down to look for it."'

When he had finished these lines, he told the man that it was his son who was intending to travel. 'May God preserve him for you,' the man replied. Shams al-Din then drew up a contract between him and 'Ala' al-Din, instructing him to look after the boy as though he was his own son and giving him a hundred dinars to spend on his servants. He bought sixty mules for his son, together with a lamp and a covering for the shrine of 'Abd al-Qadir al-Jilani. 'My son,' he said, 'I shan't be there and as this man will be your father in my place you must do everything that he tells you.' He then went off with the mules and the servants and held a feast that night in honour of Shaikh 'Abd al-Qadir al-Jilani at which the whole of the Quran was recited. Next morning, he gave his son ten thousand dinars, telling him: 'If you find the price of material favourable when you come to Baghdad, sell the stuff, but if things are stagnant, then you can spend the dinars.'

The mules were then loaded, farewells were said and the party set out from the city. Meanwhile, Mahmud al-Balkhi had made his own preparations to go to Baghdad. He had brought out his baggage and pitched his tents outside Cairo, saying to himself: 'It is in the desert that you will be able to enjoy this boy, with no telltales or observers to spoil things for you.' He had a thousand dinars left over from a business deal which he owed Shams al-Din and so he went to him and said goodbye. Shams al-Din told him to give the thousand dinars to 'Ala' al-Din, asking him to look after the boy and saying: 'He will be like a son for you.' 'Ala' al-Din then met Mahmud . . .

Night 254

Morning now dawned and Shahrazad broke off from what she had been allowed to say. Then, when it was the two hundred and fifty-fourth night, SHE CONTINUED:

I have heard, O fortunate king, that 'Ala' al-Din then met Mahmud, who had told his cook not to prepare any food, and he himself then produced food and drink both for 'Ala' al-Din and his men, after which they set out on their journey. Mahmud owned four houses, one in Cairo, one in Damascus, one in Aleppo and one in Baghdad. The caravan continued on its way through the desert wastes until it came within sight of Damascus. Then Mahmud sent his slave to 'Ala' al-Din, whom he found sitting and reading. When the slave came up and kissed his hands, 'Ala' al-Din asked what he wanted. 'My master sends you his greetings,' replied the slave, 'and invites you to dine with him in his house.' 'Ala' al-Din said that he would have to consult Kamal al-Din, the leader of the caravan, and when he did, Kamal al-Din told him not to go.

The caravan left Damascus and reached Aleppo, where Mahmud held another banquet, again sending an invitation to 'Ala' al-Din. He again consulted Kamal al-Din, who again stopped him going. They then left Aleppo and when they were within one stage of Baghdad, Mahmud renewed his invitation. 'Ala' al-Din consulted Kamal al-Din, who tried to keep him from going, but this time 'Ala' al-Din said that he had to.

He got up, belted on his sword under his robes and went to Mahmud. Mahmud rose to meet him, greeted him and then produced an enormous feast. They ate, drank and then washed their hands, after which Mahmud leaned over to take a kiss from 'Ala' al-Din. 'Ala' al-Din received this on his hand and said: 'What do you want to do?' 'I have brought you here,' said Mahmud, 'so that I may enjoy myself with you in this place, and we may interpret the poet's lines:

> Can you come to me for one short moment,
> As long as it takes to milk a small ewe or fry an egg?
> You may eat what you can of a little bit of bread, and
> Take what you can collect of a little bit of silver,
> And bear what you want without difficulty,
> A span long, half a span, or a small handful.'

Mahmud's intention was to ravish 'Ala' al-Din, but the boy got up, drew his sword and exclaimed: 'Shame on your white hairs! Are you not afraid of the All-Powerful God? God have mercy on the poet who wrote:

> Guard your white hairs from the shame that may defile them;
> White hairs are quick to show the dirt.'

After finishing this line, he added: 'This merchandise is held in trust for God and is not for sale. Were I to sell it to someone else for gold, I would sell it to you for silver, but I shall not stay in your company ever again, you filthy fellow.' He went back to Kamal al-Din, the caravan leader, and said: 'This man is a pervert. I shall never again keep company with him or walk on the same road as him.' 'My son,' said Kamal al-Din, 'didn't I tell you not to go to him? But if we part from him, we shall have reason to fear for our lives, so let us stay as one caravan.' 'I can never travel along with him,' said 'Ala' al-Din, and so he loaded up his merchandise and went off with his men until he came to a wadi where he wanted to halt. 'Don't stop here,' said Kamal al-Din, 'but press on with the journey so that we may perhaps get to Baghdad before the gates close. The Baghdadis only open and shut them in daylight lest the city fall into the hands of the Rafidi heretics, who would then throw the books of wisdom into the Tigris.' 'My father,' said 'Ala' al-Din, 'I've not come out and brought these goods here as a matter of business but in order to see the sights of the various lands.' Kamal al-Din replied: 'My son, I'm afraid lest the Bedouin attack you and plunder your goods.' 'Man,' replied 'Ala' al-Din, 'are you master or servant? For my part, I shall not enter Baghdad until it is morning, when the people there can see my merchandise and learn to recognize me.' 'Do what you want,' said Kamal al-Din. 'I have given you my advice, but you know what is best for yourself.'

On 'Ala' al-Din's orders the mules were unloaded and his tent was pitched. They stayed there until midnight, when 'Ala' al-Din, on getting up to relieve himself, saw something glinting in the distance. He asked Kamal al-Din what this could be. Kamal al-Din sat up, and after looking carefully, recognized that this was the gleam of Bedouin spear points, steel and swords. These were, in fact, Bedouin led by a man named 'Ajlan Abu Na'ib, the *shaikh* of the Bedouin. When they got near the caravan and saw the loads, they exclaimed to each other that this was a night of plunder. 'Ala' al-Din's men heard this and Kamal al-Din shouted at 'Ajlan, calling him 'the least of the Bedouin'. 'Ajlan then struck him in the breast with a spear whose point emerged gleaming from his back. He fell dead at the entrance to the tent, and when the water carrier also shouted: 'Vilest of the Bedouin,' he was cut down by a sword which struck his shoulder and emerged from the tendons of his neck. As 'Ala' al-Din watched, the Bedouin then wheeled around and attacked the caravan, killing every single one of his men. They loaded the bales of merchandise on to the mules and left. 'Ala' al-Din said to himself: 'What is going to get me killed is my mule and my clothes.' He got up and stripped off his clothes, which he threw on to the back of his mule, leaving himself only in his shirt and drawers. He looked ahead towards the entrance of the tent, where he saw a pool of blood that had streamed from the corpses. In this he plunged what he was wearing until he looked like a dead man, drowned in blood.

So much for him, but as for 'Ajlan, the Bedouin *shaikh*, he asked his men whether the caravan had been coming from Cairo or leaving Baghdad.

Night 255

Morning now dawned and Shahrazad broke off from what she had been allowed to say. Then, when it was the two hundred and fifty-fifth night, SHE CONTINUED:

I have heard, O fortunate king, that the Bedouin leader asked his men whether the caravan had been coming from Cairo or leaving Baghdad.

'It was on its way from Cairo to Baghdad,' they told him. 'Go back to the corpses,' he told them, 'for I don't believe that its owner is dead.' The Bedouin did as they were told and began thrusting and striking at the corpses until they came to 'Ala' al-Din, who had thrown himself down among them. When they reached them, they said: 'You're only pretending to be dead, but we'll finish the job.' A Bedouin drew out his spear and was about to plunge it into 'Ala' al-Din's breast when 'Ala' al-Din cried: 'Oh for your blessing, my lord 'Abd al-Qadir al-Jilani,' and he saw a hand that turned the spear aside into the breast of the caravan leader, Kamal al-Din, striking him rather than 'Ala' al-Din himself.

The Bedouin then went off with the bales that they had loaded on the mules. When 'Ala' al-Din saw that these birds had flown off with their spoils, he sat up and then started to run. 'Ajlan, however, said to his companions: 'I can see something in the distance.' One of them went back and, seeing 'Ala' al-Din running, he called to him: 'It won't do you any good to run away. We're on your track,' and, kicking his horse, he hurried after him. 'Ala' al-Din had seen a water trough in front of him with a cistern beside it. He climbed up to a grille in the cistern, stretched out on it and pretended to be asleep, praying: 'Kind Shelterer, grant me Your shelter, which cannot be removed.' Just then, the Bedouin stood up on his stirrups under the cistern and put out a hand to seize him. 'Oh for your blessing, Lady Nafisa!' exclaimed 'Ala' al-Din. 'This is the time for you to help me!' At that, a scorpion stung the Bedouin on the palm of his hand. He shrieked and called for his companions to come and help him, as he had been stung. He dismounted from his mare, and when the others came they remounted him and asked him what had happened. 'A young scorpion stung me,' he told them, after which they took the spoils of the caravan and made off.

So much for them. 'Ala' al-Din stayed and slept on the grille of the cistern, while as for Mahmud al-Balkhi, he had ordered his goods to be loaded up and had travelled on until he came to the Lion's Wood. Here he was pleased to find all 'Ala' al-Din's servants lying dead. He dismounted and walked on to the cistern and the trough, where his mule, which was thirsty, bent its head to drink. In the water it saw 'Ala' al-Din's reflection. It started away, and when Mahmud looked up, he saw 'Ala' al-Din lying there, dressed only in his shirt and drawers. 'Who has done this to you, leaving you in so bad a state?' he asked. 'The Bedouin,' 'Ala' al-Din told him. 'My son,' said Mahmud, 'the mules and the merchandise served as your ransom. Console yourself with these lines:

If a man's head has escaped destruction,
His money is no more than the clipping of a nail.

Come down, my son, and fear no harm.'

When 'Ala' al-Din had come down from the grille, Mahmud mounted him on a mule and they went on to Baghdad, where they entered Mahmud's house. He then told 'Ala' al-Din to go to the baths, and repeated: 'The wealth and the goods served as your ransom, my son, and if you obey me, I'll give you twice as much again.' When he left the baths, Mahmud brought him into a hall embellished with gold, from which four rooms opened out. On his orders, a meal of all kinds of food was produced. They ate and drank and Mahmud then leaned towards 'Ala' al-Din to snatch a kiss from him. 'Ala' al-Din received this on his hand and said: 'Are you still following your evil ways with me? Didn't I tell you that, were I to sell this merchandise to others for gold, I would sell it to you for silver?' 'It's only for this that I am going to give you trade goods, a mule and clothes,' said Mahmud, 'for I am madly in love with you. How eloquently the poet expressed it:

Abu Bilal, our *shaikh* without a peer,
Quoting from one of his own associates, has said:
"A lover's passion is not to be cured
By kisses or embraces until he copulates."'

'This can never be,' said 'Ala' al-Din. 'Take your clothes and your mule and open the door for me so that I can leave.' Mahmud did this and 'Ala' al-Din went out, with the dogs barking behind him. While he was walking off in the darkness he caught sight of the door of a mosque, and going into the entrance hall he took shelter there. Suddenly, he saw a light coming towards him, and when he looked at it closely, he made out two lanterns being carried by two slaves in front of two merchants, one an old man with a handsome face and the other a youth. He heard the youth saying to his companion: 'For God's sake, uncle, give me back my cousin.' 'How many times did I tell you to stop,' said the old man, 'when you were repeating the formula of divorce as though it was your copy of the Quran?' He then turned to his right and saw the young 'Ala' al-Din looking like a sliver of the moon. They exchanged greetings and the old man asked 'Ala' al-Din who he was. 'I am 'Ala' al-Din, son of Shams al-Din, the syndic of the merchants of Cairo. I asked my father for some merchandise and he gave me fifty loads of materials and goods . . .'

Night 256

Morning now dawned and Shahrazad broke off from what she had been allowed to say. Then, when it was the two hundred and fifty-sixth night, SHE CONTINUED:

I have heard, O fortunate king, that 'Ala' al-Din said: 'My father gave me fifty loads of goods, together with ten thousand dinars. I got as far as the Lion's Wood when I was attacked by Bedouin who took my money and my goods, so I came into the city and, not knowing where to spend the night, I saw this place and took shelter here.' 'My boy,' said the old man, 'what would you say to my giving you a thousand dinars, as well as a suit of clothes and a mule, each worth a thousand dinars?' 'Why would you do that, uncle?' asked 'Ala' al-Din. 'This young man who is with me,' replied the other, 'is my brother's only son, and I have an only daughter. My daughter is a beautiful girl, known as Zubaida, the lute player. I married her to him, but whereas he loves her, she dislikes him. After swearing by triple divorce,* he broke his oath, and no sooner was she sure of this than she left him. He got everyone to plead with me to give her back to him, but I said that the only way in which this can be done is by giving her an interim husband. My nephew and I agreed that this should be a stranger, so that nobody could reproach him about it, and as you are a stranger, come with us, so that we can draw up a contract for you to marry her and spend the night with her. In the morning, you can divorce her and I shall give you what I promised.'

'Ala' al-Din said to himself: 'To pass the night with a bride on a bed in a house is better than to pass it in lanes and entrance halls.' So he went with them to the *qadi*, who, when he saw him, felt love for him enter his heart. 'What is it that you want?' he asked the girl's father. 'I want you to draw up a marriage contract making this young man an interim husband for my daughter. It is to be written into the contract that the dowry is ten thousand dinars. If he spends the night with her and divorces her in the morning, I shall give him clothes worth a thousand dinars, a mule worth a thousand dinars, and a thousand dinars in cash, but if he doesn't divorce her, he is to pay over the ten thousand dinars.'

The contract was drawn up on these terms and the girl's father kept a

---

* An Islamic procedure whereby if a man says 'I divorce you' three times, the divorce is legal and final.

record of it. He then took 'Ala' al-Din with him, gave him a suit of clothes and brought him to the girl's house. He left 'Ala' al-Din at the door while he went to his daughter and told her: 'Take the record of your dowry, for I have drawn up a marriage contract between you and a handsome young man named 'Ala' al-Din Abu'l-Shamat, and I would ask you to treat him well.' After giving her the document, he went back to his own house. His nephew, however, had a housekeeper to whom he was kind and who was in the habit of visiting Zubaida, the lute player. He told this woman: 'When my cousin Zubaida sees this handsome young man she won't be prepared to accept me, and I want you to use some wile to keep her away from him.' She swore to him that she wouldn't let the man approach her, and she then went to 'Ala' al-Din and said: 'My son, I am going to give you some advice for the sake of Almighty God, so please accept it. I am afraid for you because of that girl. Let her sleep on her own; don't touch her or go near her.' 'Why?' he asked. 'Her body is filled with leprosy and I'm afraid that she may infect you, handsome youth that you are,' she told him. 'I have no need of her,' he replied, after which she went to the girl and told her the same story. 'I have no need of him,' the girl said. 'I shall let him sleep on his own and in the morning he can go on his way.'

She summoned a slave girl and told her to fetch 'Ala' al-Din an evening meal. The girl brought food and placed it in front of him. He ate his fill and then recited the *Sura* Ya-Sin in a melodious voice. To the listening Zubaida it seemed as though David's household were singing the Psalms. She said to herself: 'May God curse this old woman who said that he suffers from leprosy. That's not the voice of a leper, and what she said must have been a lie.' She then took in her hands a lute of Indian workmanship, tuned the strings and sang to it in a voice sweet enough to halt the birds in the middle of the sky. These were the lines she chanted:

> I fell in love with a fawn with a languid black eye,
> Who, when he walks, moves *ban* branches to envy.
> Another enjoys his union as he repulses me.
> God grants His grace to whom He wills.

When 'Ala' al-Din heard her chanting these lines after he had finished the *sura*, he, too, chanted:

> My greetings to the form hidden within its clothes,
> And to the roses in the gardens of the cheeks.

Zubaida's love for him increased; she raised the curtain, and at the sight of her, 'Ala' al-Din recited:

> She came out as a moon,
> Swaying as the branch of a *ban* tree,
> Spreading the scent of ambergris,
> And looking with the eyes of a gazelle.
> It is as though grief is in love with my heart
> And when she leaves, it finds its chance of union.

Zubaida walked, shaking her haunches and swaying, a masterwork of Him Whose favours are hidden, and each looked at the other with glances followed by a thousand sighs. When the arrow of her glances was lodged in 'Ala' al-Din's heart, he recited these lines:

> She saw the moon in the sky and reminded me
> Of the nights of our union at al-Raqmatain.
> Each one of us was looking at a moon;
> I saw one mirrored in her eyes and she saw one in mine.

She came nearer him, and when she was only two paces away, he recited:

> She spread out three locks of her hair one night,
> And so showed me four nights.
> She turned to face the heavenly moon,
> So showing me two moons at once.

When she approached 'Ala' al-Din, he said: 'Keep your distance from me, lest you infect me.' She uncovered the upper and under side of her wrist, with its white clear as silver. Then she told him to keep away from her lest he infect her with his leprosy. 'Who told you that I was a leper?' he asked, and when she told him that it was the old woman, he said: 'I, too, was told by her that you were leprous.' He uncovered his forearm for her, and she found that his flesh was like pure silver.

She then clasped him to her bosom and he clasped her to his breast. They embraced each other and she took him and lay back, undoing her drawers. The tool that his father had bequeathed him moved and he called out: 'Help me, Shaikh Zacharias, father of veins.' He put his hands on her hips and, setting the vein of sweetness to the Gate of the Cleft, he pushed until it reached the Lattice Gate and passed through the Gate of Victories. After that, he entered the Monday market, the Tuesday market, the Wednesday market and the Thursday market. He found that the carpet filled the room and he moved the tuber round against its covering until the two met.

In the morning, he said to the girl: 'Before our joy has been completed, the crow has taken it and flown away.' 'What do you mean?' she asked. 'Lady,' he answered, 'I can only stay with you for this one hour.' 'Who says so?' she asked. He replied: 'Your father drew up a contract requiring me to pay ten thousand dinars as your dowry. If I don't pay it over today, they will imprison me for its non-payment in the house of the *qadi*, but I can't even pay the smallest fraction of this sum.' 'Do you hold the marriage contract or do they?' she asked. 'I have the contract,' he said, 'but I have nothing else.' 'This is easy,' she told him, 'and there is nothing to be afraid of. Take these hundred dinars, and if I had more I would give you what you want. Because of his love for his nephew, my father moved all his own goods from mine to his nephew's house, and he even took all my jewellery. When he sends you a messenger from the *shari'a* court tomorrow . . .'

Night 257

Morning now dawned and Shahrazad broke off from what she had been allowed to say. Then, when it was the two hundred and fifty-seventh night, SHE CONTINUED:

I have heard, O fortunate king, that Zubaida told 'Ala' al-Din: 'When they send you a messenger from the *shari'a* court tomorrow, and the *qadi* and my father tell you to divorce me, say: "What school of law allows me to marry in the evening and divorce in the morning?" Then kiss the *qadi*'s hand and give him a douceur. Kiss the hands of the witnesses and give them ten dinars each. They will all talk with you and when they ask why you won't consent to a divorce and take the thousand dinars, the mule and the clothes following the condition that they agreed with you, tell them: "Every hair of her head is worth a thousand dinars to me. I shall never divorce her and take the clothes or anything else." When the *qadi* then tells you to pay over the dowry, tell him that you are short of money at the moment. The *qadi* and the witnesses will be reluctant to press you and will allow you a delay.'

While they were talking, the *qadi*'s envoy knocked on the door and when 'Ala' al-Din went out to meet him, he told 'Ala' al-Din to come and speak to the effendi, as his father-in-law wanted him. 'Ala' al-Din gave the usher five dinars and asked him which school of law sanctioned an evening marriage followed by a morning divorce. 'We do not hold this permissible at all,' said the man, 'and if you are ignorant of the law, I shall act as your attorney.' When they got to the court, the *qadi* asked: 'Why don't you divorce the woman and take what is due to you by the conditions of the agreement?' 'Ala' al-Din went up to him and kissed his hand, into which he put fifty dinars. 'O *qadi*,' he said, 'my master, what school of law sanctions an evening marriage followed in the morning by compulsory divorce?' The reply was: 'A forced divorce is not permitted by any of the Muslim schools of law.' The girl's father then said: 'If you're not going to divorce her, then pay me the ten-thousand-dinar dowry.' 'Give me three days' grace,' said 'Ala' al-Din. 'That is not a long enough delay,' said the *qadi*. 'He should allow you ten days.' They agreed on this, the condition being that after ten days 'Ala' al-Din should either pay the dowry or divorce Zubaida.

On these terms 'Ala' al-Din left, and after buying meat, rice, butter and what other foodstuffs he needed, he set off to the house and, going in, he told Zubaida all that had happened to him. 'Marvels can happen between a day and a night,' she told him, adding: 'How eloquent was the poet who said:

Show gentleness when you are angry,
And patience when misfortune visits you.
Time leaves the nights heavily pregnant;
They will give birth to wonders of all kinds.'

She got up, prepared the food and brought out the table. They ate, drank and enjoyed themselves, after which 'Ala' al-Din asked her for some music. Zubaida took the lute and played a tune that would move the solid rocks with delight and cause the strings to cry out in ecstasy: 'O David!' Then she quickened the tempo, but while she and 'Ala' al-Din were enjoying themselves in cheerful relaxation, there was a sudden knock on the door. 'Get up and see who it is,' Zubaida told 'Ala' al-Din, and so he went down and opened the door to find four dervishes standing there. When he asked them what they wanted, they said: 'Master, we are dervishes from foreign parts. Music and the subtleties of poetry are the food of our souls and we would like to spend the night relaxing with you until morning, when we shall be on our way. Almighty God will reward you. We love music and each one of us knows by heart odes, poems and *muwashshahat*.' 'I shall have to consult,' 'Ala' al-Din said, and he then went and told Zubaida, who told him to open the door for the visitors. He did this and after having brought them up, he gave them seats and made them welcome.

He produced food for them but they did not eat, telling him: 'Master, our food is the repetition of the Name of God in our hearts, and listening to music with our ears. How eloquent was the poet who said:

Our only purpose is to meet together;
Eating is the mark of beasts.

We were listening to beautiful music coming from your house, but when we came up, it stopped. Was it a slave, white or black, who was playing, or a well-born girl?' 'That was my wife,' said 'Ala' al-Din, and he told them everything that had happened to him, adding: 'My father-in-law wants me to pay a dowry of ten thousand dinars, and has allowed me a delay of ten days.' One of the dervishes said: 'Be cheerful rather than sad. I am the *shaikh* of a monastery and under my control and authority are forty dervishes. I shall collect ten thousand dinars for you from them to pay off the dowry that you owe your father-in-law. So tell your wife to play us an enjoyable tune to revive us. To some people music is food, to others medicine, and to others cheerfulness.'

These dervishes were, in fact, the caliph Harun al-Rashid, Ja'far the Barmecide, his vizier, Abu Nuwas al-Hasan ibn Hani' and Masrur, the executioner. They had passed by Zubaida's house because the caliph, in a melancholy mood, had told his vizier that he wanted to go out and stroll through the city as he was feeling depressed. They dressed as dervishes, went down to the city and passed the house, from which they heard music coming, prompting them to find out what was happening. They passed the night in harmonious enjoyment, exchanging stories until morning came. The caliph put a hundred dinars under the prayer rug, took leave of 'Ala' al-Din, and then he and the others went on their way.

When Zubaida lifted up the rug, she saw the money lying beneath it and she said to 'Ala' al-Din: 'Take these hundred dinars that I found under the prayer rug. The dervishes must have put them there without our knowledge before they left.' 'Ala' al-Din took the money and bought meat, rice, butter and everything else he needed. The following night, he lit the candles and said to Zubaida: 'The dervishes have not brought the ten thousand dinars that they promised me, but they are poor men.' As they were talking, the 'dervishes' knocked on the door. Zubaida told 'Ala' al-Din to go down and open up for them, and when they had come up, he asked them whether they had brought the promised dinars. They told him: 'We couldn't get hold of any, but have no fear. If God Almighty wills it, tomorrow we will concoct an alchemical brew for you. Now tell your wife to let us hear some splendid piece of music to revive our spirits, as music is what we love.' So she played them a tune on her lute that would make the solid rocks dance. They passed a pleasant and happy night in joyful conversation until dawn broke and the light spread. After the caliph had again slipped a hundred dinars under the prayer rug, he and his companions took leave of 'Ala' al-Din and left him, going off on their way.

They kept on coming back to him in this way for nine nights, on each of which the caliph left a hundred dinars under the prayer rug. On the tenth night, they did not arrive. The reason was that the caliph had sent a message to one of the leading merchants, saying: 'Bring me fifty loads of materials from Cairo . . .'

Night 258

Morning now dawned and Shahrazad broke off from what she had been allowed to say. Then, when it was the two hundred and fifty-eighth night, SHE CONTINUED:

I have heard, O fortunate king, that the caliph had told the merchant: 'Bring me fifty loads of materials from Cairo, each worth a thousand dinars, with its price marked on it, and bring me also an Abyssinian slave.' When the merchant had produced all this, the caliph handed the slave a basin and ewer of gold, together with a present and the fifty loads. He wrote a letter purporting to come from Shams al-Din, the syndic of the Cairene merchants. He told the slave: 'Take these loads and the other things; go to such-and-such a quarter in which the syndic of the merchants has his house and ask for 'Ala' al-Din Abu'l-Shamat. The people will direct you to the right quarter and to his house.'

The slave took what he was told to bring and set off as the caliph had ordered him. So much for him, but as for Zubaida's cousin, he went to her father and said: 'Come on, let us go to 'Ala' al-Din and get him to divorce Zubaida.' Her father came down and the two of them set off to see 'Ala' al-Din. When they got to the house, they found fifty mules with fifty loads of materials and a slave riding on another mule. 'Whose are these loads?' they asked him, and he replied: 'They belong to my master, 'Ala' al-Din Abu'l-Shamat. His father had provided him with merchandise and sent him off to Baghdad, but he was intercepted by Bedouin who took his money and his goods. When his father heard of this, he sent me to bring him replacement loads and he also sent with me a mule laden with fifty thousand dinars, a bundle of valuable clothes, a sable coat and a ewer and basin of gold.' 'Ala' al-Din is my son-in-law,' said Zubaida's father, 'and I will direct you to his house.'

While 'Ala' al-Din was sitting plunged in gloom, there was a knock on the door. 'Zubaida,' he said, 'I am sure that your father has sent me a messenger either from the *qadi* or from the *wali*.' 'Go down,' she said, 'and find out what is happening.' So he went down, opened the door and saw his father-in-law, the syndic of the merchants, together with a dusky-coloured, pleasant-faced Abyssinian slave mounted on a mule. This man dismounted and kissed his hands. 'What do you want?' asked 'Ala' al-Din. 'I am the slave of my master 'Ala' al-Din Abu'l-Shamat, the son of Shams al-Din, syndic of the Cairene merchants,' he replied, 'whose father has sent me to him in charge of this.' He then handed over the letter, which 'Ala' al-Din took, opened and read. In it he found written the lines:

> Letter, when my beloved sees you,
> Kiss the ground and kiss his shoes.
> Go slowly; don't be hasty.
> My rest and my life are in his hands.*

The letter continued: 'Greetings and honourable salutations from Shams al-Din to his son Abu'l-Shamat. Know, my son, that I have heard the news of the slaughter of your men and the plunder of your wealth and your goods. In their place I have sent you fifty loads of Egyptian material, a suit of clothes, a sable coat and a ewer and basin of gold. There is no cause for fear; the money was your ransom, and you should never be sad. Your mother and the rest of the household are in good health and are doing well. They send you many greetings. News has reached me that you were made an interim husband for Zubaida the lute player, whose dowry was set at fifty thousand dinars. This sum is sent to you with the loads of merchandise, together with your slave, Salim.'

When 'Ala' al-Din had finished reading the letter, he took charge of the loads, and then, turning to his father-in-law, he told him to take the

---

* Play on *raha* (rest) and *ruh* (life).

dinars for his daughter's dowry and to dispose of the merchandise, keeping any profit for himself but returning the capital cost. 'By God,' replied his father-in-law, 'I shall not take anything, and as for your wife's dowry, you and she must settle the matter between yourselves.' He and 'Ala' al-Din entered the house, after the merchandise had been taken in, and Zubaida asked her father: 'To whom does all this belong?' He replied: 'These goods belong to your husband, 'Ala' al-Din, and they were sent by his father to make up for the ones that the Bedouin stole from him. He also sent fifty thousand dinars, a bundle of clothes, a sable coat, a mule, and a ewer and basin made of gold. It is for you to decide what you want to do about the dowry.' Zubaida's cousin said: 'Uncle, make 'Ala' al-Din divorce my wife for me.' 'That's no longer at all possible,' said his uncle, 'as it is he who holds the contract.'

The young man went off depressed and dejected. He was ill when he went to bed and death then overtook him. As for 'Ala' al-Din, he took the loads of merchandise and went to the market, where he bought what he needed in the way of food, drink and butter. He set out a meal, as he had done every night, but he said to Zubaida: 'Look at these lying dervishes. They made us a promise and then broke it.' She replied: 'You are the son of the syndic of the merchants, and if you couldn't raise half a *fidda*, how would these poor dervishes manage?' 'Almighty God enabled us to do without them,' he said, 'but I shall not open the door for them again if they come to us.' 'Why?' she said. 'It was only through their coming that fortune visited us, and every night they used to put a hundred dinars under the prayer rug. If they do come, you must certainly open up for them.'

When daylight began to fade and night to fall, the candles were lit and 'Ala' al-Din asked Zubaida to play something for him. Just then, there was a knock on the door and Zubaida told 'Ala' al-Din to go and see who was there. He went down, opened the door and saw the 'dervishes'. 'Welcome to the liars,' he said. 'Come up.' They went up with him and he seated them and brought them a meal. They ate, drank and enjoyed themselves; and then they said: 'Master, we are concerned for you. What happened to you with your father-in-law?' 'Ala' al-Din replied: 'In exchange for my losses, God gave me more than I had wished for.' 'By God,' they said, 'we were afraid for you . . .'

Night 259

Morning now dawned and Shahrazad broke off from what she had been allowed to say. Then, when it was the two hundred and fifty-ninth night, SHE CONTINUED:

I have heard, O fortunate king, that the dervishes told 'Ala' al-Din: 'By God, we were afraid for you, and we only stayed away because we couldn't find the money.' 'Ala' al-Din told them: 'Quick relief came to me from my Lord. My father sent me fifty thousand dinars, fifty loads of materials, each worth a thousand dinars, a suit of clothes, a sable coat, a mule, a slave and a ewer and basin of gold. I have made my peace with my father-in-law and am now legally married, praise be to God.' The caliph got up to relieve himself and Ja'far, the vizier, leaned over to 'Ala' al-Din and said: 'Be sure to mind your manners, for you are in the presence of the Commander of the Faithful.' 'What rudeness have I shown in the presence of the Commander of the Faithful and which of you is he?' Ja'far replied: 'The man who was speaking to you and who got up to relieve himself was the Commander of the Faithful, the caliph Harun al-Rashid. I am Ja'far, the vizier; this is Masrur, the executioner, and this is Abu Nuwas al-Hasan ibn Hani'. Use your intelligence, 'Ala' al-Din. How many days do you think it takes to travel from Cairo to Baghdad?' 'Forty-five,' replied 'Ala' al-Din. 'It is only ten days since your goods were plundered,' said Ja'far, 'so how could the news have reached your father, and these loads been packed for you, and a forty-five-day journey been completed in ten days?' 'Where did this come from then, sir?' asked 'Ala' al-Din. 'From the caliph, the Commander of the Faithful,' said Ja'far, 'because of the great love he has for you.'

While they were talking, the caliph came back. 'Ala' al-Din got up, kissed the ground before him, and said: 'May God preserve you, Commander of the Faithful, and prolong your life. May the people never be deprived of your grace and bounty.' ''Ala' al-Din,' said the caliph, 'let Zubaida play us a tune as a sweetener to mark your well-being.' Zubaida then played on her lute a tune of such rare beauty that the solid rocks were moved with joy and the lute itself cried out in ecstasy: 'O David!' They spent the night in the happiest of states until morning came. At that point, the caliph told 'Ala' al-Din to come to his court the next day. 'To hear is to obey,' said 'Ala' al-Din. 'I shall come, God willing, if you are well.' He then took ten salvers, setting on each a splendid gift, and the next day he brought them to the court.

The caliph was sitting there on his throne when 'Ala' al-Din came in through the door reciting these lines:

> May glorious fortune greet you every morning
> And may the envious be humbled.
> May your days continue to be white,
> While those of your enemies are black.

The caliph welcomed him, and 'Ala' al-Din then said: 'Commander of the Faithful, the Prophet, may God bless him and give him peace, accepted gifts, and these ten salvers and what is on them are a gift from me to you.' The caliph accepted the gift and ordered that 'Ala' al-Din be given a robe of honour, after which he appointed him as syndic of the merchants and gave him a seat in his court. While he was sitting there, Zubaida's father came in to find him sitting in his own place, wearing his robe of honour. 'Commander of the Faithful, king of the age,' he said, 'what is this man doing sitting in my place, wearing this robe?' The caliph said: 'I have appointed him syndic of the merchants, for offices are conferred by appointment and not held for life. You are deposed.' 'He is in every way one of ours,' said Zubaida's father. 'How excellent is your action, Commander of the Faithful! May God place the best of us in charge of our affairs and how many a small man has become great.' The caliph then wrote a decree of appointment for 'Ala' al-Din which he gave to the *wali*, who, in turn, gave it to the crier. The crier called out in the court: 'The syndic of the merchants is 'Ala' al-Din Abu'l-Shamat. His orders are to be obeyed and his dignity respected. He is to be treated with the honour and esteem owed to his high rank.' When the court had been dismissed, the *wali* and the crier walked in front of 'Ala' al-Din and the crier began to proclaim: 'The syndic of the merchants is my lord 'Ala' al-Din Abu'l-Shamat.' The people in the streets of Baghdad flocked around him as the crier kept repeating his proclamation.

Next morning, 'Ala' al-Din opened a shop for the slave Salim, and would leave him sitting there to look after the business while he himself rode off to take his place at the caliph's court.

Night 260

Morning now dawned and Shahrazad broke off from what she had been allowed to say. Then, when it was the two hundred and sixtieth night, SHE CONTINUED:

I have heard, O fortunate king, that 'Ala' al-Din would ride off to take his place at the caliph's court. One day, as he was seated there as usual, a messenger came to say to the caliph: 'Commander of the Faithful, may your life be extended in exchange for that of So-and-So, your boon companion. He has been gathered to the mercy of Almighty God, but may your own life be preserved.' The caliph asked for 'Ala' al-Din and when he came before him, he presented him with a splendid robe of honour, installed him as one of his boon companions and gave him a monthly allowance of a thousand dinars. 'Ala' al-Din continued to fill this role and then one day, when he was seated as usual in attendance on the caliph, an emir, armed with sword and shield, came into the court and said: 'Commander of the Faithful, may your life be extended at the expense of the hexarch,* for he has died today.' The caliph ordered that 'Ala' al-Din be given a robe of honour and appointed his hexarch. The dead man had left no son, daughter or wife. 'Ala' al-Din took charge of his estate and the caliph told him to arrange the funeral and then to take all that the man had left in the way of wealth, slaves, slave girls and eunuchs. He then waved his handkerchief to dismiss the court and 'Ala' al-Din went down with Ahmad al-Danaf, captain of the right wing of the caliph's guard, with the captain's forty men riding at his stirrup, and on the other side Hasan Shuman, captain of the left wing, with his men. 'Ala' al-Din asked the latter to intercede for him with Ahmad al-Danaf, so that he might accept him as a son according to God's covenant. Ahmad agreed to this and said: 'I and my forty men will march in front of you to court every day.'

After this, 'Ala' al-Din remained for some time in the caliph's service. Then, one day, he came back home from court and dismissed Ahmad and his men, after which he sat with his wife, Zubaida, the lute player. He had lit the candles and Zubaida had got up to relieve herself, but while he was seated there, he heard a great cry. He sprang up to find out who it was who had made the cry, only to discover that it was his wife,

---

* 'Hexarch' means literally 'leader of sixty'.

who was now lying stretched out on the ground; and when he put his hand on her breast, he found that she was dead. Her father's house was opposite his own and when her father heard the cry he asked 'Ala' al-Din what the matter was. 'May your life be extended, father, in exchange for that of your daughter, Zubaida, the lute player. To show honour to the dead is to bury them.'

The funeral was held the next morning, and 'Ala' al-Din and her father consoled each other. So much for Zubaida, the lute player, but as for 'Ala' al-Din, he put on mourning clothes and absented himself from court, being tearful and sad at heart. The caliph asked Ja'far, his vizier, the reason for his absence, and Ja'far said: 'He is grieving for the loss of his wife, Zubaida, and is preoccupied with mourning her.' 'We must console him,' said the caliph, to which the vizier answered: 'To hear is to obey.' The caliph, together with the vizier and a number of servants, left the palace, mounted and rode off to 'Ala' al-Din's house. He was sitting there when they came and he got up to meet them, kissing the ground before the caliph. 'May God compensate you with good,' said the caliph. 'And may He grant you long life, Commander of the Faithful,' replied 'Ala' al-Din. ''Ala' al-Din,' asked the caliph, 'why do you keep away from court?' 'Because of my sorrow for my wife, Zubaida, Commander of the Faithful.' 'Banish this grief from your heart,' said the caliph. 'She has gone to the mercy of Almighty God, and sorrow does no good at all.' 'Commander of the Faithful,' he replied, 'I shall only stop grieving when I die and they bury me beside her.' The caliph said: 'In God is found a recompense for everything that has been lost. No stratagem and no wealth can save a man from death, and how eloquent was the poet who said:

Although a son of woman may live long,
One day he will be carried on a humped bier.
How can he feel delight and pleasure in this life,
Over whose cheeks dust will be poured?'

When the caliph had finished his visit of condolence, he set off home after having told 'Ala' al-Din not to cut himself off from the court. So next morning, 'Ala' al-Din rode off there and kissed the ground in front of the caliph. The caliph left his throne to come and welcome him and, after greeting him, he seated him in his place, saying: ''Ala' al-Din, you will be my guest tonight.' Later, he took him to the women's quarters, where he summoned a slave girl named Qut al-Qulub. He told her that

'Ala' al-Din had had a wife named Zubaida who had dispelled his cares and griefs, but who had died. 'I want you,' he added, 'to play some tune . . .'

Night 262*

Morning now dawned and Shahrazad broke off from what she had been allowed to say. Then, when it was the two hundred and sixty-second night, SHE CONTINUED:

I have heard, O fortunate king, that the caliph told his slave girl Qut al-Qulub: 'To play some tune on your lute for him to drive away cares and griefs.' When she had got up and done this, he asked 'Ala' al-Din: 'What do you think of the girl's voice?' 'Zubaida had a better voice,' replied 'Ala' al-Din, 'but this is an accomplished lute player who could delight the solid rocks.' 'Does she please you?' asked the caliph, and when 'Ala' al-Din said that she did, the caliph told him: 'I swear by my head and the graves of my ancestors that she is a present from me to you, both she and her maids.' 'Ala' al-Din thought that this was a joke, but in the morning the caliph went to Qut al-Qulub and told her that he had given her to 'Ala' al-Din. She was delighted, as when she had seen 'Ala' al-Din she had fallen in love with him. On leaving the seraglio, he went to the court, where he summoned porters and told them to transport Qut al-Qulub's possessions, carrying her and her maids by palanquin and taking them to 'Ala' al-Din's house. This they did, bringing her to 'Ala' al-Din's house. The caliph, meanwhile, sat in his judgement hall until the end of the day, after which he dismissed the court and retired to his palace.

So much for him, but as for Qut al-Qulub, when she entered 'Ala' al-Din's pavilion with her maids, of whom there were forty, in addition to the eunuchs, she told two of these latter to sit on chairs, one on each side of the door, with instructions that when 'Ala' al-Din came they were to kiss his cheeks and say: 'Our mistress Qut al-Qulub invites you to come in, as the caliph has given her to you, together with her maids.' 'To hear is to obey,' they said, and they took their seats as she had ordered them. When 'Ala' al-Din arrived, he was surprised to find two of the caliph's eunuchs sitting by the door. He said to himself: 'Perhaps this isn't my house – otherwise, what has happened?'

* There is no Night 261 in the Calcutta II text.

When the eunuchs saw him, they got up and kissed his hands. 'We are servants of the caliph and mamluks belonging to Qut al-Qulub,' they told him. 'She sends her greetings to you and says that the caliph has given her to you, together with her maids, and asks you to come to her.' He replied: 'Welcome her for me but tell her that as long as she is with me I shall not enter the pavilion in which she is, for what was the master's should not belong to the servant. Ask her, too, what her daily expenditure was while she was with the caliph.' The eunuchs went to Qut al-Qulub and told her what he had said, and she answered that she used to spend a hundred dinars a day. 'Ala' al-Din said to himself: 'There was no need for the caliph to give me Qut al-Qulub so that I should have to spend all this money on her, but there is nothing to be done about it.'

Qut al-Qulub stayed with him for some days, on each of which he supplied her with a hundred dinars. Then, one day, when he was absent from court, the caliph said to Ja'far, the vizier: 'I only gave Qut al-Qulub to 'Ala' al-Din to console him for the loss of his wife, so why is he still absenting himself from us?' Ja'far replied: 'It is a true saying that whoever meets his beloved forgets his friends.' 'It may be that he has some reason for staying away, but we shall go to visit him,' the caliph said. Some days earlier, 'Ala' al-Din had said to Ja'far: 'I complained to the caliph of the sorrow that I feel for the loss of my wife, Zubaida, and he gave me Qut al-Qulub.' 'He wouldn't have done this unless he loved you,' said Ja'far, who then asked: 'Have you slept with her?' 'No, by God,' said 'Ala' al-Din. 'I know nothing at all about her body,' and when Ja'far asked him why this was, he repeated: 'What is suitable for the master is not suitable for the servant.'

The caliph and Ja'far went in disguise to visit 'Ala' al-Din and when they came to him, he recognized them and rose to kiss the caliph's hands. Looking at him, the caliph could see the traces of sorrow and he asked the reason for this, adding: 'Have you not slept with Qut al-Qulub?' 'Commander of the Faithful,' he replied, 'what is suitable for the master is not suitable for the servant. Up till now I have not lain with her and I know nothing of her body. Please take her back from me.' 'I want to meet her and to question her,' said the caliph, to which 'Ala' al-Din answered: 'To hear is to obey.'

When the caliph came to the girl . . .

Night 263

Morning now dawned and Shahrazad broke off from what she had been allowed to say. Then, when it was the two hundred and sixty-third night, SHE CONTINUED:

I have heard, O fortunate king, that when the caliph came to Qut al-Qulub, she rose at the sight of him and kissed the ground in front of him. He then asked her whether 'Ala' al-Din had slept with her. 'No, Commander of the Faithful,' she replied. 'I sent a message to ask him to come to me, but he wouldn't consent.' The caliph ordered that she should be taken back to the seraglio and, after telling 'Ala' al-Din not to absent himself from the court, he set off for his palace.

The next morning, 'Ala' al-Din mounted and rode off to the *diwan*, where he took his place as a hexarch. The caliph then told the treasurer to give ten thousand dinars to the vizier Ja'far, and when this had been done, he told Ja'far: 'You are to go down to the market of the slave girls and buy a girl for 'Ala' al-Din at a price of ten thousand dinars.' Ja'far went obediently, taking 'Ala' al-Din with him to the market. As it happened, the caliph's *wali* of Baghdad, an emir called Khalid, had gone to the market that day to buy a slave girl for his son. Khalid's wife, Khatun, had borne him an ugly son named Habzalam Bazaza who had reached the age of twenty without having learned how to ride a horse, although his father was a doughty champion, a rider ready to plunge into unknown dangers.

One night it happened that Habzalam Bazaza had a polluting dream. His mother was pleased when she heard of this and she told his father, adding: 'I want us to find him a wife, as he is now ready for marriage.' Khalid replied: 'He has an ugly face, foul breath and is a filthy brute whom no woman would accept.' 'Then we shall buy him a slave girl,' she said. As Almighty God had decreed, on the day that Ja'far and 'Ala' al-Din went to the market, the emir Khalid and his son went, too. While they were there, a beautiful girl with a perfect figure was led in by an auctioneer. After Ja'far had offered a thousand dinars for her, the auctioneer went on to Khalid. Habzalam had looked at the girl with a glance that was followed by a thousand sighs, and he fell passionately and deeply in love with her. 'Father,' he said, 'buy this girl for me.' His father called the auctioneer over and then asked the girl her name. 'My name is Yasmin,' she told him, and he said to his son: 'If you admire her, put in a higher bid.' 'What price have you been offered?' Habzalam asked the auctioneer. 'A thousand dinars,' the man told him. 'I will bid a thousand and one,' Habzalam said. The auctioneer approached 'Ala' al-Din, who went up to two thousand dinars. Every time Habzalam raised the bidding by a dinar, 'Ala' al-Din raised it by a thousand. This angered Habzalam and he asked the auctioneer who was bidding against him for the girl. The auctioneer told him: 'The vizier Ja'far wants to buy her for 'Ala' al-Din Abu'l-Shamat.'

When 'Ala' al-Din had raised the price to ten thousand dinars, the girl's owner accepted and took the money. 'Ala' al-Din then took Yasmin and said to her: 'I free you for the sake of Almighty God.' He then wrote a marriage contract for her and set off for his house. The auctioneer was going back with his commission when Habzalam called to him: 'Where is the girl?' The man told him: ''Ala' al-Din bought her for ten thousand dinars, freed her and drew up a marriage contract for her.' This saddened Habzalam, who became more and more distressed until, when he got back home, he was sick with love for Yasmin. He threw himself down on his bed and stopped eating as his passionate love grew ever more extreme. When his mother saw him in this state, she said: 'God bring you health, my son, what has caused your sickness?' He replied: 'Buy Yasmin for me, mother.' She promised him: 'When the flower seller passes, I will buy you a basket of jasmine.'

'I don't want scented jasmine,' he told her. 'Yasmin is the name of a slave girl whom my father didn't buy for me.' She asked her husband why that was, and he explained: 'What is suitable for the master is not suitable for the servant. I couldn't get her because the man who bought her was the hexarch, 'Ala' al-Din.'

His son's illness grew worse; he could neither sleep nor eat and his mother tied mourning bands round her forehead. While she was sitting at home grieving for him, in came an old woman, the mother of Ahmad Qamaqim, the master thief, a man who could bore through inner walls, climb up the outsides of buildings and steal kohl from eyes. These were the evil habits that he had followed at the start of his career and although later he had been made chief of police, he was found stealing money, seized by the *wali* and taken before the caliph, who ordered him to be taken to the place of execution and put to death. He asked the vizier to protect him and the vizier, whose intercession the caliph never rejected, pleaded for him. 'How can you intercede for a plague who brings harm on the people?' the caliph asked. 'Put him in prison, Commander of the

Faithful,' replied the vizier. 'It was a wise man who built the first prison, as this is a tomb for the living and brings pleasure to their enemies.' So the caliph ordered that Ahmad should be chained up and it was to be written on his fetters that they should stay in place until he died, only to be removed when his corpse was laid out on a slab for washing. This was done and he was imprisoned.

His mother used to go again and again to the house of the *wali* Khalid, and to visit her son in his dungeon. 'Didn't I tell you to repent of evil-doing?' she would say, and he would tell her that this was God's decree and ask her, when she visited the *wali*'s wife, to get her to intercede for him with her husband. Now, on finding the *wali*'s wife wearing mourning bands, Ahmad's mother asked her the reason. 'It is because of the loss of my son, Habzalam Bazaza,' she replied. 'May he recover,' the old woman said, going on to ask what was wrong with him. The *wali*'s wife told her the story and she asked: 'What would you say about someone who could play a trick that would save your son?' 'What do you mean to do?' said the other, and the old woman told her: 'I have a son, Ahmad Qamaqim, the master thief, who is chained up in prison with a note on his fetters to say that they are to stay on him until he dies. Get up, put on your most splendid clothes and your finest ornaments. Then go to meet your husband, smiling cheerfully, and when he tries to get from you what men do try to get from women, hold yourself back and don't allow him to have you. Tell him: "By God, it is remarkable that when a man wants something from his wife he goes on pestering her until he gets it, but when she wants something from him, he won't give it to her." He will ask you what it is that you want, but refuse to tell him until he has sworn to do it. If he takes an oath by his head or by God, tell him to swear to divorce you if he refuses and don't allow him to have you unless he does. When he has done it, then tell him: "You have in your prison an officer called Ahmad Qamaqim, with a poor mother who has importuned me to approach you, asking me to get you to intercede for him with the caliph so that he may repent and you may be rewarded by God."'

The *wali*'s wife agreed and he then approached her . . .

Night 264

Morning now dawned and Shahrazad broke off from what she had been allowed to say. Then, when it was the two hundred and sixty-fourth night, SHE CONTINUED:

I have heard, O fortunate king, that when he approached her, she said what she had been told to say to him, and after he had sworn the oath of divorce, she allowed him to have her and he spent the night with her. In the morning, after he had performed the ablution and the dawn prayer, he went to the prison and said: 'Ahmad Qamaqim, you thief, do you repent of your way of life?' 'I offer my repentance to God,' Ahmad replied, 'and in penitence I ask His pardon with heart and tongue.' The emir then released him and brought him, still in chains, to the *diwan*. After approaching the caliph, he kissed the ground before him, and, when the caliph asked what he wanted, he brought Ahmad up to him in his chains. 'Are you still alive, Qamaqim?' asked the caliph. 'The life of the unfortunate goes slowly, Commander of the Faithful,' the man replied. 'Why have you brought him here?' the caliph asked the emir. 'He has a poor, lonely mother,' the emir replied, 'who has no one but him. She has approached me, your servant, asking me to intercede with you to release him from his chains and give him back his old post as chief of the watch, as he repents of his evil ways.' 'Have you done this?' the caliph asked him, and when Ahmad said that he had offered repentance to God, the caliph ordered a smith to be fetched. The chains were struck off on the slab used for washing corpses; Ahmad was reappointed as chief of the watch and told by the caliph to behave well and uprightly. He kissed the caliph's hands and left dressed in his robe of office, with a proclamation being made of his appointment.

After he had held his post for some time, his mother went to the *wali*'s wife, who said to her: 'Praise be to God, Who has brought your son safe and sound out of prison. Why don't you tell him to produce some scheme for bringing the slave girl, Yasmin, to my son Habzalam Bazaza?' 'I'll speak to him,' the old woman replied and she then left the *wali*'s wife and went to her son, whom she found drunk. 'My son,' she told him, 'it was only thanks to the *wali*'s wife that you got out of prison. She wants you to find some way to kill 'Ala' al-Din Abu'l-Shamat and to fetch Yasmin, the slave girl, for her son Habzalam Bazaza.' 'This is the easiest possible thing,' said Ahmad, 'and I shall certainly find some way of doing it tonight.'

It happened to be the first night of the new month and the Commander of the Faithful was in the habit of spending it with the Lady Zubaida in order to free a slave girl or a mamluk or something of the kind. It was also his custom to take off his royal robe, together with his rosary, his dagger and his royal signet ring, all of which he would leave on his throne in his audience chamber. He also had a gold lamp to which three jewels were attached by a gold chain and by which he set great store. He left the robe, the lamp and the rest of his things in the charge of the eunuchs and then entered the Lady Zubaida's apartments. Ahmad Qamaqim, the master thief, waited until midnight, when, at the rising of Canopus, everyone was asleep, shrouded in the Creator's covering night. It was then that, with a sword in his right hand and a grapnel in his left, he came to the caliph's audience chamber. He got ready a rope ladder and threw his grapnel over the chamber. It caught there and, using his ladder, he climbed on to the roof, where he lifted the trapdoor and let himself down. Finding the eunuchs asleep, he drugged them and then took the caliph's robe along with the rosary, the dagger, his kerchief, the signet ring and the jewelled lamp. From the place from which he had climbed up he went down to the house of 'Ala' al-Din Abu'l-Shamat.

It happened that that night 'Ala' al-Din was busy celebrating his marriage with Yasmin, and after he had lain with her, she conceived. Ahmad climbed down into his room, from the lower part of which he removed a marble slab. Beneath this he dug a hole and into the hole he put some of the caliph's belongings, keeping the rest himself. He put the slab back in its place, fixing it with plaster, and left by the way that he had come, saying to himself: 'I can now put the lamp down in front of me and sit and get drunk by its light.' He then went off to his own house.

Next morning the caliph went to his audience chamber, where he found his eunuchs drugged. He roused them but when he put his hand down he could not find his robe or his ring, his rosary, his dagger, his kerchief or his lamp. He was furiously angry and, after putting on his red robe of rage, he took his seat in the *diwan*. The vizier came forward, kissed the ground before him and said: 'May God protect the Commander of the Faithful from evil.' 'Evil has overflowed, vizier,' said the caliph and, when the vizier asked what had happened, he told him the whole story.

At that point the *wali* arrived, with Ahmad Qamaqim in his train, to find the caliph in a rage. The caliph looked at him and asked him how things were in Baghdad. 'Peaceful and secure,' he replied. 'You're lying,' said the caliph, and when the *wali* asked him why he had said that, the caliph told him what had happened and added: 'I require you to produce all that was stolen.' The *wali* replied: 'It is vinegar that produces vinegar worms, and it is there that they are found. No stranger could ever get into this place.' 'If you fail to produce these things, I shall kill you,' said the caliph. 'Before you kill me, kill Ahmad Qamaqim,' said the *wali*, 'as it is the chief of the watch who should know robbers and traitors.' Ahmad Qamaqim then interceded with the caliph for the *wali* and said: 'I guarantee to bring you the thief and I shall continue to track him until I find out who he is. But give me two *qadis* and two notaries, for the man who did this has no fear of you or of the *wali* or of anyone else.' 'You can have what you want,' said the caliph, 'but start your search in my palace, and then in those of the vizier and of the hexarch.' 'That's right, Commander of the Faithful. It may be that whoever did this was brought up in the royal palace or in the palace of one of your intimates.' 'By my head,' swore the caliph, 'I shall kill whoever is proved to have done this, even if it is my own son.' So Ahmad Qamaqim got what he wanted, together with written authorization to break into houses and search them.

Night 265

Morning now dawned and Shahrazad broke off from what she had been allowed to say. Then, when it was the two hundred and sixty-fifth night, SHE CONTINUED:

I have heard, O fortunate king, that Ahmad Qamaqim got what he wanted, together with written authorization to break into houses and search them. He went off carrying in his hand a rod made up in equal parts of bronze, copper, iron and steel. He searched the caliph's palace and that of Ja'far, the vizier; he went round the houses of the chamberlains and the deputies, and then he came by the house of 'Ala' al-Din Abu'l-Shamat. When 'Ala' al-Din heard the noise in front of his house he got up and went down, leaving his wife Yasmin. On opening the door he found the *wali* with a disorderly mob, and when he asked what had happened, the *wali*, Khalid, told him the whole story. 'Come in and search my house,' he said. 'Forgive me, sir,' said Khalid. 'You are a trustworthy man and God forbid that such a one should turn traitor.' 'Ala' al-Din insisted that his house be searched and so Khalid went in with the *qadis* and the notaries. Ahmad Qamaqim then went to the lower part of the room and came to the marble slab under which he had buried the goods. He then struck it so violently with his rod that it broke and there, beneath it, was something that gleamed. 'In God's Name,' he said. 'God's will is done and, thanks to the blessing of our coming, we have discovered a treasure. I shall go down and investigate what is there.' The *qadi* and the notaries inspected the place and after finding everything there, they drew up a document to say that the goods had been found in the house of 'Ala' al-Din, and affixed their seals to it. They ordered 'Ala' al-Din to be arrested; they took his turban from his head and drew up an inventory of all his wealth and goods.

Ahmad Qamaqim, the master thief, then seized the slave girl Yasmin, who was carrying 'Ala' al-Din's child, and gave her to his mother, telling her to hand her over to the *wali*'s wife, Khatun. His mother took the girl and brought her to Khatun. When Habzalam Bazaza saw her, he was restored to health and, getting up immediately, he approached her with delight, but she drew a dagger from her belt and said: 'Get away from me or else I shall kill you and then kill myself.' 'You whore,' said his mother, Khatun, 'let my son have his way with you.' 'Bitch,' she replied, 'what school of law permits a woman to marry two husbands and what can bring dogs into the dens of lions?' Habzalam Bazaza's passion increased; he fell ill with lovesickness and, giving up food, he took to his bed. 'Whore,' said Khatun, 'how is it that you make me grieve for my son? I am going to have to punish you, while as for 'Ala' al-Din, he will certainly be hanged.' 'Then I shall die of love for him,' replied Yasmin.

Khatun got up and, after stripping Yasmin of her jewels and her silken clothes, she made her wear drawers of coarse cloth and a hair shirt, after which she took her to the kitchen and made her act as a serving girl. 'This is your reward,' she told her. 'You will split wood, peel onions and light the fire under the cooking pots.' 'I am willing to put up with any punishment,' said Yasmin, 'and to perform any service, but I am not willing to see your son.' God filled the hearts of the maids with sympathy for her and they started to do her kitchen tasks for her.

So much, then, for Yasmin, but as for 'Ala' al-Din Abu'l-Shamat, he was taken to the *diwan*, along with the caliph's possessions. The caliph was sitting on his throne when 'Ala' al-Din was brought in with them, and when the caliph asked where they had been found he was told: 'In the middle of the house of 'Ala' al-Din Abu'l-Shamat.' The caliph, filled with rage, took his treasures and, on failing to see the lamp among them, he asked 'Ala' al-Din where it was. 'I didn't steal; I know nothing; I haven't seen the lamp and I have no knowledge of it.' 'Traitor!' exclaimed the caliph. 'How is it that I took you as a companion, but you shunned me and, while I trusted you, you betrayed me?' The caliph then ordered 'Ala' al-Din to be hanged, and the *wali* left with a herald, who proclaimed: 'This is the punishment, and the least of the punishments, of those who betray the caliphs who follow the true faith.' Crowds collected around the gallows.

So much, then, for 'Ala' al-Din, but as for Ahmad al-Danaf, his adoptive father, he was in a garden with his followers and while they were sitting there, pleasantly enjoying themselves, one of the water carriers from the caliph's court came in. He kissed Ahmad's hand and, addressing him as 'captain', said: 'You are happily sitting here with the water flowing beneath your feet, knowing nothing of what has happened.' 'What is the news?' asked Ahmad. 'Your son, 'Ala' al-Din, whom you adopted according to God's covenant, has been brought to the gallows,' said the man. Ahmad asked Hasan Shuman whether he had any scheme to propose and he said: ''Ala' al-Din is innocent in this affair and some enemy has played a trick on him.' 'What do you advise me to do?' asked Ahmad. 'God willing, we shall save him,' said Hasan.

Hasan then went to the prison and said to the gaoler: 'Give me someone who deserves to die.' The man provided him with someone who closely resembled 'Ala' al-Din. His head was covered and he was taken out between Ahmad al-Danaf and 'Ali al-Zaibaq, the Egyptian. 'Ala' al-Din had been brought to the gallows when Ahmad al-Danaf came up and put his foot on that of the hangman. 'Give me room to do my job,' said the man. 'Damn you,' said Ahmad. 'Take this fellow and hang him instead of 'Ala' al-Din, who has been wrongly condemned. We are ransoming Isma'il with the ram.'* The hangman took the substitute and hanged him in place of 'Ala' al-Din, who was taken by Ahmad al-Danaf and 'Ali al-Zaibaq to Ahmad's house.

When he was brought in, he said: 'Master, may God reward you well,' and Ahmad then asked him: 'What did you do?'

---

* A reference to the story of Abraham, Genesis 22.

Night 266

Morning now dawned and Shahrazad broke off from what she had been allowed to say. Then, when it was the two hundred and sixty-sixth night, SHE CONTINUED:

I have heard, O fortunate king, that Ahmad asked him: 'What did you do? May God have mercy on the man who said: "Even if you are a traitor, do not betray one who has trusted you." The caliph gave you a position at his court and called you faithful and trusty, so how could you act like this towards him and take his things?' 'Master,' replied 'Ala' al-Din, 'I swear by the greatest Name of God that this wasn't my doing. I am not at fault here and I don't know who did it.' 'Clearly an enemy of yours must have done it, but the doer of any deed will be paid back for it. As for you, you can't stay in Baghdad, my son, for kings don't pass matters over and those they pursue must for long face hardships.' 'Where should I go, master?' asked 'Ala' al-Din, and Ahmad replied: 'I shall take you to Alexandria, a blessed place, whose threshold is green and where life is easy.' 'To hear is to obey,' said 'Ala' al-Din.

Ahmad al-Danaf told Hasan Shuman: 'If the caliph asks about me, take care to say that I have gone off on a tour of the lands.' He then took 'Ala' al-Din and brought him out of Baghdad and the two of them walked on until they reached the vineyards and orchards. Here they found two Jews, employed by the caliph as tax collectors, mounted on a pair of mules. 'Give me the protection money,' Ahmad demanded, and when they asked why, he told them that this valley was in his charge. Each of them gave him a hundred dinars and after that he killed them and took their mules, riding on one himself with 'Ala' al-Din on the other. They travelled to the city of Ayas, where they stabled the mules in a *khan* and spent the night there. The next morning, 'Ala' al-Din sold his mule and entrusted Ahmad al-Danaf's to the gatekeeper, after which the two of them embarked on a ship in the port of Ayas and sailed to Alexandria.

When they had disembarked, they walked into the market and here they came across an auctioneer who was advertising the sale of a shop, together with living quarters, for a price of nine hundred and fifty dinars. 'Ala' al-Din offered a thousand, a price accepted by the vendor as the shop was treasury property, and he then took the keys and opened up both the shop itself and the living quarters. He found them furnished with rugs and cushions, and stored there he discovered sails, spars, ropes and chests, together with bags filled with beads, shells, stirrups, axes, maces, knives, scissors and other such things, as the previous owner had been a second-hand dealer. 'Ala' al-Din sat there in the shop and Ahmad al-Danaf said to him: 'My son, the shop, the room and their contents are yours, so stay here, buy and sell and don't repine, for Almighty God has given His blessing to trade.' Ahmad al-Danaf stayed with 'Ala' al-Din for three days and on the fourth he took his leave, saying: 'Stay here until I come back from my journey with news that the caliph has pardoned you, and I have found out who played this trick on you.'

Ahmad then set out and, on arriving at Ayas, he took the mule from the *khan* and went on to Baghdad. Here he met Hasan Shuman and his followers, and when he asked Hasan whether the caliph had enquired about him, Hasan told him: 'No, he didn't think of you.' So he remained in the caliph's service, sniffing out news. One day he found the caliph asking the vizier Ja'far about 'Ala' al-Din. Ja'far replied: 'You had him hanged by way of punishment for what he did to you, and this fate was his reward.' 'Vizier,' said the caliph, 'I want to go down and look at him hanging there.' 'As you wish, Commander of the Faithful,' said Ja'far, and so the two of them went down to the gallows. The caliph looked up and saw that the corpse was not that of 'Ala' al-Din Abu'l-Shamat, the trusty and faithful. When he pointed this out, the vizier asked: 'How can you tell that it is not him?' ''Ala' al-Din was a small man,' said the caliph, 'and this one is tall.' 'A hanged man is stretched,' Ja'far pointed out, but the caliph said: ''Ala' al-Din was fair while this man's face is black.' 'Don't you know, Commander of the Faithful,' said Ja'far, 'that corpses turn black?' On the caliph's orders the corpse was then taken down from the gallows and when this had been done, they found written on his heels the names of Abu Bakr and 'Umar. The caliph pointed out to Ja'far that 'Ala' al-Din had been a Sunni while this man must have been a *rafidi*.* 'Praise be to God, Who knows all secrets,' said Ja'far. 'As for us, we don't know whether this is 'Ala' al-Din or someone else.' On the caliph's orders the body was buried, and 'Ala' al-Din was then completely forgotten.

So much for him, but as for Habzalam Bazaza, the *wali*'s son, his

---

* As a *rafidi*, a kind of Shi'ite heretic, the man whose corpse is discovered on the gallows would have had the names of the first two caliphs Abu Bakr and 'Umar tattooed on his heels so that he could dishonour them by treading on their names. No Sunni would have done such a thing.

infatuation continued until he died and was buried. Yasmin, for her part, reached the term of her pregnancy, went into labour and gave birth to a baby boy like a full moon. 'What are you going to call him?' asked the maids. 'Were his father still alive,' she said, 'he would have named him, but I shall call him Aslan.' She suckled him for the next two years and then weaned him, after which he began to crawl and to walk. One day when, as it happened, his mother was busy with her duties in the kitchen, he walked off, and seeing the stairs leading to the sitting room, he climbed up them. The emir Khalid, the *wali*, was sitting there. He took the child, sat him on his lap and gave praise to God for having created and fashioned him. Then, looking at his face, he saw that he was very like 'Ala' al-Din Abu'l-Shamat.

The boy's mother, Yasmin, looked for him and, failing to find him, went up to the sitting room, where she saw the emir Khalid sitting there with the boy playing on his lap, God having filled his heart with love for him. The boy turned, and seeing his mother, would have thrown himself on her, but the emir held him back in his arms and said to her: 'Come here, girl.' When she came, he said: 'Whose child is this?' 'He is my son and the fruit of my heart,' she answered. 'And who is his father?' he asked. 'His father was 'Ala' al-Din Abu'l-Shamat,' she said, 'and now he has become your son.' ''Ala' al-Din was a traitor,' said Khalid. 'God preserve him from the charge of treason,' she said. '"The Trusty" could never be a traitor,' Khalid told her: 'When the child grows up and asks you who his father was, tell him: "You are the son of the emir Khalid, the *wali*, the chief of police."' 'To hear is to obey,' she replied.

The emir had Aslan circumcised and gave him the best possible upbringing. He provided him with a *faqih*, who was also a calligrapher and who taught him to read and write. He read through the Quran a first and then a second time, and memorized the whole of it, and he grew up addressing the emir as 'my father'. The emir used to take him to the training ground where he collected horsemen and taught him the arts of war and how to thrust and strike until he became a brave and accomplished horseman, and when he was fourteen years old he was appointed to the rank of emir.

As it happened, one day Aslan fell in with Ahmad Qamaqim, the master thief, and they became companions. Aslan followed Ahmad to a drinking den, where Ahmad produced the jewelled lamp that he had stolen from the caliph's treasures, and he drank by its light until he became drunk. Aslan then asked him to give him the lamp, but he said:

'I can't give it to you.' 'Why not?' asked Aslan and Ahmad told him: 'Lives have been lost because of it.' 'Whose life was that?' asked Aslan and Ahmad told him: 'A man named 'Ala' al-Din Abu'l-Shamat came here and was appointed hexarch. It was he who died because of this lamp.' Aslan asked to be told the story and why it was that 'Ala' al-Din had died. Ahmad said: 'You had a brother named Habzalam Bazaza. When he was sixteen years old he was ready to marry and his father wanted to buy him a slave girl.' He then went over the story from beginning to end, telling Aslan of Habzalam Bazaza's illness and 'Ala' al-Din's unjust fate. 'It may be,' said Aslan to himself, 'that this slave girl was my mother Yasmin and that my father was 'Ala' al-Din Abu'l-Shamat.'

He left Ahmad sorrowfully and came across Ahmad al-Danaf, who, catching sight of him, exclaimed: 'Glory be to God, Who has no match!' 'What are you marvelling at, master?' Hasan Shuman asked him. 'At the appearance of this boy, Aslan,' he replied, 'because he very closely resembles 'Ala' al-Din Abu'l-Shamat.' He then called out to Aslan, and when Aslan answered, Ahmad asked him the name of his mother. 'She is called Yasmin,' Aslan told him. 'Joy and happiness be yours,' said Ahmad, 'for your father is 'Ala' al-Din Abu'l-Shamat. Go to your mother and ask her about your father.' Aslan did this and his mother told him: 'The emir Khalid is your father.' He contradicted her and said: ''Ala' al-Din Abu'l-Shamat is my father,' at which his mother wept and asked him: 'Who told you that?' When he said that it was Ahmad al-Danaf, she told him everything that had happened. 'My son,' she went on, 'the truth has come out and falsehood has disappeared. Know that your father was indeed 'Ala' al-Din Abu'l-Shamat, but that it was the emir Khalid who brought you up and who took you as his son. If you meet Ahmad al-Danaf say to him: "Master, I ask you in God's Name to take vengeance for me on the killer of my father, 'Ala' al-Din."'

Aslan left her and went off . . .

Night 267

Morning now dawned and Shahrazad broke off from what she had been allowed to say. Then, when it was the two hundred and sixty-seventh night, SHE CONTINUED:

I have heard, O fortunate king, that Aslan left her and went off, and on coming to Ahmad al-Danaf, he kissed his hand. 'What is it, Aslan?' Ahmad asked. 'I now know for certain that 'Ala' al-Din Abu'l-Shamat was my father and I want you to avenge me on his killer.' When Ahmad asked who this was, Aslan told him that it was Ahmad Qamaqim, the master thief. 'Who told you that?' Ahmad asked, and Aslan replied: 'I saw in his possession the jewelled lamp that went missing from the caliph's treasures. When I asked him to give it to me, he refused, telling me that lives had been lost because of it. He then said that it was he who had gone down, stolen the things and put them in my father's house.' Ahmad told him: 'When you see the *wali*, Khalid, putting on his armour, ask him to give you armour as well, and when you go out with him, perform some act of courage in the presence of the Commander of the Faithful, who will then allow you to wish for what you want. Say to him: "I wish that you would avenge my father on his killer." He will then say: "Your father, the emir Khalid, the *wali*, is still alive," and you must then say: "My father was 'Ala' al-Din Abu'l-Shamat, and I am only indebted to the emir Khalid for having nurtured me." Then tell him all that happened between you and Ahmad Qamaqim, the master thief, and say: "Give orders that he be searched, Commander of the Faithful, and I will produce the lamp from his pocket."' 'To hear is to obey,' said Aslan.

He then went off and found the emir Khalid getting ready to go up to the caliph's court. 'I would like you to dress me in armour like yours,' he said, 'and to take me to court with you.' Khalid agreed to this, and the caliph left the city with his troops and, after setting up pavilions and tents, they drew up in ranks and started exercising with balls and polo mallets. One rider would strike the ball with his stick and another would hit it back to him. It happened that among the soldiers there was a spy who had been induced to try to kill the caliph. This man got the ball and hit it with his stick straight at the caliph's face. Aslan, however, intercepted it in front of the caliph and hit it back at the spy so that it struck him between the shoulders and he fell to the ground. 'God bless you, Aslan!' exclaimed the caliph, and after they had all dismounted and taken their seats, he ordered that the man who had struck the ball be brought to him. When he came, the caliph asked him: 'Who induced you to do this and are you friend or foe?' 'I am a foe,' replied the man, 'and I was intending to kill you.' 'Why?' the caliph asked. 'Are you not a Muslim?' 'No,' said the man. 'I am a *rafidi*,' and at that the caliph ordered him to be killed.

The caliph then told Aslan to make a wish and Aslan said: 'I wish that you would take vengeance for my father on his killer.' 'But your father is alive and standing on his feet,' objected the caliph. 'Who is my father?' asked Aslan. 'The emir Khalid, the *wali*,' said the caliph. 'Commander of the Faithful,' said Aslan, 'the emir is not my father except in so far as he brought me up. My real father is 'Ala' al-Din Abu'l-Shamat.' 'Then your father was a traitor,' the caliph said. 'God forbid that "the Trusty" should be a traitor, Commander of the Faithful,' said Aslan. 'How did he betray you?' 'He stole my robe and all that went with it,' said the caliph. 'God forbid that my father should have been a traitor,' repeated Aslan and he went on to ask: 'When you lost your robe and it was then restored to you, did you find that the lamp came back as well?' 'We never discovered it,' said the caliph, at which Aslan told him: 'I saw it in the possession of Ahmad Qamaqim, and when I asked him for it he did not give it to me, saying that lives had been lost because of it. He then told me of the illness of Habzalam Bazaza, the son of the emir Khalid, of his love for Yasmin, the slave girl, and of how he himself had been released from his fetters, adding that it was he who had stolen the robe and the lamp. So take revenge for my father on his killer, Commander of the Faithful.'

On the caliph's orders Ahmad Qamaqim was seized. The caliph asked: 'Where is Ahmad al-Danaf, the captain?' and when Ahmad presented himself, the caliph told him to search Qamaqim. He did so and, putting his hand in Qamaqim's pocket, he drew out the jewelled lamp. 'Come here, traitor,' ordered the caliph. 'Where did you get this lamp?' 'I bought it, Commander of the Faithful,' Qamaqim replied. 'Where did you buy it and who would have been able to sell you such a thing?' He was then beaten until he confessed that it was he who stole the robe and the lamp. 'Why did you do this, traitor, bringing about the destruction of 'Ala' al-Din Abu'l-Shamat, "the Trusty"?' the caliph asked, and he then ordered his arrest and that of the *wali*. The *wali* complained: 'I am being treated unjustly. It was you who ordered me to hang 'Ala' al-Din. I didn't know anything about this trick and it was the old woman together with Ahmad Qamaqim and my wife who planned it without my knowledge. I appeal to you, Aslan, for protection.' Aslan interceded for him with the caliph, who then asked the *wali* what he had done with Aslan's mother. 'She is still with me,' the *wali* told him, and the caliph said: 'I command you to order your wife to dress Yasmin in her robes, returning her jewellery and restoring her to her former status. Then remove the seal from 'Ala' al-Din's house and give his son his property and his goods.' 'To hear is to obey,' said the *wali* and he then went off and gave orders to his wife, who dressed Yasmin in her robes, while he himself removed the seal from 'Ala' al-Din's house and gave the keys to Aslan.

After this the caliph told Aslan to make a wish. 'My wish is for you to allow me to meet my father,' Aslan said. The caliph shed tears and said: 'It is most likely that your father was the man who was hanged and so is dead, but I swear by the lives of my ancestors that if anyone brings me the good news that he is still alive, I shall give him all he asks for.' At that Ahmad al-Danaf came forward and said: 'Grant me indemnity, Commander of the Faithful.' When the caliph had promised him this, he said: 'I give you the good news that 'Ala' al-Din Abu'l-Shamat, the trusty and faithful, is alive and well.' 'What are you saying?' exclaimed the caliph. 'I swear by your head that what I say is true,' said Ahmad. 'I saved him by providing a man, who deserved to be killed, in his place, and I took him to Alexandria, where I opened a second-hand shop for him.' 'You must bring him to me,' said the caliph.

Night 268

Morning now dawned and Shahrazad broke off from what she had been allowed to say. Then, when it was the two hundred and sixty-eighth night, SHE CONTINUED:

I have heard, O fortunate king, that when the caliph told Ahmad al-Danaf to fetch 'Ala' al-Din, he said: 'To hear is to obey,' and after the caliph had ordered him to be given ten thousand dinars, he set off for Alexandria.

So much for Aslan, but as for his father, 'Ala' al-Din Abu'l-Shamat, he had sold all but a small amount of the contents of his shop. There remained one bag, and when he shook it, out fell a jewel big enough to fill the palm of the hand, fastened to a golden chain. It had five facets and was inscribed with writing like ants' trails with names and talismans. 'Ala' al-Din rubbed the facets but without any response, and so he told himself that it was probably a piece of onyx. He hung it up in his shop, and a foreign consul who happened to be passing by on the road looked up and saw it there. He sat down in the shop and asked 'Ala' al-Din if it was for sale. 'Everything that I have is for sale,' said 'Ala' al-Din and the man then asked: 'Will you sell it to me for eighty thousand dinars?'

'Come, come,' said 'Ala' al-Din. 'For a hundred thousand?' asked the man. 'Ala' al-Din agreed to this and said: 'Hand me over the cash.' 'I can't carry this with me,' the man said, 'as there are robbers and rogues in Alexandria, but if you come with me to my ship, I shall hand over the price and give you a bale of Angora wool, together with another of satin, one of velvet and one of broadcloth.'

'Ala' al-Din got up and closed up his shop, handing over the jewel to his customer and giving the keys to his neighbour, telling him: 'Keep these in trust for me until I go to the ship with this consul and come back with the money for the jewel. If I'm slow in returning and Captain Ahmad al-Danaf, the man who settled me in here, arrives, hand over the keys to him and tell him what has happened.' He then set off for the ship together with the consul, and when he came on board this man got him a chair and seated him on it. He told his men to fetch the money, which he then paid to Ahmad, together with the five bales he had promised him. 'Do me the honour of taking a bite of food or a drink of water,' he said. 'If you have some water,' answered Ahmad, 'then give me a drink.' The man ordered sherbet to be fetched, but he drugged it with *banj*, and when 'Ala' al-Din drank it, he fell over backwards. The sailors stowed the chairs, put away the poles and unfurled the sails, after which favourable winds took them out to sea.

The captain now ordered 'Ala' al-Din to be brought up from the cabin, and when this was done they gave him a sniff of the antidote to *banj*. He opened his eyes and said: 'Where am I?' 'You are with me,' replied the captain, 'and I'm holding you as a prisoner. Had you gone on saying: "Come, come," I would have offered you more.' 'What is your trade?' asked Ahmad. 'I am a sea captain,' the man replied, 'and I want to bring you to the darling of my heart.'

While the two of them were talking a ship came in sight carrying forty Muslim merchants. The captain laid his ship against theirs and fastened grapnels to it, after which he and his men boarded it, plundered it and took it as a prize to Genoa. Taking 'Ala' al-Din with him, he went to the sea gate of a palace where a girl, her face covered by a mouth-veil, came down to him and said: 'Have you brought the jewel and its owner?' 'I have both of them here,' replied the captain. 'Give me the jewel,' she said, and when he had done so he went off to the harbour and fired the ship's guns to announce his safe return.

When the king of the city learned of his arrival he came out to meet him and asked what kind of a voyage he had had. 'A very good one,'

replied the captain. 'I captured a ship with forty Muslim merchants.'
'Land them on the dockside,' said the king, and the captain had them
brought out in chains, with 'Ala' al-Din among them. The king and the
captain rode while the prisoners were made to walk in front of them
until they came to the *diwan*. There the Genoese took their seats and
when the first of the prisoners was brought forward the king asked:
'Where do you come from, Muslim?' 'From Alexandria,' the man
answered. 'Executioner, kill him,' ordered the king. The executioner
struck off his head and the same happened to the second, the third and
then the others, until all forty were dead. 'Ala' al-Din, who was at the
end of the line, shared their distress and said to himself: 'May God have
mercy on you, 'Ala' al-Din. Your life is ended.' 'And you,' asked the
king, 'where are you from?' 'Alexandria,' said 'Ala' al-Din, and the king
said: 'Executioner, kill him.' The executioner, holding the sword, had
raised his arm and was about to strike at 'Ala' al-Din's neck when a
venerable-looking old woman came before the king, who rose respect-
fully. 'Didn't I tell you, O king, that when the captain brought in prisoners, you were to remember to assign one or two of them to serve in
the monastery church?' 'Mother,' said the king, 'I wish you had come
earlier, but you can take the one who is left.' She then turned to 'Ala'
al-Din and asked: 'Will you serve in the church or shall I let the king kill
you?' 'I will serve in the church,' he told her.

Taking 'Ala' al-Din, she left the *diwan* and set off for the church. 'Ala'
al-Din asked her what his duties would be and she said: 'After getting
up in the morning you have to take five mules, drive them to the forest,
cut dry wood, split it and bring it to the monastery kitchen. After that,
take up the carpets and clean and wipe the tiles and the marble before
putting the carpets back in their place. Next, take half an *ardabb*'s
measure of wheat, sieve it, grind it, knead it and make it into biscuits
for the monastery. Then take a *waiba*'s measure of lentils, sieve them,
crush them and cook them. You must then fill up the four fountains with
water, bringing it in barrels, and fill three hundred and sixty wooden
bowls with the biscuits, which you have broken up, and the lentils, after
which you are to carry a bowl to each of the monks and the patriarchs.'
'Take me back to the king,' exclaimed 'Ala' al-Din, 'and let him kill me,
as I'd find that easier than this service!' 'If you serve and perform your
duties properly,' said the old woman, 'you will escape death, but if not,
I shall let the king execute you.' So 'Ala' al-Din sat there full of care.

In the church there were ten blind cripples. One of these told 'Ala' al-Din to bring him a pot, and when he did the man relieved himself into it and told 'Ala' al-Din to throw away the excrement, which he did. 'May the Messiah bless you, servant of the church,' the man said. At that point the old woman came in and asked him why he had not finished his duties in the church. 'How many hands have I got with which to do all this?' he exclaimed. 'Madman,' she said, 'it was only as a servant that I brought you here.' Then she told him: 'Take this rod, my son' – it was of brass, topped with a cross – 'and go out into the street. When you come across the *wali* of the city, say to him: "I summon you to the service of the church for the sake of our Lord, the Messiah." He will not disobey you and you can let him take the wheat, sieve it, grind it, knead it and make it into biscuits. If anyone does disobey you, beat him and have no fear of anyone.' 'To hear is to obey,' said 'Ala' al-Din and, acting on her instructions, he continued to press both high and low into service for seventeen years.

While he was sitting in the church the old woman came in and told him to leave. 'Where am I to go?' he asked. 'Pass the night in a wine shop or with one of your companions,' she told him, and when he asked why she was turning him out she said: 'Husn Maryam, the daughter of Yuhanna, the king of Genoa, wants to make a pilgrimage to this church and no one must be sitting here when she comes.' 'Ala' al-Din obediently got up and pretended to the old woman that he was leaving the church, but he said to himself: 'Do you suppose that this princess is like our women or more beautiful? I'm not going to leave until I have had a look at her.' He then hid in a little room which had a window opening on to the church. While he was gazing in that direction, in came the princess and he looked at her with a glance that was followed by a thousand sighs, as he found her to be like a full moon breaking through the clouds.

The princess was accompanied by a girl . . .

Night 269

Morning now dawned and Shahrazad broke off from what she had been allowed to say. Then, when it was the two hundred and sixty-ninth night, SHE CONTINUED:

I have heard, O fortunate king, that when 'Ala' al-Din looked at the princess, he saw that she was accompanied by a girl, to whom she was saying: 'You are good company, Zubaida.' 'Ala' al-Din looked closely at the girl and saw that she was his former wife, Zubaida, the lute player, who was supposedly dead. 'Come, play me a tune on your lute,' the princess told her. 'Not until you do what I want and keep the promise you made me,' replied Zubaida. 'What promise was that?' asked the princess. 'You promised to reunite me with my husband, 'Ala' al-Din Abu'l-Shamat, the trusty and faithful,' said Zubaida. 'You have cause for happiness,' the princess told her, 'so play a tune to celebrate your reunion with your husband.' 'Where is he?' asked Zubaida. 'In that little room, listening to us,' replied the princess, and so Zubaida played a melody that would cause the solid rocks to dance. When 'Ala' al-Din heard it, he could not control his emotions; he came out of the room and rushed towards the two women, throwing his arms around his wife, Zubaida. She recognized him, and after the two of them had embraced they fell fainting on to the ground. The princess sprinkled them with rosewater and brought them back to consciousness. 'God has reunited you,' she said. 'Through your kindness, my lady,' said 'Ala' al-Din.

'Ala' al-Din then turned to Zubaida, his wife, and said: 'You died and were buried, Zubaida, so how is it that you came back to life and arrived here?' 'Master,' she told him, 'I didn't die; rather, I was kidnapped by a powerful *jinni* who flew off with me and brought me here. What you buried was a *jinniya* who had taken my shape and pretended to be dead. When you had buried her, she broke out of the tomb and went off to serve her mistress, Husn Maryam, the king's daughter. As for me, when I opened my eyes after my shock, it was to find myself with this lady, who is the Princess Husn Maryam. I asked her why she had had me brought here and she told me that she was destined to marry my husband, 'Ala' al-Din Abu'l-Shamat. She asked if I would accept her as a fellow wife, promising to share you with me on alternate nights. I agreed, but asked: "Where is my husband?" She said: "The fate decreed for him by God is inscribed on his forehead, and when he has fulfilled his destiny he will very certainly come here. Meanwhile, let us console ourselves in his absence with songs and music until God unites us with him." I have stayed with her for all this while until God brought us together in this church.'

Husn Maryam then turned to 'Ala' al-Din and asked: 'My lord, are you willing to accept me as your wife and be my husband?' 'I am a Muslim, lady,' he replied, 'and, as you are a Christian, how can I marry you?' 'God forbid that I should be an unbeliever!' she exclaimed. 'No, I am a Muslim and for eighteen years I have held to the religion of Islam

and I have had no dealings with any religion that runs counter to it.'
'My lady,' he said, 'I want to go back to my own country.' She replied:
'Know that I have seen written on your forehead what you have to fulfil
before you get what you want.' Then she added: 'I congratulate you,
'Ala' al-Din, that you have a son named Aslan, who occupies your former
place at the caliph's court and is now eighteen years old. Know that the
truth has become known and falsehood has disappeared, as our Lord
has revealed who it was who stole the caliph's treasures. This was Ahmad
Qamaqim, the treacherous thief, who is now chained up in prison. You
should also know that it was I who sent you the jewel and arranged for
you to find it in the bag in your shop. It was I who sent the captain, who
fetched you together with the jewel. He is deeply in love with me and
wants me to sleep with him, but I have not given myself to him, telling
him that I would not do that unless he brought me the jewel and its
owner. I gave him a hundred purses of money and sent him off in the
guise of a trader, whereas he is in fact the captain of a man-of-war.
When they were about to kill you after having killed the forty prisoners
who were with you, I sent you the old woman.' 'May God reward you
well on my behalf,' said 'Ala' al-Din. 'How excellently you have acted!'

Husn Maryam now renewed her profession of Islam at 'Ala' al-Din's
hands and, when he realized her sincerity, he asked her to tell him the
virtues of the jewel and where it had come from. She said: 'It comes from
a talismanic treasure hoard and it possesses five virtues to help us in
times of need. My paternal grandmother was a sorceress who could
unravel secret signs and steal from treasure hoards, and it was in one of
these that she got hold of it. When I was fourteen I read the Gospel together
with other books and I found the name of Muhammad, may God bless
him and give him peace, in four of them, the Torah, the Gospel, the
Psalms and the Quran. I believed in him and accepted Islam, being
convinced in my mind that the only true object of worship is Almighty
God and that the Lord of mankind approves of no other religion apart
from Islam. When my grandmother fell ill, she made me a present of the
jewel and taught me its five virtues. Before she died my father asked her
to forecast the future for him by means of geomancy and to tell him
what his end would be. She told him that he would be killed by a prisoner
from Alexandria, as a result of which he swore to kill every captive
coming from there. He told this to the captain and ordered him to attack
and seize Muslim ships, killing everyone who came from Alexandria or
bringing them to him. The captain did as he was told and killed as many

men as he has hairs on his head. My grandmother then died and I decided to forecast my own future to find out who would marry me. So I discovered that my husband would be none other than 'Ala' al-Din Abu'l-Shamat, the trusty and faithful. This astonished me, but I waited until the appointed time had come and then I met you.'

'Ala' al-Din now married Husn Maryam, after which he told her that he wanted to go back to his own country. 'In that case, come with me,' she said. She took him and hid him in a small room in the palace. She then went in to see her father, who told her: 'I am feeling very sad today. Sit down and let us get drunk.' She sat down, and after he had called for wine to be brought, she started pouring it out and filling up his glass until he lost his senses. At that, she drugged a glass with *banj* and when he had drunk it he fell over backwards, at which she went to 'Ala' al-Din and fetched him from his room, telling him: 'Your enemy is flat on his back. Do what you want with him, for I have made him drunk and drugged him.' 'Ala' al-Din went in, and seeing the king in this state, he tied his hands tightly and fettered him. He then gave him an antidote to the *banj* and when he recovered his senses . . .

Night 270

Morning now dawned and Shahrazad broke off from what she had been allowed to say. Then, when it was the two hundred and seventieth night, SHE CONTINUED:

I have heard, O fortunate king, that 'Ala' al-Din gave the king an antidote to the *banj* and when he recovered his senses he found 'Ala' al-Din together with his daughter sitting on his chest. 'Are you really doing this to me, daughter?' he asked. 'If I am your daughter,' she told him, 'then turn to Islam, for I have become a Muslim. The truth has been made clear to me and I have followed it, turning aside from falsehood. I have submitted myself to God, the Lord of all things, and have no dealings with any religion that runs counter to it in this world and the next. If you accept Islam, you will be welcome, but if not, then it is better for us to kill you than for you to live.' 'Ala' al-Din also admonished him, but he arrogantly refused and 'Ala' al-Din drew his dagger and cut his throat from one side to the other. He then wrote a note to say what had happened, after which he took whatever precious things were light to carry and he and the princess left the palace and went to the church.

The princess now brought out the jewel and placed her hand on the facet on which a couch was engraved. She rubbed it and a couch appeared in front of her. She took her seat on this, together with 'Ala' al-Din and his wife Zubaida, the lute player, and then she said: 'I conjure you, couch, by the names, the talismans and the hieroglyphs inscribed on this jewel to carry us up and away.' The couch rose up with them and carried them to a valley in which there was nothing growing. She turned the other four facets of the jewel up towards the sky, but reversed the one inscribed with the couch and the couch itself came down to earth. The princess now turned over the facet engraved with the picture of a pavilion and struck it, saying: 'Let a pavilion be set up in this valley.' A pavilion appeared and the three took their seats in it. The valley itself was barren, without plants or water, and so she turned the jewel's four facets towards the sky and said: 'By the truth of the Names of God, let trees grow and let a stream run beside them.' Trees immediately sprouted, and a noisy stream with clashing waves ran at their side. The three used this for their ritual ablution and then prayed and drank. The princess turned over the remaining three facets until she came to the one on which a table of food was engraved. 'By the truth of the names,' she said, 'let a meal be provided,' and instantly there was a meal comprising splendid foods of all kinds, and the three ate, drank and enjoyed themselves happily.

So much for them, but as for the king's son, he went into his father's room and found him lying dead. He also found the note written by 'Ala' al-Din, which he read, and after noting what was in it he looked for his sister but failed to find her. He then went and found the old woman in the church, but when he asked her about his sister, she told him that she had not seen her since yesterday. After this he went back and ordered his horsemen to mount, telling them what had happened. They mounted and rode off until they came near the pavilion, and Husn Maryam, who had got up, saw a dust cloud covering the horizons and rising into the air. When it had blown away and dispersed, she saw her brother and his men, who were calling out: 'Where are you heading? We are on your heels.' She asked 'Ala' al-Din whether he could hold his ground in battle and he told her: 'I am as weak as a tent peg fixed in bran. I know nothing of war and combat, swords or spears.' She took out the jewel and rubbed the facet engraved with the picture of a horse and rider. Instantly a rider appeared from the hinterland and attacked the Genoese, striking them with his sword until he had broken and routed them. Husn Maryam now asked 'Ala' al-Din whether he would prefer to go to Cairo or to Alexandria, and when he said: 'Alexandria,' they got on the couch and she pronounced a spell over it. In the twinkling of an eye, it had taken them there.

'Ala' al-Din left the women in a cave and went off to fetch them clothes from the city. After they had put these on, he took them off to the living quarters of his shop and brought them food. He then saw Ahmad al-Danaf, who was on his way from Baghdad, and, meeting him on the road, he embraced him and greeted him warmly. Ahmad al-Danaf gave him the good news that he had a son, Aslan, who was now twenty years old, after which 'Ala' al-Din astonished him by telling him his story from beginning to end and took him to his shop, where they passed the night. The next morning 'Ala' al-Din sold the shop, adding the money that he got for it to what he had with him. He was told by Ahmad al-Danaf that he was wanted by the caliph, but he said: 'I am going to Cairo to greet my father and mother and my family.' So they all got on the couch and set off for Cairo, the Fortunate City, landing in al-Darb al-Asfar, because the house of 'Ala' al-Din's family was in that quarter. He knocked on its door and his mother said: 'Who is at the door, now that I have lost my dear one?' 'It is I, 'Ala' al-Din,' he replied, and his family came down and embraced him. He brought in his wife and what he had with him, after which Ahmad al-Danaf came in with him and there they rested for three days.

'Ala' al-Din then decided to go to Baghdad and, although his father asked him to stay with him, he said: 'I cannot bear to be separated from my son, Aslan.' So he took his father and mother and went to Baghdad. There Ahmad al-Danaf gave the caliph the good news of 'Ala' al-Din's arrival and told him his story. The caliph came to greet him, taking with him Aslan, his son, and they met and embraced. The caliph ordered Ahmad Qamaqim to be produced and when this was done, he told 'Ala' al-Din: 'Here is your enemy.' 'Ala' al-Din drew his sword and cut off the thief's head, after which the caliph organized a great feast. The *qadis* and notaries attended and drew up a marriage contract for Husn Maryam. 'Ala' al-Din consummated the marriage and found his bride to be an unpierced pearl. Aslan was appointed as hexarch and the caliph gave them splendid robes of honour. They led the most pleasant and delightful of lives until they were visited by the destroyer of delights and the parter of companions.

There are very many stories of generous men, among them being one told of Hatim of Tayy. It is said that when he died, he was buried

on the summit of a mountain. By his tomb two stone water troughs
were constructed, beside which were stone statues of girls with unbound
hair. Beneath the mountain a river flowed and when wayfarers
halted there they would hear cries all night long, but in the morning
the only thing that they would find would be the stone statues. When
Dhu'l-Kura', the king of Himyar, on a journey from his tribe, spent the
night there . . .

Night 271

Morning now dawned and Shahrazad broke off from what she had been
allowed to say. Then, when it was the two hundred and seventy-first
night, SHE CONTINUED:

I have heard, O fortunate king, that when Dhu'l-Kura', the king of
Himyar, on a journey from his tribe, spent the night there and
approached that place, he heard the cries from the top of the mountain
and asked what this was. He was told: 'This is the grave of Hatim of
Tayy. There are two stone water troughs there and stone statues of girls
with unbound hair and every night people who halt here hear weeping
and wailing.' The king, in mockery of Hatim, said: 'We are your guests
tonight, Hatim, and we are hungry.'

He then fell asleep, but later woke in a panic, calling to his men for
help and telling them to look to his riding camel. When they came, they
found the camel in convulsions and so they slaughtered it, roasted its
flesh and ate it. When they asked the king about this he said: 'I closed
my eyes and then in a dream I saw Hatim approaching me with a sword.
"You have come to me," he said, "but I have no provisions." He then
struck my camel with his sword and, had you not come and cut its
throat, it would still have died.' Next morning the king mounted a camel
belonging to one of his companions, taking the man up behind him. At
midday they saw a rider leading a spare riding camel. When they asked
him who he was, he told them that he was 'Adi, the son of Hatim of
Tayy. He then asked: 'Where is Dhu'l-Kura', the king of Himyar?' 'This
is he,' they told him, and he said to the king: 'Mount this camel in place
of your own, which my father slaughtered for you.' 'Who told you that?'
asked the king. 'Adi replied: 'When I was asleep last night my father
came to me in a dream and said: "Dhu'l-Kura', the king of Himyar,
asked me for hospitality and so I slaughtered his camel for him. Take

him another camel to ride, for I had no provisions.'' 'Dhu'l-Kura' accepted the camel, wondering at Hatim's generosity both in life and after his death.

Another story of generous men is told about Ma'n ibn Za'ida. One day, it is said, he became thirsty while out hunting and found that his servants had brought no water with them. At this point three girls appeared carrying three water skins.

Night 272

Morning now dawned and Shahrazad broke off from what she had been allowed to say. Then, when it was the two hundred and seventy-second night, SHE CONTINUED:

I have heard, O fortunate king, that the girls approached carrying three water skins. He asked them for a drink, which they gave him, and he then asked his servants for something that he could give them. Then, when it turned out that the servants had no money with them, he gave each of the girls ten arrows from his quiver, the arrows' heads being made of gold. One of the girls said to the others: 'Generous qualities like this can only belong to Ma'n ibn Za'ida, so let each of you recite some poetry in his praise.'

The first recited:

He sets heads of gold on his arrows
And shoots generosity and bounty at his enemies.
He provides a cure for those who suffer from wounds,
And shrouds for those who are buried in their graves.

The second recited:

There is a warrior whose generous hands dispense bounty to both
      friends and foes.
His arrow heads are made of gold, lest war restrain his liberality.

The third recited:

Such is his generosity that he shoots his foes
With arrows whose heads are of pure gold,
So that the wounded may spend it on a cure,
And those he kills may buy a shroud.

It is also told that Ma'n ibn Za'ida went out with a hunting party. A troop of gazelles approached them and the hunters scattered in pursuit. Ma'n was left alone chasing a gazelle, which he caught and killed. He then saw a man riding on a donkey coming from the desert. He mounted his horse, rode up to the man and, after greeting him, asked where he had come from. 'From the territory of Quda'a,' the man replied. 'For some years it has suffered from drought, but this year it has been fertile and so I sowed cucumbers, which have come up early. I've picked the best of them and am on my way to the emir Ma'n ibn Za'ida, because of his well-known reputation for generosity.' 'How much are you hoping to get from him?' asked Ma'n. 'A thousand dinars,' said the man. 'And if he tells you that this is too much?' 'Five hundred dinars.' 'And if he tells you that this is too much?' 'Three hundred dinars.' 'And if he tells you that this is too much?' 'Two hundred dinars.' 'And if he tells you that this is too much?' 'Fifty dinars.' 'And if he tells you that this is too much?' 'Thirty dinars.' 'And if he tells you that this is too much?' 'I shall get my donkey to put its legs into his harem and then go back disappointed and empty-handed to my family.' Ma'n laughed at him and then rode away and rejoined his men.

When he got back home he told his chamberlain: 'When a man comes here on a donkey bringing cucumbers, take him in to me.' After some time the Bedouin arrived and the chamberlain brought him into the emir's presence. When he entered, he didn't recognize Ma'n as the man who had met him in the desert, because of the dignity and awe which now surrounded him, together with the number of his servants and retainers. For Ma'n was seated in the middle of the room on his throne of state, with servants to the left and right and in front of him. The Bedouin greeted him and Ma'n asked him why he had come. 'In hopes of the emir's generosity I have brought him some early cucumbers,' the man answered. 'How much do you hope to get from me?' Ma'n asked. 'A thousand dinars,' said the man. 'That is too much.' 'Five hundred dinars.' 'Too much.' 'Three hundred dinars.' 'Too much.' 'Two hundred dinars.' 'Too much.' 'Fifty dinars.' 'Too much.' 'Thirty dinars.' 'Too much.' 'By God,' said the man, 'that fellow who met me in the desert brought me bad luck. I shan't take less than thirty.' Ma'n laughed and then stayed silent. The Bedouin now realized that he was the man who had met him and said: 'If you don't give me thirty, then here is my donkey tethered at your door.' Ma'n, sitting on his throne, laughed until he fell over and then he called for his steward and said: 'Give this man a thousand dinars, then five hundred, then three hundred, then two hundred, then a hundred, then fifty, then thirty, and leave the donkey tethered where it is.' The astonished Bedouin received two thousand, one hundred and eighty dinars. May God's mercy be on all these men.

A city named Labtit was the royal capital of the land of Rum.* In it was a tower that was always kept locked, and whenever a king died and another Rumi succeeded him, the newcomer added a strong bolt, until there were twenty-four bolts on its door, one for each king. These kings were succeeded by someone who was not from the royal family, and this man wanted to remove the bolts so as to see what was in the tower. The leaders of the state strongly disapproved and tried to prevent him, but he refused to listen and insisted on opening the tower, and in spite of the fact that they offered him all the treasures and valuables that they had to stop him, he wouldn't draw back.

Night 273

Morning now dawned and Shahrazad broke off from what she had been allowed to say. Then, when it was the two hundred and seventy-third night, SHE CONTINUED:

I have heard, O fortunate king, that they offered him all the treasures and valuables that they had to keep him from opening it, but he would not draw back. He removed the bolts, opened the door and found inside the tower pictures of Arabs mounted on horses and camels, with long turbans and sword belts, carrying spears in their hands. He also found a written document and, on taking and reading this, he found that it said: 'When this door is opened this land will be conquered by an Arab people resembling those pictured here, so beware, beware of opening it.'

That city was in al-Andalus and it was captured in that year by Tariq ibn Ziyad in the reign of the Umaiyad caliph al-Walid ibn 'Abd al-Malik.† The king was put to the cruellest of deaths; his lands were ravaged and the women and children taken as captives. Wealth was plundered and vast amounts of treasure were found there, including more than one

---

* This story was originally told about the Visigothic capital of Toledo in Spain and the circumstances of its capture by the Arab and Berber army in 711.
† Caliph AD 705–15.

hundred and seventy crowns set with pearls, sapphires and other precious stones. A hall was discovered, big enough to allow spearsmen to gallop in it, and here there were vessels of gold and silver in indescribable quantities. They also found the table that had belonged to the prophet Solomon, son of David, upon both of whom be peace, made, it is said, from a green emerald, a table that is in the city of Rome to this day. The vessels were of gold and the dishes of chrysolite. A copy of the Psalms was found, written in Greek script on leaves of gold studded with gems, together with a book of gold and silver, listing the uses of stones, plants and minerals, together with talismans and the science of alchemy. There was another book dealing with how to set sapphires and other precious stones, how to prepare poisons and theriacs, together with a map showing the land, the sea, countries, cities and towns. There was another great hall filled with an elixir, one dirham's weight of which would turn a thousand dirhams of silver into gold. In addition, there was a huge circular mirror of remarkable composition that had been made for the prophet Solomon, son of David, in which whoever looked could see the seven climes, while yet another room contained carbuncles that surpassed all description. Tariq had all these carried on camels to al-Walid ibn 'Abd al-Malik. The Arabs spread through all the cities of this, one of the greatest of lands. This is the end of the story of Labtit.

Another tale told is that one day Hisham ibn 'Abd al-Malik was out hunting when he caught sight of a gazelle. He followed it with his dogs and while he was in pursuit of it he saw a Bedouin boy pasturing his sheep. 'Boy,' he shouted, 'follow that gazelle as it's got away from me.' The boy looked up and said: 'You don't know what good men are worth. You have looked at me slightingly and spoken scornfully, talking like a tyrant and acting like a donkey.' 'Damn you,' said Hisham, 'don't you know who I am?' The boy replied: 'Your bad manners made you known to me when you began to speak without greeting me.' 'Damn you,' repeated Hisham, 'I am Hisham ibn 'Abd al-Malik.' 'May God not show favour to your lands or bless the places you visit. You speak a lot but show little in the way of good manners,' replied the boy.

Before he had finished speaking he was surrounded by the caliph's men, all of whom were saying: 'Peace be upon you, Commander of the Faithful.' 'Cut this short,' Hisham told them, 'and hold this boy.' So they laid hands on him and when he saw the many chamberlains, viziers and officers of state, he showed no concern and asked no questions, but rested his chin on his chest, looking to see where to plant his feet, until he came and stood before Hisham. Then he bent his head towards the ground and neither greeted him nor spoke. One of Hisham's servants said: 'Bedouin dog, what stops you from greeting the Commander of the Faithful?' 'You donkey's pack saddle,' said the boy, 'it was the long way that I had to come and the sweaty climb that kept me from greeting him.' Hisham grew even more angry and said: 'Boy, you have reached your last day; there is no hope for you and your life is over.' 'However little or much you say can do me no harm if my life span is cut short and my fate is not delayed.' 'Vilest of Bedouin,' said the chamberlain, 'do you in your position dare to answer back to the Commander of the Faithful?' 'May madness be quick to seize you and may misery and distress never leave you,' the boy said. 'Have you never heard the words of Almighty God: "There will be a day on which every soul will come to argue its own case"?'*

At this point Hisham got up in a fury and told the executioner: 'Bring me the head of this boy, for what he has said is more than anyone could have imagined.' The executioner took the boy and brought him to the execution mat. Drawing his sword, he set it against his head. 'Commander of the Faithful,' he then said, 'here is a servant of yours whose arrogance is bringing him to his grave. If I cut off his head, shall I be guiltless of his blood?' 'Yes,' replied Hisham. The executioner asked again and received the same answer. He then asked for a third time and the boy realized that if Hisham said yes this time, the man would kill him. So he laughed, showing all his teeth, and Hisham, even angrier than before, said: 'I think you are out of your mind, boy. Don't you realize that you are about to leave this world? Why do you laugh, as if to mock yourself?' 'If I am given an extension of life, nothing, small or great, can harm me, but some lines have come to mind. Listen to them, for you will be able to kill me when you want.' 'Produce them, but be brief,' Hisham said, and the boy recited the following lines:

> I have heard that once, through the decree of fate, a hawk captured
>   a country sparrow.
> As the hawk flew off with it clutched in its talons, the sparrow spoke:
> 'There is not enough of me to fill you, and even if you eat me, I am
>   not worth it.'
> The great hawk smiled proudly and the sparrow was allowed to escape.

* Quran 16.112.

For his part, Hisham smiled and said: 'I swear by my relationship to the Apostle of God, may God bless him and give him peace, that had he said this to start with and asked for anything short of the caliphate, I would have given it to him.' He told his servant to 'fill the boy's mouth with jewels' and to give him a splendid reward. The man gave him a magnificent gift, which he took and went off on his way.

The end.

Another pleasant tale is that of Ibrahim ibn al-Mahdi. Ibrahim was the brother of Harun al-Rashid, and when the caliphate passed to his nephew al-Ma'mun, he did not swear allegiance to him but went to Rayy, where he claimed the caliphate for himself. He stayed there for one year, eleven months and twelve days. Al-Ma'mun kept expecting him to resume his allegiance and rejoin him, but eventually, despairing of his return, he moved into Rayy with his horse and foot to search for him. When news of this reached Ibrahim he had no alternative but to go into hiding in Baghdad, in fear of his life. Al-Ma'mun offered a reward of a hundred thousand dinars to anyone who would inform on him.

Ibrahim said: 'On hearing of this I was afraid . . .'

Night 274

Morning now dawned and Shahrazad broke off from what she had been allowed to say. Then, when it was the two hundred and seventy-fourth night, SHE CONTINUED:

I have heard, O fortunate king, that IBRAHIM SAID:

On hearing this I was afraid, and, not knowing what to do, I left my house at noon in disguise, with no idea of where to go. I went into a street which turned out to be a dead end, and I recited the formula: 'We belong to God and to Him do we return.' I then told myself that I was in mortal danger and that if I retraced my steps, people would become suspicious of me in my disguise.

At the head of the street I saw a black slave standing by the door of a house. I went up to him and asked him if he had a place where I could stay for a time. 'Yes,' he said, and when he opened the door I entered a pleasant room furnished with carpets, rugs and leather cushions. After he had let me in he shut the door on me and went off. I thought that he must have heard of the reward and that he had gone out to inform on me, and so I remained simmering in agitation like a pot boiling on the fire as I thought over my position.

While I was in this state, the man came back with a porter who was carrying everything that could be needed, bread, meat, new pots and utensils, together with a new jar and new jugs. After he had unloaded what the porter was carrying he turned to me and said: 'My life be your ransom. I'm a barber surgeon and I know that you will shrink from me because of my trade, so do what you want with these things, which I have not touched.' I needed food and so I took a pot and cooked myself a meal such as I never remember having eaten before. When I had eaten my fill, the man said: 'May God make me your ransom, master. Would you like some wine to drink, for it delights the soul and dispels care?' 'I would not dislike that,' I agreed, for I wanted to be on friendly terms with him. So he brought me a set of new glasses, untouched by hand, and a jar of spiced wine. 'Strain it for yourself as you like it,' he told me and, after I had strained some excellent wine, he brought me a new cup together with fruit and flowers in new earthenware containers and said: 'May I have your permission to sit beside you and drink my own wine by myself because of my pleasure in you and for you?' 'Do so,' I told him, and as we both drank I could feel the effect of the wine creeping through us.

The man then got up and, going to a cupboard, he brought out a wide-bodied lute and said: 'Master, it is not for me to ask you to sing, and it is for you in your great generosity to acknowledge any obligation to me, but if you think it right to honour your servant, the decision will be yours alone.' I did not believe that he had recognized me and so I said: 'Why should you think that I can sing well?' 'Glory be to God!' he exclaimed. 'You are more famous than that, lord. You are my master, Ibrahim ibn al-Mahdi, who used to be our caliph. Al-Ma'mun has offered a reward of a hundred thousand dinars to anyone who informs on you to him, but with me you are safe.'

When he said that, he made the greatest impression on me and I was convinced of his noble qualities. So I agreed to his request and, taking the lute, I tuned it and started to sing. Thinking of how I had been parted from my children and my family, I began with the words:

It may be that He who guided Joseph's family to him
And brought him glory as a captive prisoner

Will answer our prayers and reunite us,
For He, the Lord of mankind, is Omnipotent.

SHAHRAZAD CONTINUED:

The man experienced intense pleasure and the greatest of delight, for it
used to be said that Ibrahim's neighbours were transported with joy when
they heard him say: 'Boy, bridle the mule.' In his joy and happiness the
barber said: 'Master, will you allow me to recite what occurs to me, even
though this is not my craft?' 'Do so,' said Ibrahim, 'as this will be an extension of your courtesy and generosity.' So, taking the lute, the man sang:

We complained to our beloveds of the lengthy night,
But they said: 'How short we found the night.'
That was because sleep had quickly closed their eyes,
Although it had not closed our eyes at all.
When night is near that brings the lover harm,
We grieve, while they rejoice at its approach.
Were they to feel the pain that comes to us,
Like us they would be restless in their beds.

'That was excellently done, you talented man,' said Ibrahim. 'You
have dispelled my sorrows, so let me hear more such delicate lines.' The
barber then recited:

When a man's honour is not tainted by reproach
Whatever cloak he wears is beautiful.
She finds it a fault that there are few of us,
But I reply that noble men are few.
How does our lack of numbers do us harm?
Our clients are respected and those of most clans despised.
We think it no disgrace to fall in fight,
Though that is what 'Amir and Salul believe.
Love of death hurries on our fate,
While their fates loathe death and are slow to come.
We have some fault to find with what men say,
But when we speak no fault is to be found.

IBRAHIM WENT ON:

When I heard these lines I was filled with admiration and deeply
moved. I fell asleep and didn't wake until after evening. Then I washed
my face and thought again of the high worth of this barber surgeon and

his good manners. I woke him up and, taking a bag that I had with me containing a considerable number of dinars, I threw it over to him saying: 'I entrust you to God's keeping, for I am going to leave you. Please use what is in this bag for your own purposes, and when I am freed from my present fear, I shall give you a greater reward.' The man handed the bag back to me and said: 'Poor wretches like me are of no value to you, but how can it accord with my honour to accept a price for the chance that God has given me to meet you and to have you stay with me? If you say this to me again and throw the purse to me once more, I shall kill myself.' So I put the bag, which was heavy to carry, in my sleeve . . .

Night 275

Morning now dawned and Shahrazad broke off from what she had been allowed to say. Then, when it was the two hundred and seventy-fifth night, SHE CONTINUED:

I have heard, O fortunate king, that IBRAHIM SAID:

I put the bag, which was heavy to carry, in my sleeve and turned away, but when I got to the house door he said to me: 'Master, there is no better hiding place for you than here and it is no hardship for me to provide for you. Stay with me until God clears away your difficulties.' So I went back and said that I would remain on condition that he used the contents of the bag for my expenses. He pretended to agree, and I stayed with him on those terms for several days, enjoying every luxury, but as he spent nothing from the bag I was ashamed to go on living there at his expense and to be a burden on him. So I got up and left him, disguising myself as a woman with yellow boots and a veil.

After I had left the house and come out on to the road, I became extremely frightened. I was intending to cross the bridge, but when I had come to a place that had been sprinkled with water a trooper who had once been in my service recognized me and called out: 'This is the man wanted by al-Ma'mun.' He held on to me, but for dear life's sake I pushed him and his horse, overturning them in that slippery place, so that the man became an object lesson for those prepared to learn. People rushed up to him but I hurried on and crossed the bridge. On entering a street I found a house door open and a woman standing in its hall. 'Lady,' I said, 'take pity on me and save me, for I am a man in fear.' She welcomed me and told me to come in. She then took me up to a room, spread bedding for me, brought me food and said: 'Calm yourself, for no one knows that you are here.' While this was happening there was a violent knocking on the door and she went out to open it. In came my acquaintance, the man whom I had pushed over by the bridge, with a bandaged head and blood running over his clothes. He was without his horse and the woman asked him what had happened to him. He said: 'I had got hold of the young man but he escaped,' and he then told her the story. She produced some tinder, wrapped it in a rag and used this to bandage his head. She then spread bedding for him and he lay there injured.

She herself now came up to me and said: 'I think that you must be the man he was talking about.' When I agreed that I was, she told me that no harm would come to me and renewed her kindness to me, but after I had stayed with her for three days, she said: 'I am afraid for you, lest this man find out about you and betray your secret, as you fear, so make your escape.' I asked to be allowed to stay until nightfall, and she told me: 'There is no harm in that.' When night came, I put on a woman's dress and left her, making for the house of a freed-woman who had been a slave of mine. When she saw me, she wept for sorrow, praised Almighty God for my safety and left the house, pretending to be going to the market to lay in guest provisions for me. I thought that all was well, but before I knew it, there was Ibrahim al-Mausili coming with his servants and his troopers, led by a woman who, when I looked at her, turned out to be the one in whose house I was. She walked ahead of them and handed me over to them, leaving me staring death in the face.

I was taken to al-Ma'mun, wearing my disguise. He convened a general assembly and when I was brought in I greeted him as caliph. 'May God not give you safety or life,' he replied. 'Slowly, slowly, Commander of the Faithful,' I said. 'The man who is owed blood revenge is entitled to punish or to forgive, but forgiveness is closer to piety. God has set your forgiveness above that of all others, just as he has set my crime above the rest. If you punish me, you are within your rights, and if you forgive me, it is through your graciousness.' I then recited these lines:

My offence against you is great, but you are greater than it.
Either take your rightful revenge or not;
In your clemency, forgive what I have done.
If I have not acted as a noble man, do you yourself be noble.

Al-Ma'mun raised his head and looked at me and I hurried to recite three more lines:

My sin is great, but you are a man of mercy.
If you forgive, this is an act of kindness
While if you punish me, that is justice.

He then looked down and recited:

When a friend tries to anger me
And choke me with rage on my own spittle,
I forgive his offence and pardon him
For fear lest I might live without any friend.

When I heard that, I could scent that he was disposed towards mercy. He turned to his son, al-'Abbas, Abu Ishaq, his brother, and his other intimates who were there, and consulted them about what should be done with me. Every one of them advised him to put me to death, although they differed as to how this should be done. He then asked Ahmad ibn Khalid for his advice. 'Commander of the Faithful,' said Ahmad, 'if you kill him, we can find others like you who have killed others like him, but if you forgive him, then we cannot find anyone like you who has forgiven someone like him.'

Night 276

Morning now dawned and Shahrazad broke off from what she had been allowed to say. Then, when it was the two hundred and seventy-sixth night, SHE CONTINUED:

I have heard, O fortunate king, that when al-Ma'mun heard what Ahmad had to say, he bent his head and then recited:

Umaima, my own clan has killed my brother,
And the arrows that I shoot strike me.

He continued with more lines:

Forgive your brother when, thanks to him, right is mixed with
    wrong.
Continue to treat him well, whether he shows gratitude or not.
Fear to treat him harshly whether he acts unfairly or fairly.
Do you not see that your likes and dislikes are of the same stamp?
Pleasure in long life is spoilt when hair turns white.
Blossoms appear on branches with fruit that must be picked.

Who has never done wrong and whose deeds are always good?
Were you to test mankind, you would find that most of them are
    worthless.

IBRAHIM CONTINUED:

When I heard these verses, I took the woman's veil from my head and
called out loudly: 'God is greater!' I then added: 'By God, the Commander of the Faithful has pardoned me!' 'No harm shall come to you,
uncle,' the caliph said. 'My crime is too great for me to voice an excuse,'
I told him, 'and your mercy is too great for me to be able to express
thanks.' Then I chanted these lines:

God, Who created noble qualities,
United them in Adam's loins for the seventh imam.
The people's hearts are filled with awe for you,
And you protect them all with a humble heart.
I disobeyed you, being led astray,
But this was only as I craved your mercy.
You forgave the unforgivable,
A man for whom no one had made a plea.
You pitied children like the sandgrouse's young,
Together with a yearning mother's anxious heart.

Al-Ma'mun said: 'In the words of Joseph (may God bless him as well
as our Prophet and give them peace): "No blame is attached to you
today. May God forgive you, as He is the most merciful of the merciful."*
I pardon you, uncle, and restore your wealth and your lands to you. No
harm will come to you.' I invoked blessings on him and recited these
lines:

You have restored my wealth ungrudgingly to me and spared my life.
Were I to spill my blood to win your favour,
Giving all I have, even the shoes from my feet,
That would merely return a loan to you, for which,
Had you refused it, you could not be blamed.
Were I to show ingratitude for this favour,
My own blameworthiness would outweigh your nobility.

Al-Ma'mun treated me with respect and said: 'Abu Ishaq and al-'Abbas
advised me to kill you, uncle.' 'It was sound advice that they gave you,

---

* Quran 12.9.

Commander of the Faithful,' I replied, 'but you acted in a manner worthy of yourself and warded off what I feared with what I hoped for.' The caliph said: 'You killed my anger by the liveliness of your excuse and so I pardoned you without making you swallow the bitterness of having to rely on the favour of intercessors.' He then prostrated himself for a long time in prayer and, when he raised his head, he asked me if I knew why he had been praying. 'Perhaps in gratitude to God for having put your enemy in your hands?' I said. 'That is not what I had in mind,' he replied, 'but, rather, I wanted to thank God for having inspired me to forgive you and to free my mind of hatred towards you.'

He then asked me to tell him my story and I explained things to him, telling him of my experiences with the barber surgeon, the trooper and his wife, and with my freed-woman, who had informed on me. Al-Ma'mun sent for this woman, who had been waiting in her house expecting the reward to be sent to her. When she came before the caliph, he asked her what had led her to do what she had done with her master. 'I wanted the money,' she told him. He asked her whether she had a child or a husband and when she said no, he sentenced her to a hundred lashes and life imprisonment. He then sent for the trooper and his wife and for the barber surgeon. When they came, he asked the trooper why he had acted as he did and when he said that it was for the money, the caliph said: 'You must become a barber surgeon,' and he put him in charge of someone who was to place him in the barber's booth so that he might learn the trade. He treated the man's wife with honour, bringing her to the palace and saying: 'This is an intelligent woman suitable for employment in matters of importance.' To the barber surgeon he said: 'The manly qualities that you showed deserve a great reward.' He ordered that the trooper's house be handed over to the barber surgeon with all its contents. He also gave him a robe of honour and, in addition to that, an annual salary of fifteen thousand dinars.

It is said that 'Abd Allah ibn Abi Qilaba went out to look for a she-camel of his that had strayed. While he was going through the deserts of Yemen in the territory of Saba', he came across a huge city on whose perimeter was a vast fortress, around which palaces towered into the sky. When he got near it he thought that it would have inhabitants whom he could ask about his camel, and so he made for it, but on reaching it he found it empty, with no living soul inside. He said: 'I dismounted from the camel that I was riding . . .'

Night 277

Morning now dawned and Shahrazad broke off from what she had been allowed to say. Then, when it was the two hundred and seventy-seventh night, SHE CONTINUED:

I have heard, O fortunate king, that 'ABD ALLAH IBN ABI QILABA SAID:

I dismounted from the camel that I was riding and tethered it. Then, after having calmed my fears, I went into the city and approached the fortress. It had, I found, two huge doors, in size and height greater than any to be seen in the world. They were studded with sapphires and gems, white, red and green, and, when I saw this, I was amazed at such magnificence.

Although I was frightened and apprehensive, I entered the fortress and found that it was a huge place, covering as much ground as the city itself, and in it were lofty pavilions, all containing chambers made of gold and silver, studded with sapphires, coloured gems, chrysolite and pearls, and the leaves of their doors were as beautiful as those of the fortress itself. The floors were strewn with huge pearls, together with globules of musk, ambergris and saffron. I then penetrated into the city, but when I could still see no single living soul, I was almost stunned and ready to die of fear. When I looked down from the topmost chambers and the pavilions, I could see streams flowing beneath and streets lined with fruit trees and towering palms. The buildings were made of alternate gold and silver bricks. I said to myself: 'This must be the Paradise that we are promised in the next world.' I carried off what I could of the gems that were there in place of pebbles, and the musk that was its soil, and I then went back to my own land and told people about it.

News of the city reached Mu'awiya ibn Abi Sufyan, who was at that time caliph in the Hijaz, and he wrote to his governor in the Yemeni town of San'a', telling him to summon me and ask me about the truth of the story. He did this and he asked me about my adventure and what had happened to me. After I had told him what I had seen, he sent me to Mu'awiya, to whom I repeated everything. When Mu'awiya refused to believe it, I showed him some of the pearls, together with the sweet-scented globules of musk, ambergris and saffron. The pearls, however, had changed colour and turned yellow.

Night 278

Morning now dawned and Shahrazad broke off from what she had been allowed to say. Then, when it was the two hundred and seventy-eighth night, SHE CONTINUED:

I have heard, O fortunate king, that 'Abd Allah ibn Abi Qilaba said: 'The pearls had changed colour and turned yellow.'

Mu'awiya was astonished to see what Ibn Abi Qilaba showed him. He sent for Ka'b al-Ahbar and told him on his arrival: 'I have sent for you, Ka'b, as there is something that I want to have confirmed and I hope that you may be able to tell me the true facts about it.' When Ka'b asked what this was, Mu'awiya said: 'Do you know anything about the existence of a city built of gold and silver, whose columns are of chrysolite and sapphire, whose pebbles are pearls, and where there are globules of musk, ambergris and saffron?' 'Yes indeed, Commander of the Faithful,' answered Ka'b. 'This is Iram, City of the Columns, whose match was never found in any other land and which was built by Shaddad ibn 'Ad the elder.' 'Tell me something about him,' said Mu'awiya. KA'B WENT ON:

This king had two sons, Shadid and Shaddad. When their father died, these two ruled in his place and there was no king on earth who did not owe them allegiance. When Shadid died, Shaddad took sole power over the whole world. He was passionately fond of studying old books and when he came across a reference to the next world and Paradise, with its palaces, chambers, trees, fruits and so on, he conceived the ambition of building its exact replica in this world. He ruled over a hundred thousand kings, each of whom, in their turn, controlled a hundred thousand stewards, each of whom had a hundred thousand men. He brought them all together and told them: 'I have found in accounts given in old books a description of the Paradise that is to be found in the world to come and I want to make something like it in this world. Go to the best and broadest stretch of open country on earth and build me a city of gold and silver there. Its pebbles are to be chrysolites, sapphires and pearls; its arches are to be supported on pillars of chrysolite; it is to be filled with palaces whose upper storeys must be filled with chambers. Under these palaces, in the lanes and streets, there are to be trees producing varieties of ripe fruits, with streams running beneath them through conduits of gold and silver.' 'How can we produce something like this?'

they all asked. 'And how can we get the chrysolites, sapphires and pearls that you have talked about?' 'Don't you know,' he replied, 'that all the kings of the world are subject to me and under my command? Not one of them can disobey my orders.' When they agreed that that was so, he told them: 'Go to the mines of chrysolites, sapphires, gold and silver and to the pearl beds, extract the gems and collect all that is to be found in the world, sparing no effort. In addition to that, take whatever of these is to be found in people's possession, leaving nothing at all behind. Take care not to disobey me.'

Shaddad then wrote to all the kings in every district in the world, ordering them to collect whatever gems of these kinds their peoples had, and to go to the mines and excavate all their precious stones, even if they had to be fetched from the depths of the sea. In twenty years the three hundred and sixty kings who ruled the world had collected them all. Shaddad then gathered together architects, men of wisdom, artisans and craftsmen from all lands and parts. They spread out through the open country, deserts, regions and districts until they came to a wide plain of clear country, without hills or mountains, where there were gushing springs and flowing streams. 'This fits the description of what the king ordered us to find and for which he sent us to prospect,' they told themselves, and so they set about building the city following the instructions that the king had given them. Streams were made to flow in conduits, and foundations were laid in accordance with Shaddad's measurements. The rulers of every land sent gems, valuable stones, pearls both large and small, together with carnelian and gold. All this was carried by camels through the desert wastes and by great ships across the seas. The quantities of these that reached the builders were more than could be described, counted or quantified.

Three hundred years were spent on the work and, when it was finished, the builders came to the king and told him that it was done. He then ordered them to build a strong fortress towering high over the city, around which there were to be a thousand palaces, each supported on a thousand pillars, every one the residence of a vizier. The builders left at once and spent twenty years on the work, after which they returned to Shaddad and told him that they had done what he wanted. He then ordered his thousand viziers, his principal officers and the soldiers on whom he relied, together with others, to be ready to travel in order to move to Iram, City of the Columns, in the train of the king of the world, Shaddad ibn 'Ad. Similar instructions were given to those whom he chose from among his wives and his harem, such as slave girls and eunuchs. Twenty years were spent in making these preparations, after which Shaddad, happy at having achieved his purpose, set out with his entourage.

Night 279

Morning now dawned and Shahrazad broke off from what she had been allowed to say. Then, when it was the two hundred and seventy-ninth night, SHE CONTINUED:

I have heard, O fortunate king, that Shaddad, happy at having achieved his purpose, set out with his entourage. Ka'b went on: 'When he was at a single stage's distance from the city, God sent against him and his fellow unbelievers a cry from heaven, where He reigns in power, and the terrible sound killed them all. Neither Shaddad nor any of his companions reached the city or came within sight of it. God blotted out all traces of the road that led to it, but the city itself is still where it was built and will remain there until the Last Judgement.'

Mu'awiya was filled with astonishment at what Ka'b had told him and asked whether any mortal man could reach the city. 'Yes,' replied Ka'b, 'one of the companions of Muhammad, may God bless him and give him peace, can do so and there is no doubt at all that his description fits this man who is sitting here.'

Al-Sha'bi has quoted Himyaritic scholars from Yemen as saying that when Shaddad and his companions were killed by the cry, he was succeeded by his son Shaddad the younger, whom he had left to rule his lands in Hadramaut and Saba' when he went on his expedition to Iram, City of the Columns. On hearing that his father had died before reaching it, he ordered his body to be brought back to Hadramaut from the desert and that a grave be dug for him in a cave. When this was done, the body was placed in it on a golden couch over which were placed seventy robes of woven gold, studded with precious stones. At his father's head his son set a gold tablet on which were inscribed the following lines:

Be warned, you who have been deceived by length of life.
I am Shaddad ibn 'Ad, lord of the strong castle,
A ruler of power, might and great strength.
All the world obeyed me, in fear of force and threats.

Through the greatness of my power I held both east and west.
We were summoned to the true way by a rightly guided man,
But we did not obey and called out: 'Is there no refuge?'
Then came a cry out of the far horizon;
We were cut down as though we were a harvest field.
Shut in our graves, we wait for Judgement Day.

According to al-Tha'alabi, it happened that two men went into this cave, at the far end of which they found steps, and when they went down they found an excavation a hundred cubits long by forty in width and a hundred in height. In the centre of this was a golden couch on which lay a man so huge that he filled its length and breadth. He was wearing ornaments and robes embroidered with gold and silver and at his head was an inscribed tablet of gold. They took this and removed from the place as many bars of gold and silver as they could carry, together with other treasures.

ISHAQ AL-MAUSILI IS QUOTED AS SAYING:

One night I left al-Ma'mun and set off home, but feeling the need to relieve myself I went into an alley, where I stood up to urinate, as I was afraid that I might come to some harm if I squatted beside the wall. Then I saw something hanging down from one of the houses and when I felt it to see what it was, I found that it was a large basket with four handles, covered with brocade. 'There must be some reason for this,' I told myself, and in my state of confusion, drunkenness prompted me to sit down in it. Before I knew it, the people in the house drew it up, with me inside it, thinking that I was the person whom they had been expecting. When they had pulled it up to the top of the house wall, I found myself confronted by four slave girls who welcomed me warmly and told me to come in. A girl with a candle walked in front of me as I went down into a house whose rooms were furnished with such luxury as I had only seen before in the caliph's palace. I sat down and after a time I noticed that the curtains hanging by the wall had been raised. In came maids with candles in their hands and braziers in which *qaqulla* wood was burning to produce incense, and between the maids was a girl like a full moon rising. I got up and she welcomed me as a visitor before telling me to be seated. She asked me about myself and I said: 'I was coming away from a friend's house when I was caught out on my way by the need to relieve myself. I came to this alley and found a basket which had been let down.

The wine that I had drunk induced me to sit down in it and it was lifted up to this house with me in it. This is my story.'

'No harm shall come to you,' the girl said, adding: 'And I hope that you may bless the result of your adventure.' She then asked me my trade and I told her that I was a trader in the market of Baghdad. 'Can you recite any poetry?' she asked. 'A very little,' I replied. 'Tell me some,' she said, 'and recite something.' 'Visitors tend to be at a loss,' I said, 'so you should begin.' 'You are right,' she said, and she then recited some delicate lines, the choicest passages from poets both old and new. Listening, I could not make up my mind which to admire more, her grace and beauty or the excellence of her recitation. She then asked me: 'Have you now lost your bewilderment?' 'Yes, by God,' I told her. 'Then would you like to recite me something?' she said, and so I recited a sufficient number of lines from a number of old poets. She approved of this, exclaiming: 'By God, I didn't think that culture like this was to be found among market traders.' She then ordered food to be brought.

Dunyazad praised the sweetness and excellence of her sister Shahrazad's pleasant and agreeable story, but Shahrazad replied that it could not compare to what she would tell on the following night if the king were to spare her life.

Night 280

Morning now dawned and Shahrazad broke off from what she had been allowed to say. Then, when it was the two hundred and eightieth night, she repeated that it could not compare to what she would tell on the following night if the king were to spare her life. The king told her to finish the story. 'To hear is to obey,' she said, AND CONTINUED:

I have heard, O fortunate king, that according to Ishaq al-Mausili, when food had been brought, as the girl had ordered, she began to take it and set it in front of him. HE SAID:

In the room were all kinds of scented plants, together with exotic fruits such as were only to be found in royal palaces. The girl called for wine, and after drinking a cup she passed another to me and said: 'This is the time for conversation and anecdotes.' I began, telling her: 'I have heard that such-and-such happened and that someone said such-and-such,' and going on until I had told her a number of pleasant tales. She was delighted and said: 'It astonishes me that a trader knows stories like these, for they are kings' tales.' 'I had a neighbour who used to talk and drink with kings,' I explained, 'and when he was at leisure I used to go to his house, so it may be that what I have told you came from him.'

She congratulated me on how well I had remembered the stories and we then began to talk. Whenever I fell silent she would take up the conversation and in this way we passed the greater part of the night, enjoying the perfumed scent of the aloes wood. I was in a state of such pleasure that, had al-Ma'mun imagined it could be found, his longing for it would have made him rush off instantly. 'You are the most refined and witty of men,' she told me, 'and a man of outstanding culture. There is only one thing left.' 'What is that?' I asked. 'The ability to chant poetry to the lute,' she said. 'I used to be very fond of that in the old days,' I told her, 'but as I had no natural skill, I gave it up. I am still enthusiastic about it, however, and I would like now to perform well so as to bring this night to a perfect end.' 'You seem to be hinting that you would like a lute fetched,' she said. 'It is up to you,' I answered. 'You are doing the favours and it is to you that I owe thanks for this.'

She ordered a lute to be brought and when it came she sang elegantly with the sweetest of voices, plucking the strings with consummate skill. 'Do you know whose tune this is,' she asked, 'and who the poet was?' When I said no, she told me that the poet was So-and-So and that the air was by Ishaq al-Mausili. 'Bless you,' I said, 'is Ishaq really as good as this?' 'Oh, oh!' she exclaimed. 'Ishaq is the outstanding artist in this field.' 'Praise to be God,' I said, 'Who has given to this man what He has not given to anyone else!' 'Think how it would be if you could hear him sing this himself,' she said, and we went on talking like this until at daybreak an old woman, who seemed to be her nurse, came in and said: 'It is time.' At that, the girl got up and said: 'Keep our encounter secret, for meetings must be held in confidence.'

Night 281

Morning now dawned and Shahrazad broke off from what she had been allowed to say. Then, when it was the two hundred and eighty-first night, SHE CONTINUED:

I have heard, O fortunate king, that the girl said: 'Keep our encounter

secret, for meetings must be held in confidence.' ISHAQ AL-MAUSILI
WENT ON:

'May I be your ransom,' I told her. 'I didn't need to be told that.' Then
I took my leave of her and she sent a slave girl to lead me to the door of
the house. When the girl had opened it for me I left and went off to my
house, where I performed the dawn prayer and then fell asleep.

A messenger arrived from al-Ma'mun and I went off and spent the
day with him. When it was evening I thought over what had happened
on the day before, as this was an experience which none but a fool would
willingly forgo. So, after leaving the palace, I went and took my seat in
the basket and was pulled up to where I had been the day before. 'You
are zealous,' said the girl. 'No, heedless,' I replied, and we started to
talk as we had done on the previous evening, exchanging conversation,
recitations and strange tales until it was dawn. I then left, went home,
performed the dawn prayer and fell asleep. I was again summoned by
al-Ma'mun, with whom I spent the day. When it was evening, he told
me to sit where I was until he had come back from doing something.
When he had gone, leaving me, I found myself tempted by memories of
what I had enjoyed and so, ignoring the fact that I was supposed to stay
with him, I jumped up and ran off back to the basket. When I had been
pulled up and gone to her room, the girl said: 'Are you really my friend?'
'Yes, by God,' I replied. 'And are you treating this as your own house?'
'May I be your ransom,' I answered. 'The dues of hospitality extend for
three days and if I come back after that, you have the right to shed my
blood.'

We sat there as before, but when it was nearly time for me to leave I
realized that al-Ma'mun would ask me questions and would not be
satisfied unless I explained the whole story to him. So I said to the girl:
'I see that you have a great fondness for singing. I have a cousin who is
more handsome than I am, nobler and more cultured. He knows more
about Ishaq al-Mausili than any other of God's creation.' 'Are you
making importunate requests like a parasite?' she asked. 'It is for you to
decide this,' I replied, and she said: 'If your cousin is as you describe him
then I would not object to making his acquaintance.'

When the time had come for me to go, I got up and set off back to my
own house, but before I had got there al-Ma'mun's messengers pounced
on me and carried me off by force.

Night 282

Morning now dawned and Shahrazad broke off from what she had been allowed to say. Then, when it was the two hundred and eighty-second night, SHE CONTINUED:

I have heard, O fortunate king, that ISHAQ SAID:

Before I reached my house, al-Ma'mun's messengers pounced on me and carried me off by force. They brought me to him and I found him sitting on a throne. He was angry with me and asked me whether I had abandoned my allegiance to him. 'No, by God, Commander of the Faithful,' I replied. 'Then what do you have to say?' he went on. 'Tell me the truth.' 'I shall,' I promised, 'but in private.' He made a sign to those who were there and when they had retired I told him the story, adding: 'I promised her that you would visit her.' 'Well done,' he said. We spent the day enjoying our pleasures, but al-Ma'mun's heart was set on the girl and when it was time we went off. I kept warning him to avoid addressing me by name in front of her and adding: 'In her presence I shall act as your attendant.' We agreed on that and walked on to the place where the basket was. In fact, there were two baskets there and so we took our seats in them and were hauled up to the usual place. The girl came and greeted us and when al-Ma'mun saw her he was bewildered by her beauty and grace. She began to tell him stories and recite poems for him, after which she had wine brought, from which we drank. She showed interest and pleasure in him and he did the same with her. Then, after she had taken the lute and sung an air, she asked me whether 'my cousin', pointing to al-Ma'mun, was also a trader. 'Yes,' I said. 'You are very like one another,' she told me.

After al-Ma'mun had drunk three *ratls*, he was filled with joy and delight. 'O Ishaq,' he said, and I replied: 'Here I am, Commander of the Faithful.' 'Sing this air,' he told me, but when the girl realized that he was the caliph, she went off into another room. When I had finished singing, the caliph told me to find out who the owner of the house might be. An old woman quickly answered that the house belonged to al-Hasan ibn Sahl. 'Bring him to me,' ordered the caliph. The old woman went off for a time and then al-Hasan came in. 'Do you have a daughter?' the caliph asked him. 'Yes,' he said, 'she is called Khadija.' The caliph then asked if she was married, and when her father said no, he said: 'I ask you for her hand.' 'She is your slave,' her father said, 'and it is for you to dispose of her, Commander of the Faithful.' 'I will pay you thirty thousand dinars as her dowry to be brought to you this coming morning. After you have got the money, bring Khadija to me tomorrow night.' 'To hear is to obey,' said al-Hasan.

The caliph and I then left. 'Ishaq,' he said to me, 'don't tell this story to anyone,' and I kept it secret until he died. I never had such good company as I had in those four days, sitting with al-Ma'mun by day and with Khadija at night. By God, I never saw any man to match al-Ma'mun or any woman to match Khadija or to come near her in understanding, intelligence or powers of expression. God knows better.

A story is also told that at the time of the pilgrimage, when the pilgrims were circumambulating the Ka'ba in a closely packed throng, a man took hold of its covering, uttering a heartfelt prayer: 'O God, I ask You to see that she becomes angry with her husband so that I may lie with her.' A number of the pilgrims who heard this laid hands on the man and, after soundly beating him, they took him to the emir in charge of the pilgrimage. 'Emir,' they told him, 'we found this man in the holy places saying such-and-such.' The emir ordered him to be hanged, but he said: 'Emir, by the truth of the Apostle of God, may God bless him and give him peace, listen to my story and then do what you want with me.'

The emir told him to speak, and THE MAN SAID:

You must know, emir, that I am a cleaner, working in the slaughter-houses of sheep, and taking the blood and filth to the rubbish dumps. One day, when I was going with my laden donkey, I found people running away and one of them told me: 'Go into this lane or else you'll be killed.' When I asked why they were running, a eunuch told me: 'A great man's wife is coming and the eunuchs are clearing people out of the way in front of her, and are striking them with no thought for who they are.' I took my donkey into a blind alley . . .

Night 283

Morning now dawned and Shahrazad broke off from what she had been allowed to say. Then, when it was the two hundred and eighty-third night, SHE CONTINUED:

I have heard, O fortunate king, that THE MAN SAID:

I took my donkey into a blind alley and stood there waiting for the crowds to clear away. I saw eunuchs carrying sticks and with them were

about thirty women, among whom was one like the branch of a *ban* tree
or a thirsty gazelle, perfectly endowed with beauty, grace and coquetry.
The others were her attendants.

When she got to the mouth of the alley where I was standing, she
turned right and left and then summoned a eunuch. When he came, she
whispered something in his ear, after which he went up and laid hold of
me, while the people ran away. Another eunuch then came and took my
donkey away, after which my captor tied me with a rope and pulled me
along after him. I had no idea what was going on and behind us the
people were shouting: 'God does not permit this! This is a poor cleaner;
why should he be tied up with ropes?' They were telling the eunuchs:
'Show him mercy, that God may show mercy to you, and let him go.'

I said to myself: 'The eunuchs must have seized me because their
mistress was disgusted by the smell of the filth, or she may be pregnant
or sick. There is no might and no power except with God, the Exalted,
the Omnipotent.' I walked on behind the eunuchs until they arrived at
the door of a large house. They went on in and I followed until I came
to a great hall whose beauties I cannot describe, except to say that it was
furnished with magnificence. The women came in while I was still tethered to the eunuch and I told myself that they were certain to beat me
to death there and that no one would know of my fate.

After that, however, they brought me to a fine bath that was in the
hall, and while I was there, three slave girls came and sat around me.
'Take off your rags,' they told me, and so I took them off and one of the
girls started to rub my feet, while another washed my head and the third
massaged me. When they had finished, they set down a bundle of clothes
for me and told me to put them on. 'By God,' I said, 'I don't know how,'
and so they came and dressed me, laughing at me as they did it. After
that they brought flasks of rosewater, which they sprinkled over me. I
then went with them to another hall, indescribably beautiful in its pictures and furnishings. On entering I found a lady, attended by a number
of slave girls, sitting on a couch made of cane . . .

Night 284

Morning now dawned and Shahrazad broke off from what she had been
allowed to say. Then, when it was the two hundred and eighty-fourth
night, SHE CONTINUED:

I have heard, O fortunate king, that THE MAN SAID:

On entering the hall, I found a lady sitting on a couch made of cane with ivory legs. When she saw me she got up, and after she had called me to her I joined her, and when she told me to sit down I took my place beside her. She instructed the maids to bring food and they produced for me splendid dishes of all kinds of food. In all my life I had never known their names, let alone what they were like. I ate my fill, and after the plates had been cleared away and we had washed our hands, the lady ordered fruit to be brought. It was instantly produced and she told me to eat, which I did. When we had finished, she had a set of drinking glasses of varied colours brought in, and incense of all kinds was wafted from braziers. A girl like a moon got up and poured us wine to the notes of a lute's strings, and as a result I became drunk and so did the lady sitting beside me.

While all this was going on I thought that I must be dreaming, but afterwards the lady gestured to one of the girls to spread us a couch, which she did, putting it where her mistress wanted. The lady then got up and, taking me by the hand, she led me to the couch, where she and I slept together until morning. Every time I pressed her to my breast, I could smell the scent of musk and perfume coming from her, leading me to think that I was either dreaming or in Paradise.

In the morning, she asked me where I lived and I told her where it was. She then told me to leave and gave me a kerchief embroidered with gold and silver in which something was tied up. 'Use this for a visit to the baths,' she told me, and I said to myself happily: 'If there are five *flus* here, this is today's meal.' I left her as though I was leaving Paradise, and when I got to my lodging I undid the knotted kerchief and there I found fifty *mithqals* of gold. I buried this and bought bread and condiments for two *flus*, after which I ate my meal and sat by my door, thinking over what had happened to me. While I was doing this, a slave girl came up to me and said: 'My mistress wants you.' I went with her to the door of the lady's house, and after the girl had asked permission for me to enter, I went in and kissed the ground in front of the lady. She told me to be seated and, as before, she ordered food and drink to be fetched, and, as on the previous night, I slept with her.

In the morning, she gave me another kerchief containing another fifty *mithqals* of gold. I took it, left the house and went back to my lodgings, where I buried the gold. This went on for eight days; I would go to her every day in the afternoon and leave at daybreak. On the eighth night, however, while I was sleeping with her, a slave girl came running in. 'Get up,' she told me, 'and go into this room.' I did that and found that the room overlooked the road. While I was sitting there, I suddenly heard a great noise and a clatter of horses' hooves in the alley. I looked out of a window over the door and from this I saw a horse ridden by a young man like the rising moon on the night it becomes full. He was accompanied by mamluks, and attended by soldiers on foot. On reaching the door he dismounted and entered the hall, where he found the lady seated on a couch. He kissed the ground before her, and then went up and kissed her hands. She did not speak to him, but he continued to humble himself before her until he won her over, after which he slept with her that night.

Night 285

Morning now dawned and Shahrazad broke off from what she had been allowed to say. Then, when it was the two hundred and eighty-fifth night, SHE CONTINUED:

I have heard, O fortunate king, that when the lady had been won over by her husband, he slept with her that night. THE MAN WENT ON:

In the morning his men came for him and he mounted and rode out of the gate. The lady then came to me and asked: 'Did you see him?' 'Yes,' I replied. 'He is my husband,' she said, 'but I have to tell you what happened between us. One day, he and I were sitting in the garden of the house when all of a sudden he got up and left me. After a long time, finding him slow to return, I got up and went to the lavatory, thinking that he might be there. When I couldn't find him I went into the kitchen, where I asked a girl whom I found there, and she showed me my husband lying with one of the kitchen maids. At that I swore a solemn oath that I would commit adultery with the filthiest and dirtiest of men. By the time the eunuch laid hands on you, I had spent four days going round the town looking for someone to fit this description, and I hadn't come across anyone who fitted it better than you, and that was why I sought you out. What happened was decreed for us by God and I have fulfilled the oath that I swore.' Then she added: 'If my husband takes the kitchen maid and lies with her again, I'll restore to you the favours that you have enjoyed.'

When I heard what she had to say, as the arrows of her glances pierced my heart, I wept so bitterly that my eye sockets became ulcerated and I recited the following lines:

> Let me kiss your left hand ten times;
> I know how much better it is than the right.
> When you wash away your excrement,
> Your left hand is closer to the place you clean.

She then told me to leave, and this was after I had got a total of four hundred *mithqals* of gold from her, which I use for my expenses. I came here to pray to God, Glorious and Almighty, that her husband might go back again to the kitchen maid and I might go back to her.

When the emir in charge of the pilgrimage heard the man's story he let him go and told the bystanders: 'I conjure you in God's Name to pray for him, for he is to be excused.'

The story is told that one night the caliph Harun al-Rashid was very restive. He summoned his vizier, Ja'far the Barmecide, and told him that he was feeling depressed and that he wanted to go out that night to inspect the streets of Baghdad and investigate the affairs of his subjects. The two of them were to go disguised as traders so that no one might recognize them. 'To hear is to obey,' said the vizier, and getting up immediately and taking off their splendid robes, they dressed as traders. There were three of them in all, the caliph, Ja'far and Masrur, the executioner, and they walked from place to place until they came to the Tigris. There, seeing an old man sitting in a boat, they went up to him and, after greeting him, they said: 'Would you be so good as to take us for a trip in your boat in exchange for the fee of a dinar?'

Night 286

Morning now dawned and Shahrazad broke off from what she had been allowed to say. Then, when it was the two hundred and eighty-sixth night, SHE CONTINUED:

I have heard, O fortunate king, that they said to the old man: 'We would like you to take us for a trip in your boat in exchange for the fee of a dinar.'

'Who can go for a trip,' he asked them, 'when every night the caliph

Harun al-Rashid sails down the Tigris in a little barge with a herald who calls out to everyone, great and small, high and low, boys or young men, that whoever takes out a boat to sail on the Tigris will have his head struck off or will be hanged from his own mast? You can see him now, for here is his barge coming.'

The caliph and Ja'far said: '*Shaikh*, take these two dinars and bring us under one of these arches until the caliph's boat has passed.' 'Produce the gold; I put my trust in Almighty God,' he said before taking the money, and he had rowed them for a short distance when a barge came down the middle of the stream, lit with candles and lanterns. 'Didn't I tell you that the caliph sails on the river every night?' exclaimed the old man, and he prayed: 'God the Shelterer, do not remove our shelter.' He brought them under an arch and covered them with some black cloth. The three of them looked out from under this and saw in the bow of the boat a man holding a lantern of red gold in which scented aloes wood was burning. He was wearing a gown of red satin with a turban capped with Mosuli silk. He had yellow brocade on one shoulder, while hanging over the other was a bag of green silk filled with scented aloes wood, which he used instead of firewood to keep the lamp burning. At the stern was another man dressed in the same costume with a similar lamp in his hand. In the barge the caliph saw two hundred mamluks standing to the right and the left of a throne of red gold, on which sat a young man beautiful as the moon, wearing a black robe embroidered with yellow gold. In front of him was a double of the vizier Ja'far, while standing at his head was a double of Masrur, holding a drawn sword in his hand. With him were twenty companions.

When the caliph saw this, he called to Ja'far. 'Here I am, Commander of the Faithful,' Ja'far answered. 'Perhaps this is one of my sons, al-Ma'mun or al-Amin,' the caliph said. He stared at the young man seated on the throne and noted the perfection of his beauty and grace, allied to a symmetry of form. He called again to Ja'far, and when Ja'far replied he said: 'The man sitting there has all the appearance of the caliph; the one in front of him is just like you, and the other is like Masrur, while his companions are like mine. This affair baffles me . . .'

Night 287

Morning now dawned and Shahrazad broke off from what she had been allowed to say. Then, when it was the two hundred and eighty-seventh night, SHE CONTINUED:

I have heard, O fortunate king, that when the caliph saw this, he was astonished and said: 'By God, this affair astonishes me.' 'Me too, by God,' said Ja'far.

The barge passed out of sight and the old man rowed his boat out from under cover, exclaiming: 'Praise be to God that we're safe and that nobody found us!' '*Shaikh*,' asked Harun, 'does the caliph do this every night?' 'Yes, master,' said the man, 'and he has been doing it for a whole year.' Harun then asked him if he would be good enough to wait there for them on the following night in return for five gold dinars, adding: 'We are strangers who want an excursion and we are staying in the al-Khandaq quarter.' The man agreed willingly, after which the caliph, Ja'far and Masrur left him and set off for the palace. They took off their traders' clothes, and after putting on their official robes each sat down in his own place. In came the emirs, viziers, chamberlains and deputies, and the public assembly was convened.

At the end of the day, when the people of all classes had dispersed, every one going off on his own way, Harun said: 'Ja'far, come with me to look at "the second caliph".' Ja'far and Masrur laughed, and then, having dressed as merchants, they went out cheerfully, leaving by the private door. When they got to the Tigris they found the old boatman sitting waiting for them. They boarded his boat and before they had been sitting there long, the barge of 'the second caliph' came towards them. They turned and on close inspection saw that, while the torchbearers were calling out the same proclamation, the two hundred mamluks were not the same ones as before. Harun said to Ja'far: 'Had I heard of this, I wouldn't have believed it, but now I have seen it with my own eyes.' Then he said to the boatman: 'Take these ten dinars, *shaikh*, and row us on a parallel course, for they are in the light while we shall be in the darkness, and we shall be able to look at them as much as we want but they won't be able to see us.' The old man took the ten dinars and rowed alongside them in the shadow of the barge . . .

Night 288

Morning now dawned and Shahrazad broke off from what she had been allowed to say. Then, when it was the two hundred and eighty-eighth night, SHE CONTINUED:

I have heard, O fortunate king, that the caliph told the boatman to take ten dinars and row them on a parallel course to that of the barge, the boatman saying: 'To hear is to obey.' He rowed on in the shadow until he and his passengers arrived opposite orchards.

When they got there, they saw that the barge had anchored by an enclosure, where there were servants standing with a mule saddled and bridled. 'The second caliph' disembarked and after mounting the mule he moved off surrounded by his companions, with linkmen shouting and servants busying themselves in attendance on him. Harun, Ja'far and Masrur went ashore and, after making their way through the mamluks, they got ahead of them. The linkmen turned towards them, and seeing three strangers dressed as traders they pointed to them angrily. The three were brought before 'the second caliph', who looked at them and asked: 'How did you get here and what has brought you at this time?' 'Master,' they answered, 'we are traders and are strangers in these parts. We arrived today and were out for an evening stroll when we saw you coming, and then these people came and laid hands on us and brought us before you. This is our story.' 'The second caliph' said: 'Since you are strangers, no harm shall come to you, but if you were from Baghdad I would cut off your heads.' He then turned to his vizier and said: 'Take these people with you for they are our guests tonight.' 'To hear is to obey, master,' said the vizier, and he took the three to a lofty palace, magnificent and splendidly built, such as no sultan ever possessed, rising from the ground and touching the edges of the clouds. It had a door of teak inlaid with gleaming gold, leading to a hall with a tinkling fountain, and in it were carpets and pillows, together with brocaded cushions and mattresses; there were also hanging curtains and furnishings to dazzle the mind and baffle description. On the door were inscribed these lines:

Greetings and peace be to a palace
Which the days have invested with their loveliness.
In it are wonders and marvels of all kinds,
Before whose diversity pens are bewildered.

'The second caliph' entered with his entourage and sat down on a golden throne studded with jewels and covered with a rug of yellow silk. While his companions took their own seats, the executioner stood before him. Tables were spread and after they had eaten, the dishes were removed and they washed their hands. Then drinking vessels were brought; bottles and glasses were ranged in order and wine was passed around. When it reached Harun al-Rashid he refused it and 'the second caliph' asked Ja'far: 'Why isn't your friend drinking?' 'For a long time he has not drunk wine, master,' answered Ja'far. 'I have another kind of drink, made from apples, which may suit him,' the host said, and on his instructions this was immediately fetched. The man then came to Harun and told him: 'Whenever the wine comes round to you, drink from this.'

The company continued to enjoy themselves as the wine cups were passed around until the drink went to their heads and took over their wits.

Night 289

Morning now dawned and Shahrazad broke off from what she had been allowed to say. Then, when it was the two hundred and eighty-ninth night, SHE CONTINUED:

I have heard, O fortunate king, that 'the second caliph' and his companions continued to drink until the wine had gone to their heads and taken over their wits.

The caliph said to Ja'far: 'By God, we don't have cups like these. I wish I knew about this young man.' While the two of them were whispering, the man turned and, noticing what they were doing, he said: 'It's unsociable to whisper.' 'We weren't being unsociable,' said Ja'far. 'My friend here was saying that, although we have visited many lands, been intimate with great kings and associated with soldiers, we have never seen anything better organized or more splendid than what we have come across tonight. However, it is a saying of the Baghdadis that wine without music may lead to a headache.' When 'the second caliph' heard this he smiled and relaxed before striking a round gong with a staff that he held in his hand. At this a door opened and through it came a eunuch carrying an ivory chair inlaid with gleaming gold. He was followed by a girl of outstanding beauty, grace, splendour and perfection. The eunuch set the chair down and she took her seat on it like the bright sun in a cloudless sky. In her hand she was holding a lute made by Indian crafts-

men, and she placed this in her lap, bending over it like a mother with
her child. She sang to it, playing twenty-four airs with variations in such
a way as to astonish the minds of the listeners. Then she returned to the
first of these and sang the following lines as she played:

> The voice of love speaks to you from my heart,
> Telling of me that I love you.
> The burning pains of a tortured heart witness for me,
> Together with my wounded eyes and my quick-flowing tears.
> Before I loved you I did not know what love might be,
> But the fate of His creation is preordained by God.

When 'the second caliph' heard her sing these lines, he gave a great
cry and tore the robe that he was wearing down to its hem. The curtain
was lowered and his servants brought him another, more splendid than
the first, which he put on, and he sat down as before, resuming the
conversation. When the wine cup reached him he again struck the gong
with his staff and again a door opened. Out came a eunuch carrying a
golden chair, followed by another girl even more lovely than the first.
She took her seat on the chair, holding a lute that would distress the
heart of the envious and, to its accompaniment, she sang the following
lines:

> How can I endure it when my heart is on fire with longing,
> And a perpetual flood of tears flows from my eyes?
> By God, there is no pleasure in life to rejoice me.
> How can a heart be happy that is filled up with my grief?

When the young man heard these lines, he again gave a great cry and
tore his robe down to its hem. The curtain was lowered and they brought
him another one and, after having put it on, he took his seat as before
and began to talk at his ease. The next time the wine cup came to him,
he struck the gong. A eunuch came out with a chair, followed by a girl
more beautiful than the one before. She sat down holding a lute, to
which she sang these lines:

> Cut short this separation; treat me less roughly;
> I swear to you that my heart cannot forget you.
> Have pity on the emaciated lover, sad and grieving,
> Passionate and enslaved by love for you.
> Worn away by sickness through the excess of passion,

He beseeches God for your approval.
Full moon, whose place is in my heart,
How can I choose any other but you among mankind?

On hearing this, the young man again cried out and tore his robe. The curtain was lowered; he was brought a new robe and again he returned to his companions. The wine cups were passed around and when the wine reached him he struck the gong. When the door opened a servant came out with a chair. A girl, who had followed, sat down, took up a lute, tuned it and sang these lines:

How long will this separation and this hatred last
Until the joy that has passed returns to me again?
We lived together in the same country;
In our enjoyment we thought the envious paid no heed.
But time betrayed us, forcing us to part;
Leaving our dwellings like a barren waste.
You censure me; do you want me to be consoled?
My heart, I see, will not obey your voice.
Abandon blame and leave me with my love.
For love is not yet emptied from my heart.
You broke your oath and chose another love,
But, though you are away, my heart will not forget.

'The second caliph' gave a loud cry when he heard these lines, tore his clothes . . .

Night 290

Morning now dawned and Shahrazad broke off from what she had been allowed to say. Then, when it was the two hundred and ninetieth night, SHE CONTINUED:

I have heard, O fortunate king, that when 'the second caliph' heard these lines, he gave a loud cry and tore his clothes and fell down in a faint. The attendants were about to lower the curtain as usual, but its cords stuck and Harun al-Rashid had the chance to turn and look at him. On his body he saw scars of a whipping, and when he was certain of what he had seen, he exclaimed: 'By God, Ja'far, this is a handsome young man but he is also a foul thief!' 'How do you know that, Commander of the Faithful?' asked Ja'far, and the caliph replied that he had seen scars left by a flogging on his sides. The curtain was then lowered, new robes were fetched and the young man returned to sit as before with his companions.

He then turned and noticed that Harun and Ja'far were whispering together. He asked them what the matter was and Ja'far replied: 'Nothing is wrong, master, but you must know that my companion here is a merchant who has travelled through all cities and regions and has associated with kings and men of excellence. He was telling me that our lord, the caliph, has been guilty of great extravagance tonight and that he has never seen anyone else act as he has done in any other part of the world. He has torn such-and-such a number of robes, each worth thousands of dinars, and this is excessive extravagance.' 'The second caliph' replied: 'Man, the money is mine and the materials are mine. This is one of the favours that I confer on my servants and my attendants, for every robe that I tear goes to one of my companions here, and with each robe I make them a payment of five hundred dinars.' 'That is excellently done, master,' said the vizier Ja'far, and he then recited these lines:

Generous deeds have built their home in the palm of your hand,
And you have allowed all of mankind to share your wealth.
The doors of good deeds may be shut;
Your hands are a key to open them again.

When the young man heard these lines, he presented Ja'far with a thousand dinars and a robe. As the wine cups then circulated among the company and the wine was enjoyed, Harun told him to ask the young man about the marks of a beating on his body in order to see what answer he would give. 'Don't be hasty, master,' said Ja'far. 'Go gently, for patience is better.' 'By my head and by the tomb of al-'Abbas,' replied Harun, 'if you don't ask him I will have the life choked out of you.' 'Why are you and your companion whispering together?' asked the young man, turning to Ja'far. 'Tell me what is the matter with you.' 'All is well,' said Ja'far, but the young man told him: 'I ask you in the Name of God to tell me about yourselves without concealing anything.' 'Master,' replied Ja'far, 'my friend saw on your body the marks of whips and scourges. He was astonished at that, wondering how the caliph could possibly have been beaten, and he wants to know the reason for it.'

The young man smiled and said: 'Know that my story is a strange one and that the affair is so remarkable that, were it written with needles on the inner corners of the eye, it would serve as a warning to those who take heed.' Then he sighed deeply and recited these lines:

My tale is wonderful, beyond all wonders
I swear by the truth of love that the paths are closed to me.
If you wish to listen, then lend me your ears,
And let this company stay silent on every side.
Listen to these words of mine, which bear a message.
My words are true, and in them are no lies.
I am a victim of love and passion;
My murderess is more beautiful than any swelling-breasted girl.
Her dark eyes are like an Indian sword,
And from the bows of her eyebrows she shoots arrows.
My heart senses that among you is our imam,
The caliph of our age, descendant of the best of men.
The second of you is called Ja'far,
Vizier and counsellor, son of a counsellor.
The third is Masrur, sword of the caliph's vengeance.
If it turns out these words of mine are not false,
Then I have what I hoped for from this whole affair
And joy of heart arrives from every side.

When they heard this, Ja'far swore to him, using ambiguous terms, that he and his companions were not the persons mentioned, at which the young man laughed. HE SAID:

Know, sirs, that I am not the Commander of the Faithful and that I only called myself this to get what I want from the people of Baghdad. In fact, my name is Muhammad 'Ali, the jeweller. When my father, who was one of the leading men in the city, died he left me great wealth, comprising gold, silver, pearls, corals, sapphires, chrysolite, gems, landed property, baths, gardens and orchards, shops and brick works, slaves, male and female, together with servants. One day, I happened to be sitting in my shop surrounded by eunuchs and attendants when a girl came up riding on a mule, attended by three maids like moons. When she came close, she dismounted by my shop and, on taking her seat there, she asked: 'Are you Muhammad, the jeweller?' 'Yes,' I said, 'I am Muhammad, your mamluk and your slave.' 'Have you a jewelled necklace that would suit me?' she asked. 'My lady,' I answered, 'I'll show you what I have and bring it out for you. If there is anything there that you like, that will be my good fortune and if not it will be my bad luck.'

I had a hundred jewelled necklaces, all of which I showed her and none of which she liked. 'I want something finer than any of these that I have seen,' she said. As it happened, I had a small necklace that my father had bought for a hundred thousand dinars, whose like was not owned by any of the great rulers. 'My lady,' I told her, 'I still have one necklace of gemstones and jewels and no one, high or low, possesses anything to match it.' 'Show it to me,' she said. Then, when she had seen it, she said: 'This is what I am looking for and what I have wanted all my life.' She asked me the price and I said: 'My father bought it for a hundred thousand dinars.' She offered me a five-thousand-dinar profit and I said: 'My lady, the necklace and its owner are at your service, and I shall not dispute the price.' 'You have to make a profit,' she said, 'and I am deeply indebted to you.'

She then got up and, after quickly mounting her mule, she said: 'Sir, I ask you in God's Name to be good enough to come with me to fetch the purchase price, for this day that I have spent with you has been as delicious as milk.' I got up, locked the shop and went off peacefully with her until we got to her house, which, as I found, displayed all the signs of prosperity. Its door was inlaid with gold, silver and lapis lazuli and on it were inscribed these lines:

House, may no sorrow enter you, and may your owner never be
    betrayed by Time.
How good a house you are to guests, when they find shortages
    elsewhere.

My companion dismounted and went in, telling me to wait on the bench by the door for the money-changer to come. I sat there for a while until a girl came out and told me to enter the hall, adding that it was not proper for me to have to sit at the door. I got up and went in, taking my seat on a bench. Then another girl approached me and said: 'Master, my lady tells you to come in and sit by the door of the sitting room until your money is paid to you.' I followed her instructions, and after I had been sitting there for a brief moment I suddenly saw a golden chair shrouded by a silken drape, and when this was lifted, I saw beneath it the lady who had bought the necklace from me. She had unveiled a face like a rounded moon; on her neck was the necklace and at the sight of such great beauty and grace my wits left me and astonishment filled me. When she saw me she got up from the chair and hurried towards me. 'Light of my eyes,' she said, 'are all those who are as handsome as you so pitiless to those they love?' 'Lady,' I replied, 'all beauty is in you and it is part of your qualities.' 'Jeweller,' she told me, 'know that I love you but I never believed that I could get you to come to me.'

Then she bent towards me; she kissed me and I kissed her; she drew me towards her and pressed me to her breast.

Night 291

Morning now dawned and Shahrazad broke off from what she had been allowed to say. Then, when it was the two hundred and ninety-first night, SHE CONTINUED:

I have heard, O fortunate king, that THE JEWELLER SAID:

The lady bent towards me, kissed me and, drawing me towards her, she pressed me to her breast. From my condition she realized that I wanted to lie with her, but she said: 'Master, do you want to take me unlawfully? By God, may those perish who commit such sins and who take pleasure in unclean words! I am a virgin whom no man has ever approached, and I am not unknown in the city. Do you know who I am?' 'No, by God, lady,' I told her and she said: 'I am the Lady Dunya, daughter of Yahya ibn Khalid the Barmecide and my brother is Ja'far, the caliph's vizier.'

When I heard what she said, I flinched away from her and said: 'Lady, it was not my fault that I was so intrusive; it was you who made me hope for union by bringing me to you.' 'You shall come to no harm,' she replied, 'and you must have what you want, but in a way that pleases God. I am my own mistress; the *qadi* will draw up my marriage contract and it is my intention to become your wife and to have you as my husband.' She then summoned the *qadi* and the notaries and busied herself with preparations. When the officials had come she told them: 'Muhammad 'Ali, son of 'Ali the jeweller, has asked for my hand in marriage and has given me this necklace as a dowry. I am pleased to consent.' They drew up the marriage contract between us and then I went off with her.

Wine flasks were produced and the wine cups circulated in the best and most orderly sequence. When the sparkling wine had gone to our heads, the Lady Dunya told a lute girl to sing and the girl took her lute and chanted these lines to the most delightful of airs:

The beloved appeared and showed to me
In his own person a gazelle, a branch and a full moon.
Woe be to any heart he does not tempt.
God wished to quench temptation's fire
On the cheek of this handsome youth,
But another, fresh temptation then appeared.
When they talk of him I try to deceive my censurers,
Pretending that I do not like to hear his name.
When they talk of something else I listen,
But thoughts of him have caused my heart to melt.
He is the prophet of beauty, with every part a miracle,
But the supreme sign is in his face.
The mole on the surface of his cheek serves as Bilal,
Announcing the dawn prayer thanks to his gleaming face.
In their folly, the censurers want me to forget,
But I have confessed my faith and wish no infidelity.

The notes of the girl's lute strings and the delicacy of the poetry
delighted us and, one after the other, the girls performed until ten of
them had sung and recited poetry. At that point the Lady Dunya herself
took the lute and, striking up an air, she chanted these lines:

I swear by the softness of your swaying form
That I suffer fire from your parting.
Pity these entrails burning with your love,
You who are the full moon shining in dark night.
Grant me your union, for I have not ceased
To unveil your beauty in the wine glass's light,
While roses of all colours surround us,
Whose beauties bloom among the myrtle leaves.

When she had finished her poem, I took the lute from her, struck up
a strange air and sang these lines:

Praise be to God, Who has given you all beauty,
So that I have remained among your prisoners.
You whose glance enslaves all of mankind,
Pray that I may be saved from the arrows that you shoot.
Two opposites, water and a burning flash of fire,
Are found combined as a marvel in your cheeks.

For my heart you are hellfire and the delight of Paradise.
How bitter and how sweet you are for it!

My singing delighted the Lady Dunya. She dismissed her maids and we went to a most beautiful room with multi-coloured furnishings. There she took off her clothes and she and I were alone as lovers. I found her to be an unbored pearl and a filly that had never been mounted; I enjoyed her and never in my life had I experienced a sweeter night.

Night 292

Morning now dawned and Shahrazad broke off from what she had been allowed to say. Then, when it was the two hundred and ninety-second night, SHE CONTINUED:

I have heard, O fortunate king, that THE JEWELLER SAID:

When I lay with the Lady Dunya, I found her to be an unbored pearl and a filly that had never been mounted. So I recited these lines:

My arms encircled the beloved like a ringdove's collar,
And my hands made free with her veil.
This was my greatest triumph; our embrace went on;
We never wanted it to end.

I spent a whole month with her, abandoning my shop, my family and my own house. Then one day she said to me: 'My lord Muhammad, light of my eyes, today I intend to go to the baths. You must stay here on this couch and don't move from your place until I come back to you.' She made me swear to that and I said: 'To hear is to obey.' When I had taken my oath, she left with her maids for the baths. By God, my brothers, she had not got to the head of the lane before the door opened and in came an old woman who said: 'Sir, the Lady Zubaida summons you, because she has heard of your culture and wit and the beauty of your singing.' 'By God,' I told her, 'I cannot leave here until the Lady Dunya returns.' 'Don't allow the Lady Zubaida to become angry with you,' said the old woman, 'lest she become your enemy. Get up and talk to her, and then come back to your place.' So I got up immediately and set off, with the old woman leading the way, until she had brought me to the Lady Zubaida. When I came to her she said: 'Light of my eyes, are you the Lady Dunya's beloved?' 'I am your mamluk and your slave,'

I answered. 'He who described you as handsome, graceful, cultured and perfect was right. You surpass all description. Sing something so that I may listen to you.' 'To hear is to obey,' I said, and so she brought me a lute to which I sang these lines:

> The lover's heart is distressed by the beloved;
> His body is plunder seized by the hand of sickness.
> When the camels have been loaded, in the caravan
> Is a lover whose beloved is there with the travellers.
> Among your tents I entrust to God a moon
> That my heart loves although veiled from my eyes.
> She consents; she is angry; how sweet is her coquetry!
> Everything the beloved does I love.

When I had finished singing, the Lady Zubaida exclaimed: 'May God grant you health and enjoyment in your life! You combine perfection in beauty, culture and singing. So now get up and go home before the Lady Dunya comes back and becomes angry with you when she cannot find you there.' I kissed the ground before her and left, preceded by the old woman, until I reached the door from which I had left. I went in and came to the couch, to find that Dunya had returned from the baths and was asleep on it. I sat down by her feet and stroked them, but when she opened her eyes and saw me, she put her feet together and kicked me, knocking me off the couch. 'Traitor,' she said, 'you have betrayed your oath and perjured yourself. You promised me not to move from here and you broke your word by going off to the Lady Zubaida. By God, if I did not fear public disgrace, I would bring down her palace over her head.' Then she told her black slave, Sawab: 'Get up and cut off this false liar's head, for I have no need of him.' The slave came forward and blindfolded me with a strip that he had torn from the bottom of his robe. He was about to strike off my head . . .

Night 293

Morning now dawned and Shahrazad broke off from what she had been allowed to say. Then, when it was the two hundred and ninety-third night, SHE CONTINUED:

I have heard, O fortunate king, that THE JEWELLER SAID:

The slave came up and blindfolded me with a strip that he had torn from the bottom of his robe. He was about to strike off my head when the Lady Dunya's maids, old and young, went to her and said: 'Lady, he is not the first man to do something wrong. He doesn't know your nature and he has done nothing that deserves death.' 'By God,' she said, 'I must very certainly leave my mark on him.' She then gave orders that I was to be beaten. They beat me on my ribs and these were the marks of this beating that you saw.

On her orders I was then removed. They took me out of the palace and threw me down. I pulled myself together and walked a few steps at a time until I got back home. Then I sent for a surgeon and, when I had shown him my stripes, he gave me gentle treatment and did his best to cure me. I recovered and after visiting the baths, when my pains had left me, I went to my shop, where I collected all its contents and sold them. With the money that I had collected I bought four hundred mamluks such as no king had ever gathered together, two hundred of whom used to ride out with me each day. Then I had this boat built, on which I spent five thousand gold dinars. I called myself the caliph and I arranged that each one of my servants should duplicate the roles played by the caliph's own followers, seeing to it that they looked like them. I had it proclaimed that if anyone cruised on the Tigris, I would immediately have him executed. I have been doing this for a whole year now, but I have heard no news of the Lady Dunya, nor have I found any trace of her.

He then burst into floods of tears and recited these lines:

> By God, never throughout all time can I forget her,
> Nor approach anyone who cannot bring her near.
> She is formed like the full moon;
> Glory be to her Creator; glory be to Him, Who formed her.
> She has left me sad, sleepless and sick;
> My heart is at a loss to grasp her inner self.

Harun al-Rashid, on hearing this, realized the passionate intensity of Muhammad's love and was himself distracted by this. His astonishment left him bewildered and he exclaimed: 'Praise be to God, Who has assigned everything a cause!' He and his companions asked Muhammad for leave to go, and when this was granted they went off to the palace, with Harun having made up his mind to see justice done to Muhammad and to ensure that he was given the greatest gift for which he could hope.

When they had exchanged the clothes they were wearing for their court robes, he and Ja'far took their seats, with Masrur, the executioner, standing before them. He then told Ja'far: 'Fetch me the young man . . .'

Night 294

Morning now dawned and Shahrazad broke off from what she had been allowed to say. Then, when it was the two hundred and ninety-fourth night, SHE CONTINUED:

I have heard, O fortunate king, that the caliph told the vizier to 'fetch the young man whom we were with this last night'. 'To hear is to obey,' said Ja'far, who then went to the young Muhammad and ordered him to obey the summons of the caliph Harun al-Rashid. Muhammad went with him to the palace in a state of fear because he was being taken under escort, and when he entered the caliph's presence he kissed the ground before him and prayed for the perpetuation of his glory, for his good fortune, the attainment of his hopes, the continuation of his blessings and the removal of distress and misfortune. He expressed himself with the greatest eloquence, closing with the words: 'Peace be on you, Commander of the Faithful and defender of the sanctity of religion,' after which he recited these lines:

> May your door always be a Ka'ba, the goal of your people's hopes,
> And may the earth of this Ka'ba be seen on their foreheads,
> So it may be proclaimed throughout all lands:
> 'Here is the place of Abraham; the caliph is Abraham himself.'

The caliph smiled at him and returned his greeting, looking at him with favour and telling him to come nearer, after which he seated him before him. 'Muhammad,' he said to him, 'I would like you to tell me what happened to you last night, for it was a strange and marvellous affair.' Muhammad replied: 'Forgive me, Commander of the Faithful, and give me a token of security, to allay my fears and put my heart at rest.' When the caliph had promised him this, Muhammad told the whole story of what had happened from beginning to end. The caliph, realizing that here was a lover who had been parted from his beloved, asked him if he wanted his wife restored to him. 'That would be a gracious action on the part of the Commander of the Faithful,' Muhammad replied, and he recited the lines:

Kiss his fingers, for they are not fingers but keys to fortune.
Thank him for his good works, which are not good works but
　　necklaces.

Turning to Ja'far, the caliph told him to fetch his sister, the Lady
Dunya, the daughter of Yahya ibn Khalid, the vizier. 'To hear is to obey,'
said Ja'far, and he fetched her immediately. When she appeared before
the caliph, he asked her: 'Do you recognize who this is?' 'How can
women recognize men?' she said. The caliph smiled and said: 'Dunya,
this is your lover, Muhammad, son of the jeweller. I know the position:
I have heard the story from beginning to end and have understood what
lies on the surface and what is beneath it. Whatever was hidden is no
longer a secret.' The Lady Dunya said: 'That was written in the book of
fate. I ask pardon from Almighty God for what I did, and I ask you of
your grace to forgive me.' The caliph laughed and after summoning the
qadi and the notaries, he had her wedding contract to her husband
Muhammad renewed. She and he enjoyed the highest good fortune; the
envious were confounded and Muhammad became one of the caliph's
companions. They continued in the enjoyment of delectation, pleasure
and delight until they were visited by the destroyer of delights and the
parter of companions.

A story is also told that one night, when the caliph Harun al-Rashid was
feeling restless, he summoned his vizier, Ja'far the Barmecide. When he
came, the caliph said: 'Ja'far, I am very restive tonight and in a bad
humour. I want you to fetch me something to cheer and relax me.'
'Commander of the Faithful,' said Ja'far, 'I have a friend, 'Ali al-'Ajami,
who has a fund of entertaining stories that raise the spirits and remove
sorrow from the heart.' 'Bring him to me,' said the caliph, to which
Ja'far replied: 'To hear is to obey.' He left the caliph's presence to look
for 'Ali, and sent a messenger to fetch him. When 'Ali had come, Ja'far
told him of the caliph's summons. 'To hear is to obey,' 'Ali replied . . .

The story of Ali Baba and the forty thieves killed by a slave girl

In a city of Persia, on the borders of your majesty's realms, there were two brothers, one called Qasim and the other Ali Baba. These two had been left very little in the way of possessions by their father, who had divided the inheritance equally between the two of them. They should have enjoyed an equal fortune, but fate was to dispose otherwise. Qasim married a woman who, shortly after their marriage, inherited a well-stocked shop and a warehouse filled with fine goods, together with properties and estates, which all of a sudden made him so well off that he became one of the wealthiest merchants in the city. By contrast, Ali Baba had married a woman as poor as himself; he lived in great poverty and the only work he could do to help provide for himself and his children was to go out as a woodcutter in a neighbouring forest. He would then load what he had cut on to his three donkeys – these being all that he possessed – and sell it in the city.

One day, while he was in the forest and had finished chopping just enough wood to load on to his donkeys, he noticed a great cloud of dust rising up in the air and advancing straight in his direction. Looking closely, he could make out a large crowd of horsemen coming swiftly towards him. Although there was no talk of thieves in the region, nonetheless it struck him that that was just what these could be. Thinking only of his own safety and not of what could happen to his donkeys, he climbed up into a large tree, where the branches a little way up were so densely intertwined as to allow very little space between them. He positioned himself right in the middle, all the more confident that he could see without being seen, as the tree stood at the foot of an isolated rock much higher than the tree and so steep that it could not be climbed from any direction.

The large and powerful-looking horsemen, well mounted and armed, came close to the rock and dismounted. Ali Baba counted forty of them and, from their equipment and appearance, he had no doubt they were thieves. He was not mistaken, for this was what they were, and although they had caused no harm in the neighbourhood, they had assembled there before going further afield to carry out their acts of brigandage. What he saw them do next confirmed his suspicions.

Each horseman unbridled his horse, tethered it and then hung over its neck a sack of barley which had been on its back. Each then carried off his own bag and most of these seemed so heavy that Ali Baba reckoned they must be full of gold and coins.

The most prominent of the thieves, who seemed to be their captain, carried his bag like the rest and approached the rock close to Ali Baba's tree. After he had made his way through some bushes, this man was clearly heard to utter the following words: 'Open, Sesame.' No sooner had he said this than a door opened, and after he had let all his men go in before him, he too went in and the door closed.

The thieves remained for a long time inside the rock. Ali Baba was afraid that if he left his tree in order to escape, one or all of them would come out, and so he was forced to stay where he was and to wait patiently. He was tempted to climb down and seize two of the horses, mounting one and leading the other by the bridle, in the hope of reaching the city driving his three donkeys in front of him. But, as he could not be sure what would happen, he took the safest course and remained where he was.

At last the door opened again and out came the forty thieves. The captain, who had gone in last, now emerged first; after he had watched the others file past him, Ali Baba heard him close the door by pronouncing these words: 'Shut, Sesame.' Each thief returned to his horse and remounted, after bridling it and fastening his bag on to it. When the captain finally saw they were all ready to depart, he took the lead and rode off with them along the way they had come.

Ali Baba did not climb down straight away, saying to himself: 'They may have forgotten something which would make them return, and were that to happen, I would be caught.' He looked after them until they went out of sight, but he still did not get down for a long time afterwards until he felt completely safe. He had remembered the words used by the captain to make the door open and shut, and he was curious to see if they would produce the same effect for him. Pushing through the shrubs, he spotted the door which was hidden behind them, and going up to it, he said: 'Open, Sesame.' Immediately, the door opened wide.

He had expected to see a place of darkness and gloom and was surprised to find a vast and spacious manmade chamber, full of light, with a high, vaulted ceiling into which daylight poured through an opening in the top of the rock. There he saw great quantities of foodstuffs and bales of rich merchandise all piled up; there were silks and brocades, priceless carpets, and, above all, gold and coins in heaps or heaped up in sacks or in large leather bags that were piled one on top of the other. Seeing all these things, it struck him that for years, even centuries, the cave must have served as a refuge for generation upon generation of thieves. He had no hesitation about what to do next: he entered the cave and immediately the door closed behind him, but that did not worry him, for he knew the secret of how to open it again. He was not interested in the rest of the money but only in the gold coins, particularly those that were in the sacks, so he removed as much as he could carry away and load on to his three donkeys. He next rounded up the donkeys, which had wandered off, and when he had brought them up to the rock he loaded them with the sacks, which he hid by arranging firewood on top of them. When he had finished, he stood in front of the door and as soon as he uttered the words 'Shut, Sesame', the door closed, for it had closed by itself each time he had gone in and had stayed open each time he had gone out.

Having done this, Ali Baba took the road back to the city, and when he got home, he brought the donkeys into a small courtyard, carefully closing the door behind him. He removed the small amount of wood which covered the sacks and these he then took into the house, putting them down and arranging them in front of his wife, who was sitting on a sofa.

She felt the sacks and, realizing they were full of money, she suspected him of having stolen it. So when he had finished bringing them all to her, she could not help saying to him: 'Ali Baba, you can't have been so wicked as to . . . ?' 'Nonsense, wife!' Ali Baba interrupted her. 'Don't be alarmed: I'm not a thief, or at least only a thief who robs thieves. You will stop thinking ill of me when I tell you about my good fortune.' He then emptied the sacks, making a great heap of gold which quite dazzled his wife, and having done this, he told her the story of his adventure from beginning to end. When he had finished, he told her to keep everything secret.

Once his wife had recovered from her fright, she rejoiced with her husband at the good fortune which had come to them and she wanted to count all the gold that was in front of her, coin by coin. 'Wife,' said Ali Baba, 'that's not very clever: what do you think you are going to do and how long will it take you to finish counting? I am going to dig a trench and bury the gold there; we have no time to lose.' 'But it would be good if we had at least a rough idea of how much there is there,' she told him. 'I'll go and borrow some small scales from the neighbours and use them to weigh the gold while you are digging the trench.' Ali Baba objected: 'There is no point in that, and, believe me, you should leave well alone. However, do as you like, but take care to keep the secret.'

To satisfy herself, however, Ali Baba's wife went out to the house of her brother-in-law, Qasim, who lived not very far away. Qasim was not at home and so, in his absence, she spoke to his wife, asking her to lend her some scales for a short while. Her sister-in-law asked her if she wanted large scales or small scales, and Ali Baba's wife said she wanted small ones. 'Yes, of course,' her sister-in-law replied. 'Wait a moment and I will bring you some.' The sister-in-law went off to look for the scales, which she found, but knowing how poor Ali Baba was and curious to discover what sort of grain his wife wanted to weigh, she thought she would carefully apply some candle grease underneath them, which she did. She then returned and gave them to her visitor, apologizing for having made her wait and saying she had had difficulty finding them.

When Ali Baba's wife got home, she placed the scales by the pile of gold, filled them and then emptied them a little further away on the sofa, until she had finished. She was very pleased to discover how much gold she had weighed out and told her husband, who had just finished digging the trench.

Whilst Ali Baba was burying the gold, his wife, in order to show her sister-in-law how meticulous and correct she was, returned her scales to her, not noticing that a gold coin had stuck to the underside of the scales. 'Dear sister-in-law,' she said to her as she returned them to her, 'you see, I didn't keep your scales very long. I'm bringing you them back, and I'm very grateful to you.' As soon as her back was turned, Qasim's wife looked at the underside of the scales and was astonished beyond words to find a gold coin stuck there. Immediately her heart was filled with envy. 'What!' she exclaimed. 'Ali Baba has gold enough to be weighed! And where did the wretch get it from?'

As we have said, her husband, Qasim, was not at home but in his shop, from which he would only get back in the evening. So the time she had to wait for him seemed like an age, so impatient was she to tell him news which would surprise him no less than it had surprised her. When Qasim did come home, his wife said to him: 'Qasim, you may think you are rich, but you are wrong; Ali Baba has infinitely more than you; he doesn't count his money, like you – he weighs it!' Qasim demanded an explanation of this mystery and she then proceeded to enlighten him, telling him of the trick she had used to make her discovery; and she showed him the gold coin that she had found stuck to the underside of the scales – a coin so ancient that the name of the prince stamped on it was unknown to him.

Qasim, far from being pleased at his brother's good fortune, which would relieve his misery, conceived a mortal jealousy towards him and scarcely slept that night. The next morning, before even the sun had risen, he went to his brother, whom he did not treat as a real brother, having forgotten the very word since he had married the rich widow. 'Ali Baba,' he said, 'you don't say much about your affairs; you act as though you were poor, wretched and poverty-stricken but yet you have gold enough to weigh!' 'Brother,' replied Ali Baba, 'I don't know what you are talking about. Explain yourself.' 'Don't pretend to be ignorant,' said Qasim, showing him the gold coin his wife had handed to him. 'How many more coins do you have like this one, which my wife found stuck to the underside of the scales that your wife came to borrow yesterday?'

On hearing this, Ali Baba realized that, thanks to his wife's persistence, Qasim and his wife already knew what he had been so eager to keep concealed; but the damage was done and could not be repaired. Without showing the least sign of surprise or concern, he admitted everything to his brother and told him by what chance he had discovered the thieves' den and where it was, offering to give him a share in the treasure if he kept the secret. 'I will indeed claim my share,' said Qasim arrogantly, then added: 'But I also want to know precisely where this treasure is, the signs and marks of its hiding place, and how I can get in if I want to; otherwise, I shall denounce you to the authorities. If you refuse, not only will you have no hope of getting any more of it, but you will lose what you have already removed, as this will be given to me for having denounced you.' Ali Baba, more thanks to his own good nature than because he was intimidated by the insolent threats of so cruel a brother, told him everything he wanted to know, even the words to use when entering or leaving the cave.

Qasim asked no more questions but left, determined to get to the treasure before Ali Baba. Very early the next morning, before it was even light, he set out, hoping to get the treasure for himself alone. He took with him ten mules carrying large chests which he planned to fill, and he had even more chests in reserve for a second trip, depending on the number of loads he found in the cave. He took the path following Ali Baba's instructions and, drawing near to the rock, he recognized the signs and the tree in which Ali Baba had hidden. He looked for the door, found it, and said 'Open, Sesame' to make it open. When it did, he went in, and immediately it closed again. Looking around the cave, he was amazed at the sight of riches far greater than Ali Baba's account had led him to expect. The more closely he examined everything, the more his astonishment increased. Being the miser he was and fond of wealth and riches, he would have spent the whole day feasting his eyes on the sight of so much gold had he not remembered that he had come to remove it and load it on to his ten mules. He then took as many sacks as he could carry and went to open the door, but his mind was filled with thoughts far removed from what should have been of more importance to him. He found he had forgotten the necessary word and so instead of saying 'Open, Sesame', he said 'Open, Barley' and was very surprised to see that the door, rather than opening, remained shut. He went on naming various other types of grain, but not the one he needed, and still the door did not open.

Qasim had not expected this. In the great danger in which he found himself, he was so terror-stricken that, in his efforts to remember the word 'Sesame', his memory became more and more confused and soon it was as though he had never ever heard of the word. He threw down his sacks and began to stride around the cave from one side to another, no longer moved by the sight of all the riches around him. So let us now leave Qasim to bewail his fate – he does not deserve our compassion.

Towards midday, the thieves returned to their cave, and when they were a little way off, they saw Qasim's mules by the rock, laden with chests. Disturbed by this unusual sight, they advanced at full speed, scaring away the ten mules, which Qasim had neglected to tether. They had been grazing freely, and they now scattered so far into the forest that they were soon lost from sight. The thieves did not bother to run after them – it was more important for them to discover their owner. While some of them went round the rock to look for him, the captain, together with the rest, dismounted and went straight to the door, sword in hand; he pronounced the words and the door opened.

Qasim, who had heard the sound of the horses from the middle of the cave, was in no doubt that the thieves had arrived and that his last hour had come. Resolved at least to make an effort to escape from their hands and save himself, he was ready to hurl himself through the door immediately it opened. As soon as he saw it open and hearing the word 'Sesame', which he had forgotten, he rushed out headlong, flinging the captain to the ground. But he did not escape the other thieves who were standing sword in hand and who killed him on the spot.

After they had killed him, the first concern of the thieves was to enter the cave. Next to the door they found the sacks which Qasim had begun to carry off in order to load on to his mules. These they put back in their place, failing to notice what Ali Baba had previously removed. They consulted each other and discussed what had just happened, but although they could see how Qasim might have got out of the cave, what they could not imagine was how he had entered it. It struck them that he might have come down through the top of the cave, but there was nothing to show that this was what he had done, and the opening which let in the daylight was so high up and the top of the rock so inaccessible from outside that they all agreed it was incomprehensible. They could not believe that he had come in through the door, unless he knew the secret of making it open, and they were certain that no one else knew this. In this they were mistaken, unaware as they were that Ali Baba had found it out by spying on them.

They then decided that, however it was that Qasim had managed to get into the cave, it was now a question of protecting their communal riches and so they should chop his body in four and place the four pieces inside the cave near the door, two on each side, so as to terrify anyone who was bold enough to try the same thing. They themselves would only come back some time later, when the stench of the corpse had passed off. They carried out their plan, and as there was nothing else to keep them there, they left their den firmly secured, remounted their horses and went off to scour the countryside along the caravan routes, attacking and carrying out their usual highway robberies.

Qasim's wife, meanwhile, was in a state of great anxiety when she saw that night had come and her husband had not returned home. In her alarm, she went to Ali Baba and said to him: 'Brother-in-law, I believe you know well enough that your brother, Qasim, went to the forest and you know why he went there. He hasn't come back yet and as it has been dark for some time, I'm afraid that some misfortune may have befallen him.'

After the conversation that Ali Baba had had with his brother, he had suspected that he would make this trip into the forest and so he had not gone there himself that day so as not to alarm him. Without reproaching his visitor in any way which could cause offence to her or to her husband, if he was alive, he told her not to be worried yet, explaining that Qasim might well have thought fit not to come back to the city until well after dark.

Qasim's wife believed him all the more readily when she realized how important it was that her husband should act in secret. So she went home and waited patiently until midnight, but after that her fears increased and her suffering was all the more intense because she could not give vent to it nor relieve it by crying out loud, for she knew well enough that the reason for it had to remain concealed from the neighbours. The damage had been done, but she repented the foolish curiosity and blameworthy impulse which had led her to meddle in the affairs of her in-laws. She spent the night in tears, and as soon as it was light, she rushed to Ali Baba's house and told him and his wife – more through her tears than her words – what had brought her there.

For his part, Ali Baba did not wait for his sister-in-law to appeal to his kindness to find out what had happened to Qasim. Telling her to calm down, he then immediately set out with his three donkeys and made for the forest. He found no trace of his brother or of the ten mules along the way, but when he drew near the rock, he was astonished to see a pool of blood near the door. He took this for an evil omen and, standing in front of the door, he pronounced the words 'Open, Sesame'. When the door opened, he was confronted by the sorry sight of his brother's corpse, cut into four pieces. Forgetting what little fraternal love his brother had shown him, he did not hesitate in deciding to perform the last rites for his brother. He made up two bundles from the body parts that he found in the cave and these he loaded on to one of his donkeys, with firewood on top to conceal them. Then, losing no more time, he loaded the other two donkeys with sacks filled with gold, again with firewood on top, as before. As soon as he had done this and had commanded the door to shut, he set off on the path leading back to the city, but he took the precaution of stopping long enough at the edge of the forest so as to enter it only when it was dark. When he arrived home, he brought in only the two donkeys laden with the gold, leaving his wife with the job of unloading them. He told her briefly what had happened to Qasim, before leading the other donkey to his sister-in-law's house.

When he knocked at the door, it was opened by Marjana. Now this girl Ali Baba knew to be a very shrewd and clever slave who could always find a way to solve the most difficult of problems. When he had entered the courtyard, Ali Baba unloaded the firewood and the two bundles from the donkey and, taking Marjana aside, said to her: 'Marjana, the first thing I am going to ask you is an inviolable secret – you will see how necessary this is for us both, for your mistress as well as for myself. In these two bundles is the body of your master; he must be buried as though he died a natural death. Let me speak to your mistress, and listen carefully to what I say to her.'

After Marjana had told her mistress that he was there, Ali Baba, who had been following her, entered and his sister-in-law immediately cried out impatiently to him: 'Brother-in-law, what news have you of my husband? Your face tells me you have no comfort to offer me.' 'Sister-in-law,' replied Ali Baba, 'I can't tell you anything before you first promise me you will listen to me, from beginning to end, without saying a word. It is no less important to you than it is to me that what has happened should be kept a deadly secret, for your good and your peace of mind.' 'Ah!' exclaimed Qasim's wife, although without raising her voice. 'You are going to tell me that my husband is dead, but at the same time I must control myself and I understand why you are asking me to keep this a secret. So tell me; I am listening.'

Ali Baba told his sister-in-law what had happened on his trip, right up to his return with Qasim's body, adding: 'This is all very painful for you, all the more so because you so little expected it. However, although the evil cannot be remedied, if there is anything capable of comforting you, I offer to marry you and join the little God has given me to what you have. I can assure you that my wife won't be jealous and you will live happily together. If you agree, then we must think how to make it appear that my brother died of natural causes: this is something it seems to me you can entrust to Marjana, and I for my part will do everything that I can.'

What better decision could Qasim's widow take than to accept Ali Baba's proposal? With all the wealth she had inherited through the death of her first husband she had yet found someone even wealthier than herself, a husband who, thanks to the treasure he had discovered, could become richer still. So she did not refuse his offer but, on the contrary, considered the match as offering reasonable grounds for consolation. The fact that she wiped away the copious tears she had begun to shed

and stifled the piercing shrieks customary to the newly widowed made
it clear enough to Ali Baba that she had accepted his offer.

He left her in this frame of mind and returned home with his donkey,
after having instructed Marjana to carry out her task as well as she
could. She, for her part, did her best and, leaving the house at the same
time as Ali Baba, she went to a nearby apothecary's shop. She knocked
on the door and when it was opened she went in and asked for some kind
of tablets which were very effective against the most serious illnesses. The
apothecary gave her what she had paid for, asking who was ill in her
master's house. 'Ah!' she sighed heavily. 'It's Qasim himself, my dear
master! They don't know what's wrong with him; he won't speak and
he won't eat.' So saying, she went off with the tablets – which Qasim
was in no state to use.

The next morning, Marjana again went to the same apothecary and,
with tears in her eyes, asked for an essence which one usually gives the
sick only when they are at death's door. 'Alas!' she cried in great distress
as the apothecary handed it to her. 'I am very much afraid that this
remedy will have no more effect than the tablets! Ah, that I should lose
such a good master!'

For their part, Ali Baba and his wife could be seen, with sorrowful
faces, making frequent trips all day long to and from Qasim's house, so
that it was no surprise to hear, towards evening, cries and lamentations
coming from Qasim's wife, and especially from Marjana, which told of
Qasim's death.

Very early the next day, when dawn was just breaking, Marjana
left the house and went to seek out an elderly cobbler on the square
who, as she knew, was always the first to open his shop every day, long
before everyone else. She went up to him, greeted him and placed a gold
coin in his hand. Baba Mustafa, as he was known to all and sundry,
being of a naturally cheerful disposition and always ready with a joke,
looked carefully at the coin because it was not yet quite light and,
seeing it was indeed gold, exclaimed: 'That's a good start to the day!
What's all this for? And how can I help you?' 'Baba Mustafa,' Marjana
said to him, 'take whatever you need for sewing and come with me
immediately, but I will have to blindfold you when we reach a certain
place.'

When he heard this, Baba Mustafa became squeamish, saying: 'Aha!
So you want me to do something that goes against my conscience and
my honour?' Placing another gold coin in his hand, Marjana went on:

'God forbid that I should ask you to do anything which you couldn't do in all honour! Just come, and don't be afraid.'

The man allowed himself to be led by Marjana, who, after she had placed a handkerchief over his eyes at the place she had indicated, took him to the house of her late master, only removing the handkerchief once they were in the room where she had laid out the body, each quarter in its proper place. When she had removed the handkerchief, she said to him: 'Why I have brought you here is so that you can sew these pieces together. Don't waste any time, and when you have done this, I will give you another gold coin.'

When Baba Mustafa had finished, Marjana blindfolded him once more in the same room and then, after having given him the third gold coin that she had promised him, telling him to keep the secret, she took him back to the place where she had first blindfolded him. There she removed the handkerchief and let him return to his shop, watching him until he was out of sight in order to stop him retracing his steps out of curiosity to keep an eye on her.

She had heated some water with which to wash the body, and Ali Baba, who arrived just after she returned, washed it, perfumed it with incense and then wrapped it in a shroud with the customary ceremonies. The carpenter brought the coffin which Ali Baba had taken care to order, and Marjana stood at the door to receive it, to make sure that the carpenter would not notice anything. After she had paid him and sent him on his way, she helped Ali Baba to put the body into the coffin, and when Ali Baba had firmly nailed down the planks on top of it, she went to the mosque to give notice that everything was ready for the burial. The people at the mosque whose business it was to wash the bodies of the dead offered to come and perform their duty, but she told them it had already been done.

No sooner had Marjana returned than the imam and the other officials of the mosque arrived. Four neighbours had assembled there who then carried the bier on their shoulders to the cemetery, following the imam as he recited the prayers. Marjana, as the dead man's slave, followed bare-headed, weeping and wailing pitifully, violently beating her breast and tearing her hair. Ali Baba also followed, accompanied by neighbours who would step forward from time to time to take their turn to relieve the four who were carrying the bier, until they arrived at the cemetery.

As for Qasim's wife, she stayed at home grieving and uttering pitiful cries with the women of the neighbourhood who, as was the custom, hurried there whilst the funeral was taking place, adding their lamenta-tions to hers and filling the whole quarter and beyond with grief and sadness. In this way, Qasim's grisly death was carefully concealed and covered up by Ali Baba, his wife, Qasim's widow and Marjana, so that no one in the town knew anything about it or was in the least suspicious.

Three or four days after the funeral, Ali Baba moved the few items of furniture he had, together with the money he had taken from the thieves' treasure – which he brought in only at night – to the house of his brother's widow in order to set up house there. This was enough to show that he had now married his former sister-in-law, but no one showed any surprise, as such marriages are not unusual in our religion.

As for Qasim's shop, Ali Baba had a son who some time ago had finished his apprenticeship with another wealthy merchant who had always testified to his good conduct. Ali Baba gave him the shop, with the promise that if he continued to behave well, he would soon arrange an advantageous marriage for him, in keeping with his status.

Let us now leave Ali Baba to start enjoying his good fortune, and talk about the forty thieves. When they returned to their den in the forest at the time they had agreed on, they were astonished first at the absence of Qasim's body but even more so by the noticeable gaps among their piles of gold. 'We've been discovered, and if we don't take care we'll be lost,' said the captain. 'We must do something about this immediately, for otherwise bit by bit we shall lose all the riches which we and our fathers amassed with so much trouble and effort. What our loss teaches us is that the thief whom we surprised learned the secret of how to make the door open and that fortunately we arrived at the very moment he was going to come out. But he wasn't the only one – there must be someone else who found out about this. Quite apart from anything, the fact that the corpse was removed and some of our treasure taken is clear proof of this. There is nothing to show that more than two people knew the secret, however, and so now that we have killed one of them we shall have to kill the other as well. What do you think, my brave men? Isn't that what we should do?'

The band of thieves were in complete accord with their captain, and finding his proposal perfectly reasonable, they all agreed to abandon any other venture and to concentrate exclusively on this and not to give up until they had succeeded. 'I expected no less of your courage and bravery,' their captain told them. 'But before anything else, one of you who is bold, clever and enterprising must go to the city, unarmed and dressed as a traveller from foreign parts. He is to use all his skill to discover if there is any talk about the strange death of the wretch we so rightly slaughtered, in order to find out who he was and where he lived. That's what is most important for us to know, so that we don't do anything we might regret or show ourselves in a country where for a long time no one has known about us and where it is very important for us to stay unknown. Were our volunteer to make a mistake and bring back a false report rather than a true one, this could be disastrous for us. Don't you think, then, that he had better agree that, if he does this, he should be killed?'

Without waiting for the rest to vote on this, one of the thieves said: 'I agree and I glory in risking my life by taking on this task. If I don't succeed, remember at least that, for the common good of the band, I lacked neither the goodwill nor the courage.' He was warmly praised by the captain and his comrades, after which he then disguised himself in such a way that no one would take him for what he was. Leaving his comrades behind, he set out that night and saw to it that he entered the city as day was just breaking. He made for the square, where the one shop that he found open was that of Baba Mustafa.

Baba Mustafa was seated on his chair, his awl in his hand, ready to ply his trade. The robber went up to him to bid him good morning and, seeing him to be of great age, said to him: 'My good fellow, you start work very early, but you cannot possibly see clearly at your age, and even when it gets lighter, I doubt that your eyes are good enough for you to sew.' 'Whoever you are,' replied Baba Mustafa, 'you obviously don't know me. However old I may seem to you, I still have excellent eyes and you will realize the truth of this when I tell you that not long ago I sewed up a dead man in a place where the light was hardly any better than it is at the moment.' The thief was delighted to find that after his arrival he had come across someone who, as seemed certain, had, immediately and unprompted, given him the very information for which he had come.

'A dead man!' the thief exclaimed in astonishment, adding, in order to make him talk: 'What do you mean, "sewed up a dead man"? You must mean that you sewed the shroud in which he was wrapped?' 'No, no,' insisted Baba Mustafa, 'I know what I mean. You want to make me talk, but you're not going to get anything more out of me.'

The thief needed no further enlightenment to be persuaded that he had discovered what he had come to look for. Pulling out a gold coin, he placed it in Baba Mustafa's hand, saying: 'I don't want to enter into your secret, although I can assure you that I would not reveal it if you confided it to me. The only thing I ask is that you be kind enough to tell me or show me the house where you sewed up the dead man.' 'Even if I wanted to, I could not,' replied Baba Mustafa, ready to hand back the gold coin. 'Take my word. The reason is that I was led to a certain place where I was blindfolded and from there I let myself be taken right into the house. When I had finished what I had to do, I was brought back in the same way to the same place, and so you see that I cannot be of any help to you.' 'You ought at least to remember something of the path you took with your eyes blindfolded,' the thief went on. 'Come with me, I beg you, and I will blindfold you in that place, and we will go on together by the same path, taking the turns that you can remember. As every effort deserves a reward, here is another gold coin. Come, do me the favour I ask of you.' On saying this, he placed another gold coin in his hand.

Baba Mustafa was tempted by the two gold coins; he gazed at them in his hand for a while without uttering a word, thinking over what he should do. Finally, he pulled out a purse from his breast and put them there, saying to the thief: 'I can't guarantee I will remember the precise path I was led along, but since that's what you want, let's go. I will do what I can to remember it.'

To the thief's great satisfaction, Baba Mustafa rose and, without closing his shop – where there was nothing of consequence to lose – he led the thief to the place where Marjana had blindfolded him. When they arrived there, he said: 'Here is where I was blindfolded and I was turned like this, as you see.' The thief, who had his handkerchief ready, bound his eyes and then walked beside him, sometimes leading him and sometimes letting himself be led, until he came to a halt. 'I don't think I went any further,' said Baba Mustafa, and indeed he was standing before Qasim's house where Ali Baba was now living. Before he removed the handkerchief from his eyes, the thief quickly put a mark on the door with a piece of chalk which he had ready in his hand. He then removed it and asked Baba Mustafa if he knew to whom the house belonged. But Baba Mustafa replied that he could not tell him as he was not from that quarter. Seeing that he could not learn anything more, the thief thanked him for his trouble, and after he had left him to return to his shop, he himself took the path back to the forest, certain that he would be well received.

Shortly after the two of them had parted, Marjana came out of Ali Baba's house on some errand and when she returned, she noticed the mark the thief had made and stopped to examine it. 'What does this mark mean?' she asked herself. 'Does someone intend to harm my master, or is it just children playing? Well, whatever the reason, one must guard against every eventuality.' So she took a piece of chalk and, as the two or three doors on either side were similar, she marked them all in the same spot and then went inside, without telling her master or mistress what she had done.

The thief, meanwhile, had gone on until he had reached the forest, where he quickly rejoined his band. He told them of his success, exaggerating his good luck in finding right at the start the only man who would have been able to tell him what he had come to discover. They listened to what he said with great satisfaction and the captain, after praising him for the care that he had taken, addressed them all. 'Comrades,' he said, 'we have no time to lose; let us go, well armed but without making this too obvious. We must enter the town separately, one after the other, so as not to arouse suspicion, and meet in the main square, some of us coming from one side, some from the other. I myself will go and look for the house with our comrade who has just brought us such good news, in order to decide what we had better do.'

The thieves applauded their captain's speech and were soon ready to set out. They went off in twos and threes, and by walking at a reasonable distance from one another, they entered the town without arousing any suspicions. The captain and the thief who had gone there that morning were the last of them. The latter led the captain to the street where he had marked Ali Baba's house, and on coming to one of the doors which had been marked by Marjana, he pointed it out to him, telling him that that was the house. However, as they continued on their way without stopping so as not to look suspicious, the captain noticed that the next door had the same mark in the same spot. When he pointed this out to his companion and asked him if that was the door or the first one, the other was confused and did not know what to reply. His confusion increased when the two of them saw that the next four or five doors were marked in the same way. The scout swore to the captain that he had marked only one door, adding: 'I don't know who can have marked the others all in the same way, but I admit that I am too confused to be sure which is the one I marked.' The captain, seeing his plan had come to nothing, went to the main square and told his men through the first man he encountered that all their trouble had been wasted: their expedition had been useless and all they could do now was to return to their den in the forest. He led the way and they all followed in the same order in which they had set out.

When they had reassembled in the forest, he explained to them why he had made them come back. With one voice, they all declared that the scout deserved to be put to death; and indeed, he even condemned himself by admitting that he should have taken greater precautions, stoically offering his neck to the thief who came forward to cut off his head.

Since the preservation of the group meant that the wrong that had been done to them should not go unavenged, a second thief, who vowed he would do better, came forward and asked to be granted the favour of carrying out their revenge. They did this and he set out. Just as the first thief had done, he bribed Baba Mustafa, who, with his eyes blindfolded, showed him where Ali Baba's house was. The thief put a red mark on it in a less obvious spot, reckoning that this would surely distinguish the house from those which had been marked in white. But a little later, just as she had done on the day before, Marjana came out of the house and, when she returned, her sharp eyes did not fail to spot the red mark. For the same reasons as before, she made the same mark with red chalk in the same spot on all the other doors on either side.

The scout, on returning to his companions in the forest, made a point of stressing the precaution he had taken which, he claimed, was infallible and would ensure that Ali Baba's house could not be confused with the rest. The captain and his men agreed with him that this would succeed, and they made for the city in the same order, taking the same precautions as before, armed and ready to pull off the planned coup. When they arrived, the captain and the scout went straight to Ali Baba's street but encountered the same difficulty as before. The captain was indignant, while the scout found himself as confused as his predecessor had been. The captain was again forced to go back with his men, as little satisfied as on the previous day, and the scout, as the man responsible for the failure, suffered the same fate, to which he willingly submitted himself.

The captain, seeing how his band had lost two of its brave men, was afraid that more still would be lost and his band would diminish further if he continued to rely on others to tell him where the house really was. The example of the two made him realize that on such occasions his men were far better at using physical force rather than their heads. So he decided to take charge of the matter himself and went to the city, where Baba Mustafa helped him in the same way as he had helped the other two. He wasted no time placing a distinguishing mark on Ali Baba's house but examined the place very closely, passing back and forth in front of it several times so that he could not possibly mistake it.

Satisfied with his expedition and having learned what he wanted to find out, he went back to the forest. When he reached the cave where his band was waiting for him, he addressed them, saying: 'Comrades, nothing can now stop us from exacting full vengeance for the harm that has been done to us. I now know for sure the house of the man on whom revenge should fall, and on my way back I thought of such a clever way of making him experience it that no one will ever again be able to discover our hideaway or where our treasure is. This is what we have to aim for, as otherwise, instead of being of use to us, the treasure will be our downfall. To achieve this, here is what I thought of and if, when I finish explaining it, any one of you can think of a better way, he can tell us.' He went on to explain to them what he intended to do; and as they had all given him their approval, he then told them to disperse into the towns, surrounding villages and even the cities, where they were to buy nineteen mules and thirty-eight leather jars for transporting oil, one full of oil and the others empty.

Within two or three days, the thieves had collected all these. As the empty jars were a little too narrow at the top, the captain had them widened. Then, after he had made one of his men enter each of the jars, with such weapons as he thought they needed, he left open the sections of the jars that had been unstitched to allow each man to breathe freely. After that he closed them in such a way that they appeared to be full of oil. To disguise them further, he rubbed them on the outside with oil taken from the filled jar.

When all this had been done, the mules were loaded with the thirty-seven thieves – not including the captain – each hidden in one of the jars, together with the jar which was filled with oil. With the captain in the lead, they took the path to the city at the time he had decided upon and arrived at dusk, about one hour after the sun had set, as he had planned. He entered the city and went straight to Ali Baba's house, with the intention of knocking on the door and asking to spend the night there with his mules, if the master of the house would agree to it. He had no need to knock for he found Ali Baba at the door, enjoying the fresh air after his supper. After he brought his mules to a halt, the captain said to

Ali Baba: 'Sir, I have come from far away, bringing this oil to sell tomorrow in the market. I don't know where to stay at this late hour, so if it is not inconvenient to you, would you be so kind as to let me spend the night here? I would be very obliged to you.' Although in the forest Ali Baba had seen the man who was now speaking to him and had even heard his voice, how could he have recognized him as the captain of the forty thieves in his disguise as an oil merchant? 'You are very welcome, come in,' he replied, standing aside to let him in with his mules. When the man had entered, Ali Baba summoned one of his slaves and ordered him to put the mules under cover in the stable after they had been unloaded, and to give them hay and barley. He also took the trouble of going to the kitchen and ordering Marjana quickly to prepare some supper for the guest who had just arrived and to make up a bed for him in one of the rooms.

Ali Baba did even more to make his guest as welcome as possible: when he saw that the man had unloaded his mules, that the mules had been led off into the stable as he had ordered, and that he was looking for somewhere to spend the night in the open air, he went up to him in the hall where he received guests, telling him he would not allow him to sleep in the courtyard. The captain firmly refused his offer of a room, under the pretext of not wishing to inconvenience him, although in reality this was so as to be able to carry out what he planned in greater freedom, and he only accepted the offer of hospitality after repeated entreaties.

Not content with entertaining someone who wanted to kill him, Ali Baba went on to talk with him about things which he thought would please him, until Marjana brought him his supper, and he left his guest only when he had eaten his fill, saying: 'I will leave you as the master here; you have only to ask for anything you need: everything in my house is at your disposal.' The captain got up at the same time as Ali Baba and accompanied him to the door, and while Ali Baba went into the kitchen to speak to Marjana, he entered the courtyard under the pretext of going to the stable to see if his mules needed anything. Ali Baba once more told Marjana to take good care of his guest and to see he lacked for nothing, adding: 'I am going to the baths early tomorrow morning. See that my bath linen is ready – give it to Abdullah; and then make me a good beef stew to eat when I return.' Having given these orders, he then retired to bed.

Meanwhile, the captain came out of the stable and went to tell his men what they had to do. Beginning with the man in the first jar and carrying on until the last, he said to each one: 'As soon as I throw some pebbles from the room in which they have put me, cut open the jar from top to bottom with the knife you have been given and, when you come out, I shall be there.' The knives he meant were pointed and had been sharpened for this purpose.

He then returned and Marjana, seeing him standing by the kitchen door, took a lamp and led him to the room which she had prepared for him, leaving him there after having asked him if there was anything else he needed. Soon afterwards, so as not to arouse any suspicion, he put out the lamp and lay down fully dressed, ready to get up as soon as he had taken a short nap.

Marjana, remembering Ali Baba's orders, prepared his bath linen and gave it to the slave Abdullah, who had not yet gone to bed. She then put the pot on the fire to prepare the stew, but while she was removing the scum, her lamp went out. There was no more oil in the house nor were there any candles. What should she do? She had to see clearly to remove the scum, and when she told Abdullah of her quandary, he said to her: 'Don't be so worried: just take some oil from one of the jars here in the courtyard.'

Marjana thanked him for his advice and while he went off to sleep near Ali Baba's room so as to be ready to follow him to the baths, she took the oil jug and went into the courtyard. When she approached the first jar she came across, the thief hidden inside it asked: 'Is it time?' Although the man had spoken in a whisper, Marjana could easily hear his voice because the captain, as soon as he had unloaded his mules, had opened not only this jar but also all the others, to give some air to his men who, though they could still breathe, had felt very uncomfortable. Any other slave but Marjana, surprised at finding a man in the jar instead of the oil she was looking for, would have caused an uproar that could have done a lot of harm. But Marjana was of superior stock, immediately realizing the importance of keeping secret the pressing danger which threatened not only Ali Baba and his family but also herself. She grasped the need to remedy the situation swiftly and quietly, and thanks to her intelligence, she saw at once how this could be done. Restraining herself and without showing any emotion, she pretended to be the captain and replied: 'Not yet, but soon.' She went up to the next jar and was asked the same question, and she went on from jar to jar until she reached the last one, which was full of oil, always giving the same reply to the same question. In this way she discovered that her master, Ali Baba, who thought he was merely offering hospitality to an oil merchant, had let in to his house thirty-eight thieves, including the bogus oil merchant, their captain. Quickly filling her jug with oil from the last jar, she returned to the kitchen where she filled the lamp with the oil and lit it. She then took a large cooking pot and returned to the courtyard where she filled it with oil from the jar and brought the pot back and put it over the fire. She put plenty of wood underneath because the sooner the pot boiled the sooner she could carry out her plan to save the household, as there was no time to spare. At last the oil boiled; taking the pot, she went and poured enough boiling oil into each jar, from the first to the last, to smother and kill the thieves – and kill them she did.

This deed, which was worthy of Marjana's courage, was quickly and silently carried out, as she had planned, after which she returned to the kitchen with the empty pot and closed the door. She put out the fire she had lit, leaving only enough heat to finish cooking Ali Baba's stew. Finally, she blew out the lamp and remained very quiet, determined not to go to bed before watching what happened next, as far as the darkness allowed, through a kitchen window which overlooked the courtyard.

She had only to wait a quarter of an hour before the captain awoke. He got up, opened the window and looked out. Seeing no light and as the house was completely quiet, he gave the signal by throwing down pebbles, several of which, to judge by the sound, fell on the jars. He listened but heard nothing to tell him that his men were stirring. This worried him and so he threw some more pebbles for a second and then a third time. They fell on the jars and yet not one thief gave the least sign of life. He could not understand why and, alarmed by this and making as little noise as possible, he went down into the courtyard. When he went up to the first jar, intending to ask the thief, whom he thought to be alive, whether he was asleep, he was met by a whiff of burning oil coming from the jar. He then realized that his plan to kill Ali Baba and pillage his house and, if possible, carry back the stolen gold had failed. He moved on to the next jar and then all the others, one after the other, only to discover that all his men had perished in the same way. Then, on seeing how the jar which he had brought full of oil had been depleted, he realized just how he had lost the help he had been expecting. In despair at the failure of his attempt, he slipped through Ali Baba's garden gate, which led from the courtyard, and made his escape by passing from garden to garden over the walls.

After she had waited a while, Marjana, hearing no further sound and seeing that the captain had not returned, was in no doubt about what he had decided to do, as he had not tried to escape by the house door which was locked with a double bolt. She went to bed at last and fell asleep, delighted and satisfied at having so successfully ensured the safety of the whole household.

Ali Baba, meanwhile, set out before daybreak and went to the baths, followed by his slave, quite unaware of the astonishing events which had taken place in his house while he was asleep. For Marjana had not thought that she should wake him and tell him about them, as she had quite rightly realized she had no time to lose at the moment of danger and that it was pointless to disturb him after the danger had passed.

By the time Ali Baba had returned home from the baths, the sun had already risen, and when Marjana came to open the door for him, he was surprised to see that the jars of oil were still in their place and that the merchant had not gone to the market with his mules. He asked her why this was, for Marjana had left things just as they were for him to see, so that the sight of them could explain to him more effectively what she had done to save him. 'My good master,' Marjana replied, 'may God preserve you and all your household! You will understand better what you want to know when you have seen what I have to show you. Please come with me.' Ali Baba followed her and, after shutting the door, she led him to the first jar. 'Look inside,' she said, 'and see if there is any oil there.' Ali Baba looked, but seeing a man in the jar, he drew back in fright, uttering a loud cry. 'Don't be afraid,' said Marjana. 'The man you see won't do you any harm. He has done some damage but is no longer in a condition to do any more, either to you or to anyone else – he's no longer alive.' 'Marjana,' exclaimed Ali Baba, 'what is all this that you have just shown me? Explain to me.' 'I will tell you,' she replied, 'but control your astonishment and don't stir up the curiosity of your neighbours, lest they find out something that is very important for you to keep secret. But come and see the other jars first.'

Ali Baba looked into the other jars one after the other, from the first to the last one, in which he could see that the oil level was now much lower. After looking, he stood motionless, saying not a word but staring now at the jars, now at Marjana, so great was his astonishment. At last, as if he had finally recovered his speech, he asked: 'But what has become of the merchant?' 'The merchant,' replied Marjana, 'is no more a merchant than I am. I will tell you who he is and what has become of him. But you will learn the full story more comfortably in your own room, as it's time, for the sake of your health, to have some stew after your visit to the baths.'

While Ali Baba returned to his room, Marjana went to the kitchen to fetch the stew. When she brought it to him, he said to her before eating it: 'Satisfy my impatience and tell me this extraordinary story at once and in every detail.'

Obediently, Marjana began: 'Master, last night, when you had gone to bed, I prepared your linen for the bath, as you had told me, and I gave it to Abdullah. I then put the stew pot on the fire, but while I was removing the scum, the lamp suddenly went out for lack of oil. There was not a drop of oil left in the jug, and so I went to look for some candle ends but couldn't find any. Seeing me in such a fix, Abdullah reminded me of the jars in the courtyard which we both believed, as you did yourself, were full of oil. I took the jug and ran to the nearest one, but when I got to it, a voice came from inside, asking: "Is it time?" I wasn't startled, for I realized at once the bogus merchant's malicious intent, and I promptly replied: "Not yet, but soon." I went to the next jar and a second voice asked me the same question, to which I gave the same reply. I went from jar to jar, one after the other, and each time came the same question and I gave the same answer. It was only in the last jar that I found any oil and I filled my jug from it. When I considered that there were thirty-seven thieves in the middle of your courtyard, just waiting for the signal from their captain – whom you had taken for a merchant and had received so warmly – to set your house alight, I lost no time. I took the jar, lit the lamp and, taking the largest cooking pot in the kitchen, I went and filled it with oil. I put the pot over the fire and when the oil was boiling hot, I went and poured some into each of the jars where the thieves were. This was enough to stop them carrying out their plan to destroy us, and when my plan succeeded, I went back to the kitchen and put out the lamp. Then, before going to bed, I quietly went and stood by the window to see what the bogus oil merchant would do. A short time later, I heard him throw some pebbles from his window down on to the jars, as a signal. He did this twice or thrice and then, as he could neither see nor hear any movement coming from below, he came down and I saw him go from jar to jar, until after he had reached the last one, I lost sight of him because of the darkness. I kept watch for some time after that and, when he didn't return, I was sure he must have escaped through the garden, in despair at his failure. Convinced that the household was now quite safe, I went to bed.'

Having completed her account, Marjana added: 'This is the story you asked me to tell you and I am certain it all follows from something I noticed two or three days ago which I didn't think I needed to tell you. Early one morning, as I came back from the city, I saw that there was a white mark on our street door and next day there was a red mark next to it. I didn't know why this was and so on both occasions I went and marked two or three doors next to us up and down the street in the same way and in the same spot. If you add this to what has just happened, you will see that it was all a plot by the thieves of the forest who, for some reason, have lost two of their number. Be that as it may, they have now been reduced to three, at the most. This goes to show that they have sworn to do away with you and that you had better be on your guard as long as we can be sure that there is even one left alive. For my part,' she concluded, 'I will do everything I can to watch over your safety, as is my duty.'

When she had finished, Ali Baba, realizing how much he owed to her, said: 'I will not die before rewarding you as you deserve, for I owe my life to you. As a token of my gratitude, I shall start by giving you your freedom as of this moment, until I can reward you properly in the way I have in mind. I, too, am persuaded that the forty thieves set this ambush up for me, but through your hands God has saved me. May He continue to preserve me from their wickedness and, by warding off their wickedness from me, may He deliver the world from their persecution and their vile breed. What we must now do is immediately to bury the bodies of these pests of the human race, in complete secrecy, so that no one will suspect what has happened. That's what I'm going to work on with Abdullah.'

Ali Baba's garden was very long and at the end of it were some large trees. Without further delay, he went with Abdullah and together they dug a trench under the trees, long enough and wide enough for all the bodies they had to bury. The earth was easy to work, so that the job was soon completed. They then pulled the bodies out of the jars and, after removing the weapons with which the thieves were armed, they took the bodies to the bottom of the garden and laid them in the trench. After they had covered them with the soil from the trench, they scattered the rest of it around so that the ground seemed the same as before. Ali Baba carefully hid the oil jars and the weapons; while, as for the mules, for which he had no further use, he sent them at different times to the market, where he got his slave to sell them.

While Ali Baba was taking all these measures to stop people discovering how he had become so rich in such a short time, the captain of the thieves had returned to the forest in a state of unimaginable mortification. In his agitation, confused by so unexpected a disaster, he returned to the cave, having come to no decision about how or what he should or should not do to Ali Baba.

The solitude in which he found himself in this place seemed horrible to him. 'Brave lads,' he cried out, 'companions of my vigils, my struggles and adventures, where are you? What will I do without you? Have I chosen you and collected you together only to see you perish all at once by a fate so deadly and so unworthy of your courage? Had you died sword in hand like brave men, I would regret your death. When will I ever be able to get together another band of hardy men like you again? And even if I wanted to, could I do so without exposing so much gold, silver and riches to the mercy of someone who has already enriched himself with part of it? No, I could not and should not think of it before I have first got rid of him. I shall do by myself what I have not been able to do with such powerful assistance. When I have seen to it that this treasure is no longer exposed to being plundered, I will ensure that after me it will stay neither without successor nor without a master; rather, that it may be preserved and increase for all posterity.' Having made this resolution, he did not worry about how to carry it out; and so, full of hope and with a quiet mind, he went to sleep and spent a peaceful night.

The next morning, having woken up very early as he had intended, he put on new clothes of a kind suitable for his plan and went to the city, where he took up lodgings in a *khan*. Expecting that what had happened at Ali Baba's house might have caused some uproar, he asked the doorkeeper in the course of his conversation what news there was in the city, to which the doorkeeper replied by telling him all sorts of things, but not what he needed to know. From that, he decided that Ali Baba must be guarding his great secret because he did not want the fact that he knew about the treasure and how to get to it to be spread abroad. Ali Baba, for his part, was well aware that it was for this reason that his life was in jeopardy.

This encouraged the captain to do everything he could to get rid of Ali Baba by the same secret means. He provided himself with a horse and used it to transport to his lodgings various kinds of rich cloths and fine fabrics which he brought from the forest in several trips, taking the necessary precautions to conceal the place from where he was taking them. When he had got what he thought enough, he looked for a shop and having found one, he hired it from the proprietor, filled it with his stock and established himself there. Now the shop opposite this one used to belong to Qasim and had recently been occupied by Ali Baba's son. The captain, who had taken the name of Khawaja Husain, soon exchanged courtesies with the neighbouring merchants, as was the custom. Since Ali Baba's son was young and handsome and did not lack intelligence, the captain frequently had occasion to speak to him, as he did to the other merchants, and soon made friends with him. He even took to cultivating him more assiduously when, three or four days after he had established himself there, he recognized Ali Baba, who had come to see his son and talk with him, as he did from time to time. He later learned from the son, after Ali Baba had left, that this was his father. So he cultivated him all the more, flattered him and gave him small gifts, entertaining him and on several occasions inviting him to eat with him.

Ali Baba's son did not want to be under so many obligations to Khawaja Husain without being able to return them. But his lodgings were cramped and he was not well off enough to entertain him as he wished. He talked about this to his father, pointing out to him that it was not proper to let Khawaja Husain's courtesies remain unrecognized for much longer.

Ali Baba was delighted to take on the task of entertaining him himself. 'My son,' he said, 'tomorrow is Friday. As it is a day when the big merchants like Khawaja Husain and yourself keep their shops closed, arrange to take a stroll with him after dinner; when you return, arrange it so that you bring him past my house and make him come in. It's better to do it this way than if you were to invite him formally. I shall go and order Marjana to prepare the supper and have it ready.'

On Friday, Ali Baba's son and Khawaja Husain met after dinner at their agreed rendezvous and went on their walk. As they returned, Ali Baba's son carefully made Khawaja Husain pass down the street where his father lived, and when they came to the house door, he stopped and said to him, as he knocked: 'This is my father's house. When I told him about the friendship with which you have honoured me, he told me to see to it that you honoured him with your acquaintance. I beg you to add this pleasure to all the others for which I am already indebted to you.' Although Khawaja Husain had got what he wanted, which was to enter Ali Baba's house and murder him without endangering his own life and without causing a stir, nevertheless he made his excuses and pretended to be about to take leave of the son. But as Ali Baba's slave had just opened the door, the son seized him by the hand and, going in first, pulled him forcibly after him, as if in spite of himself.

Ali Baba met Khawaja Husain with a smiling face and gave him all the welcome he could wish for. He thanked him for the kindness he had shown to his son, adding: 'The debt he and I owe you is all the greater, since he is a young man still inexperienced in the ways of the world and you are not above helping instruct him in these.' Khawaja Husain returned the compliment by assuring him that though some old men might have more experience than his son, the latter had enough good sense to serve in place of the experience of very many others.

After talking for a short while on unimportant matters, Khawaja Husain wanted to take his leave, but Ali Baba stopped him, saying: 'My dear sir, where do you want to go? Please do me the honour of dining with me. The meal I would like to offer you is much inferior to what you deserve but, such as it is, I hope that you will accept it in the same spirit in which I offer it to you.' 'Dear sir,' Khawaja Husain rejoined, 'I know you mean well. If I ask you not to think ill of me for leaving without accepting this kind offer of yours, I beg you to believe me that I don't do this out of disrespect or discourtesy. I have a reason which you would appreciate, if you knew it.' 'And may I ask what this can be?' said Ali Baba. 'Yes, I can tell you what it is: it is that I don't eat meat or stew which contains salt. Just think how embarrassed I would be, eating at your table.' 'If that's the only reason,' Ali Baba replied, 'it should not deprive me of the honour of having you to supper, unless you wish it. First, there's no salt in the bread which we have in my house; and as for the meat and the stews, I promise you there won't be any in what will be served you. I shall go and give the order, and so, please be good enough to stay, as I shall be back in a moment.'

Ali Baba went to the kitchen and told Marjana not to put any salt on the meat she was going to serve and immediately to prepare two or three extra stews, in addition to those he had ordered, and these were to be unsalted. Marjana, who was ready to serve the meal, could not stop herself showing annoyance at this new order and having it out with Ali Baba. 'Who is this awkward fellow, who doesn't eat salt? Your supper will no longer be fit to eat if I serve it later.' 'Don't be angry, Marjana,' Ali Baba continued. 'He's perfectly all right. Just do as I tell you.'

Marjana reluctantly obeyed, and, curious to discover who this man was who did not eat salt, when she had finished and Abdullah had set the table, she helped him to carry in the dishes. When she saw Khawaja Husain, she immediately recognized him as the captain of the thieves, in spite of his disguise. Looking at him closely, she noticed that he had a dagger hidden under his clothes. 'I am no longer surprised the wretch doesn't want to eat salt with my master,' she said to herself, 'for he is his bitterest enemy and wants to murder him, but I am going to stop him.'

When Marjana had finished serving and letting Abdullah serve, she used the time while they were eating to make the necessary preparations to carry out a most audacious scheme. She had just finished by the time Abdullah came to ask her to serve the fruit, which she then brought and served as soon as Abdullah had cleared the table. Next to Ali Baba she placed a small side table on which she put the wine together with three cups. As she went out, she took Abdullah with her as though they were going to have supper together, leaving Ali Baba, as usual, free to talk, to enjoy the company of his guest and to give him plenty to drink.

It was then that the so-called Khawaja Husain, or rather the captain of the thieves, decided that the moment had come for him to kill Ali Baba. 'I shall get both father and son drunk,' he said to himself, 'and the son, whose life I am willing to spare, won't stop me plunging the dagger into his father's heart. I will then escape through the garden, as I did earlier, before the cook and the slave have finished their supper, or it may be that they will have fallen asleep in the kitchen.'

Instead of having supper, however, Marjana, who had seen through his evil plan, gave him no time to carry out his wicked deed. She put on a dancer's costume, with the proper headdress, and around her waist she tied a belt of gilded silver to which she attached a dagger whose sheath and handle were of the same metal. Finally, she covered her face with a very beautiful mask. Disguised in this manner, she said to Abdullah: 'Abdullah, take your tambourine and let us offer our master's guest and his son's friend the entertainment we sometimes give our master.' Abdullah took the tambourine and began to play as he walked into the room in front of Marjana. Marjana, who followed him, made a deep bow with a deliberate air so as to draw attention to herself, as though asking permission to show what she could do. Seeing that Ali Baba wanted to say something, Abdullah stopped playing his tambourine. 'Come in, Marjana, come in,' said Ali Baba. 'Khawaja Husain will judge what you are capable of and will tell us his opinion. But don't think, sir,' he said, turning to his guest, 'that I have put myself to any expense in offering you this entertainment. I have it in my own home, and as you can see, it is my slave and my cook and housekeeper who provide me with it. I hope you won't find it disagreeable.'

Khawaja Husain, who had not expected Ali Baba to add this entertainment to the supper, was afraid that he would not be able to use the opportunity he thought he had found. But he consoled himself with the hope that, if that happened, another opportunity would arise later if he continued to cultivate the friendship of the father and son. So, although he would have preferred to have done without what was being offered, he still pretended to be grateful, and he courteously indicated that what pleased his host would please him too.

When Abdullah saw that Ali Baba and Khawaja Husain had stopped talking, he began to play his tambourine again and accompanied his playing by singing a dance tune. Marjana, who could dance as well as any professional, performed so admirably that she would have aroused the admiration of any company and not only her present audience, although the so-called Khawaja Husain paid very little attention. After she had danced several dances with the same charm and vigour, she finally drew out the dagger. Holding it in her hand, she then performed a dance in which she surpassed herself with different figures, light movements, astonishing leaps of marvellous energy, now holding the dagger in front, as though to strike, now pretending to plunge it into her own chest. At last, now out of breath, with her left hand she snatched the tambourine from Abdullah and, holding the dagger in her right, she went to present the tambourine to Ali Baba, its bowl uppermost in imitation of the male and female professional dancers who do this to ask for contributions from their spectators.

Ali Baba threw a gold coin into Marjana's tambourine and, following his father's example, so did his son. Khawaja Husain, seeing she was coming to him too, had already pulled out his purse from his breast to present his offering and was putting his hand out at the very moment that Marjana, with a courage worthy of the firmness and resolve she had shown up till then, plunged the dagger right into his heart and did not pull it out again until he had breathed his last. Terrified by this, Ali Baba and his son both cried out. 'Wretched girl, what have you done?' shouted Ali Baba. 'Do you want to destroy us, my family and myself?' 'I didn't do it to destroy you,' replied Marjana. 'I did it to save you.'

Opening Khawaja Husain's robe, Marjana showed Ali Baba the dagger with which he was armed. 'See what a fine enemy you've been dealing with!' she said. 'Look carefully at his face and you will recognize the bogus oil merchant and the captain of the forty thieves. Remember how he didn't want to eat salt with you – do you need anything more to convince you that he was planning evil? The moment you told me you had such a guest, before I had even seen him I became suspicious. I then set eyes on him and you can see how my suspicions were not unfounded.'

Ali Baba, recognizing the new obligation he was under to Marjana for having saved his life a second time, embraced her and said: 'When I gave you your freedom, I promised you that my gratitude would not stop there but that I would soon add the final touch to my promise. The time has now come and I will make you my daughter-in-law.' Turning to his son, he said: 'I believe you are a dutiful enough son not to find it strange that I am giving you Marjana as a wife without consulting you. You are no less obliged to her than I am. You can see that Khawaja Husain only made friends with you in order to make it easier for him to murder me treacherously. Had he succeeded, you can be sure that you also would have been sacrificed to his vengeance. Consider, too, that if you take Marjana you will be marrying someone who, as long as we both live, will be the prop and mainstay of my family and yours.' Ali Baba's son, far from showing any displeasure, gave his consent, not only because he did not want to disobey his father but because his own inclinations led in that direction.

Their next concern was to bury the body of the captain by the corpses of the thirty-seven thieves. This was done so secretly that no one knew about it until many years later, when there was no longer any interest in this memorable tale becoming known.

A few days later, Ali Baba celebrated the wedding of his son to Marjana, with a solemn ceremony and a sumptuous banquet which was accompanied by the customary dances, spectacles and entertainments. The friends and neighbours whom he had invited were not told the real reason for the marriage, but they were well acquainted with Marjana's many excellent qualities and Ali Baba had the great satisfaction of finding that they were loud in their praises for his generosity and good-heartedness.

After the wedding, Ali Baba continued to stay away from the cave in the forest. He had not been there since he had taken away the body of his brother, Qasim, together with the gold, which he had loaded on to his three donkeys. This had been out of fear that he would find the thieves there and would fall into their hands. Even after thirty-eight of them, including their captain, had died, he still did not go back, believing that the remaining two, of whose fate he was ignorant, were still alive. But when a year had gone by, seeing that nothing had occurred to cause him any disquiet, he was curious enough to make the trip, taking the necessary precautions to ensure his safety. He mounted his horse and, on approaching the cave, he took it as a good sign that he could see no trace of men or horses. He dismounted, tied up his own horse and, standing in front of the door, he uttered these words – which he had not forgotten: 'Open, Sesame.' The door opened and he entered. The state in which he found everything in the cave led him to conclude that, since around the time when the so-called Khawaja Husain had come to rent a shop in the city, no one had been there and so the band of forty thieves must all since have scattered and been wiped out. He was now certain that he was the only person in the world who knew the secret of how to open the cave and that its treasure was at his disposal. He had a bag with him which he filled with as much gold as his horse could carry, and then returned to the city.

Later he took his son to the cave and taught him the secret of how to enter it and, in time, the two of them passed this on to their descendants. They lived in great splendour, being held in honour as the leading dignitaries in the city. They had profited from their good fortune but used it with restraint.

When she had finished telling this story to King Shahriyar, Shahrazad, seeing it was not yet light, began to recount the story we are now going to hear.

Glossary

Many of the Arabic terms used in the translation are to be found in *The Oxford English Dictionary*, including 'dinar', 'ghazi' and 'jinn'. Of these the commonest – 'emir' and 'vizier', for instance – are not entered in italics in the text and, in general, are not glossed here. Equivalents are not given for coins or units of measure as these have varied throughout the Muslim world in accordance with time and place. The prefix 'al-' (equivalent to 'the') is discounted in the alphabetical listing; hence 'al-Mansur' is entered under 'M'. Please note that only the most significant terms and figures, or ones mentioned repeatedly, are covered here.

al-ʿAbbas   *see* ʿAbbasids.

ʿAbbasids   the dynasty of Sunni Muslim caliphs who reigned in Baghdad, and for a while in Samarra, over the heartlands of Islam, from 750 until 1258. They took their name from al-ʿAbbas (d. 653), uncle of the Prophet. From the late ninth century onwards, ʿAbbasid rule was nominal as the caliphs were dominated by military protectors.

ʿAbd Allah ibn Abi Qilaba   the discoverer of the legendary city of Iram.

ʿAbd al-Malik ibn Marwan   the fifth of the Umaiyad caliphs (r. 685–705).

ʿAbd al-Qadir al-Jilani   (*c.*1077–1166) a Sufi writer and saint.

Abu Bakr al-Siddiq   after the death of the Prophet, Abu Bakr was the first to become caliph (r. 632–4). He was famed for his austere piety.

Abu Hanifa   (699–767) a theologian and jurist; founder of the Hanafi school of Sunni religious law.

Abu Hazim   an eighth-century preacher and ascetic.

Abu Jaʿfar al-Mansur   *see* al-Mansur.

Abu Muhammad al-Battal   a legendary hero of popular tales, in which he plays the part of a master of wiles.

Abu Murra   literally, 'the father of bitterness', meaning the devil.

Abu Nuwas   Abu Nuwas al-Hasan ibn Hani (*c.*755–*c.*813), a famous, or notorious, poet of the ʿAbbasid period, best known for his poems devoted to love, wine and hunting.

Abu Tammam   (*c.*805–45) a poet and anthologist of the ʿAbbasid period.

ʿAd   the race of ʿAd were a pre-Islamic tribe who rejected the prophet Hud and who consequently were punished by God for their impiety and arrogance.

'Adi ibn Zaid (d. *c.*600) a Christian poet in Hira.

Ahmad ibn Hanbal (780–855) a *hadith* scholar (student of traditions concerning the Prophet) and a legal authority; founder of the Hanbali school of Sunni religious law.

al-Ahnaf al-Ahnaf Abu Bakr ibn Qais, a *shaikh* of the tribe of Tamim. A leading general in the Arab conquests of Iran and Central Asia in the seventh century, he also had many wise sayings attributed to him.

'A'isha (d. 687) the third and favourite wife of the Prophet.

'Ali 'Ali ibn Abi Talib, cousin of the Prophet and his son-in-law by virtue of his marriage to Fatima. In 656, he became the fourth caliph and in 661 he was assassinated.

'Ali Zain al-'Abidin Zain al-'Abidin meaning 'Ornament of the Believers' (d. 712), the son of Husain and grandson of the caliph 'Ali, he was recognized as one of the Shi'i imams.

alif the first letter of the Arabic alphabet. It takes the shape of a slender vertical line.

Allahu akbar! 'God is the greatest!' A frequently used exclamation of astonishment or pleasure.

aloe aloe was imported from the Orient and the juice of its leaves was used for making a bitter purgative drug.

aloes wood the heartwood of a South-east Asian tree, it is one of the most precious woods, being chiefly prized for its pleasant scent.

al-Amin Muhammad al-Amin ibn Zubaida (d. 813), the son of Harun al-Rashid, succeeding him as caliph and reigning 809–13. He had a reputation as an indolent pleasure lover.

al-Anbari Abu Bakr ibn Muhammad al-Anbari (855–940), *hadith* scholar and philologist.

'Antar 'Antar ibn Shaddad, legendary warrior and poet of the pre-Islamic period who became the hero of a medieval heroic saga bearing his name.

ardabb a dry measure.

Ardashir the name of several pre-Islamic Sasanian kings of Persia. A great deal of early Persian wisdom literature was attributed to Ardashir I (d. 241) and there were many legends about his early years and his reign.

al-Asma'i (740–828?) an expert on the Arabic language and compiler of a famous anthology of Arabic poetry. Harun al-Rashid brought him from Basra to Baghdad in order to tutor his two sons, al-Amin and al-Ma'mun.

'Atiya *see* Jarir ibn 'Atiya.

'aun a powerful *jinni*.

Avicenna the Western version of the Arab name Ibn Sina (980–1037), a Persian physician and philosopher, the most eminent of his time, whose most famous works include *The Book of Healing* and *The Canon of Medicine*.

balila stewed maize or wheat.

ban tree Oriental willow.

banj   frequently used as a generic term referring to a narcotic or knock-out drug, but sometimes the word specifically refers to henbane.

banu   literally, 'sons of', a term used to identify tribes or clans, e.g. the Banu Quraish.

Barmecides   *see* Harun al-Rashid, Ja'far.

Bilal   an Ethiopian contemporary of the Prophet and early convert to Islam. The Prophet appointed him to be the first muezzin.

Bishr al-Hafi   al-Hafi meaning 'the man who walks barefoot' (767–841), a famous Sufi.

bulbul   Eastern song thrush.

Chosroe   in Persian 'Khusraw', in Arabic 'Kisra' – the name of several pre-Islamic Sasanian kings of Persia, including Chosroe Anurshirwan – 'the blessed' (r. 531–79).

Dailamis   Dailam is a mountainous region to the south of the Caspian Sea whose men were celebrated as warriors.

daniq   a medieval Islamic coin equivalent to a sixth of a dirham.

dhikr   a religious recitation, particularly a Sufi practice.

dhimmi   a non-Muslim subject, usually a Christian or a Jew, living under Muslim rule.

Di'bil al-Khuza'i   (765–860) a poet and philologist who lived in Iraq and who was famous for his satirical and invective poetry.

dinar   a gold coin. It can also be a measure of weight.

dirham   a silver coin, approximately a twentieth of a dinar.

diwan   council of state, council hall or reception room.

fals   plural *flus*, a low-value copper coin.

faqih   a jurisprudent, an expert in Islamic law.

faqir   literally, 'a poor man', the term also is used to refer to a Sufi or Muslim ascetic.

al-Fath ibn Khaqan   (d. 861) the caliph al-Mutawwakil's adoptive brother, chief scribe and general.

Fatiha   literally, the 'opening'; the first *sura* (chapter) of the Quran.

Fatima   (d. 633) daughter of the Prophet. She married 'Ali ibn Abi Talib. The Fatimid caliphs of Egypt, whose dynasty lasted from 909 to 1171, claimed descent from her.

fidda   silver, a small silver coin.

flus   see fals.

ghazi   a holy warrior, a slayer of infidels or participant on a raiding expedition.

ghul   a cannibalistic monster. A *ghula* is a female *ghul*.

Gog and Magog   evil tribes dwelling in a distant region. According to legend, Alexander the Great built a wall to keep them from invading the civilized parts of the earth, but in the Last Days they will break through that wall.

hadith   a saying concerning the words or deeds of the Prophet or his companions.

Hafsa daughter of 'Umar ibn al-Khattab, she married the Prophet in 623 and died in 665.

hajj the annual pilgrimage to Mecca.

al-Hajjaj ibn Yusuf al-Thaqafi (*c.*661–714) a governor of Iraq for the Umaiyad caliph 'Abd al-Malik ibn Marwan, he was notorious for his harshness, but famous for his oratory.

al-Hakim bi-amri-'llah Fatimid caliph in Egypt (r. 996–1021), he was notorious for his eccentricities and capricious cruelty. After his murder, he became a focus of Druze devotion.

al-Hariri (1054–1122) a poet, prose writer and government official. He is chiefly famous for his prose masterpiece, the *Maqamat*, a series of sketches involving an eloquently plausible rogue.

Harun al-Rashid (766–809) the fifth of the 'Abbasid caliphs, reigning from 786. In Baghdad, he presided over an efflorescence of literature and science and his court became a magnet for poets, musicians and scholars. Until 803, the administration was largely in the hands of a Persian clan, the Barmecides, but in that year, for reasons that are mysterious, he had them purged. After his death, civil war broke out between his two sons, al-Amin and al-Ma'mun. In retrospect, Harun's caliphate came to be looked upon as a golden age and in the centuries that followed numerous stories were attached to his name.

Harut a fallen angel who, together with another fallen angel, Marut, instructed men in the occult sciences (Quran 2.102).

Hasan of Basra Hasan ibn Abi'l-Hasan of Basra (642–728), a preacher and early Sufi ascetic to whom many moralizing sayings were attributed.

Hatim of Tayy a pre-Islamic poet of the sixth century, famed for his chivalry and his generosity. Many anecdotes and proverbs have been attributed to him.

hijri **calendar** the Muslim calendar, dating from the Hijra, or year of Muhammad's emigration from Mecca to Medina, each year being designated AH – *anno Hegirae* or 'in the year of the Hijra'.

Himyar a pre-Islamic kingdom in southern Arabia.

Hind India.

Hisham ibn 'Abd al-Malik the tenth of the Umaiyad caliphs (r. 724–43).

houri a nymph of the Muslim Paradise. Also a great beauty.

Iblis the devil.

Ibn 'Abbas 'Abd Allah ibn al-'Abbas (625–86 or 688), a cousin of the Prophet and transmitter of many traditions concerning him.

Ibn Zubair 'Abd Allah ibn Zubair (624–92), a grandson of the Prophet and a leading opponent of the Umaiyads. He was besieged by the Umaiyad caliph 'Abd al-Malik in Mecca (where the Ka'ba is situated) and he was eventually killed.

Ibrahim Abu Ishaq al-Mausili (742–804) a famous musician and father of the no less famous musician Ishaq al-Mausili. Like his son, he features in a number of *Nights* stories.

Ibrahim ibn Adham (730–77) a famous Sufi ascetic.

Ibrahim ibn al-Mahdi (779–839) the son of the caliph al-Mahdi and brother of Harun al-Rashid. From 817 to 819, Ibrahim set himself up as the rival of his nephew al-Ma'mun for the caliphate. He was famous as a singer, musician and a poet and as such he features in several *Nights* tales.

'Id al-Adha the Feast of Immolation, also known as Greater Bairam, is celebrated on the 10th of Dhu'l-Hijja (the month of *hajj* or pilgrimage). During this festival those Muslims who can afford it are obliged to sacrifice sheep, cattle or camels.

'Id al-Fitr the Feast of the Fast Breaking, marking the end of Ramadan.

Ifranja Europe; literally, 'the land of the Franks'.

'ifrit a kind of *jinni*, usually evil; an *'ifrita* is a female *jinni*.

imam the person who leads the prayers in a mosque.

Iram 'Iram, City of the Columns' is referred to in the Quran. Shaddad, king of the Arab tribe of 'Ad, intended Iram to rival Paradise, but God punished him for his pride and ruined his city.

Ishaq ibn Ibrahim al-Mausili (757–850) was the most famous composer and musical performer in the time of Harun al-Rashid. Like his father, Ibrahim al-Mausili, he features in a number of *Nights* stories.

Ja'far the Barmecide a member of a great Iranian clan which served the 'Abbasid caliphs as viziers and other funcrionaries. In the stories, he features as Harun's vizier, though in reality it was his father, Yahya, who held this post. For reasons that are mysterious, Ja'far and other members of his clan were executed in 803.

Jamil Buthaina Jamil ibn Ma'mar al-'Udhri (d. 701), a Hijazi poet who specialized in elegiac love poetry, famous for his chastely unhappy passion for Buthaina.

Jarir ibn 'Atiya (d. 729) a leading poet of the Umaiyad period, famous for his panegyric and invective verse.

Jawarna Zara, a port on the east coast of the Adriatic.

jinni a (male) spirit in Muslim folklore and theology; *jinniya* is a female spirit. *Jinn* (the collective term) assumed various forms: some were servants of Satan, while others were good Muslims and therefore benign.

Joseph features in the Quran as well as the Bible. In the Quran, he is celebrated for his beauty.

jubba a long outer garment, open at the front, with wide sleeves.

Ka'b al-Ahbar (d. *c.*653) a Jew who converted to Islam and a leading transmitter of religious traditions and an expert on biblical lore.

Ka'ba the cube-shaped holy building in Mecca to which Muslims turn when they pray.

kaffiyeh a headdress of cloth folded and held by a cord around the head.

khalanj **wood** tree heath (*Erica arborea*), a hard kind of wood.

Khalid ibn Safwan (d. 752) a transmitter of traditions, poems and speeches, famous for his eloquence.

khan an inn, caravanserai or market.

al-Khidr 'The Green Man', features in the Quran as a mysterious guide to Moses as well as appearing in many legends and stories. In some tales, this immortal servant of God is guardian of the Spring of Life, which gives eternal life to those who drink from it.

Khurasan in the medieval period, this designated a large territory that included eastern Persia and Afghanistan.

Kuthaiyir (660–723) a Hijazi poet who specialized in the theme of unfulfilled love, since the object of his passion, 'Azza, was married to another man.

Luqman a pre-Islamic sage and hero famed for his longevity. Many fables and proverbs were attributed to him.

Magian a Zoroastrian, a fire worshipper. In the *Nights*, the Magians invariably feature as sinister figures.

al-Mahdi (b. *c.*743) the 'Abbasid caliph who reigned from 775 to 785.

mahmal the richly decorated empty litter sent by a Muslim ruler to Mecca during the *hajj* (pilgrimage).

maidan an exercise yard or parade ground; an open space near or in a town.

maisir a pre-Islamic game of chance involving arrows and in which the stakes were designated parts of slaughtered camels.

Majnun Qais ibn Mulawwah al-Majnun ('the mad'), a (probably) legendary Arabian poet of the seventh century, famous for his doomed love for Laila. After she was married to another man, Majnun retired into the wilderness to live among wild beasts.

Malik the angel who is the guardian of hell.

Malik ibn Dinar an eighth-century Basran preacher and moralist.

mamluk slave soldier. Most mamluks were of Turkish origin.

al-Ma'mun (786–833) son of Harun al-Rashid and the 'Abbasid caliph from 813 until his death. He was famous for his patronage of learning and his sponsorship of the translation of Greek and Syriac texts into Arabic.

Ma'n ibn Za'ida (d. 769) a soldier, administrator and patron of poets under the late Umaiyads and early 'Abbasids.

mann a measure of weight.

al-Mansur (r. 754–75) 'Abbasid caliph.

marid a type of *jinni*.

Maslama ibn 'Abd al-Malik (d. 738) son of the Umaiyad caliph 'Abd al-Malik ibn Marwan and a leading general who headed a series of campaigns against the Byzantines.

Masrur the eunuch who was sword-bearer and executioner to Harun al-Rashid.

al-Mausili *see* Ibrahim Abu Ishaq al-Mausili *and* Ishaq ibn Ibrahim al-Mausili.

mithqal a measure of weight.

months of the Muslim year from the first to the twelfth month, these are: (1) al-Muharram, (2) Safar, (3) Rabi' al-awwal, (4) Rabi' al-akhir, (5) Jumada al-ula, (6) Jumada al-akhira, (7) Rajab, (8) Sha'ban, (9) Ramadan, (10) Shawwal, (11) Dhu'l-Qa'da, (12) Dhu'l-Hijja.

Mu'awiya Mu'awiya ibn Abi Sufyan, first of the Umaiyad caliphs (r. 661–80). He came to power after the assassination of 'Ali.

al-Mubarrad Abu al-'Abbas al-Mubarrad (c.815–98), a famous Basran grammarian and philologist.

muezzin the man who gives the call to prayer, usually from the minaret or roof of the mosque.

muhtasib market inspector with duties to enforce trading standards and public morals.

Munkar and Nakir two angels who examine the dead in their tombs and, if necessary, punish them.

al-Muntasir 'Abbasid caliph (r. 861–2).

al-Musta'in 'Abbasid caliph (r. 862–6).

al-Mustansir bi'llah 'Abbasid caliph (r. 1226–42).

al-Mutalammis sixth-century pre-Islamic poet and sage.

al-Mu'tatid bi'llah 'Abbasid caliph (r. 892–902).

al-Mutawakkil (822–61) 'Abbasid caliph, and great cultural patron, who reigned from 847 until he was assassinated by murderers probably hired by his son, who became the caliph al-Muntasir.

muwashshahat strophic poetry, usually recited to a musical accompaniment. This form of verse originated in Spain, but spread throughout the Islamic world.

nadd a type of incense consisting of a mixture of aloes wood with ambergris, musk and frankincense.

Nakir *see* Munkar and Nakir.

naqib an official whose duties varied according to time and place. The term was often used to refer to the chief representative of the *ashraf*, i.e. the descendants of 'Ali.

Al-Nu'man ibn al-Mundhir a fifth-century Arab ruler of the pre-Islamic Christian kingdom of Hira in Iraq.

nusf literally, 'a half'; a small coin.

parasang an old Persian measure of length, somewhere between three and four miles.

qadi a Muslim judge.

Qaf Mount Qaf was a legendary mountain located at the end of the world, or in some versions one that encircles the earth.

qintar a measure of weight, variable from region to region, equivalent to 100 *ratls*.

qirat a dry measure, but the term could also be used of a certain weight; also a coin, equivalent to a twenty-fourth of a dinar.

Quraish the dominant Arab clan in Mecca at the time of the Prophet.

rafidi literally, 'a refuser', a term applied to members of various Shi'i sects.

rak'a in the Muslim prayer ritual, a bowing of the body followed by two prostrations.

Ramadan   the ninth month of the Muslim year, in which fasting is observed from sunrise to sunset. *See also* months of the Muslim year.

ratl   a measure of weight, varying from region to region.

Ridwan   the angel who is the guardian of the gates of Paradise.

Rudaini spear   *see* Samhari spear.

rukh   a legendary bird of enormous size, strong enough to carry an elephant (in English 'roc').

Rum/Ruman   theoretically designates Constantinople and the Byzantine lands more generally, but in some stories the name is merely intended to designate a strange and usually Christian foreign land.

Rumi   of Byzantine Greek origin.

Safar   *see* months of the Muslim year.

Said ibn Jubair   a pious Muslim and Quran reader of the Umaiyad period.

Sakhr   an evil *jinni* whose story is related by commentators on the Quran.

Saladin   (1138–93), Muslim political and military leader, famed for his chivalry and piety and for opposing the Crusaders. He took over Egypt and abolished the Fatimid caliphate in 1171; in 1174 he also became sultan of most of Syria. In 1187 he invaded the kingdom of Jerusalem, occupying the city and many other places. Thereafter he had to defend his gains from the armies of the Third Crusade.

salam   meaning 'peace', the final word at the end of a prayer, similar to the Christian 'amen'.

Samhari spear   opinions varied as to whether Samhar was the name of a manufacturer of spears, or whether it was the place where they used to be made. A 'Samhari spear' was a common metaphor for slenderness; likewise 'Rudaini spear', said to be related to Rudaina, the supposed wife of Samhar.

Sasanian   the Sasanians were the Persian dynasty who ruled in Persia and Iraq from 224 until 637, when Muslim armies overran their empire.

Serendib   the old Arab name for Ceylon or Sri Lanka.

Sha'ban   *see* months of the Muslim year.

Shaddad ibn 'Ad   legendary king of the tribe of 'Ad who attempted to build the city of Iram as a rival to Paradise and was punished by God for his presumption.

al-Shafi'i   Muhammad ibn Idris al-Shafi'i (767–820), jurist and founder of the Shafi'i school of Sunni religious law, whose adherents are know as Shafi'ites.

shaikh   a tribal leader, the term also commonly used to refer to an old man or a master of one of the traditional religious sciences or a leader of a dervish order. Similarly, a *shaikha* is an old woman or a woman in authority.

Shaikhs of the Fire   Zoroastrian priests or elders.

shari'a   *shari'a* law is the body of Islamic religious law.

sharif   meaning 'noble', often used with specific reference to a descendant of the Prophet.

Shi'i an adherent of that branch of Islam that recognizes 'Ali and his descendants as the leaders of the Muslim community after the Prophet.

Sufi a Muslim mystic or ascetic.

Sufyan al-Thauri (716–78) born in Kufa, theologian, ascetic and transmitter of *hadiths* (sayings of the Prophet). He wrote on law and was a leading spokesman of strict Sunnism.

sunna the corpus of practices and teachings of the Prophet as collected and transmitted by later generations of Muslims, the *sunna* served as the guide to the practice of the Sunni Muslims and as one of the pillars of their religious law, supplementing the prescriptions of the Quran.

sura a chapter of the Quran.

sycamore a type of fig; also known as the Egyptian fig.

taghut a term designating pagan idols or idolatry. By extension, the word was used to refer to soothsayers, sorcerers and infidels.

tailasan a shawl-like garment worn over head and shoulders. It was commonly worn by judges and religious high functionaries.

Thamud an impious tribe in pre-Islamic Arabia whom Allah destroyed when they refused to pay heed to his prophet Salih.

'Udhri love this refers to the Banu 'Udhra. Several famous 'Udhri poets were supposed to have died from unconsummated love.

Umaiyads a dynasty of Sunni Muslim caliphs who ruled the Islamic lands from 661 until 750. The Umaiyads descended from the powerful Meccan tribe of the Quraish. In 750, they were overthrown by a revolution in favour of the 'Abbasids. One member of the family succeeded in escaping to Spain, where he set up an Umaiyad empire.

'Umar 'Umar ibn 'Abd al-'Aziz, eighth Umaiyad caliph (r. 717–20), famed for his piety.

'Umar ibn al-Khattab (581–644) the second of the caliphs to succeed the Prophet (r. 634–44).

'umra the minor pilgrimage to Mecca, which, unlike the *hajj*, can be performed at any time of the year.

al-'Utbi (d. 1022) famous author of prose and poetry, worked in the service of the Ghaznavid court. (The Ghaznavids were a Turkish dynasty who ruled in Afghanistan, Khurasan and north-western India from the late tenth till the late twelfth century.)

waiba a dry measure.

wali a local governor.

witr a prayer, performed between the evening and the dawn prayers, which is recommended but not compulsory.

Yahya ibn Khalid the Barmecide a Persian who was a senior government official under the 'Abbasid caliphs al-Mansur and Harun. He was disgraced and executed in 805 for reasons that remain mysterious.

Zaid ibn Aslam a freed slave of 'Umar ibn al-Khattab.

Ziyad ibn Abihi   ibn Abihi meaning 'Son of his Father' – the identity of his father being unknown – (d. 676), governor of Iraq under Mu'awiya.

Zubaida   (762–831) the granddaughter of the 'Abbasid caliph al-Mansur and famous for her wealth. She became chief wife of the caliph Harun al-Rashid and was mother to al-Amin and al-Ma'mun, both later caliphs.

al-Zuhri   Muhammad ibn Muslim al-Zuhri (d. 742), the transmitter of traditions concerning the Prophet and legal authority. He frequented the Umaiyad courts, where, among other things, he was a tutor.

Chronology

622   Year one of the Muslim *hijri* calendar (dating from the Hijra, or year of Muhammad's emigration from Mecca to Medina).

630   Mecca submits to Muhammad.

661   Beginning of the Umaiyad dynasty of caliphs.

750   Beginning of the 'Abbasid dynasty of caliphs.

762–6   Baghdad is founded and becomes the 'Abbasid capital.

786–809   reign of Harun al-Rashid, caliph in Baghdad.

*c.*800–900   *Kitab Hadith Alf Layla* ('The Book of the Tale of One Thousand Nights'), a lost precursor of *The Arabian Nights*, is put together.

*c.*850?   Earliest surviving fragment of the Arabic *Nights* written.

1085   Somadeva's *Kathasaritsagara*.

1171   Saladin overthrows the Fatimid caliphate in Egypt.

1250–60   Collapse of Aiyubid principalities in Egypt and Syria and their replacement by the Mamluk sultanate.

1258   Mongols sack Baghdad. Execution of the last 'Abbasid caliph.

1353   Boccaccio's *Decameron*.

1387   Chaucer begins *The Canterbury Tales*.

*c.*1450–1500   Probable date of *Alf Layla wa-Layla* ('The Thousand and One Nights'), the manuscript translated by Antoine Galland and the oldest substantially surviving Arabic version of the *Nights*.

1516   Ariosto's *Orlando furioso* published.

1704   Galland begins publishing his translation *Les Mille et une nuits*, the last volume appearing in 1717.

1708   Probable date of first chapbook translation of Galland into English.

1814–18   Calcutta I edition of the *Nights*.

1824–43   Breslau edition.

1835   Bulaq edition.

1838–42   Edward William Lane's translation.

1839–42   Calcutta II edition.

1882–4   John Payne's translation.

1885–8   Richard Burton's translation.

1899–1904   Joseph Charles Mardrus's French translation.

1921–8   Enno Littmann's German translation.

1984   Muhsin Mahdi's edition of the *Alf Layla wa-Layla* manuscript formerly translated by Galland.

Further Reading

Ballaster, Ros, *Fabulous Orients: Fictions of the East in England 1622–1785* (Oxford University Press, Oxford, 2005). Ballaster's book explores the impact of *The Arabian Nights* and other Oriental fictions on British and, to a lesser extent, French literature.

Burton, Richard F. (tr.), *A Plain and Literal Translation of the Arabian Nights' Entertainments*, 10 vols. (Karma Shastra Society, London, 1885). A full translation of the Calcutta II Arabic text of *The Arabian Nights*, this work was impressive for its time, but there are many errors in it and Burton's contorted literary style makes it heavy going for the modern reader.

Byatt, A. S., *The Djinn in the Nightingale's Eye: Five Fairy Stories* (Chatto, London, 1994). Despite its fictional status, Byatt's title story in this collection contains some serious and penetrating observations about the characteristics of storytelling in the *Nights*.

Caracciolo, Peter L. (ed.), *The Arabian Nights in English Literature: Studies in the Reception of The Thousand and One Nights into British Culture* (Macmillan, London, 1988). A collection of essays by various hands. Caracciolo's lengthy introductory survey is a masterpiece of intelligently directed erudition.

Clute, John, and Grant, John (eds.), *The Encyclopedia of Fantasy* (Orbit, London, 1997). This mighty work of reference is 1,049 double-columned pages long. Apart from the article 'Arabian Fantasy', it contains many entries on authors and works influenced by the *Nights*. It also has serious analytical articles about the literary tropes and devices of fantastic and magical fiction.

El-Shamy, Hasan M., *A Motif Index of The Thousand and One Nights* (Indiana University Press, Bloomington, Indiana, 2006). Weighing in at 680 pages, this classification of thousands of motifs in the *Nights* serves as an index to themes, people, animals, objects and social practices in the stories. The motifs are cross-referenced to the Burton translation and to Victor Chauvin's *Bibliographie des ouvrages arabes ou relatifs aux arabes; publiés dans l'Europe chrétienne de 1810 à 1885*, 12 vols. (Bibliothèque de la Faculté de Philosophie et Lettres de l'Université de Liège, Liège, 1892–1922). They include such topics as 'series of living corpses to serve as phantom guards', 'compulsion to steal', 'severed head speaks', 'taste of food eaten in a dream still in the mouth next day', 'fool recognized by his long beard', 'wish for exalted husband realized' and 'woman thinking lover dead erects cenotaph and mourns before it'.

Haddawy, Husain (tr.), *The Arabian Nights* (Everyman's Library Classics, London, 1992). This is a (good) translation of Muhsin Mahdi's scrupulously edited text of a Syrian manuscript dating from the fourteenth or fifteenth century. The manuscript in question was used by Antoine Galland for his eighteenth-century French translation. However, it contains only thirty-five stories.

Irwin, Robert, *The Arabian Nights: A Companion*, 2nd edition (I. B. Tauris, London and New York, 2004). A survey of the composition, collection and translation of the stories, the leading themes of the tales (including sex and magic), structuralist classifications of the tales, medieval storytelling techniques, the influence of the *Nights* on European and American literature, and much else besides.

—, *The Penguin Anthology of Classical Arabic Literature* (Penguin, London, 2006). The *Nights* are placed in the broader context of medieval Arabic prose and poetry.

Marzolph, Ulrich (ed.), *The Arabian Nights Reader* (Wayne State University Press, Detroit, Michigan, 2006). A collection of key twentieth-century essays by various academic hands, on such matters as the dating, structure and contents of the *Nights*.

—, and van Leeuwen, Richard (eds.), *The Arabian Nights Encyclopedia*, 2 vols. (ABC Clio, Santa Barbara, California, 2004). The essential reference work for *Nights* scholars and fanatics. Volume 1 contains fourteen essays by experts on such matters as literary style, oral features, illustrations, manuscripts and cinema. It also has individual articles on every story found in the Calcutta II text, Galland and other versions of the *Nights*. Volume 2 has articles on a wide range of *Nights*-related topics, such as George Eliot, Richard Burton, Harun al-Rashid, Shahrazad, camels, slaves and music. It also has tables of concordances, international tale types and narrative motifs.

Yamanaka, Yuriko, and Nishio, Tetsuo (eds.), *The Arabian Nights and Orientalism: Perspectives from East and West* (I. B. Tauris, London and New York, 2006). Essays by various scholars, the majority of them Japanese, on such subjects as the reception and translation of *The Arabian Nights* in Japan, Alexander the Great in the *Nights*, and the *Nights* in folklore research and in illustration.

Zipes, Jack (ed.), *The Oxford Companion to the Fairy Tale* (Oxford University Press, Oxford, 2000). Apart from an article on *The Arabian Nights*, there are also entries on 'Aladdin', 'Ali Baba', 'The Thief of Baghdad', Shahrazad, Galland, Edmund Dulac and Salman Rushdie.

Maps

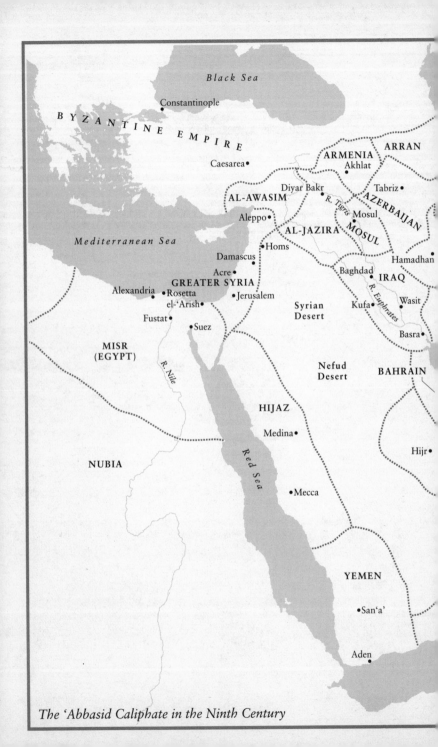

The 'Abbasid Caliphate in the Ninth Century

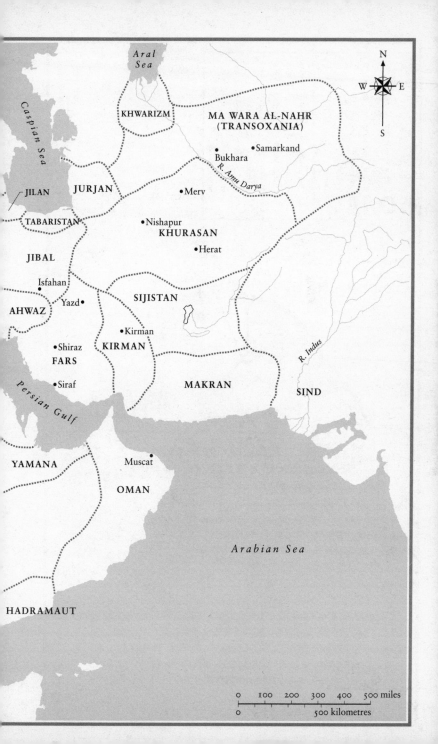

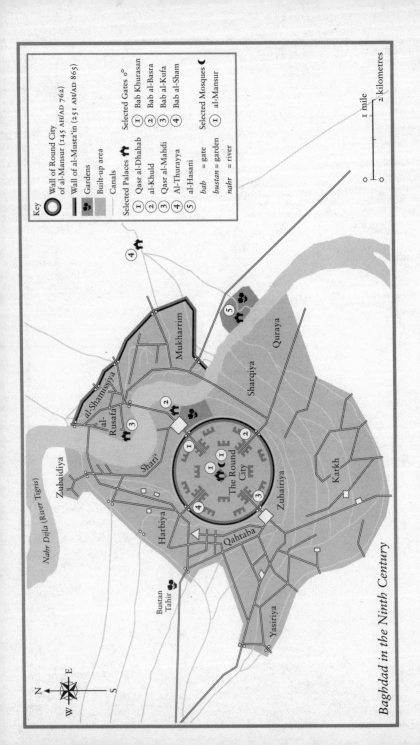

Baghdad in the Ninth Century

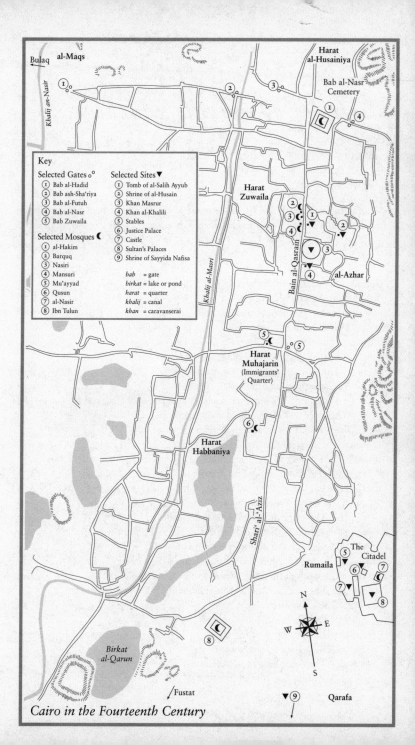

Cairo in the Fourteenth Century

Index of Nights and Stories

Bold numbers indicate the Night, or series of Nights, over which a story is told.
Stories told within a story are presented in brackets.

Volume One